Research on Technology and the Teaching and Learning of Mathematics: Volume 2

Cases and Perspectives

a volume in
Research on Technology and the Teaching and Learning of
Mathematics: Syntheses, Cases, and Perspectives

Series Editors:
M. Kathleen Heid and Glendon W. Blume
The Pennsylvania State University

Research on Technology and the Teaching and Learning of Mathematics: Syntheses, Cases, and Perspectives

M. Kathleen Heid and Glendon W. Blume, Series Editors

Research on Technology and the Teaching and Learning of Mathematics:
Volume 1. Research Syntheses (2008)
edited by M. Kathleen Heid and Glendon W. Blume

Research on Technology and the Teaching and Learning of Mathematics:
Volume 2. Cases and Perspectives (2008)
edited by Glendon W. Blume and M. Kathleen Heid

Research on Technology and the Teaching and Learning of Mathematics: Volume 2

Cases and Perspectives

edited by

Glendon W. Blume and M. Kathleen Heid
The Pennsylvania State University

Information Age Publishing, Inc.
Charlotte, North Carolina
www.infoagepub.com

NATIONAL COUNCIL OF
TEACHERS OF MATHEMATICS

Library of Congress Cataloging-in-Publication Data

Cases and perspectives / edited by Glendon W. Blume and M. Kathleen Heid.
　　p. cm. — (Research on technology and the teaching and learning of mathematics)
Includes bibliographical references.
　　ISBN 1-931576-20-3 (pbk.) — ISBN 1-931576-21-1 (hardcover) 1. Mathematics—Study and teaching—Evaluation—Case studies. 2. Technology—Study and teaching—Evaluation—Case studies. 3. Mathematics—Research. I. Blume, Glendon W. II. Heid, Mary Kathleen.
　　QA11.2.C375 2008
　　510.71—dc22

　　　　　　　　　　　　　　　　　　　　　　　　　　　　　　　　　　　　　2008017762

ISBN 13: 978-1-931576-20-8 (paperback)
ISBN 13: 978-1-931576-21-5 (hardcover)

Printed in the United States of America

CONTENTS

PREFACE

Glen Blume and M. Kathleen Heid

Almost 70 years ago, J. Abner Peddiwell (under the tutelage of Harold Benjamin) spun the tale of the Saber-Tooth Curriculum (1939), the hypothesized curriculum that defined education in an era once dominated by cave dwellers, wooly mammoths, and saber-toothed tigers. The story recounted the ways in which our hypothetical ancestors taught fish-grabbing (even after fishing nets were available and waters were too muddy to make it possible to see the fish) and tiger scaring with fire (even after the saber-toothed tiger grew to extinction because it had succumbed to pneumonia due to a glacier). The study of fish grabbing and of tiger scaring remained a part of the curriculum long after they had outlived their initial usefulness, not for the purposes of catching fish and protecting the community from tigers, but for retroactively contrived purposes of building character, agility, and bravery.

The tale of the Saber-Tooth Curriculum serves to alert curriculum developers and educators to the nonpermanent nature of the content of curricula in schools, the tenacity with which we maintain curricula that are in place no matter whether they are serving their intended purpose, and the difficulty of embracing new curricula with learning goals that have changed based on newly available technology. In the story of the incorporation of technology into mathematics curricula, we hear echoes of the Saber-Tooth Curriculum. We have new tools and we need to learn how best to use them in pursuit of educational goals that best reflect the opportunities afforded education in a technology-present environment.

The stage has been set for the systematic examination of the impact of technology on the teaching and learning of mathematics that is the purpose of these volumes. Knowledge of that impact will enable the creation and implementation of curricula that capitalize on technology and will help teachers orchestrate the use of technological tools in school mathematics classrooms.

According to the National Council of Teachers of Mathematics' *Principles and Standards for School Mathematics* (2000), "Technology is essential in teaching and learning of mathematics; it influences the mathematics that is taught and enhances students' learning" (p. 24). The first part of this principle is a value statement; the second part is a claim the support for which is open to examination. How does research inform this call for technology in mathematics teaching and learning? In response to the need to craft appropriate roles for technology in school mathematics, new technological approaches have been applied to the teaching and learning of mathematics, and the effects of these technological approaches have been examined by researchers worldwide.

The technologies with which these volumes deal are what have come to be called cognitive technologies (technologies that transcend the limitations of the mind) and mathematics-specific technologies (technologies that are used primarily for mathematics or are particularly amenable to mathematics uses). In individual chapters, authors make other distinctions important to their particular uses of technology. At times authors of research articles do not specify versions of software that were used in their studies. In those cases and when the software is commonly used, we do not include publication information for the software (e.g., Logo, Maple).

Volumes 1 and 2 of *Research on Technology and the Teaching and Learning of Mathematics: Syntheses, Cases, and Perspectives* are the products of a multi-year effort to gather and analyze what the field has learned through research on technology and the teaching and learning of mathematics. Technological approaches to school mathematics have not as yet been widely adopted largely due to a general impression by both practitioners and researchers that technology-intensive mathematics education is untested. These volumes are intended to bring the community of mathematics education researchers to a greater awareness of theory and research on the impact of technology on mathematics learning and teaching. *Volume 1: Research Syntheses* provides insight into what research suggests about the nature of mathematics learning in technological environments. Included in this volume are syntheses of research on technology in the learning of specific areas of mathematics (rational number, algebra, elementary and secondary geometry, mathematical modeling, and calculus) in addition to research syntheses of the more global issues of equity and the process of incorporating technology into mathematics teaching. The authors provide thoughtful analyses of bodies of research with the goal of understanding the ways in which technology affects what and how students learn. Each of the chapters in this volume is written by a team of experts whose own research has provided important guidance to the field.

Volume 2: Cases and Perspectives has a dual focus. It features descriptive cases that provide accounts of the development of technology-intensive curricula and technological tools. In these cases the writers describe and analyze various roles that research played in their development work and ways in which research, curriculum development, and tool development can inform each other. These thoughtful descriptions and analyses will provide documentation of how this process can and does occur. Each of these chapters is written by individuals who were intimately involved in the development of leading-edge mathematics-specific technology or technology-intensive mathematics curricula and who saw research as an essential part of that development. The remaining chapters in the second volume address overarching research-related issues and perspectives on the use of technology in the teaching and learning of mathematics. Each of these perspectives is written by a leading scholar who accounts for a global issue with the potential for providing overall guidance to research that involves technology and the teaching and learning of mathematics.

CONTENT OF VOLUME 2

We have included in this volume what we have called "cases." By "cases" in the context of these volumes we mean instances of the creation or use of technology in mathematics instruction that either are informed by or help inform research. These cases are not defined by a type of research—in particular, they are not "case studies." We were motivated to use cases of the development of technological tools and technology-intensive curricula as a major focus for this volume because, in spite of the popular impression that much tool and technology-intensive curriculum development has little relationship to research, we and our colleagues were aware that research often played a central role in the creation, testing, and revision of tools or technology-intensive curricula. We called on, as authors, those who worked at the nexus of research and creation of technological tools.

The cases in this volume are written by researchers who have been involved both in the trenches and at the vanguard of the movement toward innovative and leading-edge uses of technology in mathematics instruction. In her two chapters, Sharon Dugdale, whose work in technology-based mathematics education started with the PLATO computer-based education system and the development of the landmark software Green Globs, reflects on her 3 decades of involvement in the field. In her first chapter she recounts the varied roles of research in her early fractions project, and in her second chapter she describes the evolution of principles of software design including the importance of classroom-based testing. The chapter by Colette and Jean-Marie Laborde and the chapter by Paul Goldenberg, Daniel Scher, and Nannette Feurzeig recount the development of the first dynamical geometry software from a mathematical perspective and from an historical perspective. The next three chapters describe the role of research in the development of mathematics education software, with Julie Sarama and Douglas Clements describing the development of software for primary students, Michael Battista describing the development of middle school geometry software, and the Carnegie Learning team (Steven Ritter, Lisa Haverty, Kenneth Koedinger, William Hadley, and Albert Corbett) describing the role of cognitive science in the development of an intelligent tutor for algebra. The final three chapters in the "Cases" section deal with the role of multiple representations in the development of technology-intensive tools and technology-intensive curricula. Jere Confrey and Alan Maloney demonstrate how multirepresentational software can support the exploration and understanding of fundamental mathematical ideas and simultaneously help clarify students' mathematical thinking about those ideas. Jim Kaput and Roberta Schorr elaborate on the implications of changing fundamental representational infrastructures through the use of multirepresentational software. Thomas Dick and Barbara Edwards describe the use of the CAS in the creation of a multirepresentational calculus curriculum.

The next seven chapters are what we call "Perspectives" chapters. They reflect overarching issues that the authors have identified as critical to understanding the use of technology in the teaching and learning of mathematics. Susan Friel takes on an underdeveloped area of research—she provides a background document on technology-related research on the learning of data analysis and statistics. Thomas Dick turns his attention to the tool developer in his presentation of principles for design of technology for use in mathematics education. Michael Battista reflects on critical relationships between mathematical understandings and use of representations. Paul Drijvers and Luc Trouche describe instrumental genesis and the teacher's role in promoting it, while Carolyn Kieran and Luis Saldanha describe the codevelopment of conceptual and technical knowledge in a CAS environment. Patricia Wilson directs our attention to understanding the knowledge and understandings needed by those who prepare teachers. In the final Perspectives chapter, Joan Ferrini-Mundy and Glenda Breaux situate the issue of technology and research on its effects in the unpredictably dynamic educational policy environment. We end the volume with a chapter laying out overarching themes that arose throughout the volume.

ACKNOWLEDGMENTS

Early versions of the chapters in these two volumes were discussed at two conferences held at The Pennsylvania State University. Those conferences were sponsored by the Conferences on Research on Technology and the Teaching and Learning of Mathematics Grant # ESI-0087447 from the National Science Foundation. We thank the participants in those conferences (researchers, teacher educators, teachers, policymakers, software developers, and curriculum developers) for the insights they offered—insights that have undoubtedly made the collection of chapters richer. Of course, any opinions, findings, and conclusions or recommendations that drew on those discussions are those of the authors and editors and do not necessarily reflect the views of the National Science Foundation.

We are grateful to all of those who have made the production of these volumes possible. First, we thank the authors for their generosity in sharing the kinds of expertise that can only come from contributing leading insights for so long in such an important area. The chapters benefited greatly from the contributions of the dozens of reviewers (who shall remain anonymous). We, and the authors, thank them.

We thank our colleague Rose Mary Zbiek who offered her encouragement and patient support when work on these volumes overtook our lives. We thank Vincent Lunetta, whose collaboration with us on the NSF Graduate Research Traineeship program led to the idea of writing a monograph (now two large volumes) and holding a conference that engaged our doctoral students with researchers from around the world. We thank George Bright for his encouragement and support in bringing the conferences into being. We are thankful for the work of Jim Renney, Kristen Hall, Tracy Scala, and Linda Haffly who helped plan and orchestrate the conferences at which chapters were discussed and who coordinated the travel for attendees from 10 countries. We could not have coordinated the production of these volumes without the help of three special individuals. Thanks go to Gulseren Karagoz Akar for her diligent editorial assistance, to Linda Haffly for always being there to support in whatever way was helpful, and to Tracy Scala for the countless ways in which she helped us manage the task of coordinating and communicating about these two volumes of scholarly contributions. We also wish to thank our families, especially Ruth Blume, for their patience during the long process of preparing these volumes.

REFERENCES

National Council of Teachers of Mathematics (2000). *Principles and Standards for School Mathematics*. Reston, VA: Author.

Peddiwell, J. A. (1939). *The Saber-Tooth Curriculum*. New York: McGraw-Hill Book Company, Inc.

PART I

CASES

CHAPTER 1

RESEARCH IN A PIONEER CONSTRUCTIVIST NETWORK-BASED CURRICULUM PROJECT FOR CHILDREN'S LEARNING OF FRACTIONS

Sharon Dugdale

My involvement in technologically intensive curriculum development and technological tool development has been a journey through multiple projects, collectively spanning 3 decades. Research has played various roles, and findings from each project have informed the next. This chapter distills some of the research influence and activity from the first of these projects. A subsequent chapter continues the story into later work and highlights the continuity and influence from one project to another.

My work with technologically intensive curriculum development began in 1972 at the Computer-based Education Research Laboratory (CERL) at the University of Illinois. With funding from the National Science Foundation,[1] CERL launched extensive curriculum development initiatives from primary grades through university level for its PLATO[2] (Programmed Logic for Automated Teaching Operations) computer-based

Research on Technology and the Teaching and Learning of Mathematics:
Vol. 2. Cases and Perspectives, 3–30
Copyright © 2008 by Information Age Publishing
All rights of reproduction in any form reserved.

education system (Lyman, 1984; Smith & Sherwood, 1976). One of the areas designated for development was elementary school mathematics.

Robert B. Davis, well known for his curriculum development work with the Madison Project (Davis, 1964), was hired to initiate the elementary mathematics effort. An early decision was to focus on Grades 4 through 6, commonly referred to as the "intermediate grades." Davis selected three curricular areas for the project to address, and characterized them as follows:

1. Whole numbers, an area of fundamental importance that was considered relatively successful in existing curricula;
2. Fractions, a problematic area of intermediate grades curricula that was generally regarded as difficult to teach and to learn;
3. Graphs (coordinate geometry), a topic that was not typically included in intermediate grade mathematics, and to which that Davis and his colleagues had given substantial attention at this grade level in the Madison Project.

The elementary mathematics project formed three teams of developers, one for each of these curricular areas. My team was responsible for design and development of the fractions curriculum (Dugdale & Kibbey, 1980), and it is in this context that I begin my account of the role of research in technologically intensive curriculum development.

In thinking about the involvement of research in this and subsequent projects, it is convenient to consider three somewhat distinct roles:

1. A foundational role: Research defines the theoretical and practical foundations of the development.
2. A formative role: Research shapes the development and contributes to the knowledge base.
3. A summative role: Research evaluates the products and implementations of the development project and contributes further to the knowledge base.

These three roles are discussed below in the context of the project's foundations, its development process, and its summative evaluation stage.

FOUNDATIONS

Learning Theory

The pedagogical approach of the PLATO fractions curriculum was rooted in the ideas and perspectives that formed the basis of the constructivist movement, a movement that gained momentum and clarity in mathematics education over the ensuing decades. Consistent with Piaget's developmental theory (Piaget, 1973), we assumed that learners construct their own mathematical knowledge from personal experience, and that experience with concrete models is beneficial in building understandings as a basis for mathematical abstractions. Consistent with Dewey's work, we subscribed to the importance of developing mathematical activity in a mathematical community, that is, a social construction of mathematical ideas (Dewey, 1963). We also drew from the problem-solving heuristics of George Polya (1957), although this was not a pervading theme fundamental to the curriculum.

Concurrently with my team's development of the PLATO fractions curriculum, Davis and two of his colleagues from the earlier Madison Project created the PLATO graphs curriculum as an extension of the Madison Project work. A "discovery" approach had been prominent in the Madison Project philosophy and activities (Davis, 1967). Although each of the three elementary mathematics development teams (whole numbers, fractions, and graphs) had its own style in many ways, all subscribed to a fundamentally activity-based, constructivism-consistent learning environment.

The remainder of this chapter describes many additional factors that developed and honed my own team's perspective on children's learning. The chapter conclusion relates this perspective, which evolved as we worked closely with children in a technologically intensive environment, to more recent descriptions of constructivism in mathematics education.

Student Observations and Interviews

Beyond the overall project philosophy, my own work with seventh- and eighth-grade students shaped the character of the fractions curriculum. As a teacher of mathematics in these grades, I had had ample opportunity to observe students' work with fractions, to solicit students' explanations of their work and thinking, and to grapple with some troubling perceptions and habits of thought among these students. From these years of observation, interviews, and analysis, I had gleaned not only an awareness of students' algorithm dependence and the lack of mathematical sense associated with these algorithms, but also a far more troubling awareness of the deeply ingrained persistence of these habits of thought.

My students were accustomed to having an example to remind them of the appropriate algorithm at the beginning of a problem set. Given a fraction problem outside of the context of a problem set with an example, many students would piece together fragments of various algorithms. Having performed a combination of manipulations, there was likely to be something worth at least partial credit, and students often seemed to be demonstrating "at least I know a lot of things that can be done with fraction problems." What was missing was the sense of the quantities and the operations, or at least any habit of engaging such sense, or any other basis for making mathematical sense of the situation.

Firmly convinced that all they needed was a quick reminder of algorithms before tackling problems, students generally resisted any serious engagement in work with concrete experiences to make sense of problems or algorithms. I speculated that work with concrete models and other sense-making efforts could be more successful with, and acceptable to, students in earlier grades while they were initially building understandings about fractions and operations with fractions, rather than later as a supplement to algorithms already introduced and practiced.

When the PLATO project launched its curriculum effort, I was eager to work with children in earlier grades in the context of developing a fractions curriculum. It was an opportunity to test the hypothesis that a more extensive concrete experience with fractions, coupled with a learner-centered transition from models to algorithms, could develop a better sense of fractions and the mathematics of fractions, as well as fundamental habits of making sense of mathematics, and habits of *expecting* mathematics to make sense.

Development Environment

In any technologically intensive curriculum development, the capabilities of the specific technology play a fundamental role in determining what can be done and how the technology will be used. The ensuing curriculum is in some ways an interaction among the developer's learning theory and goals, the mathematical content, and the capabilities of the technology.

In 1972, the availability of graphics-capable computers for instruction posed new possibilities for computer-based learning environments (Tenczar, 1974). In particular, the PLATO system offered networked workstations with graphics, animation, touch-sensitive display, superimposed microfiche slide projection, and random-access recorded audio.

Coupling the instantaneously responsive, patient, individual interactiveness already valued in early CAI implementations with these recent advances enabled new and potentially richer modes of interaction between curriculum and learner. The familiar routine of computer prompt, followed by student response, followed by computer feedback, could be transformed into a host of new and exciting possibilities. For example, the computer prompt could be graphic (not just alphanumeric), the student response could be a manipulation of particular aspects of the graphic, and the computer feedback could be the graphic outcome of the student-initiated manipulation. We take these capabilities for granted today, and such interactions have been fundamental to high quality software for years, but in 1972 these were new frontiers with unknown potential.

Of course, a development environment consists of more than hardware capability. In contrast to some systems at the time, the PLATO project overall had no prescribed curriculum structure.[3] Its curriculum developers encountered a wide-open, creative atmosphere, with individuals and teams encouraged to "think outside the box," explore new features and possibilities, and challenge the potential of the system. With hardware developers, system software developers, and curriculum developers all within the same campus unit, there was opportunity for daily interaction. The curriculum developers and the students and teachers with whom we piloted materials were the end users of the system, and as such we found hardware and system software developers quite interested in collaboration on design of system features. Needless to say, this was a stimulating and enjoyable place to be in the 1970s. As might be predicted, development style, pedagogical strategy, team organization, and product quality varied widely among the PLATO curriculum development projects and teams. However, there was at least potential for substantial innovation that would likely have been precluded by a more regimented environment.

DEVELOPMENT PROCESS

Initial Planning and Development

In light of the foundations noted above, development of the fractions curriculum began with the following hypothesis:

> A more effective working knowledge of fractions could be developed by (1) more extensive work with a variety of models, in an exploratory, student-centered, active learning environment; (2) development of algorithms by students, with manipulations embedded in familiar models to maintain not only a sense of the quantities and operations, but also a sense of what results are within the bounds of reason; and (3) formalization and practice of algorithms after students become comfortable and facile performing operations in the context of familiar models.

As we constructed tentative charts of topics and potential learning activities, we discussed appropriateness of a variety of models to represent fractions. We considered what each model might add to a child's conceptualization of fractions, as well as the potential of each basic model to extend into meaningful activity with equivalent fractions and operations with fractions and mixed numbers. Although models varied considerably in their suitability for developing operations and algorithms, we resisted the temptation to pursue one "best" model. We hypothesized that an appropriately general concept of fractions would be more likely to develop from substantial interactive experience with a range of different models of fractions. Concentration on a single model seemed unlikely to achieve the degree of generalization necessary for children to relate their developing concept of fractions to the variety of contexts encountered in life.

We began development of prototype activities with some standard fractions models (e.g., sets of objects, sectors of circles, etc.) and some unusual models, such as the Skywriting activity discussed later in this chapter, in which the unit is one full trip around the circumference of a circle. Our initial development differed from standard curricula in the variety of models explored, the interactivity of those models, and the depth to which we had children pursue the models. We assumed that in order to engage children's attention sufficiently to develop a comfortable working knowledge of fractions, we needed to go far beyond the common introductory experiences offered in standard curricula of the time. Some of the examples that follow illustrate this depth of children's engagement.

Formative Research

Prototype activities were developed in conjunction with continuous micro-assessment (Davis & Dugdale, 1976). Children using the prototype activities were observed carefully to ascertain level of engagement, apparent understanding of the content, and any need for improvement in either the interface or the content treatment. It soon became evident that observation of children working together was usually more productive than observation of individuals working alone. Interactions between children working together revealed much about their thinking, in a more spontaneous and candid way than could be obtained by questions from an adult. Further, observers who were accustomed to interviewing children during mathematical activities found children less responsive to adult interruptions during their engagement in the computer activities. As one experienced observer remarked, "I usually find that children doing mathematics welcome an interruption and a chance to talk with me about it, but these children seem so intent on what they are doing that they almost resent the intrusion. They give me a short answer and want to go back to the activity."

As development proceeded, design decisions were made daily, based on work with individual children, pairs, small groups, and classes testing prototype activities. This ongoing formative research shaped the curriculum, from small details to major pedagogical decisions. A few examples are shared here to illustrate the process and its overriding influence on the curriculum design.

Diagnostic Branching

Early in the project, there was much discussion of the power of the computer's interactive environment to process each student response or action and make branching decisions based on diagnostic interpretations of these student inputs. Misconceptions could be diagnosed, conceptual breakthroughs could be detected, and children could be channeled into appropriate learning sequences. In the prevailing climate of computer-based curriculum development at the time, this level of individualization was considered a desirable goal and a natural use of the medium, though admittedly a complex challenge to implement well. While we were pilot testing prototype models for engaging children in working with fractions, we were also mapping out potential logic for individually adaptive branching to refine some of our prototypes.

However, it soon became apparent that our thinking in this direction was not compatible with various aspects of what we were seeing in our pilot test classrooms. First, a fairly typical scene around the computers is shown in Figure 1.1, with several children contributing ideas to an interaction with the software. At any time, one child might leave and another might join the interaction. Even though one child usually controlled the keyboard, the software was often not interacting with one child with one set of perceptions, but rather with a "committee" of kibitzers, each contributing suggestions and sometimes taking the interaction into new directions. We began to rethink our notions of what a program could conclude reliably from children's computer interactions without continuous monitoring of the scene around the computer.

Second, given a sensible model with which to work and a task at a reasonable level, children (individually or collectively) often proved quite facile at diagnosing their own errors. For example, given a rectangle on the screen and the request to "paint 3/5 of the box," a child might first mark off three small sections of the box and paint them. (Drawing lines and painting were done by touching the screen, somewhat like clicking a mouse today.) The program might respond: "You painted 3/10 of the box. Now paint 3/5 of the box." Observation of children in such circumstances suggested that this simple feedback was sufficient to prompt a redrawing

Figure 1.1.   Children's use of the computer was naturally social.

of lines and a successful representation of 3/5 on the next try. Although it could have been fairly straightforward in this case for a program to diagnose the difficulty and provide explicit corrective instructions, activities designed to encourage and support children's inherent talent for self-diagnosis appeared more successful in fostering healthy habits of making sense of mathematics.

Third, our observations of children indicated that even with only one child participating, it was often not possible to deduce a child's thinking or intent from what was entered into the computer. For example, Figure 1.2 shows a display from Darts (Dugdale & Kibbey, 1980), an activity that enlists children in exploring the placement of rational numbers on the number line.[4] Balloons are tied to a number line, and children shoot darts at the balloons by estimating their positions on the line. Fractions, decimals, mixed numbers, and expressions using operations are all acceptable inputs. In response to each input, a dart flies across the screen at the specified height and lodges in the number line, breaking a balloon if it hits one.

In Figure 1.2, the first dart was shot at 1/2, and a second dart has been shot at 1/3. No balloons have been hit, and some curriculum designers might think that this is an appropriate time for the computer to intervene with help. But how can we guess what help is needed? If the intended target for the shot at 1/3 was the plain balloon, perhaps the child meant to enter 1 1/3 but left off the whole number part. On the other hand, taking

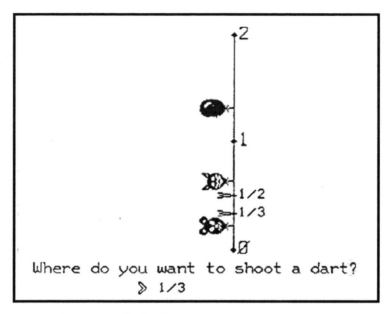

Figure 1.2.   Screen display from Darts.

into account the previous shot at 1/2, perhaps the intent was to hit the cat balloon, and there is a misconception that larger denominators make larger numbers. However, if the intended target was the mouse balloon, then the child may be homing in with successively smaller fractions, and the next shot will probably be a hit. These three possibilities were common occurrences in our observations, and in each of these scenarios, placement of the dart (in this case at 1/3) was sufficient for children to diagnose the error or confirm progress.

However, in observing a particular child's interaction with the display in Figure 1.2, we might well find that *none* of our guesses above come close to what the child had in mind. For example, in shooting the second dart at 1/3, the child might have been simply asking "How big is 1/3?" in order to use that distance to measure off 2/3, 3/3, 4/3, and so forth, to see which balloons might be hit by thirds. Indeed, this specific strategy was observed during the early classroom testing of Darts. A child using this strategy entered fractions of the form $1/n$, for successively larger integer values of n (and hence, successively *smaller* values of $1/n$). After shooting each $1/n$ dart, she placed her thumb on 0 and her index finger on $1/n$ to measure the distance from 0 to $1/n$. Keeping this distance between thumb and index finger and making a matching distance with the thumb and index finger of her other hand, she went hand-over-hand counting intervals up the number line (1/n, 2/n, 3/n, etc.), searching for balloons that could be hit with fractions of denominator n. If there were balloons remaining after she shot these, she increased n by 1, and began again. She was using the computer to locate 1/n, using the idea that m/n corresponds to m intervals of size 1/n, and defining a general algorithm for hitting all of the balloons. Hence, even the basic assumption that a child intended a particular shot to hit a balloon could be wrong. To respond as if the child *should* have been trying to hit a balloon (e.g., asking "What balloon are you aiming at?") could discourage some of the more novel and mathematically interesting approaches that we observed.

In sum, children's interactions with our prototype fractions models were both more social and more mathematically diverse than initially anticipated. Serious diagnosis and branching based on keypresses might be realistic in a more tightly controlled curricular environment, but not within the sort of learner-centered exploration we sought to encourage. Plans to test extensive diagnostic branching were abandoned, not because of the difficulty of implementation, but because they were not compatible with the children's learning and interaction styles.

Interaction and Feedback

As we observed increasingly many children engaged in computer activities, we honed our sense of what program characteristics were most effective in fostering the thoughtful engagement and comfortable working knowledge of mathematics that we sought. We were most encouraged by our observations of children's manipulation of models that were direct expressions of the mathematics. In particular, we became very interested in the apparent advantages of responding to children's input by simply interpreting that input in terms of the mathematical model and leaving the diagnostic analysis to the children, as noted in the preceding painting and number line examples.

For example, in the Darts activity discussed above, the graphic, non-judgmental feedback of the dart placement simply reflects a child's input. It essentially says, "Here is what you did," and leaves the child to decide how that relates to what was intended. Because the mathematics is intrinsic to the model, a manipulation of the model provides its own feedback. This feedback is both clear and open to personal interpretation. As evidenced above in the discussion of Figure 1.2, for any given interaction, a particular child's interpretation of the resulting display depends on what the child was thinking and trying to do. I suppose it could be argued that individual perception occurs for any type of feedback, and perhaps the difference here is that the feedback is *invariably relevant* to whatever the child had in mind.

The strategies children developed and used to approach such mathematical models were numerous and varied. For example, it was common to see a child measure the distance between integers on the Darts number line by counting finger widths from one integer to the next (thus establishing a denominator). This was usually done with the index fingers of both hands, alternately placing one index finger above the other while counting how many it took to reach from one integer to the next. The child would then use the same technique to measure the distance to each balloon (for the numerator). With this strategy children were frequently observed to use fractions like 9/13 or 11/17 as naturally and meaningfully as 1/2 or 1/3. They were clearly operating with a general notion of fractions that extended comfortably and naturally to any denominator.

One particularly careful child counting finger widths between integers found her thirteenth finger placement directly on an integer, half above and half below. She paused momentarily, and as the observer, I suspected she was considering whether to use twelfths or thirteenths. To my surprise and delight, she used twenty-fifths, mentally combining her final half-finger width with the preceding twelve finger widths (or 24 half-finger widths) to get 25 half-finger widths between integers. She expressed her numerator in half-finger widths as well (i.e., doubling the number of finger widths she counted) for a successful shot.

In applying their beginning knowledge of fractions to a mathematically accurate interactive model, children early in the study of fractions were able to pursue their own thought paths to arrive at ideas well beyond what was usually anticipated or supported at this stage. They seemed also to be building a comfortable working familiarity with rational numbers that could serve them well in later work.

As an aside, "learner control" was a popular topic in curriculum development at the time, and the term typically referred to explicit choices offered to students. For example, there might be a choice of the type of problem on which to work, or whether to see an example or a rule before proceeding with solution of a problem. Children's work with Darts and other models of similar characteristics seemed to exemplify a more subtle form of learner control. Children set their own goals and pursued their own strategies. Graphic feedback, reflecting the input and leaving the diagnostic thinking to the child, provided a wide bandwidth of information from which the child noticed only that which related to his or her particular intent.

Even when offering verbal feedback, as noted in the box-painting activity earlier, we were more satisfied with children's engagement and apparent thought processes when the feedback simply reflected in mathematical terms what the child had done. In the example cited previously, the feedback, "You painted 3/10 of the box. Now paint 3/5 of the box," seemed to give adequate and appropriate guidance without usurping the child's responsibility to solve the problem.

Of course, this is not the only type of interaction or learning experience needed to develop understanding of and facility with mathematics. However, such activities represented a dramatic departure from previous computer-learning environments, and they used the capabilities of the technology especially well to accommodate children's differing thought paths and to add a new and positive dimension to children's learning experience.

Mathematical Community

A common concern of the time was that children working on computers would be isolated from their peers and not develop normal social skills. For us, this translated into a concern that children having a substantial part of their mathematical activity on a computer might lose out on the important human interaction characteristic of active learning environments in which mathematical meaning is negotiated, misconceptions are dealt with, and shared understanding is developed.

Our early observations, however, suggested that it was not the natural tendency of children to become solitary learners in a computer context. Given the opportunity, children engaged readily in peer interaction as they pursued tasks presented by the computer. Even in classrooms in which a teacher assigned each child individually to a computer workstation and allowed no extra participants in the area, children showed interest in what was happening on neighboring screens, shared their successes, and relied on each other for assistance. Further, the overt physical activity that helped us as observers to understand children's problem-solving processes were easily noticed and imitated by other children, as well. For example, a child measuring number-line distances in finger widths would soon have several classmates using the same or similar techniques.

We were encouraged by children's propensity to interact with each other in the context of our computer-based prototype activities. Beyond this, we recognized that the system's network capabilities offered potential for other types of interaction, and we set out to investigate ways in which these capabilities might be used to expand children's involvement in a mathematical community (Dugdale, 1979).

Libraries

One of our efforts to exploit the system's network capabilities consisted of "libraries" associated with some of the activities.[5] For example, the

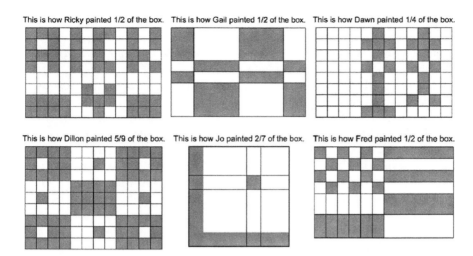

This is how Ricky painted 1/2 of the box.   This is how Gail painted 1/2 of the box.   This is how Dawn painted 1/4 of the box.

This is how Dillon painted 5/9 of the box.   This is how Jo painted 2/7 of the box.   This is how Fred painted 1/2 of the box.

Note: Although these six isolated examples may seem to be a disjoint collection, in the actual library, each was accompanied by numerous other contributions that constituted children's creative variations of the same theme.

Figure 1.3.   Six children's contributions to the Paintings Library representing some of the many "themes" that appeared in the library.

Paintings Library was created as a follow-up to the initial box-painting activity mentioned earlier. In the Paintings Library, when a finished painting represented correctly the requested fraction of the box, it could be saved in the program's electronic library for others to see. This enabled an ongoing exchange of ideas among children in many different classrooms, even in different schools and communities. Figure 1.3 shows a few such paintings from the pilot trials of the fractions curriculum.

Our pilot trials of this program indicated that the number of children participating in a library can be a critical factor in its success. The Paintings Library was first piloted with only four children. Although they could be described as bright, creative children from an open classroom environment, their paintings were unimaginative. Each child contributed some paintings and looked at the paintings stored by the other three, but new ideas were few and enthusiasm was only mild. The stored paintings were not noticeably different from what these same children had done in the initial box-painting activity in which the goal was simply to represent correctly each fraction the program presented.

However, during a later 3-week period when 300 children participated in the Paintings Library, it exploded with new ideas daily as children examined each other's work and responded with their own. The interaction of children's ideas was quite apparent as fads spread through the library. For example, one child's painting showed his own name, "Ricky," as seen in Figure 1.3. Within a few days, there were numerous paintings showing other children's names and initials. This was followed by an exchange of the message "Hi" in an array of styles and fractions until someone contributed a painting that said "Bye!" One child removed some of the lines from her painting before storing it in the library, and the removal or addition of lines quickly became a popular artistic variation. For example, for her painting in Figure 1.3, Jo most likely divided the box into sevenths horizontally and vertically (creating a 7×7 grid) then painted the leftmost column and the bottom row, plus one square. Before storing her painting, she removed all lines except the four that delineate the small painted square.

Given the incentive for creative contributions to the library, while still meeting the challenge of painting the designated fraction of a box, children were observed to engage in lines of mathematical reasoning that had not been apparent in the initial painting activity. For example, some children would begin with a simple representation of a fraction and then move pieces around for a more creative presentation, as Dillon appears to have done in Figure 1.3. Others partitioned the box and dealt with the parts separately, making sure the designated fraction of each part was painted, as Fred may have done in Figure 1.3. For fractions like 1/2 or 1/4, children often divided the box into small squares, figured out the total number of squares (often by multiplying), and then divided the number of squares by two or four to decide how many squares to paint. Paintings similar to Dawn's in Figure 1.3 were usually done by this method.

Observation of children's participation in the Paintings Library suggested potential for a productive classroom discussion and activity based on their various methods of verifying what fraction of a box was painted. Asking "How can we be sure that the right amount is painted?" for each of several of the children's paintings might have led to a class collection of methods that would have enhanced the learning experience for all of the children. Readers can no doubt imagine such a collection of rationales for the examples in Figure 1.3. My own favorite from Figure 1.3 is Gail's painting, which can be folded in half either vertically or horizontally to see that one half of the box is painted. (Regardless of which direction it is folded, the painted areas of one half are superimposed exactly onto the unpainted areas of the other half.)

Jo's contribution to Figure 1.3 is representative of a theme that persisted for some time in the library. To represent 2/7, she painted 1/7 of the box horizontally and 1/7 vertically, then painted another square to make up for the overlapping area. Of course, each example can be thought about in multiple ways. We initiated promising preliminary discussions with one fourth-grade teacher about piloting such a class activity, but we did not have time to pursue this opportunity further at the time. The Paintings Library clearly engaged children, and a well-organized follow-up might have been quite fruitful in making explicit for all children the habits of mathematical thinking that were developing for some.

Encouraged by children's positive response to the Paintings Library, we included a Paint Addition Library later in the curriculum. Here children used two kinds of paint to illustrate an addition problem. Children could ask the program for a problem to illustrate or they could create their own. In either case, after representing each of the addends correctly, the child had to tell how much of the box was painted altogether. Children sometimes approached this last step by drawing lines on the box until it was divided into some number of equal pieces, each of which was either all painted or all unpainted (a visual method of finding a common denominator for the two fractions). Figure 1.4 shows two children's representations of additions.

The most nonstandard of our initial interactive fraction models is Skywriting. Designed specifically to interject a model different from the usual fraction representations of lengths, regions, and sets, this activity invites children to write a simple program to move an airplane around the screen. The programming language originally had three commands: one to move the airplane forward, one to turn the airplane through an arc specified as a fraction of a circle, and one to repeat the program. The airplane leaves two types of smoke trails:

- It leaves one puff of smoke for each unit of forward motion, so, for example, the command "8f" moves the plane eight units forward and leaves a straight trail of 8 puffs of smoke.

This is Ruth's painting: 2/5 + 1/2 = 9/10   This is Karen's painting: 40/81 + 5/81 = 5/9

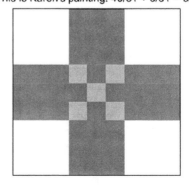

Figure 1.4.   Two children's contributions to the Paint Addition Library.

- It leaves an arc of puffs for each turn. For example, given the command $\frac{1}{2}t$, the plane proceeds in a counterclockwise arc through one-half of a circle and leaves a semicircle of smoke puffs to mark the path. Turns are of fixed radius, the command "1t" executes a full circle, and negative numbers produce clockwise turns.

Based on initial testing with children, we added a choice of either spot turns or arcs and a command to turn the smoke trail on and off. Of course, it would not be appropriate to have an airplane making spot turns. After some thought about what sort of moving object could reasonably make spot turns and leave a trail, we settled on a spider. The program became Skywriting and Spider Web, with the type of turn dependent on children's choice of an airplane or a spider.[6]

When we added libraries to facilitate children's exchange of creative work using fractions, Skywriting and Spider Web was an obvious candidate for which to include a library. Figure 1.5 shows four children's contributions to the library. In each frame, the child's program appears at the top of the screen. As the program runs, a moving pointer marks the step that is executing. At the bottom of the screen is the child's name and the title he or she entered to identify the work in the library. When the airplane or spider goes off an edge of the screen, it automatically "wraps around" to the opposite edge and continues its path, as shown in Jennifer's and Julie's library contributions in Figure 1.5.

Children's activity in the Skywriting and Spider Web Library had a decidedly experimental aspect. After entering several commands and achieving a shape they liked, most children would ask the program to repeat and see what happened. (The repeat option was popular, and most stored programs included it.) As is apparent in Figure 1.5, the titles children chose to identify their work in the library were often descriptive of the resulting pattern. Although children exhibited a sense of what would happen as they entered each command and watched it execute, it was not common to see children anticipate the pattern that would result when the program repeated. Their open experimentation with the repeat option was a natural and appropriate stage in exploring a new model, and we were encouraged to see the extent of children's enthusiasm and involvement as they contributed to the library and viewed each other's contributions.

We also recognized a wealth of further mathematical reasoning that could be pursued, and we hoped for more of this to emerge in children's sharing of examples in the library and in their consequent discussions with classmates. For example, it is a simple matter to recognize that programs of the form "n forward, $1/m$ turn, repeat" always run m iterations

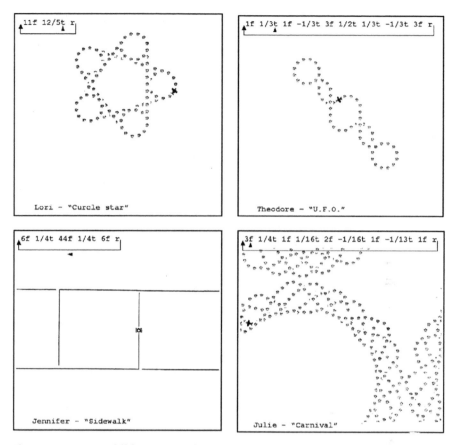

Figure 1.5.   Four children's contributions to the Skywriting and Spider Web Library.

before retracing their paths, and that the resulting figure has m "corners." In fact, even if the numerator is an integer other than 1, as long as the numerator and denominator are relatively prime, the resulting figure still takes m iterations and has m corners (as seen in Lori's library contribution in Figure 1.5).

Relationships between the fractions in the program and the number of repeats and corners in the resulting pattern become more interesting for programs that include more than one turn. Proceeding systematically from programs with one turn to programs with two turns, and experimenting with combinations of denominators for the two fractions in those turns is a productive next step on the route to understanding the relationship between the fractions and the resulting pattern. A legitimate question at some point is whether all programs eventually retrace their paths, regardless of the number of turns or the fractions used. Although children were not observed to initiate this sort of analysis on their own, many of their contributions to the library could have formed the basis of a well-planned class project. Like the Paintings Library, given some well-structured classroom follow-up, the children's work in the Skywriting and Spider Web Library could have been the starting point for more serious investigation of the mathematics involved.

In the final analysis, it was apparent that programs like the Paintings Library, Paint Addition Library, and Skywriting and Spider Web Library increased dramatically (a) the amount of time children chose to invest in working with a particular fractions model, (b) the intensity and depth of their engagement with the model, and (c) the variety and creativity of experiences they pursued with the model. Hence, it seems reasonable to infer that libraries contributed to children's understanding of and working familiarity with fractions. Even if this had been the limit of their usefulness, the libraries proved well worth supporting. As a bonus, the children's exchange of ideas in library programs could have set the stage for mathematical pursuits well beyond the basic work with fractions and fractions operations that was our primary charge in creating the fractions curriculum. There were abundant examples in the children's libraries suitable for initiating such discussions. Classroom activities specifically designed to tap this potential would have been likely in the next version of the curriculum, if resources had permitted investment in such a venture.

Real-Time Interaction

In addition to the rich exchange of ideas through stored examples facilitated by libraries, the computer network enabled interaction in "real time." Children at different workstations, even in geographically remote locations, could engage in the same activity at the same time, seeing the same display, and interacting through that display. For example, Torpedo! (see Figure 1.6) provides practice estimating distances on a number line. One player controls a boat, and the other controls a submarine. The object is to move to a point above (or below) the opponent's piece and shoot it. Sea animals are obstacles behind which one's boat can hide.

The two players take turns, and at first glance this could appear to offer nothing beyond having two children participating at the same workstation. Observation of children, however, revealed benefits that could not be duplicated by two children sharing a workstation. First, with the activity accessible from multiple classrooms, children could find someone to challenge to a game of Torpedo! even when no one in their own room was available to participate.

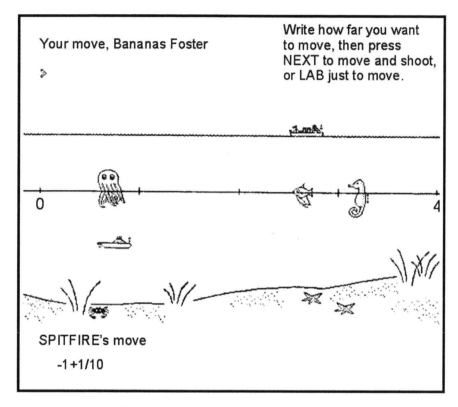

Note: A player using the name "Bananas Foster" controls the battleship. The object is to move the battleship to a position above the opponent's submarine and shoot the submarine, avoiding the sea animals in between. The opponent, "SPITFIRE," has just moved the submarine a distance of "-1+1/10" to hide under the octopus. One might speculate that SPITFIRE's thinking was that a move of -1 would be a little too far to the left, so adding 1/10 might be sufficient.

Figure 1.6.   Screen display from Torpedo!

Second, because each game typically lasted only a minute or two, children could play many different opponents in a short time. With the opponent's move specifications shown on the screen, children were likely to see a variety of methods using common fractions, decimals, or expressions with operations. A simple example of the resulting exchange of ideas is shown in Figure 1.7. Our observations indicated that children who were new to this activity did not think of entering zero as a distance to move. Even when a child found his or her game piece positioned ready to shoot the opponent's piece, the child would enter a small nonzero number rather than zero. (Adults did this, too.) Sometimes, much to the child's

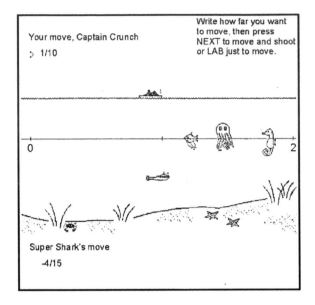

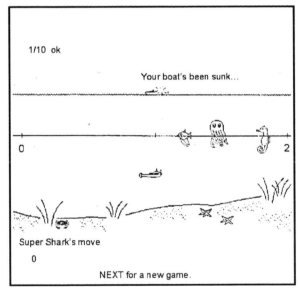

Note: In the first frame, a player who has chosen the name "Captain Crunch" is positioned so that a move of zero would win the game, but has instead entered a move of 1/10, hoping that this will be a small enough move to still hit the opponent's submarine. As the second frame shows, 1/10 was not only too big of a move (the weapon is on the front of the ship), it left the battleship directly over the submarine's weapon. "Super Shark," a more experienced player, has ended the game with a move of zero.

Figure 1.7.   Two frames from Torpedo!

TORPEDO!

1.	available	Bananas Foster	
2.	playing 4	Big Bad John	
3.	playing 16	Mermaid One	
4.	playing 2	King of the Sea	
5.	challenged by 7	Egg Fu Yung	
6.	available	The Shadow	
7.	challenging 5	Captain Crunch	
8.	available	Super Shark	
9.	playing Plato	Green Ghost	
10.	playing 13	Daffy Duck	
11.	playing Plato	The Hawk	
12.	challenging 15	Miss Piggy	
13.	playing 10	Captain Kirk	
14.	available	Celery Ltd.	
15.	challenged by 12	AQUAMAN	
16.	playing 3	Cap'n Nemo	

DATA   to update screen
LAB to play Plato

Note: Players are identified by pseudonyms they have entered. Players may challenge someone on the list, wait for a challenge from someone, or play against the computer.

Figure 1.8.   Choosing an opponent for Torpedo!

distress, the small nonzero move not only missed the target, but left the child's piece where a more experienced opponent could shoot it with a move of zero. It required few such experiences for the new player to realize that zero is a legitimate number that measures a sometimes-useful distance.

Third, Torpedo! players entered pseudonyms to identify themselves (see Figure 1.8). Players were free to use their real names, but they almost never did. Besides being considered fun, this anonymity avoided embarrassment over mistakes and encouraged participation of those children most in need of the experience. Children often changed their names after a losing streak. It was an easy matter to shed the "loser" identity and quickly show up on the challenge board looking (and perhaps feeling) like a new arrival.

The anonymity also made it possible for us to enter the children's world in ways that we could not do face-to-face. I occasionally entered Torpedo! when I was in my office. Using a pseudonym, I could participate along with the children to see what strategies they were using and to test the influence of an opponent's moves. For example, I sometimes initiated an exchange like that shown in Figure 1.7. Moving my piece into a position where it could be hit with a move of zero (like the submarine in the first frame of Figure 1.7), I waited to see what my opponent would do. My move looked like I had tried to hit my opponent's piece, but missed by just a little. If my opponent moved a little forward and missed as in Figure 1.7, I could end the game with a move of zero. I would quickly challenge the same player again and set up a similar opportunity. It often took two or even three rounds before my opponent learned from my game moves and began making effective use of zero. From the frequency with which I could lead an opponent to pick up a strategy, it was clear that children were paying attention to the moves that had defeated them and were adapting those moves successfully to apply to their own game situations.

We deliberately avoided time pressure in our activities because we valued the thoughtful and exploratory learning in which children so often engaged. However, observation of children using Torpedo! led us to add a timer option, so that children did not have to wait too long for an unseen opponent to move. Grumbling "Hurry up!" was unsatisfying and ineffective when the opponent was not within earshot, and not being able to observe the opponent's strategizing and screen-measuring activities made for an uninformative wait. In response to the timing dilemma inherent in Torpedo!, we created another real-time-interactive game. In this game, Obstacle Course, players working their way through a number line track on a shared screen display could interact if they chose to by bumping each other's game pieces, and no one had to wait for anyone else to move. (It felt somewhat like a game of lawn croquet without taking turns.) Obstacle Course allowed up to four players at different workstations to interact on identical screen displays. Although it eliminated the waiting for an opponent without imposing time pressure, it never gained the high level of popularity of Torpedo! The direct competition was apparently worth whatever time pressure or waiting time it entailed.

These early experiments with libraries and real-time interaction reinforced our enthusiasm for the computer network's potential to encourage and support mathematical activity in a mathematical community. The network linked children in widely separated locations and thus dramatically increased the number of children contributing to an activity. The influence of children on each other's work was obvious and positive, and the resulting variety of experience, richness of expression, and degree of motivation made this type of interaction an important aspect of the curriculum.[7]

Curriculum Structure and Management

The development of the curriculum structure and management was similar to the formative process employed with children's use of the computer-based activities. We developed the details of overall curriculum structure, teachers' curriculum management options, and off-line materials for children and teachers, in conjunction with ongoing classroom observation, interviews with children and teachers, and pilot tests of successive versions.

SUMMATIVE EVALUATIONS

In 1974, the PLATO fractions curriculum (Dugdale & Kibbey, 1980) included approximately 100 computer programs, a teacher's manual, and booklets and worksheets for children. The management system enabled teacher assignment of topics or individual activities, constructed personalized student sessions based on individual background information stored by the programs during interaction or entered by the teacher, and provided an extensive on-line data reporting facility for teachers and children to follow individual progress.[8]

External Evaluation

In the 1974-1975 school year, and again in 1975-1976, investigators from Educational Testing Service (ETS) conducted an external evaluation of the PLATO elementary mathematics materials, in accordance with a contract from the National Science Foundation. Each year's study included about a dozen PLATO classes and a dozen non-PLATO classes. These classes, at the fourth-, fifth-, and sixth-grade levels in eight different schools, included children from a wide range of scholastic achievement levels and socioeconomic backgrounds.

A major component of each year's ETS study was measurement of attitude and performance gains in each of the three content areas (whole numbers, fractions, and graphs) by means of pre- and posttests. Data from these studies indicated significant (in fact, large) positive achievement and attitudinal effects for the fractions curriculum at all three grade levels (Swinton, 1978).

Internal Evaluation

With the ETS evaluation in progress, we did not pursue an overall summative evaluation internally. However, the large, 2-year implementation provided opportunities beyond the earlier smaller-scale testing of parts of the curriculum. For example, the success of libraries and real-time-interactive programs became most apparent with large numbers of participants.

As with the introduction of any curriculum innovation, the quality and completeness of the implementation in a given classroom can play a large part in the impact of the innovation. In one fourth-grade classroom that had a high degree of integration of children's computer-based experience and the classroom mathematics curriculum overall, the teacher reported a startling change in children's response to learning about fractions. By mid-winter, her children were usually tired of fractions, negative about the topic, and needed to do something different for the rest of the year. After many years of this experience, her reasonable assumption was that fourth graders were simply not ready to progress further with fractions. During the 1974-1975 trial year, when this veteran teacher approached the time when she usually had to abandon work with fractions, she noted that her students had progressed further than ever before, were enjoying working with fractions, and were eager to do more. The teacher reported enthusiastically, "I will have to think about how to teach topics I have never covered before!"

CONCLUSION

This chapter has outlined the roles of research in the planning, development, and evaluation stages of a curriculum project. In the planning stage, it has featured the influences of several factors, including the developers' pedagogical assumptions and learning theory, the capabilities of the technology, and the structure of the development environment. In the development stage, the project's decisions were driven by extensive observation of children's interaction with software prototypes and careful examination of the products of that interaction. Examples in the chapter have illustrated the overriding influence of this formative research on the design of the curriculum. When children's learning and interaction styles contradicted initial assumptions, the assumptions were discarded or adapted to fit classroom reality. It is important to take an open-minded approach to a new medium. Relying on pedagogical methods from a familiar medium or designing around initial perceptions of the potential of the new medium may result in awkward, ineffective use of the medium and cause developers to overlook important opportunities for new learning modes.

The curriculum discussed in this chapter addresses fractions, a problematic area of intermediate grade mathematics that has been generally regarded as difficult to teach and to learn. Our initial development differed from standard curricula in the variety of models explored, the interactivity of those models, and the depth to which we had children pursue the models. Examples presented in the chapter illustrate the depth and intensity of children's mathematical engagement. The curriculum provides an exploratory, student-centered, active learning environment, and it proceeds with development of algorithms by students, based on manipulations embedded in familiar models.

Formative research refined our sense of what software characteristics were most effective in fostering the thoughtful engagement and comfortable working knowledge of mathematics we sought. We were most encouraged by our observations of children's manipulation of models that were direct expressions of the mathematics. In particular, we noted advantages of responding to children's input by simply interpreting that input in terms of the mathematical model and leaving the diagnostic analysis to the children. This type of learning environment played a central role in this and subsequent development projects.

Our experiences with children's mathematical interaction through libraries of stored work and real-time communication reinforced our enthusiasm for the potential of a computer network to encourage and support mathematical activity in a mathematical community. Children's influence on each other's work was obvious and positive, and the resulting variety of experience, richness of expression, and degree of motivation made this type of interaction an important aspect of the curriculum. Our later development projects also sought to establish the rich exchange of students' ideas and techniques that had proved so engaging and fruitful in the fractions curriculum.

Our perspective on how children learn mathematics evolved and sharpened as we interacted with children in a technologically intensive environment. Our perspective was influenced particularly by our observations of:

1.   children's abilities to interact with a mathematically consistent computer model, to interpret the results of their manipulations of

the model, and to use those interpretations to construct mathematical understandings consistent with the model; and

2.   children's propensity to involve other children in their mathematical activity, to share the products of their mathematical activity, and to learn the strategies and techniques apparent in the work of other children.

We observed children's learning to be interactive and constructive, with both individual and social components. In their compelling description of mathematics as both an individual constructive activity and a human social activity, Cobb, Wood, and Yackel (1990), note that "opportunities for children to construct mathematical knowledge arise as they interact with both the teacher and their peers," and that "their constructions are constrained by an obligation to develop interpretations that fit with those of other members of the classroom community" (p. 137). In our technologically intensive environment, children interacted not only with the teacher and their peers, but also with computer-based mathematical models. These models served as a test bed for children's mathematical constructions and provided an additional constraint to shape those constructions. Constructions that led to successful manipulation of a model thrived, and constructions that proved inconsistent with the mathematical model did not. For example, increasing a denominator in hopes of making a larger fraction was not successful in Darts, and the visual feedback provided by the model consistently indicated that increasing the denominator, in fact, resulted in a *smaller* fraction.

Overall, we developed a perspective consistent with that expressed by Davis, Maher, and Noddings (1990) in their distillation of areas in which constructivists are in general agreement about the nature of learners, the nature of mathematics, and appropriate forms of pedagogy. In brief, constructivists agree that learning mathematics is nonlinear and involves active manipulation of meanings to achieve conceptual understanding, that students should be led to challenge their own faulty conceptions, and that teachers should make contact with students' ways of thinking and help them develop more powerful ways of thinking.

Even during the summative evaluation years, we considered the fractions curriculum a "work in progress." Based on observation of children and classrooms, interviews with children and teachers, and collection of on-line data, we continued to improve the software, the curriculum structure, and the classroom support materials. When the project officially ended, we still saw potential for further development, such as classroom follow-up activities to exploit more fully the mathematical potential of children's work in the library programs. From this perspective, the culminating stage of the project might be viewed as the process of applying what we had learned to further development efforts. A subsequent chapter describes how the experience gained and the design principles distilled from the development of the PLATO fractions curriculum influenced the development of Green Globs and related microcomputer materials to support high school students' understanding of functional relationships.

NOTES

1. Grant number US NSF C 723.
2. The PLATO system is a development of the University of Illinois. PLATO is a service mark of Control Data Corporation.
3. For a more prescribed development environment of the time, see the rule-example-practice format of TICCIT (Rappaport & Olenbush, 1975).
4. I initially designed Darts in 1972 to demonstrate a more mathematically accurate alternative to children's learning activities that associated numbers with spaces or intervals on a "number line," for example, games in which children moved a game piece from space to space along a numbered track. I chose a dart to indicate more clearly a "point" on a number line, and a balloon to represent an interval that could be hit with multiple darts shot at different numbers within the interval. Several versions of the game have appeared subsequently, with varying resemblances to the original.
5. The idea of libraries was originated by David Kibbey. Work was begun in 1973 and first reported by Robert B. Davis at the NATO Advanced Study Institute of Machine Representations of Knowledge Conference, University of California, Santa Cruz, California, July, 1975. The resulting paper was published in *Machine Representations of Knowledge* (Davis, Dugdale, Kibbey, & Weaver, 1977).
6. Skywriting and Spider Web was originated by David Kibbey in 1973. Although the activity shares some characteristics with Turtle Logo, which was developed concurrently in the early 1970s at MIT (Papert, 1980), the two developments were independent. Both projects were well underway before interaction occurred between the two.
7. Unfortunately, such network-based activities were not supported by the stand-alone microcomputer environment that subsequently dominated the 1980s and early 1990s until the more recent dramatic growth of the Internet.
8. The individual programs that comprised the fractions curriculum have been available through NovaNET Learning, Inc. The support materials and management system are not currently available.

REFERENCES

Cobb, P., Wood, T., & Yackel, E. (1990). Classrooms as learning environments for teachers and researchers. In R. B. Davis, C. A. Maher, & N. Noddings (Eds.),

Constructivist views on the teaching and learning of mathematics (JRME Monograph Number 4) (pp. 125-146). Reston, VA: National Council of Teachers of Mathematics.

Davis, R. B. (1964). The Madison Project's approach to theory of instruction. *Journal of Research in Science Teaching, 2*, 146-162.

Davis, R. B. (1967). *Exploration in mathematics*. Palo Alto, CA: Addison-Wesley.

Davis, R. B., & Dugdale, S. (1976). The use of micro-assessment in CAI lesson design. *Journal of Children's Mathematical Behavior, 1*(Suppl. 1), 85-102.

Davis, R. B., Dugdale, S., Kibbey, D., & Weaver, C. (1977). Representing knowledge about mathematics for computer-aided teaching: Part II—The diversity of roles that a computer can play in assisting learning. In E. W. Elcock & D. Michie (Eds.), *Machine representations of knowledge* (pp. 387-421). Dordrecht, The Netherlands: D. Reidel.

Davis, R. B., Maher, C. A., & Noddings, N. (1990). Suggestions for the improvement of mathematics education. In R. B. Davis, C. A. Maher, & N. Noddings (Eds.), *Constructivist views on the teaching and learning of mathematics* (JRME Monograph Number 4) (pp. 187-191). Reston, VA: National Council of Teachers of Mathematics.

Dewey, J. (1963). *Experience and education*. New York: Collier.

Dugdale, S. (1979). Using the computer to foster creative interaction among students. In *Proceedings of the Association for Educational Data Systems* (pp. 153-159). New York: AEDS. (An adaptation of this work was published as CERL Report E-9, Computer-based Education Research Laboratory, University of Illinois, Urbana).

Dugdale, S., & Kibbey, D. (1980). *The fractions curriculum of the PLATO elementary school mathematics project* (2nd ed., CERL Report E-17). Urbana, IL: Computer-based Education Research Laboratory.

Lyman, T. (1984). CBI research and development centers—Computer-based education research laboratory, University of Illinois. *Journal of Computer-Based Instruction, 11*, 129-130.

Papert, S. (1980). *Mindstorms: Children, computers, and powerful ideas*. New York: Basic Books.

Piaget, J. (1973). *To understand is to invent*. New York: Grossman.

Polya, G. (1957). *How to solve it: A new aspect of mathematical method*. New York: Doubleday.

Rappaport, W., & Olenbush, E. (1975). Tailor-made teaching through TICCIT. *Mitre Matrix, 8*(4).

Smith, S., & Sherwood, B. (1976). Educational uses of the PLATO computer system. *Science, 192*, 344-352.

Swinton, S. (1978, March). *Outcomes of the PLATO elementary demonstration*. Paper presented at the annual meeting of the American Educational Research Association, Toronto, Canada.

Tenczar, P. (1974, May). TUTOR graphic capabilities. *Digest of Technical Papers*, Society for Information Display.

CHAPTER 2

THE DEVELOPMENT OF A DYNAMICAL GEOMETRY ENVIRONMENT

Cabri-Géomètre

Colette Laborde and Jean-Marie Laborde

THE DESIGN OF CABRI-GRAPH: A GRAPH THEORY ENVIRONMENT WITH DIRECT MANIPULATION

A major event in the history of computers and computer interface took place at the end of the 1970s. Rank Xerox invented the idea of direct manipulation for the management of an "electronic" desktop (Smith, Irby, Kimball, Verplank, & Harslem, 1982). Instead of the user entering commands in the usual symbolic way, direct manipulation makes it possible to physically manipulate files on the computer screen (opening, trashing, printing, mailing, sorting, and so on) by simply using a mouse. The Star machine was the implementation of the Xerox scientists' revolutionary ideas, ideas that were not recognized at that time, even within their company, as having any possible future.

Research on Technology and the Teaching and Learning of Mathematics:
Vol. 2. Cases and Perspectives, 31–52
Copyright © 2008 by Information Age Publishing
All rights of reproduction in any form reserved.

Just 2 or 3 years after this invention (in 1981), a group of French researchers in combinatorics and graph theory, all of whom were familiar with mainframe computing power and working in computer science departments, wanted to develop a computer environment to help research in graph theory take advantage of new graphical devices. They launched a national project focusing on the design of a computer environment supporting exploration in graph theory. Some members of the project, especially those in Grenoble at IMAG (Institut d'Informatique et Mathématiques Appliquées de Grenoble), encountered the Lisa[1] machine and realized how revolutionary it would be to base a mathematical computer tool on direct manipulation. It was revolutionary in that some computer environments for graph theory already existed, but all were based on symbolic communication with the computer. The goal of the project was to offer the power of technology to noncomputer scientists for their research work and to put technology in their hands as a tool for exploring and conjecturing.

Why Graph Theory?

For a long time, conjecturing in graph theory has been common in this field's research community and to some extent officially sanctioned: It is accepted procedure to publish conjectures with only partial support (usually because counterexamples have not yet been found). The elaboration of conjectures is supported by exploration of examples by means of diagrams as a tool for exploring and conjecturing (J. -M. Laborde, 1995).

Research in a paper-and-pencil environment suffers from limitations such as: the large size of the examples and counterexamples to be found, computed, and checked; and computation that is hardly tractable even for relatively small graphs (graphs with less than 20 vertices). At that time having access to a computer for performing computation was not common, and the people initiating the project had only dreamed of combining the ease of paper-and-pencil work and the computational power of the computer.[2] These researchers in graph theory believed that looking at the same graph in different configurations (varying the position of the vertices) could lead to very different mathematical interpretations, for example, in terms of graph structure. The example in Figure 2.1 shows how the complete bipartite graph on four vertices, $K_{4,\,4}$, minus a perfect matching (the vertical edges), can be changed into the graph of the three-dimensional cube (Tallot, 1985). This was the starting point of the project for a "**Ca**hier de **Br**ouillon **I**nformatique for Graph Theory" (Computerized Sketchpad for Graph Theory) called Cabri-graph.

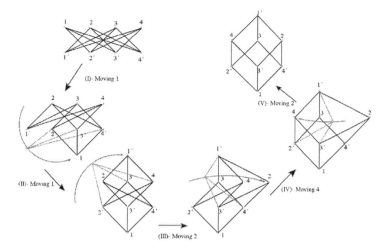

Figure 2.1.   From Graph $K_{4,4} - PM$ to the ordinary cube Q_3 in five drag and drop actions.

Design Choices

Two options for developing a Cabri for Graph Theory were possible. The first one involved taking advantage of the newly introduced raster devices (e.g., by Tektronics) working as a terminal connected to some, possibly remote, mainframe computer. The second option was to establish the feasibility of the concept by developing it as part of the concept of "personal computer" that was emerging at that time (soon thereafter IBM introduced the extremely popular PC). Because one of the aims of the project was to make the tools available to nonexperts in computer science, the second option was finally chosen.

The Development of Cabri-Graph

One year (1981-1982) was devoted to brainstorming about a computerized sketchpad for graph theory. During the 1982-1983 year, the decision was made to adopt the Lisa platform for the development of the project in Grenoble. The first phase ended in 1984 with the production of a prototype running on 6502-based machines (machines similar to the Apple II computer). Simultaneously, a psychologist in Montpellier investigated the ergonomics of direct manipulation and wrote a doctoral dissertation (Nanard-Brochot, 1990) that remains a widely quoted reference. Nanard-

Brochot developed the idea of "direct engagement" of the user. Some of her ideas are now considered classical and are often mentioned in treatises about computer interface (Schneidermann, 1998).

THE BIRTH AND DEVELOPMENT OF CABRI-GEOMETRY

Geometry and graph theory share a common feature: the importance of visualization. In 1985, Jean-Marie Laborde, one of the founders of the Cabri-graph project,[3] proposed the idea of using the drag capability for visualization in geometry. The specifications for a computerized sketchpad for geometry were given to two groups: (a) prospective engineers in computer science and applied mathematics (students in the last year of a "Grande Ecole of ingénieurs" ENSIMAG) to be developed as a project (J. -M. Laborde, 1985), and (b) the Apple Computer company.

Timeline of the Development of the Cabri-Geometry Project

End of 1984. Informal specifications for a computerized sketchpad for geometry (Cabri-géomètre) were proposed in May, 1985, to Apple. Apple provided older Lisa computers to the project.

November, 1985. Coding of Cabri-géomètre began on Macintosh and Lisa computers using Lightspeed C, an integrated environment. At that time Lightspeed C was the first programming environment to have implemented the concept of dynamic linking. This shortened the duration of the cycle (edit-compile-link-test-analyze-reedit-recompile …) to several minutes as compared to 5 to 10 minutes for previous systems.

June, 1986. The first prototype of Cabri-géomètre, developed by engineers Baulac and Cayet who were later joined by PhD student Bellemain, was produced. It was tested over the period of 1 month (May, 1987) in the classroom (Grade 9) of Bernard Capponi, a mathematics teacher in a school in the vicinity of Grenoble.

July, 1987. A technological preview of Cabri-geometry occurred at the conference of the International Group for the Psychology of Mathematics Education (PME 11) in Montreal.

1988. A working prototype was produced, and its use slowly spread among teachers, particularly in Switzerland, where schools at that time were widely equipped with Macintosh-type computers.

The first public presentation of Cabri-geometry (Laborde & Bellemain, 1988) occurred at the International Congress on Mathematical Education (ICME 6) in Budapest in August.

Cabri-geometry was awarded the Apple Trophy for the best educational software program in France. The Apple Trophy served as a catalyst for making Cabri known to a wider community and promoted the immediate, and at least partial, acceptance of the project by the computer science community.

Proposals for publishing Cabri came simultaneously from several software publishers in France.

Cabri-geometry was officially adopted by all schools of the canton de Vaud in Switzerland.

1989. Cabri was published in France.

The research group carrying out the Cabri project organized an international meeting in Grenoble on the use of computer environments for learning geometry.

1990. Cabri was acknowledged as an official IMAG project. (IMAG is the Grenoble CNRS University Institute for Computer Science and Applied Mathematics. The institute houses 700 researchers in computer science and applied mathematics.)

1994. Cabri II (Cabri's second generation) was released for the Macintosh.

January, 1995. A technological preview of the Texas Instruments TI-92 calculator was given at the joint meeting of the Mathematical Association of America and the American Mathematical Society in San Francisco.

1998. Cabri II for Windows was released.

2000. A Java-based version of Cabri was disseminated for use on the World Wide Web.

April, 2002. A preview of Cabri-Junior, a new version of Cabri for the Texas Instruments TI-83 Plus calculator, took place at the annual meetings of the National Council of Supervisors of Mathematics and the National Council of Teachers of Mathematics in Las Vegas.

Comments Related to the Chronology

The preceding chronology exemplifies how long it takes for a new idea to be widely adopted. Some reasons for the length of the acceptance process will be offered in the next section.

A second comment deals with the dialectic between continuity and change according to which the project developed. In all versions, there was a continuous effort to implement a user-centered interface and to extend the direct manipulation. The second version of Cabri offered a greater number of feedback messages to scaffold the user's actions. After the user selects a tool, as soon as the user moves the pointer close to an object that can be designated as an argument of the action performed by

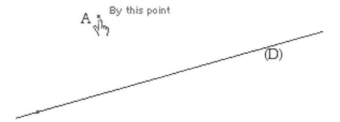

Figure 2.2.   Designating point *A*.

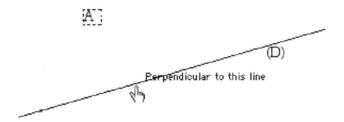

Figure 2.3.   Designating line (*D*).

the tool, Cabri displays a message indicating the role that the object could play in the action to be performed. Figures 2.2 and 2.3 show the messages displayed when designating the point and the line involved in the construction of the line perpendicular to line (*D*) passing through point *A*.

The messages in Figures 2.2 and 3.2 scaffold the use of the software in part because they express the nature of the designated objects. More importantly, however, they specify the type of relation between the object and the perpendicular line by using prepositions: "By this point" means that the perpendicular line is passing by (through) the point, whereas "Perpendicular to this line" clearly expresses the relation between the line to be constructed and given line (*D*). If no message appears when the pointer is close to an object, it means that the object cannot enter into the construction of the perpendicular line. Note that the message "On this circle" (Figure 2.4) appears when the tool "Perpendicular line" is selected: The only possible interpretation is that the user wants *a point on* the circle through which the perpendicular line should pass.

An example of the extension of direct manipulation from the first version of Cabri to the second can be seen in the construction of the intersection points of two objects. In the first version of Cabri, the user had to designate the two objects by means of the mouse. This turned out to be tedious when constructing a complex figure. It also created difficulties for

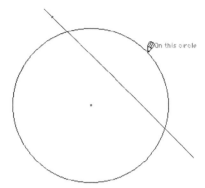

Figure 2.4.   Designating a circle on which a point will be constructed in the process of constructing a perpendicular line.

students who wanted only to show the location of the intersection point instead of showing the two objects. This behavior on the part of students revealed the conceptual difficulty of having a functional view of the geometric objects. The teachers appreciated that the use of Cabri required such a view and were opposed to easing the students' struggles by allowing construction of the intersection point solely by indicating the location of the point. In the design of Cabri II a decision had to be made about these conflicting views. The decision was made to allow the user to choose the interface: The user can construct the point by showing the two objects (by selecting a preference in the Preferences menu) or the user can show the location of the intersection point using the default option. This allows teachers to ask novice students to show both objects when first using Cabri and later to move to the quicker option. However, almost a decade of experience with Cabri II shows that teachers generally do not use this way of configuring the interface.

All of the previous examples illustrate the complexity of choices in the design of suitable interfaces from the point of view of learning and ease of use. In research done in psychology on the ease of use of software, few studies have examined interface effects specifically in the domain of mathematics.

The question of order, "selection then action" or "action then selection," has raised a heated debate for several years on the Math Forum Web site.[4] Action refers to the operation to be performed, while selection refers to the choice of the objects on which the tool should act. The question being discussed was whether action should precede selection or vice versa. For example, the Geometer's Sketchpad (GSP) (Jackiw, 2001) is based on selection then action, except for simple objects (line, line segment, or circle), whereas Cabri is based on action then selection. Blanc-

Brude (2000) contrasted the use of Geometer's Sketchpad and Cabri on construction tasks by novice users (10th-grade students) of both software programs. He observed that students exhibited no speed difference in basic constructions between the two programs, but that for more complex constructions their planning time was greater in Sketchpad than in Cabri. Two features, the way in which action and selection are ordered and the influence of mathematics, might explain this difference:

- The consistent use of action then selection for the construction of objects in Cabri might reduce planning time, whereas planning time might be greater with the Geometer's Sketchpad because the user has to change the point of view when passing from basic objects to more complex ones (such as line perpendicular to, midpoint of); and

- In mathematics what is important are the functional dependencies between objects more than the objects themselves; they are what constitutes the essence of the meaning of the object to be constructed. When constructing the line perpendicular to line (D) passing through A, the meaning resides mainly in the word *perpendicular*. So perpendicular may become the goal of the action to be performed. Furthermore, the objects in a dynamical geometry environment are variable, whereas the relations remain invariant. These reasons may lead to the assumption that there is a hierarchical order of thought when considering the process of constructing an object that depends on other objects, such as a line perpendicular to a given line. The first consideration is the goal of the action that expresses the relation and then the objects on which it operates.

Another instance of changes in the move from Cabri I to Cabri II was the extension of tools that served to enhance the relationship with mathematical activity and facilitate the teaching of mathematics. Cabri I was purely geometrical in that it did not contain any measurement capability. Because of requests coming from teachers, new capabilities were introduced in Cabri II: measurement, transferring measurement, and locus of points as an object. These capabilities allow students to relate geometry and real-valued functions. They also allow one to give a geometrical meaning to the notion of the graph of a function. The introduction of coordinates and equations of lines and conics also established a link between geometry and algebra. Even if these changes were partly due to expectations about teaching with Cabri, some new ways of using the tools introduced in Cabri II were discovered by the users—teachers or researchers in mathematics education—as they used the tools.

Changes in the software were driven by the continual goal of increasing the directness of the interface (Hutchins, Hollan, & Norman, 1986) and improving the opportunities for learning by keeping a user-centered view. This goal of the Cabri developers was the result of interactions with various research and teaching communities. This stance must be stressed. No educational software can be developed without such interactions. In particular, attention to research on teaching and learning is necessary to support such development.

CABRI IN THE RESEARCH AND TEACHING COMMUNITIES

We have identified four phases with respect to the types of reactions to and uses of Cabri by the research community and the teaching community. Although there is a chronological order to these phases, they developed in parallel to some extent (e.g., phases three and four). However, we mention dates for each phase in order to give an estimate of the period of time during which they were most prominent.

Phase One: Skepticism (1985-1990)

The idea to use the drag mode for geometry was due to the importance of visualization and of the appearance of drawings in both graph theory and geometry. The fact that the research team in graph theory and the research team in *didactique des mathématiques* (mathematics education) belonged to the same laboratory (Laboratory of Discrete Structures and Didactics–LSD2) certainly contributed to the development of reflections and research about the use of dynamical geometry for learning geometry. However, we must note that the idea of using technology, and especially the drag capability, initially was not well accepted by three communities: (a) the community of mathematicians, (b) the computer science community, and (c) the mathematics education community. The mathematics community thought that a dynamical geometry environment (DGE) eliminated creativity in mathematics because it allowed one to see immediately the properties that usually were discovered after long, hard work. Computer scientists did not see any research issues in the development of software for PCs, especially user-centered software. The mathematics education community did not view this kind of software as an object of study in the absence, at that time, of a substantial theoretical framework for such research. However, the views of these communities do not reflect simply the expression of a spontaneous rejection, since anyone might have an initial aversion to a novel idea in his/her field of activity that changes deeply the way of working. Rather than being a spontaneous rejection, these views stem from a deeper epistemological belief in each community about its particular scientific field.

The fear of loss of creativity expressed by mathematicians could be linked to the point of view that mathematics differs in its essence from the experimental sciences:

> *Les objets dont traitent les mathématiciens ne sont pas du tout de même nature que ceux des ingénieurs et des physicians.* (Dieudonné, 1987, p. 30) [The objects of work of the mathematicians are not at all of the same nature as those of engineers or physicists.] (translated by Colette Laborde)

Experimental sciences are aimed at describing observed phenomena while mathematics is building its own world within a system of rules developed only by the mathematics community. So mathematicians may have the feeling that they enjoy greater freedom and imagination than their counterparts in experimental sciences, as Dieudonné (1987) wrote:

> *Il y a toute une partie importante des mathématiques, qui a pris naissance pour fournir des modèles aux autres sciences, et il n'est pas question de les minimiser. Mais elles ne constituent certainement pas plus de 30 à 40% de l'ensemble des mathématiques contemporaines, comme il est facile de s'en rendre compte en parcourant la publication mensuelle Mathematical Reviews.... On peut dire avec Hardy que la raison principale qui pousse un mathématicien à faire de la recherche, c'est la curiosité intellectuelle, l'attrait des énigmes, le besoin de connaître la vérité.* (p. 39) [There is an important part of mathematics that was developed to provide models to the other sciences, and it is not the point to minimize them. But they constitute no more than 30% or 40% of all contemporary mathematics, as it is easy to perceive by reading the monthly publication Mathematical Reviews.... One can say with Hardy that the main reason that compels mathematicians to carry out research is intellectual curiosity, the attraction for enigmas, the need to know the truth.] (translated by Colette Laborde)

Externalizing abstract mathematical objects and their interrelations might appear as reducing the creative work of a mathematician to an observable work of reality. We interpret this as a fear, one linked to an epistemological view of mathematics as detached from reality and differing from a modeling activity. Noss and Hoyles (1996) stress that there has always been a dichotomy in the philosophical perspective on mathematics between "mathematics as a self-contained formal system, or mathematics as a way of conceptualizing the world: an opportunity to consider the place in mathematics of referential meaning, the practical, the 'real'" (p. 13). This dichotomy occurs in mathematics itself, and in parts of mathematics like graph theory (as explained previously) progress results from a dialectic between theoretical development and experiments or trials on external representations.

For mathematicians reluctant to use dynamical geometry diagrams, it is as if the process of elaborating a proof should deal with theoretical objects unrelated to their representations, not modified by actions on these representations. Bosch and Chevallard (1999) argue that mathematicians have always considered their work as dealing with nonostensive objects, and that the treatment of ostensive objects (expressions, diagrams, formulas, graphical representations) plays just an auxiliary role for them. This conception, according to which mathematical concepts exist independently of their representations, and which does not take into account interactions and mutual controls between nonostensive and ostensive objects, seems to underpin this dichotomy.

At the beginning of its development, Cabri was considered by computer scientists as essentially a graphical editor of diagrams for geometry. Computer scientists did not view the drag mode's preservation of geometrical relations as having any additional value. The fact that Cabri was developed for what at that time were called "micro computers" did not increase computer scientists' interest in it.

During the first years of the Cabri-geometry project, the French mathematics education research community had not yet developed theoretical approaches about the use of tools in mathematical work, perhaps because they were influenced unconsciously by the mathematicians' dichotomy between ostensive and nonostensive objects. Some investigations had been carried out in the Soviet Union after the World War II about the treatment of diagrams by students (Zykova, 1969) and about their difficulties in recognizing geometrical properties when diagrams were positioned in certain ways. These Soviet studies were followed by North American research in the 1970s and 1980s on the role of visual variables on the recognition of geometrical objects such as right angle or square, and in construction tasks of the image of objects through transformations such as reflection or rotation (Lesh & Mierkewicz, 1978). But no theoretical framework for the status and role of diagrams in geometry and geometry learning existed at that time. Some research on the learning of programming languages existed, but software in which actions were essentially performed without symbolic expression was a new type of object and mathematics educators had no theoretical means for dealing with this type of tool. It was only at the end of the 1980s and beginning of the 1990s that research on the use of diagrams in geometry emerged in France (Duval, 1988; Parzysz, 1988). In particular, Duval (1988) developed a theory to describe and explain the cognitive processes involved in solving a geometry problem, related to the perceptual activity of graphical representation. He showed how these processes are important for solving geometry problems (a more recent paper in English is Duval, 2000).

Phase Two: Dynamical Geometry as Posing and Solving Mathematical Problems (Beginning About 1990)

After some years of DGE existence, dynamical geometry posed theoretical problems in the three fields (mathematics, computer sciences and mathematics education) and therefore attracted growing interest in the three communities, although there was still strong resistance in some places.

One of the first core problems identified in dynamical geometry was the following: The construction of the symmetrical image of a line segment carried out in a step-by-step "manual construction" of intersection of lines and circles is not easy to manage in a "continuous" way. (The construction process in Cabri is illustrated in Figures 2.5, 2.6, and 2.7.)

To obtain a construction valid in the drag mode when A and B are not on the same side of the line of reflection requires some complex programming based on a fine geometrical analysis. The small number of software programs providing a construction for this case that remains valid in the drag mode shows that choices have to be made in the development of a software program among sometimes conflicting issues, such as maintain-

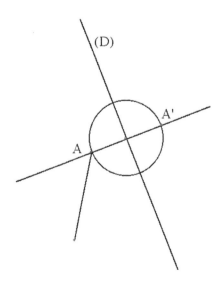

Figure 2.5.   Construction of A', the reflection of A.

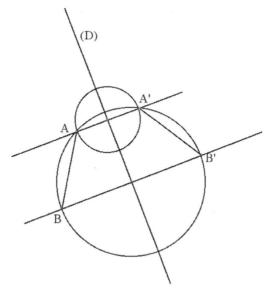

Figure 2.6.   The same construction process for *B'* and joining of *A* and *B* and *A'* and *B'*.

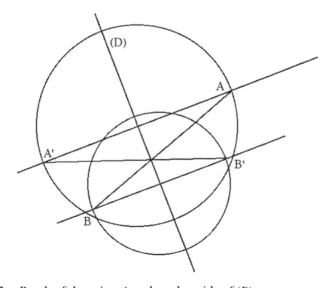

Figure 2.7.   Result of dragging *A* to the other side of (*D*).

ing mathematical validity while maintaining reasonable programming costs.

By identifying such core problems, one could determine how dynamical geometry differs from Euclidean geometry and the extent to which it represents a new type of geometry. Dynamical geometry is not only about geometry in the classical, static sense but also about the behavior of objects when they vary in the plane. The initial intention of the DGE authors was to create an environment for geometry that enhanced in a decisive way the visual possibilities of geometric diagrams. As part of this creation process, they had to make design decisions never before encountered about the behavior of moving objects. A classic example of such decisions deals with the behavior of a point on an object. What should be the behavior of point P belonging to segment AB when A or B is dragged? One decision could be to assign a random behavior to point P. From a theoretical point of view, this is completely valid because the only condition on P is that P is anywhere on segment AB. But from a visual point of view it could be surprising for the user to see jumps in the position of P on segment AB. So a decision ensuring continuity in the movement of P is to keep the ratio PA/PB invariant. Decisions on similar issues have been made according to the best judgment of the designers.

Instead of considering these problems solely as design problems, the researchers involved in the Cabri project recognized these problems as theoretical problems about a new kind of geometry, a dynamical geometry with its own objects and relations. A new field of research about the fundamentals of such a geometry was established. In particular, the theoretical problems pertaining to the axiomatic development of dynamical geometry remain under discussion at present. Contributions are being made, some of which were discussed specifically in a vibrant European meeting in Germany in December, 2000 (Gawlick & Henn, 2001).

In mathematics the idea of dynamic objects in geometry is very old (C. Laborde, 1992). The Greeks decided to consider movement as belonging to mechanics; movement was forbidden by convention in geometry more for metaphysical than scientific reasons (Bkouche, 1991). Later in the nineteenth century, the importance of imagining geometrical objects as moving objects was expressed by several mathematicians: Lobatchevski, Poincaré, and authors of several treatises, Méray (1874) in France and Treutlein (1911) in Germany.

In his introduction to the *New Principles of Geometry* Lobatchevski (1837) wrote:

En réalité dans la nature nous ne connaissons que le mouvement, c'est ce qui rend possible la perception de nos sens. Tous les autres concepts, par exemple ceux de la Géométrie, sont produits artificiellement par notre esprit et tirés des propriétés du mouvement et, pour cette raison, l'espace lui-même, pris à part, n'existe pas pour nous. [In fact in nature, we only know motion, it is what makes possible the perception. All other concepts, for instance those of Euclidean Geometry, are produced artificially by our mind and taken from the properties of motion. For this reason, space itself, and conceived as a separate entity, does not exist for us.] (translated by Colette Laborde)

The existence of dynamical geometry was revealed to an international audience in 1989 at a conference in Grenoble on artificial intelligence and education that was organized by the Cabri team: "Intelligent Learning Environments: The Case of Geometry" (J. -M. Laborde, 1996). This conference was a milestone in the story of dynamical geometry. Developers from the Cabri project and the Geometer's Sketchpad Visual Geometry Project recognized that their approaches, both of which emphasized continuity through direct manipulation using the drag mode, were reciprocal approaches that differed from what other groups supported—the power of randomly generated static snapshots.

Dynamic geometry was simultaneously used by various researchers in mathematics to create complex and dynamic representations of difficult problems, allowing them to solve these previously unsolved problems. Using Cabri, Dickey (1995) discovered new configurations of conics introduced by Steiner in connection with Pascal's famous theorem. Mollard and Payan (1990) improved the packing of circles by creating in Cabri a model in which they could change the configuration of the circles with very small variations produced by means of simulated levers (see Figure 2.8). The levers in the diagram are the segments of fixed length to which a circle is attached (by one of the endpoints of the lever). When the other endpoint is dragged, the endpoint attached to a circle moves and modifies the configuration of the circles. It is interesting to note that the same improvement was independently achieved by a numerical model requiring 2 hours of computing with a CRAY X-MP (de Groot, Peikert, & Würtz, 1990).

New theoretical problems related to the interaction between diagrams and geometrical objects also emerged in the field of research in mathematics education. Dynamical geometry highlighted the drawing/figure distinction already expressed by Parzysz (1988) and later refined by Sträßer (1992) and C. Laborde (1995). This distinction led to several reflections and empirical studies. In an important paper in 1993, Fishbein addressed the specific nature of geometrical concepts that he called *figural concepts*. Although his paper did not refer to dynamical geometry explicitly, he presented several ideas that were consistent with the theory surrounding DGE.

At about the same time numerous international researchers initiated empirical investigations of the use of Cabri, as evidenced in the proceed-

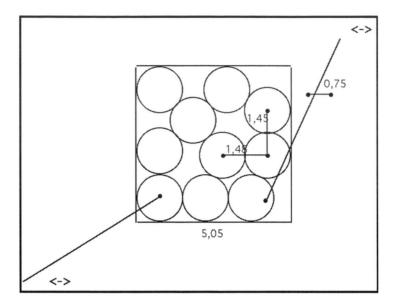

Figure 2.8.   A representation of the configuration of circles and levers that allow continuous movement of the circles and adjustments to the square.

ings of the 1992, 1993, and 1994 annual meetings of the International Group for the Psychology of Mathematics Education. These studies analyzed students' strategies when faced with construction tasks and investigated the use of the drag mode by secondary school students. Also, several doctoral theses in several countries were written at that time on the effect of the use of Cabri on the learning of geometry. DGEs were considered as an element of the "milieu" (Brousseau, 1998; Hollebrands, Laborde, & Sträßer, 2006), offering ways and means of actions in a constrained environment as well as feedback allowing evolution of the students' solution strategies.

Phase Three: Wide Dissemination and Integration Into Teaching

This phase differs from the preceding ones because it entailed widespread dissemination of Cabri and its integration into mathematics and physics teaching. In 1995 the availability of a handheld device (the TI-92 calculator) was the seed of future wider dissemination of advanced software technology. Several countries followed the example of the canton of Vaud in Switzerland, which equipped all schools with Cabri in 1988. Cabri became a tool for teaching geometry. An enquiry carried out by the French Ministry of Education showed that Cabri was used by students in activities while analogous software was used by teachers in their instruction. This can be interpreted as an indication of the effect of the efforts to create a friendly and direct manipulation interface in which the principle was to meet the possible expectations and interpretations of the users. A series of research questions follow: To what extent is there a link between the interface of a software program and the type of uses by teachers in their everyday practice? To what extent is it possible to distinguish user-centered software from teacher-centered software? and To what extent does the use of the software depend only on the teacher? During this phase several clones were developed in various countries. This was interpreted to mean that DGEs were having an increasing impact in mathematics education.

Phase Four: Institutionalization

The broad use of Cabri in France and many other countries and the adoption of GSP by many teachers in the United States gave rise to the creation of forums, summer institutes, and workshops for teachers. As a consequence this movement produced reflections on the use of DGEs in the curriculum. These reflections led to the recommended use of DGE in the curricula (and in some cases compulsory use) by institutions or ministries of education.

A typical example is the integration of DGE or geometry construction software programs into the curriculum in France beginning in 1996 at the middle school level and emphasized in the new curricula for senior high school in 2000. The curricula argue that introducing computers or calculators affects the very nature of mathematical activity and therefore the learning processes:

> L'outil informatique multiplie considérablement les possibilités d'expérimentation dans le champ des nombres et des figures du plan et de l'espace.... Cet outil élargit les possibilités d'observation et de manipulation.... L'environnement informatique peut permettre aux élèves de s'engager plus personnellement dans une situation ou une résolution de problème. De plus, il donne presque toujours la possibilité d'étudier une même notion ou propriété sous une plus grande diversité d'aspects; cela contribue à la démarche d'abstraction propre aux mathématiques et conduit à une meilleure compréhension. (Ministère de l'Education, 2001, pp. 8-9) [Computers multiply considerably the experimentation possibilities in the field of numbers and figures of the plane and of space.... Computers enlarge the possibilities for

observation and manipulation.... Computer environments can allow students to engage more personally in a situation or in solving a problem. Computer environments almost always allow the study of the same notion under a greater diversity of aspects; they contribute to the process of abstraction specific to mathematics and lead to a deeper reflection and better understanding.] (translated from the Grade 10 high school curriculum by Colette Laborde)

As reflected in the preceding quotation, a specific epistemological approach and learning hypothesis underlies the French national curriculum: Mathematics by essence is abstract, and to acquire mathematical concepts, students must themselves achieve these abstraction processes by manipulating, experimenting, and observing. Mathematical objects will be constructed by students as emerging from these experiments in a process of abstraction, eliminating all irrelevant aspects linked to the context of emergence. Technologies like computers favor abstraction processes in that they allow multiple experiments and thus may help distinguish the common relevant aspects from (irrelevant) aspects attached to the context. This view of mathematics as an experimental science is very new in the French institutional discourse and stands in contrast to the mathematicians' epistemological position mentioned in Phase One. Phase Four could be defined as the phase in which the existence of DGE affected the nature of taught mathematics, at least in the intentions of the curriculum designers. This is consistent with the *Principles and Standards for School Mathematics* (National Council of Teachers of Mathematics, 2000), which states, "Technology is essential in teaching and learning mathematics; it influences the mathematics that is taught and enhances students' learning" (p. 24).

DGEs are mentioned by the French curricula as supporting the move from an empirical geometry to a theoretical one and as preparing students for proof.

Ils permettent une approche plus dynamique des figures. En cela ils contribuent à initier les élèves au type de raisonnement que l'on propose de mener sur les objets théoriques de la géométrie. (Ministère de l'Education, 2001, p. 9) [They allow a more dynamic approach of the diagrams. They contribute thus to introduce students to the type of reasoning that we propose to carry out on theoretical objects of geometry]. (translated by Colette Laborde)

Ils permettent de donner une vision plus générale de la figure. (Ministère de l'Education, 2001, p. 9) [They give a more general vision of the diagram.] (translated by Colette Laborde).

This must be stressed since proof is a very controversial point in the debate among pros and cons about the use of DGEs.

Following the recommendations of the national program of studies, authors of French schoolbooks have introduced exercises using Cabri. Simultaneously the development of a Cabri Java version allowed the development of many Internet sites and resources for teachers, contributing to more widespread use of DGEs by teachers. Several books for teachers were written to help them to integrate technology into their teaching and in particular Cabri (both in its embodiments as a software program and as a calculator application) (e.g., Oldknow & Taylor, 2000).

The extensive use of Cabri in classrooms and general incorporation of instructional computing technologies provided evidence of numerous changes suggesting a genuine integration of new technologies into teaching. An important change required of teachers deals with the types of tasks they give to students with technology. Traditional tasks, as they are given in Cabri may make little contribution to learning if they do not pose a real mathematical problem. With Cabri, teachers must have access to new kinds of tasks that may be very fruitful for learning. This enterprise is not easy for them even if such tasks are described in research reports or books for teachers, since they require teachers to be aware of students' potential difficulties and solution strategies: They require of teachers a different management of the class (C. Laborde, 2001). Teacher education, both prospective and in-service, is needed to support the effort of society to integrate technology into the classroom. A new type of research about teacher education is thus now emerging: What is the impact of teacher education on the incorporation of DGEs into everyday practice in mathematics classrooms?

CONCLUSION

The Cabri project began more than 20 years ago. One of the important features of Cabri is its strong interrelation with mathematics throughout its development. It originated from the needs of a community of researchers in mathematics. Although Cabri was not immediately accepted by the teaching and research communities, it became accepted over time and the development process was able to take advantage of innovative uses of Cabri by teachers and researchers in mathematics education. This is certainly one of the reasons for the ongoing improvement and continuous evolution of the project. From the Cabri story emerges a question: How can a project strike a balance between pure innovation and attention to the expectations of the various communities linked with education, in order to have a substantial impact on education, that is, to change education itself?

NOTES

1. The Lisa machine became the first commercially available mouse-driven machine after Steve Jobs from Apple discovered the Star machine and realized its power. Unfortunately (for Apple) this first machine, the ancestor of the Macintosh, turned out not to be appropriately targeted from a marketing point of view and was not a commercial success.

2. Since graph theory requires visualization, it makes sense to experiment with graphs using the artistic and intuitive motions for construction with a screen pointer rather than with syntactically demanding verbal commands.

3. Other cofounders include Michel Habib (St. Etienne, Montpellier), Michel Chein (Paris, Montpellier), André Bouchet (Paris, LeMans), Claude Benzaken (Grenoble).

4. The Math Forum Web site was retrieved from http://www.mathforum.org on December 30, 2005.

REFERENCES

Bkouche, R. (1991). Variations autour de la réforme de 1902/1905 [Variations about the 1902/1905 reform]. *Cahiers d'histoire & de philosophie des sciences, 34*, 180-213.

Blanc-Brude, T. (2000). *"Action d'abord" vs "Sélection d'abord": Analyse comparative de deux méthodes syntaxiques dans deux logiciels de géomètrie dynamique (Geometer's Sketchpad et Cabri-géomètre)* ["Action first" versus "Selection first": A comparative analysis of two syntactic methods in two dynamic geometry software programs (Geometer's Sketchpad and Cabri-géomètre)]. Mémoire de DEA de Sciences Cognitives. Grenoble: Institut Polytechnique de Grenoble.

Bosch, M., & Chevallard, Y. (1999). La sensibilité de l'activité mathématique aux-Ostensifs [The sensitivity of mathematical activity to ostensive objects]. *Recherches en didactique des mathématiques, 19*, 77-124.

Brousseau, G. (1998). *Theory of didactical situations in mathematics, didactique des mathématiques 1970-1990*. Dordrecht, The Netherlands: Kluwer Academic.

de Groot, C., Peikert, R., & Würtz, D. (1990). *The optimal packing of ten equal circles in a square* (IPS Research Report No. 90-12). IPS, ETH-Zentrum, CH-8092, Zurich.

Dickey, L. (1995, January). *On a family of conics associated with the configurations of Pappus and Pascal*. Paper presented at the Joint Mathematics Meetings of the MAA-AMS, San Francisco.

Dieudonné, J. (1987). *Pour l'honneur de l'esprit humain* [For the honor of the human mind]. Paris: Hachette.

Duval, R. (1988). Pour une approche cognitive des problèmes de géométrie en termes de congruences Cabri [For a cognitive approach of geometry problems in terms of congruence]. *Annales de didactique et de sciences cognitives*, IREM et Université Louis Pasteur, *1*, 57-74.

Duval, R. (2000). Basic issues for research in mathematics education. In T. Nakahara & M. Koyama (Eds.), *Proceedings of the 24th conference of the International*

Group for the Psychology of Mathematics Education (Vol. 1, pp. 55-69). Hiroshima, Japan: Hiroshima University.

Fishbein, E. (1993). The theory of figural concepts. *Educational Studies in Mathematics, 24*, 139-162.

Gawlick, T., & Henn, H. -H. (2001). *Zeichnung-figur-zugfigur, mathematische und didaktische aspekte dynamischer geometrie software* [Diagram-figure-dragfigure, mathematical and didactical aspects of dynamical geometry software]. Hildesheim, Berlin: Verlag Franzbzecker.

Hollebrands, K. F., Laborde, C., & Sträßer, R. (2008). Technology and the learning of geometry at the secondary level. In M. K. Heid & G. W. Blume (Eds.), *Research on technology and the teaching and learning of mathematics: Vol. 1. Research syntheses* (pp. 155-206). Charlotte, NC: Information Age.

Hutchins, E. L., Hollan, J. D, & Norman, D. A. (1986). Direct manipulation interfaces. In D. A. Norman & S. W. Draper (Eds.), *User centered system design: New perspectives on human-computer interaction* (pp. 87-124). Hillsdale, NJ: Erlbaum.

Jackiw, N. (2001). The Geometer's Sketchpad, (Version 4.0) [Computer software]. Emeryville, CA: Key Curriculum Press.

Laborde, C. (1992). Enseigner la géométrie: permanences et révolutions, conférence plénière invitée [Teaching geometry: Permanence and revolution]. In C. Gaulin, B. Hodgson, D. Wheeler, & J. Egsgard (Eds.), *Proceedings of the 7th International Congress of Mathematical Education* (Vol. 1, pp. 47-75). Quebec, Canada: Presses de l'Université Laval.

Laborde, C. (1995). Designing tasks for learning geometry in a computer based environment. In L. Burton & B. Jaworski (Eds.), *Technology in mathematics teaching: A bridge between teaching and learning* (pp. 35-68). London: Chartwell-Bratt.

Laborde, C. (2001). Integration of technology in the design of geometry tasks with Cabri-geometry. *International Journal of Computers for Mathematical Learning, 6*, 283-317.

Laborde, J. -M. (1985). *Projet de cahier de brouillon informatique pour la géométrie, Archives of the Laboratory of discrete structures and didactique* (LSD2) [Project for a computerized sketchpad for geometry]. Grenoble: University Joseph Fourier.

Laborde, J. -M. (1995). Des connaissances abstraites aux réalités artificielles, le concept de micromonde Cabri [From abstract knowledge to the artificial reality of the Cabri microworld]. In M. Baron, D. Guin, & J. -F. Nicaud (Eds.), *Actes des 4 èmes journées francophones Environnements Interactifs d'Apprentissage avec Ordinateur* (pp. 29-40). Paris: Hermès.

Laborde, J. -M. (1996). *Intelligent learning environments: The case of geometry* (NATO ASI Series). Heidelberg: Springer-Verlag.

Laborde, J. -M., & Bellemain, F. (1988). Cabri-Geometry [Computer software]. Dallas, TX: Texas Instruments.

Lesh, R., & Mierkewicz, D. (1978). *Recent research concerning the development of spatial and geometric concepts.* Columbus, OH: ERIC.

Lobatchevski, N. (1837). *Nouveaux Principes de géométrie* [New principles of geometry], traduits du russe, Mémoires de la Société Royale de Liège, 3ème année, t.2, 1900.

Méray, C. (1874). *Nouveaux Eléments de Géométrie* [New elements of geometry]. Paris: F. Savy.

Ministère de l'Education. (2001). *Accompagnement des programmes, Lycée, Voie générale et technologique, Mathématiques, Classe de Seconde* [Accompanying booklet of the program of studies for high school technological and general track, Mathematics, 10th grade]. Paris: Centre National de Documentation Pédagogique.

Mollard, M., & Payan, C. (1990). Some progress in the packing of equal circles in a square. *Discrete Mathematics, 84,* 303-307.

Nanard-Brochot, J. (1990). *La manipulation directe en interface homme-machine* [Direct manipulation in human machine interface]. Thèse d'état, Université des Sciences et Techniques du Languedoc, Montpellier II.

National Council of Teachers of Mathematics. (2000). *Principles and standards for school mathematics*. Reston, VA: Author.

Noss, R., & Hoyles, C. (1996). *Windows on mathematical meanings: Learning cultures and computers*. Dordrecht, The Netherlands: Kluwer.

Oldknow, A., & Taylor, R. (2000). *Teaching mathematics with ICT*. London: Continuum.

Parzysz, B. (1988). Knowing vs. seeing: Problems of the plane representation of space geometry figures. *Educational Studies in Mathematics, 19,* 79-92.

Schneiderman, B. (1998). *Designing the user interface, strategies for effective human-computer interaction* (3rd ed.). Reading, MA: Addison Wesley.

Smith, D. C., Irby, C., Kimball, R., Verplank, W., & Harslem, E. (1982). Designing the Star User interface. *Byte, 74,* 242-282.

Sträßer, R. (1992). Didaktische perspektiven auf werkzeug-software im geometrieuntericht der sekundarstufe I [Didactic perspectives about tool software in geometry teaching at middle school]. *Zentralblatt für Didaktik der Mathematik, 24,* 197-201.

Tallot, D. (1985). *Quelques propositions pour la mise en œuvre d'algorithmes combinatoires* [Some proposals for implementing combinatorial algorithms], Thèse de troisième cycle, Université des Sciences et Techniques du Languedoc, Montpellier.

Treutlein, P. (1911). *Der geometrische anschauungsunterricht* [Geometry intuitive teaching]. Berlin, Germany: B. G. Teubner.

Zykova, V. I. (1969). The psychology of sixth-grade pupils' mastery of geometric concepts. In J. Kilpatrick & I. Wirszup (Eds.), *Soviet studies in the psychology of learning and teaching mathematics* (Vol. 1, pp.149-188). Chicago: University of Chicago.

CHAPTER 3

WHAT LIES BEHIND DYNAMIC INTERACTIVE GEOMETRY SOFTWARE?

E. Paul Goldenberg, Daniel Scher, and Nannette Feurzeig

If graphing software and then graphing calculators were the major mathematics education technologies of the 1980s, then dynamic interactive geometry environments (DGEs)[1] were among the most significant advances of the 1990s. Articles on DGEs appeared in nearly every issue of *Mathematics Teacher*, DGEs form the basis of numerous Java geometry web pages, and a whole volume on DGEs (King & Schattschneider, 1996) has been published by the Mathematical Association of America.

DRAWING AND DRAGGING

Dynamic interactive geometry software allows students to create geometric constructions and then manipulate them easily. Dragging, the "dynamic" feature of DGEs, allows users to move certain elements of a drawing freely and to observe other elements responding to the altered conditions. The display gives the impression that the drawing is being

Research on Technology and the Teaching and Learning of Mathematics:
Vol. 2. Cases and Perspectives, 53–87
Copyright © 2008 by Information Age Publishing

continuously deformed throughout the dragging, while maintaining relationships that were specified as essential constraints of the original construction. Although these tools captured many imaginations right from the start, the vision that people now have of the potential impact of this kind of interactive geometry on students' mathematical learning is far broader than it was at first. Initially, these tools appear to have been seen almost exclusively in terms of geometry, as reflected in their names. Their advertising, the activities used for illustrating the tools, and the earliest articles about the tools, all treated DGEs as if they were a vitamin for Euclid. That has changed dramatically over time, as people began to realize the potential of this kind of interactive geometry on students' learning in many other domains, from early algebra through differential equations and physics. Given the versatility and impact of these tools—and the radical changes in even the designers' perceptions of the utility of their tools—it seemed important to learn what parts of the designers' vision antedated the software. What goals, intellectual climate, educational or mathematical principles, research questions, biases, or personal whims drove the design and determined what was and was not built into the tools?

Why are we writing this history? There are at least two reasons. One reason is quite general: History helps us understand how ideas—in this case, clever and powerful educational software ideas—come into being. Understanding the evolution of a brilliant tool can spur future development efforts. To function in this role, the history must expose software ideas in their infancy, together with a trajectory of the tools' development. The other reason is more specific. A history of the mathematical and pedagogical intent of the developers helps shape our investigation and interpretation of the ideas that are tacitly bound into the software. It is these ideas that define the behaviors of the software, which, in turn, create the environment in which students derive new experience and on which they construct new mathematical ideas. Creators of mathematics curriculum and pedagogy need a thorough understanding of these ideas if they are to make informed use of DGEs. The same is true for researchers who want to develop focused and pedagogically useful studies of learning in DGEs.

This chapter describes the evolution of two DGE software programs—Cabri Geometry (Baulac, Bellemain, & Laborde, 1992, 1994) and The Geometer's Sketchpad (Jackiw, 2001)—with a focus on dragging and its consequences. We use early design documents and interviews with the developers to understand the decision-making process that led to such powerful educational software.

IS DRAGGING OBVIOUS?

In an age when we are surprised if something on our computer screen fails to move, it might seem natural, even obvious, that the static figures from Euclidean geometry should give way to dynamic ones. But "obvious" would be an inappropriate word to describe the foundations of dynamic interactive geometry. Despite the similarity of ruler-and-compass geometry to its software counterpart, the crafting of Sketchpad and Cabri was not a straightforward matter of transporting Euclid's axioms to the computer. Jean-Marie Laborde, creator of Cabri, explains that some departures from Euclidean axioms were inevitable:

> The general principle was to make the distance [between Cabri and Euclid] as small as possible, but at the very beginning I was not aware that it would remain finally at some distance.... People weren't happy at all [with the] expression "Cabri geometry." But we decided nevertheless to introduce that concept to make definite the point that what comes from the screen is not Euclidean geometry, it's not projective geometry.... It has to be different. (personal communication, April 8-12, 1993)

Nicholas Jackiw (1994), the designer and programmer of Sketchpad, echoes these comments:

> "Why hasn't anyone done this before?" is the most common initial reaction to seeing something like Sketchpad. But then ... one realizes something strange is going on behind the curtain—something that may seem intuitive, but which is by no means obvious, and by no means predetermined by the geometry and mathematics we understood before the advent of these programs.

Dragging does not behave the same way in all of the different implementations of DGEs. A post facto characterization of each piece is not sufficient to tell us what we need to know about dragging. We need also to understand the principles that led to a particular implementation—the prior thinking of the designers.[2]

PARTIAL HISTORIES OF TWO DGE TOOLS: CABRI GEOMETRY AND THE GEOMETER'S SKETCHPAD

Sketchpad and Cabri were, in their earliest stages, independently conceived designs whose teams were unaware of the existence of each other. Sketchpad began as an outgrowth of the Visual Geometry Project (VGP) at Swarthmore College, directed by Eugene Klotz and Doris Schattschneider. In the mid 1980s, the project proposed the development of a videotape series that would focus on three-dimensional geometry. Gene[3] says that as an "article of blind faith" he included interactive computer programs in the proposal description, as he felt video was a transient medium that would one day be replaced by the computer.

For programming, Gene turned to Nicholas Jackiw, a student he had advised during his freshman year. Nick's interests included both English and computer science (he began programming at the age of 9) but, perhaps surprisingly, not mathematics. In fact, he avoided mathematics courses entirely in college. Nick's first work for the VGP was a software program called Cavalieri. Nick describes the program as a foreshadowing of the dynamic element of Sketchpad. It allowed users to take a shaping tool—a virtual bulldozer—and "plow" into a figure from the left or right, reconfiguring its shape dynamically while preserving its area (see Figure 3.1). The original aim of the VGP was to accompany each videotape of a three-dimensional geometry concept with its own computer program. But given the time it took to complete just Cavalieri and the difficulty of programming three-dimensional models, Klotz and Schattschneider decided to shift their focus and create a single, two-dimensional graphics program. One of the earliest vector graphics programs to showcase the graphical capabilities of the computer was Ivan Sutherland's "Sketchpad" (1963). A hand-held light pen allowed the user to draw and manipulate points, line segments, and arcs on a monitor (Franklin Institute Online, 2000). Gene also wanted to mine the graphics potential of the computer; in honor of Sutherland's work, he named their new program-to-be "The Geometer's Sketchpad."

The first prototype version of Cabri Geometry was built in 1986, as a collaboration of Jean-Marie Laborde primarily with Franck Bellemain and Yves Baulac. Its roots lay in CabriGraph,[4] a tool developed even earlier (though first released in 1990), and in a French conception of geometric learning reflected in, for example, the work of Parzysz (1988) and C. Laborde and Capponi (1994).[5] CabriGraph (Cabri Project, 1990) allowed the user to create vertices, interconnect them with edges, and perform useful operations (like pruning) and computations (like finding the number of edges in minimal paths between vertices) on the resulting trees and networks. In this environment, the lengths of segments and the placement of vertices were merely cosmetic features, not mathematical ones. Still, dragging was a useful analytic tool, as it helped the mathematician make visual sense out of the potential tangle of edges, while the software maintained the topological invariants—the number of vertices and the way they were connected.

Jean-Marie had an original design document, "one page ... not going into detail."[6] From it, and from ideas gleaned from interviews with the designers of both DGEs we are describing, one can identify five principles

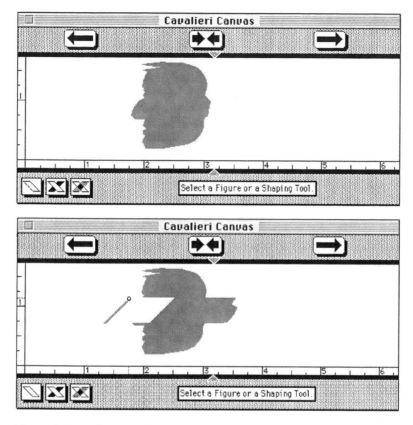

Figure 3.1. Using Cavalieri to "bulldoze" a face.

that guided much of their thinking: dragging, minimal distance from Euclid's geometry, reversibility, continuity, and minimal user surprise.

DRAGGING

The ability to "drag" objects and manipulate them dynamically is perhaps the most defining feature of Sketchpad and Cabri. Yet from a historical perspective, the ideas behind dragging and motion did not arise in a vacuum. Colette Laborde (1994) writes:

> The idea of movement in geometry is not new—the Greek geometers devised various instruments to describe mechanically defined curves—but the use of movement was nonetheless "prohibited in strict geometric reasoning" for reasons that were more metaphysical than scientific. The 17th

century marked a break with Greek tradition, and the use of movement to establish a geometric property or carry out a geometric construction became explicit. One can find numerous examples starting then....

This idea was first expressed in school geometry by the replacement of the geometry of Euclid's Elements by the geometry of transformations (which continues to be the only kind of geometry taught in some countries)—quite some time, one must point out, after the characterization of geometry as the study of the invariants of transformation groups, and also quite some years after a daring proposition made in France by Meray (*Nouveaux éléments de géométrie*, first edition, 1874).... Meray's idea was to teach geometry through movement: Translational movement allowed for the introduction of the notion of parallelism; rotational movement led to perpendicularity. (pp. 61-62, French original, translated by Paul Goldenberg)

Writing in 1945, Syer describes the ability of film to create "continuous" geometric images. His advocacy of the moving picture reads much like a modern-day justification for dynamic interactive geometry:

In addition to true-life demonstrations of solid geometry, it would be interesting to make greater use of the peculiar advantage of moving pictures over ordinary models. In plane geometry films, we used figures that changed shapes, position, and color without distracting pauses or outside aid. This continuous and swift succession of illustrations is fast enough to keep up with a spoken description, or even as fast as the thought processes that are developing the idea. Thus no time is lost erasing pictures from the blackboard, changing lantern slides, or holding up illustrations, because the illustrations and thought move simultaneously. (p. 344)

It is tempting to view the historical antecedents of a DGE's dragging feature as factors pivotal in its creation. The actual development of dragging, however, tells otherwise.

Early design plans for Sketchpad did not include a dragging component. Klotz envisioned the program as a way for students to draw accurate, static figures from Euclidean geometry:

Basic motor skills were keeping [students] from being able to draw. I thought we needed to have something that allowed people to make the basic constructions. So to me, [Sketchpad] was a drawing tool. You'd make a geometric drawing that was precise and accurate, and scroll over the page to see what was going on. (personal communication, January 5, 1995)

Drawing and selecting objects was to occur via the mouse or by issuing menu commands. Many of the proposed menu items and selection methods would be unfamiliar to today's user of Sketchpad. Table 3.1 lists several of them.

Table 3.1.   Drawing and Selection Methods

Drawing Options	*Selection Options*
• Draw point by typing coordinates	• Select point by giving coordinates
• Draw line segment by giving a point, direction, and distance	• Select circle by giving name (its label)
• Draw circle by giving the coordinates of three noncollinear points	• Select figure by listing part names

These options were sufficiently different from the standard Macintosh user interface to make Nick wonder whether there might be a better alternative. With the Macintosh, one could select objects and drag them directly with a mouse. Nick wanted to extend this notion to Sketchpad. His interest and experience in programming video games for the Macintosh helped inform his sense of what a computer geometry program could be:

> It's the video game aspect that gives me my sense of interactivity when dealing with geometry.... Looking at the input devices of video games is a tremendously educational experience. In the old days, you had games with very interesting controls that were highly specific.... [The video game] Tempest had a marvelous input device.... The types of games they would write to suit this bizarre and unique device were always interesting experiments in what does this hand motion transport you to in your imagination. I wanted to have a good feel in all of my games. (N. Jackiw, personal communication, January 4, 1995)

The Macintosh mouse was not an ideal input device for games, but it was suitable for manipulable environments where objects could be dragged. The illustration program MacDraw, in particular, contained the rudimentary features of DGE, as one could draw and move a segment with the mouse and change its length. When Nick took the basic premise of MacDraw and applied it (with considerable reworking) to Euclidean geometry, Gene found the results striking:

> I remember how shocked I was when I first saw it. [Nick] had played with a Macintosh long enough to know that you should be able to drag the vertex or a side [of a triangle] and protrude the figure. I was flabbergasted. I mean, he made the connection, and I didn't. (G. Klotz, personal communication, January 5, 1995)

Once Nick had decided to make Sketchpad "dynamic," he did not want any of its elements—even something as seemingly innocuous as labels—to suggest a static state. He says:

> I resisted labeling for a long time because I wanted the user to be engaged in the world of graphics. I didn't want things that made [the program] seem like it was representational, which labels seemed to me to do. They turned it into an illustration, whereas I wanted it to be a world. (N. Jackiw, personal communication, January 4, 1995)

Cabri had a similar history. Asked whether the dynamic feature was in any way a reaction to the Geometric Supposer (Schwartz & Yerushalmy, 1983-1991),[7] Jean-Marie said that at the time he had not even known about that software.

> In CabriGraph ... this dragging was a key feature of the software, as in Cabri later, without any [prior] command [to access it]. You just pick a point and move the point somewhere else on the screen. The idea was just to do the same in an environment where geometry would play a more important role than just the ... relationship between points and edges ... [I never even] considered any other alternatives. (J.-M. Laborde, personal communication, April 8-12, 1993)

While "drag mode" was an agreed-upon aspect of that new tool, its status was not immediately clear. For Jean-Marie, it was central—he had a strong interest in the "desk" metaphor and direct manipulation concept[8] as a way of replacing particular diagrams with an infinity of diagrams—but others were not at first convinced that it should be the default behavior. The first implementation of Cabri did not, in fact, make it a default; one had to access the menu to drag a point. The elevation of dragging to default status followed experience with the new tool: As people played with the early version, they nearly always wanted to drag points dynamically.

In fact, based on the history of these two pieces of software and some related cases, it is tempting to draw a conclusion that goes far beyond saying how dragging became a part of these tools. What determines whether a software conception remains merely a clever tool or becomes a brilliant work of art seems to be, in large part, how well the designers observe users as they interact with a prototype, and how thoughtfully they respond to what they see.

Independent Invention

The designers of Cabri and Sketchpad were both well along, with very similar ideas, before either knew of the other! Klotz (personal communication, January 5, 1995) said he had heard Judah Schwartz describe the Supposer concept at a conference—"it was '88, maybe"—and came back "bubbling over" with the idea of looking at various instances of a geometric construction. Some ideas behind Sketchpad were thus influenced by the Supposer, but the drag feature was not a reaction against or a conscious addition to the design of the Supposer. According to both Klotz (personal communication, January 5, 1995) and Jackiw (personal communication, January 4, 1995), dragging was already designed into predecessors to Sketchpad, and so, as with Cabri, no alternative to dragging was ever considered. Klotz says:

> We had just that Fall got into our dragging bit, and were very proud of what we had. We thought ... people are going to really love this. But [Cabri] had scooped us, and we had scooped them. It was one of these, you know, just amazing things where ... maybe you can sort out the exact moment, maybe there was a passing meteor, or something.[9] (personal communication, January 5, 1995)

Pedagogy

Unlike the Supposer, neither Cabri nor Sketchpad was motivated by pedagogy. No curricular goal, specific learning theory, or educational research agenda sparked the original idea or even guided development during the earliest phases. Asked whether he was thinking of Cabri pedagogically, Jean-Marie replied:

> No, at the very beginning it was just for fun, to have such a tool in geometry.... For myself, it was just thinking back to those figures from [high school or university] geometry and thinking it would be nice to [explore those figures] in the dragging mode, just "for fun," in quotation marks. (personal communication, April 8-12, 1993)

Of course, no idea springs up in a vacuum. Part of Jean-Marie's vision was that direct manipulation in geometry "would be nice." And what it would be nice *for* was influenced, in part, by a long-standing emphasis in French education on the distinction between a drawing and the class of related drawings of which it was a particular instance. This distinction, given the terms "drawing" and "figure" by Parzysz (1988), was refined into a tripartite taxonomy by Colette Laborde and Bernard Capponi (1994). Briefly, they identify

- a geometric object—an abstract mathematical object defined by a set of relationships;
- a drawing, which necessarily contains both too much information (e.g., details such as size and orientation are often irrelevant) and too little information (one cannot usually tell how much generalization of the drawing is intended); and

- a figure—the set of psychological features, interpretations, and extra baggage (see Vinner, 1983) relating the mathematical object to the particular drawing.

This way of thinking motivated the idea of Cabri Geometry, according to Jean-Marie, in that the new environment required one to specify to the computer the underlying relationships (the mathematical object) while leaving surface features (the drawing) completely malleable (within the constraints of the built-in relationships).

Nevertheless, this intellectual context and a set of clear design principles, while reflecting both mathematical and learning (or human-factors) points of view, are not ones that might properly be called pedagogical *intent* in the conventional senses. In fact, except for one other member of the Cabri team, it could not even be said that there was any interest, at first, in Cabri as an educational tool.

Jean-Marie explained:

> People started to be interested in this from a pedagogical point of view, just after *more than one year* [after the first] existence of Cabri geometry.... From the very beginning, we had Franck Bellemain in our team, who had completed a degree in mathematical didactics with Colette, so what I just said is not *completely* true, because he had some influence on the development. (J.-M. Laborde, personal communication, April 8-12, 1993)

Neither did Jean-Marie start with a background or focused interest in pedagogy (despite "one or two people, very close to me who were interested in didactics"), nor was that a truly controlling force during the early development of Cabri. When the tool was shown, "Other people ... teachers, were just looking at this as a curiosity... and only *much* later with genuine pedagogical interest" (J.-M. Laborde, personal communication, April 8-12, 1993). Gene also denies educational intent:

> My interest ... was simply to make an easy-to-use geometry drawing tool. The draggability was not in my head at all before starting out.... [In the] absence of motor coordination ... cool but hairy constructions in Euclidean geometry [are] often hard to draw with adequate precision.... Just making accurate drawings would have been a major achievement. Nick's embellishments made it spectacular. (G. Klotz, personal communication, November 23, 2001)

So, if pedagogy did not shape the design, what, other than a desire for dragging, did? The interviews reveal that each designer was motivated by his own set of principles—mathematical, aesthetic, and human-factors, among others. The following sections discuss some of these principles.

Minimal Distance From Euclid's Geometry

Jean-Marie knew from the start that his software did not produce Euclidean geometry. After all, this is already apparent in the property that the ratio of parts of a line segment subdivided by a point remains invariant as the segment is stretched. But his goal was to minimize the distance between the behavior of his system and the behavior of a microworld-according-to-Euclid.

> The general principle was to make the distance as small as possible, but at the very beginning I was not aware that it would remain finally at some distance. I now have some strong arguments to show you that this distance *cannot* be set to zero. (J.-M. Laborde, personal communication, April 8-12, 1993)

To varying extents, any DGE software must share features of projective geometry with the Euclidean base. Consider, for example, the construction of a circle through three points (elaborated subsequently in the section on Continuity). The dragging feature means that any one of these points can subsequently be moved so that it is collinear with the other two. At that moment, the circle becomes a straight line (or ceases to exist), and its center moves to infinity (or ceases to exist). But, no matter how the *display* is handled, the underlying mathematics must account for the challenging moment and not treat it as an error. As the point is moved further in the same direction, the circle (and center) must appear appropriately. This use of "points at infinity" (even if their effects are not displayed) is one element of projective geometry that must supplement the Euclidean base. To take full advantage of the continuous nature of dragging, the designs of both Geometer's Sketchpad and Cabri evolved in the direction of analytic geometry as well, incorporating loci, elements of coordinate geometry, equations for various objects on the screen, and graphing capabilities.

Continuity

DGEs strive to represent mathematical continuity. Jean-Marie said:

> We want mappings to have some continuity properties.... This was the second principle. If two configurations seem to the user to be "close," then if you make a small variation, you should just have a small variation of the image, if it's possible. (J.-M. Laborde, personal communication, April 8-12, 1993)

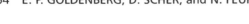

Figure 3.2.   In the Euclidean plane, the intersection's movement is discontinuous.

In some cases, small variation is not possible. For example, consider the intersection point I of a fixed line (horizontal) and a movable line that passes through a fixed point P and a movable point M (see Figure 3.2). As M is moved closer to the fixed line, that intersection will move rapidly "out to infinity" toward the left and "in from infinity" from the right. The discontinuity is unavoidable.

Likewise, consider a circle passed through three points, A, B, and P. When P is moved from one side to the other side of the segment $\overline{AB}$ (in Figure 3.3, it followed the path of the slanted dotted arrow), the center O of the circle makes a discontinuous move (from O to the right along the dotted arrow out to infinity, and then back in from the left along the dotted arrow to O'). But, in both cases, the geometry of the situation leaves a psychological sense of continuity. For example, in the second case, while the center of the circle travels out one side of the screen and back in the other side, the tracing of the circle seems entirely well behaved. Students in another context (see, for example, Goldenberg, Lewis, & O'Keefe, 1992) have described the same visual phenomenon in terms of a continuous change. In other situations, there is less of a sense of continuity. Intersection points can sometimes move in a continuous way, and at other times cease to exist, potentially causing parts of the construction to vanish. Such behavior is catastrophic, but its cause is readily understood.

The drive for continuity can easily be seen in a feature common to all DGEs with which we are familiar: the behavior of points placed on stretchy segments or resizable circles. A truly arbitrary point, whose only constructed characteristic is that it is a member of some other geometric object, has no place-determining information attached to it.[10] How should it move as its parent object is stretched? One alternative is for it to relocate arbitrarily as the containing object is altered. That would be consistent with its arbitrarily assigned original placement; it is consistent with the notion of a random draw out of a set (it is a randomly drawn point, a member of a set of points that constitutes the segment or circle or other geometric object). But such a behavior, as a default, would violate the continuity principle. Much more seriously, from a user-acceptability standpoint, it would violate the principle of minimal user surprise.

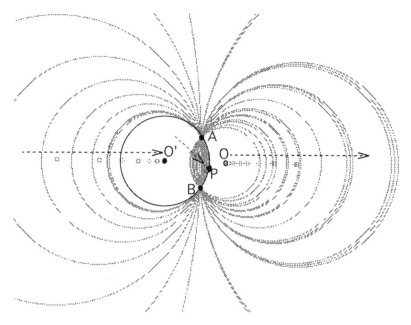

Figure 3.3.   A discontinuity in the Euclidean plane is resolved in the projective plane.

Minimal User Surprise

A general principle in software design is to have both the system and interface behave exactly the way people would naively expect them to behave, insofar as is possible without causing outright conflict with the purpose or integrity of the system. For example, consider again the case of the point placed arbitrarily on a stretchy segment. The definition requires that it stay on the segment when the segment is rotated or translated. No mathematical inconsistency would derive from having the point remain a fixed distance from the unmoved endpoint (or even the moved one), but a conflict arises if both endpoints are moved apart. Moreover, even if only one endpoint is moved, if it approaches sufficiently close to the other, the arbitrary point could be "shoved off" the segment on which it was created, a conflict with naive expectation. Choosing ratio rather than distance as the invariant under stretching resolves the conflict, and also conforms to the experiential physics of elastic bands: The point behaves the way a colored mark on an elastic band would behave, and the transformation is perceived as a kind of dilation of the entire segment around the fixed endpoint. In this case, conforming to expectations emphasizes certain mathematical ideas while leaving the user unaware that there even were alternatives. This example illustrates that choices must sometimes be made in which psychological rather than mathematical factors are primary in designing the software. It also shows that the psychological and mathematical interpretations can sometimes be in conflict. But it is also a case in which it would seem that the designers really have no other reasonable choices.

In fact, there are more complex situations, and some of these leave considerable room for choice. For example, what should happen to a point D placed arbitrarily on a perpendicular to segment AB through B, as A is moved (see Figure 3.4)? As A is moved, segment AB rotates around B, and perhaps stretches or shrinks as well. Because D must remain on the line, which is always perpendicular to segment AB, the rotational component of the transformation must be applied to D: That is, D must rotate around B as A is rotated around B. If the apparent dilation δ of C around B—the stretchy segment phenomenon—is perceived along with the apparent rotation ρ of the entire system around B, then it is certainly possible that the entire transformation is interpreted (not necessarily consciously or explicitly) as $\delta \circ \rho$. The rotational component must be applied to D, but the dilation component is not required. It is unknown what people would expect, but there is certainly room for choice. If people do perceive the transformation of A to be what we would characterize mathematically as $\delta \circ \rho$, then consistency might dictate that the same transformation be applied to D. Again, we hypothesize that this is not consciously analyzed as a composition of rotation and dilation, but perceived as a kind of scaled-down analogous movement.

Alternatively, simplicity might dictate that only what is required—and therefore, only the rotation—be applied to D. In fact, the different dynamic interactive geometries do not make the same choice here. Cabri, like Geometry Inventor (Brock, Cappo, Dromi, Rosin, & Shenkerman, 1994), applies only the rotation to D. Sketchpad, in effect, builds in similarity: It preserves $\triangle BCD$, up to scale, for all movements of A and B. This

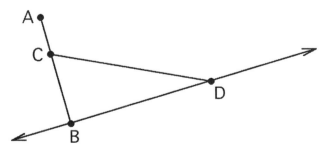

Figure 3.4.   How should D move when A is moved?

forward propagation of both rotational and dilational information is true for subsequent generations of points and certain[11] constructed lines, so a quite complex Sketchpad construction can behave as if transformations were performed on all points in the plane. The behavior exhibited by Sketchpad (in this example) represents an important point of view for certain mathematical environments, one that can evoke a particular way of thinking about the transformations that students often have a difficult time seeing.[12] The Cabri implementation is determined totally by the expressed goal of minimal user surprise. To understand the design process of a particular piece of software, one must know the history of its evolution, which cannot always be inferred reliably from the final product. Though it seemed entirely reasonable to assume that the Sketchpad decision was made on mathematical/pedagogical grounds, in contrast to the human-factors accommodation of Cabri, Nick explicitly states that this is not the case. The Sketchpad behavior happens to be particularly easily computable and therefore makes for a very smoothly working product. That it can also have pedagogical benefit is a byproduct that prudent users can exploit.[13]

Menu Items—Many or Few?

Constructing a parallelogram and building a circle through three given points are both multi-step procedures with a ruler and compass. Transporting geometry to a computer presents the possibility of bypassing some of these steps. Generating parallelograms, squares, three-point circles, and so on, could be menu options. These figures could then be altered in ways that preserve their essential character—the shape of the parallelogram, for example, could be changed—but the actual work of building parallel sides, constructing the center of the circle, and so on, would already have been done. In fact, these options appear in some geometry programs, for example, Geometry Inventor. Depending on one's purpose, these high-level constructions may even be seen as suppressing irrelevant and distracting detail, much as calculators are (sometimes!) used to allow one to get one past the low-level details of a computation and get on with the big ideas.

But the decision does, in part, depend on one's purpose. For the Sketchpad designers it was not clear that more tools meant a better program. According to Klotz:

> I sort of wore two hats; one of them was minimalist Euclid and the other was trying to make things user convenient. Depending on what hat I wore, I said, "Well, let them construct [it] ..., and you learn something from that."

On the other hand, I realized, even then, you've got to listen to user interests and so forth. (personal communication, January 5, 1995)

Nick faced this issue from both a programmer's and a learner's perspective. Providing menu options to automate an assortment of geometric construction tasks meant that Sketchpad would become a hefty program. All totaled, Nick faced a daunting wish list of nearly 400 menu items—an amount, he joked, that would require 21 volumes of documentation. In a memo (Jackiw, personal communication, 1987) to the Sketchpad project staff, he explains:

> I and the other students in my geometry class would far rather have sat down with graph paper, a pencil, and a protractor and meticulously done by hand just about anything that could reasonably be assigned to us than to have read the instruction manual for a program that does everything listed here.... I don't think that having 40 items in a tool palette and another 60 in menus is either logical or intuitive.

By advocating for a leaner Sketchpad, Nick aimed to trim the construction commands down to their "atoms" and eliminate the majority of automated constructions that could be accomplished by more primitive techniques. Even as he pared down the number of special-case figures, Nick felt that students should not have to rebuild frequently used figures from scratch each time they were needed; he created the scripting feature of Sketchpad as a way for students to start from the "atoms" and gradually build their own collection of reusable, multi-step constructions. He writes:

> In my ideal vision, students author their own tools, which forces them to confront and think through the geometry implicit in a construction before making the result available to them in the future, as a magic recipe for achieving their larger construction goals. (Jackiw, 1995)

This structure is not merely a time- and work-saver for students, nor is it just a pedagogical device, forcing students through basic steps before they have the convenience of larger units. It embodies an important mathematical idea—most likely first known to Nick as a programming idea. This kind of extensibility—using processes (e.g., functions, algorithms) to combine little building blocks into more complex objects, and then using these more complex objects as the building blocks, via yet other processes, of yet more complex objects—is a central feature of mathematics.

Ultimately, the scripting feature in Versions 1 and 2 of Sketchpad did not receive heavy use. To construct a square using a script, the user needed to match two points on the screen with the two "givens" of the script—a multi-step procedure. Version 3 of Sketchpad streamlined the process by allowing the user to create a script tool button, which, in Version 4, became "custom tools." With this new design, clicking two points on the screen automatically constructed a square with the points as neighboring vertices. The actual use of this feature, however, depends not only on its convenience but also on the focus of the mathematics classes in which Sketchpad is used.

A Visual Spreadsheet

As Nick refined his model of how geometric objects would respond to dragging, he developed a deeper sense of Sketchpad's underlying structure. He comments:

> The birth of dynamic geometry as a concept, as opposed to just an artifact of trying to be like the Mac, consisted of two sorts of parallel understandings of what Sketchpad would be. One was the notion that it was a spreadsheet, but a spreadsheet that worked with graphics.
>
> In the traditional spreadsheet paradigm, visualization—graphing or plotting the data set—comes as an optional postscript to an often-tedious exercise in data generation. Could Sketchpad dispense with the externalization of numeric data, and allow users to work at all times directly with a visual model? (N. Jackiw, personal communication, April 26, 1996)

Sketchpad, as a visual spreadsheet, would share some of the characteristics of a traditional numerical spreadsheet. With an Excel spreadsheet, a user might indicate that cell Z = cell Y + 1. Any changes then made to the value of cell Y would affect the value of cell Z. Such dependencies exist in Sketchpad, too, but in graphical form. For an arbitrary $\triangle ABC$, dragging vertex A affects the location of segments AB and AC.

Geometric Reversibility

The spreadsheet analogy worked well for Nick, but it was not as robust as he would have liked it to be. His other desire for Sketchpad was that it allow for *reversibility*. In the previous formula (cell Z = cell Y + 1), a user cannot input the value of cell Z and ask the spreadsheet to work backwards to calculate cell Y. Put another way, imagine a user has entered a formula that calculates profit in terms of two variables: number of widgets sold and price per widget. The spreadsheet operates in only one direction—given values of the two variables, it calculates profit. Nick imagined what would happen if the program had a reversibility feature built in:

> The spreadsheet is sort of the most interesting software genre that the microcomputer has come up with. [But] the spreadsheet is a constraint system that only works one way. So another way of thinking about Sketchpad early on for me was as a graphical spreadsheet in which you could specify your business plan and then say not "what happens if I sell a million widgets," but "how do I make a million dollars," and have it reverse your business plan into reasonable scenarios. (personal communication, January 4, 1995)

Of course, the solution might not be unique. There could be more than one combination of widget quantity and cost that produces the desired profit.

How does this notion of reversibility apply to a geometric setting? Nick offers an acoustics example to explain. Imagine you are in a room with two stereo speakers placed on the floor. Somewhere in the room is a location where the music reaching your ears will provide the optimum listening experience—what's commonly known as the "sweet spot." While the music plays, you move the speakers by trial and error, attempting to get the sweet spot to coincide with the location of your easy chair. By contrast, suppose you are resting comfortably on the easy chair and have no intention of moving about to fiddle with the speakers. If every location of the speakers defines a sweet spot, then why not reverse that logic and say that every location of the sweet spot defines a (possibly non-unique) placement of the stereo speakers. So relax in your chair—from a logical standpoint, the speakers should be able to relocate themselves! To get an idea of what this might mean in a geometry environment, consider the following investigation. Construct a circle with center A, place three arbitrary points, C, D, and E, on the circle, and connect the points to form $\triangle CDE$. Then construct the three medians. The medians meet at the triangle's centroid, point I, as shown in Figure 3.5. By experimenting with this construction, what can you say about $\triangle CDE$ when points I and A coincide? One approach, the "forward-engineering" approach, is to vary the locations of C, D, and E in an attempt to get I to move onto A. This method treats points C, D, and E as independent variables whose placements on the circle determine the location of the dependent point I. Their motion is analogous to the motion of the speakers in the stereo example. We move C, D, and E to land I at A as we move the speakers to reposition the sweet spot to land at our easy chair.

But Nick wanted to apply the reverse-engineering idea in cases like this so that point I could become the independent variable. To find out what happens when I coincides with A, drag I onto A and watch! (See Figure 3.6.) This reverses the notion that the points C, D, and E must determine I, and instead examines how I's location can affect the shape of $\triangle CDE$. Because, for a given location of point I, the placements of C, D, and E on

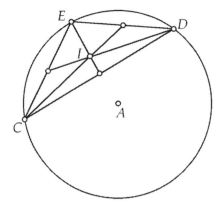

Figure 3.5.   A circle with inscribed
triangle *CDE* and triangle centroid *I*.

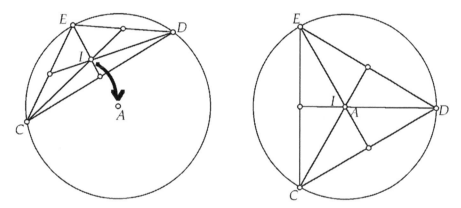

Figure 3.6.   Dragging *I* onto *A* causes Δ*CDE* to become equilateral.

the circle are not uniquely determined,[14] programming decisions need to
be made about how points *C*, *D*, and *E* will move. This means that the
behavior that students ultimately see is only partly determined by the
geometry; it is also influenced by the decisions of the programmer. As it
turns out, such a hybrid geometry is unavoidable in any dynamic interactive geometry software. Too great a departure from Euclid's geometry
would surely render the behavior of software obscure and educationally
dubious, but the departures that we see in Cabri and Sketchpad are relatively modest. Educationally, it may not matter which particular choices
the software designers have made. In any event, the effects (if any) of
extra-geometric behaviors of the software on students may be significantly

influenced by curriculum and teaching. For Nick, this "reversibility" was, essentially, the implementation of a kind of inverse geometric function. The "function" in the previous example took the positions of points C, D, and E as inputs, and produced the position of point I as output. Nick's goal was to let the same construction behave as the inverse of that function, taking the location of point I as input, and outputting C, D, and E.

Reversibility had a very different meaning for Jean-Marie.

> Jean-Marie: A second general thing about dragging in the Cabri interface [is] the principle of reversibility. If you drag and come back to the same position, things must be the same. Most of the cases where different implementations could be realized, [our own choice was] just to realize this reversibility. We really want this reversibility. That's explicit.
>
> Paul: What you're... saying is, the position of any point on the screen is a function of position of the moved point, and not of the history of the moved point, [any information about the path through which the point was dragged between its original position and its return to that position].
>
> Jean-Marie: Right. (personal communication, April 8-12, 1993)

Paul's rephrasing was intended, at the time, to check his understanding of what Jean-Marie had meant, yet, as we discovered later despite Jean-Marie's immediate assent, the two characterizations do not represent the same mathematical perspective (or pedagogical focus). Both characterizations suggested a notion of functions and their arguments, but for Jean-Marie, the visible object (a construction) on the screen, was the argument to a transformation that was applied by displacing some point (through dragging). Like Nick, his thinking emphasized the algebraic idea of inverse operations, but with a very different idea of what the function and variables were. For Jean-Marie, the inverse meant that any deformation to that screen object can be undone by returning the dragged point to the position it had occupied before the transformation. Paul had yet a third image: He saw the construction on the screen not as the argument to a function, but as the function itself—a piece of apparatus that specified a function from $\Re^2$ to $\Re^2$ geometrically, serving in place of the more familiar algebraic definition of the relationship between input and output. The dragged point, from this point of view, is the independent variable, and the construction determines how some other feature—a measurement or some other point—changes in response to movements of the input variable. Paul's characterization "the position of any [other] point on the screen is a function of position of the moved point" suggested only a definition of the domain of the functions that

Paul saw as represented by the screen behavior, and said nothing about reversibility or inverses!

As it turns out, the screen behavior is not adequately characterized as functions on $\mathfrak{R}^2$, as Jean-Marie quickly pointed out.

> I can show you also cases where it's not true.... some spatial configurations where, even [with the intent on reversibility], you have a *history* ... [and] where mathematically, it cannot be otherwise.

His construction was a projection from a circle to an ellipse, with an arbitrary point P subsequently placed on the ellipse. As the projection point is moved back and forth horizontally, the aspect of the ellipse changes from vertically oblique through circular through horizontally oblique and back. The location of P on the ellipse is not fully defined by this construction, and is therefore not stable. A far simpler construction is a conic passed through five arbitrary points (A through E in Figure 3.7), with a sixth point P placed on it. The location of P cannot be related solely to the position of the original five points. As A is moved across the line through B and E, the conic changes from an ellipse to a hyperbola. P generally moves in a continuous way, but its position is really bistable. Moving A just across $\overline{BE}$ and back shifts P to P'. A repeat of the procedure returns P to its original position.

A Democracy of Points and Segments

A user who draws an arbitrary polygon *ABCDE* with Sketchpad can construct it in several ways. Vertex A might get drawn first, or it could very well be the last point placed on the screen. In this simple example, the

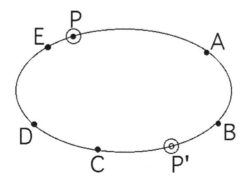

Figure 3.7. The location of an arbitrary point on a conic may be unstable.

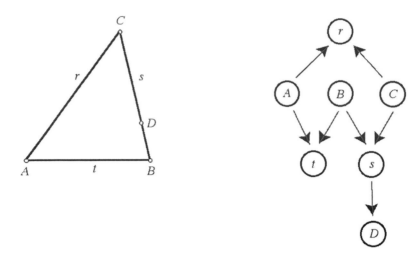

Figure 3.8.   Δ*ABC* with its acyclic graph representation.

order of the construction does not confer any hierarchy or special behavior on the vertices. The user expects to be able to drag any vertex of the polygon and deform the figure into different shapes. Nick refers to this behavior as the "democracy" of vertices in a polygon. While Nick found this democracy desirable, it was not simple to achieve. One way to reflect the equal nature of the triangle's vertices was to represent them internally as a looping cyclic graph with no beginning and end. But in such a model, programming the constraints of the triangle meant representing them algebraically as a system of simultaneous linear equations. The time it took for the computer to solve the equations would not have allowed the program to be interactive.

As another option, Nick considered using an acyclic graph (a directed graph containing no directed cycles). Figure 3.8 shows a triangle *ABC* with point *D* on side *BC*, along with its acyclic graph representation on the right. In this model, each geometric object in the triangle—each vertex, segment, and point on a segment—becomes a node of the graph. Arrows flow from node to node, indicating the logical precedence and dependence of various parts of the diagram. Vertices *A* and *B*, for example, define segment *t*, and thus their nodes come together with an arrow pointing toward node *t*.

An acyclic graph did have its problems: Nick wanted a motion on segment *r* to percolate to *A* and *C*, but the directionality of the arrows did not allow it. Dispensing with the arrows altogether was also troublesome, as an action on a node would then propagate throughout the graph without a clear idea of where to end. After thinking through these issues, Nick devised a variation on the acyclic graph that gave him the desired behavior. He viewed the graph as a tree whose roots and dependencies could change:

> Imagine this computational tree was composed out of thread and objects. If I picked up *C*, everything would hang from it, and I could make *C* become essentially the new root of the tree. And that's the algorithm Sketchpad uses, which is very different than simply saying, "Here's the graph implied by the chronology of how the user put things together, and I'm always going to follow the arrows in the same direction he did." (N. Jackiw, personal communication, April 26, 1996)

Sketchpad does not use this algorithm in every situation, but the notion of being able to move any component of a figure is a defining feature of the program. Thus, when you construct the centroid of an arbitrary triangle inscribed in a circle, you can drag that (highly constructed) centroid onto the circle's center, in turn reshaping your triangle into an equilateral one (since circumcenters and centroids coincide only in equilateral triangles). Or, when you define an object to be a mirror reflection of another, changes to either pre-image or image generate corresponding changes in the other—there is no distinction between "input" and "output" in the program's transformations.

Cabri does not allow the user to drag constructed objects and have the effect propagate back to the objects that define them (except in the trivial case of dragging a segment whose defining objects are a pair of points). As it is perfectly possible to offer this capability, why should Cabri not do so? And, if Cabri has a good reason not to, why then does Sketchpad persist? The answer is not a simple matter of whether the feature is or is not a "good one," but for what it is good. The designers may have their own independent reasons—this analysis is not from their perspective—but, from an outsider's view, the two tools are optimized for somewhat different purposes. Sketchpad's attempts to invert almost any function optimize it for experimentation. It is the reverse engineering that Nick wanted for the spreadsheet that did his widget business plan and for adjusting the speakers to place the sweet spot wherever he chose. Its only disadvantage is that, because many of the geometric functions he allows one to invert do not have well-defined inverses, he must apply rules outside of geometry to select among solutions that are not unique. As a result, the behavior is less predictable to the user, and the mathematical trail is not necessarily transparent.

By contrast, the mathematical consequences of an action in Cabri are much easier to analyze. There appear to be fewer instances in which the behavior on the screen is governed by anything other than the explicit geometric rules one has specified, but the consequence is that certain kinds of experiments are harder to perform. From this perspective—and with regard to this single design feature—one program is optimized for experimentation, whereas the other is optimized for mathematical clarity. Does this choice, by itself, affect the student? Given the large role played by curriculum and teaching, it would hardly seem to be, by itself, more than a matter of taste, though it might well influence the character of the problems best suited to the tool.

EVOLUTIONARY FORCES AT WORK?

It is, of course, impossible to know fully what forces influenced the development of DGE tools after they began to win broad acceptance and enthusiasm. Collegial sharing of ideas, not-always-collegial product competition, researchers' inflow of ideas, the developers' own experience playing with their tools and making personal wish lists, feedback from classroom trials and teachers—all of these contribute. But what role each played, and how great a role, remains difficult to sort out. While one might expect to see a certain amount of more-or-less deliberate incorporation of the features found in the competition, this mechanism for product growth does not seem to be borne out by the interview data, at least as regards the development of the two pieces of software described here. Even where one can see a convergence of features—something that might easily and naturally be attributed to playing catch-up with the competition—deliberate emulation does not seem to be much of a factor. In fact, while it is clear that, except at the earliest stages, each designer came to know the other's product, the interview data show that each designer knew less about the other's product than the other had imagined! In many ways, it would seem that ideas evolved naturally, as if existing capabilities "forced" the evolution of ideas in much the same direction in the different laboratories.

In fact, not only did Cabri and Sketchpad arise, at the outset, out of such a parallel evolution, but similar ideas were arising elsewhere as well. Before having seen or heard of any version of DGE, Education Development Center (EDC) had produced a videotape showing geometric constructions responding dynamically and in continuous fashion as the user dragged a variable element. The video was merely an animation of computer generated frames, but more than merely an example of the use of computer animation in film, which was by then a well-known reality. It embodied the idea of animated response to continuous mouse movement, yet another version of a fully dynamic interactive geometry system. Though this example of dragging remained a concept without the actual interactive software, it stands as another bit of evidence that the growing capabilities of computers at the time functioned, in a way, as an evolutionary force.

The effect of the "force" depended on the environment in which it was exerted. At EDC, at that time, a team was engaged in research[15] on how students learn when working with the then-still-new graphing software. That research showed that, faced with an expression like $f(x) = ax^2 + bx + c$ in the context of computer-aided graphing tools, students had little idea of what made x so special. It was called "the variable," but they never varied it! On the contrary, what they varied were a, b, and c, which were called parameters or, even more mysteriously, constants! Phil Lewis, a member of that research team, saw many mathematical advantages to putting the variable directly in students' hands, via the computer mouse. He suggested several versions of graphing that made use of this dynamic interface. In one, the standard Cartesian graph was produced, except that the student could "drag" the variable (x) right or left, or back and forth, rather than merely watching as a picture appeared mysteriously on the screen. The physical sensation of interacting with the drawing, all by itself, was quite clarifying to some students. Another representation, more novel and in many ways more educationally rich, came to be called DynaGraphs (see Goldenberg, 1995; Goldenberg et al., 1992). In that representation, the variable (in $\Re$, $\Re^2$, or $\mathbb{C}$) lived in its own space (line or plane) and the function value (in any of those domains) lived in a separate appropriate space. EDC did produce interactive (prototype) software for one part of the concept illustrated on the videotape—functions from $\Re$, $\Re^2$, or $\mathbb{C}$ to $\Re$, $\Re^2$, or $\mathbb{C}$, described with the language of algebra. What led to a consideration of geometric objects was the observation that students' concepts of function were extremely narrow. The team began to think of ways to make accessible the idea of functions on nonnumeric spaces, including geometric spaces. The video was created for the purpose of presenting the idea of "dynamic visualization" of functions, as the group named it, to potential funders of a project to develop the appropriate software. In the group's expanded view of functions, the variable could still be the x in some algebraic representation of a function on $\Re$, or the (x, y) in a function on $\Re^2$, but it could also be an angle (or other variable element) in a geometric construction. As it was dragged about, the function value—some other number, point, or feature of a geometric construction—would respond dynamically. The group described (though without implementation except as an animation) the notion of defining functions using geometric rather than algebraic specifications, and treating geometric objects as variables, but—and here is the relevant point for this history—even this did not lead the group to conceive of its invention as a "geometry" environment. This imagined interactive world was, for that team at EDC, explicitly and only a world of functions defined on a continuous domain, with the variable—embodied by the mouse—put directly in the student's hand.

It was only natural that when the EDC group first saw Sketchpad and Cabri, they saw functions, not a new interface for investigating Euclidean Geometry. In fact, given the incredible power of these new tools that not only "scooped" but vastly extended the geometric part of the EDC concept, it was quite a surprise to the EDC team[16] that the inventors of DGEs had not (yet) taken the final step to obliterate the boundary between synthetic and analytic geometry, and between geometry and the world of functions. The research on DGEs subsequently conducted at EDC (e.g., Hazzan & Goldenberg, 1996-1997) continued to focus centrally on the DGE as a rich source of experience for building the concept of function. Perhaps this completely non-geometric point of view (even about geometric objects) coming out of EDC played a role as yet another force in the evolution of the DGEs. Or perhaps it was inevitable—another "natural" evolutionary force—that smart people playing with rich and engaging tools would come to find more in them than had been designed in. Whatever the cause, attention broadened over time and moved beyond Euclidean geometry to include a host of mathematical ideas, from early algebra, to group theory, differential equations, and, of course, other geometries. From this point of view, the addition of conics and loci as full objects, the ability of the user to manipulate analytic descriptions of all objects (except loci) on a translatable, nonhomogeneously scalable, rotatable, and shearable coordinate system, and so on, seem quite natural.

This sense that the tool, itself, leads (in the hands of a perceptive user) to its own evolution can be seen in the way that Jean-Marie's play with Cabri software led him to evolve the notion of direct manipulation into what he calls "direct engagement" (J.-M. Laborde, personal communication, April 8-12, 1993).

> Direct engagement is a more complex thing, and a more global thing than just direct manipulation.... Direct manipulation is when the user can have the impression that he is not interacting with a representation of the object, but with the object itself.
>
> Direct engagement was designed as a concept later, I think in '78 or '79, or even at the beginning of the Eighties... you can speak about direct engagement where you have an interface that continuously facilitates and delimits the distance between your expectation and what's going on the screen. For instance, every time that a dialog box comes in front of your world, it breaks the direct engagement, because it suddenly makes you answer a special question....
>
> [There are other examples.] The way that we [implemented] the line segment and the line [in the first Cabri] wasn't compatible with the direct engagement, because... at that time, [after the user placed the first end-

point] and as long as the second point wasn't somewhere on the screen, there was no feedback, no trace of what the user is doing. And now, when you start to draw a line segment, you have something at the cursor... as soon as you start, you have your line segment [and it follows the cursor until you fix it with a second point].

The obvious value of an extension to three-dimensional geometry was certainly hampered, at first, by purely technological considerations— computers grew phenomenally in speed since DGEs were first introduced. Thus it is impossible to know what evolutionary course would have been followed if (almost implausibly) no version of plane DGE appeared until full-motion 3D graphics were ubiquitous. But, to us, it appears fortunate that coordinate and analytic geometry came first. We see dragging as inherently connected with the world of analysis and functions defined on a domain endowed with the topology of the real numbers. Had the DGE tools delved first into three dimensions, they might well have—at least for a while—continued the isolation of geometry, an isolation that DGEs seemed destined to destroy.

WHAT HAVE WE LEARNED?

This overview of the evolution of two DGEs, from the origins of dragging to the nature of menu items, suggests that very little about the programs was inevitable from the start. The underlying mathematics of geometry and algebra certainly guided their development, but did not dictate how features would operate, nor even which features to include. Nick emphasizes this point when characterizing the overall nature of the program:

> The totality of [my] decisions forms, to my mind, more of an aesthetic entity than a mathematical one. We should not lose sight of that. Part of the reason students respond so well to these environments has nothing to do with the [software's] mathematics; it has to do with the functional, balanced appeal of their industrial design. (Jackiw, 1995)

Neither program's designer was working to meet specific educational or industrial goals. Both simply followed their mathematical and aesthetic inclinations, which led them to produce two software environments that users agree are elegant, functional, and valuable both in schools and in mathematical and mathematics education research. Because the programs' design features invite exploration and play, users sense their own role in shaping and crafting their understanding of mathematics. What we all see as we watch children or adults "play" with this software is often a change of perception of mathematics, from mathematics as a collection of rules and procedures to mathematics as an intellectual game, a response to curiosity, a human endeavor.

WHERE ARE WE NOW?

C. Laborde and Capponi (1994) see dynamic interactive geometry as an environment to help students develop the ability and inclination to attend to underlying relationships rather than to the particulars of a specific drawing. Their idea is, in part, that any picture created on a DGE is, by its very nature, not a specific drawing, but a malleable one, a single instance of a class of pictures that can be navigated by dragging some point. The fact that students need help attending to underlying relationships rather than to the particulars is well enough known but what they make of the dynamic pictures—their readiness to experiment, their flexibility of experimentation, what they attend to as the screen objects morph in front of their eyes, and how they interpret what they see—is still only partially understood. The level of generality or particularity that students apply in their interpretation of drawings is not so well known. When they create what they think of as a quadrilateral *ABCD* with connected midpoints (Figure 9, frame 1) and then drag *D* as shown in frames 2 through 5, do they continue to think of all of the resulting versions of *ABCD* as a single object deformed in various ways, or as multiple objects? Is the one object (or are the multiple objects) a quadrilateral? Or do students, despite the sense of continuity and (Jean-Marie's notion of) reversibility, see frames 3 and 5 as "not like" the others? The picture may be malleable, but are the concept definitions and images (Vinner, 1983) they carry in their heads as malleable (Goldenberg & Cuoco, 1998)?

Of course, it is no surprise that we do not yet know how students glean geometric ideas from complexly moving figures—the issue, after all, has arisen only recently. How do they develop a sense of where to look, what objects to track, what questions to ask, what experiments to perform? In fact, with so many degrees of freedom, how do they learn what experiments not to perform? Our preliminary observations of college mathematics majors suggest that students who are deforming a figure tend not to let go of the point that they are dragging when the result would be a "monster" (like the cross-quadrilateral in frame 5 of Figure 3.9) but, instead, return points to tame positions before letting go. If so, are they truly ignoring the continuity of the change and treating the screen data as discrete tame cases that just happen to be connected? And, if so, might they not be better off with the discrete experiments in the first place? In fact, the shock and delight that students often express at some unexpected behavior seems a pretty good indicator that they are not ignoring

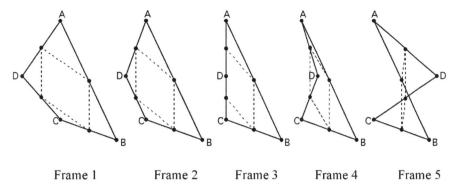

| Frame 1 | Frame 2 | Frame 3 | Frame 4 | Frame 5 |

Figure 3.9.   Five successive stages of the deformation of "quadrilateral" *ABCD*.

the monster cases. The avoidance of stopping at these cases might then be interpreted as evidence that students truly are attending to the variables and degrees of freedom, and trying to manage them while they come to understand the geometry and the display better.

What is quite clear is that geometry on a computer is different from geometry on paper. Colette Laborde (1992) remarked that geometric tools like Logo, DGE, and the Supposers differ from drawing tools like MacPaint in that "the process of construction of the drawing [with the latter] involves only action and does not require a description." What she is referring to is the fact that the geometric tools require one to describe intended relationships: Two lines are parallel or two segments are congruent because they are declared to be, not just because they happened to be drawn to look that way. The details of such specification vary greatly among tools like Logo, DGEs, and the Supposers. Those details influence how one interacts with the tool, and plausibly influence how one learns with it. But the common feature is that one is interacting both with the visual elements and with a declarative description of the visual. In fact, except for what one does in one's head, paper-and-pencil geometry also "involves only action and does not require a description." Part of what students learn in geometry is, as Poincaré put it, the art of applying good reasoning to bad drawings—adding the descriptions that specify which features or relationships in the drawings are intended, which are incidental, and which are to be totally ignored as one attempts to draw inferences about the figure depicted.

It is also clear that a "plastic" geometry is quite different from a geometry that is fixed. Movable points cause segments (and circles, conics, and so on) to stretch and deform, giving rides—sometimes very surprising rides—to points that reside upon them. This cascade of consequences of movable points creates new mathematical raw materials for students to observe. This chapter, including the brief look at the intent behind Cabri, shows just a few of the new mathematical and pedagogical issues that a dynamic interactive geometry raises. Teachers and curriculum developers readily recognize the appeal of these various tools, and their value for experimentation and demonstration, but they do not make full use of the learning potential inherent in the fact that these tools must somehow exploit, or at least account for, the fact that the geometries themselves—and not just the medium through which they are encountered—are actually *different* from a purely static paper geometry. This, as far as we know, remains to be explored.

Finally, if the potential hazards and pitfalls seem larger and more numerous than one might have imagined, it is also clear that the opportunities to make new and important mathematical connections between classical geometric content and big ideas from other mathematical areas are too intriguing to ignore. So is the evidence in students' eyes and on their faces. We must come to understand the new terrain well, so that its roughness becomes a part of, and not a detraction from, its beauty. The use of DGEs in schools might benefit from research on the student-cognition questions raised earlier in this section. Research into specific features of the software and interface also makes sense. After all, it is better to attempt to understand what is going on than to proceed blindly. At the same time, researchers and educators alike should remember and take comfort from the robustness of students' ability to learn in a variety of environments. The richness of the learning tasks may be far more important than the details that distinguish one implementation of DGE from another; perhaps the greatest research effort should focus on the development of these tasks. The DGE tools themselves have already amply demonstrated their mathematical and pedagogical worth.

ACKNOWLEDGMENT

Portions of this chapter appeared in the Winter 2000 issue of *The Mathematics Educator*, *10*(1), 42–48. Some excerpts from "What is Dynamic Geometry?" that appeared in R. Lehrer and D. Chazan (Eds.), *Designing Learning Environments for Developing Understanding of Geometry and Space*, Hillsdale, NJ: Erlbaum, have been adapted for this chapter with permission from Lawrence Erlbaum Associates. The perspective, rationale, planning, and writing of this chapter were supported in part by development funds from Education Development Center, Inc. (EDC), with additional support from the National Center for Research in Mathematical Sciences Education (NCRMSE) and EDC's Connected Geometry project, funded by the National Science Foundation (grants MDR-9252952 and RED-

9453864). Major funding for the interviews with Jean-Marie and Colette Laborde and others at Institute Mathématique Appliquées de Grenoble (IMAG) was provided by NCRMSE, with additional support from Connected Geometry. Interviews with Nick Jackiw, Eugene Klotz, Judah Schwartz, and Michal Yerushalmy and the final preparation of this chapter were supported in part by NSF grant RED-9453864. We are particularly grateful to Jean-Marie and Colette, and to Nick, for the time they spent not only during our initial discussions, but also in reviewing the manuscript, and in responding to many follow-up questions. We also acknowledge the contributions of Nicolas Balacheff, Bernard Capponi, and James King. Opinions (and errors) are ours, and do not necessarily reflect the views of any of the funders or contributors.

NOTES

1. Implementations of DGE discussed in this chapter include Geometer's Sketchpad (Jackiw, 2001), Cabri (Baulac, Bellemain, & J.-M. Laborde, 1992, 1994), Geometry Inventor (Brock, Cappo, Dromi, Rosin, & Shenkerman, 1994), and, in a partial way, superSupposer (Schwartz & Yerushalmy, 1992). More recent developments include Cabri 3D (Bainville & Laborde, 2004).

2. In fact, the implications of dragging cannot be fully evaluated without an understanding of why one might choose not to make dragging the favored mode of experimentation (or click and drag the favored mode of construction) even when it is technically feasible. For pedagogical reasons, one might prefer a linguistic interface, having students specify objects through their labels and actions upon those objects through their names. Also, in checking a conjecture, one might reasonably argue that there is a big difference, both logical and psychological, between cases that are "distant" from one another—discrete and arbitrarily selected cases—and those that feel "near" and connected, arrived at by dragging a vertex locally and in a continuous fashion.

   These highly abbreviated reasons are abstracted from a more complex and thorough argument made by Judah Schwartz and Michal Yerushalmy (personal communication, 1993). It is, alas, outside the scope of this chapter to present a full discussion of these issues.

3. While first names are not generally used in academic documents, they seem natural here to convey the immediacy of contemporary "history" as well as of personal connection. The authors are contemporaries, colleagues, and interviewers of the software developers whose work is described here.

4. This was also developed by J.-M. Laborde and several of his colleagues, Jerome Bordier significant among them.

5. See the section on Pedagogy for additional discussion.

6. The history presented here is based heavily on interviews with Cabri's principal designer, Jean-Marie Laborde, augmented with conversations with Colette Laborde, Bernard Capponi, and Nicolas Balacheff, and sup-

plemented by readings of early and recent writings about Cabri (see also J.-M. Laborde, 1985).

7.   These pioneering geometry programs—developed before computers had mouse inputs—offered a menu-driven system for creating geometric constructions based on an initial starting object (e.g., a triangle), and the option of replaying the same construction on a new instance of the starting object, arbitrarily selected by the machine or, optionally, specified by the user. Measurements and observations based on a construction could thus be checked for invariance with respect to the particular properties of the starting object.

8.   This was researched at Xerox PARC and implemented ("for the rest of us") on the Apple Macintosh.

9.   Shortly after the two projects learned of each other, the programmers began collaborating electronically, testing each other's code, offering interface design feedback, and reporting bugs and their potential fixes.

10.   In fact, ascribing placement information based on the *drawing* is in direct violation of the distinction between drawing and figure that Parzysz (1988) articulated and that Cabri researchers, in particular, elaborated.

11.   Such constructed lines include lines through, perpendicular to, or parallel to and rotational transformations of such lines. Sketched lines through B are not affected at all by movements of A, and lines constructed through B by copying angles or, for example, by bisecting the angle between $\overline{AB}$ and a perpendicular to it at B necessarily propagate the rotational component of $\delta \circ \rho$ but do not carry the additional feature of propagating scale information.

12.   Of course, no DGE can remain fully consistent with such a plan. In tools such as these, independent objects—stray points on the screen, unattached or partially arbitrary circles or lines—should not and do not respond in any way to displacements of A or B.

13.   To extend this consistent view to parallel lines, yet another behavior is practically forced upon one, one that is much harder to interpret. In this construction (a line through C parallel to segment AB, with D arbitrarily placed), the rotational component ρ of a transformation $\delta \circ \rho$ of A (or B) is reflected in a change of slope of the parallel line, but that line must continue to pass through the arbitrarily placed point C.

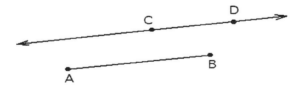

Figure: D's response to shifts of A or B is complex.

Consequently, D rotates around C and not around A (or B). Neither Cabri nor Inventor creates any expectation that δ will be applied to points off of segment AB, but the expectation that is generated in Sketchpad practically forces one to apply the dilation component about C. Visually, the behavior one sees when moving A is quite different from what one sees when moving B.

14. To see this, mark the locations of C, D, and E when I does not coincide with A. Drag I onto point A, release the mouse. Now drag I away from A, back to its original location. Most likely, the locations of C, D, and E will have changed.

15. The mandate to do the research was a subcontract from Harvard's Educational Technology Center, then directed by Judah Schwartz and Jim Kaput. The design and direction of the research were left up to Paul Goldenberg and the EDC research team.

16. The surprise sometimes led to garbled communications. In his first interview with Jean-Marie, Paul saw the distinguishing feature of a DGE as the property of continuous variation of the position of some point in a construction. In casual talk, the distinction was between discrete experimentation, as one might perform with Logo or the Supposer (in two very different ways), and continuous variation.

   Paul viewed DGE software as tools that visualized certain kinds of functions on points in the plane (functions defined on $\Re^2$), geometrically defined, where the variable was represented as (the location of) a point on the plane, and the function value was some other aspect of the construction (the location of some other point, the shape of some point set, some length, some angle, ...). Paul's language, but not Jean-Marie's, initially failed to distinguish between the dragging property—continuous variation in a domain that (ignoring properties of the computer) has the topology of the real numbers—and continuity of the functions themselves. For Jean-Marie, continuity was, as we have described previously, an important principle, but he was thinking about the continuity of the functions, not about the topology of the domain of the function.

REFERENCES

Bainville, E., & Laborde, J. -M. (2004). Cabri 3D [Computer software]. Grenoble, France: Cabrilog.

Baulac, Y., Bellemain, F., & Laborde, J. -M. (1992). Cabri: The interactive geometry notebook. Cabri Géomètre [Computer software]. Pacific Grove, CA: Brooks-Cole.

Baulac, Y., Bellemain, F., & Laborde, J. -M. (1994). Cabri II [Computer software]. Dallas, TX: Texas Instruments.

Brock, C. F., Cappo, M., Dromi, D., Rosin, M., & Shenkerman, E. (1994). Tangible Math: Geometry Inventor [Computer software]. Cambridge, MA: Logal Educational Software and Systems.

Cabri Project. (1990). CabriGraph (Version 3.0) [Computer software]. Grenoble, France: Laboratoire de Structures Discrètes et de Didactique (IMAG), Université Joseph Fourier.

Franklin Institute Online. (2000). *Dr. Ivan E. Sutherland.* Retrieved May 3, 2005, from http://sln.fi.edu/tfi/exhibits/sutherland.html

Goldenberg, E. P. (1995). Ruminations about dynamic imagery **(and a strong plea for research)**. In R. Sutherland & J. Mason (Eds.), *Proceedings of NATO*

Advanced Research Workshop: Exploiting mental imagery with computers in mathematics education (pp. 202-204). Berlin, Germany: Springer.

Goldenberg, E. P., & Cuoco, A. (1998). What is dynamic geometry? In R. Lehrer & D. Chazan (Eds.), *Designing learning environments for developing understanding of geometry and space* (pp. 351-367). Hillsdale, NJ: Erlbaum.

Goldenberg, E. P., Lewis, P. G., & O'Keefe, J. (1992). Dynamic representation and the development of an understanding of functions. In G. Harel & E. Dubinsky (Eds.), *The concept of function: Aspects of epistemology and pedagogy* (MAA Notes Number 25, pp. 235-260). Washington, DC: Mathematical Association of America.

Hazzan, O., & Goldenberg, E. P. (1996/1997). Students' understanding of the notion of function in dynamic geometry environments. *International Journal of Computers for Mathematical Learning, 3,* 263-291.

Jackiw, N. (1991). The Geometer's Sketchpad [Computer software]. Berkeley, CA: Key Curriculum Press.

Jackiw, N. (1994). Dynamics of a point on a line and interesting triangle behavior. Retrieved May 1, 2005, from http://mathforum.org/kb/message.jspa?messageID=1094730&tstart=690

Jackiw, N. (1995). Tool, then object. Retrieved May 23, 1995, from http://mathforum.org/kb/message.jspa?messageID=1094677&tstart=630)

Jackiw, N. (2001). The Geometer's Sketchpad, (Version 4.0) [Computer software]. Emeryville, CA: Key Curriculum Press.

King, J., & Schattschneider, D. (Eds.). (1996). *Geometry turned on: Dynamic software in learning, teaching, and research,* MAA Notes Number 41. Washington, DC: Mathematical Association of America.

Laborde, C. (1992). Solving problems in a computer-based geometry environment: The influence of the features of the software. *Zentralblatt für Didaktik der Mathematik, 4,* 128-135.

Laborde, C. (1994). Enseigner la géométrie: Permanences et révolutions (Teaching geometry: Permanences and revolutions). In C. Gaulin, B. Hodgson, D. Wheeler, & J. Egsgard (Eds.), *Proceedings of the 7th International Congress on Mathematical Education* (pp. 47-75). Sainte-Foy, PQ, Canada: Les Presses de L'Université Laval.

Laborde, C., & Capponi, B. (1994). Cabri-Géomètre constituant d'un milieu pour l'apprentissage de la notion de figure géométrique. *DidaTech Seminar, 150,* 175-218.

Parzysz, B. (1988). 'Knowing' versus 'seeing': Problems of the plane representation of space geometry figures. *Educational Studies in Mathematics, 19,* 79-92.

Schwartz, J., & Yerushalmy, M. (1983-1991). The Geometric Supposers [Computer software]. Pleasantville, NY: Sunburst Communications.

Schwartz, J., & Yerushalmy, M. (1992). The Geometric superSupposer [Computer software]. Pleasantville, NY: Sunburst Communications.

Sutherland, I. (1963). Sketchpad: *A man-machine graphical communications system.* Unpublished doctoral dissertation, Massachusetts Institute of Technology, Cambridge.

Syer, H. W. (1945). Making and using motion pictures for the teaching of mathematics. In W. D. Reeve (Ed.), *Multi-sensory aids in the teaching of mathematics* (pp. 325-345). New York: Teachers College, Bureau of Publications.

Vinner, S. (1983). Concept definition, concept image and the notion of function. *International Journal of Mathematical Education in Science and Technology, 14,* 293-305.

CHAPTER 4

FROM NETWORK TO MICROCOMPUTERS AND FRACTIONS TO FUNCTIONS

Continuity in Software Research and Design

Sharon Dugdale

My work in developing technologically intensive learning environments in mathematics has evolved throughout the past 30 years, in the course of multiple projects, each of which has generated findings (and often questions) that have influenced the next. In a previous chapter (Dugdale, 2008) I described some of the research activity from the first of these projects, the development of the PLATO[1] fractions curriculum (Dugdale & Kibbey, 1980). My goal in the present chapter is to highlight the continuity from that first project into the second and subsequent projects. To that end, this chapter describes how the experience gained and the design principles distilled from the development of the PLATO fractions curriculum influenced the development of microcomputer materials to support high school students' understanding of functional relationships.

Research on Technology and the Teaching and Learning of Mathematics:
Vol. 2. Cases and Perspectives, 89–112

Following a summary of the formative and summative research stages of the project that addressed functional relationships, the chapter outlines how the results of that project laid the foundation for a subsequent project that took a substantially different approach to engaging students in mathematical thought and creativity. The experience gained from each of these contrasting approaches has guided my more recent work. The chapter concludes with reflections about realistic roles for technology and classroom teachers in maximizing the effectiveness of open-ended explorations and fostering a learning environment conducive to healthy habits of mathematical thinking.

FOUNDATIONS FROM EARLIER DEVELOPMENT

Our work with children in the context of the PLATO fractions curriculum left us especially enthusiastic about the potential of computer-based interactive models in which (a) both the mathematics and the motivation are intrinsic, and (b) the feedback to the learner is a mathematical reflection of the learner's manipulation of the model. Not only did models of this sort emerge as natural applications of computer technology, they also engaged children in formulating and using mathematical strategies in ways that we had not observed before computers entered the classroom. This type of computer-interactive learning environment played a central role in our subsequent work with equations and graphs. We also sought to establish with equations and graphs the sense of mathematical community and the rich exchange of students' ideas and techniques that had proved so engaging and fruitful in the fractions curriculum.

INITIAL PLANNING AND DEVELOPMENT

Development Environment

Our earlier work, beginning in 1972, had taken place in the network environment of the PLATO system. The introduction of microcomputers in the late 1970s posed new opportunities, as well as new challenges. The microcomputer's stand-alone environment eliminated the need to maintain connections to a network. However, we found it difficult to give up that network capability, which had been so productive in establishing and maintaining a sense of mathematical community through real-time interaction and children's creative work shared in "libraries."

In 1979 we began experimenting with educational uses of the newly-developed Color MicroPLATO computer (Stifle, Smith, & Andersen, 1979). Then in 1980, with support from the National Science Foundation,[2] we launched development of materials to improve students' understanding of functional relationships. This project was a pioneering effort in the use of microcomputers to involve students in the exploration of graphical representations of functions. This is an area for which the calculational and display capabilities of computer technology proved especially well suited, and the ensuing decades have seen a great deal of activity in this area. High-quality examples and thoughtful analyses appear in the literature (e.g., Confrey, 1993; Demana, Schoen, & Waits, 1993; Kieran, 1993; Moschkovich, Schoenfeld, & Arcavi, 1993; Yerushalmy & Schwartz, 1993).

The project produced materials to address qualitative interpretation of graphs, as well as equation-graphing materials more closely related to standard high school algebra content. The qualitative interpretation materials (Dugdale & Kibbey, 1986a) relate to concerns raised at the time by Karplus (1979). In a study of secondary school students' conceptualization of functional relationships in which continuous variables such as time, distance, and temperature depend on one another, Karplus reported that few students were aware of continuous functional relationships. He concluded that mathematics instruction should include extensive qualitative representations of functions by graphs. Other researchers raised similar concerns about university students' difficulty conceptualizing functional relationships and expressing them graphically (Arons, 1982; Peters, 1982). The work on computer-based laboratories reported by Mokros and Tinker (1987) soon launched a movement that established technology more prominently in addressing qualitative understanding of functional relationships. This chapter focuses on the other side of our project—the materials related to graphing equations. In particular, it highlights the development of the software package Green Globs and Graphing Equations (Dugdale, 1982; Dugdale & Kibbey, 1986b).

Design Considerations

Within our fundamental framework of developing intrinsically motivating, interactive mathematical models and fostering mathematical community, we began planning materials for high school algebra. Based on our substantial experience with computers in classrooms, we had not only an appreciation of their potential, but also an awareness of their limitations and a willingness to go to considerable lengths to compensate for these. For example, display and interaction conventions most readily implemented on computers were not necessarily those most familiar or helpful to students and teachers in classrooms. As prototype materials took shape and underwent classroom testing with students and teachers, we formulated the following design details specific to working with equations and graphs.

Ease of Use

Algebraic notation is sufficiently challenging to students without interjecting the rules of computer conventions and formats. We sought to minimize ways in which the user must adapt to the computer. A major consideration was a well-planned interface to handle equations entered by students and teachers.[3]

Students and teachers were accustomed to writing "3x," rather than "3*x," they expected exponents to be positioned like exponents, and they used the symbol "π" (not "pi" or a numerical approximation). Further, they were accustomed to arbitrary conventions such as writing $\tan^2 x$ to mean $(\tan x)^2$. To accommodate these expectations and customs, the graphing interface was developed to accept expressions in forms natural to these users. For example, students can enter

$$y = 2\sin^2(x - \pi/2)$$

instead of the more awkward

$$y = 2*(\sin(x - 3.14/2))**2$$

which has been typical of many graphing programs developed in the ensuing years.

Refinements continued as new features were added and classroom testing revealed areas that could be improved. For example, in the initial design, pressing the "p" key placed the symbol π into the equation. Later, when exponential functions were added, the "p" key had to be processed more selectively, echoing a "p" if preceded by "ex" to make "exp," or a "π" symbol otherwise. This selective processing seemed preferable to requiring that students distinguish the two cases by using a different key (or a combination of keys) to represent π. Students' use of the "p" key in both contexts proved successful, and the computer's selective processing consistently reflected a student's intent.

As another example, students were accustomed to writing single-character function arguments without using parentheses, for example, "sin x" rather than "sin(x)." Again, selective processing was developed to accommodate users' conventions. When a user begins entering a function argument without the parentheses, the program automatically inserts a left parenthesis and gives a reminder message about this while the user continues to enter the function argument. This avoids confusion in interpreting the entry and at the same time minimizes inconvenience to the user.

Mathematical Accuracy

In our early experimentation with computerized function graphing, we noted the limitations of simply incrementing the independent variable, evaluating the function at each increment, plotting these points, and connecting the graph. First, this technique represents all functions as continuous, and for example, inappropriately connects diverging asymptotic branches. Further, when functions are steep relative to the increment of the independent variable, asymptotes and other features can be completely lost. To avoid these mathematical inaccuracies, our graphing routine was developed to monitor the function's behavior as it graphed, noting steepness and discontinuities, so that it could represent these important features accurately. We considered this accuracy of representation particularly important in materials intended for high school students developing a beginning understanding of functions and graphs.

As function graphing software became a more common pursuit, many developers overlooked these problems. Some dealt productively with the loss of asymptotes and other features by using it as a learning experience or discussion opportunity (see, e.g., Demana & Waits, 1990). Subsequently, "dot mode" (plotting only those points specifically calculated and not connecting them) became a common technique to avoid incorrect representations of functions (see, e.g., Texas Instruments, 1990, for one of the first widely-marketed implementations of this technique). It is still unusual to see technological tools developed to identify asymptotes and handle them accurately.

Mathematical Authenticity and Consistency

Some of the relations and graphs common in high school algebra do not fit conveniently into the same computer graphing routine as functions of the form $y = f(x)$ or $x = f(y)$. Notably, conics (other than the parabola) necessitate different treatment. Of course, one can require that, for example, the equation for a circle be entered as two functions, one for each half of the circle. Or it is possible to offer the option of a separate input format specifically for conics. Some software packages have done this, so that students can fill in, for example, the h, k, and r values for the equation of a circle, $(x - h)^2 + (y - k)^2 = r^2$, in order to graph the circle. This essentially asks students to specify the coordinates of the circle's center and the length of its radius.

Although it is important for students to recognize the general form of a conic equation and understand how particular numbers affect the relation and its graph, we were not comfortable having students enter functions of the form $y = f(x)$ or $x = f(y)$ in an open-ended format and enter conics by filling in blanks in a formula. The two procedures seemed qualitatively different, and an unnatural mix. We thought it most natural and least restrictive to handle conics and general functions so that the two were distinguished only by the equation entered by the student, not by the format offered in the software. In short, we considered it important to avoid compromising mathematical goals for the sake of programming convenience. To this end, the graphing interface was designed to accept functions such as $y = 3x + 5$ and conics such as $0.5x^2 - (y + 1)^2 = 16$ at the same prompt and to process each appropriately.

Implementation Considerations

In the early 1980s computer technology was still new in most classrooms. We observed that teachers varied widely in their preparedness and comfort in using this new medium to support their mathematics classes. To accommodate this broad range of classroom realities, and particularly to support those teachers least ready to take an active role, we sought to make the software accessible and motivating for students, regardless of the extent to which a teacher chose to participate. As in our earlier work, it was clear that the optimal learning environment included an involved teacher, setting goals and connecting the software experience to textbook topics and any related classroom work in progress. We wanted to encourage and support teacher involvement, but not require it in order for the materials to be useful. Based on these observations and principles, we proceeded with development and formative evaluation.

FORMATIVE RESEARCH

Prototype activities were developed in conjunction with continuous micro-assessment, which had proved most productive with the earlier fractions curriculum. Students in two public high schools worked with prototype materials in pairs or groups of three or more, actively discussing what they were doing and sharing ideas. Some students became deeply engrossed in pursuing particular techniques and seemed more intensely involved when working alone. Observation indicated that individual and small group work each provided different important learning and exploration opportunities for students and afforded useful information for us as observers.

Each prototype activity was piloted with students as soon as the activity was sufficiently functional for students to interact with it, to explore the options, and to tell us what they thought of it. During this formative stage, observations proceeded on an informal, as-needed basis, involving whatever students a teacher elected to send to the computers. During the course of developing an activity, both the observers and the teachers made an effort to involve all students in a class. For the observers, this inclusiveness was important to assure the appropriateness of the materials for the complete spectrum of students; and for the teachers, the issue was fairness in access to a learning opportunity.

The first few observations for each prototype activity usually determined whether an idea warranted further development, as well as some directions that development might take. As a prototype was refined, successive observations of students either verified the appropriateness of revisions or suggested a need to rethink particular features. Observers were free to interact with the students as they deemed appropriate, for example, to ask about a student's line of reasoning in a particular situation. In this intentionally informal atmosphere, students also spoke up when they found something confusing or had ideas for improvements in an activity.

One Case: Green Globs

In our earlier development of fractions materials, many of our computer-based activities related to standard textbook models and exercises. For example, naming points on a number line and coloring fractions of a region formed the foundations of our Darts and Paintings Library, two intrinsically motivating, interactive mathematical models with which children exhibited a remarkable range of creativity and mathematical thinking.

Similarly, in considering interactive models for algebra, we surveyed algebra texts as one potential source of material on which to base work with equations and graphs. For example, while perusing a page of linear equation exercises, with instructions to use the two-point formula to determine the equation of a graph through each of numerous given pairs of points, I wondered what students would do with a similar, more open-ended task: Given all of the points from all of the exercises, decide how to put graphs through all of the points, perhaps using as few equations as possible. I speculated that this open-endedness might invite creative approaches and leave students feeling that they had done something uniquely their own, maybe even something clever and worth sharing with classmates. This seemed to have potential, especially if we expanded students' options by allowing more than linear equations and by replacing the points with areas large enough to be hit without going directly through the center point. As it developed, the activity began to feel a bit like a two-dimensional version of the earlier Darts program, with the coordinate plane in place of the number line, and graphs (specified by equations) serving the purpose of darts (specified by rational numbers). If the model showed potential during pilot testing, I thought we might eventually add a space theme or some other fantasy context.

In readying the first pilot version of this idea for classroom trial in 1980, I added a quick, simple title page. Lacking any better name for a prototype that was essentially a coordinate grid full of green spots, on the spur of the moment I dubbed the model Green Globs. The title turned out to be a hit with the high school students, who repeated the word "globs" to each other, rolling it out into a long and graphic sound, with obvious enjoyment. Plans to develop any other theme or title fell by the wayside as users expressed their enthusiasm for Green Globs. Figure 4.1 shows a representative screen display from this program. Thirteen "globs" are scattered on the coordinate grid. The object is to hit all of the globs with graphs defined by entering equations. When a glob is hit, it explodes and disappears. In Figure 4.1, a parabola has hit three globs, for a score of $1 + 2 + 4 = 7$. Each glob hit by the graph scores twice as many points as the previous glob, so hitting an additional glob on a shot more than doubles the total score for the shot. The game continues until all of the globs have been hit.

All prototype programs underwent repeated rounds of classroom testing and revisions. For example, in the case of Green Globs, the scoring

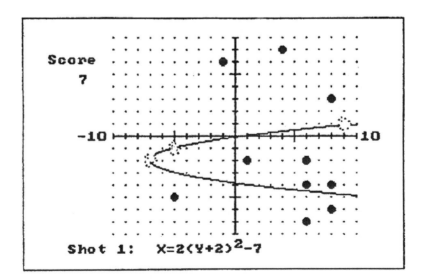

Figure 4.1.   A display from Green Globs.

algorithm was developed, the "hit range" for globs was refined, the "randomness" of the glob placement was adjusted, and the "Expert Section" was added and then redesigned. The Expert Section was initially designed to increase the challenge by displaying smaller globs and centering them at noninteger coordinates. However, students who tried this Expert Section soon returned to the Novice Section. The larger globs centered at integer coordinates provided sufficient challenge, even to the most avid players. Students preferred to seek greater challenge by increasing their own repertoire of techniques and honing their skills to capture more globs with each shot, rather than by facing a more difficult game layout.

Based on student response, we probably would have eliminated the Expert Section altogether if we had not faced the dilemma of whether to allow trigonometric functions. The periodic nature of trigonometric functions makes them especially effective in hitting large numbers of globs. For example, $y = 10\sin(10x)$ could reliably hit all of the globs regardless of their placements. Although this would undoubtedly provide an exciting opportunity for the first students who tried the technique, it was a potential detriment to the continuing success of the game overall if students could copy a single equation to finish any game in one shot. To permit use of trigonometric functions without compromising the challenge of the game, we designed a new Expert Section to allow trigonometric functions. Along with the 13 globs, we scattered five "shot absorbers" on the coordinate grid. A graph ends when it hits a shot absorber, so the challenge is to avoid the absorbers while hitting the globs. Figure 4.2 shows thoughtful use of a trigonometric function in the Expert Section. This new Expert Section format proved popular and led to students' development of techniques particularly well suited to avoiding the shot absorbers. One of these techniques is discussed later.

Feedback to Students

Consistent with our earlier experience in designing software to promote thoughtful engagement with mathematics, Green Globs responds to student input by simply interpreting that input in terms of the mathematical model. This leaves the diagnostic analysis to the student. The only criterion of correctness is whether the graph did what the student wanted it to do.

This style of graphic feedback, inherent in the model, was unusual in software design at the time. Many developers considered written congratulatory or corrective responses to student input an essential feature of good software design. More than once another software developer

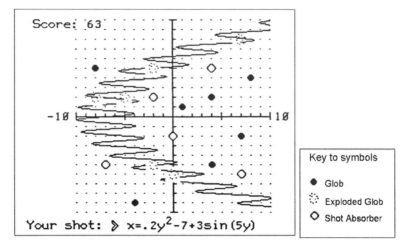

Figure 4.2.   A student in the Expert Section has constructed a parabola and then added 3sin(5y) to the equation to make the graph cover a wider path while avoiding the five shot absorbers.

expressed puzzlement about the seeming lack of feedback in programs like Green Globs. For example, during a small conference that brought together software developers from the contrasting traditions of Intelligent Tutoring Systems (ITS) and the more loosely defined area of Computer-based Education (Larkin & Chabay, 1992), my presentation of Green Globs precipitated a spate of animated whispering among a group of ITS colleagues. I overhead the word "feedback" several times before one of the participants spoke up with, "I've got it! The graph is the feedback!" This launched a productive discussion of the potential for responding to student input with a wider range of feedback than verbal comment.

Verbal comment can provide explicit guidance and point out things that might otherwise be overlooked by a student. However, in my experience, particularly with open-ended mathematical models, verbal feedback often misses the mark in assuming what a student is trying to do. A graphical interpretation of the student's input, on the other hand, is invariably relevant to what the student intended, and it often provides sufficient information for a student to diagnose errors and refine techniques.

Engagement and Mathematical Community

A major goal for Green Globs and our other programs was to encourage the type of intense engagement that had captured children's attention in the fractions curriculum and had kept them interacting with a particular model long enough and at sufficient depth to establish a comfortable working familiarity with the mathematics involved. In an effort to replicate the success of children's exchange of ideas in the fractions curriculum libraries, we added a Records Section to Green Globs. The prospect of storing solutions for classmates to examine increased students' incentive for producing and sharing clever, creative, and highly personal mathematical strategies. Further, techniques learned from classmates' stored solutions enhanced many students' performance in formulating their own solutions.

The move from the network environment of the PLATO system to microcomputers placed more stringent limits on storage space for student work and further limited the exchange of ideas to those students using the same floppy diskette. Because there was no longer space for every user to store favorites, we had to be more selective about what could be stored. Students whose scores ranked in the top ten games on a diskette were invited to store their games in the Records Section. All students could view the list of top ten scores, and more importantly, they could select any game on the list and see a shot-by-shot "replay" to glean techniques from the highest scoring players. Although this did not provide the wide-ranging interaction available through a network, each classroom shared several diskettes, and the result was a substantial exchange of techniques.

SUMMATIVE EVALUATIONS

The formative research process resulted in a set of programs that were ready for a more formal implementation and evaluation. Green Globs was one of the project's four programs related to equations and their graphs. In addition to collecting extensive observational data, we used a criterion-referenced test at one site to assess students' learning of some topics related to high school algebra. The 22-item test dealt with linear and quadratic graphs. Most items involved writing an equation for a given linear or parabolic graph, or matching a given equation (presented in standard textbook form) with an appropriate graph. One item requested an equation for a graph through two given points on a coordinate grid; two other items asked students to sketch a parabola and write its equation, given a coordinate grid with the vertex and two or more other points identified on the parabola.

Four microcomputers were placed in a mathematics classroom in a school where the materials had not been used previously. Observation of students continued, though observers in this classroom did not interact with students as they had during the formative process. We had access to an Algebra II class and a geometry class taught by the same teacher. The teacher was comfortable having the geometry students invest some of their class time in topics that could benefit them the following year when they would enroll in Algebra II. Both groups of students were given the criterion-referenced test before the microcomputer work began and three weeks later at the end of the school year. Although the situation was far from ideal, any gains among the geometry students could reasonably be attributed to the use of our materials. For comparison, the Algebra II class provided a measure of performance for students who were a year ahead of the geometry students and studying in class the topics covered by the test.

Due to some personnel issues within the school, it took longer than expected to determine which teacher would be using the microcomputers, so the program was begun several weeks later than planned. Starting the program three weeks from the end of the school year prevented most students from progressing as far as we would have liked. The geometry students used our materials for about 2.5 to 3 hours per student, with the exception of one student who chose to come in during nonclass hours to complete a total of about 10 hours with the materials.

The Algebra II students were expected not to use our materials. However, as sometimes happens when attractive materials are introduced into a classroom, it was difficult to limit use only to the students who were expected to use them. The teacher reported that the Algebra II students were exposed to the materials for an average of about 1.5 hours per student, in somewhat less organized fashion than the geometry students.

Forty-nine students were present for both the pretest and posttest: 25 in the geometry class and 24 in the Algebra II class. The Algebra II students' greater prior exposure to linear and quadratic graphs was apparent on the pretest, for which the mean score for the 24 Algebra II students was 35%, compared to a mean score of only 8% for the 25 geometry students on the pretest. Because the topics covered in our materials were a part of the Algebra II curriculum, we expected that gains from pretest to posttest for those students in the last 3 weeks of the school year would reflect whatever preparation they had made for their final exam. Posttest performance was on the average fairly comparable for the two groups, with mean scores of 52% for the Algebra II students and 50% for the geometry students. The geometry students' posttest performance was particularly encouraging in light of the short amount of treatment time that limited their progress through the materials. The one geometry student who used nonclass hours for additional time with the materials went from a pretest score of 9% to a posttest score of 100%.

Qualitative Observations

Ongoing observation of and interaction with students, as well as examination of their work stored on disks, helped shed light on students' development and use of techniques in working with equations and graphs. Participating students were enrolled in a range of classes, primarily introductory algebra through advanced algebra. One particular focus of the observations was students' development of strategies in Green Globs, including the evolution of individual students' techniques, as well as the spread of strategies among students through direct contact or review of games stored in the Records Section.

Some students became very creative in their approach to Green Globs. These students invented a variety of mathematical techniques and built on the techniques used by their classmates. Two popular techniques involved factored polynomial functions and rational functions. Students' experimentation with these functions persisted from one year to the next and from one group of students to the next. Figure 4.3 shows a use of a factored polynomial function in Green Globs. In this example, students have constructed a function to cross the x-axis at –8, –2, and 4. Using the coordinates of a glob centered at (–5, 4), they have computed an appropriate transformation factor to contract the graph vertically in order to hit five globs.

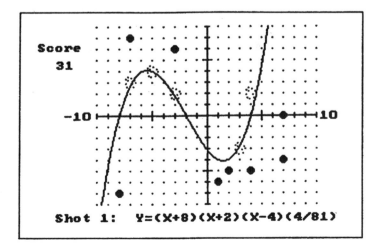

Figure 4.3.   Use of a factored polynomial function.

Use of factored polynomial functions gained widespread popularity when students extended the technique to as many factors as could be fit onto the screen. With a sufficiently large coefficient, the function could be stretched vertically so that what appeared in the viewing window on the screen was essentially a series of vertical lines, one for each factor in the function, as shown in Figure 4.4. This provided a relatively simple technique to hit all of the globs centered at a specific selection of x-coordinates. The factored polynomial technique could have been used to hit all of the globs with one shot, except that the space available for typing the equation is limited by the edge of the screen. Facing this limitation, some resourceful students used the identity $(x + a)(x - a) = x^2 - a^2$ to shorten their equations and make room for more factors. For example, $(x + 3)(x - 3)$ could be replaced by $(x^2 - 9)$. The factored polynomial technique was easy to learn, and it produced high scores in Green Globs. Hence, it was the most widely used of the techniques devised by students.

Students playing Green Globs used rational functions to produce asymptotic behavior in their graphs. This technique was particularly rewarding in the Expert Section, where successful graphs must avoid the shot absorbers while hitting the globs. Figure 4.5 illustrates students' use of rational functions combined with other techniques. Starting with the vertical line $x = 1$, these students in an Algebra II class have added three rational terms to their function to produce discontinuities in specific places, and they have carefully constructed each term to maximize its

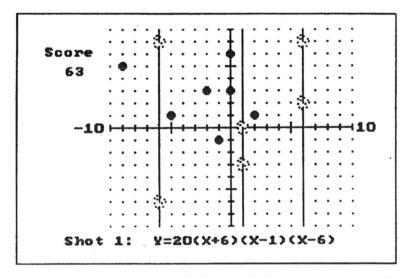

Figure 4.4.   A factored polynomial function has been stretched vertically so that what appears on the screen is essentially a set of vertical lines.

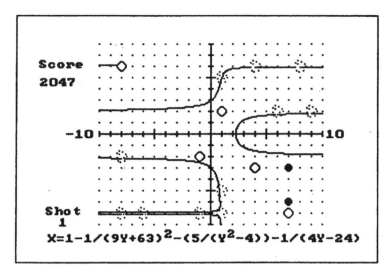

Figure 4.5.   Students in the Expert Section have combined rational functions and various algebraic techniques to hit eleven globs with one shot. Their shot ends in a shot absorber at (–8, 6).

effectiveness in hitting the globs. They have squared the denominator of the first rational term to make both branches of the graph go the same direction, thus hitting globs at (–1, –7), (–6, –7), and (–8, –7) while avoiding a shot absorber at (7, –7). In the second rational term they have combined factors $(y - 2)$ and $(y + 2)$ into $(y^2 - 4)$ to save space and produce two discontinuities with one term. Further, they have carefully chosen their coefficients to cause the "corners" of their graph to be more nearly square near (1, –7), where there was a glob to hit, and more rounded near (1, 2) and (–1, –2), where shot absorbers were to be avoided.

Characteristics of Students' Representations of Functions

As in our earlier work with fractions, the techniques that emerged from students' experimentation differed from those usually found in textbooks. Students formulated their ideas in ways that best suited their immediate needs. Representations devised by students were natural to the medium. Functions were cast in formats that isolated the essential features of the graphs and facilitated graphical manipulation. For example, textbooks typically present rational functions as quotients of two polynomial functions, whereas students' development of rational functions resulted in a basic function to define the overall shape of the graph, plus several individual rational terms, each used to insert a discontinuity and control the behavior of the function near that discontinuity. The students' representation isolated the effect of each term of the function, so that transformations on individual terms could be used to manipulate the graph near specific x-values.

Similarly, students' construction of polynomial functions in factored form facilitated manipulation of the zeros and extrema more directly than the conventional expression of a polynomial function as a sum of terms of the form ax^n. Given the expanding capability of computers for algebraic symbol manipulation, the difficulty of translating between different forms of an algebraic expression may no longer be as big an issue as choosing a form that best reveals the features that are essential for the current application.

FURTHER DEVELOPMENT

Students' Work as a Basis for New Design

Among the students involved in Green Globs, there were relatively few true pioneers who initiated explorations in substantially new directions. A larger number of participants used the strategies of their pioneering classmates or constructed variations of those strategies. There were also students who remained on the periphery of the creative activity, successfully playing the game with primarily linear and quadratic graphs, and not participating in the invention of new techniques or in the adaptation of classmates' novel strategies. Further, students who participated in inventing and refining new techniques usually proceeded experimentally, often by trial and error, and it was often not clear to what extent they formalized their understanding of the mathematics they were using. This observation raised the question of whether students' experiences could be enhanced by more direct attention to formalizing and generalizing the mathematics inherent in their techniques.

The suggestion that more attention be paid to formalization and generalization is not to dismiss the value of experimentation and observation as a route to conceptualizing mathematical ideas and techniques. Rather it is to emphasize the value of following up observations by describing what happens, generalizing the findings, and testing the generalizations in other contexts. There is inherent reward in doing this, because techniques may be extendable, and therefore more powerful, if they are formalized. In order to establish a comfortable familiarity and working facility with mathematical concepts, a cycle of *alternately* experimenting and formalizing may be the optimal approach.

Our observations of students' range of participation styles, combined with an interest in encouraging students to formalize and generalize their techniques, led directly to a subsequent software development effort. Under a grant from the National Science Foundation,[4] selected techniques devised by students in Green Globs were used as a basis for new software designed to encourage more students to construct their own mathematical ideas and techniques, utilize a wider variety of algebraic techniques, and formalize the mathematics inherent in their techniques.

The intent of this development was to devise appropriate learning incentives and opportunities to enhance the mathematical experience for the full range of creative pioneers, involved followers, and peripheral participants. We wanted to provide sufficient guidance to ensure students' use of various techniques, and at the same time require enough thinking and strategizing to compel students to explore beyond what they had been shown explicitly how to do. Learning how to approach new problem situations and conceive new techniques was considered at least as important as learning the techniques themselves. Student-invented techniques were considered especially appropriate because they were ideas that lent well to experimenting and observing, they were related to fundamental ideas covered in algebra texts, and they differed sufficiently from the usual textbook approaches to require some "new" thinking and adaptation of basic algebra content.

Software Design

The resulting software, titled Slalom, ZOT, ZigZag (Dugdale, Kibbey, & Wagner, 1991) was designed to provide an informal, exploratory introduction to polynomial and rational functions and related algebraic ideas.[5] The software approaches each type of function with a sequence of challenges whose solutions require use of a range of techniques. Each challenge builds on the previous ones in the set, and the set of challenges concludes with a game in which students combine and extend the techniques addressed in the challenges. The challenges and games treat functions and graphs in an exploratory, sometimes whimsical, spirit, as can be seen in the examples that follow.

Each challenge has one or more hints available to help students develop strategies useful in solving the challenge. The structure of challenges with hints is intended to accomplish the following:

- Reverse the traditional approach of introducing techniques and then providing problems for practice. Instead, a problem is posed, a technique must be devised, and hints (not solutions) are available upon request.

- Encourage independence in developing strategies. The hints offer thought-provoking suggestions and encourage students to develop their own problem-solving strategies. A hint generally requires some mathematical thinking to apply it to the given problem.
- Accommodate a wide range of student learning styles. Given the observed differences in students' inclinations to experiment with new functions and techniques in Green Globs, we anticipated that students would require different levels of assistance in developing new techniques.
- Relate new techniques to more general mathematical ideas. The hints develop a mathematical basis for the needed techniques.

The model of challenges, hints, and games supports a combination of inductive and deductive learning strategies. The hints provide focused assistance to students who are unsure of how to approach the challenges, and the challenges are carefully sequenced to build techniques applicable to the more open-ended games. However, by having thought-provoking hints available only through the challenges, rather than having straightforward tutorials directly accessible, Slalom, ZOT, ZigZag exhibits a preference for an inductive approach.

Treatment of Factored Polynomial Functions

The first challenge dealing with factored polynomial functions asks students to construct a function whose graph passes through two given points on the x-axis without passing through a block between them. If a student requests a hint, the hint guides an interactive discussion about how to construct a function whose graph crosses the x-axis at any two given points. Succeeding challenges extend this idea to more than two factors, asking students to construct functions whose graphs cross the x-axis in three or more given places. Vocabulary is introduced as these crossing places are referred to as *zeros* of the functions. The final two challenges in this section add constraints of keeping the graph within a limited range between the zeros (see Figure 4.6) and making it go through a specified target located away from the x-axis. The hints for these two challenges offer suggestions for transforming the function to stretch and contract the graph vertically in order to meet specified constraints.

The challenges are followed by a game, Slalom, in which students construct functions with appropriate zeros, maxima, and minima to determine a skier's path through a course of flags or gates. When an equation is entered, a skier proceeds along the specified path, leaving the graph as a trail, as shown in Figure 4.7. The entire graph plots, regardless of whether the run is successful. This gives students the "whole picture" as

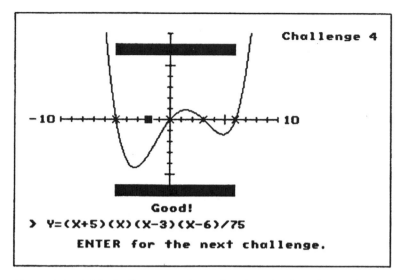

Figure 4.6.   This challenge requires a function that has given zeros (marked by X's) and whose graph stays within a limited range between the zeros. The challenge has been successfully completed.

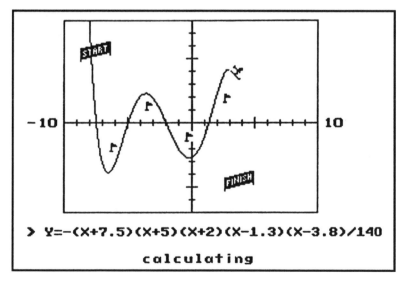

Figure 4.7.   The skier clears the fourth flag in a successful game of Slalom. The skier must enter through the START banner, go alternately below and above the flags, and exit through the FINISH banner, without leaving the course bounds before the run is complete.

diagnostic information to use in adjusting the function after an unsuccessful run. When students choose gates instead of flags on the ski slope, the skier must go *through* the gates (not just above and below them), so more precision is necessary. Students can attempt a Slalom course as many times as they like. It usually takes several tries to adjust the graph to an appropriate shape.

Treatment of Rational Functions

The activities for rational functions are structured similarly to those for polynomial functions. A sequence of challenges requires construction of ideas and techniques, and hints are available by request. The challenges are followed by a game, ZOT!, in which students combine and extend their techniques to hit targets located in a system of tunnels. Each tunnel pattern is a horizontal or diagonal path with vertical side tunnels. The vertical tunnels may go up only, down only, or both ways. Some intersections may have diagonal obstructions, so that the direction of the graph branches must be planned carefully.

Students may choose to have the targets in the tunnels be ants or abstract rectangular objects. If ants are chosen, the main character of the game is the anteater with an incredible tongue (see Figure 4.8). The anteater's tongue is capable of leaving the screen, wrapping all the way around infinity (that's incredible!), and reentering the screen from the

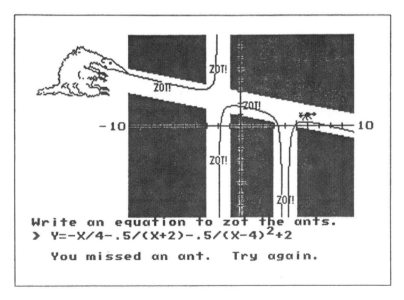

Write an equation to zot the ants.
> $Y=-X/4-.5/(X+2)-.5/(X-4)^2+2$

You missed an ant.   Try again.

Figure 4.8.   A game of ZOT! The anteater has hit five ants, but has missed the sixth.

other direction. However, it must avoid any blocks in the tunnels, and it cannot go through the ground around the tunnels. Students usually need several tries to construct an appropriate graph and adjust it to navigate the tunnels. The example in Figure 4.8 requires a function with a linear term and two rational terms. Further, in order to stay inside the tunnels, the second rational term must have negative function values on both sides of the asymptote, so the denominator of this term has been squared and a negative coefficient has been used.

Results

As with previous software projects, Slalom, ZOT, ZigZag was developed in conjunction with classroom use. Observations and interviews of students contributed to the design and revision of the materials. Working in pairs or small groups and sometimes using the hints provided in the software, students mastered the challenges and succeeded in the games. As anticipated, students showed a variety of individual learning styles in their approaches to the challenges, hints, and games. For example, some students were determined to create appropriate responses for the challenges without using the hints, whereas others readily accessed the hints, sometimes before giving the challenge a serious try. Still others bypassed the challenges and hints altogether and worked diligently to master the games without help. Some of these occasionally retreated to the challenges in search of specific techniques, much as one would access a reference manual.

In general, students broadened their variety of techniques and developed a more interactive approach to constructing mathematical knowledge, experimenting and refining techniques as needed to succeed with a given task. The development effort, software, and results are described in more detail in Dugdale (1994). The synopsis provided here illustrates the continuity from one development project to the next and the influence of classroom-based testing on the direction of further development.

Reflections

Slalom, ZOT, ZigZag tested the feasibility of structuring software to channel students toward mathematical discoveries. In retrospect, although it was successful in many ways, the effort probably crossed the boundary of what is better left to a teacher in face-to-face interactions with students. Teachers still vary widely in their preparedness and comfort in using technological tools to support mathematics instruction.

However, in comparison with their counterparts of previous decades, today's classroom teachers are more likely to be actively and knowledgeably engaged in guiding their students' interactions with technology. Hence, there is less need for computer-based models to try to bring closure to a mathematical experience independent of teacher involvement. My subsequent work (see, e.g., Dugdale 1998a, 1998b) has focused on using versatile tools, such as equation graphers and spreadsheets, for explorations that rely on teacher guidance to direct students' attention and formalize the mathematics gleaned from the exploration.

CONCLUSION

In this chapter, I have attempted to present a perspective of development, not as a one-project or one-product venture, but rather as a continuing journey. The chapter highlights the continuity from each development project to the next and the influence of classroom-based testing on the direction of further development. Although the development of a particular program or curriculum may come to closure, the experience gained, theories built, questions raised, and the like, form the basis of further development and, in turn, are refined through that development.

Within each cycle, the most rewarding aspect has been observing students' interactions with mathematical models, and the products of their mathematical thought and creativity, as exemplified by some of their work described in this chapter and my previous chapter (Dugdale, 2008). Technological tools have proved particularly adept at providing students rich interactive mathematical models, the motivation to explore and learn from those models, and the facility to share with other students their creative solutions and approaches to mathematics.

One persistent challenge in my work has been the desire to involve all students in the creative spirit and habits of mathematical thinking that have been exhibited by some. Our experiences suggest that this aspect is best facilitated by a talented teacher who is both mathematically well grounded and technologically knowledgeable. Such teachers are best able to monitor students' creative solution processes, selectively draw attention to mathematical breakthroughs, and guide students in formalizing and reflecting on the mathematics they are learning. Teacher support and development are promising areas of investment as we seek to realize the full potential of the rich array of technological tools available to support mathematics learning today.

NOTES

1. The PLATO® system is a development of the University of Illinois. PLATO® is a service mark of Control Data Corporation.
2. Grant No. SED-8012449.
3. Features reported here were developed by David Kibbey, who designed and programmed the equation-graphing interface. Kibbey ported these features to a 48K Apple II in the early 1980s, and subsequently to other microcomputers. They make the current Macintosh and Windows versions of the software among the more user-friendly and mathematically accurate graphing options available yet today.
4. Grant No. MDR 84-70608.
5. The software also addresses absolute value functions and parallel and perpendicular lines. However, the treatment of these topics is not as directly related to student-initiated techniques, so they are not discussed here.

REFERENCES

Arons, A. B. (1982). Phenomenology and logical reasoning in introductory physics courses. *American Journal of Physics*, *50*, 13-20.

Confrey, J. (1993). The role of technology in reconceptualizing functions and algebra. In J. R. Becker & B. J. Pence (Eds.), *Proceedings of the fifteenth annual meeting of the North American Chapter of the International Group for the Psychology of Mathematics Education* (Vol. 1, pp. 47-74). San Jose, CA: San Jose State University, The Center for Mathematics and Science Education.

Demana, F., Schoen, H. L., & Waits, B. (1993). Graphing in the K-12 curriculum: The impact of the graphing calculator. In T. A. Romberg, E. Fennema, & T. P. Carpenter (Eds.), *Integrating research on the graphical representation of functions* (pp. 11-39). Hillsdale, NJ: Erlbaum.

Demana, F., & Waits, B. (1990). *Precalculus mathematics: A graphing approach*. Reading, MA: Addison-Wesley.

Dugdale, S. (1982). Green Globs: A microcomputer application for graphing of equations. *Mathematics Teacher*, *75*, 208-214.

Dugdale, S. (1994). Using students' mathematical inventiveness as a foundation for software design: Toward a tempered constructivism. *Educational Technology Research and Development*, *42*, 57-73.

Dugdale, S. (1998a). A spreadsheet investigation of sequences and series for middle grades through precalculus. *Journal of Computers in Mathematics and Science Teaching*, *17*, 203-222.

Dugdale, S. (1998b). Newton's method for square root: A spreadsheet investigation and extension into chaos. *Mathematics Teacher*, *91*, 576-585.

Dugdale, S. (2008). Research in a pioneer constructivist network-based curriculum project for children's learning of fractions. In G. W. Blume & M. K. Heid (Eds.), *Research on technology and the teaching and learning of mathematics: Vol. 2. Cases and perspectives* (pp. 3-30). Charlotte, NC: Information Age.

Dugdale, S., & Kibbey, D. (1980). *The fractions curriculum of the PLATO elementary school mathematics project* (2nd ed., CERL Report E-17). Urbana, IL: Computer-based Education Research Laboratory.

Dugdale, S., & Kibbey, D. (1986a). Interpreting Graphs [Computer software]. Pleasantville, NY: Sunburst Communications.

Dugdale, S., & Kibbey, D. (1986b). Green Globs and Graphing Equations [Computer software]. Pleasantville, NY: Sunburst Communications.

Dugdale, S., Kibbey, D., & Wagner, L. J. (1991). Slalom, ZOT, ZigZag: Challenges in Graphing Equations [Computer software]. Pleasantville, NY: Sunburst Communications.

Karplus, R. (1979, October-December). Continuous functions: Students' viewpoints. *European Journal of Science Education, 1*, 397-415.

Kieran, C. (1993). Functions, graphing, and technology: Integrating research on learning and instruction. In T. A. Romberg, E. Fennema, & T. P. Carpenter (Eds.), *Integrating research on the graphical representation of functions* (pp. 11-39). Hillsdale, NJ: Erlbaum.

Larkin, J. H., & Chabay, R. W. (Eds.). (1992). *Computer assisted instruction and intelligent tutoring systems: Shared issues and complementary approaches*. Hillsdale, NJ: Erlbaum.

Mokros, J. R., & Tinker, R. F. (1987). The impact of microcomputer-based labs on children's ability to interpret graphs. *Journal of Research in Science Teaching, 24*, 369-383.

Moschkovich, J., Schoenfeld, A. H., & Arcavi, A. A. (1993). Aspects of understanding: On multiple perspectives and representations of linear relations and connections among them. In T. A. Romberg, E. Fennema, & T. P. Carpenter (Eds.), *Integrating research on the graphical representation of functions* (pp. 69-100). Hillsdale, NJ: Erlbaum.

Peters, P. C. (1982). Even honors students have conceptual difficulties with physics. *American Journal of Physics, 50*, 501-508.

Stifle, J., Smith, S., & Andersen, D. (1979). Microprocessor delivery of PLATO courseware. In *Proceedings of the annual convention of the Association for the Development of Computer-based Instructional Systems* (Vol. III, pp. 1027-1035). San Diego, CA: ADCIS.

Texas Instruments. (1990). *TI-81 guidebook*. Dallas, TX: Author.

Yerushalmy, M., & Schwartz, J. L. (1993). Seizing the opportunity to make algebra mathematically and pedagogically interesting. In T. A. Romberg, E. Fennema, & T. P. Carpenter (Eds.), *Integrating research on the graphical representation of functions* (pp. 41-68). Hillsdale, NJ: Erlbaum.

CHAPTER 5

LINKING RESEARCH AND SOFTWARE DEVELOPMENT

Julie Sarama and Douglas H. Clements

We posit that one reason that educational software has not realized its full potential to facilitate and encourage students' mathematical thinking and learning is that it has not been adequately linked with research. In the majority of cases, testing the software with target users is rare or limited to simple interface or motivational issues. Instead, we propose that software development be comprehensively linked to research to increase both the software's educational effectiveness and the contribution the software development process makes to educational research. To accomplish these goals, software development and research must be dynamically interacting, tightly linked processes. In this chapter, we briefly describe principles for comprehensive research-based curriculum and software development and describe and illustrate one model for integrated development that is consistent with these principles.

PRINCIPLES FOR COMPREHENSIVE RESEARCH-BASED CURRICULUM AND SOFTWARE DEVELOPMENT

Practices in developing and pilot testing software vary widely. Formative research is often minimal, for example, involving polling of convenience

Research on Technology and the Teaching and Learning of Mathematics:
Vol. 2. Cases and Perspectives, 113–130
Copyright © 2008 by Information Age Publishing

samples. "Beta" testing is sometimes conducted, but it usually occurs late enough in the process that changes are minimal, given the time and resources already dedicated to the project and the limited budget and pressing deadlines that remain (Char, 1989). Such inadequate practices would be improved by comprehensively linking the development of an educational innovation to research methods, including evaluation of the innovation's specific contributions to students' learning and development. Some projects have done just that (Battista & Clements, 2000; Clements & Battista, 2000; Cobb & McClain, 2002; Gravemeijer, 1994b; Lewis & Tsuchida, 1998; Yerushalmy, 1997). In a review of those projects, we abstracted principles for comprehensive research-based curriculum and software development (Clements, 2002; Clements & Battista, 2000). These and the guidelines are summarized here; the focus of this chapter is to illustrate their use in a current software development process.

Connect Research and Curriculum/Software Development and Treat Them as Integrated, Interactive Processes

Curriculum and software development might be "based" on research in several ways (Clements, 2002). Developers might consider broad philosophies, theories, and empirical results on learning and teaching when first planning curriculum, structure activities to be consistent with empirically-based models of children's thinking and learning, or evaluate their efforts formatively or summatively (Schauble, 1990). We believe that the development of quality software requires the inclusion of not one, but all of these strategies. These and many other connections between research and curriculum must be forged and maintained throughout the development process.

Use Learning Trajectories Based on Models of Cognition and Models of Mathematics

Learning trajectories consist of rich descriptions of children's thinking and learning in a specific mathematical domain and a conjectured instructional route for that learning (Gravemeijer, 1999; Simon, 1995). In more detail, we define learning trajectories as follows:

> descriptions of children's thinking and learning in a specific mathematical domain, and a related, conjectured route through a set of instructional tasks designed to engender those mental processes or actions hypothesized to move children through a developmental progression of levels of thinking,

created with the intent of supporting children's achievement of specific goals in that mathematical domain. (Clements & Sarama, 2004b, p. 83)

Thus, learning trajectories have three components: a goal, a developmental sequence specifying levels through which children grow toward the goal, and instructional activities that facilitate that growth. The developmental sequence is based on models of children's cognition. In contrast to other approaches, such as those based on the historical development of a mathematical idea or anticipatory thought experiments (Gravemeijer, 1994b), we believe that existing research should be a primary means of constructing the first draft of these developmental sequences. This is especially true for the development of software, which, compared to the construction of print-based curriculum materials, often demands that more elements be specified in detail.

In addition, the instructional activities often externalize the mental concepts and processes as software objects and actions hypothesized to move children from one level to the next. That is, students are guided to operate on specific screen objects with specific actions so as to build and internalize the goal concepts and processes. Thus, the software activities frequently use a different type of model: a model of mathematics used to support children's cognition. Gravemeijer (1999) describes how such models undergo a transition in which such a model initially emerges as a *model of* informal mathematical activity (a "model of" a situation, such as people getting on and off a bus as a concrete model of arithmetic) and then gradually develops into a *model for* more formal mathematical reasoning (symbolic descriptions of the bus situations becoming a "model for" more formal, yet personally meaningful, mathematical reasoning). Both are important; in our approach, the two are coordinated and synthesized, which we believe provides additional explanatory and instructional power (Clements, 2002; Clements & Battista, 2000).

Curriculum Must Also Be Informed by Ecological Perspectives, Including Research on Teachers and the Social and Cultural Context

Curriculum and software development, and the research that informs that development, do not stand apart from teachers. Teachers' knowledge, theories, and belief systems influence their instructional plans, decisions, and actions, including their implementation of curricula (especially because teachers affect the way software is used by, and influences, children more than the reverse [Sarama & Clements, 2002]). Developers must consider these factors, as well as the classroom social context.

Document and Describe the Development, Implementation, and Evaluation Procedures in Detail for Each Phase

Any scientific research carefully documents the procedures used. This requirement is especially intense for research-based curriculum and software development, when myriad decisions of many types are made on a variety of bases.

RESEARCH-BASED SOFTWARE DEVELOPMENT: A MODEL

As an example of an approach that embodies these principles, we describe and illustrate our own model for integrated research and curriculum development, emphasizing the development of software (Clements, 2002; Clements & Battista, 2000). The model moves through phases, but is not rigidly linear. Results in one phase can suggest a return to previous phases. The methodologies are complex and interwoven.

Phase 1: Draft the Initial Goals

The first phase begins with the identification of a significant domain of mathematics. The learning of the domain should make a substantive contribution to students' mathematical development. Learning about students' mathematical activity in the domain should make a similar contribution to research and theory.

As we began our NSF-funded project, Building Blocks, we determined that a basic, often neglected, area of children's mathematics was the composition and decomposition of two-dimensional geometric figures (other domains in geometry include shapes and their properties, transformations/congruence, and measurement). The geometric composition domain was determined to be significant for students. In the process of working with two- and three-dimensional shapes, children often decompose those shapes into familiar shapes and recombine the component shapes in ways that maintain such attributes as area, perimeter, and volume. This is a basic geometric competence that develops as preschoolers work with blocks and continues to be central to sophisticated interpretation and analysis of geometric situations in high school and beyond (Clements, Battista, Sarama, & Swaminathan, 1997; Reynolds & Wheatley, 1996; Steffe & Cobb, 1988). The domain is significant to research and theory in that there is a paucity of research on the trajectories students might follow in developing these ideas.

Phase 2: Build an Explicit Model of Students' Knowledge, Including Hypothesized Learning Trajectories

In this phase, developers build a sufficiently explicit cognitive model of students' learning that describes the processes involved in the construction of the goal mathematics concepts. Although extant models may be available, they vary in degree of specificity. Developers build these models, or fill in details of existing models, by using clinical interviews and observations to examine students' knowledge of the content domain, including intuitive ideas, and informal strategies used to solve problems. These cognitive models are then synthesized into hypothesized learning trajectories (Cobb & McClain, 2002; Gravemeijer, 1999; Simon, 1995).

As an example, our synthesis of research for the Building Blocks project posits the following developmental sequence describing children's development of strategies for composing and decomposing geometric shapes. The basic structure of this sequence was determined by observations made in the context of early research (Sarama, Clements, & Vukelic, 1996) and was later refined through a research review and a series of clinical interviews and focused observations conducted by research staff and teachers (Clements, Sarama, & Wilson, 2001). Observations were made using two tasks, creating free-form pictures with shapes and completing outline puzzles with well-defined shape sets, such as pattern blocks or tangram shapes. The levels identified in these observations are encapsulated in the following list.

Precomposer

Children manipulate shapes as individual entities, but are unable or unwilling to combine them to compose a larger shape. In making free-form pictures, they lay out separate shapes, one for each object in their picture.

Piece Assembler

Children behave similarly to those at Level 1, but can concatenate shapes to form pictures. In free-form "make a picture" tasks, for example, each shape used represents a unique role, or function in the picture, for example, one shape for a body of a horse, another for a head, another for each leg, and so forth. Children can fill simple frames using trial and error (Mansfield & Scott, 1990; Sales, 1994) and use turns or flips to do so, but again by trial and error; they cannot use motions to see shapes from different perspectives (Sarama et al., 1996). Thus, children at Levels 1 and 2 view shapes only as wholes and see no geometric relationship between shapes or between parts of shapes (i.e., properties of the shape).

Picture Maker

In creating free-form pictures, children can concatenate shapes to form pictures in which several shapes play a single role, but use trial and error and do not anticipate creation of a new geometric shape. For example, they may lay down several squares for the leg of a horse, but without knowing that this will produce a rectangle. They choose shapes using gestalt configuration or one component such as side length (Sarama et al., 1996). If several sides of the existing arrangement form a partial boundary of a shape (instantiating a schema for it), children can find and place that shape. If such cues are not present, children match by a side length. They may attempt to match corners, but do not possess angle as a quantitative entity, so will try to match shapes into corners of existing arrangements in which their angles do not fit. Rotating and flipping are used, usually by trial and error, to try different arrangements (a "picking and discarding" strategy). Thus, children at this level can complete frames whose structure strongly suggests the placement of individual shapes, but in which several shapes together may play a single semantic role in the picture.

Shape Composer

Children combine shapes to make new shapes or fill frames, with growing intentionality and anticipation ("I know what will fit"). For example, they purposely use different pattern blocks to make hexagons, just for the variety of colors this produces. They choose shapes using angles as well as side lengths. Eventually they consider several alternative shapes with angles equal to the existing arrangement. They use rotation and flipping intentionally (and mentally, i.e., with anticipation) to select and place shapes (Sarama et al., 1996). They can fill complex frames (Sales, 1994) or cover regions (Mansfield & Scott, 1990). Imagery and systematicity grow within this and the next levels. In summary, there is intentionality and anticipation, based on shapes' attributes, and thus, children have imagery of the component shapes, although imagery of the composite shape develops within this level (and throughout the next levels).

Substitution Composer

Children deliberately form composite units of shapes (Clements et al., 1997) and recognize and use substitution relationships among these shapes (e.g., two pattern block trapezoids can make a hexagon).

Shape Composite Iterator

Children construct and operate on composite units intentionally. They can continue a pattern of shapes that leads to a "good covering," but without coordinating units of units.

Shape Composer With Units of Units

Children build and apply units of units (superordinate units). For example, in constructing spatial patterns, children extend their patterning activity to create a tiling with a new unit shape—a (higher order) unit of unit shapes that they recognize and consciously construct; that is, children conceptualize each unit as being constituted of multiple singletons and as being one higher order unit (Clements et al., 1997).

In summary, the result of this phase is an explicit cognitive model of students' learning of mathematics in the target domain. Ideally, such models specify knowledge structures, the development of these structures, including mechanisms or processes related to this development, and trajectories that specify hypothetical routes that children might take in learning the mathematics.

Phase 3: Create an Initial Design for Software and Activities

In this phase, developers create a basic design to describe the objects that will constitute the software environment and the actions that may be performed on these objects based on the model of students' learning generated in Phase 2. These actions-on-objects should mirror the hypothesized mathematical activity of students. Offering students such objects and actions to be performed on these objects is consistent with the Vygotskian theory that mediation by tools and signs is critical in the development of human cognition (Steffe & Tzur, 1994). Further, designs based on objects and actions force the developer to focus on explicit actions or processes and what they will mean to the students.

In Building Blocks, for example, we wish to allow students to work with both shapes and composite shapes as objects. We wish them to act on these objects—to create, duplicate, position (with geometric motions), combine, and break apart both individual shapes (units) and composite shapes (units). Thus, we created environments that included many palettes of 2D shapes and tools that could be used to act on these shapes. In Figure 5.1, the objects are shapes in a palette along the left side of the screen. Users perform actions on these shapes with tools, such as the turn and flip tools.

The developers next create a sequence of instructional activities (that use objects and actions) to move students through the hypothesized learning trajectories. These activities are created by considering the professional literature—from reform recommendations to activities—as well as the developers' own experiences. The unique potential of technology for providing cognitive tools, "concrete mathematics," and "situated abstractions" (Clements, 1994, 2000; Hoyles, 1993) should be considered. They

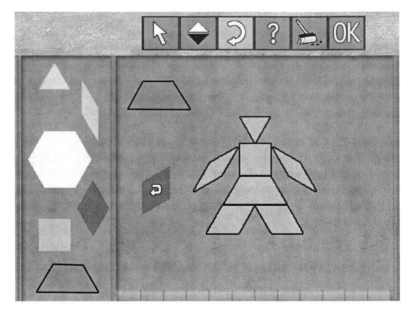

Source: Clements and Sarama (n.d.).

Figure 5.1. Building Blocks software, "Piece Puzzler."

also seek extensive advice from teachers. In Building Blocks, for example, teacher meetings were conducted monthly.

Ample opportunity for student-led, student-designed, open-ended projects must be included in the set of activities. Design activity on the part of students is frequently the best way for students to express their creativity and integrate their learning, and the computer can especially offer support for such projects (Clements, 2000).

Returning to the Building Blocks example, we initially created a sequence of activities aligned with the learning trajectory. An essential task is combining shapes to produce composite shapes (e.g., to fill a frame or create an imagined design or picture). Research shows this type of activity to be motivating for young children (Sales, 1994; Sarama et al., 1996). For the purposes of brief illustration of the essential features, only the mathematically significant basic elements are described in the following (further, all activities allow for open-ended projects using the objects and actions). Objects are well-structured geometric shapes, such as screen versions of pattern blocks or tangram shapes. At the early levels, actions include creation and duplication of shapes, deletion of shapes, and geometric motions (slides, flips, and turns). Figures 5.2A and 5.2B illustrate tasks for each level of the learning trajectory.

Level and Description of Task	Example Puzzle
Level 2. Piece Assembler. Child completes a picture given a frame that suggests the placement of the shapes, each of which plays a separate semantic role in the picture and that requires no flips or turns, such as the simple animal puzzle at the right.	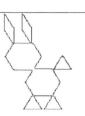
Level 3. Picture Maker. Child completes a picture given a frame that suggests the placement of the individual shapes but in which several shapes together may play a single semantic role in the picture. As the child succeeds, she is given pictures that include such combinations more frequently and that require applying (small) turn actions to the shapes. Note that the computer environment helps bring this action to an explicit level of awareness because the child must consciously choose the turn tool and because sound effects and speech are used to explicate the turning action. The child is challenged to fill an open region and is provided shapes in which matching side lengths is a useful strategy.	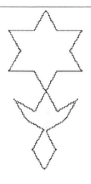
Level 4. Shape Composer. The child must use given shapes to completely fill a region that consists of multiple corners, requiring selecting and placing shapes to match angles (as in the puzzle to the right). Later tasks challenge children to fill complex frames or regions in which shape placement is ill defined, allowing for multiple solutions. These tasks require use of turning and flipping and eventually discrimination of these (e.g., the parallelogram in tangram tasks).	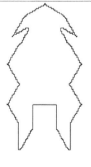

Figure 5.2A.   Descriptions and example "Piece Puzzler" tasks for Levels 2, 3, and 4 of the learning trajectory.

Level 5. Substitution Composer. The child is challenged to find as many different ways as possible to fill in a frame or region, emphasizing substitution relationships (as the child is doing to the hexagons) and angle equivalence (in the finish the wallpaper activity at the far right).

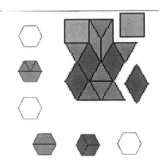
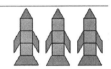
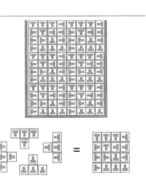

Level 6. Shape Composite Iterater. The child works in a toy factory, learning to use the glue and duplicate tools to make several copies of the same (composite) toy. The child then completes a toy puzzle using the glue, duplicate, and "do it again" tools to make and iterate composite units in filling space.

Level 7. Shape Composer with Superordinate Units. The child covers regions by building superordinate units of tetrominoes (arrangements of four squares with full sides touching) with the glue tool that are then duplicated, slid, turned, and flipped, and iterated systematically to tile the plane. For example, she might fill the rectangle at the right with a strategy that combines four "T" tetrominoes into a superordinate square.

Note: Figures 5.2A and 5.2B provide descriptions and illustrations of tasks for each level of the learning trajectory. Note that the levels constitute the *goal level* for the child, thus we begin with Level 2, the Piece Assembler level.

Figure 5.2B.   Descriptions and example "Piece Puzzler" tasks for Levels 5, 6, and 7 of the learning trajectory.

We complete this section with two caveats. First, designers and researchers should remain sensitive to additional features made possible by new technologies. However, research indicates that technological "bells and whistles" should not become a central concern. Although they can affect motivation, they rarely emerge as critical to children's learning. Instead, the critical feature is the degree to which the computer environment successfully implements education principles developed from research on the teaching and learning of specific mathematical topics (Sarama, 2000).

Second, basic research principles must be elaborated and refined by ongoing research and development work that tracks the effectiveness of specific implementations. This means that curriculum and software are not only based on research a priori. Research also must be conducted throughout the development process.

Phase 4: Investigate the Components

This phase is especially interwoven with the previous one. Components of the software are tested using clinical interviews and observations of a small number of students. A critical issue concerns how children interpret and understand the screen design, objects, and actions. A mix of model (or hypothesis) testing and model generation (e.g., a microethnographic approach, see Spradley, 1979) is used to understand the meaning that students give to the objects and actions. To accomplish this, developers may use paper or physical material mock-ups of the software or early prototype versions.

A small example of such testing used in the Building Blocks project is our research on children's initial interpretation of the actions that each icon might engender. For the decomposition of units, we had created a hammer icon. Even with minor prompting, children did not interpret this tool as breaking things apart, but instead as "nailing down" items ("It will hammer the shapes down harder") or "hammering it off" the paper or screen. We therefore created new icons (an axe "chops" shapes apart). More significant is our work with individual students using the tools. We have found that the use of these tools encourages children to become explicitly aware of the actions they perform on the shapes. Refining the tool interface for younger children while keeping the benefits previously identified through research is a continuing challenge.

Phase 5: Assess Prototypes and Curriculum

In this phase, the developers continue to evaluate the prototype, rendered in a more complete form. A major goal is to test hypotheses concerning features of the computer environment that are designed to correspond to students' thinking. Do their actions on the objects substantiate the actions of the researchers' model of children's mathematical activity? If not, should the developers change the model or should they change the way in which this model is instantiated in the software? Do students use the tools to perform the actions only with prompting? If so, what type of prompting is successful? In all cases, are students' actions-on-objects enactments of their cognitive operations (Steffe & Wiegel, 1994) in the way the learning trajectory hypothesizes, or do they merely constitute trial-and-error manipulation that is less likely to engender learning? A vivid example of this at the high school level is Dugdale's (1994) observation of children using mainly trial-and-error and "end run" methods to earn high scores on her Green Globs (Dugdale & Kibbey, 1986) computer game. A new version, Slalom, ZOT, ZigZag (Dugdale, Kibbey, & Wagner, 1991), introduced hints and sequenced tasks. It supported learning more successfully. However, it did not achieve the commercial success of the original software. Too often, externally funded and publisher-driven products do not allow the time to observe students' thinking and revise prototypes so that the final version includes research-based scaffolding support such as this.

Similarly, the developers test the learning trajectories and adjust them as needed. Using the cognitive model and learning trajectories as guides, and the software and activities as catalysts, the developer creates more refined models of particular students' cognition. Simultaneously, the developer describes what observed elements of the teaching and learning environment contributed to student learning. The theoretical model may involve disequilibrium, modeling, internalization of social processes, practice, and combinations of these and other processes. The connection of these processes with specific environmental characteristics, teaching strategies, and student learning is critical.

With so many research and development processes happening, and so many possibilities, extensive documentation is vital. Videotapes (for later microgenetic analysis), audiotapes, and field notes are collected. This documentation also should be used to evaluate and reflect on those components of the design that were based on intuition, aesthetics, and subconscious beliefs. Sometimes, focused studies are necessary, and these should be carefully documented. For example, we wished to maximize both ease of use and pedagogical advantages. We evaluated four interfaces regarding their ability to facilitate both the computer task of turning shapes and learning: tool, button, direct manipulation with continuous motion, and direct manipulation with discrete units (Sarama, Clements, Spitler, Wilson, Suresh, & Bardsley, 2002). We examined frustration levels, evidence of quantification, evidence of child's association/disassociation between the interface and the turn action, and time needed to learn to use each interface. Thirty-two 3- and 4-year-old children from two preschools were randomly assigned to using one interface mode to solve on-screen geometric puzzles. All turn modes were somewhat problematic for young children who had poor mouse control. Both tool and button interfaces were easier for children to understand and master, caused less frustration for children, and resulted in children being able to quantify their turn actions. To allow the use of "sticky drag"—an easier interface for very young children's sliding of objects, in which they click once to "pick it up" and click again to "drop it" (as opposed to needing to "click and hold" to drag it)—we chose the tool interface.

In the Building Blocks project, for example, we found that children using the computer tools develop compositional imagery. Off-computer, kindergartner Mitchell gave himself the task of making multiple hexagons. He used a trial-and-error strategy, not checking to see whether he had a hexagon until a shape was completed. On computer, Mitchell started making a hexagon out of triangles. After placing two, he counted with his finger on the screen around the center of the incomplete hexagon, imaging the other triangles. He announced that he would need four more. After placing the next one, he said, "Whoa! Now, three more!" The intentional and deliberate actions on the computer led him to form images (decomposing the hexagon mentally) and predict each succeeding placement.

As a second example, consider Alyssa, whose work is illustrated in the first picture of Level 5 (the six hexagons) in Figure 5.2B. As Alyssa fills the hexagons, she demonstrates understanding of both anticipatory use of geometric motions and substitution relationships and therefore notions of area, equivalence, and congruence.

Phase 6: Conduct Pilot Tests in a Classroom

Teachers are involved in all phases of the design model. Starting with this phase, a special emphasis is placed on the process of curricular enactment (Ball & Cohen, 1996). There are two research thrusts. First, teaching experiments continue, but in a different form. The researchers conduct classroom-based teaching experiments (including what we call interpretive case studies) with one or two children. The goal is making sense of the curricular activities as they were experienced by individual students (Gravemeijer, 1994a). Such interpretive case studies serve similar research purposes as teaching experiments but are conducted in a naturalistic classroom setting. Videotapes and extensive field notes are required so that students' performance can be examined repeatedly for evidence of their interpretations and learning.

Second, and simultaneously, the entire class is observed for information concerning the usability and effectiveness of the software and curriculum. Ethnographic participant observation is used heavily because we wish to study the teacher and students as they construct new types of classroom cultures and interactions together (Spradley, 1980). The focus is on how the materials are used and how the teacher guides students through the activities. (For our preschool materials, child-care providers and parents are also involved; classroom dynamics cannot be taken as a given.) Attention is given to how software experiences reinforce, complement, and extend learning experiences with manipulatives or print (Char, 1989) as well as the diversity in the practices of the different early childhood settings.

This pilot test phase usually involves teachers working closely with the developers. The class is taught either by a team including one of the developers and the teacher, or by a teacher familiar with and intensively involved in the development of the software and curriculum in which it is embedded.

In our Building Blocks project, several teachers in multiple settings have volunteered to be a part of this phase of testing. It is important not to choose classrooms based on convenience, especially considering access to technology. We need to be able to identify what supports, both curricular and material, teachers will need to successfully and comfortably use the materials in their school environments. Therefore, teachers from diverse backgrounds, education, years of experience, and situations (e.g., Head Start, public school) must be included.

Phase 7: Conduct Field Tests in Multiple Classrooms

We gradually expand the range of size and scope of our studies, from studies of students' learning (1 to 10 students) to studies of different kinds of teaching and their effects on student learning (10 to 100 students) to studies of what can be achieved with typical teachers under realistic circumstances (100 to 1,000 students). These field tests are conducted with teachers not initially connected intimately with development.

We completed the first of these studies in four classrooms (Clements & Sarama, 2004a, 2005). Findings most relevant to our example include significant differences on the geometry test, with effect sizes ranging from 1.47 to 2.26, and the identification of the composition subtest as having the largest positive difference between the Building Blocks and comparison groups. This confirms the power of the approach described there. In addition, we subsequently undertook two large-scale evaluations involving many more classrooms.

Phase 8: Publish

Publication is an important and often difficult process that, ideally, is begun in an earlier phase, so that concerns of the publisher are identified as soon as possible. The software and curricula may be disseminated through a variety of channels, from commercial publishers to the Internet. As simple as this seems, this phase often is problematic for both curriculum and software development and research.

Regarding curriculum, negotiations and cooperation with a commercial publisher can have a substantive influence on the final software and print materials. Multimedia-based materials often require more support and cooperation from publishers than do print materials, and there is far less financial support for innovative software materials, especially in proportion to what is required. Therefore, there may be less freedom for developers to publish their own version of their materials. These pressures often are exerted regardless of the research base for the materials. This often results in software, originally designed to support in-depth problem solving and student evaluation of mathematical strategies and products, shifting towards activities characterized by simpler problems and feedback.

There are constraints to publication of research related to curriculum and software development. Many interesting pieces of software have been created; however, the expertise developed during the production of that software too often has not been disseminated. Whether this is because resources are exhausted (finances, time, and emotional energy) or because there is no interest, nonpublication has a strong deleterious effect on the field of curriculum development and research.

CONCLUSIONS

We believe that implementing a model of curriculum and software development such as the one described here is essential to building a research base for curriculum and software development as scientific enterprises, and for moving toward a time when a solid research basis is demanded of all curricula that are used widely. At present in the United States, this is far from the case. If software is going to impact students' engagement with and understanding of central mathematical ideas, and if software development is to contribute to mathematics education research, then research needs to be embedded in all phases of the development and testing of the software.

ACKNOWLEDGMENTS

This chapter was supported in part by the National Science Foundation under Grants No. ESI-9730804, "Building Blocks—Foundations for Mathematical Thinking, Pre-Kindergarten to Grade 2: Research-based Materials Development;" REC-9903409, "Technology-Enhanced Learning of Geometry in Elementary Schools;" and ESI-98-17540: "Conference on Standards for Preschool and Kindergarten Mathematics Education." Work on the research was also supported in part by the Interagency Educational Research Initiative (NSF, DOE, and NICHHD) Grant No. REC-0228440 to D. H. Clements, J. Sarama, A. Klein, and P. Starkey, "Scaling Up the Implementation of a Pre-Kindergarten Mathematics Curricula: Teaching for Understanding with Trajectories and Technologies." Any opinions, findings, and conclusions or recommendations expressed in this material are those of the authors and do not necessarily reflect the views of the National Science Foundation.

REFERENCES

Ball, D. L., & Cohen, D. K. (1996). Reform by the book: What is–or might be–the role of curriculum materials in teacher learning and instructional reform? *Educational Researcher, 16*, 6-8, 14.

Battista, M. T., & Clements, D. H. (2000). Mathematics curriculum development as a scientific endeavor. In A. E. Kelly & R. A. Lesh (Eds.), *Handbook of research design in mathematics and science education* (pp. 737-760). Mahwah, NJ: Erlbaum.

Char, C. A. (1989, March). *Formative research in the development of mathematics software for young children.* Paper presented at the meeting of the American Educational Research Association, San Francisco, CA.

Clements, D. H. (1994). The uniqueness of the computer as a learning tool: Insights from research and practice. In J. L. Wright & D. D. Shade (Eds.), *Young children: Active learners in a technological age* (pp. 31-50). Washington, DC: National Association for the Education of Young Children.

Clements, D. H. (2000). From exercises and tasks to problems and projects: Unique contributions of computers to innovative mathematics education. *Journal of Mathematical Behavior, 19*, 9-47.

Clements, D. H. (2002). Linking research and curriculum development. In L. D. English (Ed.), *Handbook of international research in mathematics education* (pp. 599-630). Mahwah, NJ: Erlbaum.

Clements, D. H., & Battista, M. T. (2000). Designing effective software. In A. E. Kelly & R. A. Lesh (Eds.), *Handbook of research design in mathematics and science education* (pp. 761-776). Mahwah, NJ: Erlbaum.

Clements, D. H., Battista, M. T., Sarama, J., & Swaminathan, S. (1997). Development of students' spatial thinking in a unit on geometric motions and area. *The Elementary School Journal, 98*, 171-186.

Clements, D. H., & Sarama, J. (2004a). Building Blocks for early childhood mathematics. *Early Childhood Research Quarterly, 19*, 181-189.

Clements, D. H., & Sarama, J. (2004b). Learning trajectories in mathematics education. *Mathematical Thinking and Learning, 6*, 81-89.

Clements, D. H., & Sarama, J. (2005). *Effects of a preschool mathematics curriculum: Summary research on the Building Blocks project.* Manuscript submitted for publication.

Clements, D. H., & Sarama, J. (n.d.). *Real math building blocks pre-K.* Columbus, OH: SRA/McGraw-Hill.

Clements, D. H., Sarama, J., & Wilson, D. C. (2001). Composition of geometric figures. In M. v. d. Heuvel-Panhuizen (Ed.), *Proceedings of the 21st Conference of the International Group for the Psychology of Mathematics Education* (Vol. 2, pp. 273-280). Utrecht, The Netherlands: Freudenthal Institute.

Cobb, P., & McClain, K. (2002). Supporting students' learning of significant mathematical ideas. In G. Wells & G. Claxton (Eds.), *Learning for life in the 21st century: Sociocultural perspectives on the future of education* (pp. 154-166). Oxford, England: Blackwell.

Dugdale, S. (1994). Using students' mathematical inventiveness as a foundation for software design: Toward a tempered constructivism. *Educational Technology Research and Development, 42*, 57-73.

Dugdale, S., & Kibbey, D. (1986). Green Globs and Graphing Equations [Computer software]. Pleasantville, NY: Sunburst Communications.

Dugdale, S., Kibbey, D., & Wagner, L. J. (1991). Slalom, ZOT, ZigZag: Challenges in Graphing Equations [Computer software]. Pleasantville, NY: Sunburst Communications.

Gravemeijer, K. P. E. (1994a). *Developing realistic mathematics instruction.* Utrecht, Netherlands: Freudenthal Institute.

Gravemeijer, K. P. E. (1994b). Educational development and developmental research in mathematics education. *Journal for Research in Mathematics Education, 25*, 443-471.

Gravemeijer, K. P. E. (1999). How emergent models may foster the constitution of formal mathematics. *Mathematical Thinking and Learning, 1*, 155-177.

Hoyles, C. (1993). Microworlds/schoolworlds: The transformation of an innovation. In C. Keitel & K. Ruthven (Eds.), *Learning from computers: Mathematics education and technology* (pp. 1-17). Berlin, Germany: Springer-Verlag.

Lewis, C. C., & Tsuchida, I. (1998). A lesson is like a swiftly flowing river: How research lessons improve Japanese education. *American Educator, 12*, 14-17, 50-52.

Mansfield, H. M., & Scott, J. (1990). Young children solving spatial problems. In G. Booker, P. Cobb, & T. N. deMendicuti (Eds.), *Proceedings of the 14th annual conference of the International Group for the Psychology of Mathematics Education* (Vol. 2, pp. 275-282). Oaxlepec, Mexico: International Group for the Psychology of Mathematics Education.

Reynolds, A., & Wheatley, G. H. (1996). Elementary students' construction and coordination of units in an area setting. *Journal for Research in Mathematics Education, 27,* 564-581.

Sales, C. (1994). *A constructivist instructional project on developing geometric problem solving abilities using pattern blocks and tangrams with young children.* Unpublished master's thesis, University of Northern Iowa, Cedar Falls.

Sarama, J. (2000). Toward more powerful computer environments: Developing mathematics software on research-based principles. *Focus on Learning Problems in Mathematics, 22,* 125-147.

Sarama, J., & Clements, D. H. (2002). Learning and teaching with computers in early childhood education. In O. N. Saracho & B. Spodek (Eds.), *Contemporary perspectives in early childhood education* (pp. 171-219). Greenwich, CT: Information Age.

Sarama, J., Clements, D. H., Spitler, M. E., Wilson, D. C., Suresh, R., & Bardsley, M. E. (2002, April). *Evaluation and comparison of four geometric turn interfaces.* Paper presented at the meeting of the American Educational Research Association, New Orleans, LA.

Sarama, J., Clements, D. H., & Vukelic, E. B. (1996). The role of a computer manipulative in fostering specific psychological/mathematical processes. In E. Jakubowski, D. Watkins, & H. Biske (Eds.), *Proceedings of the eighteenth annual meeting of the North American Chapter of the International Group for the Psychology of Mathematics Education* (Vol. 2, pp. 567-572). Columbus, OH: ERIC Clearinghouse for Science, Mathematics, and Environmental Education.

Schauble, L. (1990). Formative evaluation in the design of educational software at the Children's Television Workshop. In B. N. Flagg (Ed.), *Formative evaluation for educational technologies* (pp. 51-66). Hillsdale, NJ: Erlbaum.

Simon, M. A. (1995). Reconstructing mathematics pedagogy from a constructivist perspective. *Journal for Research in Mathematics Education, 26,* 114-145.

Spradley, J. P. (1979). *The ethnographic interview.* New York: Holt, Rinehart & Winston.

Spradley, J. P. (1980). *Participant observation.* New York: Holt, Rinehart & Winston.

Steffe, L. P., & Cobb, P. (1988). *Construction of arithmetical meanings and strategies.* New York: Springer-Verlag.

Steffe, L. P., & Tzur, R. (1994). Interaction and children's mathematics. *Journal of Research in Childhood Education, 8,* 99-116.

Steffe, L. P., & Wiegel, H. G. (1994). Cognitive play and mathematical learning in computer microworlds. *Journal of Research in Childhood Education, 8,* 117-131.

Yerushalmy, M. (1997). Emergence of new schemes for solving algebra word problems. In E. Pehkonen (Ed.), *Proceedings of the 21st conference of the International Group for the Psychology of Mathematics Education* (Vol. 1, pp. 165-178). Lahti, Finland: University of Helsinki.

CHAPTER 6

DEVELOPMENT OF THE SHAPE MAKERS GEOMETRY MICROWORLD

Design Principles and Research

Michael T. Battista

In this chapter, I discuss various design issues and research/theoretical frameworks that have guided my development, use, and analysis of the Shape Makers (Battista, 1998, 2003) computer environment for teaching middle school geometry. To help the reader understand the design process, historical glimpses of the creation of the environment are included in the discussion. I first briefly describe the Shape Makers environment. Then I discuss conceptual frameworks used in the design of the environment, various design considerations, the nature of student thinking as students work in the environment, and finally, subsequent theory development resulting from research on students' learning in the environment.

Research on Technology and the Teaching and Learning of Mathematics:
Vol. 2. Cases and Perspectives, 131–156
Copyright © 2008 by Information Age Publishing

THE SHAPE MAKERS:
A DYNAMIC GEOMETRY MICROWORLD

To understand the Shape Makers microworld, it is helpful to examine the physical apparatus on which it is based. Consider two pairs of equal-length rods hinged together at their ends (see Figure 6.1). As students manipulate this "parallelogram maker," the visual and kinesthetic experiences they abstract from their actions, along with their reflections on those actions, are integrated to form a mental model of the apparatus that can be used in reasoning about the geometric concept of parallelogram.

The Shape Makers computer microworld, a special add-on to the dynamic geometry program The Geometer's Sketchpad (Jackiw, 1995), provides students with screen manipulable shape-making objects similar to, but more versatile than, this physical parallelogram maker (Battista, 1998). For instance, the computer Parallelogram Maker can be used to make any desired parallelogram that fits on the computer screen, regardless of its shape, size, or orientation—but only parallelograms. Dragging the Parallelogram Maker's vertices changes its angles and side lengths—and thus its visual appearance—but the transformed shape is always a parallelogram (see Figure 6.2).

The Shape Makers instructional environment consists of computer Shape Makers for each common type of quadrilateral and triangle as well as a carefully designed sequence of instructional activities. In ini-

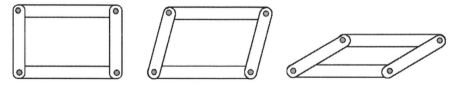

Figure 6.1.   Hinged rod "Parallelogram Maker."

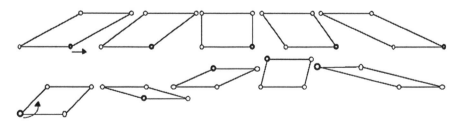

Figure 6.2.   Shape Makers Parallelogram Maker.

tial activities, students use the various Shape Makers to make their own pictures, then to duplicate given pictures. These activities familiarize students with the movement possibilities of the Shape Makers. Students are then involved in activities that require more careful analyses of shapes; they are guided to formulate and describe geometric properties of the shapes. To help students conduct these more accurate and precise analyses of shape properties, students are given Measured Shape Makers, which display angle measures and side lengths that are instantaneously updated as the Shape Makers are manipulated. Measured Shape Makers also include parallelism- and symmetry-testing capabilities. Finally, students focus on classification issues as they compare the sets of shapes that can be made by the various Shape Makers. (See Battista, 1998, 2003 for a complete description of the instructional activities.) For instance, in an early activity students are asked to use the Shape Makers to make a design (see Figure 6.3). In a later activity, for each type of special quadrilateral maker (such as a Rhombus Maker), students are asked to predict which of six quadrilaterals can be made by that quadrilateral maker. Students then check their predictions with the appropriate measured quadrilateral maker (see Figure 6.4).

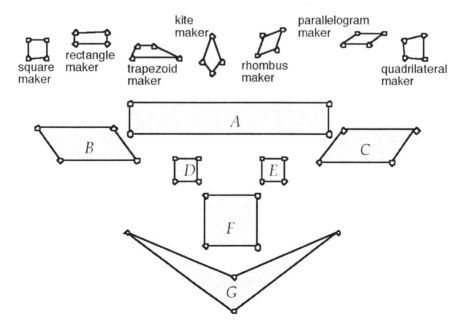

Figure 6.3.   Quadrilateral Makers and design to be made by them.

Length(AB) = 123 pixels
Length(BC) = 67 pixels
Length(CD) = 123 pixels
Length(AD) = 67 pixels

Angle(A) = 90°
Angle(B) = 90°
Angle(C) = 90°
Angle(D) = 90°

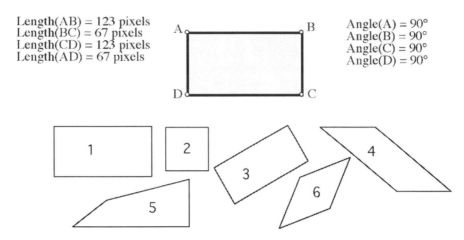

Figure 6.4.   Activity: Which shapes (1-6) can be made by the Rectangle Maker?

CONCEPTUAL FRAMEWORKS FOR THE DESIGN AND USE OF THE SHAPE MAKERS MICROWORLD

Three conceptual frameworks are valuable for reflecting on the design and use of the Shape Makers. The first is an analysis of the subject of geometry to determine instructional goals. The second consists of a general view of learning and teaching. The third is a research-based description of students' geometry learning. These three frameworks are now briefly reviewed.

Proper Goals for Geometry Instruction

In studying Euclidean geometry, we discuss only facts that are the same for all geometrically equivalent figures, that is, properties which are invariant under congruence. These are the properties which do not depend on the vagaries of the location of the figure, or the direction it is facing, or its orientation. Rather, they depend only on the intrinsic relations between the various parts of the figure—for example, the distance between two points of the figure, or the length of some segment, or the size of an angle. These are the geometric properties of the figure. (Howe & Barker, 1998, C 5, p. 3)

One of the major goals of proper geometry instruction is for students to develop fluency in purposefully and meaningfully using the geometric *conceptual system*[1] that supports reasoning about shape and space (Battista, 2001a). For instance, when students study quadrilaterals and triangles, it is essential that they understand and learn to employ an appropriate property-based conceptual system to analyze these shapes. The classic system used by mathematicians for this purpose utilizes basic concepts such as angle and length measurement, congruence, and parallelism to conceptualize spatial relationships within and among shapes. Indeed, when mathematicians define a square to be a four-sided figure that has four right angles and all sides the same length, they create an idealized property-based concept that helps us describe, reason about, and even "see" a certain class of shapes. Thus, an essential goal for geometry instruction is not, as happens in traditional curricula, for students merely to learn lists of properties that others have derived from the system, but to enable students to effectively, meaningfully, and purposefully employ this system. To do this, instruction must involve students in developing and using the system in meaningful and purposeful contexts.

A CONSTRUCTIVIST PERSPECTIVE ON MATHEMATICS LEARNING AND TEACHING

My design of the Shape Makers environment and analysis of students' work within it is founded on a constructivist view of learning and teaching mathematics (Battista, 2001b). The sections that follow describe learning and teaching from the constructivist perspective.

Learning

In the constructivist view to which I subscribe, as individuals purposefully and actively interact with their physical and sociocultural environments, their minds construct, out of their existing cognitive structures, new sets of cognitive structures that enable them to conceptualize, reason about, and manage these interactions. Among the mechanisms used in this mental construction process, abstraction is critical. Abstraction is the process that (a) isolates items in the experiential flow and grasps them as objects (perceptual abstraction); (b) enables material to be represented in the absence of perceptual input (internalization); and (c) enables material to be freely operated on in imagination so that it can be decomposed into parts and analyzed, "projected" into other perceptual material, and utilized in novel situations (interiorization). Abstraction leads to the formation of mental models, which are nonverbal recall-of-experience-like mental representations of situations that have structures isomorphic to the perceived structures of the situations they represent. Mental models consist of integrated sets of abstractions that are activated to interpret and reason about situations with which one is dealing in action or thought.

Also critical in the mental constructive process is reflection, which is the conscious process of representing experiences, actions, and mental processes and considering their results or how they are composed—leading to further, higher-level abstractions. My view of constructivism suggests that meaningful mathematics learning comes about as individuals recursively cycle through phases of action (physical and mental), reflection, and abstraction in a way that enables them to develop ever more sophisticated mental models, ways of acting, and reasoning.

Teaching

Although taking a constructivist perspective on studying learning does not specify a particular approach to teaching, many leading constructivists advocate a particular approach to teaching that they call "constructivist teaching" (Steffe & D'Ambrosio, 1995). To develop powerful mathematical thinking in students, constructivist teaching attempts to carefully guide and support students' personal construction of ideas. It encourages students to build mathematical meanings that are more complex, abstract, and powerful than they currently possess, guiding and supporting students to construct personal meaning for the important mathematical ideas of our culture. In the spirit of inquiry, problem solving, and sense making, constructivist instruction encourages students to invent, test, and refine their own ideas rather than unquestioningly follow procedures given to them by others. Because constructivists see learning as resulting from accommodations students make to their current mental structures, constructivist teaching attempts to promote such accommodations by using carefully selected sequences of problematic tasks to provoke appropriate perturbations in students' thinking.

However, unlike instruction that focuses only on inquiry and problem solving, in the constructivist paradigm, selection of instructional tasks is based on detailed knowledge of students' mathematics (Steffe & D'Ambrosio, 1995). The choice of these tasks is "grounded in detailed analyses of children's mathematical experiences and the processes by which they construct mathematical knowledge" (Cobb, Wood, & Yackel, 1990, p. 130). Constructivist teaching not only is inquiry focused, but it is based on an understanding of (a) the general stages through which students pass in acquiring the concepts and procedures for particular mathematical topics, (b) the strategies that students use to solve different problems at each stage, and (c) the mental processes and the nature of the knowledge that underlie these strategies.

GEOMETRY LEARNING

The van Hiele Levels

Consistent with the constructivist need to understand students' construction of geometric knowledge, the van Hiele theory provides descriptions of levels of students' geometric thinking and indications of strategies used within these levels (see Clements & Battista, 1992 and van Hiele, 1986 for more detail). This theory is quite helpful for understanding the progress students make as their geometric thinking develops.

- Level 0 (Prerecognition). Students attend only to part of a shape's visual characteristics and are unable to identify many common shapes.
- Level 1 (Visual). Students recognize and mentally represent shapes such as squares and triangles as visual wholes. Their reasoning is dominated by imagery and visual perception rather than by analysis of geometric properties. When identifying shapes, students often use visual prototypes, saying that a figure is a rectangle, for instance, because "it looks like a door."
- Level 2 (Descriptive/Analytic). Students recognize and characterize shapes by their geometric properties, that is, by explicitly describing spatial relationships between shape parts. For instance, students might think of a rectangle as a figure that has opposite sides equal and four right angles. While still important, the holistic appearance of shapes becomes secondary because students identify shapes by formal properties rather than mere reference to visual prototypes.
- Level 3 (Abstract/Relational). Students interrelate geometric properties, form abstract definitions, distinguish between necessary and sufficient sets of properties for a class of shapes, and understand and sometimes even provide logical arguments in the geometric domain. They meaningfully classify shapes hierarchically and give arguments to justify their classifications (e.g., a square is identified as a rhombus because it has the defining property of a rhombus, all sides congruent).
- Level 4 (Formal Axiomatic). Students formally prove theorems within an axiomatic system. That is, they produce a sequence of statements that logically justifies a conclusion as a consequence of the "givens." Thus, by necessity, thinking at Level 4 is required for meaningful and full participation in a proof-oriented high school geometry course.

Structuring

Although much of my original thinking about the Shape Makers was guided by the van Hiele theory, I have been developing another, more general perspective on geometric reasoning. It focuses on the concept of structuring.

Spatial Structuring

Vital in the construction of appropriate mental models for geometric thinking is a special type of abstraction, spatial structuring. Spatial structuring is the mental act of constructing an organization or form for an object or set of objects. Spatial structuring determines a person's perception/conception of an object's nature or shape by identifying its spatial components, combining components into spatial composites, and establishing interrelationships between and among components and composites. For example, different spatial structurings of a quadrilateral might cause it to be seen visually as a closed path consisting of four straight sections, as a composite of four segments connected at their endpoints, or as a composite of four connected angles.[2] As a spatial structuring is incorporated into a person's mental model for a spatial object, it determines the person's mental representation of the object's spatial essence, and it enables the person to imagine manipulating it and to reflect on and analyze it so as to understand it.

Geometric Structuring

Geometric structurings describe spatial structurings in terms of formal geometric concepts. That is, in geometrically structuring a spatial situation, a person uses geometric concepts such as angles, slope, parallelism, length, rectangle, coordinate systems, and geometric transformations to conceptualize and operate on the situation. So, for example, and as will be explained in more detail later, a parallelogram might be spatially structured as a *visual configuration* consisting of two pairs of "even" opposite sides—the spatial structuring is a visual mental model. A geometric structuring of this same characteristic is an explicit, verbally stated conceptualization of this imagistic relationship in terms of geometric concepts—opposite sides are parallel and congruent.

For a geometric structuring to make sense to a person, it must evoke an appropriate spatial structuring for the person. Further, to geometrically structure a spatial situation, a person must have interiorized the spatial structuring that is captured by the geometric structuring. That is, the spatial structuring described by the geometric concept must have reached a generalized level of abstraction, detaching it from its original context so it is applicable to new situations, and making it accessible to decomposition and analysis.

Logical/Axiomatic Structuring

A logical/axiomatic structuring formally organizes geometric concepts (i.e., geometric structurings) into a system and specifies that interrelationships must be described and established through logical deduction. The system can be "local" in the sense that there is little or no explicit attention to basic assumptions—certain notions are simply taken as true based on intuition or experience. Or, the system can be "global" in the sense that assumptions are explicitly and systemically stated as axioms.

To operate at the logical/axiomatic level, relevant spatial structurings must achieve "symbol" status for individuals (von Glasersfeld, 1995), that is, they must reach the second level of interiorization. At this level, verbal/symbolic statements of spatial relationships can act as substitutes for, or "pointers" to, the actual process of creating spatial structurings, with individuals able to reason meaningfully about these symbols without having to represent the actual spatial structurings for which they stand (i.e., without visualizing the situations). Furthermore, to accomplish a logical/axiomatic structuring, individuals must logically organize sets of properties, seeing, for instance, that a square possesses the defining property "opposite sides parallel" of a parallelogram and thus must be a parallelogram. This requires that properties and sets of properties (geometric structurings) be interiorized so that they can be meaningfully decomposed, analyzed, and applied to various shapes.

DESIGN OF THE SHAPE MAKERS

There were both theoretical and practical considerations that directly affected my design of the Shape Makers microworld. (Because much of my previous curriculum development and research had been with Logo, I often make comparisons between the Logo and the Shape Makers environments.)

Theoretical Considerations

- *The Shape Makers microworld should encourage and support students' movement through the first three van Hiele levels—from the visual, to the descriptive/analytic, and into the abstract/relational.* Both the van Hiele and the constructivist theories suggest that instruction begin at students' current levels of functioning. Because students' initial use of the Shape Makers occurs when they are in van Hiele Level 1, the Shape Makers microworld initially engages students at the visual level (unlike Logo, which requires students to be somewhere between Levels 1 and 2). Indeed, the Shape Makers environment allows students to start with visual tasks and progress to more analytic tasks (via measure), all within the same basic environment, promoting the all-important integration of the visual and analytic modes of thinking.

- *The Shape Makers microworld should promote in students the development of powerful mental models that they can use for reasoning about geometric shapes.* These models allow flexible imagery constrained by increasingly sophisticated knowledge of the properties of shapes (Battista, 1994).

- *The Shape Makers microworld should support students' use of sophisticated learning mechanisms that they have previously developed for learning "natural" categories as they explore and attempt to manage their environments.* This is in contrast to the traditional formal logical approach that is beyond the capability of most middle school students.[3]

- *The Shape Makers microworld should be consistent with the constructivist view of learning and teaching.* Consistent with this view, geometry instruction must get students purposefully involved in reflecting on, formulating, abstracting, and using those spatial relationships that form the core of the standard property-based conceptual system for two-dimensional shapes. Such instruction must promote and support students' development and refinement of personal theories about shapes and spatial relationships. In the Shape Makers, this is often accomplished by involving students with "predict and check" activities. Because students' predictions are based on their mental models, making predictions encourages them to reflect on and refine those mental models, which, with proper guidance, leads to increasingly sophisticated geometric reasoning. (The effectiveness of this approach depends heavily on students' ability to independently check the viability of their predictions—that is, to check their theories through the process of sense making rather than reference to authority.) Student theory building is also supported by the representational aspect of the Shape Makers microworld—it provides a powerful representation system for thinking about shape categories and their defining properties. For instance, in initial activities, students quickly conceptualize that there are rules that specify how Shape Makers can and cannot move. These rules become attentional foci and conceptual objects that students gradually refine and come to describe using standard geometric property-based concepts.

- *The Shape Makers microworld should lead students to the more classic approach to geometry most prevalent in high school.* This approach is different from the "path-based" approach taken in Logo (an approach that also has great value).

Practical Considerations

- *The Shape Makers microworld should be easy for students and teachers to use.* My experience with Logo indicates that Logo requires a significant amount of time and effort for both teachers and students to learn the programming syntax—much of this time is not spent on learning mathematics. (Of course, it might be argued that there is mathematical value in learning to program.)

- *The geometry microworld to which students are introduced in early middle school should be able to "grow" with students during their mathematical careers.* This is the major reason that I decided not to make the Shape Makers a separate stand-alone application. Although the separate-application approach would have allowed more freedom to make the Shape Makers behave exactly as I wished, by making the Shape Makers environment part of the more powerful Geometer's Sketchpad environment, students are introduced to a tool, the Geometer's Sketchpad, that they can use productively throughout their mathematical careers.

- *The Shape Makers microworld should be interesting enough to engage students fully in inquiry and reflection.* It is clear that we learn a tremendous amount without explicitly intending to learn. In fact, we learn as we try to master our environment in personally important ways, as we purposefully solve problems. This is the most natural and powerful form of learning. I designed the Shape Makers to promote this type of learning of geometry. Traditional instruction fails to help students see any intrinsic value for the standard geometric property-based conceptual system; instead, it simply demands, in unmotivated ways, that students learn results obtained with this system. In designing the Shape Makers, I wanted to present students with an interesting and motivating environment in which developing and using the property-based conceptual system would arise naturally. I wanted to put students in an environment in which "mastery of the environment" required them to construct increasingly sophisticated geometric concepts, concepts that, with appropriate instructional guidance, form the core of the classic geometric structuring of two-dimensional shapes. The Shape Makers achieve this goal because they are interesting manipulable phenomena whose behavior can best be explained using formal geometric concepts. Indeed, the Shape Makers are inherently interesting to students; students' first comments in activating the Shape Makers are often exclamations such as "cool" or "neat."

RECURSIVE DESIGN AND INTERPRETATION

Recursive thinking was an essential element not only in the design of the Shape Makers microworld, but in the analysis of student thinking within the microworld.[4] On the design side, for example, originally, students used the Shape Makers to make pictures shown to them only on activity sheets, not the computer screen. But students' inaccuracy in comparing what they made on the computer screen with what was on the activity sheets allowed them to overlook many of their errors, reducing the opportunities for perturbations that could cause reflection and accommodation. In subsequent versions, the target figures were put on the computer screen, resulting in more accurate comparisons by students, and more productive perturbations.

Another change that arose from early observations of students' Shape Maker work was the creation of the Measured Shape Makers. In the initial version of the microworld, after several days of working with the Shape Makers, to test their conjectures and conceptualizations with more precision, students began, without instructional guidance, to use rulers and protractors for measuring computer screen figures. Consequently, and in keeping with the ease-of-use tenet, I created the Measured Shape Makers that show all the important measures that students need (see Figure 6.4). This approach enabled the Shape Makers curriculum to introduce measurements, as one teacher commented, "At the perfect time, just when students see a need for them." Similarly, early on, students attended to symmetry and parallelism in their analyses of shapes. But originally, there was no way for them to test their ideas on the computer screen, an essential component in refining their thinking. This violated a basic design tenet that students need to be able to test their ideas themselves, rather than ask an authority figure. Thus, I built into the Measured Shape Makers parallelism-testers and symmetry-testers.

On the learning-analysis side, originally, I conceived of the Shape Makers as representations for classes of shapes. Although, for me, particular Shape Makers did represent such classes, I found this conception inadequate for productively reflecting on students' construction of knowledge while using the Shape Makers microworld. Initially, students simply viewed the Shape Makers as interesting, manipulable, visual-mechanical objects. But because geometric properties are "built-into" the movement possibilities of Shape Makers, to understand these movement possibilities for a particular Shape Maker, students must construct conceptualizations of at least some inter-part spatial relationships that remain invariant with that shape maker's movement. As will be illustrated subsequently, with proper instructional support and guidance, students' personal conceptualizations mature into standard geometric concepts for shape properties. Thus, as I continued my analysis of students' learning within the Shape Makers environment, I came to see that the real instructional power of the Shape Makers microworld derives from its capacity to involve students in the difficult but critical process of inventing and purposefully using a property-based conceptual system for two-dimensional shapes.

THE NATURE OF STUDENT THINKING IN THE SHAPE MAKERS MICROWORLD

The episodes below illustrate the nature of student thinking and learning while working in the Shape Makers microworld. All students were fifth graders in a class taught by a teacher who is highly skilled at implementing problem-based constructivist instruction. All episodes occurred in the teacher's normal classroom instruction (except that the research team was present).

The episodes and accompanying analyses strongly suggest that one of the most important areas of research on students' geometric thinking—for instructional practice, design, and theory—is describing precisely how students move from their idiosyncratic, self-invented spatial structurings to powerful formal geometric structurings. This movement requires not only a recursive refinement of students' informal spatial structurings but the accessibility of appropriate geometric concepts. And this conceptual accessibility depends (a) on students' having abstracted structurings and concepts at appropriate levels, and (b) on social interactions in the classroom culture, including appropriate communication of ideas and instructional scaffolding.

Episode 1. Three students were investigating the Square Maker at the beginning of their Shape Maker work.

MT: I think maybe you could have made a rectangle.
JD: No; because when you change one side, they all change.

ER: All the sides are equal.

MT, JD, and ER abstracted different things from their Shape Maker manipulations. MT noticed the visual similarity between squares and rectangles, causing him to conjecture that the Square Maker could make a rectangle. JD abstracted a movement regularity—when one side changes length, all sides change (thus, he could not get the sides to be different lengths, which he thought was necessary for a rectangle). Only ER conceptualized the movement regularity with complete precision by expressing it in terms of a traditional geometric property.

From the van Hiele perspective, we might say that MT's reasoning on this task was at Level 0, JD's was at Level 1, and ER's was at Level 2. From the structuring perspective, MT and JD had developed spatial structurings for the Square Maker, with JD's more sophisticated than MT's. ER, in contrast, had constructed a geometric structuring for the Square Maker. In fact, I conjecture that ER described a geometric structuring of the spatial structuring described by JD. An even higher level of sophistication that was not represented in this episode, but has been shown by students who have had a significant amount of work with the Shape Makers, is exhibited by students who say that the Square Maker can make one type of rectangle, the special type we call "square."

Episode 1 also illustrates another important aspect of constructivist instructional environments—they should permit students who are at different levels of sophistication in their geometric thinking to work together productively. In this episode, it was beneficial for the students to hear each other's comments as they worked on this problem (Battista, 1999). The fact that JD and ER disagreed with MT, and explained why, encouraged MT to further reflect on his reasoning and make accommodations to it. ER's response presented JD with the opportunity to reformulate his rather vague spatial structuring in terms of ER's more sophisticated geometric structuring, an important step in moving JR toward Level 2 thinking. Finally, by reflecting on the statements of his group mates, ER was presented with the opportunity to compare his sophisticated conceptualization with less sophisticated conceptualizations, solidifying and deepening ER's conceptualization.

Episode 2. NL is using the seven quadrilateral Shape Makers to make the design shown in Figure 6.3. A researcher (Res) is observing and asking questions as NL tries to make Shape C with the Rhombus Maker. (NL's partner is absent.)

NL: The Rhombus Maker on [shape] B. It doesn't work. I think I
      might have to change the Rhombus Maker to [shape] C.
Res: Why C?

NL: The Rhombus Maker is like leaning to the right. On B, the shape is leaning to the left. I couldn't get the Rhombus Maker to lean to the left, and C leans to the right so I'm going to try it. (after her initial attempts to get the Rhombus Maker to fit exactly on shape C) I don't think that is going to work.

Res: Why are you thinking that?

NL: When I try to fit it on the shape, and I try to make it bigger or smaller, the whole thing moves. It will never get exactly the right size. (manipulating the Rhombus Maker) Let's see if I can make the square with this. Here's a square. I guess it could maybe be a square. But I'm not sure if this is exactly a square. It's sort of leaning. The lines are a little diagonal. (continuing to manipulate the Rhombus Maker) Yeah, I think this is a square maybe.

Res: You said the Rhombus Maker could make the same shape as shape C, what do you mean by that?

NL: It could make the same shape. It could make this shape, the one with two diagonal sides and two straight sides that are parallel. It could have been almost that shape and it got so close I thought it was that shape.

NL: (continuing to manipulate the Rhombus Maker) Oh, I see why it didn't work, because the four sides are even and this [shape C] is more of a rectangle.

Res: How did you just come to that?

NL: All you can do is just move it from side to side and up. But you can't get it to make a rectangle. When you move it this way it is a square and you can't move it up to make a rectangle. And when you move this, it just gets a bigger square.

Res: So what made you just notice that?

NL: Well I was just thinking about it. If it [the Rhombus Maker] was the same shape, then there is no reason it couldn't fit in to C. But I saw when I was playing with it to see how you could move it and things like that, that whenever I made it bigger or smaller, it was always like a square, but sometimes it would be leaning up, but the sides are always equal.

This episode clearly shows how a student's manipulation of a Shape Maker and reflection on that manipulation can enable the student to move from thinking holistically to thinking about interrelationships between a shape's parts, that is, about its geometric properties. Indeed, NL began the episode thinking about the Rhombus Maker and shapes holistically and vaguely, saying that she was trying to make the Rhombus Maker "lean to the right" and get "bigger or smaller," and that "the whole

thing moves." The fact that NL could not make the nonequilateral parallelogram with the Rhombus Maker evoked a perturbation that caused her
to reevaluate the spatial structuring contained in her mental model of the
Rhombus Maker. Originally, because her model did not include the constraint "all sides equal," her mental simulations of changing the shape of
the Rhombus Maker included transforming it into nonequilateral parallelograms. Her subsequent attempts to make a nonequilateral parallelogram with the Rhombus Maker tested her model, showing her that it was
not viable. As she continued to analyze why the Rhombus Maker would
not make the parallelogram—why it would not elongate—her attention
shifted to its side lengths. This new focus of attention enabled her to
abstract the regularity that all the sides of the Rhombus Maker were the
same length. As she incorporated this abstraction into her mental model
for the Rhombus Maker, she was able to infer that the Rhombus Maker
could not make Shape C.

This activity encouraged and enabled NL to progress from a spatial
structuring that was incomplete, imprecise, and did not explain the
Rhombus Maker's movement to a geometric structuring that did explain
that movement. A combination of two factors may have spurred and supported NL's progress. First, during the episode, NL abstracted the "all
sides equal" property to a sufficiently high (interiorized) level that
enabled her to apply it in various situations. Previous observations indicated that NL had already concluded that squares have all sides the same
length; in Episode 2 she raised this notion to a higher level of abstraction.
Second, it is highly likely that NL's conclusions about the Rhombus Maker
came about partly because she had previously made a square with it; she
viewed the Rhombus Maker as a transformed square. I conjecture that
NL's transforming the Rhombus Maker into a square, a shape that she
conceptualized as having all sides equal in length, made a critical connection that eventually (but not easily) enabled her to transfer the concept of
equal side length to the new shape of Rhombus Maker (via reaching a
higher level of abstraction). I will discuss later how the transformation
facility of the Shape Makers is a major component of their instructional
efficacy.

Episode 2 also illustrates how students using the Shape Makers move
toward more sophisticated, property-based conceptions of shapes
because of the inherent power these conceptions give to their analyses
of spatial phenomena. In the current situation, NL developed a property-based conception of the Rhombus Maker because it enabled her to
understand why the Rhombus Maker could not make Shape C—something that truly puzzled her. Only when NL conceptualized the movement of the Rhombus Maker in terms of a geometric structuring did
she feel that she really understood its movement. NL acquired this

property-based conception not because someone told her to learn it, but because it helped her achieve a goal that she was trying to achieve—understanding why the Rhombus Maker would not make Shapes B or C. (Of course, she took this goal as personally worthwhile not only because it interested her but because of the structure of the instructional activities and because she was a willing participant in an effective inquiry-based classroom culture.)

Finally, this episode illustrates how geometry learning with the Shape Makers is much richer and more powerful than that which occurs in traditional curricula. First, because NL's learning of properties was purposeful—connected at the outset with attaining a personal goal—it is highly likely that henceforth she would see that knowledge as being applicable and useful. (In fact, NL used this and other properties with increasing regularity in her subsequent work.) Second, because NL constructed her property-based reasoning from her already-existing cognitive structures, the newly constructed knowledge was "well-connected" in the sense that it was firmly anchored in her knowledge web, making it more likely not only to be applied in problem solving but to be used in further acts of knowledge construction. Third, and finally, it is highly likely that this episode increased NL's overall appreciation for the power of formal geometric reasoning in understanding the environment, again making it more likely that, in the future, NL would seek to use geometry in understanding the world.

Episode 3. The task was to determine which of Shapes 1-7 could be made by the Rectangle Maker (explaining and justifying each conclusion) (see Figure 6.4). Fifth-grade students M and T predicted that the Rectangle Maker could make shapes 1-3, but not 4-6. They are now checking and discussing their results with the teacher (Tchr) present. (The entire episode took about 25 minutes.)

After using the Rectangle Maker to check Shapes 1-3, M and T move on to Shape 4.

    T: I'm positive it can't do this one.

    M: It [the Rectangle Maker] has no slants. We had enough experience with number 3, that it can't make a slant.

    T: Yes it can, it has a slant in the other one [Shape 3]. It's has a slant right now....

Tchr: What do you mean by slant?

    M: Like this. See how this is shaped like a parallelogram (motioning along the perimeter of Shape 4).

    T: This is in a slant right now (points at the Rectangle Maker, which is rotated from the horizontal). (Note that "slant" means nonperpendicular sides for M, but rotated from the horizontal for T.) ...

M: It can't make that kind of a shape (pointing to Shape 4).... It can't make something that has a slant at the top and stuff.

T: Do you mean it has to have a *straight* line right here (pointing to Shape 6), like coming across? (T now uses "straight" to mean horizontal.)

M: I know they are *straight*, but they are at a slant and it [the Rectangle Maker] always has lines that aren't at a slant....

Tchr: (after several failed attempts to unobtrusively get students to reconceptualize the "slant" conception in terms of angles) Keep on really looking at what makes these different. And maybe some of the information on the screen will help you. Watch the numbers up there and see if that will help you....

T: (manipulating the Rectangle Maker after the teacher leaves) Oh, this [the Rectangle Maker] always has to be a 90° angle. And that one [Shape 4] does not have 90° angles. And so this one [Shape 3] has to have a 90° angle, because we made this with that [Rectangle Maker]. So there is one thing different. A 90° angle is a right angle, and this [Shape 4] does not have any right angles.

M and T were trying to find a way to conceptualize and describe the spatial relationship that sophisticated users of geometry would describe by saying that the sides of the Rectangle Maker are perpendicular. In so doing, and typical of students at van Hiele Level 1, they developed several vague and incomplete spatial structurings, all of which were inadequate. They used familiar terminology and concepts like "slanted" and "straight" that inadequately described the idea with which they were grappling.

While interacting with M and T, the teacher recognized that they had not yet constructed a proper geometric structuring that captured what they were attempting to conceptualize with their vague spatial structurings of the situation. She saw that, at that time, M and T were unable to conceptualize the situation in terms of the formal geometric concepts of perpendicularity or right angles. Though she asked numerous questions that she thought might activate a formal, property-based geometric structuring, M and T were unable to make the required restructuring during the teacher-student interaction.

However, after the teacher left the boys, T manipulated the Rectangle Maker, focusing on its measurements. Through this manipulation, he discovered and abstracted that the Rectangle Maker always has four 90° or right angles. Furthermore, he abstracted this property sufficiently so that he was able to use it to analyze the differences between Shapes 3 and 4. He subsequently conceptualized that the Rectangle Maker could not make Shapes 4, 5, and 6 because they do not have four right angles. In fact, by the end of the class period, the boys saw that the spatial relationship to which they were attending could be described in terms of the formal mathematical concept of right angle. They had constructed a geometric structuring, a van Hiele Level 2 analysis, that enabled them to solve the problem they had embraced.

This episode illustrates how difficult it can be for students to reformulate unrefined spatial structurings of Shape Maker movements in terms of traditional geometric concepts.[5] It is only after much guidance, reflection, and experimentation that students can construct formal geometric conceptualizations of Shape Maker movement constraints. However, once students meaningfully move from their initial vague spatial structurings to appropriate geometric structurings, they embrace the latter because of their inherent power.

Students' Evolving Conceptions of Shape Maker Constraints

As students attempt to manipulate the Shape Makers, they encounter certain physical constraints—the Shape Makers can only be manipulated in certain ways. Because succeeding in the instructional tasks requires students to understand these constraints, students are naturally inclined to describe and understand the constraints. At first, students' constraint conceptualizations tend to be negative, describing what a Shape Maker cannot do. For instance, NL said, "The Rhombus Maker on [shape] B. It doesn't work.... When I try to fit it on the shape, and I try to make it bigger or smaller, the whole thing moves. It will never get exactly the right size." Only gradually, and with proper instructional encouragement and support, do students' conceptualizations become positively stated, not as what a Shape Maker cannot do, but as what regularities or invariants hold for Shape Maker movements: NL, "Oh, I see why it [the Rhombus Maker] didn't work, because the four sides are even and this [shape C] is more of a rectangle." Students progress beyond describing what the Shape Makers cannot do, to trying to make sense of Shape Maker constraints, namely, they look for causes. Indeed, the formal geometric properties that students eventually develop become, for students, concise causal explanations of Shape Maker movement constraints.

DEEPENING THE THEORY:
A TRANSFORMATIONAL PERSPECTIVE ON
SPATIAL STRUCTURING

Although the previous episodes clearly show how the Shape Maker environment encourages and supports students' movement toward property-based conceptualizations of geometric shapes, description of the mental mechanisms by which this happens is elusive. Understanding the role that the dynamic nature of the Shape Makers plays in students' construction of increasingly sophisticated geometric knowledge is particularly important in this analysis. One conceptual avenue that might lead to better understanding of the impact of this dynamic nature is using transformational geometry to understand students' mental processes in reasoning about shapes and Shape Makers. There are two interrelated components in my theory—transformations as structuring, and the "transformational-saliency hypothesis."

Geometric Transformations as
Psychological Mechanisms for Spatial Structuring

The first component of this new theory is that unconscious visual transformations are one of the mental mechanisms by which we spatially structure shapes. For example, but differing in detail from Leyton (1992), I posit that in a parallelogram, seeing opposite sides parallel might be based on mentally (but unconsciously) translating one side onto the opposite side. Similarly, seeing that opposite angles in a parallelogram are congruent may be based on an unconscious 180° rotation.

This analysis is consistent with my empirical finding that parallelism is much more difficult for students to "see" in the Trapezoid Maker than it is in the Rectangle and Parallelogram Makers. Seeing parallelism in scalene trapezoids cannot be accomplished using the same mental transformation that establishes this property for rectangles and parallelograms because, in a scalene trapezoid, one side is not the translation image of its opposite side. Also consistent with this hypothesis is the common student belief that the property "opposite sides parallel" goes with "opposite sides equal" because the first property is established with a translation that also establishes the second. To disassociate these two properties, parallelism might need to be established, for example, with a translation and stretch. The following episode illustrates students' confusion in this regard.

Episode 4. A class of fifth-grade students working on the Shape Makers is discussing the concept of parallelism.

Tchr: When you think of parallel, what do you think of?

T: Two lines that are almost beside each other but one's … a little further up.

M: It's like taking two rulers that are the same length and putting them, like right on top of each other.

Tchr: So like this (holds two different length rulers in horizontal parallel positions, one above the other).

M: Yeah except the same length.

J: [For] parallel lines, I think of lines that are exactly opposite from each other (holds hands vertically and directly across from each other). They're the same length exactly.

B: Well I think that maybe they have to be even length. But they can be like, um, one of them could be ahead of the other one (has her right hand horizontal above her parallel left hand, then moves her right hand to the right). Like um, I think with the parallelogram you can like make it kinda at a slant. And, the top line is like farther ahead than the other one. But, they're still the same lengths.

This episode clearly shows students' confounding the ideas of parallelism and congruence, which makes sense, given students' initial instructional exposure to these ideas. Generally, as students first formally encounter parallelism in parallelograms or rectangles in "standard position," they see parallel congruent segments "directly" across from each other vertically or horizontally. This "seeing" can be accomplished with simple vertical or horizontal mental translations. Like B in Episode 4, students then enlarge their conceptualizations to congruent parallel segments that are askew, those that can be seen with oblique translations (which are more difficult to visualize than vertical or horizontal translations). Finally, with further refinement in thinking, students separate and disambiguate the notions of parallel and congruent as they attempt to apply their notion of parallelism to shapes such as scalene trapezoids. This conceptual reformulation involves both explicit logical analysis and implicit visual imagery that supports the new parallelism conceptualization—a mental transformation consisting of a translation then a stretch.

The Transformational-Saliency Hypothesis

Although the above explanation describes how mental transformations spatially structure shapes, it does not explain why the dynamic nature of the Shape Makers is such a powerful way for students to investigate shapes. The second component of my theory does. It suggests that, as a Shape Maker is manipulated, students' minds naturally notice what stays invariant. This increases the likelihood that students will realize that the part-to-part transformations that establish spatial relations within Shape Makers are preserved during Shape Maker manipulations. The basis for this hypothesis is connected to a deeper and more mathematically sophisticated aspect of transformational geometry.

In the nineteenth century, mathematicians gained significant insights into the nature of geometry when they reconceptualized it as the study of invariants under various transformation groups (Yaglom, 1988). They found that the essences of different geometries were, in fact, determined by their transformation groups. For instance, the intrinsic spatial relations between parts of shapes that define the properties studied in classic Euclidean Geometry are the invariants under the group of isometries (actually the group of similarities).

Similar reasoning can be applied to the Shape Makers. For example, the invariants under the group generated by all possible movements of the Rectangle Maker are precisely the properties of the class of rectangles. I conjecture, therefore, that investigating shapes through Shape Maker transformations makes the essence of their properties more psychologically salient to students than simply comparing examples of shapes as is done in traditional instruction. Although I devised this "transformational-saliency hypothesis" post hoc from my observation of and reflection on students' Shape Maker work, there is precedent for such thinking.

For instance, Cassirer (1944) suggested that transformational invariants might be the perceptual mechanism that enables an individual to perceive a succession of images as a single perceptual form.

> The "possibility of the object" depends upon the formation of certain invariants in the flux of sense-impressions, no matter whether these be invariants of perception or of geometrical thought.... The positing of something endowed with objective existence and nature depends on the formation of constants.... *[The] search for constancy, the tendency toward certain invariants, constitutes a characteristic feature and immanent function of perception.* (p. 21)

Cassirer continued,

> The peculiar kind of "identity" that is attributed to apparently altogether heterogeneous figures in virtue of their being transformable into one another by means of certain operations defining a group, is thus seen to exist also in the domain of perception. *This identity permits us not only to single out elements but also to grasp "structure" in perception.* (p. 25)

Several modern cognitive psychologists have similarly posited a connection between formal transformation-based geometric analysis and perceptual mechanisms (Leyton, 1992; Shepard, 1994). Indeed, transformation-based perception might explain students' tendency to compare shapes using transformations, both rigid and nonrigid (Battista, 1994; Lehrer et al., 1998).

There are several additional points of support for the transformational-saliency hypothesis. First, with proper mental coordination, movement of a Shape Maker can cause students to form spatial composites out of synchronously moving Shape Maker parts. Indeed, a considerable amount of research has shown that objects that move together are seen as part of the same object (e.g., Driver & Baylis, 1989; Regan & Hamstra, 1991). So, for instance, because of the way the Quadrilateral Maker moves, one might see it as a set of four connected "angle composites," each of which includes two sides with common endpoint. Or, because in the Parallelogram Maker the opposite sides move together in a way that maintains their parallelism and congruence, such movement might encourage the formation of two "opposite-sides-parallel" composites (each maintained by a separate mental translation). Furthermore, students might not only unite synchronously moving parts, they might also abstract the movement of this unit and mentally attach the movement to the composite. For instance, in Episode 1, JD saw that the sides of the Rhombus Maker "move together" in a way that maintained their congruence; he thus structured the Rhombus Maker as four connected same-length sides growing uniformly. Thus, I am suggesting that Shape Maker manipulations that cause synchronous movements of subsets of shape components encourage students to form "specially behaving" composites out of these subsets. The special behavior of these subsets is an invariant of the transformation group for that Shape Maker, and represents, in an informal and intuitively accessible form, a geometric property of the class of shapes made by that Shape Maker.

A second line of support for the transformational-saliency hypothesis is that, if properties are established at some deep level through transformations, then because the Shape Maker environment focuses students' attention on transformation and change, working with the Shape Makers puts students' attention in a "transformational mode," making it more likely that they will notice transformational invariants. Indeed, because the Shape Maker environment highlights transformational shape change, and because the mind's attentional system is especially alert and sensitive to change (Ornstein, 1991), Shape Maker manipulations might activate the attentional system to these changes, causing students' minds to actively attempt to make sense of the transformational changes and invariants.

CONCLUSION

In this chapter, I have attempted to make evident the design process for my development of the Shape Makers learning environment. Although I have touched upon several "nuts-and-bolts" factors that all software and curriculum designers must face, far more importantly, I have tried to illustrate a software/curriculum-design effort strongly grounded in and integrated with research on students' learning. Indeed, my scientific research on students' learning of geometry continued throughout the development of the Shape Makers learning environment, providing both empirical data and theoretical constructs for understanding the effects of the environment on students' learning. Maintaining such a strong connection between research on learning and software/curriculum development is absolutely critical to improving the quality of mathematics instruction and curricula and should become the norm, not the exception, in design efforts (Battista & Clements, 2000; Clements & Battista, 2000).

ACKNOWLEDGMENT

Partial support for this work was provided by grants REC-8954664 and IMD 0099047 from the National Science Foundation. The opinions expressed, however, are those of the author and do not necessarily reflect the views of that foundation.

NOTES

1. Most previous elementary school geometry curricular, instructional, and research efforts have failed to recognize the systemic nature of the set of concepts mathematicians use to reason about shape. Conceptualizing this set of ideas as a system, rather than discretely, helps us better appreciate the nature of the learning task that students must face.

2. My verbal descriptions are actually examples of geometric structurings—I am describing shapes in terms of geometric concepts. Spatial structurings are imagistic organizational abstractions that are incorporated into mental models.

3. Research suggests that people form two kinds of categories (Pinker, 1997). Fuzzy or natural categories, such as games, are formed in everyday activity. Such categories generally have no clear definitions, fuzzy boundaries, and are conceptualized mainly in terms of stereotypes and family-like resemblances—so some examples are deemed "better" than others. Identification of instances seems to be the major goal. The second type of category

consists of formal, explicitly defined categories, such as odd numbers, in which all instances are logically equivalent as representative of the class.

4. The major portion of the research and development for the Shape Makers environment was conducted over a period of 3 years. In each year, the researcher/designer, along with project staff observed students working on the Shape Makers in an inquiry-based classroom (videotaping small-group work, whole-class discussions, "shadowing" of case-study pairs of students who were working together, and individual interviews with case-study students). The amount of classroom time spent on the Shape Makers grew from about 2½ weeks the first year to over 6 weeks the final year (in which students also studied a Shape Makers unit on triangles). Thus, conducting integrated curriculum-design research work is time- and person-intensive.

5. The difficulty students have with this process points out just how deficient traditional cursory memorization-based approaches to this topic are. It takes a great deal of thought and appropriate experience for students to use the formal geometric conception-based system with genuine understanding.

REFERENCES

Battista, M. T. (1994). On Greeno's environmental/model view of conceptual domains: A spatial/geometric perspective. *Journal for Research in Mathematics Education, 25*, 86-94.

Battista, M. T. (1998). *Shape Makers: Developing geometric reasoning with the Geometer's Sketchpad.* Berkeley, CA: Key Curriculum Press.

Battista, M. T. (1999). The importance of spatial structuring in geometric reasoning. *Teaching Children Mathematics, 6,* 170-177.

Battista, M. T. (2001a). A research-based perspective on teaching school geometry. In J. Brophy (Ed.), *Subject-specific instructional methods and activities. Advances in research on teaching* (Vol. 8, pp. 145-185). Amsterdam, Holland: JAI Press.

Battista, M. T. (2001b). How do children learn mathematics? Research and reform in mathematics education. In T. Loveless (Ed.), *The great curriculum debate: How should we teach reading and math?* (pp. 42-84). Washington, DC: Brookings Press.

Battista, M. T. (2003). *Shape Makers: Developing geometric reasoning with the Geometer's Sketchpad.* Berkeley, CA: Key Curriculum Press.

Battista, M. T., & Clements, D. H. (2000). Mathematics curriculum development as a scientific endeavor. In A. E. Kelly & R. A. Lesh (Eds.), *Handbook of research design in mathematics and science education* (pp. 737-760). Mahwah, NJ: Erlbaum.

Cassirer, E. (1944). The concept of group and the theory of perception. *Philosophy and Phenomenological Research, 5,* 1-35.

Clements, D. H., & Battista, M. T. (1992). Geometry and spatial reasoning. In D. Grouws (Ed.), *Handbook of research on mathematics teaching and learning* (pp. 420-464). New York: National Council of Teachers of Mathematics/Macmillan.

Clements, D. H., & Battista, M. T. (2000). Designing effective software. In A. E. Kelly & R. A. Lesh (Eds.), *Handbook of research design in mathematics and science education* (pp. 761-776). Mahwah, NJ: Erlbaum.

Cobb, P., Wood, T., & Yackel, E. (1990). Classrooms as learning environments for teachers and researchers. In R. B. Davis, C. A. Maher, & N. Noddings (Eds.), *Constructivist views on the teaching and learning of mathematics. Journal for Research in Mathematics Education Monograph Number 4* (pp. 125-146). Reston, VA: National Council of Teachers of Mathematics.

Driver, J., & Baylis, G. C. (1989). Movement and visual attention: The spotlight metaphor breaks down. *Journal of Experimental Psychology: Human Perception and Performance, 15,* 448-456.

Howe, R., & Barker, W. (1998). *Undergraduate notes, 1998 Summer Park City Mathematics Institute.* Unpublished manuscript, Park City, UT.

Jackiw, N. (1995). Geometer's Sketchpad (Version 3.0) [Computer software]. Berkeley, CA: Key Curriculum Press.

Lehrer, R., Jacobson, C., Thoyre, G., Kemeny, V., Strom, D., Horvath, J., et al. (1998). Developing understanding of geometry and space in the primary grades. In R. Lehrer & D. Chazan (Eds.), *Designing learning environments for developing understanding of geometry and space* (pp. 169-200). Mahwah, NJ: Erlbaum.

Leyton, M. (1992). *Symmetry, causality, mind.* Cambridge, MA: MIT Press.

Ornstein, R. (1991). *The evolution of consciousness.* New York: Touchstone.

Pinker, S. (1997). *How the mind works.* New York: W. W. Norton.

Regan, D., & Hamstra, S. (1991). Shape discrimination for motion-defined and contrast-defined form: *Squareness is special. Perception, 20,* 315-336.

Shepard, R. N. (1994). Peceptual-cognitive universals as reflections of the world. *Psychonomic Bulletin & Review, 1,* 2-28.

Steffe, L. P., & D'Ambrosio, B. S. (1995). Toward a working model of constructivist teaching: A reaction to Simon. *Journal for Research in Mathematics Education, 26,* 146-159.

van Hiele, P. M. (1986). *Structure and insight.* Orlando, FL: Academic Press.

von Glasersfeld, E. (1995). *Radical constructivism: A way of knowing and learning.* London: The Falmer Press.

Yaglom, I. M. (1988). *Felix Klein and Sophus Lie: Evolution of the idea of symmetry in the nineteenth century.* Boston: Birkhauser.

CHAPTER 7

INTEGRATING INTELLIGENT SOFTWARE TUTORS WITH THE MATHEMATICS CLASSROOM

Steven Ritter, Lisa Haverty, Kenneth R. Koedinger, William Hadley, and Albert T. Corbett

Education and the learning sciences have a long history, filled with periods of academic competition and those of collaboration (see Lagemann, 2000). For both practical and social reasons, the application of science about how people learn to educational practice has been limited. Issues of scale, lack of adequate implementation blueprints, the difficulties of translation from the environment of a research laboratory to a live classroom full of students, and a simple failure of communication and awareness of relevant results all hinder this transfer. In this chapter we discuss one recent instance of a successful transition from cognitive science research to educational practice: the Cognitive Tutors, developed at Carnegie Mellon University and currently produced by Carnegie Learning (Carnegie Learning, 2005). Cognitive Tutors are so named to reflect their basis in cognitive science research and their use of intelligent tutoring systems to guide student problem solving. Products following this approach have addressed high school mathematics (Algebra I, geometry, and Alge-

Research on Technology and the Teaching and Learning of Mathematics:
Vol. 2. Cases and Perspectives, 157–181
Copyright © 2008 by Information Age Publishing

bra II) and represent a unique approach to the use of technology in mathematics education (Aleven, Koedinger, Sinclair, & Snyder, 1998; Corbett, Trask, Scarpinatto, & Hadley, 1998; Koedinger, Anderson, Hadley, & Mark, 1997). Each Tutor curriculum consists of software, print materials (equivalent to a textbook, homework assignments, teacher's guide, etc.) and teacher training. The intent is to provide teachers with sufficient materials and support to teach an entire mathematics course.

The design of the Cognitive Tutors represents a shift in the use of educational technology. In many cases in the past, technology, although often paired with the main curriculum, was used as a supplement, either for students who needed extra practice or for those who could benefit from enrichment. In contrast, the Cognitive Tutor software is an integral part of a full curriculum. Students work with the software in a computer lab[1] during their regular class period in the same way that students in a science course would have a lab component for some fraction of their regular classroom time. This arrangement addresses many goals that are not typically found in a curriculum. For example, different skills are emphasized in many different modalities—some in the software, some in the classroom, and many in both. A student can, for example, discuss, present, and write about a problem, and present its relations graphically, symbolically, or in table form. The integration of the Cognitive Tutor lab and classroom components provides to teachers an opportunity to capitalize on the pedagogical affordances of two venues. In the classroom the teacher can offer direct instruction and monitor and guide students verbally, noting their weaknesses and areas of difficulty. In the lab the teacher can move from one student to another, focusing on those who are most in need of attention, while the software guides class instruction, student by student. The format of the problems in the software and in the texts is similar, the skills being covered in the two settings are complementary, the instructional approach is similar, and the software provides extensive information for the teacher about the progress of each of the students in the classroom. This configuration of features is designed to ensure that the full benefits of both the software and the text are realized. Neither is marginalized because of an awkward or difficult fit with the other.

Typically, students in the Cognitive Tutor courses spend 40% of their time in the computer lab. This substantial allocation of the students' time in the course reflects a commitment to relying heavily on the cognitive science that is instantiated in the Tutor software. The software automatically tracks the progress of student understanding[2] over time and uses that information to control pacing through the software curriculum. Students entering the lab can begin working where they had stopped at the end of their previous session and proceed through the materials at their own pace. Because the software comes to "know" (in the sense of artificial intelligence) the student over the course of a full year, it can effectively drive the pace and focus of the classroom implementation.

The print materials used in the classroom, the software used in the lab, and the initial teacher training and ongoing support are in keeping with Honey, Culp, and Carigg's (2000) argument that, if technology is to have a significant impact on learning, the technology must be part of a broader systemic change. While we cannot claim to have influenced the educational environment outside of mathematics, our broader influence on how this subject is presented in the school may account for a large part of our success. In this chapter, we will explore how we came to believe in this novel approach to the implementation of educational technology in the classroom and why we believe it is a successful model for the deployment of educational technology.

THE COGNITIVE TUTORS

Research History

The Cognitive Tutors grew out of research conducted at Carnegie Mellon University. The theory of learning developed by John Anderson and his collaborators is one that encompasses much of what we know about cognition from years of empirical research (Anderson, 1990, 1993; Anderson & Lebiere, 1998). To wit, "ACT-R consists of a theory of the nature of human knowledge, a theory of how this knowledge is deployed, and a theory of how this knowledge is acquired" (Anderson & Lebiere, 1998, p. 5). However, what is most extraordinary about the ACT-R theory is that it exists in a concrete physical manifestation—a software system that embodies the various constraints of, for example, human memory. This computer architecture of an ACT-R simulation mimics the (presumed) architecture of the brain.

One of the important distinctions in this cognitive architecture is that it considers knowledge to come in two basic forms: declarative and procedural. Facts about the world (including sounds and images) are classified as *declarative*. Knowledge about how to do things is classified as *procedural*. The two types of knowledge are very much interconnected. Procedural knowledge tells us how and when to utilize our declarative knowledge. The ACT-R cognitive architecture enables researchers to computationally model various aspects of human behavior and problem solving with these tools. Building an ACT-R model involves defining the relevant knowledge, skills, subskills, potential misconceptions, and strategies for the target domain. The precision required to create a computer model of human behavior requires and enables researchers to articulate clearly their theories of thinking and learning.

An accurate theory of human learning, when put to the ultimate test, should be able to produce a blueprint for very effective instruction. A *computational* model of human learning that concretely specifies learning mechanisms should suggest a concrete set of effective instructional techniques. Thus, the ultimate test of the ACT-R theory was to see if it could give rise to effective instruction. Researchers began to create ACT-R based intelligent tutoring systems as a way to test and refine the theory while collecting further learning data for basic cognitive science research (Anderson, Boyle, Corbett, & Lewis, 1990; Anderson, Boyle, & Reiser, 1985). Before long the intelligent tutoring systems came to be viewed not only as a research tool but as a way to increase student achievement. These precursors to today's Cognitive Tutors included ANGLE, an intelligent tutoring system for geometric proof (Koedinger & Anderson, 1990), and the Lisp tutor, which taught the Lisp programming language (Corbett & Anderson, 1989). These had both proven successful in real-world use (Anderson, Corbett, Koedinger, & Pelletier, 1995; Corbett & Anderson, 1992; Corbett, Anderson, & Patterson, 1990) and encouraged extension to yet more practical environments.

The first Cognitive Tutors designed for high school were implemented in the Pittsburgh public schools both to test the validity of ACT-R as a computational theory of learning and to examine its effectiveness with students. Proper implementation of the early tutors was closely guided by the researchers. However, as the number of implementations increased, the researchers could not be involved as closely and therefore could not govern the conditions under which the tutors would be used. To safeguard the goal of successful implementation and to ensure that the tutors were compatible with the target setting, the development of the tutors now required (a) a fully specified curriculum environment, and (b) collaboration with people who knew the high school mathematics classroom best, namely, teachers (e.g., Koedinger & Anderson, 1993a). Consequently, high school mathematics teachers were engaged in all stages of the development, and the exchange of ideas between researchers and practitioners led to tutors that were of higher quality and more appropriate for broad dissemination. Indeed, early research indicated substantial student improvements with the tutors when compared to traditional approaches of instruction (e.g., Koedinger et al., 1997). This success eventually led to a commercial model that would enable wide dissemination of the tutor curricula.

THE CURRICULUM EXPERIENCE

Software

The Cognitive Tutor software presents a problem and a set of tools that is appropriate for solving that problem. This approach parallels the view of tasks presented in Hiebert and colleagues (Heibert et al., 1997). As the student works through his or her problem solution, the system "watches" the steps that the student is performing. If the student's actions suggest that the student is confused or harboring a misconception, the system will intervene and present a message to get the student back on track. The student can also ask for a hint at any step in the problem-solving process, and the system will respond with suggestions that are specific to the student's solution path and to the particular problem that the student is solving. Otherwise, the student can proceed without interruption.

Figures 7.1A, 7.1B, 7.1C, and 7.1D show screen shots from a typical problem in the Algebra I Cognitive Tutor. (This problem is presented in Unit 2 of 30 units in the curriculum and would typically be encountered by a student at the end of the first month of class.) The initial statement of the problem is in the "scenario" window (see Figure 7.1A). Generally students will begin the problem by reading the problem scenario and then completing the associated table in the worksheet window. In Figure 7.1B, the student has already identified the independent and dependent variables (in this case, *time* and *number of square miles of rain forest*) and needs to enter their corresponding units of measure. The data rows in the worksheet table correspond to the numbered questions in the scenario window, which ask about specific instances of the relation between *time* and *number of square miles of rain forest*. In the final row, the student will express the function in algebraic language, picking a variable to represent the *time* and an expression in terms of that variable to represent the *number of square miles of rain forest*. Finally, the student must also use the grapher window (see Figure 7.1C) to graph the function described in the scenario. The student needs to label the axes appropriately, set appropriate bounds and intervals, plot points corresponding to rows in the worksheet, and draw the curve representing the function.

In this problem, a cell in the worksheet window (representing *time* in Question 4) is initially inactive (and colored gray). Students are directed to "use the graph" to answer this question. That is, for this question, the student would plot the graph of the linear function on the coordinate grid using points from Questions 1 to 3 and then plot the point corresponding to the situation and the specific value given in Question 4 ("2400 square miles"). When this point is plotted on the graph, the corresponding cell in the worksheet becomes active and the student can read the coordinate

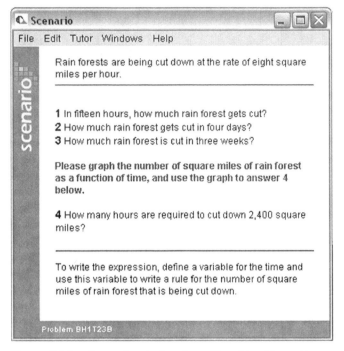

Figure 7.1A.   Scenario window from Cognitive Tutor Algebra I software.

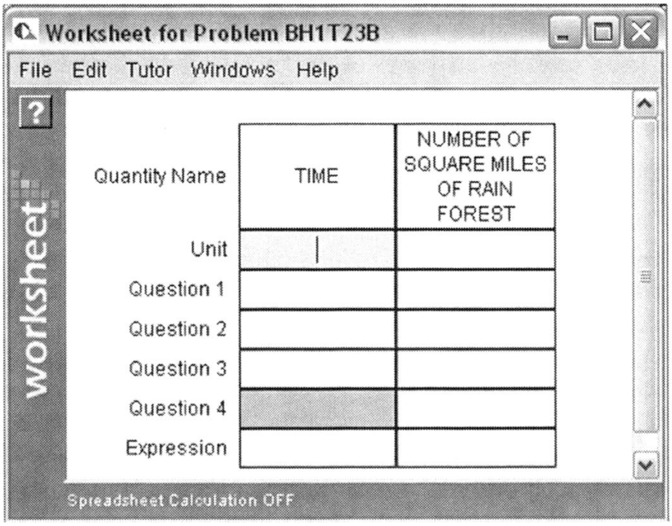

Figure 7.1B.   Worksheet table from Cognitive Tutor Algebra I software.

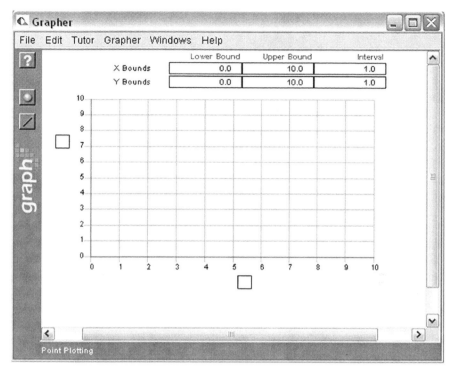

Figure 7.1C.   Grapher window from Cognitive Tutor Algebra I software.

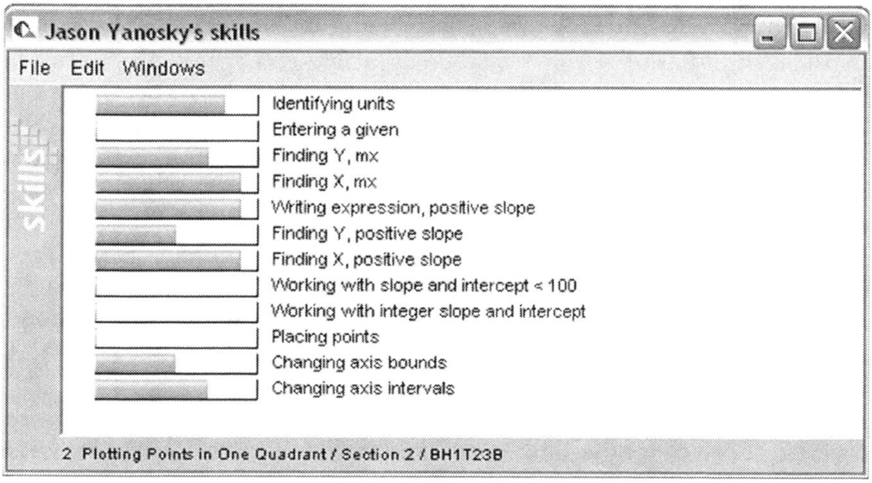

Figure 7.1D.   Skill mastery chart from Cognitive Tutor Algebra I software.

of the plotted point on the graph and fill in the worksheet with the appropriate value.

The remaining window (see Figure 7.1D) displays a measure of the student's mastery of each of the skills entailed in the current problem. The bars in this graph increase and decrease as students complete each step of a problem. A more complete bar signifies a strong grasp of the skill. When a bar reaches a threshold, that skill is considered "mastered," and the bar turns gold. Many students perceive their goal to be getting their gold bars, and this can be highly motivating. From a cognitive modeling perspective, the bars are a direct reflection of the tutor's assessment of each of the skills underlying problems of this type. We will return to this dynamic assessment later.

In later sections of the curriculum, new tools are introduced, and the functionality of some tools changes. For example, in some later sections, students graph linear functions by identifying the slope and intercept, rather than by plotting points. Also, as the coefficients in the expression get more complicated students are encouraged to use an equation-solving tool (Ritter & Anderson, 1995) to find the value of a variable when given values for other variables, or to solve a system of equations. There are also lessons devoted to solving linear and quadratic equations in the absence of a problem context. In this way, the curriculum helps students recognize situations in which symbolic mathematics is valuable in solving real-world problems and also gives students enough practice with symbolic mathematics skills that they become proficient in applying these skills both in and out of context.

Text materials and classroom activities. The Cognitive Tutor student texts and class activities were developed to complement the Cognitive Tutor software. As such, the classroom materials parallel the software's approach in asking students to consider relationships between different mathematical representations (text, tables, equations, and graphs). This curricular focus is not unique and is similar to that taken in several texts (e.g., *Concepts in Algebra: A Technological Approach*, Fey, Heid, Good, Sheets, Blume, & Zbiek, 1995, 1999). As the example text pages shown in Figure 7.2 illustrate, the Cognitive Tutor text contains relatively little declarative instruction. Most of the instruction is embedded in the problems themselves. The tasks require students to scrutinize the mathematics they are using and to articulate their knowledge and problem-solving methods. Students are thus expected to develop conceptual knowledge and procedural skills by grappling with these real-world problem situations.

The topics covered in the classroom are complementary to the units covered in the computer lab, but are not tied to students' progress in the lab. This permits students to proceed at their own pace with the software in the lab but to be working on the same unit as the other students in

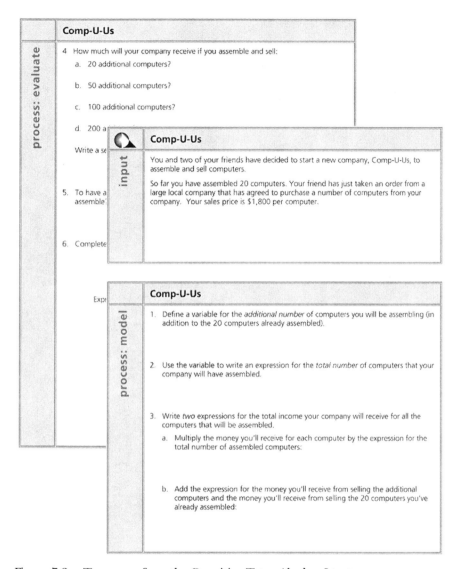

Figure 7.2.   Two pages from the Cognitive Tutor Algebra I text.

terms of classroom work and any homework assignments. Consider, for example, that the Algebra I Cognitive Tutor software has 32 units, but the student text has only seven units. Indeed, the software and the text will sometimes offer instruction on different topics. As shown in Figure 7.3, some text assignments ask students to engage in activities that are similar to those that the software asks students to do, while other text assign-

Assignment 14

Name: _____

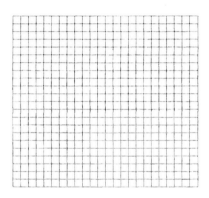

PROBLEM SITUATION You are going on vacation by airplane. You will be traveling at an average
speed of 325 miles per hour.

Make a table showing how far you will travel in various time periods from 1
to 20 hours. Use this information to construct a line graph and find the
algebraic formula.

	Time in the Air	Distance Traveled
Labels		
Units		
Formula		
	1	
	2	
	5	
	11	
	15	
	18	
	20	

Cognitive Tutor™ algebra 1 © 2001   29
Assignments

Figure 7.3.   Assignments from student text.

ments relate to topics or approaches not addressed in the software. The
relationship between the text and software is often confusing to teachers
initially. Part of the experience of teaching this curriculum is coming to
realize that the spread of student achievement in the computer lab is
reflective of the spread of student achievement and understanding in any
classroom. The Cognitive Tutor software just makes this range of understanding more obvious to the teacher. Once teachers gain that under-

standing, they can use their knowledge of students' achievement in the lab to guide their emphasis and pacing in the classroom.

This parallel structure is supported by classroom emphasis on problem solving. Many classroom activities are designed to be conducted in small groups, which provides an environment in which students with different levels of understanding can participate. More advanced students may be more articulate and use formal methods in their problem solving. Students who have not progressed as far in the lab will, likewise, have less formal methods of problem solving in their skill set, such as expressing a relation between two variables in words rather than in a formal equation, or plotting individual points to construct the graph of a function rather than using an equation to inform the plotting of the graph. Furthermore, as students are working together, the relative skills that they collectively bring will be shared with other students in group problem solving and presentations, and this not only reinforces the skills for all students involved but also provides, in a different modality, a learning opportunity for the student who has yet to grasp a particular concept being used. Taking advantage of this opportunity may assist the student when he returns to the computer lab to grapple with that concept again.

Training and support. With its emphasis on group activities, problem solving, and class presentations, the Cognitive Tutor course represents a major shift in pedagogy for mathematics teachers (Stigler & Hiebert, 1999). It became evident very early on that, to grow the program beyond a closely watched research project, a robust training program would need to be developed to prepare teachers to skillfully implement the program. Teacher training facilitates the transition from teaching a traditional curriculum to the integration of Cognitive Tutor software and classroom activities. In today's commercial model of the Cognitive Tutor course, teachers new to the Cognitive Tutors take a 4-day training class. Most teachers go into this class thinking that they will primarily be learning how to use the software. This is partly true—teachers make extensive use of the student software as part of the training so that they can become familiar with the general approach and with the particular lessons that students will be completing. Teachers also learn how to perform administrative tasks related to the course, such as entering class rosters and printing reports. However, the true focus of the training is elsewhere—on how best to implement the pedagogical approach and objectives of the curriculum and on how to help students who are struggling with the mathematics.

The reliance on active problem solving in the Cognitive Tutor text, emphasis on group activities, and the relationship between the computer lab and the classroom are all major concerns that are addressed in the training. Teachers learn both practical strategies for implementing new instructional methods and the pedagogical reasons for approaching instruction in this way. For example, they learn how to use the information from the software to learn which students will be most likely to need help with a particular concept during classroom work and to set overall pacing for the classroom portion of the course. To the extent possible, the training itself is conducted in the format of a Cognitive Tutor class so that teachers (a) see the instructional technique in action, (b) experience first-hand some of the issues that arise, and (c) observe how experienced instructors manage those events.

ARTIFICIAL INTELLIGENCE

Having discussed how the finished product looks, feels, and works, we now discuss the technology guiding and assessing students in the background. A fundamental belief behind the Cognitive Tutor approach is that a detailed and accurate model of student thinking allows for better instructional decisions for individual students. Although the close relationship between our cognitive modeling efforts and the ACT-R theory is unique, the general idea that instruction benefits from knowledge about student thinking is not new. Cognitively Guided Instruction (Carpenter, Fennema, Franke, Levi, & Empson, 1999), for example, emphasizes understanding students' current knowledge and problem-solving strategies. CGI stresses that teachers can make better decisions when their instruction is informed by knowledge about student strategies and concepts in the domain of concern.

The Cognitive Tutor curricula rely on knowledge about student problem solving that has been culled from years of research in cognitive psychology. The classroom materials are built on research on how students learn and on methods of task analysis that minutely specify the skills and knowledge involved in solving or understanding any given mathematical problem or concept. But the cognitive models actually instantiate that knowledge of student learning.

Cognitive Models in Action

Tracing student knowledge. The Cognitive Tutor software employs two cognitive models. The first is a complete model of what a proficient student knows about the domain, the skills that that student would have, and the strategies that that student would likely employ in any given problem situation. In the intelligent tutoring literature, this is often referred to as the "expert module" (see Anderson, 1988). Here, we use the term "proficient" to emphasize the fact that it is really representing a proficient student (the target at the end of the class), not necessarily full mastery. The proficient model includes many different strategies for solving mathematics problems as well as common misconceptions that students may harbor. The second cognitive model is one that is being built to represent the individual student using the Cognitive Tutor. This model is equipped to become as fully realized as the first model. However, the collection of skills, strategies, and knowledge in the proficient model are not yet attributed to the student being modeled and are therefore not assumed in this second cognitive model. These bits of knowledge will gradually augment the student model as the student herself evidences that she has attained that knowledge. To a large extent, the student model is a subset of the proficient model.

The proficient model is used to distinguish and identify the knowledge being displayed by a student. When students take an action in the software, the model relates that action to what it knows about the strategies that students might employ in solving the problem. Because the proficient cognitive model contains information about likely misconceptions, it is able to recognize student actions that indicate misconceptions, and it presents students with feedback when they take such actions. For example, if a student is in the midst of solving an equation and subtracts a constant from both sides of the equation, the proficient model will compare that action to its own stores of knowledge and infer that the student must possess particular knowledge elements in order to have selected that action. Through this process, called *model tracing*, the system matches the actions of a student to the knowledge that the proficient model would use when completing a similar action. That knowledge is then strengthened in the emerging cognitive model of the student, and via *knowledge tracing* the Cognitive Tutor monitors the strength of the student's grasp on a particular skill, strategy, or piece of knowledge.

Thus, model tracing is critical to identifying mental processes that a student is using, given the student's actions. This process affects the knowledge attributed to the student in the emergent student model. The student model is then used to accomplish knowledge tracing, to (a) monitor a student's progress in mastering this knowledge and estimate the student's proficiency on each skill included in the curriculum, and (b) adapt the curriculum in such a way that the student is called upon to reinforce and strengthen that knowledge, in conjunction with other skills being learned. The system uses information in the student model to choose problems for students that emphasize skills that they have not yet mastered. When a student demonstrates sufficient mastery of some unit of knowledge (i.e., the student model matches the proficient model with respect to that piece of knowledge), the Cognitive Tutor will fully attribute that knowledge to the student model and the curriculum will proceed without the necessity of practicing that skill further. When a student demonstrates mastery of all of the skills introduced in a particular section of the curriculum, the student is allowed to proceed to the next section of the curriculum, which introduces new skills.

Subgoal reification. One final word about model tracing and knowledge tracing is that their effectiveness is directly reliant on the quality and specificity of the software interface. For model and knowledge tracing to be effective, the cognitive model's identification of a student's actions and its deductions about the student's knowledge must correspond to what the student actually knows. In practice this means that, as much as possible, the student's thought processes and problem-solving activities must be made visible to the cognitive model through the software interface (Corbett & Anderson, 1995; Koedinger & Anderson, 1993b). If many of the significant aspects of problem solving are performed without interacting with the computer, then the computer will not know how the student is thinking about the problem.

In many ways, this situation is not much different from the one facing a teacher in the classroom. One of the reasons a teacher may ask students to show their work or to talk about how they reached a particular solution is so that the teacher can understand how the students are thinking about the problem. The challenge for the computer program, relative to the teacher, comes from two considerations. First, the program's insight into a student's thoughts is limited to information about the student's keyboard and mouse input. Teachers have the luxury of also relying on body language, tone of voice, and so forth. Second, although the Cognitive Tutors are reasonably proficient at using the data they have to infer how students are thinking about a problem, the system's reasoning facilities in this area are much more limited than that of a human being.[3]

For all of these reasons it is critical to make a student's thinking evident in the interface to the greatest extent possible so that the cognitive models are not left to infer a great deal about the knowledge that a student is using to solve a problem. The practice of capturing in the interface as much as possible of a student's thinking is called "subgoal reification."[4] If each problem-solving step requires an interaction with the software interface, then the models will not have to "guess" what the student is thinking—it will be possible to "directly observe" the knowledge being used.

The success of the cognitive models, and the artificial intelligence, inside the Cognitive Tutors is symbiotic with the strength of the software interface (Koedinger & Anderson, 1993b). This is an important lesson for any developer of educational software based on cognitive models. A well-designed interface feeds stronger information back to the cognitive models, making their deductions more accurate and occasionally even contributing to refinements in their knowledge structure. Correspondingly, improved cognitive models inform the software interface by providing yet more specific information about the skills required to master various mathematical concepts.

Development

Naturally, the effectiveness of any educational technology based on artificial intelligence depends on how well understood student thinking about the domain is and how well that thinking is represented in the cognitive models. In the case of the Cognitive Tutors, cognitive models directly affect the tasks, feedback, and instructional material that a student sees in the classroom. However, the *process* of cognitive modeling itself informs the curriculum structure and content by enhancing our understanding of how students think and of what makes particular tasks difficult. This modeling process involves basic research on student thinking, and both the modeling and the research depend greatly on describing the task, or domain, in sufficient detail that a computer model can be built to simulate student behavior.

At the most fundamental level, the ACT-R theory serves as a guide for curriculum sequencing. An ACT-R model specifies a collection of procedural skills that are required to complete a particular task. Performance on a later task will be similar to that on the earlier task to the extent that the two tasks share skills (Singley & Anderson, 1989). We can predict student performance on a particular task if we know the student's knowledge of the skills that compose the task. Decomposition of a task into component skills therefore provides a concrete metric for deciding which tasks belong together in a section of the curriculum and which build on skills learned in earlier tasks.

Cognitive models are developed using a mixture of formal and informal techniques. An important emphasis in the use of these methods is to maintain frequent contact with teachers and students. This leads to an iterative development process in which one cognitive modeling technique suggests a particular approach which is then tested in the classroom, refined, and enhanced by results from another modeling technique. This development methodology fits well with the description by Sabelli and Dede (2001) of "implementation research." Some of the more important techniques used in the development of the cognitive models behind the Cognitive Tutors are "difficulty factors assessments," formative experimentation, focused testing, and skill refinement.

Difficulty factors assessment. The difficulty factors assessment (DFA) technique (Nathan, Koedinger, & Tabachneck, 1996) provides a relatively simple way to understand the particular dimensions of a task that pose difficulties to students. A DFA takes the form of a paper-and-pencil assessment, with test items constructed to vary along a small number of fixed dimensions. Early in the development of the Algebra I Cognitive Tutor, Nathan and colleagues (1996) found, using a DFA, that students were better able to solve word problems than corresponding equations. Presumably the effect would not have occurred if students had been solving the word problems using the normative approach (translate the problem into an equation and then solve the equation). In fact, it appears that students were using situational reasoning to solve these problems. This type of data provides insight into the kinds of problem-solving strategies that students are able to implement successfully and was fundamental to the approach to algebraic symbolization that is used in the Algebra I Cognitive Tutor curriculum.

Formative experimentation. In some cases, it is possible to construct two variants of a Cognitive Tutor lesson (either in software or in classroom activities) and to study whether one is more effective than the other. As discussed earlier, one general principle is to work from what students know to what they need to know. The DFA data showing that students could solve problems in context more easily than solving decontextualized equations suggested that having students reason about a problem situation would help to scaffold their use of more formal algebraic representations. Koedinger and Anderson (1998) tested two versions of the Cognitive Tutor. In one version, the expression row was at the top of the worksheet, encouraging students to work on the algebraic formalization of the problem before completing specific instances. In the other variant, the expression row was at the bottom of the worksheet, so students worked on specific instances before attempting to induce the algebraic expression. The results showed that students were better able to find the algebraic expression after having calculated specific instances. This data led to the tutor's presentation of the "expression" row at the bottom of the worksheet.

Focused testing. Pretesting and posttesting of a unit of instruction helps identify areas in which the curriculum can be improved. In developing an Algebra II unit concerned with general linear form problems, Corbett, McLaughlin, Scarpinatto, and Hadley (2000) discovered that while students were able to solve problems requiring them to compute numeric answers, they were much less proficient at building an equation to represent the calculations they had performed. Furthermore, given an equation representing the situation, they were unable to identify which quantities were represented by particular variables in that equation. For example, if told that movie theater popcorn costs $2 and a beverage costs $1.50 and that one has a total of $10, students could, with high accuracy, determine how many beverages they could buy if they were buying two boxes of popcorn. On this type of question, students performed substantially better than they had on the pretest.

When asked to produce an equation corresponding to the movie theater situation (e.g., $2x + 1.5y = 10$), students were less successful. Similarly, when given an equation equivalent to the situation in general linear form, students were less successful at saying which term represented, for example, the total money spent on popcorn. It was clear that the skills required to solve general linear form problems were different from those required to articulate algebraic equations in that form. As a result, the Cognitive Tutor now represents the skill of articulating the meanings of expressions as separate from the skill of being able to compose and use those expressions. The curriculum now includes a tool that focuses on associating abstract algebraic expressions with their problem-specific meanings—a tool that significantly improves student performance on this kind of task (Corbett et al., 2000).

Skill refinement. As students work through a problem, the model and knowledge-tracing processes continually adjust the Tutor's assessment of how likely it is that a student has acquired each of the component skills (Anderson, Conrad, & Corbett, 1989). In essence, the tutor is comparing the proficient and student models to make a prediction about student performance. If the system rates the student's level of knowledge on a skill as high, then it should be likely that the student will correctly complete tasks requiring that skill.

Because we collect such data across a large group of students, we can test whether the cognitive model's predictions for particular skills turn out to be true. If they are not, this is evidence that the cognitive model does not accurately reflect student thinking (Corbett, 2001). For example, in an early version of the equation-solving tutor, the tutor had a single skill related to "removing" the coefficient of a variable in an equation of the form $ax = b$. When we examined the data from student use of the tutor, it was clear that there were some cases in which the tutor predicted that students would perform better than they actually did. The data showed that, in many cases, these overpredictions corresponded to cases in which a equaled -1. Because the convention for writing a coefficient of -1 is to use only the negative sign, some students were not able to apply the same knowledge to operating on a -1 coefficient as they did to operating on other coefficients. Essentially, some students had learned a procedure corresponding to "divide by the number in front of the variable." Since there was no number in front of the variable (just a negative sign), these students did not know how to proceed. The refined cognitive model treats operating on -1 coefficients (or, more accurately, representing the relationship between the negative sign and the coefficient, -1) as a separate skill. As a result, student performance on that skill is now traced independent of performance on the more general "operate-on-coefficient" skill.

Effectiveness

A strong foundation in cognitive theory gives products like the Cognitive Tutors a good chance at success, but continual testing and refinement in vivo is the ultimate measure of success. Through the years, the Cognitive Tutors have been subjected to several controlled evaluations (Anderson et al., 1995; Koedinger et al., 1997; Morgan & Ritter, 2002) that confirm that success.

Evaluating any educational program in vivo presents many practical and methodological problems, and for the Cognitive Tutors there are added scientific challenges. A Cognitive Tutor course differs from a traditional mathematics course on several dimensions. It uses software as part of its primary instruction, it emphasizes small-group classroom activities, and it focuses on active learning. In addition, the Cognitive Tutor emphasis on mathematical problem solving, communication, and translation between multiple representations differs somewhat from the goals of many traditional mathematics courses.

Any of these differences could become the focus of an evaluation to determine the independent effect of that component or feature on student achievement. Instead, our evaluations have taken the course as a whole (text, software, and training) as a single treatment. This reflects our belief that each aspect of the course reinforces the others, so that the whole is greater than the sum of the parts. To address different curricular emphases, evaluations of the Cognitive Tutor course have used both standardized exams, which typically emphasize mathematics skills given more emphasis in traditional courses, and problem-solving exams, which more closely match the objectives of the Cognitive Tutor course.

Three recent independent studies examined the effectiveness of the Cognitive Tutor in its full implementation. In the 2001-2002 school year the Moore (Oklahoma) Independent School District conducted a within-teacher experiment (Morgan & Ritter, 2002[5]). Eight teachers at four junior high schools taught using both Cognitive Tutor Algebra I and McDougal Littell's Heath Algebra I curriculum. On the ETS End-of-course Algebra exam, students taking the Cognitive Tutor curriculum ($n = 224$) scored significantly higher than students taking the traditional McDougal Littell curriculum ($n = 220$) ($F(1,442) = 8.8$, $p < .01$). Cognitive Tutor students also earned higher course grades (first semester $F(1,367) = 4.0$,

$p < .05$; second semester $F(1,362) = 5.5, p < .02$, where a grade of "A" is assigned 4 points and a grade of "F" 0 points).

In the 2002-2003 school year Miami-Dade County public schools commissioned an independent research evaluation of the effectiveness of the Cognitive Tutor Algebra I curriculum with students in 10 high schools (Sarkis, 2004). A total of 6,395 students participated, including 4,649 mainstream students, 770 exceptional education students (ESE), and 976 limited English proficient (LEP) students. Students took either a conventional Algebra I course or the Cognitive Tutor curriculum. The Florida Comprehensive Assessment Test (FCAT) (Florida Department of Education, 2003) was used as a measure of student achievement, and mainstream Cognitive Tutor students scored significantly higher than students using the conventional curriculum (279.1 scaled score versus 274.7 scaled score, $p < .001$, see Figure 7.4). For ESE and LEP students the results were even more striking. Cognitive Tutor ESE students scored 44 points higher on the FCAT than ESE students using the conventional curriculum ($p < .001$, see Figure 7.5). LEP students using the Cognitive Tutor also

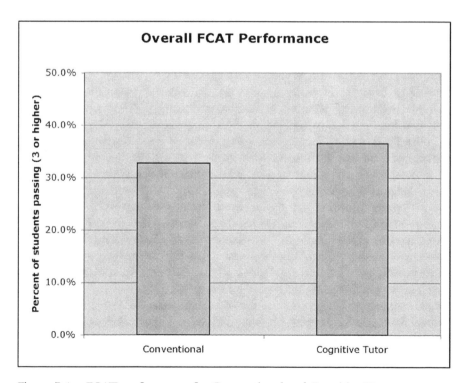

Figure 7.4.   FCAT performance for Conventional and Cognitive Tutor groups.

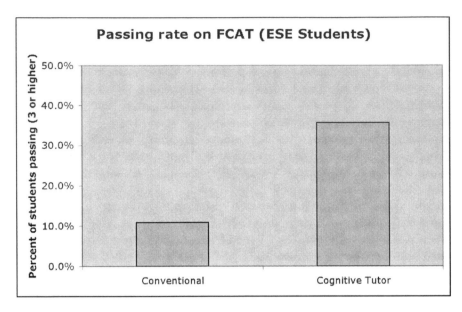

Figure 7.5. FCAT performance for ESE students in Conventional and Cognitive Tutor groups.

showed a dramatic effect, scoring 16 points higher than LEP students who used the conventional curriculum ($p < .001$).

Finally, a doctoral study conducted by Gary Plano (2004) at Kent School District (in the state of Washington) echoes the results described above (Carnegie Learning, 2004). Students taking the Cognitive Tutor Algebra I curriculum outperformed students in a conventional Algebra I curriculum on the Achievement Levels Test (ALT) developed by the Northwest Evaluation Association. The study used a regression discontinuity design (Shadish, Cook, & Campbell, 2002) and used student mathematics grades from the prior year as the basis for a cutoff. Students with grades below "C" were assigned to the Cognitive Tutor curriculum and students with grades above "C" were assigned to the conventional curriculum in use in the district. The pre-post gains for Cognitive Tutor students were significantly higher than those for students using the conventional curriculum (12.3 versus 9.5 point gains, $p < .05$, see Figure 7.6). Even more striking were the results for ELL students, who improved 31.4 points from pre to posttest, in comparison to a gain of only 11.7 points for ELL students using the conventional curriculum ($p < .001$, see Figure 7.7). In fact, all subgroups showed a positive effect of Cognitive Tutor, and the effect was statistically significant for students with free or reduced lunch, males, females, White, Asian, and Hispanic students.

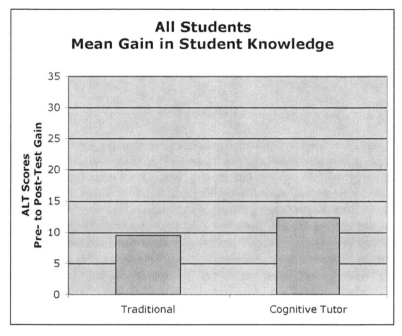

Figure 7.6.   Knowledge gains for Traditional and Cognitive Tutor students.

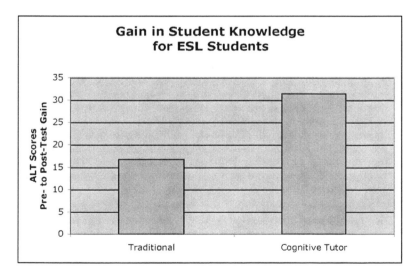

Figure 7.7.   Knowledge gains for Traditional and Cognitive Tutor ESL students.

There is a rich and ongoing research tradition regarding the Cognitive Tutors, and experimental studies continue to show its effectiveness with students of all races and ability levels, and even to reveal new strengths of the Tutor curricula (e.g., exceptional effectiveness with LEP students).

CONCLUSION

The Cognitive Tutor programs represent a unique approach to the use of technology in the classroom. The basis in cognitive science research, the embodiment of that knowledge in cognitive models, the use of artificial intelligence to trace students' learning and to tailor instruction to individual needs, the seamless integration of software use in the lab and use of a text in the classroom, and the continual evaluation of the program in scientific studies—both in the lab and in the classroom, all combine to yield a strong educational instantiation of cognitive science. Incorporating scientific findings from many varied fields of research, the Cognitive Tutors serve as a successful example of transforming research evidence into full, practical applications in the field of education.

NOTES

1. The authors use the informal term "computer lab" to refer to a school computer laboratory.

2. The editors note that there is considerable variation in the literature in use of the term "understanding."

3. Consider the significant computational limitations on processing natural language: A teacher can ask students why they performed certain actions or what they are thinking about (and understand the response); a computer system has limited capabilities for engaging in dialogue with students. Such limitations are being addressed in various research programs. In particular, eye movement studies (e.g., Gluck, 1999) provide one way of increasing the density of data about what pieces of information students are considering in their problem solving. Research on dialog-based tutoring systems (e.g., Aleven, Popescu, & Koedinger, 2001; Heffernan & Koedinger, 2000) is also making progress in including more natural language abilities in tutoring systems.

4. This term arises from the ACT-R practice of characterizing problem solving as a series of goals and subgoals. If, for example, the goal is to solve a linear equation, then one of the subgoals is to isolate the variable. As is discussed in the Development section on Skill Refinement, our cognitive model did not initially recognize that removing a coefficient of "-1" was a skill separate from removing a positive coefficient. This was a subgoal that our model had not at that point included, and that could now be "reified" in the software interface by making a tool available for dividing or multi-

plying by -1 so that this particular problem-solving step could be observed directly when applied by a student.

5. This study was conducted by Morgan, of the Moore Independent School District. After completion of data collection, Ritter was informed of the study and asked to assist with data analysis.

REFERENCES

Aleven, V., Koedinger, K. R., Sinclair, H. C., & Snyder, J. (1998). Combatting shallow learning in a tutor for geometry problem solving. In B. P. Goettl, H. M. Halff, C. L. Redfield, & V. J. Shute (Eds.), *Intelligent tutoring systems: Proceedings of the fourth international conference* (pp. 364-373). Berlin, Germany: Springer-Verlag.

Aleven, V., Popescu, O., & Koedinger, K. R. (2001). Towards tutorial dialog to support self-explanation: Adding natural language understanding to a cognitive tutor. In J. D. Moore, C. L. Redfield, & W. L. Johnson (Eds.), *Artificial intelligence in education: AI-ED in the wired and wireless future: Proceedings of AI-ED 2001* (pp. 246-255). Amsterdam: IOS Press.

Anderson, J. R. (1988). The expert module. In M. Polson & J. Richardson (Eds.), *Handbook of intelligent training systems* (pp. 21-53). Hillsdale, NJ: Erlbaum.

Anderson, J. R. (1990). *The adaptive character of thought*. Hillsdale, NJ: Erlbaum.

Anderson, J. R. (1993). *Rules of the mind*. Hillsdale, NJ: Erlbaum.

Anderson, J. R., Boyle, C. F., Corbett, A., & Lewis, M. W. (1990). Cognitive modelling and intelligent tutoring. *Artificial Intelligence, 42*, 7-49.

Anderson, J. R., Boyle, C. F., & Reiser, B. J. (1985). Intelligent tutoring systems. *Science, 228*, 456-462.

Anderson, J. R., Conrad, F. G., & Corbett, A. T. (1989). Skill acquisition and the LISP tutor. *Cognitive Science, 13*, 467-505.

Anderson, J. R., Corbett, A. T., Koedinger, K. R., & Pelletier, R. (1995). Cognitive tutors: Lessons learned. *The Journal of the Learning Sciences, 4*, 167-207.

Anderson, J. R., & Lebière, C. (1998). *The atomic components of thought*. Mahwah, NJ: Erlbaum.

Carnegie Learning. (2004, September). *Results from Kent, WA*. (Cognitive Tutor Research Report WA-04-01). Retrieved April 14, 2005, from http://www .carnegielearning.com/research/research_reports/WA-04-01.pdf

Carnegie Learning. (2005). *Cognitive Tutor® Algebra I, Cognitive Tutor® Geometry, Cognitive Tutor® Algebra II* [Computer software]. Pittsburgh, PA: Carnegie Learning.

Carpenter, T. P., Fennema, E., Franke, M. L., Levi, L., & Empson, S. B. (1999). *Children's mathematics: Cognitively guided instruction*. Portsmouth, NH: Heinemann.

Corbett, A. T. (2001). Cognitive computer tutors: Solving the two-sigma problem. In M. Bauer, P. Gmytrasiewicz, & J. Vassileva (Eds.), *User modeling 2001: Proceedings of the eighth international conference* (pp. 137-147). Berlin, Germany: Springer-Verlag.

Corbett, A. T., & Anderson, J. R. (1989). Feedback timing and student control in the LISP Intelligent Tutoring System. In D. Bierman, J. Breuker, & J. Sandberg (Eds.), *Artificial intelligence and education: The Proceedings of the fourth international conference on AI and education* (pp. 64-72). Springfield, VA: IOS.

Corbett, A. T., & Anderson, J. R. (1992). The Lisp Intelligent Tutoring System: Research in skill acquisition. In J. H. Larkin & R. W. Chabay (Eds.), *Computer assisted instruction and intelligent tutoring systems: Shared goals and complementary approaches* (pp. 73-109). Hillsdale, NJ: Erlbaum.

Corbett, A. T., & Anderson, J. R. (1995). Knowledge decomposition and subgoal reification in the ACT programming tutor. In J. Greer (Ed.), *Artificial intelligence and education, 1995: The proceedings of AI-ED 95* (pp. 469-476). Charlottesville, VA: Association for the Advancement of Computing in Education.

Corbett, A. T., Anderson, J. R., & Patterson, E. G. (1990). Student modeling and tutoring flexibility in the Lisp Intelligent Tutoring System. In C. Frasson & G. Gauthier (Eds.), *Intelligent tutoring systems: At the crossroads of artificial intelligence and education* (pp. 83-106). Norwood, NJ: Ablex.

Corbett, A. T., McLaughlin, M. S., Scarpinatto, K. C., & Hadley, W. S. (2000). Analyzing and generating mathematical models: An Algebra II cognitive tutor design study. In G. Gauthier, C. Frasson, & K. VanLehn (Eds.), *Intelligent tutoring systems: Proceedings of the fifth international conference* (pp. 314-323). Berlin, Germany: Springer-Verlag.

Corbett, A. T., Trask, H. J., Scarpinatto, K. C., & Hadley, W. S. (1998). A formative evaluation of the PACT Algebra II Tutor: Support for simple hierarchical reasoning. In B. P. Goettl, H. M. Halff, C. L. Redfield, & V. J. Shute, (Eds.), *Intelligent tutoring systems: Proceedings of the fourth international conference* (pp. 374-383). Berlin, Germany: Springer-Verlag.

Fey, J. T., Heid, M. K., Good, R. A., Sheets, C., Blume, G. W., & Zbiek, R. M. (1995). *Concepts in algebra: A technological approach*. Dedham, MA: Janson Publications.

Fey, J. T., Heid, M. K., Good, R. A., Sheets, C., Blume, G. W., & Zbiek, R. M. (1999). *Concepts in algebra: A technological approach*. Chicago: Everyday Learning Corporation.

Florida Department of Education. (2003). *Florida Comprehensive Assessment Test.* Retrieved April 14, 2005, from http://www.firn.edu/doe/sas/fcat.htm

Gluck, K. (1999). *Eye movements and algebra tutoring*. Unpublished doctoral dissertation, Carnegie Mellon University, Pittsburgh, PA.

Heffernan, N. T., & Koedinger, K. R. (2000). Intelligent tutoring systems are missing the tutor: Building a more strategic dialog-based tutor. In C. P. Rose & R. Freedman (Eds.), *Proceedings of the AAAI fall symposium on building dialogue systems for tutorial applications* (pp. 14-19). Menlo Park, CA: AAAI Press.

Hiebert, J., Carpenter, T. R, Fennema, E., Fuson, K. C., Wearne, D., Murray, H. et al. (1997). *Making sense: Teaching and learning mathematics with understanding.* Portsmouth, NH: Heinemann.

Honey, M., Culp, K. M., & Carrigg, F. (2000). Perspectives on technology and education research: Lessons from the past and present. *Journal of Educational Computing Research, 23,* 5-14.

Koedinger, K., & Anderson, J. (1990). Abstract planning and perceptual chunks: Elements of expertise in geometry. *Cognitive Science, 14*, 511-550.

Koedinger, K. R., & Anderson, J. R. (1993a). Effective use of intelligent software in high school math classrooms. In P. Brna, S. Ohlsson, & H. Pain (Eds.), *Proceedings of the sixth world conference on artificial intelligence in education* (pp. 241-248). Charlottesville, VA: Association for the Advancement of Computing in Education.

Koedinger, K. R., & Anderson, J. R. (1993b). Reifying implicit planning in geometry: Guidelines for model-based intelligent tutoring system design. In S. Lajoie & S. Derry (Eds.), *Computers as cognitive tools* (pp. 14-45). Hillsdale, NJ: Erlbaum.

Koedinger, K. R., & Anderson, J. R. (1998). Illustrating principled design: The early evolution of a cognitive tutor for algebra symbolization. *Interactive Learning Environments, 5*, 161-180.

Koedinger, K. R., Anderson, J. R., Hadley, W. H., & Mark, M. A. (1997). Intelligent tutoring goes to school in the big city. *International Journal of Artificial Intelligence in Education, 8*, 30-43.

Lagemann, E. C. (2000). An elusive science: *The troubling history of education research*. Chicago: The University of Chicago Press.

Morgan, P., & Ritter, S. (2002). *An experimental study of the effects of Cognitive Tutor® Algebra I on student knowledge and attitude.* Retrieved April 14, 2005, from http://www.carnegielearning.com/wwc/originalstudy.pdf

Nathan, M. J., Koedinger, K. R., & Tabachneck, H. J. M. (1996, April). *Difficulty factors in arithmetic and algebra: The disparity of teachers' beliefs and students' performances.* Paper presented at the annual meeting of the American Educational Research Association, New York.

Plano, G. S. (2004). The effects of the Cognitive Tutor Algebra on student attitudes and achievement in a 9th-grade algebra course. (Doctoral dissertation, Seton Hall University). *Dissertation Abstracts International, 65*(04), 1291A. (UMI No. 3130130)

Ritter, S., & Anderson, J. R. (1995). Calculation and strategy in the equation solving tutor. In J. D. Moore & J. F. Lehman (Eds.), *Proceedings of the seventeenth annual conference of the Cognitive Science Society* (pp. 413-418). Hillsdale, NJ: Erlbaum.

Sabelli, N., & Dede, C. (2001, July). *Integrating educational research and practice: Reconceptualizing goals and policies: How to make what works, work for us?* Retrieved April 14, 2005, from http://www.virtual.gmu.edu/ss_research/cdpapers/policy.pdf

Sarkis, H. (2004, May). *Cognitive Tutor Algebra I Program Evaluation: Miami-Dade County Public Schools.* Retrieved July 1, 2004, from http://relgroup.net/

Shadish, W. R., Cook, T. D., & Campbell, D. T. (2002). *Experimental and quasi-experimental designs for generalized causal inference.* Boston: Houghton Mifflin.

Singley, M. K., & Anderson, J. R. (1989). *The transfer of cognitive skill.* Cambridge, MA: Harvard University Press.

Stigler, J. W., & Hiebert, J. (1999). *The teaching gap.* New York: The Free Press.

CHAPTER 8

RESEARCH-DESIGN INTERACTIONS IN BUILDING FUNCTION PROBE SOFTWARE

Jere Confrey and Alan Maloney

Over the period of 15 years, our research team[1] designed and built Function Probe,[2] a multirepresentational software for teaching introductory functions to students in Grades 4 to 14. Originally developed to support a precalculus course at Cornell University and the mathematics classes at the Apple Classroom of Tomorrow (ACOT) in Columbus, Ohio, Function Probe was designed to support student thinking about, and exploration and understanding of families of functions, including linear, quadratic, exponential, polynomial, rational, and trigonometric. The software was built to permit students to explore the contrasting and complementary appearance and behavior of these functions using different representations. With research and development support from numerous sources,[3] we designed the software to respond to students' own inclinations to act in applied problem-solving settings and to permit them to explore the results of their actions. Fortunately the design work coincided with a very active research field to produce opportunities to experiment with novel approaches and to assess the results. A group of talented graduate stu-

Research on Technology and the Teaching and Learning of Mathematics:
Vol. 2. Cases and Perspectives, 183–209

dents undertook a variety of studies that made such investigations possible. Function Probe was constructed through multiple rounds of design and research, which served to clarify how students thought about functions, how they can learn about functions in improved ways, and thence to inform subsequent rounds of design of the software's features. In this chapter, we review some of the more original design innovations in the software and discuss their interactions with the research process.

In discussing these interactions between the software and our research, we can illustrate how our own content knowledge developed as researchers and as teacher educators, both in terms of pedagogical content knowledge and in terms of generative domain knowledge. Both types of knowledge are necessary changes to teachers' content knowledge. The distinction between them is that pedagogical content knowledge relates to the content required to know how to teach a topic, namely, its pedagogy, while generative domain knowledge refers to how the content itself needs to be restructured in light of new approaches to technology, learning, and applications of mathematics—hence the term "generative." For example, pedagogical content knowledge is necessary to guide teachers in choosing examples, anticipating student strategies and misconceptions, and in generating convincing and understandable explanations. Generative domain knowledge refers to how one's own content knowledge is transformed substantively in the context of problem solving and multiple representations. This transformation of knowledge is necessary for teachers to become flexible and adaptable, to recognize innovative student approaches, to generate and identify novel applications and representational possibilities, and to link mathematical topics in new ways (Confrey, 1999).

We will illustrate how two of our design principles affected the software's development and revision. First, we regularly conducted careful study of student use of software prototypes and tasks, and revised our designs to respond to the students' documented approaches—a "learner-centered design approach" (Confrey, 1996). Second, we built representations that independently supported the pursuit of mathematical actions consistent with the functionality of the representation, while working for compatibility across them. This led us to develop unique tools and generate interesting mathematical possibilities within "an epistemology of multiple representations" (Confrey & Smith, 1994).

INTRODUCTION TO FUNCTION PROBE

Function Probe is Java-based, cross-platform software which opens with three separate but linked windows: a Table window, a Graph window, and a Calculator window. It has been used with a range of students, from fourth graders, to college students enrolled in precalculus courses.

The Function Probe software includes a series of sample problems that support students' understanding of different families of functions. These are excerpted and expanded from problems in *Learning About Functions Through Problem Solving* (Confrey, 1998). The software is in use in many colleges and community colleges in the United States as well as in countries around the world.

Although we will primarily discuss the features of the Table, Graph, and Calculator windows separately, one of the major features of the software is that points, values, and equations can be moved from one window to another with ease. This further strengthens students' capabilities of working with multiple representations in constructing and solving mathematical problems.

THE TABLE WINDOW

The Table window was the first area in which we explored innovations. Unlike other software, for which spreadsheet architecture was selected for exploring table behavior (Sutherland & Rojano, 1993), Function Probe was built with a column-oriented structure that makes actions on columns, instead of actions on individual cells, the elementary unit of action for a user. Data in the columns can be entered in four ways: direct keyboard entry of individual values, import of data from other applications, a "Fill command," and the entry of a formula. Above the columns are three rows of cells, one (icon row) for determining which columns of data will be graphed, one for a formal variable name or equation, and one (labels row) for an informal text description of the quantities that vary in each column (see Figures 8.1A and 8.1B).

As we watched students use Function Probe's Table, we observed that it was important that students be provided time to use the Table. Often, students entered a few values and struggled to see how the values could be ordered and organized. This process frequently occurred before students named the variable, either formally or informally. An instance of this occurred with the "Cliff Problem," in which a house is located at a certain distance from an eroding cliff, and students are asked to predict the position of the cliff edge in subsequent years. The students struggled to decide whether to enter data in feet or inches, whether to measure from the back, middle, or front of the house (and what those terms mean in the context of the safety of the house as the cliff erodes) and whether to enter the date as the number of years since the starting year or to use the entire date. Variations in these decisions proved to be important: They resulted

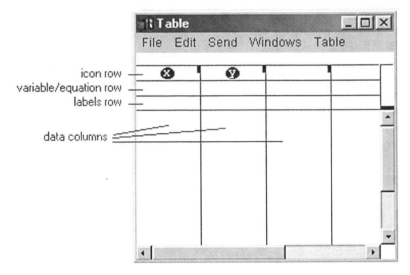

Figure 8.1A.   Function Probe default Table window.

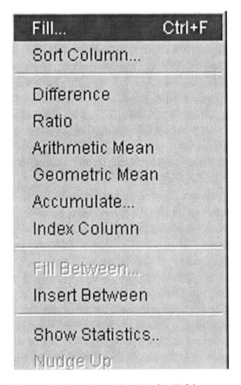

Figure 8.1B.   Function Probe Table menu.

in differences in the equations students developed to solve the problem, and they promoted interesting opportunities to generate natural transformations of those equations which themselves later became a major topic of exploration. Working directly with the numbers often provided students with a sense of the kinds of quantities with which they were working and how these changed relative to each other. As a result, their naming of variables was not just a pro forma identification process, but rather a constructive choice leading to concept and strategy development.

The "Fill" command was designed to support viewing functions as the "covariation" of two sequences. Design of the Fill command was generated by concern for students' conceptual development of rates of change for linear and exponential functions. It was influenced by our earlier software, Function Finder, which was designed as a version of "Guess My Rule" in which students chose values of x for which the values of y were automatically produced, and were challenged to produce the function as a form of $y = mx + b$. We documented that students' strategies with Function Finder evolve from the selection of random values for x, to systematic use of zero, consecutive values, and values symmetric about zero. Using an x-value of zero permitted them to isolate the value of the added term (b), while the use of consecutive x-values and values symmetric about zero permitted them to deduce the value of the multiplier (m). Note that in discussing the Table, we refrain from using the terms, "y-intercept" and "slope," because these have a different meaning in the context of the graph. In the context of the Table, the operational qualities of the function are paramount, that is, how the combination of operations on an x-value produces the corresponding y-value.

The concept of slope itself provides an excellent example of this distinction. In the context of a table, the concept of slope does, of course, apply as the ratio of the difference in y over the difference in x. The primary conceptual challenge experienced by students, however, was to determine how and why a constant additive change between y-values, corresponding to consecutive x-values, becomes a multiplicative quality in describing the equation that relates x to y. Consistently, large numbers of students predicted that the function defined by the equation $y = 2x + 5$ would be described as $y = x + 2$ as they attempted to code the pattern in the y-values (noting the difference of 2 between consecutive y-values) rather than the method of transforming an x-value into a y-value. This captures the essence of the distinction between correspondence and covariation in functions. A correspondence approach tells how to go from an x-value to a y-value, whereas a covariation approach specifies how, in the vertical direction, the y-values vary as the x-values change by a consistent additive amount. In a covariation approach to linear functions, students are working to co-vary two arithmetic sequences. By watching students learn to coordinate these two approaches and consider a linear function as a correspondence of x to y, we found that it is better for many students to view a linear function as a certain number of "units of m" (that is, x units of m) which is translated by its additive initial amount, b. One student developed the strategy (in Function Finder) of putting in large values of x in order to distinguish the multiplier from the adder. For example, if the function were $y = 2x + 5$, then the x-values of 10, 100, and 1000 produce corresponding y-values of 25, 205, and 2005. This clearly reveals the differential impact of the two parameters in a clever way. Contrasting the concept of m as a constant ratio with m as an operational multiplier of x illustrates how one might design "learner-centered" software to support a student strategy and to highlight the contrasting character of different representations. Too often in mathematics, the "generalization" (across representations, in the form of a single abstract term) is held in higher esteem than the particularization (the distinctions in the behavior and meaning of those terms in different representations), whereas in our design principles, we sought to make both the generalization and the particularization a source of intellectual delight.

In her research, Rizzuti (1991) examined students' work with Function Probe in an urban school in Columbus, Ohio. Drawing on the distinction between covariation and correspondence (Marcovits, Eylon, & Bruckheimer, 1986), Rizutti documented that students often preferred to describe how the dependent values of a function changed as the independent variable was incremented by one unit. In the context of the kinds of problems given, this evolved into a rate-of-change approach to describing functions.

Our design of the Fill command was also influenced by our research on exponential functions, in which we witnessed students' isomorphic tendency to attempt to focus on the pattern of repeated multiplication in values in the y-column corresponding to a pattern of repeated addition in the x-column (Confrey, 1990; Confrey & Smith, 1995). To support this we built the Fill command so, in filling a column, a user could as easily multiply or divide by a constant amount as add or subtract a constant amount (see Figure 8.2). In a growth problem based on doubling a number of objects per unit time, students would observe the pattern in the y-values and tend to describe the function iteratively as $y = 2x$ rather than as $y = 2^x$. In fact, if one codes the linear function as $y = b + xm$, one notes its parallel structure to the coding of the exponential as $y = C*2^x$. These approaches were further supported by the design of the Difference and Ratio commands in the Table window. From our work with quadratic (Afamasaga-Fuata'i, 1992) and quadratic and linear functions (Rizutti, 1991), we were convinced of the power of first and second differences and built these into our designs. However, having also exploited the parallel struc-

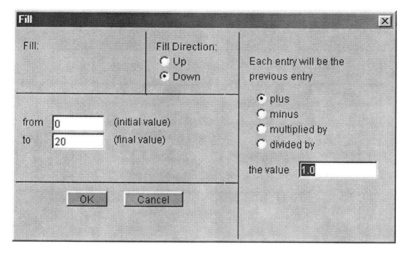

Figure 8.2.   Fill command's dialog box, with an additive entry pattern selected.

ture between the linear and exponential function in the Fill command, we developed a Ratio command, symbolized by ®, to reveal the change or constancy in the ratios of consecutive values in a column. We were thrilled to be able to invent a symbol for this operation, having scoured the litera- ture and failed to find one. Students tend to treat exponential growth with two separate actions—computing the *change* in a population's size, and then adding this change to the population size. The Ratio command (see Figure 8.3) has proven powerful in helping students curtail this tendency and instead compute exponential growth with a single action—multiply- ing the population size by the quantity (1 + growth rate).

One area of development of the Table has yet to be adequately pursued and revised. We developed a "Nudge" command which would permit a set of values generated by the Difference or Accumulate command, and which were therefore "off line" from the original set, to be nudged to move into position at the same height as the original data set. (The Accu- mulate command iteratively generates the sum of the values in a column.) A critical element in developing the nudge capability came from the examination of history of the development of calculus and functions. Two trends profoundly influenced our work. One is relevant to the develop- ment of the Table and the other to the Graph and to the use of Geome- ter's Sketchpad. We studied the period between the time of Descartes and the time of Newton and Leibniz. During that period, the mathematician John Wallis undertook significant study of mathematics using tables. Wal- lis developed some impressive results by examining tables and creating

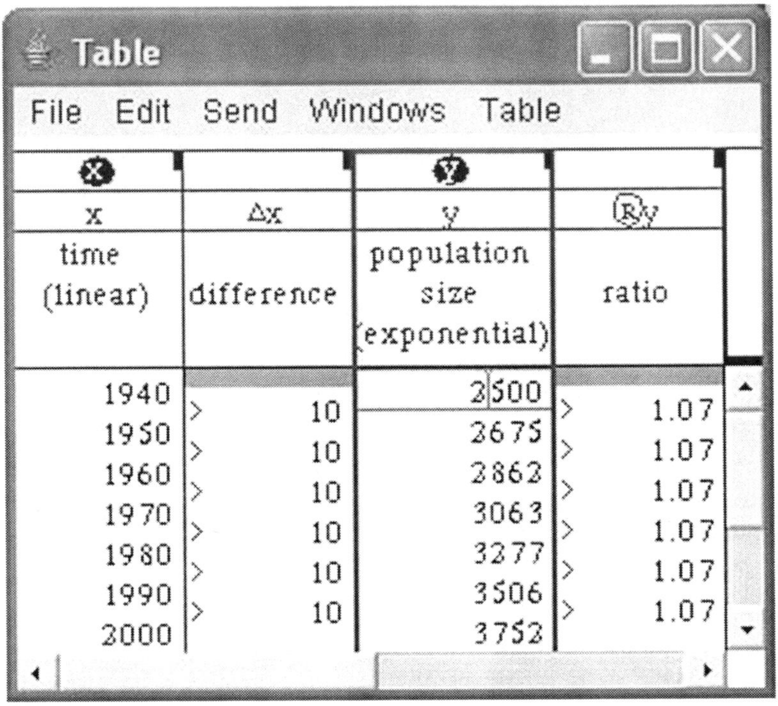

x	Δx	y	®y
time (linear)	difference	population size (exponential)	ratio
1940	> 10	2500	> 1.07
1950	> 10	2675	> 1.07
1960	> 10	2862	> 1.07
1970	> 10	3063	> 1.07
1980	> 10	3277	> 1.07
1990	> 10	3506	> 1.07
2000		3752	

Note: The x- and y-columns represent 10-year census figures for a hypothetical population, growing at a constant intrinsic growth rate of 7% each 10 years. Change in the time column is illustrated with the Difference command (Δx); change in the population size column is illustrated with the Ratio command (®x).

Figure 8.3.   Example of the Table's Difference and Ratio commands.

sums of sequences to approximate mathematical quantities such as the value of π (Dennis & Confrey, 1996). Interestingly, in research with economics majors, we found that they were adept in scanning tables to find patterns and preferred these to looking at the more compact form of equations. This historical work and subsequent study of students with different majors made us realize that tools to make it easy to examine data, rate of change, and accumulation are a potentially powerful but largely overlooked part of mathematics.

We found additionally that Newton was also extraordinarily facile in his use of tables. He studied the relationships between first, second, and third differences, not just by looking at patterns in the values, but also by graphing the patterns in relation to the original functions. To do this, one needed to index the *differences* between the values in a column, not just the values of the original functions. This led us to develop the Nudge command in Function Probe. Using it allows one either (a) to treat the differences as bars spanning the intervals of the original index (see Figure 8.4A) or (b) to treat the unit changes as averages in the Table or point values in the Graph by nudging them to be on line with the original indexing and plotting these approximations of the derivative as their own graphs (see Figure 8.4B).

We surmise that history made the use of tables in mathematics nearly obsolete for a time. The inventions of more compact notations by Newton and Leibniz made it possible for students of mathematics to "master" the notation while overlooking or circumventing the cumbersome demands of numeric particulars, and hence avoid tables. Unfortunately, by reducing mathematics to "mere child's play" notationally, even Leibniz feared he had inadvertently undermined the development of the mathematical mind (Confrey, 1995). We believe that use of the table may experience a rebirth with appropriate design and use of automatic commands that permit easy manipulation of columns of data and their operational transformations, such as the commands built into Function Probe. This work with tables becomes afforded by the medium in novel ways, and we see it as

x	$y=x^3$	Δy
0	0	
1	1	1
2	4	3
3	9	5
4	16	7
5	25	9
6	36	11
7	49	13
8	64	15
		17

Figure 8.4A.   Difference column, which can be plotted as bars (areas) on the Graph.

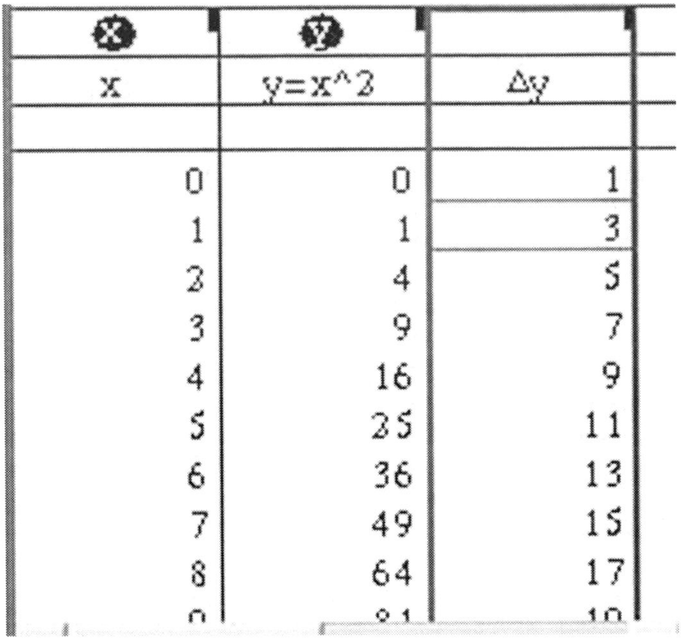

x	y=x^2	Δy
0	0	1
1	1	3
2	4	5
3	9	7
4	16	9
5	25	11
6	36	13
7	49	15
8	64	17
0	8 1	1 0

Figure 8.4B.   Difference column nudged up, suggesting values to be plotted as points.

another example of generative domain knowledge rather than an example of pedagogical content knowledge.

THE GRAPH WINDOW

The impetus for developing the Graph window was to build an environment to support visual reasoning in the context of learning about functions. In doing this, we learned a great deal about students' visual reasoning. This work conveniently coincided with an increased emphasis on modeling using real data and curve fitting. In our design, we decided to incorporate the ability to transform functions visually and then register the symbolic impact of the transformations. Because of increasing flexibility with programming graphical interfaces, we designed direct actions on the graphs. This is in contrast to other functions software that drove transformations algebraically or numerically, such as Function Supposer (Schwartz & Yerushalmy, 1992), and Grapher (Schoenfeld, 1988).

Because transformations often involved multiple iterative actions—as does curve fitting—we designed the Function Probe Graph window to generate a history of the graph actions. Originally we saw this as a research decision as well as a design consideration, because it created a record for examining student work. We have since found it to be a useful instructional tool as well. Its use as a tool for student reflection was studied most extensively by Haarer (1999), who also designed the software's capacity to permit students to reflect on their work and to enter "pictures" of their graphs in laboratory reports.

Design of the translation and reflection commands was relatively intuitive. However, design of the stretch command was particularly difficult, in part because its treatment in textbooks is typically oversimplified. There were two challenges involved, one in design and the other conceptual. Stretching involves two distinct actions. The first is to determine where the line of invariance is, and the second concerns the impact of a stretch on the value of individual points. To simplify the explanation of these conceptual and design issues, we will discuss only vertical stretches, though the argument applies to both vertical and horizontal stretches. (Note, in the case of horizontal stretches, the stretch factor appears in the equation as its multiplicative inverse on x, a topic that requires careful and distinct conceptual development.)

To understand stretching, consider vertically stretching a rubber sheet that is attached to horizontal poles at its top and bottom. Imagine pulling the poles smoothly away from each other, thereby stretching the plane vertically. Notice that there is always one horizontal line of invariance, a single horizontal line that does not move while all other horizontal lines migrate away from that invariant line. In the Function Probe software, a graph or curve lies on the sheet (or plane) to be stretched, while the original coordinate plane and axes remain fixed. The two sheets, or planes, can be seen as connected at the line of invariance.

In most software, this line of invariance is placed automatically at the x-axis, where y equals zero. This makes sense for symbolic ease, as it permits the impact of the stretch on the original function to be simply and solely multiplicative ($y = x^2$ becomes $y = ax^2$ with a stretch factor of a). However, in a visual environment, we claimed that this line of invariance should be manipulable: The line of invariance determines which points remain invariant under the transformation, and if software is to be used effectively to model real phenomena, the position of the line of invariance is established by the context of the problem. Although one could simply adjust one's reference axis (to avoid a nonzero line of invariance), doing so can be awkward, and impede a visual operation. In response to this design challenge, we invented the idea of an "anchor" line, and required that the user place it prior to stretching a curve. Once the direction of stretch is selected, the user places the anchor line using the same action as for translating. We included a notation in the history window to indicate the equation of the anchor line.

An example of using an anchor line off the axis was spontaneously generated in a summer workshop. A classroom teacher was working on one of our problems in which a set of stepping stones must be placed with equal spacing to create a path from a house to a bird feeder. In the problem, the final stone is required to be adjacent to the feeder, but the placement of the first stone was not specified and could be varied. The teacher wanted to show the set of all possible solutions on a graph of stone number versus distance from the house. After creating one possible configuration, she placed the line of invariance at the distance of the bird feeder, and the stretched and contracted the point-set to illustrate all possible solutions. Our Graph window design readily permitted this manipulation (see Figure 8.5).

The second conceptual challenge in stretching a function is to understand the relationship of the stretch to multiplication. Most textbooks treat stretching as a non-problematic multiplicative action. In our research, we found that students need to engage with why, for example,

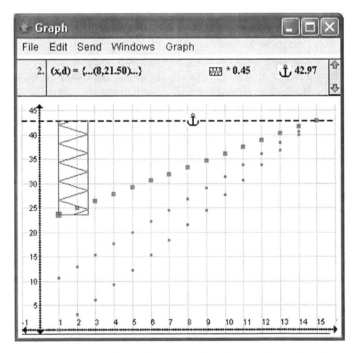

Figure 8.5.   Stretching of stone path points, with anchor line at $d = 43$, position of feeder.

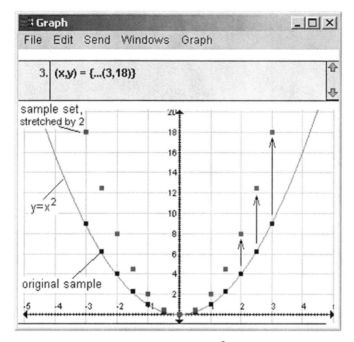

Figure 8.6.   Point set sampled on $y = x^2$, then stretched vertically by 2.

multiplying a function like $y = x^2$ by 2, so it becomes $y = 2x^2$, results in a stretch of the function, and vice versa. To understand this, one needs to recognize that, upon stretching, the magnitudes of the y-values corresponding to large values of x change more than those corresponding to small values of x. However, visualizing this on a continuous function is difficult, because it is not possible to show the specific mapping for each point. We found that by developing a graph-sampling capability (see Figure 8.6), and acting on the sample as a discrete set, we could facilitate students' transition through this conceptual obstacle (Borba, 1993). Arrows were added to the visual stretch features (see Figure 8.6) to emphasize differences in the changes in y-coordinates that correspond to the position of the original points on the curve.

As previously stated, one of our design principles was to build representations that would be "true" to the actions a student could take, while facilitating contrasts and similarities among the different representations and conventions. By taking this perspective, our research work highlighted many examples of representational issues that are unsatisfactorily resolved in conventional treatments. This occurred particularly frequently in relation to visual reasoning, which is traditionally devalued in teaching high

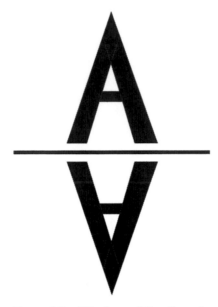

Figure 8.7.   The letter "A" reflected
horizontally, as in Ascher (1991).

school algebra. For example, in a summer workshop with high school teachers, we debated whether a reflection across a horizontal line should be referred to as a "horizontal reflection"—based on the line of reflection's directionality—or a "vertical reflection"—based on the direction of motion of the curve (LaChance, 1999). We subsequently examined many text-books and found that most of them label a reflection about a horizontal line a "horizontal reflection." For instance, in *Ethnomathematics*, Marcia Ascher (1991) refers to the reflection in Figure 8.7 as being horizontal.

However, in stretching a function vertically, one can produce this same action by stretching through the anchor line. Thus, a vertical stretch of –1 is equivalent to a horizontal reflection. Such inconsistent use of language is disconcerting and, to our knowledge, has not been resolved in the research literature. In our documentation, we finessed the problem by referring to reflections as "mirroring along" either a horizontal or vertical line of reflection, rather than as horizontal or vertical reflection per se, although this is not an entirely satisfying resolution either.

Not all such tensions are easily identified. All of us, researchers and teachers, were surprised by the results displayed in one teacher workshop. During the session, we worked on a problem called "Parking Garage," in which a parking garage pricing structure, with incremental costs for dif-ferent blocks of time a vehicle is parked, is modeled and then varied by the students. The greatest integer function is a powerful tool in conceptual development, to help students grasp the distinction between horizontal and vertical stretches prior to learning about trigonometric functions. Understanding that, compared to $y = [x]$, $y = 3[x]$ will make the steps taller by a factor of three, whereas $y = [3x]$ will make the steps narrower by a factor of 3 is a significant and challenging insight for students. In the context of a parking garage fee structure, the vertical stretch represents a change in the pricing structure by increasing or decreasing the increments of cost, for each unit of time, whereas the horizontal stretch represents a change in the pricing structure by increasing or decreasing the unit time intervals at which the pricing changes. Because Function Probe permits one to observe and manipulate these differences visually, and because the problem context reinforces understanding of these differences because they are affecting different quantities, students learn the material effectively. However, it was in the context of combining stretches and translations into multiple linked transformations that we were all surprised by the following outcome.

Most textbooks ignore the impact of carrying out multiple transformations as a sequence of actions. When they do treat multiple transformations, they do so by giving an expression such as $y = Af(B(x - C)) + D$, or some variation of this, in a single simple order; the only emphasis made in most texts is to determine the direction of the translation and whether a stretch is a dilation or contraction. They neglect working with a visual order of transformations, which produced the conceptual obstacle that surprised us all. To understand the issue, consider the following sequence of transformations and predict the resulting equation:

1. Stretch a step function horizontally by half (or shrink it by 2), relative to the y-axis.
2. Translate the function 0.25 units to the right.

What equation would you expect to see produced? Now reverse the order of the two transformations and again predict the equation.

In the first case, the first transformation (the horizontal stretch) produces $y = [2x]$, and the second transformation (the translation) then produces $y = [2(x - 0.25)]$. In the second case, the final equation is $y = [2(x) - 0.25]$. In our experience, most people reverse these two predictions to reflect the order in which they visually carried out the transformations. Resolving the conflict between the algebraic order of operations and the visual order of transformations led to an interesting challenge.

Using Function Probe and sets of contextual problems, we studied six different ways to introduce students to transformations (Confrey, 1994). Most textbooks use an approach of *parameter substitution*. However, this approach hides as much as it reveals. As demonstrated with the Parking

Garage problem, the order of transformations does not correspond to one's usual understanding of the rules that apply to the algebraic order of operations. By choosing only a single form of the transformed equation, the texts identify a set of actions, but provide little help for variations from these forms. We developed a number of alternative forms including:

1. *Function Building*: One begins with $y = x$ as a form of a basic identity function and applies transformations first to x, such as stretching and translating to produce $y = mx + b$ and then applying the prototype function, f, to produce $y = f(mx + b)$. Then by transforming this function, using only vertical translations, reflections, and stretches, one produces the final form $y = a f(mx + b) + c$.

2. *Symmetric Descriptions*: One works with the form $B(y - C) = f(D(x - E))$, in which f is a function and B, C, D, and E are parameters. By using this form, one sees the vertical transformations exactly as one sees the horizontal transformations, thus eliminating the need for different explanations for the behavior of the translations in different directions. The disadvantage of this approach is that many applications, including Function Probe, require functions to be entered as "$f(x) =$" or "$y =$".

3. *The Horseshoe Display:* In this approach, a two-dimensional display is used to code the actions that are carried out visually, starting with a prototype function, such as $y = x$, $y = x^2$ or $y = \sin x$. Transformations are recorded in order (but separately for transformations on the x- and y-variables) in a two-column list (see Figure 8A). If a transformation is carried out on the x-variable, it is coded in one column (i.e., on one side of the "horseshoe"). If the action is performed on the y-variable, it is coded in the other column (i.e., on the other side of the "horseshoe").

With the actions recorded in the horseshoe diagram, one constructs the final equation by linking x'' to y'', carrying out a series of substitutions beginning on the bottom right and solving for x in terms of x''. Then, using the resulting x-value (in terms of x''), the substitutions on the y-side are carried out sequentially to get y'' in terms of x'' down the left column. For the diagram in Figure 8.8A, the substitutions would be those shown in Figure 8B.

Learning transformations well, as supported by Function Probe, is an increasingly important skill set for students, especially in the context of modeling and applications. The software has permitted us to reveal the inadequacies of the traditional treatments, but also to begin to map out strategies to remedy those inadequacies, especially in the context of visualization.

Type of transformation	Transformations on y	Prototype function	Transformations on x	Type of transformation
		$y = \sin x$		
VS: vertical stretch (by 0.5)	$y' = 0.5y$		$x' = 2x$	HS: horizontal stretch (by 2)
VT: vertical translation (by 1)	$y'' = y' + 1$		$x'' = x' + .25$	HT: horizontal translation (by 0.25)

Note: The diagram assumes all stretches are anchored on the x- or y-axis.

Figure 8.8A.   Horseshoe Diagram of transformations of $y = \sin x$.

Description of Action	Transformations	Sequential substitutions, in reverse order of graph action, for x in terms of x'' and for y'' in terms of y.
Transformation on x (HT)	$x'' = x' + 0.25$	$x' = x'' - 0.25$
Transformation on x (HS)	$x' = 2x$	$x = 0.5(x'' - 0.25)$
Prototype function	$y = \sin x$	$y = \sin[0.5(x'' - 0.25)]$
Transformation on y (VS)	$y' = 0.5y$	$y' = 0.5 \sin[0.5(x'' - 0.25)]$
Transformation on y (VT)	$y'' = y' + 1$	$y'' = 0.5 \sin[0.5(x'' - 0.25)] + 1$

Figure 8.8B.   Sequential solution of transformations for final equation.

Additional major design challenges evolved from our interest in the transition to calculus. In considering how to build intuitive links to differentiation and integration, we were intrigued by the relationship among points on a curve, samples of points, and their relationship to slope triangles and bars. (Slope triangles and bars are illustrated in Figure 8.9.) Driven in part by the capabilities of Function Probe's Table to create first and second differences and to accumulate values, we were challenged as designers and educators to build parallel capabilities in graphical representation. Structuring these so that the ideas would be compatible and elegant proved to be an interesting challenge.

In handling and sampling points on a curve, we provided means for students to progress through various levels of examining and analyzing functions and rates of change. Rather than focus solely on a line or curve as a representation of the solution set for an equation, we designed tools for viewing points as values that satisfy a particular function, as well as to scan changes in the points' locations and coordinates. Students can dynamically and qualitatively begin to understand the implications of change from one pair of coordinates to another over different intervals along a curve. We designed the software to permit three methods of working with points or point sets: making individual points in "freehand," hooking a point to a curve then dragging and watching its coordinates change, and creating sequences of points either on or not on a curve.

Along with this, we designed a sampling tool to permit users to carry out more systematic analysis of functions and rates of change. We designed our sampling tool to permit a user to create a sample of a curve using one of four methods: (a) creating a set by clicking manually on points on a curve with the mouse, (b) specifying a list of x-values from the Table, (c) creating a sequence of x-values using a command identical to the Fill command in the Table, and (d) partitioning an interval evenly into m parts. Sampling on y was much more problematic, as we could not always compute the corresponding inverse of a function to obtain x-values, so we relied on screen-level accuracy for this process, which is not an elegant or satisfying solution.

Point sets constructed on a curve can then be sent back to the table as data for further analysis of patterns and number. In addition, however, slope triangles and areas represented as bars are also critical tools for developing ideas of change and the basis for calculus. As we worked with the ideas of slope triangles and bars, we found that the same resources we designed for working with points and point samples could be adapted for slope triangles and bars. Thus, we designed Function Probe to permit one to draw a free-standing slope triangle or bar, to link a single triangle or bar to a curve and drag it, observing changes in its values, or to create slope or bar sets. Each of these new tools required the development of new forms of notation to support them. Each had small variations that posed challenges to be solved. For instance, in the case of the slope triangle, we added a tangent tool to "take the slope triangle to its logical extreme." Figure 8.9 shows examples of all three types of sample sets (points, triangles, and bars) on a single sine curve. These design extensions in Function Probe await further refinement. However, as it is, Function Probe already has the resources to support an intuitive calculus, starting in the early grades, which is clearly consistent with the National Council of Teachers of Mathematics (NCTM) mathematics standards (NCTM, 2000) and with work such as that undertaken by Kaput and Roschelle (2000) in SimCalc and Nemirovsky and Monk (2000) at TERC.

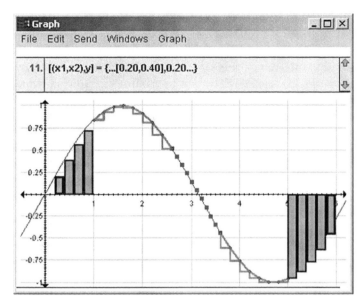

Figure 8.9.   Graph of $y = \sin x$, showing sets of bars, points, and slope triangles.

A final example of a design challenge in a visual environment involves our design of a linear regression tool. Because Function Probe is a pedagogical tool, we designed a regression tool with three attributes. In the first, the student is given a line tool, which the student can drag and tilt to "fit" to a set of points and display the equation for the line. This dynamic tool permits students to experiment with the notion that a scatter plot of data can be described better by some lines than others. Then we provide a tool that dynamically displays the distances between each point and the line, as well as the sum of squares (or the absolute value) of those differences, to permit students to get a feel for minimizing the sum of the squares. Finally students can use a full-blown regression tool to automatically produce the best-fit regression line using either least squares or least absolute deviation as the method. We provide this as an example of how one can design a tool to help students progressively gain an insight into a complex process instead of confronting them initially with an automated black box.

THE CALCULATOR WINDOW

The calculator on Function Probe is the representation that has been least researched. At the time the software was initially built, the calculator was essentially a resource rather than a full representational form: the calculator resource permitted one to compute particular values of functions, but it was not designed as a full environment for acting on functions and relations.

Computationally, the calculator in Function Probe has two unique characteristics overlooked in most other calculator layouts. First, it permits one to use degree measures of angles as the inputs to trigonometric functions while offering a notation for distinguishing the inputs. Thus, the $\sin_d$ key accepts degree measures of angles for inputs and the $\sin_r$ key accepts radians. In a study of mathematical modeling, Doerr (1994) demonstrated that students often come to view the trigonometric functions as calculator-button pushes, but fail to recognize that trigonometric functions describe ratios of the sides of similar right triangles. This suggests that more work needs to be undertaken in this area.

The second unique feature of the Function Probe calculator is its support for the use of any base for logarithms. We contend that most calculators lack this capability because they use a notation for exponentials of the form y^x. This does not yield an inverse, because one does not know whether to take the inverse of a polynomial to yield a power function with a rational exponent (for example, $y = x^3$ vs. $y = x^{1/3}$), or to take the inverse of an exponential to yield a logarithmic function (for example, $y = 2^x$ vs. $y = \log_2 x$). Partly as a result of this design feature in most calculators, we find that both students and teachers typically fail to distinguish adequately between quadratic functions and exponentials.

Therefore, we designed Function Probe's exponential key to be separate from the power key. The a^x key takes its first input as x (the exponent), and then requires a declaration for a (the base). Conversely, the x^a key takes its first input as x (the base), and then requires a declaration for a (the exponent). Either of these keys can be used to compute a number raised to a power. However, depressing the inverse (INV) key produces two distinct inverses: $x^{1/a}$ (for the x^a key), and $\log_a x$ (for the a^x key). Figure 8.10 illustrates the use of these keys.

Because Function Probe's calculator permits the user to build a button, the a^x and x^a keys and their inverses can be used to create functions of any base and export them to the Table or to the Graph. This is a strong resource for teaching students to work with compound interest, or with logs of any other base.

Another innovation in the calculator involves its use of a keystroke record, also shown in Figure 8.10. As in the Graph, the calculator keystroke history is maintained to support collaboration and student reflection, and to allow review of students' approaches by teachers and researchers. However, the keystroke record has also been useful in teaching particular topics. For instance, if a function is computed for a particular value, such as, $f(3)$ for $f(x) = 4x^2 + 2$, the keystroke record will look

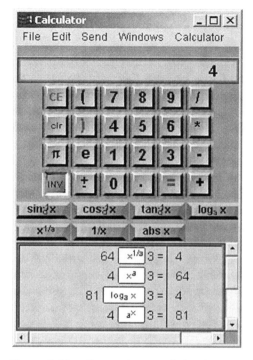

Figure 8.10.   Keystroke record showing
use of a^x and x^a keys and their inverses.

like "3 x^a 2 * 4 + 2". The student can then understand the inverse function as a reversal of the process. The inverse would be to subtract 2,
divide by 4, and then take the square root. Because the keystroke history makes the order of operations clear, its inverse is clarified. It can
also help the students to understand why the inverse of a polynomial
can produce two numerical results, one of which is not consistent with
the value entered. Another feature that strengthens the Calculator's
visual environment is a matrix tool, which includes capabilities to execute row operations rather than simply producing numeric solutions of
systems of linear equations. This is another example of how to build a
pedagogically sound tool that promotes conceptual development along
with technological fluency. We plan to merge the calculator with a new
design for symbolic manipulation and for rendering functional notation
graphically. In the future, we will also add more statistical power and
link this to Function Probe's other resources, such as the linear regression tool in the Graph window.

LIMITING FACTORS

The use of Function Probe has been heavily curtailed by the widespread use of the graphing calculator. Major publishers have been reluctant to distribute Function Probe because they wish to avoid competing with the aggressive marketing of the graphing calculator and its saturation of the field. The graphing calculator has advantages in that students and schools can purchase individual calculators inexpensively. It is durable. Test makers have even permitted its use on high-stakes examinations such as advanced placement tests.

The graphing calculator is an engineer's or accountant's *short cut* in that it is compact and efficient, but it can be an intellectual and pedagogical *short circuit* for a student. Every button serves three or more purposes; once the operation of its less-than-intuitive interface is learned, people are reluctant to abandon it. A number of characteristics limit its usefulness as a robust support for mathematical learners, however. The graphing calculator lacks the kind of screen space desirable for effective visualization. Though it can be operated with probes, it produces poor quality displays. Students are not able to save their work, except in the form of programs, nor can they easily print calculation results. Though the graphing calculator can be linked to computers, it is neither easily interfaced nor extensible to the web. In classroom use, it tends to drive mathematics towards the symbolic, and only marginally supports the previously discussed kinds of cross-representational capabilities discussed previously in Function Probe. Finally, there is little published evidence that its designers have carefully studied student strategies, or that they have designed in response to student strategies.

We have observed teachers using the graphing calculator creatively to develop discovery lessons, and a few studies indicate that well-integrated graphing calculator use by experienced teachers skilled with the use of the graphing calculator can lead to creation of important mathematical meaning by students (Doerr & Zangor, 2000; Van Streun, 2000). The majority of teachers, however, apparently continued to use graphing calculators primarily for display of graphs and computation of solutions to equations, which may not contribute importantly to robust student mathematical learning (Guerrero, Walker, & Dugdale, 2004). Frequently, we have observed teachers using graphing calculators to teach students to compute results algorithmically, but avoiding study of the underlying mathematical structure or derivation of the algorithms. It is a simple matter for students to see mastery of the complicated sequence of calculator commands, rather than mathematical structure and reasoning, as the goal of mathematical participation. We are led to propose that there are weaknesses in the design of the hardware and software of the graphing calculator. One begins to suspect that the graphing calculator is in widespread use due to its market penetration and timing at least as much as its inherent educational value. Economic feasibility, portability, and durability are considerations, but as the price point on computers continues to become lower, computer-based options should become increasingly attractive.

Technological tools must be examined for their pedagogical and content-based design qualities and evaluated according to how intuitive, intellectually valid, and conceptually sound those designs are. The most important consideration should be the intellectual development of sound and flexible mathematical thinkers. We believe that it is important to elucidate the conditions under which different combinations of technology, curriculum, and teacher professional development are likely to have optimal benefit for students' learning. Studies are needed to compare the impact of calculator and software use on the development of mathematical thinking, while accounting for the technology design, teacher technology experience, content knowledge, and pedagogical/curricular approaches.

The second limiting factor with Function Probe is teacher use in the context of typical school organization. We have found that many mathematics teachers lag behind their counterparts in science in developing facility with computers. Once they are proficient in basic computer use, they find Function Probe intuitive and easy to use. However, getting teachers to move from novice to expert use is often more problematic, as the issues often reside in the ways in which their content knowledge must be revised, adapted, and/or remediated. Unfortunately, schools dedicate few resources to this kind of professional development. Often we witness greater proficiency in students' use of technologies and willingness to explore and conjecture, while teachers themselves are too often hesitant, easily overwhelmed by the increased demands of eager student activity, and inadequately supported in relation to equipment maintenance and regular access. When provided appropriate and sufficient professional development and adequate technological resources and support, teachers have undergone remarkable intellectual growth and excitement using Function Probe. It changes their relationship to their students, as novel approaches and surprises occur more frequently than before (Castro-Filho, 1999; Doerr, 1994; LaChance, 1999; Piliero, 1994).

We have experimented with helping schools and departments become more effective in organizing to engage in technologically innovative practices. We have learned that they must incorporate opportunities for teachers to collaborate, to support each other, and to have regular, reliable technology access. Inservice programs should provide a combination of opportunities for teachers, in the context of practice, to learn the mathematics itself in the context of problem solving and technology, and to learn to work with students effectively. And finally, a stable cadre of tools needs to be selected so that learning to use software does not take up disproportionate and repeated amounts of time. Explicit formative and summative assessments must be carefully linked to high-stakes testing in order to avoid having technology squeezed out of the instructional program (Castro-Filho, 1999; LaChance, 1999). Finally, we know that more research must be conducted in partnership with schools if such challenges are to be solved in scaleable and sustainable ways (Confrey, Bell, & Carrejo, 2001; Confrey, Castro-Filho, & Wilhelm, 2000).

CONCLUSION

Function Probe is a software application that is meant to accomplish certain design and learning goals. It is student-centered, and designed for use from novice to expert levels. It was designed to strengthen the distinctions among its representations of functions with the assumptions that robust understanding requires one to be able to examine mathematical ideas in different representations and then work to coordinate and contrast those results. It is an analytic tool in that it permits one to create a history of one's actions and to reflect back on those actions, either alone or with peers, with instructors, or with or by researchers.

A software application can be likened to a combination of a piece of scientific equipment and an artistic composition. In such a perspective, a designer is both a scientist and a craftsperson. Each software piece affords some conceptual development and hinders others. Each piece of software expresses its authors' ideas of how to access certain resources, which resources are most important, and how to support a variety of levels of sophistication of users—novice, intermediate, or expert—within the limitations and opportunities afforded by the medium in which the designer works. With a student-centered software such as Function Probe, software also has pedagogical intentions—to teach and address students' conceptual challenges.

A question can be raised about the generalizability of results on student cognition from such research and design contexts. It is true that the results of the kinds of studies reported herein are inextricably tied to the design characteristics of this particular piece of software. Yet, so too are studies with students in settings using traditional artifacts such as paper and pencil, computational devices, or other software. The medium of learning unavoidably influences intellectual results (Pea, 1987). In the case of the traditional setting, results are more easily recognized and accommodated, as they are more likely to converge with a teacher's own experience of learning and teaching. Yet, such an approach will leave instruction stagnant. To gain validity and generalizability for the research with new technologies, one must seek generalization across similar use of and purposes for particular media. One must carefully evaluate what is learned by students in these new approaches, such as those prepared and revised by the National Council of Teachers of Mathematics 2000). One must anticipate the changes in the students' future work prospects and environments. It seems clear that in the future, students will need to be able to use mathematics to model and explore various phenomena, to build, display, and interpret vast quantities of data that are presented visually and symbolically, and to integrate across disciplines previously regarded as independent. In addition, we will continue to need to prepare students to study complex problems and build new technologies to address them. These three factors—comparing results across similar media, evaluating compatibility to current content standards, and anticipating emerging trends in work and society—make research and development in this arena both particularly challenging and intellectually intriguing.

NOTES

1. Our research and development team included primary programmers, Forrest Carroll, Francisco Garcia, and Pedro Larios. Other team members are cited throughout the text.

2. For further information about availability of Function Probe, please contact author Maloney at alan_maloney@ncsu.edu.

3. Funding for our software and equipment came from the National Science Foundation, the Apple Classrooms of Tomorrow, Intel Corporation, and Microsoft Corporation.

REFERENCES

Afamasaga-Fuata'i, K. (1992). *Students' strategies for solving contextual problems on quadratic functions*. Unpublished doctoral dissertation, Cornell University, Ithaca, NY.

Ascher, M. (1991). *Ethnomathematics: A multicultural view of mathematical ideas*. Pacific Grove, CA: Brooks/Cole.

Borba, M. (1993). *Students' understanding of transformations of functions using multirepresentational software*. Unpublished doctoral dissertation, Cornell University, Ithaca, NY.

Castro-Filho, J. A. (1999). *Teachers, math, and reform: An investigation of learning in practice*. Unpublished doctoral dissertation, Cornell University, Ithaca, NY.

Confrey, J. (1990). The concept of exponential functions: A student's perspective. In L. Steffe (Ed.), *Epistemological foundations of mathematical experience* (pp. 124-159). New York: Springer-Verlag.

Confrey, J. (1994). Six approaches to transformation of functions using multi-representational software. In J. P. d. Ponte & J. F. Matos (Eds.), *Proceedings of the eighteenth annual conference of the International Group for the Psychology of Mathematics Education* (Vol. 2, pp. 217-224). Lisbon, Portugal: GRAFIS, Coop. de Artes Graficias, CRL.

Confrey, J. (1995). A theory of intellectual development, Part III. *For the Learning of Mathematics: An International Journal of Mathematics Education, 15*, 36-45.

Confrey, J. (1996). The role of new technologies in designing mathematics education. In C. Fisher, K. Dwyer, & K. Yocam (Eds.), *Education and technology: Reflections on computing in classrooms* (pp. 129-149). San Francisco: Apple Corp./Jossey-Bass.

Confrey, J. (1998). *Learning about functions through problem solving.* Ithaca, NY: Cornell University.

Confrey, J. (1999, April). Generative domain knowledge: *An epistemological taxonomy for rethinking content knowledge in mathematics.* Paper presented at the annual meeting of the American Educational Research Association, Montreal, Canada.

Confrey, J., Bell, K., & Carrejo, D. (2001). *Systemic crossfire: What implementation research reveals about urban reform in mathematics.* Unpublished manuscript, University of Texas at Austin.

Confrey, J., Castro-Filho, J., & Wilhelm, J. (2000). Implementation research as a means to link systemic reform and applied psychology in mathematics education. *Educational Psychologist, 35*, 179-191.

Confrey, J., & Smith, E. (1994). Comments on James Kaput's chapter "Democratizing access to calculus: New routes to old roots." In A. Schoenfeld (Ed.), *Mathematical thinking and problem solving* (pp. 172-192). Hillsdale, NJ: Erlbaum.

Confrey, J., & Smith, E. (1995). Splitting, covariation, and their role in the development of exponential functions. *Journal for Research in Mathematics Education, 26*, 66-86.

Dennis, D., & Confrey, J. (1996). The creation of continuous exponents: A study of the methods and epistemology of John Wallis. *Conference Board of the Mathematical Sciences: Issues in Mathematics Education, 6*, 33-60.

Doerr, H. (1994). *Building computational models: An effective approach to constructing student understandings.* Unpublished doctoral dissertation, Cornell University, Ithaca, NY.

Doerr, H. M., & Zangor, R. (2000). Creating meaning for and with the graphing calculator. *Educational Studies in Mathematics, 41*, 143-163.

Guerrero, S., Walker, N., & Dugdale, S. (2004). Technology in support of middle grades mathematics: What have we learned? *Journal of Computers in Mathematics and Science Teaching 23*, 5-20.

Haarer, S. (1999). *Student reflection and the use of software tools for recording students' actions and constructing verbal models.* Unpublished doctoral dissertation, Cornell University, Ithaca, NY.

Kaput, J. J., & Roschelle, J. (2000, October). *Shifting representational infrastructures and reconstituting content to democratize access to the math of change & variation: Impacts on cognition, curriculum, learning and teaching.* Paper presented at a workshop to Integrate Computer-based Modeling and Scientific Visualization into K-12 Teacher Education Programs, Ballston, VA.

LaChance, A. M. (1999). *Promoting reform in mathematics education by building content knowledge, technological skills, and teacher community.* Unpublished doctoral dissertation, Cornell University, Ithaca, NY.

Markovits, Z., Eylon, B. -S., & Bruckheimer, M. (1986). Functions today and yesterday. *For the Learning of Mathematics, 6*, 18-28.

National Council of Teachers of Mathematics. (2000). *Principles and standards for school mathematics.* Reston, VA: Author.

Nemirovsky, R., & Monk, S. (2000). "If you look at it the other way ...": An exploration into the nature of symbolizing. In P. Cobb, E. Yackel, & K. McClain (Eds.), *Symbolizing and communicating in mathematics classrooms* (pp. 17-36). Mahwah, NJ: Erlbaum.

Pea, R. D. (1987). Cognitive technologies for mathematics education. In A. Schoenfeld (Ed.), *Cognitive science and mathematics education* (pp. 89-122). Hillsdale, NJ: Erlbaum.

Piliero, S. (1994). *An investigation of teacher knowledge, beliefs and practices in the implementation of a problem-based curriculum using multi-representational software in a technology-rich classroom.* Unpublished doctoral dissertation, Cornell University, Ithaca, NY.

Rizzuti, J. (1991). *High school students' uses of multiple representations in the conceptualization of linear and exponential functions.* Unpublished doctoral dissertation, Cornell University, Ithaca, NY.

Schoenfeld, A. (1990). GRAPHER: A case study of educational technology, research, and development. In M. Gardner, J. Greeno, F. Reif, A. Schoenfeld, A. diSessa, & E. Stage (Eds.), *Toward a scientific practice of science education* (pp. 281-300). Hillsdale, NJ: Erlbaum.

Schwartz, J., & Yerushalmy, M. (1992). The Function Supposer [Computer software]. Windsor, ON: Sunburst Communications.

Sutherland, R., & Rojano, T. (1993). A spreadsheet approach to solving algebra problems. *Journal of Mathematical Behavior, 12*, 351-383.

Van Streun, A. (2000). Representations in applying functions. *International Journal of Mathematical Education in Science and Technology, 31*, 703-725.

CHAPTER 9

CHANGING REPRESENTATIONAL INFRASTRUCTURES CHANGES MOST EVERYTHING

The Case of SimCalc, Algebra, and Calculus

Jim Kaput and Roberta Schorr

OVERVIEW OF THE CASE

Epistemic level research and development that changes representational infrastructure must confront highly interconnected and deeply institutionalized expectations involving all aspects of mathematics education: curriculum and content, learning, teaching, teacher education, assessment, implementation of change, policy, and even the economics of education. We will treat as a specific case the SimCalc Project, whose goal is to democratize access to the mathematics of change and variation, including the ideas underlying calculus beginning at the middle school and early high school levels, gradually spreading upward in traditional mathemati-

Research on Technology and the Teaching and Learning of Mathematics:
Vol. 2. Cases and Perspectives, 211–253
Copyright © 2008 by Information Age Publishing
All rights of reproduction in any form reserved.

cal level and outward to the more contemporary iterative and visual mathematics of dynamical systems. The core means of achieving this goal involve building and testing webs of representational and simulation tools coupled with teaching and learning activities that exploit broadly available kinesthetic, visualization, linguistic, and other sociocultural resources for organizing human experience. From the outset, it seemed clear to the researchers that they were unwrapping a series of fundamental representational innovations whose implications would require the better part of a generation to unfold.

The starting points for our representation-intensive strategy were (a) an historical analysis that revealed the representational origins of the status quo relative to the mathematics of change and calculus (Kaput, 1994); (b) acknowledgement of the intimate connections between thought and notation (e.g., Cobb, Yackel, & McClain, 2000; Kaput, 1991; among many others); and (c) a realization that the constraints of static, inert media on the kinds of notations possible had been radically relaxed (Kaput, Noss, & Hoyles, 2002).

Access to the Mathematics of Change and Variation had for centuries been limited in the United States to a small intellectual elite comprising at most 5 to 10% of the population in recent years because the mathematics was assumed to require a long series of algebraic prerequisites that effectively filtered out most of the population, especially those from less advantaged families, neighborhoods, and schools (National Center for Education Statistics, 1994). Two broad representational approaches were therefore exploited to facilitate broad entry to this critically important domain of mathematics: (a) interactive simulations hot-linked to new forms of visually editable graphs and visualization tools, and (b) building in the fundamental relationships between rates and accumulations (embodying in computational form what is normally referred to as the "Fundamental Theorem of Calculus") into both the structure of the software and the associated curriculum. The second representational approach is akin to the way the extraordinarily powerful hierarchical structure of the number system is built into efficient base-ten representations that rapidly became the standard means by which numbers could be expressed, used, and operated upon using the standard algorithms that have defined the elementary school mathematics curriculum since the sixteenth century (Swetz, 1987). Indeed, this number system representational infrastructure dramatically enlarged access to computation. Prior to its development, computation that we would regard as routine, say multiplication of two numbers now represented by three characters apiece, would have required a level of expertise available only to a small group of mathematical specialists (Dantzig, 1954).

Historically, changes in representational infrastructures, for example, writing systems and even the base-ten placeholder system for arithmetic, and changes in associated communities of practice (and literacy) as well as supporting social institutions were slow, and, more importantly, on the same time scale. This consonance in timescales no longer prevails, which creates new tensions and new opportunities, as changes in representation and its learnability are occurring on much shorter timescales than changes in the surrounding social systems, especially formal educational systems. Research of the sort described in these volumes is necessarily done in relation to expectations defined by preexisting social systems—whether or not those expectations are appropriate to changed representational infrastructure, for example, whether core ideas in calculus can be expressed and learned in graphical ways apart from character-string algebra.

Thus, change in representational infrastructure requires us to encounter deeply institutionalized patterns of belief and practice regarding the nature of mathematics in general and the Mathematics of Change and Variation in particular, as well as who might learn it and how it can be learned. It needs to confront long-standing curriculum structures built into American education, and the assessment practices separating different levels of schooling, for example, the special place of algebra as a gateway course for secondary mathematics and the assessment assumptions built into college admissions. Working through this deep change is a generation-long process that the SimCalc Project continues today, complicated even further recently by strong accountability constraints now codified in the form of legal and political documents (U.S. Department of Education, 2002).

OVERVIEW OF THE CHAPTER

We begin in Part I with an outline of the specific representational strategies employed by SimCalc. Then, to illustrate our starting points, in Part II we offer a series of vignettes taken from studies involving middle-grade students from an extremely low-SES population in an unusually challenged middle school in New Jersey—typical of the contexts in which early SimCalc work transpired. With these student-performance images of the specific instantiations of the representational strategies, in Part III we reflect on the patterns of design research that led to those specific innovations. In Part IV, we describe ongoing research into the issues of implementation that is intended to inform the implementation of deep change. In Part V, we reflect upon the very long-term historical context for the representational approaches in order to contextualize the research issues that have arisen—in effect we contrast research in this case that involves change in representational infrastructure to research that involves change within the existing representational infrastructure. Finally, in Part VI, we return to focus on epistemic level changes in curriculum and content, closing with concrete illustrations of how core ideas of mean value and the Fundamental Theorem of Calculus are reconstituted when representational infrastructure is changed.

AN OVERVIEW OF
THE SIMCALC REPRESENTATION-INTENSIVE STRATEGY

Summary of SimCalc Representational Strategies and Their Research-Based Origins

Before looking at students' work, we will summarize the core web of five representational strategies employed by the SimCalc Project, all of which require a computational medium for their realization. Although the fourth and fifth representational strategies do not play a role in this chapter, they are included for the sake of completeness.

1. *Definition and direct graphical manipulation of graphically defined functions, especially piecewise-defined functions*, with or without algebraic descriptions. Included is "Snap-to-Grid" control, whereby the allowed values can be constrained as needed—to integers, for example. This allows a new balance between complexity and computational tractability whereby key rate and accumulation quantitative relationships traditionally requiring difficult computational and conceptual prerequisites can be explored using whole number arithmetic and basic geometry. Such functions also make possible sufficient variation to model interesting situations, avoid the degeneracy of constant rates of change, while postponing (but not ignoring!) the messiness and conceptual challenges of continuous change.

This deep representational shift combined the recent technological affordance of direct graphical manipulation with micro-analytic research by Nemirovsky (a Principal Investigator of the SimCalc Project) and colleagues (Monk & Nemirovsky, 1994; Nemirovsky, 1996) showing that people tend to interpret time-based change phenomena on an interval basis, whereby they break a situation into time-interval based parts for which some common and relatively salient property is shared across an interval that is not common on adjacent intervals ("the car is speeding up for the first 4 seconds, and then it goes at a constant speed ...").

2. *Direct connections between the representational innovations and simulations*—especially motion simulations—to allow immediate construction and execution of a wide variety of variation phenomena. This puts phenomena at the center of the representation experience, reflecting the purposes for which traditional representations were designed initially. Most importantly, it enables substantial tightening of the feedback loop between model and phenomenon.

The well-established idea of computer simulations as rapidly manipulable models of phenomena and surrogate for physical experience was initially conceived in terms of bringing the experience of automobile driving into the service of mathematics education, where speed (speedometer) and distance (odometer) would (a) be represented graphically, and (b) treated as directly controllable in a "first person" style via an onscreen "accelerator" (see, for example, Kaput, 1992). This was recognized to be too narrow an experiential base to appeal to both genders and insufficiently flexible to support generalization across different kinds of change situations. However, three other factors helped convince us that motion should be used as a root metaphor for change: (a) historical analyses of the role of motion in generating the ideas underlying calculus among the Scholastics well before Newton and Leibniz, the roles of dynamic variation in Newton's thinking, as well as certain dynamic styles of thinking among the Greeks (reviewed in Kaput, 1994); (b) from a linguistic perspective, the generality of motion-based language across nonmotion situations, for example, "the rate of inflation is speeding up," suggested that patterns of description of motion situations would readily extend to non-motion situations; and (c) a newly developing body of research, based in the use of computer-based laboratory motion sensors, suggested that students' kinesthetic sense played an important role in their thinking and learning about motion situations, both correct and incorrect (Brasell, 1987; Clement, 1989; McCloskey, 1983; Nemirovsky, 1992; Thompson, 1994; Thornton, 1992; Thornton & Sokolow, 1990; Tierney & Nemirovsky, 1991; Tierney, Nemirovsky, Wright, & Ackerman, 1993). In addition, there was a classic body of work rooted in Piaget (1970).

3. *Direct, hot-linked connections between graphically editable functions and their derivatives or integrals.* Traditionally, connections between descriptions of rates of change (e.g., velocities) and accumulations (positions) are mediated through the algebraic symbol system as sequential procedures employing derivative and integral formu-

las—but they need not be. Through direct, hot-linked connections provided by the computational medium, the fundamental idea, expressed in the Fundamental Theorem of Calculus, is built into the representational infrastructure from the start, enabling a student to change a rate function and see instantly the graphical consequences of that change in the corresponding accumulation function, and vice versa. This was unprecedented, although a version of this idea had been suggested by W. W. Sawyer (1961/1975).

4. *Importing physical motion-data via MBL/CBL and reenacting it in simulations, and exporting function-generated data to drive physical phenomena.* Through the importing and then reanimating of students' physical motions, this representational innovation plays an especially important role in SimCalc instructional materials to anchor the visual experience of the simulations in students' kinesthetic experience.[1] In the other direction, LBM (Line Becomes Motion) is based on work by Nemirovsky and colleagues and enables students to define functions graphically or algebraically that then drive physical phenomena, including cars on tracks (Nemirovsky, Kaput, & Roschelle, 1998). In this context there is a two-way connection between physical phenomena and varieties of mathematical notations. This work draws upon the previously cited research on students' kinesthetic sense.

5. *Use of hybrid physical/cybernetic devices embodying dynamical systems,* whose inner workings are visible and open to examination and control with rich feedback, and whose quantitative behavior is symbolized with real-time graphs generated on a computer screen (Nemirovsky, 1993a, 1993b).

The result of using this array of functionality over an extended period of time is a qualitative transformation in the mathematical experience of change and variation. This is particularly true for the first three representational strategies, on which the work in this chapter is focused. Moreover, in the short term, using some combination of rate or totals describing the quantities involved, as early as sixth to eighth grade a student can construct and examine, in less than a minute, a variety of interesting change phenomena that relate to direct experience of daily phenomena. And in more extended investigations, students can make connections among physical, linguistic, kinesthetic, cognitive, and symbolic experience. For convenience, we summarize the SimCalc approaches in Table 9.1, adapted from Roschelle, Tatar, & Kaput (in press).

Table 9.1.   SimCalc's Approach

SimCalc's Approach	Integrates These Three Perspectives		
	Learner Strengths	Representation-Intensive Technology	Restructured
Foregrounding the relation of mathematical representations to phenomenological motion	Perceiving, describing, and reasoning about motion in the concrete	Linked animation and mathematical notations make tangible the connection between formalism and common sense	Emphasizes phenomena as tools for building understanding
Formalisms are introduced to help consolidate and extend knowledge previously established	Natural progression from case-based specific learning to more integrative, general understanding	Unites and reifies mathematical formalism and more intuitive expressive notations in one medium	Provides substantial informal learning opportunities before introducing formal concepts
Piecewise functions	Reasoning about intervals, can leverage arithmetic and simple geometric skills to compute quantitative aspects	Can visually represent and allow purposeful manipulation of piecewise-defined motions	Uses piecewise functions as an essential building block for all calculus concepts
Emphasizing reasoning across rate (velocity) and accumulation (position) descriptions	Build on ability to think about "same" object in "different" views	Dynamic links among different representational views of the mathematical object	Focuses on rate-accumulatiion relationships expressed qualitatively and arithmetically
Primary focus on graph-based and linguistic reasoning	Making sense of and guiding action within graphical, visual forms	Supports visual presentation and direct editing of graphical forms in newly expressive ways	Shifts the emphasis from symbol manipulation to more democratically accessible forms of expression
Inquiry cycle of plan, construct, experience, reflect	Ability to understand a challenge, hypothesize possible solutions, and distinguish success from failure	Computational apparatus allows for many, quick, iterative feedback cycles	A more playful, expressive micro-worlds approach to mathematics

AN ILLUSTRATION OF STUDENTS EXPLOITING THE SIMCALC REPRESENTATIONAL STRATEGIES

Context for the Following Vignettes

We have concentrated our work in middle schools and high schools that have a long-established pattern of very low academic achievement. Our underlying assumption has been that if students in these contexts can learn these ideas, then we have a foundation for expanding to wider, and more broadly based populations. In these contexts, we have seen that as early as sixth grade, young children can build powerful understandings of the Mathematics of Change and Variation when provided with appropriate learning environments, pedagogical practices, and curriculum materials. For example, middle school children in one of New Jersey's lowest performing middle schools,[2] have developed and are able to articulate meaningful insights into the velocity-position relationships embodied in the fundamental theorem of calculus. In fact, one student developed and then confirmed for himself (via generic reasoning from well-chosen special cases) a hypothesis about generating velocity graphs by using the slope of a corresponding position graph, and alternatively, generating position graphs by calculating the area under the curve in a corresponding velocity graph. He noted that, "this should be in books." He had come up with an idea that does indeed appear in books—books written by the greatest geniuses of western civilization and then appearing in calculus textbooks over the ages that few, if any, students from his school community would study until reaching college—if and when that might ever occur. This work is reported on in Schorr (2003).

The context for the following vignettes is an after-school program in which approximately 15 students met 1.5 hours per week for 18 weeks and were taught by the second author with the cooperation and assistance of the school's science teacher. The excerpts below are taken from the fourth session and demonstrate Representational Strategies 1 and 2. They also document how the students were able to extrapolate ideas relating to stepwise-varying velocity to linearly varying velocity and were able to compare motions of a character by comparing its velocity across different intervals.

Concrete Introduction to the Core Representational Strategies Employed

In Figure 9.1 the (red) staircase-shaped velocity graph drives the (red) elevator on the left side of the building appearing to the left of

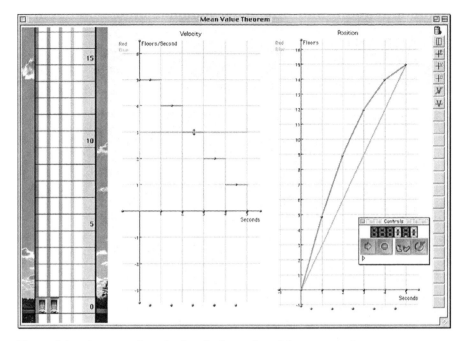

Figure 9.1.   Averages from both velocity and position perspectives.

the graphs.[3] The (blue) constant velocity graph drives the (blue) elevator immediately to the left of the graphs (embodying Representational Strategies 1 and 2). By pointing, clicking and dragging, the user can create or visually edit any of the segments in the graphs as well as add or delete them. For the stepwise-varying velocities initially used by the students, the flat segments are constrained to be draggable vertically or stretchable horizontally, thereby enabling changes in velocity (height) and duration (width) of the respective segments. This ensures that area computations are restricted to rectangular regions, and hence the total area is a sum of products. Moreover, by turning on "Snap-to-Grid" the values appearing in these sums of products can be made to fit those appearing in the tic marks on the axes—integers in this case—further simplifying computations. The two corresponding position graphs are shown on the right side of the figure simply to illustrate how Representational Strategy 3, the hot connection between heights of velocity graph segments and slopes of position graph segments, can appear in certain activities. Importantly, the contents of the tool bar on the far right (e.g., function types, coordinate axes, editability of functions) can be configured by the teacher or curriculum author (via drag and drop) to fit the students or activities at hand.

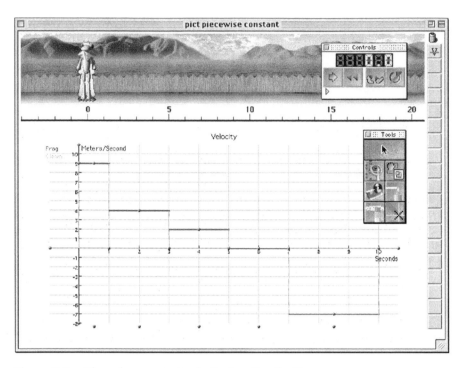

Figure 9.2.   Piecewise constant velocity function for Frog.

In Figure 9.2, the velocity graph—which "drives" the frog that is situated in the "world" just above the graph, with horizontal motion instead of the vertical motion of the Elevator World—also has an additional character, the clown, who was not used in the vignettes that follow. By pointing, clicking, and dragging, the students created or visually edited any of the segments. However, for the stepwise-varying velocities initially used by the students, only vertical or horizontal stretches were allowed for segments. This ensured that area computations are sums of products, and, because Snap-to-Grid was turned on, the values were limited to whole numbers.

During previous sessions, the students had been given opportunities to make predictions about the motion of elevators (vertical motion) or characters (horizontal motion) based upon given velocity graphs, and, conversely, had constructed velocity graphs to make the elevators and characters move in ways described verbally. For example, students had determined the graph for a pizza delivery person who had to deliver pizzas to various floors, waiting to be paid at each delivery (zero velocity). They had also defined motion functions for two or more characters that were to patrol a given region in a periodic fashion. In all instances, students were encouraged to make predictions and explain the graphs or motions of the characters before, during, and after each animation. The students had also explored the concept of average velocity as they built graphical representations for an elevator that had variable velocities (using piecewise-constant velocity functions) throughout a trip, compared with an elevator that traveled at a constant velocity, where both elevators traveled for the same amount of time and had the same starting and ending positions using a version of the configuration in Figure 9.1 involving elevators. Such investigations allowed the students to consider the relationship between a graphical representation and its associated motion; consider how area under the curve is related to the position of a character; and explore the idea of an average, or mean, velocity for a given set of motions.

Vignette 1. The first vignette documents how students used area-based reasoning with piecewise-constant velocity graphs to determine the position of the character at a given point in time, and how the students were able to extrapolate ideas relating to stepwise-varying velocity to linearly varying velocity as well as to compare motions of a character by comparing its velocity across different intervals. In this case, students were given a piecewise-constant velocity function (depicted in Figure 9.2) and asked to determine where the character ("frog") would be at the end of several different time periods, for example, after 8 seconds. They were also challenged to talk about the motion of the character at different intervals during the trip, for example, whether he was going faster or slower than in another interval. Typically, the students would work in pairs at their own computers and then come together to share insights, observations, ideas, and solutions. In this vignette, eight students were gathered around the front of the room to discuss their ideas as they viewed the graph and motions on the overhead projection system. The researcher controlled the computer for most of the interactions, using the software in accordance with student requests. The following quote relates to Figure 9.2 and is in response to the researcher's question, Where will the frog be at the end of 8 seconds?

Student: I say it's huh, 14. Because right here on the 1st second ... on the middle of the 2nd ... right here he's on the 9th floor [referring to the character's position at one second] ... right here he's gonna go on the 13 [referring to the character's position at 2 seconds] ... 17 (at 3 seconds) ... 19 (at 4 seconds) ... 21 (at 5 seconds) ... he's gonna stop here for 2 seconds (pointing to the interval from 5 to 7 seconds)...and then ... take 21 from 7 ... it leaves you 14.

The reference that this student makes to the position of the frog at the end of the first segment, ("9th floor") is in the language of the first motion system that the student had experienced, which is an indication that the student has already abstracted away from certain particulars, such as the physical context for the motion, and is focusing on the displacement in terms of areas under the graph. She calculated the area below the curve, when the curve was above the horizontal axis, and she, informally representing the consensus of the group, also noted that when the velocity was 0, the character would stop. She then subtracted the area below the curve, when the segment was below the horizontal axis, explaining that she did so "because it's a negative [velocity]," thereby inferring what others had said in previous sessions regarding negative velocity, which in this instance meant that the character was moving toward the left and therefore going backwards. This excerpt highlights how the students were able to calculate position by computing net area between the velocity graph and the horizontal axis.

The students were also able to determine the relative speed of the character across different intervals by examining the graph. For example, a different student offered the following explanation to justify why he felt that the character would be going faster during the second segment than during the third (again referring to Figure 2):

> Student: He slowed down cause he is going 4 meters, right …
> Researcher: … 4 meters per second?
> Student: … for 2 seconds. He goes 8, 8 meters. But here it goes 2 meters … yeah 2 meters per second for 2 seconds … 4 meters. It will just be four and he will go faster here cause he will go 4 meters in just 1 second … it's just 2 in 1 second.

In this case, the student compared the distance that the frog would travel in one second for two different segments to determine the relative speed of each.

The researcher then decided to see if these types of understandings could be generalized to linearly (as opposed to stepwise) changing velocity, which would help determine both the generality of the arguments and the extent to which they were truly area based. Hence a linearly increasing function was displayed. The students saw, on the overhead projection system, a velocity graph increasing from 0 to 4 m/s over 5 seconds depicted in Figure 9.3, and the researcher asked them to make predictions about the motion and the final position of the character. Several students suggested that they would find the area under the graph to figure out where the frog would end his trip, even though the graph was not horizontal.

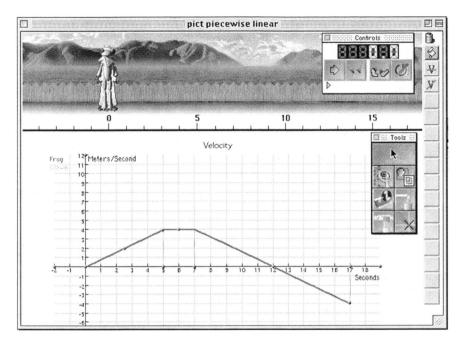

Figure 9.3.   Linearly varying velocity.

These types of predictions appeared to show that the students were able, to some extent, to extrapolate from their experience with piecewise functions. In addition to noting where the character would end up, one student also commented that, "I think it is going to go from slow to fast because it is a slant … so it is going to change, it is going to change throughout its trip." In effect, this student is generalizing the stepwise variation to continuous variation.

The researcher then extended the velocity graph to include two additional segments (up to 12 seconds—as depicted in the positive part of the graph in Figure 9.3) and repeated the questions, to see whether the students would extend their area-based reasoning to this situation, and to see how the students would describe the motion of the character. Various students were able to develop their own methods for calculating the area of the regions formed by the graph and the horizontal axis. The researcher then added the third segment (extending the graph from 7 to 12 seconds), whereupon students used different strategies for determining the area of the enclosed region. One girl, for example, noted that she could find the final position by imagining that the region that enclosed the segments was cut into three parts. She then said that the frog would end up at the 28-meter mark "because the first beginning is 10 and at the end is 10 and in the middle is 8, and if you add it up, it's 28 [meters]." Other students counted the "boxes" while others developed their own version of the traditional algorithm for finding the area of a triangle by finding the area of an enclosing rectangle and then taking one-half of it.

The researcher then asked the students to discuss the motion of the frog. One student—reflecting the consensus of the group—said, "He gonna go slow to fast, then keep his pace and then gonna go down fast to slow again." While the individual students varied in their understanding of the increasingly complex situations of this vignette, the overall understanding of the group was clearly exhibited in their responses to the researcher's probes, understandings that were then further developed in subsequent work in pairs on comparable problem situations following the next vignette.

Vignette 2. Now the researcher added the last, negative velocity, segment as depicted in Figure 9.3, (extending from 12 to 17 seconds) in order to investigate how the students would interpret linearly changing velocity in the region below the horizontal axis.

The students of the entire class were challenged to determine the motion during the last segment. At the outset, many of the students shouted out that the frog would be going backward because the velocity was negative. The researcher then challenged them to talk among themselves about where the frog would end up, and why. Unfortunately, while the sound quality of the video recordings could not capture all of the dialogue, we have a clear record of the "public" discussion that occurred within the group of eight located at the front of the room.

Student: He's going back to 18. He's going back to 18 because if you look at it, there is going to be an invisible line right there to make that 10 (gesturing to indicate a line perpendicular to the horizontal axis, extending upward from the end of the last segment to the horizontal axis). And then 28 (28 had been calculated as the position before the last segment had been added) minus 10 is 18.

Researcher: So your prediction is what?
    Student: It's an invisible line right there where the 12 is just goes down and you equal it up with the line over there by the...
Researcher: Can you show me? I don't see what you mean. Yeah, go ahead you had a good idea that you were about to share.
    Student: Right here, if you put an invisible line and equal it up with that, it will be the same as that and when it goes down, it is a negative. So subtract it.

In this exchange, the student was pointing to the positive-area section of the graph that was congruent to the new section that had just been formed. The positive-area section is in the time interval from 7 to 12 seconds, and the new section is in the 12 to17 seconds. This student imagined the two as having the same (numerical) area, and therefore came up with an answer of 18 by subtracting. Several other students echoed this solution. The student went on to state that this last region indicated that, "It's gonna go backwards." The student also indicated that the character would turn around at the 28-meter mark. It is important to note the use of imagery that occurred throughout these sessions. The students repeatedly used their hands and arms, and in some cases, whole bodies (as the next excerpt will demonstrate) to imagine what amounted to segments, regions, and motions to help them as they reasoned about the situations.

The researcher then asked the students to discuss the motion of the frog. One student stated, "As soon as he gets to 12 (seconds), he is gonna turn around, but he is gonna be walking slower." Not only did this student notice when the Frog would turn around, she also predicted that he would be walking slower. A boy, who became very excited about sharing his thinking jumped in (referred to here as Student 1):

Student 1:	… when it go to the end it's gonna be fast. Because if you look upside down (he turns his head toward the floor, as he literally looks "upside down"), it's going up, it's going fast.
Researcher:	So over here, is he going faster or slower than over here (first pointing to the graph at 13–14 seconds, and then 15–16 seconds)?
Student 1:	Over there (at about 13 seconds) he is going slower than over there (referring to about 16 seconds) because …
Researcher:	Wait, wait, wait … I don't know what you meant. Do you want to just point to where …
Student:	Wait, look upside down (he tugs on the Researcher to turn her head upside down as he does the same) … if you look upside down it goes from downward to upward. So that means it's going faster.
Researcher:	So he is going faster … is he going faster here (at about 13 seconds) …
Student 1:	Yes.
Researcher:	… than here (at about 15 seconds)?…
Student 1:	Yes.

In this vignette, the student literally turned his head "upside down," so that he could look at the graph "upside down." He also pulled on the researcher's arm in an effort to get her to do the same. He noted, with considerable emphasis, that if "you look upside down it goes from downward to upward, so that means it's going faster." This student appears to be making sense of the situation by visualizing the graphical representation from another perspective. He appears to be building upon what he had seen to be true of linearly increasing functions that were in the region above the horizontal axis. He reasoned that if this particular segment had been viewed from another angle or perspective, it would look just like the first segment (from 0 to 5 seconds), and therefore be increasing in velocity. He verified this by later stating that "Since it's going down, it's almost the same thing but it's down. But if you tilt it up, it will be going up."

Several of his peers spontaneously joined in the conversation. One girl stated that she thought that, "it's the opposite." In a commonly seen misgeneralization from the positive case (the farther "down," the slower the motion), she reasoned that the frog would have to be slowing up, not going faster. This student noted that in the third segment (from 7 to 12 seconds) the frog was slowing up, and this segment looked very similar to that. Space limits prevent discussion of her thinking and its interaction with that of the other students.

Reflections on the Vignettes

These excerpts provide a glimpse into the types of very grounded reasoning and imagery that students used during these sessions and that have repeatedly occurred across other instructional contexts in which students have had the opportunity to learn. Not only could these middle school students from extremely low socioeconomic backgrounds discuss complex mathematical ideas after a relatively brief intervention (in this case, four sessions on the Mathematics of Motion) they could also fluently move between and among different representational systems—including those involving symbols. Representational Strategies 1 and 2 appear to work under these circumstances in the sense of providing the means by which students could begin with very simple functions and motions that tapped into their simplest intuitions about motion and leveraged their arithmetic and geometric competencies. Note also that we have repeatedly seen that motion (Strategy 1) quickly fades from attention and is called upon only as a potentially useful representation when the situation is ambiguous and/or the functions increase in complexity. For example, after using SimCalc-based instructional materials for a 5-week period (four sessions per week with 1.5 hours per session) in a summer course designed for a group of 17 precollege economically disadvantaged students, not a single student used any technological resources on their posttest to solve problems similar to those previously described, despite the fact that they took the test at their computer with the software loaded and running. This is a frequently reported phenomenon among users and helps answer the frequently voiced concern that students in such technological environments would become so dependent upon the technology that they simply would not, or could not, solve the problems without it. The opposite appears to be the case.

We have repeatedly seen that this approach feeds back into and intensely engages their prior mathematical skills and understandings—in the aforementioned case, notions of area were contextualized and enriched, particularly to include signed areas, which were examined in more detail in later vignettes. In effect, the approach becomes a vehicle for teaching core mathematics such as signed number arithmetic, signed areas, dimensional analysis (especially when non-motion rates are considered), rate and ratio, among others. These mathematical experiences also lead directly into algebraic formalizations, especially linear, quadratic, and periodic functions.

The young students whose work we sketched previously articulated their mathematical thinking with fluency and fluidity despite test scores suggesting otherwise. When fully engaged with challenging ideas, they were able to marshal linguistic resources to match the task. Recent work deliberately mixing writing with these kinds of mathematical activities suggests that the same positive feedback and engagement that occurs with other mathematical ideas may apply to the development of reading, writing, and speaking capacities (Hegedus & Kaput, 2002). Other work by Schorr has shown robustness of learning revealed in interviews 2 or more years following the preceding kind of intervention.

HOW DID THE REPRESENTATIONAL STRATEGIES ARISE AND STABILIZE? STAGES OF DESIGN RESEARCH

The kinds of research depicted in the previously described vignettes were common in the middle SimCalc years, after the base representational systems had been developed. SimCalc research has evolved through four stages. Prior to the research depicted in the vignettes, in its earliest years (1992–96) the task was to define the representational opportunities technologically. However, the foundations and democratization of access to the Mathematics of Change and Variation goals of the work had been developed earlier through historical analyses of the evolution of calculus ideas and a critical examination of the standard curriculum relative to those ideas (Kaput, 1994) and an analysis of the role of technology in exploiting cognitive resources (Kaput, 1992). Early design required applying the best available development resources of the day to produce a flexible environment that would support cycles of trials and changes to the underlying technology, including such innovations as drag-and-drop configuration of the interface, scriptability of the software that enabled non-software engineers to make substantive changes to the software so that a broader group could contribute to the rapid design cycles, and so on (Roschelle, DeLaura, & Kaput, 1996; Roschelle & Kaput, 1996).

This early design research attempted to answer the question of what could work. It was in the spirit of strongly innovation-oriented design research described by Cobb, Confrey, Lehrer, diSessa, and Schauble (2002). Many alternatives were weeded out, including, among others: game-like approaches; two-dimensional variation; and dynamic, iteratively defined functions. The participants at this stage were primarily the researchers and students either in their classes or in pull-out situations, after school clinical studies, and situations in which all the constraints of schools and schooling were not a factor.

As the technological platform and representations stabilized, the focus turned in the next phase, 1996–98, to establishing sets of activities that could exploit the representational affordances most fully and make sense to students at various grade levels. The initial group of researchers began to recruit local teachers and engaged researchers at other universities, including the second author, but continued to do most of their testing cycles outside of regular classrooms. The kinds of activities depicted in the vignettes were largely unprecedented in school mathematics and amounted to a radical departure from the ways the core ideas of calculus had been approached. Indeed, they amount to a reconstitution of the subject matter at an epistemic level (Kaput, 1997) and embodied in very concrete terms the idea that representational infrastructure determines what mathematics is possible (Kaput, 1991; Kaput, Noss, & Hoyles, 2002) and that the representations and the mathematics coconstitute each other (Cobb, Gravemeijer, Yackel, McClain, & Whitenack, 1997; Gravemeijer, Cobb, Bowers, & Whitenack, 2000; Lehrer, Schauble, Carpenter, & Penner, 2000; Sfard, 2000). The research methods were again design studies, but the cycles of improvement were directed towards improving the activities and optimally exploiting the representational options, with the use of both clinical methods and pretesting and posttesting of small groups of students on critical tasks (Roschelle, Kaput, & Stroup, 2000).

The third stage, 1998–2002, involved taking the innovations to school with a curricular focus, to classrooms taught by teachers as part of their standard instruction. The enhanced community of researchers now engaged teachers in their respective regions (Doerr in Syracuse, Bowers and Nickerson in San Diego, Schorr in New Jersey, Nemirovsky and Stroup in the Boston area, as well as the original core of researchers in

Southeastern Massachusetts). Most of this work took place in the kinds of low SES school contexts reflected in the vignettes. The focus became how to integrate these deeply different approaches to mathematics into the existing school curriculum, and needed to confront the constraints of existing curricula, especially the role of the first algebra course. This course dominates attention in Grades 7 to 10 in the United States, and has increasingly become a pivot point in the accountability systems that are being put in place in recent years. The SimCalc representations differ substantially from the algebraically defined standard linear functions and equations studied in typical algebra courses, in which the idea of slope is treated procedurally as "rise over run," and the ideas of rate and proportion are likewise treated in procedural "rule of three" and unit-rate styles. The Mathematics of Change and Variation is treated as a strand in curricular standards statements (National Council of Teachers of Mathematics, 2000) and, to some extent, in many standards-based curricula.

In collaboration with participating teachers in Grades 7 to 10 at the various locations, a variety of lessons were produced that made strong use of animations and visually editable piecewise-defined functions to build concepts of time-based rate as multiplicative relations between changes in quantity and changes in time (especially velocity, which is rate of change of position with respect to change in time), and emphasizing the core idea of slope-as-rate. The latter provides an approach to a key idea in the algebra course that extends as a key idea through calculus, as does the idea of average rate of change. The development of these ideas makes intense use of the first two representational strategies, particularly the ability to create variations in rate of change (and hence slope) that both provide interesting and rich modeling activities as well as avoiding what Stroup (2002) refers to as the degeneracy of linear functions. These lessons lead carefully towards the algebraic description of linear functions (both slope-intercept and point-slope forms) in a highly contextualized style, where the parameters have strong interpretations in terms of velocities, initial position, and so on. Similarly, a phenomenon-based approach to simultaneous equations using motion ("simultaneous" means "same place at the same time") provides a strongly grounded experience of simultaneous equations. More generally, the theme was (and continues to be) that mathematics needs to be about something, and that it is insufficient simply to link representations as in computer algebra systems (CASs)—they need to be seen as representing something other than simply each other. As Thompson and Sfard (1994) put it, if they only represent each other, then the emperor is *only* clothes.

However, because of what amounts to a lack of curricular space, relatively little use is made of the connection between rate and accumulation functions, the third representational strategy. The first two strategies supported an integration with existing content that was more transformative than additive, although the inevitable constraint is time, especially in teachers' minds, and hence the curricular integration is tightly constrained. While design research continued to be the mode of inquiry, the "What *could* work?" question took on a different meaning, because it was no longer focused solely on the learning of students, but included the curricular dimension, namely, what could work in terms of existing school curricula.

THE BROADER ISSUE OF IMPLEMENTATION: TEACHERS, ASSESSMENT, REFORM CONSTRAINTS, AND AVAILABLE SCHOOL TECHNOLOGIES

The fourth stage of SimCalc research, post-2000 (overlapping with the previous stage), began the process of confronting more fully the matter of implementation, in which, of course, teachers are in the center of the critical path. The third stage employed teachers who tended to be early adopters, pedagogically sophisticated, and were closely supported by researchers, especially in terms of curriculum design (Bowers & Doerr, 2001; Nickerson, Nydam, & Bowers, 2000). At this stage, we not only need to concern ourselves with teacher learning and teacher knowledge, we must also deal with issues of accountability performance measures and assessments, and issues of school and even school district and wider contexts for reform. Furthermore, we must also concern ourselves with the forms of the technologies in schools and the means by which the representational innovations are physically instantiated in school-available materials and technologies. Hence, the initial design experiment foci on student learning and curriculum suddenly open out to a plethora of critical issues that previously were not directly addressed. Moreover, as the activities and technologies further stabilized, we needed to concern ourselves with their effectiveness, both in our own terms and in terms of more broadly recognized measures of success. After approximately a decade, the real interaction between deep representational innovation and the existing education system is engaged—the matter of scaling up.

The penetrating historical analysis of reform efforts by Elmore (1996) reveals that reform efforts seldom change what he describes as the "core"—the daily classroom practice of teachers—in either a sustained way or across significant portions of the population. And, since the SimCalc innovations are centered on core classroom instruction on core mathematical topics, his story is highly relevant to planning for scale-up. Another very relevant line of analysis has been provided by Cohen and associates (Cohen & Ball, 1999; Cohen, Raudenbush, & Ball, 2003). They applied their extensive analyses of reform efforts in the United States, especially in California in the late 1990s, to formulate a theory of scaling up classroom innovations that takes into account the many competing forces at work in determining the success of an implementation, and the levels of "ambition" of the reform in question. Space limitations prevent a full analysis, but an essential element is the tradeoff between the degree of ambition in an innovation and its degree of elaboration and specification of that innovation. Innovations that are near to today's classroom practice need little specification, whereas ambitious innovations such as SimCalc's deep changes in representational infrastructure, on the other hand require a great deal of specification. Although we had specified curriculum materials in the prior phase, we needed to describe in detail how those might be used in various curricular contexts (especially textbook series), but, more importantly, we needed to elaborate the process of developing teacher capacity to use the materials, to provide assessments that enabled teachers and their administrators to determine the effectiveness of the materials and their specific implementation. In effect, we needed to concern ourselves with the complex interactions among teachers, students, and resources. Further, since these support materials specifying these interactions would not be implemented by the researchers, we needed to specify to third-party implementers how to build teacher and school capacity. These are enormous tasks and are continuing as of this writing.

In particular, we have embarked on a series of implementation studies that shift away from design research methods towards more quantitative studies that specify critical implementation variables, especially at the teacher and school levels, and that depend on sufficiently stable interventions that can support replication across importantly varying sites. This is a shift from "What *could* work?" questions towards "What *does* work?" questions—and their essential follow-up questions, "Why?" or "Why not?"

Consequently, we decided—because of the critical role of teachers—to build a study that examined critical teacher variables and school variables, especially, but not exclusively, as reflected in student demographics. As part of this study, we had to make choices regarding which SimCalc materials to test and at what grade levels (we chose a 2–3 week replacement module approach in Grades 7 and 8 focusing on ratio, rate, slope-as-rate and linear functions), and finally, we needed to develop standardized professional development materials and practices to use with the participating teachers in a reasonable time frame (a 1-week workshop was developed). New forms of research required vastly different resources and expertise in addition to all the prior expertise that had been embodied in the materials and technologies being implemented, which helps to explain why relatively few technology-intensive projects succeed at, or even attempt, scale-up research.

As of this writing, a pilot study involving 25 seventh-grade teachers has been completed, with intriguingly strong relationships appearing between teacher and student learning, and substantially positive results in a SimCalc-Controls comparison. A fuller story of the implementation study, including the pilot results, can be found in work by Roschelle and colleagues (Roschelle et al., in press; Roschelle, Tatar, Kaput, & Hopkins, 2005).

Simultaneously, a major investment in making the technologies affordable and accessible was required. This meant shifting from a reliance on the expensive and inadequately available technology of desktop computers used mainly in computer laboratories, to the popularly available, at-hand technology of the graphing calculator. Fortunately, by the early part of this decade, the graphing calculator, particularly the Texas Instruments (TI) TI-83 model, had become an almost-standard technology in algebra courses in the United States, and comparable devices were also popular in other countries. In the terms of Cohen and colleagues (1999), it involved relatively low-ambition changes. Teachers could use it without major changes to daily practice (although many experienced it as a major innovation) because it offered the ability to graph functions that typically already were the subject of algebra and precalculus courses, and to make tables and do computations that allowed for more realistic data and applications (Fey, 1989). They also enabled more numeric approaches to problem solving and modeling (a huge descriptive literature has been generated around these affordances, as well as a number of research studies, a number of which are represented in these volumes and will not be reviewed here). Additionally, for those teachers whose pedagogy tended to be more exploratory and activity-centered, these devices provided opportunity for rapid student constructions and input to the classroom pedagogical process, and as such, they aligned with teachers' practices. In approximately 2002, a change in the base device occurred that transformed it from a "closed box" with relatively fixed and open functionality (in the sense that all its capabilities were always available through the fixed keypad) to a fully programmable device in essentially the same sense that larger computers are fully programmable—it could be adapted to accommodate the designers' needs. Hence, running Cabri Junior (Laborde, 2003) it is a geometry device, and, running SimCalc MathWorlds, it becomes a Mathematics of Change device. With the support of Texas Instruments, we developed a version of the desktop software for this nearly ubiquitous device, made agreements that made TI a distributor of curriculum materials and software for their devices (see, for example, http://www.simcalc.umassd.edu), and also rewrote the desktop software to be cross platform. The result was a base of software and curriculum resources that could be used in conjunction with most of the available underlying technologies. This was a necessary, but far from sufficient, step towards the long-term goal of democratizing access to the mathematics of change and variation.

STEPPING BACK FOR THE VERY LONG VIEW: THE EVOLUTION OF REPRESENTATIONAL INFRASTRUCTURES AND THEIR MATERIAL TECHNOLOGIES

Our focus in this chapter is on changes in representational infrastructures. An understanding of these issues from an historical perspective helps to contextualize work on implementation, especially the depth and complexity of the change that is involved, by helping to expose how much of our current situation has been determined by the representational infrastructures that we have inherited.

Kaput (2000/2001) offers an analogy that relates the evolution of western writing systems and corresponding change in the representational infrastructures of mathematics.[4] The deep impact of the writing system changes on human expressivity and learnability of expressive writing systems, as well as their physical availability, can be compared to changes in the representational infrastructures of mathematics as they have become increasingly visual, expressive, and learnable. We will first look at learnability.

Learnability of Writing Systems

Over a period of several thousand years in the Middle East, early writing (based in the need to create external records of quantitative information [Schmandt-Besserat, 1978, 1992]) evolved from the ideographic to the phonetic/acoustic and eventually to the alphabetic. In its early ideographic forms, writing was a specialist's tool, requiring a lengthy apprenticeship. Those who would write had to learn the subtleties of 600 or more signs and highly context-dependent, nonlinear interpretation processes. Such writing systems made large demands on human memory and interpretive skill, and hence were laboriously learned and used only by specialists—scribes. For example, approximately 15% of all the 100,000 existing cuneiform tablets were used to train scribes (Davies, 1987; Walker, 1987). Moreover, the complex nonphonetic system and the lexical lists used to train scribes during the third millennium B.C.E. remained essentially unchanged for more than 600 years—a hint that the conservative nature of education is not a recent phenomenon.

As (Western) writing gradually transitioned from ideographic to phonetic, it tapped into highly expressive sound-based systems of meaning-making and communicating that had been evolving for the previous several hundred thousand years and that was well supported physically and neurophysiologically (Deacon, 1997; Donald, 1991). Writing tapped into a powerful preexisting meaning-making and meaning-communicating system that was universally available within the population. However, although the writing systems became more expressive, they remained difficult to learn and hence remained a specialist's endeavor.

But then, in the 2 millennia B.C.E., phonetic syllabaries evolved into alphabetic writing systems in several languages (Arabic, Hebrew, Aramaic, and Phoenician). The Phoenecian alphabet was adopted and modified by the Greeks to become the system that is used in all western languages today (Woodard, 1996). This extraordinary achievement allows an extremely efficient and learnable bidirectional mapping between the sound stream and sequences of two-dimensional characters that amounts to one of the supreme achievements of the species (Ong, 1982). Roughly two-dozen characters are all that is needed, an optimization that has never been improved upon. In Greece, anyone who wanted to learn these mappings (reading and writing), and was allowed to by virtue of social class, could do so at a relatively young age (Havelock, 1982).

Writing, as a fundamental representational infrastructure, changed the means by which humans constructed their world individually (Nelson, 1996) and culturally (e.g., Cole, 1997; Donald, 1991; Havelock, 1982; Olson, 1976; Shaffer & Kaput, 1999). Humans became able to communicate, build, and accumulate knowledge (and all that comes with knowledge—including power and control) across time and space.

Physical Availability of Writing Systems

Another level of the analogy between writing and mathematics as evolving representational infrastructures involves changes in their physical availability, as precipitated by the technological innovation of the printing press (Eisenstein, 1979). Two millennia passed before reading and writing became widely distributed across the populations of the west, when written documents became widely available via the printing press. As argued by Haas (1996), this technology was slow to develop into a broadly useable form and hence its impacts required some 2 to 3 centuries to be realized (see Kaput, 2000/2001 for more detail).

It is important to keep in mind the distinction—between a change in representational infrastructure, such as alphabetic writing, and a change in the material means by which that infrastructure can be embodied, such as the printing press and inexpensive paper—which participates in a different kind of infrastructure, a combined technological, physical, and social infrastructure. We now turn to the other side of our dual analogy, the mathematics and mathematics learning side.

The Representational Infrastructures—Operative Systems— of Arithmetic and Algebra

We will not recount the histories of these systems here (see Kaput, Noss, & Hoyles, 2002 for a more detailed account). However, the evolution of each was a lengthy process, covering thousands of years before the achievement of an efficient symbol system upon which a human could operate. Unlike written language, which supported the creation of fixed records in static, inert media, the placeholder system of arithmetic that stabilized representationally in the thirteenth and fourteenth centuries supported rule-based actions by an appropriately trained human. These actions, which are performed upon the physical symbols, are taken to be quantitative operations on the numbers that are taken to be represented by those symbols. This system, and the algorithms built on it, seems to be optimal in an evolutionary sense similar to the way the alphabetic phonetic writing systems seem to be optimal. Each has remained relatively stable for many centuries and has spread widely across the world. The arithmetic system, although initially a specialist's tool—for accounting purposes—came to be part of the general cultural tool-set as needs for numerical computation arose in Western societies. Interestingly, the early algorithms developed for accounting in the fourteenth and fifteenth centuries and that appeared in the first arithmetic training books at that time have remained essentially unchanged to this day, and continue to dominate elementary school mathematics (Swetz, 1987).

Algebra had begun by the time of the Egyptians in the second millennium B.C.E. as evidenced in the famous Ahmes Papyrus (Kline, 1972, for example provides detail on the history of algebra; see Cajori, 1929, Volume 2 for specific details on the history of the symbols). The Egyptians used available writing systems to express quantitative relationships—especially to "solve equations," that is, to determine unknown quantities based on given quantitative relationships. This so-called "rhetorical algebra" continued to Diophantus' time in the third century, when the process of abbreviation of natural language statements and the introduction of special symbols began to accelerate. Algebra written in this way is normally referred to as "syncopated algebra." Importantly, achievement to that point was primitive, with little generalization of methods across cases and little theory to support generalization.

But, in a slow, millennium-long struggle involving the coevolution of underlying concepts of number, algebraic symbolism gradually freed itself from written language in order to support techniques that increasingly depended on working with the symbols themselves according to systematic rules of substitution and transformation rather than with the quantitative relations for which they stood (Kaput, Blanton, & Moreno, in press). Just as symbolism for numbers evolved to yield support for rule-based operations on symbols taken to denote numbers, where attention and actions are focused on the physical notations rather than on their assumed referents, the system for acting upon physical symbols for unknowns and variables developed. Bruner (1973) refers to this use of symbolic notation as an "opaque" use of the notations rather than "transparent" use, in which the actions are guided by reasoning about the entities to which the notations are assumed to refer. In effect, algebraic symbolism gradually freed itself from natural language's ambiguities, inefficiencies (relative to the mathematical purposes), and complexity so that very general statements of quantitative relations could be very efficiently expressed.

However, the more important aspects of the new representational infrastructure are those that involve the rules—the syntax—for guiding operations on these expressions of generality (see Kaput, Blanton, & Moreno, in press, for descriptions of how these can be constituted as the "lifting out" of structures of actions). These emerged in the seventeenth century as the symbolism became more compact and standardized in the intense attempts to mathematize the natural world that reached such triumphant fruition in the "calculus" of Newton and Leibniz. In the words of Bochner (1966):

> Not only was this algebra a characteristic of the century, but a certain feature of it, namely the "symbolization" inherent to it, became a profoundly distinguishing mark of all mathematics to follow.... (T)his feature of algebra has become an attribute of the essence of mathematics, of its foundations, and of the nature of its abstractness on the uppermost level of the "ideation" a la Plato. (pp. 38–39)

Beyond this first aspect of algebra, its role in the expression of abstraction and generalization, Bochner also pointed out the critical new ingredient:

> that various types of "equalities," "equivalences," "congruences," "homeomorphisms," etc. between objects of mathematics must be discerned, and

strictly adhered to. However this is not enough. In mathematics there is the second requirement that one must know how to "operate" with mathematical objects, that is, to produce new objects out of given ones. (p. 313)

Indeed, Mahoney (1980) points out that this development made possible an entirely new mode of thought "characterized by the use of an operant symbolism, that is, a symbolism that not only abbreviates words but represents the workings of the combinatory operations, or, in other words, a symbolism with which one operates" (p. 142). This second aspect of algebra, the syntactically guided transformation of symbols while holding in abeyance their potential interpretation, flowered in the eighteenth century, particularly in the hands of such masters as Euler, to generate powerful new systems of understanding human experience, systems written in this new representational infrastructure of algebra.

But this operative aspect of algebra is both a source of that power of mathematics and a source of difficulty for learners. Another factor that impacts the difficulty of learning algebra is its relations with natural language. These include the fact that it shares notational elements such as letters, and, as illustrated by the "Student-Professors Problem," it conflicts with phonetically common locutions (e.g., the pronunciation of "6S" which in natural language treats the "6" as an adjectival modifier of the "S" that is taken as a noun-abbreviation of "students"—as opposed to the algebraic pronunciation as "6 times the number of students") (Clement, 1982; Kaput & Sims-Knight, 1983). For many good reasons, traditional character-string-based algebra is not easy to learn—analogous to the difficulty of the learnability of ideographic writing. And, it should be noted, algebra is an ideographic system, despite its roots in phonetic writing.

Until relatively late in the twentieth century, algebra was regarded as a specialist's tool. Indeed, in contrast with the arithmetic system, the algebra system evolved within a small and specialized intellectual elite at whose hands, quite literally, it extended the power of human understanding far beyond what was imaginable without it—without regard for its learnability by the population at large. The effect of these learnability factors was not felt until the latter part of the twentieth century, when education systems around the world began to attempt to teach algebra to the general population (Chick & Stacy, 2004). Prior to the middle of the twentieth century, the community that was algebra-literate was quite small, quite analogous to the small literacy-specialist communities associated with early writing.

By the end of the twentieth century, with the growth of the knowledge economies, the need for quantitative insight spread across the population of industrialized countries in a fashion that resembled the earlier spread of arithmetic skill. This general need combined with the politically driven need to democratize opportunity to learn higher mathematics, typically assumed to require knowledge and skill in algebra, has produced considerable tension in many democracies, especially the United States, where access to algebra learning has come to be seen as political right (Moses, 1995).

Computationally Mediated Changes in the Nature of the Representational Infrastructure—Writing and Algebra Linking Into Existing Powerful Visual Systems of Seeing and Acting

Just as writing gradually tapped into oral language, a previously established, neurophysiologically grounded human system of meaning making and communicating, and changed radically in the process as it became phonetic, algebra may likewise be in the process of doing so. In this case, instead of tapping into the auditory-narrative system of oral language, it taps into the visual-graphic system. Although it may not have been Descartes' intent, anticipated by Oresme (Clagett, 1968), he (and Fermat) laid the base for tapping into humans' visual perceptual and cognitive capacities previously employed only by geometry. Recall Joseph Lagrange's prescient comment:

> As long as algebra and geometry proceeded along separate paths, their advance was slow and their applications limited. But when these sciences joined company, they drew from each other fresh vitality and thenceforward marched on a rapid pace towards perfection. (cited in Kline, 1953, p. 159)

From the coordinate geometry of 350 years ago to our contemporary graphs of quantitative relationships, we see an analogy to the gradual transition that occurred as Western writing became more phonetic—the newer ways of graphing with computational technology, for example, in the use of CASs, coexist with the old in various combinations as we graph functions which are defined and input into our graphing systems via character strings—and dynamically link these as well.

Can we make the next transition that might make the representation and manipulation of quantitative relationships broadly learnable in a way analogous to the invention of the alphabet? In what follows, we shall propose an analogous step. But before doing so, we reflect on the larger change in media that makes the new alphabet possible.

Both writing and mathematical symbol systems were instantiated in, and hence subject to, the constraints of the static, inert media of the previous several millennia. But, the computational medium is neither static nor inert. Rather, it is dynamic and interactive, exploiting the great new advance of the twentieth century, autonomously executable symbolic processes—that is, operations on symbol systems not requiring a human partner (Kaput & Shaffer, 2002). The longer term development of the computational medium is reviewed in Shaffer & Kaput (1999).

An Alphabet for Graphing Quantitative Relationships and Functions

Nemirovsky (1996; Monk & Nemirovsky, 1994) has suggested a starting point in the analysis, which, in fact, informed the development of the piecewise-defined and graphically editable functions described in Part II (An Illustration of Exploiting the SimCalc Representational Strategies). In his cognitive analysis of how people interpret graphs of phenomena, he referred to an "algebra of shapes" (Nemirovsky, 1996). The first representational strategy listed earlier, is a concrete, physical instantiation of this idea. Moreover, it not only acts as an efficient way to express functions and quantitative relationships, it supports direct graphical editing as well via clicking and dragging of the notational elements—which makes it an operative system in the same sense that algebra and arithmetic are operative systems.

Importantly, as expressed in the computational medium, the system employs the user's previously developed visual capacities: remembering and recognizing shapes and their spatial orientations; basic actions on them such as extending, stretching, and reorienting them; and relating two or more sets of shapes to one another such as in parallelism, intersection, perpendicularity, and so on. All these are based in extremely well developed human neurophysiological capacities (and indeed are shared by most other species of animals to at least some extent) and employ eye-hand coordination that is more readily learned than handwriting of either natural language or mathematical symbolism.

The second representational strategy, hot linking to motion phenomena, may be regarded as either an extension in expressivity, or as the inclusion of new notational elements, especially when used in schematic form (where the graphical features of the motion system are suppressed and the motion takes the form of dots moving on scalable number lines—SimCalc MathWorlds has a "Hide/Show World" viewing option that enables users to toggle between the conditions). From this latter point of view, the importing of physical motion and the use of graphs to drive physical phenomena (the fourth and fifth representational strategies) may be regarded as forms of "writing" in this enlarged system.

In terms of our larger analogy, the third representational strategy, hot-linking functions to their derivatives or integrals when applied to piece-wise-defined functions, amounts to extending the alphabet to different languages, in one case, the language of rates of change (describing "how fast"), and the other the language of accumulation (describing "how much"), and exploiting the fact that they are mutually equivalent descriptions (the content of the Fundamental Theorem of Calculus).

To summarize, we have argued that we are entering an era in which the historically received representational infrastructures, the product of evolution in static inert media, are expanded to include a much more learnable set of representational infrastructures. But we have not yet addressed their physical availability.

The Development of Material Means by Which Access to Learnable Representational Infrastructures Might Be Democratized—Analogy With the Printing Press

With the emergence of physical computers, we are involved in an extended process analogous to the evolution associated with the development of the printing press. The first stages involved expensive, and hence rare, central computers, what we have known as "mainframes" and "mini-computers." Then came the microcomputer and networks—connectivity, local and global. More recently, we have seen the emergence of hand-helds and, even more recently, connectivity across device types. We are moving towards the kind of ubiquitous access and full integration into life and work that was achieved by printed materials that eventually occurred by the time of the Industrial Revolution. But, as our previous cursory examination of the printing press evolution suggests, the process will take time and will depend on many other changes taking place along the way. We should note that the desktop software described earlier has both been translated to the ubiquitous hand-held graphing calculator and made fully network compatible, so that objects produced on one platform move fluently to other platforms (Hegedus & Kaput, 2003; Kaput & Hegedus, 2002; Roschelle, Vahey, Tatar, & Hegedus, 2003).[5] We regard the changes associated with classroom connectivity as at least as important as those associated with changes in representational infrastructure, and a second branch of the SimCalc Project is actively investigating the synergistic interactions between representational and communicational affordances of technology.

EPISTEMIC CHANGES IN CONTENT AND CURRICULUM

Deeper Assumptions Linked to Representation-Based Curricular Assumptions

Our comment earlier that the basic mathematical representational infrastructures coevolved with our system of education is especially vividly illustrated by the elementary school mathematics curriculum, which is based upon the base-ten placeholder system of numbers, which was used to create the standard algorithms for whole number arithmetic in the reckoning schools of northern Italy in the sixteenth century (Swetz, 1987) (expanded later to support actions on decimals). Elementary mathematics education has been defined by that system and its algorithms—the numerical representational infrastructure, just as the quantitative core of secondary mathematics education has been defined by the algebraic representational infrastructure. Interestingly, these two have remained separate historically and in school curricula, especially in the United States (Kaput, Carraher, & Blanton, 2008).

The algebraic representational infrastructure, through its embodiment in school algebra, has had a long-established relationship with calculus wherein algebra has been universally regarded as a prerequisite for calculus—because, after all, calculus is written in algebra. In fact, a significant part of school algebra was invented in the process of developing and applying calculus (Boyer, 1959; Edwards, 1979).

The Matter of Content: The Impacts of New Representational Infrastructures

We see three profound types of consequences of the development of the new medium for carrying representational infrastructures: (a) re-instantiating traditional notation systems in the new medium, and adding built-in computation that previously required a human partner (Shaffer & Kaput, 1999) and linkages among them, as illustrated by CASs, for example; (b) creating new representational infrastructures such as in SimCalc, or in geometry by Cabri Géomètre and Geometer's Sketchpad, in which new actions and new ways of representing structures and constraints become possible; and (c) creating new systems of knowledge employing new computationally intensive representational infrastructures—for example, modeling of complex systems with emergent behavior—each of which has multiple forms of notations and relationships with phenomena (Kaput & Roschelle, 1998) yielding a profound shift in the nature of mathematics and science previously beyond the reach of classical analytic methods (Bar-Yam, 1997; Coveney & Highfield, 1995; Lewin, 1992; Pagels, 1988). Tracing any of these types of consequences is a challenging endeavor, particularly since they overlap in substantive ways and is beyond the scope of this paper (see Kaput, 2000/2001 for further discussion). Instead, we will focus on item b and the reconstitution of key ideas underlying Calculus using the new representational infrastructure introduced in Part II. But first we set the historical context.

What came to be called "Calculus" evolved historically, beginning with the work of the Scholastics in the 1300s, through attempts to mathematize change in the world (see Kaput, 1994 for a review of this history). The resulting body of theory and technique that emerged in the seventeenth and eighteenth centuries, most notably, of course, in the work of Newton and Leibniz, which was extended in algebraic style in the eighteenth century by Euler and others, and then cleaned up for logical hygiene in the nineteenth century, is now institutionalized as a capstone course for students in many parts of the world, and especially in the United States. These ultimately successful mathematizing attempts were undertaken by the intellectual giants of Western civilization, who also developed the representational infrastructure of algebra as part of the process. Their work, done in static and inert media, directed to a small audience of peers, led to profoundly powerful understandings of the different ways quantities can vary, how these differences in variation relate to the ways the quantities accumulate, and the fundamental connections between varying quantities and their accumulation. These efforts also gave rise to the eventual formalization of such basic mathematical ideas as function, series, limit, continuity, and the like (Boyer, 1959; Edwards, 1979).

Over the past 2 centuries or so this elite community's intellectual tools, methods, and products became the foundations of the science and technology upon which we utterly depend. The tools and methods of calculus were institutionalized as the structure and core content of school and university mathematics curricula in most industrialized countries and taken as the epistemological essence of mathematics (Bochner, 1966; Mahoney, 1980). This content has also been taken as the subject of computerization as reflected in several chapters in Blume and Heid (2006). With this extremely abbreviated historical context, let us now turn to a review of the SimCalc approach to calculus, which involves an epistemic-level reformulation of the content exploiting the representational strategies outlined earlier.

The Reconstitution of Core Calculus Ideas Exploiting the SimCalc Representational Strategies—Some Illustrations

The representational strategies listed at the outset are not merely a series of software functionalities supporting some curriculum activities, but amount to a reconstitution of key ideas of the Mathematics of Change and Variation, including ideas underlying calculus. Hence we are not merely treating the underlying ideas of calculus in a new way, treating them as the focus of school mathematics beginning in the early grades and rooting them in children's everyday experience (see Table 9.1), especially their kinesthetic experience, but we are reformulating them in an epistemic way. We continue to address such familiar fundamentals as variable rates of changing quantities, the accumulation of those quantities, the connections between rates and accumulations, approximations, relations between discrete and continuous change, and so on, but they are intended to be experienced in profoundly different ways and are related to each other in new ways.

These approaches are not intended to eliminate the need for eventual use of formal notations for some students, and perhaps some formal notations for all students. Rather, they are intended to provide a substantial mathematical experience for the 90% of students in the United States who have not had substantive access to the Mathematics of Change and Variation, including the ideas underlying calculus. They also provide a conceptual foundation for the 5% to 10% of the population who need to learn more formal calculus. Finally, these strategies are intended to lead into the mathematics of dynamical systems and its use in modeling nonlinear phenomena of the sort that is growing dramatically in importance in the twenty-first century (Cohen & Stewart, 1994; Hall, 1992; Kaput & Roschelle, 1998; Stewart, 1990).

Mean values and continuity from rate and accumulation perspectives. To illustrate the contrast to traditional approaches, we refer the reader again to Figure 9.1, where we will initially focus on the velocity graphs of two functions, respectively controlling one of the two elevators on the left of the figure. (We return to the position functions later.) The downward-stepping, but positive, velocity function, which controls the left elevator, typically leads to a conflict with expectations, because most students associate it with a downward motion. However, by constructing it and observing the associated motion (often with many deliberate repetitions and variations), the conflicts lead to new and deeper understandings of both graphs and motion ("the elevator is not *going* down, it is *slowing* down!") This is a discrete version of the idea that the values of the function can be positive, while its slope is negative. The second, flat, constant-velocity function in Figure 9.1 that controls the elevator on the right generates constant velocity (objects are color coded to match their graphs). It is depicted in Figure 9.1 (without color) in the midst of being adjusted (by vertically dragging a hotspot in its center) to satisfy the constraint of "getting to the same floor at exactly the same time." This amounts to constructing the average velocity of the left-hand elevator, which has the (stepwise) variable velocity.

Determining the average in turn reduces to finding a constant velocity segment with the same area under it as does the staircase graph. In this case, the total area under the staircase is 15 and the number of seconds of the "trip" is five, so the mean value is a whole number, namely, three. We have "Snap-to-Grid" turned on in this case so that, as dragging occurs, the pointer jumps from point to point in the discrete coordinate system. Note that if we had provided six steps for the left elevator instead of five, the constraint of getting to the same floor at exactly the same time (from the same starting floor) could not be satisfied with a whole-number constant velocity, hence could not be reached with "Snap-to-Grid" turned on. This helps make problematic the issue of "having numbers where you need them"—an opportunity to pursue the continuity of the number line.

The standard mean value theorem, of course, asserts that if a function is continuous over an interval, then its mean value will exist and will be the value of that function at some point in that interval. But, of course, the stepwise-varying function is *not* continuous, and so the mean value theorem conclusion might fail—as it would if the average were not a whole number matching a step-height. However, if we had used imported data from a student's physical motion (or perhaps a falling body) then the velocity would necessarily equal the average velocity at one or more times in the interval. Other activities involve a second student walking in parallel whose responsibility is to walk at an estimated average speed of her partner. Then the differences between same-velocity and same-position begin to become kinesthetically apparent as well. Additional activities involve the two students in importing their motion data into the computer (or calculator) *serially* and replaying them *simultaneously*. In these activities, the velocity-position distinction becomes even more apparent due to the availability of the respective velocity and position graphs alongside the cybernetically replayed motion.

The fundamental rate-accumulation connection. The dual perspectives of the velocity and position functions, both illustrated in Figure 9.1, show two different views of the average value situation, and they are hot-linked, so that a change in one is immediately reflected in its counterpart. In the left-hand graph, we see the connection as a matter of equal areas under respective velocity graphs. In the right-hand graph, we see it through position graphs as a matter of getting to the same place at the same time, one with variable velocity and slope and the other with constant velocity and slope.

Depending on the goals of the activity, the system can be configured so that one or the other of the graphs might not be viewable or, if viewable, not editable. For example, another version of this activity involves giving the piecewise-defined position function on the right and asking the student to construct its velocity-function mean value on the left, phrasable as "getting to the same place at the same time, but with constant velocity." This makes the area-slope connection explicit and testable (by running the animation). By reversing the roles of velocity and position in terms of which is given and which is requested, the area-slope connection is experienced in an opposite way. Importantly, by building in the connections between rate (velocity) and accumulation (position) quantities throughout, the underlying idea of the Fundamental Theorem of Calculus is always at hand, built into the experience of the user at every stage.

Target averages and area balancing—concrete versions of highly general ideas. Another set of activities that illustrates the deep reformulation of content involves *Target Averages*: Given that I am behind my target pace by a certain amount after 6 minutes in an 8 minute time-trial race, how fast must I travel for the last 2 minutes to achieve my target average speed for the race (20 ft/sec)? See Figure 9.4 where we have depicted average rates for the first three 2-minute segments of the race indicating that I am averaging about 16 ft/sec and have 2 minutes to make up the shortfall. Thinking in terms of areas above and below the target average, in the interval from 2 to 4 minutes I squandered the pace advantage I accumulated in the first

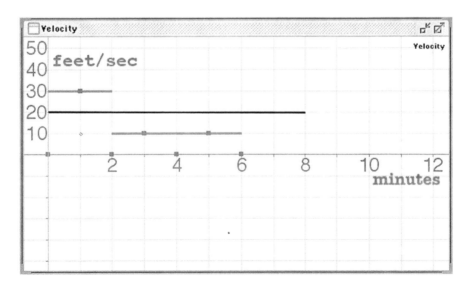

Figure 9.4.   Average rates (in ft/sec) as a function of number of minutes traveled.

2 minutes, and then in the next 2 minutes, fell behind as much as I was ahead earlier. So (using the geometric simplicity and ignoring computational details) I need to match my initial 30 ft/sec pace for 2 minutes to balance out my deficit. But what if I had to make up the shortfall in only 1 minute, how fast would I need to go? Answer: Twice as fast, because, from an area-balancing point of view, the shorter the time interval, the taller the balancing area-rectangle needs to be.

The matter of generality and shift in the roles of computation. Importantly, the same arguments apply to a company trying to meet an annual revenue target: How much do I need to sell in the last quarter to hit my annual target? Or, in a variable pay-rate situation: Given a base rate of $8/hr for the first 8 hours, how many hours must I work at time-and-a-half (1.5 times one's usual pay) to average $10/hr for the day? In fact, they even apply to that bane of students and teachers, "Mixture Problems," in which the rates are such things as cost per pound (e.g., of peanuts, walnuts, and the mixture)—thereby providing a graphical way of modeling such situations. The area approach also applies to weighted averages in, say, grade-point averages, in which the grade in a course is its (vertical axis) "rate" and its number of credits determines an interval on the horizontal axis so then the GPA is the constant rate across all credits earned that has the same area as the variable rates in the different courses.

Thus the area arguments are very general, despite their concrete instantiations here. At least as important is the fact that they apply to continuously varying functions. The only difference is in computational complexity. However, the stepwise-varying rate functions are typically the same as those used for approximations of continuous functions, so that what is learned earlier applies directly to the more general cases. This reflects in yet another way the fact that the reconstitution of content is differently aligned with the "capstone mathematics" of calculus, namely in conceptual terms rather than in the usual computational procedural prerequisite terms centered on algebraic syntax.

Another important consequence of the representational strategies illustrated in the previous accounts is a shift in the role of computation. The idea of "average" in school mathematics is usually treated as some kind of total divided by a number of instances in discrete contexts, or in continuous contexts, motion for example, it is a net change divided by the elapsed variable, for example, time. However, this radically underplays the richness of the situations and of the idea itself as indicated in the target-average examples. Computation remains important, but its role is changed to one in which it is more explicitly a tool of analysis and insight than merely a tool to yield a single-number characterization of a situation.

ACKNOWLEDGMENT

This chapter is dedicated, in loving memory, to Jim Kaput, a mentor, colleague, role model, and friend who continues to inspire me, and countless others, to reach higher than we ever thought possible. He was a visionary, a modern-day genius, who was willing to challenge deep-rooted patterns of belief and practice regarding the nature of mathematics and who could learn it. In an often unreasonable world, Jim did good beyond reason. May his dream of democratizing access to powerful ideas become a reality in our time.

—Roberta Schorr

NOTES

1. Evaluation versions of SimCalc MathWorlds for computers and calculators can be downloaded from http://www.simcalc.umassd.edu
2. This school was one of the lowest performing middle schools in New Jersey as measured by state mathematics and reading tests. For example, in the year prior to the study, only 2.9% of the school's eighth-grade students passed the state-mandated mathematics test. The school not only underperformed the average for eighth-grade students in the district, but was also the fourth-lowest-scoring school in the state. It should be noted that in many districts, particularly suburban districts, passing rates reach close to 100%.
3. We use graphics depicting the software (except for color) as it appeared to students in the vignettes. The software's appearance and functionalities have evolved since that time. Colors are described as they appeared in the software.
4. In Kaput (2000) we develop this analogy in full as part of a more elaborated version of this section of this chapter. That paper was republished in the *New Zealand Mathematics Magazine, 38*(3), December, 2001.
5. This software and associated curriculum materials are described in detail at http://www.simcalc.umassd.edu/ and samples are available there.

REFERENCES

Bar-Yam, Y. (1997). *Dynamics of complex systems*. Reading, MA: Addison-Wesley.

Blume, G. W., & Heid, M. K. (Eds.). (2008). *Research on technology and the teaching and learning of mathematics: Vol. 2. Cases and perspectives*. Charlotte, NC: Information Age.

Bochner, S. (1966). *The role of mathematics in the rise of science*. Princeton, NJ: Princeton University Press.

Bowers, J. S., & Doerr, H. M. (2001). An analysis of prospective teachers' dual roles in understanding the mathematics of change: Eliciting growth with technology. *Journal of Mathematics Teacher Education, 4*, 115–137.

Boyer, C. (1959). *The history of calculus and its historical development.* New York: Dover.

Brasell, H. (1987). The effect of real-time laboratory graphing on learning graphic representations of distance and velocity. *Journal of Research in Science Teaching, 24,* 385–395.

Bruner, J. (1973). *Beyond the information given.* New York: Norton.

Cajori, F. (1929). *A history of mathematical notations, Vol. 2: Notations mainly in higher mathematics.* La Salle, IL: The Open Court.

Chick, H., & Stacy, K. (Eds.). (2004). *The future of the teaching and learning of algebra: The 12th ICMI study.* Norwood, MA: Kluwer Academic.

Clagett, M. (1968). *Nicole Oresme and the medieval geometry of qualities and motions.* Madison, WI: University of Wisconsin Press.

Clement, J. (1982). Algebra word problem solutions: Thought processes underlying a common misconception. *Journal for Research in Mathematics Education, 13,* 16–30.

Clement, J. (1989). The concept of variation and misconceptions in Cartesian graphing. *Focus on Learning Problems in Mathematics, 11*(1-2), 77–87.

Cobb, P., Confrey, J., diSessa, A., Lehrer, R., & Schauble, L. (2002). Design experiments in educational research. *Educational Researcher, 32*(1), 9–13.

Cobb, P., Gravemeijer, K., Yackel, E., McClain, K., & Whitenack, J. (1997). Mathematizing and symbolizing: The emergence of chains of signification in one first-grade classroom. In D. Kirshner & J. A. Whitson (Eds.), *Situated cognition theory: Social, semiotic, and neurological perspectives* (pp. 151–233). Hillsdale, NJ: Erlbaum.

Cobb, P., Yackel, E., & McClain, K. (2000). *Symbolizing and communicating in mathematics classrooms.* Mahwah, NJ: Erlbaum.

Cohen, D. K., & Ball, D. L. (1999). *Instruction, capacity, and improvement* (CPRE Research Report No. RR-043). Philadelphia: University of Pennsylvania, Consortium for Policy Research in Education.

Cohen, D. K., Raudenbush, S., & Ball, D. L. (2003). Resources, instruction, and research. *Educational Evaluation and Policy Analysis, 25,* 1–24.

Cohen, J., & Stewart, I. (1994). *The collapse of chaos: Discovering simplicity in a complex world.* New York: Viking Books.

Cole, M. (1997). Cultural-historical psychology: A Meso-genetic approach. In L. Martin, K. Nelson, & E. Toback (Eds.), *Socio-cultural psychology: Theory and practice of knowing and doing* (pp. 168–204). New York: Cambridge University Press.

Coveney, P., & Highfield, R. (1995). *Frontiers of complexity: The search for order in a chaotic world.* New York: Addison-Wesley.

Dantzig, T. (1954). *Number: The language of science.* New York: Macmillan.

Davies, W. V. (1987). *Egyptian hieroglyphs.* London: British Museum.

Deacon, T. (1997). *The symbolic species: The co-evolution of language and the brain.* New York: W. W. Norton.

Donald, L. (1991). *The origins of the modern mind.* Cambridge, MA: Harvard University Press.

Edwards, C. (1979). *The historical development of the calculus.* New York: Springer-Verlag.

Eisenstein, E. (1979). *The printing press as an agent of change* (Vols. 1 & 2). Cambridge, England: Cambridge University Press.

Elmore, R. F. (1996). Getting to scale with good educational practice. *Harvard Educational Review, 66,* 1–26.

Fey, J. (1989). Technology and mathematics education: A survey of recent developments and important problems. *Educational Studies in Mathematics, 20,* 237–272.

Gravemeijer, K., Cobb, P., Bowers, J., & Whitenack, J. (2000). Symbolizing, modeling, and instructional design. In P. Cobb, E. Yackel, & K. McClain (Eds.), *Symbolizing and communicating in mathematics classrooms* (pp. 225–274). Mahwah, NJ: Erlbaum.

Haas, C. (1996). *Writing technology: Studies on the materiality of literacy.* Mahwah, NJ: Erlbaum.

Hall, N. (1992). *Exploring chaos: A guide to the new science of disorder.* New York: W. W. Norton.

Havelock, E. (1982). *The literate revolution in Greece and its cultural consequences.* Princeton, NJ: Princeton University Press.

Hegedus, S., & Kaput, J. (2002, October). Exploring the phenomena of classroom connectivity. In D. Mewborn & L. Hatfield (Eds.), *Proceedings of the 24th annual meeting of the North American chapter of the International Group for the Psychology of Mathematics Education* (Vol. 1, pp. 422–432). Columbus, OH: ERIC Clearinghouse.

Hegedus, S., & Kaput, J. (2003, July). The effect of SimCalc connected classrooms on students' algebraic thinking. In N. A. Pateman, B. J. Dougherty, & J. Zilliox (Eds.), *Proceedings of the 27th conference of the International Group For The Psychology Of Mathematics Education held jointly with the 25th conference of the North American chapter of the International Group For The Psychology Of Mathematics Education* (Vol. 3, pp. 47–54). Honolulu, HI: University of Hawaii, College of Education.

Kaput, J. (1991). Notations and representations as mediators of constructive processes. In E. von Glaserfeld (Ed.), *Constructivism and mathematics education* (pp. 53–74). Boston: Reidel.

Kaput, J. (1992). Technology and mathematics education. In D. Grouws (Ed.), *Handbook of research on mathematics teaching and learning* (pp. 515–556). New York: Macmillan.

Kaput, J. (1994). Democratizing access to calculus: New routes to old roots. In A. Schoenfeld (Ed.), *Mathematical thinking and problem solving* (pp. 77–156). Hillsdale, NJ: Erlbaum.

Kaput, J. (1997). Rethinking calculus: Learning and thinking. *The American Mathematical Monthly, 104,* 731–737.

Kaput, J. (2001). Implications of the shift from isolated, expensive technology to connected, inexpensive, ubiquitous, and diverse technologies. *New Zealand Mathematics Magazine, 38*(3), 1–26. (Original work published 2000)

Kaput, J., Carraher, D., & Blanton, M. (Eds.). (2008). *Algebra in the early grades.* Mahwah, NJ: Erlbaum.

Kaput, J., & Hegedus, S. (2002). Exploiting classroom connectivity by aggregating student constructions to create new learning opportunities. In A. D. Cockburn & E. Nardi (Eds.), *Proceedings of the 26th conference of the International Group for the Psychology of Mathematics Education* (Vol. 3, pp. 177–184). University of East Anglia: Norwich, UK.

Kaput, J., Blanton, M., & Moreno, L. (2008). Algebra from a symbolization point of view. In J. J. Kaput, D. W. Carraher, & M. L. Blanton (Eds.), *Algebra in the early grades* (pp. 19-56). Mahwah, NJ: Erlbaum.

Kaput, J. J. (2000). Implications of the shift from isolated, expensive technology to connected, inexpensive, ubiquitous, and diverse technologies. In M. O. J. Thomas (Ed.), *TIME 2000: An international conference in mathematics education* (pp. 1–25). Auckland, New Zealand: University of Auckland and the Auckland University of Technology.

Kaput, J., Noss, R., & Hoyles, C. (2002). Developing new notations for a learnable mathematics in the computational era. In L. D. English (Ed.), *Handbook of international research on mathematics education* (pp. 51–75). Mahwah, NJ: Erlbaum.

Kaput, J., & Roschelle, J. (1998). The mathematics of change and variation from a millennial perspective: New content, new context. In C. Hoyles, C. Morgan, & G. Woodhouse (Eds.), *Mathematics for a new millennium* (pp. 155–170). London: Springer-Verlag.

Kaput, J., & Shaffer, D. (2002). On the development of human representational competence from an evolutionary point of view: From episodic to virtual culture. In K. Gravemeijer, R. Lehrer, B. van Oers, & L. Verschaffel (Eds.), *Symbolizing, modeling and tool use in mathematics education* (pp. 277–293). London: Kluwer Academic.

Kaput, J., & Sims-Knight, J. (1983). Errors in translations to algebraic equations: Roots and implications. *Focus on Learning Problems in Mathematics, 5*(3), 63–78.

Kline, M. (1953). *Mathematics in western culture.* New York: Oxford University Press.

Kline, M. (1972). *Mathematical thought from ancient to modern times.* New York: Oxford University Press.

Laborde, J. -M. (2003). *Cabri Junior.* Dallas, TX: Texas Instruments. Retrieved May 15, 2006, from http://education.ti.com/us/product/apps/cabrijr.html

Lehrer, R., Schauble, L., Carpenter, S., & Penner, D. (2000). The interrelated development of inscriptions and conceptual understanding. In P. Cobb, E. Yackel, & K. McClain (Eds.), *Symbolizing and communicating in mathematics classrooms* (pp. 325–360). Mahwah, NJ: Erlbaum.

Lewin, R. (1992). *Complexity: Life at the edge of chaos.* New York: Macmillan.

Mahoney, M. (1980). The beginnings of algebraic thought in the seventeenth century. In S. Gankroger (Ed.), *Descartes: Philosophy, mathematics and physics.* Sussex, England: Harvester Press.

McCloskey, M. (1983). Naive theories of motion. In D. Gentner & A. Stevens (Eds.), *Mental models* (pp. 299–324). Hillsdale, NJ: Erlbaum.

Monk, S., & Nemirovsky, R. (1994). The case of Dan: Student construction of a functional situation through visual attributes. *CBMS Issues in Mathematics Education, 4,* 139–168.

Moses, R. (1995). Algebra, the new civil right. In C. Lacampagne, W. Blair, & J. Kaput (Eds.), *The algebra initiative colloquium* (pp. 53–67). Washington, DC: U.S. Department of Education.

National Center for Education Statistics. (1994). *A profile of the American high school sophomore in 1990* (NCES No. 95-086). Washington, DC: Author.

National Council of Teachers of Mathematics. (2000). *Principles and standards for school mathematics*. Washington, DC: Author.

Nelson, K. (1996). *Language in cognitive development: Emergence of the mediated mind*. Cambridge, England: Cambridge University Press.

Nemirovsky, R. (1992). *Students' graphical representations of motion: A basic vocabulary of shapes* (TERC Technical Report). Cambridge, MA: TERC.

Nemirovsky, R. (1993a). *Motion, flow, and contours: The experience of continuous change*. Unpublished doctoral dissertation, Harvard University, Cambridge, MA.

Nemirovsky, R. (1993b). Students making sense of chaotic behavior. *Interactive Learning Environments, 3,* 151–175.

Nemirovsky, R. (1996). Mathematical narratives. In N. Bednarz, C. Kieran, & L. Lee (Eds.), *Approaches to algebra: Perspectives for research and teaching* (pp. 197–223). Dordrecht, Netherlands: Kluwer Academic.

Nemirovsky, R., Kaput, J., & Roschelle, J. (1998). Enlarging mathematical activity from modeling phenomena to generating phenomena. In A. Oliver & K. Newstead (Eds.), *Proceedings of the 22nd conference of the International Group for the Psychology of Mathematics Education conference* (Vol. 3, pp. 287–294). Stellenbosch, South Africa: Conference Committee.

Nickerson, S., Nydam, C., & Bowers, J. S. (2000). Linking algebraic concepts and contexts: Every picture tells a story. *Mathematics Teaching in the Middle School, 6,* 92–98.

Olson, D. (1976). Culture, technology, and intellect. In L. Resnick & R. Glaser (Eds.), *The nature of intelligence* (pp. 189–202). Potomac, MD: Erlbaum.

Ong, W. J. (1982). *Orality and literacy: The technologizing of the word*. London: Methuen.

Pagels, H. (1988). *The dreams of reason: The rise of the sciences of complexity*. New York: Bantam Books.

Piaget, J. (1970). *The child's conception of movement and speed*. New York: Basic Books.

Roschelle, J., DeLaura, R., & Kaput, J. (1996). Scriptable applications: Implementing open architectures in learning technology. In P. Carlson & F. Makedon (Eds.), *Proceedings of Ed-Media 96: World conference on educational multimedia and hypermedia* (pp. 599–604). Charlottesville, VA: American Association of Computers in Education.

Roschelle, J., & Kaput, J. (1996). SimCalc MathWorlds for the Mathematics of Change. *Communications of the ACM, 39*(8), 97–99.

Roschelle, J., Kaput, J., & Stroup, W. (2000). SimCalc: Accelerating student engagement with the mathematics of change. In M. J. Jacobsen & R. B. Kozma (Eds.), *Learning the sciences of the 21st century: Research, design, and implementing advanced technology learning environments* (pp. 47–75). Hillsdale, NJ: Erlbaum.

Roschelle, J., Tatar, D., & Kaput, J. (in press). Getting to scale with innovations that deeply restructure how students come to know mathematics. In A. E. Kelly, R. A. Lesh, & J. Y. Baek (Eds.), *Handbook of design research methods in edu-*

cation: Innovations in science, technology, engineering, and mathematics learning and teaching. Mahwah, NJ: Erlbaum.

Roschelle, J., Tatar, D., Kaput, J., & Hopkins, B. (2005, April). *Scaling up innovative technology-based mathematics with a wide variety of 7th grade teachers.* Paper presented at the research presession of the National Council for Teachers of Mathematics, Anaheim, CA.

Roschelle, J., Vahey, P., Tatar, D., Kaput, J., & Hegedus, S. (2003, July). Five key considerations for networking in a handheld-based mathematics classroom. In N. A. Pateman, B. J. Dougherty, & J. Zilliox (Eds.), *Proceedings of the 27th conference of the International Group for the Psychology of Mathematics Education held jointly with the 25th conference of the PME-NA* (Vol. 4, pp. 71–78). Honolulu, HI: University of Hawaii.

Sawyer, W. W. (1975). *What is calculus about?* New Haven, CT: Yale University Press. (Original work published 1961)

Schmandt-Besserat, D. (1978). The earliest precursor of writing. *Scientific American, 238,* 50–59.

Schmandt-Besserat, D. (1992). *Before writing: From counting to cuneiform* (Vol. 1). Houston, TX: University of Texas Press.

Schorr, R. Y. (2003). Motion, speed, and other ideas that "should be put in books". *Journal of Mathematical Behavior, 22,* 467–479.

Sfard, A. (2000). Symbolizing mathematical reality into being: Or how mathematical discourse and mathematical objects create each other. In P. Cobb, E. Yackel, & K. McClain (Eds.), *Symbolizing and communicating in mathematics classrooms* (pp. 37–98). Mahwah, NJ: Erlbaum.

Shaffer, D., & Kaput, J. (1999). Mathematics and virtual culture: An evolutionary perspective on technology and mathematics education. *Educational Studies in Mathematics, 37,* 97–119.

Stewart, I. (1990). Change. In L. Steen (Ed.), *On the shoulders of giants: New approaches to numeracy* (pp. 183–219). Washington, DC: National Academy Press.

Stroup, W. M. (2002). Understanding qualitative calculus: A structural synthesis of learning research. *International Journal of Computers for Mathematical Learning, 7,* 167–215.

Swetz, F. (1987). *Capitalism and arithmetic: The new math of the 15th century.* La Salle, IL: Open Court.

Thompson, P. (1994). The development of the concept of speed and its relationship to concepts of rate. In G. Harel & J. Confrey (Eds.), *The development of multiplicative reasoning in the learning of mathematics* (pp. 179–234). Albany, NY: State University of New York Press.

Thompson, P. W., & Sfard, A. (1994). Problems of reification: Representations and mathematical objects. In D. Kirshner (Ed.), *Proceedings of the sixteenth annual meeting of the North American Chapter of the International Group for the Psychology Of Mathematics Education: Plenary sessions* (Vol. 1, pp. 3–34). Baton Rouge, LA: Louisiana State University.

Thornton, R. (1992). Enhancing and evaluating students' learning of motion concepts. In A. Tiberghien & H. Mandl (Eds.), *Physics and learning environments: NATO science series* (pp. 265–283). New York: Springer-Verlag.

Thornton, R., & Sokolow, D. (1990). Learning motion concepts using real time microcomputer-based tools. *American Journal of Physics, 58*, 858–866.

Tierney, C., & Nemirovsky, R. (1991). Children's spontaneous representations of changing situations. *Hands On!, 14*(2), 7–10.

Tierney, C., Nemirovsky, R., Wright, T., & Ackermann, E. (1993). Body motion and children's understanding of graphs. In J. R. Becker & B. J. Pence (Eds.), *Proceedings of the fifteenth annual meeting of the North American Chapter of the International Group for the Psychology of Mathematics Education* (Vol. 1, pp. 192–198). San Jose, CA: San Jose State University, The Center for Mathematics and Computer Science Education.

U.S. Department of Education. (2002). *No child left behind.* Retrieved March 22, 2006, from http://www.ed.gov/nclb/landing.jhtml

Walker, C. B. F. (1987). *Cuneiform.* London: British Museum.

Woodard, R. (1996). Writing systems. In B. Comrie, S. Matthews, & M. Polinksy (Eds.), *The atlas of languages: The origin and development of languages throughout the world.* London: Quarto.

CHAPTER 10

MULTIPLE REPRESENTATIONS AND LOCAL LINEARITY

Research Influences on the Use of Technology in Calculus Curriculum Reform

Thomas P. Dick and Barbara S. Edwards

Curriculum development tends to be a process of gradual evolution punctuated with more active periods of revolution. The term "calculus reform" refers to such a period recently in the history of calculus curricula.

THE CALCULUS REFORM MOVEMENT

After several decades of publisher-driven development based on user surveys resulting in textbooks with constantly increasing numbers of pages, a groundswell of interest in changing the calculus curriculum arose in the mid 1980s. The Sloan Conference (held at Tulane University, 1986) and the Calculus for a New Century Conference (held in Washington, DC, 1987) sounded the call for reform of the calculus curriculum, and the

---

Research on Technology and the Teaching and Learning of Mathematics:
Vol. 2. Cases and Perspectives, 255–275
Copyright © 2008 by Information Age Publishing
All rights of reproduction in any form reserved.

National Science Foundation (NSF) provided funding for a variety of curriculum development efforts.

The proceedings of the original Sloan Conference was given the title "Toward a Lean and Lively Calculus," reflecting the discussions about both curricular and instructional reform (Douglas, 1986). The call for leanness was to concentrate on fewer, well-chosen, central concepts rather than an encyclopedic collection of topics seemingly representing the union of all instructors' wish lists. The call for liveliness was to invigorate the teaching of calculus and to get students to *think* about those central ideas. The Calculus for a New Century Conference (see Steen, 1988) also marked the involvement of the National Science Foundation as a willing funding partner for a wide range of reform projects at the collegiate level. Some of the funded projects were multiyear, large-scale curriculum development efforts, but the NSF also funded a wide variety of other projects.

It is grossly simplistic to suggest that the calculus reform movement represented a single coherent vision of what calculus curriculum and instruction should be.[1] For example, it would be patently false to think of the use of technology as a defining characteristic of calculus reform efforts. Some calculus reform projects made no use of technology while other projects were essentially embedded in the use of technology (for example, as a collection of electronic notebooks within a computer algebra system). However, it is clear that technology was a powerful catalyst for calculus reform. As powerful computer algebra systems and graphing calculators with numerical differentiation and integration routines made new tools widely accessible, the surrounding landscape of calculus instruction changed. The advance of technology was, for many, the key impetus to genuinely reflect and reexamine which calculus topics should be taught and how they should be taught.

The Calculus Connections Curriculum Project

The Calculus Connections Curriculum Project was one of the early NSF-funded efforts. An assumption from the beginning in the writing of this curriculum was that each student would have constant access to technology capable of function graphing and extensive numerical calculation capabilities, including equation solving and definite integration. Most computer algebra systems (CASs) possess these capabilities as well as additional symbolic algebra operations.

However, the actual catalyst inspiring the direction of the Calculus Connections Curriculum Project was the (then) recent appearance of the requisite capabilities in a hand-held device, the graphing calculator. This development removed a major obstacle to widespread accessibility to graphing capability. The authors of the curriculum (Dick & Patton, 1993) kept that basic assumption of technological access in mind throughout the writing.

The proper uses of these tools were of great concern in the development of the curriculum. Gratuitous use of the technology was shunned. Rather, the intent was to make use of the technology in ways that would provide either more powerful insights or new approaches to a concept that were impossible without the availability of technology. Mathematics education research played an important part in guiding the role of technology in this curriculum (Heid, 1988; Palmiter, 1991).

THEMES OF CALCULUS CURRICULUM REFORM

In this chapter, we will examine two themes—multiple representations and local linearity—that were central not only to the Calculus Connections Curriculum Project but were common to many of the other reform projects as well. Indeed, these themes influenced the College Board to incorporate significant changes into the Advanced Placement Calculus course descriptions in 1998. In this section, we will highlight the particular mathematics education research that profoundly influenced the development of the Calculus Connections curriculum and discuss the particular ways that this research guided the use of technology.

Connecting Multiple Representations of Function

Perhaps the most frequently stated goal of curricular and instructional reform is the improvement of students' conceptual knowledge. Hiebert and Lefevre (1986) describe conceptual knowledge entirely in terms of relationships:

> Conceptual knowledge is characterized most clearly as knowledge that is rich in relationships. It can be thought of as a connected web of knowledge, a network in which the linking relationships are as prominent as the discrete pieces of information. Relationships pervade the individual facts and propositions so that all pieces of information are linked to some network. In fact, a unit of conceptual knowledge cannot be an isolated piece of information; by definition it is a part of conceptual knowledge only if the holder recognizes its relationship to other pieces of information. (pp. 3-4)

One means of building rich webs of relationships for mathematical phenomena is through multiple representations of mathematical objects.

Mathematical actions taken on these objects have representational consequences. In other words, the results of an action are reflected in some discernible way in a corresponding change in the representation of the object. The activities of describing patterns in these changes and making predictions based on those patterns are the lifeblood of learning mathematics.

Examining and re-examining the consequences of a mathematical action when the object is represented in multiple ways potentially increases the possible conceptual connections exponentially. The Soviet psychologist, Krutetskii (1976) studied mathematically gifted children from 1955 to 1966 and observed that "more able" children exhibited a characteristic of flexibility in switching between and among representations while engaging in problem-solving activities. This flexibility worked as an advantage for these students over "average" or "below-average" students. Since different goals or contexts of a particular problem often are more easily addressed through different representations, students should be flexible enough to allow the goal or context to determine which representation is most appropriate (Schoenfeld, 1990). Although it is clear that the mere availability of multiple representations of mathematical entities does not automatically create this flexibility for students or make the deep conceptual connections for them, their absence certainly hinders the facilitation of this important skill. (See Goldin, 1998, for a more complete discussion of these issues.)

A theme adopted by many calculus curriculum reform efforts focused on playing out a multiple representation instructional strategy on the central idea of function in calculus—examining key concepts such as limit, derivative, and integral in symbolic, graphic, and tabular representations. An understanding of the concept of function is a central piece in understanding limit, derivative, and integral. Furthermore, each representation of the functions involved can reveal different aspects of the concept in question. A student who comes to see the connection between the various representations can thus build richer and more complex understandings. It should be noted that this theme was wholly compatible with the call for a multiple representation approach highlighted in the original National Council of Teachers of Mathematics (1989) standards.

Many pedagogical and epistemological questions remain concerning the connections students make between and among multiple representations of functions. For instance, considering a graphical representation of a function seems to require different psychological processes from those that are required when considering that function in its symbolic form (Bell & Janvier, 1981; Goldenberg, 1988).

The Rule of Three and Rule of Four

The Harvard Consortium Project used the phrase "Rule of Three" (Hughes-Hallett et al., 1992) to capture this notion of multiple representations of function—analytic (symbolic formula), graphic, and numeric. Later this was expanded to include a fourth representation—verbal. The central tenet of the approach is to examine each important concept in calculus through multiple representations. We will illustrate with a particular example.

Even and Odd Functions in Multiple Representations

Formally, a function f is called *even* if the outputs satisfy the property $f(x) = f(-x)$ for every real number input x in the domain of f. A function g is called *odd* if the outputs satisfy the property $g(x) = -g(-x)$ for every real number input x in the domain of g. What are the consequences of these definitions in the numeric, graphic, and symbolic representations of a function? It is instructive (and motivates the terminology) to consider $f(x) = x^2$ and $g(x) = x^3$ as the (canonical) examples of an even and an odd function. Numerically, an even function produces equal outputs for opposite inputs. An odd function produces opposite outputs for opposite inputs. If $f(x) = x^2$, then $f(-2) = (-2)^2 = 4$ and $f(2) = 2^2 = 4$, so $f(-2) = f(2)$. Also, $f(5) = (5)^2$ 25 and $f(-5) = (-5)^2 = 25$, so $f(5) = f(-5)$. On the other hand, if $g(x) = x^3$, then $g(-2) = (-2)^3 = -8$, and $g(2) = 2^3 = 8$, so $g(-2) = -g(2)$. Similarly, $g(5) = 5^3 = 125$ and $g(-5) = (-5)^3 = -125$, so $g(5) = -g(-5)$.

Graphically, an even function (with y as a function of x) will have a graph that is symmetric about the y-axis, that is, the graph of an even function over its positive inputs will appear to be a mirror image of the graph over its negative inputs, with the y-axis (the output axis) as the line of reflection for the graph of an even function. The graph of an odd function has symmetry with respect to the origin. If we rotate the graph of an odd function 180 about the origin, the rotated graph will coincide with the original graph. Another way to think of g as a function with a graph symmetric with respect to the origin is that, for any input value x, a line segment connecting the points $(x, g(x))$ and $(-x, g(-x))$ will always have its midpoint at the origin. Figure 10.1 illustrates these two symmetry properties of even and odd function graphs for the examples $f(x) = x^2$ and $g(x) = x^3$.

Symbolically, replacing x by $-x$ in the formula of an even function produces the same formula, while replacing x by $-x$ in the expression for an odd function produces the opposite of the original expression. Note that $f(-x) = (-x)^2 = x^2 = f(x)$ for all real values x. On the other hand, $g(-x) = (-x)^3 = -g(x)$ for all real values x.

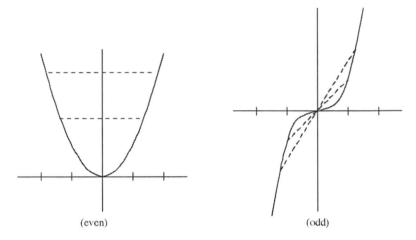

Figure 10.1.   Examples of symmetries of even and odd function graphs.

Certainly one could find a similar explanation of these representational qualities of even and odd functions in many textbooks, but often the exercises following such a treatment would concentrate on the symbolic representation. In a multiple representation curricular approach, it is imperative that not only the exposition but also the exercise and problem sets should reflect the approach. An example of such a problem follows.

Problem 1

Suppose *f* and *g* are differentiable functions with *f* even and *g* odd. Explain (a) analytically, and (b) graphically, why *f′* is odd and *g′* is even.

Solution to Problem 1

(a) Analytically, the chain rule can be applied. For *f* even, we have

$$f'(x) = \frac{d}{dx}(f(x)) = \frac{d}{dx}(f(-x)) = f'(-x) \cdot (-1) = -f'(-x).$$

Thus *f′* satisfies the property to be odd.

For *g* odd, we have

$$g'(x) = \frac{d}{dx}(g(x)) = \frac{d}{dx}(-g(-x)) = -g'(-x) \cdot (-1) = g'(-x).$$

Thus *g′* satisfies the property to be even.

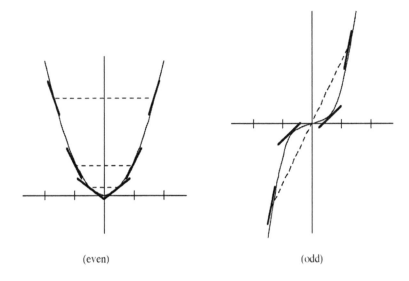

(even)   (odd)

Figure 10.2.   Symmetries in slopes of graphs of even and odd functions.

(b) More geometric insight is afforded by considering the graphs of even and odd functions. Figure 10.2 illustrates how the defining symmetry of the graph of an even function results in its tangent slopes having an odd symmetry (the slopes at x and at $-x$ are opposites). Similarly, the symmetry with respect to the origin in the graph of an odd function results in tangent slopes having an even symmetry (the slopes at x and at $-x$ are the same).

An example of a task employing tabular representations follows.

Problem 2

Which of the following tables of values could belong to a function f whose first and second derivatives are both negative for all real numbers?

x	$f(x)$		x	$f(x)$		x	$f(x)$		x	$f(x)$
-4	-2		-4	-12		-4	-2		-4	-12
-2	-6		-2	-11		-2	-3		-2	-8
0	-9		0	-9		0	-5		0	-5
2	-11		2	-6		2	-8		2	-3
4	-12		4	-2		4	-12		4	-2

The solution of this problem could take several different paths. One could reason that the values of $f(x)$ must be decreasing (first derivative negative) and the decrements must be getting larger (second derivative negative) to conclude that the third table is the only possibility. Another strategy might be to plot the points indicated and draw a smooth curve through them to use a concavity interpretation of the second derivative.

Consideration of alternative representations can both reinforce student thinking and help them monitor their thinking. Yet students exhibit reluctance to exploit other representations, especially for tasks posed in symbolic format. The results of a study by Dick (1988) reported in Eisenberg and Dreyfus (1990) highlighted how profound that reluctance can be, and served as a great motivator for pursuing the multiple representation approach of the Calculus Connections project. In that study, subjects were given the following problem near the end of a semester-long course on probability and statistics:

Problem 3

Let $f(x) = \begin{cases} |x - 2| & 1 < x < 3 \\ 0 & otherwise \end{cases}$ describe a probability density

function.

(a) Graph $y = f(x)$.

(b) Find $\text{Prob}(X > \frac{3}{2})$ if X is a continuous random variable with probability density function given by $f(x)$.

Note: A grid was provided for part a. Students were given no special instructions regarding the use of part a in calculating the probability value in part b.

Students' work was examined for the following: (1) correct graph in part a, (2) correct formulation of $\text{Prob}(X > \frac{3}{2})$ as $\int_{3/2}^{3} f(x)dx$, and (3) correct computation of $\text{Prob}(X > \frac{3}{2})$, either by direct analysis of the graph or by computation of $\int_{3/2}^{2}(2 - x)dx + \int_{2}^{3}(x - 2)dx$. Of the 36 subjects, 33 (91.7%) correctly graphed the probability density function, and 32 (88.9%) had both the correct graph and the correct formulation of $\text{Prob}(X > \frac{3}{2})$. However, only 14 of these 32 students correctly computed this probability—10 by integration and four by direct graphical analysis. The other 18 students incorrectly integrated the function, many of them "ignoring" the absolute value signs. There was no evidence of graphical interpretation of any kind on any of the 18 incorrect papers.

To be sure, if students are asked for a graphical interpretation of a definite integral, "area under the curve" is the overwhelmingly most common response. However, consideration of the results of this study warns us that a student's ability to parrot a phrase from lecture does not imply that the student can use that interpretation in a meaningful way to solve a problem.

A Framework for Multiple Representations— The Work of Claude Janvier

Janvier's work on representations is particularly relevant to implementing a multiple representation approach to the abstract concept of function, and it beautifully anticipated the "Rule of Four" idea. Janvier used a 4 x 4 table to illustrate the translation processes between different representations of a situation. Figure 10.3 is adapted from his chapter "Translation Processes in Mathematics Education" in his book *Problems of Representation in the Teaching and Learning of Mathematics* (Janvier, 1987, p. 29).

For example, in translating from a graphic representation to a symbolic representation (formula), one could fit a curve to a given graph. In moving from a physical situation to a tabular representation, one could gather paired measurements and compile them. For the purposes of curriculum guidance in calculus, we view Janvier's table as applied to the "situation" presented by an abstract function. How can we re-present that abstraction in various forms (formulae, graphs, tables, words)? How can we translate from one of those forms to another? What are the inherent limitations and advantages of each form?

An examination of traditional curricula reveals an overwhelming emphasis on working with symbolic forms, and any translations among representations in those curricula tend to start with symbolic forms and move to tables and/or graphs. Janvier's table provides a useful framework for curricular development, drawing attention to the richer set of mathematical tasks necessary to truly adopt a multiple representation approach. (Later in this chapter we will suggest some possible modifications to this framework.) Note that reversing the direction of a translation between function representations is not simply a matter of "inverting" the steps in an algorithm. Each of the activities Janvier identifies in his table has its own unique set of cognitive skills and understandings associated with it. At the same time as calculus curriculum reform efforts intensified, so did research on translation processes between representations, particularly

To From	Situations, Verbal Description	Tables	Graphs	Formulae
Situations, Verbal Description		Measuring	Sketching	Modelling
Tables	Reading		Plotting	Fitting
Graphs	Interpretation	Reading off		Curve Fitting
Formulae	Parameter Recognition	Computing	Sketching	

Figure 10.3. Janvier's 4 × 4 table of translation processes between representations.

those involving moves to and from graphical representations (see Leinhardt, Zaslavsky, & Stein, 1990; Romberg, Fennema, & Carpenter, 1993).

It is tempting to add diagonal entries to Janvier's 4 × 4 table to also indicate activities or transformations within a representation. Figure 10.4 shows such an augmented table of representational processes. In the language of this table, taking a multiple representation approach to calculus means moving from activities dominated by those in the bottom row and including activities from throughout the grid.

Local Linearity and Local Straightness—Tall's Cognitive Root

Notion of a Cognitive Root

Tall (1992) uses the term cognitive root to refer to an idea that can be used as a basis for mathematical concept building. According to Tall, a cognitive root must have the attributes of being developmentally appropriate while also having long-term mathematical relevance. It is the naive or "common sense" idea behind what later becomes a more precise and formal mathematical concept. In his chapter "The Transition to Advanced Mathematical Thinking: Functions, Limits, Infinity, and Proof"

From \ To	Situations, Verbal Description	Tables	Graphs	Formulae
Situations, Verbal Description	Rewording	Measuring	Sketching	Modelling
Tables	Reading	Data Transforming	Plotting	Fitting
Graphs	Interpretation	Reading off	Rescaling	Curve Fitting
Formulae	Parameter Recognition	Computing	Sketching	Algebraic Manipulation

Figure 10.4.   A 4 × 4 table of translation and transformation processes for representations.

(Tall, 1992) in the *Handbook of Research on Mathematics Teaching and Learning* (Grouws, 1992), Tall asserts the importance of cognitive roots:

> A cognitive root is different from a mathematical foundation; whereas a mathematical foundation is an appropriate starting point for a logical development of the subject, a cognitive root is more appropriate for curriculum development. (p. 497)

Local Straightness as a Cognitive Root for Derivative

The usual introduction to the concept of derivative in calculus involves a sequence of secant lines to a function graph (i.e., lines determined by two points on the graph) converging to a unique tangent line (provided, of course, that the function is differentiable). Close to the point of tangency, the tangent line is a good approximation to the original function graph; and very close to the point of tangency, the tangent line is almost indistinguishable from the function graph. (How close are "close" and "very close"? These are relative terms depending on the function and point of tangency.) It is this property of differentiability that Tall proposes to exploit as a cognitive root, namely, over suitably small intervals a differentiable function graph appears straight (and in contrast, non-differentiable functions fail in some way to "straighten out" upon magnification).

The Calculus Connections project pursued the idea of local linearity in developing its curriculum, examining its implications in its approach to topics involving differentiable functions. From the highly visual notion of local straightness as a cognitive root, one can introduce analytic consequences through a more mathematical notion of approximate local linearity. This strategy is also consistent with the multiple representation approach, for it provided a way to repeatedly appeal directly to a simple but powerful graphical interpretation of an analytic definition.

ROLE OF TECHNOLOGY

For both the multiple representation approach to function and the cognitive root of local straightness there were existing theoretical frameworks from mathematics education research for guiding the efforts of calculus curriculum developers, especially efforts to make sensible use of technology.

CAS as Representational Toolkit

A computer algebra system or graphing calculator provides a toolkit for creating numerical tables, plots of function graphs, and possibly some facility for manipulating symbols in formulae. As such it can be viewed as a means of moving between representations of a function that provide new opportunities for students to develop the translation processes that Janvier discusses. Figure 10.5 illustrates how common features found in a CAS package or a graphing calculator provide technological tools that can aid in "Rule of Three" translations. Special software, such as Function Probe (see Confrey & Maloney, 2008, for a discussion of Function Probe), would even allow some movement from Graphic to Symbolic (the missing arrow in Figure 10.5).

Perhaps the most profound curricular shift that the technology facilitates in terms of representations is in making a table of function values or a graph of a function a feasible starting point in approaching a mathematical problem. Indeed, one could argue that the "real world" rarely presents functions to us in any other way. If assessment is overly dominated by tasks presenting symbolic formulae, students can become conditioned to see that as the only "legitimate" means of specifying a function.

Tall and Vinner (cf. Tall & Vinner, 1981; Vinner, 1983; Vinner & Dreyfus, 1989) use the term *compartmentalization* to capture such self-imposed cognitive restrictions that students create. Hart (1992) used Tall and Vinner's concept image framework in a study comparing students using the

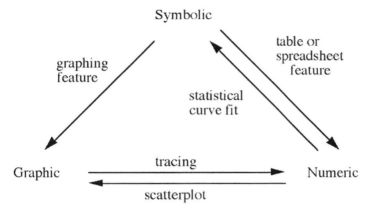

Figure 10.5.   Technology aids to representational translations.

Calculus Connections curriculum with students using a "traditional" calculus curriculum. She found that even very good students using a traditional curriculum were often at a loss when presented with a task that involved working directly with a function graph for which they were not provided a formula. For example, when presented with the graph of a derivative $y = f'(x)$ and asked to sketch a possible graph of $y = f(x)$, these students struggled with the absence of a specific algebraic formulation that could be manipulated. Some students would go so far as to claim that the task was ill-posed and did not present enough information. The best of the students managed some success on the task by (a) introducing an algebraic formulation of a function that shared some of the attributes of the given graph, (b) formally manipulating this formulation using symbolic rules for antidifferentiation, and (c) sketching the graph of this result. While this was a mathematically defensible strategy, it was clearly not nearly as efficient as using the graphical slope information that was directly presented. In contrast, students with experience in dealing with multiple representations of functions had much less difficulty.

Bringing Local Linearity Alive Through Technology

A cognitive root can provide both a powerful organizational theme for a concept image as well as a foundation for intuitive reasoning. Tall's notion of local straightness as a good cognitive root for derivative can be exploited in curriculum and instruction through graphing technology. The usual graphical introduction of the idea of a locally linear approximation makes use of an additional geometric construct, the tangent line to a graph.

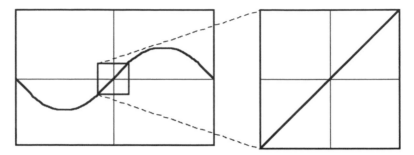

Figure 10.6. Zooming in to see local linearity.

However, a much simpler way to illustrate the idea of local linearity is to just zoom in on the graph of the function (with equal scale factors horizontally and vertically)[2] as illustrated in Figure 10.6. Repeated magnifications of a differentiable function's graph centered at a particular point reveal quite strikingly this *characteristic property* of differentiability without the extra cognitive burden of dealing with the additional notion of a tangent line. (To be sure, we consider the tangent line to be still a very important topic to be developed, but here we are talking about the student's first introduction to the idea of derivative and how the nature of local linearity can be powerfully and simply demonstrated.)

We want to emphasize that this illustration of using zooming to introduce a graphical interpretation of derivative is not just a flashy device to be employed once at the beginning of differential calculus. A cognitive root should have an appeal that can be drawn on for insight—a "hook" to which to return time and again and on which to hang new encounters with its manifestations.

A New Look at an Old Rule

It is a relatively simple algebra exercise to note that if two (nonvertical) lines both cross the *x*-axis at the same point *a*, then the ratio of the ordinates at any other point $b \neq a$ will be the same as the ratio of the slopes of the two lines. Now consider the same observation applied to the graphs of two differentiable functions with a common zero. In light of local linearity, the simple algebra exercise can become a compelling motivation for L'Hôpital's rule (Figure 10.7).

Slope Fields

In making the transition from differential to integral calculus and ultimately the Fundamental Theorem of Calculus, local linearity can be used to provide a highly visual means to thinking qualitatively about antideriv-

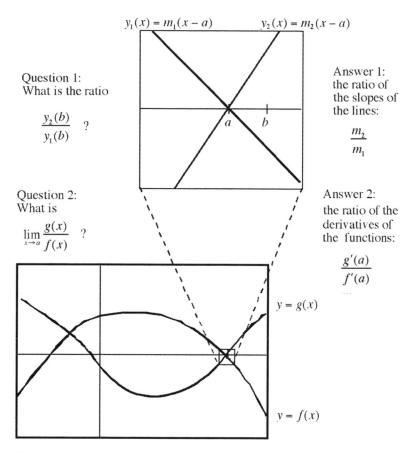

Question 1:
What is the ratio

$$\frac{y_2(b)}{y_1(b)} \ ?$$

Answer 1:
the ratio of
the slopes of
the lines:

$$\frac{m_2}{m_1}$$

Question 2:
What is

$$\lim_{x \to a} \frac{g(x)}{f(x)} \ ?$$

Answer 2:
the ratio of the
derivatives of
the functions:

$$\frac{g'(a)}{f'(a)}$$

Figure 10.7.   Local linearity and L'Hôpital's Rule.

atives (and more generally, solutions to differential equations). The mathematical statement of the antiderivative problem is:

Given $\frac{dy}{dx} = f(x)$, find functions of the form $y = F(x)$ satisfying $F'(x) = f(x)$.

In bringing local linearity to bear on the problem, we can recognize that the derivative provides us with abundant information about the *local slope* of the graph of $y = F(x)$ If the point (x, y) is on the graph of F, then we can visualize at least a very small part of the graph—namely, the graph should look like a straight line passing through (x, y) with slope given by $f(x)$. A *slope field* is generated by taking this idea and exploiting it for a grid or lattice of points. The result is a mosaic of small local pictures that

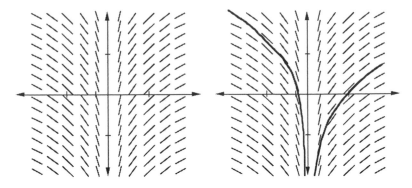

Figure 10.8.   A slope field for $\frac{dy}{dx} = \frac{1}{x}$ and possible solution curves.

when viewed globally can provide powerful visual cues to the shape of the graph of the antiderivative F. Figure 10.8 illustrates a slope field generated by the differential equation $\frac{dy}{dx} = \frac{1}{x}$ along with some candidates for the graphs of an antiderivative. While simple, the procedure can be somewhat tedious to perform by hand but carrying out such simple, repetitive procedures is a natural candidate for the use of technology.[3] Newer versions of graphing calculators have included slope field features, indicating the reciprocal influence that curriculum development has had on software designers.

A New Look at an Old relationship

It is not hard to extend the use of slope fields to more general differential equations of the form $\frac{dy}{dx} = G(x, y)$, where $G(x, y)$ could be any expression in x and y. New insights into old relationships are possible by taking advantage of this technique. For example, the fundamental differential equations underlying exponential growth and decay are of the form $\frac{dy}{dx} = ky$, where k is a constant.

The most natural case to consider is when $k = 1$: $\frac{dy}{dx} = y$. Figure 10.9 shows slope fields for both $\frac{dy}{dx} = \frac{1}{x}$ and $\frac{dy}{dx} = y$ side by side. Note that one slope field could be obtained from the other by reflecting across the line $y = x$. This suggests that solutions to these two differential equations might enjoy some special relationship.

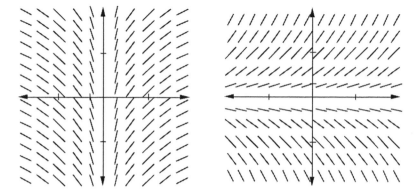

Figure 10.9. Slope fields for $\frac{dy}{dx} = \frac{1}{x}$ and $\frac{dy}{dx} = y$.

A Glimpse to the Future: Revisiting Janvier— A Fifth Representation?

Janvier seems to have considered contextual "situations" to be inter-twined with verbal representations. For example, to translate from a graphical representation to a physical situation, one would interpret in words how the physical circumstances are reflected in the graphical behavior. In this final section, we look to future uses of technology in teaching calculus and suggest that it is reasonable to think of physical sit-uations as a fifth representation. Microcomputer-based and calculator-based laboratory probes and virtual computer environments introduce a new set of representational possibilities, in which a physical situation is directly monitored or even driven by the technology in ways that allow for direct examination of the connection to other representations. Thus, we suggest that one could think of the physical embodiment of an abstract mathematical concept as being itself a representation.

In calculus, a function $y = f(x)$ may be presented in terms of dependent and independent variables having no units of measurement. The idea of the derivative as capturing the "instantaneous" rate of change of the dependent variable with respect to the independent variable suggests that we metaphorically endow the dimensionless variables with units, most notably the independent variable with units of time. Indeed, Monk (1988) notes that a key shift in students' understanding of function that must take place in calculus is to move from a pointwise perspective of function to an "across time" perspective (i.e., from function value at a point to function behavior over intervals of points). Adopting this view for the

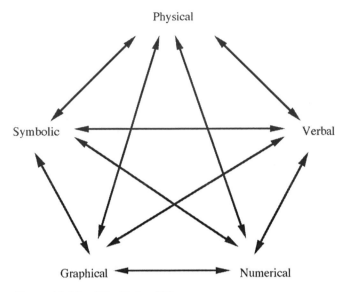

Figure 10.10.   The Rule of Five.

moment, and positing new translation moves to and from this fifth representation, we offer the multiple representation model in Figure 10.10, in which each arrow represents a translational move from one representation to another. One might ask if all of these arrowheads even make sense. For example, we can imagine moving directly from a physical representation to a table or graph using a data collection probe paired with appropriate software. This is exactly the situation afforded by the use of microcomputer-based laboratories (MBLs) or calculator-based laboratories (CBLs): Consider the activity of a student altering her walking pattern while being tracked by a motion detector hooked up to a real-time graphical display of position, velocity, or acceleration. A change made in the physical situation results in corresponding changes in the table or graph and provides a fertile field for discussion of the meanings of these connections in terms of calculus.

But what would it mean to make a graphical transformation and have that translate to a real-time change in a physical situation? We submit that this is exactly the type of activity captured in the work of researchers such as Kaput in his SimCalc work (see the Web site http://www .simcalc.umassd.edu/[4] and Kaput & Schorr, 2008) or Nemirovsky, Tierney, and Wright (1998) in their work at TERC. On the horizon there are new uses of stylus-based computer technology allowing students to directly manipulate function graphs on touch-sensitive screens while viewing real-time changes in the symbolic and tabular representations. These new technological advances in educational software and hardware are providing exciting ways to incorporate a multiple representation approach to the concept of function more fully in curriculum and instruction. The translational processes suggested by the arrows of the Rule of Five diagram may also provide researchers with a framework for investigating students' development of representational knowledge, both in terms of procedural facility and conceptual connections.

NOTES

1. The authors wish to express sincere appreciation for the helpful comments and critiques received on an earlier draft of this chapter when it was discussed at the Research on Technology and the Teaching and Learning of Mathematics Conference held on the campus of The Pennsylvania State University.
2. It would be just as erroneous to label "traditional" calculus as if it were a monolithic, universally recognized standard. Nevertheless, a number of methodologically ill-conceived treatment/control studies were conducted purporting to judge the effects of "reform" versus "traditional" calculus.
3. It is critically important that equal scale factors be used in zooming for illustrations of local linearity. "Square zooms," as we suggest they be called, preserve scale in a way that does not distort slope. For example, repeated zooming in with a horizontal factor that exceeds the vertical factor will result in a continuous function's graph (such as the absolute value function) appearing to be horizontal. However, using square zooms cannot straighten out the sharp corner in the graph of $y = |x|$.
4. We do suggest that it is instructive to have students create a few simple slope fields by hand.
5. Retrieved January 15, 2006.

REFERENCES

Bell, A., & Janvier, C. (1981). The interpretation of graphs representing situations. *For the Learning of Mathematics, 1*, 34-42.

Confrey, J., & Maloney, A. (2008). Research-design interactions in building function probe software. In G. W. Blume & M. K. Heid (Eds.), *Research on technology and the teaching and learning of mathematics: Vol. 2. Cases and perspectives* (pp. 183-210). Charlotte, NC: Information Age.

Dick, T. P. (1988). The development of graphical sense. *Sixth International Congress on Mathematical Education: Abstracts of short communications, 1. Oral presentations*. Budapest, Hungary: International Commission on Mathematical Instruction.

Dick, T. P., & Patton, C. M. (1993). *Calculus*. Boston: International Thomson.

Douglas, R. G. (Ed.). (1986). *Toward a lean and lively calculus, MAA Notes 6*. Washington, DC: Mathematical Association of America.

Eisenberg, T., & Dreyfus, T. (1990). On the reluctance to visualize in mathematics. In W. Zimmerman & S. Cunningham (Eds.), *Visualization in teaching and learning mathematics, MAA Notes 19* (pp. 25-37). Washington, DC: Mathematical Association of America.

Goldin, G. A. (1998). Representational systems, learning, and problem solving in mathematics. *Journal of Mathematical Behavior, 17*, 135-165.

Goldenberg, P. (1988). Mathematics, metaphors, and human factors: Mathematical, technical, and pedagogical challenges in the educational use of graphical representations of functions. *Journal of Mathematical Behavior, 7*, 135-173.

Grouws, D. A. (Ed.). (1992). *Handbook of research on mathematics teaching and learning*. New York: Macmillan.

Hart, D. K. (1992). *Building concept images–Supercalculators and students' use of multiple representations in calculus*. Unpublished doctoral dissertation, Oregon State University, Portland.

Heid, M. K. (1988). Resequencing skills and concepts in applied calculus using the computer as a tool. *Journal for Research in Mathematics Education, 19*, 3-25.

Hiebert, J., & Lefevre, P. (1986). Conceptual and procedural knowledge in mathematics: An introductory analysis. In J. Hiebert (Ed.), *Conceptual and procedural knowledge: The case of mathematics* (pp. 1-27). Hillsdale, NJ: Erlbaum.

Hughes-Hallett, D., Gleason, A. M., McCallum, W., Lomen, D., Lovelock, D., Pasquale, A., et al. (1994). *Calculus*. Toronto, Canada: Wall & Emerson.

Janvier, C. (1987). Translation processes in mathematics education. In C. Janvier (Ed.), *Problems of representation in the teaching and learning of mathematics* (pp. 27-32). Hillsdale, NJ: Erlbaum.

Kaput, J., & Schorr, R. (2008). Changing representational infrastructures changes most everything: The case of SimCalc, algebra, and calculus. In G. W. Blume & M. K. Heid (Eds.), *Research on technology and the teaching and learning of mathematics: Vol. 2. Cases and perspectives* (pp. 211-254). Charlotte, NC: Information Age.

Krutetskii, V. A. (1976). *The psychology of mathematical abilities in schoolchildren* (J. Teller, Trans., J. Kilpatrick & I. Wirzup, Eds.). Chicago: University of Chicago.

Leinhardt, G., Zaslavsky, O., & Stein, M. K. (1990). Functions, graphs, and graphing: Tasks, learning, and teaching. *Review of Educational Research, 60*, 1-64.

Monk, G. S. (1994, February). Students' understanding of functions in calculus courses. *Humanistic Mathematics Network Journal, 9*, 21-27.

National Council of Teachers of Mathematics. (1989). *Curriculum and evaluation standards for school mathematics*. Reston, VA: Author.

Nemirovsky, R., Tierney, C., & Wright, T. (1998). Body motion and graphing. *Cognition and Instruction, 16*, 119-172.

Palmiter, J. (1991). Effects of computer algebra systems on concept and skill acquisition in calculus. *Journal for Research in Mathematics Education, 22*, 151-156.

Romberg, T., Fennema, E., & Carpenter, T. (Eds.). (1993). *Integrating research on the graphical representation of functions*. Hillsdale, NJ: Erlbaum.

Schoenfeld, A. H. (1990). GRAPHER: A case study in educational technology, research, and development. In A. diSessa, M. Gardner, J. Greeno, F. Reif, A. H. Schoenfeld, & E. State (Eds.), *Toward a scientific practice of science education* (pp. 281-300). Hillsdale, NJ: Erlbaum.

Steen, L. A. (Ed.). (1988). *Calculus for a new century: A pump not a filter. Mathematical Association of America Notes 8.* Washington, DC: Mathematical Association of America.

Tall, D. (1992). The transition to advanced mathematical thinking: Functions, limits, infinity, and proof. In D. A. Grouws (Ed.), *Handbook of research on mathematics teaching and learning* (pp. 495-511). New York: Macmillan.

Tall, D., & Vinner, S. (1981). Concept image and concept definition in mathematics with particular reference to limits and continuity. *Educational Studies in Mathematics, 12,* 151-169.

Vinner, S. (1983). Concept definition, concept image and the notion of function. *International Journal of Mathematical Education in Science and Technology, 14,* 293-305.

Vinner, S., & Dreyfus, T. (1989). Images and definitions for the concept of function. *Journal for Research in Mathematics Education, 20,* 356-366.

PART II

PERSPECTIVES

CHAPTER 11

THE RESEARCH FRONTIER

Where Technology Interacts With the Teaching and Learning of Data Analysis and Statistics

Susan N. Friel

Data analysis and statistics[1] have emerged as major topics in primary and secondary school (K–12) mathematics curricula during the 1990s (National Council of Teachers of Mathematics, NCTM, 1989, 2000). Statistics—a discipline addressed primarily at the postsecondary level prior to the *Curriculum and Evaluation Standards for School Mathematics* (NCTM, 1989)—has lacked definition at the kindergarten through 12th grade (K–12) levels. The lack of clarity about what content to address has resulted in initial work focusing on how to take traditional statistics and translate the content—or more specifically, techniques—for use with younger students. Instructional practices have not been well defined. Increased attention has been given by researchers and curriculum developers to setting better directions for what K–12 students need to know and be able to do with respect to data analysis and statistics and with respect to defining the nature of instruction needed to support these directions.

Research on Technology and the Teaching and Learning of Mathematics:
Vol. 2. Cases and Perspectives, 279–331
Copyright © 2008 by Information Age Publishing
All rights of reproduction in any form reserved.

More recently, new directions have arisen from the interaction of technology with efforts to redefine both the content and instructional practices regarding data analysis and statistics in K–12. Educational technology affords a greater variety of strategies for *teaching* statistics and, at the same time, offers new ways of *doing* statistics (Garfield & Burrill, 1997). Today, computers, software, and the Internet are essential tools for practice in this domain. As a new content area with this kind of technological support is incorporated into school mathematics curricula, the definition and teaching of this content area must be grounded in research.

This chapter provides an overview related to this need by addressing the following questions:

Section I: Content Recommendations and Technological Enhancements

- What should students in grades K–12 know and be able to do with respect to statistics and data analysis?
- In what ways can technological tools be used to enhance learning statistics and data analysis?

Section II: Research and Teaching and Learning of Statistics and Data Analysis

- What is known from ongoing literature about clarifying the interactions between software use and the teaching and learning of the recommended content in data analysis and statistics in grades K–12?

Section III: Research Agenda for Statistics Education and the Use of Technology

- What knowledge is needed about the interaction of technology with the teaching and learning of content in data analysis and statistics in grades K–12 to provide directions for an ongoing research agenda?

CONTENT RECOMMENDATIONS
AND TECHNOLOGICAL ENHANCEMENT

In addressing statistics and data analysis education in grades K–12, we need to clarify what content is to be taught and learned. The clearer we are about what it is we want students to know, understand, and be able to do, the better able we will be to articulate what we need to know (research) about their initial knowledge and their growth in knowledge over time with respect to this content. The use of technology is an important piece of this puzzle. Again, developing a perspective on its applications in teaching and learning statistics and data analysis is needed in order to be able to identify research directions.

Content Recommendations

Statistics, stochastics, data analysis, data handling—whatever the name—is a vital, albeit relatively new, part of U.S. mathematics curricula in grades K–12. Since the publication of the *Curriculum and Evaluation Standards* (NCTM, 1989), statistics and probability have become recognized topics in K–12 curricula. (See Appendix A for a description of efforts to establish a direction for the content of statistics education.) Before 1989, most statistics and probability coursework and research occurred at the postsecondary levels, and research focused primarily on the understanding of probability concepts (Shaughnessy, 1992; Shaughnessy, Garfield, & Greer, 1996). More recently, the *Principles and Standards for School Mathematics* (*PSSM*) (NCTM, 2000) provided broad standards grounded in research (Konold & Higgins, 2003) for a data analysis and probability strand for pre-kindergarten through 12th grades (preK–12):

Instructional programs from preK–12 should enable students to:

- formulate questions that can be addressed with data and collect, organize, and display relevant data to answer them;
- select and use appropriate statistical methods to analyze data;
- develop and evaluate inferences and predications that are based on data; and
- understand and apply basic concepts of probability (NCTM, 2000, p. 48).

PSSM (NCTM, 2000) contains recommendations about specific expectations for each of four grade ranges (preK–2, 3–5, 6–8, 9–12). Scheaffer (2000, 2002) summarizes additional recommendations for content across K–12 curricula from the NAEP 2004 Framework[2] and adds his own suggestions. Finally, content recommendations from the NAEP 2005 Framework (National Assessment Governing Board, 2004) are available. There is general agreement among the various sets of recommendations. In the elementary grades, there is an emphasis on a process of statistical investigation, on using and constructing data representations, including line plots, pictographs, bar graphs, and tables, and on describing characteristics of data sets using measures of center (median and mode) and spread (range). In the middle grades, emphasis continues on these topics, with more sophisticated uses of data representations, including histograms, line graphs, box plots, and frequency distributions, and more sophisticated ways of describing characteristics of data sets using all three measures of center (mean, median, and mode), additional measures of spread (range, interquartile range, and outliers) and their relationships to the shape of a distribution. Students at this level also are introduced to the concepts of association and sampling. At the high school level, students continue and deepen their work with ideas begun in middle grades at more sophisticated levels. They regularly work with both univariate and bivariate data situations, with covariation and correlation, and with distinctions between sample statistics and population statistics. The content at this level is characterized by an emphasis on simulation and modeling and the integration of data analysis with other areas of mathematics such as algebra.

While *PSSM* and other documents set directions for the content at K-12, there is need for greater elaboration in order to provide sufficient detail so that a cohesive and coherent curriculum strand can be articulated (Franklin et al., 2005). A "fleshing out" of the *PSSM* Statistics and Data Analysis Standards is being provided through the work of a subcommittee of the American Statistical Association (ASA). The document, currently in draft form, is titled *A Curriculum Framework for Pre-K–12 Statistics Education* (Franklin et al., 2005). The main content of the framework is divided into three levels, labeled A, B, and C. While naming these as levels instead of grade ranges, the authors intend that they be somewhat equivalent to elementary (Pre-K–5), middle (6–8), and secondary (9–12) designations. However, the Framework levels are based on experience, not age. So, for example, middle school students with no prior experience (or no rich experiences) with statistics will need to begin with Level A concepts and activities before moving to Level B. This holds true for secondary students as well.

How might work in data analysis at these different levels look? The authors offer a number of examples. One way to think about the levels is in terms of the nature of the statistical investigations in which students might engage. Distinctions are drawn about the depth of understanding and sophistication of methods used across the levels. For example, Level A students may collect data to answer questions about their class (take a census of their classroom). Level B students may collect data to answer questions about their school (making a transition to using a simple random sample within the school). Finally, Level C students may collect data to answer questions about the community and then use statistics to model the relationships they notice between, say, housing prices and geographic variables such as the location of schools.

The authors seek to articulate with more detail the expected development of a concept at each level. For example, when thinking about the mean, we might think about models being used and relationships to conceptual ideas being emphasized.

Level A: The mean is conceptualized as using fair shares or evening out, thus providing a model for the algorithm and foreshadowing the conceptualization of the mean as a balance point in a distribution.

Level B: The mean is conceptualized as a balance point or "fulcrum" in a distribution; this conceptualization helps focus attention on the relationship between shape of a distribution and location of the mean when the distribution is represented graphically.

Level C: The mean is conceptualized as an estimate of a population mean, determined from a sample and used to make an inference about a population; this focuses attention on understanding the concepts of sampling distribution and using data from a sample to estimate the population mean.

Clearly, this kind of elaboration, if done well, will help in detailing the content more specifically across levels.

There are several big ideas in data analysis and statistics that can benefit from having this level of elaboration specified. Of primary importance is *doing statistics*.[3] Statistical analysis is an investigatory activity characterized as an iterative, four-stage process that includes asking a question, collecting the data, analyzing the data, and forming and communicating conclusions (Friel & Joyner, 1997; Franklin et al., 2005; Konold & Higgins, 2003). The process of data analysis is dynamic with ongoing interactions among the various stages occurring throughout the process. Beyond *doing statistics*, there are several other big ideas related to statistics and data analysis that must be considered (see Appendix B).

Central to work within data analysis and statistics is the need to focus on statistical reasoning and thinking. Traditional approaches to teaching and learning statistics involve an emphasis on skills, procedures, and computations without a resulting competence in knowing how to reason or think statistically (Ben-Zvi & Garfield, 2004a; Chance, 2002; Garfield, 2002; Rumsey, 2002). Ben-Zvi and Garfield (2004a) characterize statistical reasoning "as the way people reason with statistical ideas and make sense of statistical information" (p. 7).

This involves making interpretations based on sets of data, representations of data, or statistical summaries of data. Statistical reasoning may involve connecting one concept to another (e.g., center and spread), or it may combine ideas about data and chance. Reasoning means understanding and being able to explain statistical processes and being able to fully interpret statistical results. (p. 7)

Thus, learning statistics includes two central components: the concepts and conventions of the discipline itself (Konold, 2002a) and the ability to apply this knowledge in a broader, more flexible, and skeptical manner when interpreting and/or communicating results obtained by statistical analysis. There appears to be a kind of "statistical gestalt" in reasoning and thinking that is both difficult to capture descriptively and challenging to learn.

While statistics has entered school curricula via the route of mathematics instruction, there is considerable debate about whether statistics is part of mathematics. delMas (2004) provides a very thorough analysis and comparison of mathematical and statistical reasoning. Gal and Garfield (1997a; Garfield, 2003) suggest a number of key differences between mathematics and statistics as disciplines, including two points that seem important to highlight here:

1. Context matters: Data are viewed as numbers with a context. In statistics, unlike mathematics, the context motivates procedures and is the source of meaning and basis for interpretation of results of such activities.

2. Ambiguity exists: A primary goal of statistics education is to enable students to be able to render reasoned descriptions, judgments, inferences, and opinions about data, or argue about the interpretation of data, using various mathematical tools only to the degree needed. [Unlike mathematics,] judgments and inferences expected of students often cannot be characterized as "right" or "wrong." Rather they need to be evaluated in terms of the quality of the reasoning, adequacy of methods employed, and the nature of data and evidence used (Gal & Garfield, 1997a, p. 6).

There is strong consensus that statistics is a practical subject, students need to become competent in carrying out statistical investigations, and people, in general, need to be "intelligent consumer(s) of data" (Schaeffer, Watkins, & Landwehr, 1998, as cited in Greer, 2000a, p. 6).

Technology Enhancements

The use of technology is included in the earlier-noted recommendations, but assumptions about its appropriate use and availability to support teaching and learning in the past have been limited by vision, versatility of software, and accessibility to hardware. Most school-appropriate technology tools used for data analysis and statistics fall into the category of spreadsheet software (e.g., Appleworks, Excel) or graphing tools (e.g., graphing calculator; DeltaGraph, 2005) that offer similar functions, including plotting, graphing, and analysis capabilities. Further, these kinds of software restrict the user to conventional displays and emphasize numerical over categorical data. Graphs, tables, and plots are treated as static end products rather than as dynamic aids to inquiry (Hancock, 2002). Some sources for information about the kinds, needs, and changes in statistics and data analysis software options available over the past 10 years include: Biehler (1994, 1997a); Garfield, Chance, and Snell (2001); Huntley, Zucker, and Esty (2000); and Shaughnessy et al. (1996). More recently, tools have been developed that are more dynamic and are able to support inquiry of a kind not possible with earlier software tools (e.g., TinkerPlots, Konold & Miller, 2005; Tabletop, 1995; Fathom, Finzer, 2005).

With the increased capabilities and availability of technological tools, it is important to consider what uses may be most appropriate in facilitating students' learning of statistics. Ben-Zvi (2000) describes how technological data tools are now being designed to support data analysis and statistics learning by engaging students actively in constructing knowledge by both "doing" and "seeing" statistics. In addition, students have opportunities to reflect on observed phenomena and on their own thought processes.

School-appropriate, technology-based data tools that are now being used in data analysis and statistics instruction fall into the following categories:

1. *Statistical packages* for analyzing data and constructing visual representations of data. Examples include:

    (a) *Spreadsheets* (e.g., AppleWorks, Excel, StatTools: Statistics for Excel, 2005) which have plotting, graphing, and analysis capability, with focus on the use of a set of conventional displays that support graphing numerical over categorical data. These programs automatically generate graphs with default assignments of attributes to axes; there is limited control available to the user.

    (b) *Graphing tools* (e.g., DeltaGraph) offer a range of functions similar to spreadsheets but are removed from the spreadsheet context. Like spreadsheets, these programs treat graphs and plots as relatively inert end products; again, the user has limited control of the structure and how the final product looks.

   (c) *Data analysis tools* (e.g., Fathom, Tabletop, TinkerPlots) pro-
      vide greater flexibility than spreadsheets or graphing tools for
      analysis and visualization, and they facilitate inquiry as a pro-
      cess. They support opportunities for in-depth inquiry in sta-
      tistics and data analysis through statistical and plotting
      capabilities that give the user greater overall control in struc-
      turing and representing data.

2. *Web-based or computer-based applets*, including simulations, to demonstrate and visualize statistical concepts. Applets may be characterized as "little applications"—single-purpose computer
programs—designed to enhance learning. They can provide a
visual approach and more active learning that can improve the
effectiveness of teaching (Bakker, 2002; Bright, Brewer, McClain, &
Mooney, 2003; Darius, Michiels, & Raymaekers, 2002; Mittag,
2002; Tinker, 1996).

3. *Graphing calculators* for computation, graphing or simulation.
These calculators allow students to work when and where they
choose and to experiment with data representation and analysis.
While the student has limited control over structure and look of
final products, he or she has easy and immediate access to statistical power (Burrill, 2002; Herweyers, 2002).

4. *Internet browsing* for access to data and information. More of a
resource than a tool, the Internet provides a vast and growing
library that students can access for all kinds of material, in particular, data. The user needs to be aware that some information on the
Internet may be misleading or simply wrong. Often it is "undi-
gested," that is, raw data that requires careful study, sorting, and
manipulating in order to organize it into a useful form. The data
may also be biased; students need to develop ways to assess what
they extract from the Internet (Tinker, 1996).

Bakker (2002) has articulated the need to distinguish between software
used to *do* statistics and data analysis work and software used to *learn* the
content and process of statistics and data analysis. He observes that professional statistical software packages are not suitable for use by students
when they are learning data analysis.[4] He argues that a user cannot
choose among histograms, box plots, or circle graphs if he or she does
not yet understand what these representations are and when they would
be useful. The creation of special software (e.g., applets and data analysis
tools previously noted) designed to enhance learning suggests that software designers are developing some knowledge about the critical issues of
learning data analysis and statistics in the classroom and the ways technol-

ogy can assist. The intent of these tools "is to allow students to start with what they can invent themselves and work towards the use of more conventional graphs and statistical notions" (Bakker, 2002, p. 1).

Bakker (2002) takes on the challenge of characterizing the distinctions between the use of a well-designed set of computer applets and the use of a well-designed software package, both of which are intended to support the learning of data analysis. He characterizes the former as "route-type" software (e.g., Minitools 1 to 3 designed, in part, to focus students' attention on the overarching notion of distributions represented graphically using a single type of plot in each of the Minitools[5] [Cobb, 1999]) and the latter as "landscape-type" software (e.g., TinkerPlots designed as a construction tool that offers students many possibilities for making their own often-unconventional graphs).

The Minitools were designed to support an explicit learning trajectory that influences the development of activities designed to guide students in reinventing conventional plots such as value bar graphs, dot plots, histograms, and scatter plots (see also McClain, Cobb, & Gravemeijer, 2005). In teaching experiments, problems were typically solved using one Minitool, with a single type of plot that was thought to be meaningful for students at that stage of the hypothesized learning trajectory (Bakker & Gravemeijer, 2004; Cobb, 1999; McClain et al., 2005).

TinkerPlots is a flexible, multipurpose software package with a number of options and actions. For example, students can separate, stack, and order data vertically and horizontally. They can make a variety of representations beyond those found in conventional software packages like spreadsheets. Students can switch between different representations without having to use a different tool (which is not an option with the Minitools). They can also switch between plots that represent individual case data values (e.g., dot plots) and plots that allow aggregation of cases (e.g., histograms, pie charts). The design of TinkerPlots does not assume a particular learning trajectory as do the Minitools. Rather it resembles a landscape that allows many routes while the Minitools accommodate specific routes that focus on just one type of plot thought to be meaningful for students at the given stage of learning (Bakker, 2002).

Such a distinction is not trivial. On the one hand, as Bakker (2002) discusses, there are reasons to want the Minitools to be a bit more flexible and connected in design so students might move among representations more fluidly. On the other hand, Bakker (2002) points out that the flexibility and options available with TinkerPlots and the multiplicity of learning routes might lead to an unworkable number of possibilities, making it difficult for teachers to support students in the variety of explorations that can emerge when investigating a problem using TinkerPlots. Bakker (2002) suggests that software like the Minitools is particularly helpful when the goal is to guide students toward understanding specific statistical notions, such as graphs (in this case). TinkerPlots may be more appropriate when the goal is broadly defined as genuine data analysis with multivariate data sets.

Roy Pea's (1987) characterization of computers as cognitive tools that serve as amplifiers and reorganizers of the human mind has provided a useful structure to thinking about computer use in statistics instruction as well. Cognition tends to be situated in context; cognitive development involves both the individual mind and the development of knowledge through socially structured activities. With this distinction in mind, Ben-Zvi (2000) applies Pea's characterizations of educational uses of technology to the teaching of statistics. Ben-Zvi's list is consistent with earlier characterizations of the potential effects of technology in a range of other areas of mathematics (Fey et al., 1984):

1. *Technology is an amplifier of statistical power*: In learning environments that are not based on the use of technological tools, graphs or tables are either presented to students or constructed by students according to prescriptive instructions. The resulting representations are often identical for students learning in the same class. The focus on instruction is on translation skills between representations with mastery of these skills being the goal. With the use of multirepresentational technological tools, many of the standard data manipulations are automatic operations. Students produce a variety of different representations, ones that often reflect their emerging understandings of the data and the context in which the data are situated. Such tools enable students to do what they already do but faster, more often, more accurately, and with fewer errors.

2. *Technology as a reorganizer of physical and mental work:* In addition to amplifying human capabilities, the appropriate use of technology has the potential to bring about structural changes in the system of students' cognitive and sociocultural activities. Such powerful tools bring about reorganization of physical or mental work in a variety of ways, including:

    (a) Shifting activity to higher cognitive levels. For example, computer use makes it possible to shift students' attention from steps in making a graph to problems of scaling and designing graphs to support statistical claims.

    (b) Changing the "objects" on which an activity may focus. For example, a focus on graphs as objects of study can be enlarged to include consideration of tables, data cards, and graphs as

linked representations that are possible with a tool such as
TinkerPlots. Or a focus on the mean as an object (i.e., a number) that is an attribute of a distribution can be enlarged to
include mean, median, and mode as objects, the locations of
each in a distribution (an object), the relationship to data values (objects) of a distribution, and so on.

(c) Focusing on transforming and analyzing representations. For
example, the use of computer-created representations instead
of representations created by paper and pencil allows for easy
and interactive changes as well as saving, recalling, and editing representations and their construction.

(d) Supporting a situated cognition perspective. For example,
data analysis becomes a dynamic process that involves entering data from an experiment as it is conducted, observing "in
the moment" graphing of the data, and experimenting with
"what if" changes to see the effect immediately on an initial
"model."

(e) Understanding statistical concepts dynamically through the
use of graphics. For example, the use of a slider permits
adjusting the bin widths on a histogram in order to explore
the effects on the shape of the data, and the availability of a
"by a technology hand" adjustment of the position of a line on
a scatter plot highlights experimenting with fitting a line to
describe a relationship.

(f) Confronting "representative ambiguity." For example, individual representations often provide only partial information
about the data when some of the critical properties are displayed; changes in or transformations of graphs permit highlighting other aspects of critical properties.

In a more general way, Tinker (1996) highlights the use of information
technologies (such as we have been discussing) "primarily as tools that help
students accomplish more" (p. 2). He distinguishes among four levels of
impact on the curriculum that may result from the capacities of the information technology tools used in mathematics and science education. His
levels (Tinker, 1996, pp. 2-3), representative of the long history of research
on innovations (technological or nontechnological) in instruction are quite
pertinent to our consideration of statistical information technologies.[6]
(Hall and Hord's, 2001, Levels of Use[7] also are relevant here.)

Level 1.   *Substitution*. At the first level, information technologies are
used to accomplish the existing curriculum goals but doing
them better or to a higher level of student comprehension.

Level 2. *Addition*. At this level, technology makes it possible to achieve new curriculum goals, usually by adding new material to an existing course.

Level 3. *Disciplinary restructuring*. At this level, the capacity of information technologies makes it possible to redesign a course or series of courses within a discipline.

Level 4. *Interdisciplinary restructuring*. At this level technology supports the redesign of courses across disciplines.

Level 1 is the simplest to implement, because an improved, technology-based approach is easily substituted for a less effective approach. More difficult to implement, Level 2 involves adding, which implies something has to be dropped. Levels 3 and 4 represent large-scale changes that are generally untried and unstudied. It is at these levels of use that Ben-Zvi's (2000) observations about what it means to reorganize physical or mental work become important. In addition to consideration of the levels, it is also necessary to recognize that an "investment in familiarity" with a tool is necessary.

Even with the best user interfaces, information technologies take time to master because they usually embody new concepts that take time to appreciate. This requires a substantial investment of time. Students need time to learn how to operate generalized tools and then more time to master them with sufficient skill to appreciate their generality. (Tinker, 1996, p. 5)

Such an investment is as important when using technology to support learning and/or doing data analysis work as it is in other areas in which information technologies are applied.

RESEARCH ON TEACHING AND LEARNING OF STATISTICS AND DATA ANALYSIS

Research on statistical thinking with students in grades K–12 has been nonexistent or sparse for quite some time (Shaughnessy, 1992; Shaughnessy et al., 1996). However, since the release of the *Curriculum and Evaluation Standards for School Mathematics* (NCTM, 1989) and the shift in emphasis in the professional practice community (see Appendix A), research about students' statistical thinking has emerged as an exciting opportunity and has begun to yield models of students' conceptions that are detailed enough to have practical, pedagogical implications even at the K–12 levels (e.g., Jones, Langrall, Mooney, & Thornton, 2004). Further, powerful new software tools designed explicitly for statistics education could make statistical thinking accessible to students in K–12 in ways not previously considered.

However, identifying and summarizing new directions in research in statistics and data analysis (with or without the inclusion of technological applications) is challenging. As is often the case with "emerging" fields, special interest initiatives occur through professional organizations, for example, the ISI and the ASA (see Appendix A). When this happens, these interest groups extend themselves to include other related professional organizations. In the case of statistics education, because of its attachment to mathematics, research reports and special sessions now occur regularly at meetings such as those of the International Group for the Psychology of Mathematics Education (PME), International Congress on Mathematical Education (ICME), the Research Presessions at the NCTM Annual Meetings, and the American Education Research Association (AERA). Dissertations related to relevant research topics in statistics education are being completed. Tracking the literature involves some detective work in order to identify materials, many of which are only now becoming more readily available through mainstream channels (e.g., well established research journals such the *Journal for Research in Mathematics Education* or *Mathematical Thinking and Learning* or newly established journals such as the *Statistics Education Research Journal*). Also, various synthesis books have been published (e.g., Ben-Zvi & Garfield, 2004b; Gal & Garfield, 1997b; Lajoie, 1998) that attempt to assemble collections of related work that can be used both to inform the field and to provide directions for next steps and needed research. As a field of research, statistics education is not well defined, and there can be a sense of fragmentation as one looks for themes and well-articulated directions. Unlike more established fields, statistics education is in a state of flux and change. It is both an exciting time because opportunities to contribute to setting directions related to statistics education K–12 are many, and it is a challenging time in that it is hard to be sure about what we do know.

Much of the literature (see Appendix C for a description of the literature review conducted for this chapter) currently available with respect to statistics education and the use of technology is not research-based. The majority of the articles report results of observation and experience, explorations that are not empirical research, conceptual and theoretical perspectives, discussions of software design, or reasoned arguments about technology use in teaching and learning in statistics education. Some of this literature addresses specific research projects related to the use of technology in statistics education. In choosing the literature to review for this chapter, the focus was on the teaching and learning of statistics K–12 that involves the use of technology.

The discussion that follows will not provide a traditional review of the literature, with extensive commentary on results from a variety of research-based and nonresearch-based articles. This kind of review does not seem valuable, in part, because themes have not emerged from the literature at this time and, in part, because there is limited literature that addresses statistics education and the use of technology in K–12 statistics education. This section is organized in two parts: (a) teaching and learning statistics using technology, and (b) instruction and student learning. Exemplars from the literature reviewed will be highlighted as they contribute to the major points that seem necessary to make in each of these parts.

Teaching and Learning Statistics Using Technology

Much of the literature (both research-based and nonresearch based) focuses on the use of technology in statistics and data analysis at the secondary or the postsecondary levels and discusses teaching practices that center on using software to address conceptual learning of one or more big ideas. Initially, this literature was read from the perspective of what computers and calculators allow students to do that they are unlikely to be able to do as easily, if at all, by hand. At the same time, the major content areas addressed in this literature were noted and were used to identify and summarize what appear to be many of the essential "big ideas" (see Appendix B) on which most instruction centers. A variety of different software tools was used in the contexts reported in the literature that was reviewed, including: DataScope (Konold, Pollatsek, Well, & Gagnon, 1997), Fathom (Finzer, 2005), TinkerPlots (Konold & Miller, 2005), Microsoft Excel, Minitab, graphing calculators, or the Minitools (Bakker, 2002; Cobb, 1999).

From this review, we[8] identified a number of points that were made about what computer and calculator tools allowed students to do, including the following:

- organize data in different ways, including structuring data by experimenting with tools before being presented with conventional methods;
- represent sets of data in different ways, including providing easy access to displays, multiple-linked representations, simulations, and animated and/or interactive demonstrations of statistical concepts;
- experience technology-enhanced access to data, including being able to use larger and more complex data sets than those that are feasible when work is done by hand; and

- expedite analysis and problem solving, including being able to solve problems without being able to execute, by hand, complex calculations.

These summary points provide information about ways technology can contribute—on a surface level—to students' access to and learning of data analysis and statistics. They also are more of an itemization of behaviors and actions than of the development of statistical understandings. For example, statements focused more substantively on big ideas were not the norm, such as a *possible* statement that might emerge about students' actions and thinking about lines of best fit supported by explorations using technology:

> The use of a movable line on a scatter plot helped students explore what finding a line of best fit might mean. Students focused on the clustering or lack of clustering of points around a line that had been positioned to "fit" the data and what this might mean for the relationship between the two variables being investigated.[9]

However, there are nuggets of information in the reviewed literature related to software use that appear to pertain to student thinking:

- Software tools with ready-made methods influence the way a subject matter problem is understood and is transformed into a "statistical problem" and into a "problem for the software," that is, a problem that is reframed in such a way that permits using the software tool to help in its solution (Biehler, 1997b).
- Students working in pairs on problems dealing with graphing are better able to make the critical inferences crucial to learning from problem-solving experiences than their classmates working alone (Jackson, Edwards, & Berger, 1993b[10]).
- On a project, students used more mathematics, and took less time, largely because technology took care of graphing and laborious calculations (Erickson, 2002).
- The graphing facilities of the more standard types of graphing programs (e.g., Microsoft Works [now known as Appleworks] or Cricket Graph [no longer being updated but similar to DeltaGraph]) can be overwhelming and confusing to students, as when students are faced with a menu that involves choosing a graph from a large number of simultaneous choices, thus requiring much advanced planning (Jackson, Edwards, & Berger, 1993a), or when the first choice made by the user, the type of graph, is irrevocable.[11] Many students find this frustrating, because they are still learning about

how to choose an appropriate graph, and they do not want to start from the very beginning again. In these kinds of technology contexts, many students may end up choosing the default representation in the software without thinking about their choices (Jackson, Edwards, & Berger, 1993a).

- Certain sequences of actions (e.g., sort the data, regraph, move or resize, choose a different graph type) taken by students were correlated either positively or negatively, depending on the choice of actions, with the quality (basically good or poor) of the resulting graph (Jackson, Edwards, & Berger, 1992).

  1. Students, characterized as "Lost at Sea," were distracted by extraneous possibilities for the general form of graph that is appropriate and tended to make more cosmetic changes and make more new graph types.
  2. Students, characterized as "Right on Target," produced graphs appropriate to the task and tended to do more sorting to make fewer new graph types and to make better graphs.
  3. Students, characterized as "Wild Goose Chasers," concentrated only on one often-ineffective way to solve the problem, that of making changes in the axis scale of the graph by adjusting increment values or minimum or maximum values. They did not experiment with sorting data or with making different types of graphs, seemingly being unable to think about other ways to solve the problem.

- Students might spend most of their time learning to use the software rather than doing significant statistical thinking (Bantanero, Estepa, & Godino, 1997; Jackson et al., 1993a).
- Ideas learned may be overly connected to specific tools (i.e., learning the tool rather than learning the concepts to be learned through use of the tool) (Galmacci & Cicchitelli, 1998).
- Students often use the display methods that are offered by the software rather than thinking through the best representations for the purpose of the investigation (Biehler, 1997b; Jackson et al., 1992).

Clearly, the preceding points provide some insights into what must be considered when integrating technology in statistics instruction. However, these points do not get at the heart of what would seem to be a central concern: Once we are clear about the content to be addressed and the "big ideas" with which we are working, what is the instructional program that integrates the use of technology that can be used to support learning the content?

Instruction and Student Learning

Much of the early research on K–12 statistics education has sought to establish what students appear to know without reference to whether or in what ways instruction may have occurred and had an impact, often because prior instruction, if it has occurred, may have been difficult to characterize. More and more, researchers want to know what students understand about different statistical "big ideas" as the result of some reasonably well-designed set of instructional interventions (e.g., Bakker & Gravemeijer, 2004; Ben-Zvi, 2004, Biehler, 1997b; Cobb, 1999; Cobb & McClain, 2004; Konold et al., 1997; McClain et al., 2005). Much of this research has focused on students' reasoning about data analysis, often associated with the process of statistical investigation or *doing statistics*. In a few cases, the research has focused either more specifically on a single concept or big idea (e.g., distributions as in Bakker & Gravemeijer, 2004) or on statistical reasoning used in relation to a selected set of big ideas (e.g., Cobb, 1999; Cobb & McClain, 2004; McClain et al., 2005). The research involving instructional interventions cited here involves middle grades students or high school students.

Konold and colleagues (1997) and Biehler (1997b) jointly engaged in a project (i.e., the Barriers Project) focused on identifying critical barriers to students' effectively analyzing data. Each reports the results of a study that explored high school students' statistical reasoning behaviors (using technology) after a yearlong course covering probability and statistics. The statistics component of this course involved several concepts including the median, mean, standard deviation, interquartile range, and the use of stem plots, box plots, histograms, scatter plots, and frequency tables. The software used was DataScope; this software is designed as an educational tool rather than as a professional tool. The purpose of the study was to explore difficulties encountered by students conducting fairly rudimentary data analysis using the computer.

Konold and his colleagues (1997) point out that in much prior research students have had little or no instruction in statistics. They highlight the need to better understand the kinds of problems and the nature of the problems that emerge during, and persist throughout, instruction as students encounter new concepts, methodologies, representational systems, and forms of argument. Their study (Konold et al., 1997) examined the work of two pairs of students who were in the statistics and probability class described previously. After the class was completed, the students worked to solve a problem and were interviewed during the process. The researchers wanted to see "how students with some background in statistics made use of the computer to analyze a set of real data" (p. 153). A set of questions was posed to the pairs of students concerning a data set the students had explored during the course. The set included a number of attributes from data collected about the students and their classmates:

1.   Students were asked to use DataScope to give a brief summary of the dataset in order to characterize the students included in the survey. Researchers were interested in the information on which students would focus, which plots and summaries they would elect to use, and how they would interpret them.

2.   Each student pair was reminded of one of the questions each student in that pair had explored as part of class project and was asked to use the computer to show what she had found (the students were all female).

3.   Students were asked a question not posed during the course— whether having curfews affects school performance (i.e., Does having a curfew make you have better grades? [Biehler, 1997b]). They were asked to investigate the question and, if possible, arrive at a conclusion. Analysis included the variable, *hours of homework*, and the variable, *having a curfew* (yes/no).

After a year-long course in which students used a number of statistics including means, medians, and percents to make group comparisons, students did not, without prompting, make use of these methods during the assessment. The students seemed to be thinking about and comparing properties of individual cases or properties of homogeneous cases but not comparing *group propensities*. Konold and his colleagues raise an interesting point: The methods that are used to compare groups are dependent on the reasons for comparing the groups. The researchers observed that students could either consider the comparisons they were making in light of a "contest" framework (i.e., Did those with curfews do more homework than those without curfews?) or in light of the "fairness" criteria (i.e., How much more time did students with curfews spend studying than students without curfews?). The researchers noted the need to define the task for students as one not only of deciding, for example, whether those with curfews study more than those without curfews (contest), but also of determining measures of how much different groups study in order to induce a more statistical approach.

Essentially, the observed results from this one interaction appear to be discouraging to the researchers; the students' work seems to reflect the most recent content they had studied with respect to statistics instruction (i.e., the use of frequency tables), and they seemed not to have the ability to reflect in a more global way about either the problem context or how to analyze the data in order to respond to the question posed. A number of issues and questions arise about the details of the investigation. One might wonder whether the task was too open-ended. Would there be some way of sequencing problems in which we want students to initiate the process of statistical investigation so that it is more manageable? Did this happen during instruction or was this one of the first times that students encountered a problem that was presented in such a fashion? Why was the original task selected in the first place? How might the researchers have approached analyzing this problem? Would thinking through their own approaches and their expectations for these students at this point in their experience have helped the researchers articulate the task in a different way that might have resulted in students drawing on different knowledge? Or is this just "where students are" at this point, suggesting a need to better understand what might be expected of students after one course in statistics and probability?

Biehler (1997b) investigated the same problem[12] under similar conditions in Germany; his analysis of the ways students responded identified 25 problem areas related to elementary data analysis and, by default, provided definition for what he considers properties of genuine statistical problem solving. As with Konold and his colleagues (1997), there seems to be a tension between the expectations of how the students might have solved this problem and their work. Their work appeared to be narrower than expected in its demonstration of an understanding of the process of statistical investigation and the interactions of the many statistical ideas that are used when engaged in such a process. Again, one wonders about the impact of the task that was chosen on the extent to which one could be able to see students demonstrate some level of comprehensive knowledge about *doing statistics*.

Ben-Zvi and others (Ben-Zvi, 2002, 2004; Ben-Zvi & Arcavi, 1998; Ben-Zvi & Friedlander, 1997) have developed a junior high statistics curriculum—known as Statistics Curriculum—focused on Exploratory Data Analysis (EDA) and integrating the use of spreadsheets. This curriculum (Ben-Zvi, 2004, p. 125) has the following features:

1. It stresses students' active participation in organization, description, interpretation, representation, and analysis of data situations (on topics related to the student's world, such as sport records, lengths of people's names in different countries, labor conflicts, and car brands).
2. It incorporates technology tools for easy use in creating various data representations and transformations.

The scope of the curriculum involves 30 instructional sessions spread out over 2 and a half months. There is a student book and a teacher book, using Excel as the spreadsheet program. The general task design is reported as being that of the creation of small scenarios in which students could experience some of the processes involved in experts' practice of data-based inquiry. In reading the reports of research, it is possible to get a flavor of the kinds of tasks that are used. However, no table of contents or other information about the sequencing and flow of the tasks appears to be readily available. The authors report research that addresses both the iterative cycle of the curriculum development process and its interaction with student knowledge and, later, results from investigating specific research questions with students once the curriculum was completed.

Ben-Zvi and his colleagues use a case-based approach and focus on presenting analyses of student thinking from a qualitative perspective; hence, their studies generally involve a limited number of subjects. However, they seek to generalize ways to characterize what is occurring. For example, Ben-Zvi and Friedlander characterize levels of reasoning processes observed in students' handling of data representations as follows:

(a) *Uncritical thinking*, in which the technological power and statistical methods are used randomly or uncritically rather than "targeted";
(b) *Meaningful use of a representation*, in which students use an appropriate graphical representation or measure in order to answer their research questions and interpret their findings;
(c) *Meaningful handling of multiple representations*, in which students are involved in an ongoing search for meaning and interpretation to achieve sensible results as well as in monitoring their processes; and
(d) *Creative thinking*, in which students decide that an uncommon representation or method would best express their thoughts, and they manage to produce an innovative graphical representation, or self-invented measure, or method of analysis previously described (Ben-Zvi & Friedlander, 1997, as cited in Ben-Zvi, 2004, p. 123).

Revisiting Jackson and colleagues' (1992) previously described characterizations of student behaviors, possibly their "Lost at Sea" students or "Wild Goose Chasers" correspond to Ben-Zvi and Friedlander's category of "uncritical thinking" and their "Right on Target" students correspond to Ben-Zvi and Friedlander's category of "meaningful use of a representation."

In later research, Ben-Zvi (2004), reports results from an investigation of students' development of reasoning about variability, again using the spreadsheet (Excel) as the technology. The students in the study were in three classes that had experienced instruction using the Statistics Curriculum. The students were engaged in the Surname Activity, an activity in which they were asked to compare the name lengths of a set of surnames collected in their own class (35 Hebrew names) with a set of surnames from an American class that was given to them (35 English names). Again, this study is case-based and qualitative, and the work of only one pair of students' with this one problem is analyzed. However, an outcome of the study was identification of seven developmental stages of these students' reasoning about variability:

Stage 1. Identifying focus, beginning from irrelevant and local information;

Stage 2. Describing variability informally in raw data;

Stage 3. Formulating a statistical hypothesis that accounts for variability;

Stage 4. Accounting for variability when comparing groups using frequency tables;

Stage 5. Using center and spread measures to compare groups;

Stage 6. Modeling variability informally through handling outlying values; and

Stage 7. Noticing and distinguishing the variability within and between the distributions in a graph.

The idiosyncratic aspects of this study (i.e., two students studied) limit its potential for broad recommendations. The initial summary of stages, however, provides direction for others who may want to do further work in this area. Also, as Ben-Zvi notes (and this is relevant for all of his and his colleagues' work), the students are engaged in a well-structured learning environment designed to promote the kinds of thoughtful and deep analyses that Ben-Zvi highlights. This environment includes the following:

- a curriculum built on the basis of expert views of EDA as a sequence of semistructured, yet open, questions designed to foster learning within the context of extended meaningful problem situations;

- timely and nondirective interventions by the teacher as a representative of the discipline in the classroom; and

- computerized tools that enable students to handle complex actions (change of representations, scaling, deletions, restructuring of tables, etc.) without having to engage in a great amount of technical work, leaving time and energy for conceptual discussions (Ben-Zvi, 2004, p. 59).

It is helpful to have these kinds of syntheses, as long as we realize the limitations on generalizability. Such summary points help structure ways to look at other situations that involve the development, in this case, of ways of reasoning about variability.

While Ben-Zvi and colleagues have designed a Statistics Curriculum that can be used to address a number of big ideas related to statistics education, Bakker and Gravemeijer (2004) focus on a single big idea—that of distribution—and how informal reasoning about distributions can be developed in a technological environment with middle grades students. They use "design research," a type of research that has been used by Cobb, Gravemeijer, McClain, and colleagues. Design research cycles consist of three main phases: the design of instructional materials (based on a well-articulated theoretical framework), classroom-based teaching experiments, and retrospective analysis (Bakker & Gravemeijer, 2004).

Focusing on the concept of distribution highlights the essential characteristic of statistical data analysis: It is mainly about describing and predicting aggregate features of data sets. A key element to consider with middle grades students is distinguishing between data as individual values and distribution as a conceptual entity. Measures of center (mean, median, midrange, etc.), spread (range, interquartile range, standard deviation, etc.), density (actual or relative frequencies, majority, and quartiles), and skewness (position of the majority of the data) are considered characteristics of a distribution. Bakker and Gravemeijer suggest that focusing on informal aspects of shape of a distribution can help students engage with many other statistical ideas along the way as various statistical aspects of the data set influence the shape of a distribution.

Their study involved teaching experiments conducted in each of four seventh-grade classes (the number of students in a class ranged from 23 to 28), with each class completing 12 to 15 lessons, each of which was 50 minutes in length. The collected data included audio recordings, student work, field notes, and final tests in all classes, as well as videotapes and pretests in the last two experiments (each class was considered a teaching experiment). An essential component was a set of mini-interviews that were carried out during the lessons; the interviews varied in length from 20 seconds to 4 minutes.

The intent of the research was to find out how seventh-grade students could learn to reason about distributions in informal ways, not whether teaching the sequence of instructional activities could be used in other seventh-grade classes and lead to the same results. The researchers were able to identify patterns of students' answers that were similar in all teaching experiments and categorized a developing learning trajectory that evolved in three stages according to students' reasoning with the representations used. The authors designed an instructional sequence that was supported by computer tool use (Minitools) and the invention of graphs that stimulated students to reason about aspects of distributions.

Stage 1:   Representing Data Using Bars: Minitool 1 presents each data value as an individual bar that extends horizontally from the *y*-axis; this kind of graph is called a case-value bar graph. When students solved problems with Minitool 1, they used informal words such as *majority, outliers, reliability,* and *spread out.* Students not only reasoned about aspects of distribution, they were also asked to invent data sets in Minitool 1 that matched certain characteristics of a described distribution.

Stage 2:   Replacing Bars With Dots: Minitool 2 displays data in dot plots so students can see the frequencies of occurrence of data values, where data cluster, and so on. It also permits students to mark sections of the distribution. Students developed qualitative notions of more advanced properties of distribution including *frequency, spread, quartiles, median,* and *density.* With the dot plot representation, students could also choose to structure data into two equal groups, four equal groups, fixed-size groups, and groups with fixed-interval widths.

Stage 3:   Symbolizing Data as a "Bump": It was at this stage that students appeared to reason explicitly with the shape of the distribution with a focus on a majority or "modal" clump and, eventually, moved to reasoning about the whole shape using other statistical notions such as outliers and sample size.

As part of the framework for instructional task design, Bakker and Gravemeijer began engaging students in back-and-forth movement between interpreting graphs and constructing graphs according to specified statistical notions (e.g., students were asked to invent a case value plot for battery life span data in which data for brand A are "bad but reliable" and data for brand B are "good but unreliable"). The authors comment on the effectiveness of this instructional strategy, noting that when students invent their own data and graphs, teachers and researchers can better assess what the students understand. Students' work demonstrates the ability to think reversibly in conceptualizing a big idea; this kind of thinking seems to help students become more flexible thinkers (Rachlin, 1998).

This research involved teaching experiments. Instructional tasks were designed but not with the intention of producing a curriculum for others to use. Readers do not know the nature or sequencing of the explicit tasks that were used to facilitate students' understanding of the concept of distribution, with the exception of the few tasks that are reported in order to characterize how the students' reasoning developed. The research of Bakker and Gravemeijer, which clearly involves task design, is focused on student understandings so that, in part, they can articulate an instructional trajectory that is a starting place for thinking about curriculum design.

Cobb, McClain, and Gravemeijer (Cobb, 1999; Cobb & McClain, 2004; McClain & Cobb, 2001; McClain, Cobb, & Gravemeijer, 2000) have used the context of middle grade students learning data analysis and the methodology of design research in ways that are similar to that reported by Bakker and Gravemeijer (2004). Indeed, the results from their initial work are reflected in the work of Bakker and Gravemeijer (2004). There are a number of publications that provide the details of the work by Cobb and colleagues; their focus of instruction was broader than that of Bakker and Gravemeijer, addressing ways of supporting students' developing understandings of statistical data analysis in contexts of exploratory data analysis and data generation. The concept of distribution was considered to be an overarching statistical idea to be developed as part of the instructional work. The researchers conducted two sets of teaching experiments with classes of seventh-grade students and one teaching experiment with eighth-grade students. What is of interest for the purposes of this chapter is a proposal for a set of principles for instructional design (Cobb & McClain, 2004) that has grown out of the design research work that has been the focus of several years of study. These principles will be addressed in more depth in the next section:

1. The big or central statistical ideas, such as distribution, can provide an orientation for the design of instruction.

2. Instructional activities need to make it possible for students to engage in the investigative nature of data analysis and enable teachers to build on the variety of data-based arguments that result from students' statistical investigations.

3. Classroom activity structures that support the development of students' reasoning about data generation as well as data analysis need to be in place.

4. Students need to use data analysis tools that support and fit with their statistical reasoning as the tools are introduced in an instructional sequence and can be used to support their development of increasingly sophisticated forms of statistical reasoning.

5. The characteristics of classroom discourse involve creating statistical arguments that "explain why the way in which the data have been organized gives rise to insights into the phenomenon under investigation" (p. 392) and engaging students in sustained exchanges that focus on central statistical ideas.

As Cobb and McClain point out, these principles are highly interrelated. Cobb and McClain characterize the various principles as providing an orientation about the design of productive classroom *activity systems*—systems designed to produce the learning of significant statistical ideas. This approach to design goes far beyond the traditional focus on curriculum, and acknowledges the "vital, mediating role of the teacher" (p. 393).

Eventually, most K–12 teachers will want to have sequences of selected tasks (collected, developed and/or provided via curriculum materials), access to available technology, and knowledge of appropriate pedagogy in order to teach statistics and data analysis with some reasonable success. Clearly, the statistics education community needs to be able to help define these components for teachers' and students' use and to provide evidence of effectiveness in terms of learning that has occurred. This issue is addressed in more detail in the following section.

RESEARCH AGENDA FOR
STATISTICS EDUCATION AND THE USE OF TECHNOLOGY[13]

We have just begun to understand what it means to know and be able to do data analysis and statistics at the K–12 grade levels. With a shift away from statistics instruction whose content is premised on the automatic transfer of traditional content from postsecondary to K–12 and a move toward reconceptualizing this content and how it is learned, we find the field in a state of flux. When we add to this the need to consider the interactions among technology, content, and learning, given the new kinds of software being developed, there are rich opportunities for framing a research agenda.

Knowing What We Know: What Is the Literature Related to Research in Statistics Education?

As was noted previously, identifying and summarizing new directions in research in statistics and data analysis (with or without the inclusion of technological applications) is challenging. Tracking the literature involves detective work. Jolliffe (2003) notes that there are relatively few outlets for publication and presentation of statistics education research[14] activities and results so that finding out what others are doing is partly a matter of chance. As a consequence, important research findings do not always get as widely disseminated. It is possible that researchers are doing similar studies, unaware of duplication and without the benefits of comparison and pooling of results for purposes of replication.

There are some resources that attempt to have reasonably up-to-date links (e.g., International Association for Statistical Education (IASE) (http://www.stat.auckland.ac.nz/~iase/ [Retrieved May 5, 2005]) and CAUSEweb (http://www.causeweb.org/ [Retrieved May 5, 2005]) to a number of available resources that provide information about research but they are not comprehensive (e.g., there are few links to work being presented and/or published in fields such as mathematics education that are outside statistical education research). Other resources, such as the What Works Clearinghouse (http://www.whatworks.ed.gov/ [Retrieved May 5, 2005]) are too narrow in their goals, purposes, and content addressed to be of much use in assembling information about what is being done with respect to statistical education research and, more particularly, with respect to the design and use of technology as it relates to statistics education.

The ideal would be to have available an annotated bibliographic electronic database—a repository of abstracts of research (e.g., Huntley et al., 2000; Sharma & Begg, 2003) or a more comprehensive database upon which to build a resource bank of related research references and resources. It would be helpful for those doing research in these areas to have access to an annotated resource of research references that would serve as an evidence-based repository that could be used to inform research directions and could be updated to reflect results of new work as it is added to the field.

Jolliffe (2003) provides an excellent overview with respect to this very need; he discusses what is necessary in order to move toward a database of research in statistical education. He first addresses statistical education research and whether and how it might be defined. He then elaborates on the nature of the database that could be developed. He also proposes strategies for locating researchers and research. Clearly, this would be a very welcome addition to the research efforts in statistics education.

SETTING A RESEARCH AGENDA

There are different ways to approach making recommendations for a research agenda in statistics education research, particularly as it relates to the inclusion of the use of technology. For purposes here, the focus will be on statistics education and the need for research involving instructional design and learning, specifically using several of the points discussed by Cobb and McClain (2004) to provide direction for the recommendations. Curriculum design and development seems to be a very important next step for statistics educators; this topic was the focus of the 2004 IASE Roundtable, "Curriculum Development in Statistics Education" (Burrill, 2004). Questions that framed the discussion at this roundtable included:

- What is important to teach, when should it be taught, and how should it be taught?
- What do we know about when concepts should be taught and how they should be taught?
- How do we carefully structure the curriculum?
- How does research link to practice?

From the presentations and discussions that occurred, the role of frameworks was identified as a way to guide thinking about curriculum development, assessment, trajectories in concept development, and the nature of teachers' practice (see Franklin et al., 2005, as an exemplar). A general trend that also emerged concerned students' lack of ability, at all levels, from elementary to tertiary, to reason and think statistically. Reported research and observations indicate that students master technical skills but are unable to use these skills in meaningful ways (e.g., Konold et al., 1997 as well as other research articles cited previously that involved use of instructional activities, i.e., Bakker & Gravemeijer, 2004; Biehler, 1997b; Ben-Zvi, 2004; Ben-Zvi & Friedlander, 1997; Konold et al., 1997). The use of technology both as a means to develop understanding of concepts and to enable students to apply their knowledge and skills in problem-solving situations also was addressed as an area of special interest (Burrill, 2004).

The selected exemplars of the kinds of current research that involve investigating students' thinking in the context of instructional interventions (Bakker & Gravemeijer, 2004; Biehler, 1997b; Ben-Zvi, 2004; Ben-Zvi & Friedlander, 1997; Konold et al., 1997) do not provide much insight about either the instructional tasks that were used or about the kinds of ongoing assessment of student learning that was used. Rather, some of the research reports on the nature of student reasoning related to students' work on a single specific task that, in one case, is part of a curriculum (Ben-Zvi, 2004) and, in the other case, is intended to assess more broadly the nature of student reasoning after instruction using a particular curriculum (Biehler, 1997b; Konold et al., 1997). In other instances, the research provides some general observations about the nature of student thinking that develops from use of a curriculum (Ben-Zvi & Friedlander, 1997) or about the nature of kinds of instructional tasks used (Bakker & Gravemeijer, 2004; Cobb & McClain, 2004). However, currently, there appears to be no research with K–12 students that examines interactions among curricula, outcomes, and students' thinking. Such research should examine student progress through a sequenced set of instructional tasks and should document outcomes of student thinking and learning related to the completion of the instructional tasks. Assuming that the use of technology is an integral part of such an instructional sequence, this kind of research would also document the use of the technology and its impact on students' thinking related to the content they are learning. This must be a central research focus if we are to enhance what we know about what students know and are able to do with respect to the content and processes of statistics education.

Central Statistical Ideas

To begin the instructional design process, it is essential that "the 'big ideas' that are at the heart of the discipline, that have enduring value beyond the classroom and that offer potential for engaging students" (Cobb & McClain, 2004, p. 318) be identified. Given the shifts and changes in work in statistics education, this area is probably still in development. A review of current literature suggests what the statistics education and research communities seem to consider to be the big ideas (see Appendix B). These big ideas certainly provide directions for researchers about content (e.g., Cobb & McClain, 2004, discuss their focus on distribution as an overarching statistical idea).

However, deciding on which "big idea(s)" to focus research requires a certain amount of additional clarity about the statistics content that is involved in addressing each big idea under consideration. Cobb and McClain (2004) comment that, given the overarching idea of distribution, one of the primary goals they had was to have students come to reason about data sets as "entities that are distributed with a space of possible values" (p. 381). Notions such as center, spread, skewness, and relative density (Bakker & Gravemeijer, 2004) provide ways of characterizing how specific data sets are distributed. Various graphs and other representations provide ways of structuring data distributions so that students might identify relevant trends or patterns (i.e., by focusing on relative density [frequency] of the data points within a distribution).

Cobb and McClain (2004) extend the focus on distribution to the analysis of bivariate data and, eventually, to the key idea of sampling distributions as explored at the university level, thus proposing the beginnings of a long-term learning trajectory that addresses the overarching statistical idea of distribution. Statistical covariation involves the coordination of the distributions of two sets of measures within a data set. Cobb and McClain

(2004) comment that scatter plots do not provide direct perceptual support in helping the viewer focus on the distribution of each of the two sets of measures (variables) being explored. It is difficult to identify the relative frequency or density and to see the shape of the distribution for either data set when examining data displayed using a scatter plot (see Figure 11.1). However, some of the newer software offers possibilities in this area that engage students quite differently in looking at how two distributions may covary (e.g., Konold, 2002b). One example is shown in Figure 11.2; the "slices" of distributions continue to help students focus on how each of the variables is distributed, while, at the same time, highlighting the nature of the relationship between the two variables.

In research involving tertiary students' statistics learning with respect to sampling distributions (e.g., Chance, delMas, & Garfield, 2004; Lipson, 1997), prerequisite knowledge for learning about sampling distributions included understanding the central statistical ideas of variability, distribution (including normal distribution), and sampling. In addition, Chance and her colleagues (2004) detail a number of key points concerning the central statistical idea of sampling distributions that students must understand and how they might demonstrate this knowledge, as well as

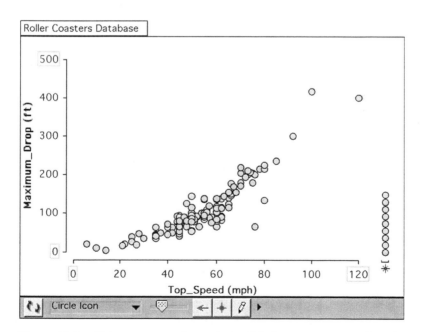

Figure 11.1.   Using a scatter plot: relationship between top speeds and maximum drops of roller coasters.

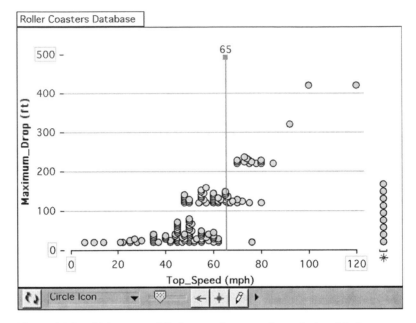

Figure 11.2.   Using a modified type of scatter plot: relationship between top speeds and maximum drops of roller coasters.

common student misconceptions. This level of detail provides the kind of needed elaboration of statistics content that underlies and is related to the central statistical idea of distribution as well as variability and sampling.

In order to do research that addresses instructional design with respect to these central statistical ideas and the resulting assessments of what students learn, this kind of articulation of central ideas and possible content trajectories is essential. Franklin and her colleagues (2005) allude to this in their designations of Level A, Level B, and Level C work. However, Cobb and McClain (2004) and Bakker and Gravemeijer (2004) possibly have "pushed the edge" in terms of asking that we rethink how we talk about statistical content (e.g., overarching statistical ideas) and articulate the connectivity and development of these ideas from the K–12 level to the tertiary level of statistics education. To do this requires both opportunities for the statistics education community to work together to articulate this content and a great deal of research (e.g., Bakker & Gravemeijer, 2004) that addresses instructional design and assessment issues. This research needs to involve determining how these central statistical ideas may be developed through instruction (with the use of technology as part of this instruction), understanding the outcomes of such instruction (e.g., Bakker & Gravemeijer's three stages in coming to understand the idea of distribution or Ben-Zvi and Friedlander's (1997) four levels of reasoning in the context of a statistical investigation, both involving use of technology), and finding ways to document—through assessment—the demonstration, growth, and achievement of students' knowledge of these central ideas.

One way to begin to build this level of detailed understanding of overarching statistical ideas would be to have available reviews of the literature focused on a "big idea" or related set of "big ideas" and written to include the context of technology use. Hammerman and Rubin (2004), in reporting research about the ways learners use new software tools to deal with variability in analyzing data in the context of comparing groups, include the beginnings of a review of the literature that models these directions. Hammerman and Rubin address individual and aggregate properties of distributions, a trajectory of different ways of viewing data, ways of thinking about comparing groups, the importance of proportional reasoning in relation to reasoning about variability between groups, and ways students and teachers appear to explore and manage variability using the TinkerPlots software. Any of these central ideas would benefit from more elaboration, but all of them are interrelated in terms of the work the authors are doing. What sets this initial review apart is the more extensive discussion of how the use of software contributes to developing the central ideas being addressed in their work. Bakker and Gravemeijer (2004), Cobb (1999), and McClain and colleagues (2005) also include similar kinds of discussions of technology use as it contributes to understanding selected "big ideas" in statistics while, at the same time, elaborating, in more detail, the content of the particular "big idea" (i.e., distribution in the case of Bakker & Gravemeijer, 2004, and Cobb, 1999) about which they are designing instruction. We need to have these kinds of summaries available to the broader research and software development communities. There are a few reviews of the literature that provide some of this direction (e.g., Friel, Curcio, & Bright, 2001; Meletiou, 2002), but we found no published reviews that included a reasonable integration of the role of technology in exploring, understanding, and learning about one or more central ideas.

Instructional Design

Increasingly, at levels of elementary statistics instruction (i.e., possibly both Levels A and B as proposed by Franklin et. al, 2005), more attention is being given to exploratory data analysis (EDA). Cobb and McClain

(2004) note that the use of an exploratory or investigative orientation is central to data analysis and constitutes an important instructional goal in its own right (p. 383). As a consequence, the instructional activities on which they focus all involve analyzing data sets for purposes that, for the students, are viewed as realistic (e.g., compare two drug treatment groups for AIDS or compare the speeds of drivers before and after a speed trap has been set up). Coupled with the attention to EDA is the need to attend to certain central statistical ideas that are intended to emerge during whole-class discussions. This involves a tension between the process of involving students in an investigative orientation and the goal of "systematically supporting the emergence and development of key statistical ideas" (p. 383). In order to have this happen, the actual and various data-based arguments that students produced have to be a primary resource on which the teacher can draw to initiate and orchestrate a whole-class discussion that addresses a central statistical idea. Consequently, instructional activities need to be developed that, when used, will catalyze such student analyses and, as a result, would be available as a resource for the teacher. The design process involves detailed instructional planning which includes the development of tasks and the identification, modification, or design of data sets, all the while attempting to anticipate the kinds of data-based arguments students might produce and the directions for development of the central statistical ideas that are likely to emerge as part of any instructional activity. The design process, in their work, is actually a cyclic one of testing and revising instructional activities, often making minor but important changes.

Cobb and McClain (2004) want students to have a deep understanding of the context of the data situation and its relevance to the question they are addressing. This means that an understanding of the data-generation process is essential; for their work, Cobb and McClain (2004) primarily use provided data sets as opposed to having students collect their own data. Particularly by middle school, time to collect data is often not available, the topics to be investigated may be ones about which students would not easily be able to collect data (e.g., results of AIDS drug treatments), and, more importantly, using provided data sets assures the presence of particular characteristics that the teacher can use to guide students in addressing issues that will further the instructional agenda. However, Cobb and McClain contend that "it is important for students to talk through the data generation process whether or not they actually collect the data" (p. 386).

A primary purpose for engaging students in these phases is to enable them to remain cognizant of the purposes underpinning their inquiries and, eventually, to appreciate the influence of data generation on the legitimacy of the conclusions they can draw from the data they collect. In an approach of this type, the series of methodological decisions that make the collection of data possible are not assumed to be transparent to students, but instead become an explicit focus of discussion in the course of which students engage in all phases of the data generation process. (p. 386) One might assert that the tasks in which students engage frame both what and how students learn in a statistics classroom. The intent in detailing some of the instructional design practices used by Cobb and McClain (2004) is to raise awareness about what may be a "missing factor" in research in statistics education—the articulation and in-depth discussion of the tasks selected for instruction, how they are used, and what occurs with students during their use. As was noted earlier, when research related to curriculum use (e.g., Ben-Zvi & Friedlander, 1997; Friel, 2002; Konold et al., 1997) is reported, it often is in light of how students respond to a particular task that was part of an instructional sequence (that is not detailed) or ways in which students appear to think when asked to investigate a statistical problem *after* instruction is completed. However, it would seem productive to spend time analyzing tasks and identifying and accumulating ways students respond to a sequence of instructional tasks, using a type of Lesson Study model (Lewis, 2002) that engages those involved in instructional development in a more extensive process of planning and testing. It would seem that the research reported by Chance and colleagues (2004) is an exemplar of this kind of process of instructional design involving the use of technology that addresses the central statistical idea of sampling distribution.

It might be productive to have opportunities for those engaged in instructional design in statistics education to talk through individual tasks or sequences of instructional tasks, their use, and the resulting student responses. A product from Lesson Study can be the development of a library of tasks developed and refined over time with input from those who engage in using the task(s) in a process of analysis, testing, and accumulation of evidence of student response. The focus might be one of working with a proposed set of stages or sequence of ways of thinking (e.g., Bakker & Gravemeijer, 2004; Ben-Zvi & Friedlander, 1997) and gaining an understanding of the sets of tasks that support the emergence of these identified stages or ways of thinking. Others could then make use of these tasks as well and add to what we know about ways students respond.

There is a growing literature that addresses the issues of students "comparing groups" in order to address a few central statistical ideas including distribution and variability. There are many tasks that have been developed and used that can be found both in the literature and in published curricula. One possible scenario would be to pull together the tasks that address "comparing groups," and work on refining and clarifying what is to be addressed with respect to statistics content. The use of these tasks and related technology and the ways students respond can be investigated in order to develop hypotheses about both content and developmental trajectories associated with instructional tasks and technology use. Moreover, such investigations can lead to additional or refined tasks and technology use that are needed to "fill in developmental holes." From here, research involving an instructional sequence of activities and technology use would be carried out and the results used to characterize more specifically the nature of the tasks and technology use that appear to support student learning of the desired content. In a sense, something of this nature happens with the International Research Forum on Statistical Reasoning, Thinking and Literacy (SRTL) (see Appendix A). Themes are selected (the SRTL 2004 focus was on the central idea of distribution, and the focus for SRTL 2003 was on the central idea of variability) and researchers meet to engage in substantive discussions about one another's research in progress related to this theme. This idea might be extended to the creation of an *International Research Forum on Instructional Design in Statistics Education* (IDSE) at which the same kind of in-depth consideration would be given to task design that includes the use of technology and the nature of student thinking that occurs when a particular set of tasks and technology occur within a given instructional scenario.

Tool Use

Throughout this discussion of recommendations for a research agenda, the integration of technology use is assumed. As Cobb and McClain (2004) note, "the use of computer-based tools to create and manipulate graphical representations of data is central to exploratory data analysis" (p. 386). A design principle with respect to the use of technological tools is that the particular tool or tools should fit with students' reasoning at a particular point in the instructional sequence (p. 387). This issue was addressed previously in Bakker's (2002) discussion of route-type and landscape-type computer tools. Clearly, the work of Cobb and his colleagues involved the use of route-type Minitool applets, specially designed for specific instructional purposes.

Three main software programs in the United States (i.e., Fathom, TinkerPlots, and Tabletop) and the various styles of graphing calculators with statistics capabilities including graphing tools seem to serve as appropriate technological tools to support statistics instruction. These tools would be classified as landscape-type tools. The tension in their use becomes one of deciding whether to, and if so, how to, loosely define instructional routes in the use of any of these software tools. This tension surfaces because (a) many curricula are designed with specific instructional goals that need to be accomplished, (b) the *time* needed for students to experience truly the "landscape" of learning within any one of these software environments is not always available in more traditional school settings, and (c) expectations for teacher facility and knowledge both in terms of statistics content and its investigation within any one of these technology environments may not be realistic. So instructional design within the context of the use of any of these software tools involves thought not only about the choice and sequencing of tasks but also about the routes that students might follow in solving these problems using any one of these tools.

Two kinds of information are needed to help the statistics community better understand how to conceptualize using these software tools in instructional design. The first is to have a better understanding of the ways each tool might be used to address central statistical ideas; these ideas would come from knowledgeable statistics educators with expertise in using the software and would include the software designers themselves. We have some examples of this kind of literature (that is not research-based per se). Konold (2002b) discusses technological alternatives to the use of the scatter plot using TinkerPlots to explore covariation. Many of the recent articles written by Konold and other colleagues include ways to use TinkerPlots to explore important statistical ideas. Similarly, for example, Lock (2002) discusses ways to use Fathom in the context of promoting interactive statistical explorations addressing central statistical ideas.

The second kind of information needed involves conducting research in order to identify how the learners who are engaged in the instructional activities make use of the technological tool(s) to explore the intended content. Hammerman and Rubin (2004) provide a good example of research that has focused on how middle grades and secondary students and teachers explore variability within different contexts using Tinker-Plots. McClain and her colleagues (2005) also provide the same kinds of insights about the use of the Minitools. Clearly, one needs to consider both theoretical "expert" strategies and the strategies students actually used. As with the process of instructional design discussed earlier, it is the testing and revision of tasks resulting from feedback about how students approach each task using a given technology tool that needs to be addressed.

There also is a need to be aware of the ways in which the use of technology is cognitively shifting the nature of the content and ways in which students might reason statistically (Ben-Zvi, 2000). Part of what it means to address the idea of cognitive interactions with the software tool includes identifying and addressing situations that may occur simply because of

"There's a dip at 0.7 because its ... like.... all up around it (i.e., 0.7)."

Graph 1: Icon Size = 16

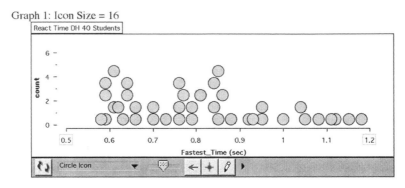

Graph 2: Icon Size = 8

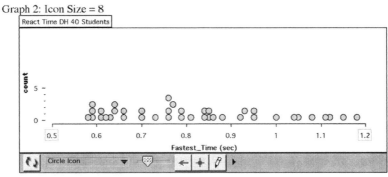

Graph 3: Icon size < 8

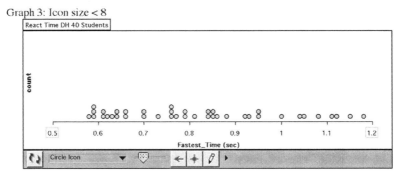

Figure 11.3.   Does icon size matter?

the way the software is designed. For example, Figure 11.3 shows a situation that occurred during students' use of TinkerPlots. The problem involved describing 40 students' fastest reaction times in a computer reaction-time game. The graphs show the reaction times of all the students. The first graph in the series is the graph that a student made. The quoted comment before the Graph 1 in the sequence of three graphs shown in Figure 11.3 is from a student who is interpreting the data in Graph 1 based on how the visual representation appears when using a specific (default) icon size. It turns out, as the icon size is made smaller (Graph 2 and then Graph 3), that the shape of the distribution emerges more clearly and the initial student observations appear to need to be revised. For purposes of research, it might be useful to see what happens if this feature is discussed with students, that is, do students come to understand how size of the icon may impact the visual display of a distribution of data? Once they are made aware of this effect, do they use other strategies (e.g., reduce icon size) to make sure they can more accurately visualize the shape of the distribution?

On the other hand, part of what it means to consider the cognitive implications of a tool such as TinkerPlots involves students in making use of special features of the software such as dividers. Figure 11.4 displays a "separated" graph that shows the distributions of fastest computer reaction time trials for 40 students using their dominant hands and using their nondominant hands. There are a number of ways that students might proceed to compare these distributions. One way, shown here, involves choosing a "benchmark" time—in this case 1 second—and partitioning both distributions in order to examine the percent of reaction times that are below one second and the percent of reaction times that are at or above one second. The ability to partition distributions and obtain frequencies is not something that would be done with "by hand" graphs. It is the power of the software that permits students to explore a strategy of partitioning the distribution into two groups and use the results to make comparisons that go beyond finding means, or medians, or ranges.

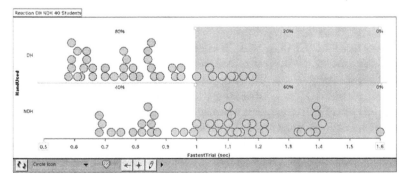

Figure 11.4.   Comparison of fastest reaction times using dominant and nondominant hands.

Assessment

Cobb and McClain (2004) place a great deal of emphasis on the use of whole-class discussions in which students' analyses are shared and critiqued as a way to support students' learning. These discussions address central statistical ideas and are used to move the teacher's instructional agenda forward; that is, the statistics to be learned drives the direction of the discussion that is intended and orchestrated by the teacher. Such whole-class discussions engage the teacher in issues of assessment. In fact, Cobb and McClain comment that, in their research, it was often the case that students carried out their analyses and wrote reports in one class period and then the whole-class discussion was conducted in the next class period. This gave the teacher an opportunity to review the students' work prior to the discussion in order to (a) get a sense of the ways in which students reasoned about the data and (b) develop his or her own conjectures about the content issues that might emerge—and possibly could be encouraged—during the whole-class discussion in order to promote substantive statistical conversations. Clearly, this kind of planning involves a teacher who is knowledgeable about assessing what students know and/or are able to do and then to be able to build on this knowledge to create a productive classroom discussion that moves all learners forward in their statistical growth.

Chance and Garfield (2002) indicate the need for research on the effects of instructional materials that includes:

> documenting evidence of the effects on students of these instructional changes, trying to identify the most effective instructional techniques, while also developing models of how students come to understand statistics [i.e., the big ideas] which will help foster additional reform and be closely tied to practice. (p. 39)

Formulating strategies for assessment in this context can be a challenge. Only recently has serious attention been directed toward assessment (e.g., Gal & Garfield, 1997b; Garfield & Chance, 2000). If we have instructional options for use with students that we believe fit within conceptual and instructional frameworks that are well-articulated, and if we have well-designed vehicles for supporting and assessing students' knowledge development as they progress through instructional sequences, then we are well on our way to being able to claim not only what we think students should know and be able to do with respect to statistics but also that we have evidence that they have attained this knowledge. However, we have not yet achieved this. And when technology use is included, greater complexity with regard to any part of this sequence is introduced. Clearly, a major focus of research needs to be assessment as it relates to student knowledge within a context that makes use of technology tools to support learning.

CONCLUSION

Data analysis and statistics, as a content strand, is new to K–12 curriculum. Much of the research prior to the publication of the NCTM (1989) standards has focused on conceptual understandings of postsecondary students and has not necessarily looked at how this knowledge develops through instruction. It is only recently that research foci have developed concerning K–12 students' understanding of the concepts of statistics and data analysis. The use of technology for *doing* and *learning* statistics and data analysis is a natural extension when planning instruction in statistics and data analysis, yet, again, it is only recently that appropriate tools (e.g., Minitools, Fathom, TinkerPlots, and Tabletop) have become available for *learning* statistics and data analysis. Our knowledge about the design and use of instruction in statistics education that incorporates the use of technology is still in its infancy. A research frontier truly awaits our exploration.

There are many ways that the journey to and settling of this frontier might occur. For purposes here, the focus has been on instructional design with the focus of research being on what students learn and are able to do concerning K–12 statistics and data analysis content knowledge and application. While there continue to be efforts to clarify and articulate the big ideas or central statistical concepts that should occur in grades K–12 and, more specifically, what and how content trajectories might play out for students in grades K–12 (e.g., at Levels A, B, & C in Franklin et al., 2005, or grade ranges Pre-K-2, 3–5, 6–8, and 9–12 in NCTM, 2000), we do know more now about what content needs to be addressed. Indeed, there have been a number of curriculum initiatives that involve the development of instructional materials to teach statistics and data analysis that incorporate the use of technology and provide possible curricular directions (e.g., Bakker & Gravemeijer, 2004; Ben-Zvi & Friedlander, 1997; Burrill, Clifford, Errtum, Kranendonk, Mastromatteo, & O'Connor, 1999; Lappan, Fey, Fitzgerald, Friel, & Phillips, in press).

What we do not know well is how the learning of statistics and data analysis develops in these instructional contexts that include technology use by students. In developing a statistics unit for middle grades, this author hypothesized that there may be stages of research that are involved (e.g., reflecting a process like that of the developmental research of Gravemeijer, 1994, or the conjecture-driven research of Confrey & Lachance, 2000). Initially, as tasks are designed, the tasks reflect a sequence of expectations about learning for which there may be little concrete evidence. This is an exploratory stage of research; the interactions of students with tasks and with technology are experienced and analyzed by the teacher and the developers. Theories are revised along with the tasks and additional "rounds" of exploration are carried out in order to ground in some reality the expectations for what might happen using the instructional tasks. At some point, instructional design "settles into" a series of tasks that have promise for developing a given set of central statistical ideas.

A second stage of research emerges. Strategic points in the instructional sequence may be identified that include tasks, the completion of which have the potential to serve as assessment benchmarks that will provide information about students' conceptual knowledge. A more comprehensive assessment of students' knowledge needs to occur. This knowledge comes from analysis of written work, class discussions, student interactions with technology, and interviews to assess students' ways of thinking in selected problem contexts. This needs to happen with large numbers of students who are using a curriculum. This second stage can be used to inform additional work in instructional design that may involve modifications of tasks and sequences of tasks and that may inform assessment strategies.

At this stage, information gathered might also be used to inform software developers about changes needed in their programs. While Clements and Battista (2000) articulate a process of software development that includes a research component, in statistics education software development has not occurred in this fashion. However, software developers appear to be interested in and willing to listen to "from the classroom" feedback that they will incorporate as they construct upgrades of the software.[15]

Additional stages of research have yet to be defined that can address more general assessments of knowledge and abilities with respect to the identified central statistical concepts that are the focus of instruction. It is not clear that work has progressed beyond the more exploratory stages of research to a stage that involves assessment benchmarks with respect to identifying the learning that has occurred and that permits both comparison among different groups of students and replication on a larger scale with greater numbers of students.

This kind of research certainly is not straightforward or easily designed and implemented. However, it does seem that what we are most interested in knowing is what students know and understand and are able to do—both in order to report successes in terms of instruction and to inform ongoing theories about what and how students are learning about data analysis and statistics. This kind of research also will inform our evolving theories about how statistical knowledge develops and help us articulate learning, content, and instructional trajectories.

APPENDIX A: DEVELOPMENT OF DIRECTIONS FOR THE CONTENT OF STATISTICS EDUCATION

Interest in giving definition to the content and directions for statistics education also has emerged in the statisticians' community as an important area of focus. The American Statistical Association (ASA) (http://www.amstat.org [Retrieved May 5, 2005]) has been involved in statistics education for many years. In 1967, the ASA/NCTM Joint Committee on the Curriculum in Statistics and Probability for grades K–12 was created by these two organizations. One of this committee's highly successful endeavors was the Quantitative Literacy Project, followed by the Elementary Quantitative Literacy, Data Driven Mathematics, and Science Education and Quantitative Literacy. The committee supports a newsletter, *The Statistics Teacher Network*, meant for precollege teachers.

The International Statistical Institute (ISI) (http://www.cbs.nl/isi/ [Retrieved May 5, 2005]) is one of the oldest international scientific associations; its purpose is to develop and improve statistical methods and their application through the promotion of international activity and cooperation. In 1991, the International Association for Statistical Education (IASE) (http://www.stat.auckland.ac.nz/~iase/ [Retrieved May 5, 2005]), a section of the ISI and an outgrowth of the ISI Education Committee, was established to advance statistical education at all levels, from primary school through training of professionals. The IASE has a number of publications including ICOTS (International Conference on Teaching of Statistics) Proceedings (with ICOTS-5 (Pereria-Mendoza, 1998) and ICOTS-6 (Phillips, 2002) being more relevant for our technology considerations here) as well as other books and conference proceedings. The *International Statistical Review* includes a number of articles related to statistics education. More recently, the *Statistics Education Research Journal* was established (2002) by the IASE to encourage research activity in statistics education. In addition, The *International Research Forum on Statistical Reasoning, Thinking and Literacy* (SRTL) occurs every 2 years; forums are focused on current research studies that examine the nature and development of statistical literacy, reasoning, and thinking. SRTL–4 (July 2005, New Zealand) addressed reasoning about distribution as a key concept. Participation was by invitation and based on proposals that were submitted for review. The November 2004 issue of the SERJ includes a number of the papers first presented at SRTL-3 on the topic of variability.

APPENDIX B: DESCRIPTION OF SELECTED BIG IDEAS
IN K–12 DATA ANALYSIS AND STATISTICS[16]

Data provide measures of particular aspects or features of a real situation and are collected because they are judged to be relevant for use in addressing a specific question or issue that involves that situation.

A *distribution* of a single data set summarizes the possible values for a given variable and their frequencies of occurrence. Distributions highlight "data as an aggregate" and have properties such as center (e.g., mean, median, mode), shape (particularly the location of the majority of the data), density (e.g., actual or relative frequency, majority, quartiles), and spread (e.g., outliers, range, standard deviation).

Representations may be used to help visualize the structure of a distribution. The relative value of any kind of representation depends on its intended purpose. Often-used representations for the K–12 curriculum include tables, line plots, bar graphs, histograms, box plots, line graphs, and scatter plots.

Measures of central tendency are summary statistics that mark where a collection of data values (i.e., distribution) is centered and include the mode (most frequently occurring data value or values), median (the midpoint of a distribution), and mean (the "balance point" of a distribution).

Variability addresses how a collection of data values is distributed. It refers to similarities and differences found among data values or found between data values and a measure of center of a distribution. There are different kinds of variability: (a) measurement variability that comes from measurement errors, (b) natural variability that is inherent in nature, (c) induced variability that may be the result of experimental design, and (d) sampling variability that occurs when different (random) samples from the same population are selected and used.

Measures of spread provide information about the degree of variability or scatter of individual data values and their differences (deviations) from other data values or from a measure of center and include range, standard deviation, interquartile range, and percentiles.

Association involves examining two variables in a data set to see how they may *covary* in order to decide whether and in what ways data from one variable may help explain or predict data from the other variable.

Samples are subsets of a larger group (population). *Sampling* involves the process of identifying a sample and using the data from a sample to make estimates about a population. There are several ways to select a sample, including using random sampling techniques.

A *trend* characterizes group propensities or pattern(s) that emerge during the process of statistical investigation. For example, changes over time when examining time-series data can provide evidence of possible trends or making a line of best fit when examining bivariate data can characterize possible trends.

Statistical inference involves ways of estimating and drawing conclusions about populations based on analysis of data from one or more samples. With K–12 students, statistical inference is addressed informally and involves analyzing shapes of graphs and computing simple statistics to characterize single distributions, extending work with single distributions to compare and contrast two or more distributions (both equal-size or unequal-size groups), or characterizing associations between two variables in a data set.

Statistical models of a real situation are the results obtained from translating properly collected data into graphical representations, summary statistics, and so on, in order to search for meaning from the data. Judgments resulting from these analyses need to be framed in a way that makes sense in terms of the real situation being investigated.

APPENDIX C: DESCRIPTION OF LITERATURE REVIEW

The primary sources for literature reviewed are the Proceedings of the 1996 IASE Round Table Conference on Research on the Role of Technology in Teaching and Learning Statistics (Garfield & Burrill, 1997) and the Proceedings from the Fifth and Sixth International Conferences on Teaching of Statistics (ICOTS). For both ICOTS-5 (Pereira-Mendoza, 1998) and ICOTS-6 (Phillips, 2002), three strands were reviewed for relevance, namely, Topic 2 in ICOTS-6 or Topic 3 in ICOTS-5: Statistics Education at the School Level; Topic 6: Research in Statistics Education; and Topic 7: Technology in Statistics Education. Ben-Zvi and Garfield (2004a), which includes a number of chapters addressing the development of statistical reasoning, also was reviewed. Relevance involved having a focus on K–12 statistics education (although work addressing tertiary levels was considered if it could provide insights and directions for research at the K–12 level), on the design for and/or use of technology in teaching and learning statistics, on research studies in order to highlight both results of such studies and issues of methodology, and on perspectives that appear to provide insights into setting directions for a research agenda.

Two other sources were also reviewed for relevance: the special issue of *Mathematical Thinking and Learning* on statistical thinking and learning (Greer, 2000b) and the focus issue of *Statistics Education Research Journal* on variation (Ben-Zvi & Garfield, 2004c). In addition, the work of the Statistics Education Research Groups at Vanderbilt University (e.g. Cobb, 1999; Cobb et al., 2003; McClain et al., 2000, 2005) involving teaching experiments focused on statistics and data analysis and the use of computer applets (i.e., Minitools) and the work of the Statistics Education Research Group at University of Massachusetts, Amherst (e.g., Konold, 2002a, 2002b; Konold et al., 1997; Konold & Higgins, 2002, 2003; Konold & Pollatsek, 2002), which includes TinkerPlots, were reviewed. Earlier research in the use of technology and statistics education reported by Jackson and colleagues (1992, 1993a, and 1993b) and by Hancock and colleagues (1992) was also considered. Finally, a publication by Ben-Zvi and Garfield (2004b) also has been an invaluable resource for synthesizing some of the themes that are highlighted herein.

NOTES

1. The terms data analysis and statistics are often bundled together in the literature. The terms may be used individually but with the implication that they involve the same content. Definitions for statistics focus attention on data, for example, "the science of reasoning from data" (Rossman, 1997, p. 222), "the study of the theory and practice of data collection, data description and analysis, and the making of statistical inferences" (Glencross & Binyavanga, 1997, p. 302), or "the science of gaining information from data, where data are 'numbers with a context'" (Moore, 1992, as cited in Greer, 2000a, p. 4). The term data analysis describes a major part of what is involved in reasoning about data, and the science of statistics relies heavily on data analysis. For purposes here, statistics and data analysis are considered synonymous and used interchangeably.

    Beyond statistics, the important role of probability is recognized as part of the framework of what students need to know and be able to do. However, given space limitations and the timeliness of the relationships among technology and data analysis and statistics, the focus in this chapter is on that connection.

2. Examination of curriculum frameworks from a few other countries (Curriculum Council of Western Australia, 2003; National Curriculum for England, 2003; South Australian Curriculum Standards and Accountability, 2003) indicates the same increased emphases and directions across pre-university education.

3. Different kinds of mathematical tasks require different kinds and levels of student thinking. Stein, Smith, Henningsen, and Silver (2000) refer to the kinds of thinking needed to solve tasks as the tasks' *cognitive demands* (p. 3). These authors have characterized levels of mathematical instructional tasks (p. 16) by examining their cognitive demands. Applying their ideas to statistics education, we can contrast tasks that offer lower-level cognitive demands (e.g., memorization or using procedures without connections to understanding, meaning, or concepts) with those that offer higher-level cognitive demands (i.e., using procedures in ways that build connections to

understanding, meaning, or concepts or doing statistics) to make the point that it is possible to think about differentiating the levels of cognitive demand associated with the problems or tasks used with students to promote their statistical reasoning. Specifically, *doing statistics* requires more complex and nonprocedural thinking that engages students in exploring and understanding the nature of the statistical and data analysis concepts, skills, and relationships as they engage in statistical reasoning (e.g., Konold, Pollatsek, Well, & Gagnon, 1997).

4. The Minitools and TinkerPlots described by Bakker (2002) are designed for learning statistics and data analysis; while these software can be used to do data analysis work, it is probable that an experienced statistics user would choose an alternative software program. For example, a more experienced statistics user probably would not want to be bothered having to create graphs from scratch in every investigation—a characteristic feature of TinkerPlots.

5. The Minitools are commercially available as applets on CD with Bright, Brewer, McClain, & Mooney, 2003.

6. Tinker deliberately chooses the term "information technologies" to distinguish computer technologies from any other kind of learning technology. The modifier "information" is intended to provide a clue to what makes these technologies unique and important to education (Tinker, 1996, p. 20).

7. Hall and Hord (2001) characterize eight classifications, or levels, of behaviors of people as they learn about how to use new practices (innovations) for their classroom and schools. Three levels pertain to nonusers and five levels (mechanical use, routine use, refinement, integration, and renewal) pertain to the user. Since these levels deal with behavior, they can be defined operationally. For the user, the key in making distinctions involves the type of adaptations being made in using the innovation (e.g., technology in teaching statistics).

8. Ms. Trista Stearns, a graduate student at UNC-Chapel Hill, worked with the author to summarize the articles reviewed. Her help was invaluable to completing this task.

9. This statement is hypothetical; there is no evidence for its validity in any research reviewed although there are software options that make this kind of investigation of student understanding a realistic option.

10. The work of Jackson, Berger, and Edwards (1992) and Jackson, Edwards, and Berger (1993a, 1993b) focused on a curriculum development and research project involving the Detroit Public Schools and the School of Education at the University of Michigan. A unit on computer-assisted graphing was implemented as part of the district's Computer Applications Program. The unit involved two phases conducted over six to seven class sessions: direct group instruction to introduce the principles of graph design and interpretation and how to use the graphing software followed by problem-solving session in which the students or student pairs graphically analyzed spreadsheet-based data. This graph unit was taught several

times over several years in the school district. The student population generally was several hundred inner city high school students. In the first study (1992), students used Cricket Graph. Following this study, the authors designed their own software called CAPGraph (1993a) and then carried out another study (with the sixth iteration of the graphing unit and using the new software) about which they reported their results (1993b).

11.   This finding supports Bakker's (2002) observation that the use of professional statistical software packages is not a good idea because a user who is *learning* about statistics and data analysis does not have the necessary "graph knowledge framework" to guide choices among histograms, box plots, or circle graphs if he or she does not yet understand what these representations are and when they would be useful.

12.   Biehler reports on two studies, one of them being the Barriers Project. The other study involved similar work completed with preservice teachers. His summary points (in addition to his report of results from each study) are drawn from his analysis of both studies. For purposes here, we focus only on the specific study conducted with secondary students that was part of the Barriers Project.

13.   The reader is encouraged to read Garfield and Ben-Zvi's (2004) chapter, "Research on Statistical Literacy, Thinking: Issues, Challenges, and Implications" and Jolliffe's (1998) chapter, "What Is Research in Statistical Education?" in order to develop a more general overview about research in statistics education.

14.   Jolliffe (2003) distinguishes between statistics education research and statistical education research. In the literature, both of the terms tend to be used with similar meaning. "However, statistical education research includes research into such topics as statistical reasoning and thinking and so is wider in scope than statistics education research, which implies research into education in statistics" (p. 47).

15.   The author had interactions with the developers of the Fathom who made some modifications of the software during its recent revision to reflect some needs that arose from classroom use. This author also provided feedback, grounded in classroom use of the software with a curriculum, during the development of TinkerPlots.

16.   These ideas are discussed in a variety of sources (Bakker & Gravemeijer, 2004; Cobb, 1999; Cobb, McClain, & Gravemeijer, 2003; Franklin et al., 2005; Garfield & Ben-Zvi, 2004; Hancock, Kaput, & Goldsmith, 1992; Konold & Higgins, 2002, 2003; Konold & Pollatsek, 2002; Pfannkuch & Wild, 2004).

REFERENCES

Bakker, A. (2002). Route-type and landscape-type software for learning statistical data analysis. In B. Phillips (Ed.), *Developing a statistically literate society: Pro-*

ceedings of the sixth International Conference on Teaching Statistics [CD]. Voorburg, The Netherlands: International Statistical Institute.

Bakker, A., & Gravemeijer, K. P. E. (2004). Learning to reason about distribution. In D. Ben-Zvi & J. Garfield (Eds.), *The challenge of developing statistical literacy, reasoning and thinking* (pp. 147-168). Boston: Kluwer Academic.

Batanero, C., Estepa, A., & Godino, J. (1997). Evolution of students' understanding of statistical association in a computer-based teaching environment. In J. Garfield & G. Burrill (Eds.), *Research on the role of technology in teaching and learning statistics: Proceedings of the 1996 International Association for Statistical Education (IASE) Round Table Conference* (pp. 198-212). Voorburg, The Netherlands: International Statistical Institute.

Ben-Zvi, D. (2000). Toward understanding the role of technological tools in statistical learning. *Mathematical Thinking and Learning, 2,* 127-155.

Ben-Zvi, D. (2002). Seventh grade students' sense making of data and data representations. In B. Phillips (Chief Ed.), *Developing a statistically literate society: Proceedings of the sixth International Conference on Teaching Statistics* [CD]. Voorburg, The Netherlands: International Statistical Institute.

Ben-Zvi, D. (2004). Reasoning about data analysis. In D. Ben-Zvi & J. Garfield (Eds.), *The challenge of developing statistical literacy, reasoning and thinking* (pp. 121-145). Boston: Kluwer Academic.

Ben-Zvi, D., & Arcavi, A. (1998). Toward a characterization and understanding of students' learning in an interactive statistics environment. In L. Pereira-Mendoza (Ed.), *Statistical education—Expanding the network: Proceedings of the fifth International Conference on Teaching Statistics* (Vol. 2, pp. 647-653). Voorburg, The Netherlands: International Statistical Institute.

Ben-Zvi D., & Friedlander, A. (1997). Statistical thinking in a technological environment. In J. B. Garfield & G. Burrill (Eds.), *Research on the role of technology in teaching and learning statistics: Proceedings of the 1996 International Association for Statistical Education (IASE) Round Table Conference* (pp. 45-55). Voorburg, The Netherlands: International Statistical Institute.

Ben-Zvi, D., & Garfield, J. (2004a). Statistical literacy, reasoning, and thinking: Goals, definitions, and challenges. In D. Ben-Zvi & J. Garfield (Eds.), *The challenge of developing statistical literacy, reasoning and thinking* (pp. 3-15). Boston: Kluwer Academic.

Ben-Zvi, D., & Garfield, J. (Eds.). (2004b). *The challenge of developing statistical literacy, reasoning and thinking*. Boston: Kluwer Academic.

Ben-Zvi, D., & Garfield, J. (Guest Eds.). (2004c). *Statistics Education Research Journal, 3*(2). Retrieved May 5, 2005, from http://www.stat.auckland.ac.nz/~iase/publications.php?show=serj#archives/

Biehler, R. (1994). Software tools and mathematics education: The case of statistics. In C. Keitel & K. Ruthven (Eds.), *Learning from computers: Mathematics education and technology* (pp. 68-100). Berlin, Germany: Springer-Verlag.

Biehler, R. (1997a). Software for learning and doing statistics. *International Statistical Review, 65,* 167-189.

Biehler, R. (1997b). Students' difficulties in practicing computer-supported data analysis: Some hypothetical generalizations from results of two exploratory studies. In J. B. Garfield & G. Burrill (Eds.), *Research on the role of technology in teaching and learning statistics: Proceedings of the 1996 International Association for Statistical Education (IASE) Round Table Conference* (pp. 176-197). Voorburg, The Netherlands: International Statistical Institute.

Bright, G. W., Brewer, W., McClain, K., & Mooney, E. S. (2003). Navigating through data analysis in grades 6-8 [book and CD with applets]. Reston, VA: National Council of Teachers of Mathematics.

Burrill, G. (2002). Simulation as a tool to develop statistical understanding. In B. Phillips (Ed.) *Developing a statistically literate society: Proceedings of the sixth International Conference on Teaching Statistics* [CD]. Voorburg, The Netherlands: International Statistical Institute.

Burrill, G. (2004). International Association for Statistical Education (IASE) 2004 Roundtable Conference on Curricular Development in Statistics Education. Retrieved May 5, 2005, from http://hobbes.lite.msu.edu/~IASE_2004_Roundtable/

Burrill, J., Clifford, M., Errthum, E., Kranendonk, H., Mastromatteo, M., & O'Connor, V. (1999). *Data-driven mathematics: Mathematics in a world of data*. White Plains, NY: Dale Seymour.

Chance, B. (2002). Components of statistical thinking and implications for instruction and assessment. *Journal of Statistics Education, 10*. Retrieved May 5, 2005, from www.amstat.org/publications/jse/v10n3/chance.html

Chance, B. L., & Garfield, J. B. (2002). New approaches to gathering data on student learning for research in statistics education. *Statistics Education Research Journal, 1*, 38-41. Retrieved May 5, 2005, from http://www.stat.auckland.ac.nz/~iase/publications.php?show=serj#archives/

Chance, B., delMas, R., & Garfield, J. (2004). Reasoning about sampling distributions. In D. Ben-Zvi & J. Garfield (Eds.), *The challenge of developing statistical literacy, reasoning and thinking* (pp. 295-323). Boston: Kluwer Academic.

Clements, D. H., & Battista, M. T. (2000). Designing effective software. In A. E. Kelly & R. A. Lesh (Eds.), *Handbook of research design in mathematics and science education* (pp. 761-776). Mahwah, NJ: Erlbaum.

Cobb, P. (1999). Individual and collective mathematical development: The case of statistical data analysis. *Mathematical Thinking and Learning, 1*, 5-43.

Cobb, P., & McClain, K. (2004). Principles of instructional design for supporting the development of students' statistical reasoning. In D. Ben-Zvi & J. Garfield (Eds.), *The challenge of developing statistical literacy, reasoning and thinking* (pp. 375-395). Boston: Kluwer Academic.

Cobb, P., McClain, K., & Gravemeijer, K. (2003). Learning about statistical covariation. *Cognition and Instruction, 21*, 1-78.

Confrey, J., & Lachance, A. (2000). Transformative teaching experiments through conjecture-driven research design. In A. E. Kelly & R. A. Lesh (Eds.), *Handbook of research design in mathematics and science education* (pp. 231-265). Mahwah, NJ: Erlbaum.

Curriculum Council of Western Australia. (n.d.). *The curriculum framework*. Retrieved May 5, 2005, from http://www.curriculum.wa.edu.au/default.htm

Darius, P., Michiels, S., Raeymaekers, B., Ottoy, J. -P., & Thas, O. (2002). Applets for experimenting with statistical concepts. In B. Phillips (Ed.), *Developing a statistically literate society: Proceedings of the Sixth International Conference on*

Teaching Statistics [CD]. Voorburg, The Netherlands: International Statistical Institute.

delMas, R. C. (2004). A comparison of mathematical and statistical reasoning. In D. Ben-Zvi & J. Garfield (Eds.), *The challenge of developing statistical literacy, reasoning and thinking* (pp. 79-95). Boston: Kluwer Academic.

DeltaGraph. (2005). (Version 5, MacIntosh) (Version 5.4, Windows) [Computer software]. Golden, CO: RockWare.

Erickson, T. (2002). Technology, statistics, and subtleties of measurement: bridging the gap between science and mathematics . In B. Phillips (Ed.) *Developing a statistically literate society: Proceedings of the Sixth International Conference on Teaching Statistics* [CD]. Voorburg, The Netherlands: International Statistical Institute.

Fey, J. T., Atchison, W. F., Good, R. A., Heid, M. K., Johnson, J., Kantowski, M. G., et al. (1984). *Computing & mathematics: The impact on secondary school curricula*. Reston, VA: National Council of Teachers of Mathematics.

Finzer, W. (2005). Fathom Dynamic Data Software™ (Version 2.0) [Computer software]. Emeryville, CA: Key Curriculum Press.

Franklin, C., Kader, G., Mewborn, D., Moreno, J., Peck, R., Perry, M., et al. (2005). *A curriculum framework for pre-K-12 statistics education*. Retrieved May 5, 2005, from http://it.stlawu.edu/~rlock/gaise/ and currently located at http://www.amstat.org/education/gaise/GAISEPreK-12.htm

Friel, S. N. (2002). Wooden or steel roller coasters: What's the choice? *New England Mathematics Journal, 34*, 45-54.

Friel, S. N., Curcio, F. R., & Bright, G. W. (2001). Making sense of graphs: Critical factors influencing comprehension and instructional implications. *Journal for Research in Mathematics Education, 32*, 124-58.

Friel, S. N., & Joyner, J. M. (1997). *Teach-Stat for teachers: Professional development manual*. Palo Alto, CA: Dale Seymour.

Gal, I., & Garfield, J. B. (1997a). Curricular goals and assessment challenges in statistics education. In I. Gal & J. B. Garfield, (Eds.), *The assessment challenge in statistics education* (pp. 1-13). Voorburg, The Netherlands: The International Statistical Institute.

Gal, I., & Garfield, J. B. (Eds.). (1997b). *The assessment challenge in statistics education*. Voorburg, The Netherlands: The International Statistical Institute.

Galmacci, G., & Cicchitelli, G. (1998). Network facilities for teaching statistics: A data archive driven by interactive software. In L. Pereira-Mendoza (Chief Ed.), *Statistical education expanding the network: Proceedings of the fifth international conference on teaching statistics* (pp. 961-968, 2). Singapore: ISI-IASE.

Garfield, J. (2002). The challenge of developing statistical reasoning. *Journal of Statistics Education, 10*. Retrieved May 5, 2005, from www.amstat.org/publications/jse/v10n3/garfield.html

Garfield, J. (2003). Assessing statistical reasoning. *Statistics Education Research Journal, 2*, 22-38. Retrieved May 5, 2005, from http://www.stat.auckland.ac.nz/~iase/publications.php?show=serj#archives/

Garfield, J. B., & Ben-Zvi, D. (2004). Research on statistical literacy, reasoning, and thinking: Issues, challenges, and implications. In D. Ben-Zvi & J.

Garfield (Eds.), *The challenge of developing statistical literacy, reasoning and thinking* (pp. 397-409). Boston: Kluwer Academic.

Garfield, J. B., & Burrill, G. (Eds.). (1997). *Research on the role of technology in teaching and learning statistics: Proceedings of the 1996 International Association for Statistical Education (IASE) Round Table Conference.* Voorburg, The Netherlands: International Statistical Institute.

Garfield, J., & Chance, B. (2000). Assessment in statistics education: Issues and challenges. *Mathematical Thinking and Learning, 2,* 99-125.

Garfield, J., Chance, B., & Snell, J. L. (2001). Technology in college statistics courses. In D. Holton (Ed.), *The teaching and learning of mathematics at university level: An ICMI study* (pp. 357-370). Boston, MA: Kluwer Publishers.

Glencross, M. J., & Binyavanga, K.W. (1997). The role of technology in statistics education: A view from a developing region. In J. B. Garfield & G. Burrill, (Eds.), *Research on the role of technology in teaching and learning statistics: Proceedings of the 1996 International Association for Statistical Education (IASE) Round Table Conference* (pp. 301-308). Voorburg, The Netherlands: International Statistical Institute.

Gravemeijer, K. (1994). Educational development and developmental research in mathematics education. *Journal for Research in Mathematics Education, 25,* 443-471.

Greer, B. (2000a). Statistical thinking and learning. *Mathematical Thinking and Learning, 2,* 1-9.

Greer, B. (Ed.). (2000b). Statistical thinking and learning [Special issue]. *Mathematical Thinking and Learning, 2.*

Hall, G. E., & Hord, S. M. (2001). *Implementing change.* Boston: Allyn & Bacon.

Hammerman, J., & Rubin, A. (2004). Strategies for managing statistical complexity with new software tools. *Statistics Education Research Journal, 3,* 17-41. Retrieved May 5, 2005, from http://www.stat.auckland.ac.nz/~iase/publications.php?show=serj#archives/

Hancock, C. (2002). *Foundational tools for data literacy.* Proposal submitted to the National Science Foundation (Funded June, 2003).

Hancock, C., Kaput, J. J., & Goldsmith, L. T. (1992). Authentic inquiry with data: Critical barriers to classroom implementation. *Educational Psychologist, 27,* 337-364.

Herweyers, G. (2002). Simulating experiments with the graphic calculator TI83Plus. In B. Phillips (Ed.), *Developing a statistically literate society: Proceedings of the sixth International Conference on Teaching Statistics* [CD]. Voorburg, The Netherlands: International Statistical Institute.

Huntley, M. A., Zucker, A. A., & Esty, E. T. (2000, January). *A review of research on computer-based tools (spreadsheets, graphing, data analysis, and probability tools), with an annotated bibliography.* Arlington, VA: SRI International, Center for Technology and Learning.

Jackson, D., Berger, C., & Edwards, B. (1992). Computer-assisted thinking tools: Problem solving in graphical data analysis. *Journal of Educational Computing Research, 8,* 43-67.

Jackson, D., Edwards, B., & Berger, C. (1993a). The design of software tools for meaningful learning by experience: Flexibility and feedback. *Journal of Educational Computing Research, 9*, 413-443.

Jackson, D., Edwards, B., & Berger, C. (1993b). Teaching the design and interpretation of graphs through computer-aided graphical data analysis. *Journal of Research in Science Teaching, 30*, 483-501.

Jolliffe, F. (1998). What is research in statistical education? In L. Pereira-Mendoza (Chief Ed.), *Statistical education—Expanding the network: Proceedings of the fifth International Conference on Teaching Statistics* (Vol. 2, pp. 801-806). Voorburg, The Netherlands: International Statistical Institute.

Jolliffe, F. (2003). Towards a database of research in statistical education. *Statistics Education Research Journal, 2*, 47-58. Retrieved May 5, 2005, from http://www.stat.auckland.ac.nz/~iase/publications.php?show=serj#archives/

Jones, G. A., Langrall, C. W., Mooney, E. S., & Thornton, C. A. (2004). Models of development in statistical reasoning. In D. Ben-Zvi & J. Garfield (Eds.), *The challenge of developing statistical literacy, reasoning and thinking* (pp. 97-117). Boston: Kluwer Academic.

Konold, C. (2002a). Teaching concepts rather than conventions. *New England Mathematics Journal, 34*, 69-81.

Konold, C. (2002b). Alternatives to scatter plots. In B. Phillips (Ed.), *Developing a statistically literate society: Proceedings of the sixth International Conference on Teaching Statistics* [CD]. Voorburg, The Netherlands: International Statistical Institute.

Konold, C., & Higgins, T. (2002). Highlights of related research. In S. J. Russell, D. Schifter, & V. Bastable (Eds., with C. Konold & T. L. Higgins), *Developing mathematical ideas: Working with data* [CD]. Parsippany, NJ: Dale Seymour.

Konold, C., & Higgins, T. L. (2003). Reasoning about data. In J. Kilpatrick, W. G. Martin, & D. Schifter (Eds.), *A research companion to Principles and Standards for School Mathematics* (pp. 193-215). Reston, VA: National Council of Teachers of Mathematics.

Konold, C., & Miller, C. D. (2005). TinkerPlots: Dynamic Data Exploration™ [Computer software]. Emeryville, CA: Key Curriculum Press.

Konold, C., & Pollatsek, A. (2002). Data analysis as the search for signals in noisy processes. *Journal for Research in Mathematics Education, 33*, 259-289.

Konold, C., Pollatsek, A., Well, A., & Gagnon, A. (1997). Students analyzing data: Research of critical barriers. In J. B. Garfield & G. Burrill (Eds.), *Research on the role of technology in teaching and learning statistics: Proceedings of the 1996 International Association for Statistical Education (IASE) Round Table Conference* (pp. 151-167). Voorburg, The Netherlands: International Statistical Institute.

Lajoie, S. P. (1998). *Reflections on statistics: Learning, teaching, and assessment in grades K-12.* Mahwah, NJ: Erlbaum.

Lappan, G., Fey, J. T., Fitzgerald, W. M., Friel, S. N., & Phillips, E. D. (in press). *Data distributions.* Needham, MA: Prentice Hall.

Lewis, C. C. (2002). *Lesson study: A handbook of teacher-led instructional change.* Philadelphia: Research for Better Schools.

Lipson, K. (1997). What do students gain form computer simulation exercises? An evaluation of activities designed to develop an understanding of sampling distribution of a proportion. In J. B. Garfield & G. Burrill (Eds.), *Research on the role of technology in teaching and learning statistics: Proceedings of the 1996 International Association for Statistical Education (IASE) Round Table Conference* (pp. 137-150). Voorburg, The Netherlands: International Statistical Institute.

Lock, R. (2002). Using Fathom to promote interactive explorations of statistical concepts. In B. Phillips (Ed.), *Developing a statistically literate society: Proceedings of the sixth International Conference on Teaching Statistics* [CD]. Voorburg, The Netherlands: International Statistical Institute.

McClain, K., & Cobb, P. (2001). Supporting students' ability to reason about data. *Educational Studies in Mathematics, 45,* 103-129.

McClain, K., Cobb, P., & Gravemeijer, K. (2000). Supporting students' ways of reasoning about data. In M. J. Burke & F. R. Curcio (Eds.), *Learning mathematics for a new century* (2000 Yearbook of the National Council of Teachers of Mathematics) (pp. 174-187). Reston, VA: National Council of Teachers of Mathematics.

McClain, K., Cobb, P. & Gravemeijer, K. (2005). Statistical data analysis: A tool for learning. In T. A. Romberg, T. P. Carpenter, & F. Dremock (Eds.), *Understanding mathematics and science matters* (pp. 127-157). Mahwah, NJ: Erlbaum.

Meletiou, M. (2002). Concepts of variation: A literature review. *Statistics Education Research Journal, 1,* 46-52. Retrieved May 5, 2005, from http://www.stat.auckland.ac.nz/~iase/index.php

Mittag, H. -J. (2002). Java applets and multimedia catalogues for statistics education. In B. Phillips (Ed.), *Developing a statistically literate society: Proceedings of the sixth International Conference on Teaching Statistics* [CD]. Voorburg, The Netherlands: International Statistical Institute.

National Assessment Governing Board. (2004). *Mathematics framework for the 2005 National Assessment of Educational Progress.* Washington, DC: Author. Retrieved May 5, 2005, from http://nces.ed.gov/nationsreportcard/frameworks.asp

National Council of Teachers of Mathematics. (1989). *Curriculum and evaluation standards for school mathematics.* Reston, VA: Author.

National Council of Teachers of Mathematics. (2000). *Principles and standards for school mathematics.* Reston, VA: Author.

National Curriculum for England. (n.d.). Retrieved May 5, 2005, from http://www.nc.uk.net/Ma-4-4-POS.html.

Pea, R. (1987). Beyond amplification: Using the computer to reorganize mental functioning. In A. H. Schoenfeld (Ed.), *Cognitive science and mathematics education* (pp. 89-122). Hillsdale, NJ: Erlbaum.

Pereiria-Mendoza, L. (Ed.). (1998). *Statistical education—Expanding the network: Proceedings of the fifth International Conference on Teaching Statistics* [CD]. Voorburg, The Netherlands: International Statistical Institute.

Pfannkuch, J., & Wild, C. (2004). Towards an understanding of statistical thinking. In D. Ben-Zvi & J. Garfield (Eds.), *The challenge of developing statistical literacy, reasoning and thinking* (pp. 17-46). Boston: Kluwer Academic.

Phillips, B. (Ed.). (2002). *Developing a statistically literate society: Proceedings of the sixth International Conference on Teaching Statistics* [CD]. Voorburg, The Netherlands: International Statistical Institute.

Rachlin, S. (1998). Learning to see the wind. *Mathematics Teaching in the Middle School, 3*, 470-473.

Rossman, A. (1997). Workshop statistics: Using technology to promote learning by self-discovery. In J. B. Garfield & G. Burrill (Eds.), *Research on the role of technology in teaching and learning statistics: 1996 Proceedings of the 1996 International Association for Statistical Education (IASE) Round Table Conference* (pp. 226-237). Voorburg, The Netherlands: International Statistical Institute.

Rumsey, D. J. (2002). Statistical literacy as a goal for introductory statistics courses. *Journal of Statistics Education, 10*. Retrieved May 5, 2005, from www.amstat.org/publications/jse/v10n3/rumsey2.html

Scheaffer, R. L. (2000). Statistics for a new century. In M. J. Burke & F. R. Curcio (Eds.), *Learning mathematics for a new century* (2000 Yearbook of the National Council of Teachers of Mathematics) (pp. 158-173). Reston, VA: National Council of Teachers of Mathematics.

Scheaffer, R. L. (2002). Data analysis in the K-12 curriculum: Teaching teachers. *New England Mathematics Journal, 34*(2), 6-25.

Sharma, S., & Begg, A. (2003). *Statistics education bibliography.* Hamilton, New Zealand: University of Waikato, Centre for Science, Mathematics and Technology Education Research.

Shaughnessy, J. M. (1992). Research in probability and statistics: Reflections and directions. In D. Grouws (Ed.), *Handbook of research on mathematics teaching and learning* (pp. 465-494). New York: Macmillian.

Shaughnessy, J. M., Garfield, J., & Greer, B. (1996). Data handling. In A. J. Bishop, K. Clements, C. Keitel, J. Kilpatrick, & C. Laborde (Eds.), *International handbook of mathematics education* (Vol. 1, pp. 205-237). Dordrecht, The Netherlands: Kluwer.

South Australian Curriculum Standards and Accountability Framework. (n.d.). Retrieved May 5, 2005, from http://www.sacsa.sa.edu.au/index_fsrc.asp?t= HOME

StatTools: Statistics for Excel. (2005). [Computer software]. Golden, CO: Rock-Ware.

Stein, M. K., Smith, M. S., Henningsen, J. A., & Silver, E. A. (2000). *Implementing standards-based mathematics instruction.* New York: Teachers College Press.

Tabletop™. (1995). [Computer software]. Elgin, IL: Sunburst Technology.

Tinker, R. (1996). *Information technologies in science and mathematics education.* (ENC-007682, out of print). Retrieved May 5, 2005, from http://www.concord.org/newsletter/pdf/enc-v7.pdf

CHAPTER 12

KEEPING THE FAITH

Fidelity in Technological Tools for Mathematics Education

Thomas P. Dick

There are many different audiences that can benefit from the insights that can arise from thoughtful research on the use of technology in the teaching and learning of mathematics. These audiences include classroom mathematics teachers, mathematics curriculum developers, educational policymakers, and the designers of the technological tools. The purpose of this chapter is to consider, from the perspective of the tool designer, the lessons that can be learned from research.

As the title indicates, the theme of this chapter is *fidelity*—technology designed for use in mathematics education should be faithful to some basic principles. We will refer to these principles as *pedagogical fidelity*, *mathematical fidelity*, and *cognitive fidelity*.

Before providing specifics of what we mean by "keeping the faith" pedagogically, mathematically, and cognitively, it is important to note that these remarks are aimed at designers of technological tools intended primarily to facilitate the *learning* of mathematics. There are, of course, tools

Research on Technology and the Teaching and Learning of Mathematics:
Vol. 2. Cases and Perspectives, 333–339
Copyright © 2008 by Information Age Publishing

that are designed primarily for the *application* of mathematics that enjoy extensive use in mathematics classrooms. For example, a computer spreadsheet is a tool that has been heavily adapted for use in the mathematics classroom, in ways that likely were never imagined by the designers of the first spreadsheets. For a tool such as a spreadsheet, the lessons to be learned from research are actually intended for the educational adapters (classroom teachers, curriculum developers, etc.), not the spreadsheet designers.

We will not go so far as to say that our distinction between designed and adapted tools is universally easy to apply. For example, the suite of features found on some computer algebra systems (CASs) could be argued to be a mix of tools for mathematics learning and mathematics applications.

PEDAGOGICAL FIDELITY

At the risk of invoking an educational cliché, we take as axiomatic that students learn mathematics by doing mathematics. But what does it mean to "do mathematics?" Suppose we make our axiom a bit more explicit.

> *Axiom:* Students learn mathematics by taking mathematical actions (e.g., transforming, representing, manipulating) on mathematical objects (e.g., symbolic expressions, graphs, geometric figures, physical models), observing the mathematical consequences of those actions, and reflecting on their meanings.

Students' reflections on mathematical consequences of mathematical actions on mathematical objects are the fuel for feeding the cycle of prediction-conjecture-testing that ultimately leads to proofs or refutations.

A technological tool stays true to this pedagogical axiom to the degree that its use is perceived transparently by the student to further these purposes. That is, for a tool to be pedagogically faithful, the student should perceive the tool as (a) facilitating the creation of mathematical objects, (b) allowing mathematical actions on those objects, and (c) providing clear evidence of the consequences of those actions.

Keeping the pedagogical faith is evidenced most clearly in the organization of the user interface of a technological tool. For example, consider something as mundane as the menu organization of a software package. Clearly the software will have general commands common to almost all packages (file management, editing functions such as cut/copy/paste, etc.). We would also expect the software to have commands that correspond to creating mathematical objects, taking actions on those objects, and displaying or reporting information. There is no single best way to organize this mix, but if the designer stays faithful to the pedagogy principle, then that organization should be made with the clear goal of facilitating the mathematical moves with as few distractions as possible. For example, a graphing software package should not mix parameter controls that are cosmetic with those having mathematical substance. Font characteristics for labels or measurements are user preferences that should be quite separate from window scaling options.

The pedagogical faithfulness of a technological tool can be reflected in how a user would typically describe the steps in an activity or procedure. A pedagogically faithful tool will lend itself to describing moves in terms of interactions with the mathematics (e.g., "I graphed this function," "I created this triangle," or "I measured this area") rather than in terms of interactions with the tool (e.g., "I went to this menu," "I changed this mode," or "I set the preferences to").

MATHEMATICAL FIDELITY

A technological tool must stay true to the mathematics. If a student perceives that a virtual mathematical object has been created through the use of a tool, then the characteristics and behavior of that object in the technological arena should reflect accurately the mathematical characteristics and behavior that the idealized object should have. (Platonism is not a bad philosophy for the technological tool designer!)

While the goal of mathematical fidelity may seem obvious, in practice it can be quite difficult to implement. Some of the obstacles are inherent and due to technological limitations. Other problems are due to conscious design choices that put ease of use at a higher priority than faithfulness to mathematical structure.

For example, design choices made in the handling of implicit multiplication in algebraic expressions may make life easier for the user in certain circumstances, but betray mathematical conventions in other circumstances. To allow users to enter an expression such as $\sin 2x$ as the conventional shorthand for $\sin(2x)$ means that implicit multiplication must have a higher precedence than function application. This convenience puts us in a bizarre situation in which explicit multiplication notation has an entirely different mathematical interpretation from implicit multiplication: $\sin 2*x$ would mean $(\sin(2))*x$, since the evaluation of the sine function (at 2) would take precedence over the explicit multiplication by x.

A common technological limitation has to do with the modeling of continuous phenomena with discrete structures. This goes far beyond the usual caveats of interpreting displayed numerical results represented as finite precision terminating decimals. The hidden traps are encountered when the results of such computations are generated and used but are not seen by the student.

For example, suppose a geometry tool that provides features for the creation and manipulation of lines in the plane uses the Cartesian slope of the line as one of the underlying defining parameters. That is, the tool stores a line internally using two pieces of data: the slope of the line and a reference point (such as the y-intercept). Of course, the case of a vertical line would need to be handled differently by such a tool. The tool could use this very compact bundle of data not only to generate a visual display of the line in a given window but also to perform actions such as creating a parallel or perpendicular line to a given line or testing for the parallelism or perpendicularity of two given lines. The real problems arise when dealing with lines that are *nearly* vertical or horizontal. Precision limitations could result in gross (and visually obvious) errors. Indeed, my first experience attempting to create a perpendicular to a very steep (visually almost vertical) line on an early dynamic geometry package resulted in a line that was nowhere near horizontal visually.

Perhaps the worst "conscious" offenses have been made with how technological tools deal with functions. The mathematical concept of function is arguably the single most important in all of mathematics, so this lack of faithfulness is particularly troubling. In most cases, the fundamental error made with functions is to treat them as expressions rather than mappings with *domains*. The mathematics community itself is somewhat to blame for the situation, given the common convention of adopting implicit domains for functions in certain contexts. For example, it is typical in calculus to assume that a functional expression $y = f(x)$ defines a real-valued mapping having as its domain the largest subset of real numbers x for which the expression $f(x)$ results in a real number. Thus, one can "define" a function simply by writing $y = \dfrac{1}{x-2}$, provided it is understood that the implied domain of the function is $\{x : x \varepsilon \Re, x \neq 2\}$.

We are already on shaky ground pedagogically with such conventions, for while the expert may be careful to account for these implicit domains in composing functions, a student may be blissfully unaware of them. The risk is compounded when a student uses a technological tool that "defines" functions without reference to any domain. For example, the equations $y = 2\ln(x)$ and $y = \ln(x^2)$ would define different functions having different implicit domains using the usual calculus convention. The domain of the first is the set of positive real numbers and the domain of the second is the set of nonzero real numbers, although it is true that the two functions take on the same values at each point in the intersection of their domains.

Now consider the function $y = |\ln(x)|$. What is its domain? If we follow the chain of compositions, $x \to \ln(x) \to |\ln(x)|$, the implicit domain would be the set of positive real numbers. However, many computer and calculator graphers will plot this function as if its domain were the set of all nonzero real numbers, since the *modulus (absolute value)* of the complex number $\ln(x)$ that results for $x < 0$ gives a final result of a real number.

The algebraic "simplification" of an expression can effectively change the domain (and hence change the definition of the function). Consider the function $y = \arctan\left(\dfrac{1}{x}\right)$, implicitly defined on the domain of all nonzero real numbers. Its derivative is given by $\dfrac{dy}{dx} = \dfrac{1}{1 + \left(\dfrac{1}{x}\right)^2} \cdot \dfrac{-1}{x^2} = -\dfrac{1}{x^2 + 1}$.

The final simplification of the algebraic expression for the derivative function results in an expression whose implied domain is the set of *all* real numbers, including $x = 0$. Clearly, the derivative of a function cannot be defined at a point that is not in the domain of the function! At this point, we must make the domain of nonzero real numbers *explicit* in order to maintain the mathematical fidelity of our actions (differentiation followed by simplification). This particular example is sometimes used as a test of the integrity of computer algebra systems.

It is unrealistic to expect the mathematics community to suddenly drop conventions that have the inertia of historical usage behind them. Human users of symbols must be aware of the implicit assumptions and contexts for their usage (Is $f(x) = 3$ an equation or a definition of a constant function?) and ignore them at their own risk. To use technological tools intelligently in arenas in which implicit assumptions and contexts lurk, there need to be ways of explicitly informing the machine. One strategy has been the setting of modes or preferences that correspond to these explicit assumptions. However, for tools that aim to handle many different possible mathematical contexts, the number of mode/preference settings can quickly become unwieldy.

COGNITIVE FIDELITY

Technological tools for mathematics education should be faithful to students' cognitive processes. Unlike the application of a technological tool in the "real world," there should be more emphasis on illuminating mathematical thinking processes than simply arriving at "black box" final results as efficiently as possible.

In the context of intelligent tutoring systems, Beeson (1989) has used the term "cognitive fidelity" to refer to the degree to which the computer's method of solution resembles a person's method of solution. In that same context, Beeson discusses the idea of a "glass box"—a computer program that allows the user to see *how* the answer is produced, meaning that a program is most useful in instruction if its (visible) inner workings are cognitively faithful. (We would note that this usage of the term "glass box" applied to a computer program is a bit different from the term "white box" used to describe instructional activity with a CAS (see, for example Cedillo & Kieran, 2003). The machine algorithms used by a tool to accomplish a result may bear little resemblance to conceptually based procedures a person typically would use. For example, the numeric root finder or equation solver found on most graphing calculators generally uses techniques far more sophisticated than those with which its users (students) would be familiar.

Some of the calculus reform projects funded by the National Science Foundation did not have to do so much with curriculum development as they did with the building of a glass box front end (i.e., an additional interface layer through which the user works instead of the usual interface) to a CAS. A CAS generally uses some very sophisticated "black box" symbolic integration techniques to produce antiderivatives. A classical integration by parts ($\int u\,dv = uv - \int v\,du$) completed "by hand" could be performed quite differently by a CAS. A glass box for integrating by parts might require the student to choose the u and dv, calculate the corresponding du and v (with the help of the CAS, perhaps) and then instruct the CAS to perform the integration by parts using the student's choices.

CHALLENGES FOR THE FUTURE: THE NEED FOR AUTHORING TOOLS

The greatest unrealized challenge is to bridge the gap between the vision of the educational practitioners and the technical expertise of the educational tool designer. Specifically, how do we efficiently move from the idea for a mathematics learning activity to the implementation of a technological tool that facilitates that activity and remains faithful to it? Currently, the vast majority of classroom teachers and curriculum developers find themselves adapting their ideas and activities to the available tools. In the process, the original ideas may be compromised. In some rare cases, the practitioner may have the technological savvy or programming knowledge (or sufficient communication access to those who do) to design or adapt the tool to the activity in a way that does not compromise the original vision.

What we need to move toward is the notion of authoring tools—that is, tools for building tools—that provide a kind of "macro" construction kit for practitioners to create their own learning microworlds for students, complete with user-friendly interfaces and robust operational integrity. We have seen some exciting possibilities for how technology can be used to aid mathematics learning and teaching that have emerged in the hands of a few developers who share both educational vision and technical expertise. Now think about a future in which the number of such developers is multiplied literally by the thousands. Authoring tools that could truly enable the classroom teacher or curriculum developer to implement their ideas directly into reliable ready-to-use technological tools for mathematics learning would shift our language from technological innovation to educational innovation.

In terms of the fidelity principles discussed in this chapter, the structure of the authoring tools themselves could help practitioners who are developers adhere to those principles.

A dream perhaps? Keep the faith!

REFERENCES

Beeson, M. (1989). Logic and computation in MATHPERT: An expert system for learning mathematics. In E. Kaltofen & S. Watt (Eds.), *Computers and mathematics* (pp. 202-214). New York/Heidelberg: Springer-Verlag.

Cedillo, T., & Kieran, C. (2003). Initiating students into algebra with symbol-manipulatingcalculators. In J. T. Fey, A. Cuoco, C. Kieran, L. McMullin, & R. Zbiek (Eds.), *Computer algebra systems in secondary school mathematics education* (pp. 219-239). Reston, VA: National Council of Teachers of Mathematics.

CHAPTER 13

REPRESENTATIONS AND COGNITIVE OBJECTS IN MODERN SCHOOL GEOMETRY

Michael T. Battista

It is widely recognized that Dynamical Geometry Environments (DGEs) such as the Geometer's Sketchpad (GSP) (Jackiw, 1995) and Cabri (Baulac, Bellemain, & Laborde, 1994) are powerful tools for learning and doing geometry. However, DGEs also can play an important role in research on students' geometry learning. As an additional medium for geometric reasoning, DGEs provide to researchers a new window for viewing students' learning. This window can be especially valuable for investigating the nature of the representations and cognitive objects that students use in geometric thought. The goal of this chapter is to highlight some of the critical issues involved in understanding the objects and representations utilized in geometric reasoning, first in general, then for DGEs.

PRELIMINARIES

First, a *cognitive object* is a mental entity that is operated on (consciously or unconsciously) during reasoning. Second, a *representation* is something

Research on Technology and the Teaching and Learning of Mathematics:
Vol. 2. *Cases and Perspectives*, 341–362

that "stands for" something else (Goldin & Kaput, 1996). Third, in general, in geometric thought, we reason *about* objects; we reason *with* representations.

Also preliminary to analyzing the nature of geometric objects and representations is a recognition that the analysis could consider multiple dimensions, only some of which will be addressed in this chapter. For instance, the objects reasoned about in geometry can be physical things (including drawings or dynamic computer constructions) or formal concepts. Representations can be internal (i.e., mental) or external (e.g., a paper-and-pencil or dynamic drawing), and they can be imagistic or verbal. And the same entity might be a representation for one person but an object for another. For instance, a drawing of a geometric figure in a mathematics textbook might be a representation of a concept for the book's authors, but merely a single instance of a visual graphic for a student. Furthermore, external representations, such as drawings, might serve different purposes. For instance, when considering the validity of a proposition, an individual might draw several examples in an attempt to understand what the proposition means and get a "feel" for whether it is valid. Or, an individual might draw a single "generic" example that somehow encapsulates pertinent spatial relationships, thereby reducing the load on working memory to make reflection and analysis easier. In the former case, each drawing represents one instantiation (or class of instantiations) of a general relationship; in the latter case, the single drawing represents the general relationship.

WHAT IS THE NATURE OF THE COGNITIVE OBJECTS IN GEOMETRIC REASONING?

Numerous researchers in geometry education distinguish between two types of cognitive objects that occur in geometric reasoning: "Drawing refers to the material entity while figure refers to a theoretical object" (Laborde, 1993, p. 49).[1] However, the complexity of identifying the objects of geometric reasoning is inadequately captured by the drawing-figure dichotomy. Indeed, Jones argues that learners in DGEs "can get 'stuck' somewhere between a drawing and a figure" (Jones, 2000, p. 58). Furthermore, research in psychology and neuroscience suggests that finer distinctions are needed. For instance, some researchers characterize the difference between physical and perceptual objects in terms of distal and proximal stimuli: "A distal stimulus is an actual object or event 'out there' in the world; a proximal stimulus is the information our sensory receptors receive about that object" (Coren, Ward, & Enns, 1994, p. 485). Other researchers distinguish between perceptual and conceptual objects. Perception is nonconscious and operates on signals from the outside world received by the body's receptors, whereas conception is conscious and operates on the activity of those portions of the brain that record signals from the outside world (Edelman, 1992). Smith (1995) distinguishes between a category, which is a group of objects in the world that belong together, and a concept which is a mental representation for such a group. Thus, the study of students' geometric reasoning would benefit greatly from further analysis of the nature of objects that exist "between" drawing and figure.

As an initial attempt at elaborating the range of geometric objects, we might distinguish four types of objects instead of two. A physical object is a "concrete" entity such as a door, box, ball, picture, drawing, or dynamic, draggable computer figure. Laborde's "drawing" is this type of object. A perceptual object is the mental entity "sensed" when viewing a physical object. A conceptual object (or conceptualization) is a mental model[2] that is activated when an object is perceived, when an entity is recalled for reflection and analysis, or when a verbal description is encountered. A geometric concept is an explicit formal verbal description of (a) a spatial relationship or (b) the defining characteristics of a category of shapes (Laborde's "figure" is this type of object). To understand students' geometric reasoning and learning, we must understand their cognitions about these four types of objects and relationships between them.

COMPLICATION: DIFFICULTIES IN DISENTANGLING CONCEPTUALIZATION FROM PERCEPTION

Separating conceptualization from perception is difficult for several reasons. First of all, individuals seem to naturally form categorical conceptualizations (Pinker, 1997), especially under of the influence of culture and language. And once a conceptualization is formed, that conceptualization dominates consciousness, so the individual is unaware of perceptual objects. As an example, consider a rectangle briefly flashed on a screen. Schooled individuals beyond the primary grades will generally say they saw a rectangle (a geometric conceptualization) as opposed to four line segments in a particular configuration (which is, relatively speaking, "closer" to a description of a perception).[3] A second complicating factor is that conceptualization affects perception. To illustrate, consider Figure 13.1 (Coren et al., 1994, p. 497). Amazingly, the two dark vertical segments are congruent; but our conceptualization of the physical world, and the resulting mental models created to represent it, cause us to perceive the two segments as very different in length. Thus, what we perceive can be dramatically affected by context and conceptualizations.

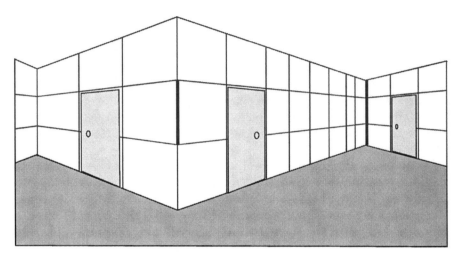

Figure 13.1.   Perception affected by conceptualization.

The notion that conceptualization affects perception extends directly to geometry. For instance, the up-down orientation that is critical to maneuvering within the world is a conceptual context that affects individuals' conceptualization of shape (Pinker, 1997). Thus, many young children view a square with vertical and horizontal sides as a square, but the same shape rotated 45° as a diamond—and it is often difficult for children to move beyond this conceptualization. One possible explanation for this phenomenon is research suggesting that context can influence the stimulus information to which an individual attends (Ross, 1996). For instance, a square turned 45° might be perceived as a diamond because the up-down context causes a student to attend not to relationships that exist among angles or sides of the figure but to the position of the overall shape, including how opposite angles line up vertically and horizontally.

Another way that context can affect perception is through language—verbal labeling can affect how one perceives and conceives of objects or shape. For instance, an ambiguous figure that is called a broom when it is presented is drawn by subjects to look like a broom, whereas if it is called a rifle when presented, it is drawn as a rifle (Coren et al., 1994). The verbal label seems to activate a particular assimilating conceptualization. Might a similar phenomenon occur in geometry—does calling the same shape by different names (e.g., square, rhombus, diamond) affect a student's perception and conceptualization (and drawing) of the shape?

CREATING AND USING PERCEPTUAL AND CONCEPTUAL
GEOMETRIC OBJECTS: LEVELS OF ABSTRACTION

The process of abstraction is critical to spatial perception, geometric conceptualization, and geometric reasoning. The following levels of abstraction indicate major landmarks in constructing and using geometric objects. Each level permits increasingly powerful mental operations to be performed on the objects.

Perceptual Abstraction

At the perceptual/recognition level, abstraction isolates an item in the experiential flow and grasps it as an object: "Focused attention picks a chunk of experience, isolates it from what came before and from what follows, and treats it as a closed entity" (von Glasersfeld, 1991, p. 47). When items are perceptually abstracted, we become conscious of them, entering them into working memory. Perceptual abstraction isolates those sensory properties of an experience that are needed to recognize further instantiations of the experience. However, items that have been abstracted only at this level cannot be re-presented (visualized) and cannot be operated on unless they are physically present.

Internalization

When material has been sufficiently abstracted so that it can be re-presented in the absence of perceptual input, it has been internalized. Internalization is "the process that results either in the ability to re-present a sensory item without relevant sensory signals being available in actual perception or in the ability to reenact a motor activity without the presence of the kinesthetic signals from actual physical movement. Internalization leads to 'visualization' in all sensory modalities" (Steffe & Cobb, 1988, p. 337).

Interiorization

To re-present to oneself an activity that one has carried out is quite different from reflecting upon the results of a re-presentation and considering how that is composed. Reflecting upon the results of a re-presentation requires detachment and placing the re-presented activity at a distance in order to analyze its structure and composition. (Steffe & Cobb, 1988, p. 17)

To do so requires interiorization, which makes material sufficiently separable[4] from its experiential sensory particulars so that it can be used for a new purpose. That is, to use an abstracted item for thinking about a new situation requires that the item be reprocessed, not simply recalled as it has been encountered in the past (Steffe, 1998).

Second Level of Interiorization

When material reaches the second level of interiorization, operations can be performed on the material without representing it and symbols can be used to substitute for it.

OBJECTS, REPRESENTATIONS, AND DIAGRAMS

Diagrams and physical objects play two major roles in geometric reasoning. On the one hand, particular instances of diagrams and objects can be thought of as the *data* for the formation of geometric conceptualizations—it is through analysis of instances that geometric concepts are derived. On the other hand, diagrams and objects can be used to *represent* formal geometric concepts (e.g., a rectangular figure can be used to represent the concept of rectangle).[5] However, instruction, curricula, and research in mathematics education generally neglect the process of forming concepts from instances, and instead focus on the "representational" perspective. Consider the following statements by researchers:

- "Diagrams are intended as models ... meant to be understood as representing a class of objects" (Yerushalmy & Chazan, 1993, pp. 25).
- "Every diagram has characteristics that are individual and not representative of the class" (Yerushalmy & Chazan, 1993, p. 25).
- "Students often attribute characteristics of a drawing to the geometric object it represents" (Clements & Battista, 1992, p. 448).

Chazan and Yerushalmy (1998) argue that what I have called the representational perspective on diagrams is rooted in the traditional axiomatic approach to geometry instruction. Geometric "objects" are either undefined or are defined formally in terms of undefined terms; "diagrams are aids for intuition and are not the objects of study themselves" (p. 70). These researchers seem to conceptualize diagrams and physical objects in representational terms: "Geometry has as its object the spatial forms and relations of actual bodies, *removed from their other properties and considered from the purely abstract point of view*" (Aleksandrov as quoted in Chazan & Yerushalmy, 1998, p. 70) [italics added].

The representational perspective focuses on abstract, general mathematical concepts as the objects of study. A diagram, as a representation of an abstract mathematical concept, can be used: (a) to represent classes of shapes (e.g., the *set* of rectangles); and (b) to represent geometric relationships (e.g., the bisectors of the angles of a triangle meet at the incenter of the triangle). Students, however, have difficulty with both types of representational uses of diagrams. One difficulty occurs when students attribute irrelevant characteristics of a diagram to the geometric concept it is intended to represent (Clements & Battista, 1992; Yerushalmy & Chazan, 1993). For instance, students might not identify right triangles drawn in nonstandard orientations (having unconsciously and erroneously abstracted orientation as an attribute). Another difficulty occurs when students use diagrams in proofs (Clements & Battista, 1992; Presmeg, 1997; Yerushalmy & Chazan, 1993). For example, students may assume that sides that look parallel in an accompanying diagram are parallel (adding unintended relationships to hypotheses). Or, students might link a theorem too tightly to the example diagram given with the theorem statement. For instance, students might believe that a theorem originally accompanied by a diagram of an acute triangle does not apply to obtuse triangles, or it might not occur to them to apply the theorem to obtuse triangles. Still another type of difficulty occurs when drawings do not capture appropriate geometric relationships, for example, a tangent to a circle might be drawn freehand so that it is not perpendicular to the radius it intersects. Also, students might mistake geometric diagrams for pictures of objects, profoundly changing their interpretation. For instance, a bright fourth-grade student identified nonrectangular parallelograms as rectangles because he interpreted them as pictures of rectangles viewed "sideways" (Clements & Battista, 1992).

It could be that many of the above-mentioned errors can be attributed to students not understanding the representational use of diagrams. In fact, Laborde (1998) argues that teaching often "confuses drawings and the theoretical geometrical objects that the former represent" (p. 115). She argues that student difficulties in geometry often arise because students reason about material drawings (physical objects) when they are expected to reason about figures (concepts) (Laborde, 1993). Said differently, students construe the drawings, not the concepts, as the *objects* of analysis. Even more, students might not possess the cognitive processes required to support the representational use of diagrams. For instance, when using a drawing as a representation, an individual might mentally operate on the drawing as physical object, then think about what that operation suggests about the represented conceptual object, in essence, switching attention back and forth between the drawing-as-object and the conceptual object that is being represented. Alternatively, one might use the drawing to think directly about the represented conceptual object—in effect, the representation acts as a "transparent" manifestation of the represented object. (How one deals with representations in this regard might depend on one's level of expertise in a field.) In both the "switching" or "transparent" modes, however, the mind must establish and maintain a structure-preserving mapping between the elements and relations mentally constructed for the representation and those constructed for the object being represented (cf., Gentner & Markman, 1994, 1997).

Though the representational use of diagrams is critical to geometric reasoning, the representational perspective fails to give proper consideration to the fact that formal geometric concepts are usually abstractions of characteristics of *particular* figures.[6] Too often, mathematics education research has treated diagrams only as imperfect representations of idealized abstract geometric concepts, neglecting the fact the diagrams themselves can be construed as geometrically analyzable graphic objects. Thus, in addition to investigating how students can properly interpret and productively utilize external representations, research must also investigate two additional crucial areas: (a) the mental mechanisms that enable students to progress from analysis of particular figures to general abstractions about classes of figures, and (b) the mental mechanisms that enable students to utilize formal abstract geometric concepts to analyze particular figures. These questions are critical to understanding how students construct understanding of abstract geometric concepts that are applicable not only within mathematics but to real-world problems. For example, on the one hand, researchers should investigate what mental mechanisms enable a student who has not been exposed to definitions of perpendicularity or right angles to construct the notion of perpendicularity when viewing examples of perpendicular and nonperpendicular lines (Battista, 2006). On the other hand, researchers should also analyze the mental processes that enable a student to use a definition of perpendicularity to conceptualize perpendicularity in novel and complex situations. The process of abstraction is key to understanding the mechanisms for both situations.

DYNAMICAL GEOMETRY: REPRESENTATIONS OR NEW KINDS OF OBJECTS?

I now consider some of the critical issues previously discussed in the context of dynamical geometry environments. First, what are the objects? According to Jones (2000), Laborde's distinction between a drawing as a material entity and a figure as a theoretical object manifests itself in a DGE as,

> A drawing can be a juxtaposition of geometrical objects resembling closely the intended construction (something that can be made to "look right"). In contrast, a figure ... captures the relationships between the objects in such a way that the figure is invariant when any basic object used in the construction is dragged (in other words, that it passes the drag test). (p. 58)

So, a DGE rectangular "drawing" would not remain a rectangle when its vertices are dragged, whereas a DGE rectangular "figure" would. However, as pointed out in my earlier discussion and as will be further illustrated, this dichotomous formulation is inadequate. Second, both DGE "drawings" and "figures" can be representations or objects, so we have to look carefully at what function these dynamic entities serve for students.

Two Perspectives on DGE "Draggable Drawings"

There are two major theoretical perspectives on draggable drawings, that is, DGE drawings that, by virtue of their construction, have certain relationships between their components "built in." In the first perspective, draggable drawings are seen as generating numerous examples. For instance, Marrades and Gutierrez (2000) made the following claim:

> The main advantage of DGS learning environments ... is that students can construct complex figures and can easily perform in real time a very wide range of transformations on those figures, so students have access to a variety of examples that can hardly be matched by non-computational or static computational environments. (p. 95)

Such researchers posit that DGE representations might remedy one of the difficulties students face with paper-and-pencil representations, that a picture or diagram is one concrete case that can be too restricted for the general kind of reasoning required in most mathematics (Presmeg, 1986). The first theoretical perspective on draggable drawings is consistent with the representational perspective described earlier because to talk about examples raises the question, Of what (geometric concept or relationship) are these examples?

In the second theoretical perspective, draggable drawings are seen as interesting, manipulable, visual-mechanical objects that have movement constraints that can be conceptualized and analyzed geometrically (Battista, 2006). In this view, "Geometrical relationships can be visualized as invariants in the continuous moving of the [draggable] figure" as opposed to characteristics abstracted from a set of examples (Laborde, 1992, p. 130). This approach is taken in Battista's Shape Makers environment in which students explore GSP draggable constructions for various types of quadrilaterals and triangles (Battista, 2008). For instance, the Rectangle Maker can be used to make any desired rectangle that fits on the computer screen, no matter what its shape, size, or orientation. Dragging the Rectangle Maker's vertices changes its side lengths—and thus its visual appearance—but the transformed shape is always a rectangle. This approach is also taken in Laborde's "black-box" activities in which students are given a Cabri-draggable drawing without being told how it was constructed and are asked to construct a draggable drawing that behaves in the same way (Laborde, 1998). Producing a duplicate draggable drawing requires students to conceptualize the behavior of the figure in terms of DGE constructions (which, depending on the student, can represent varying degrees of understanding of geometrically formulated spatial relationships). Thus, rather than examining *a set of figures* to conceptualize how they are the same, with Shape Makers or black box constructions, students investigate how an interesting manipulable "geometric" object works (which can, with proper instructional guidance, support the construction of meaningful conceptualizations of geometric properties).

What complicates matters, however, is that there may be a mismatch between how researchers and students conceptualize draggable dynamic drawings. For instance, Chazan and Yerushalmy (1998) seem to view them as representations: "Computers allow users to treat screen representations of Euclidean objects as tangible and manipulable objects" (p. 70). Battista, although starting with this view, abandoned it as he observed students' work (Battista, 2008). At least initially, the fifth-grade students with whom he was working viewed the Shape Makers not as representations, but as interesting visual-geometric objects. Seemingly consistent with this view, some researchers argue that DGEs should not be conceptualized as a device to merely "enable us to do what we already do faster, better or to a larger extent or degree," but as an environment requiring a fundamentally different cognitive view than has been taken in traditional approaches to geometry instruction (Dörfler, 1993, p. 161).

In considering the aforementioned theoretical perspectives on DGE-draggable drawings, which guide both research and curriculum development, several questions arise. First, it is important to test the theories and determine empirically how students conceptualize draggable drawings (which might differ depending on whether they or the teacher constructed the drawing). Do students see the various configurations of a draggable drawing as a set of examples of a geometric concept or do they see a draggable drawing as a geometrically interesting manipulable object? How are students' views on this matter affected by instruction?

Should instruction promote one view over the other, and does this vary by student age, experience, and level of expertise in geometry?

Second, do the conceptualizations that students construct as they are thinking about DGE figures as manipulable objects "transfer" to reasoning about corresponding geometric concepts? Battista's Shape Makers research suggests that, with appropriate instruction, such transfer does occur. For instance, after struggling to conceptualize precisely the kinds of shapes that can be made by the Rectangle Maker, one student used the concept of right angle not only to describe a property of the Rectangle Maker, but also to describe the characteristics of shapes that appeared on a student sheet (Battista, 2008, pp. 147-148). In another episode in the same class (but not cited in Battista, 2008), another student used Shape Makers to reason about categories of shapes: K said, "The Parallelogram Maker can only make parallelograms. And, it can make a rectangle [using his fingers to make the outline of a rectangle], so a rectangle has to be a parallelogram." To reason in this way, K had to distinguish between three types of *objects*: a Parallelogram Maker, instances of parallelograms, and the category of parallelograms (a distinction that is difficult for many students to make). Although there is no evidence in this episode that K used the Parallelogram Maker as a representation of the concept of parallelogram, his experience with the DGE objects of Parallelogram Maker and Rectangle Maker enabled him to reason productively about the parallelogram and rectangle concepts as objects.

Finally, we should ask, more generally, if DGE-draggable drawings are viewed differently by students who have already attained strong conceptualizations of the underlying geometric concepts, as opposed to students who are constructing meaning for these concepts for the first time in a DGE. That is, for an expert, a Parallelogram Maker might indeed be a representation for the class of parallelograms, whereas for the novice it might be simply an interesting dynamic object whose movement is constrained in particular ways. Or, for some students, like K, it might be a device for making parallelograms.

The "Transparency" of DGE Representations

Jones (2000) has conducted research that focuses on students' interpretation of the syntax of DGE representations (e.g., understanding which objects can be dragged and which cannot). He argues that such investigation is needed to understand how the DGE medium affects students' mental construction of geometric conceptualizations, how students "progressively mathematise the sense they made of the software environment and how this impacts on their developing mathematical reasoning" (Jones, 2000, p. 73). For instance, Jones suggests that to construct correct draggable DGE drawings, students must understand the "essence" of the particular DGE within which they are working (Jones, 2000). In particular, Jones states that in Cabri, although basic points, points on object, and points of intersection look identical on the screen, basic points and points on objects are draggable, whereas intersection points are not because they move only as a consequence of their dependence on the intersecting objects. As another example, Jones states, "the sequential organisation of actions necessary to produce a figure in Cabri introduces an explicit order of construction where, for most users, order is not normally expected or does not even matter" (Jones, 2000, pp. 58-59).

In pursuing this line of inquiry, Jones found that students often have difficulty developing appropriate understanding of the DGE medium. For instance, he reports instances in which students developed nonmathematical conceptualizations of the draggability of figures. In particular, asked why their constructed figure could not be "messed up" (i.e., why it was draggable), one student replied, "They stay together because of the intersections ... a bit like glue really. It just glued them together" (Jones, 2000, p. 71). This student seemed to focus on the operation of the DGE construction as a "mechanical," not mathematical, object. Thus, there is a real danger that DGE mechanical knowledge can replace or confound mathematical knowledge, that is, learning about representational objects can interfere with learning about geometric objects. In essence, students working in a DGE need to see beyond the mechanical operational syntax of the environment (i.e., the representation must become "transparent"). But Jones' research suggests that this is not happening for many students, which raises a number of research questions. For instance, what are the cognitive mechanisms and instructional experiences that permit students to use a DGE as a representational system for reasoning about formal geometric concepts, without being distracted by the operational syntax of the environment? That is, how can students "distinguish fundamental characteristics of geometry from features that are the result of the particular design of the DGE" (Jones, 2000, pp. 58-59)?

Additionally, we need to investigate exactly what knowledge of the mechanical aspects of DGE representational systems students must learn to use DGE representations effectively for geometric reasoning. Although Hoyles and Jones (1998) also found that few students understood the mechanical dependencies implicit in DGE constructions, they reported that appropriately designed DGE instructional contexts helped students develop better understanding of the properties of geometric figures. So apparently, appropriate instruction can prevent students' lack of understanding of the mechanical aspects of DGEs from thwarting geometric learning (see also Battista, 2008).

In summary, pedagogical use of DGEs introduces a whole new set of representational artifacts that are distinct from geometric concepts. Because these artifacts are not legitimate geometric concepts, learning about them must be considered "investment overhead" for understanding how to represent and manipulate geometric ideas in a DGE. Consequently, researchers must investigate how these artifacts can be pushed into the background for students. Of course, some of these difficulties can be avoided if DGE draggable drawings are treated as objects that can be understood with geometric analyses, not as representations of traditional mathematical concepts. But then, how does instruction ensure that conceptualizations constructed in a DGE get transformed or generalized to encompass standard geometric concepts?

Conceptualizing DGE Constructions

How do students conceptualize DGE constructions? In what situations do DGE constructions represent geometric relations for students? For instance, what is involved conceptually when a student constructs a parallel to a given line through a point not on that line? What does the construction mean to the student? Is it a rote procedure for constructing a visual configuration, or is it a representation of a formal geometric concept? How does learning to use the DGE construction change, supplement, or supplant a student's conceptualization of parallelism? Conversely, what kinds of conceptualizations enable students to employ DGE construction tools productively? Is the nature of conceptualizations created through use of DGE construction tools the same as those learned through verbal definitions or drawing?

An example: What happens when constructing a DGE-draggable drawing? Many instructional treatments involving DGEs introduce "a specific criterion of validation for the solution of a construction problem: a solution is valid if and only if it is not possible to 'mess it up' by dragging" (Jones, 2000, p. 58). The notion is that if the figure is draggable, the appropriate properties have been built into it. So some sufficient set of geometric properties is represented by draggability. But let us more carefully examine the process of constructing a draggable figure. For instance, two students were attempting to make a draggable rectangle in Cabri (Hölzl, Healy, Hoyles, & Noss, 1994). After drawing segment AB, they constructed a perpendicular to segment AB passing through B and put a point, C, on it, constructed a perpendicular to line BC and put a point, D, on it, then constructed another perpendicular to line CD through D (see

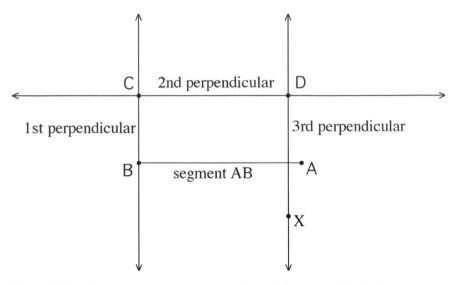

Figure 13.2.   Students' attempt to make a draggable rectangle in Cabri.

Figure 13.2). The students then joined points A, B, C, and D with line segments and hid the lines, forming a trapezoid with two adjacent right angles, and dragged A so that it looked like a rectangle. The girls realized that they had not created a draggable rectangle, but got confused with Cabri operations when trying to fix their error. For instance, the students attempted to change the nature of point A to be a "point on object [DX]." Finally, when the students were told that this could not be done, they completed their rectangle by creating an intersection point on line DX and segment BA.

A number of questions must be asked about this episode. First, the authors claim that the students "were clearly aware of the properties of rectangles and the need to construct perpendicular lines to obtain right angles" (Hölzl et al., 1994, p. 9). However, exactly which properties of rectangles did the students know? For instance, the only property for which the students evidenced knowledge was that the sides of a rectangle are perpendicular. There was no explicit evidence in their construction that they knew that opposite sides were congruent and parallel or that they learned about these properties by doing the DGE construction. We might even ask what the students really understood about the perpendicularity of sides. For instance, it could be that the students constructed the rectangle visually, using perpendicularity as a tool for making lines meet in a particular visual configuration. That is, they might have "understood" perpendicularity as a DGE procedure for making "square" line intersections, not as a geometric concept involving right angles. Thus, it is important to understand precisely what DGE constructions mean to students and how students recognize properties that arise implicitly in such constructions. What exactly did this construction represent for students?

The claim by Hölzl and colleagues (1994) that students working in DGEs "ran up against some fundamental aspects of *its [Cabri] geometry*" (p. 11) raises additional issues. First, does Cabri really have its own "geometry?" If so, what is it and how is it related to traditional mathematical geometry? For instance, as has already been mentioned, unlike mathematical geometry, Cabri "geometry" has different kinds of points—they behave differently. As another example, the idea of "point on object," as implemented in a DGE, may promote student conceptualizations that are very different from the corresponding mathematical concept. In Birkoff's formulation of geometry (Moise, 1963), the statement, "let X be a point on segment AB" means that X is any of the points that are elements of the point-set that is segment AB. However, the way the point concept is implemented in a DGE might lead some students to conceptualize a point on a segment as an object "on top of" or separate from the segment, not as part of the segment. In this case, the DGE concept and mathematical concept would be inconsistent. In contrast, in Hilbert's formulation of geometry (Wallace & West, 1992), "point," "line," and "on" are undefined terms, and there is no requirement that individual points be elements of sets of points called lines. In this case, there seems to be no inconsistency between the DGE and mathematical concepts. Again, the question is, How does the DGE representation affect students' construction of geometric concepts?

Student-Intended Versus Researcher-Intended DGE Representations

Healy and Hoyles (2001) asked students to construct a quadrilateral in which the bisectors of two adjacent angles intersect at right angles, then to discover and prove other properties of this quadrilateral. Tim and Richard created quadrilateral *ABCD*, then the bisectors of angles *ABC* and *BCD* (see Figure 13.3). They measured the angle at the intersection of the two bisectors and dragged the vertices of the quadrilateral until this angle measured 90°. At this time they noticed that segment *BA* was parallel to segment *CD* and conjectured that whenever the two angle bisectors were at right angles, segment *BA* would be parallel to segment *CD*. They dragged the vertices for further empirical validation of their conjecture. Then, with the angle bisectors intersecting at right angles, the boys used Cabri's "check-property tool" to test whether segment *BA* and segment

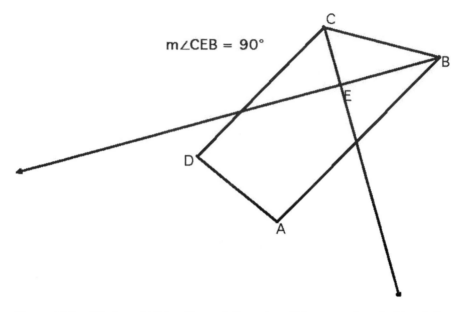

Figure 13.3. Tim's and Richard's quadrilateral and bisectors of angles B and C.

CD were parallel. The boys were "disappointed and puzzled that the property that the two lines were parallel was declared *not* to be true in general" (p. 244). However, since in the counterexamples presented by Cabri's check-property tool, the angle bisectors did *not* intersect at right angles, the boys decided that the parallel property had been declared invalid because the condition of 90° between the angle bisectors had not been retained by the construction. Note that the boys' reasoning required sophisticated knowledge about the nature of DGE representations. This is knowledge about Cabri, not about geometry. Students in this situation who do not sufficiently understand the functioning of Cabri will likely be thwarted in their geometric investigations.

Tim and Richard continued investigating their conjecture by constructing a line parallel to segment CD passing through B. They found that whenever point A was dragged onto this line, the two angle bisectors intersected at right angles, but if A was not on this line, the angle bisectors were no longer perpendicular. In searching for a proof for their conjecture, the boys returned to manipulating the quadrilateral, with A always on the line parallel to segment CD. They measured angles and looked for angles that remained equal when dragging vertices. The boys noticed that the alternate interior angles where the bisector of angle ABC intersected segments BA and CD were always "the same," then realized that proof of this equality would show that the two line segments are parallel.

However, before Tim and Richard moved away from their Cabri construction to a strictly formal analysis of the situation, they used their construction to further explore their conjectures. But this was complicated by the fact that the angle bisectors did not always intersect the sides of the quadrilateral, so the relevant angles could not always be measured. The issue was resolved when the teacher suggested that they construct lines through the sides of the quadrilateral, which allowed the boys to measure the relevant angles in all draggable positions. At this point, the boys stopped manipulating the figure. The researchers claimed that the boys had "used the figure they had generated with its specific measurements as a generic example, to help them to formulate a general argument" (Healy & Hoyles, 2001, p. 246).

The DGE construction played two important roles in Tim and Richard's work. First, it provided them with a representation that allowed them to investigate the situation empirically so that they could formulate a valid conjecture about a geometric property. Second, the boys' manipulations of their DGE representation, including the accurate measurements of angles, helped guide their construction of a proof.

However, several caveats must accompany this success story. First, Tim and Richard encountered several difficulties with the DGE representation for which the teacher had to help them. Second, on this same task, many other students failed to see the parallel relationship between the sides of the resulting quadrilateral. Third, the construction expected by the researchers—a draggable quadrilateral having angle bisectors of two adjacent angles intersecting at right angles—was not the construction created by successful students. Constructing a general quadrilateral that satisfied the given conditions proved too difficult for students. Because students could not use the Cabri tools available to them to construct such a quadrilateral, they became frustrated and failed to solve the problem. In fact, like Tim and Richard, all students who were successful on this problem constructed a general quadrilateral with adjacent angle bisectors and manipulated it to find when the bisectors were perpendicular.

Thus, we see that having students use DGE constructions as representations can be powerful, but sometimes daunting. And there can be a large discrepancy between how students and teachers or researchers represent geometric ideas in DGEs—the draggability criterion may at times be unreasonable. Research needs to determine which kinds of DGE representations are best for students to construct and in which situations it makes sense to construct them.

Representational Explicitness of Geometric Relationships

One essential feature that has been claimed for computer environments for representing and exploring school geometry is that they require students to provide explicit descriptions of geometric relationships and shapes, for example, menu selections and constructions in Geometric Supposers and DGEs, and command lists in Logo (Clements & Battista, 1992). The claim is that students cannot make drawings in such environments without some level of *conceptual* explicitness, as they can with paper and pencil. In particular, Laborde (2001) claimed that,

> In constructing a square with a given side.... With paper and pencil the ... task is controlled by perception.... The same task in Cabri ... cannot be obtained by eye ... but uses a circle as a tool for transferring a given distance. The task in Cabri requires more mathematical knowledge about the properties of a square and the characteristic property of a circle. (p. 294)

A number of researchers have argued that this "representational" explicitness promotes and supports reflection on and abstraction of geometric concepts (Clements & Battista, 1992).

However, understanding the nature of the conceptual explicitness required in constructing DGE drawings requires much additional research. For instance, one can "draw" a rectangle by creating four line segments in a rectangular configuration in such a way that the drawing does not remain rectangular when its vertices are dragged (creating what Jones (2000) and Laborde (1993) refer to as a "drawing"). Little conceptual explicitness is required. Alternately, one can use DGE commands to "construct" a rectangle that is preserved with dragging (creating what Jones and Laborde refer to as a "figure"). In this case, it can be argued that each step in the construction requires some conceptual explicitness. The question is, how much? For instance, as previously mentioned, are students' conceptualizations of such constructions merely proceduralized methods for creating visual configurations, or are they abstract mathematical concepts? Another difficulty with DGEs is that access to commands given in a construction is not straightforward, making the commands less explicit. That is, if students do not manually record all the steps in their GSP construction, they may not be able to recall and productively reflect on what they did. For instance, the construction description that GSP displays for a draggable rectangle may not include a specification of right angles. Thus, the conceptual explicitness that occurs in computer environments for geometry learning depends on a complex interaction between the task, the commands given in constructing figures, the availability of those commands to inspection, and the reasoning of the student. Further investigations of conceptual explicitness are critical to understanding the pedagogical usefulness of DGE representations for learning geometric concepts.

CONCLUSIONS

Dynamical geometry environments can be marvelous instructional tools for the development of students' geometric reasoning. Such environments can also provide an analytic window that leads to new insights into students' geometric reasoning. However, as has been pointed out in this chapter, there are numerous questions that need to be answered to realize the potential of these environments, both for pedagogy and for research. This chapter has attempted to raise relevant issues and point to potentially fruitful directions for addressing these issues.

ACKNOWLEDGMENT

Partial support for this work was provided by grants REC-8954664 and IMD 0099047 from the National Science Foundation. The opinions expressed, however, are those of the author and do not necessarily reflect the views of that foundation.

NOTES

1. Unless I am referring directly to statements made by other researchers, I use the terms *figure* and *drawing* interchangeably.
2. Mental models are nonverbal recall-of-experience-like mental versions of situations that have structures isomorphic to the perceived structures of the situations they represent (Battista, 1994; Greeno, 1991; Johnson-Laird, 1983; Johnson-Laird, 1998). That is, "the parts of the model correspond to the relevant parts of what it represents, and the structural relations between the parts of the model are analogous to the structural relations in the world" (Johnson-Laird, 1998, p. 447). Individuals reason about a situation by activating mental models that enable them to simulate interactions within the situation so that they can explore possible scenarios and solutions to problems. When using a mental model to reason about a situation, a person can mentally move around, move on or into, combine, and transform objects, as well as perform other operations like those that can be performed on objects in the physical world. Students reason by manipulating objects in mental models and observing the results. "The behavior of objects in the model is similar to the behavior of objects that they represent, and inferences are based on observing the effects of the operations" (Greeno, 1991, p. 178). Importantly, individuals use of mental models is constrained by their knowledge and beliefs (Kosslyn, 1983). That is, much

of what happens when we form and manipulate a mental model reflects our underlying knowledge and beliefs about what would happen if we were dealing with the objects they represent. So the properties and behavior of objects in a mental model simulate the properties and behavior we believe the objects they represent possess.

3.   However, even to describe the configuration as four segments requires the conceptualization of the notion of segment. In fact, it might be argued that perception without conceptualization rarely occurs beyond infancy.

4.   To be applied in a new situation, some type of structure must be "lifted" out of the originally abstracted experiential context and the new situation assimilated into it.

5.   Geometric concepts can also be used to *represent* the shapes of objects (e.g., in the utterance "that door is a rectangle," the conceptualization of rectangle mentally "stands in for" the actual shape of the door).

6.   Of course, one can take a purely axiomatic approach in which concepts do not refer to any physical referents.

REFERENCES

Battista, M. T. (1994). On Greeno's environmental/model view of conceptual domains: A spatial/geometric perspective. *Journal for Research in Mathematics Education, 25*, 86-94.

Battista, M. T. (2008). Design and theory for the Shape Makers geometry microworld. In G. W. Blume & M. K. Heid (Eds.), *Research on technology and the teaching and learning of mathematics: Vol. 2. Cases and perspectives* (pp. 131-156). Charlotte, NC: Information Age.

Baulac, Y., Bellemain, F., & Laborde, J.-M. (1994). Cabri II [Computer software]. Dallas, TX: Texas Instruments.

Chazan, D., & Yerushalmy, M. (1998). Charting a course for secondary geometry. In R. Lehrer & D. Chazan (Eds.), *Designing learning environments for developing understanding of geometry and space* (pp. 67-90). Mahwah, NJ: Erlbaum.

Clements, D. H., & Battista, M. T. (1992). Geometry and spatial reasoning. In D. A. Grouws (Ed.), *Handbook of research on mathematics teaching and learning* (pp. 420-464). New York: Macmillan.

Coren, S., Ward, L. M., & Enns, J. T. (1994). *Sensation and perception*. Fort Worth, TX: Harcourt Brace College.

Dörfler, W. (1993). Computer use and views of the mind. In C. Keitel & K. Ruthven (Eds.), *Learning from computers: Mathematics education and technology* (pp. 161-186). Grenoble Cedex, France: NATO ASI Series, Computer and Systems Sciences.

Edelman, G. M. (1992). *Bright air, brilliant fire*. New York: BasicBooks.

Gentner, D., & Markman, A. B. (1994). Structural alignment in comparison: No difference without similarity. *Psychological Science, 5*, 152-158.

Gentner, D., & Markman, A. B. (1997). Structure mapping in analogy and similarity. *American Psychologist, 52*, 45-56.

Goldin, G. A., & Kaput, J. J. (1996). A joint perspective on the idea of representation in learning and doing mathematics. In L. P. Steffe, P. Nesher, P. Cobb, G. A. Goldin, & B. Greer (Eds.), *Theories of mathematical learning* (pp. 397-430). Mahwah, NJ: Erlbaum.

Greeno, J. G. (1991). Number sense as situated knowing in a conceptual domain. *Journal for Research in Mathematics Education*, *22*, 170-218.

Healy, L., & Hoyles, C. (2001). Software tools for geometrical problem solving: Potentials and pitfalls. *International Journal of Computers for Mathematical Learning*, *6*, 235–256.

Hölzl, R., Healy, L., Hoyles, C., & Noss, R. (1994). Geometrical relationships and dependencies in Cabri. *Micromath*, *10*, 8-11.

Hoyles, C., & Jones, K. (1998). Proof in dynamic geometry contexts. In C. Mammana & V. Villani (Eds.), *Perspectives on the teaching of geometry for the 21st century* (pp. 121-128). Dordrecht, The Netherlands: Kluwer.

Jackiw, N. (1995). Geometer's Sketchpad (Version 3.0) [Computer software]. Berkeley, CA: Key Curriculum Press.

Johnson-Laird, P. N. (1983). *Mental models: Towards a cognitive science of language, inference, and consciousness*. Cambridge, MA: Harvard University Press.

Johnson-Laird, P. N. (1998). Imagery, visualization, and thinking. In J. Hochberg (Ed.), *Perception and cognition at century's end* (pp. 441-467). San Diego, CA: Academic Press.

Jones, K. (2000). Providing a foundation for deductive reasoning: Students' interpretations when using dynamic geometry software and their evolving mathematical explanations. *Educational Studies in Mathematics*, *44*, 55-85.

Kosslyn, S. M. (1983). *Ghosts in the mind's machine*. New York: W. W. Norton.

Laborde, C. (1992). Solving problems in computer-based geometry environments: The influence of the features of the software. *Zentralblatt für Didaktik der Mathematik*, *4*, 128-135.

Laborde, C. (1993). The computer as part of the learning environment: The case of geometry. In C. Keitel & K. Ruthven (Eds.), *Learning from computers: Mathematics education and technology* (Vol. 121, pp. 48-67). Grenoble Cedex, France: NATO ASI Series, Computer and Systems Sciences.

Laborde, C. (1998). Visual phenomena in the teaching/learning of geometry in a computer-based environment. In C. Mammana & V. Villani (Eds.), *Perspectives on the teaching of geometry for the 21st century* (pp. 113-121). Dordrecht, Country: Kluwer.

Laborde, C. (2001). Integration of technology in the design of geometry tasks with Cabri-geometry. *International Journal of Computers for Mathematical Learning*, *6*, 283-317.

Marrades, R., & Gutierrez, A. (2000). Proofs produced by secondary school students learning geometry in a dynamic computer environment. *Educational Studies in Mathematics*, *44*, 87-125.

Moise, E. E. (1963). *Elementary geometry from an advanced standpoint*. Reading, MA: Addison-Wesley.

Pinker, S. (1997). *How the mind works*. New York: W. W. Norton.

Presmeg, N. C. (1986). Visualization in high school mathematics. *For the Learning of Mathematics*, *6*, 42-46.

Presmeg, N. C. (1997). Generalization using imagery in mathematics. In L. D. English (Ed.), *Mathematical reasoning* (pp. 299-312). Mahwah, NJ: Erlbaum.

Ross, B. H. (1996). Category representations and the effects of interacting with instances. *Journal of Experimental Child Psychology: Learning, Memory and Cognition, 22,* 1249-1265.

Smith, E. E. (1995). Concepts and categorization. In D. N. Osherson & E. E. Smith (Eds.), *An invitation to cognitive science* (Vol. 3, pp. 3-33). Cambridge, MA: MIT Press.

Steffe, L. P. (1998, April). *Principles of design and use of TIMA software.* Paper presented at the research presession to the annual meeting of the National Council of Teachers of Mathematics, Washington, DC.

Steffe, L., & Cobb, P. (1988). *Construction of arithmetical meanings and strategies.* New York: Springer-Verlag.

von Glasersfeld, E. (1991). Abstraction, re-presentation, and reflection: An interpretation of experience and Piaget's approach. In L. P. Steffe (Ed.), *Epistemological foundations of mathematical experience* (pp. 45-67). New York: Springer-Verlag.

Wallace, E. C., & West, S. F. (1992). *Roads to geometry.* Englewood Cliffs, NJ: Prentice Hall.

Yerushalmy, M., & Chazan, D. (1993). Overcoming visual obstacles with the aid of the Supposer. In J. L. Schwartz, M. Yersushalmy, & B. Wilson (Eds.), *The geometric supposer: What is it a case of?* (pp. 25-56). Hillsdale, NJ: Erlbaum.

CHAPTER 14

FROM ARTIFACTS TO INSTRUMENTS

A Theoretical Framework Behind the Orchestra Metaphor

Paul Drijvers and Luc Trouche

The large-scale distribution of PCs and handheld devices made software for use in mathematics education available to both students and teachers. Currently, programming languages, graphing software, spreadsheets, geometry software, computer algebra systems, and other kinds of new tools for the learning of mathematics are widely disseminated. Originally, optimism dominated the debate: Technology would free the student from calculation and procedural drudgery, and would enable mathematics education to focus on more relevant issues such as realistic applications, modeling, conceptual understanding, and higher-order skills. An—often implicit—underlying idea was that technical skills and conceptual understanding could be separated in the learning.

At present, the optimism has taken on additional nuances. The research survey of Lagrange, Artigue, Laborde, and Trouche (2003) indicates that difficulties arising while using technology for learning mathe-

Research on Technology and the Teaching and Learning of Mathematics:
Vol. 2. Cases and Perspectives, 363–391
Copyright © 2008 by Information Age Publishing

matics have gained considerable attention. These difficulties on the one hand recognize the complexity of teaching and learning in general, but on the other hand reveal the subtlety of using tools for educational purposes. For example, Drijvers (2002) addresses obstacles that students encountered while working in a computer algebra environment. Balacheff (1994) sees *computational transposition* as part of the complexity of using computerized environments. He describes computational transposition as the "work on knowledge which offers a symbolic representation and the implementation of this representation on a computer-based device" (p. 16). Artigue (1997) brings to light two phenomena linked to this process, the phenomenon of *pseudotransparency*, linked to the gap between what a student writes on the keyboard and what appears on the screen, and the phenomenon of *double reference*. The latter refers to the double interpretation that students and teachers may have of tasks. Whereas teachers want the task to address the mathematical concepts involved, students may perceive the task as one of finding the typical way in which the computerized learning environment deals with these concepts and represents them. Techniques that are used within the computer algebra environment differ from the traditional paper-and-pencil techniques (Lagrange, 2005), a phenomenon that again may lead to conceptual difficulties. As an example of the non-trivial character of the use of technological tools for mathematics, we refer to an example presented by Guin and Trouche (1999). Students were asked to answer the question: Does the function f, defined by $f(x) = \ln(x) + 10 \cdot \sin(x)$, have an infinite limit as x tends to $+\infty$? The answers depended strongly on the working environment (even though elementary theorems make it possible to answer "yes" to this question). In a non-CAS graphing calculator environment, 25% of students answered "no," appealing to the oscillation of the observed graphic representation (Figure 14.1); in a paper-and-pencil environment, only 5% of students answered "no."

Apparently, the use of *cognitive technological tools*—in the sense of Lajoie (1993)—for the learning of mathematics, such as applets, graphing calculators, geometry software, and computer algebra systems, is not as easy as it might seem. Current research on the integration of technology in mathematics education, which aims at taking into account the complexity of the issue, uses a variety of perspectives, such as psychological, didactical, and sociocultural perspectives. However, the articulation of the different perspectives, and their integration into a more comprehensive framework is missing. Therefore, we look for a theoretical approach that allows for:

1. an analysis of the learning process in technological environments of increasing complexity, which takes into account the non-trivial

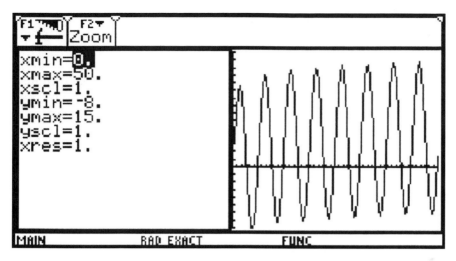

Figure 14.1.   The graph of $f(x) = ln(x) + 10 \cdot \sin(x)$ on the screen of a graphing calculator.

character of using technological tools and goes beyond simplistic views on "leaving work to the tool";

2. a set of cues for the organization of the teaching in such environments, concerning both pedagogical resources and classroom settings; and

3. a trajectory for conception, development, and evolution of pedagogical resources for teachers' professional development as well as software, and more generally, computerized learning environments.

Furthermore, such a framework should, as suggested by Arnon and Dubinsky (2001), have predictable as well as explanatory power, help to organize our thinking, and be applicable to a broad range of phenomena. Our main claim in this chapter is that the *instrumental approach* to using technology in mathematics education is a promising "candidate" for such a comprehensive framework.

The aim of this chapter is to present the main ideas of the instrumental approach, to apply it to the use of technology in mathematics education, to illustrate it by means of some examples, and to discuss its merits and limitations. Although the examples mainly concern the use of graphing calculators and computer algebra, we do want to stress the more general character of the instrumental approach, and that its scope goes beyond these specific kinds of technology. For example, the instrumental approach has been applied to using spreadsheets (Haspekian, 2003) and dynamical geometry software (Hollebrands, Laborde, & Sträßer, 2008). Furthermore, we explain how the approach encompasses both an individual and a collective perspective.

We consider the metaphor of the students in a classroom as instrumentalists, and the teacher as the conductor of this classroom orchestra, and we first address the learning process of the soloist musician. The main ideas of the instrumental approach concerning the individual learner using tools and developing instruments are explained in the next section, thus addressing criterion 1 in the preceding list. In the third section, which corresponds to criterion 2, we take the "orchestra perspective" and consider the notion of instrumental orchestration. The fourth section addresses the question of resources for professional development mentioned in item 3.

THE INSTRUMENTAL APPROACH: THE SOLOIST LEARNING PERSPECTIVE

As stated previously, we believe that the theoretical framework of the instrumental approach allows for an analysis of the learning process in technological environments of increasing complexity, and takes into account the non-trivial character of using computerized environments. In this section, we review the principles of the instrumental approach to the individual learner who uses technological tools for mathematical tasks.

Artifact and Instrument

The principles of the instrumental approach can be characterized by the following keywords: *artifact, instrument, instrumental genesis, instrumentation, instrumentalization*, and *scheme*. These keywords are addressed in the general description that follows.

The basis of the instrumental approach is formed by the ideas of Vygotsky (1930/1985). He noted that an instrument constitutes "a new intermediary element situated between the object and the psychic operation directed at it" (p. 42) and thus mediates the activity. A tool, which has been developed in a specific cultural and historical context, can be a material artifact, such as a violin, a calculator, or a computer, but also a nonmaterial cognitive tool such as language or an algebraic symbol. An "instrumental act" for Vygotsky includes a problem that needs to be solved, the mental processes involved in solving, and the (psychological) tools that are used to carry out and to coordinate these processes. The interesting thing here is the active role attributed to the tools, which influence the mental processes. The notion that tools are not just passively "waiting to be used" is an important one when considering tool use and learning.

To illustrate with an example of the role of the tool in the instrumental act, we can think of a hammer. A hammer can be considered as an extension of the body, which allows us to hit a nail much more efficiently and with less effort and pain than would be the case if we did so by hand. However, the availability of a hammer may lead us to try to solve all kinds of problems—including problems for which a screwdriver would be more appropriate—by using the hammer. In some cases, this may be adequate, but in others it may just be a matter of using the tools at hand. In that sense, the availability of the tool guides the choice of the problem-solving strategy. An effective use of a hammer requires skills, experience, and insight into the way it can contribute to solving the problem or carrying out the task at hand.

Rabardel and his colleagues elaborate on Vygotsky by distinguishing an artifact from an instrument (Rabardel, 2002; Vérillon & Rabardel, 1995). The *artifact* is the "bare tool," the material or abstract object, which is available to the user to sustain a certain kind of activity, but which may be a meaningless object to the user as long as that person does not know what kinds of tasks the "thing" can support in which ways. Only after the user has become aware of how the artifact can extend one's capacities for a given kind of relevant task, and after the user has developed means of using the artifact for this specific purpose, does the artifact become part of a valuable and useful instrument that mediates the activity.

If the artifact is the tool that is used, such as a hammer, a violin, a calculator, or a computer, it is not automatically a mediating instrument. What is the instrument? Following Rabardel, we speak of an *instrument* when there exists a meaningful relationship between the artifact and the user for dealing with a certain type of task—in our case a mathematical task—which the user has the intention to solve. As the interaction between user and artifact requires mental processes, we see that the main "players" here, the mental processes of the user, the artifact, and the task, are the same as was the case for Vygotsky's previously described instrumental act. Particularly for mathematical tools, which can be considered to be "extensions of the mind" rather than extensions of the body, these mental processes are essential. Therefore, the instrument consists of both the artifact and the accompanying mental schemes that the user develops to use it for performing specific kinds of tasks. This notion of instrument is illustrated in Figure 14.2 and can be summarized as:

$$\text{Instrument} = \text{Artifact} + \text{Scheme}$$

for a class of tasks.

Reflecting on Figure 14.2, one can wonder whether the type of task should be included in the oval that represents the instrument. Furthermore, we point out that the artifact is not always the material object as a whole. For example, the graphing module of a symbolic calculator can be seen as an artifact on its own, or even the submodule for setting the dimensions of the viewing window of the graph can be seen as an artifact. Finally, it is worthwhile to stress that the meaning of the word "instrument" here is more subtle than it is in daily life: The artifact develops into an instrument only in combination with the development of mental schemes.

Now that we have distinguished between artifacts and instruments, the question is how the availability of an artifact can lead to the development of an instrument. To do so, the user has to develop mental schemes, which involve skills to use the artifact in a proficient manner and knowledge about the circumstances in which the artifact is useful. The "birth" of an instrument requires a process of appropriation, which allows the artifact to mediate the activity. This complex process is called the *instrumental genesis*. The example in the first section on the interpretation of a graph (Figure 14.1) indicates that the instrumental genesis is far from a trivial process, which requires time and effort of both students and teachers. As the double arrows in Figure 14.2 indicate, instrumental genesis is a bidirectional process. On the one hand, the possibilities and constraints of the artifact shape the techniques and the

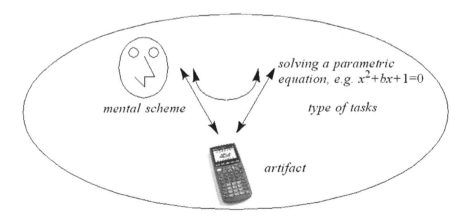

Figure 14.2.   Instrument for solving parametric quadratic equations, composed of artifact and mental scheme for this type of task.

conceptual understanding of the user. Some approaches are quite natural in a specific environment, while others are discouraged because of the peculiarities of the artifact. This is called the *instrumentation* process: The artifact shapes the thinking of the user. On the other hand, the conceptions and preferences of the user change the ways in which he or she uses the artifact, and may even lead to changing or customizing it. For example, one may update the version of the word-processing software on a computer, and in this way change its functionality. A student who enters into the graphing calculator a program that calculates the zeros of a quadratic function, also extends the artifact. If a game is downloaded, the primary functionality of the artifact—at least as the teacher perceives it—is changed. The artifact is shaped by the user, and this is called *instrumentalization*. The difference between instrumentation and instrumentalization, therefore, consists of the bidirectional interaction, in which the student's thinking is shaped by the artifact, but also shapes the artifact (Hoyles & Noss, 2003).

The instrumental genesis thus involves the development of mental schemes, which organize the problem-solving strategy, and induce the concepts that form the basis of the strategy. Meanwhile, techniques co-evolve, consisting of means for using the artifact in an efficient way to complete the intended types of tasks. The questions now are: What is such a scheme? and How can we identify it and observe its development? As a first approach to the notion of scheme, we follow Vergnaud, who elaborated on Piaget. Vergnaud defines a *scheme* as "une organisation invariante de la conduite pour une classe donnée de situations." (Vergnaud, 1996, p. 177) [An invariant organization of behavior for a given class of situations.] (translated by Paul Drijvers). In the context of tool use, we speak of a *utilization scheme*, which we consider as a more or less stable mental organization, including both technical skills and supporting concepts for a way of using the artifact for a given class of tasks. In the case of a mathematical problem, a mental scheme involves the global solution strategy, the technical means that the artifact offers, and the mathematical concepts that underpin the strategy. It contains *operational invariants* that consist of—explicit or implicit—knowledge in the form of concepts-in-action or theorems-in-action (Trouche, 2005a). The relationship of the co-evolving technical and conceptual elements in a mental scheme is characteristic for instrumental genesis. As a consequence, the technical work with the artifact—in our case technological tools for mathematics—is connected to conceptual insights. The teacher must exploit this relationship for the sake of learning.

Consider an example outside of mathematics. Moving a text block while writing a chapter like this in a word-processing environment can be done with a technique called "cut-and-paste." An experienced user applies this cut-and-paste scheme quickly, accurately, and without thinking by means of a sequence of keystrokes and/or mouse clicks. But do you remember the first time you did this? You had to find your way through some menus, and also accept the somewhat frightening fact that the text block that needed to be moved elsewhere, seemed to have disappeared after it had been cut. Some insight into the difference between what is on the screen and what is in the memory of the computer is a conceptual aspect of the accompanying scheme. Without that notion, the instrumental genesis is not completed and applying the technique will remain difficult; meanwhile, the technique may evoke this insight, as the text block reappears after the command "paste" is executed.

Two types of utilization schemes are distinguished, *usage schemes* and *instrumented action schemes*. The cut-and-paste scheme described above is a basic, elementary scheme, directly related to the artifact. Such schemes are called usage schemes. The usage schemes can serve as building blocks for schemes of a higher order, the instrumented action schemes. Instrumented action schemes focus on carrying out specific kinds of transformations on the objects of activity, which in our case are mathematical objects such as formulas, graphs, and so on. Instrumented action schemes are coherent and meaningful mental schemes, and are built up from elementary usage schemes by means of instrumental genesis. This articulation of usage schemes may involve new technical and conceptual aspects, which are integrated in the scheme.

A well-known example of an instrumented action scheme concerns scaling the viewing window of a graphing calculator (Goldenberg, 1988). The technical skills that the instrumental genesis of this instrumented action scheme requires are not very difficult: It is a matter of finding the window-setting menu and knowing the meaning of the different fields that need to be filled in. The use of negative numbers and the corresponding difference between the minus sign for negative numbers and the minus sign for subtractions can be considered as one of the component usage schemes. However, more is needed. The student should be able to perceive the calculator screen as a relatively small viewing window, through which we look at part of an infinite plane, theoretically speaking. The position and the dimensions of our window determine whether the window includes some part of the graph. In fact, in most cases no window can show the entire graph. The student needs skills to determine appropriate window settings. Based on our classroom observations, we claim that it is the incompleteness of these conceptual aspects of the scheme rather than the technical aspects that cause the difficulties that many students experience with graphing on a graphing calculator.

The difference between elementary usage schemes and higher order instrumented action schemes is not always obvious. Sometimes, it is merely a matter of the level of the user and the level of observation: What at first may seem an instrumented action scheme for a particular user, may later act as a building block in the genesis of a higher order scheme.

The examples of the cut-and-paste scheme and the viewing window scheme illustrate that a utilization scheme involves an interplay between acting and thinking, and that it integrates machine techniques and mental concepts. In the case of mathematical information technology tools, the conceptual part of utilization schemes therefore includes both mathematical objects and insight into the "mathematics of the machine." As a consequence, seemingly technical obstacles that students experience while using a computerized environment for mathematics often turn out to have an important conceptual background.

A difficulty is that we cannot observe mental schemes directly. Our observations are limited to techniques that students carry out with the artifact, and to the way they report on this in a written or oral form. From these data we try to reconstruct the schemes, but it is important to keep in mind that they are no more than our reconstructions.

We already argued that the construction of schemes, the instrumental genesis, is not straightforward in practice. Students may construct schemes that are not appropriate, not efficient, or that are based on inadequate conceptions. The elaborated example in the next section illustrates the difficulty of the instrumental genesis of a scheme for solving equations.

Example: Solving Equations With a Computer Algebra Device

As an example, described in more detail in Drijvers (2003), we now consider a scheme for solving equations in a computer algebra environment. At a first glance, this seems to be a trivial task: One just types in "Solve" and everything works. However, further examination shows that things are more complex.

The following assignment is presented to a tenth-grade, high-achieving student called Maria (Figure 14.3). Let us consider Task ii. Maria uses a Texas Instruments TI-89 symbolic calculator, a handheld device, which offers facilities for graphing as well as for symbolic manipulation. She first enters $Solve(x^2+b*x+1, x)$, which results in an error message from the TI-89, because the first argument of the *Solve* command should be an equation instead of an expression. She comments:

Below you see a sheaf of graphs of the family $y = x^2 + b \cdot x + 1$
We pay attention to the extreme points of the parabola
(the points that have maximum or minimum y-values for the
parabolas).

i.   Mark and connect the extreme points. What kind of curve do
      you seem to get?
ii.   Express the coordinates of the extreme value of a "family
      member" in b.
      Hint: the minimum lies between the zeros, if there are zeros.
iii. Find the equation of the curve through all the extreme points.

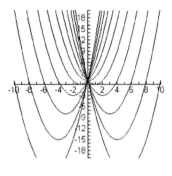

Figure 14.3.   The sheaf of graphs assignment.

M: It hates me, that calculator.

Then she considers substituting a value for x with the substitution bar:
$Solve(x^2+b*x+1, x \mid$. However, she clears this and enters $Solve(x^2+b*x+1, b)$. Apparently, she is not sure about the unknown with respect to which
the equation should be solved, and about the role of the different literal
symbols in the problem situation.

Next she enters $Solve(x^2+b*x+1 = y, b)$, which results in the solution
$b = -\dfrac{x^2 - y + 1}{x}$. She seems to think that this is not a valid result, and
wishes to substitute the value 5 for b. Besides the substitution operator, $\mid$,
she also uses the $Solve$ command: $Solve(b = -(x\char`\^2-y+1)/x \mid b=5)$. Once
more, this leads to an error message.

The observer passes by and Maria complains:

M: So you cannot solve that, you don't have x and you don't have y. Only b.

In fact, this is not true, we do know that $y = 0$.

M: Maybe x is zero, it should pass by the zeros, do you have to fill in zero for x?

The observer indicates that $y = 0$. Maria enters $Solve(b=-(x \wedge 2-0+1)/x, x)$, which expresses x in terms of b instead of b in terms of x.

M: But then you have to fill in a value for b?

Maria seems to think that an equation should have a numerical solution, and that an expression cannot be considered as a solution. Furthermore, she confuses "express in b" with "solving with respect to b." The observer suggests solving $x^2 + b * x + 1 = 0$ with respect to x, but Maria comments:

M: But it is of no use if it lies between two zeros if you cannot calculate it?

Once more, solutions to her should be numerical. However, after some more discussion with the participating observer, she solves the equation with respect to x and seems to understand why. However, while copying the result into her notebook, she does not realize the scope of the square root symbol, which results in an error (Figure 14.4).

How do we interpret these observations in light of the instrumental approach? The tasks here involve solving parametric quadratic equations. The artifact is the algebraic application within the symbolic calculator. The instrumented action consists of solving the parametric equation with the artifact. The mental scheme that Maria is developing can be seen as an instrumented action scheme, as it involves the transformation of mathematical formulas. In this case, however, the scheme is not built up from other elementary usage schemes. As such, it can be seen as an elementary usage scheme itself, but because of the conceptual components in the instrumental genesis that obviously cause many difficulties, we prefer to see it as an instrumented action scheme here.

Our claim now is that the instrumental genesis of the scheme for the application of the Solve technique in the handheld computer algebra device interacts with several conceptual aspects and therefore illustrates how technical and conceptual aspects interfere with each other and co-develop during the instrumental genesis. In fact, the problem situation and the artifact use force Maria to sharpen and to extend her conception

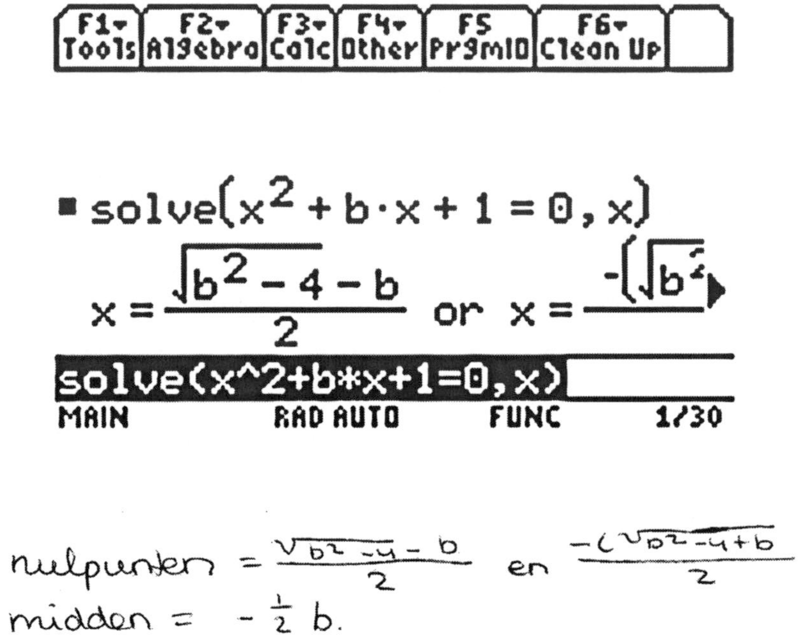

F1▾	F2▾	F3▾	F4▾	F5	F6▾
Tools	Algebra	Calc	Other	Prgmio	Clean Up

$$\blacksquare \; \text{solve}\left(x^2 + b\cdot x + 1 = 0, x\right)$$

$$x = \frac{\sqrt{b^2 - 4} - b}{2} \quad \text{or} \quad x = \frac{-\left(\sqrt{b^2}\right.}{}\blacktriangleright$$

`solve(x^2+b*x+1=0,x)`

MAIN   RAD AUTO   FUNC   1/30

$$\text{nulpunten} = \frac{\sqrt{b^2 - 4} - b}{2} \quad \text{en} \quad \frac{-(\sqrt{b^2 - 4} + b}{2}$$

$$\text{midden} = -\tfrac{1}{2}\, b.$$

Figure 14.4.   The artifact's output and Maria's copy in her notebook.

of solving equations in several ways, which are part of the instrumental genesis of an appropriate instrumented action scheme for solving parameterized equations. We distinguish the following aspects, which are depicted in Figure 14.5:

1. knowing that the Solve command can be used to express one of the variables in a parameterized equation in other variables. This is an extension of the notion of solving, and requires expressions to be considered as solutions.

2. knowing where to find the Solve command on the TI-89, remembering its syntax and knowing the difference between an expression and an equation.

3. realizing that an equation is solved with respect to an unknown, being able to identify the unknown in the parameterized problem situation and not forget to add it at the end of the command Solve(equation, unknown).

4. being able to accept the result, particularly when it is an expression, as a solution, to interpret it with some "symbol sense," and to relate it to graphical representations.

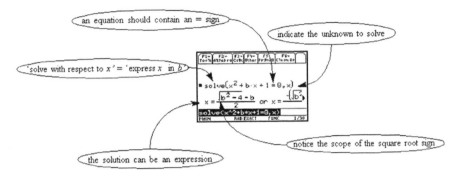

Figure 14.5. Conceptual elements encountered while solving a parametric equation with computer algebra.

Of course, the observation reveals no more than one student's behavior. Meanwhile, it may clarify how the instrumental approach, and the identification of instrumented action schemes in particular, may help us to see the complexity of tool use, and to understand the obstacles and opportunities that emerge during the instrumental genesis.

Discussion

We conclude this section on the instrumental approach of the "soloist" learning process. For what does the instrumental approach to learning mathematics using technological tools allow? It allows for an analysis of the learning process in technological environments of increasing complexity, and takes into account the non-trivial character of using computerized environments. Furthermore, it stresses the subtle relationship between machine technique and mathematical insight, and provides a conceptual framework for investigating the development of schemes, in which both aspects are included. This is helpful for designing student activities, for observing the interaction between students and the computer algebra environment, for interpreting it and for understanding what works well and what does not. The seemingly technical obstacles that students encounter while working in the computer algebra environment often have conceptual components, and the instrumental framework helps one to be conscious of this and to turn such obstacles into opportunities for learning.

Essentially, the instrumental approach reflects "old" ideas, already reflected in the notions of tool use by Vygotsky and others. Its originality lies in the fact that these ideas have been appropriated for the case of using technology in mathematics education mainly by French researchers (Artigue, Laborde, Lagrange, Guin, and Trouche) during the most recent decade.

We also consider the articulation of the instrumental approach with other theoretical perspectives. For example, many research studies on mathematics education focus on semiotics, symbolizing, modeling, and tool use (e.g., Cobb, Gravemeijer, Yackel, McClain, & Whitenack, 1997; Gravemeijer, 1999; Gravemeijer, Cobb, Bowers, & Whitenack, 2000; Meira, 1995; Nemirovsky, 1994; Roth & Tobin, 1997). These approaches stress the dialectic relation between symbolizing and development of meaning in increasing levels of formalism. This relation may be problematic if the artifact imposes specific symbolizations. For example, computer algebra environments offer limited possibilities for the student to develop individual informal symbolizations and related meanings in a process of "symbolic genesis." Meanwhile, instrumental genesis includes a signification process of giving meaning to algebraic objects and procedures. Therefore, we think that an articulation of the instrumental approach with the perspective of symbolizing, both within and apart from the technological environment, might be fruitful.

So far, we examined the instrumental genesis of utilization schemes as an individual process. Different students may develop different schemes for the same type of task, or for using a similar command in the technological environment. However, instrumental genesis also has a social dimension. The students develop mental schemes in the context of the classroom community, in which the guidance of the teacher is one of the factors. The next section, therefore, addresses the social perspective of the instrumental approach.

THE INSTRUMENTAL APPROACH:
THE CONDUCTOR'S TEACHING PERSPECTIVE

In contrast to the individual learning perspective of the previous section, this section takes a more collective, classroom-oriented teaching view. Its main goal is to address criterion 2 in the introduction, and to illustrate the complexity of the role of the teacher when the use of technology is an integrated part of his/her teaching.

From a Set to an Orchestra of Instruments

We agree with the point of view of Hollebrands and colleagues (2008): "We do not take the learner as an isolated individual facing the world, but take the learner as deeply embedded in his/her environment which is highly structured and defines the ways the individual is learning" (p. 157). The way the environment, within the classroom, is structured greatly depends on the teacher. As stated by Zbiek and Hollebrands (2008), "teachers play a central role in the technology-based mathematics learning experiences of children of all ages" (p. 287). The role of a teacher, in such an environment, is rather complex, because s/he always has to manage *a set of instruments*, from two points of view:

- Each student builds a personal set of instruments (for example, in a CAS environment, an instrument for solving equations, an instrument for studying function behavior, etc.); and
- In a classroom seen as a *community of practice* (Wenger, 1998), mobilized instruments are built by each student for each task; these instruments are not necessarily the same. We have shown (Trouche, 2005b) that the more complex the environment, the greater the diversity of the instruments.

Therefore the question is: How can the teacher help each student as well as the class as a whole to articulate or fine-tune these sets of instruments, namely, to build coherent *systems of instruments*, working as an orchestra, with each student building his or her own orchestra? Asking this question means conceiving of instrumental geneses as individual as well as social processes. As a result, utilization schemes also acquire the character of social schemes: "[S]chemes are elaborated and shared in communities of practice and may give rise to an appropriation by subjects, or even result from explicit training processes" (Rabardel & Samurçay, 2001, p. 20).

We do insist here on one aspect of the answer to the question above, often a blind spot in research studies: The constitution of systems of instruments strongly depends on the organization of the artifactual environment the teacher establishes. In order to describe this organization, we have introduced the notion of *instrumental orchestration*[1] (Trouche, 2004). An instrumental orchestration is the intentional and systematic organization of the various artifacts available in a computerized learning environment by the teacher for a given mathematical situation, in order to guide students' instrumental genesis. An instrumental orchestration is defined by

- *didactic configurations* (i.e., arrangements of the artifactual environment, according to various stages of the mathematical situation), and
- *exploitation modes* of these configurations.

Example: Configuration and Exploitation Modes in a Calculator Environment

Designing a configuration first depends on the given technological environment. For example, in a calculator environment, the small screen of this kind of artifact particularly raises the issue of the socialization of students' actions and productions. There is a particular artifact—a viewscreen or a data projector—that allows one to project the calculator's small screen onto a big screen, which the entire class can see. This device is probably designed to project the teacher's calculator screen (the cable linking this artifact to a calculator is rather short and the connection requires a special plug on the calculator). Although in some instances students' calculators have this special plug, the plug often is reserved for the teacher's calculator.

In the Artifact and Instrument section we explained that a subject, while using an artifact, always transforms it through a process of instrumentalization. This transformation can sometimes be in directions that are unplanned by the designer. This is all the more true in a teaching environment: Teachers have to organize the use of artifacts according to their pedagogical goals. We have thus presented (Trouche, 2004) a *configuration* integrating the viewscreen and students' calculators (instead of teacher's calculator) with the main objective of socializing—to a certain extent—students' instrumental genesis.

This configuration (Figure 14.6) rests on the devolution of a particular role to one student: This student, called the *sherpa-student*,[2] handles the overhead-projected calculator. This configuration has several advantages:

- It favors the collective management of a part of the instrumentation and instrumentalization processes. What a student does with her/his calculator—traces of her/his activity—is seen by all and can be the subject of classroom discussions.
- The teacher can guide, through the student's calculator, the calculators of the whole class (the teacher does not perform the instrumented gesture but checks how it is performed by the sherpa-student). The teacher thus fulfils the functions of an orchestra conductor rather than a one-person band.[3]
- For teaching, the teacher can combine paper-and-pencil results obtained on the board, and results obtained by the sherpa-student's calculator on the class screen. For the student, this facilitates the combination of paper-and-pencil work and calculator work at his or her own desk, as well as the articulation of the different sets of instruments.

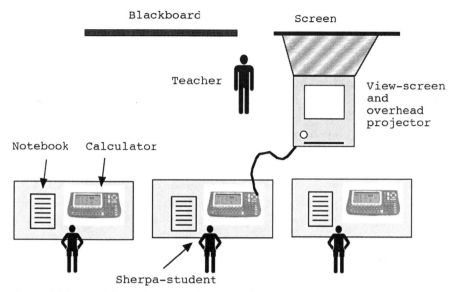

Figure 14.6.   Configuration with sherpa-student.

- It favors debates within the class and the elucidation of procedures. The existence of another point of reference distinct from the teacher's allows new relationships to develop between the students in the class and the teacher as well as between this sherpa-student and the teacher—concerning a mathematical result, a conjecture, a gesture, or a technique—and it can give the teacher means through which to reintegrate lower achieving students into the class. The sherpa-student function gives lower achieving students a different status and forces the teacher to tune teaching procedures with the work of the student who is supposed to follow the teacher's guidelines. Follow-up of the work by this student shown on the big work-screen allows very quick feedback from both teacher and class.

Several exploitation modes of this structure may be considered. The teacher may organize work phases of different kinds:

- Sometimes calculators are shut off (and so is the overhead projector); it is then a matter of work in a paper-and-pencil environment.
- Sometimes calculators as well as the overhead projector are on and work is strictly guided by the sherpa-student under the guidance of the teacher (students are supposed to have exactly the same thing on their calculator screens as is on the big screen in front of the

class). Instrumentation and instrumentalization processes are then strongly constrained.

- Sometimes calculators are on as well as the overhead projector and work is free over a given time. Instrumentation and instrumentalization processes are then relatively constrained (by the type of activities and by referring to the sherpa-student's calculator which remains visible on the big screen) and sometimes calculators are on and the projector is off. Instrumentation and instrumentalization processes are then only weakly constrained.

These various modes seem to illustrate what Healy (2002) named *filling out* and *filling in*,[4] during classroom social interaction. When the sherpa-student's initiative is free, it is possible for mathematically significant issues *to arise out of* the student's own constructive efforts (this is a filling out approach); and when the teacher guides the sherpa-student, it is possible for mathematically significant issues to be *appropriated during* students' own constructive efforts (this is a filling in approach).

Other questions must also be answered: Will the same student play the role of the sherpa-student during the whole lesson or, depending on the results, should another student's calculator be connected to the projector? Do all students have to play this role in turn or must only some of them be privileged?

In the frame of this configuration, teachers and students play new roles. The sherpa-student can be considered, for both class and teacher, as a reference, a guide, an auxiliary, or a mediator. The function of orchestra conductor, for the teacher, combines the various roles pinpointed by Zbiek and Hollebrands (2008): technical assistant, resource, catalyst and facilitator, explainer, task setter, counselor, collaborator, evaluator, planner and conductor, allocator of time, and manager. The predominant role, for the sherpa-student as well for the teacher and for the other students, strongly depends on the exploitation modes chosen for this configuration. Following the orchestra metaphor, the relationships between musicians and between conductor and musicians are not the same in a jazz band and in a symphonic orchestra.

In the same environment, different configurations can be conceived, based on different relationships between students, teacher, and artifacts. More generally, we (Trouche, 2004) gave examples of configurations at several levels: the level of the artifacts (concerning internal arrangement of software itself), the level of the instruments (as the sherpa-student configuration), and the meta-level of the relationship a subject maintains with an instrument (aiming to develop self analysis of subjects' activity).

Orchestration and Mathematical Situations

Following the metaphor once more, we can say that designing an orchestration obviously requires a musical frame. Actually, an instrumental orchestration is to be designed related to both a particular environment and a *mathematical situation* (Brousseau, 1997). The choice of the situations is crucial. As stated by Rabardel (2001), "activity mediated by instruments is always situated and situations have a determining influence on activity" (p. 18). For the case of a CAS environment, Artigue (2005) gives several examples of mathematical situations aiming "to manage jointly and coherently the development of both mathematical and instrumental knowledge" (p. 233).

Chevallard (1992) distinguishes, within a computerized learning environment, three kinds of elements, whose interaction is essential to successfully integrate artifacts in the teaching process:

- environment components: various artifacts (calculators, overhead projectors, teaching software, …), but also instructions for use, technical sheets, and so on;
- mathematical situations; and
- *didactic exploitation system*: an essential element concerned with making relevant use of the potential resources of a given environment and with achieving both the coordination and integration of the environment components and the mathematical situations.

Instrumental orchestrations can be positioned in this schema. A didactic exploitation system can be described as a set of *didactical exploitation scenarios* (one for a given environment and for each mathematical situation). A didactical exploitation scenario (Figure 14.7) contains both the mathematical management of different stages of the situation and an instrumental orchestration (with successive configurations and their exploitation modes, according to the mathematical treatment and the teacher's pedagogical goals). From this perspective, teachers have to build scenarios that are fitting for their personal teaching environment and for the mathematical situations they want to introduce.

Obviously, building such new pedagogical resources requires time and experience. We agree with the conclusion of Zbiek and Hollebrands (2008): "If we give teachers mathematical technology as nets, but provide no personal learning experiences and no support, we should not be surprised when they prefer to catch their mathematical and pedagogical fish by hand" (p. 338). The question of how to generate personal experiences and how to support teachers will be addressed in the next section.

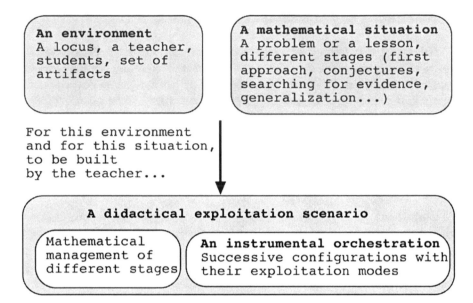

Figure 14.7   Orchestration, part of a didactical exploitation scenario.

INSTRUMENTAL APPROACH FOR PROFESSIONAL DEVELOPMENT

In this section, we address the question of professional development—criterion 3 in the introduction—and particularly the evolution of professional practices in computerized learning environments, from a single person's band practice into an orchestra conductor practice. In a sense, we will take a metaperspective here by using the instrumental approach as a framework for the learning of the teacher.

New Pedagogical Resources, New Teachers' Communities of Practice

In a previous section, we stressed the crucial point of pedagogical resources helping the teacher to organize the technological environment. For this purpose, the idea of conceiving *usage scenarios* (Vivet, 1991) has proved particularly relevant: These scenarios consist of the presentation of a unit with its objectives, student materials, and supporting notes for teachers to help put the unit into practice. This idea acknowledges the necessity of taking into account the available artifacts, the pedagogical organization of a class, and the role of the teacher. Such usage scenarios may be considered as a first approach of didactical exploitation scenarios, as previously described. Usage scenarios have also been developed for teachers wanting to produce teaching units integrating dynamical geometry software (Laborde, 1999).

Using and, moreover, conceiving such scenarios requires teachers' communities of practice to exist or to be built. The idea of building an evolving network of teachers to develop usage scenarios for geometry software was introduced in the United States (Allen, Wallace, Cederberg, & Pearson, 1996). Similar training mechanisms have been developed around units integrating a lesson presentation, a usage scenario, and reports of experimentations with these units by a group of teachers in training, aiming at assisting management of the unit by the teacher and at promoting collaborative work both in the class around a scientific debate and within the group of teachers (Guin, Delgoulet, & Salles, 2000).

This approach to organization has been extended through the use of a distance platform to conduct both collaborative workshops aimed at providing pedagogical resources and continuous long-term support for integration by teachers (Guin, Joab, & Trouche, 2003). The structure of these pedagogical resources was devised with the aim of facilitating both their implementation in classrooms and their evolution in response to teachers' ideas, experiments, and experiences. Thus pedagogical resources evolve through usages in the classrooms and discussions in the community of teachers (see Figure 14.8). Such an approach aims at creating learning and training conditions for teachers in which technological environments can provide spaces for discovery with flexible tutorial assistance. It appears that this mechanism may help teachers to make the transition to pedagogical action.

An Instrumental Approach to Creating Pedagogical Resources

In fact, the process shown in Figure 14.8 is more complex than it might seem. It is not a linear process, and what makes it interesting is precisely that not only the resources but also teachers' practices evolve through the process. The instrumental approach, as presented earlier, affords a better description of such a process. In order to use this approach, we have to consider not only one teacher and one resource, because the interaction in that case is quite limited. One can not say that one resource deeply modifies one teacher's practice. Moreover, there is not, between a given teacher and a given resource, a cycle of interactions.

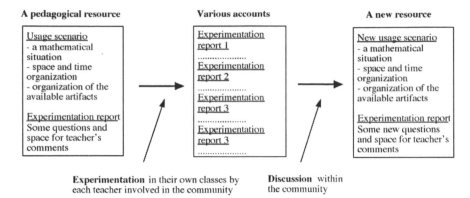

Figure 14.8.   A pedagogical resource in progress.

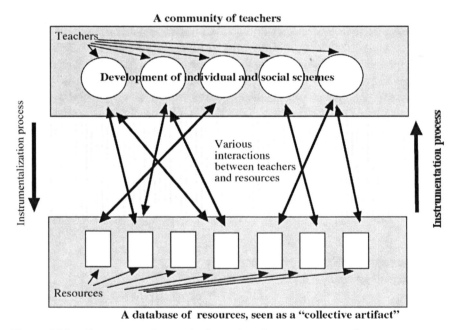

Figure 14.9.   Instrumental genesis, from virtual resources to ready-to-use resources integrated into teachers' practice.

So, consider a database of resources (seen as a "*collective artifact*") and a community of teachers (see Figure 14.9). This community will use this database in order to perform a particular *type of task* (for example, teaching algebra at a given school level in a given technological environment).

When integrating this artifact, teachers develop individual and social schemes. Through the process of instrumental genesis instruments develop. The interaction between teachers and resources can be analyzed as the two components of the instrumental genesis:

- Teachers, when experimenting with resources in their classes, modify these resources, incorporating in them their own experiences (Guin & Trouche, 2005). This is the instrumentalization process.
- Resources, when implemented by teachers in their classes, contribute to modify their practices. This is the instrumentation process.

There are obviously some conditions for such a process to succeed:

- The resources have to be rather flexible, putting in evidence possible didactical choices for the teacher.

- The resources have to include a scenario in use, in order to assist teachers when putting this situation in place in their classes.
- The resources have to allow experimentation reports to be completed, in order to transmit and socialize each teacher's experience.
- Last but not least, there is a need for an instrumental orchestration (as introduced in a previous section), organizing the relationships within the community and the interaction between teachers and resources.

In the context of a distance training organization, Guin and Trouche (2005) thus stress the importance of making rights and duties explicit for all actors (trainers and trainees) involved in this organization through the use of *charts*. These charts are reference texts explaining in detail tasks and working modes in the community, both for trainers and trainees, interacting modes with others and modes of using resources. Charts illustrate that distance working modes require agreement to a strict schedule and the unavoidable act of putting into written form (and consequently, making explicit) didactical choices which usually remain tacit for teachers. Under these conditions, the database of resources may give birth to instruments integrated into each teacher's practice. This is an endless process. Usages as well as technologies evolve, and no database of resources is completely and definitively closed. New resources (through the Internet, for example) always can be added and can enter into this process of instrumental genesis.

An Instrumental Approach to Software Design

The process we described in the previous section for conception, development and evolution of pedagogical resources may be applied to the design of software and computerized learning environments. As stated by Sarama and Clements (2008): "[C]urriculum and software are not only based on research a priori. Research also must be conducted throughout the development process" (p. 123). Linking research and software development is not only a matter of a technical, sequential procedure in which computer scientists, mathematicians, and researchers in mathematics education first conceive a product, and teachers later use it. Rather, from an instrumental point of view, this requires *multidisciplinary teams*, in which researchers and teachers collaborate in an iterative and bidirectional way. Such an approach is needed in order to conceptualize and develop software that takes into account users' experiments and experiences.

CONCLUSION

In the introduction to this chapter, three essential issues were raised: the need for the analysis of the learning process in technological environments, the question of how the teacher can organize the teaching in such an environment, and the need to describe the development of resources for professional development of new teaching practices. As a conclusion, we would like to stress three essential points.

First, the transformation of an artifact—particularly if it is a complex one—into an instrument for mathematics requires time. The instrumental genesis, the construction of an instrument, depends on several factors, such as the affordances and constraints of the artifact, the type of tasks, the learning ecology as a whole, and the inventiveness of the student. A general feature of the instrumental genesis, however, is that it is a time-consuming and laborious process.

Second, the notion of *system of instruments* is essential, on the one hand to describe the "ensemble" of artifacts that a student has to integrate during the learning process, and on the other hand as the set of instruments that are developed within a class of students, which the teacher has to manage in the process of teaching.

Third, the metaphor of *orchestration* is appropriate to describe the organization of the available artifacts by the teacher. The importance of the metaphor is that it expresses the idea of articulation or fine-tuning of a system of instruments, including the guidance by the conductor as well as the improvisations by the soloist players and adaptability for different styles of music.

In this chapter we first applied the instrumental approach to technological artifacts, but also to pedagogical resources and even to the development of software, indicating that this development can only take place effectively if it is *related to its use* in the classroom. Finally, one could apply this perspective to the instrumental approach itself. If we apply the instrumental approach to different situations, and confront it with other theoretical frameworks, it will further develop within the community of researchers. In fact, this chapter illustrates this process. The diversity of the situations in which the instrumental approach can be used illustrates its potential.

NOTES

1. The word "orchestration" is quite natural when speaking of a set of instruments, in the sense of "the art to put in action various sonorities of the collective instrument which one names orchestra by means of infinitely varying combinations" (Lavignac, French musicographer, 1900).

2. On the one hand, the word sherpa refers to the person who guides and who carries the load during expeditions in the Himalaya, and on the other hand, to diplomats who prepare international conferences.

3. This advantage is not a minor one. Teachers, in complex technological environments, are strongly prone to perform alone all mathematical and technical tasks linked to the problem solving in the class.

4. Healy (2002) identified a major difference between instructional theories drawing from constructivist perspectives and those guided by sociocultural ideologies, which related to the primacy assigned to the individual or the cultural in the learning process. Constructivist approaches emphasize a *filling-outwards* (FO) flow in which personal understandings are moved gradually towards institutionalized knowledge. A reverse *filling-inwards* (FI) flow of instruction described in sociocultural accounts stresses moving from institutionalized knowledge to connect with learners' understandings. Teaching interventions in Healy's study were therefore designed to allow investigation of these two different instructional approaches: the FO approach aimed to encourage the development of general mathematical models from learners' activities, and the FI approach intended to support learners in appropriating general mathematical models previously introduced.

REFERENCES

Allen, R., Wallace, M., Cederberg, J., & Pearson, D. (1996). Teachers empowering teachers: Vertically-integrated, inquiry-based geometry in school classrooms. *Mathematics Teacher, 90,* 254-255.

Arnon, I., & Dubinsky, E. (2001, February). *Research on technology and other dangerous pedagogical considerations.* Paper presented at the Conference on Research on Technology and the Teaching and Learning of Mathematics, University Park, PA.

Artigue, M. (1997). Le logiciel 'Derive' comme révélateur de phénomènes didactiques liés à l'utilisation d'environnements informatiques pour l'apprentissage [The software Derive revealing didactical phenomena related to the use of technological environments for learning]. *Educational Studies in Mathematics, 33*, 133-169.

Artigue, M. (2005). The integration of symbolic calculators into secondary education: some lessons from didactical engineering. In D. Guin, K. Ruthven, & L. Trouche (Eds.), *The didactical challenge of symbolic calculators: Turning a computational device into a mathematical instrument*. Dordrecht: Kluwer Academic.

Balacheff, N. (1994). Didactique et intelligence artificielle [Didactique and artificial intelligence]. *Recherches en Didactique des Mathématiques 14*, 9-42.

Brousseau, G. (1997). *Theory of didactical situations in mathematics*. Dordrecht: Kluwer Academic Publishers.

Chevallard, Y. (1992). Intégration et viabilité des objets informatiques, le problème de l'ingénierie didactique [Integration and viability of computer objects, the problem of didactical engineering]. In B. Cornu (Ed.), *L'ordinateur pour enseigner les mathématiques*, (pp. 183-203). Paris: Presses Universitaires de France.

Cobb, P., Gravemeijer, K. P. E., Yackel, E., McClain, K., & Whitenack, J. (1997). Mathematizing and symbolising: The emergence of chains of signification in one first-grade classroom. In D. Kirshner & J. A. Whitson (Eds.), *Situated cognition theory: Social, semiotic, and neurological perspectives* (pp. 151-233). Hillsdale, NJ: Erlbaum.

Drijvers, P. (2002). Learning mathematics in a computer algebra environment: Obstacles are opportunities. *Zentralblatt für Didaktik der Mathematik, 34*, 221-228.

Drijvers, P. (2003). *Learning algebra in a computer algebra environment. Design research on the understanding of the concept of parameter*. Unpublished doctoral dissertation, Freudenthal Institute ,Utrecht, the Netherlands. Retrieved February 19, 2006 from www.fi.uu.nl/~pauld/dissertation

Goldenberg, E. P. (1988). Mathematics, metaphors, and human factors: Mathematical, technical and pedagogical challenges in the educational use of graphical representation of functions. *Journal of Mathematical Behavior, 7*, 135-173.

Gravemeijer, K. (1999). How emergent models may foster the constitution of formal mathematics. *Mathematical Thinking and Learning, 1*, 155-177.

Gravemeijer, K., Cobb, P., Bowers, J., & Whitenack, J. (2000). Symbolising, modeling and instructional design. In P. Cobb, E. Yackel, & K. McClain (Eds.), *Symbolising and communicating in mathematics classrooms: Perspectives on discourse, tools, and instructional design* (pp. 225-273). Hillsdale, NJ: Erlbaum.

Guin, D., Delgoulet, J., & Salles, J. (2000, July). *Formation aux TICE: concevoir un dispositif d'enseignement autour d'un fichier rétroprojetable* [Preparing teachers training for ICT in education: conceive a tool for teaching around a projected file]. Paper presented at the L'enseignement des mathématiques dans les pays francophones, EM 2000, Grenoble, France.

Guin, D., Joab, M., & Trouche, L. (2003). *SFoDEM (Suivi de Formation à Distance pour les Enseignants de Mathématiques), bilan de la phase expérimentale* [SFoDEM (Series of distant in-service training for mathematics teachers), results of the experimental phase]. Montpellier: Institut de Recherche sur l'Enseignement des Mathématiques, Université Montpellier II.

Guin, D., & Trouche, L. (1999). The complex process of converting tools into mathematical instruments: The case of calculators. *International Journal of Computers for Mathematical Learning, 3,* 195-227.

Guin, D., & Trouche, L. (2005, February). *Distance training: A key mode to support teachers in the integration of ICT? Towards collaborative conception of living pedagogical resources.* Paper presented at the Fourth Conference of the European Society for Research in Mathematics Education, Sant Feliu de Guíxols, Spain.

Haspekian, M. (2003, March). *Between arithmetic and algebra: A space for the spreadsheet? Contribution to an instrumental approach. Tools and technologies in mathematical didactics.* Paper presented at the Third Conference of the European Society for Research in Mathematics Education, Italy. Retrieved March 24, 2005, from http://www.dm.unipi.it/~didattica/CERME3/proceedings/Groups/TG9/TG9_Haspekian_cerme3.pdf

Healy, L. (2002). *Iterative design and comparison of learning systems for reflection in two dimensions.* Unpublished doctoral dissertation, University of London.

Hollebrands, K., Laborde, C., & Sträßer, R. (2008). Technology and the learning of geometry at the secondary level. In M. K. Heid & G. W. Blume (Eds.), *Research on technology and the teaching and learning of mathematics: Vol. 1. Research syntheses* (pp. 155-206). Charlotte, NC: Information Age.

Hoyles, C., & Noss, R. (2003). What can digital technologies take from and bring to research in mathematics education? In A. J. Bishop, M. A. Clements, C. Keitel, J. Kilpatrick, & F. Leung (Eds.), *Second international handbook of mathematics education* (Vol. 1, pp. 323-349). Dordrecht: Kluwer Academic.

Laborde, C. (1999). Vers un usage banalisé de Cabri-Géomètre en classe de seconde: analyse des facteurs de l'intégration [Towards an ordinary use of Cabri-Géomètre in grade 10: analysis of integrating factors]. In D. Guin (Ed.), *Calculatrices symboliques et géométriques dans l'enseignement des mathématiques, colloque francophone européen* (pp. 79-94). Montpellier: Institut de Recherche sur l'Enseignement des Mathématiques, Université Montpellier II.

Lagrange, J. B. (2005). Using symbolic calculators to study mathematics. In D. Guin, K. Ruthven, & L. Trouche (Eds.), *The didactical challenge of symbolic calculators: Turning a computational device into a mathematical instrument* (pp. 113-135). Dordrecht: Kluwer Academic.

Lagrange, J. B., Artigue, M., Laborde, C., & Trouche, L. (2003). Technology and mathematics education: A multidimensional study of the evolution of research and innovation. In A. J. Bishop, M. A. Clements, C. Keitel, J. Kilpatrick, & F. K. S. Leung (Eds.), *Second international handbook of mathematics education* (Vol. 1, pp. 239-271). Dordrecht: Kluwer Academic.

Lajoie, S. P. (1993). Cognitive tools for enhancing learning. In S. P. Lajoje & S. J. Derry (Eds.), *Computers as cognitive tools* (pp. 261-289). Hillsdale, NJ: Erlbaum.

Meira, L. (1995). The microevolution of mathematical representations in children's activity. *Cognition and Instruction, 13*, 269-313.

Nemirovsky, R. C. (1994). On ways of symbolizing: The case of Laura and the velocity sign. *Journal of Mathematical Behavior, 13*, 389-422.

Rabardel, P. (2001). Instrument mediated activity in situations. In A. Blandford, J. Vanderdonckt, & P. Gray (Eds.), *People and computers XV—Interactions without frontiers* (pp. 17-30). Berlin: Springer-Verlag.

Rabardel, P. (2002). *People and technology—a cognitive approach to contemporary instruments*. Retrieved March 1, 2005, from http://ergoserv.psy.univ-paris8.fr

Rabardel, P., & Samurçay, R. (2001, March). *From artifact to instrument-mediated learning: New challenges to research on learning*. Retrieved March 1, 2005, from http://ergoserv.psy.univ-paris8.fr/Site/default.asp?Act_group=1

Roth, W., & Tobin, K. (1997). Cascades of inscriptions and the re-presentation of nature: How numbers, tables, graphs, and money come to re-present a rolling ball. *International Journal of Science Education, 19*, 1075-1091.

Sarama, J., & Clements, D. H. (2008). Linking research and software development. In G. W. Blume & M. K. Heid (Eds.), *Research on technology and the teaching and learning of mathematics: Vol. 2. Cases and perspectives* (pp. 113-130). Charlotte, NC: Information Age.

Trouche, L. (2004). Managing complexity of human/machine interactions in computerized learning environments: Guiding student's command process through instrumental orchestrations. *International Journal of Computers for Mathematical Learning, 9*, 281-307.

Trouche, L. (2005a). An instrumental approach to mathematics learning in symbolic calculator environments. In D. Guin, K. Ruthven, & L. Trouche (Eds.), *The didactical challenge of symbolic calculators: Turning a computational device into a mathematical instrument* (pp. 137-162). Dordrecht: Kluwer Academic.

Trouche, L. (2005b). Instrumental genesis, individual and social aspects. In D. Guin, K. Ruthven, & L. Trouche (Eds.), *The didactical challenge of symbolic calculators: Turning a computational device into a mathematical instrument* (pp. 197-230). Dordrecht: Kluwer Academic.

Vergnaud, G. (1996). Au fond de l'apprentissage, la conceptualisation [At the heart of learning—the conceptualization]. In R. Noirfalise & M. J. Perrin (Eds.), *Actes de l'école d'été de didactique des mathématiques* (pp. 174-185). Clermont-Ferrand, France: Institut de Recherche sur l'Enseignement des Mathématiques, Université de Clermont-Ferrand II.

Vérillon, P., & Rabardel, P. (1995). Cognition and artefacts: A contribution to the study of though [sic] in relation to instrumented activity, *European Journal of Psychology of Education, 10*, 77-103.

Vivet, M. (1991). Usage des tuteurs intelligents: prise en compte du contexte, rôle du maître [Use of intelligent systems taking into account the context and the role of the teacher]. In M. Baron, R. Gras, & J. F. Nicaud (Eds.), *Deuxièmes journées Environnements informatiques d'apprentissage avec l'ordinateur* (pp. 239-246). Cachan: Ecole Nationale Supérieure.

Vygotsky, L. S. (1930/1985). La méthode instrumentale en psychology [The instrumental method in psychology]. In B. Schneuwly & J. P. Bronckart (Eds.), *Vygotsky auhourd'hui* (pp. 39-47). Neufchâtel: Delachaux et Niestlé.

Wenger, E. (1998). *Communities of practice*. New York: Cambridge University Press.

Zbiek, R. M., & Hollebrands, K. (2008). A research-informed view of the process of incorporating mathematics technology into classroom practice by inservice and prospective teachers. In M. K. Heid & G. W. Blume (Eds.), *Research on technology and the teaching and learning of mathematics: Vol. 1. Research syntheses* (pp. 287-344). Charlotte, NC: Information Age.

CHAPTER 15

DESIGNING TASKS FOR THE CODEVELOPMENT OF CONCEPTUAL AND TECHNICAL KNOWLEDGE IN CAS ACTIVITY

An Example From Factoring

Carolyn Kieran and Luis Saldanha

In this chapter we describe a classroom instructional activity that integrates the use of Computer Algebra Systems (CAS) in a manner aimed at engaging high school students in substantive mathematical reasoning. The activity draws on students' prior knowledge of factoring and pushes them to use and develop this knowledge beyond what is usual for high-school-level algebra. In particular, we discuss the attendant design and mathematical principles of the activity at some length, explicating the intended role of the CAS. We then highlight aspects of engagement and student reasoning that emerged with the unfolding of the activity in a

Research on Technology and the Teaching and Learning of Mathematics:
Vol. 2. Cases and Perspectives, 393–414
Copyright © 2008 by Information Age Publishing
393

high school mathematics classroom. Three features of the design of the activity are considered to have played important roles in the further development of students' conceptual and technical knowledge of factoring: reconciling the forms generated by the CAS in relation to the forms they had generated with paper and pencil, reflecting on the objects they had reconciled, and proving the relations they had generalized.

THEORETICAL FRAMEWORK

One of the contributions of the French didactique research community (e.g., Artigue, 2002; Guin & Trouche, 1999; Lagrange, 2000) has been the notion that both conceptual and technical knowledge can co-develop within mathematical activity involving technological tools, as long as the technical aspects of that activity are not neglected. According to Vérillon and Rabardel (1995), tools exist as both artifacts (physical objects) and instruments (psychological constructions). These researchers suggest that, when students appropriate tools for themselves, and thereby transform artifacts into instruments, they are not simply learning tool-techniques in response to given tasks. They are actually developing conceptually while they are perfecting their techniques with the tool.

Lagrange (2003) has described research in which French teachers initially used Derive (1996) in their algebra classrooms with the intention that the symbol manipulation software would lighten the technical load, and so they emphasized conceptual activity. The result, however, was that neither the conceptual nor the technical developed. The research team began to look upon techniques in a different light and to view them as a link between tasks and conceptual reflection. Further, Lagrange (2003) points out the following:

> A technique is generally a mixture of routine and reflection. It plays a pragmatic role when the important thing is to complete the task or when the task is a routine part of another task. Technique plays an epistemic role by contributing to an understanding of the objects it handles, particularly during its elaboration. It also serves as an object for a conceptual reflection when compared with other techniques. (p. 271)

But, for technique to be a link between tasks and conceptual reflection, an immediate question arises: What is the nature of the tasks that support this potential conceptualizing role of technique?

THE NATURE OF TASK-SITUATIONS[1] THAT PROVIDE FOR THE CODEVELOPMENT OF CONCEPTUAL AND TECHNICAL KNOWLEDGE

CAS-Related Literature

In the Derive study mentioned previously, Lagrange noted that the easier calculation afforded by the tool did not automatically enhance students' reflection and understanding. Teachers had

> encouraged students to jump directly from tasks to conceptual reflection … not seeing that techniques specific to the use of symbolic computation are useful, that the techniques are not obvious to students, and that these techniques may be a topic for reflection. (Lagrange, 2003, p. 271)

In contrast, two experienced teachers, who assigned to their class of 16- to 18-year-old college students the long-term problem of working on the factorization of $x^n - 1$, did recognize the epistemic value of developing techniques of factorization with Derive (Mounier & Aldon, 1996). According to the teachers, as reported by Lagrange, the students learned a great deal at a conceptual level about finding a general factored form that is true for every integer n.

But how can one make "techniques a topic for reflection"? What kinds of situations, in which a task such as the previous one is embedded, could potentially lead to the codevelopment of both conceptual and technical aspects of mathematical activity? This was a central question we faced as we began our CAS research project in 2004 and were confronted with the need to design a set of CAS task-situations for use by tenth-grade students within their algebra course of study. Of equal import to us as researchers was our need to ensure that these tasks would also function as productive vehicles for generating rich data on the codevelopment of conceptual and technical knowledge.

We combed the CAS research literature regarding the nature of tasks susceptible to playing this dual role, looking specifically for design frameworks, or basic principles, for constructing such tasks. Hoyles (2002) had emphasized that a focus on the design of task-situations is at the heart of the "transformative potential of [technological] tools in activities" and that, with this focus, "knowledge and epistemology are brought back to center stage" (p. 284). But the search for design frameworks proved elusive. In fact, Zbiek (2003) found that the "absence of detail in research reports causes difficulty in using the reports to develop deeper insights into the kind of CAS-related mathematical experiences that best support student learning. Writers who wish to have a greater impact on classroom practice should consider ways to include in their research reports more information about the mathematical tasks and CAS activities used in the classroom" (p. 212).

However, we were able to glean relevant information from various research reports that provided a basis for getting started on our own task construction. For example, Drijvers (2003) emphasized that,

> While designing instructional activities, the key question is what meaningful problems may foster the students' cognitive development according to the goals of the hypothesized learning trajectory, ... three design principles guided the design process: guided reinvention, didactical phenomenology, and mediating models. (p. 26)

Especially useful was Drijvers' suggestion that more attention needed to be paid to the roles of both paper-and-pencil work throughout CAS activity and focused classroom discussions. Artigue, Defouad, Duperier, Juge, and Lagrange (1998) provided several examples of novel CAS tasks, pointing out that they had used three types of situations in their study: guided manipulation, problem solving, and teaching of a specific notion—each with different degrees of teacher intervention. Artigue (2002) also pointed out that some of the levers on which one can capitalize with respect to CAS activity playing an epistemic role include "the surprise effect that can occur when one obtains results that do not conform to expectations and that can destabilize erroneous conceptions, and the multiplicity of results that can be obtained in a short space of time when exploring and trying to understand a certain phenomenon" (p. 344) (translated by Carolyn Kieran and Luis Saldanha). Guin and Trouche (1999) added that situations should aim at fostering investigation and anticipation.

Zehavi and Mann (2003) described how they set out to develop tasks that, in their view, could not be handled practically and effectively without CAS—tasks that had the potential to intertwine student work, CAS performance, and student reflection. The tasks were to highlight the fundamental ideas within a mathematical topic, and were to extend the topic at hand by connecting it with previously learned topics or with topics that would be learned at a later stage. Often they were based on the identification of persistent learning difficulties in current non-CAS practice, and sometimes involved replicating and completing examples. Ball and Stacey (2003), who raised the question as to what students should record when working in CAS environments, suggested that, "Our goal is to shift the focus of students' written records from principally providing the detail to principally providing the overview and emphasizing the reasoning" (p. 290). Finally, Lagrange (1999) proposed that task-situations ought to be created in such a way as to "bring about a better comprehension of mathematical content" (p. 63) via the progressive acquisition of techniques in the achievement of a solution to the task.

Relevant Non-CAS-Related Literature

In addition to the research cited above, which deals specifically with the design and implementation of CAS-based tasks, another perspective on instructional design, relevant to the present discussion, is that developed by Thompson (2002). His is a more general perspective that involves conceptual analyses of mathematical ideas and their contribution to the design of mathematical learning experiences that aim to support learners' conceptual advances. In Thompson's view, doing conceptual analyses entails imagining students having *something* in mind in the context of *discussing* that something.

Toward this end, according to Thompson, instructional activities should be designed with two central aims in mind: (a) to create opportunities for students and teacher to discuss particular things, objects, or ideas that need to be understood and to discuss how to imagine such things; and (b) to create opportunities for the instructor to ensure that specific conceptual issues will arise for students as they engage in discussions with her or him. When goals a and b are realized with regard to a particular idea, they can produce *instructional conversations* (interactions) around that idea.

At the core of this design perspective, then, is a vision of students purposefully participating in conversations that foster reflection on some mathematical *thing*—an object, an idea, or a way of thinking. Thompson (2002) employs the term *didactic object* to refer to "a thing to talk about that is designed to support reflective mathematical discourse involving specific mathematical ideas or ways of thinking" (p. 210). In our view, a didactic object is akin to a tool for a designer or a teacher who conceives using it in ways that enable student engagement and conversations that foster productive reflection on specific mathematical things.

Drawing on the notion of didactic object, we view the CAS as a *didactical tool* in that we intended that it be used in our task-situations as a means for leveraging the kinds of instructional interactions envisioned by Thompson. More specifically, the *things* generated by the CAS in the context of the activity within which it is integrated—for example, the expressions it produces and displays as a result of students' interaction with it in the context of some goal-directed sequence of activities—could be taken as objects of explicit and substantive reflection and classroom discussions.

DESIGNING CAS TASK-SITUATIONS: AN EXAMPLE FROM FACTORING

With the preceding prior experiences of other CAS researchers as a pool from which to draw, and with Thompson's perspective of didactic objects in mind as a background instructional design heuristic, the members of our research team began to think about the nature of the task-situations that might be integrated into our own study of tenth-grade algebra classes. It was clear to the team from the outset that CAS technology was not intended to replace paper-and-pencil work as a technical tool. Nor would it be simply a means for checking paper-and-pencil work. It was, however, seen as a didactical tool for pushing students to come to grips with underlying theoretical ideas in algebra.

Some of the components of our activities that were intended to make CAS a didactical tool were questions that drew on the machine to occasion discussions that do not normally happen in mathematics classes. Tasks that asked students to write about how they were interpreting their work and the related CAS displays aimed to bring mathematical notions to the surface, making them objects of explicit reflection and discourse in the classroom, and clarifying ideas and distinctions, in ways that simply "doing algebra" may not require. The design team decided that, if CAS is to be effective at the high school level, it is precisely this kind of usage that needs to be considered—usage that involves a mix of paper-and-pencil work, CAS activity, reflection questions, and classroom discussions of a substantive nature in which the teacher draws out from the students the ideas upon which they are reflecting.

One of the several task-situations that we developed was an elaboration of the $x^n - 1$ factoring task[2] previously referenced in the Lagrange (2003) report.[3] We shall use it as the vehicle for presenting the principles on which we drew as we designed the various questions of the task-situations, a process that involved several refinement loops. (See the Appendix for the task-situation in its entirety—Activity 6: Factoring.[4]) After presenting the aims and design principles of each of the main parts of the factoring task-situation, we briefly describe some of the highlights of its unfolding within one of the classes that we observed and conclude by pointing toward those design principles and features of CAS that supported students' engagement in substantive mathematical reasoning and the codevelopment of their conceptual and technical knowledge.

Overview of the Task-Situation and Its Design Principles

The particular task-situation discussed here as an illustrative example is one that involves seeing patterns in the factorization of an expression. We designed the task-situation with the intention that students would engage in the following meta-level processes of mathematical activity: anticipating, verifying, conjecturing, generalizing, and proving (Kieran, 1996). We structured the situation so as to unfold in phases of student work that would correspond more or less with these processes.

Students had already learned to factor the difference of squares (e.g., $x^2 - 1$) and the sum and difference of cubes (e.g., $x^3 - 1$). As a first design principle, we wished for them to *link their past work* involving these identities with the generalization toward which they would be working regarding the factoring of $x^n - 1$. We aimed to support students' construing a factoring pattern that they might not have noticed before when using only 2 and 3 as values of n.

An additional design principle involved students' *predicting* a factorization for $x^n - 1$, using the symbol n for the exponent, rather than specific numerical values. This principle, which reflected our intention that students would move toward an algebraic formalization of the patterns they noticed, would be invoked within the context of yet another principle—that of *focused substantive classroom discussion* in which the teacher attempts to elicit student thinking rather than give them answers a little too quickly.

Then, activity with the systematic replacement of n by ever-increasing integral values in $x^n - 1$ was intended to provide an arena for making conjectures and working toward and refining the generalization taking place. To facilitate both the process of generalization and the identification of the constraints on the form of the complete factorization of $x^n - 1$, we elaborated as a design principle the student practice of *reconciling* the factored form obtained by paper and pencil with the unexpected form of the CAS output. This design principle is described more fully in Part II of the Task-Situation: Conjecturing and Moving Toward a More Refined Generalization.

The last design principle to be called on was one that we adapted for use with CAS task-situations that aim at supporting the development of conceptual knowledge within technical activity. It involves the *mobilization of the emerging conceptual knowledge* within the multifaceted activity of proving—an activity that has only rarely figured explicitly in CAS research at the secondary school level.

We now present some details of the three main parts of the factoring task situation. We also include brief reference to the suggestions offered for teacher intervention so as to give some indication of the classroom context for which we attempted to provide.

Part I of the Task-Situation: Anticipating and Verifying

The activity begins with a brief review of paper-and-pencil factoring of differences of squares and cubes, accompanied by CAS verification (see Item 1a of the Appendix). The activity entails prompts to suggest that this preliminary work be followed by the teacher asking students to look at the factored forms of $x^2 - 1$ and $x^3 - 1$ to see whether they detect some signs of a pattern. Students might remark that $(x - 1)$ is a factor of both. The teacher could then write the factored forms on the board, while posing the question, "So what do we obtain when we multiply out these factored forms?" In this way the teacher could be helping students to relate explicitly both the factored and expanded forms of the two examples:

$(x - 1)(x + 1) =$ _____ and $(x - 1)(x^2 + x + 1) =$ _____ .

Students then return to the activity sheets (Items 1b, 2a–2d) where they are asked to write the result they anticipate for $(x - 1)(x^3 + x^2 + x + 1)$, without doing any paper-and-pencil or CAS manipulation. They then verify their anticipated result by means of CAS. They are asked subsequently to note what the three expressions $[(x - 1)(x + 1), (x - 1)(x^2 + x + 1)$, and $(x - 1)(x^3 + x^2 + x + 1)]$ have in common, as well as to explain why it is that a binomial results as the product in all three cases. The next section of Part I (Items 2e–2g) presents an item requiring prediction: "On the basis of the expressions we have found so far, predict a factorization of the expression $x^5 - 1$," followed by a few more items of an anticipatory or explanatory nature.

The classroom discussion that brings this first part of the activity to a close focuses on whether students have been able to anticipate a general factorization of the expression $x^n - 1$, for integral values of n. We considered it important that students try to generate the general formulation themselves, tackling issues such as representing decreasing powers of the variable with a general notation. At this point, we suggested that the discussion could address the importance of the factor $x - 1$ and the fact that in multiplying this binomial by any polynomial of the form $x^{n-1} + x^{n-2} + \ldots x^2 + x + 1$, the result is the sum of the first and last terms of the product. This result is obtained by distributing the factor x, then the factor -1, throughout all the terms of the second polynomial, thereby leading to the pair-wise cancellation of all "inner" terms. In sum, for integral values of n we have $(x - 1)(x^{n-1} + x^{n-2} + \ldots x^2 + x + 1) = x^n - 1$.

Part II: Toward a generalization (activity with __paper & pencil__ and with __calculator__).

II(A) In this activity each line of the table below must be filled in completely (all three cells), one row at a time. Start from the top row (the cells of the three columns) and work your way down.

If, for a given row, the results in the left and middle columns differ, reconcile the two by using algebraic manipulations in the right hand column.

Factorization using paper and pencil	Result produced by FACTOR command	Calculation to reconcile the two, if necessary
$x^2 - 1 =$		

Figure 15.1.   First line of table requesting the systematic replacement of n in $x^n - 1$ by 2, 3, 4, 5, and 6.

Part II of the Task-Situation: Conjecturing and Moving Toward a More Refined Generalization

The second part of the activity focuses, first, on the systematic replacement of n by the integers from 2 through 6 in $x^n - 1$. Students are asked to fill in a table, of which only the first line is shown in Figure 15.1, according to the given instructions.

We anticipated that students might factor $x^4 - 1$ as $(x - 1)(x^3 + x^2 + x + 1)$, according to the pattern they had generalized up to this point, not realizing that the second factor could be further factored. In fact, several students might be initially surprised by the factored form produced by the CAS for $x^4 - 1$, until perhaps noting that they were dealing with a difference of squares or that the second factor could be refactored by grouping. Thus, a reconciliation of the versions they had produced with paper-and-pencil and with CAS would be in order. We also considered it important that the reconciling be done after each example of $x^n - 1$, which explains why students are asked to fill in all three cells of a given row before moving down to the next row of the table.

We conjectured that the reconciling part of the activity would be a crucial factor in students' evolving conceptual development. Not only was the completely-factored CAS output intended to provoke them into thinking more deeply about what it meant to be "fully factored," but also how they might be able to tell, or test, whether a given expression could be factored differently or whether the "factors" they had produced could be further factored. Indeed, the prompt to reconcile is that part of the activity that aims to engage students in the act of reflecting on the "things" (forms, in this case) generated by the CAS in relation to the forms generated by them.

After filling in the table for $x^2 - 1$ through $x^6 - 1$, students are asked to do some conjecturing (Item II.A.2): "Conjecture, in general, for what numbers n will the factorization of $x^n - 1$: (i) contain exactly two factors? (ii) contain more than two factors? (iii) include $x + 1$ as a factor? Please explain."

The discussion following this first section of Part II was intended to touch upon the different ways of factoring $x^6 - 1$, that is, an expression in which n is a multiple of both 3 and 2, before asking students about the conjectures they had made regarding the factorization of $x^n - 1$. We anticipated that students would first distinguish the cases of n even and n odd. We also thought that many of them would (incorrectly) conjecture that there are more than two factors for even numbers $n > 2$ and only two factors when n is odd. At this point, it was suggested that the teacher might want to offer $x^9 - 1$ as a counterexample to this conjecture, for which the factored form contains three factors. Then students would be urged to work either individually or in groups, in order to revise their conjectures. They would then be prompted to go on to the second section, which involves completing a table as before, but this time for $x^7 - 1$ through $x^{13} - 1$.

The same conjecturing question is repeated after students have completed the table with the extended integral values for n, in order to give them the opportunity to revise and elaborate their initial conjectures (Item II.B.2). The final item of Part II involves applying the generalizations they have formed to a few numerical examples (Items II.C.1–II.C.3): "Does $x^{2004} - 1$ (followed by $x^{3003} - 1$, and then $x^{853} - 1$) (i) contain more than two factors? (ii) include $x + 1$ as a factor? Please explain."

The aim of Part II is to stimulate students to discover the general relationship: $x^n - 1 = (x - 1)(x^{n-1} + x^{n-2} + \ldots x^2 + x + 1)$, for integral values of n. More specifically, we intended to encourage the realization that for n prime, the factorization will be of this form; while for n even, the form of the complete factorization, which involves a refactorization of the second factor, will include both $(x - 1)$ and $(x + 1)$ as factors. In the discussion following the first section of Part II, the counterexample

$$x^9 - 1 = (x - 1)(x^8 + x^7 + x^6 + x^5 + x^4 + x^3 + x^2 + x + 1)$$
$$= (x - 1)(x^6 + x^3 + 1)(x^2 + x + 1)$$

aims at promoting distinctions among the cases of n prime, even $n > 2$, and odd n not prime (see Figure 15.2 for examples of the cases of n prime and even $n > 2$).

If n is even and $n > 2$, then $(x - 1)$ and $(x + 1)$ are two factors of the factored polynomial.

$$x^4 - 1 = (x^2 - 1)(x^2 + 1) = (x - 1)(x + 1)(x^2 + 1)$$

$$x^6 - 1 = (x^3 - 1)(x^3 + 1) = (x - 1)(x + 1)(x^2 + x + 1)(x^2 - x + 1)$$

$$x^8 - 1 = (x^4 - 1)(x^4 + 1) = (x^2 - 1)(x^2 + 1)(x^4 + 1) = (x - 1)(x + 1)(x^2 + 1)(x^4 + 1)$$

$$x^{10} - 1 = (x^5 - 1)(x^5 + 1) = (x - 1)(x^4 + x^3 + x^2 + x + 1)(x^5 + 1)$$
$$= (x - 1)(x + 1)(x^4 + x^3 + x^2 + x + 1)(x^4 - x^3 + x^2 - x + 1)$$

If n is a prime number, the factored expression contains only two factors:

$$x^2 - 1 = (x - 1)(x + 1)$$

$$x^3 - 1 = (x - 1)(x^2 + x + 1)$$

$$x^5 - 1 = (x - 1)(x^4 + x^3 + x^2 + x + 1)$$

$$x^7 - 1 = (x - 1)(x^6 + x^5 + x^4 + x^3 + x^2 + x + 1)$$

$$x^{11} - 1 = (x - 1)(x^{10} + x^9 + x^8 + \ldots + x^3 + x^2 + x + 1)$$

Figure 15.2.   Factoring $x^n - 1$ for cases of n prime and even $n > 2$.

Part III of the Task-Situation: Proving

Part III contains a single item: "Explain why $(x + 1)$ is always a factor of $x^n - 1$ for even values of $n \geq 2$." When we included this item, we were not sure what tenth-grade students would be able to do with it. They had not had any prior experience with proofs such as the following:

$$
\begin{aligned}
x^n - 1 &= x^{2k} - 1 \qquad \text{(for n even)} \\
&= (x^2)^k - 1 \\
&= (x^2 - 1)(x^{2^{k-1}} + x^{2^{k-2}} + \ldots + 1) \\
&= (x + 1)(x - 1)(\ \ldots\ )
\end{aligned}
$$

What we observed was a surprise, both to ourselves and to the classroom teacher.

SOME HIGHLIGHTS OF THE UNFOLDING OF
THE FACTORING ACTIVITY WITHIN ONE OF THE CLASSES[5]

The activity unfolded over two 1-hour class periods occurring on consecutive days. Students engaged in the activity, following the intended structure that we elaborated in the previous section, each part concluding with a whole-class discussion of ideas addressed within that part. Our aim in this section is not to provide a detailed research report of what transpired within this unfolding. Rather, we focus on two highlights that illustrate how engagement with the activity brought issues of substantive mathematical reasoning to the fore and pushed students to reason in seemingly new directions. The first highlight, emerging in the classroom discussion at the end of Part I, concerns issues related to the symbolic formalization of the general relationship that we intended for students to broach. The second highlight concerns a creative and elegant proof of the general relationship, advanced by a particular pair of students at the activity's conclusion.

The emergence of these highlights was driven by students' attending to the subtle but important requirement, built into particular parts of the activity, that they reconcile the forms produced by the CAS with their own paper-and-pencil factorizations of expressions of the form $x^n - 1$ for increasing integral values of n. By helping to orient students toward constructing complete factorizations of these expressions, the reconciling requirement thus played a central role in pushing them to conjecture, generalize, and formalize a proof.

Dealing With *n*s in the General Formulation

After the students had shared their thinking with respect to the three given examples of Item 2c in Part I [$(x - 1)(x + 1)$, $(x - 1)(x^2 + x + 1)$, and $(x - 1)(x^3 + x^2 + x + 1)$, along with their expanded forms], the teacher asked them to predict the factorization of $x^n - 1$. It seemed clear to the researcher-observers that this was the first time that the students had been asked to deal with a general formulation of a factored form.

One student started with the suggestion, "$(x - 1)(x^{n-1} + x^{n-2}$" but then stopped and said, "but I don't know how far to go." This was echoed by several others in the class. The teacher then offered: "down to $x^2 + x + 1$, as with the others." On examining the proposed factored form for $x^n - 1$, another student wondered whether $(x - 1)(x^{n-1} + 1)$ would be the same as $(x - 1)(x^{n-1} + x^{n-2} + \ldots x^2 + x + 1)$. We noted that even the knowledge of how to multiply x by x^{n-1} seemed precarious at this moment. One student suggested adding the exponents, 1 and $n - 1$. In the background, however, remained the question of "how far to go" in the second factor; it had not yet been satisfactorily addressed. The student asked again, "If it's decreasing, how far down do you go?" to which the teacher responded, "You go all the way to x^0, which is 1." However, the link between x^0 and x^{n-n} was not made, and the student in question seemed unsatisfied.

Even though the issue was still not resolved, the teacher asked the students to move on to Part II. So, midway through Part II, when the rest of the class had begun to work on the factoring of $x^7 - 1$ and its successor expressions, the same student went up to the board to repeat his question to the teacher: "When you go like this, going down even to $n - 1$, $n - 2$, $n - 3$, how far do you go with the ns; when will this (circling the –3) be zero?" "It depends on n," offered the teacher. Not yet convinced, the student added that he did not like the dots either (referring to the second general factor where the middle terms were represented by three dots).

Had the students not been asked to predict a general factorization for x^{n-1} and to express it in general notation, we would not have witnessed the difficulties that are inherent in such polynomial notations involving non-numerical exponents for students of this age and particular algebraic experience. It suggested an interesting area for further study.

Proving That $(x + 1)$ Is Always a Factor of $x^n - 1$ for Even Values of $n \geq 2$

After having given the class about 15 minutes to try to generate a proof of this phenomenon—that $(x + 1)$ is always a factor of x^{n-1} for even values of $n \geq 2$—and having circulated around the classroom during this time in order to see what kind of proofs the students were attempting, the teacher invited selected students to come to the board, one at a time, to present their proofs.

One of the first "proofs" that was proposed was as follows: "When n is an even number greater than or equal to 2, $(x^2 - 1)$ is always a factor, and so $(x + 1)$ is a factor." However, the student could not really show why $(x^2 - 1)$ is always a factor. Then another student came forward with what he proposed as a counterexample, $(x^{12} - 1)$, which he manipulated so as to have a sum of cubes (i.e., the first factor of the expression $(x^3 + 1)(x^3 - 1)(x^6 + 1)$), which yielded $(x + 1)$ as a factor. So, the presence of $(x^2 - 1)$, he argued, was perhaps not so crucial after all.

But the quite remarkable attempt appeared when Jane was invited to come forward to present the proof that she and her partner had constructed (see Figure 15.3). Theirs was a generic proof (Tall, 1979), in that the argument was presented as an example that embodied the structure of a more general argument. Their proof was based on noticing that for

Figure 15.3.   The beginning of the proof based on the idea of grouping the even number of terms in the second factor.

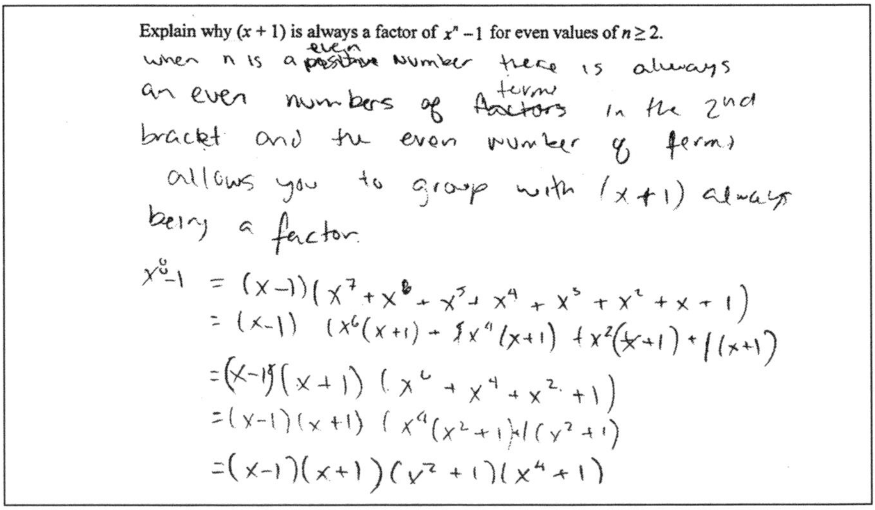

Explain why $(x + 1)$ is always a factor of $x^n - 1$ for even values of $n \geq 2$.

when n is a positive even Number there is always an even numbers of terms factors in the 2nd bracket and the even number of terms allows you to group with $(x+1)$ always being a factor.

$$x^8 - 1 = (x-1)(x^7 + x^6 + x^5 + x^4 + x^5 + x^2 + x + 1)$$
$$= (x-1)(x^6(x+1) + 5x^4(x+1) + x^2(x+1) + 1(x+1))$$
$$= (x-1)(x+1)(x^6 + x^4 + x^2 + 1)$$
$$= (x-1)(x+1)(x^4(x^2+1) + 1(x^2+1))$$
$$= (x-1)(x+1)(x^2+1)(x^4+1)$$

Figure 15.4.   Written work illustrating the proof that $(x + 1)$ is always a factor of $x^n - 1$ for even values of $n \geq 2$.

even ns in x^{n-1}, the number of terms in the second factor was even. Thus the terms of this second factor could be grouped pairwise, yielding a common factor of $(x + 1)$. See Figure 15.4 for the written work underpinning,

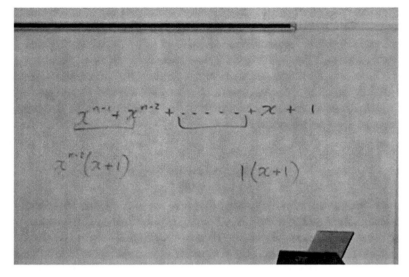

Figure 15.5.   Part of a more general notation for the "grouping" proof.

and extending, the presentation at the board. Part of a more general notation for the proof was added by the teacher (see Figure 15.5), but the elegant simplicity of the proof had already been appreciated by many in the class—as well as by the teacher and the researcher-observers.

CONCLUDING REMARKS

We offer the activity described here as an illustration of a productive way to integrate CAS into mathematical activity that at once draws upon students' prior knowledge and skills *and* pushes them to reflect on and use these in a manner that goes beyond the usual for the high school context. From our perspective, in this activity the CAS functioned as a generator of factorizations of expressions of the form $x^{n} - 1$, for different values of n.

This function, together with the important requirement that students reconcile their own paper-and-pencil work with the results produced by the CAS, provided an impetus for their generating conjectures about the form of the complete factorization of $x^{n} - 1$. This, in turn, oriented students to elaborate a general relationship and to formalize that relationship. It also led several of them to find a way of proving that $(x + 1)$ is always a factor of $x^{n} - 1$ for even values of $n \geq 2$, with novel methods that intertwined both the conceptual and technical knowledge that had been developed throughout the activity.

The coupling of students' attention to the forms produced by the CAS in comparison to their own productions, we argue, helped constitute these forms and their structure as objects of explicit reflection and classroom discussion. We hasten to add that this function was not inherent to the CAS, but rather was imposed on it within the context of the total intended activity. In other words, that the CAS served this function was very much an intended *design* feature of the activity. It is in this way that we view the CAS as a didactical tool.

ACKNOWLEDGMENTS

The authors express their appreciation to the Social Sciences and Humanities Research Council of Canada, which funded this research, and to the other members of the research team who collaborated in the design of the tasks: André Boileau, José Guzmán, Fernando Hitt, Denis Tanguay, and also Michèle Artigue who served as consultant on this project, and the participating classroom teachers who provided feedback on a regular basis throughout the successive cycles of task development.

NOTES

1. We use the term *task* to refer to a single question (with possibly one or two subquestions) and the term *task-situation* or *activity* to refer to an extended set of questions related to a given central task or mathematical idea.
2. In these activities, the assumption was made that factoring would be over the set of integers.
3. We wish to acknowledge in particular the contribution of Fernando Hitt to the design of the elaborated version of the basic task reported by Lagrange (2003).
4. Every activity that was developed had a student version, a teacher version that included ideas for classroom discussions, and an answer key that could be given to students after we had collected their activity sheets for use as one of our data sources.
5. We express our appreciation to the students and teacher of the class reported herein. They gracefully accommodated all of our videotaping, observing, and interviewing over a period of several months. We are grateful to Texas Instruments for providing the calculators used in our study.

APPENDIX

Activity 6: Factoring

Part I (Paper & Pencil, and CAS): Seeing Patterns in Factors

1. (a) Before using your calculator, try to recall the factorization of each algebraic expression listed in the left column of this table:

Factorization using _paper and pencil_	Verification using FACTOR (show result displayed by the _CAS_)
$a^2 - b^2$	
$a^3 - b^3$	
$x^2 - 1$	
$x^3 - 1$	

Classroom discussion of Part I, 1a

1. (b) Perform the indicated operations (using paper and pencil)

$(x - 1)(x + 1)$

$(x - 1)(x^2 + x + 1)$

2. (a) Without doing any algebraic manipulation, anticipate the result of the following product:

$(x - 1)(x^3 + x^2 + x + 1)$

2. (b) Verify the anticipated result above using _paper and pencil_ (in the box below), and then using the calculator.

2. (c) What do the following three expressions have in common? And, also, how do they differ?

$(x - 1)(x + 1)$, $(x - 1)(x^2 + x + 1)$, and $(x - 1)(x^3 + x^2 + x + 1)$.

2. (d) How do you explain the fact that the following products result in a binomial: two binomials, a binomial with a trinomial, and a binomial with a quadrinomial?

Classroom discussion following Question 2d

2. (e) On the basis of the expressions we have found so far, predict a factorization of the expression $x^5 - 1$.

2. (f) Explain why the product $(x - 1)(x^{15} + x^{14} + x^{13} + \ldots + x^2 + x + 1)$ gives the result $x^{16} - 1$?

2. (g) Is your explanation (in (f), above) also valid for the following equality: $(x - 1)(x^{134} + x^{133} + x^{132} + \ldots + x^2 + x + 1) = x^{135} - 1$?

Explain:

Classroom discussion of Part I, #1 #2

Part II: Toward a Generalization
(Activity With *Paper & Pencil* and With *Calculator*)

II(A) 1. In this activity each line of the table below must be filled in completely (all three cells), one row at a time. Start from the top row (the cells of the three columns) and work your way down.

If, for a given row, the results in the left and middle columns differ, reconcile the two by using algebraic manipulations in the right hand column.

Factorization using paper and pencil	*Result produced by FACTOR command*	*Calculation to reconcile the two, if necessary*
$x^2 - 1 =$		
$x^3 - 1 =$		
$x^4 - 1 =$		
$x^5 - 1 =$		
$x^6 - 1 =$		

II.(A).2. Conjecture, in general, for what numbers n will the factorization of $x^n - 1$:

        i) contain exactly two factors?
        ii) contain more than two factors?
        iii) include $(x + 1)$ as a factor?

Please explain:

Classroom discussion of Part II A

Part II Continued (With *Paper and Pencil,* and With *Calculator*)

II(B) 1. As with Part A above, each line of the table below must be filled in completely (all three cells), one row at a time before proceeding to the next row. Start from the top row and work your way down.

If, for a given row, the results in the left and middle columns differ, reconcile the two by using algebraic manipulations in the right hand column.

Factorization using *paper and pencil*	Result produced by *FACTOR command*	Calculation to reconcile the two, if necessary
$x^7 - 1 =$		
$x^8 - 1 =$		
$x^9 - 1 =$		
$x^{10} - 1 =$		
$x^{11} - 1 =$		
$x^{12} - 1 =$		
$x^{13} - 1 =$		

II.(B).2. On the basis of patterns you observe in the table II.B above, revise (if necessary) your conjecture from Part A. That is, for what numbers n will the factorization of $x^n - 1$:

  i) contain exactly two factors?
  ii) contain more than two factors?
  iii) include $(x + 1)$ as a factor?

Please explain:

II.(C). *Without using your calculator,* answer the following questions:

1. Does $x^{2004} - 1$
   i) contain more than two factors?
   ii) include $(x + 1)$ as a factor?

Please explain:

2. Does $x^{3003} - 1$
   i) contain more than two factors?
   ii) include $(x + 1)$ as a factor?

Please explain:

```
                                                                    
```

3. Does $x^{853} - 1$
   i) contain more than two factors?
   ii) include $(x + 1)$ as a factor?

Please explain:

```
                                                                    
```

Classroom discussion of Part II B and C

Part III: Challenge

Explain why $(x + 1)$ is always a factor of $x^n - 1$ for even values of $n \geq 2$.

```
                                                                    
```

REFERENCES

Artigue, M. (2002). L'intégration de calculatrices symboliques à l'enseignement secondaire: les leçons de quelques ingénieries didactiques [The integration of symbolic calculators into high school teaching: A lesson from didactic engineering]. In D. Guin & L. Trouche (Eds.), *Calculatrices symboliques—transformer un outil en un instrument du travail mathématique: un problème didactique* (pp. 277-349). Grenoble, France: La Pensée sauvage.

Artigue. M., Defouad, B., Duperier, M., Juge, G., & Lagrange, J. B. (1998). *Intégration de calculatrices complexes dans l'enseignement des mathématiques au lycée* [Integrating complex calculators into mathematics teaching at the upper high school level]. Paris: Université Denis Diderot, Équipe DIDIREM.

Ball, L., & Stacey, K. (2003). What should students record when solving problems with CAS? Reasons, information, the plan, and some answers. In J. T. Fey, A. Cuoco, C. Kieran, L. McMullin, & R. M. Zbiek (Eds.), *Computer algebra systems in secondary school mathematics education* (pp. 289-303). Reston, VA: National Council of Teachers of Mathematics.

Derive©. [Computer software]. (1996). Linz, Austria: Soft Warehouse Europe.

Drijvers, P. H. M. (2003). *Learning algebra in a computer algebra environment.* Utrecht, Netherlands: Freudenthal Institute.

Guin, D., & Trouche, L. (1999). The complex process of converting tools into mathematical instruments: The case of calculators. *International Journal of Computers for Mathematical Learning, 3,* 195-227.

Hoyles, C. (2002). From describing to designing mathematical activity: The next step in developing a social approach to research in mathematics education? In C. Kieran, E. Forman, & A. Sfard (Eds.), *Learning discourse: Discursive approaches to research in mathematics education* (pp. 273-286). Dordrecht, Netherlands: Kluwer Academic.

Kieran, C. (1996). The changing face of school algebra. In C. Alsina, J. M. Alvarez, B. Hodgson, C. Laborde, & A. Pérez (Eds.), *8th International Congress on Mathematical Education: Selected lectures* (pp. 271-290). Seville, Spain: S.A.E.M. Thales.

Lagrange, J. -B. (1999). Complex calculators in the classroom: Theoretical and practical reflections on teaching pre-calculus. *International Journal of Computers for Mathematical Learning, 4,* 51-81.

Lagrange, J. -B. (2000). L'intégration d'instruments informatiques dans l'enseignement: une approche par les techniques [The integration of technological tools into teaching: An approach focusing on techniques]. *Educational Studies in Mathematics, 43,* 1-30.

Lagrange, J. -B. (2003). Learning techniques and concepts using CAS: A practical and theoretical reflection. In J. T. Fey, A. Cuoco, C. Kieran, L. McMullin, & R. M. Zbiek (Eds.), *Computer algebra systems in secondary school mathematics education* (pp. 269-283). Reston, VA: National Council of Teachers of Mathematics.

Mounier, G., & Aldon, G. (1996). A problem story: Factorisations of $x^n - 1$. *International DERIVE Journal, 3,* 51-61.

Tall, D. O. (1979). Cognitive aspects of proof, with special reference to the irrationality of $\sqrt{2}$. In D. Tall (Ed.), *Proceedings of the third International Conference for the Psychology of Mathematics Education* (pp. 203-205). Coventry, England: PME.

Thompson, P. W. (2002). Didactic objects and didactic models in radical constructivism. In K. Gravemeijer, R. Lehrer, B. v. Oers, & L. Verschaffel (Eds.), *Symbolizing, modeling and tool use in mathematics education* (pp. 191-212). Dordrecht, Netherlands: Kluwer Academic.

Vérillon, P., & Rabardel, P. (1995). Cognition and artifacts: A contribution to the study of thought in relation to instrumented activity. *European Journal of Psychology of Education, 10,* 77-101.

Zbiek, R. M. (2003). Using research to influence teaching and learning with computer algebra systems. In J. T. Fey, A. Cuoco, C. Kieran, L. McMullin, & R. M. Zbiek (Eds.), *Computer algebra systems in secondary school mathematics education* (pp. 197-216). Reston, VA: National Council of Teachers of Mathematics.

Zehavi, N., & Mann, G. (2003). Task design in a CAS environment: Introducing (In)equations. In J. T. Fey, A. Cuoco, C. Kieran, L. McMullin, & R. M. Zbiek (Eds.), *Computer algebra systems in secondary school mathematics education* (pp. 173-191). Reston, VA: National Council of Teachers of Mathematics.

CHAPTER 16

TEACHER EDUCATION

A Conduit to the Classroom

Patricia S. Wilson

From many perspectives, the progress that has been made in developing technology for teaching and learning mathematics is amazing. We have valuable tools, strategies, capabilities, and research that give us the potential to improve the learning of mathematics on a broad scale. Curricula that incorporate and use technology wisely as well as informed and supportive educational policies will make the difficult job of reform possible. All of these components are necessary in order to take advantage of what technology brings to the teaching and learning of mathematics, but they are not sufficient. It is teachers who will make the difference between success and failure, and it is teacher education that must serve as a major conduit that connects teachers with new technologies, research, curricula, and policies. It is not enough to make technology available or even include attention to technology in the curriculum. Teacher education must meet the challenge of helping teachers come to know the appropriate and constructive uses of technology. The purpose of this chapter is to raise awareness of critical issues in teacher education with respect to technology in the teaching and learning of mathematics.

Research on Technology and the Teaching and Learning of Mathematics:
Vol. 2.Cases and Perspectives, 415–426
Copyright © 2008 by Information Age Publishing
All rights of reproduction in any form reserved.

Research on Technology and the Teaching and Learning of Mathematics: Syntheses, Cases, and Perspectives, Volumes 1 and 2 (Blume & Heid, 2008, Heid & Blume, 2008) is an essential resource for teacher education. It offers analyses of available technologies, describes existence proofs, and provides a vision of what we can do to improve the teaching and learning of mathematics as a mathematics education community. Our community has assembled a respectable collection of knowledge about technology, but we are not providing the guidance that teachers need to connect mathematical and technological ideas and make that body of knowledge relevant to their practice. This abandonment is neither fair nor wise. Zbiek and Hollebrands (2008) make a well-reasoned argument for teacher education that addresses using technology to teach mathematics, and other authors have also alluded to the importance of effective uses of tools, instruments, microworlds, hardware, and software in classrooms. Dunham and Hennessey (2008) note that teacher education programs need to address equity issues with respect to technology. Teacher education is the key to applying the results of research efforts to improve the teaching and learning of mathematics in the classroom.

We need to think strategically about teacher education. What do teachers need? Who can prepare and support teachers? What are the best opportunities for teacher education? What education do teacher educators need? What is appropriate teacher education? These broad questions apply to all teacher education, but as a community we need to address these questions informed by our research on technology in the teaching and learning of mathematics.

WHAT DO TEACHERS NEED?

The pronouncement that teachers are key to reform is certainly not new, but research addressing what teachers need and how teachers learn is relatively new. Researchers are studying teacher learning, including how and what teachers learn from professional development experiences and how that learning influences their practice (Borko, 2004; Nipper, 2004). There is a common plea for teachers to deepen their knowledge and transform their practice. If we apply that plea to the goal of learning effective uses of technology in teaching mathematics, it means a deeper knowledge of both mathematics and technology, as well as a transformed practice of mathematics teaching that incorporates technology. Zbiek and Hollebrands (2008) address the complexities of that challenge. In particular, they address teacher needs from several perspectives, including concerns, knowledge, management, and authority, and they argue for a developmental approach that attends to affect as well as action. They distinguish between technology and other innovations: "Technology can quickly assume, or open to students, roles in the classroom that were once the exclusive domain of teachers" (p. 336). This distinction is critical in considering how to support teachers as they transform their practice. Instruction and learning in a technology-rich classroom may require new learning strategies in addition to new instructional strategies.

In thinking about a deeper knowledge of mathematics and technology, we need to focus on the mathematical and technological knowledge needed for teaching, which differs substantially from general mathematical or technological knowledge (Ball, 2003; Ball & Cohen, 1999; Shulman, 1986). Teachers must understand the mathematics they teach so that they can make connections between ideas, apply mathematics, build mathematical models, and represent concepts in mathematics. The use of technology can clearly enhance this knowledge, and examples are given throughout these volumes (Blume & Heid, 2008; Heid & Blume, 2008). Teachers need to learn to differentiate between powerful instructional uses of technology and more mundane uses (e.g., checking numeric calculations, finding values in trigonometric or statistical tables). Powerful instructional uses of technology allow students to interact with mathematical representations, affording them opportunities to investigate ideas (e.g., study patterns, visualize and explore functions, form and test conjectures). Teachers also need to understand students' mathematics as well as how students construct their mathematical ideas. They need to know how to use technology to provide insights into students' learning. For example, Geometer's Sketchpad enables students to create objects such as a square or procedures such as finding a circumcenter of a triangle. As they create the object or procedure, the software captures a script that records each action. By studying a student's script, a teacher can infer ways that the student is thinking about the object or procedure. Teachers need to be aware of the dynamic nature of mathematics and the use of technology to show change, illustrate movement, or collect data over time. Technology is changing mathematics and the way mathematics can be taught, and teachers need to be aware of those changes.

WHO CAN PREPARE AND SUPPORT TEACHERS?

Teacher educators are a diverse group of people who operate in a variety of domains. It is easy to think of teacher educators as professors who reside in a college of education and whose primary teaching responsibility is to teach courses to prospective and practicing teachers, but teacher education needs to be the responsibility of a larger community that focuses on teachers' and learners' needs. For technology-supported mathematics education, teacher educators should include mathematicians, statisticians, programmers, and engineers who offer courses, materials, or software for teachers and who are interested in teacher education. The academic workforce for teacher education needs to expand to include more mathematicians and technologists who are willing to address post-secondary education, because using technology appropriately to teach mathematics is not a concern restricted to education in preschool through 12th grade (P–12). In considering those who educate teachers, we must move beyond the traditional view of educators residing at colleges and universities. We need to include curriculum developers, tool developers, software authors, and researchers who offer mathematical education for teachers. As technological innovations become available for teaching mathematics, who will educate teachers to use them effectively? Administrators, publishers, and policymakers who enable teacher education are people who are not frequently considered teacher educators, but who also are critical to the success of teacher education.

School districts provide professional development for their teachers, but often they are forced to meet a wide range of district needs and to serve broad categories of teachers. School districts struggle to provide personnel and programs to address the appropriate uses of technology in the mathematics classroom, and they increasingly turn to classroom teachers to provide teacher education for their colleagues. That education can be formal or informal. In a study of what practicing high school teachers considered good mathematics teaching, the participants explained that they acquired most of their knowledge about how to teach mathematics from colleagues or experience (Wilson, Cooney, & Stinson, 2005). We need to consider seriously teacher leaders as an important group for educating teachers in the appropriate use of technology in teaching and learning mathematics.

The responsibility for educating teachers about technology and mathematics lies with a varied group of people. Mathematicians and P–12 teachers have a strong influence on how mathematics is perceived and taught. They are influential teacher educators, and that responsibility is seldom explicit in their teaching assignments, their institutions' reward structures, or their own preparation in mathematics and technology.

WHAT ARE THE BEST OPPORTUNITIES FOR TEACHER EDUCATION?

Zbiek and Hollebrands (2008) remind us that in order to affect teachers' and students' work in the classroom, teachers need support in managing technology, developing confidence in using technologies, and securing an appropriate curriculum. These requirements are in addition to establishing a deep knowledge of mathematics and effective teaching practices. Changing technology, tools, and instruments imply that education must be continued throughout one's career, and there needs to be an emphasis on the themes or organizing principles that characterize appropriate application of technology in learning and teaching mathematics. Good initial certification and graduate programs are important in preparing teachers to use technology in their mathematics instruction, but teacher education needs to extend into more venues, just as it needs to depend on a diverse group of teacher educators.

Traditionally, we think of teacher education taking place in formal courses offered by postsecondary institutions. Many colleges, universities, and professional societies are recognizing the importance of including experiences in these courses that are designed to teach a special kind of mathematics that is needed for teaching. One way to focus on the mathematics that is needed for teaching is to focus on artifacts from the practice of teaching mathematics (Ball & Cohen, 1999). For example, mathematics courses that include a study of P–12 student work, a microworld used in instruction, or an investigation of a P–12 mathematics curriculum increase teachers' opportunities to see mathematical connections, explore various representations of mathematical concepts, see the same mathematics from different perspectives, and identify key mathematical ideas embedded in such artifacts. Software that records students' work as they use a microworld to explore mathematics offers valuable insights about students' mathematical thinking as well as highlighting subtle but important mathematical ideas that contribute to understanding a concept. These artifacts or records from the practice of teaching mathematics are valuable in *mathematics* courses as well as in courses on teaching mathematics. Instructors of mathematics courses for elementary and middle school teachers are beginning to adopt the use of records of practice. Some mathematics courses for elementary teachers introduce samples of students' mathematical work in elementary school in order to illustrate frequent mathematical misconceptions or clever solutions that highlight an important mathematical idea. Consider the power of studying the work of a student who has invented a subtraction algorithm that ignores place value and arrives at an incorrect solution. By analyzing the student's algorithm, the traditional algorithm becomes more meaningful and the role of place value can be examined.

In many high school teacher preparation programs, knowledge of mathematics comparable to that of a mathematics major is considered to be sufficient for, or at least is the major component of, the preparation of teachers. A large portion of the mathematics preparation is the responsibility of departments of mathematics, and very few mathematics courses required of prospective high school mathematics teachers focus on mathematics that is needed specifically for teaching. Mathematics courses for secondary teachers often enroll, in addition to prospective teachers, students preparing for advanced work in mathematics, engineering, or other sciences. This diversity of students may account for a treatment of mathematical ideas that does not emphasize a specific professional goal such as teaching mathematics. It is often left to the mathematics education courses to afford opportunities for the in-depth study of mathematical ideas that prepares a teacher not only to understand a concept, but also to understand it well enough to be able to help someone else understand the concept. Using examples and artifacts from the teaching of school mathematics in collegiate mathematics courses could enhance the learning of all students. Mathematics classes frequently use engineering applications for the purpose of developing students' mathematical ideas. In a similar way, analyzing the mathematics in a teacher's lesson using Geometer's Sketchpad (Jackiw, 2001) or writing constructive comments on a high school student's explanation of inverse functions could help collegiate students connect mathematical ideas. Students, regardless of their professional goals, could develop a deeper understanding of a particular function if they are asked to use various technologies such as graphing tools, spreadsheets, and tables to represent the function.

Workshops, summer institutes, and conference work sessions are popular structures for providing teacher education in mathematics and technology for practicing teachers. These venues need to connect to the practice of teachers. When instruction on the use of software or an innovative tool is tied to a teacher's work, it seems to be easier for a teacher to incorporate the technology into his or her own practice. Teachers have a legitimate concern when they ask how their professional development experiences tie to their work of teaching mathematics with technology. In educating teachers, *how* mathematics is learned is as important as *what* mathematics is learned because teachers' own learning experiences with technology and mathematics influence their teaching (Nipper, 2004).

There are advantages to the strategy of using teachers to teach teachers, but we must be cautious in increasing the responsibilities of already overburdened teachers and in assuming that having taught with technology is sufficient background for teaching others to teach with technology. If a program is to add innovations in the use of technology for teaching mathematics, a teacher who is called upon to conduct professional development must be thoroughly familiar with the technology, with how students learn mathematics, and with how the technology can improve the learning of mathematics. Otherwise, the teacher may end up promoting the status quo or a misuse of the technology.

Teachers report that they learn from their own practice, and it often occurs through trial and error (Wilson et al., 2005; Zbiek & Hollebrands, 2008). Although a persistent teacher can learn from an isolated experience, it is difficult to introduce technological innovations into one's own practice without a professional community to support those innovations. There are advantages to teachers forming professional learning communities whose members work together on their practice. Professional learning communities are difficult to build and sustain, but they have the potential of helping teachers examine their own practice (Putnam & Borko, 2000; Wilson & Berne, 1999).

Productive professional learning communities are often characterized as having shared norms and values. The community members open up their own practice to each other, collaborate on initiatives, reflect on their practice, and focus on student learning (Kruse & Louis, 1993). The degree of success of a professional learning community is related to the energy and time that teachers and administrators devote to nurturing the group.

Technology not only enhances the mathematical experiences in all of the previously described settings, it also can provide a venue for learning. Technology can be a vehicle for delivering teacher education. There are a variety of experiments with distance education that are bringing diverse groups of teacher educators and teachers together. In project InterMath (2000) the materials were designed to help teachers experience mathematical explorations using technological tools. The delivery relies heavily on those explorations and resources being available on a web page. Teacher educators can create syllabi for courses for middle school mathematics teachers by drawing from selected exercises. The technologies involved are the message and the medium. Although instructor guidance is essential, the convenient access to curriculum and materials is through a Web site.

In providing teacher education in mathematics and technology, we need to make use of a variety of venues that provide a career-long education in appropriate uses of technology to teach mathematics. Opportunities need to be tied to practice, but they need not necessarily take place in schools. Teachers need access to technologies, software, and the Internet. We need to be sensitive to the time constraints faced by practitioners, and we need to advocate for allocation of time for professional development that integrates wise uses of technology in the teaching of mathematics.

WHAT EDUCATION DO TEACHER EDUCATORS NEED?

The question of what education teacher educators need is rarely asked. In our focus on students and teachers, we may be unintentionally avoiding this critical question. The education of teacher educators is key to connecting research, technological innovations, craft knowledge, theory, effective instructional strategies, and classroom practice (Stein, Smith, & Silver, 1999).

The greatest progress we have made toward addressing this question in mathematics education can be found in our attention to doctoral programs. Some U.S. doctoral programs are striving to provide the experiences that will prepare their doctoral students to become mathematics teacher educators (Reys & Kilpatrick, 2001). Programs are beginning to provide a focus on research on teacher education and apprenticeships in working with teacher education programs. There is still much work to be done.

Although doctoral programs in mathematics education are important contributions, they are only a partial answer when one considers the vast and diverse population of individuals who provide teacher education for teachers of mathematics. How are mathematicians educated to meet the needs of the teachers that are in their classes? How are curriculum developers prepared to do teacher education? What preparation do we provide for school district personnel who must lead the mathematics education in their districts? What do we do in our teacher preparation programs that helps teachers become participants in learning communities or teachers of their colleagues? How do we help all mathematics teachers, P–12 and postsecondary, learn from their own practice?

The education of educators begins to sound like it poses a conundrum of nested education programs that continue to demand additional layers of education. We can begin to address this riddle by analyzing the type of knowledge that is needed for a particular level of mathematics education. Classroom teachers require a different kind of mathematical knowledge from that required of their students. Likewise, teacher educators need a different knowledge of mathematics and technology from that of their students who are mathematics teachers. Those who educate teacher educators need yet another kind of knowledge. They need to help teacher educators understand the nature of mathematics for teaching. They need to be able to model and critique appropriate uses of technology that enhance the learning of mathematics. They need to be able to identify and analyze topics that teachers find difficult to understand or teach, and help teacher educators to think about how to address these difficult topics. The knowledge base to support the education of teacher educators is growing (Stein et al., 1999). Research has contributed to our understanding of teachers' mathematical practices, teachers' mathematical learning, appropriate uses of technology for learning and teaching, and the mathematics needed for teaching. In the education-of-teacher-educators layer, the traditional teacher-student relationship is quite different because students and teachers are colleagues with varying degrees of knowledge related to mathematics, technology, teaching, and learning.

The last layer breaks the nesting cycle and requires collaborative work in which colleagues share their expertise and focus on improving the education of mathematics teachers. For example, the project Preparing Mathematicians to Educate Teachers (PMET),[1] funded by the National Science Foundation (NSF), has sponsored faculty development, resource dissemination, regional networks, and mini-grants in an effort to educate the teacher educators who provide mathematics instruction for teachers. The NSF-funded Center for Proficiency in Teaching Mathematics (CPTM) at the University of Georgia and the University of Michigan has a postdoctoral experience in mathematics education for mathematicians who work with teachers of mathematics. CPTM is also supporting research-practitioners who work in school districts as classroom teachers, and work with their colleagues to improve mathematics instruction in their schools. The University of Georgia offers a graduate certificate in mathematics education for PhD candidates in mathematics if they complete a 12-semester-hour program in mathematics education. These examples illustrate collaborations that encourage mathematics educators, mathematicians, practitioners, and experts in technology to work together to educate those who educate teachers of mathematics.

WHAT IS APPROPRIATE TEACHER EDUCATION IN MATHEMATICS AND TECHNOLOGY?

Despite the importance of the question of appropriateness of teacher education in mathematics and technology, definitive answers are not available. Hilda Borko offered a map of the terrain in her 2004 presidential address to the American Educational Research Association (Borko, 2004), drawing from research in mathematics education and science education as well as other fields. Her analysis of what we know and how we need to proceed provides food for thought with respect to teacher education in mathematics and technology. Citing "existence proofs" of successful teacher education, she elaborated on the needs of teachers and how they could be met. Teachers need to know their content in special ways, they need to understand their students' learning of that content, and they need to know instructional practices that help students learn. Technology adds another dimension to the terrain of teacher education. Teachers need to understand the influence of technology on the nature of mathematics and how mathematical work is done, they need to understand their students' learning of mathematics through technology, and they need to understand the instructional advantages related to a specific technology. Although technology increases the demand for and complexity of specialized teacher knowledge, it simultaneously contributes to successful teacher education. Consider a successful implementation of specific software such as Geometer's Sketchpad. As teachers struggle to understand the various commands and features of the software, they are presented with numerous opportunities for expanding their knowledge of mathematics. For example, after sketching a triangle determined by three points, the teacher can watch the orthocenter, circumcenter, and centroid move on the Euler line as they drag one vertex to create a variety of triangles. A teacher education program that capitalizes on the exploration and dynamic features of this software has the potential for increasing teachers' knowledge about the software and also about the nature of mathematics and geometric concepts. Preparing teachers to use Geometer's Sketchpad should include learning to use student sketches or software functions (e.g., measure, rotate, trace) to gain insights into students' thinking. Instruction on Geometer's Sketchpad should prepare teachers to use a variety of instructional approaches offered by that technology (e.g., dynamic demonstrations, conjecture testing, quick calculations, table building, easy generation of examples).

Appropriate teacher education attends not only to meeting teachers' needs with respect to mathematical and technological knowledge, but also to connecting what teachers are learning to their practice. For example, as teachers learn a new technology they also need to learn ways to use that technology within the constraints in their own classrooms. They need to think about how the technology could enhance their students' thinking or what problems might arise as students begin using the technology. Teacher education needs to help teachers learn to work in communities that share information, allow risk taking, and lessen teacher isolation. For example, many of the hardware challenges associated with using technology in the classroom can be addressed better by a community of users than by one individual. A group of technology users can generate clever instructional uses when they are working together and discussing ideas or solving instructional problems faced by the group.

Research on technology in teaching and learning mathematics offers knowledge and insights that are needed to provide high quality teacher education for teachers of mathematics and to prepare the teacher educators who plan and implement teacher education programs. The use of technology provides ways for future and practicing teachers to investigate not only mathematical concepts but also the ways in which their students think about those mathematical concepts. Appropriate teacher education models the use of innovations in technology that allow students and teachers to explore ideas leading to mathematical connections that are not evident when instruction is organized by compartmentalized, static topics or courses. Pedagogy and learning can be transformed by appropriate uses of technology. Examples of research bases for these claims appear throughout these volumes (Blume & Heid, 2008; Heid & Blume, 2008) and provide the scaffolding for effective teacher education. In order to meet the challenge of creating and implementing appropriate teacher education, we must prepare teacher educators to use technology for exploring mathematics, focusing on student learning, integrating mathematical ideas, and using research to inform their teaching.

Teacher education can be a valuable conduit connecting research and innovations in technology with the practice and curricula in mathematics lessons if we address the issues that have been described in this chapter. We must think creatively about opportunities for educating teachers of mathematics and realize that those who educate teachers to use technology to teach mathematics need education themselves. Just as teachers must be proficient in using technologies to teach mathematics, teacher educators must be proficient users of technology. In addition, teacher educators must be knowledgeable about research on technology in the teaching and learning of mathematics and model the best practices. Teacher education must address teachers' immediate needs, but it also has the responsibility to prepare teachers who will continue to learn and to adopt innovations in technology wisely. Those who prepare teachers of mathematics have the responsibility of moving the research on optimal uses of technology into the practice of learning and teaching mathematics.

NOTE

1.   The description of PMET was retrieved from http://www.maa.org/pmet/ on December 29, 2005.

REFERENCES

Ball, D. (2003, February). *What mathematical knowledge is needed for teaching mathematics?* Paper presented at the Secretary's Summit on Mathematics, U.S. Department of Education, Washington, DC.

Ball, D., & Cohen, D. (1999). Developing practice, developing practitioners: Toward a practice-based theory of professional education. In L. Darling-Hammond & G. Sykes (Eds.), *Teaching as the learning profession: A handbook of policy and practice* (pp. 3-31). San Francisco: Jossey-Bass.

Blume, G. W., & Heid, M. K. (Eds.). (2008). *Research on technology and the teaching and learning of mathematics: Vol. 2. Cases and perspectives*. Charlotte, NC: Information Age.

Borko, H. (2004). Professional development and teacher learning: Mapping the terrain. *Educational Researcher, 33*(8), 3-15.

Dunham, P., & Hennessy, S. (2008). Equity and use of educational technology in mathematics. In M. K. Heid & G. W. Blume (Eds.), *Research on technology and the teaching and learning of mathematics: Vol. 1. Research syntheses* (pp. 345-418). Charlotte, NC: Information Age.

Heid, M. K., & Blume, G. W. (Eds.). (20068. *Research on technology and the teaching and learning of mathematics: Vol. 1. Research syntheses.* Charlotte, NC: Information Age.

InterMath. (2000). *InterMath: Technology and the teaching and learning of middle grades mathematics.* Retrieved March 24, 2005, from The University of Georgia and CEISMC-Georgia Institute of Technology Web site: http://www.intermath-uga.gatech.edu

Jackiw, N. (2001). The Geometer's Sketchpad (Version 4.06) [Computer program]. Berkeley, CA: Key Curriculum Press.

Kruse, S., & Louis, K. (1993, April). *An emerging framework for analyzing school-based professional community.* Paper presented at the annual meeting of the American Educational Research Association, Atlanta, GA.

Nipper, K. (2004). *Mathematics teacher development: Making sense of teacher development.* Unpublished doctoral dissertation. University of Georgia, Athens.

Putnam, R. T., & Borko, H. (2000). What do new views of knowledge and thinking have to say about research on teacher learning? *Educational Researcher, 29*(1), 4-15.

Reys, R. E., & Kilpatrick, J. (Eds.). (2001). *One field, many paths: U. S. doctoral programs in mathematics education.* Washington, DC: Conference Board of the Mathematical Sciences.

Shulman, L. (1986). Those who understand: Knowledge growth in teaching. *Educational Researcher, 15*(2), 4-14.

Stein, M. K., Smith, M. S., & Silver, E. A. (1999). The development of professional developers: Learning to assist teachers in new settings in new ways. *Harvard Educational Review, 69,* 237-269.

Wilson, P., Cooney, T., & Stinson, D. (2005). What constitutes good mathematics teaching and how it develops: Nine high school teachers' perspectives. *Journal of Mathematics Teacher Education, 8,* 83-111.

Wilson, S. M., & Berne, J. (1999). Teacher learning and the acquisition of professional knowledge: An examination of research on contemporary professional development. In A. Iran-Nejad & P. D. Pearson (Eds.), *Review of research in education* (Vol. 24, pp. 173-209). Washington, DC: American Educational Research Association.

Zbiek, R. M., & Hollebrands, K. (2008). A research-informed view of the process of incorporating mathematics technology into classroom practice by inservice and preservice teachers. In M. K. Heid & G. W. Blume (Eds.), *Research on technology and the teaching and learning of mathematics: Vol. 1. Research syntheses* (pp. 287-344). Charlotte, NC: Information Age.

CHAPTER 17

PERSPECTIVES ON RESEARCH, POLICY, AND THE USE OF TECHNOLOGY IN MATHEMATICS TEACHING AND LEARNING IN THE UNITED STATES

Joan Ferrini-Mundy and Glenda A. Breaux

This chapter addresses four areas of policy that seem especially relevant to the role of technology in the teaching and learning of mathematics. Specifically, this chapter focuses on policies that relate to curriculum, to allowable and expected uses of technology, and to access to technology. In addition, the chapter discusses policies that influence educational research (which informs the design and implementation of technology-infused approaches to mathematics education).

For our purposes, we use an encompassing meaning of policy that is operationally defined as "a plan of action adopted by an individual or social group" (WordNet Electronic Lexical Database[1]). Although the phrase, "educational policy" is so broad that it risks being rendered

Research on Technology and the Teaching and Learning of Mathematics:
Vol. 2. Cases and Perspectives, 427–448
Copyright © 2008 by Information Age Publishing

meaningless, we contend that, given almost any construal of its meaning, there are important implications for educational researchers, developers, and practitioners. Such implications are especially powerful for those who have particular interest in the role and impact of technology in the teaching and learning of mathematics. In this chapter we provide our view of the implications of trends in technology policy for researchers and developers concerned with the use of various technologies in the service of mathematics teaching and learning. Although we recognize that our national policies regarding technology might significantly differ from, or be similar to, technology-related policies in other countries, we restrict our scope to U.S. education policy.

In the U.S., education policies are formed by government at the state and federal level, as well as by local entities such as school boards. These policies often have implications for the role and place of educational technology in K-12 schooling. For example, Public Law 107-110, also known as the No Child Left Behind (NCLB) Act of 2001 (see U.S. Department of Education [USDE], 2001), is a U.S. federal policy that includes a number of components that are relevant for those interested in advancing the use of technology in learning.

In mathematics education, many consider the plans and proposals that are produced by national professional societies and organizations to be policy documents. We contend that the National Council of Teachers of Mathematics (NCTM) standards documents (NCTM, 1989, 1991, 1995, 2000), the International Technology Education Association (ITEA) *Standards for Technological Literacy* (ITEA, 2000), and the International Society for Technology in Education (ISTE) *National Educational Technology Standards (NETS)* (1998, 2000) are policies in the sense that they are authoritative statements offered by professionals in the field that sometimes influence curriculum, state and local standards, and teacher education.[2] These policies, however, are voluntary. Unlike many policies formulated by government entities, there are no consequences for failing to implement them.

Another type of policy captured in our definition is that of funding programs offered by federal or state agencies or by private foundations. The programs offered by the National Science Foundation (NSF), such as the Mathematics and Science Partnerships (MSPs), or the Centers for Learning and Teaching, are plans of action, and thus are policies.[3] In addition, reports and recommendations offered by various entities of the government, such as the *Report to the President on the Use of Technology to Strengthen K-12 Education in the United States* (President's Committee of Advisors on Science and Technology [PCAST], 1997), and the *National Education Technology (NET) Plan* (USDE, 2004) are sometimes quite influential regarding the allocation of resources and effort.

The examples provided above illustrate the ways in which our operational definition of policy affects the scope and content of this perspectives chapter. In the chapter we focus selectively on key policies from the four arenas identified at the outset and address implications of those policies for the role of technology in the teaching and learning of mathematics. The chapter is organized in sections that present information on: policy about curriculum, policy about technology use, policy about technology access, and policy that affects education research. For each policy presented herein, we provide some background information on the policy (e.g., its goals, excerpts of the content of the relevant document, information about its formulation and effects, etc.) as well as some commentary explaining why the policy warrants inclusion in this overview.

POLICY ABOUT CURRICULUM

Curriculum policy that involves technology comes from many sources. Policy documents about curriculum come from the academic disciplines, such as mathematics, as well as from technology education organizations. Such documents comment on the role of technologies in learning particular disciplines at the K-12 level. For example, NCTM's *Principles and Standards for School Mathematics* (NCTM, 2000) includes a technology principle. This principle states, "Technology is essential in teaching and learning mathematics; it influences the mathematics that is taught and enhances students' learning" (p. 24). A statement such as this is more a statement of values than of empirically justified fact, although its inclusion was based on warrants from research that show how technology can support students' mathematics learning. Technology education policy documents, such as the *Standards for Technological Literacy* (ITEA, 2000) and the *National Educational Technology Standards (NETS)* (ISTE, 1998, 2000) express similar goals. For example, the primary goal of the ISTE NETS Project is "to enable stakeholders in PreK-12 education to develop national standards for educational uses of technology that facilitate school improvement in the United States" (http://cnets.iste.org/ [Retrieved January 19, 2006]). These standards, and others like them, address related issues such as technology support needs, assessment, and the evaluation of the impact of technology use on student learning. These documents also sometimes include discipline-specific recommendations, as embodied in the following from the NETS secondary-level mathematics activity, *Chaos and Beyond* (ISTE, 2000).[4]

The purposes of this activity are to:

- Introduce students to nonlinear models and dynamic chaos;
- Provide an example of mathematics that is possible only because of technology; and
- Introduce students to the ideas of self-similarity, recursion, and fractals. (ISTE, 2000, p. 122)

For those concerned about the integration of technology into the teaching and learning of mathematics, the standpoints offered both in disciplinary standards and in technology standards seem challenging. The NCTM Technology Principle, which asserts that technology is *essential* in the teaching and learning of mathematics, is a bold statement that begs for more elaborated discussion and justification of technology use. Similarly, the assumption implicit in the NETS document about the value in introducing mathematics that cannot be introduced without technology needs more careful consideration. Researchers, developers, and mathematics education scholars concerned with curriculum coherence and justified mathematical goals might be especially well situated to illuminate the nuances and considerations involved in implementing such technology policies in a manner consistent with these aims.

POLICY ABOUT TECHNOLOGY USE

As discussed with regard to curriculum, voluntary and mandatory policies are set and elaborated by a variety of governmental and nongovernmental institutions and organizations. Some policies regarding technology use are set by the same entities that set and elaborate curriculum policies related to technology, while other technology use policies are set within the context of assessment policy. This section focuses on policies that describe expectations for technology use in classroom settings and during assessment. The content in this section that relates to technology use in classrooms is derived from the policies of the NCTM as expressed in the *Curriculum and Evaluation Standards for School Mathematics* (NCTM, 1989) and in the *Principles and Standards* (NCTM, 2000), while the content related to technology use during assessment is derived from the National Assessment Governing Board (NAGB) calculator policy for the National Assessment of Educational Progress,[5] the College Board's policy for the SAT and AP exams,[6] and the policy for calculator use on the ACT Mathematics Test.[7]

In the *Curriculum and Evaluation Standards*, the NCTM advocates mathematics education reforms that respond to the shift from an industrial society to an information society (NCTM, 1989, p. 3). They attribute this shift partly to the increasing availability of low-cost technology, such as calculators and computers, which has reduced the labor involved in basic computation and created an appropriate context for emphasizing higher order conceptual and procedural skills. The ideas about technology in this document lay the groundwork for current discussions.

At each grade-level band (K-4, 5-8, and 9-12), the *Curriculum and Evaluation Standards* presents the assumptions and contextual conditions on which the standards for that grade level are based. These assumptions are presented in the document prior to the presentation of the standards and serve as a guide for understanding the intent of the standards and the expectations for implementation. The clearest description of NCTM's policy about technology use is embedded within the assumptions that precede the K-4 standards, while the descriptions that precede the 5-8 and 9-12 standards elaborate on, rather than restate, these expectations.

With regard to grades K-4, the *Curriculum and Evaluation Standards* states:
The K-4 curriculum should make appropriate and ongoing use of calculators and computers. Calculators must be accepted at the K-4 level as valuable tools for learning mathematics. Calculators enable children to explore number ideas and patterns, to have valuable concept-development experiences, to focus on problem-solving processes, and to investigate realistic applications. The thoughtful use of calculators can increase the quality of the curriculum as well as the quality of children's learning.

Calculators do not replace the need to learn basic facts, to compute mentally, or to do reasonable paper-and-pencil computation. Classroom experience indicates that young children take a commonsense view about calculators and recognize the importance of not relying on them when it is more appropriate to compute in other ways. The availability of calculators means, however, that educators must develop a broader view of the various ways computation can be carried out and must place less emphasis on complex paper-and-pencil computation. Calculators also highlight the importance of teaching children to recognize whether computer results are reasonable.

The power of computers also needs to be used in contemporary mathematics programs. Computer languages that are geometric in nature help young children become familiar with important geometric ideas. Computer simulations of mathematical ideas, such as modeling the renaming of numbers, are an important aid in helping children identify the key features of the mathematics. Many software programs provide interesting problem-solving situations and applications.

The thoughtful and creative use of technology can greatly improve both the quality of the curriculum and the quality of children's learning. Integrating calculators and computers into school mathematics programs is critical in meeting the goals of a redefined curriculum. (NCTM, 1989, p. 19)

With regard to grades 5-8, the *Curriculum and Evaluation Standards* states:
Technology, including calculators, computers, and videos, should be used when appropriate. These devices and formats free students from tedious computations and allow them to concentrate on problem solving and other important content. They also give them new means to explore content. As paper-and-pencil computation becomes less important, the skills and understanding required to make proficient use of calculators and computers become more important. (NCTM, 1989, p. 67)

The standards for grades 5-8 assume that:
All students will have a calculator with functions consistent with the tasks envisioned in this curriculum. Calculators should include the following features: algebraic logic including order of operations; computation in decimal and common fraction form; constant function for addition, subtraction, multiplication, and division; and memory, percent, square root, exponent, reciprocal, and +/- keys. (NCTM, 1989, p. 68)
Every classroom will have at least one computer available at all times for demonstrations and student use. Additional computers should be available for individual, small-group, and whole-class use. (NCTM, 1989, p. 68)

With regard to grades 9-12, the *Standards* assume:
Scientific calculators with graphing capabilities will be available to all students at all times. (NCTM, 1989, p. 124)
A computer will be available at all times in every classroom for demonstration purposes, and all students will have access to computers for individual and group work. (NCTM, 1989, p. 124)
The integration of ideas from algebra and geometry is particularly strong, with graphical representation playing an important connecting role. Thus, frequent reference to graphing utilities will be found throughout these standards; by this we mean a computer with appropriate graphing software or a graphing calculator. (NCTM, 1989, p. 125)
Computer software can be used effectively for class demonstrations and independently by students to explore additional examples, perform independent investigations, generate and summarize data as part of a project, or complete assignments. (NCTM, 1989, p. 128)

In addition to these statements, NCTM further clarifies the expectations for technology use for K-12 teachers by highlighting the need for increased attention to use of calculators for *complex* [emphasis added] calculations (p. 20), for 5-8 teachers by highlighting the need to use appropriate technology for computation and exploration, and for 9-12 teachers by highlighting the need for increased attention to using technology to promote the development of conceptual understanding.

Presumably, in Grades 5-8 technology is also expected to be used for computations that are complex by these grade-level standards (not in lieu of applying previously learned basic arithmetic skills), however, this is a point that easily may have been lost on middle grades teachers who acquired only a fragmented understanding of NCTM's policy on technology use. A similar outcome may also have occurred at the high school level, at which, by virtue of sound preparation, computation should have ceased to be a complex issue so technology use was expected to focus more intensely on deepening and expanding conceptual understanding.

Unfortunately, misinterpretations and errors made at the middle and high school levels led to faulty implementations of the policy on technology use that were not evident at the K-4 level, at which the *Curriculum and Evaluation Standards* presented the clearest description of the policy's intent and at which, possibly as a result, the skill levels of K-4 students, as a whole, were essentially unimpaired by the integration of calculation technology in mathematics teaching and learning (Hembree & Dessart, 1992).

The *Principles and Standards* (NCTM, 2000) addressed the fragmentation issue that impaired the clear communication of NCTM's policy on technology use by presenting all of the policy expectations before presenting any of the standards. These expectations, referred to in the document as *principles,* have a more compact format, reducing the cognitive demand of understanding the threads-within-bands-within-strands that characterized the 1989 version. By eliminating the need to attend to, for instance, the technology thread within the 5-8 grade band within the geometry strand, the *Principles and Standards* document more clearly communicates the role technology is expected to play across the K-12 mathematics curriculum and elaborates the policy on appropriate uses of technology before presenting the content standards.

As noted previously, the Technology Principle states, "Technology is essential in teaching and learning mathematics; it influences the mathematics that is taught and enhances students' learning" (NCTM, 2000, p. 24). In the section devoted to explaining this principle, NCTM describes the ways in which technology enhances mathematics learning, supports effective teaching, and influences course content. In essence, these descriptions present the NCTM policy on technology use.

With regard to technology use, first and foremost, teachers are expected to be knowledgeable enough about mathematics, about their students, and about the features of the technology they are using to exercise good judgment regarding the potential learning benefits of specific uses of technology. They are supposed to use technology to connect the development of skills and procedures to the more general development of mathematical understanding, and use it in ways that encourage students to work at higher levels of generalization or abstraction (NCTM, 2000). Specifically teachers and students are expected to use technology to do the following:

- to rapidly create multiple additional examples or representational forms, more than would be feasible by hand, so that students can compare and contrast them and explore or further explicate the underlying mathematics concepts and principles;
- to provide students with instant individualized feedback that they can use to check the accuracy of their conjectures and mental or paper-and-pencil calculations; and
- to replicate quickly solution procedures used by others in preparation for discussing the range of appropriate strategies for solving a problem and the advantages and disadvantages of various representations.

The Assessment Principle in the *Principles and Standards* echoes the policy on assessment in the *Curriculum and Evaluation Standards,* which states, "Assessment of student learning should be viewed as an integral part of instruction and should be aligned with key aspects of instruction, such as the use of technology" (NCTM, 1989, p. 128). Unfortunately, the simplified format of the 2000 standards unbraids the assessment and technology policies, and the text that elaborates the Technology Principle makes no mention of assessment. However, various organizations that set assessment policy have recognized and responded to the misalignment that resulted from disallowing the use of calculators during exams for students who have completed curricula in which technology use is integrated with content and plays an integral role in learning activities.

Assessment-related policies about technology use include policies about whether calculators may be used on high-stakes assessments such as advanced placement exams, graduation examinations, college entrance exams, university placement exams, or state-level assessments used to determine whether schools are attaining adequate yearly progress under NCLB provisions.

Policies allowing calculator use on high-stakes tests are becoming increasingly prevalent. For instance, students are allowed to use specified models of scientific or graphing calculators on designated sections of the Advanced Placement (AP) exams in calculus and statistics (see www.collegeboard.com/student/testing/ap/exday_cal.html [Retrieved January 13, 2006]). They are allowed to use the same set of specified calculator models on the entire mathematics section of the SAT Reasoning Test (see www.collegeboard.com/student/testing/sat/about/sat/math.html [Retrieved January 13, 2006]), and SAT Subject Tests for Mathematics Level 1 (see www.collegeboard.com/student/testing/sat/lc_two/math1c/math1c .html?math1c [Retrieved January 17, 2006]) and Level 2 (see www .collegeboard.com/student/testing/sat/lc_two/math2c/math2c.html? match2c [Retrieved January 17, 2006]). On the ACT exam (see www

.actstudent.org/faq/answers/calculator.html [Retrieved January 13, 2006]), students also can use scientific or graphing calculators for the entire mathematics exam, provided that the calculators are not on the list of prohibited models and do not have certain prohibited features that cannot be modified (e.g., sound features that cannot be turned off).

Similar to the AP calculator policy, students are allowed to use calculators only on portions of the NAEP. According to the Mathematics Framework for the 2005 NAEP, students could use calculators on one-third of the mathematics portion, and the type of calculator allowed varies by grade. For example, at Grade 4 students could use only a four-function calculator that was supplied by NAEP, whereas eighth-grade students were supplied a scientific calculator (see www.nagb.org/pubs/m_framework_05/chap1.html [Retrieved January 13, 2006]). The calculator policy for 12th-grade students was similar to that for the ACT. Calculators with built-in computer algebra systems are prohibited, but students can bring any other type of calculator that they are accustomed to using, provided it does not have features that violate test security (e.g., wireless communication capability).

While policies about technology use on high-stakes assessments are increasingly prevalent, they are also increasingly controversial. They have enormous implications for educational equity (see Dunham & Hennessy, 2008), and, depending on the specific policies, they either help or hinder the prospects of certain technologies becoming embedded fully in K-12 mathematics classrooms. At the level of states and districts, there are also policies in place that affect use of various technologies. Similarly, policies about use exist in institutions of higher education, among which there are major research universities that do not allow the use of calculators on exams in calculus courses, and in K-12 schools, among which there are middle schools and high schools that require courses in keyboarding and computer literacy.

In general, policy about technology use is quite varied, and seems to be based largely in local opinions, values, and perspectives about whether technology can support learning effectively. It is perhaps in this area that the concerted efforts of researchers stand a chance of having the most impact. Contentious questions have centered around the use of calculators in mathematics classrooms in the elementary grades. An example of the debate and views from both sides appears in a 2001 article in *American Teacher*, "Should we curb calculator use by younger students?" (Klein & Cicci, 2001). Lee Stiff, NCTM President in 2001, presented his perspective on the issue in a presidential address posted on the organization's *News Bulletin* (NCTM, April 2001).[8]

This debate continued unabated (see www.usatoday.com/news/education/2004-04-14-calculators_x.htm [Retrieved January 13, 2006], also see Klein, Braams, Parker, Quirk, Schmid, & Wilson, 2005), suggesting that the research community needs to continue to find ways to synthesize, present, and articulate its findings in forms that are compelling for the concerned parents and community members, business leaders, and school board members who often govern the local policies about technology use. In response, NCTM released a position statement in May of 2005 that further clarified the organization's view on the role of technology in K-12 mathematics education. This position statement, entitled *Computation, Calculators, and Common Sense,*[9] expressed the following opinion and went on to situate it with reference to the Technology Principle and NCTM's expectations for computational facility, problem-solving skills, and rich learning experiences:

> School mathematics programs should provide students with a range of knowledge, skills, and tools. Students need an understanding of number and operations, including the use of computational procedures, estimation, mental mathematics, and the appropriate use of the calculator. A balanced mathematics program develops students' confidence and understanding of when and how to use these skills and tools. Students need to develop their basic mathematical understandings to solve problems both in and out of school.
>
> A skillful teacher knows how to help students develop these abilities in a balanced program that focuses on mathematical understanding, proficiency, and thinking. The teacher should help students learn when to use a calculator and when not to, when to use pencil and paper, and when to do something in their heads. Students should become fluent in making decisions about which approach to use for different situations and proficient in using their chosen method to solve a wide range of problems.
>
> Responding to the expectations in the *Standards* and position statement will require additional and continued attention to teacher education and professional development. Teachers need to learn to teach mathematics, both with and without technology, in ways that enhance students' mathematical understanding as well as their ability to use a range of available tools in support of mathematical pursuits.

POLICY ABOUT TECHNOLOGY ACCESS

Policy about technology access, though not necessarily a primary concern for researchers and developers interested in questions related to mathematics teaching and learning, is likely to have significant impact on whether the approaches, tools, and findings of their work will stand a chance of widespread implementation and institutionalization in schools. The kinds of policy recommendations and issues that appear within this arena tend to be global considerations related to access and broader learning questions rather than to the kinds of questions about learning in focused mathematical areas that have been the domain of many mathematics education researchers and developers. For instance, Title V of the NCLB legislation includes a provision for Community Technology Centers, which states:

> Increasing community access to technology and opportunities to enhance technological proficiency supports learning inside and outside the classroom as well as broader community improvement. Access to computers and the Internet in the community is particularly important for low-income students and adults. (USDE, 2002, p. 100)

Three-year grants were available to organizations interested in leading this sort of technology expansion. Similarly, at the level of states and local school districts, through budgeting priorities, local policymakers can also have significant influence on students' and teachers' access to technology.

The U.S. Department of Education's (2004) NET Plan reiterates its recommendation to consider innovative budgeting as a means to increase technology access. The document states:

> Needed technology often can be funded successfully through innovative restructuring and reallocation of existing budgets to realize efficiencies and cost savings. The new focus begins with the educational objective and evaluates funding requests—for technology or other programs—in terms of how they support student learning. Today, every program in *No Child Left Behind* is an opportunity for technology funding—but the focus is on how the funding will help attain specific educational goals.

Funding and budgetary recommendations for states, schools and districts include:

- Determine the total costs for technology as a percentage of total spending.
- Consider a systemic restructuring of budgets to realize efficiencies, cost savings and reallocation. This can include reallocations in expenditures on textbooks, instructional supplies, space and computer labs.
- Consider leasing with 3-5 year refresh cycles.
- Create a technology innovation fund to carry funds over yearly budget cycles. (p. 40)

Unfortunately, there seems to be little research on how access questions relate to the potential for technology to have a major impact on mathematics teaching and learning. Information available from various sources indicates that, in the absence of professional development on instructional technology and curriculum materials that integrate technology use into the lesson content, teachers are not particularly likely to embed technology-based or technology-rich activities into their courses. In addition, the absence of guidance on appropriate uses of technology in mathematics learning often leads to uses of technology that are limited to checking answers or other versions of computation replacement. Questions remain regarding the degree to which providing greater access to technology motivates teachers both to seek out resources for enhancing instruction through technology and to implement what they learn in their classrooms.

We also include here policies that are specifically designed to provide support to enable teachers to become expert users of technology, both in general ways and for the learning of specific subject matter areas. The U.S. Department of Education's *Preparing Tomorrow's Teachers to Use Technology* (PT3)10 grants program, funded from 1999 through 2005, had the goal of addressing "a growing challenge in modern education: nearly all elementary and secondary schools are now 'wired' to the Internet, but most teachers still feel uncomfortable using technology in their teaching" (www.ed.gov/programs/teachtech/index.html).

Since 1999, PT3 has awarded over 400 grants to education consortia to help address this gap between access to technology and the integration of technology into classroom instruction. These grants include projects designed to transform teaching and learning through: "faculty development, course restructuring, certification policy changes, online teacher preparation, enriched-networked-virtual materials, video case studies, electronic portfolios, mentoring triads, and embedded assessments" (www.ed.gov/programs/teachtech/index.html).

Embedded within many of these projects is a focus on supporting mathematics teachers in their use of technology. This area is arguably crucial for continued research and development as members of the "digital generation" now populate our schools of education and, increasingly, professional development programs for inservice teachers.

Recent discussions about technology access also focus on virtual learning opportunities. With regard to e-learning and virtual schools, the NET Plan offers the following observations:

> In the past five years there has been significant growth in organized online instruction (e-learning) and "virtual" schools, making it possible for students at all levels to receive high quality supplemental or full courses of instruction personalized to their needs. Traditional schools are turning to these services to expand opportunities and choices for students and professional development for teachers. (USDE, 2004, pp. 41-42)

These aspects of policy have important ramifications for the ultimate impact and implementation of innovative technological supports for mathematics learning. It seems that implementation research, designed by mathematics educators concerned with issues of resources and access, might be important for ensuring the longer-term availability of such technological supports.

EDUCATIONAL RESEARCH POLICY

The final area of policy that we propose has direct bearing on the prospects of technology-based or technology-supported mathematics learning, and the one that we would like to discuss in more depth in the remainder of this chapter, is educational research policy. Since its inception in 1950, the National Science Foundation has, through its funding offerings, provided a policy orientation relative to educational research, which of course has, in more recent years, afforded researchers and developers access to funds to support design, exploration, implementation, and evaluation of various instructional tools and materials, including technologies of various types, through the Research in Teaching and Learning program and the Applications of Advanced Technology program. This support has been crucial in funding some of the long-term, sustained programs that are discussed in these volumes.

This kind of funding history and availability has given way to a new paradigm that is emerging for federal funding for research. Some U.S. federal policy initiatives have included the reauthorization of the Office of Educational Research and Improvement (OERI), which resulted in the Institute of Education Sciences;[11] the NCLB legislation (U.S. Department of Education, 2001); and current funding decisions about NSF programs in education. All of these initiatives suggest that the oncoming perspectives on educational research are somewhat different from the research and development (R&D), design experiment, and proof-of-concept and engineering models that have prevailed in the area of educational tools and development. In this section we describe these stances, point to other key reports that help to illuminate and amplify the issues that they raise, and then discuss the challenges that we see emerging for the community of scholars, researchers, developers, and teachers concerned with the role of technology in mathematics education.

"RND" is a new three-letter acronym that has emerged on the educational scene; it means "results not demonstrated." In the U.S. Office of Management and Budget's program evaluation report (based on the Program Assessment Rating Tools), this designation was assigned to 35 of the 56 programs funded through the U.S. Department of Education.[12] Programs that received RND ratings comprised 10 of the 17 for which funding recommendations were cut to $0 in the FY 06 budget (see www.govexec.com/dailyfed/ 0205/020705chart.htm [Retrieved January 13, 2006]).

This kind of clear connection between demonstration of results and subsequent funding and policy decisions is evident in a number of places throughout key policy documents that are currently in place. In No Child Left Behind (USDE, 2002), for example, consider the following:

> The NCLB Act puts a special emphasis on determining what educational programs and practices have been clearly demonstrated to be effective through rigorous scientific research. Federal funding will be targeted to support these programs and teaching methods that improve student learning and achievement. (p. xiii)
>
> The NCLB Act will support scientifically based reading instruction programs in the early grades under the new Reading First program and in preschool under the new Early Reading First program. (p. xiii)
>
> The program [Title I: Improving the Academic Achievement of Educationally Disadvantaged Students] focuses on promoting schoolwide reform in high-poverty schools and ensuring students' access to scientifically based instructional strategies and challenging academic content. (p. 1)
>
> All activities supported with Title II (Teacher and Principal Training and Recruiting Fund) funds must be based on a review of scientifically based research that shows how such interventions are expected to improve student achievement. (p. 38)

The NCLB Principles for Effectiveness, which incorporate the expectation for scientifically-based or research-based activities and programs, also apply to grants funding under Title III: Language Instruction for Limited English Proficient and Immigrant Children (p. 62) and Title IV: Safe and Drug-Free Schools and Communities (p. 66). For continued funding, all programs funded under Titles I-V (note: Title V funds Innovative Programs) must submit research reports regarding their effectiveness annually or biannually (USDE, 2002).

This orientation towards scientifically based and evidence-based initiatives was foreshadowed in the OERI reauthorization language, in which scientific research was defined as:

(A) The term "scientifically based research standards" means research standards that:

   (i)   apply rigorous, systematic, and objective methodology to obtain reliable and valid knowledge relevant to education activities and programs; and

(ii)   present findings and make claims that are appropriate to and supported by the methods that have been employed.

(B)   The term includes, appropriate to the research being conducted:

(i)   employing systematic, empirical methods that draw on observation or experiment;

(ii)   involving data analyses that are adequate to support the general findings;

(iii)   relying on measurements or observational methods that provide reliable data;

(iv)   making claims of causal relationships only in random assignment experiments or other designs (to the extent such designs substantially eliminate plausible competing explanations for the obtained results);

(v)   ensuring that studies and methods are presented in sufficient detail and clarity to allow for replication or, at a minimum, to offer the opportunity to build systematically on the findings of the research;

(vi)   obtaining acceptance by a peer-reviewed journal or approval by a panel of independent experts through a comparably rigorous, objective, and scientific review; and using research designs and methods appropriate to the research question posed. (107th Congress Report 99-006, section 181, Public Law 107-404)

This definition is consistent with the National Research Council (NRC) report *Scientific Research in Education* (NRC, 2002), which provides a useful perspective on what constitutes scientific research. This report offers six principles for educational research:

Scientific Principle 1: Pose significant questions that can be investigated empirically.

Scientific Principle 2: Link research to relevant theory.

Scientific Principle 3: Use methods that permit direct investigation of the question.

Scientific Principle 4: Provide a coherent and explicit chain of reasoning.

Scientific Principle 5: Replicate and generalize across studies.

Scientific Principle 6: Disclose research to encourage professional scrutiny and critique. (NRC, 2002, pp. 3-5)

The authors also argue the importance of the accumulation of research results—another goal that seems especially worthwhile in the technology area.

The NRC report, *On Evaluating Curricular Effectiveness: Judging the Quality of K-12 Mathematics Evaluations* (NRC, 2004), is an important resource for the educational research community that addresses some of the challenges in moving in the directions that are represented in the current federal research policy. This report includes a chapter that specifies a framework for curricular evaluation. Although it is intended for use primarily with print instructional materials, we believe that the principles that it includes apply equally well to the evaluation of technological tools and technologically based materials used in mathematics teaching and learning.

The framework presented in *On Evaluating Curricular Effectiveness* is intended to guide researchers and evaluators in their efforts to define "a rigorous standard to which programs should be held to be *scientifically established as effective* (NRC, 2004, p. 5, Executive Summary)—a standard which, we might hope, would remove the label of "RND" from so many of the promising, but not rigorously evaluated, instructional materials and technologies for mathematics teaching.

Note that to amass the kind of high-quality research and evaluation that is described in the NRC report would probably require either a significant shift of research interest on behalf of mathematics educators currently working in technology design, development, and small-scale implementation, or the involvement of researchers and evaluators who might come from other interest domains into the territory of mathematics education and technology. In either case, we contend that without such efforts to conduct rigorous evaluation on the impact of technological innovations for mathematics learning, the possibilities for continued development funding, at least in the federal sector, might be limited in the near term. Moreover, if it is our hope that these innovations that have been so carefully designed, tested, refined, and implemented in controlled settings might be taken up by teachers and students in a wider way for the improvement of mathematics teaching and learning, then such evaluation research is essential.

The main elements of the NRC framework call for a collection of studies that demonstrate improvement in student learning that can be attributed to the curricular innovation in order to judge that a curricular innovation is "effective enough to adopt" (NRC, 2004, pp. 5-6, Executive Summary). It recommends four key elements of such research: content analyses, comparative studies involving experimental or quasi-experimental designs, at least one case study, and a final report that is made public (pp. 5-6). Other advice provided in this report, although challenging for researchers, seems wise and worth adapting and implementing in a next generation of research about technology that is more squarely aimed at documenting its impact on student learning of mathematics, including the need to work with representative samples of students, the need for careful documentation of students' opportunity to learn under the curricular innovation, the importance of measures that have curricular validity, and the need to employ multiple student outcome measures. These considerations are not necessarily those that are consistently visible in the current body of research about the role of technology in mathematics teaching and learning. Our understanding of the current policy environment leads us to the suggestion that such considerations would be well worth researchers' attention in future work.

We note that the research recommendations relative to technology made by the federal government as long as eight years ago, when the PCAST report was produced, at least in part foreshadowed the contemporary climate. The recommendations in the PCAST report included an extensive statement on educational research, summarized here:

> While research in a wide range of areas could directly or indirectly facilitate the effective utilization of educational technology within our nation's K-12 schools, much of the research that the Panel believes to be most important falls into one of the following three categories:
>
> 1. Basic research in various learning-related disciplines and fundamental work on various educationally relevant technologies;
>
> 2. Early-stage research aimed at developing new forms of educational software, content, and technology-enabled pedagogy; and
>
> 3. Empirical studies designed to determine which approaches to the use of technology are in fact most effective. (PCAST, 1997, Executive Summary)[13]

Certainly the third category is especially consistent with current directions; the emphasis on basic research and early-stage research remains equally critical to the advancement of this field. In providing rationale for the first two categories (areas that are less salient as priorities in the current research funding environment), PCAST notes the importance of underlying research in cognitive and developmental psychology, neuroscience, artificial intelligence, and cognitive science.

It is interesting to note that PCAST argued that the later stages of implementation research and associated evaluation might more properly be the province of the industrial sector, with private sector R&D financing rather than federal government financing. The report provides an interesting rationale for why federal funding is better suited to the early-stage research, discussing issues of intellectual property, profitability, and "free-rider" problems that might emerge if public funds were applied to the later stages.

> In the Panel's view, such economic externalities, combined with the potential "multiplier effect" that can be realized when carefully targeted early-stage government research funds are used to seed later-stage private sector R&D, provide a strong case for the federal funding of early-stage research aimed at developing new forms of educational software, content, and technology-enabled pedagogy. To date, the level of federal support for such research has been quite low relative to the associated potential returns, and such funding as has been available has been concentrated largely in the areas of mathematics and science education (where grants from the National Science Foundation have made a significant impact). (PCAST, 1997, Section 8.3: Priorities for Future Research)

In contrast to current discussion, there is strong support in the PCAST report for early-stage development work more consistent with much of what is reported in this volume, and/or what served as a basis for the work described here. PCAST also supports the need for a balanced portfolio of research, aimed not only at the question of demonstrating results, but at other key early-stage issues.

> In the Panel's judgment, the principal goal of such empirical work should not be to answer the question of whether computers can be effectively used within the school. The probability that elementary and secondary education will prove to be the one information-based industry in which computer technology does not have a natural role would at this point appear to be so low as to render unconscionably wasteful any research that might be designed to answer this question alone. (PCAST, 1997, Section 8.3: Priorities for Future Research)

PCAST also describes the challenge of effectiveness research, and argues on its behalf.

CONCLUSION

It is clearly daunting to balance the sometimes contradictory needs to continue to develop innovative technologies that can support, enhance, and advance mathematics learning; to study the impact of those technological tools on student learning in ways that both inform ongoing development and improvement of the tools and that generalize adequately to inform curricular decisions in schools and districts; and to employ research designs and methodological approaches that can offer insights to developers as well as to practitioners—all in the midst of an unpredictably dynamic educational policy environment. Nonetheless, as we have noted, we believe that unless leaders in the mathematics education technology research and development community confront these challenges and address them, the prospects for implementation and institutionalization of technology in mathematics teaching, as well as the establishment of a place for ongoing innovation in technology within the K-12 community, are less than promising.

The U.S. Department of Education's recent policy statement about educational technology is the *National Education Technology Plan* (USDE, 2004). This plan offers recommendations in the following seven areas:

1. Strengthen leadership;
2. Consider innovative budgeting;
3. Improve teacher training;
4. Support e-learning and virtual schools;
5. Encourage broadband access;
6. Move toward digital content; and
7. Integrate data systems. (pp. 39-44)

This document is meant to guide thinking about the role of technology in schools—it addresses several areas that have come into prominence with the advent of newly available technologies, such as e-learning, virtual schools, broadband access, and digital content. We ask how the base of research that currently exists relative to technology in mathematics education can serve as a foundation for the ongoing, needed research in these areas, and whether R&D that has mathematics as a focus will continue to inform these innovations.

This suggests that the development work, design studies, and small-scale proof-of-concept work must still go on—much of what is in this volume represents the best of that kind of work—and the case for such research is available in the policy documents we have discussed here. But, as we have suggested, another layer of work—the scaling up, the larger tests, and yes, even randomized, controlled trials—must also go on, and must be embraced eagerly by either some subset of this community, or some new group of researchers that can partner with them. For research to inform and influence policy requires an extraordinary confluence of conditions, including the existence of a league of scholars who are willing to write for different audiences and participate in activities and initiatives that relate to policy-making (such as design of standards for curriculum, or programmatic design for teacher preparation and professional development). Judging from the incredible array of scholarship in these volumes, this kind of energy, commitment, and expertise is certainly available in the mathematics educational technology community, and the policy community could benefit from it.

NOTES

1. The Princeton University Cognitive Science Laboratory WordNet® Electronic Lexical Database is located at http://wordnet.princeton.edu/ (Retrieved October 27, 2005).

2. The ISTE is currently in the process of producing *Educational Technology Support Standards*, which describes standards for professional development, systems, access, and support services essential to support effective use of technology; and *Standards for Student Assessment and Evaluation of Technology Use*, which describes various means of assessing student progress and evaluating the use of technology in learning and teaching.

3. For further elaboration of these ideas, see Ferrini-Mundy and Floden (2007).

4. http://cnets.iste.org/students/pf/pf_chaos_beyond.html (Retrieved October 28, 2005)

5. The National Assessment Governing Board Calculator Policy can be found in the Mathematics Framework for the 2005 NAEP, available at www.nagb.org/pubs/m_framework_05/chap2.html#calc (Retrieved October 28, 2005).

6. The College Board's Calculator Policy for Advanced Placement Mathematics can be found at www.collegeboard.com/student/testing/ap/exday_cal.html (Retrieved October 28, 2005); for SAT 1 Mathematics at www.collegeboard.com/student/testing/sat/about/sat/math.html (Retrieved October 28, 2005); for the SAT Subject Test Mathematics Level 1 at www.collegeboard.com/student/testing/sat/lc_two/math1c/math1c.html?math1c (Retrieved October 28, 2005); and policy for the SAT Subject Test Mathematics Level 2 can be found at www.collegeboard.com/student/testing/sat/lc_two/math2c/math2c.html?match2c (Retrieved October 28, 2005).

7. The ACT policy on calculator use can be found at www.actstudent.org/faq/answers/calculator.html (Retrieved January 13, 2006).

8. A reprint of this article is available at the NCTM Web site: www.nctm.org/news/pastpresident/2001-04 president.htm (Retrieved January 13, 2006).

9. A copy of this NCTM position statement is available at www.nctm.org/about/position_statements/ computation.htm (Retrieved January 17, 2006).

10. More Information on *Preparing Tomorrow's Teachers to Use Technology* (PT3) grants program can be found at www.ed.gov/programs/teachtech/index.html (Retrieved January 13, 2006).

11.   The creation of the Institute of Education Sciences was authorized by the passage of the Education Sciences Reform Act of 2002, Title I of Public Law 107-279.

12.   Sixteen of the 56 programs received ratings of adequate ($n = 14$) or effective ($n = 2$). Five programs were deemed ineffective. For a list of programs, program descriptions, and an explanation of the ratings see www.whitehouse.gov/omb/budget/fy2006/pma/education.pdf (Retrieved January 13, 2006).

13.   The PCAST report is available online via the Office of Science and Technology Policy website at www.ostp.gov/PCAST/k-12ed.html

REFERENCES

Dunham, P., & Hennessy, S. (2008). Equity and use of educational technology in mathematics. In M. K. Heid & G. W. Blume (Eds.), *Research on technology and the teaching and learning of mathematics: Vol. 1. Research syntheses* (pp. 345-418). Charlotte, NC: Information Age.

Ferrini-Mundy, J., & Floden, R. (2007). Research on policy and mathematics education. In F. Lester, Jr. (Ed.), *Second handbook of research on mathematics teaching and learning* (pp. 1247-1279). Charlotte, NC: Information Age.

Hembree, R., & Dessart, D. J. (1992). Research on calculators in mathematics education. In J. T. Fey (Ed.), *Calculators in mathematics education: 1992 yearbook of the National Council of Teachers of Mathematics* (pp. 22-31). Reston, VA: NCTM.

International Society for Technology in Education. (1998). *Technology foundation standards for students.* Eugene, OR: International Society for Technology in Education. Retrieved October 31, 2005, from http://cnets.iste.org/students/s_stands.html

International Society for Technology in Education. (2000). *National educational technology standards (NETS) for students: Connecting curriculum and technology.* Eugene, OR: International Society for Technology in Education. Retrieved October 31, 2005, from http://cnets.iste.org/students/s_book.html

International Technology Education Association. (2000). *Standards for technological literacy: Content for the study of technology.* Reston, VA: Author. Retrieved October 31, 2005, from www.iteaconnect.org/TAA/PDFs/xstnd.pdf

Klein, D., Braams, B., Parker, T., Quirk, W., Schmid, W., & Wilson, S. (2005). *State of the state math standards.* Washington, DC: Fordham Foundation.

Klein, D., & Cicci, F. (2001, March). Should we curb calculator use by younger students? *American Teacher.* Retrieved October 31, 2005, from www.aft.org/pubsreports/american_teacher/mar01/ speakout.html

National Council of Teachers of Mathematics. (1989). *Curriculum and evaluation standards for school mathematics.* Reston, VA: Author.

National Council of Teachers of Mathematics. (1991). *Professional teaching standards for school mathematics.* Reston, VA: Author.

National Council of Teachers of Mathematics. (1995). *Assessment standards for school mathematics.* Reston, VA: Author.

National Council of Teachers of Mathematics. (2000). *Principles and standards for school mathematics*. Reston, VA: Author.

National Research Council. (2002). *Scientific research in education*. Committee on Scientific Principles for Education Research. R. J. Shavelson & L. Towne (Eds.) Center for Education: Division of Behavioral and Social Sciences and Education. Washington, DC: National Academies Press.

National Research Council. (2004). *On evaluating curricular effectiveness: Judging the quality of K-12 mathematics evaluations*. Committee for a Review of the Evaluation Data on the Effectiveness of NSF-Supported and Commercially Generated Mathematics Curriculum Materials. Mathematical Sciences Education Board, Center for Education, Division of Behavioral and Social Sciences and Education. Washington, DC: The National Academies Press.

President's Committee of Advisors on Science and Technology, Panel on Educational Technology. (1997). *Report to the President on the use of technology to strengthen K-12 education in the United States*. Retrieved October 31, 2005, from www.ostp.gov/PCAST/k-12ed.html

United States Department of Education. (2001). *No Child Left Behind Act of 2001*. Washington, DC: Author. Retrieved October 31, 2005 from www.ed.gov/nclb/

United States Department of Education. (2002). *No child left behind: A desktop reference*. Washington, DC: Author.

United States Department of Education. (2004). *Toward a new golden age in American education: How the Internet, the law, and today's students are revolutionizing expectations*. Retrieved October 31, 2005, from www.nationaledtechplan.org/theplan/ NETP_Final.pdf

CHAPTER 18

THE ROLE OF RESEARCH AND THEORY IN THE INTEGRATION OF TECHNOLOGY IN MATHEMATICS TEACHING AND LEARNING

Glendon W. Blume and M. Kathleen Heid

The incorporation of technology into teaching and learning mathematics makes new demands on teachers, teacher educators, and curriculum developers. Likewise, it makes new demands on researchers, since it introduces new representations, new ways in which students demonstrate their understandings, and new mathematics. One of the tasks facing anyone who designs technology-intensive curricula or technological mathematics tools is to be mindful of the lessons of research while capitalizing on the new representations, new manifestations of student understanding, and new mathematics. Software and curriculum development efforts of the past have produced tools and curricula whose features have been shaped by research and theory and whose impact on mathematics teaching and learning has been documented by research, both formative and summative. The insights about such research that are available from the cases

Research on Technology and the Teaching and Learning of Mathematics:
Vol. 2. Cases and Perspectives, pp. 449–464
Copyright © 2008 by Information Age Publishing
All rights of reproduction in any form reserved.

developed in chapters 1–10 and from the perspectives offered in chapters 11–17 can collectively serve to inform the mathematics education community about appropriate directions that the teaching and learning of mathematics might take as well as ways in which the development of software and technological tools might be improved.

As Dugdale (2008b) points out in Chapter 1, research can play three major roles in the development of technological tools and curricula: a foundational role, in which research provides a theoretical or methodological basis for such work; a formative role, in which research provides data of various types that contribute to subsequent iterations during the development process; and a summative role, in which research examines various outcomes from the use of technological tools and curricula. Each of the cases described in Chapters 1 through 10 provides illustrations of research having played one or more of these roles in contributing insights about the teaching and learning of mathematics in technology-intensive environments.

THE CONTRIBUTIONS OF RESEARCH AND THEORY TO THE CASES AND THE CASES' CONTRIBUTIONS TO RESEARCH AND THEORY IN DEVELOPMENT OF TECHNOLOGY AND TECHNOLOGY-INTENSIVE CURRICULA

Sharon Dugdale's work in chapters 1 and 4 (Dugdale, 2008a, 2008b) highlights the importance of formative uses of research and provides examples of ways in which formative research can inform software development or curriculum development. Dugdale's formative research included observation of students' interactions while at the computer and revealed that those interactions were more social and less predictable than was expected. This had design implications—it suggested that it was not wise to base computer interactions with the user on the assumption that it was possible to deduce a student's thinking from what was input, nor on the assumption that only one student's input was guiding the interaction with the computer. This formative research also provided evidence that a student (or group of students) could diagnose his or her (their) errors from computer feedback that, instead of being a verbal reply, was simply a direct result of the student's manipulation of the mathematical model. This expression of feedback directly in terms of the mathematical model left the error diagnosis and correction to the student rather than embedding it in the tool. Another implication of the research conducted in conjunction with Dugdale's work is that research is more powerful when it is sensitive to the interactive nature of the environment, for example, examining the interactions within a group of students and probing to identify students' reasons for their actions rather than inferring them only from the actions themselves. Dugdale's research also established that, in both small-group interaction and in a network setting, children benefited from the participation of other students. Because the Internet and within-classroom networks of tools offer possibilities for interactions between and among students that are not available with stand-alone use of tools, teachers need to consider such uses of tools in their practice and researchers need to determine the advantages and disadvantages of learning in these settings.

Some implications for teachers' practice that follow from this type of formative research include provision of feedback that is based within the mathematical activity—allowing the student to make sense of what they have done—and encouragement of children to learn from each other through direct interaction or examination of each other's approaches and strategies. This formative research also informs practice in that it suggests that teachers should pay attention to students' thinking by reacting to their work—monitoring unusual solution processes, pointing out to students important advances in their mathematical thinking, and assisting students in reflecting on and formalizing their ideas—without presuming that one knows what the child was thinking.

The type of teacher-student interaction suggested by Dugdale's work contrasts to the approach used by intelligent tutors, as described by Ritter, Haverty, Koedinger, Hadley, and Corbett (2008) in chapter 7. Intelligent tutors also pay close attention to students' performance, but they make data-based inferences about students' thinking that guide the interaction between student and tutor. A theory of learning, coupled with extensive observations of students' knowledge, skills, and strategies, as well as inferences about their misconceptions, guided development of the tutor, making the tutor capable of guiding the development of subsequent learners' knowledge, skills, and strategies. That guidance depends on models of students' declarative and procedural knowledge—a data-based model of a student's thinking is constantly compared to a model of proficient performance.

The intelligent tutor's use of a theory of learning and models of student cognition represents one use of theory to guide the development of tools; other uses of theory are illustrated in chapters 5 and 6. Sarama and Clements (2008) in chapter 5 and Battista (2008a) in Chapter 6 emphasize ways in which theory can inform technological tool and curriculum development, and, ultimately, teachers' classroom practice. A strong research message from both of these chapters is that software and curriculum developers can use analysis of a mathematics content domain and research-based theory—either a theory pertinent to the mathematical domain of interest or a general theory of learning or teaching—to build models of students' thinking and learning in that domain.

Sarama and Clements (2008) argue that research and curriculum or tool development need to be integrated and interactive. They present an example of a model of students' knowledge concerning composition of two-dimensional geometric figures and hypothesized progression through levels of that knowledge, and subsequent use of that model to design software. Such models allow researchers to test hypotheses concerning features of the tool environment that are designed to correspond to students' thinking. Because software or curriculum developers can make use of research from which models of students' thinking can be developed, researchers need to conduct research that leads to the development of learning trajectories.

Sarama and Clements lament the lack of dissemination of research related to curriculum and software development and note that lack of interest in and lack of resources for research can act as constraints to such dissemination. In addition, rapidly changing technology hampers dissemination of research. In some instances tools become outdated and are no longer used in schools, or tools are revised so that they provide different capabilities, making it difficult to study effects of their use over long periods of time. In other instances researchers' attention may prematurely be drawn away from existing tools to newly developed tools whose potential contribution to students' learning may be more compelling.

Battista (2008a) provides a somewhat different example of use of theory—one in which tool design drew on three different types of conceptual frameworks: one that was an analysis of subject matter, one that addressed learning and teaching in general, and one that specifically addressed students' learning of geometry. This suggests that developers can successfully draw on research and theory from a variety of perspectives, not just a single perspective. Battista identifies theoretical considerations that affected the design of the Shape Makers software. He posits that the software should support students' movement through levels predicted by theory and it should promote development in students of increasingly sophisticated mental structures for reasoning about geometric shapes. In addition, Battista notes that several practical considerations, as well as theoretical ones, received attention during the design process. These included software that was easy to use (for both teacher and student), a tool that was structured in such a way that it could grow with students throughout their study of mathematics, and a tool context that was interesting enough to encourage inquiry and reflection. Both the theoretical and practical considerations, coupled with formative research, informed revisions of the software.

The accounts of the development of dynamical geometry software in chapters 2 and 3 (Goldenberg, Scher, & Feurzeig, 2008; Laborde & Laborde, 2008) call attention to the importance of learning from the history of the design process as it unfolded for various tools. Doing so requires explicit documentation of foundational bases for tool and curriculum development, findings from informal and formal research efforts, and reasons for design decisions and modifications. The historical account constructed by Goldenberg and colleagues captures five principles that guided the developers' thinking: dragging, minimal distance from Euclid's geometry, reversibility, continuity, and minimal user surprise. The recognition of principles underpinning the creation of interactive geometry tools suggests foci for researchers' work in understanding student thinking in dynamical geometry environments.

It is clear that important tool and curriculum design features need to be based on theory and empirical research and that subsequent research should study the effects of those design features on students' learning. An example of this is direct manipulation, as described by Laborde and Laborde (2008), in which the user acts directly on mathematical objects rather than selecting menu commands that carry out actions. This important feature is one of many that merits researchers' attention—more needs to be learned about how students use this feature, what it contributes to students' mathematical understanding, and how teachers can take advantage of such features in their work with students.

An important message in both chapters 2 and 3 is that dynamic tools can embody mathematics that differs from the mathematics that students experience in other settings: "What is quite clear is that geometry on a computer is different from geometry on paper" (Goldenberg et al., 2008, p. 81). Because of that difference, researchers need, for example, to study what students glean from complicated figures when those figures are dragged, identify that to which students attend when using dynamical geometry software, characterize the ways in which students experiment within the context of a dynamical geometry sketch, and examine how students interpret the mathematical relationships that are embedded in a sketch. As Laborde and Laborde (2008) point out, researchers must recognize how mathematics in dynamic tools differs from mathematics in other settings and address the mathematics teaching and learning questions that arise from that difference: "Instead of considering these problems solely as design problems, the researchers involved in the Cabri project recognized these problems as theoretical problems about a new kind of geometry, a dynamical geometry with its own objects and relations" (p. 44). Dynamical geometry thus offers a site for studying potentially new teaching and learning issues that result when a new area of mathematics is being studied.

Research on representation is addressed in various ways in chapters 8, 9, and 10 (Confrey & Maloney, 2008; Dick & Edwards, 2008; Kaput & Schorr, 2008). These chapters underscore the importance of tool designers' and curriculum designers' attention to the potential of representations to influence mathematics learning and the role of representations in studying mathematical objects. Confrey and Maloney (2008) describe the evolution of the Function Probe software and its basis in theory and empirical research. Key issues addressed included covariation as opposed to correspondence, additive as opposed to multiplicative strategies, and the history of the development of calculus and functions (particularly with respect to the use of tables). Function Probe is a good example of software that was designed to have distinctions among its representations of functions that would enable students to coordinate and contrast results from different representations, and thus it provides a clear message on issues related to mathematical representations that research ought to continue to address:

> One of our design principles was to build representations that would be "true" to the actions that a student could take, while facilitating contrasts and similarities among the different representations and conventions ... our research work highlighted many examples of representational issues that are unsatisfactorily resolved in conventional treatments. (p. 195)

In particular, Confrey and Maloney question the soundness of the graphing calculator as a pedagogical device and call for research that examines the impact of calculator use and software use on students' mathematical thinking.

In the case of SimCalc in chapter 9, Kaput and Schorr (2008) use its development to illustrate four stages of research that they and others conducted as part of the development of SimCalc. Their experiences closely parallel those described by Sarama and Clements (2008) and suggest a changing focus for research as the development process proceeds. Initial design research focuses on identifying technological opportunities to address the identified goals for the technological tool (for Kaput and Schorr these were representational opportunities). A second stage entails creating activities that exploit the features of the tool and can meaningfully engage students at various levels (for Kaput and Schorr this meant activities that exploited the representational affordances of SimCalc). A third stage involves a shift to a curricular focus—use by teachers as part of standard instruction (for Kaput and Schorr this included testing by an expanded set of researchers and teachers "local" to each of them). Finally, in a fourth stage, research confronts implementation and scale-up issues (for Kaput and Schorr this meant addressing, among other things, the existing accountability and assessment climate in schools as well as issues such as larger-scale professional development and district-wide reform). Kaput and Schorr aptly characterize the foci of these stages of research as moving from "What could work?" to "What does work?" to "Why does it work, or why does it not work?" For the accountability concerns of the fourth-stage research, it seems that the questions might be "What support is necessary for it to work with all teachers?" and "How can the impact of innovative tools and activities be studied in the context of district-wide assessment?"

Dick and Edwards (2008) show in chapter 10 how Janvier's (1987) framework for representation not only guided calculus curriculum development but was extensible by them to a "Rule of Five" (graphical, numeric, symbolic, verbal, physical) framework that encompassed more types of representations. This case illustrates how theory can be used to develop technology-intensive curricula and how, in turn, insights from the curriculum development process can serve to further develop theory. Dick and Edwards also note how empirical research was used to guide the role of technology in the curriculum.

RESEARCH DIRECTIONS FROM THE CASES AND PERSPECTIVES

A number of important themes emerge from the cases and perspectives on technology use that appear in this volume (Blume & Heid, 2008). The themes we have selected are not intended to be exhaustive, rather, they are illustrations of key ideas on which there is agreement (and sometimes disagreement) across the chapters in this volume. Among these themes are:

- the importance of research on students' thinking for technological tool and curriculum development, formative research, and summative research;
- attention to both technical and conceptual aspects during tool use;
- the importance of representations in technological environments;
- integration of on-computer and off-computer activities;
- the significance of policy issues;
- the interaction of empirical research and theory with tool design and development;
- direct expression of key mathematical ideas and mathematical fidelity; and
- technology's capability to engage students with mathematics beyond that which is typical for their level.

Each of these themes arises from the role that research played in several of the cases. In some instances the themes echo conclusions presented in the research syntheses in the first of these two volumes (Heid & Blume, 2008). In other instances they represent insights gleaned from the research that occurs during the lengthy and intensive process of developing tools—tools that engage students in thinking mathematically, take advantage of technological capabilities that were not previously available, and enable students to interact with mathematics in new ways.

The Importance of Research on Students' Thinking for Technological Tool and Curriculum Development

A number of chapters in this volume highlight the importance of research on students' thinking in the development of technological tools. Sarama and Clements (2008) focus on the importance of using models of student thinking as a basis for software development, namely, building on theory that provides a trajectory that describes students' evolving understanding of the content domain. Models of students' cognition also are paramount to the work of Ritter and colleagues (2008), but in this case, intelligent tutors incorporate well-specified cognitive models that can be used to guide students' development of competence in a domain. Yet another focus on students' thinking involves designing tools in response to students' strategies (Confrey & Maloney, 2008; Dugdale, 2008a, 2008b), and, as Confrey and Maloney note, building tools with the intent of addressing students' conceptual challenges. Wilson (2008) points out that use of technology provides a rich venue for prospective and practicing teachers and researchers to conduct investigations on how students think about mathematical concepts. Research on students' thinking in technological environments can impact teacher educators' practice and provide rich illustrations of students' thinking.

Attention to Both Technical and Conceptual Aspects During Tool Use

Confrey and Maloney (2008), Drijvers and Trouche (2008), and Kieran and Saldanha (2008) all highlight the importance of simultaneous attention to technical and conceptual knowledge—in research, in tool and curriculum development, and in classroom practice. In chapter 8, Confrey and Maloney illustrate this with respect to building a pedagogically sound tool that promotes both conceptual understanding and technical fluency. Drijvers and Trouche point out in chapter 14 how technical and conceptual aspects can interfere with each other but also codevelop during the process of instrumental genesis. Explicit attention to a task's technical and conceptual potential during task design is one message from Kieran and Saldanha in chapter 15; their students' work illustrates the intertwined conceptual and technical knowledge that can be developed through comparing CAS-produced symbolic forms and student-produced symbolic forms.

The Importance of Representations in Technological Environments

Representations often receive attention in technological environments, in part because they provide a venue for studying students' thinking and in part because they offer a variety of ways of communicating mathematical ideas, some of which are unavailable without technology. In particular, these new representations (e.g., slope triangles and bars in Confrey & Maloney, 2008, and technologically generated slope fields in Dick and Edwards, 2008) that provide alternatives to the usual representations are worthy of researchers' interest.

Kaput and Schorr (2008) in chapter 9 and Battista (2008b) in chapter 13 make important distinctions concerning objects and representations of those objects. Kaput and Schorr argue that mathematics needs to be about objects, and that various representations need to represent the object being represented rather than representing each other. Battista identifies four types of geometric objects—physical, perceptual, conceptual, and formal geometric concepts—and contends that from a representational perspective geometric diagrams often are seen as representing a class of objects rather than being objects of study themselves. This representational perspective fails to focus on the formation of concepts from instances. Battista argues that research on representations in geometry should have more of a conceptual focus. He points out that in addition to investigating how students interpret and use external representations, research should address both the mechanisms by which students progress from analysis of particular figures to general abstractions about classes of figures and the mechanisms that enable students to use formal geometric concepts to analyze particular figures.

Integration of On-Computer and Off-Computer Work

Several of the reviews of research in Volume 1 conclude that coordinated on-computer and off-computer work are beneficial for learning (for example, see Clements, Sarama, Yelland, & Glass, 2008; Olive & Lobato,

2008). The cases and perspectives in this volume (Blume & Heid, 2008) provide additional evidence of the importance of learning more about the complementary nature of on-tool and off-tool work. The instrumental approach to using technology presented by Drijvers and Trouche (2008) in chapter 14 acknowledges the complexity of technology-intensive learning environments that goes far beyond delegating the work to the tool. Drijvers and Trouche describe different ways of organizing tool use within the classroom that vary in the extent to which they constrain instrumentation and instrumentalization. This suggests that it is imperative for researchers studying instrumental orchestration to examine both on-tool and supporting off-tool work. Drijvers and Trouche also suggest a particular focus for research: "We think that an articulation of the instrumental approach with the perspective of symbolizing, both within and apart from the technological environment, might be fruitful" (p. 376).

Kieran and Saldanha (2008) provide in chapter 15 an extensive classroom example of coordinated on-tool and off-tool work—a mix of paper-and-pencil work, CAS use, reflection questions, and classroom discussions. They selected an activity involving factorization of $x^n - 1$ that was designed to make techniques a topic for reflection and that would generate rich data on the codevelopment of conceptual and technical knowledge. The studies they cite about the selection of such tasks coupled with their experience with this task suggest that a fruitful direction for research can be to examine, in an environment in which on-tool and off-tool tasks are coordinated, the codevelopment of conceptual and technical knowledge.

In chapter 5, Sarama and Clements (2008) also direct researchers' attention to on-tool and off-tool work. They emphasize the need, during classroom pilot testing, for research that examines how children's experiences with software reinforce, complement, and extend their learning experiences with physical manipulatives or print materials.

The Importance of Policy Issues

The policy considerations related to technology presented by Ferrini-Mundy and Breaux (2008) in chapter 17 become extremely important for implementation of existing technology, examination of the effectiveness of innovative tools and curricula, development of new technologies, and development of curricula that take advantage of emerging technologies. The authors make recommendations for research based on the implications from policy concerning curriculum, technology use, technology access, and educational research. Ferrini-Mundy and Breaux suggest that because of contentious debate about technology use (e.g., use of calculators in the elementary grades), research that addresses technology use is likely to have vast potential for impact. Also, the authors note that few research studies have investigated the relationship between access to technology and its potential to impact mathematics teaching and learning, for example, whether increased access might lead to teachers seeking technological resources to enhance instruction. This seems to be another potentially informative direction for research. Finally, given the current funding climate for educational research, they recommend that rigorous evaluation research examining impact on learning is essential if the technological innovations that have been carefully designed and tested in controlled settings are to be implemented more broadly.

Ferrini-Mundy and Breaux are not alone in addressing policy issues related to the use of technology in the teaching and learning of mathematics and policy issues related to research on such use—a number of the cases and perspectives chapters in this volume also directly or indirectly address policy and underscore its importance. For example, in their account of development and implementation of SimCalc, Kaput and Schorr (2008) discuss a number of issues that have major policy implications, ranging from democratization of access to ideas normally encountered only in advanced mathematics to affordability and accessibility in the scaling-up of technological innovations. Policy that supports an innovation can be heavily dependent on the degree of acceptance of that innovation, and acceptance, in turn, can depend heavily on research issues. In chapter 2, Laborde and Laborde (2008) point out the initial lack of acceptance of Cabri by various communities—mathematicians (due to fears about loss of creativity), computer scientists (due to a perceived lack of research issues in software development), and mathematics educators (due to lack of a theoretical framework for studying such software)—noting some of the underlying research issues that contributed to that initial lack of acceptance. Wilson (2008) also notes the importance of involvement of multiple communities (including curriculum developers and tool developers) as participants in teacher education related to technology in the teaching and learning of mathematics. By broadening the definition of teacher educator we can better ensure that teachers receive education that prepares them to use technological tools and curricula effectively.

The Interaction of Empirical Research and Theory With Tool Design and Development

Because of the nature of associated research activity, technology design, conceptualization, pilot testing, revision, field testing, and so on, should be thought of as educational research endeavors. The development of technological tools and curricula needs to be intimately connected with theory, formative empirical research, and summative empirical research. Roschelle and Jackiw (2000) make the case that, as educational research, technology design should incorporate three thrusts for research: imagination (in conceptualization and development of new tools), inquiry (examining the consequences of technology for new methods of teaching and learning), and impact (in mainstream curricula). They argue for including a research focus on impact rather than focusing primarily on imagination and inquiry.

Throughout the cases and perspectives of this volume the theme of research is reinforced. The cases in chapters by Battista (2008a), Confrey and Maloney (2008), Dugdale (2008a, 2008b), Goldenberg and colleagues (2008), and Sarama and Clements (2008), are just some of the instances of theory and empirical research playing a central role in the development of technological tools and curricula. In addition, because of its relative infancy, the body of research on tools and curricula for data analysis and statistics (see Friel, 2008) is poised to take advantage of the lessons of these cases as it matures into a more coherent and elaborated body of research. To begin this process, Friel suggests a research agenda with a focus on the central ideas of statistics and tool use.

Direct Expression of Key Mathematical Ideas and Mathematical Fidelity

Several of the cases (Dugdale, 2008a; Laborde & Laborde, 2008) illustrate the importance of direct expression of mathematical ideas in technological tools. In chapter 1, Dugdale (2008a) describes how students' varied input (fractions, decimals, mixed numbers, and expressions using operations) simply was interpreted in terms of the number-line mathematical model (a dart lodging somewhere in the number line, possibly breaking a balloon in the process), causing students to engage directly with the mathematical idea. Furthermore, the use of dragging to manipulate on-screen geometric entities directly in Cabri enables students to engage directly with mathematical relationships.

Of course, mathematical ideas that are expressed directly in technological tools must be correct. In chapter 12, Dick (2008) makes a strong case for attention to *mathematical fidelity*, the extent to which the characteristics and behavior of a mathematical object in a technological environment accurately reflects the characteristics and behavior of the idealized mathematical object. This is illustrated in several of the cases, for example, in chapter 4 Dugdale (2008b) relates how mathematical goals were not compromised for programming convenience in the creation of the means for entering equations that defined conics, and in chapter 8 Confrey and Maloney (2008) describe how knowledge of students' difficulties in distinguishing between quadratic functions and exponential functions led to Function Probe's distinction between the exponential key and the power key, a distinction that yields fidelity when one produces inverses.

Technology's Capability to Engage Students With Mathematics Beyond That Which Is Typical for Their Level

Technological tools, when properly designed, often can enable students to engage with ideas that are typically believed to be beyond the grasp of students at their particular grade level. Dugdale (2008a, 2008b) provides several striking examples of this. She illustrates how students, when interacting with a mathematically accurate model during their initial work with fractions, could generate ideas well beyond what was usually expected during such initial learning, and she relates quite creative solutions from students who used Green Globs. Kaput and Schorr (2008) also provide illustrations of student engagement with mathematical ideas often encountered only by students in more advanced courses, such as those chronicling how students from low-performing middle schools developed meaningful insights into the velocity-position relationships embodied in the Fundamental Theorem of Calculus. Likewise, a student unexpectedly was able to offer an elegant proof for one of the factoring tasks in Kieran and Saldanha (2008). Just as teachers need to anticipate in their practice that, when using technological tools and curricula, students may engage with ideas that are well beyond what might be expected of them, researchers need to be mindful of the possibility of such unexpected outcomes and anticipate them in the selection of tasks, interactions with subjects, and interpretations of their results.

CONCLUSION

One might argue that technology makes new demands on research because, as Noss and Hoyles (1996) have pointed out, technology provides new windows on mathematical thinking. So, when technological tools are used we have different sources of knowledge about students' thinking. Since the relationship between technological tools and students' thinking is a reciprocal relationship, our enhanced understanding of and ability to examine students' thinking also has powerful implications for how software and tools might be structured.

Part of our reason for collecting the works in this second volume was that many people did not believe that research was involved extensively in technological tool and curriculum development. We were interested in making visible the extent to which research related to the creation of technological tools and curricula went far beyond the often-minimal market research associated with commercial products. We found that the tool and curriculum developers whose chapters are included in this volume thought carefully about the relationship between students' thinking, mathematical content, and tool and curriculum development, and they made extensive use of theory and empirical research when designing and revising tools and curricula.

In the spirit of the life's work of Jim Kaput, the mathematics education community (including researchers, teachers, tool and curriculum developers, and teacher educators) needs to be proleptic (Kaput, 1993) in its vision and goals—much as the authors of the cases in this volume were at the time their development activities occurred. Researchers need deliberately to anticipate the future—a future in which quite different technological tools and curricula are available and the circumstances under which teaching and learning occur are different as well. This anticipation requires attention both to what Kaput referred to as practice-extending research (extending and improving current practice) and future-defining research (testing the boundaries of what is possible outside the constraints of current technology and practice). We sincerely hope that his multi-faceted, continuously proleptic vision is realized in the work that builds on the accumulated knowledge of these two volumes.

REFERENCES

Battista, M. T. (2008a). Development of the Shape Makers geometry microworld: Design principles and research. In G. W. Blume & M. K. Heid (Eds.), *Research on technology and the teaching and learning of mathematics: Vol. 2. Cases and perspectives* (pp. 131-156). Charlotte, NC: Information Age.

Battista, M. T. (2008b). Representations and cognitive objects in modern school geometry. In G. W. Blume & M. K. Heid (Eds.), *Research on technology and the teaching and learning of mathematics: Vol. 2. Cases and perspectives* (pp. 341-362). Charlotte, NC: Information Age.

Blume, G. W., & Heid, M. K. (Eds.). (2008). *Research on technology and the teaching and learning of mathematics: Vol. 2. Cases and perspectives*. Charlotte, NC: Information Age.

Clements, D. H., Sarama, J., Yelland, N. J., & Glass, B. (2008). Learning and teaching geometry with computers in the elementary and middle school. In M. K. Heid & G. W. Blume (Eds.), *Research on technology and the teaching and learning of mathematics: Vol. 1. Research syntheses* (pp. 109-154). Charlotte, NC: Information Age.

Confrey, J., & Maloney, A. (2008). Research–design interactions in building Function Probe software. In G. W. Blume & M. K. Heid (Eds.), *Research on technology and the teaching and learning of mathematics: Vol. 2. Cases and perspectives* (pp. 183-209). Charlotte, NC: Information Age.

Dick, T. P. (2008). Keeping the faith: Fidelity in technological tools for mathematics education. In G. W. Blume & M. K. Heid (Eds.), *Research on technology and the teaching and learning of mathematics: Vol. 2. Cases and perspectives* (pp. 333-339). Charlotte, NC: Information Age.

Dick, T. P., & Edwards, B. (2008). Multiple representations and local linearity—Research influences on the use of technology in calculus curriculum reform. In G. W. Blume & M. K. Heid (Eds.), *Research on technology and the teaching and learning of mathematics: Vol. 2. Cases and perspectives* (pp. 255-275). Charlotte, NC: Information Age.

Drijvers, P., & Trouche, L. (2008). From artifacts to instruments: A theoretical framework behind the orchestra metaphor. In G. W. Blume & M. K. Heid (Eds.), *Research on technology and the teaching and learning of mathematics: Vol. 2. Cases and perspectives* (pp. 363-391). Charlotte, NC: Information Age.

Dugdale, S. (2008a). From network to microcomputers and fractions to functions: Continuity in software research and design. In G. W. Blume & M. K. Heid (Eds.), *Research on technology and the teaching and learning of mathematics: Vol. 2. Cases and perspectives* (pp. 89-112). Charlotte, NC: Information Age.

Dugdale, S. (2008b). Research in a pioneer constructivist network-based curriculum project for children's learning of fractions. In G. W. Blume & M. K. Heid (Eds.), *Research on technology and the teaching and learning of mathematics: Vol. 2. Cases and perspectives* (pp. 3-30). Charlotte, NC: Information Age.

Ferrini-Mundy, J., & Breaux, G. A. (2008). Perspectives on research, policy, and the use of technology in mathematics teaching and learning in the United States. In G. W. Blume & M. K. Heid (Eds.), *Research on technology and the teaching and learning of mathematics: Vol. 2. Cases and perspectives* (pp. 427–448). Charlotte, NC: Information Age.

Friel, S. N. (2008). The research frontier: Where technology interacts with the teaching and learning of data analysis and statistics. In G. W. Blume & M. K. Heid (Eds.), *Research on technology and the teaching and learning of mathematics: Vol. 2. Cases and perspectives* (pp. 279-331). Charlotte, NC: Information Age.

Goldenberg, E. P., Scher, D., & Feurzeig, N. (2008). What lies behind dynamic interactive geometry software? In G. W. Blume & M. K. Heid (Eds.), *Research on technology and the teaching and learning of mathematics: Vol. 2. Cases and perspectives* (pp. 53-87). Charlotte, NC: Information Age.

Heid, M. K. & Blume, G. W. (Eds.). (2008). *Research on technology and the teaching and learning of mathematics: Vol. 1. Research syntheses*. Charlotte, NC: Information Age.

Janvier, C. (Ed.). (1987). Translation processes in mathematics education. In *Problems of representation in the teaching and learning of mathematics* (pp. 27-32). Hillsdale, NJ: Erlbaum.

Kaput, J. (1993). The urgent need for proleptic research in the representation of quantitative relationships. In T. A. Romberg, E. Fennema, & T. P. Carpenter (Eds.), *Integrating research on graphical representation of functions* (pp. 279-312). Hillsdale, NJ: Erlbaum.

Kaput, J., & Schorr, R. (2008). Changing representational infrastructures changes most everything: The case of SimCalc, algebra, and calculus. In G. W. Blume & M. K. Heid (Eds.), *Research on technology and the teaching and learning of mathematics: Vol. 2. Cases and perspectives* (pp. 211-253). Charlotte, NC: Information Age.

Kieran C., & Saldanha, L. (2008). Designing tasks for the co-development of conceptual and technical knowledge in CAS activity: An example from factoring. In G. W. Blume & M. K. Heid (Eds.), *Research on technology and the teaching and learning of mathematics: Vol. 2. Cases and perspectives* (pp. 393-414). Charlotte, NC: Information Age.

Laborde, C., & Laborde, J. -M. (2008). The development of a dynamical geometry environment: Cabri-géomètre. In G. W. Blume & M. K. Heid (Eds.), *Research on technology and the teaching and learning of mathematics: Vol. 2. Cases and perspectives* (pp. 31-52). Charlotte, NC: Information Age.

Noss, R., & Hoyles, C. (Eds.). (1996). *Windows on mathematical meanings—Learning cultures and computers.* Dordrecht, Netherlands: Kluwer Academic.

Olive, J., & Lobato, J. (2008). The learning of rational number concepts using technology. In M. K. Heid & G. W. Blume (Eds.), *Research on technology and the teaching and learning of mathematics: Vol. 1. Research syntheses* (pp. 1-53). Charlotte, NC: Information Age.

Ritter, S., Haverty, L., Koedinger, K. R., Hadley, W., & Corbett, A. T. (2008). Integrating intelligent software tutors with the mathematics classroom. In G. W. Blume & M. K. Heid (Eds.), *Research on technology and the teaching and learning of mathematics: Vol. 2. Cases and perspectives* (pp. 157-181). Charlotte, NC: Information Age.

Roschelle, J., & Jackiw, N. (2000). Technology design as educational research: Interweaving imagination, inquiry, and impact. In A. E. Kelly & R. A. Lesh (Eds.), *Handbook of research design in mathematics and science education* (pp. 777-797). Mahwah, NJ: Erlbaum.

Sarama, J., & Clements, D. H. (2008). Linking research and software development. In G. W. Blume & M. K. Heid (Eds.), *Research on technology and the teaching and learning of mathematics: Vol. 2. Cases and perspectives* (pp. 113-130). Charlotte, NC: Information Age.

Wilson, P. S. (2008). Teacher education: A conduit to the classroom. In G. W. Blume & M. K. Heid (Eds.), *Research on technology and the teaching and learning of mathematics: Vol. 2. Cases and perspectives* (pp. 415-426). Charlotte, NC: Information Age.

LIST OF CONTRIBUTORS

Michael T. Battista
Professor
Ohio State University
School of Teaching & Learning
209 Arps
1945 N High Street
Columbus, Ohio 43210
battista.23@osu.edu

Glenda A. Breaux
Research Associate
Michigan State University
Division of Science and Mathematics
    Education
221 North Kedzie
East Lansing, MI 48824
breauxgl@msu.edu

Glendon W. Blume
Professor of Mathematics Education
The Pennsylvania State University
269 Chambers Building
University Park, PA 16802-3205
gblume@psu.edu

Douglas H. Clements
Professor
University at Buffalo, State University
    of New York
Department of Learning and
    Instruction Graduate School of
    Education
505 Baldy Hall,
Buffalo, NY 14260
clements@buffalo.edu

Jere Confrey
Joseph D. Moore
Distinguished Professor
Department of Mathematics, Science,
    and Technology Education
North Carolina State University
jere_confrey@ncsu.edu

Albert T. Corbett
Associate Research Professor
Carnegie Mellon University
Human-Computer Interaction
    Institute
5000 Forbes Avenue
3605 Newell-Simon Hall
Pittsburgh, PA 15213
corbett@cmu.edu

Thomas P. Dick
Professor
Oregon State University
Department of Mathematics
108D Kidder Hall
Corvallis, OR 97331
tpdick@math.orst.edu

Paul Drijvers
Assistant Professor in Mathematics
    Education
Freudenthal Institute
Utrecht University
PO Box 9432
NL3506 GK Utrecht
The Netherlands
p.drijvers@fi.uu.nl

Sharon Dugdale
Professor of Education
University of California at Davis
School of Education
One Shields Avenue
Davis, CA 95616-8579
ssdugdale@ucdavis.edu

Barbara Edwards
Associate Professor
Oregon State University
Department of Mathematics
Kidder Hall 363
Corvallis, OR 97331
    edwards@math.orst.edu

Joan Ferrini-Mundy
University Distinguished Professor
    and Associate Dean
Michigan State University
Division of Science and Mathematics
    Education
211 N. Kedzie Lab
East Lansing MI 48824-1031
jferrini@msu.edu

Nannette Feurzeig
Freelance Writer
13 White Pine Lane
Lexington, MA 02421
NanniF@comcast.net

Susan N. Friel
Professor of Mathematics Education
University of North Carolina at
    Chapel Hill
School of Education
201b Peabody Hall
Chapel Hill, NC 27599-3500
sfriel@email.unc.edu

E. Paul Goldenberg
Distinguished Scholar
Education Development Center Inc.
    (EDC)
Center for Mathematics Education
Division of Mathematics Learning and
    Teaching
55 Chapel Street
Newton, MA 02458-1060
PGoldenberg@edc.org

William Hadley
Cofounder and Advisor
Carnegie Learning
Frick Building, 20th Floor
437 Grant Street
Pittsburgh, PA 15219
bhadley@carnegielearning.com

Lisa Haverty
Cognitive Scientist
Arnold Worldwide
101 Huntington Avenue
Boston, MA 02199
haverty@alum.dartmouth.org

M. Kathleen Heid
Distinguished Professor of
    Mathematics Education
The Pennsylvania State University
271 Chambers Building
University Park, PA, 16802-3205
mkh2@psu.edu

Jim Kaput
(Deceased)
Chancellor Professor of Mathematics
University of Massachusetts-
    Dartmouth

Carolyn Kieran
Professor
Université du Québec à Montréal
    Département de Mathématiques
CP 8888, succ. Centre-Ville
Montreal, QC H3C 3P8, Canada
kieran-suave.carolyn@uqam.ca

Kenneth R. Koedinger
Professor
Carnegie Mellon University
5000 Forbes Avenue
3601 Newell-Simon Hall
Pittsburgh, PA 15213
koedinger@cmu.edu

Colette Laborde
Professeure Emérite
Institut Universitaire de Formation
    des Maitres (IUFM)
Equipe IAM
Laboratoire d' Informatique de
    Grenoble - LIG
46 Avenue Félix Viallet
38 031 Grenoble Cedex, France
Colette.Laborde@imag.fr

Jean-Marie Laborde
President, Cabrilog
6 place Robert Schuman
38000 Grenoble France
Jean-Marie.Laborde@cabri

Alan Maloney
Extension Associate Professor
Department of Mathematics, Science,
    and Technology Education
North Carolina State University
2310 Stinson Drive
Raleigh, NC 27695-7801
alan_maloney@ncsu.edu

Steven Ritter
Cofounder and Chief Scientist
Carnegie Learning
Frick Building, 20th Floor
437 Grant Street
Pittsburgh, PA, 15219
steve@carnegielearning.com

Luis Saldanha
Assistant Professor
Portland State University
Department of Mathematics and
    Statistics
Office 329NH
P.O. Box 751
Portland, OR 97207
saldanha@pdx.edu

Julie Sarama
Associate Professor
University at Buffalo, State University
    of New York
Department of Learning and
    Instruction
Graduate School of Education
593 Baldy Hall
Buffalo, NY
14260 jsarama@buffalo.edu

Daniel Scher
Curriculum Developer
KCP Technologies, Inc.
1150 65th Street
Emeryville, CA 94608
dscher@keypress.com

Roberta Schorr
Associate Professor of Mathematics
    Education
Rutgers University-Newark
Room 171, Bradley Hall
110 Warren Street
Newark, NJ 07102
schorr@rci.rutgers.edu

Luc Trouche
Professor
National Institute for Pedagogical
    Research
19 allée de Fontenay
BP 17424
69347 Lyon cedex 07
France
luc.trouche@inrp.fr

Patricia S. Wilson
Professor
University of Georgia
Department of Mathematics and
    Science Education
105 Aderhold Hall
Athens, GA 30602
pswilson@uga.edu
Institute of Education
University of London
dpratt@ioe.ac.uk

Julie Sarama
Associate Professor
University at Buffalo
State University of New York
Department of Learning and
    Instruction
Graduate School of Education
593 Baldy Hall, Buffalo, NY 14260
jsarama@buffalo.edu

David Smith
Associate Professor Emeritus
Duke University
1408 Shepherd Street
Durham, NC 27707
das@math.duke.edu

Rudolf Sträßer
Professor
Justus Liebig University
Karl-Gloeckner-Str. 21 C
D- 35394 Giessen
Germany
Rudolf.Straesser@math.uni-giessen.de

David Tall
Emeritus Professor in Mathematical
    Thinking
Institute of Education
University of Warwick
Coventry, CV4 7AL UK
david.tall@warwick.ac.uk

Nicola J. Yelland
Professor of Education
Victoria University
School of Education
Ballarat Road, Footscray 3011
Victoria, Australia
nicola.yelland@vu.edu.au

Rose Mary Zbiek
Associate Professor
The Pennsylvania State University
272 Chambers Building
University Park, PA 16802-3205
rmz101@psu.edu

Amelia

Henry Fielding

CONTENTS
INTRODUCTION.
DEDICATION.

AMELIA.

1

2

INTRODUCTION.

Fielding's third great novel has been the subject of much more discordant judgments than either of its forerunners. If we take the period since its appearance as covering four generations, we find the greatest authority in the earliest, Johnson, speaking of it with something more nearly approaching to enthusiasm than he allowed himself in reference to any other work of an author, to whom he was on the whole so unjust. The greatest man of letters of the next generation, Scott (whose attitude to Fielding was rather undecided, and seems to speak a mixture of intellectual admiration and moral dislike, or at least failure in sympathy), pronounces it "on the whole unpleasing," and regards it chiefly as a sequel to Tom Jones, showing what is to be expected of a libertine and thoughtless husband. But he too is enthusiastic over the heroine. Thackeray (whom in this special connection at any rate it is scarcely too much to call the greatest man of the third generation) overflows with predilection for it, but chiefly, as it would seem, because of his affection for Amelia herself, in which he practically agrees with Scott and Johnson. It would be invidious, and is noways needful, to single out any critic of our own time to place beside these great men. But it cannot be denied that the book, now as always, has incurred a considerable amount of hinted fault and hesitated dislike. Even Mr. Dobson notes some things in it as "unsatisfactory;" Mr. Gosse, with evident consciousness of temerity, ventures to ask whether it is not "a little dull." The very absence of episodes (on the ground that Miss Matthews's story is too closely connected with the main action to be fairly called an episode) and of introductory dissertations has been brought against it, as the presence of these things was brought against its forerunners.

I have sometimes wondered whether Amelia pays the penalty of an audacity which, a priori, its most unfavourable critics would indignantly deny to be a fault. It begins instead of ending with the marriage-bells; and though critic after critic of novels has exhausted his indignation and his satire over the folly of insisting on these as a finale, I doubt whether the demand is not too deeply rooted in the English, nay, in the human mind, to be safely neglected. The essence of all romance is a quest; the quest most perennially and universally interesting to man is the quest of a wife or a mistress; and the chapters dealing with what comes later have an inevitable flavour of tameness, and of the day after the feast. It is not common now-a-days to meet anybody who thinks Tommy Moore a great poet; one has to encounter either a suspicion of Philistinism or a suspicion of paradox if one tries to vindicate for him even his due place in the poetical hierarchy. Yet I suspect that no poet ever put into words a more universal criticism of life than he did when he wrote "I saw from the beach," with its moral of—

"Give me back, give me back, the wild freshness of morning—Her smiles and her tears are worth evening's best light."

If we discard this fallacy boldly, and ask ourselves whether Amelia is or is not as good as Joseph Andrews or Tom Jones, we shall I think be inclined to answer rather in the affirmative than in the negative. It is perhaps a little more easy to find fault with its characters than with theirs; or rather, though no one of these characters has the defects of Blifil or of Allworthy, it is easy to say that no one of them has the charm of the best personages of the earlier books. The idolaters of Amelia would of course exclaim at this sentence as it regards that amiable lady; and I am myself by no means disposed to rank amiability low in the scale of things excellent in woman. But though she is by no means what her namesake and spiritual grand-daughter. Miss Sedley, must, I fear, be pronounced to be, an amiable fool, there is really too much of the milk of human kindness, unrefreshed and unrelieved of its mawkishness by the rum or whisky of human frailty, in her. One could have better pardoned her forgiveness of her husband if she had in the first place been a little more conscious of what there was to forgive; and in the second, a little more romantic in her attachment to him. As it is, he was son homme; he was handsome; he had broad shoulders; he had a sweet temper; he was the father of her children, and that was enough. At least we are allowed to see in Mr. Booth no qualities other than these, and in her no imagination even of any other qualities. To put what I mean out of reach of cavil, compare Imogen and Amelia, and the difference will be felt.

But Fielding was a prose writer, writing in London in the eighteenth century, while Shakespeare was a poet writing in all time and all space, so that the comparison is luminous in

4

more ways than one. I do not think that in the special scheme which the novelist set himself here he can be accused of any failure. The life is as vivid as ever; the minor sketches may be even called a little more vivid. Dr Harrison is not perfect. I do not mean that he has ethical faults, for that is a merit, not a defect; but he is not quite perfect in art. His alternate persecution and patronage of Booth, though useful to the story, repeat the earlier fault of Allworthy, and are something of a blot. But he is individually much more natural than Allworthy, and indeed is something like what Dr Johnson would have been if he had been rather better bred, less crotchety, and blessed with more health. Miss Matthews in her earlier scenes has touches of greatness which a thousand French novelists lavishing "candour" and reckless of exaggeration have not equalled; and I believe that Fielding kept her at a distance during the later scenes of the story, because he could not trust himself not to make her more interesting than Amelia. Of the peers, more wicked and less wicked, there is indeed not much good to be said. The peer of the eighteenth-century writers (even when, as in Fielding's case, there was no reason why they should "mention him with Kor," as Policeman X. has it) is almost always a faint type of goodness or wickedness dressed out with stars and ribbons and coaches-and-six. Only Swift, by combination of experience and genius, has given us live lords in Lord Sparkish and Lord Smart. But Mrs. Ellison and Mrs. Atkinson are very women, and the serjeant, though the touch of "sensibility" is on him, is excellent; and Dr Harrison's country friend and his prig of a son are capital; and Bondum, and "the author," and Robinson, and all the minor characters, are as good as they can be.

It is, however, usual to detect a lack of vivacity in the book, an evidence of declining health and years. It may be so; it is at least certain that Fielding, during the composition of Amelia, had much less time to bestow upon elaborating his work than he had previously had, and that his health was breaking. But are we perfectly sure that if the chronological order had been different we should have pronounced the same verdict? Had Amelia come between Joseph and Tom, how many of us might have committed ourselves to some such sentence as this: "In Amelia we see the youthful exuberances of Joseph Andrews corrected by a higher art; the adjustment of plot and character arranged with a fuller craftsmanship; the genius which was to find its fullest exemplification in Tom Jones already displaying maturity"? And do we not too often forget that a very short time—in fact, barely three years—passed between the appearance of Tom Jones and the appearance of Amelia? that although we do not know how long the earlier work had been in preparation, it is extremely improbable that a man of Fielding's temperament, of his wants, of his known habits and history, would have kept it when once finished long in his desk? and that consequently between some scenes of Tom Jones and some scenes of Amelia it is not improbable that there was no more than a few months' interval? I do not urge these things in mitigation of any unfavourable judgment against the later novel. I only ask—How much of that unfavourable judgment ought in justice to be set down to the fallacies connected with an imperfect appreciation of facts?

To me it is not so much a question of deciding whether I like Amelia less, and if so, how much less, than the others, as a question what part of the general conception of this great writer it supplies? I do not think that we could fully understand Fielding without it; I do not think that we could derive the full quantity of pleasure from him without it. The exuberant romantic faculty of Joseph Andrews and its pleasant satire; the mighty craftsmanship and the vast science of life of Tom Jones; the ineffable irony and logical grasp of Jonathan Wild, might have left us with a slight sense of hardness, a vague desire for unction, if it had not been for this completion of the picture. We should not have known (for in the other books, with the possible exception of Mrs. Fitzpatrick, the characters are a little too determinately goats and sheep) how Fielding could draw nuances, how he could project a mixed personage on the screen, if we had not had Miss Matthews and Mrs. Atkinson—the last especially a figure full of the finest strokes, and, as a rule, insufficiently done justice to by critics.

And I have purposely left to the last a group of personages about whom indeed there has been little question, but who are among the triumphs of Fielding's art—the two Colonels and their connecting-link, the wife of the one and the sister of the other. Colonel Bath has necessarily united all suffrages. He is of course a very little stagey; he reminds us that his author had had a long theatrical apprenticeship: he is something too much d'une pièce. But as a study of the brave man who is almost more braggart than brave, of the generous man who will sacrifice not only generosity but bare justice to "a hogo of honour," he is admirable, and up to his time almost

unique. Ordinary writers and ordinary readers have never been quite content to admit that bravery and braggadocio can go together, that the man of honour may be a selfish pedant. People have been unwilling to tell and to hear the whole truth even about Wolfe and Nelson, who were both favourable specimens of the type; but Fielding the infallible saw that type in its quiddity, and knew it, and registered it for ever.

Less amusing but more delicately faithful and true are Colonel James and his wife. They are both very good sort of people in a way, who live in a lax and frivolous age, who have plenty of money, no particular principle, no strong affection for each other, and little individual character. They might have been—Mrs. James to some extent is—quite estimable and harmless; but even as it is, they are not to be wholly ill spoken of. Being what they are, Fielding has taken them, and, with a relentlessness which Swift could hardly have exceeded, and a good-nature which Swift rarely or never attained, has held them up to us as dissected preparations of half-innocent meanness, scoundrelism, and vanity, such as are hardly anywhere else to be found. I have used the word "preparations," and it in part indicates Fielding's virtue, a virtue shown, I think, in this book as much as anywhere. But it does not fully indicate it; for the preparation, wet or dry, is a dead thing, and a museum is but a mortuary. Fielding's men and women, once more let it be said, are all alive. The palace of his work is the hall, not of Eblis, but of a quite beneficent enchanter, who puts burning hearts into his subjects, not to torture them, but only that they may light up for us their whole organisation and being. They are not in the least the worse for it, and we are infinitely the better.

{Illustration.}
{Illustration.}

DEDICATION.
To RALPH ALLEN, ESQ.

SIR,—The following book is sincerely designed to promote the cause of virtue, and to expose some of the most glaring evils, as well public as private, which at present infest the country; though there is scarce, as I remember, a single stroke of satire aimed at any one person throughout the whole.

The best man is the properest patron of such an attempt. This, I believe, will be readily granted; nor will the public voice, I think, be more divided to whom they shall give that appellation. Should a letter, indeed, be thus inscribed, DETUR OPTIMO, there are few persons who would think it wanted any other direction.

I will not trouble you with a preface concerning the work, nor endeavour to obviate any criticisms which can be made on it. The good-natured reader, if his heart should be here affected, will be inclined to pardon many faults for the pleasure he will receive from a tender sensation: and for readers of a different stamp, the more faults they can discover, the more, I am convinced, they will be pleased.

Nor will I assume the fulsome stile of common dedicators. I have not their usual design in this epistle, nor will I borrow their language. Long, very long may it be before a most dreadful circumstance shall make it possible for any pen to draw a just and true character of yourself without incurring a suspicion of flattery in the bosoms of the malignant. This task, therefore, I shall defer till that day (if I should be so unfortunate as ever to see it) when every good man shall pay a tear for the satisfaction of his curiosity; a day which, at present, I believe, there is but one good man in the world who can think of it with unconcern.

Accept then, sir, this small token of that love, that gratitude, and that respect, with which I shall always esteem it my GREATEST HONOUR to be,

Sir, Your most obliged, and most obedient humble servant,
HENRY FIELDING.
Bow Street, Dec. 2, 1751.

{Illustration.}

AMELIA.

VOL. I

BOOK I.

Chapter i. — Containing the exordium, &c.

The various accidents which befel a very worthy couple after their uniting in the state of matrimony will be the subject of the following history. The distresses which they waded through were some of them so exquisite, and the incidents which produced these so extraordinary, that they seemed to require not only the utmost malice, but the utmost invention, which superstition hath ever attributed to Fortune: though whether any such being interfered in the case, or, indeed, whether there be any such being in the universe, is a matter which I by no means presume to determine in the affirmative. To speak a bold truth, I am, after much mature deliberation, inclined to suspect that the public voice hath, in all ages, done much injustice to Fortune, and hath convicted her of many facts in which she had not the least concern. I question much whether we may not, by natural means, account for the success of knaves, the calamities of fools, with all the miseries in which men of sense sometimes involve themselves, by quitting the directions of Prudence, and following the blind guidance of a predominant passion; in short, for all the ordinary phenomena which are imputed to Fortune; whom, perhaps, men accuse with no less absurdity in life, than a bad player complains of ill luck at the game of chess.

But if men are sometimes guilty of laying improper blame on this imaginary being, they are altogether as apt to make her amends by ascribing to her honours which she as little deserves. To retrieve the ill consequences of a foolish conduct, and by struggling manfully with distress to subdue it, is one of the noblest efforts of wisdom and virtue. Whoever, therefore, calls such a man fortunate, is guilty of no less impropriety in speech than he would be who should call the statuary or the poet fortunate who carved a Venus or who writ an Iliad.

Life may as properly be called an art as any other; and the great incidents in it are no more to be considered as mere accidents than the several members of a fine statue or a noble poem. The critics in all these are not content with seeing anything to be great without knowing why and how it came to be so. By examining carefully the several gradations which conduce to bring every model to perfection, we learn truly to know that science in which the model is formed: as histories of this kind, therefore, may properly be called models of human life, so, by observing minutely the several incidents which tend to the catastrophe or completion of the whole, and the minute causes

7

whence those incidents are produced, we shall best be instructed in this most useful of all arts, which I call the art of life.

Chapter ii. — The history sets out. Observations on the excellency of the English constitution and curious examinations before a justice of peace.

On the first of April, in the year ——, the watchmen of a certain parish (I know not particularly which) within the liberty of Westminster brought several persons whom they had apprehended the preceding night before Jonathan Thrasher, Esq., one of the justices of the peace for that liberty.

But here, reader, before we proceed to the trials of these offenders, we shall, after our usual manner, premise some things which it may be necessary for thee to know.

It hath been observed, I think, by many, as well as the celebrated writer of three letters, that no human institution is capable of consummate perfection. An observation which, perhaps, that writer at least gathered from discovering some defects in the polity even of this well-regulated nation. And, indeed, if there should be any such defect in a constitution which my Lord Coke long ago told us "the wisdom of all the wise men in the world, if they had all met together at one time, could not have equalled," which some of our wisest men who were met together long before said was too good to be altered in any particular, and which, nevertheless, hath been mending ever since, by a very great number of the said wise men: if, I say, this constitution should be imperfect, we may be allowed, I think, to doubt whether any such faultless model can be found among the institutions of men.

It will probably be objected, that the small imperfections which I am about to produce do not lie in the laws themselves, but in the ill execution of them; but, with submission, this appears to me to be no less an absurdity than to say of any machine that it is excellently made, though incapable of performing its functions. Good laws should execute themselves in a well-regulated state; at least, if the same legislature which provides the laws doth not provide for the execution of them, they act as Graham would do, if he should form all the parts of a clock in the most exquisite manner, yet put them so together that the clock could not go. In this case, surely, we might say that there was a small defect in the constitution of the clock.

To say the truth, Graham would soon see the fault, and would easily remedy it. The fault, indeed, could be no other than that the parts were improperly disposed.

Perhaps, reader, I have another illustration which will set my intention in still a clearer light before you. Figure to yourself then a family, the master of which should dispose of the several economical offices in the following manner; viz. should put his butler in the coach-box, his steward behind his coach, his coachman in the butlery, and his footman in the stewardship, and in the same ridiculous manner should misemploy the talents of every other servant; it is easy to see what a figure such a family must make in the world.

As ridiculous as this may seem, I have often considered some of the lower officers in our civil government to be disposed in this very manner. To begin, I think, as low as I well can, with the watchmen in our metropolis, who, being to guard our streets by night from thieves and robbers, an office which at least requires strength of body, are chosen out of those poor old decrepit people who are, from their want of bodily strength, rendered incapable of getting a livelihood by work. These men, armed only with a pole, which some of them are scarce able to lift, are to secure the persons and houses of his majesty's subjects from the attacks of gangs of young, bold, stout, desperate, and well-armed villains.

Quae non viribus istis
Munera conveniunt.

If the poor old fellows should run away from such enemies, no one I think can wonder, unless it be that they were able to make their escape.

The higher we proceed among our public officers and magistrates, the less defects of this kind will, perhaps, be observable. Mr. Thrasher, however, the justice before whom the prisoners

above mentioned were now brought, had some few imperfections in his magistratical capacity. I own, I have been sometimes inclined to think that this office of a justice of peace requires some knowledge of the law: for this simple reason; because, in every case which comes before him, he is to judge and act according to law. Again, as these laws are contained in a great variety of books, the statutes which relate to the office of a justice of peace making of themselves at least two large volumes in folio; and that part of his jurisdiction which is founded on the common law being dispersed in above a hundred volumes, I cannot conceive how this knowledge should by acquired without reading; and yet certain it is, Mr. Thrasher never read one syllable of the matter.

This, perhaps, was a defect; but this was not all: for where mere ignorance is to decide a point between two litigants, it will always be an even chance whether it decides right or wrong: but sorry am I to say, right was often in a much worse situation than this, and wrong hath often had five hundred to one on his side before that magistrate; who, if he was ignorant of the law of England, was yet well versed in the laws of nature. He perfectly well understood that fundamental principle so strongly laid down in the institutes of the learned Rochefoucault, by which the duty of self-love is so strongly enforced, and every man is taught to consider himself as the centre of gravity, and to attract all things thither. To speak the truth plainly, the justice was never indifferent in a cause but when he could get nothing on either side.

Such was the justice to whose tremendous bar Mr. Gotobed the constable, on the day above mentioned, brought several delinquents, who, as we have said, had been apprehended by the watch for diverse outrages.

The first who came upon his trial was as bloody a spectre as ever the imagination of a murderer or a tragic poet conceived. This poor wretch was charged with a battery by a much stouter man than himself; indeed the accused person bore about him some evidence that he had been in an affray, his cloaths being very bloody, but certain open sluices on his own head sufficiently shewed whence all the scarlet stream had issued: whereas the accuser had not the least mark or appearance of any wound. The justice asked the defendant, What he meant by breaking the king's peace?——To which he answered——"Upon my shoul I do love the king very well, and I have not been after breaking anything of his that I do know; but upon my shoul this man hath brake my head, and my head did brake his stick; that is all, gra." He then offered to produce several witnesses against this improbable accusation; but the justice presently interrupted him, saying, "Sirrah, your tongue betrays your guilt. You are an Irishman, and that is always sufficient evidence with me."

The second criminal was a poor woman, who was taken up by the watch as a street-walker. It was alleged against her that she was found walking the streets after twelve o'clock, and the watchman declared he believed her to be a common strumpet. She pleaded in her defence (as was really the truth) that she was a servant, and was sent by her mistress, who was a little shopkeeper and upon the point of delivery, to fetch a midwife; which she offered to prove by several of the neighbours, if she was allowed to send for them. The justice asked her why she had not done it before? to which she answered, she had no money, and could get no messenger. The justice then called her several scurrilous names, and, declaring she was guilty within the statute of street-walking, ordered her to Bridewell for a month.

A genteel young man and woman were then set forward, and a very grave-looking person swore he caught them in a situation which we cannot as particularly describe here as he did before the magistrate; who, having received a wink from his clerk, declared with much warmth that the fact was incredible and impossible. He presently discharged the accused parties, and was going, without any evidence, to commit the accuser for perjury; but this the clerk dissuaded him from, saying he doubted whether a justice of peace had any such power. The justice at first differed in opinion, and said, "He had seen a man stand in the pillory about perjury; nay, he had known a man in gaol for it too; and how came he there if he was not committed thither?" "Why, that is true, sir," answered the clerk; "and yet I have been told by a very great lawyer that a man cannot be committed for perjury before he is indicted; and the reason is, I believe, because it is not against the peace before the indictment makes it so." "Why, that may be," cries the justice, "and indeed perjury is but scandalous words, and I know a man cannot have no warrant for those, unless you put for rioting {Footnote: Opus est interprete. By the laws of England abusive words are not punishable by the magistrate; some commissioners of the peace, therefore, when one scold hath applied to them for a warrant against another, from a too eager desire of doing justice, have

9

construed a little harmless scolding into a riot, which is in law an outrageous breach of the peace committed by several persons, by three at the least, nor can a less number be convicted of it. Under this word rioting, or riotting (for I have seen it spelt both ways), many thousands of old women have been arrested and put to expense, sometimes in prison, for a little intemperate use of their tongues. This practice began to decrease in the year 1749.} them into the warrant."

The witness was now about to be discharged, when the lady whom he had accused declared she would swear the peace against him, for that he had called her a whore several times. "Oho! you will swear the peace, madam, will you?" cries the justice: "Give her the peace, presently; and pray, Mr. Constable, secure the prisoner, now we have him, while a warrant is made to take him up." All which was immediately performed, and the poor witness, for want of securities, was sent to prison.

A young fellow, whose name was Booth, was now charged with beating the watchman in the execution of his office and breaking his lanthorn. This was deposed by two witnesses; and the shattered remains of a broken lanthorn, which had been long preserved for the sake of its testimony, were produced to corroborate the evidence. The justice, perceiving the criminal to be but shabbily drest, was going to commit him without asking any further questions. At length, however, at the earnest request of the accused, the worthy magistrate submitted to hear his defence. The young man then alledged, as was in reality the case, "That as he was walking home to his lodging he saw two men in the street cruelly beating a third, upon which he had stopt and endeavoured to assist the person who was so unequally attacked; that the watch came up during the affray, and took them all four into custody; that they were immediately carried to the round-house, where the two original assailants, who appeared to be men of fortune, found means to make up the matter, and were discharged by the constable, a favour which he himself, having no money in his pocket, was unable to obtain. He utterly denied having assaulted any of the watchmen, and solemnly declared that he was offered his liberty at the price of half a crown."

Though the bare word of an offender can never be taken against the oath of his accuser, yet the matter of this defence was so pertinent, and delivered with such an air of truth and sincerity, that, had the magistrate been endued with much sagacity, or had he been very moderately gifted with another quality very necessary to all who are to administer justice, he would have employed some labour in cross-examining the watchmen; at least he would have given the defendant the time he desired to send for the other persons who were present at the affray; neither of which he did. In short, the magistrate had too great an honour for truth to suspect that she ever appeared in sordid apparel; nor did he ever sully his sublime notions of that virtue by uniting them with the mean ideas of poverty and distress.

There remained now only one prisoner, and that was the poor man himself in whose defence the last-mentioned culprit was engaged. His trial took but a very short time. A cause of battery and broken lanthorn was instituted against him, and proved in the same manner; nor would the justice hear one word in defence; but, though his patience was exhausted, his breath was not; for against this last wretch he poured forth a great many volleys of menaces and abuse.

The delinquents were then all dispatched to prison under a guard of watchmen, and the justice and the constable adjourned to a neighbouring alehouse to take their morning repast.

Chapter iii. — Containing the inside of a prison.

Mr. Booth (for we shall not trouble you with the rest) was no sooner arrived in the prison than a number of persons gathered round him, all demanding garnish; to which Mr. Booth not making a ready answer, as indeed he did not understand the word, some were going to lay hold of him, when a person of apparent dignity came up and insisted that no one should affront the gentleman. This person then, who was no less than the master or keeper of the prison, turning towards Mr. Booth, acquainted him that it was the custom of the place for every prisoner upon his first arrival there to give something to the former prisoners to make them drink. This, he said, was what they call garnish, and concluded with advising his new customer to draw his purse upon

the present occasion. Mr. Booth answered that he would very readily comply with this laudable custom, was it in his power; but that in reality he had not a shilling in his pocket, and, what was worse, he had not a shilling in the world.—"Oho! if that be the case," cries the keeper, "it is another matter, and I have nothing to say." Upon which he immediately departed, and left poor Booth to the mercy of his companions, who without loss of time applied themselves to uncasing, as they termed it, and with such dexterity, that his coat was not only stript off, but out of sight in a minute.

Mr. Booth was too weak to resist and too wise to complain of this usage. As soon, therefore, as he was at liberty, and declared free of the place, he summoned his philosophy, of which he had no inconsiderable share, to his assistance, and resolved to make himself as easy as possible under his present circumstances.

Could his own thoughts indeed have suffered him a moment to forget where he was, the dispositions of the other prisoners might have induced him to believe that he had been in a happier place: for much the greater part of his fellow-sufferers, instead of wailing and repining at their condition, were laughing, singing, and diverting themselves with various kinds of sports and gambols.

The first person who accosted him was called Blear-eyed Moll, a woman of no very comely appearance. Her eye (for she had but one), whence she derived her nickname, was such as that nickname bespoke; besides which, it had two remarkable qualities; for first, as if Nature had been careful to provide for her own defect, it constantly looked towards her blind side; and secondly, the ball consisted almost entirely of white, or rather yellow, with a little grey spot in the corner, so small that it was scarce discernible. Nose she had none; for Venus, envious perhaps at her former charms, had carried off the gristly part; and some earthly damsel, perhaps, from the same envy, had levelled the bone with the rest of her face: indeed it was far beneath the bones of her cheeks, which rose proportionally higher than is usual. About half a dozen ebony teeth fortified that large and long canal which nature had cut from ear to ear, at the bottom of which was a chin preposterously short, nature having turned up the bottom, instead of suffering it to grow to its due length.

Her body was well adapted to her face; she measured full as much round the middle as from head to foot; for, besides the extreme breadth of her back, her vast breasts had long since forsaken their native home, and had settled themselves a little below the girdle.

I wish certain actresses on the stage, when they are to perform characters of no amiable cast, would study to dress themselves with the propriety with which Blear-eyed Moll was now arrayed. For the sake of our squeamish reader, we shall not descend to particulars; let it suffice to say, nothing more ragged or more dirty was ever emptied out of the round-house at St Giles's.

We have taken the more pains to describe this person, for two remarkable reasons; the one is, that this unlovely creature was taken in the fact with a very pretty young fellow; the other, which is more productive of moral lesson, is, that however wretched her fortune may appear to the reader, she was one of the merriest persons in the whole prison.

Blear-eyed Moll then came up to Mr. Booth with a smile, or rather grin, on her countenance, and asked him for a dram of gin; and when Booth assured her that he had not a penny of money, she replied—"D—n your eyes, I thought by your look you had been a clever fellow, and upon the snaffling lay {Footnote: A cant term for robbery on the highway} at least; but, d—n your body and eyes, I find you are some sneaking budge {Footnote: Another cant term for pilfering} rascal." She then launched forth a volley of dreadful oaths, interlarded with some language not proper to be repeated here, and was going to lay hold on poor Booth, when a tall prisoner, who had been very earnestly eying Booth for some time, came up, and, taking her by the shoulder, flung her off at some distance, cursing her for a b—h, and bidding her let the gentleman alone.

This person was not himself of the most inviting aspect. He was long-visaged, and pale, with a red beard of above a fortnight's growth. He was attired in a brownish-black coat, which would have shewed more holes than it did, had not the linen, which appeared through it, been entirely of the same colour with the cloth.

This gentleman, whose name was Robinson, addressed himself very civilly to Mr. Booth, and told him he was sorry to see one of his appearance in that place: "For as to your being without your coat, sir," says he, "I can easily account for that; and, indeed, dress is the least part which distinguishes a gentleman." At which words he cast a significant look on his own coat, as if he

11

desired they should be applied to himself. He then proceeded in the following manner:

"I perceive, sir, you are but just arrived in this dismal place, which is, indeed, rendered more detestable by the wretches who inhabit it than by any other circumstance; but even these a wise man will soon bring himself to bear with indifference; for what is, is; and what must be, must be. The knowledge of this, which, simple as it appears, is in truth the heighth of all philosophy, renders a wise man superior to every evil which can befall him. I hope, sir, no very dreadful accident is the cause of your coming hither; but, whatever it was, you may be assured it could not be otherwise; for all things happen by an inevitable fatality; and a man can no more resist the impulse of fate than a wheelbarrow can the force of its driver."

Besides the obligation which Mr. Robinson had conferred on Mr. Booth in delivering him from the insults of Blear-eyed Moll, there was something in the manner of Robinson which, notwithstanding the meanness of his dress, seemed to distinguish him from the crowd of wretches who swarmed in those regions; and, above all, the sentiments which he had just declared very nearly coincided with those of Mr. Booth: this gentleman was what they call a freethinker; that is to say, a deist, or, perhaps, an atheist; for, though he did not absolutely deny the existence of a God, yet he entirely denied his providence. A doctrine which, if it is not downright atheism, hath a direct tendency towards it; and, as Dr Clarke observes, may soon be driven into it. And as to Mr. Booth, though he was in his heart an extreme well-wisher to religion (for he was an honest man), yet his notions of it were very slight and uncertain. To say truth, he was in the wavering condition so finely described by Claudian:

labefacta cadelat
Religio, causaeque—viam non sponte sequebar
Alterius; vacua quae currere semina motu
Affirmat; magnumque novas fer inane figures
Fortuna, non arte, regi; quae numina sensu
Ambiguo, vel nulla futat, vel nescia nostri. — This way of thinking, or rather of doubting, he had contracted from the same reasons which Claudian assigns, and which had induced Brutus in his latter days to doubt the existence

of that virtue which he had all his life cultivated. In short, poor Booth imagined that a larger share of misfortunes had fallen to his lot than he had merited; and this led

him, who (though a good classical scholar) was not deeply learned in religious matters, into a disadvantageous opinion of Providence. A dangerous way of reasoning, in which our

conclusions are not only too hasty, from an imperfect view of things, but we are likewise liable to much error from partiality to ourselves; viewing our virtues and vices as

through a perspective, in which we turn the glass always to our own advantage, so as to diminish the one, and as greatly to magnify the other.

From the above reasons, it can be no wonder that Mr. Booth did not decline the acquaintance of this person, in a place which could not promise to afford him any better. He answered him, therefore, with great courtesy, as indeed he was of a very good and gentle disposition, and, after expressing a civil surprize at meeting him there, declared himself to be of the same opinion with regard to the necessity of human actions; adding, however, that he did not believe men were under any blind impulse or direction of fate, but that every man acted merely from the force of that passion which was uppermost in his mind, and could do no otherwise.

A discourse now ensued between the two gentlemen on the necessity arising from the impulse of fate, and the necessity arising from the impulse of passion, which, as it will make a pretty pamphlet of itself, we shall reserve for some future opportunity. When this was ended they set forward to survey the gaol and the prisoners, with the several cases of whom Mr. Robinson, who had been some time under confinement, undertook to make Mr. Booth acquainted.

Chapter iv. — Disclosing further secrets of the prison-house.

The first persons whom they passed by were three men in fetters, who were enjoying

themselves very merrily over a bottle of wine and a pipe of tobacco. These, Mr. Robinson informed his friend, were three street-robbers, and were all certain of being hanged the ensuing sessions. So inconsiderable an object, said he, is misery to light minds, when it is at any distance.

A little farther they beheld a man prostrate on the ground, whose heavy groans and frantic actions plainly indicated the highest disorder of mind. This person was, it seems, committed for a small felony; and his wife, who then lay-in, upon hearing the news, had thrown herself from a window two pair of stairs high, by which means he had, in all probability, lost both her and his child.

A very pretty girl then advanced towards them, whose beauty Mr. Booth could not help admiring the moment he saw her; declaring, at the same time, he thought she had great innocence in her countenance. Robinson said she was committed thither as an idle and disorderly person, and a common street-walker. As she past by Mr. Booth, she damned his eyes, and discharged a volley of words, every one of which was too indecent to be repeated.

They now beheld a little creature sitting by herself in a corner, and crying bitterly. This girl, Mr. Robinson said, was committed because her father-in-law, who was in the grenadier guards, had sworn that he was afraid of his life, or of some bodily harm which she would do him, and she could get no sureties for keeping the peace; for which reason justice Thrasher had committed her to prison.

A great noise now arose, occasioned by the prisoners all flocking to see a fellow whipt for petty larceny, to which he was condemned by the court of quarter-sessions; but this soon ended in the disappointment of the spectators; for the fellow, after being stript, having advanced another sixpence, was discharged untouched.

This was immediately followed by another bustle; Blear-eyed Moll, and several of her companions, having got possession of a man who was committed for certain odious practices, not fit to be named, were giving him various kinds of discipline, and would probably have put an end to him, had he not been rescued out of their hands by authority.

When this bustle was a little allayed, Mr. Booth took notice of a young woman in rags sitting on the ground, and supporting the head of an old man in her lap, who appeared to be giving up the ghost. These, Mr. Robinson informed him, were father and daughter; that the latter was committed for stealing a loaf, in order to support the former, and the former for receiving it, knowing it to be stolen.

A well-drest man then walked surlily by them, whom Mr. Robinson reported to have been committed on an indictment found against him for a most horrid perjury; but, says he, we expect him to be bailed today. "Good Heaven!" cries Booth, "can such villains find bail, and is no person charitable enough to bail that poor father and daughter?" "Oh! sir," answered Robinson, "the offence of the daughter, being felony, is held not to be bailable in law; whereas perjury is a misdemeanor only; and therefore persons who are even indicted for it are, nevertheless, capable of being bailed. Nay, of all perjuries, that of which this man is indicted is the worst; for it was with an intention of taking away the life of an innocent person by form of law. As to perjuries in civil matters, they are not so very criminal." "They are not," said Booth, "and yet even there are a most flagitious offence, and worthy the highest punishment." "Surely they ought to be distinguished," answered Robinson, "from the others: for what is taking away a little property from a man, compared to taking away his life and his reputation, and ruining his family into the bargain?—I hope there can be no comparison in the crimes, and I think there ought to be none in the punishment. However, at present, the punishment of all perjury is only pillory and transportation for seven years; and, as it is a traversable and bailable offence, methods are found to escape any punishment at all." {Footnote: By removing the indictment by certiorari into the King's Bench, the trial is so long postponed, and the costs are so highly encreased, that prosecutors are often tired out, and some incapacitated from pursuing. Verbum sapienti.}

Booth exprest great astonishment at this, when his attention was suddenly diverted by the most miserable object that he had yet seen. This was a wretch almost naked, and who bore in his countenance, joined to an appearance of honesty, the marks of poverty, hunger, and disease. He had, moreover, a wooden leg, and two or three scars on his forehead. "The case of this poor man is, indeed, unhappy enough," said Robinson. "He hath served his country, lost his limb, and received several wounds at the siege of Gibraltar. When he was discharged from the hospital abroad he came over to get into that of Chelsea, but could not immediately, as none of his officers

were then in England. In the mean time, he was one day apprehended and committed hither on suspicion of stealing three herrings from a fishmonger. He was tried several months ago for this offence, and acquitted; indeed, his innocence manifestly appeared at the trial; but he was brought back again for his fees, and here he hath lain ever since."

Booth exprest great horror at this account, and declared, if he had only so much money in his pocket, he would pay his fees for him; but added that he was not possessed of a single farthing in the world.

Robinson hesitated a moment, and then said, with a smile, "I am going to make you, sir, a very odd proposal after your last declaration; but what say you to a game at cards? it will serve to pass a tedious hour, and may divert your thoughts from more unpleasant speculations."

I do not imagine Booth would have agreed to this; for, though some love of gaming had been formerly amongst his faults, yet he was not so egregiously addicted to that vice as to be tempted by the shabby plight of Robinson, who had, if I may so express myself, no charms for a gamester. If he had, however, any such inclinations, he had no opportunity to follow them, for, before he could make any answer to Robinson's proposal, a strapping wench came up to Booth, and, taking hold of his arm, asked him to walk aside with her, saying, "What a pox, are you such a fresh cull that you do not know this fellow? why, he is a gambler, and committed for cheating at play. There is not such a pickpocket in the whole quad."{footnote: A cant word for a prison.}

A scene of altercation now ensued between Robinson and the lady, which ended in a bout at fisticuffs, in which the lady was greatly superior to the philosopher.

While the two combatants were engaged, a grave-looking man, rather better drest than the majority of the company, came up to Mr. Booth, and, taking him aside, said, "I am sorry, sir, to see a gentleman, as you appear to be, in such intimacy with that rascal, who makes no scruple of disowning all revealed religion. As for crimes, they are human errors, and signify but little; nay, perhaps the worse a man is by nature, the more room there is for grace. The spirit is active, and loves best to inhabit those minds where it may meet with the most work. Whatever your crime be, therefore I would not have you despair, but rather rejoice at it; for perhaps it may be the means of your being called." He ran on for a considerable time with this cant, without waiting for an answer, and ended in declaring himself a methodist.

Just as the methodist had finished his discourse, a beautiful young woman was ushered into the gaol. She was genteel and well drest, and did not in the least resemble those females whom Mr. Booth had hitherto seen. The constable had no sooner delivered her at the gate than she asked with a commanding voice for the keeper; and, when he arrived, she said to him, "Well, sir, whither am I to be conducted? I hope I am not to take up my lodging with these creatures." The keeper answered, with a kind of surly respect, "Madam, we have rooms for those who can afford to pay for them." At these words she pulled a handsome purse from her pocket, in which many guineas chinked, saying, with an air of indignation, "That she was not come thither on account of poverty." The keeper no sooner viewed the purse than his features became all softened in an instant; and, with all the courtesy of which he was master, he desired the lady to walk with him, assuring her that she should have the best apartment in his house.

Mr. Booth was now left alone; for the methodist had forsaken him, having, as the phrase of the sect is, searched him to the bottom. In fact, he had thoroughly examined every one of Mr. Booth's pockets; from which he had conveyed away a penknife and an iron snuff-box, these being all the moveables which were to be found.

Booth was standing near the gate of the prison when the young lady above mentioned was introduced into the yard. He viewed her features very attentively, and was persuaded that he knew her. She was indeed so remarkably handsome, that it was hardly possible for any who had ever seen her to forget her. He enquired of one of the underkeepers if the name of the prisoner lately arrived was not Matthews; to which he was answered that her name was not Matthews but Vincent, and that she was committed for murder.

The latter part of this information made Mr. Booth suspect his memory more than the former; for it was very possible that she might have changed her name; but he hardly thought she could so far have changed her nature as to be guilty of a crime so very incongruous with her former gentle manners: for Miss Matthews had both the birth and education of a gentlewoman. He concluded, therefore, that he was certainly mistaken, and rested satisfied without any further enquiry.

Chapter v. — Containing certain adventures which befel Mr. Booth in the prison.

The remainder of the day Mr. Booth spent in melancholy contemplation on his present condition. He was destitute of the common necessaries of life, and consequently unable to subsist where he was; nor was there a single person in town to whom he could, with any reasonable hope, apply for his delivery. Grief for some time banished the thoughts of food from his mind; but in the morning nature began to grow uneasy for want of her usual nourishment: for he had not eat a morsel during the last forty hours. A penny loaf, which is, it seems, the ordinary allowance to the prisoners in Bridewell, was now delivered him; and while he was eating this a man brought him a little packet sealed up, informing him that it came by a messenger, who said it required no answer.

Mr. Booth now opened his packet, and, after unfolding several pieces of blank paper successively, at last discovered a guinea, wrapt with great care in the inmost paper. He was vastly surprized at this sight, as he had few if any friends from whom he could expect such a favour, slight as it was; and not one of his friends, as he was apprized, knew of his confinement. As there was no direction to the packet, nor a word of writing contained in it, he began to suspect that it was delivered to the wrong person; and being one of the most untainted honesty, he found out the man who gave it him, and again examined him concerning the person who brought it, and the message delivered with it. The man assured Booth that he had made no mistake; saying, "If your name is Booth, sir, I am positive you are the gentleman to whom the parcel I gave you belongs."

The most scrupulous honesty would, perhaps, in such a situation, have been well enough satisfied in finding no owner for the guinea; especially when proclamation had been made in the prison that Mr. Booth had received a packet without any direction, to which, if any person had any claim, and would discover the contents, he was ready to deliver it to such claimant. No such claimant being found (I mean none who knew the contents; for many swore that they expected just such a packet, and believed it to be their property), Mr. Booth very calmly resolved to apply the money to his own use.

The first thing after redemption of the coat, which Mr. Booth, hungry as he was, thought of, was to supply himself with snuff, which he had long, to his great sorrow, been without. On this occasion he presently missed that iron box which the methodist had so dexterously conveyed out of his pocket, as we mentioned in the last chapter.

He no sooner missed this box than he immediately suspected that the gambler was the person who had stolen it; nay, so well was he assured of this man's guilt, that it may, perhaps, be improper to say he barely suspected it. Though Mr. Booth was, as we have hinted, a man of a very sweet disposition, yet was he rather overwarm. Having, therefore, no doubt concerning the person of the thief, he eagerly sought him out, and very bluntly charged him with the fact.

The gambler, whom I think we should now call the philosopher, received this charge without the least visible emotion either of mind or muscle. After a short pause of a few moments, he answered, with great solemnity, as follows: "Young man, I am entirely unconcerned at your groundless suspicion. He that censures a stranger, as I am to you, without any cause, makes a worse compliment to himself than to the stranger. You know yourself, friend; you know not me. It is true, indeed, you heard me accused of being a cheat and a gamester; but who is my accuser? Look at my apparel, friend; do thieves and gamesters wear such cloaths as these? play is my folly, not my vice; it is my impulse, and I have been a martyr to it. Would a gamester have asked another to play when he could have lost eighteen-pence and won nothing? However, if you are not satisfied, you may search my pockets; the outside of all but one will serve your turn, and in that one there is the eighteen-pence I told you of." He then turned up his cloaths; and his pockets entirely resembled the pitchers of the Belides.

Booth was a little staggered at this defence. He said the real value of the iron box was too inconsiderable to mention; but that he had a capricious value for it, for the sake of the person who gave it him; "for, though it is not," said he, "worth sixpence, I would willingly give a crown to any one who would bring it me again."

15

Robinson answered, "If that be the case, you have nothing more to do but to signify your intention in the prison, and I am well convinced you will not be long without regaining the possession of your snuff-box."

This advice was immediately followed, and with success, the methodist presently producing the box, which, he said, he had found, and should have returned it before, had he known the person to whom it belonged; adding, with uplifted eyes, that the spirit would not suffer him knowingly to detain the goods of another, however inconsiderable the value was. "Why so, friend?" said Robinson. "Have I not heard you often say, the wickeder any man was the better, provided he was what you call a believer?" "You mistake me," cries Cooper (for that was the name of the methodist): "no man can be wicked after he is possessed by the spirit. There is a wide difference between the days of sin and the days of grace. I have been a sinner myself." "I believe thee," cries Robinson, with a sneer. "I care not," answered the other, "what an atheist believes. I suppose you would insinuate that I stole the snuff-box; but I value not your malice; the Lord knows my innocence." He then walked off with the reward; and Booth, turning to Robinson, very earnestly asked pardon for his groundless suspicion; which the other, without any hesitation, accorded him, saying, "You never accused me, sir; you suspected some gambler, with whose character I have no concern. I should be angry with a friend or acquaintance who should give a hasty credit to any allegation against me; but I have no reason to be offended with you for believing what the woman, and the rascal who is just gone, and who is committed here for a pickpocket, which you did not perhaps know, told you to my disadvantage. And if you thought me to be a gambler you had just reason to suspect any ill of me; for I myself am confined here by the perjury of one of those villains, who, having cheated me of my money at play, and hearing that I intended to apply to a magistrate against him, himself began the attack, and obtained a warrant against me of Justice Thrasher, who, without hearing one speech in my defence, committed me to this place."

Booth testified great compassion at this account; and, he having invited Robinson to dinner, they spent that day together. In the afternoon Booth indulged his friend with a game at cards; at first for halfpence and afterwards for shillings, when fortune so favoured Robinson that he did not leave the other a single shilling in his pocket.

A surprizing run of luck in a gamester is often mistaken for somewhat else by persons who are not over-zealous believers in the divinity of fortune. I have known a stranger at Bath, who hath happened fortunately (I might almost say unfortunately) to have four by honours in his hand almost every time he dealt for a whole evening, shunned universally by the whole company the next day. And certain it is, that Mr. Booth, though of a temper very little inclined to suspicion, began to waver in his opinion whether the character given by Mr. Robinson of himself, or that which the others gave of him, was the truer.

In the morning hunger paid him a second visit, and found him again in the same situation as before. After some deliberation, therefore, he resolved to ask Robinson to lend him a shilling or two of that money which was lately his own. And this experiments he thought, would confirm him either in a good or evil opinion of that gentleman.

To this demand Robinson answered, with great alacrity, that he should very gladly have complied, had not fortune played one of her jade tricks with him: "for since my winning of you," said he, "I have been stript not only of your money but my own." He was going to harangue farther; but Booth, with great indignation, turned from him.

This poor gentleman had very little time to reflect on his own misery, or the rascality, as it appeared to him, of the other, when the same person who had the day before delivered him the guinea from the unknown hand, again accosted him, and told him a lady in the house (so he expressed himself) desired the favour of his company.

Mr. Booth immediately obeyed the message, and was conducted into a room in the prison, where he was presently convinced that Mrs. Vincent was no other than his old acquaintance Miss Matthews.

Chapter vi. — Containing the extraordinary behaviour of Miss Matthews on her meeting with Booth, and some endeavours to prove, by reason and authority, that it is possible for a woman to appear to be what she really is not.

Eight or nine years had past since any interview between Mr. Booth and Miss Matthews; and their meeting now in so extraordinary a place affected both of them with an equal surprize.

After some immaterial ceremonies, the lady acquainted Mr. Booth that, having heard there was a person in the prison who knew her by the name of Matthews, she had great curiosity to inquire who he was, whereupon he had been shewn to her from the window of the house; that she immediately recollected him, and, being informed of his distressful situation, for which she expressed great concern, she had sent him that guinea which he had received the day before; and then proceeded to excuse herself for not having desired to see him at that time, when she was under the greatest disorder and hurry of spirits.

Booth made many handsome acknowledgments of her favour; and added that he very little wondered at the disorder of her spirits, concluding that he was heartily concerned at seeing her there; "but I hope, madam," said he—

Here he hesitated; upon which, bursting into an agony of tears, she cried out, "O captain! captain! many extraordinary things have passed since last I saw you. O gracious heaven! did I ever expect that this would be the next place of our meeting?"

She then flung herself into her chair, where she gave a loose to her passion, whilst he, in the most affectionate and tender manner, endeavoured to soothe and comfort her; but passion itself did probably more for its own relief than all his friendly consolations. Having vented this in a large flood of tears, she became pretty well composed; but Booth unhappily mentioning her father, she again relapsed into an agony, and cried out, "Why? why will you repeat the name of that dear man? I have disgraced him, Mr. Booth, I am unworthy the name of his daughter."— Here passion again stopped her words, and discharged itself in tears.

After this second vent of sorrow or shame, or, if the reader pleases, of rage, she once more recovered from her agonies. To say the truth, these are, I believe, as critical discharges of nature as any of those which are so called by the physicians, and do more effectually relieve the mind than any remedies with which the whole materia medica of philosophy can supply it.

When Mrs. Vincent had recovered her faculties, she perceived Booth standing silent, with a mixture of concern and astonishment in his countenance; then addressing herself to him with an air of most bewitching softness, of which she was a perfect mistress, she said, "I do not wonder at your amazement, Captain Booth, nor indeed at the concern which you so plainly discover for me; for I well know the goodness of your nature: but, O, Mr. Booth! believe me, when you know what hath happened since our last meeting, your concern will be raised, however your astonishment may cease. O, sir! you are a stranger to the cause of my sorrows."

"I hope I am, madam," answered he; "for I cannot believe what I have heard in the prison— surely murder"—at which words she started from her chair, repeating, "Murder! oh! it is music in my ears!—You have heard then the cause of my commitment, my glory, my delight, my reparation! Yes, my old friend, this is the hand, this is the arm that drove the penknife to his heart. Unkind fortune, that not one drop of his blood reached my hand.—Indeed, sir, I would never have washed it from it.—But, though I have not the happiness to see it on my hand, I have the glorious satisfaction of remembering I saw it run in rivers on the floor; I saw it forsake his cheeks, I saw him fall a martyr to my revenge. And is the killing a villain to be called murder? perhaps the law calls it so.—Let it call it what it will, or punish me as it pleases.—Punish me!—no, no—that is not in the power of man—not of that monster man, Mr. Booth. I am undone, am revenged, and have now no more business for life; let them take it from me when they will."

Our poor gentleman turned pale with horror at this speech, and the ejaculation of "Good heavens! what do I hear?" burst spontaneously from his lips; nor can we wonder at this, though he was the bravest of men; for her voice, her looks, her gestures, were properly adapted to the sentiments she exprest. Such indeed was her image, that neither could Shakspear describe, nor Hogarth paint, nor Clive act, a fury in higher perfection.

{Illustration: She then gave a loose to her passions}

"What do you hear?" reiterated she. "You hear the resentment of the most injured of women.

17

You have heard, you say, of the murder; but do you know the cause, Mr. Booth? Have you since your return to England visited that country where we formerly knew one another? tell me, do you know my wretched story? tell me that, my friend."

Booth hesitated for an answer; indeed, he had heard some imperfect stories, not much to her advantage. She waited not till he had formed a speech; but cried, "Whatever you may have heard, you cannot be acquainted with all the strange accidents which have occasioned your seeing me in a place which at our last parting was so unlikely that I should ever have been found in; nor can you know the cause of all that I have uttered, and which, I am convinced, you never expected to have heard from my mouth. If these circumstances raise your curiosity, I will satisfy it."

He answered, that curiosity was too mean a word to express his ardent desire of knowing her story. Upon which, with very little previous ceremony, she began to relate what is written in the following chapter.

But before we put an end to this it may be necessary to whisper a word or two to the critics, who have, perhaps, begun to express no less astonishment than Mr. Booth, that a lady in whom we had remarked a most extraordinary power of displaying softness should, the very next moment after the words were out of her mouth, express sentiments becoming the lips of a Dalila, Jezebel, Medea, Semiramis, Parysatis, Tanaquil, Livilla, Messalina, Agrippina, Brunichilde, Elfrida, Lady Macbeth, Joan of Naples, Christina of Sweden, Katharine Hays, Sarah Malcolm, Con Philips,{Footnote: Though last not least.} or any other heroine of the tender sex, which history, sacred or profane, ancient or modern, false or true, hath recorded.

We desire such critics to remember that it is the same English climate, in which, on the lovely 10th of June, under a serene sky, the amorous Jacobite, kissing the odoriferous zephyr's breath, gathers a nosegay of white roses to deck the whiter breast of Celia; and in which, on the 11th of June, the very next day, the boisterous Boreas, roused by the hollow thunder, rushes horrible through the air, and, driving the wet tempest before him, levels the hope of the husbandman with the earth, dreadful remembrance of the consequences of the Revolution.

Again, let it be remembered that this is the selfsame Celia, all tender, soft, and delicate, who with a voice, the sweetness of which the Syrens might envy, warbles the harmonious song in praise of the young adventurer; and again, the next day, or, perhaps the next hour, with fiery eyes, wrinkled brows, and foaming lips, roars forth treason and nonsense in a political argument with some fair one of a different principle.

Or, if the critic be a Whig, and consequently dislikes such kind of similes, as being too favourable to Jacobitism, let him be contented with the following story:

I happened in my youth to sit behind two ladies in a side-box at a play, where, in the balcony on the opposite side, was placed the inimitable B——y C——s, in company with a young fellow of no very formal, or indeed sober, appearance. One of the ladies, I remember, said to the other— "Did you ever see anything look so modest and so innocent as that girl over the way? what pity it is such a creature should be in the way of ruin, as I am afraid she is, by her being alone with that young fellow!" Now this lady was no bad physiognomist, for it was impossible to conceive a greater appearance of modesty, innocence, and simplicity, than what nature had displayed in the countenance of that girl; and yet, all appearances notwithstanding, I myself (remember, critic, it was in my youth) had a few mornings before seen that very identical picture of all those engaging qualities in bed with a rake at a bagnio, smoking tobacco, drinking punch, talking obscenity, and swearing and cursing with all the impudence and impiety of the lowest and most abandoned trull of a soldier.

Chapter vii. — In which Miss Matthews begins her history.

Miss Matthews, having barred the door on the inside as securely as it was before barred on the outside, proceeded as follows:

"You may imagine I am going to begin my history at the time when you left the country; but I cannot help reminding you of something which happened before. You will soon recollect the

incident; but I believe you little know the consequence either at that time or since. Alas! I could keep a secret then! now I have no secrets; the world knows all; and it is not worth my while to conceal anything. Well!—You will not wonder, I believe.—I protest I can hardly tell it you, even now.——But I am convinced you have too good an opinion of yourself to be surprized at any conquest you may have made.——Few men want that good opinion—and perhaps very few had ever more reason for it. Indeed, Will, you was a charming fellow in those days; nay, you are not much altered for the worse now, at least in the opinion of some women; for your complexion and features are grown much more masculine than they were." Here Booth made her a low bow, most probably with a compliment; and after a little hesitation she again proceeded.——"Do you remember a contest which happened at an assembly, betwixt myself and Miss Johnson, about standing uppermost? you was then my partner; and young Williams danced with the other lady. The particulars are not now worth mentioning, though I suppose you have long since forgot them. Let it suffice that you supported my claim, and Williams very sneakingly gave up that of his partner, who was, with much difficulty, afterwards prevailed to dance with him. You said—I am sure I repeat the words exactly—that you would not for the world affront any lady there; but that you thought you might, without any such danger declare, that there was no assembly in which that lady, meaning your humble servant, was not worthy of the uppermost place; 'nor will I,' said you, 'suffer, the first duke in England, when she is at the uppermost end of the room, and hath called her dance, to lead his partner above her.'

"What made this the more pleasing to me was, that I secretly hated Miss Johnson. Will you have the reason? why, then, I will tell you honestly, she was my rival. That word perhaps astonishes you, as you never, I believe, heard of any one who made his addresses to me; and indeed my heart was, till that night, entirely indifferent to all mankind: I mean, then, that she was my rival for praise, for beauty, for dress, for fortune, and consequently for admiration. My triumph on this conquest is not to be expressed any more than my delight in the person to whom I chiefly owed it. The former, I fancy, was visible to the whole company; and I desired it should be so; but the latter was so well concealed, that no one, I am confident, took any notice of it. And yet you appeared to me that night to be an angel. You looked, you danced, you spoke-everything charmed me."

"Good Heavens!" cries Booth, "is it possible you should do me so much unmerited honour, and I should be dunce enough not to perceive the least symptom?"

"I assure you," answered she, "I did all I could to prevent you; and yet I almost hated you for not seeing through what I strove to hide. Why, Mr. Booth, was you not more quick-sighted?—I will answer for you—your affections were more happily disposed of to a much better woman than myself, whom you married soon afterwards. I should ask you for her, Mr. Booth; I should have asked you for her before; but I am unworthy of asking for her, or of calling her my acquaintance."

Booth stopt her short, as she was running into another fit of passion, and begged her to omit all former matters, and acquaint him with that part of her history to which he was an entire stranger.

She then renewed her discourse as follows: "You know, Mr. Booth, I soon afterwards left that town, upon the death of my grandmother, and returned home to my father's house; where I had not been long arrived before some troops of dragoons came to quarter in our neighbourhood. Among the officers there was a cornet whose detested name was Hebbers, a name I could scarce repeat, had I not at the same time the pleasure to reflect that he is now no more. My father, you know, who is a hearty well-wisher to the present government, used always to invite the officers to his house; so did he these. Nor was it long before this cornet in so particular a manner recommended himself to the poor old gentleman (I cannot think of him without tears), that our house became his principal habitation, and he was rarely at his quarters, unless when his superior officers obliged him to be there. I shall say nothing of his person, nor could that be any recommendation to a man; it was such, however, as no woman could have made an objection to. Nature had certainly wrapt up her odious work in a most beautiful covering. To say the truth, he was the handsomest man, except one only, that I ever saw—I assure you, I have seen a handsomer——but—well.—He had, besides, all the qualifications of a gentleman; was genteel and extremely polite; spoke French well, and danced to a miracle; but what chiefly recommended him to my father was his skill in music, of which you know that dear man was the most violent lover. I wish he was not too susceptible of flattery on that head; for I have heard Hebbers often greatly

commend my father's performance, and have observed that the good man was wonderfully pleased with such commendations. To say the truth, it is the only way I can account for the extraordinary friendship which my father conceived for this person; such a friendship, that he at last became a part of our family.

"This very circumstance, which, as I am convinced, strongly recommended him to my father, had the very contrary effect with me: I had never any delight in music, and it was not without much difficulty I was prevailed on to learn to play on the harpsichord, in which I had made a very slender progress. As this man, therefore, was frequently the occasion of my being importuned to play against my will, I began to entertain some dislike for him on that account; and as to his person, I assure you, I long continued to look on it with great indifference.

"How strange will the art of this man appear to you presently, who had sufficient address to convert that very circumstance which had at first occasioned my dislike into the first seeds of affection for him!

"You have often, I believe, heard my sister Betty play on the harpsichord; she was, indeed, reputed the best performer in the whole country.

"I was the farthest in the world from regarding this perfection of hers with envy. In reality, perhaps, I despised all perfection of this kind: at least, as I had neither skill nor ambition to excel this way, I looked upon it as a matter of mere indifference.

"Hebbers first put this emulation in my head. He took great pains to persuade me that I had much greater abilities of the musical kind than my sister, and that I might with the greatest ease, if I pleased, excel her; offering me, at the same time, his assistance if I would resolve to undertake it.

"When he had sufficiently inflamed my ambition, in which, perhaps, he found too little difficulty, the continual praises of my sister, which before I had disregarded, became more and more nauseous in my ears; and the rather, as, music being the favourite passion of my father, I became apprehensive (not without frequent hints from Hebbers of that nature) that she might gain too great a preference in his favour.

"To my harpsichord then I applied myself night and day, with such industry and attention, that I soon began to perform in a tolerable manner. I do not absolutely say I excelled my sister, for many were of a different opinion; but, indeed, there might be some partiality in all that.

"Hebbers, at least, declared himself on my side, and nobody could doubt his judgment. He asserted openly that I played in the better manner of the two; and one day, when I was playing to him alone, he affected to burst into a rapture of admiration, and, squeezing me gently by the hand, said, There, madam, I now declare you excel your sister as much in music as, added he in a whispering sigh, you do her, and all the world, in every other charm.

"No woman can bear any superiority in whatever thing she desires to excel in. I now began to hate all the admirers of my sister, to be uneasy at every commendation bestowed on her skill in music, and consequently to love Hebbers for the preference which he gave to mine.

"It was now that I began to survey the handsome person of Hebbers with pleasure. And here, Mr. Booth, I will betray to you the grand secret of our sex.——Many women, I believe, do, with great innocence, and even with great indifference, converse with men of the finest persons; but this I am confident may be affirmed with truth, that, when once a woman comes to ask this question of herself, Is the man whom I like for some other reason, handsome? her fate and his too, very strongly depend on her answering in the affirmative.

"Hebbers no sooner perceived that he had made an impression on my heart, of which I am satisfied I gave him too undeniable tokens, than he affected on a sudden to shun me in the most apparent manner. He wore the most melancholy air in my presence, and, by his dejected looks and sighs, firmly persuaded me that there was some secret sorrow labouring in his bosom; nor will it be difficult for you to imagine to what cause I imputed it.

"Whilst I was wishing for his declaration of a passion in which I thought I could not be mistaken, and at the same time trembling whenever we met with the apprehension of this very declaration, the widow Carey came from London to make us a visit, intending to stay the whole summer at our house.

"Those who know Mrs. Carey will scarce think I do her an injury in saying she is far from being handsome; and yet she is as finished a coquette as if she had the highest beauty to support that character. But perhaps you have seen her; and if you have I am convinced you will readily subscribe to my opinion."

Booth answered he had not; and then she proceeded as in the following chapter.

Chapter viii. — The history of Miss Matthews continued.

"This young lady had not been three days with us before Hebbers grew so particular with her, that it was generally observed; and my poor father, who, I believe, loved the cornet as if he had been his son, began to jest on the occasion, as one who would not be displeased at throwing a good jointure into the arms of his friend.

"You will easily guess, sir, the disposition of my mind on this occasion; but I was not permitted to suffer long under it; for one day, when Hebbers was alone with me, he took an opportunity of expressing his abhorrence at the thoughts of marrying for interest, contrary to his inclinations. I was warm on the subject, and, I believe, went so far as to say that none but fools and villains did so. He replied, with a sigh, Yes, madam, but what would you think of a man whose heart is all the while bleeding for another woman, to whom he would willingly sacrifice the world; but, because he must sacrifice her interest as well as his own, never durst even give her a hint of that passion which was preying on his very vitals? 'Do you believe, Miss Fanny, there is such a wretch on earth?' I answered, with an assumed coldness, I did not believe there was. He then took me gently by the hand, and, with a look so tender that I cannot describe it, vowed he was himself that wretch. Then starting, as if conscious of an error committed, he cried with a faltering voice, 'What am I saying? Pardon me, Miss Fanny; since I beg only your pity, I never will ask for more.—' At these words, hearing my father coming up, I betrayed myself entirely, if, indeed, I had not done it before. I hastily withdrew my hand, crying, Hush! for heaven's sake, my father is just coming in; my blushes, my look, and my accent, telling him, I suppose, all which he wished to know.

"A few days now brought matters to an eclaircissement between us; the being undeceived in what had given me so much uneasiness gave me a pleasure too sweet to be resisted. To triumph over the widow, for whom I had in a very short time contracted a most inveterate hatred, was a pride not to be described. Hebbers appeared to me to be the cause of all this happiness. I doubted not but that he had the most disinterested passion for me, and thought him every way worthy of its return. I did return it, and accepted him as my lover.

"He declared the greatest apprehensions of my father's suspicion, though I am convinced these were causeless had his designs been honourable. To blind these, I consented that he should carry on sham addresses to the widow, who was now a constant jest between us; and he pretended from time to time to acquaint me faithfully with everything that past at his interviews with her; nor was this faithless woman wanting in her part of the deceit. She carried herself to me all the while with a shew of affection, and pretended to have the utmost friendship for me But such are the friendships of women!"

At this remark, Booth, though enough affected at some parts of the story, had great difficulty to refrain from laughter; but, by good luck, he escaped being perceived; and the lady went on without interruption.

"I am come now to a part of my narrative in which it is impossible to be particular without being tedious; for, as to the commerce between lovers, it is, I believe, much the same in all cases; and there is, perhaps, scarce a single phrase that hath not been repeated ten millions of times.

"One thing, however, as I strongly remarked it then, so I will repeat it to you now. In all our conversations, in moments when he fell into the warmest raptures, and exprest the greatest uneasiness at the delay of his joys, he seldom mentioned the word marriage; and never once solicited a day for that purpose. Indeed, women cannot be cautioned too much against such lovers; for though I have heard, and perhaps truly, of some of our sex, of a virtue so exalted, that it is proof against every temptation; yet the generality, I am afraid, are too much in the power of a man to whom they have owned an affection. What is called being upon a good footing is, perhaps, being upon a very dangerous one; and a woman who hath given her consent to marry can hardly be said to be safe till she is married.

21

"And now, sir, I hasten to the period of my ruin. We had a wedding in our family; my musical sister was married to a young fellow as musical as herself. Such a match, you may be sure, amongst other festivities, must have a ball. Oh! Mr. Booth, shall modesty forbid me to remark to you what past on that occasion? But why do I mention modesty, who have no pretensions to it? Everything was said and practised on that occasion, as if the purpose had been to inflame the mind of every woman present. That effect, I freely own to you, it had with me. Music, dancing, wine, and the most luscious conversation, in which my poor dear father innocently joined, raised ideas in me of which I shall for ever repent; and I wished (why should I deny it?) that it had been my wedding instead of my sister's.

"The villain Hebbers danced with me that night, and he lost no opportunity of improving the occasion. In short, the dreadful evening came. My father, though it was a very unusual thing with him, grew intoxicated with liquor; most of the men were in the same condition; nay, I myself drank more than I was accustomed to, enough to inflame, though not to disorder. I lost my former bed-fellow, my sister, and—you may, I think, guess the rest—the villain found means to steal to my chamber, and I was undone.

"Two months I passed in this detested commerce, buying, even then, my guilty, half-tasted pleasures at too dear a rate, with continual horror and apprehension; but what have I paid since— what do I pay now, Mr. Booth? O may my fate be a warning to every woman to keep her innocence, to resist every temptation, since she is certain to repent of the foolish bargain. May it be a warning to her to deal with mankind with care and caution; to shun the least approaches of dishonour, and never to confide too much in the honesty of a man, nor in her own strength, where she has so much at stake; let her remember she walks on a precipice, and the bottomless pit is to receive her if she slips; nay, if she makes but one false step.

"I ask your pardon, Mr. Booth; I might have spared these exhortations, since no woman hears me; but you will not wonder at seeing me affected on this occasion."

Booth declared he was much more surprised at her being able so well to preserve her temper in recounting her story.

"O sir," answered she, "I am at length reconciled to my fate; and I can now die with pleasure, since I die revenged. I am not one of those mean wretches who can sit down and lament their misfortunes. If I ever shed tears, they are the tears of indignation.—But I will proceed.

"It was my fate now to solicit marriage; and I failed not to do it in the most earnest manner. He answered me at first with procrastinations, declaring, from time to time, he would mention it to my father; and still excusing himself for not doing it. At last he thought on an expedient to obtain a longer reprieve. This was by pretending that he should, in a very few weeks, be preferred to the command of a troop; and then, he said, he could with some confidence propose the match.

"In this delay I was persuaded to acquiesce, and was indeed pretty easy, for I had not yet the least mistrust of his honour; but what words can paint my sensations, when one morning he came into my room, with all the marks of dejection in his countenance, and, throwing an open letter on the table, said, 'There is news, madam, in that letter which I am unable to tell you; nor can it give you more concern than it hath given me.'

"This letter was from his captain, to acquaint him that the rout, as they call it, was arrived, and that they were to march within two days. And this, I am since convinced, was what he expected, instead of the preferment which had been made the pretence of delaying our marriage.

"The shock which I felt at reading this was inexpressible, occasioned indeed principally by the departure of a villain whom I loved. However, I soon acquired sufficient presence of mind to remember the main point; and I now insisted peremptorily on his making me immediately his wife, whatever might be the consequence.

"He seemed thunderstruck at this proposal, being, I suppose, destitute of any excuse: but I was too impatient to wait for an answer, and cried out with much eagerness, Sure you cannot hesitate a moment upon this matter—'Hesitate! madam!' replied he—'what you ask is impossible. Is this a time for me to mention a thing of this kind to your father?'—My eyes were now opened all at once—I fell into a rage little short of madness. Tell not me, I cried, of impossibilities, nor times, nor of my father—my honour, my reputation, my all are at stake.—I will have no excuse, no delay—make me your wife this instant, or I will proclaim you over the face of the whole earth for the greatest of villains. He answered, with a kind of sneer, 'What will you proclaim, madam?— whose honour will you injure?' My tongue faltered when I offered to reply, and I fell into a violent

agony, which ended in a fit; nor do I remember anything more that past till I found myself in the arms of my poor affrighted father.

"O, Mr. Booth, what was then my situation! I tremble even now from the reflection.—I must stop a moment. I can go no farther." Booth attempted all in his power to soothe her; and she soon recovered her powers, and proceeded in her story.

Chapter ix. — In which Miss Matthews concludes her relation.

Before I had recovered my senses I had sufficiently betrayed myself to the best of men, who, instead of upbraiding me, or exerting any anger, endeavoured to comfort me all he could with assurances that all should yet be well. This goodness of his affected me with inexpressible sensations; I prostrated myself before him, embraced and kissed his knees, and almost dissolved in tears, and a degree of tenderness hardly to be conceived—But I am running into too minute descriptions.

"Hebbers, seeing me in a fit, had left me, and sent one of the servants to take care of me. He then ran away like a thief from the house, without taking his leave of my father, or once thanking him for all his civilities. He did not stop at his quarters, but made directly to London, apprehensive, I believe, either of my father or brother's resentment; for I am convinced he is a coward. Indeed his fear of my brother was utterly groundless; for I believe he would rather have thanked any man who had destroyed me; and I am sure I am not in the least behindhand with him in good wishes.

"All his inveteracy to me had, however, no effect on my father, at least at that time; for, though the good man took sufficient occasions to reprimand me for my past offence, he could not be brought to abandon me. A treaty of marriage was now set on foot, in which my father himself offered me to Hebbers, with a fortune superior to that which had been given with my sister; nor could all my brother's remonstrances against it, as an act of the highest injustice, avail.

"Hebbers entered into the treaty, though not with much warmth. He had even the assurance to make additional demands on my father, which being complied with, everything was concluded, and the villain once more received into the house. He soon found means to obtain my forgiveness of his former behaviour; indeed, he convinced me, so foolishly blind is female love, that he had never been to blame.

"When everything was ready for our nuptials, and the day of the ceremony was to be appointed, in the midst of my happiness I received a letter from an unknown hand, acquainting me (guess, Mr. Booth, how I was shocked at receiving it) that Mr. Hebbers was already married to a woman in a distant part of the kingdom.

"I will not tire you with all that past at our next interview. I communicated the letter to Hebbers, who, after some little hesitation, owned the fact, and not only owned it, but had the address to improve it to his own advantage, to make it the means of satisfying me concerning all his former delays; which, to say the truth, I was not so much displeased at imputing to any degree of villany, as I should have been to impute it to the want of a sufficient warmth of affection, and though the disappointment of all my hopes, at the very instant of their expected fruition, threw me into the most violent disorders; yet, when I came a little to myself, he had no great difficulty to persuade me that in every instance, with regard to me, Hebbers had acted from no other motive than from the most ardent and ungovernable love. And there is, I believe, no crime which a woman will not forgive, when she can derive it from that fountain. In short, I forgave him all, and am willing to persuade myself I am not weaker than the rest of my sex. Indeed, Mr. Booth, he hath a bewitching tongue, and is master of an address that no woman could resist. I do assure you the charms of his person are his least perfection, at least in my eye."

Here Booth smiled, but happily without her perceiving it.

"A fresh difficulty (continued she) now arose. This was to excuse the delay of the ceremony to my father, who every day very earnestly urged it. This made me so very uneasy, that I at last listened to a proposal, which, if any one in the days of my innocence, or even a few days before,

had assured me I could have submitted to have thought of, I should have treated the supposition with the highest contempt and indignation; nay, I scarce reflect on it now with more horror than astonishment. In short, I agreed to run away with him—to leave my father, my reputation, everything which was or ought to have been dear to me, and to live with this villain as a mistress, since I could not be his wife.

"Was not this an obligation of the highest and tenderest kind, and had I not reason to expect every return in the man's power on whom I had conferred it? I will make short of the remainder of my story, for what is there of a woman worth relating, after what I have told you?

"Above a year I lived with this man in an obscure court in London, during which time I had a child by him, whom Heaven, I thank it, hath been pleased to take to itself.

"During many months he behaved to me with all the apparent tenderness and even fondness imaginable; but, alas! how poor was my enjoyment of this compared to what it would have been in another situation? When he was present, life was barely tolerable: but, when he was absent, nothing could equal the misery I endured. I past my hours almost entirely alone; for no company but what I despised, would consort with me. Abroad I scarce ever went, lest I should meet any of my former acquaintance; for their sight would have plunged a thousand daggers in my soul. My only diversion was going very seldom to a play, where I hid myself in the gallery, with a daughter of the woman of the house. A girl, indeed, of good sense and many good qualities; but how much beneath me was it to be the companion of a creature so low! O heavens! when I have seen my equals glittering in a side-box, how have the thoughts of my lost honour torn my soul!"

"Pardon me, dear madam," cries Booth, "for interrupting you; but I am under the utmost anxiety to know what became of your poor father, for whom I have so great a respect, and who, I am convinced, must so bitterly feel your loss."

"O Mr. Booth," answered she, "he was scarce ever out of my thoughts. His dear image still obtruded itself in my mind, and I believe would have broken my heart, had I not taken a very preposterous way to ease myself. I am, indeed, almost ashamed to tell you; but necessity put it in my head.—You will think the matter too trifling to have been remembered, and so it surely was; nor should I have remembered it on any other occasion. You must know then, sir, that my brother was always my inveterate enemy and altogether as fond of my sister.—He once prevailed with my father to let him take my sister with him in the chariot, and by that means I was disappointed of going to a ball which I had set my heart on. The disappointment, I assure you, was great at the time; but I had long since forgotten it. I must have been a very bad woman if I had not, for it was the only thing in which I can remember that my father ever disobliged me. However, I now revived this in my mind, which I artificially worked up into so high an injury, that I assure you it afforded me no little comfort. When any tender idea intruded into my bosom, I immediately raised this fantom of an injury in my imagination, and it considerably lessened the fury of that sorrow which I should have otherwise felt for the loss of so good a father, who died within a few months of my departure from him.

"And now, sir, to draw to a conclusion. One night, as I was in the gallery at Drury-lane playhouse, I saw below me in a side-box (she was once below me in every place), that widow whom I mentioned to you before. I had scarce cast my eyes on this woman before I was so shocked with the sight that it almost deprived me of my senses; for the villain Hebbers came presently in and seated himself behind her.

"He had been almost a month from me, and I believed him to be at his quarters in Yorkshire. Guess what were my sensations when I beheld him sitting by that base woman, and talking to her with the utmost familiarity. I could not long endure this sight, and having acquainted my companion that I was taken suddenly ill, I forced her to go home with me at the end of the second act.

"After a restless and sleepless night, when I rose the next morning I had the comfort to receive a visit from the woman of the house, who, after a very short introduction, asked me when I had heard from the captain, and when I expected to see him? I had not strength or spirits to make her any answer, and she proceeded thus:—'Indeed I did not think the captain would have used me so. My husband was an officer of the army as well as himself; and if a body is a little low in the world, I am sure that is no reason for folks to trample on a body. I defy the world to say as I ever was guilty of an ill thing.' For heaven's sake, madam, says I, what do you mean? 'Mean?' cries she; 'I am sure, if I had not thought you had been Captain Hebbers' lady, his lawful lady too,

you should never have set footing in my house. I would have Captain Hebbers know, that though I am reduced to let lodgings, I never have entertained any but persons of character.'—In this manner, sir, she ran on, saying many shocking things not worth repeating, till my anger at last got the better of my patience as well as my sorrow, and I pushed her out of the room.

"She had not been long gone before her daughter came to me, and, after many expressions of tenderness and pity, acquainted me that her mother had just found out, by means of the captain's servant, that the captain was married to another lady; 'which, if you did not know before, madam,' said she, 'I am sorry to be the messenger of such ill news.'

"Think, Mr. Booth, what I must have endured to see myself humbled before such a creature as this, the daughter of a woman who lets lodgings! However, having recollected myself a little, I thought it would be in vain to deny anything; so, knowing this to be one of the best-natured and most sensible girls in the world, I resolved to tell her my whole story, and for the future to make her my confidante. I answered her, therefore, with a good deal of assurance, that she need not regret telling me this piece of ill news, for I had known it before I came to her house.

"'Pardon me, madam,' replied the girl, 'you cannot possibly have known it so long, for he hath not been married above a week; last night was the first time of his appearing in public with his wife at the play. Indeed, I knew very well the cause of your uneasiness there; but would not mention—'

"His wife at the play? answered I eagerly. What wife? whom do you mean?

"'I mean the widow Carey, madam,' replied she, 'to whom the captain was married a few days since. His servant was here last night to pay for your lodging, and he told it my mother.'

"I know not what answer I made, or whether I made any. I presently fell dead on the floor, and it was with great difficulty I was brought back to life by the poor girl, for neither the mother nor the maid of the house would lend me any assistance, both seeming to regard me rather as a monster than a woman.

"Scarce had I recovered the use of my senses when I received a letter from the villain, declaring he had not assurance to see my face, and very kindly advising me to endeavour to reconcile myself to my family, concluding with an offer, in case I did not succeed, to allow me twenty pounds a-year to support me in some remote part of the kingdom.

"I need not mention my indignation at these proposals. In the highest agony of rage, I went in a chair to the detested house, where I easily got access to the wretch I had devoted to destruction, whom I no sooner found within my reach than I plunged a drawn penknife, which I had prepared in my pocket for the purpose, into his accursed heart. For this fact I was immediately seized and soon after committed hither; and for this fact I am ready to die, and shall with pleasure receive the sentence of the law.

"Thus, sir," said she, "I have related to you my unhappy story, and if I have tired your patience, by dwelling too long on those parts which affected me the most, I ask your pardon."

Booth made a proper speech on this occasion, and, having exprest much concern at her present situation, concluded that he hoped her sentence would be milder than she seemed to expect.

Her reply to this was full of so much bitterness and indignation, that we do not think proper to record the speech at length, in which having vented her passion, she all at once put on a serene countenance, and with an air of great complacency said, "Well, Mr. Booth, I think I have now a right to satisfy my curiosity at the expense of your breath. I may say it is not altogether a vain curiosity, for perhaps I have had inclination enough to interest myself in whatever concerns you; but no matter for that: those days (added she with a sigh) are now over."

Booth, who was extremely good-natured and well-bred, told her that she should not command him twice whatever was in his power; and then, after the usual apology, was going to begin his history, when the keeper arrived, and acquainted the lady that dinner was ready, at the same time saying, "I suppose, madam, as the gentleman is an acquaintance of yours, he must dine with us too."

Miss Matthews told the keeper that she had only one word to mention in private to the gentleman, and that then they would both attend him. She then pulled her purse from her pocket, in which were upwards of twenty guineas, being the remainder of the money for which she had sold a gold repeating watch, her father's present, with some other trinkets, and desired Mr. Booth to take what he should have occasion for, saying, "You know, I believe, dear Will, I never valued

money; and now I am sure I shall have very little use for it." Booth, with much difficulty, accepted of two guineas, and then they both together attended the keeper.

Chapter x. — Table-talk, consisting of a facetious discourse that passed in the prison.

There were assembled at the table the governor of these (not improperly called infernal) regions; the lieutenant-governor, vulgarly named the first turnkey; Miss Matthews, Mr. Booth, Mr. Robinson the gambler, several other prisoners of both sexes, and one Murphy, an attorney.

The governor took the first opportunity to bring the affair of Miss Matthews upon the carpet, and then, turning to Murphy, he said, "It is very lucky this gentleman happens to be present; I do assure you, madam, your cause cannot be in abler hands. He is, I believe, the best man in England at a defence; I have known him often succeed against the most positive evidence."

"Fy, sir," answered Murphy; "you know I hate all this; but, if the lady will trust me with her cause, I will do the best in my power. Come, madam, do not be discouraged; a bit of manslaughter and cold iron, I hope, will be the worst: or perhaps we may come off better with a slice of chance-medley, or se defendendo"

"I am very ignorant of the law, sir," cries the lady.

"Yes, madam," answered Murphy; "it can't be expected you should understand it. There are very few of us who profess it that understand the whole, nor is it necessary we should. There is a great deal of rubbish of little use, about indictments, and abatements, and bars, and ejectments, and trovers, and such stuff, with which people cram their heads to little purpose. The chapter of evidence is the main business; that is the sheet-anchor; that is the rudder, which brings the vessel safe in portum. Evidence is, indeed, the whole, the summa totidis, for de non apparentibus et non insistentibus eandem est ratio."

"If you address yourself to me, sir," said the lady, "you are much too learned, I assure you, for my understanding."

"Tace, madam," answered Murphy, "is Latin for a candle: I commend your prudence. I shall know the particulars of your case when we are alone."

"I hope the lady," said Robinson, "hath no suspicion of any person here. I hope we are all persons of honour at this table."

"D—n my eyes!" answered a well-dressed woman, "I can answer for myself and the other ladies; though I never saw the lady in my life, she need not be shy of us, d—n my eyes! I scorn to rap {Footnote: A cant word, meaning to swear, or rather to perjure yourself} against any lady."

"D—n me, madam!" cried another female, "I honour what you have done. I once put a knife into a cull myself—so my service to you, madam, and I wish you may come off with se diffidendo with all my heart."

"I beg, good woman," said Miss Matthews, "you would talk on some other subject, and give yourself no concern about my affairs."

"You see, ladies," cried Murphy, "the gentle-woman doth not care to talk on this matter before company; so pray do not press her."

"Nay, I value the lady's acquaintance no more than she values mine," cries the first woman who spoke. "I have kept as good company as the lady, I believe, every day in the week. Good woman! I don't use to be so treated. If the lady says such another word to me, d—n me, I will darken her daylights. Marry, come up! Good woman!—the lady's a whore as well as myself! and, though I am sent hither to mill doll, d—n my eyes, I have money enough to buy it off as well as the lady herself."

Action might perhaps soon have ensued this speech, had not the keeper interposed his authority, and put an end to any further dispute. Soon after which, the company broke up, and none but himself, Mr. Murphy, Captain Booth, and Miss Matthews, remained together.

Miss Matthews then, at the entreaty of the keeper, began to open her case to Mr. Murphy, whom she admitted to be her solicitor, though she still declared she was indifferent as to the event of the trial.

26

Mr. Murphy, having heard all the particulars with which the reader is already acquainted (as far as related to the murder), shook his head and said, "There is but one circumstance, madam, which I wish was out of the case; and that we must put out of it; I mean the carrying the penknife drawn into the room with you; for that seems to imply malice prepensive, as we call it in the law: this circumstance, therefore, must not appear against you; and, if the servant who was in the room observed this, he must be bought off at all hazards. All here you say are friends; therefore I tell you openly, you must furnish me with money sufficient for this purpose. Malice is all we have to guard against."

"I would not presume, sir," cries Booth, "to inform you in the law; but I have heard, in case of stabbing, a man may be indicted upon the statute; and it is capital, though no malice appears."

"You say true, sir," answered Murphy; "a man may be indicted contra formam statutis; and that method, I allow you, requires no malice. I presume you are a lawyer, sir?"

"No, indeed, sir," answered Booth, "I know nothing of the law."

"Then, sir, I will tell you—If a man be indicted contra formam tatutis, as we say, no malice is necessary, because the form of the statute makes malice; and then what we have to guard against is having struck the first blow. Pox on't, it is unlucky this was done in a room: if it had been in the street we could have had five or six witnesses to have proved the first blow, cheaper than, I am afraid, we shall get this one; for when a man knows, from the unhappy circumstances of the case, that you can procure no other witness but himself, he is always dear. It is so in all other ways of business. I am very implicit, you see; but we are all among friends. The safest way is to furnish me with money enough to offer him a good round sum at once; and I think (it is for your good I speak) fifty pounds is the least than can be offered him. I do assure you I would offer him no less was it my own case."

"And do you think, sir," said she, "that I would save my life at the expense of hiring another to perjure himself?"

"Ay, surely do I," cries Murphy; "for where is the fault, admitting there is some fault in perjury, as you call it? and, to be sure, it is such a matter as every man would rather wish to avoid than not: and yet, as it may be managed, there is not so much as some people are apt to imagine in it; for he need not kiss the book, and then pray where's the perjury? but if the crier is sharper than ordinary, what is it he kisses? is it anything but a bit of calf's-skin? I am sure a man must be a very bad Christian himself who would not do so much as that to save the life of any Christian whatever, much more of so pretty a lady. Indeed, madam, if we can make out but a tolerable case, so much beauty will go a great way with the judge and the jury too."

The latter part of this speech, notwithstanding the mouth it came from, caused Miss Matthews to suppress much of the indignation which began to arise at the former; and she answered with a smile, "Sir, you are a great casuist in these matters; but we need argue no longer concerning them; for, if fifty pounds would save my life, I assure you I could not command that sum. The little money I have in my pocket is all I can call my own; and I apprehend, in the situation I am in, I shall have very little of that to spare."

"Come, come, madam," cries Murphy, "life is sweet, let me tell you, and never sweeter than when we are near losing it. I have known many a man very brave and undaunted at his first commitment, who, when business began to thicken a little upon him, hath changed his note. It is no time to be saving in your condition."

The keeper, who, after the liberality of Miss Matthews, and on seeing a purse of guineas in her hand, had conceived a great opinion of her wealth, no sooner heard that the sum which he had in intention intirely confiscated for his own use was attempted to be broke in upon, thought it high time to be upon his guard. "To be sure," cries he, "Mr. Murphy, life is sweet, as you say, that must be acknowledged; to be sure, life is sweet; but, sweet as it is, no persons can advance more than they are worth to save it. And indeed, if the lady can command no more money than that little she mentions, she is to be commended for her unwillingness to part with any of it; for, to be sure, as she says, she will want every farthing of that to live like a gentlewoman till she comes to her trial. And, to be sure, as sweet as life is, people ought to take care to be able to live sweetly while they do live; besides, I cannot help saying the lady shews herself to be what she is, by her abhorrence of perjury, which is certainly a very dreadful crime. And, though the not kissing the book doth, as you say, make a great deal of difference; and, if a man had a great while to live and repent, perhaps he might swallow it well enough; yet, when people comes to be near their end (as

27

who can venture to foretel what will be the lady's case?) they ought to take care not to overburthen their conscience. I hope the lady's case will not be found murder; for I am sure I always wish well to all my prisoners who shew themselves to be gentlemen or gentlewomen; yet one should always fear the worst."

"Indeed, sir, you speak like an oracle," answered the lady; "and one subornation of perjury would sit heavier on my conscience than twenty such murders as I am guilty of."

"Nay, to be sure, madam," answered the keeper, "nobody can pretend to tell what provocation you must have had; and certainly it can never be imagined that a lady who behaves herself so handsomely as you have done ever since you have been under my keys should be guilty of killing a man without being very highly provoked to do it."

Mr. Murphy was, I believe, going to answer when he was called out of the room; after which nothing passed between the remaining persons worth relating, till Booth and the lady retired back again into the lady's apartment.

Here they fell immediately to commenting on the foregoing discourse; but, as their comments were, I believe, the same with what most readers have made on the same occasion, we shall omit them. At last, Miss Matthews reminding her companion of his promise of relating to her what had befallen him since the interruption of their former acquaintance, he began as is written in the next book of this history.

BOOK II.

Chapter i. — In which Captain Booth begins to relate his history.

The tea-table being removed, and Mr. Booth and the lady left alone, he proceeded as follows:

"Since you desire, madam, to know the particulars of my courtship to that best and dearest of women whom I afterwards married, I will endeavour to recollect them as well as I can, at least all those incidents which are most worth relating to you.

"If the vulgar opinion of the fatality in marriage had ever any foundation, it surely appeared in my marriage with my Amelia. I knew her in the first dawn of her beauty; and, I believe, madam, she had as much as ever fell to the share of a woman; but, though I always admired her, it was long without any spark of love. Perhaps the general admiration which at that time pursued her, the respect paid her by persons of the highest rank, and the numberless addresses which were made her by men of great fortune, prevented my aspiring at the possession of those charms which seemed so absolutely out of my reach. However it was, I assure you the accident which deprived her of the admiration of others made the first great impression on my heart in her favour. The injury done to her beauty by the overturning of a chaise, by which, as you may well remember, her lovely nose was beat all to pieces, gave me an assurance that the woman who had been so much adored for the charms of her person deserved a much higher adoration to be paid to her mind; for that she was in the latter respect infinitely more superior to the rest of her sex than she had ever been in the former."

"I admire your taste extremely," cried the lady; "I remember perfectly well the great heroism with which your Amelia bore that misfortune."

"Good heavens! madam," answered he; "what a magnanimity of mind did her behaviour demonstrate! If the world have extolled the firmness of soul in a man who can support the loss of fortune; of a general who can be composed after the loss of a victory; or of a king who can be contented with the loss of a crown; with what astonishment ought we to behold, with what praises

28

to honour, a young lady, who can with patience and resignation submit to the loss of exquisite beauty, in other words to the loss of fortune, power, glory, everything which human nature is apt to court and rejoice in! what must be the mind which can bear to be deprived of all these in a moment, and by an unfortunate trifling accident; which could support all this, together with the most exquisite torments of body, and with dignity, with resignation, without complaining, almost without a tear, undergo the most painful and dreadful operations of surgery in such a situation!" Here he stopt, and a torrent of tears gushed from his eyes; such tears are apt to flow from a truly noble heart at the hearing of anything surprisingly great and glorious. As soon as he was able he again proceeded thus:

"Would you think, Miss Matthews, that the misfortune of my Amelia was capable of any aggravation? I assure you, she hath often told me it was aggravated with a circumstance which outweighed all the other ingredients. This was the cruel insults she received from some of her most intimate acquaintance, several of whom, after many distortions and grimaces, have turned their heads aside, unable to support their secret triumph, and burst into a loud laugh in her hearing."

"Good heavens!" cried Miss Matthews; "what detestable actions will this contemptible passion of envy prevail on our sex to commit!"

"An occasion of this kind, as she hath since told me, made the first impression on her gentle heart in my favour. I was one day in company with several young ladies, or rather young devils, where poor Amelia's accident was the subject of much mirth and pleasantry. One of these said she hoped miss would not hold her head so high for the future. Another answered, 'I do not know, madam, what she may do with her head, but I am convinced she will never more turn up her nose at her betters.' Another cried, 'What a very proper match might now be made between Amelia and a certain captain,' who had unfortunately received an injury in the same part, though from no shameful cause. Many other sarcasms were thrown out, very unworthy to be repeated. I was hurt with perceiving so much malice in human shape, and cried out very bluntly, Indeed, ladies, you need not express such satisfaction at poor Miss Emily's accident; for she will still be the handsomest woman in England. This speech of mine was afterwards variously repeated, by some to my honour, and by others represented in a contrary light; indeed, it was often reported to be much ruder than it was. However, it at length reached Amelia's ears. She said she was very much obliged to me, since I could have so much compassion for her as to be rude to a lady on her account.

"About a month after the accident, when Amelia began to see company in a mask, I had the honour to drink tea with her. We were alone together, and I begged her to indulge my curiosity by showing me her face. She answered in a most obliging manner, 'Perhaps, Mr. Booth, you will as little know me when my mask is off as when it is on;' and at the same instant unmasked.—The surgeon's skill was the least I considered. A thousand tender ideas rushed all at once on my mind. I was unable to contain myself, and, eagerly kissing her hand, I cried—Upon my soul, madam, you never appeared to me so lovely as at this instant. Nothing more remarkable passed at this visit; but I sincerely believe we were neither of us hereafter indifferent to each other.

"Many months, however, passed after this, before I ever thought seriously of making her my wife. Not that I wanted sufficient love for Amelia. Indeed it arose from the vast affection I bore her. I considered my own as a desperate fortune, hers as entirely dependent on her mother, who was a woman, you know, of violent passions, and very unlikely to consent to a match so highly contrary to the interest of her daughter. The more I loved Amelia, the more firmly I resolved within myself never to propose love to her seriously. Such a dupe was my understanding to my heart, and so foolishly did I imagine I could be master of a flame to which I was every day adding fuel.

"O, Miss Matthews! we have heard of men entirely masters of their passions, and of hearts which can carry this fire in them, and conceal it at their pleasure. Perhaps there may be such: but, if there are, those hearts may be compared, I believe, to damps, in which it is more difficult to keep fire alive than to prevent its blazing: in mine it was placed in the midst of combustible matter.

"After several visits, in which looks and sighs had been interchanged on both sides, but without the least mention of passion in private, one day the discourse between us when alone happened to turn on love; I say happened, for I protest it was not designed on my side, and I am

as firmly convinced not on hers. I was now no longer master of myself; I declared myself the most wretched of all martyrs to this tender passion; that I had long concealed it from its object. At length, after mentioning many particulars, suppressing, however, those which must have necessarily brought it home to Amelia, I concluded with begging her to be the confidante of my amour, and to give me her advice on that occasion.

"Amelia (O, I shall never forget the dear perturbation!) appeared all confusion at this instant. She trembled, turned pale, and discovered how well she understood me, by a thousand more symptoms than I could take notice of, in a state of mind so very little different from her own. At last, with faltering accents, she said I had made a very ill choice of a counsellor in a matter in which she was so ignorant.—Adding, at last, 'I believe, Mr. Booth, you gentlemen want very little advice in these affairs, which you all understand better than we do.'

"I will relate no more of our conversation at present; indeed I am afraid I tire you with too many particulars."

"O, no!" answered she; "I should be glad to hear every step of an amour which had so tender a beginning. Tell me everything you said or did, if you can remember it."

He then proceeded, and so will we in the next chapter.

Chapter ii. — Mr. Booth continues his story. In this chapter there are some passages that may serve as a kind of touchstone by which a young lady may examine the heart of her lover. I would advise, therefore, that every lover be obliged to read it over

in the presence of his mistress, and that she carefully watch his emotions while he is reading.

"I was under the utmost concern," cries Booth, "when I retired from my visit, and had reflected coolly on what I had said. I now saw plainly that I had made downright love to Amelia; and I feared, such was my vanity, that I had already gone too far, and been too successful. Feared! do I say? could I fear what I hoped? how shall I describe the anxiety of my mind?"

"You need give yourself no great pain," cried Miss Matthews, "to describe what I can so easily guess. To be honest with you, Mr. Booth, I do not agree with your lady's opinion that the men have a superior understanding in the matters of love. Men are often blind to the passions of women: but every woman is as quick-sighted as a hawk on these occasions; nor is there one article in the whole science which is not understood by all our sex."

"However, madam," said Mr. Booth, "I now undertook to deceive Amelia. I abstained three days from seeing her; to say the truth, I endeavoured to work myself up to a resolution of leaving her for ever: but when I could not so far subdue my passion—But why do I talk nonsense of subduing passion?—I should say, when no other passion could surmount my love, I returned to visit her; and now I attempted the strangest project which ever entered into the silly head of a lover. This was to persuade Amelia that I was really in love in another place, and had literally expressed my meaning when I asked her advice and desired her to be my confidante.

"I therefore forged a meeting to have been between me and my imaginary mistress since I had last seen Amelia, and related the particulars, as well as I could invent them, which had passed at our conversation.

"Poor Amelia presently swallowed this bait; and, as she hath told me since, absolutely believed me to be in earnest. Poor dear love! how should the sincerest of hearts have any idea of deceit? for, with all her simplicity, I assure you she is the most sensible woman in the world."

"It is highly generous and good in you," said Miss Matthews, with a sly sneer, "to impute to honesty what others would, perhaps, call credulity."

"I protest, madam," answered he, "I do her no more than justice. A good heart will at all times betray the best head in the world.——Well, madam, my angel was now, if possible, more confused than before. She looked so silly, you can hardly believe it."

"Yes, yes, I can," answered the lady, with a laugh, "I can believe it.—Well, well, go on."—"After some hesitation," cried he, "my Amelia said faintly to me, 'Mr. Booth, you use me very ill; you desire me to be your confidante, and conceal from me the name of your mistress.'

"Is it possible then, madam," answered I, "that you cannot guess her, when I tell you she is one of your acquaintance, and lives in this town?"

"'My acquaintance!' said she: 'La! Mr. Booth—In this town! I—I—I thought I could have guessed for once; but I have an ill talent that way—I will never attempt to guess anything again.' Indeed I do her an injury when I pretend to represent her manner. Her manner, look, voice, everything was inimitable; such sweetness, softness, innocence, modesty!—Upon my soul, if ever man could boast of his resolution, I think I might now, that I abstained from falling prostrate at her feet, and adoring her. However, I triumphed; pride, I believe, triumphed, or perhaps love got the better of love. We once more parted, and I promised, the next time I saw her, to reveal the name of my mistress.

"I now had, I thought, gained a complete victory over myself; and no small compliments did I pay to my own resolution. In short, I triumphed as cowards and niggards do when they flatter themselves with having given some supposed instance of courage or generosity; and my triumph lasted as long; that is to say, till my ascendant passion had a proper opportunity of displaying itself in its true and natural colours.

"Having hitherto succeeded so well in my own opinion, and obtained this mighty self-conquest, I now entertained a design of exerting the most romantic generosity, and of curing that unhappy passion which I perceived I had raised in Amelia.

"Among the ladies who had expressed the greatest satisfaction at my Amelia's misfortune, Miss Osborne had distinguished herself in a very eminent degree; she was, indeed, the next in beauty to my angel, nay, she had disputed the preference, and had some among her admirers who were blind enough to give it in her favour."

"Well," cries the lady, "I will allow you to call them blind; but Miss Osborne was a charming girl."

"She certainly was handsome," answered he, "and a very considerable fortune; so I thought my Amelia would have little difficulty in believing me when I fixed on her as my mistress. And I concluded that my thus placing my affections on her known enemy would be the surest method of eradicating every tender idea with which I had been ever honoured by Amelia.

"Well, then, to Amelia I went; she received me with more than usual coldness and reserve; in which, to confess the truth, there appeared to me more of anger than indifference, and more of dejection than of either. After some short introduction, I revived the discourse of my amour, and presently mentioned Miss Osborne as the lady whose name I had concealed; adding, that the true reason why I did not mention her before was, that I apprehended there was some little distance between them, which I hoped to have the happiness of accommodating.

"Amelia answered with much gravity, 'If you know, sir, that there is any distance between us, I suppose you know the reason of that distance; and then, I think, I could not have expected to be affronted by her name. I would not have you think, Mr. Booth, that I hate Miss Osborne. No! Heaven is my witness, I despise her too much.—Indeed, when I reflect how much I loved the woman who hath treated me so cruelly, I own it gives me pain—when I lay, as I then imagined, and as all about me believed, on my deathbed, in all the agonies of pain and misery, to become the object of laughter to my dearest friend.—O, Mr. Booth, it is a cruel reflection! and could I after this have expected from you—but why not from you, to whom I am a person entirely indifferent, if such a friend could treat me so barbarously?'

"During the greatest part of this speech the tears streamed from her bright eyes. I could endure it no longer. I caught up the word indifferent, and repeated it, saying, Do you think then, madam, that Miss Emily is indifferent to me?

"'Yes, surely, I do,' answered she: 'I know I am; indeed, why should I not be indifferent to you?'

"Have my eyes," said I, "then declared nothing?"

"'O! there is no need of your eyes' answered she; 'your tongue hath declared that you have singled out of all womankind my greatest, I will say, my basest enemy. I own I once thought that character would have been no recommendation to you;—but why did I think so? I was born to deceive myself.'

"I then fell on my knees before her; and, forcing her hand, cried out, O, my Amelia! I can bear no longer. You are the only mistress of my affections; you are the deity I adore. In this stile I ran on for above two or three minutes, what it is impossible to repeat, till a torrent of contending

31

passions, together with the surprize, overpowered her gentle spirits, and she fainted away in my arms.

"To describe my sensation till she returned to herself is not in my power."—"You need not," cried Miss Matthews.—"Oh, happy Amelia! why had I not been blest with such a passion?"—"I am convinced, madam," continued he, "you cannot expect all the particulars of the tender scene which ensued. I was not enough in my senses to remember it all. Let it suffice to say, that that behaviour with which Amelia, while ignorant of its motive, had been so much displeased, when she became sensible of that motive, proved the strongest recommendation to her favour, and she was pleased to call it generous."

"Generous!" repeated the lady, "and so it was, almost beyond the reach of humanity. I question whether you ever had an equal."

Perhaps the critical reader may have the same doubt with Miss Matthews; and lest he should, we will here make a gap in our history, to give him an opportunity of accurately considering whether this conduct of Mr. Booth was natural or no; and consequently, whether we have, in this place, maintained or deviated from that strict adherence to universal truth which we profess above all other historians.

Chapter iii. — The narrative continued. More of the touchstone.

Booth made a proper acknowledgment of Miss Matthew's civility, and then renewed his story. "We were upon the footing of lovers; and Amelia threw off her reserve more and more, till at length I found all that return of my affection which the tenderest lover can require.

"My situation would now have been a paradise, had not my happiness been interrupted with the same reflections I have already mentioned; had I not, in short, concluded, that I must derive all my joys from the almost certain ruin of that dear creature to whom I should owe them.

"This thought haunted me night and day, till I at last grew unable to support it: I therefore resolved in the strongest manner, to lay it before Amelia.

"One evening then, after the highest professions of the most disinterested love, in which Heaven knows my sincerity, I took an occasion to speak to Amelia in the following manner:—

"Too true it is, I am afraid, my dearest creature, that the highest human happiness is imperfect. How rich would be my cup, was it not for one poisonous drop which embitters the whole! O, Amelia! what must be the consequence of my ever having the honour to call you mine!—You know my situation in life, and you know your own: I have nothing more than the poor provision of an ensign's commission to depend on; your sole dependence is on your mother; should any act of disobedience defeat your expectations, how wretched must your lot be with me! O, Amelia! how ghastly an object to my mind is the apprehension of your distress! Can I bear to reflect a moment on the certainty of your foregoing all the conveniences of life? on the possibility of your suffering all its most dreadful inconveniencies? what must be my misery, then, to see you in such a situation, and to upbraid myself with being the accursed cause of bringing you to it? Suppose too in such a season I should be summoned from you. Could I submit to see you encounter all the hazards, the fatigues of war, with me? you could not yourself, however willing, support them a single campaign. What then; must I leave you to starve alone, deprived of the tenderness of a husband, deprived too of the tenderness of the best of mothers, through my means? a woman most dear to me, for being the parent, the nurse, and the friend of my Amelia.—-But oh! my sweet creature, carry your thoughts a little further. Think of the tenderest consequences, the dearest pledges of our love. Can I bear to think of entailing beggary on the posterity of my Amelia? on our—Oh, Heavens!—on our children!—On the other side, is it possible even to mention the word—I will not, must not, cannot, cannot part with you.——What must we do, Amelia? It is now I sincerely ask your advice."

"'What advice can I give you,' said she, 'in such an alternative? Would to Heaven we had never met!'

"These words were accompanied with a sigh, and a look inexpressibly tender, the tears at the

same time overflowing all her lovely cheeks. I was endeavouring to reply when I was interrupted by what soon put an end to the scene.

"Our amour had already been buzzed all over the town; and it came at last to the ears of Mrs. Harris: I had, indeed, observed of late a great alteration in that lady's behaviour towards me whenever I visited at the house; nor could I, for a long time before this evening, ever obtain a private interview with Amelia; and now, it seems, I owed it to her mother's intention of overhearing all that passed between us.

"At the period then above mentioned, Mrs. Harris burst from the closet where she had hid herself, and surprised her daughter, reclining on my bosom in all that tender sorrow I have just described. I will not attempt to paint the rage of the mother, or the daughter's confusion, or my own. 'Here are very fine doings, indeed,' cries Mrs. Harris: 'you have made a noble use, Amelia, of my indulgence, and the trust I reposed in you.—As for you, Mr. Booth, I will not accuse you; you have used my child as I ought to have expected; I may thank myself for what hath happened;' with much more of the same kind, before she would suffer me to speak; but at last I obtained a hearing, and offered to excuse my poor Amelia, who was ready to sink into the earth under the oppression of grief, by taking as much blame as I could on myself. Mrs. Harris answered, 'No, sir, I must say you are innocent in comparison of her; nay, I can say I have heard you use dissuasive arguments; and I promise you they are of weight. I have, I thank Heaven, one dutiful child, and I shall henceforth think her my only one.'—She then forced the poor, trembling, fainting Amelia out of the room; which when she had done, she began very coolly to reason with me on the folly, as well as iniquity, which I had been guilty of; and repeated to me almost every word I had before urged to her daughter. In fine, she at last obtained of me a promise that I would soon go to my regiment, and submit to any misery rather than that of being the ruin of Amelia.

"I now, for many days, endured the greatest torments which the human mind is, I believe, capable of feeling; and I can honestly say I tried all the means, and applied every argument which I could raise, to cure me of my love. And to make these the more effectual, I spent every night in walking backwards and forwards in the sight of Mrs. Harris's house, where I never failed to find some object or other which raised some tender idea of my lovely Amelia, and almost drove me to distraction."

"And don't you think, sir," said Miss Matthews, "you took a most preposterous method to cure yourself?"

"Alas, madam," answered he, "you cannot see it in a more absurd light than I do; but those know little of real love or grief who do not know how much we deceive ourselves when we pretend to aim at the cure of either. It is with these, as it is with some distempers of the body, nothing is in the least agreeable to us but what serves to heighten the disease.

"At the end of a fortnight, when I was driven almost to the highest degree of despair, and could contrive no method of conveying a letter to Amelia, how was I surprised when Mrs. Harris's servant brought me a card, with an invitation from the mother herself to drink tea that evening at her house!

"You will easily believe, madam, that I did not fail so agreeable an appointment: on my arrival I was introduced into a large company of men and women, Mrs. Harris and my Amelia being part of the company.

"Amelia seemed in my eyes to look more beautiful than ever, and behaved with all the gaiety imaginable. The old lady treated me with much civility, but the young lady took little notice of me, and addressed most of her discourse to another gentleman present. Indeed, she now and then gave me a look of no discouraging kind, and I observed her colour change more than once when her eyes met mine; circumstances, which, perhaps, ought to have afforded me sufficient comfort, but they could not allay the thousand doubts and fears with which I was alarmed, for my anxious thoughts suggested no less to me than that Amelia had made her peace with her mother at the price of abandoning me forever, and of giving her ear to some other lover. All my prudence now vanished at once; and I would that instant have gladly run away with Amelia, and have married her without the least consideration of any consequences.

"With such thoughts I had tormented myself for near two hours, till most of the company had taken their leave. This I was myself incapable of doing, nor do I know when I should have put an end to my visit, had not Dr Harrison taken me away almost by force, telling me in a whisper that he had something to say to me of great consequence.—You know the doctor,

33

madam—"

"Very well, sir," answered Miss Matthews, "and one of the best men in the world he is, and an honour to the sacred order to which he belongs."

"You will judge," replied Booth, "by the sequel, whether I have reason to think him so."—He then proceeded as in the next chapter.

Chapter iv. — The story of Mr. Booth continued. In this chapter the reader will perceive a glimpse of the character of a very good divine, with some matters of a very tender kind.

"The doctor conducted me into his study, and I then, desiring me to sit down, began, as near as I can remember, in these words, or at least to this purpose:

"'You cannot imagine, young gentleman, that your love for Miss Emily is any secret in this place; I have known it some time, and have been, I assure you, very much your enemy in this affair.'

"I answered, that I was very much obliged to him.

"'Why, so you are,' replied he; 'and so, perhaps, you will think yourself when you know all.—I went about a fortnight ago to Mrs. Harris, to acquaint her with my apprehensions on her daughter's account; for, though the matter was much talked of, I thought it might possibly not have reached her ears. I will be very plain with you. I advised her to take all possible care of the young lady, and even to send her to some place, where she might be effectually kept out of your reach while you remained in the town.'

"And do you think, sir, said I, that this was acting a kind part by me? or do you expect that I should thank you on this occasion?

"'Young man,' answered he, 'I did not intend you any kindness, nor do I desire any of your thanks. My intention was to preserve a worthy lady from a young fellow of whom I had heard no good character, and whom I imagined to have a design of stealing a human creature for the sake of her fortune.'

"It was very kind of you, indeed, answered I, to entertain such an opinion of me.

"'Why, sir,' replied the doctor, 'it is the opinion which, I believe, most of you young gentlemen of the order of the rag deserve. I have known some instances, and have heard of more, where such young fellows have committed robbery under the name of marriage.'

"I was going to interrupt him with some anger when he desired me to have a little patience, and then informed me that he had visited Mrs. Harris with the above-mentioned design the evening after the discovery I have related; that Mrs. Harris, without waiting for his information, had recounted to him all which had happened the evening before; and, indeed, she must have an excellent memory, for I think she repeated every word I said, and added, that she had confined her daughter to her chamber, where she kept her a close prisoner, and had not seen her since.

"I cannot express, nor would modesty suffer me if I could, all that now past. The doctor took me by the hand and burst forth into the warmest commendations of the sense and generosity which he was pleased to say discovered themselves in my speech. You know, madam, his strong and singular way of expressing himself on all occasions, especially when he is affected with anything. 'Sir,' said he, 'if I knew half a dozen such instances in the army, the painter should put red liveries upon all the saints in my closet.'

"From this instant, the doctor told me, he had become my friend and zealous advocate with Mrs. Harris, on whom he had at last prevailed, though not without the greatest difficulty, to consent to my marrying Amelia, upon condition that I settled every penny which the mother should lay down, and that she would retain a certain sum in her hands which she would at any time deposit for my advancement in the army.

"You will, I hope, madam, conceive that I made no hesitation at these conditions, nor need I mention the joy which I felt on this occasion, or the acknowledgment I paid the doctor, who is, indeed, as you say, one of the best of men.

"The next morning I had permission to visit Amelia, who received me in such a manner, that

I now concluded my happiness to be complete.

"Everything was now agreed on all sides, and lawyers employed to prepare the writings, when an unexpected cloud arose suddenly in our serene sky, and all our joys were obscured in a moment.

"When matters were, as I apprehended, drawing near a conclusion, I received an express, that a sister whom I tenderly loved was seized with a violent fever, and earnestly desired me to come to her. I immediately obeyed the summons, and, as it was then about two in the morning, without staying even to take leave of Amelia, for whom I left a short billet, acquainting her with the reason of my absence.

"The gentleman's house where my sister then was stood at fifty miles' distance, and, though I used the utmost expedition, the unmerciful distemper had, before my arrival, entirely deprived the poor girl of her senses, as it soon after did of her life.

"Not all the love I bore Amelia, nor the tumultuous delight with which the approaching hour of possessing her filled my heart, could, for a while, allay my grief at the loss of my beloved Nancy. Upon my soul, I cannot yet mention her name without tears. Never brother and sister had, I believe, a higher friendship for each other. Poor dear girl! whilst I sat by her in her light-head fits, she repeated scarce any other name but mine; and it plainly appeared that, when her dear reason was ravished away from her, it had left my image on her fancy, and that the last use she made of it was to think on me. 'Send for my dear Billy immediately,' she cried; 'I know he will come to me in a moment. Will nobody fetch him to me? pray don't kill me before I see him once more. You durst not use me so if he was here.'—Every accent still rings in my ears. Oh, heavens! to hear this, and at the same time to see the poor delirious creature deriving the greatest horrors from my sight, and mistaking me for a highwayman who had a little before robbed her. But I ask your pardon; the sensations I felt are to be known only from experience, and to you must appear dull and insipid. At last, she seemed for a moment to know me, and cried, 'O heavens! my dearest brother!' upon which she fell into immediate convulsions, and died away in my arms."

Here Mr. Booth stopped a moment, and wiped his eyes; and Miss Matthews, perhaps out of complaisance, wiped hers.

Chapter v. — Containing strange revolutions of fortune

Booth proceeded thus:

"This loss, perhaps, madam, you will think had made me miserable enough; but Fortune did not think so; for, on the day when my Nancy was to be buried, a courier arrived from Dr Harrison, with a letter, in which the doctor acquainted me that he was just come from Mrs. Harris when he despatched the express, and earnestly desired me to return the very instant I received his letter, as I valued my Amelia. 'Though if the daughter,' added he, 'should take after her mother (as most of them do) it will be, perhaps, wiser in you to stay away.'

"I presently sent for the messenger into my room, and with much difficulty extorted from him that a great squire in his coach and six was come to Mrs. Harris's, and that the whole town said he was shortly to be married to Amelia.

"I now soon perceived how much superior my love for Amelia was to every other passion; poor Nancy's idea disappeared in a moment; I quitted the dear lifeless corpse, over which I had shed a thousand tears, left the care of her funeral to others, and posted, I may almost say flew, back to Amelia, and alighted at the doctor's house, as he had desired me in his letter.

"The good man presently acquainted me with what had happened in my absence. Mr. Winckworth had, it seems, arrived the very day of my departure, with a grand equipage, and, without delay, had made formal proposals to Mrs. Harris, offering to settle any part of his vast estate, in whatever manner she pleased, on Amelia. These proposals the old lady had, without any deliberation, accepted, and had insisted, in the most violent manner, on her daughter's compliance, which Amelia had as peremptorily refused to give; insisting, on her part, on the consent which her mother had before given to our marriage, in which she was heartily seconded

by the doctor, who declared to her, as he now did to me, 'that we ought as much to be esteemed man and wife as if the ceremony had already past between us.'

"These remonstrances, the doctor told me, had worked no effect on Mrs. Harris, who still persisted in her avowed resolution of marrying her daughter to Winckworth, whom the doctor had likewise attacked, telling him that he was paying his addresses to another man's wife; but all to no purpose; the young gentleman was too much in love to hearken to any dissuasives.

"We now entered into a consultation what means to employ. The doctor earnestly protested against any violence to be offered to the person of Winckworth, which, I believe, I had rashly threatened; declaring that, if I made any attempt of that kind, he would for ever abandon my cause. I made him a solemn promise of forbearance. At last he determined to pay another visit to Mrs. Harris, and, if he found her obdurate, he said he thought himself at liberty to join us together without any further consent of the mother, which every parent, he said, had a right to refuse, but not retract when given, unless the party himself, by some conduct of his, gave a reason.

"The doctor having made his visit with no better success than before, the matter now debated was, how to get possession of Amelia by stratagem, for she was now a closer prisoner than ever; was her mother's bedfellow by night, and never out of her sight by day.

"While we were deliberating on this point a wine-merchant of the town came to visit the doctor, to inform him that he had just bottled off a hogshead of excellent old port, of which he offered to spare him a hamper, saying that he was that day to send in twelve dozen to Mrs. Harris.

"The doctor now smiled at a conceit which came into his head; and, taking me aside, asked me if I had love enough for the young lady to venture into the house in a hamper. I joyfully leapt at the proposal, to which the merchant, at the doctor's intercession, consented; for I believe, madam, you know the great authority which that worthy mart had over the whole town. The doctor, moreover, promised to procure a license, and to perform the office for us at his house, if I could find any means of conveying Amelia thither.

"In this hamper, then, I was carried to the house, and deposited in the entry, where I had not lain long before I was again removed and packed up in a cart in order to be sent five miles into the country; for I heard the orders given as I lay in the entry; and there I likewise heard that Amelia and her mother were to follow me the next morning.

"I was unloaded from my cart, and set down with the rest of the lumber in a great hall. Here I remained above three hours, impatiently waiting for the evening, when I determined to quit a posture which was become very uneasy, and break my prison; but Fortune contrived to release me sooner, by the following means: The house where I now was had been left in the care of one maid-servant. This faithful creature came into the hall with the footman who had driven the cart. A scene of the highest fondness having past between them, the fellow proposed, and the maid consented, to open the hamper and drink a bottle together, which, they agreed, their mistress would hardly miss in such a quantity. They presently began to execute their purpose. They opened the hamper, and, to their great surprise, discovered the contents.

"I took an immediate advantage of the consternation which appeared in the countenances of both the servants, and had sufficient presence of mind to improve the knowledge of those secrets to which I was privy. I told them that it entirely depended on their behaviour to me whether their mistress should ever be acquainted, either with what they had done or with what they had intended to do; for that if they would keep my secret I would reciprocally keep theirs. I then acquainted them with my purpose of lying concealed in the house, in order to watch an opportunity of obtaining a private interview with Amelia.

{Illustration: They opened The Hamper}

"In the situation in which these two delinquents stood, you may be assured it was not difficult for me to seal up their lips. In short, they agreed to whatever I proposed. I lay that evening in my dear Amelia's bedchamber, and was in the morning conveyed into an old lumber-garret, where I was to wait till Amelia (whom the maid promised, on her arrival, to inform of my place of concealment) could find some opportunity of seeing me."

"I ask pardon for interrupting you," cries Miss Matthews, "but you bring to my remembrance a foolish story which I heard at that time, though at a great distance from you: That an officer had, in confederacy with Miss Harris, broke open her mother's cellar and stole away a great quantity of her wine. I mention it only to shew you what sort of foundations most stories have."

Booth told her he had heard some such thing himself, and then continued his story as in the

36

next chapter.

Chapter vi. — Containing many surprising adventures.

"There," continued he, "I remained the whole day in hopes of a happiness, the expected approach of which gave me such a delight that I would not have exchanged my poor lodgings for the finest palace in the universe.

"A little after it was dark Mrs. Harris arrived, together with Amelia and her sister. I cannot express how much my heart now began to flutter; for, as my hopes every moment encreased, strange fears, which I had not felt before, began now to intermingle with them.

"When I had continued full two hours in these circumstances, I heard a woman's step tripping upstairs, which I fondly hoped was my Amelia; but all on a sudden the door flew open, and Mrs. Harris herself appeared at it, with a countenance pale as death, her whole body trembling, I suppose with anger; she fell upon me in the most bitter language. It is not necessary to repeat what she said, nor indeed can I, I was so shocked and confounded on this occasion. In a word, the scene ended with my departure without seeing Amelia."

"And pray," cries Miss Matthews, "how happened this unfortunate discovery?"

Booth answered, That the lady at supper ordered a bottle of wine, "which neither myself," says he, "nor the servants had presence of mind to provide. Being told there was none in the house, though she had been before informed that the things came all safe, she had sent for the maid, who, being unable to devise any excuse, had fallen on her knees, and, after confessing her design of opening a bottle, which she imputed to the fellow, betrayed poor me to her mistress.

"Well, madam, after a lecture of about a quarter of an hour's duration from Mrs. Harris, I suffered her to conduct me to the outward gate of her court-yard, whence I set forward in a disconsolate condition of mind towards my lodgings. I had five miles to walk in a dark and rainy night: but how can I mention these trifling circumstances as any aggravation of my disappointment!"

"How was it possible," cried Miss Matthews, "that you could be got out of the house without seeing Miss Harris?"

"I assure you, madam," answered Booth, "I have often wondered at it myself; but my spirits were so much sunk at the sight of her mother, that no man was ever a greater coward than I was at that instant. Indeed, I believe my tender concern for the terrors of Amelia were the principal cause of my submission. However it was, I left the house, and walked about a hundred yards, when, at the corner of the garden-wall, a female voice, in a whisper, cried out, 'Mr. Booth.' The person was extremely near me, but it was so dark I could scarce see her; nor did I, in the confusion I was in, immediately recognize the voice. I answered in a line of Congreve's, which burst from my lips spontaneously; for I am sure I had no intention to quote plays at that time.

"'Who calls the wretched thing that was Alphonso?'

"Upon which a woman leapt into my arms, crying out—'O! it is indeed my Alphonso, my only Alphonso!'—O Miss Matthews! guess what I felt when I found I had my Amelia in my arms. I embraced her with an ecstasy not to be described, at the same instant pouring a thousand tendernesses into her ears; at least, if I could express so many to her in a minute, for in that time the alarm began at the house; Mrs. Harris had mist her daughter, and the court was presently full of lights and noises of all kinds.

"I now lifted Amelia over a gate, and, jumping after, we crept along together by the side of a hedge, a different way from what led to the town, as I imagined that would be the road through which they would pursue us. In this opinion I was right; for we heard them pass along that road, and the voice of Mrs. Harris herself, who ran with the rest, notwithstanding the darkness and the rain. By these means we luckily made our escape, and clambring over hedge and ditch, my Amelia performing the part of a heroine all the way, we at length arrived at a little green lane, where stood a vast spreading oak, under which we sheltered ourselves from a violent storm.

"When this was over and the moon began to appear, Amelia declared she knew very well

where she was; and, a little farther striking into another lane to the right, she said that would lead us to a house where we should be both safe and unsuspected. I followed her directions, and we at length came to a little cottage about three miles distant from Mrs. Harris's house.

"As it now rained very violently, we entered this cottage, in which we espied a light, without any ceremony. Here we found an elderly woman sitting by herself at a little fire, who had no sooner viewed us than she instantly sprung from her seat, and starting back gave the strongest tokens of amazement; upon which Amelia said, 'Be not surprised, nurse, though you see me in a strange pickle, I own.' The old woman, after having several times blessed herself, and expressed the most tender concern for the lady who stood dripping before her, began to bestir herself in making up the fire; at the same time entreating Amelia that she might be permitted to furnish her with some cloaths, which, she said, though not fine, were clean and wholesome and much dryer than her own. I seconded this motion so vehemently, that Amelia, though she declared herself under no apprehension of catching cold (she hath indeed the best constitution in the world), at last consented, and I retired without doors under a shed, to give my angel an opportunity of dressing herself in the only room which the cottage afforded belowstairs.

"At my return into the room, Amelia insisted on my exchanging my coat for one which belonged to the old woman's son." "I am very glad," cried Miss Matthews, "to find she did not forget you. I own I thought it somewhat cruel to turn you out into the rain."—"O, Miss Matthews!" continued he, taking no notice of her observation, "I had now an opportunity of contemplating the vast power of exquisite beauty, which nothing almost can add to or diminish. Amelia, in the poor rags of her old nurse, looked scarce less beautiful than I have seen her appear at a ball or an assembly." "Well, well," cries Miss Matthews, "to be sure she did; but pray go on with your story."

"The old woman," continued he, "after having equipped us as well as she could, and placed our wet cloaths before the fire, began to grow inquisitive; and, after some ejaculations, she cried— 'O, my dear young madam! my mind misgives me hugeously; and pray who is this fine young gentleman? Oh! Miss Emmy, Miss Emmy, I am afraid madam knows nothing of all this matter.' 'Suppose he should be my husband, nurse,' answered Amelia. 'Oh! good! and if he be,' replies the nurse, 'I hope he is some great gentleman or other, with a vast estate and a coach and six: for to be sure, if an he was the greatest lord in the land, you would deserve it all.' But why do I attempt to mimic the honest creature? In short, she discovered the greatest affection for my Amelia; with which I was much more delighted than I was offended at the suspicions she shewed of me, or the many bitter curses which she denounced against me, if I ever proved a bad husband to so sweet a young lady.

"I so well improved the hint given me by Amelia, that the old woman had no doubt of our being really married; and, comforting herself that, if it was not as well as it might have been, yet madam had enough for us both, and that happiness did not always depend on great riches, she began to rail at the old lady for having turned us out of doors, which I scarce told an untruth in asserting. And when Amelia said, 'She hoped her nurse would not betray her,' the good woman answered with much warmth—'Betray you, my dear young madam! no, that I would not, if the king would give me all that he is worth: no, not if madam herself would give me the great house, and the whole farm belonging to it.'

"The good woman then went out and fetched a chicken from the roost, which she killed, and began to pick, without asking any questions. Then, summoning her son, who was in bed, to her assistance, she began to prepare this chicken for our supper. This she afterwards set before us in so neat, I may almost say elegant, a manner, that whoever would have disdained it either doth not know the sensation of hunger, or doth not deserve to have it gratified. Our food was attended with some ale, which our kind hostess said she intended not to have tapped till Christmas; 'but,' added she, 'I little thought ever to have the honour of seeing my dear honoured lady in this poor place.'

"For my own part, no human being was then an object of envy to me, and even Amelia seemed to be in pretty good spirits; she softly whispered to me that she perceived there might be happiness in a cottage."

"A cottage!" cries Miss Matthews, sighing, "a cottage, with the man one loves, is a palace."

"When supper was ended," continued Booth, "the good woman began to think of our further wants, and very earnestly recommended her bed to us, saying, it was a very neat, though homely

one, and that she could furnish us with a pair of clean sheets. She added some persuasives which painted my angel all over with vermilion. As for myself, I behaved so awkwardly and foolishly, and so readily agreed to Amelia's resolution of sitting up all night, that, if it did not give the nurse any suspicion of our marriage, it ought to have inspired her with the utmost contempt for me.

"We both endeavoured to prevail with nurse to retire to her own bed, but found it utterly impossible to succeed; she thanked Heaven she understood breeding better than that. And so well bred was the good woman, that we could scarce get her out of the room the whole night. Luckily for us, we both understood French, by means of which we consulted together, even in her presence, upon the measures we were to take in our present exigency. At length it was resolved that I should send a letter by this young lad, whom I have just before mentioned, to our worthy friend the doctor, desiring his company at our hut, since we thought it utterly unsafe to venture to the town, which we knew would be in an uproar on our account before the morning."

Here Booth made a full stop, smiled, and then said he was going to mention so ridiculous a distress, that he could scarce think of it without laughing. What this was the reader shall know in the next chapter.

Chapter vii. — The story of Booth continued.—More surprising adventures.

"From what trifles, dear Miss Matthews," cried Booth, "may some of our greatest distresses arise!" Do you not perceive I am going to tell you we had neither pen, ink, nor paper, in our present exigency?

A verbal message was now our only resource; however, we contrived to deliver it in such terms, that neither nurse nor her son could possibly conceive any suspicion from it of the present situation of our affairs. Indeed, Amelia whispered me, I might safely place any degree of confidence in the lad; for he had been her foster-brother, and she had a great opinion of his integrity. He was in truth a boy of very good natural parts; and Dr Harrison, who had received him into his family, at Amelia's recommendation, had bred him up to write and read very well, and had taken some pains to infuse into him the principles of honesty and religion. He was not, indeed, even now discharged from the doctor's service, but had been at home with his mother for some time, on account of the small-pox, from which he was lately recovered.

"I have said so much," continued Booth, "of the boy's character, that you may not be surprised at some stories which I shall tell you of him hereafter.

"I am going now, madam, to relate to you one of those strange accidents which are produced by such a train of circumstances, that mere chance hath been thought incapable of bringing them together; and which have therefore given birth, in superstitious minds, to Fortune, and to several other imaginary beings.

"We were now impatiently expecting the arrival of the doctor; our messenger had been gone much more than a sufficient time, which to us, you may be assured, appeared not at all shorter than it was, when nurse, who had gone out of doors on some errand, came running hastily to us, crying out, 'O my dear young madam, her ladyship's coach is just at the door!' Amelia turned pale as death at these words; indeed, I feared she would have fainted, if I could be said to fear, who had scarce any of my senses left, and was in a condition little better than my angel's.

"While we were both in this dreadful situation, Amelia fallen back in her chair with the countenance in which ghosts are painted, myself at her feet, with a complexion of no very different colour, and nurse screaming out and throwing water in Amelia's face, Mrs. Harris entered the room. At the sight of this scene she threw herself likewise into a chair, and called immediately for a glass of water, which Miss Betty her daughter supplied her with; for, as to nurse, nothing was capable of making any impression on her whilst she apprehended her young mistress to be in danger.

"The doctor had now entered the room, and, coming immediately up to Amelia, after some expressions of surprise, he took her by the hand, called her his little sugar-plum, and assured her

there were none but friends present. He then led her tottering across the room to Mrs. Harris. Amelia then fell upon her knees before her mother; but the doctor caught her up, saying, 'Use that posture, child, only to the Almighty!' but I need not mention this singularity of his to you who know him so well, and must have heard him often dispute against addressing ourselves to man in the humblest posture which we use towards the Supreme Being.

"I will tire you with no more particulars: we were soon satisfied that the doctor had reconciled us and our affairs to Mrs. Harris; and we now proceeded directly to church, the doctor having before provided a licence for us."

"But where is the strange accident?" cries Miss Matthews; "sure you have raised more curiosity than you have satisfied."

"Indeed, madam," answered he, "your reproof is just; I had like to have forgotten it; but you cannot wonder at me when you reflect on that interesting part of my story which I am now relating.—But before I mention this accident I must tell you what happened after Amelia's escape from her mother's house. Mrs. Harris at first ran out into the lane among her servants, and pursued us (so she imagined) along the road leading to the town; but that being very dirty, and a violent storm of rain coming, she took shelter in an alehouse about half a mile from her own house, whither she sent for her coach; she then drove, together with her daughter, to town, where, soon after her arrival, she sent for the doctor, her usual privy counsellor in all her affairs. They sat up all night together, the doctor endeavouring, by arguments and persuasions, to bring Mrs. Harris to reason; but all to no purpose, though, as he hath informed me, Miss Betty seconded him with the warmest entreaties."

Here Miss Matthews laughed; of which Booth begged to know the reason: she, at last, after many apologies, said, "It was the first good thing she ever heard of Miss Betty; nay," said she, "and asking your pardon for my opinion of your sister, since you will have it, I always conceived her to be the deepest of hypocrites."

Booth fetched a sigh, and said he was afraid she had not always acted so kindly;—and then, after a little hesitation, proceeded:

"You will be pleased, madam, to remember the lad was sent with a verbal message to the doctor: which message was no more than to acquaint him where we were, and to desire the favour of his company, or that he would send a coach to bring us to whatever place he would please to meet us at. This message was to be delivered to the doctor himself, and the messenger was ordered, if he found him not at home, to go to him wherever he was. He fulfilled his orders and told it to the doctor in the presence of Mrs. Harris."

"Oh, the idiot!" cries Miss Matthews. "Not at all," answered Booth: "he is a very sensible fellow, as you will, perhaps, say hereafter. He had not the least reason to suspect that any secrecy was necessary; for we took the utmost care he should not suspect it.—Well, madam, this accident, which appeared so unfortunate, turned in the highest degree to our advantage. Mrs. Harris no sooner heard the message delivered than she fell into the most violent passion imaginable, and accused the doctor of being in the plot, and of having confederated with me in the design of carrying off her daughter.

"The doctor, who had hitherto used only soothing methods, now talked in a different strain. He confessed the accusation and justified his conduct. He said he was no meddler in the family affairs of others, nor should he have concerned himself with hers, but at her own request; but that, since Mrs. Harris herself had made him an agent in this matter, he would take care to acquit himself with honour, and above all things to preserve a young lady for whom he had the highest esteem; 'for she is,' cries he, and, by heavens, he said true, 'the most worthy, generous, and noble of all human beings. You have yourself, madam,' said he, 'consented to the match. I have, at your request, made the match;' and then he added some particulars relating to his opinion of me, which my modesty forbids me to repeat."—"Nay, but," cries Miss Matthews, "I insist on your conquest of that modesty for once. We women do not love to hear one another's praises, and I will be made amends by hearing the praises of a man, and of a man whom, perhaps," added she with a leer, "I shall not think much the better of upon that account."—"In obedience to your commands, then, madam," continued he, "the doctor was so kind to say he had enquired into my character and found that I had been a dutiful son and an affectionate brother. Relations, said he, in which whoever discharges his duty well, gives us a well-grounded hope that he will behave as properly in all the rest. He concluded with saying that Amelia's happiness, her heart, nay, her very reputation,

were all concerned in this matter, to which, as he had been made instrumental, he was resolved to carry her through it; and then, taking the licence from his pocket, declared to Mrs. Harris that he would go that instant and marry her daughter wherever he found her. This speech, the doctor's voice, his look, and his behaviour, all which are sufficiently calculated to inspire awe, and even terror, when he pleases, frightened poor Mrs. Harris, and wrought a more sensible effect than it was in his power to produce by all his arguments and entreaties; and I have already related what followed.

"Thus the strange accident of our wanting pen, ink, and paper, and our not trusting the boy with our secret, occasioned the discovery to Mrs. Harris; that discovery put the doctor upon his metal, and produced that blessed event which I have recounted to you, and which, as my mother hath since confessed, nothing but the spirit which he had exerted after the discovery could have brought about.

"Well, madam, you now see me married to Amelia; in which situation you will, perhaps, think my happiness incapable of addition. Perhaps it was so; and yet I can with truth say that the love which I then bore Amelia was not comparable to what I bear her now." "Happy Amelia!" cried Miss Matthews. "If all men were like you, all women would be blessed; nay, the whole world would be so in a great measure; for, upon my soul, I believe that from the damned inconstancy of your sex to ours proceeds half the miseries of mankind."

That we may give the reader leisure to consider well the foregoing sentiment, we will here put an end to this chapter.

Chapter viii. — In which our readers will probably be divided in their opinion of Mr. Booth's conduct.

Booth proceeded as follows:—

"The first months of our marriage produced nothing remarkable enough to mention. I am sure I need not tell Miss Matthews that I found in my Amelia every perfection of human nature. Mrs. Harris at first gave us some little uneasiness. She had rather yielded to the doctor than given a willing consent to the match; however, by degrees, she became more and more satisfied, and at last seemed perfectly reconciled. This we ascribed a good deal to the kind offices of Miss Betty, who had always appeared to be my friend. She had been greatly assisting to Amelia in making her escape, which I had no opportunity of mentioning to you before, and in all things behaved so well, outwardly at least, to myself as well as her sister, that we regarded her as our sincerest friend.

"About half a year after our marriage two additional companies were added to our regiment, in one of which I was preferred to the command of a lieutenant. Upon this occasion Miss Betty gave the first intimation of a disposition which we have since too severely experienced."

"Your servant, sir," says Miss Matthews; "then I find I was not mistaken in my opinion of the lady.—No, no, shew me any goodness in a censorious prude, and—"

As Miss Matthews hesitated for a simile or an execration, Booth proceeded: "You will please to remember, madam, there was formerly an agreement between myself and Mrs. Harris that I should settle all my Amelia's fortune on her, except a certain sum, which was to be laid out in my advancement in the army; but, as our marriage was carried on in the manner you have heard, no such agreement was ever executed. And since I was become Amelia's husband not a word of this matter was ever mentioned by the old lady; and as for myself, I declare I had not yet awakened from that delicious dream of bliss in which the possession of Amelia had lulled me."

Here Miss Matthews sighed, and cast the tenderest of looks on Booth, who thus continued his story:—

"Soon after my promotion Mrs. Harris one morning took an occasion to speak to me on this affair. She said, that, as I had been promoted gratis to a lieutenancy, she would assist me with money to carry me yet a step higher; and, if more was required than was formerly mentioned, it should not be wanting, since she was so perfectly satisfied with my behaviour to her daughter. Adding that she hoped I had still the same inclination to settle on my wife the remainder of her

fortune.

"I answered with very warm acknowledgments of my mother's goodness, and declared, if I had the world, I was ready to lay it at my Amelia's feet.—And so, Heaven knows, I would ten thousand worlds.

"Mrs. Harris seemed pleased with the warmth of my sentiments, and said she would immediately send to her lawyer and give him the necessary orders; and thus ended our conversation on this subject.

"From this time there was a very visible alteration in Miss Betty's behaviour. She grew reserved to her sister as well as to me. She was fretful and captious on the slightest occasion; nay, she affected much to talk on the ill consequences of an imprudent marriage, especially before her mother; and if ever any little tenderness or endearments escaped me in public towards Amelia, she never failed to make some malicious remark on the short duration of violent passions; and, when I have expressed a fond sentiment for my wife, her sister would kindly wish she might hear as much seven years hence.

"All these matters have been since suggested to us by reflection; for, while they actually past, both Amelia and myself had our thoughts too happily engaged to take notice of what discovered itself in the mind of any other person.

"Unfortunately for us, Mrs. Harris's lawyer happened at this time to be at London, where business detained him upwards of a month, and, as Mrs. Harris would on no occasion employ any other, our affair was under an entire suspension till his return.

"Amelia, who was now big with child, had often expressed the deepest concern at her apprehensions of my being some time commanded abroad; a circumstance, which she declared if it should ever happen to her, even though she should not then be in the same situation as at present, would infallibly break her heart. These remonstrances were made with such tenderness, and so much affected me, that, to avoid any probability of such an event, I endeavoured to get an exchange into the horse-guards, a body of troops which very rarely goes abroad, unless where the king himself commands in person. I soon found an officer for my purpose, the terms were agreed on, and Mrs. Harris had ordered the money which I was to pay to be ready, notwithstanding the opposition made by Miss Betty, who openly dissuaded her mother from it; alledging that the exchange was highly to my disadvantage; that I could never hope to rise in the army after it; not forgetting, at the same time, some insinuations very prejudicial to my reputation as a soldier.

"When everything was agreed on, and the two commissions were actually made out, but not signed by the king, one day, at my return from hunting, Amelia flew to me, and eagerly embracing me, cried out, 'O Billy, I have news for you which delights my soul. Nothing sure was ever so fortunate as the exchange you have made. The regiment you was formerly in is ordered for Gibraltar.'

"I received this news with far less transport than it was delivered. I answered coldly, since the case was so, I heartily hoped the commissions might be both signed. 'What do you say?' replied Amelia eagerly; 'sure you told me everything was entirely settled. That look of yours frightens me to death.'—But I am running into too minute particulars. In short, I received a letter by that very post from the officer with whom I had exchanged, insisting that, though his majesty had not signed the commissions, that still the bargain was valid, partly urging it as a right, and partly desiring it as a favour, that he might go to Gibraltar in my room.

"This letter convinced me in every point. I was now informed that the commissions were not signed, and consequently that the exchange was not compleated; of consequence the other could have no right to insist on going; and, as for granting him such a favour, I too clearly saw I must do it at the expense of my honour. I was now reduced to a dilemma, the most dreadful which I think any man can experience; in which, I am not ashamed to own, I found love was not so overmatched by honour as he ought to have been. The thoughts of leaving Amelia in her present condition to misery, perhaps to death or madness, were insupportable; nor could any other consideration but that which now tormented me on the other side have combated them a moment."

"No woman upon earth," cries Miss Matthews, "can despise want of spirit in a man more than myself; and yet I cannot help thinking you was rather too nice on this occasion."

"You will allow, madam," answered Booth, "that whoever offends against the laws of honour in the least instance is treated as the highest delinquent. Here is no excuse, no pardon; and he doth

42

nothing who leaves anything undone. But if the conflict was so terrible with myself alone, what was my situation in the presence of Amelia? how could I support her sighs, her tears, her agonies, her despair? could I bear to think myself the cruel cause of her sufferings? for so I was: could I endure the thought of having it in my power to give her instant relief, for so it was, and refuse it her?

"Miss Betty was now again become my friend. She had scarce been civil to me for a fortnight last past, yet now she commended me to the skies, and as severely blamed her sister, whom she arraigned of the most contemptible weakness in preferring my safety to my honour: she said many ill-natured things on the occasion, which I shall not now repeat.

"In the midst of this hurricane the good doctor came to dine with Mrs. Harris, and at my desire delivered his opinion on the matter."

Here Mr. Booth was interrupted in his narrative by the arrival of a person whom we shall introduce in the next chapter.

Chapter ix. — Containing a scene of a different kind from any of the preceding.

The gentleman who now arrived was the keeper; or, if you please (for so he pleased to call himself), the governor of the prison.

He used so little ceremony at his approach, that the bolt, which was very slight on the inside, gave way, and the door immediately flew open. He had no sooner entered the room than he acquainted Miss Matthews that he had brought her very good news, for which he demanded a bottle of wine as his due.

This demand being complied with, he acquainted Miss Matthews that the wounded gentleman was not dead, nor was his wound thought to be mortal: that loss of blood, and perhaps his fright, had occasioned his fainting away; "but I believe, madam," said he, "if you take the proper measures you may be bailed to-morrow. I expect the lawyer here this evening, and if you put the business into his hands I warrant it will be done. Money to be sure must be parted with, that's to be sure. People to be sure will expect to touch a little in such cases. For my own part, I never desire to keep a prisoner longer than the law allows, not I; I always inform them they can be bailed as soon as I know it; I never make any bargain, not I; I always love to leave those things to the gentlemen and ladies themselves. I never suspect gentlemen and ladies of wanting generosity."

Miss Matthews made a very slight answer to all these friendly professions. She said she had done nothing she repented of, and was indifferent as to the event. "All I can say," cries she, "is, that if the wretch is alive there is no greater villain in life than himself;" and, instead of mentioning anything of the bail, she begged the keeper to leave her again alone with Mr. Booth. The keeper replied, "Nay, madam, perhaps it may be better to stay a little longer here, if you have not bail ready, than to buy them too dear. Besides, a day or two hence, when the gentleman is past all danger of recovery, to be sure some folks that would expect an extraordinary fee now cannot expect to touch anything. And to be sure you shall want nothing here. The best of all things are to be had here for money, both eatable and drinkable: though I say it, I shan't turn my back to any of the taverns for either eatables or wind. The captain there need not have been so shy of owning himself when he first came in; we have had captains and other great gentlemen here before now; and no shame to them, though I say it. Many a great gentleman is sometimes found in places that don't become them half so well, let me tell them that, Captain Booth, let me tell them that."

"I see, sir," answered Booth, a little discomposed, "that you are acquainted with my title as well as my name."

"Ay, sir," cries the keeper, "and I honour you the more for it. I love the gentlemen of the army. I was in the army myself formerly; in the Lord of Oxford's horse. It is true I rode private; but I had money enough to have bought in quarter-master, when I took it into my head to marry, and my wife she did not like that I should continue a soldier, she was all for a private life; and so I came to this business."

"Upon my word, sir," answered Booth, "you consulted your wife's inclinations very notably;

but pray will you satisfy my curiosity in telling me how you became acquainted that I was in the army? for my dress I think could not betray me."

"Betray!" replied the keeper; "there is no betraying here, I hope—I am not a person to betray people.—But you are so shy and peery, you would almost make one suspect there was more in the matter. And if there be, I promise you, you need not be afraid of telling it me. You will excuse me giving you a hint; but the sooner the better, that's all. Others may be beforehand with you, and first come first served on these occasions, that's all. Informers are odious, there's no doubt of that, and no one would care to be an informer if he could help it, because of the ill-usage they always receive from the mob: yet it is dangerous to trust too much; and when safety and a good part of the reward too are on one side and the gallows on the other—I know which a wise man would chuse."

"What the devil do you mean by all this?" cries Booth.

"No offence, I hope," answered the keeper: "I speak for your good; and if you have been upon the snaffling lay—you understand me, I am sure."

"Not I," answered Booth, "upon my honour."

"Nay, nay," replied the keeper, with a contemptuous sneer, "if you are so peery as that comes to, you must take the consequence.—But for my part, I know I would not trust Robinson with twopence untold."

"What do you mean?" cries Booth; "who is Robinson?"

"And you don't know Robinson?" answered the keeper with great emotion. To which Booth replying in the negative, the keeper, after some tokens of amazement, cried out, "Well, captain, I must say you are the best at it of all the gentlemen I ever saw. However, I will tell you this: the lawyer and Mr. Robinson have been laying their heads together about you above half an hour this afternoon. I overheard them mention Captain Booth several times, and, for my part, I would not answer that Mr. Murphy is not now gone about the business; but if you will impeach any to me of the road, or anything else, I will step away to his worship Thrasher this instant, and I am sure I have interest enough with him to get you admitted an evidence."

"And so," cries Booth, "you really take me for a highwayman?"

"No offence, captain, I hope," said the keeper; "as times go, there are many worse men in the world than those. Gentlemen may be driven to distress, and when they are, I know no more genteeler way than the road. It hath been many a brave man's case, to my knowledge, and men of as much honour too as any in the world."

"Well, sir," said Booth, "I assure you I am not that gentleman of honour you imagine me."

Miss Matthews, who had long understood the keeper no better than Mr. Booth, no sooner heard his meaning explained than she was fired with greater indignation than the gentleman had expressed. "How dare you, sir," said she to the keeper, "insult a man of fashion, and who hath had the honour to bear his majesty's commission in the army? as you yourself own you know. If his misfortunes have sent him hither, sure we have no laws that will protect such a fellow as you in insulting him." "Fellow!" muttered the keeper—"I would not advise you, madam, to use such language to me."—"Do you dare threaten me?" replied Miss Matthews in a rage. "Venture in the least instance to exceed your authority with regard to me, and I will prosecute you with the utmost vengeance."

A scene of very high altercation now ensued, till Booth interposed and quieted the keeper, who was, perhaps, enough inclined to an accommodation; for, in truth, he waged unequal war. He was besides unwilling to incense Miss Matthews, whom he expected to be bailed out the next day, and who had more money left than he intended she should carry out of the prison with her; and as for any violent or unjustifiable methods, the lady had discovered much too great a spirit to be in danger of them. The governor, therefore, in a very gentle tone, declared that, if he had given any offence to the gentleman, he heartily asked his pardon; that, if he had known him to be really a captain, he should not have entertained any such suspicions; but the captain was a very common title in that place, and belonged to several gentlemen that had never been in the army, or, at most, had rid private like himself. "To be sure, captain," said he, "as you yourself own, your dress is not very military" (for he had on a plain fustian suit); "and besides, as the lawyer says, noscitur a sosir, is a very good rule. And I don't believe there is a greater rascal upon earth than that same Robinson that I was talking of. Nay, I assure you, I wish there may be no mischief hatching against you. But if there is I will do all I can with the lawyer to prevent it. To be sure, Mr. Murphy

is one of the cleverest men in the world at the law; that even his enemies must own, and as I recommend him to all the business I can (and it is not a little to be sure that arises in this place), why one good turn deserves another. And I may expect that he will not be concerned in any plot to ruin any friend of mine, at least when I desire him not. I am sure he could not be an honest man if he would."

Booth was then satisfied that Mr. Robinson, whom he did not yet know by name, was the gamester who had won his money at play. And now Miss Matthews, who had very impatiently borne this long interruption, prevailed on the keeper to withdraw. As soon as he was gone Mr. Booth began to felicitate her upon the news of the wounded gentleman being in a fair likelihood of recovery. To which, after a short silence, she answered, "There is something, perhaps, which you will not easily guess, that makes your congratulations more agreeable to me than the first account I heard of the villain's having escaped the fate he deserves; for I do assure you, at first, it did not make me amends for the interruption of my curiosity. Now I hope we shall be disturbed no more till you have finished your whole story.—You left off, I think, somewhere in the struggle about leaving Amelia—the happy Amelia." "And can you call her happy at such a period?" cries Booth. "Happy, ay, happy, in any situation," answered Miss Matthews, "with such a husband. I, at least, may well think so, who have experienced the very reverse of her fortune; but I was not born to be happy. I may say with the poet,

"The blackest ink of fate was sure my lot,
    And when fate writ my name, it made a blot."

"Nay, nay, dear Miss Matthews," answered Booth, "you must and shall banish such gloomy thoughts. Fate hath, I hope, many happy days in store for you."—"Do you believe it, Mr. Booth?" replied she; "indeed you know the contrary—you must know—for you can't have forgot. No Amelia in the world can have quite obliterated—forgetfulness is not in our own power. If it was, indeed, I have reason to think—but I know not what I am saying.—Pray do proceed in that story."

Booth so immediately complied with this request that it is possible he was pleased with it. To say the truth, if all which unwittingly dropt from Miss Matthews was put together, some conclusions might, it seems, be drawn from the whole, which could not convey a very agreeable idea to a constant husband. Booth, therefore, proceeded to relate what is written in the third book of this history.

BOOK III.

Chapter i. — In which Mr. Booth resumes his story.

"If I am not mistaken, madam," continued Booth, "I was just going to acquaint you with the doctor's opinion when we were interrupted by the keeper.

"The doctor, having heard counsel on both sides, that is to say, Mrs. Harris for my staying, and Miss Betty for my going, at last delivered his own sentiments. As for Amelia, she sat silent, drowned in her tears; nor was I myself in a much better situation.

"'As the commissions are not signed,' said the doctor, 'I think you may be said to remain in your former regiment; and therefore I think you ought to go on this expedition; your duty to your king and country, whose bread you have eaten, requires it; and this is a duty of too high a nature to admit the least deficiency. Regard to your character, likewise, requires you to go; for the world, which might justly blame your staying at home if the case was even fairly stated, will not deal so honestly by you: you must expect to have every circumstance against you heightened, and most of

what makes for your defence omitted; and thus you will be stigmatized as a coward without any palliation. As the malicious disposition of mankind is too well known, and the cruel pleasure which they take in destroying the reputations of others, the use we are to make of this knowledge is to afford no handle to reproach; for, bad as the world is, it seldom falls on any man who hath not given some slight cause for censure, though this, perhaps, is often aggravated ten thousand-fold; and, when we blame the malice of the aggravation we ought not to forget our own imprudence in giving the occasion. Remember, my boy, your honour is at stake; and you know how nice the honour of a soldier is in these cases. This is a treasure which he must be your enemy, indeed, who would attempt to rob you of. Therefore, you ought to consider every one as your enemy who, by desiring you to stay, would rob you of your honour.'

"'Do you hear that, sister?' cries Miss Betty.—'Yes, I do hear it' answered Amelia, with more spirit than I ever saw her exert before, and would preserve his honour at the expense of my life. 'I will preserve it if it should be at that expense; and since it is Dr Harrison's opinion that he ought to go, I give my consent. Go, my dear husband,' cried she, falling upon her knees: 'may every angel of heaven guard and preserve you!'—I cannot repeat her words without being affected," said he, wiping his eyes, "the excellence of that woman no words can paint: Miss Matthews, she hath every perfection in human nature.

"I will not tire you with the repetition of any more that past on that occasion, nor with the quarrel that ensued between Mrs. Harris and the doctor; for the old lady could not submit to my leaving her daughter in her present condition. She fell severely on the army, and cursed the day in which her daughter was married to a soldier, not sparing the doctor for having had some share in the match. I will omit, likewise, the tender scene which past between Amelia and myself previous to my departure." "Indeed, I beg you would not," cries Miss Matthews; "nothing delights me more than scenes of tenderness. I should be glad to know, if possible, every syllable which was uttered on both sides."

"I will indulge you then," cries Booth, "as far as is in my power. Indeed, I believe I am able to recollect much the greatest part; for the impression is never to be effaced from my memory."

He then proceeded as Miss Matthews desired; but, lest all our readers should not be of her opinion, we will, according to our usual custom, endeavour to accommodate ourselves to every taste, and shall, therefore, place this scene in a chapter by itself, which we desire all our readers who do not love, or who, perhaps, do not know the pleasure of tenderness, to pass over; since they may do this without any prejudice to the thread of the narrative.

Chapter ii. — Containing a scene of the tender kind.

"The doctor, madam," continued Booth, "spent his evening at Mrs. Harris's house, where I sat with him whilst he smoaked his pillow pipe, as his phrase is. Amelia was retired about half an hour to her chamber before I went to her. At my entrance I found her on her knees, a posture in which I never disturbed her. In a few minutes she arose, came to me, and embracing me, said she had been praying for resolution to support the cruellest moment she had ever undergone or could possibly undergo. I reminded her how much more bitter a farewel would be on a death-bed, when we never could meet, in this world at least, again. I then endeavoured to lessen all those objects which alarmed her most, and particularly the danger I was to encounter, upon which head I seemed a little to comfort her; but the probable length of my absence and the certain length of my voyage were circumstances which no oratory of mine could even palliate. 'O heavens!' said she, bursting into tears, 'can I bear to think that hundreds, thousands for aught I know, of miles or leagues, that lands and seas are between us? What is the prospect from that mount in our garden where I have sat so many happy hours with my Billy? what is the distance between that and the farthest hill which we see from thence compared to the distance which will be between us? You cannot wonder at this idea; you must remember, my Billy, at this place, this very thought came formerly into my foreboding mind. I then begged you to leave the army. Why would you not comply?—did I not tell you then that the smallest cottage we could survey from the mount would

be, with you, a paradise to me? it would be so still—why can't my Billy think so? am I so much his superior in love? where is the dishonour, Billy? or, if there be any, will it reach our ears in our little hut? are glory and fame, and not his Amelia, the happiness of my husband? go then, purchase them at my expence. You will pay a few sighs, perhaps a few tears, at parting, and then new scenes will drive away the thoughts of poor Amelia from your bosom; but what assistance shall I have in my affliction? not that any change of scene could drive you one moment from my remembrance; yet here every object I behold will place your loved idea in the liveliest manner before my eyes. This is the bed in which you have reposed; that is the chair on which you sat. Upon these boards you have stood. These books you have read to me. Can I walk among our beds of flowers without viewing your favourites, nay, those which you have planted with your own hands? can I see one beauty from our beloved mount which you have not pointed out to me?'—Thus she went on, the woman, madam, you see, still prevailing."—"Since you mention it," says Miss Matthews, with a smile, "I own the same observation occurred to me. It is too natural to us to consider ourselves only, Mr. Booth."—"You shall hear," he cried. "At last the thoughts of her present condition suggested themselves.—' But if,' said she, 'my situation, even in health, will be so intolerable, how shall I, in the danger and agonies of childbirth, support your absence?'—Here she stopt, and, looking on me with all the tenderness imaginable, cried out, 'And am I then such a wretch to wish for your presence at such a season? ought I not to rejoice that you are out of the hearing of my cries or the knowledge of my pains? if I die, will you not have escaped the horrors of a parting ten thousand times more dreadful than this? Go, go, my Billy; the very circumstance which made me most dread your departure hath perfectly reconciled me to it. I perceive clearly now that I was only wishing to support my own weakness with your strength, and to relieve my own pains at the price of yours. Believe me, my love, I am ashamed of myself.'—I caught her in my arms with raptures not to be exprest in words, called her my heroine; sure none ever better deserved that name; after which we remained for some time speechless, and locked in each other's embraces."—

"I am convinced," said Miss Matthews, with a sigh, "there are moments in life worth purchasing with worlds."

"At length the fatal morning came. I endeavoured to hide every pang of my heart, and to wear the utmost gaiety in my countenance. Amelia acted the same part. In these assumed characters we met the family at breakfast; at their breakfast, I mean, for we were both full already. The doctor had spent above an hour that morning in discourse with Mrs. Harris, and had, in some measure, reconciled her to my departure. He now made use of every art to relieve the poor distressed Amelia; not by inveighing against the folly of grief, or by seriously advising her not to grieve; both of which were sufficiently performed by Miss Betty. The doctor, on the contrary, had recourse to every means which might cast a veil over the idea of grief, and raise comfortable images in my angel's mind. He endeavoured to lessen the supposed length of my absence by discoursing on matters which were more distant in time. He said he intended next year to rebuild a part of his parsonage-house. 'And you, captain,' says he, 'shall lay the corner-stone, I promise you:' with many other instances of the like nature, which produced, I believe, some good effect on us both.

"Amelia spoke but little; indeed, more tears than words dropt from her; however, she seemed resolved to bear her affliction with resignation. But when the dreadful news arrived that the horses were ready, and I, having taken my leave of all the rest, at last approached her, she was unable to support the conflict with nature any longer, and, clinging round my neck, she cried, 'Farewel, farewel for ever; for I shall never, never see you more.' At which words the blood entirely forsook her lovely cheeks, and she became a lifeless corpse in my arms.

"Amelia continued so long motionless, that the doctor, as well as Mrs. Harris, began to be under the most terrible apprehensions; so they informed me afterwards, for at that time I was incapable of making any observation. I had indeed very little more use of my senses than the dear creature whom I supported. At length, however, we were all delivered from our fears; and life again visited the loveliest mansion that human nature ever afforded it.

"I had been, and yet was, so terrified with what had happened, and Amelia continued yet so weak and ill, that I determined, whatever might be the consequence, not to leave her that day; which resolution she was no sooner acquainted with than she fell on her knees, crying, 'Good Heaven! I thank thee for this reprieve at least. Oh! that every hour of my future life could be crammed into this dear day!'

"Our good friend the doctor remained with us. He said he had 'intended to visit a family in

some affliction; 'but I don't know,' says he, 'why I should ride a dozen miles after affliction, when we have enough here.'" Of all mankind the doctor is the best of comforters. As his excessive good-nature makes him take vast delight in the office, so his great penetration into the human mind, joined to his great experience, renders him the most wonderful proficient in it; and he so well knows when to soothe, when to reason, and when to ridicule, that he never applies any of those arts improperly, which is almost universally the case with the physicians of the mind, and which it requires very great judgment and dexterity to avoid.

"The doctor principally applied himself to ridiculing the dangers of the siege, in which he succeeded so well, that he sometimes forced a smile even into the face of Amelia. But what most comforted her were the arguments he used to convince her of the probability of my speedy if not immediate return. He said the general opinion was that the place would be taken before our arrival there; in which case we should have nothing more to do than to make the best of our way home again.

"Amelia was so lulled by these arts that she passed the day much better than I expected. Though the doctor could not make pride strong enough to conquer love, yet he exalted the former to make some stand against the latter; insomuch that my poor Amelia, I believe, more than once flattered herself, to speak the language of the world, that her reason had gained an entire victory over her passion; till love brought up a reinforcement, if I may use that term, of tender ideas, and bore down all before him.

"In the evening the doctor and I passed another half-hour together, when he proposed to me to endeavour to leave Amelia asleep in the morning, and promised me to be at hand when she awaked, and to support her with all the assistance in his power. He added that nothing was more foolish than for friends to take leave of each other. 'It is true, indeed,' says he, 'in the common acquaintance and friendship of the world, this is a very harmless ceremony; but between two persons who really love each other the church of Rome never invented a penance half so severe as this which we absurdly impose on ourselves.

"I greatly approved the doctor's proposal; thanked him, and promised, if possible, to put it in execution. He then shook me by the hand, and heartily wished me well, saying, in his blunt way, 'Well, boy, I hope to see thee crowned with laurels at thy return; one comfort I have at least, that stone walls and a sea will prevent thee from running away.'

"When I had left the doctor I repaired to my Amelia, whom I found in her chamber, employed in a very different manner from what she had been the preceding night; she was busy in packing up some trinkets in a casket, which she desired me to carry with me. This casket was her own work, and she had just fastened it as I came to her.

"Her eyes very plainly discovered what had passed while she was engaged in her work: however, her countenance was now serene, and she spoke, at least, with some cheerfulness. But after some time, 'You must take care of this casket, Billy,' said she. 'You must, indeed, Billy—for—' here passion almost choked her, till a flood of tears gave her relief, and then she proceeded—'For I shall be the happiest woman that ever was born when I see it again.' I told her, with the blessing of God, that day would soon come. 'Soon!' answered she. 'No, Billy, not soon: a week is an age;—but yet the happy day may come. It shall, it must, it will! Yes, Billy, we shall meet never to part again, even in this world, I hope.' Pardon my weakness, Miss Matthews, but upon my soul I cannot help it," cried he, wiping his eyes. "Well, I wonder at your patience, and I will try it no longer. Amelia, tired out with so long a struggle between variety of passions, and having not closed her eyes during three successive nights, towards the morning fell into a profound sleep. In which sleep I left her, and, having drest myself with all the expedition imaginable, singing, whistling, hurrying, attempting by every method to banish thought, I mounted my horse, which I had over-night ordered to be ready, and galloped away from that house where all my treasure was deposited.

"Thus, madam, I have, in obedience to your commands, run through a scene which, if it hath been tiresome to you, you must yet acquit me of having obtruded upon you. This I am convinced of, that no one is capable of tasting such a scene who hath not a heart full of tenderness, and perhaps not even then, unless he hath been in the same situation."

Chapter iii. — In which Mr. Booth sets forward on his journey.

"Well, madam, we have now taken our leave of Amelia. I rode a full mile before I once suffered myself to look back; but now being come to the top of a little hill, the last spot I knew which could give me a prospect of Mrs. Harris's house, my resolution failed: I stopped and cast my eyes backward. Shall I tell you what I felt at that instant? I do assure you I am not able. So many tender ideas crowded at once into my mind, that, if I may use the expression, they almost dissolved my heart. And now, madam, the most unfortunate accident came first into my head. This was, that I had in the hurry and confusion left the dear casket behind me. The thought of going back at first suggested itself; but the consequences of that were too apparent. I therefore resolved to send my man, and in the meantime to ride on softly on my road. He immediately executed my orders, and after some time, feeding my eyes with that delicious and yet heartfelt prospect, I at last turned my horse to descend the hill, and proceeded about a hundred yards, when, considering with myself that I should lose no time by a second indulgence, I again turned back, and once more feasted my sight with the same painful pleasure till my man returned, bringing me the casket, and an account that Amelia still continued in the sweet sleep I left her. I now suddenly turned my horse for the last time, and with the utmost resolution pursued my journey.

"I perceived my man at his return—But before I mention anything of him it may be proper, madam, to acquaint you who he was. He was the foster-brother of my Amelia. This young fellow had taken it into his head to go into the army; and he was desirous to serve under my command. The doctor consented to discharge him; his mother at last yielded to his importunities, and I was very easily prevailed on to list one of the handsomest young fellows in England.

"You will easily believe I had some little partiality to one whose milk Amelia had sucked; but, as he had never seen the regiment, I had no opportunity to shew him any great mark of favour. Indeed he waited on me as my servant; and I treated him with all the tenderness which can be used to one in that station.

"When I was about to change into the horse-guards the poor fellow began to droop, fearing that he should no longer be in the same corps with me, though certainly that would not have been the case. However, he had never mentioned one word of his dissatisfaction. He is indeed a fellow of a noble spirit; but when he heard that I was to remain where I was, and that we were to go to Gibraltar together, he fell into transports of joy little short of madness. In short, the poor fellow had imbibed a very strong affection for me; though this was what I knew nothing of till long after.

"When he returned to me then, as I was saying, with the casket, I observed his eyes all over blubbered with tears. I rebuked him a little too rashly on this occasion. 'Heyday!' says I, 'what is the meaning of this? I hope I have not a milk-sop with me. If I thought you would shew such a face to the enemy I would leave you behind.'—'Your honour need not fear that,' answered he; 'I shall find nobody there that I shall love well enough to make me cry.' I was highly pleased with this answer, in which I thought I could discover both sense and spirit. I then asked him what had occasioned those tears since he had left me (for he had no sign of any at that time), and whether he had seen his mother at Mrs. Harris's? He answered in the negative, and begged that I would ask him no more questions; adding that he was not very apt to cry, and he hoped he should never give me such another opportunity of blaming him. I mention this only as an instance of his affection towards me; for I never could account for those tears any otherwise than by placing them to the account of that distress in which he left me at that time. We travelled full forty miles that day without baiting, when, arriving at the inn where I intended to rest that night, I retired immediately to my chamber, with my dear Amelia's casket, the opening of which was the nicest repast, and to which every other hunger gave way.

"It is impossible to mention to you all the little matters with which Amelia had furnished this casket. It contained medicines of all kinds, which her mother, who was the Lady Bountiful of that country, had supplied her with. The most valuable of all to me was a lock of her dear hair, which I have from that time to this worn in my bosom. What would I have then given for a little picture of my dear angel, which she had lost from her chamber about a month before! and which we had the highest reason in the world to imagine her sister had taken away; for the suspicion lay only

between her and Amelia's maid, who was of all creatures the honestest, and whom her mistress had often trusted with things of much greater value; for the picture, which was set in gold, and had two or three little diamonds round it, was worth about twelve guineas only; whereas Amelia left jewels in her care of much greater value."

"Sure," cries Miss Matthews, "she could not be such a paultry pilferer."

"Not on account of the gold or the jewels," cries Booth. "We imputed it to mere spite, with which, I assure you, she abounds; and she knew that, next to Amelia herself, there was nothing which I valued so much as this little picture; for such a resemblance did it bear of the original, that Hogarth himself did never, I believe, draw a stronger likeness. Spite, therefore, was the only motive to this cruel depredation; and indeed her behaviour on the occasion sufficiently convinced us both of the justice of our suspicion, though we neither of us durst accuse her; and she herself had the assurance to insist very strongly (though she could not prevail) with Amelia to turn away her innocent maid, saying, she would not live in the house with a thief."

Miss Matthews now discharged some curses on Miss Betty, not much worth repeating, and then Mr. Booth proceeded in his relation.

Chapter iv. — A sea piece.

"The next day we joined the regiment, which was soon after to embark. Nothing but mirth and jollity were in the countenance of every officer and soldier; and as I now met several friends whom I had not seen for above a year before, I passed several happy hours, in which poor Amelia's image seldom obtruded itself to interrupt my pleasure. To confess the truth, dear Miss Matthews, the tenderest of passions is capable of subsiding; nor is absence from our dearest friends so unsupportable as it may at first appear. Distance of time and place do really cure what they seem to aggravate; and taking leave of our friends resembles taking leave of the world; concerning which it hath been often said that it is not death, but dying, which is terrible."—Here Miss Matthews burst into a fit of laughter, and cried, "I sincerely ask your pardon; but I cannot help laughing at the gravity of your philosophy." Booth answered, That the doctrine of the passions had been always his favourite study; that he was convinced every man acted entirely from that passion which was uppermost. "Can I then think," said he, "without entertaining the utmost contempt for myself, that any pleasure upon earth could drive the thoughts of Amelia one instant from my mind?

"At length we embarked aboard a transport, and sailed for Gibraltar; but the wind, which was at first fair, soon chopped about; so that we were obliged, for several days, to beat to windward, as the sea phrase is. During this time the taste which I had of a seafaring life did not appear extremely agreeable. We rolled up and down in a little narrow cabbin, in which were three officers, all of us extremely sea-sick; our sickness being much aggravated by the motion of the ship, by the view of each other, and by the stench of the men. But this was but a little taste indeed of the misery which was to follow; for we were got about six leagues to the westward of Scilly, when a violent storm arose at north-east, which soon raised the waves to the height of mountains. The horror of this is not to be adequately described to those who have never seen the like. The storm began in the evening, and, as the clouds brought on the night apace, it was soon entirely dark; nor had we, during many hours, any other light than what was caused by the jarring elements, which frequently sent forth flashes, or rather streams of fire; and whilst these presented the most dreadful objects to our eyes, the roaring of the winds, the dashing of the waves against the ship and each other, formed a sound altogether as horrible for our ears; while our ship, sometimes lifted up, as it were, to the skies, and sometimes swept away at once as into the lowest abyss, seemed to be the sport of the winds and seas. The captain himself almost gave up all for lost, and exprest his apprehension of being inevitably cast on the rocks of Scilly, and beat to pieces. And now, while some on board were addressing themselves to the Supreme Being, and others applying for comfort to strong liquors, my whole thoughts were entirely engaged by my Amelia. A

thousand tender ideas crouded into my mind. I can truly say that I had not a single consideration about myself in which she was not concerned. Dying to me was leaving her; and the fear of never seeing her more was a dagger stuck in my heart. Again, all the terrors with which this storm, if it reached her ears, must fill her gentle mind on my account, and the agonies which she must undergo when she heard of my fate, gave me such intolerable pangs, that I now repented my resolution, and wished, I own I wished, that I had taken her advice, and preferred love and a cottage to all the dazzling charms of honour.

"While I was tormenting myself with those meditations, and had concluded myself as certainly lost, the master came into the cabbin, and with a chearful voice assured us that we had escaped the danger, and that we had certainly past to westward of the rock. This was comfortable news to all present; and my captain, who had been some time on his knees, leapt suddenly up, and testified his joy with a great oath.

"A person unused to the sea would have been astonished at the satisfaction which now discovered itself in the master or in any on board; for the storm still raged with great violence, and the daylight, which now appeared, presented us with sights of horror sufficient to terrify minds which were not absolute slaves to the passion of fear; but so great is the force of habit, that what inspires a landsman with the highest apprehension of danger gives not the least concern to a sailor, to whom rocks and quicksands are almost the only objects of terror.

"The master, however, was a little mistaken in the present instance; for he had not left the cabbin above an hour before my man came running to me, and acquainted me that the ship was half full of water; that the sailors were going to hoist out the boat and save themselves, and begged me to come that moment along with him, as I tendered my preservation. With this account, which was conveyed to me in a whisper, I acquainted both the captain and ensign; and we all together immediately mounted the deck, where we found the master making use of all his oratory to persuade the sailors that the ship was in no danger; and at the same time employing all his authority to set the pumps a-going, which he assured them would keep the water under, and save his dear Lovely Peggy (for that was the name of the ship), which he swore he loved as dearly as his own soul.

"Indeed this sufficiently appeared; for the leak was so great, and the water flowed in so plentifully, that his Lovely Peggy was half filled before he could be brought to think of quitting her; but now the boat was brought alongside the ship, and the master himself, notwithstanding all his love for her, quitted his ship, and leapt into the boat. Every man present attempted to follow his example, when I heard the voice of my servant roaring forth my name in a kind of agony. I made directly to the ship-side, but was too late; for the boat, being already overladen, put directly off. And now, madam, I am going to relate to you an instance of heroic affection in a poor fellow towards his master, to which love itself, even among persons of superior education, can produce but few similar instances. My poor man, being unable to get me with him into the boat, leapt suddenly into the sea, and swam back to the ship; and, when I gently rebuked him for his rashness, he answered, he chose rather to die with me than to live to carry the account of my death to my Amelia: at the same time bursting into a flood of tears, he cried, 'Good Heavens! what will that poor lady feel when she hears of this!' This tender concern for my dear love endeared the poor fellow more to me than the gallant instance which he had just before given of his affection towards myself.

"And now, madam, my eyes were shocked with a sight, the horror of which can scarce be imagined; for the boat had scarce got four hundred yards from the ship when it was swallowed up by the merciless waves, which now ran so high, that out of the number of persons which were in the boat none recovered the ship, though many of them we saw miserably perish before our eyes, some of them very near us, without any possibility of giving them the least assistance.

"But, whatever we felt for them, we felt, I believe, more for ourselves, expecting every minute when we should share the same fate. Amongst the rest, one of our officers appeared quite stupified with fear. I never, indeed, saw a more miserable example of the great power of that passion: I must not, however, omit doing him justice, by saying that I afterwards saw the same man behave well in an engagement, in which he was wounded; though there likewise he was said to have betrayed the same passion of fear in his countenance.

"The other of our officers was no less stupified (if I may so express myself) with fool-hardiness, and seemed almost insensible of his danger. To say the truth, I have, from this and

51

some other instances which I have seen, been almost inclined to think that the courage as well as cowardice of fools proceeds from not knowing what is or what is not the proper object of fear; indeed, we may account for the extreme hardiness of some men in the same manner as for the terrors of children at a bugbear. The child knows not but that the bugbear is the proper object of fear, the blockhead knows not that a cannon-ball is so.

"As to the remaining part of the ship's crew and the soldiery, most of them were dead drunk, and the rest were endeavouring, as fast as they could, to prepare for death in the same manner.

"In this dreadful situation we were taught that no human condition should inspire men with absolute despair; for, as the storm had ceased for some time, the swelling of the sea began considerably to abate; and we now perceived the man of war which convoyed us, at no great distance astern. Those aboard her easily perceived our distress, and made towards us. When they came pretty near they hoisted out two boats to our assistance. These no sooner approached the ship than they were instantaneously filled, and I myself got a place in one of them, chiefly by the aid of my honest servant, of whose fidelity to me on all occasions I cannot speak or think too highly. Indeed, I got into the boat so much the more easily, as a great number on board the ship were rendered, by drink, incapable of taking any care for themselves. There was time, however, for the boat to pass and repass; so that, when we came to call over names, three only, of all that remained in the ship after the loss of her own boat, were missing.

"The captain, ensign, and myself, were received with many congratulations by our officers on board the man of war.—The sea-officers too, all except the captain, paid us their compliments, though these were of the rougher kind, and not without several jokes on our escape. As for the captain himself, we scarce saw him during many hours; and, when he appeared, he presented a view of majesty beyond any that I had ever seen. The dignity which he preserved did indeed give me rather the idea of a Mogul, or a Turkish emperor, than of any of the monarchs of Christendom. To say the truth, I could resemble his walk on the deck to nothing but the image of Captain Gulliver strutting among the Lilliputians; he seemed to think himself a being of an order superior to all around him, and more especially to us of the land service. Nay, such was the behaviour of all the sea-officers and sailors to us and our soldiers, that, instead of appearing to be subjects of the same prince, engaged in one quarrel, and joined to support one cause, we land-men rather seemed to be captives on board an enemy's vessel. This is a grievous misfortune, and often proves so fatal to the service, that it is great pity some means could not be found of curing it."

Here Mr. Booth stopt a while to take breath. We will therefore give the same refreshment to the reader.

Chapter v. — The arrival of Booth at Gibraltar, with what there befel him.

"The adventures," continued Booth, "which I happened to me from this day till my arrival at Gibraltar are not worth recounting to you. After a voyage the remainder of which was tolerably prosperous, we arrived in that garrison, the natural strength of which is so well known to the whole world.

"About a week after my arrival it was my fortune to be ordered on a sally party, in which my left leg was broke with a musket-ball; and I should most certainly have either perished miserably, or must have owed my preservation to some of the enemy, had not my faithful servant carried me off on his shoulders, and afterwards, with the assistance of one of his comrades, brought me back into the garrison.

"The agony of my wound was so great, that it threw me into a fever, from whence my surgeon apprehended much danger. I now began again to feel for my Amelia, and for myself on her account; and the disorder of my mind, occasioned by such melancholy contemplations, very highly aggravated the distemper of my body; insomuch that it would probably have proved fatal, had it not been for the friendship of one Captain James, an officer of our regiment, and an old acquaintance, who is undoubtedly one of the pleasantest companions and one of the best-natured men in the world. This worthy man, who had a head and a heart perfectly adequate to every office

of friendship, stayed with me almost day and night during my illness; and by strengthening my hopes, raising my spirits, and cheering my thoughts, preserved me from destruction.

"The behaviour of this man alone is a sufficient proof of the truth of my doctrine, that all men act entirely from their passions; for Bob James can never be supposed to act from any motives of virtue or religion, since he constantly laughs at both; and yet his conduct towards me alone demonstrates a degree of goodness which, perhaps, few of the votaries of either virtue or religion can equal." "You need not take much pains," answered Miss Matthews, with a smile, "to convince me of your doctrine. I have been always an advocate for the same. I look upon the two words you mention to serve only as cloaks, under which hypocrisy may be the better enabled to cheat the world. I have been of that opinion ever since I read that charming fellow Mandevil."

"Pardon me, madam," answered Booth; "I hope you do not agree with Mandevil neither, who hath represented human nature in a picture of the highest deformity. He hath left out of his system the best passion which the mind can possess, and attempts to derive the effects or energies of that passion from the base impulses of pride or fear. Whereas it is as certain that love exists in the mind of man as that its opposite hatred doth; and the same reasons will equally prove the existence of the one as the existence of the other."

"I don't know, indeed," replied the lady, "I never thought much about the matter. This I know, that when I read Mandevil I thought all he said was true; and I have been often told that he proves religion and virtue to be only mere names. However, if he denies there is any such thing as love, that is most certainly wrong.—I am afraid I can give him the lye myself."

"I will join with you, madam, in that," answered Booth, "at any time."

"Will you join with me?" answered she, looking eagerly at him—"O, Mr. Booth! I know not what I was going to say—What—Where did you leave off?—I would not interrupt you—but I am impatient to know something."

"What, madam?" cries Booth; "if I can give you any satisfaction—"

"No, no," said she, "I must hear all; I would not for the world break the thread of your story. Besides, I am afraid to ask—Pray, pray, sir, go on."

"Well, madam," cries Booth, "I think I was mentioning the extraordinary acts of friendship done me by Captain James; nor can I help taking notice of the almost unparalleled fidelity of poor Atkinson (for that was my man's name), who was not only constant in the assiduity of his attendance, but during the time of my danger demonstrated a concern for me which I can hardly account for, as my prevailing on his captain to make him a sergeant was the first favour he ever received at my hands, and this did not happen till I was almost perfectly recovered of my broken leg. Poor fellow! I shall never forget the extravagant joy his halbert gave him; I remember it the more because it was one of the happiest days of my own life; for it was upon this day that I received a letter from my dear Amelia, after a long silence, acquainting me that she was out of all danger from her lying-in.

"I was now once more able to perform my duty; when (so unkind was the fortune of war), the second time I mounted the guard, I received a violent contusion from the bursting of a bomb. I was felled to the ground, where I lay breathless by the blow, till honest Atkinson came to my assistance, and conveyed me to my room, where a surgeon immediately attended me.

"The injury I had now received was much more dangerous in my surgeon's opinion than the former; it caused me to spit blood, and was attended with a fever, and other bad symptoms; so that very fatal consequences were apprehended.

"In this situation, the image of my Amelia haunted me day and night; and the apprehensions of never seeing her more were so intolerable, that I had thoughts of resigning my commission, and returning home, weak as I was, that I might have, at least, the satisfaction of dying in the arms of my love. Captain James, however, persisted in dissuading me from any such resolution. He told me my honour was too much concerned, attempted to raise my hopes of recovery to the utmost of his power; but chiefly he prevailed on me by suggesting that, if the worst which I apprehended should happen, it was much better for Amelia that she should be absent than present in so melancholy an hour. 'I know' cried he, 'the extreme joy which must arise in you from meeting again with Amelia, and the comfort of expiring in her arms; but consider what she herself must endure upon the dreadful occasion, and you would not wish to purchase any happiness at the price of so much pain to her.' This argument at length prevailed on me; and it was after many long debates resolved, that she should not even know my present condition, till my doom either for life

or death was absolutely fixed."

"Oh! Heavens! how great! how generous!" cried Miss Matthews. "Booth, thou art a noble fellow; and I scarce think there is a woman upon earth worthy so exalted a passion."

Booth made a modest answer to the compliment which Miss Matthews had paid him. This drew more civilities from the lady, and these again more acknowledgments; all which we shall pass by, and proceed with our history.

Chapter vi. — Containing matters which will please some readers.

"Two months and more had I continued in a state of incertainty, sometimes with more flattering, and sometimes with more alarming symptoms; when one afternoon poor Atkinson came running into my room, all pale and out of breath, and begged me not to be surprized at his news. I asked him eagerly what was the matter, and if it was anything concerning Amelia? I had scarce uttered the dear name when she herself rushed into the room, and ran hastily to me, crying, 'Yes, it is, it is your Amelia herself.'

"There is nothing so difficult to describe, and generally so dull when described, as scenes of excessive tenderness."

"Can you think so?" says Miss Matthews; "surely there is nothing so charming!—Oh! Mr. Booth, our sex is d—ned by the want of tenderness in yours. O, were they all like you—certainly no man was ever your equal."

"Indeed, madam," cries Booth, "you honour me too much. But—well—when the first transports of our meeting were over, Amelia began gently to chide me for having concealed my illness from her; for, in three letters which I had writ her since the accident had happened, there was not the least mention of it, or any hint given by which she could possibly conclude I was otherwise than in perfect health. And when I had excused myself, by assigning the true reason, she cried—'O Mr. Booth! and do you know so little of your Amelia as to think I could or would survive you? Would it not be better for one dreadful sight to break my heart all at once than to break it by degrees?—O Billy! can anything pay me for the loss of this embrace?'—But I ask your pardon—how ridiculous doth my fondness appear in your eyes!"

"How often," answered she, "shall I assert the contrary? What would you have me say, Mr. Booth? Shall I tell you I envy Mrs. Booth of all the women in the world? would you believe me if I did? I hope you—what am I saying? Pray make no farther apology, but go on."

"After a scene," continued he, "too tender to be conceived by many, Amelia informed me that she had received a letter from an unknown hand, acquainting her with my misfortune, and advising her, if she ever desired to see me more, to come directly to Gibraltar. She said she should not have delayed a moment after receiving this letter, had not the same ship brought her one from me written with rather more than usual gaiety, and in which there was not the least mention of my indisposition. This, she said, greatly puzzled her and her mother, and the worthy divine endeavoured to persuade her to give credit to my letter, and to impute the other to a species of wit with which the world greatly abounds. This consists entirely in doing various kinds of mischief to our fellow-creatures, by belying one, deceiving another, exposing a third, and drawing in a fourth, to expose himself; in short, by making some the objects of laughter, others of contempt; and indeed not seldom by subjecting them to very great inconveniences, perhaps to ruin, for the sake of a jest.

"Mrs. Harris and the doctor derived the letter from this species of wit. Miss Betty, however, was of a different opinion, and advised poor Amelia to apply to an officer whom the governor had sent over in the same ship, by whom the report of my illness was so strongly confirmed, that Amelia immediately resolved on her voyage.

"I had a great curiosity to know the author of this letter, but not the least trace of it could be discovered. The only person with whom I lived in any great intimacy was Captain James, and he, madam, from what I have already told you, you will think to be the last person I could suspect; besides, he declared upon his honour that he knew nothing of the matter, and no man's honour is,

I believe, more sacred. There was indeed an ensign of another regiment who knew my wife, and who had sometimes visited me in my illness; but he was a very unlikely man to interest himself much in any affairs which did not concern him; and he too declared he knew nothing of it."

"And did you never discover this secret?" cried Miss Matthews.

"Never to this day," answered Booth.

"I fancy," said she, "I could give a shrewd guess. What so likely as that Mrs. Booth, when you left her, should have given her foster-brother orders to send her word of whatever befel you? Yet stay—that could not be neither; for then she would not have doubted whether she should leave dear England on the receipt of the letter. No, it must have been by some other means;—yet that I own appeared extremely natural to me; for if I had been left by such a husband I think I should have pursued the same method."

"No, madam," cried Booth, "it must have been conveyed by some other channel; for my Amelia, I am certain, was entirely ignorant of the manner; and as for poor Atkinson, I am convinced he would not have ventured to take such a step without acquainting me. Besides, the poor fellow had, I believe, such a regard for my wife, out of gratitude for the favours she hath done his mother, that I make no doubt he was highly rejoiced at her absence from my melancholy scene. Well, whoever writ it is a matter very immaterial; yet, as it seemed so odd and unaccountable an incident, I could not help mentioning it.

"From the time of Amelia's arrival nothing remarkable happened till my perfect recovery, unless I should observe her remarkable behaviour, so full of care and tenderness, that it was perhaps without a parallel."

"O no, Mr. Booth," cries the lady; "it is fully equalled, I am sure, by your gratitude. There is nothing, I believe, so rare as gratitude in your sex, especially in husbands. So kind a remembrance is, indeed, more than a return to such an obligation; for where is the mighty obligation which a woman confers, who being possessed of an inestimable jewel, is so kind to herself as to be careful and tender of it? I do not say this to lessen your opinion of Mrs. Booth. I have no doubt but that she loves you as well as she is capable. But I would not have you think so meanly of our sex as to imagine there are not a thousand women susceptible of true tenderness towards a meritorious man. Believe me, Mr. Booth, if I had received such an account of an accident having happened to such a husband, a mother and a parson would not have held me a moment. I should have leapt into the first fishing-boat I could have found, and bid defiance to the winds and waves.—Oh! there is no true tenderness but in a woman of spirit. I would not be understood all this while to reflect on Mrs. Booth. I am only defending the cause of my sex; for, upon my soul, such compliments to a wife are a satire on all the rest of womankind."

"Sure you jest, Miss Matthews," answered Booth with a smile; "however, if you please, I will proceed in my story."

Chapter vii. — The captain, continuing his story, recounts some particulars which, we doubt not, to many good people, will appear unnatural.

I was scarce sooner recovered from my indisposition than Amelia herself fell ill. This, I am afraid, was occasioned by the fatigues which I could not prevent her from undergoing on my account; for, as my disease went off with violent sweats, during which the surgeon strictly ordered that I should lie by myself, my Amelia could not be prevailed upon to spend many hours in her own bed. During my restless fits she would sometimes read to me several hours together; indeed it was not without difficulty that she ever quitted my bedside. These fatigues, added to the uneasiness of her mind, overpowered her weak spirits, and threw her into one of the worst disorders that can possibly attend a woman; a disorder very common among the ladies, and our physicians have not agreed upon its name. Some call it fever on the spirits, some a nervous fever, some the vapours, and some the hysterics.

"O say no more," cries Miss Matthews; "I pity you, I pity you from my soul. A man had better be plagued with all the curses of Egypt than with a vapourish wife."

"Pity me! madam," answered Booth; "pity rather that dear creature who, from her love and care of my unworthy self, contracted a distemper, the horrors of which are scarce to be imagined. It is, indeed, a sort of complication of all diseases together, with almost madness added to them. In this situation, the siege being at an end, the governor gave me leave to attend my wife to Montpelier, the air of which was judged to be most likely to restore her to health. Upon this occasion she wrote to her mother to desire a remittance, and set forth the melancholy condition of her health, and her necessity for money, in such terms as would have touched any bosom not void of humanity, though a stranger to the unhappy sufferer. Her sister answered it, and I believe I have a copy of the answer in my pocket. I keep it by me as a curiosity, and you would think it more so could I shew you my Amelia's letter." He then searched his pocket-book, and finding the letter among many others, he read it in the following words:

"'DEAR SISTER,—My mamma being much disordered, hath commanded me to tell you she is both shocked and surprized at your extraordinary request, or, as she chuses to call it, order for money. You know, my dear, she says that your marriage with this red-coat man was entirely against her consent and the opinion of all your family (I am sure I may here include myself in that number); and yet, after this fatal act of disobedience, she was prevailed on to receive you as her child; not, however, nor are you so to understand it, as the favourite which you was before. She forgave you; but this was as a Christian and a parent; still preserving in her own mind a just sense of your disobedience, and a just resentment on that account. And yet, notwithstanding this resentment, she desires you to remember that, when you a second time ventured to oppose her authority, and nothing would serve you but taking a ramble (an indecent one, I can't help saying) after your fellow, she thought fit to shew the excess of a mother's tenderness, and furnished you with no less than fifty pounds for your foolish voyage. How can she, then, be otherwise than surprized at your present demand? which, should she be so weak to comply with, she must expect to be every month repeated, in order to supply the extravagance of a young rakish officer. You say she will compassionate your sufferings; yes, surely she doth greatly compassionate them, and so do I too, though you was neither so kind nor so civil as to suppose I should. But I forgive all your slights to me, as well now as formerly. Nay, I not only forgive, but I pray daily for you. But, dear sister, what could you expect less than what hath happened? you should have believed your friends, who were wiser and older than you. I do not here mean myself, though I own I am eleven months and some odd weeks your superior; though, had I been younger, I might, perhaps, have been able to advise you; for wisdom and what some may call beauty do not always go together. You will not be offended at this; for I know in your heart, you have always held your head above some people, whom, perhaps, other people have thought better of; but why do I mention what I scorn so much? No, my dear sister, Heaven forbid it should ever be said of me that I value myself upon my face—not but if I could believe men perhaps—but I hate and despise men—you know I do, my dear, and I wish you had despised them as much; but jacta est jalea, as the doctor says. You are to make the best of your fortune—what fortune, I mean, my mamma may please to give you, for you know all is in her power. Let me advise you, then, to bring your mind to your circumstances, and remember (for I can't help writing it, as it is for your own good) the vapours are a distemper which very ill become a knapsack. Remember, my dear, what you have done; remember what my mamma hath done; remember we have something of yours to keep, and do not consider yourself as an only child; no, nor as a favourite child; but be pleased to remember, Dear sister, Your most affectionate sister,

"'and most obedient humble servant,

"'E. HARRIS.'"

"O brave Miss Betty!" cried Miss Matthews; "I always held her in high esteem; but I protest she exceeds even what I could have expected from her."

"This letter, madam," cries Booth, "you will believe, was an excellent cordial for my poor wife's spirits. So dreadful indeed was the effect it had upon her, that, as she had read it in my absence, I found her, at my return home, in the most violent fits; and so long was it before she recovered her senses, that I despaired of that blest event ever happening; and my own senses very narrowly escaped from being sacrificed to my despair. However, she came at last to herself, and I began to consider of every means of carrying her immediately to Montpelier, which was now become much more necessary than before.

"Though I was greatly shocked at the barbarity of the letter, yet I apprehended no very ill

consequence from it; for, as it was believed all over the army that I had married a great fortune, I had received offers of money, if I wanted it, from more than one. Indeed, I might have easily carried my wife to Montpelier at any time; but she was extremely averse to the voyage, being desirous of our returning to England, as I had leave to do; and she grew daily so much better, that, had it not been for the receipt of that cursed—which I have just read to you, I am persuaded she might have been able to return to England in the next ship.

"Among others there was a colonel in the garrison who had not only offered but importuned me to receive money of him; I now, therefore, repaired to him; and, as a reason for altering my resolution, I produced the letter, and, at the same time, acquainted him with the true state of my affairs. The colonel read the letter, shook his head, and, after some silence, said he was sorry I had refused to accept his offer before; but that he had now so ordered matters, and disposed of his money, that he had not a shilling left to spare from his own occasions.

"Answers of the same kind I had from several others, but not one penny could I borrow of any; for I have been since firmly persuaded that the honest colonel was not content with denying me himself, but took effectual means, by spreading the secret I had so foolishly trusted him with, to prevent me from succeeding elsewhere; for such is the nature of men, that whoever denies himself to do you a favour is unwilling that it should be done to you by any other.

"This was the first time I had ever felt that distress which arises from the want of money; a distress very dreadful indeed in a married state; for what can be more miserable than to see anything necessary to the preservation of a beloved creature, and not be able to supply it?

"Perhaps you may wonder, madam, that I have not mentioned Captain James on this occasion; but he was at that time laid up at Algiers (whither he had been sent by the governor) in a fever. However, he returned time enough to supply me, which he did with the utmost readiness on the very first mention of my distress; and the good colonel, notwithstanding his having disposed of his money, discounted the captain's draft. You see, madam, an instance in the generous behaviour of my friend James, how false are all universal satires against humankind. He is indeed one of the worthiest men the world ever produced.

"But, perhaps, you will be more pleased still with the extravagant generosity of my sergeant. The day before the return of Mr. James, the poor fellow came to me with tears in his eyes, and begged I would not be offended at what he was going to mention. He then pulled a purse from his pocket, which contained, he said, the sum of twelve pounds, and which he begged me to accept, crying, he was sorry it was not in his power to lend me whatever I wanted. I was so struck with this instance of generosity and friendship in such a person, that I gave him an opportunity of pressing me a second time before I made him an answer. Indeed, I was greatly surprised how he came to be worth that little sum, and no less at his being acquainted with my own wants. In both which points he presently satisfied me. As to the first, it seems he had plundered a Spanish officer of fifteen pistoles; and as to the second, he confessed he had it from my wife's maid, who had overheard some discourse between her mistress and me. Indeed people, I believe, always deceive themselves, who imagine they can conceal distrest circumstances from their servants; for these are always extremely quicksighted on such occasions."

"Good heavens!" cries Miss Matthews, "how astonishing is such behaviour in so low a fellow!"

"I thought so myself," answered Booth; "and yet I know not, on a more strict examination into the matter, why we should be more surprised to see greatness of mind discover itself in one degree or rank of life than in another. Love, benevolence, or what you will please to call it, may be the reigning passion in a beggar as well as in a prince; and wherever it is, its energies will be the same.

"To confess the truth, I am afraid we often compliment what we call upper life, with too much injustice, at the expense of the lower. As it is no rare thing to see instances which degrade human nature in persons of the highest birth and education, so I apprehend that examples of whatever is really great and good have been sometimes found amongst those who have wanted all such advantages. In reality, palaces, I make no doubt, do sometimes contain nothing but dreariness and darkness, and the sun of righteousness hath shone forth with all its glory in a cottage."

Chapter viii. — The story of Booth continued.

"Mr. Booth thus went on:

"We now took leave of the garrison, and, having landed at Marseilles, arrived at Montpelier, without anything happening to us worth remembrance, except the extreme sea-sickness of poor Amelia; but I was afterwards well repaid for the terrors which it occasioned me by the good consequences which attended it; for I believe it contributed, even more than the air of Montpelier, to the perfect re-establishment of her health."

"I ask your pardon for interrupting you," cries Miss Matthews, "but you never satisfied me whether you took the sergeant's money. You have made me half in love with that charming fellow."

"How can you imagine, madam," answered Booth, "I should have taken from a poor fellow what was of so little consequence to me, and at the same time of so much to him? Perhaps, now, you will derive this from the passion of pride."

"Indeed," says she, "I neither derive it from the passion of pride nor from the passion of folly: but methinks you should have accepted the offer, and I am convinced you hurt him very much when you refused it. But pray proceed in your story." Then Booth went on as follows:

"As Amelia recovered her health and spirits daily, we began to pass our time very pleasantly at Montpelier; for the greatest enemy to the French will acknowledge that they are the best people in the world to live amongst for a little while. In some countries it is almost as easy to get a good estate as a good acquaintance. In England, particularly, acquaintance is of almost as slow growth as an oak; so that the age of man scarce suffices to bring it to any perfection, and families seldom contract any great intimacy till the third, or at least the second generation. So shy indeed are we English of letting a stranger into our houses, that one would imagine we regarded all such as thieves. Now the French are the very reverse. Being a stranger among them entitles you to the better place, and to the greater degree of civility; and if you wear but the appearance of a gentleman, they never suspect you are not one. Their friendship indeed seldom extends as far as their purse; nor is such friendship usual in other countries. To say the truth, politeness carries friendship far enough in the ordinary occasions of life, and those who want this accomplishment rarely make amends for it by their sincerity; for bluntness, or rather rudeness, as it commonly deserves to be called, is not always so much a mark of honesty as it is taken to be.

"The day after our arrival we became acquainted with Mons. Bagillard. He was a Frenchman of great wit and vivacity, with a greater share of learning than gentlemen are usually possessed of. As he lodged in the same house with us, we were immediately acquainted, and I liked his conversation so well that I never thought I had too much of his company. Indeed, I spent so much of my time with him, that Amelia (I know not whether I ought to mention it) grew uneasy at our familiarity, and complained of my being too little with her, from my violent fondness for my new acquaintance; for, our conversation turning chiefly upon books, and principally Latin ones (for we read several of the classics together), she could have but little entertainment by being with us. When my wife had once taken it into her head that she was deprived of my company by M. Bagillard, it was impossible to change her opinion; and, though I now spent more of my time with her than I had ever done before, she still grew more and more dissatisfied, till at last she very earnestly desired me to quit my lodgings, and insisted upon it with more vehemence than I had ever known her express before. To say the truth, if that excellent woman could ever be thought unreasonable, I thought she was so on this occasion.

"But in what light soever her desires appeared to me, as they manifestly arose from an affection of which I had daily the most endearing proofs, I resolved to comply with her, and accordingly removed to a distant part of the town; for it is my opinion that we can have but little love for the person whom we will never indulge in an unreasonable demand. Indeed, I was under a difficulty with regard to Mons. Bagillard; for, as I could not possibly communicate to him the true reason for quitting my lodgings, so I found it as difficult to deceive him by a counterfeit one; besides, I was apprehensive I should have little less of his company than before. I could, indeed, have avoided this dilemma by leaving Montpelier, for Amelia had perfectly recovered her health;

but I had faithfully promised Captain James to wait his return from Italy, whither he was gone some time before from Gibraltar; nor was it proper for Amelia to take any long journey, she being now near six months gone with child.

"This difficulty, however, proved to be less than I had imagined it; for my French friend, whether he suspected anything from my wife's behaviour, though she never, as I observed, shewed him the least incivility, became suddenly as cold on his side. After our leaving the lodgings he never made above two or three formal visits; indeed his time was soon after entirely taken up by an intrigue with a certain countess, which blazed all over Montpelier.

"We had not been long in our new apartments before an English officer arrived at Montpelier, and came to lodge in the same house with us. This gentleman, whose name was Bath, was of the rank of a major, and had so much singularity in his character, that, perhaps, you never heard of any like him. He was far from having any of those bookish qualifications which had before caused my Amelia's disquiet. It is true, his discourse generally turned on matters of no feminine kind; war and martial exploits being the ordinary topics of his conversation: however, as he had a sister with whom Amelia was greatly pleased, an intimacy presently grew between us, and we four lived in one family.

"The major was a great dealer in the marvellous, and was constantly the little hero of his own tale. This made him very entertaining to Amelia, who, of all the persons in the world, hath the truest taste and enjoyment of the ridiculous; for, whilst no one sooner discovers it in the character of another, no one so well conceals her knowledge of it from the ridiculous person. I cannot help mentioning a sentiment of hers on this head, as I think it doth her great honour. 'If I had the same neglect,' said she, 'for ridiculous people with the generality of the world, I should rather think them the objects of tears than laughter; but, in reality, I have known several who, in some parts of their characters, have been extremely ridiculous, in others have been altogether as amiable. For instance,' said she, 'here is the major, who tells us of many things which he has never seen, and of others which he hath never done, and both in the most extravagant excess; and yet how amiable is his behaviour to his poor sister, whom he hath not only brought over hither for her health, at his own expence, but is come to bear her company.' I believe, madam, I repeat her very words; for I am very apt to remember what she says.

"You will easily believe, from a circumstance I have just mentioned in the major's favour, especially when I have told you that his sister was one of the best of girls, that it was entirely necessary to hide from her all kind of laughter at any part of her brother's behaviour. To say the truth, this was easy enough to do; for the poor girl was so blinded with love and gratitude, and so highly honoured and reverenced her brother, that she had not the least suspicion that there was a person in the world capable of laughing at him.

"Indeed, I am certain she never made the least discovery of our ridicule; for I am well convinced she would have resented it: for, besides the love she bore her brother, she had a little family pride, which would sometimes appear. To say the truth, if she had any fault, it was that of vanity, but she was a very good girl upon the whole; and none of us are entirely free from faults."

"You are a good-natured fellow, Will," answered Miss Matthews; "but vanity is a fault of the first magnitude in a woman, and often the occasion of many others."

To this Booth made no answer, but continued his story.

"In this company we passed two or three months very agreeably, till the major and I both betook ourselves to our several nurseries; my wife being brought to bed of a girl, and Miss Bath confined to her chamber by a surfeit, which had like to have occasioned her death."

Here Miss Matthews burst into a loud laugh, of which when Booth asked the reason, she said she could not forbear at the thoughts of two such nurses.

"And did you really," says she, "make your wife's caudle yourself?"

"Indeed, madam," said he, "I did; and do you think that so extraordinary?"

"Indeed I do," answered she; "I thought the best husbands had looked on their wives' lying-in as a time of festival and jollity. What! did you not even get drunk in the time of your wife's delivery? tell me honestly how you employed yourself at this time."

"Why, then, honestly," replied he, "and in defiance of your laughter, I lay behind her bolster, and supported her in my arms; and, upon my soul, I believe I felt more pain in my mind than she underwent in her body. And now answer me as honestly: Do you really think it a proper time of mirth, when the creature one loves to distraction is undergoing the most racking torments, as well

as in the most imminent danger? and—but I need not express any more tender circumstances."

"I am to answer honestly," cried she. "Yes, and sincerely," cries Booth. "Why, then, honestly and sincerely," says she, "may I never see heaven if I don't think you an angel of a man!"

"Nay, madam," answered Booth—"but, indeed, you do me too much honour; there are many such husbands. Nay, have we not an example of the like tenderness in the major? though as to him, I believe, I shall make you laugh. While my wife lay-in, Miss Bath being extremely ill, I went one day to the door of her apartment, to enquire after her health, as well as for the major, whom I had not seen during a whole week. I knocked softly at the door, and being bid to open it, I found the major in his sister's ante-chamber warming her posset. His dress was certainly whimsical enough, having on a woman's bedgown and a very dirty flannel nightcap, which, being added to a very odd person (for he is a very awkward thin man, near seven feet high), might have formed, in the opinion of most men, a very proper object of laughter. The major started from his seat at my entering into the room, and, with much emotion, and a great oath, cried out, 'Is it you, sir?' I then enquired after his and his sister's health. He answered, that his sister was better, and he was very well, 'though I did not expect, sir,' cried he, with not a little confusion, 'to be seen by you in this situation.' I told him I thought it impossible he could appear in a situation more becoming his character. 'You do not?' answered he. 'By G—— I am very much obliged to you for that opinion; but, I believe, sir, however my weakness may prevail on me to descend from it, no man can be more conscious of his own dignity than myself.' His sister then called to him from the inner room; upon which he rang the bell for her servant, and then, after a stride or two across the room, he said, with an elated aspect, 'I would not have you think, Mr. Booth, because you have caught me in this deshabille, by coming upon me a little too abruptly—I cannot help saying a little too abruptly—that I am my sister's nurse. I know better what is due to the dignity of a man, and I have shewn it in a line of battle. I think I have made a figure there, Mr. Booth, and becoming my character; by G—— I ought not to be despised too much if my nature is not totally without its weaknesses.' He uttered this, and some more of the same kind, with great majesty, or, as he called it, dignity. Indeed, he used some hard words that I did not understand; for all his words are not to be found in a dictionary. Upon the whole, I could not easily refrain from laughter; however, I conquered myself, and soon after retired from him, astonished that it was possible for a man to possess true goodness, and be at the same time ashamed of it.

"But, if I was surprized at what had past at this visit, how much more was I surprized the next morning, when he came very early to my chamber, and told me he had not been able to sleep one wink at what had past between us! 'There were some words of yours,' says he, 'which must be further explained before we part. You told me, sir, when you found me in that situation, which I cannot bear to recollect, that you thought I could not appear in one more becoming my character; these were the words—I shall never forget them. Do you imagine that there is any of the dignity of a man wanting in my character? do you think that I have, during my sister's illness, behaved with a weakness that savours too much of effeminacy? I know how much it is beneath a man to whine and whimper about a trifling girl as well as you or any man; and, if my sister had died, I should have behaved like a man on the occasion. I would not have you think I confined myself from company merely upon her account. I was very much disordered myself. And when you surprized me in that situation—I repeat again, in that situation—her nurse had not left the room three minutes, and I was blowing the fire for fear it should have gone out.'—In this manner he ran on almost a quarter of an hour before he would suffer me to speak. At last, looking steadfastly in his face, I asked him if I must conclude that he was in earnest? 'In earnest!' says he, repeating my words, 'do you then take my character for a jest?'—Lookee, sir, said I, very gravely, I think we know one another very well; and I have no reason to suspect you should impute it to fear when I tell you I was so far from intending to affront you, that I meant you one of the highest compliments. Tenderness for women is so far from lessening, that it proves a true manly character. The manly Brutus shewed the utmost tenderness to his Portia; and the great king of Sweden, the bravest, and even fiercest of men, shut himself up three whole days in the midst of a campaign, and would see no company, on the death of a favourite sister. At these words I saw his features soften; and he cried out, 'D—n me, I admire the king of Sweden of all the men in the world; and he is a rascal that is ashamed of doing anything which the king of Sweden did.—And yet, if any king of Sweden in France was to tell me that his sister had more merit than mine, by G—— I'd knock his brains about his ears. Poor little Betsy! she is the honestest, worthiest girl

that ever was born. Heaven be praised, she is recovered; for, if I had lost her, I never should have enjoyed another happy moment.' In this manner he ran on some time, till the tears began to overflow; which when he perceived, he stopt; perhaps he was unable to go on; for he seemed almost choaked: after a short silence, however, having wiped his eyes with his handkerchief, he fetched a deep sigh, and cried, 'I am ashamed you should see this, Mr. Booth; but d——n me, nature will get the better of dignity.' I now comforted him with the example of Xerxes, as I had before done with that of the king of Sweden; and soon after we sat down to breakfast together with much cordial friendship; for I assure you, with all his oddity, there is not a better-natured man in the world than the major."

"Good-natured, indeed!" cries Miss Matthews, with great scorn. "A fool! how can you mention such a fellow with commendation?"

Booth spoke as much as he could in defence of his friend; indeed, he had represented him in as favourable a light as possible, and had particularly left out those hard words with which, as he hath observed a little before, the major interlarded his discourse. Booth then proceeded as in the next chapter.

Chapter ix. — Containing very extraordinary matters.

"Miss Bath," continued Booth, "now recovered so fast, that she was abroad as soon as my wife. Our little partie quarree began to grow agreeable again; and we mixed with the company of the place more than we had done before. Mons. Bagillard now again renewed his intimacy, for the countess, his mistress, was gone to Paris; at which my wife, at first, shewed no dissatisfaction; and I imagined that, as she had a friend and companion of her own sex (for Miss Bath and she had contracted the highest fondness for each other), that she would the less miss my company. However, I was disappointed in this expectation; for she soon began to express her former uneasiness, and her impatience for the arrival of Captain James, that we might entirely quit Montpelier.

"I could not avoid conceiving some little displeasure at this humour of my wife, which I was forced to think a little unreasonable."—"A little, do you call it?" says Miss Matthews: "Good Heavens! what a husband are you!"—"How little worthy," answered he, "as you will say hereafter, of such a wife as my Amelia. One day, as we were sitting together, I heard a violent scream; upon which my wife, starting up, cried out, 'Sure that's Miss Bath's voice;' and immediately ran towards the chamber whence it proceeded. I followed her; and when we arrived, we there beheld the most shocking sight imaginable; Miss Bath lying dead on the floor, and the major all bloody kneeling by her, and roaring out for assistance. Amelia, though she was herself in little better condition than her friend, ran hastily to her, bared her neck, and attempted to loosen her stays, while I ran up and down, scarce knowing what I did, calling for water and cordials, and despatching several servants one after another for doctors and surgeons.

"Water, cordials, and all necessary implements being brought, Miss Bath was at length recovered, and placed in her chair, when the major seated himself by her. And now, the young lady being restored to life, the major, who, till then, had engaged as little of his own as of any other person's attention, became the object of all our considerations, especially his poor sister's, who had no sooner recovered sufficient strength than she began to lament her brother, crying out that he was killed; and bitterly bewailing her fate, in having revived from her swoon to behold so dreadful a spectacle. While Amelia applied herself to soothe the agonies of her friend, I began to enquire into the condition of the major, in which I was assisted by a surgeon, who now arrived. The major declared, with great chearfulness, that he did not apprehend his wound to be in the least dangerous, and therefore begged his sister to be comforted, saying he was convinced the surgeon would soon give her the same assurance; but that good man was not so liberal of assurances as the major had expected; for as soon as he had probed the wound he afforded no more than hopes, declaring that it was a very ugly wound; but added, by way of consolation, that

he had cured many much worse.

"When the major was drest his sister seemed to possess his whole thoughts, and all his care was to relieve her grief. He solemnly protested that it was no more than a flesh wound, and not very deep, nor could, as he apprehended, be in the least dangerous; and as for the cold expressions of the surgeon, he very well accounted for them from a motive too obvious to be mentioned. From these declarations of her brother, and the interposition of her friends, and, above all, I believe, from that vast vent which she had given to her fright, Miss Bath seemed a little pacified: Amelia, therefore, at last prevailed; and, as terror abated, curiosity became the superior passion. I therefore now began to enquire what had occasioned that accident whence all the uproar arose.

"The major took me by the hand, and, looking very kindly at me, said, 'My dear Mr. Booth, I must begin by asking your pardon; for I have done you an injury for which nothing but the height of friendship in me can be an excuse; and therefore nothing but the height of friendship in you can forgive.' This preamble, madam, you will easily believe, greatly alarmed all the company, but especially me. I answered, Dear major, I forgive you, let it be what it will; but what is it possible you can have done to injure me? 'That,' replied he, 'which I am convinced a man of your honour and dignity of nature, by G—, must conclude to be one of the highest injuries. I have taken out of your own hands the doing yourself justice. I am afraid I have killed the man who hath injured your honour. I mean that villain Bagillard—but I cannot proceed; for you, madam,' said he to my wife, 'are concerned, and I know what is due to the dignity of your sex.' Amelia, I observed, turned pale at these words, but eagerly begged him to proceed. 'Nay, madam,' answered he, 'if I am commanded by a lady, it is a part of my dignity to obey.' He then proceeded to tell us that Bagillard had rallied him upon a supposition that he was pursuing my wife with a view of gallantry; telling him that he could never succeed; giving hints that, if it had been possible, he should have succeeded himself; and ending with calling my poor Amelia an accomplished prude; upon which the major gave Bagillard a box in the ear, and both immediately drew their swords.

"The major had scarce ended his speech when a servant came into the room, and told me there was a fryar below who desired to speak with me in great haste. I shook the major by the hand, and told him I not only forgave him, but was extremely obliged to his friendship; and then, going to the fryar, I found that he was Bagillard's confessor, from whom he came to me, with an earnest desire of seeing me, that he might ask my pardon and receive my forgiveness before he died for the injury he had intended me. My wife at first opposed my going, from some sudden fears on my account; but when she was convinced they were groundless she consented.

"I found Bagillard in his bed; for the major's sword had passed up to the very hilt through his body. After having very earnestly asked my pardon, he made me many compliments on the possession of a woman who, joined to the most exquisite beauty, was mistress of the most impregnable virtue; as a proof of which he acknowledged the vehemence as well as ill success of his attempts: and, to make Amelia's virtue appear the brighter, his vanity was so predominant he could not forbear running over the names of several women of fashion who had yielded to his passion, which, he said, had never raged so violently for any other as for my poor Amelia; and that this violence, which he had found wholly unconquerable, he hoped would procure his pardon at my hands. It is unnecessary to mention what I said on the occasion. I assured him of my entire forgiveness; and so we parted. To say the truth, I afterwards thought myself almost obliged to him for a meeting with Amelia the most luxuriously delicate that can be imagined.

"I now ran to my wife, whom I embraced with raptures of love and tenderness. When the first torrent of these was a little abated, 'Confess to me, my dear,' said she, 'could your goodness prevent you from thinking me a little unreasonable in expressing so much uneasiness at the loss of your company, while I ought to have rejoiced in the thoughts of your being so well entertained; I know you must; and then consider what I must have felt, while I knew I was daily lessening myself in your esteem, and forced into a conduct which I was sensible must appear to you, who was ignorant of my motive, to be mean, vulgar, and selfish. And yet, what other course had I to take with a man whom no denial, no scorn could abash? But, if this was a cruel task, how much more wretched still was the constraint I was obliged to wear in his presence before you, to shew outward civility to the man whom my soul detested, for fear of any fatal consequence from your suspicion; and this too while I was afraid he would construe it to be an encouragement? Do you not pity your poor Amelia when you reflect on her situation?' Pity! cried I; my love! is pity an adequate expression for esteem, for adoration? But how, my love, could he carry this on so

secretly?—by letters? 'O no, he offered me many; but I never would receive but one, and that I returned him. Good G—! I would not have such a letter in my possession for the universe; I thought my eyes contaminated with reading it.'" "O brave!" cried Miss Matthews; "heroic, I protest.

"'Had I a wish that did not bear
The stamp and image of my dear,
I'd pierce my heart through ev'ry vein,
And die to let it out again.'"

"And you can really," cried he, "laugh at so much tenderness?" "I laugh at tenderness! O, Mr. Booth!" answered she, "thou knowest but little of Calista." "I thought formerly," cried he, "I knew a great deal, and thought you, of all women in the world, to have the greatest—of all women!" "Take care, Mr. Booth," said she. "By heaven! if you thought so, you thought truly. But what is the object of my tenderness—such an object as—" "Well, madam," says he, "I hope you will find one." "I thank you for that hope, however," says she, "cold as it is. But pray go on with your story;" which command he immediately obeyed.

Chapter x. — Containing a letter of a very curious kind.

"The major's wound," continued Booth, "was really as slight as he believed it; so that in a very few days he was perfectly well; nor was Bagillard, though run through the body, long apprehending to be in any danger of his life. The major then took me aside, and, wishing me heartily joy of Bagillard's recovery, told me I should now, by the gift (as it were) of Heaven, have an opportunity of doing myself justice. I answered I could not think of any such thing; for that when I imagined he was on his death-bed I had heartily and sincerely forgiven him. 'Very right,' replied the major, 'and consistent with your honour, when he was on his death-bed; but that forgiveness was only conditional, and is revoked by his recovery.' I told him I could not possibly revoke it; for that my anger was really gone.—'What hath anger,' cried he, 'to do with the matter? the dignity of my nature hath been always my reason for drawing my sword; and when that is concerned I can as readily fight with the man I love as with the man I hate.'—I will not tire you with the repetition of the whole argument, in which the major did not prevail; and I really believe I sunk a little in his esteem upon that account, till Captain James, who arrived soon after, again perfectly reinstated me in his favour.

"When the captain was come there remained no cause of our longer stay at Montpelier; for, as to my wife, she was in a better state of health than I had ever known her; and Miss Bath had not only recovered her health but her bloom, and from a pale skeleton was become a plump, handsome young woman. James was again my cashier; for, far from receiving any remittance, it was now a long time since I had received any letter from England, though both myself and my dear Amelia had written several, both to my mother and sister; and now, at our departure from Montpelier, I bethought myself of writing to my good friend the doctor, acquainting him with our journey to Paris, whither I desired he would direct his answer.

"At Paris we all arrived without encountering any adventure on the road worth relating; nor did anything of consequence happen here during the first fortnight; for, as you know neither Captain James nor Miss Bath, it is scarce worth telling you that an affection, which afterwards ended in a marriage, began now to appear between them, in which it may appear odd to you that I made the first discovery of the lady's flame, and my wife of the captain's.

"The seventeenth day after our arrival at Paris I received a letter from the doctor, which I have in my pocket-book; and, if you please, I will read it you; for I would not willingly do any injury to his words."

The lady, you may easily believe, desired to hear the letter, and Booth read it as follows:

"MY DEAR CHILDREN—For I will now call you so, as you have neither of you now any other parent in this world. Of this melancholy news I should have sent you earlier notice if I had thought you ignorant of it, or indeed if I had known whither to have written. If your sister hath

63

received any letters from you she hath kept them a secret, and perhaps out of affection to you hath reposited them in the same place where she keeps her goodness, and, what I am afraid is much dearer to her, her money. The reports concerning you have been various; so is always the case in matters where men are ignorant; for, when no man knows what the truth is, every man thinks himself at liberty to report what he pleases. Those who wish you well, son Booth, say simply that you are dead: others, that you ran away from the siege, and was cashiered. As for my daughter, all agree that she is a saint above; and there are not wanting those who hint that her husband sent her thither. From this beginning you will expect, I suppose, better news than I am going to tell you; but pray, my dear children, why may not I, who have always laughed at my own afflictions, laugh at yours, without the censure of much malevolence? I wish you could learn this temper from me; for, take my word for it, nothing truer ever came from the mouth of a heathen than that sentence:

'——Leve fit quod bene fertur onus.' {Footnote: The burthen becomes light by being well borne.}

"And though I must confess I never thought Aristotle (whom I do not take for so great a blockhead as some who have never read him) doth not very well resolve the doubt which he hath raised in his Ethics, viz., How a man in the midst of King Priam's misfortunes can be called happy? yet I have long thought that there is no calamity so great that a Christian philosopher may not reasonably laugh at it; if the heathen Cicero, doubting of immortality (for so wise a man must have doubted of that which had such slender arguments to support it), could assert it as the office of wisdom, Humanas res despicere atque infra se positas arbitrari. {Footnote: To look down on all human affairs as matters below his consideration.}

"Which passage, with much more to the same purpose, you will find in the third book of his Tusculan Questions.

"With how much greater confidence may a good Christian despise, and even deride, all temporary and short transitory evils! If the poor wretch, who is trudging on to his miserable cottage, can laugh at the storms and tempests, the rain and whirlwinds, which surround him, while his richest hope is only that of rest; how much more chearfully must a man pass through such transient evils, whose spirits are buoyed up with the certain expectation of finding a noble palace and the most sumptuous entertainment ready to receive him! I do not much like the simile; but I cannot think of a better. And yet, inadequate as the simile is, we may, I think, from the actions of mankind, conclude that they will consider it as much too strong; for, in the case I have put of the entertainment, is there any man so tender or poor-spirited as not to despise, and often to deride, the fiercest of these inclemencies which I have mentioned? but in our journey to the glorious mansions of everlasting bliss, how severely is every little rub, every trifling accident, lamented! and if Fortune showers down any of her heavier storms upon us, how wretched do we presently appear to ourselves and to others! The reason of this can be no other than that we are not in earnest in our faith; at the best, we think with too little attention on this our great concern. While the most paultry matters of this world, even those pitiful trifles, those childish gewgaws, riches and honours, are transacted with the utmost earnestness and most serious application, the grand and weighty affair of immortality is postponed and disregarded, nor ever brought into the least competition with our affairs here. If one of my cloth should begin a discourse of heaven in the scenes of business or pleasure; in the court of requests, at Garraway's, or at White's; would he gain a hearing, unless, perhaps, of some sorry jester who would desire to ridicule him? would he not presently acquire the name of the mad parson, and be thought by all men worthy of Bedlam? or would he not be treated as the Romans treated their Aretalogi, {Footnote: A set of beggarly philosophers who diverted great men at their table with burlesque discourses on virtue.} and considered in the light of a buffoon? But why should I mention those places of hurry and worldly pursuit? What attention do we engage even in the pulpit? Here, if a sermon be prolonged a little beyond the usual hour, doth it not set half the audience asleep? as I question not I have by this time both my children. Well, then, like a good-natured surgeon, who prepares his patient for a painful operation by endeavouring as much as he can to deaden his sensation, I will now communicate to you, in your slumbering condition, the news with which I threatened you. Your good mother, you are to know, is dead at last, and hath left her whole fortune to her elder daughter.——This is all the ill news I have to tell you. Confess now, if you are awake, did you not expect it was much worse; did not you apprehend that your charming child was dead? Far from it,

he is in perfect health, and the admiration of everybody: what is more, he will be taken care of, with the tenderness of a parent, till your return. What pleasure must this give you! if indeed anything can add to the happiness of a married couple who are extremely and deservedly fond of each other, and, as you write me, in perfect health. A superstitious heathen would have dreaded the malice of Nemesis in your situation; but as I am a Christian, I shall venture to add another circumstance to your felicity, by assuring you that you have, besides your wife, a faithful and zealous friend. Do not, therefore, my dear children, fall into that fault which the excellent Thucydides observes is too common in human nature, to bear heavily the being deprived of the smaller good, without conceiving, at the same time, any gratitude for the much greater blessings which we are suffered to enjoy. I have only farther to tell you, my son, that, when you call at Mr. Morand's, Rue Dauphine, you will find yourself worth a hundred pounds. Good Heaven! how much richer are you than millions of people who are in want of nothing! farewel, and know me for your sincere and affectionate friend."

"There, madam," cries Booth, "how do you like the letter?"

"Oh! extremely," answered she: "the doctor is a charming man; I always loved dearly to hear him preach. I remember to have heard of Mrs. Harris's death above a year before I left the country, but never knew the particulars of her will before. I am extremely sorry for it, upon my honour."

"Oh, fy! madam," cries Booth; "have you so soon forgot the chief purport of the doctor's letter?"

"Ay, ay," cried she; "these are very pretty things to read, I acknowledge; but the loss of fortune is a serious matter; and I am sure a man of Mr. Booth's understanding must think so."

"One consideration, I must own, madam," answered he, "a good deal baffled all the doctor's arguments. This was the concern for my little growing family, who must one day feel the loss; nor was I so easy upon Amelia's account as upon my own, though she herself put on the utmost chearfulness, and stretched her invention to the utmost to comfort me. But sure, madam, there is something in the doctor's letter to admire beyond the philosophy of it; what think you of that easy, generous, friendly manner, in which he sent me the hundred pounds?"

"Very noble and great indeed," replied she. "But pray go on with your story; for I long to hear the whole."

Chapter xi. — In which Mr. Booth relates his return to England.

"Nothing remarkable, as I remember, happened during our stay at Paris, which we left soon after and came to London. Here we rested only two days, and then, taking leave of our fellow-travellers, we set out for Wiltshire, my wife being so impatient to see the child which she had left behind her, that the child she carried with her was almost killed with the fatigue of the journey.

"We arrived at our inn late in the evening. Amelia, though she had no great reason to be pleased with any part of her sister's behaviour, resolved to behave to her as if nothing wrong had ever happened. She therefore sent a kind note to her the moment of our arrival, giving her her option, whether she would come to us at the inn, or whether we should that evening wait on her. The servant, after waiting an hour, brought us an answer, excusing her from coming to us so late, as she was disordered with a cold, and desiring my wife by no means to think of venturing out after the fatigue of her journey; saying, she would, on that account, defer the great pleasure of seeing her till the morning, without taking any more notice of your humble servant than if no such person had been in the world, though I had very civilly sent my compliments to her. I should not mention this trifle, if it was not to shew you the nature of the woman, and that it will be a kind of key to her future conduct.

"When the servant returned, the good doctor, who had been with us almost all the time of his absence, hurried us away to his house, where we presently found a supper and a bed prepared for us. My wife was eagerly desirous to see her child that night; but the doctor would not suffer it; and, as he was at nurse at a distant part of the town, and the doctor assured her he had seen him

in perfect health that evening, she suffered herself at last to be dissuaded.

"We spent that evening in the most agreeable manner; for the doctor's wit and humour, joined to the highest chearfulness and good nature, made him the most agreeable companion in the world: and he was now in the highest spirits, which he was pleased to place to our account. We sat together to a very late hour; for so excellent is my wife's constitution, that she declared she was scarce sensible of any fatigue from her late journeys.

"Amelia slept not a wink all night, and in the morning early the doctor accompanied us to the little infant. The transports we felt on this occasion were really enchanting, nor can any but a fond parent conceive, I am certain, the least idea of them. Our imaginations suggested a hundred agreeable circumstances, none of which had, perhaps, any foundation. We made words and meaning out of every sound, and in every feature found out some resemblance to my Amelia, as she did to me.

"But I ask your pardon for dwelling on such incidents, and will proceed to scenes which, to most persons, will be more entertaining.

"We went hence to pay a visit to Miss Harris, whose reception of us was, I think, truly ridiculous; and, as you know the lady, I will endeavour to describe it particularly. At our first arrival we were ushered into a parlour, where we were suffered to wait almost an hour. At length the lady of the house appeared in deep mourning, with a face, if possible, more dismal than her dress, in which, however, there was every appearance of art. Her features were indeed skrewed up to the very height of grief. With this face, and in the most solemn gait, she approached Amelia, and coldly saluted her. After which she made me a very distant formal courtesy, and we all sat down. A short silence now ensued, which Miss Harris at length broke with a deep sigh, and said, 'Sister, here is a great alteration in this place since you saw it last; Heaven hath been pleased to take my poor mother to itself.'—(Here she wiped her eyes, and then continued.)—'I hope I know my duty, and have learned a proper resignation to the divine will; but something is to be allowed to grief for the best of mothers; for so she was to us both; and if at last she made any distinction, she must have had her reasons for so doing. I am sure I can truly say I never wished, much less desired it.' The tears now stood in poor Amelia's eyes; indeed, she had paid too many already for the memory of so unnatural a parent. She answered, with the sweetness of an angel, that she was far from blaming her sister's emotions on so tender an occasion; that she heartily joined with her in her grief; for that nothing which her mother had done in the latter part of her life could efface the remembrance of that tenderness which she had formerly shewn her. Her sister caught hold of the word efface, and rung the changes upon it.—'Efface!' cried she, 'O Miss Emily (for you must not expect me to repeat names that will be for ever odious), I wish indeed everything could be effaced.—Effaced! O that that was possible! we might then have still enjoyed my poor mother; for I am convinced she never recovered her grief on a certain occasion.'—Thus she ran on, and, after many bitter strokes upon her sister, at last directly charged her mother's death on my marriage with Amelia. I could be silent then no longer. I reminded her of the perfect reconciliation between us before my departure, and the great fondness which she expressed for me; nor could I help saying, in very plain terms, that if she had ever changed her opinion of me, as I was not conscious of having deserved such a change by my own behaviour, I was well convinced to whose good offices I owed it. Guilt hath very quick ears to an accusation. Miss Harris immediately answered to the charge. She said, such suspicions were no more than she expected; that they were of a piece with every other part of my conduct, and gave her one consolation, that they served to account for her sister Emily's unkindness, as well to herself as to her poor deceased mother, and in some measure lessened the guilt of it with regard to her, since it was not easy to know how far a woman is in the power of her husband. My dear Amelia reddened at this reflection on me, and begged her sister to name any single instance of unkindness or disrespect in which she had ever offended. To this the other answered (I am sure I repeat her words, though I cannot mimic either the voice or air with which they were spoken)—'Pray, Miss Emily, which is to be the judge, yourself or that gentleman? I remember the time when I could have trusted to your judgment in any affair; but you are now no longer mistress of yourself, and are not answerable for your actions. Indeed, it is my constant prayer that your actions may not be imputed to you. It was the constant prayer of that blessed woman, my dear mother, who is now a saint above; a saint whose name I can never mention without a tear, though I find you can hear it without one. I cannot help observing some concern on so melancholy an occasion; it seems due to decency; but, perhaps (for I always wish to

excuse you) you are forbid to cry.' The idea of being bid or forbid to cry struck so strongly on my fancy, that indignation only could have prevented me from laughing. But my narrative, I am afraid, begins to grow tedious. In short, after hearing, for near an hour, every malicious insinuation which a fertile genius could invent, we took our leave, and separated as persons who would never willingly meet again.

"The next morning after this interview Amelia received a long letter from Miss Harris; in which, after many bitter invectives against me, she excused her mother, alledging that she had been driven to do as she did in order to prevent Amelia's ruin, if her fortune had fallen into my hands. She likewise very remotely hinted that she would be only a trustee for her sister's children, and told her that on one condition only she would consent to live with her as a sister. This was, if she could by any means be separated from that man, as she was pleased to call me, who had caused so much mischief in the family.

"I was so enraged at this usage, that, had not Amelia intervened, I believe I should have applied to a magistrate for a search-warrant for that picture, which there was so much reason to suspect she had stolen; and which I am convinced, upon a search, we should have found in her possession."

"Nay, it is possible enough," cries Miss Matthews; "for I believe there is no wickedness of which the lady is not capable."

"This agreeable letter was succeeded by another of the like comfortable kind, which informed me that the company in which I was, being an additional one raised in the beginning of the war, was reduced; so that I was now a lieutenant on half-pay.

"Whilst we were meditating on our present situation the good doctor came to us. When we related to him the manner in which my sister had treated us, he cried out, 'Poor soul! I pity her heartily;' for this is the severest resentment he ever expresses; indeed, I have often heard him say that a wicked soul is the greatest object of compassion in the world."—A sentiment which we shall leave the reader a little time to digest.

Chapter xii. — In which Mr. Booth concludes his story.

"The next day the doctor set out for his parsonage, which was about thirty miles distant, whither Amelia and myself accompanied him, and where we stayed with him all the time of his residence there, being almost three months.

"The situation of the parish under my good friend's care is very pleasant. It is placed among meadows, washed by a clear trout-stream, and flanked on both sides with downs. His house, indeed, would not much attract the admiration of the virtuoso. He built it himself, and it is remarkable only for its plainness; with which the furniture so well agrees, that there is no one thing in it that may not be absolutely necessary, except books, and the prints of Mr. Hogarth, whom he calls a moral satirist.

"Nothing, however, can be imagined more agreeable than the life that the doctor leads in this homely house, which he calls his earthly paradise. All his parishioners, whom he treats as his children, regard him as their common father. Once in a week he constantly visits every house in the parish, examines, commends, and rebukes, as he finds occasion. This is practised likewise by his curate in his absence; and so good an effect is produced by this their care, that no quarrels ever proceed either to blows or law-suits; no beggar is to be found in the whole parish; nor did I ever hear a very profane oath all the time I lived in it.

"But to return from so agreeable a digression, to my own affairs, that are much less worth your attention. In the midst of all the pleasures I tasted in this sweet place and in the most delightful company, the woman and man whom I loved above all things, melancholy reflexions concerning my unhappy circumstances would often steal into my thoughts. My fortune was now reduced to less than forty pounds a-year; I had already two children, and my dear Amelia was again with child.

"One day the doctor found me sitting by myself, and employed in melancholy contemplations

67

on this subject. He told me he had observed me growing of late very serious; that he knew the occasion, and neither wondered at nor blamed me. He then asked me if I had any prospect of going again into the army; if not, what scheme of life I proposed to myself?

"I told him that, as I had no powerful friends, I could have but little expectations in a military way; that I was as incapable of thinking of any other scheme, as all business required some knowledge or experience, and likewise money to set up with; of all which I was destitute.

"'You must know then, child,' said the doctor, 'that I have been thinking on this subject as well as you; for I can think, I promise you, with a pleasant countenance.' These were his words. 'As to the army, perhaps means might be found of getting you another commission; but my daughter seems to have a violent objection to it; and to be plain, I fancy you yourself will find no glory make you amends for your absence from her. And for my part,' said he, 'I never think those men wise who, for any worldly interest, forego the greatest happiness of their lives. If I mistake not,' says he, 'a country life, where you could be always together, would make you both much happier people.'

"I answered, that of all things I preferred it most; and I believed Amelia was of the same opinion.

"The doctor, after a little hesitation, proposed to me to turn farmer, and offered to let me his parsonage, which was then become vacant. He said it was a farm which required but little stock, and that little should not be wanting.

"I embraced this offer very eagerly, and with great thankfulness, and immediately repaired to Amelia to communicate it to her, and to know her sentiments.

"Amelia received the news with the highest transports of joy; she said that her greatest fear had always been of my entring again into the army. She was so kind as to say that all stations of life were equal to her, unless as one afforded her more of my company than another. 'And as to our children,' said she, 'let us breed them up to an humble fortune, and they will be contented with it; for none,' added my angel, 'deserve happiness, or, indeed, are capable of it, who make any particular station a necessary ingredient.'"

"Thus, madam, you see me degraded from my former rank in life; no longer Captain Booth, but farmer Booth at your service.

"During my first year's continuance in this new scene of life, nothing, I think, remarkable happened; the history of one day would, indeed, be the history of the whole year."

"Well, pray then," said Miss Matthews, "do let us hear the history of that day; I have a strange curiosity to know how you could kill your time; and do, if possible, find out the very best day you can."

"If you command me, madam," answered Booth, "you must yourself be accountable for the dulness of the narrative. Nay, I believe, you have imposed a very difficult task on me; for the greatest happiness is incapable of description.

"I rose then, madam—"

"O, the moment you waked, undoubtedly," said Miss Matthews.

"Usually," said he, "between five and six."

"I will have no usually," cried Miss Matthews, "you are confined to a day, and it is to be the best and happiest in the year."

"Nay, madam," cries Booth, "then I must tell you the day in which Amelia was brought to bed, after a painful and dangerous labour; for that I think was the happiest day of my life."

"I protest," said she, "you are become farmer Booth, indeed. What a happiness have you painted to my imagination! you put me in mind of a newspaper, where my lady such-a-one is delivered of a son, to the great joy of some illustrious family."

"Why then, I do assure you, Miss Matthews," cries Booth, "I scarce know a circumstance that distinguished one day from another. The whole was one continued series of love, health, and tranquillity. Our lives resembled a calm sea."—

"The dullest of all ideas," cries the lady.

"I know," said he, "it must appear dull in description, for who can describe the pleasures which the morning air gives to one in perfect health; the flow of spirits which springs up from exercise; the delights which parents feel from the prattle and innocent follies of their children; the joy with which the tender smile of a wife inspires a husband; or lastly, the chearful, solid comfort which a fond couple enjoy in each other's conversation?—All these pleasures and every other of

which our situation was capable we tasted in the highest degree. Our happiness was, perhaps, too great; for fortune seemed to grow envious of it, and interposed one of the most cruel accidents that could have befallen us by robbing us of our dear friend the doctor."

"I am sorry for it," said Miss Matthews. "He was indeed a valuable man, and I never heard of his death before."

"Long may it be before any one hears of it!" cries Booth. "He is, indeed, dead to us; but will, I hope, enjoy many happy years of life. You know, madam, the obligations he had to his patron the earl; indeed, it was impossible to be once in his company without hearing of them. I am sure you will neither wonder that he was chosen to attend the young lord in his travels as his tutor, nor that the good man, however disagreeable it might be (as in fact it was) to his inclination, should comply with the earnest request of his friend and patron.

"By this means I was bereft not only of the best companion in the world, but of the best counsellor; a loss of which I have since felt the bitter consequence; for no greater advantage, I am convinced, can arrive to a young man, who hath any degree of understanding, than an intimate converse with one of riper years, who is not only able to advise, but who knows the manner of advising. By this means alone, youth can enjoy the benefit of the experience of age, and that at a time of life when such experience will be of more service to a man than when he hath lived long enough to acquire it of himself.

"From want of my sage counsellor, I now fell into many errors. The first of these was in enlarging my business, by adding a farm of one hundred a year to the parsonage, in renting which I had also as bad a bargain as the doctor had before given me a good one. The consequence of which was, that whereas, at the end of the first year, I was worth upwards of fourscore pounds; at the end of the second I was near half that sum worse (as the phrase is) than nothing.

"A second folly I was guilty of in uniting families with the curate of the parish, who had just married, as my wife and I thought, a very good sort of a woman. We had not, however, lived one month together before I plainly perceived this good sort of a woman had taken a great prejudice against my Amelia, for which, if I had not known something of the human passions, and that high place which envy holds among them, I should not have been able to account, for, so far was my angel from having given her any cause of dislike, that she had treated her not only with civility, but kindness.

"Besides superiority in beauty, which, I believe, all the world would have allowed to Amelia, there was another cause of this envy, which I am almost ashamed to mention, as it may well be called my greatest folly. You are to know then, madam, that from a boy I had been always fond of driving a coach, in which I valued myself on having some skill. This, perhaps, was an innocent, but I allow it to have been a childish vanity. As I had an opportunity, therefore, of buying an old coach and harness very cheap (indeed they cost me but twelve pounds), and as I considered that the same horses which drew my waggons would likewise draw my coach, I resolved on indulging myself in the purchase.

"The consequence of setting up this poor old coach is inconceivable. Before this, as my wife and myself had very little distinguished ourselves from the other farmers and their wives, either in our dress or our way of living, they treated us as their equals; but now they began to consider us as elevating ourselves into a state of superiority, and immediately began to envy, hate, and declare war against us. The neighbouring little squires, too, were uneasy to see a poor renter become their equal in a matter in which they placed so much dignity; and, not doubting but it arose in me from the same ostentation, they began to hate me likewise, and to turn my equipage into ridicule, asserting that my horses, which were as well matched as any in the kingdom, were of different colours and sizes, with much more of that kind of wit, the only basis of which is lying.

"But what will appear most surprizing to you, madam, was, that the curate's wife, who, being lame, had more use of the coach than my Amelia (indeed she seldom went to church in any other manner), was one of my bitterest enemies on the occasion. If she had ever any dispute with Amelia, which all the sweetness of my poor girl could not sometimes avoid, she was sure to introduce with a malicious sneer, 'Though my husband doth not keep a coach, madam.' Nay, she took this opportunity to upbraid my wife with the loss of her fortune, alledging that some folks might have had as good pretensions to a coach as other folks, and a better too, as they brought a better fortune to their husbands, but that all people had not the art of making brick without straw.

"You will wonder, perhaps, madam, how I can remember such stuff, which, indeed, was a

long time only matter of amusement to both Amelia and myself; but we at last experienced the mischievous nature of envy, and that it tends rather to produce tragical than comical events. My neighbours now began to conspire against me. They nicknamed me in derision, the Squire Farmer. Whatever I bought, I was sure to buy dearer, and when I sold I was obliged to sell cheaper, than any other. In fact, they were all united, and, while they every day committed trespasses on my lands with impunity, if any of my cattle escaped into their fields, I was either forced to enter into a law-suit or to make amends fourfold for the damage sustained.

"The consequences of all this could be no other than that ruin which ensued. Without tiring you with particulars, before the end of four years I became involved in debt near three hundred pounds more than the value of all my effects. My landlord seized my stock for rent, and, to avoid immediate confinement in prison, I was forced to leave the country with all that I hold dear in the world, my wife and my poor little family.

"In this condition I arrived in town five or six days ago. I had just taken a lodging in the verge of the court, and had writ my dear Amelia word where she might find me, when she had settled her affairs in the best manner she could. That very evening, as I was returning home from a coffee-house, a fray happening in the street, I endeavoured to assist the injured party, when I was seized by the watch, and, after being confined all night in the round-house, was conveyed in the morning before a justice of peace, who committed me hither; where I should probably have starved, had I not from your hands found a most unaccountable preservation.—And here, give me leave to assure you, my dear Miss Matthews, that, whatever advantage I may have reaped from your misfortune, I sincerely lament it; nor would I have purchased any relief to myself at the price of seeing you in this dreadful place."

He spake these last words with great tenderness; for he was a man of consummate good nature, and had formerly had much affection for this young lady; indeed, more than the generality of people are capable of entertaining for any person whatsoever.

BOOK IV.

Chapter i. — Containing very mysterious matter.

Miss Matthews did not in the least fall short of Mr. Booth in expressions of tenderness. Her eyes, the most eloquent orators on such occasions, exerted their utmost force; and at the conclusion of his speech she cast a look as languishingly sweet as ever Cleopatra gave to Antony. In real fact, this Mr. Booth had been her first love, and had made those impressions on her young heart, which the learned in this branch of philosophy affirm, and perhaps truly, are never to be eradicated.

When Booth had finished his story a silence ensued of some minutes; an interval which the painter would describe much better than the writer. Some readers may, however, be able to make pretty pertinent conjectures by what I have said above, especially when they are told that Miss Matthews broke the silence by a sigh, and cried, "Why is Mr. Booth unwilling to allow me the happiness of thinking my misfortunes have been of some little advantage to him? sure the happy Amelia would not be so selfish to envy me that pleasure. No; not if she was as much the fondest as she is the happiest of women." "Good heavens! madam," said he, "do you call my poor Amelia the happiest of women?" "Indeed I do," answered she briskly. "O Mr. Booth! there is a speck of white in her fortune, which, when it falls to the lot of a sensible woman, makes her full amends for all the crosses which can attend her. Perhaps she may not be sensible of it; but if it had been my blest fate—O Mr. Booth! could I have thought, when we were first acquainted, that the most

agreeable man in the world had been capable of making the kind, the tender, the affectionate husband—happy Amelia, in those days, was unknown; Heaven had not then given her a prospect of the happiness it intended her; but yet it did intend it her; for sure there is a fatality in the affairs of love; and the more I reflect on my own life, the more I am convinced of it.—O heavens! how a thousand little circumstances crowd into my mind! When you first marched into our town, you had then the colours in your hand; as you passed under the window where I stood, my glove, by accident, dropt into the street; you stoopt, took up my glove, and, putting it upon the spike belonging to your colours, lifted it up to the window. Upon this a young lady who stood by said, 'So, miss, the young officer hath accepted your challenge.' I blushed then, and I blush now, when I confess to you I thought you the prettiest young fellow I had ever seen; and, upon my soul, I believe you was then the prettiest fellow in the world." Booth here made a low bow, and cried, "O dear madam, how ignorant was I of my own happiness!" "Would you really have thought so?" answered she. "However, there is some politeness if there be no sincerity in what you say."—Here the governor of the enchanted castle interrupted them, and, entering the room without any ceremony, acquainted the lady and gentleman that it was locking-up time; and, addressing Booth by the name of captain, asked him if he would not please to have a bed; adding, that he might have one in the next room to the lady, but that it would come dear; for that he never let a bed in that room under a guinea, nor could he afford it cheaper to his father.

No answer was made to this proposal; but Miss Matthews, who had already learnt some of the ways of the house, said she believed Mr. Booth would like to drink a glass of something; upon which the governor immediately trumpeted forth the praises of his rack-punch, and, without waiting for any farther commands, presently produced a large bowl of that liquor.

The governor, having recommended the goodness of his punch by a hearty draught, began to revive the other matter, saying that he was just going to bed, and must first lock up.—"But suppose," said Miss Matthews, with a smile, "the captain and I should have a mind to sit up all night."—"With all my heart," said the governor; "but I expect a consideration for those matters. For my part, I don't enquire into what doth not concern me; but single and double are two things. If I lock up double I expect half a guinea, and I'm sure the captain cannot think that's out of the way; it is but the price of a bagnio."

Miss Matthews's face became the colour of scarlet at those words. However, she mustered up her spirits, and, turning to Booth, said, "What say you, captain? for my own part, I had never less inclination to sleep; which hath the greater charms for you, the punch or the pillow?"—"I hope, madam," answered Booth, "you have a better opinion of me than to doubt my preferring Miss Matthews's conversation to either."—"I assure you," replied she, "it is no compliment to you to say I prefer yours to sleep at this time."

The governor, then, having received his fee, departed; and, turning the key, left the gentleman and the lady to themselves.

In imitation of him we will lock up likewise a scene which we do not think proper to expose to the eyes of the public. If any over-curious readers should be disappointed on this occasion, we will recommend such readers to the apologies with which certain gay ladies have lately been pleased to oblige the world, where they will possibly find everything recorded that past at this interval.

But, though we decline painting the scene, it is not our intention to conceal from the world the frailty of Mr. Booth, or of his fair partner, who certainly past that evening in a manner inconsistent with the strict rules of virtue and chastity.

To say the truth, we are much more concerned for the behaviour of the gentleman than of the lady, not only for his sake, but for the sake of the best woman in the world, whom we should be sorry to consider as yoked to a man of no worth nor honour. We desire, therefore, the good-natured and candid reader will be pleased to weigh attentively the several unlucky circumstances which concurred so critically, that Fortune seemed to have used her utmost endeavours to ensnare poor Booth's constancy. Let the reader set before his eyes a fine young woman, in a manner, a first love, conferring obligations and using every art to soften, to allure, to win, and to enflame; let him consider the time and place; let him remember that Mr. Booth was a young fellow in the highest vigour of life; and, lastly, let him add one single circumstance, that the parties were alone together; and then, if he will not acquit the defendant, he must be convicted, for I have nothing more to say in his defence.

71

Chapter ii. — The latter part of which we expect will please our reader better than the former.

A whole week did our lady and gentleman live in this criminal conversation, in which the happiness of the former was much more perfect than that of the latter; for, though the charms of Miss Matthews, and her excessive endearments, sometimes lulled every thought in the sweet lethargy of pleasure, yet in the intervals of his fits his virtue alarmed and roused him, and brought the image of poor injured Amelia to haunt and torment him. In fact, if we regard this world only, it is the interest of every man to be either perfectly good or completely bad. He had better destroy his conscience than gently wound it. The many bitter reflections which every bad action costs a mind in which there are any remains of goodness are not to be compensated by the highest pleasures which such an action can produce.

So it happened to Mr. Booth. Repentance never failed to follow his transgressions; and yet so perverse is our judgment, and so slippery is the descent of vice when once we are entered into it, the same crime which he now repented of became a reason for doing that which was to cause his future repentance; and he continued to sin on because he had begun. His repentance, however, returned still heavier and heavier, till, at last, it flung him into a melancholy, which Miss Matthews plainly perceived, and at which she could not avoid expressing some resentment in obscure hints and ironical compliments on Amelia's superiority to her whole sex, who could not cloy a gay young fellow by many years' possession. She would then repeat the compliments which others had made to her own beauty, and could not forbear once crying out, "Upon my soul, my dear Billy, I believe the chief disadvantage on my side is my superior fondness; for love, in the minds of men, hath one quality, at least, of a fever, which is to prefer coldness in the object. Confess, dear Will, is there not something vastly refreshing in the cool air of a prude?" Booth fetched a deep sigh, and begged her never more to mention Amelia's name. "O Will," cries she, "did that request proceed from the motive I could wish, I should be the happiest of womankind."—"You would not, sure, madam," said Booth, "desire a sacrifice which I must be a villain to make to any?"—"Desire!" answered she, "are there any bounds to the desires of love? have not I been sacrificed? hath not my first love been torn from my bleeding heart? I claim a prior right. As for sacrifices, I can make them too, and would sacrifice the whole world at the least call of my love."

Here she delivered a letter to Booth, which she had received within an hour, the contents of which were these:—

"DEAREST MADAM,—Those only who truly know what love is, can have any conception of the horrors I felt at hearing of your confinement at my arrival in town, which was this morning. I immediately sent my lawyer to enquire into the particulars, who brought me the agreeable news that the man, whose heart's blood ought not to be valued at the rate of a single hair of yours, is entirely out of all danger, and that you might be admitted to bail. I presently ordered him to go with two of my tradesmen, who are to be bound in any sum for your appearance, if he should be mean enough to prosecute you. Though you may expect my attorney with you soon, I would not delay sending this, as I hope the news will be agreeable to you. My chariot will attend at the same time to carry you wherever you please. You may easily guess what a violence I have done to myself in not waiting on you in person; but I, who know your delicacy, feared it might offend, and that you might think me ungenerous enough to hope from your distresses that happiness which I am resolved to owe to your free gift alone, when your good nature shall induce you to bestow on me what no man living can merit. I beg you will pardon all the contents of this hasty letter, and do me the honour of believing me, Dearest madam,

Your most passionate admirer,

and most obedient humble servant,

DAMON."

Booth thought he had somewhere before seen the same hand, but in his present hurry of spirits could not recollect whose it was, nor did the lady give him any time for reflection; for he

had scarce read the letter when she produced a little bit of paper and cried out, "Here, sir, here are the contents which he fears will offend me." She then put a bank-bill of a hundred pounds into Mr. Booth's hands, and asked him with a smile if he did not think she had reason to be offended with so much insolence?

Before Booth could return any answer the governor arrived, and introduced Mr. Rogers the attorney, who acquainted the lady that he had brought her discharge from her confinement, and that a chariot waited at the door to attend her wherever she pleased.

She received the discharge from Mr. Rogers, and said she was very much obliged to the gentleman who employed him, but that she would not make use of the chariot, as she had no notion of leaving that wretched place in a triumphant manner; in which resolution, when the attorney found her obstinate, he withdrew, as did the governor, with many bows and as many ladyships.

They were no sooner gone than Booth asked the lady why she would refuse the chariot of a gentleman who had behaved with such excessive respect? She looked earnestly upon him, and cried, "How unkind is that question! do you imagine I would go and leave you in such a situation? thou knowest but little of Calista. Why, do you think I would accept this hundred pounds from a man I dislike, unless it was to be serviceable to the man I love? I insist on your taking it as your own and using whatever you want of it."

Booth protested in the solemnest manner that he would not touch a shilling of it, saying, he had already received too many obligations at her hands, and more than ever he should be able, he feared, to repay. "How unkind," answered she, "is every word you say, why will you mention obligations? love never confers any. It doth everything for its own sake. I am not therefore obliged to the man whose passion makes him generous; for I feel how inconsiderable the whole world would appear to me if I could throw it after my heart."

Much more of this kind past, she still pressing the bank-note upon him, and he as absolutely refusing, till Booth left the lady to dress herself, and went to walk in the area of the prison.

Miss Matthews now applied to the governor to know by what means she might procure the captain his liberty. The governor answered, "As he cannot get bail, it will be a difficult matter; and money to be sure there must be; for people no doubt expect to touch on these occasions. When prisoners have not wherewithal as the law requires to entitle themselves to justice, why they must be beholden to other people to give them their liberty; and people will not, to be sure, suffer others to be beholden to them for nothing, whereof there is good reason; for how should we all live if it was not for these things?" "Well, well," said she, "and how much will it cost?" "How much!" answered he,—"How much!—why, let me see."—Here he hesitated some time, and then answered "That for five guineas he would undertake to procure the captain his discharge. "That being the sum which he computed to remain in the lady's pocket; for, as to the gentleman's, he had long been acquainted with the emptiness of it.

Miss Matthews, to whom money was as dirt (indeed she may be thought not to have known the value of it), delivered him the bank-bill, and bid him get it changed; for if the whole, says she, will procure him his liberty, he shall have it this evening.

"The whole, madam!" answered the governor, as soon as he had recovered his breath, for it almost forsook him at the sight of the black word hundred—"No, no; there might be people indeed—but I am not one of those. A hundred! no, nor nothing like it.—As for myself, as I said, I will be content with five guineas, and I am sure that's little enough. What other people will expect I cannot exactly say. To be sure his worship's clerk will expect to touch pretty handsomely; as for his worship himself, he never touches anything, that is, not to speak of; but then the constable will expect something, and the watchman must have something, and the lawyers on both sides, they must have their fees for finishing."—"Well," said she, "I leave all to you. If it costs me twenty pounds I will have him discharged this afternoon.—But you must give his discharge into my hands without letting the captain know anything of the matter."

The governor promised to obey her commands in every particular; nay, he was so very industrious, that, though dinner was just then coming upon the table, at her earnest request he set out immediately on the purpose, and went as he said in pursuit of the lawyer.

All the other company assembled at table as usual, where poor Booth was the only person out of spirits. This was imputed by all present to a wrong cause; nay, Miss Matthews herself either could not or would not suspect that there was anything deeper than the despair of being speedily

discharged that lay heavy on his mind.

However, the mirth of the rest, and a pretty liberal quantity of punch, which he swallowed after dinner (for Miss Matthews had ordered a very large bowl at her own expense to entertain the good company at her farewell), so far exhilarated his spirits, that when the young lady and he retired to their tea he had all the marks of gayety in his countenance, and his eyes sparkled with good humour.

The gentleman and lady had spent about two hours in tea and conversation, when the governor returned, and privately delivered to the lady the discharge for her friend, and the sum of eighty-two pounds five shillings; the rest having been, he said, disbursed in the business, of which he was ready at any time to render an exact account.

Miss Matthews being again alone with Mr. Booth, she put the discharge into his hands, desiring him to ask her no questions; and adding, "I think, sir, we have neither of us now anything more to do at this place." She then summoned the governor, and ordered a bill of that day's expense, for long scores were not usual there; and at the same time ordered a hackney coach, without having yet determined whither she would go, but fully determined she was, wherever she went, to take Mr. Booth with her.

The governor was now approaching with a long roll of paper, when a faint voice was heard to cry out hastily, "Where is he?"—and presently a female spectre, all pale and breathless, rushed into the room, and fell into Mr. Booth's arms, where she immediately fainted away.

Booth made a shift to support his lovely burden; though he was himself in a condition very little different from hers. Miss Matthews likewise, who presently recollected the face of Amelia, was struck motionless with the surprize, nay, the governor himself, though not easily moved at sights of horror, stood aghast, and neither offered to speak nor stir.

Happily for Amelia, the governess of the mansions had, out of curiosity, followed her into the room, and was the only useful person present on this occasion: she immediately called for water, and ran to the lady's assistance, fell to loosening her stays, and performed all the offices proper at such a season; which had so good an effect, that Amelia soon recovered the disorder which the violent agitation of her spirits had caused, and found herself alive and awake in her husband's arms.

Some tender caresses and a soft whisper or two passed privately between Booth and his lady; nor was it without great difficulty that poor Amelia put some restraint on her fondness in a place so improper for a tender interview. She now cast her eyes round the room, and, fixing them on Miss Matthews, who stood like a statue, she soon recollected her, and, addressing her by her name, said, "Sure, madam, I cannot be mistaken in those features; though meeting you here might almost make me suspect my memory."

Miss Matthews's face was now all covered with scarlet. The reader may easily believe she was on no account pleased with Amelia's presence; indeed, she expected from her some of those insults of which virtuous women are generally so liberal to a frail sister: but she was mistaken; Amelia was not one

Who thought the nation ne'er would thrive,
Till all the whores were burnt alive.

Her virtue could support itself with its own intrinsic worth, without borrowing any assistance from the vices of other women; and she considered their natural infirmities as the objects of pity, not of contempt or abhorrence.

When Amelia therefore perceived the visible confusion in Miss Matthews she presently called to remembrance some stories which she had imperfectly heard; for, as she was not naturally attentive to scandal, and had kept very little company since her return to England, she was far from being a mistress of the lady's whole history. However, she had heard enough to impute her confusion to the right cause; she advanced to her, and told her, she was extremely sorry to meet her in such a place, but hoped that no very great misfortune was the occasion of it.

Miss Matthews began, by degrees, to recover her spirits. She answered, with a reserved air, "I am much obliged to you, madam, for your concern; we are all liable to misfortunes in this world. Indeed, I know not why I should be much ashamed of being in any place where I am in such good company."

Here Booth interposed. He had before acquainted Amelia in a whisper that his confinement was at an end. "The unfortunate accident, my dear," said he, "which brought this young lady to

this melancholy place is entirely determined; and she is now as absolutely at her liberty as myself."

Amelia, imputing the extreme coldness and reserve of the lady to the cause already mentioned, advanced still more and more in proportion as she drew back; till the governor, who had withdrawn some time, returned, and acquainted Miss Matthews that her coach was at the door; upon which the company soon separated. Amelia and Booth went together in Amelia's coach, and poor Miss Matthews was obliged to retire alone, after having satisfied the demands of the governor, which in one day only had amounted to a pretty considerable sum; for he, with great dexterity, proportioned the bills to the abilities of his guests.

It may seem, perhaps, wonderful to some readers, that Miss Matthews should have maintained that cold reserve towards Amelia, so as barely to keep within the rules of civility, instead of embracing an opportunity which seemed to offer of gaining some degree of intimacy with a wife whose husband she was so fond of; but, besides that her spirits were entirely disconcerted by so sudden and unexpected a disappointment; and besides the extreme horrors which she conceived at the presence of her rival, there is, I believe, something so outrageously suspicious in the nature of all vice, especially when joined with any great degree of pride, that the eyes of those whom we imagine privy to our failings are intolerable to us, and we are apt to aggravate their opinions to our disadvantage far beyond the reality.

Chapter iii. — Containing wise observations of the author, and other matters.

There is nothing more difficult than to lay down any fixed and certain rules for happiness; or indeed to judge with any precision of the happiness of others from the knowledge of external circumstances. There is sometimes a little speck of black in the brightest and gayest colours of fortune, which contaminates and deadens the whole. On the contrary, when all without looks dark and dismal, there is often a secret ray of light within the mind, which turns everything to real joy and gladness.

I have in the course of my life seen many occasions to make this observation, and Mr. Booth was at present a very pregnant instance of its truth. He was just delivered from a prison, and in the possession of his beloved wife and children; and (which might be imagined greatly to augment his joy) fortune had done all this for him within an hour, without giving him the least warning or reasonable expectation of the strange reverse in his circumstances; and yet it is certain that there were very few men in the world more seriously miserable than he was at this instant. A deep melancholy seized his mind, and cold damp sweats overspread his person, so that he was scarce animated; and poor Amelia, instead of a fond warm husband, bestowed her caresses on a dull lifeless lump of clay. He endeavoured, however, at first, as much as possible, to conceal what he felt, and attempted what is the hardest of all tasks, to act the part of a happy man; but he found no supply of spirits to carry on this deceit, and would have probably sunk under his attempt, had not poor Amelia's simplicity helped him to another fallacy, in which he had much better success.

This worthy woman very plainly perceived the disorder in her husband's mind; and, having no doubt of the cause of it, especially when she saw the tears stand in his eyes at the sight of his children, threw her arms round his neck, and, embracing him with rapturous fondness, cried out, "My dear Billy, let nothing make you uneasy. Heaven will, I doubt not, provide for us and these poor babes. Great fortunes are not necessary to happiness. For my own part, I can level my mind with any state; and for those poor little things, whatever condition of life we breed them to, that will be sufficient to maintain them in. How many thousands abound in affluence whose fortunes are much lower than ours! for it is not from nature, but from education and habit, that our wants are chiefly derived. Make yourself easy, therefore, my dear love; for you have a wife who will think herself happy with you, and endeavour to make you so, in any situation. Fear nothing, Billy, industry will always provide us a wholesome meal; and I will take care that neatness and chearfulness shall make it a pleasant one."

Booth presently took the cue which she had given him. He fixed his eyes on her for a minute with great earnestness and inexpressible tenderness; and then cried, "O my Amelia, how much are

you my superior in every perfection! how wise, how great, how noble are your sentiments! why can I not imitate what I so much admire? why can I not look with your constancy on those dear little pledges of our loves? All my philosophy is baffled with the thought that my Amelia's children are to struggle with a cruel, hard, unfeeling world, and to buffet those waves of fortune which have overwhelmed their father.—Here, I own I want your firmness, and am not without an excuse for wanting it; for am I not the cruel cause of all your wretchedness? have I not stept between you and fortune, and been the cursed obstacle to all your greatness and happiness?"

"Say not so, my love," answered she. "Great I might have been, but never happy with any other man. Indeed, dear Billy, I laugh at the fears you formerly raised in me; what seemed so terrible at a distance, now it approaches nearer, appears to have been a mere bugbear—and let this comfort you, that I look on myself at this day as the happiest of women; nor have I done anything which I do not rejoice in, and would, if I had the gift of prescience, do again."

Booth was so overcome with this behaviour, that he had no words to answer. To say the truth, it was difficult to find any worthy of the occasion. He threw himself prostrate at her feet, whence poor Amelia was forced to use all her strength as well as entreaties to raise and place him in his chair.

Such is ever the fortitude of perfect innocence, and such the depression of guilt in minds not utterly abandoned. Booth was naturally of a sanguine temper; nor would any such apprehensions as he mentioned have been sufficient to have restrained his joy at meeting with his Amelia. In fact, a reflection on the injury he had done her was the sole cause of his grief. This it was that enervated his heart, and threw him into agonies, which all that profusion of heroic tenderness that the most excellent of women intended for his comfort served only to heighten and aggravate; as the more she rose in his admiration, the more she quickened his sense of his own unworthiness. After a disagreeable evening, the first of that kind that he had ever passed with his Amelia, in which he had the utmost difficulty to force a little chearfulness, and in which her spirits were at length overpowered by discerning the oppression on his, they retired to rest, or rather to misery, which need not be described.

The next morning at breakfast, Booth began to recover a little from his melancholy, and to taste the company of his children. He now first thought of enquiring of Amelia by what means she had discovered the place of his confinement. Amelia, after gently rebuking him for not having himself acquainted her with it, informed him that it was known all over the country, and that she had traced the original of it to her sister; who had spread the news with a malicious joy, and added a circumstance which would have frightened her to death, had not her knowledge of him made her give little credit to it, which was, that he was committed for murder. But, though she had discredited this part, she said the not hearing from him during several successive posts made her too apprehensive of the rest; that she got a conveyance therefore for herself and children to Salisbury, from whence the stage coach had brought them to town; and, having deposited the children at his lodging, of which he had sent her an account on his first arrival in town, she took a hack, and came directly to the prison where she heard he was, and where she found him.

Booth excused himself, and with truth, as to his not having writ; for, in fact, he had writ twice from the prison, though he had mentioned nothing of his confinement; but, as he sent away his letters after nine at night, the fellow to whom they were entrusted had burnt them both for the sake of putting the twopence in his own pocket, or rather in the pocket of the keeper of the next gin-shop. As to the account which Amelia gave him, it served rather to raise than to satisfy his curiosity. He began to suspect that some person had seen both him and Miss Matthews together in the prison, and had confounded her case with his; and this the circumstance of murder made the more probable. But who this person should be he could not guess. After giving himself, therefore, some pains in forming conjectures to no purpose, he was forced to rest contented with his ignorance of the real truth.

Two or three days now passed without producing anything remarkable; unless it were that Booth more and more recovered his spirits, and had now almost regained his former degree of chearfulness, when the following letter arrived, again to torment him:

"DEAR BILLY,

"To convince you I am the most reasonable of women, I have given you up three whole days to the unmolested possession of my fortunate rival; I can refrain no longer from letting you know that I lodge in Dean Street, not far from the church, at the sign of the Pelican and Trumpet,

where I expect this evening to see you.

"Believe me I am, with more affection than any other woman in the world can be, my dear Billy, Your affectionate, fond, doating

"F. MATTHEWS."

Booth tore the letter with rage, and threw it into the fire, resolving never to visit the lady more, unless it was to pay her the money she had lent him, which he was determined to do the very first opportunity, for it was not at present in his power.

This letter threw him back into his fit of dejection, in which he had not continued long when a packet from the country brought him the following from his friend Dr Harrison:

"Sir, Lyons, January 21, N. S.

"Though I am now on my return home, I have taken up my pen to communicate to you some news I have heard from England, which gives me much uneasiness, and concerning which I can indeed deliver my sentiments with much more ease this way than any other. In my answer to your last, I very freely gave you my opinion, in which it was my misfortune to disapprove of every step you had taken; but those were all pardonable errors. Can you be so partial to yourself, upon cool and sober reflexion, to think what I am going to mention is so? I promise you, it appears to me a folly of so monstrous a kind, that, had I heard it from any but a person of the highest honour, I should have rejected it as utterly incredible. I hope you already guess what I am about to name; since, Heaven forbid, your conduct should afford you any choice of such gross instances of weakness. In a word, then, you have set up an equipage. What shall I invent in your excuse, either to others or to myself? In truth, I can find no excuse for you, and, what is more, I am certain you can find none for yourself. I must deal therefore very plainly and sincerely with you. Vanity is always contemptible; but when joined with dishonesty, it becomes odious and detestable. At whose expence are you to support this equipage? is it not entirely at the expence of others? and will it not finally end in that of your poor wife and children? you know you are two years in arrears to me. If I could impute this to any extraordinary or common accident I think I should never have mentioned it; but I will not suffer my money to support the ridiculous, and, I must say, criminal vanity of any one. I expect, therefore, to find, at my return, that you have either discharged my whole debt, or your equipage. Let me beg you seriously to consider your circumstances and condition in life, and to remember that your situation will not justify any the least unnecessary expence. Simply to be poor, says my favourite Greek historian, was not held scandalous by the wise Athenians, but highly so to owe that poverty to our own indiscretion.

"Present my affections to Mrs. Booth, and be assured that I shall not, without great reason, and great pain too, ever cease to be, Your most faithful friend,

"R. HARRISON."

Had this letter come at any other time, it would have given Booth the most sensible affliction; but so totally had the affair of Miss Matthews possessed his mind, that, like a man in the most raging fit of the gout, he was scarce capable of any additional torture; nay, he even made an use of this latter epistle, as it served to account to Amelia for that concern which he really felt on another account. The poor deceived lady, therefore, applied herself to give him comfort where he least wanted it. She said he might easily perceive that the matter had been misrepresented to the doctor, who would not, she was sure, retain the least anger against him when he knew the real truth.

After a short conversation on this subject, in which Booth appeared to be greatly consoled by the arguments of his wife, they parted. He went to take a walk in the Park, and she remained at home to prepare him his dinner.

He was no sooner departed than his little boy, not quite six years old, said to Amelia, "La! mamma, what is the matter with poor papa, what makes him look so as if he was going to cry? he is not half so merry as he used to be in the country." Amelia answered, "Oh! my dear, your papa is only a little thoughtful, he will be merry again soon."—Then looking fondly on her children, she burst into an agony of tears, and cried, "Oh Heavens; what have these poor little infants done? why will the barbarous world endeavour to starve them, by depriving us of our only friend?—O my dear, your father is ruined, and we are undone!"—The children presently accompanied their mother's tears, and the daughter cried—"Why, will anybody hurt poor papa? hath he done any harm to anybody?"—"No, my dear child," said the mother; "he is the best man in the world, and therefore they hate him." Upon which the boy, who was extremely sensible at his years, answered, "Nay, mamma, how can that be? have not you often told me that if I was good everybody would

77

love me?" "All good people will," answered she. "Why don't they love papa then?" replied the child, "for I am sure he is very good." "So they do, my dear," said the mother, "but there are more bad people in the world, and they will hate you for your goodness." "Why then, bad people," cries the child, "are loved by more than the good."—"No matter for that, my dear," said she; "the love of one good person is more worth having than that of a thousand wicked ones; nay, if there was no such person in the world, still you must be a good boy; for there is one in Heaven who will love you, and his love is better for you than that of all mankind."

This little dialogue, we are apprehensive, will be read with contempt by many; indeed, we should not have thought it worth recording, was it not for the excellent example which Amelia here gives to all mothers. This admirable woman never let a day pass without instructing her children in some lesson of religion and morality. By which means she had, in their tender minds, so strongly annexed the ideas of fear and shame to every idea of evil of which they were susceptible, that it must require great pains and length of habit to separate them. Though she was the tenderest of mothers, she never suffered any symptom of malevolence to shew itself in their most trifling actions without discouragement, without rebuke, and, if it broke forth with any rancour, without punishment. In which she had such success, that not the least mark of pride, envy, malice, or spite discovered itself in any of their little words or deeds.

Chapter iv. — In which Amelia appears in no unamiable light.

Amelia, with the assistance of a little girl, who was their only servant, had drest her dinner, and she had likewise drest herself as neat as any lady who had a regular sett of servants could have done, when Booth returned, and brought with him his friend James, whom he had met with in the Park; and who, as Booth absolutely refused to dine away from his wife, to whom he had promised to return, had invited himself to dine with him. Amelia had none of that paultry pride which possesses so many of her sex, and which disconcerts their tempers, and gives them the air and looks of furies, if their husbands bring in an unexpected guest, without giving them timely warning to provide a sacrifice to their own vanity. Amelia received her husband's friend with the utmost complaisance and good humour: she made indeed some apology for the homeliness of her dinner; but it was politely turned as a compliment to Mr. James's friendship, which could carry him where he was sure of being so ill entertained; and gave not the least hint how magnificently she would have provided had she expected the favour of so much good company. A phrase which is generally meant to contain not only an apology for the lady of the house, but a tacit satire on her guests for their intrusion, and is at least a strong insinuation that they are not welcome.

Amelia failed not to enquire very earnestly after her old friend Mrs. James, formerly Miss Bath, and was very sorry to find that she was not in town. The truth was, as James had married out of a violent liking of, or appetite to, her person, possession had surfeited him, and he was now grown so heartily tired of his wife, that she had very little of his company; she was forced therefore to content herself with being the mistress of a large house and equipage in the country ten months in the year by herself. The other two he indulged her with the diversions of the town; but then, though they lodged under the same roof, she had little more of her husband's society than if they had been one hundred miles apart. With all this, as she was a woman of calm passions, she made herself contented; for she had never had any violent affection for James: the match was of the prudent kind, and to her advantage; for his fortune, by the death of an uncle, was become very considerable; and she had gained everything by the bargain but a husband, which her constitution suffered her to be very well satisfied without.

When Amelia, after dinner, retired to her children, James began to talk to his friend concerning his affairs. He advised Booth very earnestly to think of getting again into the army, in which he himself had met with such success, that he had obtained the command of a regiment to which his brother-in-law was lieutenant-colonel. These preferments they both owed to the favour of fortune only; for, though there was no objection to either of their military characters, yet neither of them had any extraordinary desert; and, if merit in the service was a sufficient

recommendation, Booth, who had been twice wounded in the siege, seemed to have the fairest pretensions; but he remained a poor half-pay lieutenant, and the others were, as we have said, one of them a lieutenant-colonel, and the other had a regiment. Such rises we often see in life, without being able to give any satisfactory account of the means, and therefore ascribe them to the good fortune of the person.

Both Colonel James and his brother-in-law were members of parliament; for, as the uncle of the former had left him, together with his estate, an almost certain interest in a borough, so he chose to confer this favour on Colonel Bath; a circumstance which would have been highly immaterial to mention here, but as it serves to set forth the goodness of James, who endeavoured to make up in kindness to the family what he wanted in fondness for his wife.

Colonel James then endeavoured all in his power to persuade Booth to think again of a military life, and very kindly offered him his interest towards obtaining him a company in the regiment under his command. Booth must have been a madman, in his present circumstances, to have hesitated one moment at accepting such an offer, and he well knew Amelia, notwithstanding her aversion to the army, was much too wise to make the least scruple of giving her consent. Nor was he, as it appeared afterwards, mistaken in his opinion of his wife's understanding; for she made not the least objection when it was communicated to her, but contented herself with an express stipulation, that wherever he was commanded to go (for the regiment was now abroad) she would accompany him.

Booth, therefore, accepted his friend's proposal with a profusion of acknowledgments; and it was agreed that Booth should draw up a memorial of his pretensions, which Colonel James undertook to present to some man of power, and to back it with all the force he had.

Nor did the friendship of the colonel stop here. "You will excuse me, dear Booth," said he, "if, after what you have told me" (for he had been very explicit in revealing his affairs to him), "I suspect you must want money at this time. If that be the case, as I am certain it must be, I have fifty pieces at your service." This generosity brought the tears into Booth's eyes; and he at length confest that he had not five guineas in the house; upon which James gave him a bank-bill for twenty pounds, and said he would give him thirty more the next time he saw him.

Thus did this generous colonel (for generous he really was to the highest degree) restore peace and comfort to this little family; and by this act of beneficence make two of the worthiest people two of the happiest that evening.

Here, reader, give me leave to stop a minute, to lament that so few are to be found of this benign disposition; that, while wantonness, vanity, avarice, and ambition are every day rioting and triumphing in the follies and weakness, the ruin and desolation of mankind, scarce one man in a thousand is capable of tasting the happiness of others. Nay, give me leave to wonder that pride, which is constantly struggling, and often imposing on itself, to gain some little pre-eminence, should so seldom hint to us the only certain as well as laudable way of setting ourselves above another man, and that is, by becoming his benefactor.

Chapter v. — Containing an eulogium upon innocence, and other grave matters.

Booth past that evening, and all the succeeding day, with his Amelia, without the interruption of almost a single thought concerning Miss Matthews, after having determined to go on the Sunday, the only day he could venture without the verge in the present state of his affairs, and pay her what she had advanced for him in the prison. But she had not so long patience; for the third day, while he was sitting with Amelia, a letter was brought to him. As he knew the hand, he immediately put it into his pocket unopened, not without such an alteration in his countenance, that had Amelia, who was then playing with one of the children, cast her eyes towards him, she must have remarked it. This accident, however, luckily gave him time to recover himself; for Amelia was so deeply engaged with the little one, that she did not even remark the delivery of the letter. The maid soon after returned into the room, saying, the chairman desired to know if there was any answer to the letter.—"What letter?" cries Booth.—"The letter I gave you just now,"

answered the girl.—"Sure," cries Booth, "the child is mad, you gave me no letter."—"Yes, indeed, I did, sir," said the poor girl. "Why then as sure as fate," cries Booth, "I threw it into the fire in my reverie; why, child, why did you not tell me it was a letter? bid the chairman come up, stay, I will go down myself; for he will otherwise dirt the stairs with his feet."

Amelia was gently chiding the girl for her carelessness when Booth returned, saying it was very true that she had delivered him a letter from Colonel James, and that perhaps it might be of consequence. "However," says he, "I will step to the coffee-house, and send him an account of this strange accident, which I know he will pardon in my present situation."

Booth was overjoyed at this escape, which poor Amelia's total want of all jealousy and suspicion made it very easy for him to accomplish; but his pleasure was considerably abated when, upon opening the letter, he found it to contain, mixed with several very strong expressions of love, some pretty warm ones of the upbraiding kind; but what most alarmed him was a hint that it was in her (Miss Matthews's) power to make Amelia as miserable as herself. Besides the general knowledge of

——Furens quid faemina possit,

he had more particular reasons to apprehend the rage of a lady who had given so strong an instance how far she could carry her revenge. She had already sent a chairman to his lodgings with a positive command not to return without an answer to her letter. This might of itself have possibly occasioned a discovery; and he thought he had great reason to fear that, if she did not carry matters so far as purposely and avowedly to reveal the secret to Amelia, her indiscretion would at least effect the discovery of that which he would at any price have concealed. Under these terrors he might, I believe, be considered as the most wretched of human beings.

O innocence, how glorious and happy a portion art thou to the breast that possesses thee! thou fearest neither the eyes nor the tongues of men. Truth, the most powerful of all things, is thy strongest friend; and the brighter the light is in which thou art displayed, the more it discovers thy transcendent beauties. Guilt, on the contrary, like a base thief, suspects every eye that beholds him to be privy to his transgressions, and every tongue that mentions his name to be proclaiming them. Fraud and falsehood are his weak and treacherous allies; and he lurks trembling in the dark, dreading every ray of light, lest it should discover him, and give him up to shame and punishment.

While Booth was walking in the Park with all these horrors in his mind he again met his friend Colonel James, who soon took notice of that deep concern which the other was incapable of hiding. After some little conversation, Booth said, "My dear colonel, I am sure I must be the most insensible of men if I did not look on you as the best and the truest friend; I will, therefore, without scruple, repose a confidence in you of the highest kind. I have often made you privy to my necessities, I will now acquaint you with my shame, provided you have leisure enough to give me a hearing: for I must open to you a long history, since I will not reveal my fault without informing you, at the same time, of those circumstances which, I hope, will in some measure excuse it."

The colonel very readily agreed to give his friend a patient hearing. So they walked directly to a coffee-house at the corner of Spring-Garden, where, being in a room by themselves, Booth opened his whole heart, and acquainted the colonel with his amour with Miss Matthews, from the very beginning to his receiving that letter which had caused all his present uneasiness, and which he now delivered into his friend's hand.

The colonel read the letter very attentively twice over (he was silent indeed long enough to have read it oftener); and then, turning to Booth, said, "Well, sir, and is it so grievous a calamity to be the object of a young lady's affection; especially of one whom you allow to be so extremely handsome?" "Nay, but, my dear friend," cries Booth, "do not jest with me; you who know my Amelia." "Well, my dear friend," answered James, "and you know Amelia and this lady too. But what would you have me do for you?" "I would have you give me your advice," says Booth, "by what method I shall get rid of this dreadful woman without a discovery."—"And do you really," cries the other, "desire to get rid of her?" "Can you doubt it," said Booth, "after what I have communicated to you, and after what you yourself have seen in my family? for I hope, notwithstanding this fatal slip, I do not appear to you in the light of a profligate." "Well," answered James, "and, whatever light I may appear to you in, if you are really tired of the lady, and if she be really what you have represented her, I'll endeavour to take her off your hands; but I insist upon it that you do not deceive me in any particular." Booth protested in the most solemn

manner that every word which he had spoken was strictly true; and being asked whether he would give his honour never more to visit the lady, he assured James that he never would. He then, at his friend's request, delivered him Miss Matthews's letter, in which was a second direction to her lodgings, and declared to him that, if he could bring him safely out of this terrible affair, he should think himself to have a still higher obligation to his friendship than any which he had already received from it.

Booth pressed the colonel to go home with him to dinner; but he excused himself, being, as he said, already engaged. However, he undertook in the afternoon to do all in his power that Booth should receive no more alarms from the quarter of Miss Matthews, whom the colonel undertook to pay all the demands she had on his friend. They then separated. The colonel went to dinner at the King's Arms, and Booth returned in high spirits to meet his Amelia.

The next day, early in the morning, the colonel came to the coffee-house and sent for his friend, who lodged but at a little distance. The colonel told him he had a little exaggerated the lady's beauty; however, he said, he excused that, "for you might think, perhaps," cries he, "that your inconstancy to the finest woman in the world might want some excuse. Be that as it will," said he, "you may make yourself easy, as it will be, I am convinced, your own fault, if you have ever any further molestation from Miss Matthews."

Booth poured forth very warmly a great profusion of gratitude on this occasion; and nothing more anywise material passed at this interview, which was very short, the colonel being in a great hurry, as he had, he said, some business of very great importance to transact that morning.

The colonel had now seen Booth twice without remembering to give him the thirty pounds. This the latter imputed intirely to forgetfulness; for he had always found the promises of the former to be equal in value with the notes or bonds of other people. He was more surprized at what happened the next day, when, meeting his friend in the Park, he received only a cold salute from him; and though he past him five or six times, and the colonel was walking with a single officer of no great rank, and with whom he seemed in no earnest conversation, yet could not Booth, who was alone, obtain any further notice from him.

This gave the poor man some alarm; though he could scarce persuade himself that there was any design in all this coldness or forgetfulness. Once he imagined that he had lessened himself in the colonel's opinion by having discovered his inconstancy to Amelia; but the known character of the other presently cured him of his suspicion, for he was a perfect libertine with regard to women; that being indeed the principal blemish in his character, which otherwise might have deserved much commendation for good-nature, generosity, and friendship. But he carried this one to a most unpardonable height; and made no scruple of openly declaring that, if he ever liked a woman well enough to be uneasy on her account, he would cure himself, if he could, by enjoying her, whatever might be the consequence.

Booth could not therefore be persuaded that the colonel would so highly resent in another a fault of which he was himself most notoriously guilty. After much consideration he could derive this behaviour from nothing better than a capriciousness in his friend's temper, from a kind of inconstancy of mind, which makes men grow weary of their friends with no more reason than they often are of their mistresses. To say the truth, there are jilts in friendship as well as in love; and, by the behaviour of some men in both, one would almost imagine that they industriously sought to gain the affections of others with a view only of making the parties miserable.

This was the consequence of the colonel's behaviour to Booth. Former calamities had afflicted him, but this almost distracted him; and the more so as he was not able well to account for such conduct, nor to conceive the reason of it.

Amelia, at his return, presently perceived the disturbance in his mind, though he endeavoured with his utmost power to hide it; and he was at length prevailed upon by her entreaties to discover to her the cause of it, which she no sooner heard than she applied as judicious a remedy to his disordered spirits as either of those great mental physicians, Tully or Aristotle, could have thought of. She used many arguments to persuade him that he was in an error, and had mistaken forgetfulness and carelessness for a designed neglect.

But, as this physic was only eventually good, and as its efficacy depended on her being in the right, a point in which she was not apt to be too positive, she thought fit to add some consolation of a more certain and positive kind. "Admit," said she, "my dear, that Mr. James should prove the unaccountable person you have suspected, and should, without being able to alledge any cause,

withdraw his friendship from you (for surely the accident of burning his letter is too trifling and ridiculous to mention), why should this grieve you? the obligations he hath conferred on you, I allow, ought to make his misfortunes almost your own; but they should not, I think, make you see his faults so very sensibly, especially when, by one of the greatest faults in the world committed against yourself, he hath considerably lessened all obligations; for sure, if the same person who hath contributed to my happiness at one time doth everything in his power maliciously and wantonly to make me miserable at another, I am very little obliged to such a person. And let it be a comfort to my dear Billy, that, however other friends may prove false and fickle to him, he hath one friend, whom no inconstancy of her own, nor any change of his fortune, nor time, nor age, nor sickness, nor any accident, can ever alter; but who will esteem, will love, and doat on him for ever." So saying, she flung her snowy arms about his neck, and gave him a caress so tender, that it seemed almost to balance all the malice of his fate.

And, indeed, the behaviour of Amelia would have made him completely happy, in defiance of all adverse circumstances, had it not been for those bitter ingredients which he himself had thrown into his cup, and which prevented him from truly relishing his Amelia's sweetness, by cruelly reminding him how unworthy he was of this excellent creature.

Booth did not long remain in the dark as to the conduct of James, which, at first, appeared to him to be so great a mystery; for this very afternoon he received a letter from Miss Matthews which unravelled the whole affair. By this letter, which was full of bitterness and upbraiding, he discovered that James was his rival with that lady, and was, indeed, the identical person who had sent the hundred-pound note to Miss Matthews, when in the prison. He had reason to believe, likewise, as well by the letter as by other circumstances, that James had hitherto been an unsuccessful lover; for the lady, though she had forfeited all title to virtue, had not yet so far forfeited all pretensions to delicacy as to be, like the dirt in the street, indifferently common to all. She distributed her favours only to those she liked, in which number that gentleman had not the happiness of being included.

When Booth had made this discovery, he was not so little versed in human nature, as any longer to hesitate at the true motive to the colonel's conduct; for he well knew how odious a sight a happy rival is to an unfortunate lover. I believe he was, in reality, glad to assign the cold treatment he had received from his friend to a cause which, however injustifiable, is at the same time highly natural; and to acquit him of a levity, fickleness, and caprice, which he must have been unwillingly obliged to have seen in a much worse light.

He now resolved to take the first opportunity of accosting the colonel, and of coming to a perfect explanation upon the whole matter. He debated likewise with himself whether he should not throw himself at Amelia's feet, and confess a crime to her which he found so little hopes of concealing, and which he foresaw would occasion him so many difficulties and terrors to endeavour to conceal. Happy had it been for him, had he wisely pursued this step; since, in all probability, he would have received immediate forgiveness from the best of women; but he had not sufficient resolution, or, to speak perhaps more truly, he had too much pride, to confess his guilt, and preferred the danger of the highest inconveniences to the certainty of being put to the blush.

Chapter vi. — In which may appear that violence is sometimes done to the name of love.

When that happy day came, in which unhallowed hands are forbidden to contaminate the shoulders of the unfortunate, Booth went early to the colonel's house, and, being admitted to his presence, began with great freedom, though with great gentleness, to complain of his not having dealt with him with more openness. "Why, my dear colonel," said he, "would you not acquaint me with that secret which this letter hath disclosed?" James read the letter, at which his countenance changed more than once; and then, after a short silence, said, "Mr. Booth, I have been to blame, I own it; and you upbraid me with justice. The true reason was, that I was ashamed of my own folly.

D—n me, Booth, if I have not been a most consummate fool, a very dupe to this woman; and she hath a particular pleasure in making me so. I know what the impertinence of virtue is, and I can submit to it; but to be treated thus by a whore—You must forgive me, dear Booth, but your success was a kind of triumph over me, which I could not bear. I own, I have not the least reason to conceive any anger against you; and yet, curse me if I should not have been less displeased at your lying with my own wife; nay, I could almost have parted with half my fortune to you more willingly than have suffered you to receive that trifle of my money which you received at her hands. However, I ask your pardon, and I promise you I will never more think of you with the least ill-will on the account of this woman; but as for her, d—n me if I do not enjoy her by some means or other, whatever it costs me; for I am already above two hundred pounds out of pocket, without having scarce had a smile in return."

Booth exprest much astonishment at this declaration; he said he could not conceive how it was possible to have such an affection for a woman who did not shew the least inclination to return it. James gave her a hearty curse, and said, "Pox of her inclination; I want only the possession of her person, and that, you will allow, is a very fine one. But, besides my passion for her, she hath now piqued my pride; for how can a man of my fortune brook being refused by a whore?"—"Since you are so set on the business," cries Booth, "you will excuse my saying so, I fancy you had better change your method of applying to her; for, as she is, perhaps, the vainest woman upon earth, your bounty may probably do you little service, nay, may rather actually disoblige her. Vanity is plainly her predominant passion, and, if you will administer to that, it will infallibly throw her into your arms. To this I attribute my own unfortunate success. While she relieved my wants and distresses she was daily feeding her own vanity; whereas, as every gift of yours asserted your superiority, it rather offended than pleased her. Indeed, women generally love to be of the obliging side; and, if we examine their favourites, we shall find them to be much oftener such as they have conferred obligations on than such as they have received them from."

There was something in this speech which pleased the colonel; and he said, with a smile, "I don't know how it is, Will, but you know women better than I."—"Perhaps, colonel," answered Booth, "I have studied their minds more."—"I don't, however, much envy your knowledge," replied the other, "for I never think their minds worth considering. However, I hope I shall profit a little by your experience with Miss Matthews. Damnation seize the proud insolent harlot! the devil take me if I don't love her more than I ever loved a woman!"

The rest of their conversation turned on Booth's affairs. The colonel again reassumed the part of a friend, gave him the remainder of the money, and promised to take the first opportunity of laying his memorial before a great man.

Booth was greatly overjoyed at this success. Nothing now lay on his mind but to conceal his frailty from Amelia, to whom he was afraid Miss Matthews, in the rage of her resentment, would communicate it. This apprehension made him stay almost constantly at home; and he trembled at every knock at the door. His fear, moreover, betrayed him into a meanness which he would have heartily despised on any other occasion. This was to order the maid to deliver him any letter directed to Amelia; at the same time strictly charging her not to acquaint her mistress with her having received any such orders.

A servant of any acuteness would have formed strange conjectures from such an injunction; but this poor girl was of perfect simplicity; so great, indeed, was her simplicity, that, had not Amelia been void of all suspicion of her husband, the maid would have soon after betrayed her master.

One afternoon, while they were drinking tea, little Betty, so was the maid called, came into the room, and, calling her master forth, delivered him a card which was directed to Amelia. Booth, having read the card, on his return into the room chid the girl for calling him, saying "If you can read, child, you must see it was directed to your mistress." To this the girl answered, pertly enough, "I am sure, sir, you ordered me to bring every letter first to you." This hint, with many women, would have been sufficient to have blown up the whole affair; but Amelia, who heard what the girl said, through the medium of love and confidence, saw the matter in a much better light than it deserved, and, looking tenderly on her husband, said, "Indeed, my love, I must blame you for a conduct which, perhaps, I ought rather to praise, as it proceeds only from the extreme tenderness of your affection. But why will you endeavour to keep any secrets from me? believe me, for my own sake, you ought not; for, as you cannot hide the consequences, you make me

83

always suspect ten times worse than the reality. While I have you and my children well before my eyes, I am capable of facing any news which can arrive; for what ill news can come (unless, indeed, it concerns my little babe in the country) which doth not relate to the badness of our circumstances? and those, I thank Heaven, we have now a fair prospect of retrieving. Besides, dear Billy, though my understanding be much inferior to yours, I have sometimes had the happiness of luckily hitting on some argument which hath afforded you comfort. This, you know, my dear, was the case with regard to Colonel James, whom I persuaded you to think you had mistaken, and you see the event proved me in the right." So happily, both for herself and Mr. Booth, did the excellence of this good woman's disposition deceive her, and force her to see everything in the most advantageous light to her husband.

The card, being now inspected, was found to contain the compliments of Mrs. James to Mrs. Booth, with an account of her being arrived in town, and having brought with her a very great cold. Amelia was overjoyed at the news of her arrival, and having drest herself in the utmost hurry, left her children to the care of her husband, and ran away to pay her respects to her friend, whom she loved with a most sincere affection. But how was she disappointed when, eager with the utmost impatience, and exulting with the thoughts of presently seeing her beloved friend, she was answered at the door that the lady was not at home! nor could she, upon telling her name, obtain any admission. This, considering the account she had received of the lady's cold, greatly surprized her; and she returned home very much vexed at her disappointment.

Amelia, who had no suspicion that Mrs. James was really at home, and, as the phrase is, was denied, would have made a second visit the next morning, had she not been prevented by a cold which she herself now got, and which was attended with a slight fever. This confined her several days to her house, during which Booth officiated as her nurse, and never stirred from her.

In all this time she heard not a word from Mrs. James, which gave her some uneasiness, but more astonishment. The tenth day, when she was perfectly recovered, about nine in the evening, when she and her husband were just going to supper, she heard a most violent thundering at the door, and presently after a rustling of silk upon her staircase; at the same time a female voice cried out pretty loud, "Bless me! what, am I to climb up another pair of stairs?" upon which Amelia, who well knew the voice, presently ran to the door, and ushered in Mrs. James, most splendidly drest, who put on as formal a countenance, and made as formal a courtesie to her old friend, as if she had been her very distant acquaintance.

Poor Amelia, who was going to rush into her friend's arms, was struck motionless by this behaviour; but re-collecting her spirits, as she had an excellent presence of mind, she presently understood what the lady meant, and resolved to treat her in her own way. Down therefore the company sat, and silence prevailed for some time, during which Mrs. James surveyed the room with more attention than she would have bestowed on one much finer. At length the conversation began, in which the weather and the diversions of the town were well canvassed. Amelia, who was a woman of great humour, performed her part to admiration; so that a by-stander would have doubted, in every other article than dress, which of the two was the most accomplished fine lady.

After a visit of twenty minutes, during which not a word of any former occurrences was mentioned, nor indeed any subject of discourse started, except only those two above mentioned, Mrs. James rose from her chair and retired in the same formal manner in which she had approached. We will pursue her for the sake of the contrast during the rest of the evening. She went from Amelia directly to a rout, where she spent two hours in a croud of company, talked again and again over the diversions and news of the town, played two rubbers at whist, and then retired to her own apartment, where, having past another hour in undressing herself, she went to her own bed.

Booth and his wife, the moment their companion was gone, sat down to supper on a piece of cold meat, the remains of their dinner. After which, over a pint of wine, they entertained themselves for a while with the ridiculous behaviour of their visitant. But Amelia, declaring she rather saw her as the object of pity than anger, turned the discourse to pleasanter topics. The little actions of their children, the former scenes and future prospects of their life, furnished them with many pleasant ideas; and the contemplation of Amelia's recovery threw Booth into raptures. At length they retired, happy in each other.

It is possible some readers may be no less surprized at the behaviour of Mrs. James than was Amelia herself, since they may have perhaps received so favourable an impression of that lady

from the account given of her by Mr. Booth, that her present demeanour may seem unnatural and inconsistent with her former character. But they will be pleased to consider the great alteration in her circumstances, from a state of dependency on a brother, who was himself no better than a soldier of fortune, to that of being wife to a man of a very large estate and considerable rank in life. And what was her present behaviour more than that of a fine lady who considered form and show as essential ingredients of human happiness, and imagined all friendship to consist in ceremony, courtesies, messages, and visits? in which opinion, she hath the honour to think with much the larger part of one sex, and no small number of the other.

Chapter vii. — Containing a very extraordinary and pleasant incident.

The next evening Booth and Amelia went to walk in the park with their children. They were now on the verge of the parade, and Booth was describing to his wife the several buildings round it, when, on a sudden, Amelia, missing her little boy, cried out, "Where's little Billy?" Upon which, Booth, casting his eyes over the grass, saw a foot-soldier shaking the boy at a little distance. At this sight, without making any answer to his wife, he leapt over the rails, and, running directly up to the fellow, who had a firelock with a bayonet fixed in his hand, he seized him by the collar and tript up his heels, and, at the same time, wrested his arms from him. A serjeant upon duty, seeing the affray at some distance, ran presently up, and, being told what had happened, gave the centinel a hearty curse, and told him he deserved to be hanged. A by-stander gave this information; for Booth was returned with his little boy to meet Amelia, who staggered towards him as fast as she could, all pale and breathless, and scarce able to support her tottering limbs. The serjeant now came up to Booth, to make an apology for the behaviour of the soldier, when, of a sudden, he turned almost as pale as Amelia herself. He stood silent whilst Booth was employed in comforting and recovering his wife; and then, addressing himself to him, said, "Bless me! lieutenant, could I imagine it had been your honour; and was it my little master that the rascal used so?—I am glad I did not know it, for I should certainly have run my halbert into him."

Booth presently recognised his old faithful servant Atkinson, and gave him a hearty greeting, saying he was very glad to see him in his present situation. "Whatever I am," answered the serjeant, "I shall always think I owe it to your honour." Then, taking the little boy by the hand he cried, "What a vast fine young gentleman master is grown!" and, cursing the soldier's inhumanity, swore heartily he would make him pay for it.

As Amelia was much disordered with her fright, she did not recollect her foster-brother till he was introduced to her by Booth; but she no sooner knew him than she bestowed a most obliging smile on him; and, calling him by the name of honest Joe, said she was heartily glad to see him in England. "See, my dear," cries Booth, "what preferment your old friend is come to. You would scarce know him, I believe, in his present state of finery." "I am very well pleased to see it," answered Amelia, "and I wish him joy of being made an officer with all my heart." In fact, from what Mr. Booth said, joined to the serjeant's laced coat, she believed that he had obtained a commission. So weak and absurd is human vanity, that this mistake of Amelia's possibly put poor Atkinson out of countenance, for he looked at this instant more silly than he had ever done in his life; and, making her a most respectful bow, muttered something about obligations, in a scarce articulate or intelligible manner.

The serjeant had, indeed, among many other qualities, that modesty which a Latin author honours by the name of ingenuous: nature had given him this, notwithstanding the meanness of his birth; and six years' conversation in the army had not taken it away. To say the truth, he was a noble fellow; and Amelia, by supposing he had a commission in the guards, had been guilty of no affront to that honourable body.

Booth had a real affection for Atkinson, though, in fact, he knew not half his merit. He acquainted him with his lodgings, where he earnestly desired to see him.

{Illustration: He seized him by the collar.}

Amelia, who was far from being recovered from the terrors into which the seeing her

husband engaged with the soldier had thrown her, desired to go home: nor was she well able to walk without some assistance. While she supported herself, therefore, on her husband's arm, she told Atkinson she should be obliged to him if he would take care of the children. He readily accepted the office; but, upon offering his hand to miss, she refused, and burst into tears. Upon which the tender mother resigned Booth to her children, and put herself under the serjeant's protection; who conducted her safe home, though she often declared she feared she should drop down by the way; the fear of which so affected the serjeant (for, besides the honour which he himself had for the lady, he knew how tenderly his friend loved her) that he was unable to speak; and, had not his nerves been so strongly braced that nothing could shake them, he had enough in his mind to have set him a trembling equally with the lady.

When they arrived at the lodgings the mistress of the house opened the door, who, seeing Amelia's condition, threw open the parlour and begged her to walk in, upon which she immediately flung herself into a chair, and all present thought she would have fainted away. However, she escaped that misery, and, having drank a glass of water with a little white wine mixed in it, she began in a little time to regain her complexion, and at length assured Booth that she was perfectly recovered, but declared she had never undergone so much, and earnestly begged him never to be so rash for the future. She then called her little boy and gently chid him, saying, "You must never do so more, Billy; you see what mischief you might have brought upon your father, and what you have made me suffer." "La! mamma," said the child, "what harm did I do? I did not know that people might not walk in the green fields in London. I am sure if I did a fault, the man punished me enough for it, for he pinched me almost through my slender arm." He then bared his little arm, which was greatly discoloured by the injury it had received. Booth uttered a most dreadful execration at this sight, and the serjeant, who was now present, did the like.

Atkinson now returned to his guard and went directly to the officer to acquaint him with the soldier's inhumanity, but he, who was about fifteen years of age, gave the serjeant a great curse and said the soldier had done very well, for that idle boys ought to be corrected. This, however, did not satisfy poor Atkinson, who, the next day, as soon as the guard was relieved, beat the fellow most unmercifully, and told him he would remember him as long as he stayed in the regiment.

Thus ended this trifling adventure, which some readers will, perhaps, be pleased at seeing related at full length. None, I think, can fail drawing one observation from it, namely, how capable the most insignificant accident is of disturbing human happiness, and of producing the most unexpected and dreadful events. A reflexion which may serve to many moral and religious uses.

This accident produced the first acquaintance between the mistress of the house and her lodgers; for hitherto they had scarce exchanged a word together. But the great concern which the good woman had shewn on Amelia's account at this time, was not likely to pass unobserved or unthanked either by the husband or wife. Amelia, therefore, as soon as she was able to go up-stairs, invited Mrs. Ellison (for that was her name) to her apartment, and desired the favour of her to stay to supper. She readily complied, and they past a very agreeable evening together, in which the two women seemed to have conceived a most extraordinary liking to each other.

Though beauty in general doth not greatly recommend one woman to another, as it is too apt to create envy, yet, in cases where this passion doth not interfere, a fine woman is often a pleasing object even to some of her own sex, especially when her beauty is attended with a certain air of affability, as was that of Amelia in the highest degree. She was, indeed, a most charming woman; and I know not whether the little scar on her nose did not rather add to than diminish her beauty.

Mrs. Ellison, therefore, was as much charmed with the loveliness of her fair lodger as with all her other engaging qualities. She was, indeed, so taken with Amelia's beauty, that she could not refrain from crying out in a kind of transport of admiration, "Upon my word, Captain Booth, you are the happiest man in the world! Your lady is so extremely handsome that one cannot look at her without pleasure."

This good woman had herself none of these attractive charms to the eye. Her person was short and immoderately fat; her features were none of the most regular; and her complexion (if indeed she ever had a good one) had considerably suffered by time.

Her good humour and complaisance, however, were highly pleasing to Amelia. Nay, why should we conceal the secret satisfaction which that lady felt from the compliments paid to her person? since such of my readers as like her best will not be sorry to find that she was a woman.

Chapter viii. — Containing various matters.

A fortnight had now passed since Booth had seen or heard from the colonel, which did not a little surprize him, as they had parted so good friends, and as he had so cordially undertaken his cause concerning the memorial on which all his hopes depended.

The uneasiness which this gave him farther encreased on finding that his friend refused to see him; for he had paid the colonel a visit at nine in the morning, and was told he was not stirring; and at his return back an hour afterwards the servant said his master was gone out, of which Booth was certain of the falsehood; for he had, during that whole hour, walked backwards and forwards within sight of the colonel's door, and must have seen him if he had gone out within that time.

The good colonel, however, did not long suffer his friend to continue in the deplorable state of anxiety; for, the very next morning, Booth received his memorial enclosed in a letter, acquainting him that Mr. James had mentioned his affair to the person he proposed, but that the great man had so many engagements on his hands that it was impossible for him to make any further promises at this time.

The cold and distant stile of this letter, and, indeed, the whole behaviour of James, so different from what it had been formerly, had something so mysterious in it, that it greatly puzzled and perplexed poor Booth; and it was so long before he was able to solve it, that the reader's curiosity will, perhaps, be obliged to us for not leaving him so long in the dark as to this matter. The true reason, then, of the colonel's conduct was this: his unbounded generosity, together with the unbounded extravagance and consequently the great necessity of Miss Matthews, had at length overcome the cruelty of that lady, with whom he likewise had luckily no rival. Above all, the desire of being revenged on Booth, with whom she was to the highest degree enraged, had, perhaps, contributed not a little to his success; for she had no sooner condescended to a familiarity with her new lover, and discovered that Captain James, of whom she had heard so much from Booth, was no other than the identical colonel, than she employed every art of which she was mistress to make an utter breach of friendship between these two. For this purpose she did not scruple to insinuate that the colonel was not at all obliged to the character given of him by his friend, and to the account of this latter she placed most of the cruelty which she had shewn to the former.

Had the colonel made a proper use of his reason, and fairly examined the probability of the fact, he could scarce have been imposed upon to believe a matter so inconsistent with all he knew of Booth, and in which that gentleman must have sinned against all the laws of honour without any visible temptation. But, in solemn fact, the colonel was so intoxicated with his love, that it was in the power of his mistress to have persuaded him of anything; besides, he had an interest in giving her credit, for he was not a little pleased with finding a reason for hating the man whom he could not help hating without any reason, at least, without any which he durst fairly assign even to himself. Henceforth, therefore, he abandoned all friendship for Booth, and was more inclined to put him out of the world than to endeavour any longer at supporting him in it.

Booth communicated this letter to his wife, who endeavoured, as usual, to the utmost of her power, to console him under one of the greatest afflictions which, I think, can befal a man, namely, the unkindness of a friend; but he had luckily at the same time the greatest blessing in his possession, the kindness of a faithful and beloved wife. A blessing, however, which, though it compensates most of the evils of life, rather serves to aggravate the misfortune of distressed circumstances, from the consideration of the share which she is to bear in them.

This afternoon Amelia received a second visit from Mrs. Ellison, who acquainted her that she had a present of a ticket for the oratorio, which would carry two persons into the gallery; and therefore begged the favour of her company thither.

Amelia, with many thanks, acknowledged the civility of Mrs. Ellison, but declined accepting her offer; upon which Booth very strenuously insisted on her going, and said to her, "My dear, if you knew the satisfaction I have in any of your pleasures, I am convinced you would not refuse

the favour Mrs. Ellison is so kind to offer you; for, as you are a lover of music, you, who have never been at an oratorio, cannot conceive how you will be delighted." "I well know your goodness, my dear," answered Amelia, "but I cannot think of leaving my children without some person more proper to take care of them than this poor girl." Mrs. Ellison removed this objection by offering her own servant, a very discreet matron, to attend them; but notwithstanding this, and all she could say, with the assistance of Booth, and of the children themselves, Amelia still persisted in her refusal; and the mistress of the house, who knew how far good breeding allows persons to be pressing on these occasions, took her leave.

She was no sooner departed than Amelia, looking tenderly on her husband, said, "How can you, my dear creature, think that music hath any charms for me at this time? or, indeed, do you believe that I am capable of any sensation worthy the name of pleasure when neither you nor my children are present or bear any part of it?"

An officer of the regiment to which Booth had formerly belonged, hearing from Atkinson where he lodged, now came to pay him a visit. He told him that several of their old acquaintance were to meet the next Wednesday at a tavern, and very strongly pressed him to be one of the company. Booth was, in truth, what is called a hearty fellow, and loved now and then to take a chearful glass with his friends; but he excused himself at this time. His friend declared he would take no denial, and he growing very importunate, Amelia at length seconded him. Upon this Booth answered, "Well, my dear, since you desire me, I will comply, but on one condition, that you go at the same time to the oratorio." Amelia thought this request reasonable enough, and gave her consent; of which Mrs. Ellison presently received the news, and with great satisfaction.

It may perhaps be asked why Booth could go to the tavern, and not to the oratorio with his wife? In truth, then, the tavern was within hallowed ground, that is to say, in the verge of the court; for, of five officers that were to meet there, three, besides Booth, were confined to that air which hath been always found extremely wholesome to a broken military constitution. And here, if the good reader will pardon the pun, he will scarce be offended at the observation; since, how is it possible that, without running in debt, any person should maintain the dress and appearance of a gentleman whose income is not half so good as that of a porter? It is true that this allowance, small as it is, is a great expense to the public; but, if several more unnecessary charges were spared, the public might, perhaps, bear a little encrease of this without much feeling it. They would not, I am sure, have equal reason to complain at contributing to the maintenance of a sett of brave fellows, who, at the hazard of their health, their limbs, and their lives, have maintained the safety and honour of their country, as when they find themselves taxed to the support of a sett of drones, who have not the least merit or claim to their favour, and who, without contributing in any manner to the good of the hive, live luxuriously on the labours of the industrious bee.

Chapter ix. — In which Amelia, with her friend, goes to the oratorio.

Nothing happened between the Monday and the Wednesday worthy a place in this history. Upon the evening of the latter the two ladies went to the oratorio, and were there time enough to get a first row in the gallery. Indeed, there was only one person in the house when they came; for Amelia's inclinations, when she gave a loose to them, were pretty eager for this diversion, she being a great lover of music, and particularly of Mr. Handel's compositions. Mrs. Ellison was, I suppose, a great lover likewise of music, for she was the more impatient of the two; which was rather the more extraordinary; as these entertainments were not such novelties to her as they were to poor Amelia.

Though our ladies arrived full two hours before they saw the back of Mr. Handel, yet this time of expectation did not hang extremely heavy on their hands; for, besides their own chat, they had the company of the gentleman whom they found at their first arrival in the gallery, and who, though plainly, or rather roughly dressed, very luckily for the women, happened to be not only well-bred, but a person of very lively conversation. The gentleman, on his part, seemed highly charmed with Amelia, and in fact was so, for, though he restrained himself entirely within the

rules of good breeding, yet was he in the highest degree officious to catch at every opportunity of shewing his respect, and doing her little services. He procured her a book and wax-candle, and held the candle for her himself during the whole entertainment.

At the end of the oratorio he declared he would not leave the ladies till he had seen them safe into their chairs or coach; and at the same time very earnestly entreated that he might have the honour of waiting on them. Upon which Mrs. Ellison, who was a very good-humoured woman, answered, "Ay, sure, sir, if you please; you have been very obliging to us; and a dish of tea shall be at your service at any time;" and then told him where she lived.

The ladies were no sooner seated in their hackney coach than Mrs. Ellison burst into a loud laughter, and cried, "I'll be hanged, madam, if you have not made a conquest to-night; and what is very pleasant, I believe the poor gentleman takes you for a single lady." "Nay," answered Amelia very gravely, "I protest I began to think at last he was rather too particular, though he did not venture at a word that I could be offended at; but, if you fancy any such thing, I am sorry you invited him to drink tea," "Why so?" replied Mrs. Ellison. "Are you angry with a man for liking you? if you are, you will be angry with almost every man that sees you. If I was a man myself, I declare I should be in the number of your admirers. Poor gentleman, I pity him heartily; he little knows that you have not a heart to dispose of. For my own part, I should not be surprized at seeing a serious proposal of marriage: for I am convinced he is a man of fortune, not only by the politeness of his address, but by the fineness of his linen, and that valuable diamond ring on his finger. But you will see more of him when he comes to tea." "Indeed I shall not," answered Amelia, "though I believe you only rally me; I hope you have a better opinion of me than to think I would go willingly into the company of a man who had an improper liking for me." Mrs. Ellison, who was one of the gayest women in the world, repeated the words, improper liking, with a laugh; and cried, "My dear Mrs. Booth, believe me, you are too handsome and too good-humoured for a prude. How can you affect being offended at what I am convinced is the greatest pleasure of womankind, and chiefly, I believe, of us virtuous women? for, I assure you, notwithstanding my gaiety, I am as virtuous as any prude in Europe." "Far be it from me, madam," said Amelia, "to suspect the contrary of abundance of women who indulge themselves in much greater freedoms than I should take, or have any pleasure in taking; for I solemnly protest, if I know my own heart, the liking of all men, but of one, is a matter quite indifferent to me, or rather would be highly disagreeable."

This discourse brought them home, where Amelia, finding her children asleep, and her husband not returned, invited her companion to partake of her homely fare, and down they sat to supper together. The clock struck twelve; and, no news being arrived of Booth, Mrs. Ellison began to express some astonishment at his stay, whence she launched into a general reflexion on husbands, and soon passed to some particular invectives on her own. "Ah, my dear madam," says she, "I know the present state of your mind, by what I have myself often felt formerly. I am no stranger to the melancholy tone of a midnight clock. It was my misfortune to drag on a heavy chain above fifteen years with a sottish yoke-fellow. But how can I wonder at my fate, since I see even your superior charms cannot confine a husband from the bewitching pleasures of a bottle?" "Indeed, madam," says Amelia, "I have no reason to complain; Mr. Booth is one of the soberest of men; but now and then to spend a late hour with his friend is, I think, highly excusable." "O, no doubt! "cries Mrs. Ellison, "if he can excuse himself; but if I was a man—" Here Booth came in and interrupted the discourse. Amelia's eyes flashed with joy the moment he appeared; and he discovered no less pleasure in seeing her. His spirits were indeed a little elevated with wine, so as to heighten his good humour, without in the least disordering his understanding, and made him such delightful company, that, though it was past one in the morning, neither his wife nor Mrs. Ellison thought of their beds during a whole hour.

Early the next morning the serjeant came to Mr. Booth's lodgings, and with a melancholy countenance acquainted him that he had been the night before at an alehouse, where he heard one Mr. Murphy, an attorney, declare that he would get a warrant backed against one Captain Booth at the next board of greencloth. "I hope, sir," said he, "your honour will pardon me, but, by what he said, I was afraid he meant your honour; and therefore I thought it my duty to tell you; for I knew the same thing happen to a gentleman here the other day."

Booth gave Mr. Atkinson many thanks for his information. "I doubt not," said he, "but I am the person meant; for it would be foolish in me to deny that I am liable to apprehensions of that

sort." "I hope, sir," said the serjeant, "your honour will soon have reason to fear no man living; but in the mean time, if any accident should happen, my bail is at your service as far as it will go; and I am a housekeeper, and can swear myself worth one hundred pounds." Which hearty and friendly declaration received all those acknowledgments from Booth which it really deserved.

The poor gentleman was greatly alarmed at the news; but he was altogether as much surprized at Murphy's being the attorney employed against him, as all his debts, except only to Captain James, arose in the country, where he did not know that Mr. Murphy had any acquaintance. However, he made no doubt that he was the person intended, and resolved to remain a close prisoner in his own lodgings, till he saw the event of a proposal which had been made him the evening before at the tavern, where an honest gentleman, who had a post under the government, and who was one of the company, had promised to serve him with the secretary at war, telling him that he made no doubt of procuring him whole pay in a regiment abroad, which in his present circumstances was very highly worth his acceptance, when, indeed, that and a gaol seemed to be the only alternatives that offered themselves to his choice.

Mr. Booth and his lady spent that afternoon with Mrs. Ellison—an incident which we should scarce have mentioned, had it not been that Amelia gave, on this occasion, an instance of that prudence which should never be off its guard in married women of delicacy; for, before she would consent to drink tea with Mrs. Ellison, she made conditions that the gentleman who had met them at the oratorio should not be let in. Indeed, this circumspection proved unnecessary in the present instance, for no such visitor ever came; a circumstance which gave great content to Amelia; for that lady had been a little uneasy at the raillery of Mrs. Ellison, and had upon reflexion magnified every little compliment made her, and every little civility shewn her by the unknown gentleman, far beyond the truth. These imaginations now all subsided again; and she imputed all that Mrs. Ellison had said either to raillery or mistake.

A young lady made a fourth with them at whist, and likewise stayed the whole evening. Her name was Bennet. She was about the age of five-and-twenty; but sickness had given her an older look, and had a good deal diminished her beauty; of which, young as she was, she plainly appeared to have only the remains in her present possession. She was in one particular the very reverse of Mrs. Ellison, being altogether as remarkably grave as the other was gay. This gravity was not, however, attended with any sourness of temper; on the contrary, she had much sweetness in her countenance, and was perfectly well bred. In short, Amelia imputed her grave deportment to her ill health, and began to entertain a compassion for her, which in good minds, that is to say, in minds capable of compassion, is certain to introduce some little degree of love or friendship.

Amelia was in short so pleased with the conversation of this lady, that, though a woman of no impertinent curiosity, she could not help taking the first opportunity of enquiring who she was. Mrs. Ellison said that she was an unhappy lady, who had married a young clergyman for love, who, dying of a consumption, had left her a widow in very indifferent circumstances. This account made Amelia still pity her more, and consequently added to the liking which she had already conceived for her. Amelia, therefore, desired Mrs. Ellison to bring her acquainted with Mrs. Bennet, and said she would go any day with her to make that lady a visit. "There need be no ceremony," cried Mrs. Ellison; "she is a woman of no form; and, as I saw plainly she was extremely pleased with Mrs. Booth, I am convinced I can bring her to drink tea with you any afternoon you please."

The two next days Booth continued at home, highly to the satisfaction of his Amelia, who really knew no happiness out of his company, nor scarce any misery in it. She had, indeed, at all times so much of his company, when in his power, that she had no occasion to assign any particular reason for his staying with her, and consequently it could give her no cause of suspicion. The Saturday, one of her children was a little disordered with a feverish complaint which confined her to her room, and prevented her drinking tea in the afternoon with her husband in Mrs. Ellison's apartment, where a noble lord, a cousin of Mrs. Ellison's, happened to be present; for, though that lady was reduced in her circumstances and obliged to let out part of her house in lodgings, she was born of a good family and had some considerable relations.

His lordship was not himself in any office of state, but his fortune gave him great authority with those who were. Mrs. Ellison, therefore, very bluntly took an opportunity of recommending Booth to his consideration. She took the first hint from my lord's calling the gentleman captain; to which she answered, "Ay, I wish your lordship would make him so. It would be an act of justice,

and I know it is in your power to do much greater things." She then mentioned Booth's services, and the wounds he had received at the siege, of which she had heard a faithful account from Amelia. Booth blushed, and was as silent as a young virgin at the hearing her own praises. His lordship answered, "Cousin Ellison, you know you may command my interest; nay, I shall have a pleasure in serving one of Mr. Booth's character: for my part, I think merit in all capacities ought to be encouraged, but I know the ministry are greatly pestered with solicitations at this time. However, Mr. Booth may be assured I will take the first opportunity; and in the mean time, I shall be glad of seeing him any morning he pleases." For all these declarations Booth was not wanting in acknowledgments to the generous peer any more than he was in secret gratitude to the lady who had shewn so friendly and uncommon a zeal in his favour.

The reader, when he knows the character of this nobleman, may, perhaps, conclude that his seeing Booth alone was a lucky circumstance, for he was so passionate an admirer of women, that he could scarce have escaped the attraction of Amelia's beauty. And few men, as I have observed, have such disinterested generosity as to serve a husband the better because they are in love with his wife, unless she will condescend to pay a price beyond the reach of a virtuous woman.

END OF VOL. I.

VOL. II.

BOOK V.

Chapter i. — In which the reader will meet with an old acquaintance.

Booth's affairs were put on a better aspect than they had ever worn before, and he was willing to make use of the opportunity of one day in seven to taste the fresh air.

At nine in the morning he went to pay a visit to his old friend Colonel James, resolving, if possible, to have a full explanation of that behaviour which appeared to him so mysterious: but the colonel was as inaccessible as the best defended fortress; and it was as impossible for Booth to pass beyond his entry as the Spaniards found it to take Gibraltar. He received the usual answers; first, that the colonel was not stirring, and an hour after that he was gone out. All that he got by asking further questions was only to receive still ruder answers, by which, if he had been very sagacious, he might have been satisfied how little worth his while it was to desire to go in; for the porter at a great man's door is a kind of thermometer, by which you may discover the warmth or coldness of his master's friendship. Nay, in the highest stations of all, as the great man himself hath his different kinds of salutation, from an hearty embrace with a kiss, and my dear lord or dear Sir Charles, down to, well Mr.——, what would you have me do? so the porter to some bows with respect, to others with a smile, to some he bows more, to others less low, to others not at all. Some he just lets in, and others he just shuts out. And in all this they so well correspond, that one would be inclined to think that the great man and his porter had compared their lists together, and, like two actors concerned to act different parts in the same scene, had rehearsed their parts privately together before they ventured to perform in public.

Though Booth did not, perhaps, see the whole matter in this just light, for that in reality it is,

yet he was discerning enough to conclude, from the behaviour of the servant, especially when he considered that of the master likewise, that he had entirely lost the friendship of James; and this conviction gave him a concern that not only the flattering prospect of his lordship's favour was not able to compensate, but which even obliterated, and made him for a while forget the situation in which he had left his Amelia: and he wandered about almost two hours, scarce knowing where he went, till at last he dropt into a coffee-house near St James's, where he sat himself down.

He had scarce drank his dish of coffee before he heard a young officer of the guards cry to another, "Od, d—n me, Jack, here he comes—here's old honour and dignity, faith." Upon which he saw a chair open, and out issued a most erect and stately figure indeed, with a vast periwig on his head, and a vast hat under his arm. This august personage, having entered the room, walked directly up to the upper end, where having paid his respects to all present of any note, to each according to seniority, he at last cast his eyes on Booth, and very civilly, though somewhat coldly, asked him how he did.

Booth, who had long recognized the features of his old acquaintance Major Bath, returned the compliment with a very low bow; but did not venture to make the first advance to familiarity, as he was truly possessed of that quality which the Greeks considered in the highest light of honour, and which we term modesty; though indeed, neither ours nor the Latin language hath any word adequate to the idea of the original.

The colonel, after having discharged himself of two or three articles of news, and made his comments upon them, when the next chair to him became vacant, called upon Booth to fill it. He then asked him several questions relating to his affairs; and, when he heard he was out of the army, advised him earnestly to use all means to get in again, saying that he was a pretty lad, and they must not lose him.

Booth told him in a whisper that he had a great deal to say to him on that subject if they were in a more private place; upon this the colonel proposed a walk in the Park, which the other readily accepted.

During their walk Booth opened his heart, and, among other matters, acquainted Colonel Bath that he feared he had lost the friendship of Colonel James; "though I am not," said he, "conscious of having done the least thing to deserve it."

Bath answered, "You are certainly mistaken, Mr. Booth. I have indeed scarce seen my brother since my coming to town; for I have been here but two days; however, I am convinced he is a man of too nice honour to do anything inconsistent with the true dignity of a gentleman." Booth answered, "He was far from accusing him of anything dishonourable."—"D—n me," said Bath, "if there is a man alive can or dare accuse him: if you have the least reason to take anything ill, why don't you go to him? you are a gentleman, and his rank doth not protect him from giving you satisfaction." "The affair is not of any such kind," says Booth; "I have great obligations to the colonel, and have more reason to lament than complain; and, if I could but see him, I am convinced I should have no cause for either; but I cannot get within his house; it was but an hour ago a servant of his turned me rudely from the door." "Did a servant of my brother use you rudely?" said the colonel, with the utmost gravity. "I do not know, sir, in what light you see such things; but, to me, the affront of a servant is the affront of the master; and if he doth not immediately punish it, by all the dignity of a man, I would see the master's nose between my fingers." Booth offered to explain, but to no purpose; the colonel was got into his stilts; and it was impossible to take him down, nay, it was as much as Booth could possibly do to part with him without an actual quarrel; nor would he, perhaps, have been able to have accomplished it, had not the colonel by accident turned at last to take Booth's side of the question; and before they separated he swore many oaths that James should give him proper satisfaction.

Such was the end of this present interview, so little to the content of Booth, that he was heartily concerned he had ever mentioned a syllable of the matter to his honourable friend.

{This chapter occurs in the original edition of Amelia, between 1 and 2. It is omitted later, and would have been omitted here but for an accident. As it had been printed it may as well appear: for though it has no great value it may interest some readers as an additional illustration of Fielding's dislike to doctors.—ED.

Containing a brace of doctors and much physical matter.

He now returned with all his uneasiness to Amelia, whom he found in a condition very little adapted to relieve or comfort him. That poor woman was now indeed under very great

apprehensions for her child, whose fever now began to rage very violently: and what was worse, an apothecary had been with her, and frightened her almost out of her wits. He had indeed represented the case of the child to be very desperate, and had prevailed on the mother to call in the assistance of a doctor.

Booth had been a very little time in the room before this doctor arrived, with the apothecary close at his heels, and both approached the bed, where the former felt the pulse of the sick, and performed several other physical ceremonies.

He then began to enquire of the apothecary what he had already done for the patient; all which, as soon as informed, he greatly approved. The doctor then sat down, called for a pen and ink, filled a whole side of a sheet of paper with physic, then took a guinea, and took his leave; the apothecary waiting upon him downstairs, as he had attended him up.

All that night both Amelia and Booth sat up with their child, who rather grew worse than better. In the morning Mrs. Ellison found the infant in a raging fever, burning hot, and very light-headed, and the mother under the highest dejection; for the distemper had not given the least ground to all the efforts of the apothecary and doctor, but seemed to defy their utmost power, with all that tremendous apparatus of phials and gallypots, which were arranged in battle-array all over the room.

Mrs. Ellison, seeing the distress, and indeed distracted, condition of Amelia's mind, attempted to comfort her by giving her hopes of the child's recovery. "Upon my word, madam," says she, "I saw a child of much the same age with miss, who, in my opinion, was much worse, restored to health in a few days by a physician of my acquaintance. Nay, I have known him cure several others of very bad fevers; and, if miss was under his care, I dare swear she would do very well." "Good heavens! madam," answered Amelia, "why should you not mention him to me? For my part I have no acquaintance with any London physicians, nor do I know whom the apothecary hath brought me." "Nay, madam," cries Mrs. Ellison, "it is a tender thing, you know, to recommend a physician; and as for my doctor, there are abundance of people who give him an ill name. Indeed, it is true, he hath cured me twice of fevers, and so he hath several others to my knowledge; nay, I never heard of any more than one of his patients that died; and yet, as the doctors and apothecaries all give him an ill character, one is fearful, you know, dear madam." Booth enquired the doctor's name, which he no sooner heard than he begged his wife to send for him immediately, declaring he had heard the highest character imaginable of him at the Tavern from an officer of very good understanding. Amelia presently complied, and a messenger was despatched accordingly.

But before the second doctor could be brought, the first returned with the apothecary attending him as before. He again surveyed and handled the sick; and when Amelia begged him to tell her if there was any hopes, he shook his head, and said, "To be sure, madam, miss is in a very dangerous condition, and there is no time to lose. If the blisters which I shall now order her, should not relieve her, I fear we can do no more."—"Would not you please, sir," says the apothecary, "to have the powders and the draught repeated?" "How often were they ordered?" cries the doctor. "Only tertia quaq. hora," says the apothecary. "Let them be taken every hour by all means," cries the doctor; "and—let me see, pray get me a pen and ink."—"If you think the child in such imminent danger," said Booth, "would you give us leave to call in another physician to your assistance—indeed my wife"—"Oh, by all means," said the doctor, "it is what I very much wish. Let me see, Mr. Arsenic, whom shall we call?" "What do you think of Dr Dosewell?" said the apothecary.—"Nobody better," cries the physician.—"I should have no objection to the gentleman," answered Booth, "but another hath been recommended to my wife." He then mentioned the physician for whom they had just before sent. "Who, sir?" cries the doctor, dropping his pen; and when Booth repeated the name of Thompson, "Excuse me, sir," cries the doctor hastily, "I shall not meet him."—"Why so, sir?" answered Booth. "I will not meet him," replied the doctor. "Shall I meet a man who pretends to know more than the whole College, and would overturn the whole method of practice, which is so well established, and from which no one person hath pretended to deviate?" "Indeed, sir," cries the apothecary, "you do not know what you are about, asking your pardon; why, he kills everybody he comes near." "That is not true," said Mrs. Ellison. "I have been his patient twice, and I am alive yet." "You have had good luck, then, madam," answered the apothecary, "for he kills everybody he comes near." "Nay, I know above a dozen others of my own acquaintance," replied Mrs. Ellison, "who have all been

cured by him." "That may be, madam," cries Arsenic; "but he kills everybody for all that—why, madam, did you never hear of Mr. ——? I can't think of the gentleman's name, though he was a man of great fashion; but everybody knows whom I mean." "Everybody, indeed, must know whom you mean," answered Mrs. Ellison; "for I never heard but of one, and that many years ago."

Before the dispute was ended, the doctor himself entered the room. As he was a very well-bred and very good-natured man, he addressed himself with much civility to his brother physician, who was not quite so courteous on his side. However, he suffered the new comer to be conducted to the sick-bed, and at Booth's earnest request to deliver his opinion.

The dispute which ensued between the two physicians would, perhaps, be unintelligible to any but those of the faculty, and not very entertaining to them. The character which the officer and Mrs. Ellison had given of the second doctor had greatly prepossessed Booth in his favour, and indeed his reasoning seemed to be the juster. Booth therefore declared that he would abide by his advice, upon which the former operator, with his zany, the apothecary, quitted the field, and left the other in full possession of the sick.

The first thing the new doctor did was (to use his own phrase) to blow up the physical magazine. All the powders and potions instantly disappeared at his command; for he said there was a much readier and nearer way to convey such stuff to the vault, than by first sending it through the human body. He then ordered the child to be blooded, gave it a clyster and some cooling physic, and, in short (that I may not dwell too long on so unpleasing a part of history), within three days cured the little patient of her distemper, to the great satisfaction of Mrs. Ellison, and to the vast joy of Amelia.

Some readers will, perhaps, think this whole chapter might have been omitted; but though it contains no great matter of amusement, it may at least serve to inform posterity concerning the present state of physic.}

Chapter ii. — In which Booth pays a visit to the noble lord.

When that day of the week returned in which Mr. Booth chose to walk abroad, he went to wait on the noble peer, according to his kind invitation.

Booth now found a very different reception with this great man's porter from what he had met with at his friend the colonel's. He no sooner told his name than the porter with a bow told him his lordship was at home: the door immediately flew wide open, and he was conducted to an ante-chamber, where a servant told him he would acquaint his lordship with his arrival. Nor did he wait many minutes before the same servant returned and ushered him to his lordship's apartment.

He found my lord alone, and was received by him in the most courteous manner imaginable. After the first ceremonials were over, his lordship began in the following words: "Mr. Booth, I do assure you, you are very much obliged to my cousin Ellison. She hath given you such a character, that I shall have a pleasure in doing anything in my power to serve you.—But it will be very difficult, I am afraid, to get you a rank at home. In the West Indies, perhaps, or in some regiment abroad, it may be more easy; and, when I consider your reputation as a soldier, I make no doubt of your readiness to go to any place where the service of your country shall call you." Booth answered, "That he was highly obliged to his lordship, and assured him he would with great chearfulness attend his duty in any part of the world. The only thing grievous in the exchange of countries," said he, "in my opinion, is to leave those I love behind me, and I am sure I shall never have a second trial equal to my first. It was very hard, my lord, to leave a young wife big with her first child, and so affected with my absence, that I had the utmost reason to despair of ever seeing her more. After such a demonstration of my resolution to sacrifice every other consideration to my duty, I hope your lordship will honour me with some confidence that I shall make no objection to serve in any country."—"My dear Mr. Booth," answered the lord, "you speak like a

soldier, and I greatly honour your sentiments. Indeed, I own the justice of your inference from the example you have given; for to quit a wife, as you say, in the very infancy of marriage, is, I acknowledge, some trial of resolution." Booth answered with a low bow; and then, after some immaterial conversation, his lordship promised to speak immediately to the minister, and appointed Mr. Booth to come to him again on the Wednesday morning, that he might be acquainted with his patron's success. The poor man now blushed and looked silly, till, after some time, he summoned up all his courage to his assistance, and relying on the other's friendship, he opened the whole affair of his circumstances, and confessed that he did not dare stir from his lodgings above one day in seven. His lordship expressed great concern at this account, and very kindly promised to take some opportunity of calling on him at his cousin Ellison's, when he hoped, he said, to bring him comfortable tidings.

Booth soon afterwards took his leave with the most profuse acknowledgments for so much goodness, and hastened home to acquaint his Amelia with what had so greatly overjoyed him. She highly congratulated him on his having found so generous and powerful a friend, towards whom both their bosoms burnt with the warmest sentiments of gratitude. She was not, however, contented till she had made Booth renew his promise, in the most solemn manner, of taking her with him. After which they sat down with their little children to a scrag of mutton and broth, with the highest satisfaction, and very heartily drank his lordship's health in a pot of porter.

In the afternoon this happy couple, if the reader will allow me to call poor people happy, drank tea with Mrs. Ellison, where his lordship's praises, being again repeated by both the husband and wife, were very loudly echoed by Mrs. Ellison. While they were here, the young lady whom we have mentioned at the end of the last book to have made a fourth at whist, and with whom Amelia seemed so much pleased, came in; she was just returned to town from a short visit in the country, and her present visit was unexpected. It was, however, very agreeable to Amelia, who liked her still better upon a second interview, and was resolved to solicit her further acquaintance.

Mrs. Bennet still maintained some little reserve, but was much more familiar and communicative than before. She appeared, moreover, to be as little ceremonious as Mrs. Ellison had reported her, and very readily accepted Amelia's apology for not paying her the first visit, and agreed to drink tea with her the very next afternoon.

Whilst the above-mentioned company were sitting in Mrs. Ellison's parlour, serjeant Atkinson passed by the window and knocked at the door. Mrs. Ellison no sooner saw him than she said, "Pray, Mr. Booth, who is that genteel young serjeant? he was here every day last week to enquire after you." This was indeed a fact; the serjeant was apprehensive of the design of Murphy; but, as the poor fellow had received all his answers from the maid of Mrs. Ellison, Booth had never heard a word of the matter. He was, however, greatly pleased with what he was now told, and burst forth into great praises of the serjeant, which were seconded by Amelia, who added that he was her foster-brother, and, she believed, one of the honestest fellows in the world.

"And I'll swear," cries Mrs. Ellison, "he is one of the prettiest. Do, Mr. Booth, desire him to walk in. A serjeant of the guards is a gentleman; and I had rather give such a man as you describe a dish of tea than any Beau Fribble of them all."

Booth wanted no great solicitation to shew any kind of regard to Atkinson; and, accordingly, the serjeant was ushered in, though not without some reluctance on his side. There is, perhaps, nothing more uneasy than those sensations which the French call the mauvaise honte, nor any more difficult to conquer; and poor Atkinson would, I am persuaded, have mounted a breach with less concern than he shewed in walking across a room before three ladies, two of whom were his avowed well-wishers.

Though I do not entirely agree with the late learned Mr. Essex, the celebrated dancing-master's opinion, that dancing is the rudiment of polite education, as he would, I apprehend, exclude every other art and science, yet it is certain that persons whose feet have never been under the hands of the professors of that art are apt to discover this want in their education in every motion, nay, even when they stand or sit still. They seem, indeed, to be overburthened with limbs which they know not how to use, as if, when Nature hath finished her work, the dancing-master still is necessary to put it in motion.

Atkinson was, at present, an example of this observation which doth so much honour to a profession for which I have a very high regard. He was handsome, and exquisitely well made; and

yet, as he had never learnt to dance, he made so awkward an appearance in Mrs. Ellison's parlour, that the good lady herself, who had invited him in, could at first scarce refrain from laughter at his behaviour. He had not, however, been long in the room before admiration of his person got the better of such risible ideas. So great is the advantage of beauty in men as well as women, and so sure is this quality in either sex of procuring some regard from the beholder.

The exceeding courteous behaviour of Mrs. Ellison, joined to that of Amelia and Booth, at length dissipated the uneasiness of Atkinson; and he gained sufficient confidence to tell the company some entertaining stories of accidents that had happened in the army within his knowledge, which, though they greatly pleased all present, are not, however, of consequence enough to have a place in this history.

Mrs. Ellison was so very importunate with her company to stay supper that they all consented. As for the serjeant, he seemed to be none of the least welcome guests. She was, indeed, so pleased with what she had heard of him, and what she saw of him, that, when a little warmed with wine, for she was no flincher at the bottle, she began to indulge some freedoms in her discourse towards him that a little offended Amelia's delicacy, nay, they did not seem to be highly relished by the other lady; though I am far from insinuating that these exceeded the bounds of decorum, or were, indeed, greater liberties than ladies of the middle age, and especially widows, do frequently allow to themselves.

Chapter iii. — Relating principally to the affairs of serjeant Atkinson.

The next day, when all the same company, Atkinson only excepted, assembled in Amelia's apartment, Mrs. Ellison presently began to discourse of him, and that in terms not only of approbation but even of affection. She called him her clever serjeant, and her dear serjeant, repeated often that he was the prettiest fellow in the army, and said it was a thousand pities he had not a commission; for that, if he had, she was sure he would become a general.

"I am of your opinion, madam," answered Booth; "and he hath got one hundred pounds of his own already, if he could find a wife now to help him to two or three hundred more, I think he might easily get a commission in a marching regiment; for I am convinced there is no colonel in the army would refuse him."

"Refuse him, indeed!" said Mrs. Ellison; "no; he would be a very pretty colonel that did. And, upon my honour, I believe there are very few ladies who would refuse him, if he had but a proper opportunity of soliciting them. The colonel and the lady both would be better off than with one of those pretty masters that I see walking about, and dragging their long swords after them, when they should rather drag their leading-strings."

"Well said," cries Booth, "and spoken like a woman of spirit.—Indeed, I believe they would be both better served."

"True, captain," answered Mrs. Ellison; "I would rather leave the two first syllables out of the word gentleman than the last."

"Nay, I assure you," replied Booth, "there is not a quieter creature in the world. Though the fellow hath the bravery of a lion, he hath the meekness of a lamb. I can tell you stories enow of that kind, and so can my dear Amelia, when he was a boy."

"O! if the match sticks there," cries Amelia, "I positively will not spoil his fortune by my silence. I can answer for him from his infancy, that he was one of the best-natured lads in the world. I will tell you a story or two of him, the truth of which I can testify from my own knowledge. When he was but six years old he was at play with me at my mother's house, and a great pointer-dog bit him through the leg. The poor lad, in the midst of the anguish of his wound, declared he was overjoyed it had not happened to miss (for the same dog had just before snapt at me, and my petticoats had been my defence).—Another instance of his goodness, which greatly recommended him to my father, and which I have loved him for ever since, was this: my father was a great lover of birds, and strictly forbad the spoiling of their nests. Poor Joe was one day caught upon a tree, and, being concluded guilty, was severely lashed for it; but it was afterwards

discovered that another boy, a friend of Joe's, had robbed the nest of its young ones, and poor Joe had climbed the tree in order to restore them, notwithstanding which, he submitted to the punishment rather than he would impeach his companion. But, if these stories appear childish and trifling, the duty and kindness he hath shewn to his mother must recommend him to every one. Ever since he hath been fifteen years old he hath more than half supported her: and when my brother died, I remember particularly, Joe, at his desire, for he was much his favourite, had one of his suits given him; but, instead of his becoming finer on that occasion, another young fellow came to church in my brother's cloaths, and my old nurse appeared the same Sunday in a new gown, which her son had purchased for her with the sale of his legacy."

"Well, I protest, he is a very worthy creature," said Mrs. Bennet.

"He is a charming fellow," cries Mrs. Ellison—"but then the name of serjeant, Captain Booth; there, as the play says, my pride brings me off again."

And whatsoever the sages charge on pride,
The angels' fall, and twenty other good faults beside;
On earth I'm sure—I'm sure—something—calling
Pride saves man, and our sex too, from falling.—

Here a footman's rap at the door shook the room. Upon which Mrs. Ellison, running to the window, cried out, "Let me die if it is not my lord! what shall I do? I must be at home to him; but suppose he should enquire for you, captain, what shall I say? or will you go down with me?"

The company were in some confusion at this instant, and before they had agreed on anything, Booth's little girl came running into the room, and said, "There was a prodigious great gentleman coming up-stairs." She was immediately followed by his lordship, who, as he knew Booth must be at home, made very little or no enquiry at the door.

Amelia was taken somewhat at a surprize, but she was too polite to shew much confusion; for, though she knew nothing of the town, she had had a genteel education, and kept the best company the country afforded. The ceremonies therefore past as usual, and they all sat down.

His lordship soon addressed himself to Booth, saying, "As I have what I think good news for you, sir, I could not delay giving myself the pleasure of communicating it to you. I have mentioned your affair where I promised you, and I have no doubt of my success. One may easily perceive, you know, from the manner of people's behaving upon such occasions; and, indeed, when I related your case, I found there was much inclination to serve you. Great men, Mr. Booth, must do things in their own time; but I think you may depend on having something done very soon."

Booth made many acknowledgments for his lordship's goodness, and now a second time paid all the thanks which would have been due, even had the favour been obtained. This art of promising is the economy of a great man's pride, a sort of good husbandry in conferring favours, by which they receive tenfold in acknowledgments for every obligation, I mean among those who really intend the service; for there are others who cheat poor men of their thanks, without ever designing to deserve them at all.

This matter being sufficiently discussed, the conversation took a gayer turn; and my lord began to entertain the ladies with some of that elegant discourse which, though most delightful to hear, it is impossible should ever be read.

His lordship was so highly pleased with Amelia, that he could not help being somewhat particular to her; but this particularity distinguished itself only in a higher degree of respect, and was so very polite, and so very distant, that she herself was pleased, and at his departure, which was not till he had far exceeded the length of a common visit, declared he was the finest gentleman she had ever seen; with which sentiment her husband and Mrs. Ellison both entirely concurred.

Mrs. Bennet, on the contrary, exprest some little dislike to my lord's complaisance, which she called excessive. "For my own part," said she, "I have not the least relish for those very fine gentlemen; what the world generally calls politeness, I term insincerity; and I am more charmed with the stories which Mrs. Booth told us of the honest serjeant than with all that the finest gentlemen in the world ever said in their lives!"

"O! to be sure," cries Mrs. Ellison; "All for Love, or the World well Lost, is a motto very proper for some folks to wear in their coat of arms; but the generality of the world will, I believe, agree with that lady's opinion of my cousin, rather than with Mrs. Bennet."

97

Mrs. Bennet, seeing Mrs. Ellison took offence at what she said, thought proper to make some apology, which was very readily accepted, and so ended the visit.

We cannot however put an end to the chapter without observing that such is the ambitious temper of beauty, that it may always apply to itself that celebrated passage in Lucan,

Nec quenquam jam ferre potest Caesarve priorem, Pompeiusve parem.

Indeed, I believe, it may be laid down as a general rule, that no woman who hath any great pretensions to admiration is ever well pleased in a company where she perceives herself to fill only the second place. This observation, however, I humbly submit to the judgment of the ladies, and hope it will be considered as retracted by me if they shall dissent from my opinion.

Chapter iv. — Containing matters that require no preface.

When Booth and his wife were left alone together they both extremely exulted in their good fortune in having found so good a friend as his lordship; nor were they wanting in very warm expressions of gratitude towards Mrs. Ellison. After which they began to lay down schemes of living when Booth should have his commission of captain; and, after the exactest computation, concluded that, with economy, they should be able to save at least fifty pounds a-year out of their income in order to pay their debts.

These matters being well settled, Amelia asked Booth what he thought of Mrs. Bennet? "I think, my dear," answered Booth, "that she hath been formerly a very pretty woman." "I am mistaken," replied she, "if she be not a very good creature. I don't know I ever took such a liking to any one on so short an acquaintance. I fancy she hath been a very spritely woman; for, if you observe, she discovers by starts a great vivacity in her countenance." "I made the same observation," cries Booth: "sure some strange misfortune hath befallen her." "A misfortune, indeed!" answered Amelia; "sure, child, you forget what Mrs. Ellison told us, that she had lost a beloved husband. A misfortune which I have often wondered at any woman's surviving." At which words she cast a tender look at Booth, and presently afterwards, throwing herself upon his neck, cried, "O, Heavens! what a happy creature am I! when I consider the dangers you have gone through, how I exult in my bliss!" The good-natured reader will suppose that Booth was not deficient in returning such tenderness, after which the conversation became too fond to be here related.

The next morning Mrs. Ellison addressed herself to Booth as follows: "I shall make no apology, sir, for what I am going to say, as it proceeds from my friendship to yourself and your dear lady. I am convinced then, sir, there is a something more than accident in your going abroad only one day in the week. Now, sir, if, as I am afraid, matters are not altogether as well as I wish them, I beg, since I do not believe you are provided with a lawyer, that you will suffer me to recommend one to you. The person I shall mention is, I assure you, of much ability in his profession, and I have known him do great services to gentlemen under a cloud. Do not be ashamed of your circumstances, my dear friend: they are a much greater scandal to those who have left so much merit unprovided for."

Booth gave Mrs. Ellison abundance of thanks for her kindness, and explicitly confessed to her that her conjectures were right, and, without hesitation, accepted the offer of her friend's assistance.

Mrs. Ellison then acquainted him with her apprehensions on his account. She said she had both yesterday and this morning seen two or three very ugly suspicious fellows pass several times by her window. "Upon all accounts," said she, "my dear sir, I advise you to keep yourself close confined till the lawyer hath been with you. I am sure he will get you your liberty, at least of walking about within the verge. There's something to be done with the board of green-cloth; I don't know what; but this I know, that several gentlemen have lived here a long time very comfortably, and have defied all the vengeance of their creditors. However, in the mean time, you must be a close prisoner with your lady; and I believe there is no man in England but would exchange his liberty for the same gaol."

She then departed in order to send for the attorney, and presently afterwards the serjeant arrived with news of the like kind. He said he had scraped an acquaintance with Murphy. "I hope your honour will pardon me," cries Atkinson, "but I pretended to have a small demand upon your honour myself, and offered to employ him in the business. Upon which he told me that, if I would go with him to the Marshal's court, and make affidavit of my debt, he should be able very shortly to get it me; for I shall have the captain in hold," cries he, "within a day or two." "I wish," said the serjeant, "I could do your honour any service. Shall I walk about all day before the door? or shall I be porter, and watch it in the inside till your honour can find some means of securing yourself? I hope you will not be offended at me, but I beg you would take care of falling into Murphy's hands; for he hath the character of the greatest villain upon earth. I am afraid you will think me too bold, sir; but I have a little money; if it can be of any service, do, pray your honour, command it. It can never do me so much good any other way. Consider, sir, I owe all I have to yourself and my dear mistress."

Booth stood a moment, as if he had been thunderstruck, and then, the tears bursting from his eyes, he said, "Upon my soul, Atkinson, you overcome me. I scarce ever heard of so—much goodness, nor do I know how to express my sentiments of it. But, be assured, as for your money, I will not accept it; and let it satisfy you, that in my present circumstances it would do me no essential service; but this be assured of likewise, that whilst I live I shall never forget the kindness of the offer. However, as I apprehend I may be in some danger of fellows getting into the house, for a day or two, as I have no guard but a poor little girl, I will not refuse the goodness you offer to shew in my protection. And I make no doubt but Mrs. Ellison will let you sit in her parlour for that purpose."

Atkinson, with the utmost readiness, undertook the office of porter; and Mrs. Ellison as readily allotted him a place in her back-parlour, where he continued three days together, from eight in the morning till twelve at night; during which time, he had sometimes the company of Mrs. Ellison, and sometimes of Booth, Amelia, and Mrs. Bennet too; for this last had taken as great a fancy to Amelia as Amelia had to her, and, therefore, as Mr. Booth's affairs were now no secret in the neighbourhood, made her frequent visits during the confinement of her husband, and consequently her own.

Nothing, as I remember, happened in this interval of time, more worthy notice than the following card which Amelia received from her old acquaintance Mrs. James:—"Mrs. James sends her compliments to Mrs. Booth, and desires to know how she does; for, as she hath not had the favour of seeing her at her own house, or of meeting her in any public place, in so long time, fears it may be owing to ill health."

Amelia had long given over all thoughts of her friend, and doubted not but that she was as entirely given over by her; she was very much surprized at this message, and under some doubt whether it was not meant as an insult, especially from the mention of public places, which she thought so inconsistent with her present circumstances, of which she supposed Mrs. James was well apprized. However, at the entreaty of her husband, who languished for nothing more than to be again reconciled to his friend James, Amelia undertook to pay the lady a visit, and to examine into the mystery of this conduct, which appeared to her so unaccountable.

Mrs. James received her with a degree of civility that amazed Amelia no less than her coldness had done before. She resolved to come to an eclaircissement, and, having sat out some company that came in, when they were alone together Amelia, after some silence and many offers to speak, at last said, "My dear Jenny (if you will now suffer me to call you by so familiar a name), have you entirely forgot a certain young lady who had the pleasure of being your intimate acquaintance at Montpelier?" "Whom do you mean, dear madam?" cries Mrs. James with great concern. "I mean myself," answered Amelia. "You surprize me, madam," replied Mrs. James: "how can you ask me that question?" "Nay, my dear, I do not intend to offend you," cries Amelia, "but I am really desirous to solve to myself the reason of that coldness which you shewed me when you did me the favour of a visit. Can you think, my dear, I was not disappointed, when I expected to meet an intimate friend, to receive a cold formal visitant? I desire you to examine your own heart and answer me honestly if you do not think I had some little reason to be dissatisfied with your behaviour?" "Indeed, Mrs. Booth," answered the other lady, "you surprize me very much; if there was anything displeasing to you in my behaviour I am extremely concerned at it. I did not know I had been defective in any of the rules of civility, but if I was, madam, I ask your pardon." "Is

civility, then, my dear," replied Amelia, "a synonymous term with friendship? Could I have expected, when I parted the last time with Miss Jenny Bath, to have met her the next time in the shape of a fine lady, complaining of the hardship of climbing up two pair of stairs to visit me, and then approaching me with the distant air of a new or a slight acquaintance? Do you think, my dear Mrs. James, if the tables had been turned, if my fortune had been as high in the world as yours, and you in my distress and abject condition, that I would not have climbed as high as the monument to visit you?" "Sure, madam," cried Mrs. James, "I mistake you, or you have greatly mistaken me. Can you complain of my not visiting you, who have owed me a visit almost these three weeks? Nay, did I not even then send you a card, which sure was doing more than all the friendship and good-breeding in the world required; but, indeed, as I had met you in no public place, I really thought you was ill."

"How can you mention public places to me," said Amelia, "when you can hardly be a stranger to my present situation? Did you not know, madam, that I was ruined?" "No, indeed, madam, did I not," replied Mrs. James; "I am sure I should have been highly concerned if I had." "Why, sure, my dear," cries Amelia, "you could not imagine that we were in affluent circumstances, when you found us in such a place, and in such a condition." "Nay, my dear," answered Mrs. James, "since you are pleased to mention it first yourself, I own I was a little surprized to see you in no better lodgings; but I concluded you had your own reasons for liking them; and, for my own part, I have laid it down as a positive rule never to enquire into the private affairs of any one, especially of my friends. I am not of the humour of some ladies, who confine the circle of their acquaintance to one part of the town, and would not be known to visit in the city for the world. For my part, I never dropt an acquaintance with any one while it was reputable to keep it up; and I can solemnly declare I have not a friend in the world for whom I have a greater esteem than I have for Mrs. Booth."

At this instant the arrival of a new visitant put an end to the discourse; and Amelia soon after took her leave without the least anger, but with some little unavoidable contempt for a lady, in whose opinion, as we have hinted before, outward form and ceremony constituted the whole essence of friendship; who valued all her acquaintance alike, as each individual served equally to fill up a place in her visiting roll; and who, in reality, had not the least concern for the good qualities or well-being of any of them.

Chapter v. — Containing much heroic matter.

At the end of three days Mrs. Ellison's friend had so far purchased Mr. Booth's liberty that he could walk again abroad within the verge without any danger of having a warrant backed against him by the board before he had notice. As for the ill-looked persons that had given the alarm, it was now discovered that another unhappy gentleman, and not Booth, was the object of their pursuit.

Mr. Booth, now being delivered from his fears, went, as he had formerly done, to take his morning walk in the Park. Here he met Colonel Bath in company with some other officers, and very civilly paid his respects to him. But, instead of returning the salute, the colonel looked him full in the face with a very stern countenance; and, if he could be said to take any notice of him, it was in such a manner as to inform him he would take no notice of him.

Booth was not more hurt than surprized at this behaviour, and resolved to know the reason of it. He therefore watched an opportunity till the colonel was alone, and then walked boldly up to him, and desired to know if he had given him any offence? The colonel answered hastily, "Sir, I am above being offended with you, nor do I think it consistent with my dignity to make you any answer." Booth replied, "I don't know, sir, that I have done anything to deserve this treatment." "Look'ee, sir," cries the colonel, "if I had not formerly had some respect for you, I should not think you worth my resentment. However, as you are a gentleman born, and an officer, and as I have had an esteem for you, I will give you some marks of it by putting it in your power to do yourself justice. I will tell you therefore, sir, that you have acted like a scoundrel." "If we were not

in the Park," answered Booth warmly, "I would thank you very properly for that compliment." "O, sir," cries the colonel, "we can be soon in a convenient place." Upon which Booth answered, he would attend him wherever he pleased. The colonel then bid him come along, and strutted forward directly up Constitution-hill to Hyde-park, Booth following him at first, and afterwards walking before him, till they came to that place which may be properly called the field of blood, being that part, a little to the left of the ring, which heroes have chosen for the scene of their exit out of this world.

Booth reached the ring some time before the colonel; for he mended not his pace any more than a Spaniard. To say truth, I believe it was not in his power: for he had so long accustomed himself to one and the same strut, that as a horse, used always to trotting, can scarce be forced into a gallop, so could no passion force the colonel to alter his pace.

{Illustration with caption: Colonel Bath.}

At length, however, both parties arrived at the lists, where the colonel very deliberately took off his wig and coat, and laid them on the grass, and then, drawing his sword, advanced to Booth, who had likewise his drawn weapon in his hand, but had made no other preparation for the combat.

The combatants now engaged with great fury, and, after two or three passes, Booth run the colonel through the body and threw him on the ground, at the same time possessing himself of the colonel's sword.

As soon as the colonel was become master of his speech, he called out to Booth in a very kind voice, and said, "You have done my business, and satisfied me that you are a man of honour, and that my brother James must have been mistaken; for I am convinced that no man who will draw his sword in so gallant a manner is capable of being a rascal. D—n me, give me a buss, my dear boy; I ask your pardon for that infamous appellation I dishonoured your dignity with; but d—n me if it was not purely out of love, and to give you an opportunity of doing yourself justice, which I own you have done like a man of honour. What may be the consequence I know not, but I hope, at least, I shall live to reconcile you with my brother."

Booth shewed great concern, and even horror in his countenance. "Why, my dear colonel," said he, "would you force me to this? for Heaven's sake tell me what I have ever done to offend you."

"Me!" cried the colonel. "Indeed, my dear child, you never did anything to offend me.—Nay, I have acted the part of a friend to you in the whole affair. I maintained your cause with my brother as long as decency would permit; I could not flatly contradict him, though, indeed, I scarce believed him. But what could I do? If I had not fought with you, I must have been obliged to have fought with him; however, I hope what is done will be sufficient, and that matters may be discomodated without your being put to the necessity of fighting any more on this occasion."

"Never regard me," cried Booth eagerly; "for Heaven's sake, think of your own preservation. Let me put you into a chair, and get you a surgeon."

"Thou art a noble lad," cries the colonel, who was now got on his legs, "and I am glad the business is so well over; for, though your sword went quite through, it slanted so that I apprehend there is little danger of life: however, I think there is enough done to put an honourable end to the affair, especially as you was so hasty to disarm me. I bleed a little, but I can walk to the house by the water; and, if you will send me a chair thither, I shall be obliged to you."

As the colonel refused any assistance (indeed he was very able to walk without it, though with somewhat less dignity than usual), Booth set forward to Grosvenor-gate, in order to procure the chair, and soon after returned with one to his friend; whom having conveyed into it, he attended himself on foot into Bond-street, where then lived a very eminent surgeon.

The surgeon having probed the wound, turned towards Booth, who was apparently the guilty person, and said, with a smile, "Upon my word, sir, you have performed the business with great dexterity."

"Sir," cries the colonel to the surgeon, "I would not have you imagine I am afraid to die. I think I know more what belongs to the dignity of a man; and, I believe, I have shewn it at the head of a line of battle. Do not impute my concern to that fear, when I ask you whether there is or is not any danger?"

"Really, colonel," answered the surgeon, who well knew the complexion of the gentleman then under his hands, "it would appear like presumption to say that a man who hath been just run

101

through the body is in no manner of danger. But this I think I may assure you, that I yet perceive no very bad symptoms, and, unless something worse should appear, or a fever be the consequence, I hope you may live to be again, with all your dignity, at the head of a line of battle."

"I am glad to hear that is your opinion," quoth the colonel, "for I am not desirous of dying, though I am not afraid of it. But, if anything worse than you apprehend should happen, I desire you will be a witness of my declaration that this young gentleman is entirely innocent. I forced him to do what he did. My dear Booth, I am pleased matters are as they are. You are the first man that ever gained an advantage over me; but it was very lucky for you that you disarmed me, and I doubt not but you have the equananimity to think so. If the business, therefore, hath ended without doing anything to the purpose, it was Fortune's pleasure, and neither of our faults."

Booth heartily embraced the colonel, and assured him of the great satisfaction he had received from the surgeon's opinion; and soon after the two combatants took their leave of each other. The colonel, after he was drest, went in a chair to his lodgings, and Booth walked on foot to his; where he luckily arrived without meeting any of Mr. Murphy's gang; a danger which never once occurred to his imagination till he was out of it.

The affair he had been about had indeed so entirely occupied his mind, that it had obliterated every other idea; among the rest, it caused him so absolutely to forget the time of the day, that, though he had exceeded the time of dining above two hours, he had not the least suspicion of being at home later than usual.

Chapter vi. — In which the reader will find matter worthy his consideration.

Amelia, having waited above an hour for her husband, concluded, as he was the most punctual man alive, that he had met with some engagement abroad, and sat down to her meal with her children; which, as it was always uncomfortable in the absence of her husband, was very short; so that, before his return, all the apparatus of dining was entirely removed.

Booth sat some time with his wife, expecting every minute when the little maid would make her appearance; at last, curiosity, I believe, rather than appetite, made him ask how long it was to dinner? "To dinner, my dear!" answered Amelia; "sure you have dined, I hope?" Booth replied in the negative; upon which his wife started from her chair, and bestirred herself as nimbly to provide him a repast as the most industrious hostess in the kingdom doth when some unexpected guest of extraordinary quality arrives at her house.

The reader hath not, I think, from any passages hitherto recorded in this history, had much reason to accuse Amelia of a blameable curiosity; he will not, I hope, conclude that she gave an instance of any such fault when, upon Booth's having so long overstayed his time, and so greatly mistaken the hour of the day, and upon some other circumstances of his behaviour (for he was too honest to be good at concealing any of his thoughts), she said to him after he had done eating, "My dear, I am sure something more than ordinary hath happened to-day, and I beg you will tell me what is."

Booth answered that nothing of any consequence had happened; that he had been detained by a friend, whom he met accidently, longer than he expected. In short, he made many shuffling and evasive answers, not boldly lying out, which, perhaps, would have succeeded, but poorly and vainly endeavouring to reconcile falsehood with truth; an attempt which seldom fails to betray the most practised deceiver.

How impossible was it therefore for poor Booth to succeed in an art for which nature had so entirely disqualified him. His countenance, indeed, confessed faster than his tongue denied, and the whole of his behaviour gave Amelia an alarm, and made her suspect something very bad had happened; and, as her thoughts turned presently on the badness of their circumstances, she feared some mischief from his creditors had befallen him; for she was too ignorant of such matters to know that, if he had fallen into the hands of the Philistines (which is the name given by the faithful to bailiffs), he would hardly have been able so soon to recover his liberty. Booth at last perceived her to be so uneasy, that, as he saw no hopes of contriving any fiction to satisfy her, he

thought himself obliged to tell her the truth, or at least part of the truth, and confessed that he had had a little skirmish with Colonel Bath, in which, he said, the colonel had received a slight wound, not at all dangerous; "and this," says he, "is all the whole matter." "If it be so," cries Amelia, "I thank Heaven no worse hath happened; but why, my dear, will you ever converse with that madman, who can embrace a friend one moment, and fight with him the next?" "Nay, my dear," answered Booth, "you yourself must confess, though he be a little too much on the qui vive, he is a man of great honour and good-nature." "Tell me not," replied she, "of such good-nature and honour as would sacrifice a friend and a whole family to a ridiculous whim. Oh, Heavens!" cried she, falling upon her knees, "from what misery have I escaped, from what have these poor babes escaped, through your gracious providence this day!" Then turning to her husband, she cried, "But are you sure the monster's wound is no more dangerous than you say? a monster surely I may call him, who can quarrel with a man that could not, that I am convinced would not, offend him."

Upon this question, Booth repeated the assurances which the surgeon had given them, perhaps with a little enlargement, which pretty well satisfied Amelia; and instead of blaming her husband for what he had done, she tenderly embraced him, and again returned thanks to Heaven for his safety.

In the evening Booth insisted on paying a short visit to the colonel, highly against the inclination of Amelia, who, by many arguments and entreaties, endeavoured to dissuade her husband from continuing an acquaintance in which, she said, she should always foresee much danger for the future. However, she was at last prevailed upon to acquiesce; and Booth went to the colonel, whose lodgings happened to be in the verge as well as his own.

He found the colonel in his night-gown, and his great chair, engaged with another officer at a game of chess. He rose immediately, and, having heartily embraced Booth, presented him to his friend, saying, he had the honour to introduce to him as brave and as fortitudinous a man as any in the king's dominions. He then took Booth with him into the next room, and desired him not to mention a word of what had happened in the morning; saying, "I am very well satisfied that no more hath happened; however, as it ended in nothing, I could wish it might remain a secret." Booth told him he was heartily glad to find him so well, and promised never to mention it more to any one.

The game at chess being but just begun, and neither of the parties having gained any considerable advantage, they neither of them insisted on continuing it; and now the colonel's antagonist took his leave and left the colonel and Booth together.

As soon as they were alone, the latter earnestly entreated the former to acquaint him with the real cause of his anger; "for may I perish," cries Booth, "if I can even guess what I have ever done to offend either you, or your brother, Colonel James."

"Look'ee, child," cries the colonel; "I tell you I am for my own part satisfied; for I am convinced that a man who will fight can never be a rascal; and, therefore, why should you enquire any more of me at present? when I see my brother James, I hope to reconcile all matters, and perhaps no more swords need be drawn on this occasion." But Booth still persisting in his desire, the colonel, after some hesitation, with a tremendous oath, cried out, "I do not think myself at liberty to refuse you after the indignity I offered you; so, since you demand it of me, I will inform you. My brother told me you had used him dishonourably, and had divellicated his character behind his back. He gave me his word, too, that he was well assured of what he said. What could I have done? though I own to you I did not believe him, and your behaviour since hath convinced me I was in the right; I must either have given him the lye, and fought with him, or else I was obliged to behave as I did, and fight with you. And now, my lad, I leave it to you to do as you please; but, if you are laid under any necessity to do yourself further justice, it is your own fault."

"Alas! colonel," answered Booth, "besides the obligations I have to the colonel, I have really so much love for him, that I think of nothing less than resentment. All I wish is to have this affair brought to an eclaircissement, and to satisfy him that he is in an error; for, though his assertions are cruelly injurious, and I have never deserved them, yet I am convinced he would not say what he did not himself think. Some rascal, envious of his friendship for me, hath belyed me to him; and the only resentment I desire is, to convince him of his mistake."

At these words the colonel grinned horribly a ghastly smile, or rather sneer, and answered, "Young gentleman, you may do as you please; but, by the eternal dignity of man, if any man

breathing had taken a liberty with my character—Here, here—Mr. Booth (shewing his fingers), here d—n me, should be his nostrils; he should breathe through my hands, and breathe his last, d—n me."

Booth answered, "I think, colonel, I may appeal to your testimony that I dare do myself justice; since he who dare draw his sword against you can hardly be supposed to fear any other person; but I repeat to you again that I love Colonel James so well, and am so greatly obliged to him, that it would be almost indifferent to me whether I directed my sword against his breast or my own."

The colonel's muscles were considerably softened by Booth's last speech; but he again contracted them into a vast degree of fierceness before he cried out—"Boy, thou hast reason enough to be vain; for thou art the first person that ever could proudly say he gained an advantage over me in combat. I believe, indeed, thou art not afraid of any man breathing, and, as I know thou hast some obligations to my brother, I do not discommend thee; for nothing more becomes the dignity of a man than gratitude. Besides, as I am satisfied my brother can produce the author of the slander—I say, I am satisfied of that—d—n me, if any man alive dares assert the contrary; for that would be to make my brother himself a liar—I will make him produce his author; and then, my dear boy, your doing yourself proper justice there will bring you finely out of the whole affair. As soon as my surgeon gives me leave to go abroad, which, I hope, will be in a few days, I will bring my brother James to a tavern where you shall meet us; and I will engage my honour, my whole dignity to you, to make you friends."

The assurance of the colonel gave Booth great pleasure; for few persons ever loved a friend better than he did James; and as for doing military justice on the author of that scandalous report which had incensed his friend against him, not Bath himself was ever more ready, on such an occasion, than Booth to execute it. He soon after took his leave, and returned home in high spirits to his Amelia, whom he found in Mrs. Ellison's apartment, engaged in a party at ombre with that lady and her right honourable cousin.

His lordship had, it seems, had a second interview with the great man, and, having obtained further hopes (for I think there was not yet an absolute promise) of success in Mr. Booth's affairs, his usual good-nature brought him immediately to acquaint Mr. Booth with it. As he did not therefore find him at home, and as he met with the two ladies together, he resolved to stay till his friend's return, which he was assured would not be long, especially as he was so lucky, he said, to have no particular engagement that whole evening.

We remarked before that his lordship, at the first interview with Amelia, had distinguished her by a more particular address from the other ladies; but that now appeared to be rather owing to his perfect good-breeding, as she was then to be considered as the mistress of the house, than from any other preference. His present behaviour made this still more manifest; for, as he was now in Mrs. Ellison's apartment, though she was his relation and an old acquaintance, he applied his conversation rather more to her than to Amelia. His eyes, indeed, were now and then guilty of the contrary distinction, but this was only by stealth; for they constantly withdrew the moment they were discovered. In short, he treated Amelia with the greatest distance, and at the same time with the most profound and awful respect; his conversation was so general, so lively, and so obliging, that Amelia, when she added to his agreeableness the obligations she had to him for his friendship to Booth, was certainly as much pleased with his lordship as any virtuous woman can possibly be with any man, besides her own husband.

Chapter vii. — Containing various matters.

We have already mentioned the good-humour in which Booth returned home; and the reader will easily believe it was not a little encreased by the good-humour in which he found his company. My lord received him with the utmost marks of friendship and affection, and told him that his affairs went on as well almost as he himself could desire, and that he doubted not very

soon to wish him joy of a company.

When Booth had made a proper return to all his lordship's unparalleled goodness, he whispered Amelia that the colonel was entirely out of danger, and almost as well as himself. This made her satisfaction complete, threw her into such spirits, and gave such a lustre to her eyes, that her face, as Horace says, was too dazzling to be looked at; it was certainly too handsome to be looked at without the highest admiration.

His lordship departed about ten o'clock, and left the company in raptures with him, especially the two ladies, of whom it is difficult to say which exceeded the other in his commendations. Mrs. Ellison swore she believed he was the best of all humankind; and Amelia, without making any exception, declared he was the finest gentleman and most agreeable man she had ever seen in her life; adding, it was great pity he should remain single. "That's true, indeed," cries Mrs. Ellison, "and I have often lamented it; nay, I am astonished at it, considering the great liking he always shews for our sex, and he may certainly have the choice of all. The real reason, I believe, is, his fondness for his sister's children. I declare, madam, if you was to see his behaviour to them, you would think they were his own. Indeed he is vastly fond of all manner of children." "Good creature!" cries Amelia; "if ever he doth me the honour of another visit I am resolved I will shew him my little things. I think, Mrs. Ellison, as you say my lord loves children, I may say, without vanity, he will not see many such." "No, indeed, will he not," answered Mrs. Ellison: "and now I think on't, madam, I wonder at my own stupidity in never making the offer before; but since you put it into my head, if you will give me leave, I'll take master and miss to wait on my lord's nephew and niece. They are very pretty behaved children; and little master and miss will be, I dare swear, very happy in their acquaintance; besides, if my lord himself should see them, I know what will happen; for he is the most generous of all human beings."

Amelia very readily accepted the favour which Mrs. Ellison offered her; but Booth exprest some reluctance. "Upon my word, my dear," said he, with a smile, "this behaviour of ours puts me in mind of the common conduct of beggars; who, whenever they receive a favour, are sure to send other objects to the same fountain of charity. Don't we, my dear, repay our obligations to my lord in the same manner, by sending our children a begging to him?"

"O beastly!" cries Mrs. Ellison; "how could such a thought enter your brains? I protest, madam, I begin to grow ashamed of this husband of yours. How can you have so vulgar a way of thinking? Begging, indeed! the poor little dear things a begging! If my lord was capable of such a thought, though he was my own brother instead of my cousin, I should scorn him too much ever to enter his doors." "O dear madam!" answered Amelia, "you take Mr. Booth too seriously, when he was only in jest; and the children shall wait upon you whenever you please."

Though Booth had been a little more in earnest than Amelia had represented him, and was not, perhaps, quite so much in the wrong as he was considered by Mrs. Ellison, yet, seeing there were two to one against him, he wisely thought proper to recede, and let his simile go off with that air of a jest which his wife had given it.

Mrs. Ellison, however, could not let it pass without paying some compliments to Amelia's understanding, nor without some obscure reflexions upon Booth, with whom she was more offended than the matter required. She was indeed a woman of most profuse generosity, and could not bear a thought which she deemed vulgar or sneaking. She afterwards launched forth the most profuse encomiums of his lordship's liberality, and concluded the evening with some instances which he had given of that virtue which, if not the noblest, is, perhaps, one of the most useful to society with which great and rich men can be endowed.

The next morning early, serjeant Atkinson came to wait on lieutenant Booth, and desired to speak with his honour in private. Upon which the lieutenant and serjeant took a walk together in the Park. Booth expected every minute when the serjeant would open his mouth; under which expectation he continued till he came to the end of the mall, and so he might have continued till he came to the end of the world; for, though several words stood at the end of the serjeant's lips, there they were likely to remain for ever. He was, indeed, in the condition of a miser, whom a charitable impulse hath impelled to draw a few pence to the edge of his pocket, where they are altogether as secure as if they were in the bottom; for, as the one hath not the heart to part with a farthing, so neither had the other the heart to speak a word.

Booth at length, wondering that the serjeant did not speak, asked him, What his business was? when the latter with a stammering voice began the following apology: "I hope, sir, your honour

105

will not be angry, nor take anything amiss of me. I do assure you, it was not of my seeking, nay, I dare not proceed in the matter without first asking your leave. Indeed, if I had taken any liberties from the goodness you have been pleased to shew me, I should look upon myself as one of the most worthless and despicable of wretches; but nothing is farther from my thoughts. I know the distance which is between us; and, because your honour hath been so kind and good as to treat me with more familiarity than any other officer ever did, if I had been base enough to take any freedoms, or to encroach upon your honour's goodness, I should deserve to be whipt through the regiment. I hope, therefore, sir, you will not suspect me of any such attempt."

"What can all this mean, Atkinson?" cries Booth; "what mighty matter would you introduce with all this previous apology?"

"I am almost ashamed and afraid to mention it," answered the serjeant; "and yet I am sure your honour will believe what I have said, and not think anything owing to my own presumption; and, at the same time, I have no reason to think you would do anything to spoil my fortune in an honest way, when it is dropt into my lap without my own seeking. For may I perish if it is not all the lady's own goodness, and I hope in Heaven, with your honour's leave, I shall live to make her amends for it." In a word, that we may not detain the reader's curiosity quite so long as he did Booth's, he acquainted that gentleman that he had had an offer of marriage from a lady of his acquaintance, to whose company he had introduced him, and desired his permission to accept of it.

Booth must have been very dull indeed if, after what the serjeant had said, and after what he had heard Mrs. Ellison say, he had wanted any information concerning the lady. He answered him briskly and chearfully, that he had his free consent to marry any woman whatever; "and the greater and richer she is," added he, "the more I shall be pleased with the match. I don't enquire who the lady is," said he, smiling, "but I hope she will make as good a wife as, I am convinced, her husband will deserve."

"Your honour hath been always too good to me," cries Atkinson; "but this I promise you, I will do all in my power to merit the kindness she is pleased to shew me. I will be bold to say she will marry an honest man, though he is but a poor one; and she shall never want anything which I can give her or do for her, while my name is Joseph Atkinson."

"And so her name is a secret, Joe, is it?" cries Booth.

"Why, sir," answered the serjeant, "I hope your honour will not insist upon knowing that, as I think it would be dishonourable in me to mention it."

"Not at all," replied Booth; "I am the farthest in the world from any such desire. I know thee better than to imagine thou wouldst disclose the name of a fair lady." Booth then shook Atkinson heartily by the hand, and assured him earnestly of the joy he had in his good fortune; for which the good serjeant failed not of making all proper acknowledgments. After which they parted, and Booth returned home.

As Mrs. Ellison opened the door, Booth hastily rushed by; for he had the utmost difficulty to prevent laughing in her face. He ran directly up-stairs, and, throwing himself into a chair, discharged such a fit of laughter as greatly surprized, and at first almost frightened, his wife.

Amelia, it will be supposed, presently enquired into the cause of this phenomenon, with which Booth, as soon as he was able (for that was not within a few minutes), acquainted her. The news did not affect her in the same manner it had affected her husband. On the contrary, she cried, "I protest I cannot guess what makes you see it in so ridiculous a light. I really think Mrs. Ellison hath chosen very well. I am convinced Joe will make her one of the best of husbands; and, in my opinion, that is the greatest blessing a woman can be possessed of."

However, when Mrs. Ellison came into her room a little while afterwards to fetch the children, Amelia became of a more risible disposition, especially when the former, turning to Booth, who was then present, said, "So, captain, my jantee-serjeant was very early here this morning. I scolded my maid heartily for letting him wait so long in the entry like a lacquais, when she might have shewn him into my inner apartment." At which words Booth burst out into a very loud laugh; and Amelia herself could no more prevent laughing than she could blushing.

"Heyday!" cries Mrs. Ellison; "what have I said to cause all this mirth?" and at the same time blushed, and looked very silly, as is always the case with persons who suspect themselves to be the objects of laughter, without absolutely taking what it is which makes them ridiculous.

Booth still continued laughing; but Amelia, composing her muscles, said, "I ask your pardon,

dear Mrs. Ellison; but Mr. Booth hath been in a strange giggling humour all this morning; and I really think it is infectious."

"I ask your pardon, too, madam," cries Booth, "but one is sometimes unaccountably foolish."

"Nay, but seriously," said she, "what is the matter?—something I said about the serjeant, I believe; but you may laugh as much as you please; I am not ashamed of owning I think him one of the prettiest fellows I ever saw in my life; and, I own, I scolded my maid at suffering him to wait in my entry; and where is the mighty ridiculous matter, pray?"

"None at all," answered Booth; "and I hope the next time he will be ushered into your inner apartment."

"Why should he not, sir?" replied she, "for, wherever he is ushered, I am convinced he will behave himself as a gentleman should."

Here Amelia put an end to the discourse, or it might have proceeded to very great lengths; for Booth was of a waggish inclination, and Mrs. Ellison was not a lady of the nicest delicacy.

Chapter viii. — The heroic behaviour of Colonel Bath.

Booth went this morning to pay a second visit to the colonel, where he found Colonel James. Both the colonel and the lieutenant appeared a little shocked at their first meeting, but matters were soon cleared up; for the former presently advanced to the latter, shook him heartily by the hand, and said, "Mr. Booth, I am ashamed to see you; for I have injured you, and I heartily ask your pardon. I am now perfectly convinced that what I hinted to my brother, and which I find had like to have produced such fatal consequences, was entirely groundless. If you will be contented with my asking your pardon, and spare me the disagreeable remembrance of what led me into my error, I shall esteem it as the highest obligation."

Booth answered, "As to what regards yourself, my dear colonel, I am abundantly satisfied; but, as I am convinced some rascal hath been my enemy with you in the cruellest manner, I hope you will not deny me the opportunity of kicking him through the world."

"By all the dignity of man," cries Colonel Bath, "the boy speaks with spirit, and his request is reasonable."

Colonel James hesitated a moment, and then whispered Booth that he would give him all the satisfaction imaginable concerning the whole affair when they were alone together; upon which, Booth addressing himself to Colonel Bath, the discourse turned on other matters during the remainder of the visit, which was but short, and then both went away together, leaving Colonel Bath as well as it was possible to expect, more to the satisfaction of Booth than of Colonel James, who would not have been displeased if his wound had been more dangerous; for he was grown somewhat weary of a disposition that he rather called captious than heroic, and which, as he every day more and more hated his wife, he apprehended might some time or other give him some trouble; for Bath was the most affectionate of brothers, and had often swore, in the presence of James, that he would eat any man alive who should use his sister ill.

Colonel Bath was well satisfied that his brother and the lieutenant were gone out with a design of tilting, from which he offered not a syllable to dissuade them, as he was convinced it was right, and that Booth could not in honour take, nor the colonel give, any less satisfaction. When they had been gone therefore about half an hour, he rang his bell to enquire if there was any news of his brother; a question which he repeated every ten minutes for the space of two hours, when, having heard nothing of him, he began to conclude that both were killed on the spot.

While he was in this state of anxiety his sister came to see him; for, notwithstanding his desire of keeping it a secret, the duel had blazed all over the town. After receiving some kind congratulations on his safety, and some unkind hints concerning the warmth of his temper, the colonel asked her when she had seen her husband? she answered not that morning. He then communicated to her his suspicion, told her he was convinced his brother had drawn his sword that day, and that, as neither of them had heard anything from him, he began to apprehend the

worst that could happen.

Neither Miss Bellamy nor Mrs. Gibber were ever in a greater consternation on the stage than now appeared in the countenance of Mrs. James. "Good Heavens! brother," cries she; "what do you tell me? you have frightened me to death. Let your man get me a glass of water immediately, if you have not a mind to see me die before your face. When, where, how was this quarrel? why did you not prevent it if you knew of it? is it not enough to be every day tormenting me with hazarding your own life, but must you bring the life of one who you know must be, and ought to be, so much the dearest of all to me, into danger? take your sword, brother, take your sword, and plunge it into my bosom; it would be kinder of you than to fill it with such dreads and terrors." Here she swallowed the glass of water, and then threw herself back in her chair, as if she had intended to faint away.

Perhaps, if she had so, the colonel would have lent her no assistance, for she had hurt him more than by ten thousand stabs. He sat erect in his chair, with his eyebrows knit, his forehead wrinkled, his eyes flashing fire, his teeth grating against each other, and breathing horrour all round him. In this posture he sat for some time silent, casting disdainful looks at his sister. At last his voice found its way through a passion which had almost choaked him, and he cried out, "Sister, what have I done to deserve the opinion you express of me? which of my actions hath made you conclude that I am a rascal and a coward? look at that poor sword, which never woman yet saw but in its sheath; what hath that done to merit your desire that it should be contaminated with the blood of a woman?"

"Alas! brother," cried she, "I know not what you say; you are desirous, I believe, to terrify me out of the little senses I have left. What can I have said, in the agonies of grief into which you threw me, to deserve this passion?"

"What have you said?" answered the colonel: "you have said that which, if a man had spoken, nay, d—n me, if he had but hinted that he durst even think, I would have made him eat my sword; by all the dignity of man, I would have crumbled his soul into powder. But I consider that the words were spoken by a woman, and I am calm again. Consider, my dear, that you are my sister, and behave yourself with more spirit. I have only mentioned to you my surmise. It may not have happened as I suspect; but, let what will have happened, you will have the comfort that your husband hath behaved himself with becoming dignity, and lies in the bed of honour."

"Talk not to me of such comfort," replied the lady; "it is a loss I cannot survive. But why do I sit here lamenting myself? I will go this instant and know the worst of my fate, if my trembling limbs will carry me to my coach. Good morrow, dear brother; whatever becomes of me, I am glad to find you out of danger." The colonel paid her his proper compliments, and she then left the room, but returned instantly back, saying, "Brother, I must beg the favour of you to let your footman step to my mantua-maker; I am sure it is a miracle, in my present distracted condition, how it came into my head." The footman was presently summoned, and Mrs. James delivered him his message, which was to countermand the orders which she had given that very morning to make her up a new suit of brocade. "Heaven knows," says she, "now when I can wear brocade, or whether ever I shall wear it." And now, having repeated her message with great exactness, lest there should be any mistake, she again lamented her wretched situation, and then departed, leaving the colonel in full expectation of hearing speedy news of the fatal issue of the battle.

But, though the reader should entertain the same curiosity, we must be excused from satisfying it till we have first accounted for an incident which we have related in this very chapter, and which, we think, deserves some solution. The critic, I am convinced, already is apprized that I mean the friendly behaviour of James to Booth, which, from what we had before recorded, seemed so little to be expected.

It must be remembered that the anger which the former of these gentlemen had conceived against the latter arose entirely from the false account given by Miss Matthews of Booth, whom that lady had accused to Colonel James of having as basely as wickedly traduced his character.

Now, of all the ministers of vengeance, there are none with whom the devil deals so treacherously as with those whom he employs in executing the mischievous purposes of an angry mistress; for no sooner is revenge executed on an offending lover that it is sure to be repented; and all the anger which before raged against the beloved object, returns with double fury on the head of his assassin.

Miss Matthews, therefore, no, sooner heard that Booth was killed (for so was the report at

first, and by a colonel of the army) than she immediately concluded it to be James. She was extremely shocked with the news, and her heart instantly began to relent. All the reasons on which she had founded her love recurred, in the strongest and liveliest colours, to her mind, and all the causes of her hatred sunk down and disappeared; or, if the least remembrance of anything which had disobliged her remained, her heart became his zealous advocate, and soon satisfied her that her own fates were more to be blamed than he, and that, without being a villain, he could have acted no otherwise than he had done.

In this temper of mind she looked on herself as the murderer of an innocent man, and, what to her was much worse, of the man she had loved, and still did love, with all the violence imaginable. She looked on James as the tool with which she had done this murder; and, as it is usual for people who have rashly or inadvertently made any animate or inanimate thing the instrument of mischief to hate the innocent means by which the mischief was effected (for this is a subtle method which the mind invents to excuse ourselves, the last objects on whom we would willingly wreak our vengeance), so Miss Matthews now hated and cursed James as the efficient cause of that act which she herself had contrived and laboured to carry into execution.

She sat down therefore in a furious agitation, little short of madness, and wrote the following letter:

"I Hope this will find you in the hands of justice, for the murder of one of the best friends that ever man was blest with. In one sense, indeed, he may seem to have deserved his fate, by chusing a fool for a friend; for who but a fool would have believed what the anger and rage of an injured woman suggested; a story so improbable, that I could scarce be thought in earnest when I mentioned it?

"Know, then, cruel wretch, that poor Booth loved you of all men breathing, and was, I believe, in your commendation guilty of as much falsehood as I was in what I told you concerning him.

"If this knowledge makes you miserable, it is no more than you have made the unhappy F. MATTHEWS."

Chapter ix. — Being the last chapter of the fifth book.

We shall now return to Colonel James and Mr. Booth, who walked together from Colonel Bath's lodging with much more peaceable intention than that gentleman had conjectured, who dreamt of nothing but swords and guns and implements of wars.

The Birdcage-walk in the Park was the scene appointed by James for unburthening his mind.—Thither they came, and there James acquainted Booth with all that which the reader knows already, and gave him the letter which we have inserted at the end of the last chapter.

Booth exprest great astonishment at this relation, not without venting some detestation of the wickedness of Miss Matthews; upon which James took him up, saying, he ought not to speak with such abhorrence of faults which love for him had occasioned.

"Can you mention love, my dear colonel," cried Booth, "and such a woman in the same breath?"

"Yes, faith! can I," says James; "for the devil take me if I know a more lovely woman in the world." Here he began to describe her whole person; but, as we cannot insert all the description, so we shall omit it all; and concluded with saying, "Curse me if I don't think her the finest creature in the universe. I would give half my estate, Booth, she loved me as well as she doth you. Though, on second consideration, I believe I should repent that bargain; for then, very possibly, I should not care a farthing for her."

"You will pardon me, dear colonel," answered Booth; "but to me there appears somewhat very singular in your way of thinking. Beauty is indeed the object of liking, great qualities of admiration, good ones of esteem; but the devil take me if I think anything but love to be the object of love."

"Is there not something too selfish," replied James, "in that opinion? but, without considering

it in that light, is it not of all things the most insipid? all oil! all sugar! zounds! it is enough to cloy the sharp-set appetite of a parson. Acids surely are the most likely to quicken."

"I do not love reasoning in allegories," cries Booth; "but with regard to love, I declare I never found anything cloying in it. I have lived almost alone with my wife near three years together, was never tired with her company, nor ever wished for any other; and I am sure I never tasted any of the acid you mention to quicken my appetite."

"This is all very extraordinary and romantic to me," answered the colonel. "If I was to be shut up three years with the same woman, which Heaven forbid! nothing, I think, could keep me alive but a temper as violent as that of Miss Matthews. As to love, it would make me sick to death in the twentieth part of that time. If I was so condemned, let me see, what would I wish the woman to be? I think no one virtue would be sufficient. With the spirit of a tigress I would have her be a prude, a scold, a scholar, a critic, a wit, a politician, and a Jacobite; and then, perhaps, eternal opposition would keep up our spirits; and, wishing one another daily at the devil, we should make a shift to drag on a damnable state of life, without much spleen or vapours."

"And so you do not intend," cries Booth, "to break with this woman?"

"Not more than I have already, if I can help it," answered the colonel.

"And you will be reconciled to her?" said Booth.

"Yes, faith! will I, if I can," answered the colonel; "I hope you have no objection."

"None, my dear friend," said Booth, "unless on your account."

"I do believe you," said the colonel: "and yet, let me tell you, you are a very extraordinary man, not to desire me to quit her on your own account. Upon my soul, I begin to pity the woman, who hath placed her affection, perhaps, on the only man in England of your age who would not return it. But for my part, I promise you, I like her beyond all other women; and, whilst that is the case, my boy, if her mind was as full of iniquity as Pandora's box was of diseases, I'd hug her close in my arms, and only take as much care as possible to keep the lid down for fear of mischief. But come, dear Booth," said he, "let us consider your affairs; for I am ashamed of having neglected them so long; and the only anger I have against this wench is, that she was the occasion of it."

Booth then acquainted the colonel with the promises he had received from the noble lord, upon which James shook him by the hand, and heartily wished him joy, crying, "I do assure you, if you have his interest, you will need no other; I did not know you was acquainted with him."

To which Mr. Booth answered, "That he was but a new acquaintance, and that he was recommended to him by a lady."

"A lady!" cries the colonel; "well, I don't ask her name. You are a happy man, Booth, amongst the women; and, I assure you, you could have no stronger recommendation. The peer loves the ladies, I believe, as well as ever Mark Antony did; and it is not his fault if he hath not spent as much upon them. If he once fixes his eye upon a woman, he will stick at nothing to get her."

"Ay, indeed!" cries Booth. "Is that his character?"

"Ay, faith," answered the colonel, "and the character of most men besides him. Few of them, I mean, will stick at anything beside their money. Jusque a la Bourse is sometimes the boundary of love as well as friendship. And, indeed, I never knew any other man part with his money so very freely on these occasions. You see, dear Booth, the confidence I have in your honour."

"I hope, indeed, you have," cries Booth, "but I don't see what instance you now give me of that confidence."

"Have not I shewn you," answered James, "where you may carry your goods to market? I can assure you, my friend, that is a secret I would not impart to every man in your situation, and all circumstances considered."

"I am very sorry, sir," cries Booth very gravely, and turning as pale as death, "you should entertain a thought of this kind; a thought which hath almost frozen up my blood. I am unwilling to believe there are such villains in the world; but there is none of them whom I should detest half so much as myself, if my own mind had ever suggested to me a hint of that kind. I have tasted of some distresses of life, and I know not to what greater I may be driven, but my honour, I thank Heaven, is in my own power, and I can boldly say to Fortune she shall not rob me of it."

"Have I not exprest that confidence, my dear Booth?" answered the colonel. "And what you say now well justifies my opinion; for I do agree with you that, considering all things, it would be the highest instance of dishonour."

"Dishonour, indeed!" returned Booth. "What! to prostitute my wife! Can I think there is such

110

a wretch breathing?"

"I don't know that," said the colonel, "but I am sure it was very far from my intention to insinuate the least hint of any such matter to you. Nor can I imagine how you yourself could conceive such a thought. The goods I meant were no other than the charming person of Miss Matthews, for whom I am convinced my lord would bid a swinging price against me."

Booth's countenance greatly cleared up at this declaration, and he answered with a smile, that he hoped he need not give the colonel any assurances on that head. However, though he was satisfied with regard to the colonel's suspicions, yet some chimeras now arose in his brain which gave him no very agreeable sensations. What these were, the sagacious reader may probably suspect; but, if he should not, we may perhaps have occasion to open them in the sequel. Here we will put an end to this dialogue, and to the fifth book of this history.

BOOK VI.

Chapter i. — Panegyrics on beauty, with other grave matters.

The colonel and Booth walked together to the latter's lodging, for as it was not that day in the week in which all parts of the town are indifferent, Booth could not wait on the colonel.

When they arrived in Spring-garden, Booth, to his great surprize, found no one at home but the maid. In truth, Amelia had accompanied Mrs. Ellison and her children to his lordship's; for, as her little girl showed a great unwillingness to go without her, the fond mother was easily persuaded to make one of the company.

Booth had scarce ushered the colonel up to his apartment when a servant from Mrs. James knocked hastily at the door. The lady, not meeting with her husband at her return home, began to despair of him, and performed everything which was decent on the occasion. An apothecary was presently called with hartshorn and sal volatile, a doctor was sent for, and messengers were despatched every way; amongst the rest, one was sent to enquire at the lodgings of his supposed antagonist.

The servant hearing that his master was alive and well above-stairs, ran up eagerly to acquaint him with the dreadful situation in which he left his miserable lady at home, and likewise with the occasion of all her distress, saying, that his lady had been at her brother's, and had there heard that his honour was killed in a duel by Captain Booth.

The colonel smiled at this account, and bid the servant make haste back to contradict it. And then turning to Booth, he said, "Was there ever such another fellow as this brother of mine? I thought indeed, his behaviour was somewhat odd at the time. I suppose he overheard me whisper that I would give you satisfaction, and thence concluded we went together with a design of tilting. D—n the fellow, I begin to grow heartily sick of him, and wish I could get well rid of him without cutting his throat, which I sometimes apprehend he will insist on my doing, as a return for my getting him made a lieutenant-colonel."

Whilst these two gentlemen were commenting on the character of the third, Amelia and her company returned, and all presently came up-stairs, not only the children, but the two ladies, laden with trinkets as if they had been come from a fair. Amelia, who had been highly delighted all the morning with the excessive pleasure which her children enjoyed, when she saw Colonel James with her husband, and perceived the most manifest marks of that reconciliation which she knew had been so long and so earnestly wished by Booth, became so transported with joy, that her happiness was scarce capable of addition. Exercise had painted her face with vermilion; and the highest good-humour had so sweetened every feature, and a vast flow of spirits had so lightened

up her bright eyes, that she was all a blaze of beauty. She seemed, indeed, as Milton sublimely describes Eve,

> —Adorn'd
> With what all Earth or Heaven could bestow
> To make her amiable.

Again:—

> Grace was in all her steps, Heaven in her eye,
> In every gesture, dignity and love.

Or, as Waller sweetly, though less sublimely sings:—

> Sweetness, truth, and every grace
> Which time and use are wont to teach,
> The eye may in a moment reach,
> And read distinctly in her face.

Or, to mention one poet more, and him of all the sweetest, she seemed to be the very person of whom Suckling wrote the following lines, where, speaking of Cupid, he says,

> All his lovely looks, his pleasing fires,
> All his sweet motions, all his taking smiles;
> All that awakes, all that inflames desires,
> All that sweetly commands, all that beguiles,
> He does into one pair of eyes convey,
> And there begs leave that he himself may stay.

Such was Amelia at this time when she entered the room; and, having paid her respects to the colonel, she went up to her husband, and cried, "O, my dear! never were any creatures so happy as your little things have been this whole morning; and all owing to my lord's goodness; sure never was anything so good-natured and so generous!" She then made the children produce their presents, the value of which amounted to a pretty large sum; for there was a gold watch, amongst the trinkets, that cost above twenty guineas.

Instead of discovering so much satisfaction on this occasion as Amelia expected, Booth very gravely answered, "And pray, my dear, how are we to repay all these obligations to his lordship?" "How can you ask so strange a question?" cries Mrs. Ellison: "how little do you know of the soul of generosity (for sure my cousin deserves that name) when you call a few little trinkets given to children an obligation!" "Indeed, my dear," cries Amelia, "I would have stopped his hand if it had been possible; nay, I was forced at last absolutely to refuse, or I believe he would have laid a hundred pound out on the children; for I never saw any one so fond of children, which convinces me he is one of the best of men; but I ask your pardon, colonel," said she, turning to him; "I should not entertain you with these subjects; yet I know you have goodness enough to excuse the folly of a mother."

The colonel made a very low assenting bow, and soon after they all sat down to a small repast; for the colonel had promised Booth to dine with him when they first came home together, and what he had since heard from his own house gave him still less inclination than ever to repair thither.

But, besides both these, there was a third and stronger inducement to him to pass the day with his friend, and this was the desire of passing it with his friend's wife. When the colonel had first seen Amelia in France, she was but just recovered from a consumptive habit, and looked pale and thin; besides, his engagements with Miss Bath at that time took total possession of him, and guarded his heart from the impressions of another woman; and, when he had dined with her in town, the vexations through which she had lately passed had somewhat deadened her beauty; besides, he was then engaged, as we have seen, in a very warm pursuit of a new mistress, but now he had no such impediment; for, though the reader hath just before seen his warm declarations of a passion for Miss Matthews, yet it may be remembered that he had been in possession of her for above a fortnight; and one of the happy properties of this kind of passion is, that it can with equal violence love half a dozen or half a score different objects at one and the same time.

But indeed such were the charms now displayed by Amelia, of which we endeavoured above to draw some faint resemblance, that perhaps no other beauty could have secured him from their influence; and here, to confess a truth in his favour, however the grave or rather the hypocritical part of mankind may censure it, I am firmly persuaded that to withdraw admiration from exquisite

beauty, or to feel no delight in gazing at it, is as impossible as to feel no warmth from the most scorching rays of the sun. To run away is all that is in our power; and in the former case, if it must be allowed we have the power of running away, it must be allowed also that it requires the strongest resolution to execute it; for when, as Dryden says,

All paradise is open'd in a face,

how natural is the desire of going thither! and how difficult to quit the lovely prospect!

And yet, however difficult this may be, my young readers, it is absolutely necessary, and that immediately too: flatter not yourselves that fire will not scorch as well as warm, and the longer we stay within its reach the more we shall burn. The admiration of a beautiful woman, though the wife of our dearest friend, may at first perhaps be innocent, but let us not flatter ourselves it will always remain so; desire is sure to succeed; and wishes, hopes, designs, with a long train of mischiefs, tread close at our heels. In affairs of this kind we may most properly apply the well-known remark of nemo repente fuit turpissimus. It fares, indeed, with us on this occasion as with the unwary traveller in some parts of Arabia the desert, whom the treacherous sands imperceptibly betray till he is overwhelmed and lost. In both cases the only safety is by withdrawing our feet the very first moment we perceive them sliding.

This digression may appear impertinent to some readers; we could not, however, avoid the opportunity of offering the above hints; since of all passions there is none against which we should so strongly fortify ourselves as this, which is generally called love; for no other lays before us, especially in the tumultuous days of youth, such sweet, such strong and almost irresistible temptations; none hath produced in private life such fatal and lamentable tragedies; and what is worst of all, there is none to whose poison and infatuation the best of minds are so liable. Ambition scarce ever produces any evil but when it reigns in cruel and savage bosoms; and avarice seldom flourishes at all but in the basest and poorest soil. Love, on the contrary, sprouts usually up in the richest and noblest minds; but there, unless nicely watched, pruned, and cultivated, and carefully kept clear of those vicious weeds which are too apt to surround it, it branches forth into wildness and disorder, produces nothing desirable, but choaks up and kills whatever is good and noble in the mind where it so abounds. In short, to drop the allegory, not only tenderness and good nature, but bravery, generosity, and every virtue are often made the instruments of effecting the most atrocious purposes of this all-subduing tyrant.

Chapter ii. — Which will not appear, we presume, unnatural to all married readers.

If the table of poor Booth afforded but an indifferent repast to the colonel's hunger, here was most excellent entertainment of a much higher kind. The colonel began now to wonder within himself at his not having before discovered such incomparable beauty and excellence. This wonder was indeed so natural that, lest it should arise likewise in the reader, we thought proper to give the solution of it in the preceding chapter.

During the first two hours the colonel scarce ever had his eyes off from Amelia; for he was taken by surprize, and his heart was gone before he suspected himself to be in any danger. His mind, however, no sooner suggested a certain secret to him than it suggested some degree of prudence to him at the same time; and the knowledge that he had thoughts to conceal, and the care of concealing them, had birth at one and the same instant. During the residue of the day, therefore, he grew more circumspect, and contented himself with now and then stealing a look by chance, especially as the more than ordinary gravity of Booth made him fear that his former behaviour had betrayed to Booth's observation the great and sudden liking he had conceived for his wife, even before he had observed it in himself.

Amelia continued the whole day in the highest spirits and highest good humour imaginable, never once remarking that appearance of discontent in her husband of which the colonel had taken notice; so much more quick-sighted, as we have somewhere else hinted, is guilt than innocence. Whether Booth had in reality made any such observations on the colonel's behaviour as he had suspected, we will not undertake to determine; yet so far may be material to say, as we

can with sufficient certainty, that the change in Booth's behaviour that day, from what was usual with him, was remarkable enough. None of his former vivacity appeared in his conversation; and his countenance was altered from being the picture of sweetness and good humour, not indeed to sourness or moroseness, but to gravity and melancholy.

Though the colonel's suspicion had the effect which we have mentioned on his behaviour, yet it could not persuade him to depart. In short, he sat in his chair as if confined to it by enchantment, stealing looks now and then, and humouring his growing passion, without having command enough over his limbs to carry him out of the room, till decency at last forced him to put an end to his preposterous visit. When the husband and wife were left alone together, the latter resumed the subject of her children, and gave Booth a particular narrative of all that had passed at his lordship's, which he, though something had certainly disconcerted him, affected to receive with all the pleasure he could; and this affectation, however aukwardly he acted his part, passed very well on Amelia; for she could not well conceive a displeasure of which she had not the least hint of any cause, and indeed at a time when, from his reconciliation with James, she imagined her husband to be entirely and perfectly happy.

The greatest part of that night Booth past awake; and, if during the residue he might be said to sleep, he could scarce be said to enjoy repose; his eyes were no sooner closed, that he was pursued and haunted by the most frightful and terrifying dreams, which threw him into so restless a condition, that he soon disturbed his Amelia, and greatly alarmed her with apprehensions that he had been seized by some dreadful disease, though he had not the least symptoms of a fever by any extraordinary heat, or any other indication, but was rather colder than usual.

As Booth assured his wife that he was very well, but found no inclination to sleep, she likewise bid adieu to her slumbers, and attempted to entertain him with her conversation. Upon which his lordship occurred as the first topic; and she repeated to him all the stories which she had heard from Mrs. Ellison, of the peer's goodness to his sister and his nephew and niece. "It is impossible, my dear," says she, "to describe their fondness for their uncle, which is to me an incontestible sign of a parent's goodness." In this manner she ran on for several minutes, concluding at last, that it was pity so very few had such generous minds joined to immense fortunes.

Booth, instead of making a direct answer to what Amelia had said, cried coldly, "But do you think, my dear, it was right to accept all those expensive toys which the children brought home? And I ask you again, what return we are to make for these obligations?"

"Indeed, my dear," cries Amelia, "you see this matter in too serious a light. Though I am the last person in the world who would lessen his lordship's goodness (indeed I shall always think we are both infinitely obliged to him), yet sure you must allow the expense to be a mere trifle to such a vast fortune. As for return, his own benevolence, in the satisfaction it receives, more than repays itself, and I am convinced he expects no other."

"Very well, my dear," cries Booth, "you shall have it your way; I must confess I never yet found any reason to blame your discernment; and perhaps I have been in the wrong to give myself so much uneasiness on this account."

"Uneasiness, child!" said Amelia eagerly; "Good Heavens! hath this made you uneasy?"

"I do own it hath," answered Booth, "and it hath been the only cause of breaking my repose."

"Why then I wish," cries Amelia, "all the things had been at the devil before ever the children had seen them; and, whatever I may think myself, I promise you they shall never more accept the value of a farthing:—if upon this occasion I have been the cause of your uneasiness, you will do me the justice to believe that I was totally innocent."

At those words Booth caught her in his arms, and with the tenderest embrace, emphatically repeating the word innocent, cried, "Heaven forbid I should think otherwise! Oh, thou art the best of creatures that ever blessed a man!"

"Well, but," said she, smiling, "do confess, my dear, the truth; I promise you I won't blame you nor disesteem you for it; but is not pride really at the bottom of this fear of an obligation?"

"Perhaps it may," answered he; "or, if you will, you may call it fear. I own I am afraid of obligations, as the worst kind of debts; for I have generally observed those who confer them expect to be repaid ten thousand-fold."

Here ended all that is material of their discourse; and a little time afterwards, they both fell fast asleep in one another's arms; from which time Booth had no more restlessness, nor any

further perturbation in his dreams.

Their repose, however, had been so much disturbed in the former part of the night, that, as it was very late before they enjoyed that sweet sleep I have just mentioned, they lay abed the next day till noon, when they both rose with the utmost chearfulness; and, while Amelia bestirred herself in the affairs of her family, Booth went to visit the wounded colonel.

He found that gentleman still proceeding very fast in his recovery, with which he was more pleased than he had reason to be with his reception; for the colonel received him very coldly indeed, and, when Booth told him he had received perfect satisfaction from his brother, Bath erected his head and answered with a sneer, "Very well, sir, if you think these matters can be so made up, d—n me if it is any business of mine. My dignity hath not been injured."

"No one, I believe," cries Booth, "dare injure it."

"You believe so!" said the colonel: "I think, sir, you might be assured of it; but this, at least, you may be assured of, that if any man did, I would tumble him down the precipice of hell, d—n me, that you may be assured of."

As Booth found the colonel in this disposition, he had no great inclination to lengthen out his visit, nor did the colonel himself seem to desire it: so he soon returned back to his Amelia, whom he found performing the office of a cook, with as much pleasure as a fine lady generally enjoys in dressing herself out for a ball.

Chapter iii. — In which the history looks a little backwards.

Before we proceed farther in our history we shall recount a short scene to our reader which passed between Amelia and Mrs. Ellison whilst Booth was on his visit to Colonel Bath. We have already observed that Amelia had conceived an extraordinary affection for Mrs. Bennet, which had still encreased every time she saw her; she thought she discovered something wonderfully good and gentle in her countenance and disposition, and was very desirous of knowing her whole history.

She had a very short interview with that lady this morning in Mrs. Ellison's apartment. As soon, therefore, as Mrs. Bennet was gone, Amelia acquainted Mrs. Ellison with the good opinion she had conceived of her friend, and likewise with her curiosity to know her story: "For there must be something uncommonly good," said she, "in one who can so truly mourn for a husband above three years after his death."

"O!" cries Mrs. Ellison, "to be sure the world must allow her to have been one of the best of wives. And, indeed, upon the whole, she is a good sort of woman; and what I like her the best for is a strong resemblance that she bears to yourself in the form of her person, and still more in her voice. But for my own part, I know nothing remarkable in her fortune, unless what I have told you, that she was the daughter of a clergyman, had little or no fortune, and married a poor parson for love, who left her in the utmost distress. If you please, I will shew you a letter which she writ to me at that time, though I insist upon your promise never to mention it to her; indeed, you will be the first person I ever shewed it to." She then opened her scrutore, and, taking out the letter, delivered it to Amelia, saying, "There, madam, is, I believe, as fine a picture of distress as can well be drawn."

"DEAR MADAM,

"As I have no other friend on earth but yourself, I hope you will pardon my writing to you at this season; though I do not know that you can relieve my distresses, or, if you can, have I any pretence to expect that you should. My poor dear, O Heavens—my—lies dead in the house; and, after I had procured sufficient to bury him, a set of ruffians have entered my house, seized all I have, have seized his dear, dear corpse, and threaten to deny it burial. For Heaven's sake, send me, at least, some advice; little Tommy stands now by me crying for bread, which I have not to give him. I can say no more than that I am Your most distressed humble servant, M. BENNET."

Amelia read the letter over twice, and then returning it with tears in her eyes, asked how the

poor creature could possibly get through such distress.

"You may depend upon it, madam," said Mrs. Ellison, "the moment I read this account I posted away immediately to the lady. As to the seizing the body, that I found was a mere bugbear; but all the rest was literally true. I sent immediately for the same gentleman that I recommended to Mr. Booth, left the care of burying the corpse to him, and brought my friend and her little boy immediately away to my own house, where she remained some months in the most miserable condition. I then prevailed with her to retire into the country, and procured her a lodging with a friend at St Edmundsbury, the air and gaiety of which place by degrees recovered her; and she returned in about a twelve-month to town, as well, I think, as she is at present."

"I am almost afraid to ask," cries Amelia, "and yet I long methinks to know what is become of the poor little boy."

"He hath been dead," said Mrs. Ellison, "a little more than half a year; and the mother lamented him at first almost as much as she did her husband, but I found it indeed rather an easier matter to comfort her, though I sat up with her near a fortnight upon the latter occasion."

"You are a good creature," said Amelia, "and I love you dearly."

"Alas! madam," cries she, "what could I have done if it had not been for the goodness of that best of men, my noble cousin! His lordship no sooner heard of the widow's distress from me than he immediately settled one hundred and fifty pounds a year upon her during her life."

"Well! how noble, how generous was that!" said Amelia. "I declare I begin to love your cousin, Mrs. Ellison."

"And I declare if you do," answered she, "there is no love lost, I verily believe; if you had heard what I heard him say yesterday behind your back——"

"Why, what did he say, Mrs. Ellison?" cries Amelia.

"He said," answered the other, "that you was the finest woman his eyes ever beheld.—Ah! it is in vain to wish, and yet I cannot help wishing too.—O, Mrs. Booth! if you had been a single woman, I firmly believe I could have made you the happiest in the world. And I sincerely think I never saw a woman who deserved it more."

"I am obliged to you, madam," cries Amelia, "for your good opinion; but I really look on myself already as the happiest woman in the world. Our circumstances, it is true, might have been a little more fortunate; but O, my dear Mrs. Ellison! what fortune can be put in the balance with such a husband as mine?"

"I am afraid, dear madam," answered Mrs. Ellison, "you would not hold the scale fairly.—I acknowledge, indeed, Mr. Booth is a very pretty gentleman; Heaven forbid I should endeavour to lessen him in your opinion; yet, if I was to be brought to confession, I could not help saying I see where the superiority lies, and that the men have more reason to envy Mr. Booth than the women have to envy his lady."

"Nay, I will not bear this," replied Amelia. "You will forfeit all my love if you have the least disrespectful opinion of my husband. You do not know him, Mrs. Ellison; he is the best, the kindest, the worthiest of all his sex. I have observed, indeed, once or twice before, that you have taken some dislike to him. I cannot conceive for what reason. If he hath said or done anything to disoblige you, I am sure I can justly acquit him of design. His extreme vivacity makes him sometimes a little too heedless; but, I am convinced, a more innocent heart, or one more void of offence, was never in a human bosom."

"Nay, if you grow serious," cries Mrs. Ellison, "I have done. How is it possible you should suspect I had taken any dislike to a man to whom I have always shewn so perfect a regard; but to say I think him, or almost any other man in the world, worthy of yourself, is not within my power with truth. And since you force the confession from me, I declare, I think such beauty, such sense, and such goodness united, might aspire without vanity to the arms of any monarch in Europe."

"Alas! my dear Mrs. Ellison," answered Amelia, "do you think happiness and a crown so closely united? how many miserable women have lain in the arms of kings?—Indeed, Mrs. Ellison, if I had all the merit you compliment me with, I should think it all fully rewarded with such a man as, I thank Heaven, hath fallen to my lot; nor would I, upon my soul, exchange that lot with any queen in the universe."

"Well, there are enow of our sex," said Mrs. Ellison, "to keep you in countenance; but I shall never forget the beginning of a song of Mr. Congreve's, that my husband was so fond of that he was always singing it:—

Love's but a frailty of the mind,
     When 'tis not with ambition join'd.

Love without interest makes but an unsavoury dish, in my opinion."

"And pray how long hath this been your opinion?" said Amelia, smiling.

"Ever since I was born," answered Mrs. Ellison; "at least, ever since I can remember."

"And have you never," said Amelia, "deviated from this generous way of thinking?"

"Never once," answered the other, "in the whole course of my life."

"O, Mrs. Ellison! Mrs. Ellison!" cries Amelia; "why do we ever blame those who are disingenuous in confessing their faults, when we are so often ashamed to own ourselves in the right? Some women now, in my situation, would be angry that you had not made confidantes of them; but I never desire to know more of the secrets of others than they are pleased to intrust me with. You must believe, however, that I should not have given you these hints of my knowing all if I had disapproved your choice. On the contrary, I assure you I highly approve it. The gentility he wants, it will be easily in your power to procure for him; and as for his good qualities, I will myself be bound for them; and I make not the least doubt, as you have owned to me yourself that you have placed your affections on him, you will be one of the happiest women in the world."

"Upon my honour," cries Mrs. Ellison very gravely, "I do not understand one word of what you mean."

"Upon my honour, you astonish me," said Amelia; "but I have done."

"Nay then," said the other, "I insist upon knowing what you mean."

"Why, what can I mean," answered Amelia, "but your marriage with serjeant Atkinson?"

"With serjeant Atkinson!" cries Mrs. Ellison eagerly, "my marriage with a serjeant!"

"Well, with Mr. Atkinson, then, Captain Atkinson, if you please; for so I hope to see him."

"And have you really no better opinion of me," said Mrs. Ellison, "than to imagine me capable of such condescension? What have I done, dear Mrs. Booth, to deserve so low a place in your esteem? I find indeed, as Solomon says, Women ought to watch the door of their lips. How little did I imagine that a little harmless freedom in discourse could persuade any one that I could entertain a serious intention of disgracing my family! for of a very good family am I come, I assure you, madam, though I now let lodgings. Few of my lodgers, I believe, ever came of a better."

"If I have offended you, madam," said Amelia, "I am very sorry, and ask your pardon; but, besides what I heard from yourself, Mr. Booth told me—"

"O yes!" answered Mrs. Ellison, "Mr. Booth, I know, is a very good friend of mine. Indeed, I know you better than to think it could be your own suspicion. I am very much obliged to Mr. Booth truly."

"Nay," cries Amelia, "the serjeant himself is in fault; for Mr. Booth, I am positive, only repeated what he had from him."

"Impudent coxcomb!" cries Mrs. Ellison. "I shall know how to keep such fellows at a proper distance for the future—I will tell you, dear madam, all that happened. When I rose in the morning I found the fellow waiting in the entry; and, as you had exprest some regard for him as your foster-brother—nay, he is a very genteel fellow, that I must own—I scolded my maid for not shewing him into my little back-room; and I then asked him to walk into the parlour. Could I have imagined he would have construed such little civility into an encouragement?"

"Nay, I will have justice done to my poor brother too," said Amelia. "I myself have seen you give him much greater encouragement than that."

"Well, perhaps I have," said Mrs. Ellison. "I have been always too unguarded in my speech, and can't answer for all I have said." She then began to change her note, and, with an affected laugh, turned all into ridicule; and soon afterwards the two ladies separated, both in apparent good humour; and Amelia went about those domestic offices in which Mr. Booth found her engaged at the end of the preceding chapter.

Chapter iv. — Containing a very extraordinary incident.

In the afternoon Mr. Booth, with Amelia and her children, went to refresh themselves in the Park. The conversation now turned on what past in the morning with Mrs. Ellison, the latter part of the dialogue, I mean, recorded in the last chapter. Amelia told her husband that Mrs. Ellison so strongly denied all intentions to marry the serjeant, that she had convinced her the poor fellow was under an error, and had mistaken a little too much levity for serious encouragement; and concluded by desiring Booth not to jest with her any more on that subject.

Booth burst into a laugh at what his wife said. "My dear creature," said he, "how easily is thy honesty and simplicity to be imposed on! how little dost thou guess at the art and falsehood of women! I knew a young lady who, against her father's consent, was married to a brother officer of mine; and, as I often used to walk with her (for I knew her father intimately well), she would of her own accord take frequent occasions to ridicule and vilify her husband (for so he was at the time), and exprest great wonder and indignation at the report which she allowed to prevail that she should condescend ever to look at such a fellow with any other design than of laughing at and despising him. The marriage afterwards became publicly owned, and the lady was reputably brought to bed. Since which I have often seen her; nor hath she ever appeared to be in the least ashamed of what she had formerly said, though, indeed, I believe she hates me heartily for having heard it."

"But for what reason," cries Amelia, "should she deny a fact, when she must be so certain of our discovering it, and that immediately?"

"I can't answer what end she may propose," said Booth. "Sometimes one would be almost persuaded that there was a pleasure in lying itself. But this I am certain, that I would believe the honest serjeant on his bare word sooner than I would fifty Mrs. Ellisons on oath. I am convinced he would not have said what he did to me without the strongest encouragement; and, I think, after what we have been both witnesses to, it requires no great confidence in his veracity to give him an unlimited credit with regard to the lady's behaviour."

To this Amelia made no reply; and they discoursed of other matters during the remainder of a very pleasant walk.

When they returned home Amelia was surprized to find an appearance of disorder in her apartment. Several of the trinkets which his lordship had given the children lay about the room; and a suit of her own cloaths, which she had left in her drawers, was now displayed upon the bed.

She immediately summoned her little girl up-stairs, who, as she plainly perceived the moment she came up with a candle, had half cried her eyes out; for, though the girl had opened the door to them, as it was almost dark, she had not taken any notice of this phenomenon in her countenance.

The girl now fell down upon her knees and cried, "For Heaven's sake, madam, do not be angry with me. Indeed, I was left alone in the house; and, hearing somebody knock at the door, I opened it—I am sure thinking no harm. I did not know but it might have been you, or my master, or Madam Ellison; and immediately as I did, the rogue burst in and ran directly up-stairs, and what he hath robbed you of I cannot tell; but I am sure I could not help it, for he was a great swinging man with a pistol in each hand; and, if I had dared to call out, to be sure he would have killed me. I am sure I was never in such a fright in my born days, whereof I am hardly come to myself yet. I believe he is somewhere about the house yet, for I never saw him go out."

Amelia discovered some little alarm at this narrative, but much less than many other ladies would have shewn, for a fright is, I believe, sometimes laid hold of as an opportunity of disclosing several charms peculiar to that occasion. And which, as Mr. Addison says of certain virtues,

Shun the day, and lie conceal'd
In the smooth seasons and the calms of life.

Booth, having opened the window, and summoned in two chairmen to his assistance, proceeded to search the house; but all to no purpose; the thief was flown, though the poor girl, in her state of terror, had not seen him escape.

But now a circumstance appeared which greatly surprized both Booth and Amelia; indeed, I believe it will have the same effect on the reader; and this was, that the thief had taken nothing with him. He had, indeed, tumbled over all Booth's and Amelia's cloaths and the children's toys, but had left all behind him.

Amelia was scarce more pleased than astonished at this discovery, and re-examined the girl, assuring her of an absolute pardon if she confessed the truth, but grievously threatening her if she was found guilty of the least falsehood. "As for a thief, child," says she, "that is certainly not true;

you have had somebody with you to whom you have been shewing the things; therefore tell me plainly who it was."

The girl protested in the solemnest manner that she knew not the person; but as to some circumstances she began to vary a little from her first account, particularly as to the pistols, concerning which, being strictly examined by Booth, she at last cried—"To be sure, sir, he must have had pistols about him." And instead of persisting in his having rushed in upon her, she now confessed that he had asked at the door for her master and mistress; and that at his desire she had shewn him up-stairs, where he at first said he would stay till their return home; "but, indeed," cried she, "I thought no harm, for he looked like a gentleman-like sort of man. And, indeed, so I thought he was for a good while, whereof he sat down and behaved himself very civilly, till he saw some of master's and miss's things upon the chest of drawers; whereof he cried, 'Hey-day! what's here?' and then he fell to tumbling about the things like any mad. Then I thinks, thinks I to myself, to be sure he is a highwayman, whereof I did not dare speak to him; for I knew Madam Ellison and her maid was gone out, and what could such a poor girl as I do against a great strong man? and besides, thinks I, to be sure he hath got pistols about him, though I can't indeed, (that I will not do for the world) take my Bible-oath that I saw any; yet to be sure he would have soon pulled them out and shot me dead if I had ventured to have said anything to offend him."

"I know not what to make of this," cries Booth. "The poor girl, I verily believe, speaks to the best of her knowledge. A thief it could not be, for he hath not taken the least thing; and it is plain he had the girl's watch in his hand. If it had been a bailiff, surely he would have staid till our return. I can conceive no other from the girl's account than that it must have been some madman."

"O good sir!" said the girl, "now you mention it, if he was not a thief, to be sure he must have been a madman: for indeed he looked, and behaved himself too, very much like a madman; for, now I remember it, he talked to himself and said many strange kind of words that I did not understand. Indeed, he looked altogether as I have seen people in Bedlam; besides, if he was not a madman, what good could it do him to throw the things all about the room in such a manner? and he said something too about my master just before he went down-stairs. I was in such a fright I cannot remember particularly, but I am sure they were very ill words; he said he would do for him—I am sure he said that, and other wicked bad words too, if I could but think of them."

"Upon my word," said Booth, "this is the most probable conjecture; but still I am puzzled to conceive who it should be, for I have no madman to my knowledge of my acquaintance, and it seems, as the girl says, he asked for me." He then turned to the child, and asked her if she was certain of that circumstance.

The poor maid, after a little hesitation, answered, "Indeed, sir, I cannot be very positive; for the fright he threw me into afterwards drove everything almost out of my mind."

"Well, whatever he was," cries Amelia, "I am glad the consequence is no worse; but let this be a warning to you, little Betty, and teach you to take more care for the future. If ever you should be left alone in the house again, be sure to let no persons in without first looking out at the window and seeing who they are. I promised not to chide you any more on this occasion, and I will keep my word; but it is very plain you desired this person to walk up into our apartment, which was very wrong in our absence."

Betty was going to answer, but Amelia would not let her, saying, "Don't attempt to excuse yourself; for I mortally hate a liar, and can forgive any fault sooner than falsehood."

The poor girl then submitted; and now Amelia, with her assistance, began to replace all things in their order; and little Emily hugging her watch with great fondness, declared she would never part with it any more.

Thus ended this odd adventure, not entirely to the satisfaction of Booth; for, besides his curiosity, which, when thoroughly roused, is a very troublesome passion, he had, as is I believe usual with all persons in his circumstances, several doubts and apprehensions of he knew not what. Indeed, fear is never more uneasy than when it doth not certainly know its object; for on such occasions the mind is ever employed in raising a thousand bugbears and fantoms, much more dreadful than any realities, and, like children when they tell tales of hobgoblins, seems industrious in terrifying itself.

Chapter v. — Containing some matters not very unnatural.

Matters were scarce sooner reduced into order and decency than a violent knocking was heard at the door, such indeed as would have persuaded any one not accustomed to the sound that the madman was returned in the highest spring-tide of his fury.

Instead, however, of so disagreeable an appearance, a very fine lady presently came into the room, no other, indeed, than Mrs. James herself; for she was resolved to shew Amelia, by the speedy return of her visit, how unjust all her accusation had been of any failure in the duties of friendship; she had, moreover, another reason to accelerate this visit, and that was, to congratulate her friend on the event of the duel between Colonel Bath and Mr. Booth.

The lady had so well profited by Mrs. Booth's remonstrance, that she had now no more of that stiffness and formality which she had worn on a former occasion. On the contrary, she now behaved with the utmost freedom and good-humour, and made herself so very agreeable, that Amelia was highly pleased and delighted with her company.

An incident happened during this visit, that may appear to some too inconsiderable in itself to be recorded; and yet, as it certainly produced a very strong consequence in the mind of Mr. Booth, we cannot prevail on ourselves to pass it by.

Little Emily, who was present in the room while Mrs. James was there, as she stood near that lady happened to be playing with her watch, which she was so greatly overjoyed had escaped safe from the madman. Mrs. James, who exprest great fondness for the child, desired to see the watch, which she commended as the prettiest of the kind she had ever seen.

Amelia caught eager hold of this opportunity to spread the praises of her benefactor. She presently acquainted Mrs. James with the donor's name, and ran on with great encomiums on his lordship's goodness, and particularly on his generosity. To which Mrs. James answered, "O! certainly, madam, his lordship hath universally the character of being extremely generous-where he likes."

In uttering these words she laid a very strong emphasis on the three last monosyllables, accompanying them at the same time with a very sagacious look, a very significant leer, and a great flirt with her fan.

The greatest genius the world hath ever produced observes, in one of his most excellent plays, that

Trifles, light as air,
Are to the jealous confirmations strong
As proofs of holy writ.

That Mr. Booth began to be possessed by this worst of fiends, admits, I think, no longer doubt; for at this speech of Mrs. James he immediately turned pale, and, from a high degree of chearfulness, was all on a sudden struck dumb, so that he spoke not another word till Mrs. James left the room.

The moment that lady drove from the door Mrs. Ellison came up-stairs. She entered the room with a laugh, and very plentifully rallied both Booth and Amelia concerning the madman, of which she had received a full account below-stairs; and at last asked Amelia if she could not guess who it was; but, without receiving an answer, went on, saying, "For my own part, I fancy it must be some lover of yours! some person that hath seen you, and so is run mad with love. Indeed, I should not wonder if all mankind were to do the same. La! Mr. Booth, what makes you grave? why, you are as melancholy as if you had been robbed in earnest. Upon my word, though, to be serious, it is a strange story, and, as the girl tells it, I know not what to make of it. Perhaps it might be some rogue that intended to rob the house, and his heart failed him; yet even that would be very extraordinary. What, did you lose nothing, madam?"

"Nothing at all," answered Amelia. "He did not even take the child's watch."

"Well, captain," cries Mrs. Ellison, "I hope you will take more care of the house to-morrow; for your lady and I shall leave you alone to the care of it. Here, madam," said she, "here is a present from my lord to us; here are two tickets for the masquerade at Ranelagh. You will be so charmed with it! It is the sweetest of all diversions."

"May I be damned, madam," cries Booth, "if my wife shall go thither."

Mrs. Ellison stared at these words, and, indeed, so did Amelia; for they were spoke with great vehemence. At length the former cried out with an air of astonishment, "Not let your lady go to Ranelagh, sir?"

"No, madam," cries Booth, "I will not let my wife go to Ranelagh."

"You surprize me!" cries Mrs. Ellison. "Sure, you are not in earnest?"

"Indeed, madam," returned he, "I am seriously in earnest. And, what is more, I am convinced she would of her own accord refuse to go."

"Now, madam," said Mrs. Ellison, "you are to answer for yourself: and I will for your husband, that, if you have a desire to go, he will not refuse you."

"I hope, madam," answered Amelia with great gravity, "I shall never desire to go to any place contrary to Mr. Booth's inclinations."

"Did ever mortal hear the like?" said Mrs. Ellison; "you are enough to spoil the best husband in the universe. Inclinations! what, is a woman to be governed then by her husband's inclinations, though they are never so unreasonable?"

"Pardon me, madam," said Amelia; "I will not suppose Mr. Booth's inclinations ever can be unreasonable. I am very much obliged to you for the offer you have made me; but I beg you will not mention it any more; for, after what Mr. Booth hath declared, if Ranelagh was a heaven upon earth, I would refuse to go to it."

"I thank you, my dear," cries Booth; "I do assure you, you oblige me beyond my power of expression by what you say; but I will endeavour to shew you, both my sensibility of such goodness, and my lasting gratitude to it."

"And pray, sir," cries Mrs. Ellison, "what can be your objection to your lady's going to a place which, I will venture to say, is as reputable as any about town, and which is frequented by the best company?"

"Pardon me, good Mrs. Ellison," said Booth: "as my wife is so good to acquiesce without knowing my reasons, I am not, I think, obliged to assign them to any other person."

"Well," cries Mrs. Ellison, "if I had been told this, I would not have believed it. What, refuse your lady an innocent diversion, and that too when you have not the pretence to say it would cost you a farthing?"

"Why will you say any more on this subject, dear madam?" cries Amelia. "All diversions are to me matters of such indifference, that the bare inclinations of any one for whom I have the least value would at all times turn the balance of mine. I am sure then, after what Mr. Booth hath said—"

"My dear," cries he, taking her up hastily, "I sincerely ask your pardon; I spoke inadvertently, and in a passion. I never once thought of controuling you, nor ever would. Nay, I said in the same breath you would not go; and, upon my honour, I meant nothing more."

"My dear," said she, "you have no need of making any apology. I am not in the least offended, and am convinced you will never deny me what I shall desire."

"Try him, try him, madam," cries Mrs. Ellison; "I will be judged by all the women in town if it is possible for a wife to ask her husband anything more reasonable. You can't conceive what a sweet, charming, elegant, delicious place it is. Paradise itself can hardly be equal to it."

"I beg you will excuse me, madam," said Amelia; "nay, I entreat you will ask me no more; for be assured I must and will refuse. Do let me desire you to give the ticket to poor Mrs. Bennet. I believe it would greatly oblige her."

"Pardon me, madam," said Mrs. Ellison; "if you will not accept of it, I am not so distressed for want of company as to go to such a public place with all sort of people neither. I am always very glad to see Mrs. Bennet at my own house, because I look upon her as a very good sort of woman; but I don't chuse to be seen with such people in public places."

Amelia exprest some little indignation at this last speech, which she declared to be entirely beyond her comprehension; and soon after, Mrs. Ellison, finding all her efforts to prevail on Amelia were ineffectual, took her leave, giving Mr. Booth two or three sarcastical words, and a much more sarcastical look, at her departure.

Chapter vi. — A scene in which some ladies will possibly think Amelia's conduct exceptionable.

Booth and his wife being left alone, a solemn silence prevailed during a few minutes. At last Amelia, who, though a good, was yet a human creature, said to her husband, "Pray, my dear, do inform me what could put you into so great a passion when Mrs. Ellison first offered me the tickets for this masquerade?"

"I had rather you would not ask me," said Booth. "You have obliged me greatly in your ready acquiescence with my desire, and you will add greatly to the obligation by not enquiring the reason of it. This you may depend upon, Amelia, that your good and happiness are the great objects of all my wishes, and the end I propose in all my actions. This view alone could tempt me to refuse you anything, or to conceal anything from you."

"I will appeal to yourself," answered she, "whether this be not using me too much like a child, and whether I can possibly help being a little offended at it?"

"Not in the least," replied he; "I use you only with the tenderness of a friend. I would only endeavour to conceal that from you which I think would give you uneasiness if you knew. These are called the pious frauds of friendship."

"I detest all fraud," says she; "and pious is too good an epithet to be joined to so odious a word. You have often, you know, tried these frauds with no better effect than to teize and torment me. You cannot imagine, my dear, but that I must have a violent desire to know the reason of words which I own I never expected to have heard. And the more you have shown a reluctance to tell me, the more eagerly I have longed to know. Nor can this be called a vain curiosity, since I seem so much interested in this affair. If after all this, you still insist on keeping the secret, I will convince you I am not ignorant of the duty of a wife by my obedience; but I cannot help telling you at the same time you will make me one of the most miserable of women."

"That is," cries he, "in other words, my dear Emily, to say, I will be contented without the secret, but I am resolved to know it, nevertheless."

"Nay, if you say so," cries she, "I am convinced you will tell me. Positively, dear Billy, I must and will know."

"Why, then, positively," says Booth, "I will tell you. And I think I shall then shew you that, however well you may know the duty of a wife, I am not always able to behave like a husband. In a word then, my dear, the secret is no more than this; I am unwilling you should receive any more presents from my lord."

"Mercy upon me!" cries she, with all the marks of astonishment; "what! a masquerade ticket!"—

"Yes, my dear," cries he; "that is, perhaps, the very worst and most dangerous of all. Few men make presents of those tickets to ladies without intending to meet them at the place. And what do we know of your companion? To be sincere with you, I have not liked her behaviour for some time. What might be the consequence of going with such a woman to such a place, to meet such a person, I tremble to think. And now, my dear, I have told you my reason of refusing her offer with some little vehemence, and I think I need explain myself no farther."

"You need not, indeed, sir," answered she. "Good Heavens! did I ever expect to hear this? I can appeal to heaven, nay, I will appeal to yourself, Mr. Booth, if I have ever done anything to deserve such a suspicion. If ever any action of mine, nay, if ever any thought, had stained the innocence of my soul, I could be contented."

"How cruelly do you mistake me!" said Booth. "What suspicion have I ever shewn?"

"Can you ask it," answered she, "after what you have just now declared?"

"If I have declared any suspicion of you," replied he, "or if ever I entertained a thought leading that way, may the worst of evils that ever afflicted human nature attend me! I know the pure innocence of that tender bosom, I do know it, my lovely angel, and adore it. The snares which might be laid for that innocence were alone the cause of my apprehension. I feared what a wicked and voluptuous man, resolved to sacrifice everything to the gratification of a sensual appetite with the most delicious repast, might attempt. If ever I injured the unspotted whiteness of thy virtue in my imagination, may hell—"

"Do not terrify me," cries she, interrupting him, "with such imprecations. O, Mr. Booth! Mr. Booth! you must well know that a woman's virtue is always her sufficient guard. No husband, without suspecting that, can suspect any danger from those snares you mention; and why, if you are liable to take such things into your head, may not your suspicions fall on me as well as on any other? for sure nothing was ever more unjust, I will not say ungrateful, than the suspicions which you have bestowed on his lordship. I do solemnly declare, in all the times I have seen the poor man, he hath never once offered the least forwardness. His behaviour hath been polite indeed, but rather remarkably distant than otherwise. Particularly when we played at cards together. I don't remember he spoke ten words to me all the evening; and when I was at his house, though he shewed the greatest fondness imaginable to the children, he took so little notice of me, that a vain woman would have been very little pleased with him. And if he gave them many presents, he never offered me one. The first, indeed, which he ever offered me was that which you in that kind manner forced me to refuse."

"All this may be only the effect of art," said Booth. "I am convinced he doth, nay, I am convinced he must like you; and my good friend James, who perfectly well knows the world, told me, that his lordship's character was that of the most profuse in his pleasures with women; nay, what said Mrs. James this very evening? 'His lordship is extremely generous—where he likes.' I shall never forget the sneer with which she spoke those last words."

"I am convinced they injure him," cries Amelia. "As for Mrs. James, she was always given to be censorious; I remarked it in her long ago, as her greatest fault. And for the colonel, I believe he may find faults enow of this kind in his own bosom, without searching after them among his neighbours. I am sure he hath the most impudent look of all the men I know; and I solemnly declare, the very last time he was here he put me out of countenance more than once."

"Colonel James," answered Booth, "may have his faults very probably. I do not look upon him as a saint, nor do I believe he desires I should; but what interest could he have in abusing this lord's character to me? or why should I question his truth, when he assured me that my lord had never done an act of beneficence in his life but for the sake of some woman whom he lusted after?"

"Then I myself can confute him," replied Amelia: "for, besides his services to you, which, for the future, I shall wish to forget, and his kindness to my little babes, how inconsistent is the character which James gives of his lordship's behaviour to his own nephew and niece, whose extreme fondness of their uncle sufficiently proclaims his goodness to them? I need not mention all that I have heard from Mrs. Ellison, every word of which I believe; for I have great reason to think, notwithstanding some little levity, which, to give her her due, she sees and condemns in herself, she is a very good sort of woman."

"Well, my dear," cries Booth, "I may have been deceived, and I heartily hope I am so; but in cases of this nature it is always good to be on the surest side; for, as Congreve says,

'The wise too jealous are: fools too secure.'"

Here Amelia burst into tears, upon which Booth immediately caught her in his arms, and endeavoured to comfort her. Passion, however, for a while obstructed her speech, and at last she cried, "O, Mr. Booth! can I bear to hear the word jealousy from your mouth?"

"Why, my love," said Booth, "will you so fatally misunderstand my meaning? how often shall I protest that it is not of you, but of him, that I was jealous? If you could look into my breast, and there read all the most secret thoughts of my heart, you would not see one faint idea to your dishonour."

"I don't misunderstand you, my dear," said she, "so much as I am afraid you misunderstand yourself. What is it you fear?—you mention not force, but snares. Is not this to confess, at least, that you have some doubt of my understanding? do you then really imagine me so weak as to be cheated of my virtue?—am I to be deceived into an affection for a man before I perceive the least inward hint of my danger? No, Mr. Booth, believe me, a woman must be a fool indeed who can have in earnest such an excuse for her actions. I have not, I think, any very high opinion of my judgment, but so far I shall rely upon it, that no man breathing could have any such designs as you have apprehended without my immediately seeing them; and how I should then act I hope my whole conduct to you hath sufficiently declared."

"Well, my dear," cries Booth, "I beg you will mention it no more; if possible, forget it. I hope, nay, I believe, I have been in the wrong; pray forgive me."

"I will, I do forgive you, my dear," said she, "if forgiveness be a proper word for one whom you have rather made miserable than angry; but let me entreat you to banish for ever all such suspicions from your mind. I hope Mrs. Ellison hath not discovered the real cause of your passion; but, poor woman, if she had, I am convinced it would go no farther. Oh, Heavens! I would not for the world it should reach his lordship's ears. You would lose the best friend that ever man had. Nay, I would not for his own sake, poor man; for I really believe it would affect him greatly, and I must, I cannot help having an esteem for so much goodness. An esteem which, by this dear hand," said she, taking Booth's hand and kissing it, "no man alive shall ever obtain by making love to me."

Booth caught her in his arms and tenderly embraced her. After which the reconciliation soon became complete; and Booth, in the contemplation of his happiness, entirely buried all his jealous thoughts.

Chapter vii. — A chapter in which there is much learning.

The next morning, whilst Booth was gone to take his morning walk, Amelia went down into Mrs. Ellison's apartment, where, though she was received with great civility, yet she found that lady was not at all pleased with Mr. Booth; and, by some hints which dropt from her in conversation, Amelia very greatly apprehended that Mrs. Ellison had too much suspicion of her husband's real uneasiness; for that lady declared very openly she could not help perceiving what sort of man Mr. Booth was: "And though I have the greatest regard for you, madam, in the world," said she, "yet I think myself in honour obliged not to impose on his lordship, who, I know very well, hath conceived his greatest liking to the captain on my telling him that he was the best husband in the world."

Amelia's fears gave her much disturbance, and when her husband returned she acquainted him with them; upon which occasion, as it was natural, she resumed a little the topic of their former discourse, nor could she help casting, though in very gentle terms, some slight blame on Booth for having entertained a suspicion which, she said, might in its consequence very possibly prove their ruin, and occasion the loss of his lordship's friendship.

Booth became highly affected with what his wife said, and the more, as he had just received a note from Colonel James, informing him that the colonel had heard of a vacant company in the regiment which Booth had mentioned to him, and that he had been with his lordship about it, who had promised to use his utmost interest to obtain him the command.

The poor man now exprest the utmost concern for his yesterday's behaviour, said "he believed the devil had taken possession of him," and concluded with crying out, "Sure I was born, my dearest creature, to be your torment."

Amelia no sooner saw her husband's distress than she instantly forbore whatever might seem likely to aggravate it, and applied herself, with all her power, to comfort him. "If you will give me leave to offer my advice, my dearest soul," said she, "I think all might yet be remedied. I think you know me too well to suspect that the desire of diversion should induce me to mention what I am now going to propose; and in that confidence I will ask you to let me accept my lord's and Mrs. Ellison's offer, and go to the masquerade. No matter how little while I stay there; if you desire it I will not be an hour from you. I can make an hundred excuses to come home, or tell a real truth, and say I am tired with the place. The bare going will cure everything."

Amelia had no sooner done speaking than Booth immediately approved her advice, and readily gave his consent. He could not, however, help saying, that the shorter her stay was there, the more agreeable it would be to him; "for you know, my dear," said he, "I would never willingly be a moment out of your sight."

In the afternoon Amelia sent to invite Mrs. Ellison to a dish of tea; and Booth undertook to laugh off all that had passed yesterday, in which attempt the abundant good humour of that lady gave him great hopes of success.

Mrs. Bennet came that afternoon to make a visit, and was almost an hour with Booth and

Amelia before the entry of Mrs. Ellison.

Mr. Booth had hitherto rather disliked this young lady, and had wondered at the pleasure which Amelia declared she took in her company. This afternoon, however, he changed his opinion, and liked her almost as much as his wife had done. She did indeed behave at this time with more than ordinary gaiety; and good humour gave a glow to her countenance that set off her features, which were very pretty, to the best advantage, and lessened the deadness that had usually appeared in her complexion.

But if Booth was now pleased with Mrs. Bennet, Amelia was still more pleased with her than ever. For, when their discourse turned on love, Amelia discovered that her new friend had all the same sentiments on that subject with herself. In the course of their conversation Booth gave Mrs. Bennet a hint of wishing her a good husband, upon which both the ladies declaimed against second marriages with equal vehemence.

Upon this occasion Booth and his wife discovered a talent in their visitant to which they had been before entirely strangers, and for which they both greatly admired her, and this was, that the lady was a good scholar, in which, indeed, she had the advantage of poor Amelia, whose reading was confined to English plays and poetry; besides which, I think she had conversed only with the divinity of the great and learned Dr Barrow, and with the histories of the excellent Bishop Burnet.

Amelia delivered herself on the subject of second marriages with much eloquence and great good sense; but when Mrs. Bennet came to give her opinion she spoke in the following manner: "I shall not enter into the question concerning the legality of bigamy. Our laws certainly allow it, and so, I think, doth our religion. We are now debating only on the decency of it, and in this light I own myself as strenuous an advocate against it as any Roman matron would have been in those ages of the commonwealth when it was held to be infamous. For my own part, how great a paradox soever my opinion may seem, I solemnly declare, I see but little difference between having two husbands at one time and at several times; and of this I am very confident, that the same degree of love for a first husband which preserves a woman in the one case will preserve her in the other. There is one argument which I scarce know how to deliver before you, sir; but—if a woman hath lived with her first husband without having children, I think it unpardonable in her to carry barrenness into a second family. On the contrary, if she hath children by her first husband, to give them a second father is still more unpardonable."

"But suppose, madam," cries Booth, interrupting her with a smile, "she should have had children by her first husband, and have lost them?"

"That is a case," answered she, with a sigh, "which I did not desire to think of, and I must own it the most favourable light in which a second marriage can be seen. But the Scriptures, as Petrarch observes, rather suffer them than commend them; and St Jerom speaks against them with the utmost bitterness."—"I remember," cries Booth (who was willing either to shew his learning, or to draw out the lady's), "a very wise law of Charondas, the famous lawgiver of Thurium, by which men who married a second time were removed from all public councils; for it was scarce reasonable to suppose that he who was so great a fool in his own family should be wise in public affairs. And though second marriages were permitted among the Romans, yet they were at the same time discouraged, and those Roman widows who refused them were held in high esteem, and honoured with what Valerius Maximus calls the Corona Pudicitiae. In the noble family of Camilli there was not, in many ages, a single instance of this, which Martial calls adultery:

Quae toties nubit, non nubit; adultera lege est."

"True, sir," says Mrs. Bennet, "and Virgil calls this a violation of chastity, and makes Dido speak of it with the utmost detestation:

Sed mihi vel Tellus optem prius ima dehiscat
Vel Pater omnipotens adigat me fulmine ad umbras,
Pallentes umbras Erebi, noctemque profundam,
Ante, pudor, quam te violo, aut tua jura resolvo.
Ille meos, primum qui me sibi junxit, amores,
Ille habeat semper secum, servetque Sepulchro."

She repeated these lines with so strong an emphasis, that she almost frightened Amelia out of her wits, and not a little staggered Booth, who was himself no contemptible scholar. He expressed great admiration of the lady's learning; upon which she said it was all the fortune given her by her

father, and all the dower left her by her husband; "and sometimes," said she, "I am inclined to think I enjoy more pleasure from it than if they had bestowed on me what the world would in general call more valuable."—She then took occasion, from the surprize which Booth had affected to conceive at her repeating Latin with so good a grace, to comment on that great absurdity (for so she termed it) of excluding women from learning; for which they were equally qualified with the men, and in which so many had made so notable a proficiency; for a proof of which she mentioned Madam Dacier, and many others.

Though both Booth and Amelia outwardly concurred with her sentiments, it may be a question whether they did not assent rather out of complaisance than from their real judgment.

Chapter viii. — Containing some unaccountable behaviour in Mrs. Ellison.

Mrs. Ellison made her entrance at the end of the preceding discourse. At her first appearance she put on an unusual degree of formality and reserve; but when Amelia had acquainted her that she designed to accept the favour intended her, she soon began to alter the gravity of her muscles, and presently fell in with that ridicule which Booth thought proper to throw on his yesterday's behaviour.

The conversation now became very lively and pleasant, in which Booth having mentioned the discourse that passed in the last chapter, and having greatly complimented Mrs. Bennet's speech on that occasion, Mrs. Ellison, who was as strenuous an advocate on the other side, began to rally that lady extremely, declaring it was a certain sign she intended to marry again soon. "Married ladies," cries she, "I believe, sometimes think themselves in earnest in such declarations, though they are oftener perhaps meant as compliments to their husbands; but, when widows exclaim loudly against second marriages, I would always lay a wager that the man, if not the wedding-day, is absolutely fixed on."

Mrs. Bennet made very little answer to this sarcasm. Indeed, she had scarce opened her lips from the time of Mrs. Ellison's coming into the room, and had grown particularly grave at the mention of the masquerade. Amelia imputed this to her being left out of the party, a matter which is often no small mortification to human pride, and in a whisper asked Mrs. Ellison if she could not procure a third ticket, to which she received an absolute negative.

During the whole time of Mrs. Bennet's stay, which was above an hour afterwards, she remained perfectly silent, and looked extremely melancholy. This made Amelia very uneasy, as she concluded she had guessed the cause of her vexation. In which opinion she was the more confirmed from certain looks of no very pleasant kind which Mrs. Bennet now and then cast on Mrs. Ellison, and the more than ordinary concern that appeared in the former lady's countenance whenever the masquerade was mentioned, and which, unfortunately, was the principal topic of their discourse; for Mrs. Ellison gave a very elaborate description of the extreme beauty of the place and elegance of the diversion.

When Mrs. Bennet was departed, Amelia could not help again soliciting Mrs. Ellison for another ticket, declaring she was certain Mrs. Bennet had a great inclination to go with them; but Mrs. Ellison again excused herself from asking it of his lordship. "Besides, madam," says she, "if I would go thither with Mrs. Bennet, which, I own to you, I don't chuse, as she is a person whom nobody knows, I very much doubt whether she herself would like it; for she is a woman of a very unaccountable turn. All her delight lies in books; and as for public diversions, I have heard her often declare her abhorrence of them."

"What then," said Amelia, "could occasion all that gravity from the moment the masquerade was mentioned?"

"As to that," answered the other, "there is no guessing. You have seen her altogether as grave before now. She hath had these fits of gravity at times ever since the death of her husband."

"Poor creature!" cries Amelia; "I heartily pity her, for she must certainly suffer a great deal on these occasions. I declare I have taken a strange fancy to her."

"Perhaps you would not like her so well if you knew her thoroughly," answered Mrs.

Ellison.—"She is, upon the whole, but of a whimsical temper; and, if you will take my opinion, you should not cultivate too much intimacy with her. I know you will never mention what I say; but she is like some pictures, which please best at a distance."

Amelia did not seem to agree with these sentiments, and she greatly importuned Mrs. Ellison to be more explicit, but to no purpose; she continued to give only dark hints to Mrs. Bennet's disadvantage; and, if ever she let drop something a little too harsh, she failed not immediately to contradict herself by throwing some gentle commendations into the other scale; so that her conduct appeared utterly unaccountable to Amelia, and, upon the whole, she knew not whether to conclude Mrs. Ellison to be a friend or enemy to Mrs. Bennet.

During this latter conversation Booth was not in the room, for he had been summoned down-stairs by the serjeant, who came to him with news from Murphy, whom he had met that evening, and who assured the serjeant that, if he was desirous of recovering the debt which he had before pretended to have on Booth, he might shortly have an opportunity, for that there was to be a very strong petition to the board the next time they sat. Murphy said further that he need not fear having his money, for that, to his certain knowledge, the captain had several things of great value, and even his children had gold watches.

This greatly alarmed Booth, and still more when the serjeant reported to him, from Murphy, that all these things had been seen in his possession within a day last past. He now plainly perceived, as he thought, that Murphy himself, or one of his emissaries, had been the supposed madman; and he now very well accounted to himself, in his own mind, for all that had happened, conceiving that the design was to examine into the state of his effects, and to try whether it was worth his creditors' while to plunder him by law.

At his return to his apartment he communicated what he had heard to Amelia and Mrs. Ellison, not disguising his apprehensions of the enemy's intentions; but Mrs. Ellison endeavoured to laugh him out of his fears, calling him faint-hearted, and assuring him he might depend on her lawyer. "Till you hear from him," said she, "you may rest entirely contented: for, take my word for it, no danger can happen to you of which you will not be timely apprized by him. And as for the fellow that had the impudence to come into your room, if he was sent on such an errand as you mention, I heartily wish I had been at home; I would have secured him safe with a constable, and have carried him directly before justice Thresher. I know the justice is an enemy to bailiffs on his own account."

This heartening speech a little roused the courage of Booth, and somewhat comforted Amelia, though the spirits of both had been too much hurried to suffer them either to give or receive much entertainment that evening; which Mrs. Ellison perceiving soon took her leave, and left this unhappy couple to seek relief from sleep, that powerful friend to the distrest, though, like other powerful friends, he is not always ready to give his assistance to those who want it most.

Chapter ix. — Containing a very strange incident.

When the husband and wife were alone they again talked over the news which the serjeant had brought; on which occasion Amelia did all she could to conceal her own fears, and to quiet those of her husband. At last she turned the conversation to another subject, and poor Mrs. Bennet was brought on the carpet. "I should be sorry," cries Amelia, "to find I had conceived an affection for a bad woman; and yet I begin to fear Mrs. Ellison knows something of her more than she cares to discover; why else should she be unwilling to be seen with her in public? Besides, I have observed that Mrs. Ellison hath been always backward to introduce her to me, nor would ever bring her to my apartment, though I have often desired her. Nay, she hath given me frequent hints not to cultivate the acquaintance. What do you think, my dear? I should be very sorry to contract an intimacy with a wicked person."

"Nay, my dear," cries Booth. "I know no more of her, nor indeed hardly so much as yourself. But this I think, that if Mrs. Ellison knows any reason why she should not have introduced Mrs. Bennet into your company, she was very much in the wrong in introducing her into it."

In discourses of this kind they past the remainder of the evening. In the morning Booth rose early, and, going down-stairs, received from little Betty a sealed note, which contained the following words:

Beware, beware, beware;
For I apprehend a dreadful snare
Is laid for virtuous innocence,
Under a friend's false pretence.

Booth immediately enquired of the girl who brought this note? and was told it came by a chair-man, who, having delivered it, departed without saying a word.

He was extremely staggered at what he read, and presently referred the advice to the same affair on which he had received those hints from Atkinson the preceding evening; but when he came to consider the words more maturely he could not so well reconcile the two last lines of this poetical epistle, if it may be so called, with any danger which the law gave him reason to apprehend. Mr. Murphy and his gang could not well be said to attack either his innocence or virtue; nor did they attack him under any colour or pretence of friendship.

After much deliberation on this matter a very strange suspicion came into his head; and this was, that he was betrayed by Mrs. Ellison. He had, for some time, conceived no very high opinion of that good gentlewoman, and he now began to suspect that she was bribed to betray him. By this means he thought he could best account for the strange appearance of the supposed madman. And when this conceit once had birth in his mind, several circumstances nourished and improved it. Among these were her jocose behaviour and raillery on that occasion, and her attempt to ridicule his fears from the message which the serjeant had brought him.

This suspicion was indeed preposterous, and not at all warranted by, or even consistent with, the character and whole behaviour of Mrs. Ellison, but it was the only one which at that time suggested itself to his mind; and, however blameable it might be, it was certainly not unnatural in him to entertain it; for so great a torment is anxiety to the human mind, that we always endeavour to relieve ourselves from it by guesses, however doubtful or uncertain; on all which occasions, dislike and hatred are the surest guides to lead our suspicion to its object.

When Amelia rose to breakfast, Booth produced the note which he had received, saying, "My dear, you have so often blamed me for keeping secrets from you, and I have so often, indeed, endeavoured to conceal secrets of this kind from you with such ill success, that I think I shall never more attempt it." Amelia read the letter hastily, and seemed not a little discomposed; then, turning to Booth with a very disconsolate countenance, she said, "Sure fortune takes a delight in terrifying us! what can be the meaning of this?" Then, fixing her eyes attentively on the paper, she perused it for some time, till Booth cried, "How is it possible, my Emily, you can read such stuff patiently? the verses are certainly as bad as ever were written."—"I was trying, my dear," answered she, "to recollect the hand; for I will take my oath I have seen it before, and that very lately;" and suddenly she cried out, with great emotion, "I remember it perfectly now; it is Mrs. Bennet's hand. Mrs. Ellison shewed me a letter from her but a day or two ago. It is a very remarkable hand, and I am positive it is hers."

"If it be hers," cries Booth, "what can she possibly mean by the latter part of her caution? sure Mrs. Ellison hath no intention to betray us."

"I know not what she means," answered Amelia, "but I am resolved to know immediately, for I am certain of the hand. By the greatest luck in the world, she told me yesterday where her lodgings were, when she pressed me exceedingly to come and see her. She lives but a very few doors from us, and I will go to her this moment."

Booth made not the least objection to his wife's design. His curiosity was, indeed, as great as hers, and so was his impatience to satisfy it, though he mentioned not this his impatience to Amelia; and perhaps it had been well for him if he had.

Amelia, therefore, presently equipped herself in her walking dress, and, leaving her children to the care of her husband, made all possible haste to Mrs. Bennet's lodgings.

Amelia waited near five minutes at Mrs. Bennet's door before any one came to open it; at length a maid servant appeared, who, being asked if Mrs. Bennet was at home, answered, with some confusion in her countenance, that she did not know; "but, madam," said she, "if you will send up your name, I will go and see." Amelia then told her name, and the wench, after staying a considerable time, returned and acquainted her that Mrs. Bennet was at home. She was then

ushered into a parlour and told that the lady would wait on her presently.

In this parlour Amelia cooled her heels, as the phrase is, near a quarter of an hour. She seemed, indeed, at this time, in the miserable situation of one of those poor wretches who make their morning visits to the great to solicit favours, or perhaps to solicit the payment of a debt, for both are alike treated as beggars, and the latter sometimes considered as the more troublesome beggars of the two.

During her stay here, Amelia observed the house to be in great confusion; a great bustle was heard above-stairs, and the maid ran up and down several times in a great hurry.

At length Mrs. Bennet herself came in. She was greatly disordered in her looks, and had, as the women call it, huddled on her cloaths in much haste; for, in truth, she was in bed when Amelia first came. Of this fact she informed her, as the only apology she could make for having caused her to wait so long for her company.

Amelia very readily accepted her apology, but asked her with a smile, if these early hours were usual with her? Mrs. Bennet turned as red as scarlet at the question, and answered, "No, indeed, dear madam. I am for the most part a very early riser; but I happened accidentally to sit up very late last night. I am sure I had little expectation of your intending me such a favour this morning."

Amelia, looking very steadfastly at her, said, "Is it possible, madam, you should think such a note as this would raise no curiosity in me?" She then gave her the note, asking her if she did not know the hand.

Mrs. Bennet appeared in the utmost surprize and confusion at this instant. Indeed, if Amelia had conceived but the slightest suspicion before, the behaviour of the lady would have been a sufficient confirmation to her of the truth. She waited not, therefore, for an answer, which, indeed, the other seemed in no haste to give, but conjured her in the most earnest manner to explain to her the meaning of so extraordinary an act of friendship; "for so," said she, "I esteem it, being convinced you must have sufficient reason for the warning you have given me."

Mrs. Bennet, after some hesitation, answered, "I need not, I believe, tell you how much I am surprized at what you have shewn me; and the chief reason of my surprize is, how you came to discover my hand. Sure, madam, you have not shewn it to Mrs. Ellison?"

Amelia declared she had not, but desired she would question her no farther. "What signifies how I discovered it, since your hand it certainly is?"

"I own it is," cries Mrs. Bennet, recovering her spirits, "and since you have not shewn it to that woman I am satisfied. I begin to guess now whence you might have your information; but no matter; I wish I had never done anything of which I ought to be more ashamed. No one can, I think, justly accuse me of a crime on that account; and I thank Heaven my shame will never be directed by the false opinion of the world. Perhaps it was wrong to shew my letter, but when I consider all circumstances I can forgive it."

"Since you have guessed the truth," said Amelia, "I am not obliged to deny it. She, indeed, shewed me your letter, but I am sure you have not the least reason to be ashamed of it. On the contrary, your behaviour on so melancholy an occasion was highly praiseworthy; and your bearing up under such afflictions as the loss of a husband in so dreadful a situation was truly great and heroical."

"So Mrs. Ellison then hath shewn you my letter?" cries Mrs. Bennet eagerly.

"Why, did not you guess it yourself?" answered Amelia; "otherwise I am sure I have betrayed my honour in mentioning it. I hope you have not drawn me inadvertently into any breach of my promise. Did you not assert, and that with an absolute certainty, that you knew she had shewn me your letter, and that you was not angry with her for so doing?"

"I am so confused," replied Mrs. Bennet, "that I scarce know what I say; yes, yes, I remember I did say so—I wish I had no greater reason to be angry with her than that."

"For Heaven's sake," cries Amelia, "do not delay my request any longer; what you say now greatly increases my curiosity, and my mind will be on the rack till you discover your whole meaning; for I am more and more convinced that something of the utmost importance was the purport of your message."

"Of the utmost importance, indeed," cries Mrs. Bennet; "at least you will own my apprehensions were sufficiently well founded. O gracious Heaven! how happy shall I think myself if I should have proved your preservation! I will, indeed, explain my meaning; but, in order to disclose all my fears in their just colours, I must unfold my whole history to you. Can you have

129

patience, madam, to listen to the story of the most unfortunate of women?"

Amelia assured her of the highest attention, and Mrs. Bennet soon after began to relate what is written in the seventh book of this history.

BOOK VII.

Chapter i. — A very short chapter, and consequently requiring no preface.

Mrs. Bennet having fastened the door, and both the ladies having taken their places, she once or twice offered to speak, when passion stopt her utterance; and, after a minute's silence, she burst into a flood of tears. Upon which Amelia, expressing the utmost tenderness for her, as well by her look as by her accent, cried, "What can be the reason, dear madam, of all this emotion?" "O, Mrs. Booth!" answered she, "I find I have undertaken what I am not able to perform. You would not wonder at my emotion if you knew you had an adulteress and a murderer now standing before you."

Amelia turned pale as death at these words, which Mrs. Bennet observing, collected all the force she was able, and, a little composing her countenance, cried, "I see, madam, I have terrified you with such dreadful words; but I hope you will not think me guilty of these crimes in the blackest degree." "Guilty!" cries Amelia. "O Heavens!" "I believe, indeed, your candour," continued Mrs. Bennet, "will be readier to acquit me than I am to acquit myself. Indiscretion, at least, the highest, most unpardonable indiscretion, I shall always lay to my own charge: and, when I reflect on the fatal consequences, I can never, never forgive myself." Here she again began to lament in so bitter a manner, that Amelia endeavoured, as much as she could (for she was herself greatly shocked), to soothe and comfort her; telling her that, if indiscretion was her highest crime, the unhappy consequences made her rather an unfortunate than a guilty person; and concluded by saying—"Indeed, madam, you have raised my curiosity to the highest pitch, and I beg you will proceed with your story."

Mrs. Bennet then seemed a second time going to begin her relation, when she cried out, "I would, if possible, tire you with no more of my unfortunate life than just with that part which leads to a catastrophe in which I think you may yourself be interested; but I protest I am at a loss where to begin."

"Begin wherever you please, dear madam," cries Amelia; "but I beg you will consider my impatience." "I do consider it," answered Mrs. Bennet; "and therefore would begin with that part of my story which leads directly to what concerns yourself; for how, indeed, should my life produce anything worthy your notice?" "Do not say so, madam," cries Amelia; "I assure you I have long suspected there were some very remarkable incidents in your life, and have only wanted an opportunity to impart to you my desire of hearing them: I beg, therefore, you would make no more apologies." "I will not, madam," cries Mrs. Bennet, "and yet I would avoid anything trivial; though, indeed, in stories of distress, especially where love is concerned, many little incidents may appear trivial to those who have never felt the passion, which, to delicate minds, are the most interesting part of the whole." "Nay, but, dear madam," cries Amelia, "this is all preface."

"Well, madam," answered Mrs. Bennet, "I will consider your impatience." She then rallied all her spirits in the best manner she could, and began as is written in the next chapter.

And here possibly the reader will blame Mrs. Bennet for taking her story so far back, and relating so much of her life in which Amelia had no concern; but, in truth, she was desirous of inculcating a good opinion of herself, from recounting those transactions where her conduct was unexceptionable, before she came to the more dangerous and suspicious part of her character.

This I really suppose to have been her intention; for to sacrifice the time and patience of Amelia at such a season to the mere love of talking of herself would have been as unpardonable in her as the bearing it was in Amelia a proof of the most perfect good breeding.

Chapter ii. — The beginning of Mrs. Bennet's history.

"I was the younger of two daughters of a clergyman in Essex; of one in whose praise if I should indulge my fond heart in speaking, I think my invention could not outgo the reality. He was indeed well worthy of the cloth he wore; and that, I think, is the highest character a man can obtain.

"During the first part of my life, even till I reached my sixteenth year, I can recollect nothing to relate to you. All was one long serene day, in looking back upon which, as when we cast our eyes on a calm sea, no object arises to my view. All appears one scene of happiness and tranquillity.

"On the day, then, when I became sixteen years old, must I begin my history; for on that day I first tasted the bitterness of sorrow.

"My father, besides those prescribed by our religion, kept five festivals every year. These were on his wedding-day, and on the birthday of each of his little family; on these occasions he used to invite two or three neighbours to his house, and to indulge himself, as he said, in great excess; for so he called drinking a pint of very small punch; and, indeed, it might appear excess to one who on other days rarely tasted any liquor stronger than small beer.

"Upon my unfortunate birthday, then, when we were all in a high degree of mirth, my mother having left the room after dinner, and staying away pretty long, my father sent me to see for her. I went according to his orders; but, though I searched the whole house and called after her without doors, I could neither see nor hear her. I was a little alarmed at this (though far from suspecting any great mischief had befallen her), and ran back to acquaint my father, who answered coolly (for he was a man of the calmest temper), 'Very well, my dear, I suppose she is not gone far, and will be here immediately.' Half an hour or more past after this, when, she not returning, my father himself expressed some surprize at her stay; declaring it must be some matter of importance which could detain her at that time from her company. His surprize now increased every minute, and he began to grow uneasy, and to shew sufficient symptoms in his countenance of what he felt within. He then despatched the servant-maid to enquire after her mistress in the parish, but waited not her return; for she was scarce gone out of doors before he begged leave of his guests to go himself on the same errand. The company now all broke up, and attended my father, all endeavouring to give him hopes that no mischief had happened. They searched the whole parish, but in vain; they could neither see my mother, nor hear any news of her. My father returned home in a state little short of distraction. His friends in vain attempted to administer either advice or comfort; he threw himself on the floor in the most bitter agonies of despair.

"Whilst he lay in this condition, my sister and myself lying by him, all equally, I believe, and completely miserable, our old servant-maid came into the room and cried out, her mind misgave her that she knew where her mistress was. Upon these words, my father sprung from the floor, and asked her eagerly, where? But oh! Mrs. Booth, how can I describe the particulars of a scene to you, the remembrance of which chills my blood with horror, and which the agonies of my mind, when it past, made all a scene of confusion! The fact then in short was this: my mother, who was a most indulgent mistress to one servant, which was all we kept, was unwilling, I suppose, to disturb her at her dinner, and therefore went herself to fill her tea-kettle at a well, into which, stretching herself too far, as we imagine, the water then being very low, she fell with the tea-kettle in her hand. The missing this gave the poor old wretch the first hint of her suspicion, which, upon examination, was found to be too well grounded.

"What we all suffered on this occasion may more easily be felt than described."——"It may indeed," answered Amelia, "and I am so sensible of it, that, unless you have a mind to see me faint before your face, I beg you will order me something; a glass of water, if you please. "Mrs. Bennet

immediately complied with her friend's request; a glass of water was brought, and some hartshorn drops infused into it; which Amelia having drank off, declared she found herself much better; and then Mrs. Bennet proceeded thus:—"I will not dwell on a scene which I see hath already so much affected your tender heart, and which is as disagreeable to me to relate as it can be to you to hear. I will therefore only mention to you the behaviour of my father on this occasion, which was indeed becoming a philosopher and a Christian divine. On the day after my mother's funeral he sent for my sister and myself into his room, where, after many caresses and every demonstration of fatherly tenderness as well in silence as in words, he began to exhort us to bear with patience the great calamity that had befallen us; saying, 'That as every human accident, how terrible soever, must happen to us by divine permission at least, a due sense of our duty to our great Creator must teach us an absolute submission to his will. Not only religion, but common sense, must teach us this; for oh! my dear children,' cries he, 'how vain is all resistance, all repining! could tears wash back again my angel from the grave, I should drain all the juices of my body through my eyes; but oh, could we fill up that cursed well with our tears, how fruitless would be all our sorrow!'—I think I repeat you his very words; for the impression they made on me is never to be obliterated. He then proceeded to comfort us with the chearful thought that the loss was entirely our own, and that my mother was greatly a gainer by the accident which we lamented. 'I have a wife,' cries he, 'my children, and you have a mother, now amongst the heavenly choir; how selfish therefore is all our grief! how cruel to her are all our wishes!' In this manner he talked to us near half an hour, though I must frankly own to you his arguments had not the immediate good effect on us which they deserved, for we retired from him very little the better for his exhortations; however, they became every day more and more forcible upon our recollection; indeed, they were greatly strengthened by his example; for in this, as in all other instances, he practised the doctrines which he taught. From this day he never mentioned my mother more, and soon after recovered his usual chearfulness in public; though I have reason to think he paid many a bitter sigh in private to that remembrance which neither philosophy nor Christianity could expunge.

"My father's advice, enforced by his example, together with the kindness of some of our friends, assisted by that ablest of all the mental physicians, Time, in a few months pretty well restored my tranquillity, when fortune made a second attack on my quiet. My sister, whom I dearly loved, and who as warmly returned my affection, had fallen into an ill state of health some time before the fatal accident which I have related. She was indeed at that time so much better, that we had great hopes of her perfect recovery; but the disorders of her mind on that dreadful occasion so affected her body, that she presently relapsed to her former declining state, and thence grew continually worse and worse, till, after a decay of near seven months, she followed my poor mother to the grave.

"I will not tire you, dear madam, with repetitions of grief; I will only mention two observations which have occurred to me from reflections on the two losses I have mentioned. The first is, that a mind once violently hurt grows, as it were, callous to any future impressions of grief, and is never capable of feeling the same pangs a second time. The other observation is, that the arrows of fortune, as well as all others, derive their force from the velocity with which they are discharged; for, when they approach you by slow and perceptible degrees, they have but very little power to do you mischief.

"The truth of these observations I experienced, not only in my own heart, but in the behaviour of my father, whose philosophy seemed to gain a complete triumph over this latter calamity.

"Our family was now reduced to two, and my father grew extremely fond of me, as if he had now conferred an entire stock of affection on me, that had before been divided. His words, indeed, testified no less, for he daily called me his only darling, his whole comfort, his all. He committed the whole charge of his house to my care, and gave me the name of his little housekeeper, an appellation of which I was then as proud as any minister of state can be of his titles. But, though I was very industrious in the discharge of my occupation, I did not, however, neglect my studies, in which I had made so great a proficiency, that I was become a pretty good mistress of the Latin language, and had made some progress in the Greek. I believe, madam, I have formerly acquainted you, that learning was the chief estate I inherited of my father, in which he had instructed me from my earliest youth.

"The kindness of this good man had at length wiped off the remembrance of all losses; and I

during two years led a life of great tranquillity, I think I might almost say of perfect happiness.

"I was now in the nineteenth year of my age, when my father's good fortune removed us from the county of Essex into Hampshire, where a living was conferred on him by one of his old school-fellows, of twice the value of what he was before possessed of.

"His predecessor in this new living had died in very indifferent circumstances, and had left behind him a widow with two small children. My father, therefore, who, with great economy, had a most generous soul, bought the whole furniture of the parsonage-house at a very high price; some of it, indeed, he would have wanted; for, though our little habitation in Essex was most completely furnished, yet it bore no proportion to the largeness of that house in which he was now to dwell.

"His motive, however, to the purchase was, I am convinced, solely generosity; which appeared sufficiently by the price he gave, and may be farther inforced by the kindness he shewed the widow in another instance; for he assigned her an apartment for the use of herself and her little family, which, he told her, she was welcome to enjoy as long as it suited her conveniency.

"As this widow was very young, and generally thought to be tolerably pretty, though I own she had a cast with her eyes which I never liked, my father, you may suppose, acted from a less noble principle than I have hinted; but I must in justice acquit him, for these kind offers were made her before ever he had seen her face; and I have the greatest reason to think that, for a long time after he had seen her, he beheld her with much indifference.

"This act of my father's gave me, when I first heard it, great satisfaction; for I may at least, with the modesty of the ancient philosophers, call myself a lover of generosity, but when I became acquainted with the widow I was still more delighted with what my father had done; for though I could not agree with those who thought her a consummate beauty, I must allow that she was very fully possessed of the power of making herself agreeable; and this power she exerted with so much success, with such indefatigable industry to oblige, that within three months I became in the highest manner pleased with my new acquaintance, and had contracted the most sincere friendship for her.

"But, if I was so pleased with the widow, my father was by this time enamoured of her. She had, indeed, by the most artful conduct in the world, so insinuated herself into his favour, so entirely infatuated him, that he never shewed the least marks of chearfulness in her absence, and could, in truth, scarce bear that she should be out of his sight.

"She had managed this matter so well (O, she is the most artful of women!) that my father's heart was gone before I ever suspected it was in danger. The discovery you may easily believe, madam, was not pleasing. The name of a mother-in-law sounded dreadful in my ears; nor could I bear the thought of parting again with a share in those dear affections, of which I had purchased the whole by the loss of a beloved mother and sister.

"In the first hurry and disorder of my mind on this occasion I committed a crime of the highest kind against all the laws of prudence and discretion. I took the young lady herself very roundly to task, treated her designs on my father as little better than a design to commit a theft, and in my passion, I believe, said she might be ashamed to think of marrying a man old enough to be her grandfather; for so in reality he almost was.

"The lady on this occasion acted finely the part of a hypocrite. She affected to be highly affronted at my unjust suspicions, as she called them; and proceeded to such asseverations of her innocence, that she almost brought me to discredit the evidence of my own eyes and ears.

"My father, however, acted much more honestly, for he fell the next day into a more violent passion with me than I had ever seen him in before, and asked me whether I intended to return his paternal fondness by assuming the right of controlling his inclinations? with more of the like kind, which fully convinced me what had passed between him and the lady, and how little I had injured her in my suspicions.

"Hitherto, I frankly own, my aversion to this match had been principally on my own account; for I had no ill opinion of the woman, though I thought neither her circumstances nor my father's age promised any kind of felicity from such an union; but now I learnt some particulars, which, had not our quarrel become public in the parish, I should perhaps have never known. In short, I was Informed that this gentle obliging creature, as she had at first appeared to me, had the spirit of a tigress, and was by many believed to have broken the heart of her first husband.

"The truth of this matter being confirmed to me upon examination, I resolved not to

133

suppress it. On this occasion fortune seemed to favour me, by giving me a speedy opportunity of seeing my father alone and in good humour. He now first began to open his intended marriage, telling me that he had formerly had some religious objections to bigamy, but he had very fully considered the matter, and had satisfied himself of its legality. He then faithfully promised me that no second marriage should in the least impair his affection for me; and concluded with the highest eulogiums on the goodness of the widow, protesting that it was her virtues and not her person with which he was enamoured.

"I now fell upon my knees before him, and bathing his hand in my tears, which flowed very plentifully from my eyes, acquainted him with all I had heard, and was so very imprudent, I might almost say so cruel, to disclose the author of my information.

"My father heard me without any indication of passion, and answered coldly, that if there was any proof of such facts he should decline any further thoughts of this match: 'But, child,' said he, 'though I am far from suspecting the truth of what you tell me, as far as regards your knowledge, yet you know the inclination of the world to slander.' However, before we parted he promised to make a proper enquiry into what I had told him.—But I ask your pardon, dear madam, I am running minutely into those particulars of my life in which you have not the least concern."

Amelia stopt her friend short in her apology; and though, perhaps, she thought her impertinent enough, yet (such was her good breeding) she gave her many assurances of a curiosity to know every incident of her life which she could remember; after which Mrs. Bennet proceeded as in the next chapter.

Chapter iii. — Continuation of Mrs. Bennet's story.

"I think, madam," said Mrs. Bennet, "I told you my father promised me to enquire farther into the affair, but he had hardly time to keep his word; for we separated pretty late in the evening and early the next morning he was married to the widow.

"But, though he gave no credit to my information, I had sufficient reason to think he did not forget it, by the resentment which he soon discovered to both the persons whom I had named as my informers.

"Nor was it long before I had good cause to believe that my father's new wife was perfectly well acquainted with the good opinion I had of her, not only from her usage of me, but from certain hints which she threw forth with an air of triumph. One day, particularly, I remember she said to my father, upon his mentioning his age, 'O, my dear! I hope you have many years yet to live! unless, indeed, I should be so cruel as to break your heart.' She spoke these words looking me full in the face, and accompanied them with a sneer in which the highest malice was visible, under a thin covering of affected pleasantry.

"I will not entertain you, madam, with anything so common as the cruel usage of a step-mother; nor of what affected me much more, the unkind behaviour of a father under such an influence. It shall suffice only to tell you that I had the mortification to perceive the gradual and daily decrease of my father's affection. His smiles were converted into frowns; the tender appellations of child and dear were exchanged for plain Molly, that girl, that creature, and sometimes much harder names. I was at first turned all at once into a cypher, and at last seemed to be considered as a nuisance in the family.

"Thus altered was the man of whom I gave you such a character at the entrance on my story; but, alas! he no longer acted from his own excellent disposition, but was in everything governed and directed by my mother-in-law. In fact, whenever there is great disparity of years between husband and wife, the younger is, I believe, always possessed of absolute power over the elder; for superstition itself is a less firm support of absolute power than dotage.

"But, though his wife was so entirely mistress of my father's will that she could make him use me ill, she could not so perfectly subdue his understanding as to prevent him from being conscious of such ill-usage; and from this consciousness, he began inveterately to hate me. Of this hatred he gave me numberless instances, and I protest to you I know not any other reason for it

than what I have assigned; and the cause, as experience hath convinced me, is adequate to the effect.

"While I was in this wretched situation, my father's unkindness having almost broken ray heart, he came one day into my room with more anger in his countenance than I had ever seen, and, after bitterly upbraiding me with my undutiful behaviour both to himself and his worthy consort, he bid me pack up my alls, and immediately prepare to quit his house; at the same time gave me a letter, and told me that would acquaint me where I might find a home; adding that he doubted not but I expected, and had indeed solicited, the invitation; and left me with a declaration that he would have no spies in his family.

"The letter, I found on opening it, was from my father's own sister; but before I mention the contents I will give you a short sketch of her character, as it was somewhat particular. Her personal charms were not great; for she was very tall, very thin, and very homely. Of the defect of her beauty she was, perhaps, sensible; her vanity, therefore, retreated into her mind, where there is no looking-glass, and consequently where we can flatter ourselves with discovering almost whatever beauties we please. This is an encouraging circumstance; and yet I have observed, dear Mrs. Booth, that few women ever seek these comforts from within till they are driven to it by despair of finding any food for their vanity from without. Indeed, I believe the first wish of our whole sex is to be handsome."

Here both the ladies fixed their eyes on the glass, and both smiled.

"My aunt, however," continued Mrs. Bennet, "from despair of gaining any applause this way, had applied herself entirely to the contemplation of her understanding, and had improved this to such a pitch, that at the age of fifty, at which she was now arrived, she had contracted a hearty contempt for much the greater part of both sexes; for the women, as being idiots, and for the men, as the admirers of idiots. That word, and fool, were almost constantly in her mouth, and were bestowed with great liberality among all her acquaintance.

"This lady had spent one day only at my father's house in near two years; it was about a month before his second marriage. At her departure she took occasion to whisper me her opinion of the widow, whom she called a pretty idiot, and wondered how her brother could bear such company under his roof; for neither she nor I had at that time any suspicion of what afterwards happened.

"The letter which my father had just received, and which was the first she had sent him since his marriage, was of such a nature that I should be unjust if I blamed him for being offended; fool and idiot were both plentifully bestowed in it as well on himself as on his wife. But what, perhaps, had principally offended him was that part which related to me; for, after much panegyric on my understanding, and saying he was unworthy of such a daughter, she considered his match not only as the highest indiscretion as it related to himself, but as a downright act of injustice to me. One expression in it I shall never forget. 'You have placed,' said she, 'a woman above your daughter, who, in understanding, the only valuable gift of nature, is the lowest in the whole class of pretty idiots.' After much more of this kind, it concluded with inviting me to her house.

"I can truly say that when I had read the letter I entirely forgave my father's suspicion that I had made some complaints to my aunt of his behaviour; for, though I was indeed innocent, there was surely colour enough to suspect the contrary.

"Though I had never been greatly attached to my aunt, nor indeed had she formerly given me any reason for such an attachment, yet I was well enough pleased with her present invitation. To say the truth, I led so wretched a life where I then was, that it was impossible not to be a gainer by any exchange.

"I could not, however, bear the thoughts of leaving my father with an impression on his mind against me which I did not deserve. I endeavoured, therefore, to remove all his suspicion of my having complained to my aunt by the most earnest asseverations of my innocence; but they were all to no purpose. All my tears, all my vows, and all my entreaties were fruitless. My new mother, indeed, appeared to be my advocate; but she acted her part very poorly, and, far from counterfeiting any desire of succeeding in my suit, she could not conceal the excessive joy which she felt on the occasion.

"Well, madam, the next day I departed for my aunt's, where, after a long journey of forty miles, I arrived, without having once broke my fast on the road; for grief is as capable as food of filling the stomach, and I had too much of the former to admit any of the latter. The fatigue of my

135

journey, and the agitation of my mind, joined to my fasting, so overpowered my spirits, that when I was taken from my horse I immediately fainted away in the arms of the man who helped me from my saddle. My aunt expressed great astonishment at seeing me in this condition, with my eyes almost swollen out of my head with tears; but my father's letter, which I delivered her soon after I came to myself, pretty well, I believe, cured her surprize. She often smiled with a mixture of contempt and anger while she was reading it; and, having pronounced her brother to be a fool, she turned to me, and, with as much affability as possible (for she is no great mistress of affability), said, 'Don't be uneasy, dear Molly, for you are come to the house of a friend—of one who hath sense enough to discern the author of all the mischief: depend upon it, child, I will, ere long, make some people ashamed of their folly.' This kind reception gave me some comfort, my aunt assuring me that she would convince him how unjustly he had accused me of having made any complaints to her. A paper war was now begun between these two, which not only fixed an irreconcileable hatred between them, but confirmed my father's displeasure against me; and, in the end, I believe, did me no service with my aunt; for I was considered by both as the cause of their dissension, though, in fact, my stepmother, who very well knew the affection my aunt had for her, had long since done her business with my father; and as for my aunt's affection towards him, it had been abating several years, from an apprehension that he did not pay sufficient deference to her understanding.

"I had lived about half a year with my aunt when I heard of my stepmother's being delivered of a boy, and the great joy my father expressed on that occasion; but, poor man, he lived not long to enjoy his happiness; for within a month afterwards I had the melancholy news of his death.

"Notwithstanding all the disobligations I had lately received from him, I was sincerely afflicted at my loss of him. All his kindness to me in my infancy, all his kindness to me while I was growing up, recurred to my memory, raised a thousand tender, melancholy ideas, and totally obliterated all thoughts of his latter behaviour, for which I made also every allowance and every excuse in my power.

"But what may perhaps appear more extraordinary, my aunt began soon to speak of him with concern. She said he had some understanding formerly, though his passion for that vile woman had, in a great measure, obscured it; and one day, when she was in an ill-humour with me, she had the cruelty to throw out a hint that she had never quarrelled with her brother if it had not been on my account." My father, during his life, had allowed my aunt very handsomely for my board; for generosity was too deeply riveted in his nature to be plucked out by all the power of his wife. So far, however, she prevailed, that, though he died possessed of upwards of L.2000, he left me no more than L.100, which, as he expressed in his will, was to set me up in some business, if I had the grace to take to any.

"Hitherto my aunt had in general treated me with some degree of affection; but her behaviour began now to be changed. She soon took an opportunity of giving me to understand that her fortune was insufficient to keep me; and, as I could not live on the interest of my own, it was high time for me to consider about going into the world. She added, that her brother having mentioned my setting up in some business in his will was very foolish; that I had been bred to nothing; and, besides, that the sum was too trifling to set me up in any way of reputation; she desired me therefore to think of immediately going into service.

"This advice was perhaps right enough; and I told her I was very ready to do as she directed me, but I was at that time in an ill state of health; I desired her therefore to let me stay with her till my legacy, which was not to be paid till a year after my father's death, was due; and I then promised to satisfy her for my board, to which she readily consented.

"And now, madam," said Mrs. Bennet, sighing, "I am going to open to you those matters which lead directly to that great catastrophe of my life which hath occasioned my giving you this trouble, and of trying your patience in this manner."

Amelia, notwithstanding her impatience, made a very civil answer to this; and then Mrs. Bennet proceeded to relate what is written in the next chapter.

Chapter iv. — Further continuation.

"The curate of the parish where my aunt dwelt was a young fellow of about four-and-twenty. He had been left an orphan in his infancy, and entirely unprovided for, when an uncle had the goodness to take care of his education, both at school and at the university. As the young gentleman was intended for the church, his uncle, though he had two daughters of his own, and no very large fortune, purchased for him the next presentation of a living of near 1,200 a-year. The incumbent, at the time of the purchase, was under the age of sixty, and in apparent good health; notwithstanding which, he died soon after the bargain, and long before the nephew was capable of orders; so that the uncle was obliged to give the living to a clergyman, to hold it till the young man came of proper age.

"The young gentleman had not attained his proper age of taking orders when he had the misfortune to lose his uncle and only friend, who, thinking he had sufficiently provided for his nephew by the purchase of the living, considered him no farther in his will, but divided all the fortune of which he died possessed between his two daughters; recommending it to them, however, on his deathbed, to assist their cousin with money sufficient to keep him at the university till he should be capable of ordination.

"But, as no appointment of this kind was in the will, the young ladies, who received about each, thought proper to disregard the last words of their father; for, besides that both of them were extremely tenacious of their money, they were great enemies to their cousin, on account of their father's kindness to him; and thought proper to let him know that they thought he had robbed them of too much already.

"The poor young fellow was now greatly distrest; for he had yet above a year to stay at the university, without any visible means of sustaining himself there.

"In this distress, however, he met with a friend, who had the good nature to lend him the sum of twenty pounds, for which he only accepted his bond for forty, and which was to be paid within a year after his being possessed of his living; that is, within a year after his becoming qualified to hold it.

"With this small sum thus hardly obtained the poor gentleman made a shift to struggle with all difficulties till he became of due age to take upon himself the character of a deacon. He then repaired to that clergyman to whom his uncle had given the living upon the conditions above mentioned, to procure a title to ordination; but this, to his great surprize and mortification, was absolutely refused him.

"The immediate disappointment did not hurt him so much as the conclusion he drew from it; for he could have but little hopes that the man who could have the cruelty to refuse him a title would vouchsafe afterwards to deliver up to him a living of so considerable a value; nor was it long before this worthy incumbent told him plainly that he valued his uncle's favours at too high a rate to part with them to any one; nay, he pretended scruples of conscience, and said that, if he had made any slight promises, which he did not now well remember, they were wicked and void; that he looked upon himself as married to his parish, and he could no more give it up than he could give up his wife without sin.

"The poor young fellow was now obliged to seek farther for a title, which, at length, he obtained from the rector of the parish where my aunt lived.

"He had not long been settled in the curacy before an intimate acquaintance grew between him and my aunt; for she was a great admirer of the clergy, and used frequently to say they were the only conversible creatures in the country.

"The first time she was in this gentleman's company was at a neighbour's christening, where she stood godmother. Here she displayed her whole little stock of knowledge, in order to captivate Mr. Bennet (I suppose, madam, you already guess that to have been his name), and before they parted gave him a very strong invitation to her house.

"Not a word passed at this christening between Mr. Bennet and myself, but our eyes were not unemployed. Here, madam, I first felt a pleasing kind of confusion, which I know not how to describe. I felt a kind of uneasiness, yet did not wish to be without it. I longed to be alone, yet dreaded the hour of parting. I could not keep my eyes off from the object which caused my confusion, and which I was at once afraid of and enamoured with. But why do I attempt to

describe my situation to one who must, I am sure, have felt the same?"

Amelia smiled, and Mrs. Bennet went on thus: "O, Mrs. Booth! had you seen the person of whom I am now speaking, you would not condemn the suddenness of my love. Nay, indeed, I had seen him there before, though this was the first time I had ever heard the music of his voice. Oh! it was the sweetest that was ever heard.

"Mr. Bennet came to visit my aunt the very next day. She imputed this respectful haste to the powerful charms of her understanding, and resolved to lose no opportunity in improving the opinion which she imagined he had conceived of her. She became by this desire quite ridiculous, and ran into absurdities and a gallimatia scarce credible.

"Mr. Bennet, as I afterwards found, saw her in the same light with myself; but, as he was a very sensible and well-bred man, he so well concealed his opinion from us both, that I was almost angry, and she was pleased even to raptures, declaring herself charmed with his understanding, though, indeed, he had said very little; but I believe he heard himself into her good opinion, while he gazed himself into love.

"The two first visits which Mr. Bennet made to my aunt, though I was in the room all the time, I never spoke a word; but on the third, on some argument which arose between them, Mr. Bennet referred himself to me. I took his side of the question, as indeed I must to have done justice, and repeated two or three words of Latin. My aunt reddened at this, and exprest great disdain of my opinion, declaring she was astonished that a man of Mr. Bennet's understanding could appeal to the judgment of a silly girl; 'Is she,' said my aunt, bridling herself, 'fit to decide between us?' Mr. Bennet spoke very favourably of what I had said; upon which my aunt burst almost into a rage, treated me with downright scurrility, called me conceited fool, abused my poor father for having taught me Latin, which, she said, had made me a downright coxcomb, and made me prefer myself to those who were a hundred times my superiors in knowledge. She then fell foul on the learned languages, declared they were totally useless, and concluded that she had read all that was worth reading, though, she thanked heaven, she understood no language but her own.

"Before the end of this visit Mr. Bennet reconciled himself very well to my aunt, which, indeed, was no difficult task for him to accomplish; but from that hour she conceived a hatred and rancour towards me which I could never appease.

"My aunt had, from my first coming into her house, expressed great dislike to my learning. In plain truth, she envied me that advantage. This envy I had long ago discovered, and had taken great pains to smother it, carefully avoiding ever to mention a Latin word in her presence, and always submitting to her authority; for indeed I despised her ignorance too much to dispute with her. By these means I had pretty well succeeded, and we lived tolerably together; but the affront paid to her understanding by Mr. Bennet in my favour was an injury never to be forgiven to me. She took me severely to task that very evening, and reminded me of going to service in such earnest terms as almost amounted to literally turning me out of doors; advising me, in the most insulting manner, to keep my Latin to myself, which she said was useless to any one, but ridiculous when pretended to by a servant.

"The next visit Mr. Bennet made at our house I was not suffered to be present. This was much the shortest of all his visits; and when he went away he left my aunt in a worse humour than ever I had seen her. The whole was discharged on me in the usual manner, by upbraiding me with my learning, conceit, and poverty; reminding me of obligations, and insisting on my going immediately to service. With all this I was greatly pleased, as it assured me that Mr. Bennet had said something to her in my favour; and I would have purchased a kind expression of his at almost any price.

"I should scarce, however, have been so sanguine as to draw this conclusion, had I not received some hints that I had not unhappily placed my affections on a man who made me no return; for, though he had scarce addressed a dozen sentences to me (for, indeed, he had no opportunity), yet his eyes had revealed certain secrets to mine with which I was not displeased.

"I remained, however, in a state of anxiety near a month; sometimes pleasing myself with thinking Mr. Bennet's heart was in the same situation with my own; sometimes doubting that my wishes had flattered and deceived me, and not in the least questioning that my aunt was my rival; for I thought no woman could be proof against the charms that had subdued me. Indeed, Mrs. Booth, he was a charming young fellow; I must—I must pay this tribute to his memory. O, gracious Heaven! why, why did I ever see him? why was I doomed to such misery?" Here she

burst into a flood of tears, and remained incapable of speech for some time; during which the gentle Amelia endeavoured all she could to soothe her, and gave sufficient marks of sympathizing in the tender affliction of her friend.

Mrs. Bennet, at length, recovered her spirits, and proceeded, as in the next chapter.

Chapter v. — The story of Mrs. Bennet continued.

I scarce know where I left off—Oh! I was, I think, telling you that I esteemed my aunt as my rival; and it is not easy to conceive a greater degree of detestation than I had for her; and what may, perhaps, appear strange, as she daily grew more and more civil to me, my hatred encreased with her civility; for I imputed it all to her triumph over me, and to her having secured, beyond all apprehension, the heart I longed for.

"How was I surprized when, one day, with as much good-humour as she was mistress of (for her countenance was not very pleasing), she asked me how I liked Mr. Bennet? The question, you will believe, madam, threw me into great confusion, which she plainly perceived, and, without waiting for my answer, told me she was very well satisfied, for that it did not require her discernment to read my thoughts in my countenance. 'Well, child,' she said, 'I have suspected this a great while, and I believe it will please you to know that I yesterday made the same discovery in your lover.' This, I confess to you, was more than I could well bear, and I begged her to say no more to me at that time on that subject. 'Nay, child,' answered she, 'I must tell you all, or I should not act a friendly part. Mr. Bennet, I am convinced, hath a passion for you; but it is a passion which, I think, you should not encourage. For, to be plain with you, I fear he is in love with your person only. Now this is a love, child, which cannot produce that rational happiness which a woman of sense ought to expect.' In short, she ran on with a great deal of stuff about rational happiness, and women of sense, and concluded with assuring me that, after the strictest scrutiny, she could not find that Mr. Bennet had an adequate opinion of my understanding; upon which she vouchsafed to make me many compliments, but mixed with several sarcasms concerning my learning.

"I hope, madam, however," said she to Amelia, "you have not so bad an opinion of my capacity as to imagine me dull enough to be offended with Mr. Bennet's sentiments, for which I presently knew so well to account. I was, indeed, charmed with his ingenuity, who had discovered, perhaps, the only way of reconciling my aunt to those inclinations which I now assured myself he had for me.

"I was not long left to support my hopes by my sagacity. He soon found an opportunity of declaring his passion. He did this in so forcible though gentle a manner, with such a profusion of fervency and tenderness at once, that his love, like a torrent, bore everything before it; and I am almost ashamed to own to you how very soon he prevailed upon me to—to—in short, to be an honest woman, and to confess to him the plain truth.

"When we were upon a good footing together he gave me a long relation of what had past at several interviews with my aunt, at which I had not been present. He said he had discovered that, as she valued herself chiefly on her understanding, so she was extremely jealous of mine, and hated me on account of my learning. That, as he had loved me passionately from his first seeing me, and had thought of nothing from that time but of throwing himself at my feet, he saw no way so open to propitiate my aunt as that which he had taken by commending my beauty, a perfection to which she had long resigned all claim, at the expense of my understanding, in which he lamented my deficiency to a degree almost of ridicule. This he imputed chiefly to my learning; on this occasion he advanced a sentiment which so pleased my aunt that she thought proper to make it her own; for I heard it afterwards more than once from her own mouth. Learning, he said, had the same effect on the mind that strong liquors have on the constitution; both tending to eradicate all our natural fire and energy. His flattery had made such a dupe of my aunt that she assented, without the least suspicion of his sincerity, to all he said; so sure is vanity to weaken every fortress of the understanding, and to betray us to every attack of the enemy.

"You will believe, madam, that I readily forgave him all he had said, not only from that motive which I have mentioned, but as I was assured he had spoke the reverse of his real sentiments. I was not, however, quite so well pleased with my aunt, who began to treat me as if I was really an idiot. Her contempt, I own, a little piqued me; and I could not help often expressing my resentment, when we were alone together, to Mr. Bennet, who never failed to gratify me by making her conceit the subject of his wit; a talent which he possessed in the most extraordinary degree.

"This proved of very fatal consequence; for one day, while we were enjoying my aunt in a very thick arbour in the garden, she stole upon us unobserved, and overheard our whole conversation. I wish, my dear, you understood Latin, that I might repeat you a sentence in which the rage of a tigress that hath lost her young is described. No English poet, as I remember, hath come up to it; nor am I myself equal to the undertaking. She burst in upon us, open-mouthed, and after discharging every abusive word almost, in the only language she understood, on poor Mr. Bennet, turned us both out of doors, declaring she would send my rags after me, but would never more permit me to set my foot within her threshold.

"Consider, dear madam, to what a wretched condition we were now reduced. I had not yet received the small legacy left me by my father; nor was Mr. Bennet master of five pounds in the whole world.

"In this situation, the man I doated on to distraction had but little difficulty to persuade me to a proposal which, indeed, I thought generous in him to make, as it seemed to proceed from that tenderness for my reputation to which he ascribed it; indeed, it could proceed from no motive with which I should have been displeased. In a word, within two days we were man and wife.

"Mr. Bennet now declared himself the happiest of men; and, for my part, I sincerely declared I envied no woman upon earth. How little, alas! did I then know or suspect the price I was to pay for all my joys! A match of real love is, indeed, truly paradise; and such perfect happiness seems to be the forbidden fruit to mortals, which we are to lament having tasted during the rest of our lives.

"The first uneasiness which attacked us after our marriage was on my aunt's account. It was very disagreeable to live under the nose of so near a relation, who did not acknowledge us, but on the contrary, was ever doing us all the ill turns in her power, and making a party against us in the parish, which is always easy enough to do amongst the vulgar against persons who are their superiors in rank, and, at the same time, their inferiors in fortune. This made Mr. Bennet think of procuring an exchange, in which intention he was soon after confirmed by the arrival of the rector. It was the rector's custom to spend three months every year at his living, for which purpose he reserved an apartment in his parsonage-house, which was full large enough for two such little families as then occupied it. We at first promised ourselves some little convenience from his boarding with us; and Mr. Bennet began to lay aside his thoughts of leaving his curacy, at least for some time. But these golden ideas presently vanished; for, though we both used our utmost endeavours to please him, we soon found the impossibility of succeeding. He was, indeed, to give you his character in a word, the most peevish of mortals. This temper, notwithstanding that he was both a good and a pious man, made his company so insufferable that nothing could compensate it. If his breakfast was not ready to a moment—if a dish of meat was too much or too little done—in short, if anything failed of exactly hitting his taste, he was sure to be out of humour all that day, so that, indeed, he was scarce ever in a good temper a whole day together; for fortune seems to take a delight in thwarting this kind of disposition, to which human life, with its many crosses and accidents, is, in truth, by no means fitted.

"Mr. Bennet was now, by my desire as well as his own, determined to quit the parish; but when he attempted to get an exchange, he found it a matter of more difficulty than he had apprehended; for the rector's temper was so well known among the neighbouring clergy, that none of them could be brought to think of spending three months in a year with him.

"After many fruitless enquiries, Mr. Bennet thought best to remove to London, the great mart of all affairs, ecclesiastical and civil. This project greatly pleased him, and he resolved, without more delay, to take his leave of the rector, which he did in the most friendly manner possible, and preached his farewell sermon; nor was there a dry eye in the church, except among the few, whom my aunt, who remained still inexorable, had prevailed upon to hate us without any cause.

"To London we came, and took up our lodging the first night at the inn where the stage-

coach set us down: the next morning my husband went out early on his business, and returned with the good news of having heard of a curacy, and of having equipped himself with a lodging in the neighbourhood of a worthy peer, 'who,' said he, 'was my fellow-collegiate; and, what is more, I have a direction to a person who will advance your legacy at a very reasonable rate.'

"This last particular was extremely agreeable to me, for our last guinea was now broached; and the rector had lent my husband ten pounds to pay his debts in the country, for, with all his peevishness, he was a good and a generous man, and had, indeed, so many valuable qualities, that I lamented his temper, after I knew him thoroughly, as much on his account as on my own.

"We now quitted the inn and went to our lodgings, where my husband having placed me in safety, as he said, he went about the business of the legacy with good assurance of success.

"My husband returned elated with his success, the person to whom he applied having undertaken to advance the legacy, which he fulfilled as soon as the proper enquiries could be made, and proper instruments prepared for that purpose.

"This, however, took up so much time, that, as our fund was so very low, we were reduced to some distress, and obliged to live extremely penurious; nor would all do without my taking a most disagreeable way of procuring money by pawning one of my gowns.

"Mr. Bennet was now settled in a curacy in town, greatly to his satisfaction, and our affairs seemed to have a prosperous aspect, when he came home to me one morning in much apparent disorder, looking as pale as death, and begged me by some means or other to get him a dram, for that he was taken with a sudden faintness and lowness of spirits.

"Frighted as I was, I immediately ran downstairs, and procured some rum of the mistress of the house; the first time, indeed, I ever knew him drink any. When he came to himself he begged me not to be alarmed, for it was no distemper, but something that had vexed him, which had caused his disorder, which he had now perfectly recovered.

"He then told me the whole affair. He had hitherto deferred paying a visit to the lord whom I mentioned to have been formerly his fellow-collegiate, and was now his neighbour, till he could put himself in decent rigging. He had now purchased a new cassock, hat, and wig, and went to pay his respects to his old acquaintance, who had received from him many civilities and assistances in his learning at the university, and had promised to return them fourfold hereafter.

"It was not without some difficulty that Mr. Bennet got into the antechamber. Here he waited, or as the phrase is, cooled his heels, for above an hour before he saw his lordship; nor had he seen him then but by an accident; for my lord was going out when he casually intercepted him in his passage to his chariot. He approached to salute him with some familiarity, though with respect, depending on his former intimacy, when my lord, stepping short, very gravely told him he had not the pleasure of knowing him. How! my lord, said he, can you have so soon forgot your old acquaintance Tom Bennet? O, Mr. Bennet! cries his lordship, with much reserve, is it you? you will pardon my memory. I am glad to see you, Mr. Bennet, but you must excuse me at present, for I am in very great haste. He then broke from him, and without more ceremony, or any further invitation, went directly into his chariot.

"This cold reception from a person for whom my husband had a real friendship, and from whom he had great reason to expect a very warm return of affection, so affected the poor man, that it caused all those symptoms which I have mentioned before.

"Though this incident produced no material consequence, I could not pass it over in silence, as, of all the misfortunes which ever befel him, it affected my husband the most. I need not, however, to a woman of your delicacy, make any comments on a behaviour which, though I believe it is very common, is, nevertheless, cruel and base beyond description, and is diametrically opposite to true honour as well as to goodness.

"To relieve the uneasiness which my husband felt on account of his false friend, I prevailed with him to go every night, almost for a fortnight together, to the play; a diversion of which he was greatly fond, and from which he did not think his being a clergyman excluded him; indeed, it is very well if those austere persons who would be inclined to censure him on this head have themselves no greater sins to answer for.

"From this time, during three months, we past our time very agreeably, a little too agreeably perhaps for our circumstances; for, however innocent diversions may be in other respects, they must be owned to be expensive. When you consider then, madam, that our income from the curacy was less than forty pounds a year, and that, after payment of the debt to the rector, and

another to my aunt, with the costs in law which she had occasioned by suing for it, my legacy was reduced to less than seventy pounds, you will not wonder that, in diversions, cloaths, and the common expenses of life, we had almost consumed our whole stock.

"The inconsiderate manner in which we had lived for some time will, I doubt not, appear to you to want some excuse; but I have none to make for it. Two things, however, now happened, which occasioned much serious reflexion to Mr. Bennet; the one was, that I grew near my time; the other, that he now received a letter from Oxford, demanding the debt of forty pounds which I mentioned to you before. The former of these he made a pretence of obtaining a delay for the payment of the latter, promising, in two months, to pay off half the debt, by which means he obtained a forbearance during that time.

"I was now delivered of a son, a matter which should in reality have encreased our concern, but, on the contrary, it gave us great pleasure; greater indeed could not have been conceived at the birth of an heir to the most plentiful estate: so entirely thoughtless were we, and so little forecast had we of those many evils and distresses to which we had rendered a human creature, and one so dear to us, liable. The day of a christening is, in all families, I believe, a day of jubilee and rejoicing; and yet, if we consider the interest of that little wretch who is the occasion, how very little reason would the most sanguine persons have for their joy!

"But, though our eyes were too weak to look forward, for the sake of our child, we could not be blinded to those dangers that immediately threatened ourselves. Mr. Bennet, at the expiration of the two months, received a second letter from Oxford, in a very peremptory stile, and threatening a suit without any farther delay. This alarmed us in the strongest manner; and my husband, to secure his liberty, was advised for a while to shelter himself in the verge of the court.

"And, now, madam, I am entering on that scene which directly leads to all my misery."—Here she stopped, and wiped her eyes; and then, begging Amelia to excuse her for a few minutes, ran hastily out of the room, leaving Amelia by herself, while she refreshed her spirits with a cordial to enable her to relate what follows in the next chapter.

Chapter vi. — Farther continued.

Mrs. Bennet, returning into the room, made a short apology for her absence, and then proceeded in these words:

"We now left our lodging, and took a second floor in that very house where you now are, to which we were recommended by the woman where we had before lodged, for the mistresses of both houses were acquainted; and, indeed, we had been all at the play together. To this new lodging then (such was our wretched destiny) we immediately repaired, and were received by Mrs. Ellison (how can I bear the sound of that detested name?) with much civility; she took care, however, during the first fortnight of our residence, to wait upon us every Monday morning for her rent; such being, it seems, the custom of this place, which, as it was inhabited chiefly by persons in debt, is not the region of credit.

"My husband, by the singular goodness of the rector, who greatly compassionated his case, was enabled to continue in his curacy, though he could only do the duty on Sundays. He was, however, sometimes obliged to furnish a person to officiate at his expence; so that our income was very scanty, and the poor little remainder of the legacy being almost spent, we were reduced to some difficulties, and, what was worse, saw still a prospect of greater before our eyes.

"Under these circumstances, how agreeable to poor Mr. Bennet must have been the behaviour of Mrs. Ellison, who, when he carried her her rent on the usual day, told him, with a benevolent smile, that he needed not to give himself the trouble of such exact punctuality. She added that, if it was at any time inconvenient to him, he might pay her when he pleased. 'To say the truth,' says she, 'I never was so much pleased with any lodgers in my life; I am convinced, Mr. Bennet, you are a very worthy man, and you are a very happy one too; for you have the prettiest wife and the prettiest child I ever saw' These, dear madam, were the words she was pleased to make use of: and I am sure she behaved to me with such an appearance of friendship and

affection, that, as I could not perceive any possible views of interest which she could have in her professions, I easily believed them real.

"There lodged in the same house—O, Mrs. Booth! the blood runs cold to my heart, and should run cold to yours, when I name him—there lodged in the same house a lord—the lord, indeed, whom I have since seen in your company. This lord, Mrs. Ellison told me, had taken a great fancy to my little Charley. Fool that I was, and blinded by my own passion, which made me conceive that an infant, not three months old, could be really the object of affection to any besides a parent, and more especially to a gay young fellow! But, if I was silly in being deceived, how wicked was the wretch who deceived me—who used such art, and employed such pains, such incredible pains, to deceive me! He acted the part of a nurse to my little infant; he danced it, he lulled it, he kissed it; declared it was the very picture of a nephew of his—his favourite sister's child; and said so many kind and fond things of its beauty, that I myself, though, I believe, one of the tenderest and fondest of mothers, scarce carried my own ideas of my little darling's perfection beyond the compliments which he paid it.

"My lord, however, perhaps from modesty, before my face, fell far short of what Mrs. Ellison reported from him. And now, when she found the impression which was made on me by these means, she took every opportunity of insinuating to me his lordship's many virtues, his great goodness to his sister's children in particular; nor did she fail to drop some hints which gave me the most simple and groundless hopes of strange consequences from his fondness to my Charley.

"When, by these means, which, simple as they may appear, were, perhaps, the most artful, my lord had gained something more, I think, than my esteem, he took the surest method to confirm himself in my affection. This was, by professing the highest friendship for my husband; for, as to myself, I do assure you he never shewed me more than common respect; and I hope you will believe I should have immediately startled and flown off if he had. Poor I accounted for all the friendship which he expressed for my husband, and all the fondness which he shewed to my boy, from the great prettiness of the one and the great merit of the other; foolishly conceiving that others saw with my eyes and felt with my heart. Little did I dream that my own unfortunate person was the fountain of all this lord's goodness, and was the intended price of it.

"One evening, as I was drinking tea with Mrs. Ellison by my lord's fire (a liberty which she never scrupled taking when he was gone out), my little Charley, now about half a year old, sitting in her lap, my lord—accidentally, no doubt, indeed I then thought it so—came in. I was confounded, and offered to go; but my lord declared, if he disturbed Mrs. Ellison's company, as he phrased it, he would himself leave the room. When I was thus prevailed on to keep my seat, my lord immediately took my little baby into his lap, and gave it some tea there, not a little at the expense of his embroidery; for he was very richly drest; indeed, he was as fine a figure as perhaps ever was seen. His behaviour on this occasion gave me many ideas in his favour. I thought he discovered good sense, good nature, condescension, and other good qualities, by the fondness he shewed to my child, and the contempt he seemed to express for his finery, which so greatly became him; for I cannot deny but that he was the handsomest and genteelest person in the world, though such considerations advanced him not a step in my favour.

"My husband now returned from church (for this happened on a Sunday), and was, by my lord's particular desire, ushered into the room. My lord received him with the utmost politeness, and with many professions of esteem, which, he said, he had conceived from Mrs. Ellison's representations of his merit. He then proceeded to mention the living which was detained from my husband, of which Mrs. Ellison had likewise informed him; and said, he thought it would be no difficult matter to obtain a restoration of it by the authority of the bishop, who was his particular friend, and to whom he would take an immediate opportunity of mentioning it. This, at last, he determined to do the very next day, when he invited us both to dinner, where we were to be acquainted with his lordship's success.

"My lord now insisted on my husband's staying supper with him, without taking any notice of me; but Mrs. Ellison declared he should not part man and wife, and that she herself would stay with me. The motion was too agreeable to me to be rejected; and, except the little time I retired to put my child to bed, we spent together the most agreeable evening imaginable; nor was it, I believe, easy to decide whether Mr. Bennet or myself were most delighted with his lordship and Mrs. Ellison; but this, I assure you, the generosity of the one, and the extreme civility and kindness of the other, were the subjects of our conversation all the ensuing night, during which we neither

of us closed our eyes.

"The next day at dinner my lord acquainted us that he had prevailed with the bishop to write to the clergyman in the country; indeed, he told us that he had engaged the bishop to be very warm in our interest, and had not the least doubt of success. This threw us both into a flow of spirits; and in the afternoon Mr. Bennet, at Mrs. Ellison's request, which was seconded by his lordship, related the history of our lives from our first acquaintance. My lord seemed much affected with some tender scenes, which, as no man could better feel, so none could better describe, than my husband. When he had finished, my lord begged pardon for mentioning an occurrence which gave him such a particular concern, as it had disturbed that delicious state of happiness in which we had lived at our former lodging. 'It would be ungenerous,' said he, 'to rejoice at an accident, which, though it brought me fortunately acquainted with two of the most agreeable people in the world, was yet at the expense of your mutual felicity. The circumstance, I mean, is your debt at Oxford; pray, how doth that stand? I am resolved it shall never disturb your happiness hereafter.' At these words the tears burst from my poor husband's eyes; and, in an ecstasy of gratitude, he cried out, 'Your lordship overcomes me with generosity. If you go on in this manner, both my wife's gratitude and mine must be bankrupt' He then acquainted my lord with the exact state of the case, and received assurances from him that the debt should never trouble him. My husband was again breaking out into the warmest expressions of gratitude, but my lord stopt him short, saying, 'If you have any obligation, it is to my little Charley here, from whose little innocent smiles I have received more than the value of this trifling debt in pleasure.' I forgot to tell you that, when I offered to leave the room after dinner upon my child's account, my lord would not suffer me, but ordered the child to be brought to me. He now took it out of my arms, placed it upon his own knee, and fed it with some fruit from the dessert. In short, it would be more tedious to you than to myself to relate the thousand little tendernesses he shewed to the child. He gave it many baubles; amongst the rest was a coral worth at least three pounds; and, when my husband was confined near a fortnight to his chamber with a cold, he visited the child every day (for to this infant's account were all the visits placed), and seldom failed of accompanying his visit with a present to the little thing.

"Here, Mrs. Booth, I cannot help mentioning a doubt which hath often arisen in my mind since I have been enough mistress of myself to reflect on this horrid train which was laid to blow up my innocence. Wicked and barbarous it was to the highest degree without any question; but my doubt is, whether the art or folly of it be the more conspicuous; for, however delicate and refined the art must be allowed to have been, the folly, I think, must upon a fair examination appear no less astonishing: for to lay all considerations of cruelty and crime out of the case, what a foolish bargain doth the man make for himself who purchases so poor a pleasure at so high a price!

"We had lived near three weeks with as much freedom as if we had been all of the same family, when, one afternoon, my lord proposed to my husband to ride down himself to solicit the surrender; for he said the bishop had received an unsatisfactory answer from the parson, and had writ a second letter more pressing, which his lordship now promised us to strengthen by one of his own that my husband was to carry with him. Mr. Bennet agreed to this proposal with great thankfulness, and the next day was appointed for his journey. The distance was near seventy miles.

"My husband set out on his journey, and he had scarce left me before Mrs. Ellison came into my room, and endeavoured to comfort me in his absence; to say the truth, though he was to be from me but a few days, and the purpose of his going was to fix our happiness on a sound foundation for all our future days, I could scarce support my spirits under this first separation. But though I then thought Mrs. Ellison's intentions to be most kind and friendly, yet the means she used were utterly ineffectual, and appeared to me injudicious. Instead of soothing my uneasiness, which is always the first physic to be given to grief, she rallied me upon it, and began to talk in a very unusual stile of gaiety, in which she treated conjugal love with much ridicule.

"I gave her to understand that she displeased me by this discourse; but she soon found means to give such a turn to it as made a merit of all she had said. And now, when she had worked me into a good humour, she made a proposal to me which I at first rejected—but at last fatally, too fatally, suffered myself to be over-persuaded. This was to go to a masquerade at Ranelagh, for which my lord had furnished her with tickets."

At these words Amelia turned pale as death, and hastily begged her friend to give her a glass

of water, some air, or anything. Mrs. Bennet, having thrown open the window, and procured the water, which prevented Amelia from fainting, looked at her with much tenderness, and cried, "I do not wonder, my dear madam, that you are affected with my mentioning that fatal masquerade; since I firmly believe the same ruin was intended for you at the same place; the apprehension of which occasioned the letter I sent you this morning, and all the trial of your patience which I have made since."

Amelia gave her a tender embrace, with many expressions of the warmest gratitude; assured her she had pretty well recovered her spirits, and begged her to continue her story, which Mrs. Bennet then did. However, as our readers may likewise be glad to recover their spirits also, we shall here put an end to this chapter.

Chapter vii. — The story farther continued.

Mrs. Bennet proceeded thus:

"I was at length prevailed on to accompany Mrs. Ellison to the masquerade. Here, I must confess, the pleasantness of the place, the variety of the dresses, and the novelty of the thing, gave me much delight, and raised my fancy to the highest pitch. As I was entirely void of all suspicion, my mind threw off all reserve, and pleasure only filled my thoughts. Innocence, it is true, possessed my heart; but it was innocence unguarded, intoxicated with foolish desires, and liable to every temptation. During the first two hours we had many trifling adventures not worth remembering. At length my lord joined us, and continued with me all the evening; and we danced several dances together.

"I need not, I believe, tell you, madam, how engaging his conversation is. I wish I could with truth say I was not pleased with it; or, at least, that I had a right to be pleased with it. But I will disguise nothing from you. I now began to discover that he had some affection for me, but he had already too firm a footing in my esteem to make the discovery shocking. I will—I will own the truth; I was delighted with perceiving a passion in him, which I was not unwilling to think he had had from the beginning, and to derive his having concealed it so long from his awe of my virtue, and his respect to my understanding. I assure you, madam, at the same time, my intentions were never to exceed the bounds of innocence. I was charmed with the delicacy of his passion; and, in the foolish thoughtless turn of mind in which I then was, I fancied I might give some very distant encouragement to such a passion in such a man with the utmost safety—that I might indulge my vanity and interest at once, without being guilty of the least injury.

"I know Mrs. Booth will condemn all these thoughts, and I condemn them no less myself; for it is now my stedfast opinion that the woman who gives up the least outwork of her virtue doth, in that very moment, betray the citadel.

"About two o'clock we returned home, and found a very handsome collation provided for us. I was asked to partake of it, and I did not, I could not refuse. I was not, however, entirely void of all suspicion, and I made many resolutions; one of which was, not to drink a drop more than my usual stint. This was, at the utmost, little more than half a pint of small punch.

"I adhered strictly to my quantity; but in the quality I am convinced I was deceived; for before I left the room I found my head giddy. What the villain gave me I know not; but, besides being intoxicated, I perceived effects from it which are not to be described.

"Here, madam, I must draw a curtain over the residue of that fatal night. Let it suffice that it involved me in the most dreadful ruin; a ruin to which I can truly say I never consented, and of which I was scarce conscious when the villanous man avowed it to my face in the morning.

"Thus I have deduced my story to the most horrid period; happy had I been had this been the period of my life, but I was reserved for greater miseries; but before I enter on them I will mention something very remarkable, with which I was now acquainted, and that will shew there was nothing of accident which had befallen me, but that all was the effect of a long, regular, premeditated design.

"You may remember, madam, I told you that we were recommended to Mrs. Ellison by the

woman at whose house we had before lodged. This woman, it seems, was one of my lord's pimps, and had before introduced me to his lordship's notice.

"You are to know then, madam, that this villain, this lord, now confest to me that he had first seen me in the gallery at the oratorio, whither I had gone with tickets with which the woman where I first lodged had presented me, and which were, it seems, purchased by my lord. Here I first met the vile betrayer, who was disguised in a rug coat and a patch upon his face."

At these words Amelia cried, "O, gracious heavens!" and fell back in her chair. Mrs. Bennet, with proper applications, brought her back to life; and then Amelia acquainted her that she herself had first seen the same person in the same place, and in the same disguise. "O, Mrs. Bennet!" cried she, "how am I indebted to you! what words, what thanks, what actions can demonstrate the gratitude of my sentiments! I look upon you, and always shall look upon you, as my preserver from the brink of a precipice, from which I was falling into the same ruin which you have so generously, so kindly, and so nobly disclosed for my sake."

Here the two ladies compared notes; and it appeared that his lordship's behaviour at the oratorio had been alike to both; that he had made use of the very same words, the very same actions to Amelia, which he had practised over before on poor unfortunate Mrs. Bennet. It may, perhaps, be thought strange that neither of them could afterwards recollect him; but so it was. And, indeed, if we consider the force of disguise, the very short time that either of them was with him at this first interview, and the very little curiosity that must have been supposed in the minds of the ladies, together with the amusement in which they were then engaged, all wonder will, I apprehend, cease. Amelia, however, now declared she remembered his voice and features perfectly well, and was thoroughly satisfied he was the same person. She then accounted for his not having visited in the afternoon, according to his promise, from her declared resolutions to Mrs. Ellison not to see him. She now burst forth into some very satirical invectives against that lady, and declared she had the art, as well as the wickedness, of the devil himself.

Many congratulations now past from Mrs. Bennet to Amelia, which were returned with the most hearty acknowledgments from that lady. But, instead of filling our paper with these, we shall pursue Mrs. Bennet's story, which she resumed as we shall find in the next chapter.

Chapter viii. — Further continuation.

"No sooner," said Mrs. Bennet, continuing her story, "was my lord departed, than Mrs. Ellison came to me. She behaved in such a manner, when she became acquainted with what had past, that, though I was at first satisfied of her guilt, she began to stagger my opinion, and at length prevailed upon me entirely to acquit her. She raved like a mad woman against my lord, swore he should not stay a moment in her house, and that she would never speak to him more. In short, had she been the most innocent woman in the world, she could not have spoke nor acted any otherwise, nor could she have vented more wrath and indignation against the betrayer.

"That part of her denunciation of vengeance which concerned my lord's leaving the house she vowed should be executed immediately; but then, seeming to recollect herself, she said, 'Consider, my dear child, it is for your sake alone I speak; will not such a proceeding give some suspicion to your husband?' I answered, that I valued not that; that I was resolved to inform my husband of all the moment I saw him; with many expressions of detestation of myself and an indifference for life and for everything else.

"Mrs. Ellison, however, found means to soothe me, and to satisfy me with my own innocence, a point in which, I believe, we are all easily convinced. In short, I was persuaded to acquit both myself and her, to lay the whole guilt upon my lord, and to resolve to conceal it from my husband.

"That whole day I confined myself to my chamber and saw no person but Mrs. Ellison. I was, indeed, ashamed to look any one in the face. Happily for me, my lord went into the country without attempting to come near me, for I believe his sight would have driven me to madness.

"The next day I told Mrs. Ellison that I was resolved to leave her lodgings the moment my

lord came to town; not on her account (for I really inclined to think her innocent), but on my lord's, whose face I was resolved, if possible, never more to behold. She told me I had no reason to quit her house on that score, for that my lord himself had left her lodgings that morning in resentment, she believed, of the abuses which she had cast on him the day before.

"This confirmed me in the opinion of her innocence; nor hath she from that day to this, till my acquaintance with you, madam, done anything to forfeit my opinion. On the contrary, I owe her many good offices; amongst the rest, I have an annuity of one hundred and fifty pounds a-year from my lord, which I know was owing to her solicitations, for she is not void of generosity or good-nature; though by what I have lately seen, I am convinced she was the cause of my ruin, and hath endeavoured to lay the same snares for you.

"But to return to my melancholy story. My husband returned at the appointed time; and I met him with an agitation of mind not to be described. Perhaps the fatigue which he had undergone in his journey, and his dissatisfaction at his ill success, prevented his taking notice of what I feared was too visible. All his hopes were entirely frustrated; the clergyman had not received the bishop's letter, and as to my lord's he treated it with derision and contempt. Tired as he was, Mr. Bennet would not sit down till he had enquired for my lord, intending to go and pay his compliments. Poor man! he little suspected that he had deceived him, as I have since known, concerning the bishop; much less did he suspect any other injury. But the lord—the villain was gone out of town, so that he was forced to postpone all his gratitude.

"Mr. Bennet returned to town late on the Saturday night, nevertheless he performed his duty at church the next day, but I refused to go with him. This, I think, was the first refusal I was guilty of since our marriage; but I was become so miserable, that his presence, which had been the source of all my happiness, was become my bane. I will not say I hated to see him, but I can say I was ashamed, indeed afraid, to look him in the face. I was conscious of I knew not what—guilt I hope it cannot be called."

"I hope not, nay, I think not," cries Amelia.

"My husband," continued Mrs. Bennet, "perceived my dissatisfaction, and imputed it to his ill-success in the country. I was pleased with this self-delusion, and yet, when I fairly compute the agonies I suffered at his endeavours to comfort me on that head, I paid most severely for it. O, my dear Mrs. Booth! happy is the deceived party between true lovers, and wretched indeed is the author of the deceit!

"In this wretched condition I passed a whole week, the most miserable I think of my whole life, endeavouring to humour my husband's delusion and to conceal my own tortures; but I had reason to fear I could not succeed long, for on the Saturday night I perceived a visible alteration in his behaviour to me. He went to bed in an apparent ill-humour, turned sullenly from me, and if I offered at any endearments he gave me only peevish answers.

"After a restless turbulent night, he rose early on Sunday morning and walked down-stairs. I expected his return to breakfast, but was soon informed by the maid that he was gone forth, and that it was no more than seven o'clock. All this you may believe, madam, alarmed me. I saw plainly he had discovered the fatal secret, though by what means I could not divine. The state of my mind was very little short of madness. Sometimes I thought of running away from my injured husband, and sometimes of putting an end to my life.

"In the midst of such perturbations I spent the day. My husband returned in the evening. O, Heavens! can I describe what followed?—It is impossible! I shall sink under the relation. He entered the room with a face as white as a sheet, his lips trembling and his eyes red as coals of fire starting as it were from his head.—'Molly,' cries he, throwing himself into his chair, 'are you well?' 'Good Heavens!' says I, 'what's the matter?—Indeed I can't say I am well.' 'No!' says he, starting from his chair, 'false monster, you have betrayed me, destroyed me, you have ruined your husband!' Then looking like a fury, he snatched off a large book from the table, and, with the malice of a madman, threw it at my head and knocked me down backwards. He then caught me up in his arms and kissed me with most extravagant tenderness; then, looking me stedfastly in the face for several moments, the tears gushed in a torrent from his eyes, and with his utmost violence he threw me again on the floor, kicked me, stamped upon me. I believe, indeed, his intent was to kill me, and I believe he thought he had accomplished it.

"I lay on the ground for some minutes, I believe, deprived of my senses. When I recovered myself I found my husband lying by my side on his face, and the blood running from him. It

seems, when he thought he had despatched me, he ran his head with all his force against a chest of drawers which stood in the room, and gave himself a dreadful wound in his head.

"I can truly say I felt not the least resentment for the usage I had received; I thought I deserved it all; though, indeed, I little guessed what he had suffered from me. I now used the most earnest entreaties to him to compose himself; and endeavoured, with my feeble arms, to raise him from the ground. At length he broke from me, and, springing from the ground, flung himself into a chair, when, looking wildly at me, he cried—'Go from me, Molly. I beseech you, leave me. I would not kill you.'—He then discovered to me—O Mrs. Booth! can you not guess it?—I was indeed polluted by the villain—I had infected my husband.—O heavens! why do I live to relate anything so horrid—I will not, I cannot yet survive it. I cannot forgive myself. Heaven cannot forgive me!"

Here she became inarticulate with the violence of her grief, and fell presently into such agonies, that the frighted Amelia began to call aloud for some assistance. Upon this a maid-servant came up, who, seeing her mistress in a violent convulsion fit, presently screamed out she was dead. Upon which one of the other sex made his appearance: and who should this be but the honest serjeant? whose countenance soon made it evident that, though a soldier, and a brave one too, he was not the least concerned of all the company on this occasion.

The reader, if he hath been acquainted with scenes of this kind, very well knows that Mrs. Bennet, in the usual time, returned again to the possession of her voice: the first use of which she made was to express her astonishment at the presence of the serjeant, and, with a frantic air, to enquire who he was.

The maid, concluding that her mistress was not yet returned to her senses, answered, "Why, 'tis my master, madam. Heaven preserve your senses, madam!—Lord, sir, my mistress must be very bad not to know you!"

What Atkinson thought at this instant, I will not say; but certain it is he looked not over-wise. He attempted twice to take hold of Mrs. Bennet's hand, but she withdrew it hastily, and presently after, rising up from her chair, she declared herself pretty well again, and desired Atkinson and the maid to withdraw. Both of whom presently obeyed: the serjeant appearing by his countenance to want comfort almost as much as the lady did to whose assistance he had been summoned,

It is a good maxim to trust a person entirely or not at all; for a secret is often innocently blabbed out by those who know but half of it. Certain it is that the maid's speech communicated a suspicion to the mind of Amelia which the behaviour of the serjeant did not tend to remove: what that is, the sagacious readers may likewise probably suggest to themselves; if not, they must wait our time for disclosing it. We shall now resume the history of Mrs. Bennet, who, after many apologies, proceeded to the matters in the next chapter.

Chapter ix. — The conclusion of Mrs. Bennet's history.

"When I became sensible," cries Mrs. Bennet, "of the injury I had done my husband, I threw myself at his feet, and embracing his knees, while I bathed them with my tears, I begged a patient hearing, declaring, if he was not satisfied with what I should say, I would become a willing victim of his resentment, I said, and I said truly, that, if I owed my death that instant to his hands, I should have no other terrour but of the fatal consequence which it might produce to himself.

"He seemed a little pacified, and bid me say whatever I pleased.

"I then gave him a faithful relation of all that had happened. He heard me with great attention, and at the conclusion cried, with a deep sigh—'O Molly! I believe it all.—You must have been betrayed as you tell me; you could not be guilty of such baseness, such cruelty, such ingratitude.' He then—O! it is impossible to describe his behaviour—he exprest such kindness, such tenderness, such concern for the manner in which he had used me—I cannot dwell on this scene—I shall relapse—you must excuse me."

Amelia begged her to omit anything which so affected her; and she proceeded thus: "My

husband, who was more convinced than I was of Mrs. Ellison's guilt, declared he would not sleep that night in her house. He then went out to see for a lodging; he gave me all the money he had, and left me to pay her bill, and put up the cloaths, telling me, if I had not money enough, I might leave the cloaths as a pledge; but he vowed he could not answer for himself if he saw the face of Mrs. Ellison.

"Words cannot scarce express the behaviour of that artful woman, it was so kind and so generous. She said, she did not blame my husband's resentment, nor could she expect any other, but that he and all the world should censure her—that she hated her house almost as much as we did, and detested her cousin, if possible, more. In fine, she said I might leave my cloaths there that evening, but that she would send them to us the next morning; that she scorned the thought of detaining them; and as for the paultry debt, we might pay her whenever we pleased; for, to do her justice, with all her vices, she hath some good in her."

"Some good in her, indeed!" cried Amelia, with great indignation.

"We were scarce settled in our new lodgings," continued Mrs. Bennet, "when my husband began to complain of a pain in his inside. He told me he feared he had done himself some injury in his rage, and burst something within him. As to the odious—I cannot bear the thought, the great skill of his surgeon soon entirely cured him; but his other complaint, instead of yielding to any application, grew still worse and worse, nor ever ended till it brought him to his grave.

"O Mrs. Booth! could I have been certain that I had occasioned this, however innocently I had occasioned it, I could never have survived it; but the surgeon who opened him after his death assured me that he died of what they called a polypus in his heart, and that nothing which had happened on account of me was in the least the occasion of it.

"I have, however, related the affair truly to you. The first complaint I ever heard of the kind was within a day or two after we left Mrs. Ellison's; and this complaint remained till his death, which might induce him perhaps to attribute his death to another cause; but the surgeon, who is a man of the highest eminence, hath always declared the contrary to me, with the most positive certainty; and this opinion hath been my only comfort.

"When my husband died, which was about ten weeks after we quitted Mrs. Ellison's, of whom I had then a different opinion from what I have now, I was left in the most wretched condition imaginable. I believe, madam, she shewed you my letter. Indeed, she did everything for me at that time which I could have expected from the best of friends, She supplied me with money from her own pocket, by which means I was preserved from a distress in which I must have otherwise inevitably perished.

"Her kindness to me in this season of distress prevailed on me to return again to her house. Why, indeed, should I have refused an offer so very convenient for me to accept, and which seemed so generous in her to make? Here I lived a very retired life with my little babe, seeing no company but Mrs. Ellison herself for a full quarter of a year. At last Mrs. Ellison brought me a parchment from my lord, in which he had settled upon me, at her instance, as she told me, and as I believe it was, an annuity of one hundred and fifty pounds a-year. This was, I think, the very first time she had mentioned his hateful name to me since my return to her house. And she now prevailed upon me, though I assure you not without some difficulty, to suffer him to execute the deed in my presence.

"I will not describe our interview—I am not able to describe it, and I have often wondered how I found spirits to support it. This I will say for him, that, if he was not a real penitent, no man alive could act the part better.

"Beside resentment, I had another motive of my backwardness to agree to such a meeting; and this was—fear. I apprehended, and surely not without reason, that the annuity was rather meant as a bribe than a recompence, and that further designs were laid against my innocence; but in this I found myself happily deceived; for neither then, nor at any time since, have I ever had the least solicitation of that kind. Nor, indeed, have I seen the least occasion to think my lord had any such desires.

"Good heavens! what are these men? what is this appetite which must have novelty and resistance for its provocatives, and which is delighted with us no longer than while we may be considered in the light of enemies?"

"I thank you, madam," cries Amelia, "for relieving me from my fears on your account; I trembled at the consequence of this second acquaintance with such a man, and in such a

situation."

"I assure you, madam, I was in no danger," returned Mrs. Bennet; "for, besides that I think I could have pretty well relied on my own resolution, I have heard since, at St Edmundsbury, from an intimate acquaintance of my lord's, who was an entire stranger to my affairs, that the highest degree of inconstancy is his character; and that few of his numberless mistresses have ever received a second visit from him.

"Well, madam," continued she, "I think I have little more to trouble you with; unless I should relate to you my long ill state of health, from which I am lately, I thank Heaven, recovered; or unless I should mention to you the most grievous accident that ever befel me, the loss of my poor dear Charley." Here she made a full stop, and the tears ran down into her bosom.

Amelia was silent a few minutes, while she gave the lady time to vent her passion; after which she began to pour forth a vast profusion of acknowledgments for the trouble she had taken in relating her history, but chiefly for the motive which had induced her to it, and for the kind warning which she had given her by the little note which Mrs. Bennet had sent her that morning.

"Yes, madam," cries Mrs. Bennet, "I am convinced, by what I have lately seen, that you are the destined sacrifice to this wicked lord; and that Mrs. Ellison, whom I no longer doubt to have been the instrument of my ruin, intended to betray you in the same manner. The day I met my lord in your apartment I began to entertain some suspicions, and I took Mrs. Ellison very roundly to task upon them; her behaviour, notwithstanding many asseverations to the contrary, convinced me I was right; and I intended, more than once, to speak to you, but could not; till last night the mention of the masquerade determined me to delay it no longer. I therefore sent you that note this morning, and am glad you so luckily discovered the writer, as it hath given me this opportunity of easing my mind, and of honestly shewing you how unworthy I am of your friendship, at the same time that I so earnestly desire it."

Chapter x. — Being the last chapter of the seventh book.

Amelia did not fail to make proper compliments to Mrs. Bennet on the conclusion of her speech in the last chapter. She told her that, from the first moment of her acquaintance, she had the strongest inclination to her friendship, and that her desires of that kind were much increased by hearing her story. "Indeed, madam," says she, "you are much too severe a judge on yourself; for they must have very little candour, in my opinion, who look upon your case with any severe eye. To me, I assure you, you appear highly the object of compassion; and I shall always esteem you as an innocent and an unfortunate woman."

Amelia would then have taken her leave, but Mrs. Bennet so strongly pressed her to stay to breakfast, that at length she complied; indeed, she had fasted so long, and her gentle spirits had been so agitated with variety of passions, that nature very strongly seconded Mrs. Bennet's motion.

Whilst the maid was preparing the tea-equipage, Amelia, with a little slyness in her countenance, asked Mrs. Bennet if serjeant Atkinson did not lodge in the same house with her? The other reddened so extremely at the question, repeated the serjeant's name with such hesitation, and behaved so aukwardly, that Amelia wanted no further confirmation of her suspicions. She would not, however, declare them abruptly to the other, but began a dissertation on the serjeant's virtues; and, after observing the great concern which he had manifested when Mrs. Bennet was in her fit, concluded with saying she believed the serjeant would make the best husband in the world, for that he had great tenderness of heart and a gentleness of manners not often to be found in any man, and much seldomer in persons of his rank.

"And why not in his rank?" said Mrs. Bennet. "Indeed, Mrs. Booth, we rob the lower order of mankind of their due. I do not deny the force and power of education; but, when we consider how very injudicious is the education of the better sort in general, how little they are instructed in the practice of virtue, we shall not expect to find the heart much improved by it. And even as to the head, how very slightly do we commonly find it improved by what is called a genteel

education! I have myself, I think, seen instances of as great goodness, and as great understanding too, among the lower sort of people as among the higher. Let us compare your serjeant, now, with the lord who hath been the subject of conversation; on which side would an impartial judge decide the balance to incline?"

"How monstrous then," cries Amelia, "is the opinion of those who consider our matching ourselves the least below us in degree as a kind of contamination!"

"A most absurd and preposterous sentiment," answered Mrs. Bennet warmly; "how abhorrent from justice, from common sense, and from humanity—but how extremely incongruous with a religion which professes to know no difference of degree, but ranks all mankind on the footing of brethren! Of all kinds of pride, there is none so unchristian as that of station; in reality, there is none so contemptible. Contempt, indeed, may be said to be its own object; for my own part, I know none so despicable as those who despise others."

"I do assure you," said Amelia, "you speak my own sentiments. I give you my word, I should not be ashamed of being the wife of an honest man in any station.—Nor if I had been much higher than I was, should I have thought myself degraded by calling our honest serjeant my husband."

"Since you have made this declaration," cries Mrs. Bennet, "I am sure you will not be offended at a secret I am going to mention to you."

"Indeed, my dear," answered Amelia, smiling, "I wonder rather you have concealed it so long; especially after the many hints I have given you."

"Nay, pardon me, madam," replied the other; "I do not remember any such hints; and, perhaps, you do not even guess what I am going to say. My secret is this; that no woman ever had so sincere, so passionate a lover, as you have had in the serjeant."

"I a lover in the serjeant!—I!" cries Amelia, a little surprized.

"Have patience," answered the other;—"I say, you, my dear. As much surprized as you appear, I tell you no more than the truth; and yet it is a truth you could hardly expect to hear from me, especially with so much good-humour; since I will honestly confess to you.—But what need have I to confess what I know you guess already?—Tell me now sincerely, don't you guess?"

"I guess, indeed, and hope," said she, "that he is your husband."

"He is, indeed, my husband," cries the other; "and I am most happy in your approbation. In honest truth, you ought to approve my choice; since you was every way the occasion of my making it. What you said of him very greatly recommended him to my opinion; but he endeared himself to me most by what he said of you. In short, I have discovered that he hath always loved you with such a faithful, honest, noble, generous passion, that I was consequently convinced his mind must possess all the ingredients of such a passion; and what are these but true honour, goodness, modesty, bravery, tenderness, and, in a word, every human virtue?—Forgive me, my dear; but I was uneasy till I became myself the object of such a passion."

"And do you really think," said Amelia, smiling, "that I shall forgive you robbing me of such a lover? or, supposing what you banter me with was true, do you really imagine you could change such a passion?"

"No, my dear," answered the other; "I only hope I have changed the object; for be assured, there is no greater vulgar error than that it is impossible for a man who loves one woman ever to love another. On the contrary, it is certain that a man who can love one woman so well at a distance will love another better that is nearer to him. Indeed, I have heard one of the best husbands in the world declare, in the presence of his wife, that he had always loved a princess with adoration. These passions, which reside only in very amorous and very delicate minds, feed only on the delicacies there growing; and leave all the substantial food, and enough of the delicacy too, for the wife."

The tea being now ready, Mrs. Bennet, or, if you please, for the future, Mrs. Atkinson, proposed to call in her husband; but Amelia objected. She said she should be glad to see him any other time, but was then in the utmost hurry, as she had been three hours absent from all she most loved. However, she had scarce drank a dish of tea before she changed her mind; and, saying she would not part man and wife, desired Mr. Atkinson might appear.

The maid answered that her master was not at home; which words she had scarce spoken, when he knocked hastily at the door, and immediately came running into the room, all pale and breathless, and, addressing himself to Amelia, cried out, "I am sorry, my dear lady, to bring you ill

news; but Captain Booth"—"What! what!" cries Amelia, dropping the tea-cup from her hand, "is anything the matter with him?"—"Don't be frightened, my dear lady," said the serjeant: "he is in very good health; but a misfortune hath happened."—"Are my children well?" said Amelia.—"O, very well," answered the serjeant. "Pray, madam, don't be frightened; I hope it will signify nothing—he is arrested, but I hope to get him out of their damned hands immediately." "Where is he?" cries Amelia; "I will go to him this instant!" "He begs you will not," answered the serjeant. "I have sent his lawyer to him, and am going back with Mrs. Ellison this moment; but I beg your ladyship, for his sake, and for your own sake, not to go." "Mrs. Ellison! what is Mrs. Ellison to do?" cries Amelia: "I must and will go." Mrs. Atkinson then interposed, and begged that she would not hurry her spirits, but compose herself, and go home to her children, whither she would attend her. She comforted her with the thoughts that the captain was in no immediate danger; that she could go to him when she would; and desired her to let the serjeant return with Mrs. Ellison, saying she might be of service, and that there was much wisdom, and no kind of shame, in making use of bad people on certain occasions.

"And who," cries Amelia, a little come to herself, "hath done this barbarous action?"

"One I am ashamed to name," cries the serjeant; "indeed I had always a very different opinion of him: I could not have believed anything but my own ears and eyes; but Dr Harrison is the man who hath done the deed."

"Dr Harrison!" cries Amelia. "Well, then, there is an end of all goodness in the world. I will never have a good opinion of any human being more."

The serjeant begged that he might not be detained from the captain; and that, if Amelia pleased to go home, he would wait upon her. But she did not chuse to see Mrs. Ellison at this time; and, after a little consideration, she resolved to stay where she was; and Mrs. Atkinson agreed to go and fetch her children to her, it being not many doors distant.

The serjeant then departed; Amelia, in her confusion, never having once thought of wishing him joy on his marriage.

BOOK VIII.

Chapter i. — Being the first chapter of the eighth book.

The history must now look a little backwards to those circumstances which led to the catastrophe mentioned at the end of the last book.

When Amelia went out in the morning she left her children to the care of her husband. In this amiable office he had been engaged near an hour, and was at that very time lying along on the floor, and his little things crawling and playing about him, when a most violent knock was heard at the door; and immediately a footman, running upstairs, acquainted him that his lady was taken violently ill, and carried into Mrs. Chenevix's toy-shop.

Booth no sooner heard this account, which was delivered with great appearance of haste and earnestness, than he leapt suddenly from the floor, and, leaving his children, roaring at the news of their mother's illness, in strict charge with his maid, he ran as fast as his legs could carry him to the place; or towards the place rather: for, before he arrived at the shop, a gentleman stopt him full butt, crying, "Captain, whither so fast?"—Booth answered eagerly, "Whoever you are, friend, don't ask me any questions now."—"You must pardon me, captain," answered the gentleman; "but I have a little business with your honour—In short, captain, I have a small warrant here in my pocket against your honour, at the suit of one Dr Harrison." "You are a bailiff then?" says Booth. "I am an officer, sir," answered the other. "Well, sir, it is in vain to contend," cries Booth;

"but let me beg you will permit me only to step to Mrs. Chenevix's—I will attend you, upon my honour, wherever you please; but my wife lies violently ill there." "Oh, for that matter," answered the bailiff, "you may set your heart at ease. Your lady, I hope, is very well; I assure you she is not there. You will excuse me, captain, these are only stratagems of war. Bolus and virtus, quis in a hostess equirit?" "Sir, I honour your learning," cries Booth, "and could almost kiss you for what you tell me. I assure you I would forgive you five hundred arrests for such a piece of news. Well, sir, and whither am I to go with you?" "O, anywhere: where your honour pleases," cries the bailiff. "Then suppose we go to Brown's coffee-house," said the prisoner. "No," answered the bailiff, "that will not do; that's in the verge of the court." "Why then, to the nearest tavern," said Booth. "No, not to a tavern," cries the other, "that is not a place of security; and you know, captain, your honour is a shy cock; I have been after your honour these three months. Come, sir, you must go to my house, if you please." "With all my heart," answered Booth, "if it be anywhere hereabouts." "Oh, it is but a little ways off," replied the bailiff; "it is only in Gray's-inn-lane, just by almost." He then called a coach, and desired his prisoner to walk in.

Booth entered the coach without any resistance, which, had he been inclined to make, he must have plainly perceived would have been ineffectual, as the bailiff appeared to have several followers at hand, two of whom, beside the commander in chief, mounted with him into the coach. As Booth was a sweet-tempered man, as well as somewhat of a philosopher, he behaved with all the good-humour imaginable, and indeed, with more than his companions; who, however, shewed him what they call civility, that is, they neither struck him nor spit in his face.

Notwithstanding the pleasantry which Booth endeavoured to preserve, he in reality envied every labourer whom he saw pass by him in his way. The charms of liberty, against his will, rushed on his mind; and he could not avoid suggesting to himself how much more happy was the poorest wretch who, without controul, could repair to his homely habitation and to his family, compared to him, who was thus violently, and yet lawfully, torn away from the company of his wife and children. And their condition, especially that of his Amelia, gave his heart many a severe and bitter pang.

At length he arrived at the bailiff's mansion, and was ushered into a room in which were several persons. Booth desired to be alone; upon which the bailiff waited on him up-stairs into an apartment, the windows of which were well fortified with iron bars, but the walls had not the least outwork raised before them; they were, indeed, what is generally called naked; the bricks having been only covered with a thin plaster, which in many places was mouldered away.

The first demand made upon Booth was for coach-hire, which amounted to two shillings, according to the bailiff's account; that being just double the legal fare. He was then asked if he did not chuse a bowl of punch? to which he having answered in the negative, the bailiff replied, "Nay, sir, just as you please. I don't ask you to drink, if you don't chuse it; but certainly you know the custom; the house is full of prisoners, and I can't afford gentlemen a room to themselves for nothing."

Booth presently took this hint—indeed it was a pretty broad one—and told the bailiff he should not scruple to pay him his price; but in fact he never drank unless at his meals. "As to that, sir," cries the bailiff, "it is just as your honour pleases. I scorn to impose upon any gentleman in misfortunes: I wish you well out of them, for my part. Your honour can take nothing amiss of me; I only does my duty, what I am bound to do; and, as you says you don't care to drink anything, what will you be pleased to have for dinner?"

Booth then complied in bespeaking a dish of meat, and told the bailiff he would drink a bottle with him after dinner. He then desired the favour of pen, ink, and paper, and a messenger; all which were immediately procured him, the bailiff telling him he might send wherever he pleased, and repeating his concern for Booth's misfortunes, and a hearty desire to see the end of them.

The messenger was just dispatched with the letter, when who should arrive but honest Atkinson? A soldier of the guards, belonging to the same company with the serjeant, and who had known Booth at Gibraltar, had seen the arrest, and heard the orders given to the coachman. This fellow, accidentally meeting Atkinson, had acquainted him with the whole affair.

At the appearance of Atkinson, joy immediately overspread the countenance of Booth. The ceremonials which past between them are unnecessary to be repeated. Atkinson was soon dispatched to the attorney and to Mrs. Ellison, as the reader hath before heard from his own mouth.

Booth now greatly lamented that he had writ to his wife. He thought she might have been acquainted with the affair better by the serjeant. Booth begged him, however, to do everything in his power to comfort her; to assure her that he was in perfect health and good spirits; and to lessen as much as possible the concern which he knew she would have at the reading his letter.

The serjeant, however, as the reader hath seen, brought himself the first account of the arrest. Indeed, the other messenger did not arrive till a full hour afterwards. This was not owing to any slowness of his, but to many previous errands which he was to execute before the delivery of the letter; for, notwithstanding the earnest desire which the bailiff had declared to see Booth out of his troubles, he had ordered the porter, who was his follower, to call upon two or three other bailiffs, and as many attorneys, to try to load his prisoner with as many actions as possible.

Here the reader may be apt to conclude that the bailiff, instead of being a friend, was really an enemy to poor Booth; but, in fact, he was not so. His desire was no more than to accumulate bail-bonds; for the bailiff was reckoned an honest and good sort of man in his way, and had no more malice against the bodies in his custody than a butcher hath to those in his: and as the latter, when he takes his knife in hand, hath no idea but of the joints into which he is to cut the carcase; so the former, when he handles his writ, hath no other design but to cut out the body into as many bail-bonds as possible. As to the life of the animal, or the liberty of the man, they are thoughts which never obtrude themselves on either.

Chapter ii. — Containing an account of Mr. Booth's fellow-sufferers.

Before we return to Amelia we must detain our reader a little longer with Mr. Booth, in the custody of Mr. Bondum the bailiff, who now informed his prisoner that he was welcome to the liberty of the house with the other gentlemen.

Booth asked who those gentlemen were. "One of them, sir," says Mr. Bondum, "is a very great writer or author, as they call him; he hath been here these five weeks at the suit of a bookseller for eleven pound odd money; but he expects to be discharged in a day or two, for he hath writ out the debt. He is now writing for five or six booksellers, and he will get you sometimes, when he sits to it, a matter of fifteen shillings a-day. For he is a very good pen, they say, but is apt to be idle. Some days he won't write above five hours; but at other times I have know him at it above sixteen." "Ay!" cries Booth; "pray, what are his productions? What does he write?" "Why, sometimes," answered Bondum, "he writes your history books for your numbers, and sometimes your verses, your poems, what do you call them? and then again he writes news for your newspapers." "Ay, indeed! he is a most extraordinary man, truly!—How doth he get his news here?" "Why he makes it, as he doth your parliament speeches for your magazines. He reads them to us sometimes over a bowl of punch. To be sure it is all one as if one was in the parliament-house—it is about liberty and freedom, and about the constitution of England. I say nothing for my part, for I will keep my neck out of a halter; but, faith, he makes it out plainly to me that all matters are not as they should be. I am all for liberty, for my part." "Is that so consistent with your calling?" cries Booth. "I thought, my friend, you had lived by depriving men of their liberty." "That's another matter," cries the bailiff; "that's all according to law, and in the way of business. To be sure, men must be obliged to pay their debts, or else there would be an end of everything." Booth desired the bailiff to give him his opinion on liberty. Upon which, he hesitated a moment, and then cried out, "O 'tis a fine thing, 'tis a very fine thing, and the constitution of England." Booth told him, that by the old constitution of England he had heard that men could not be arrested for debt; to which the bailiff answered, that must have been in very bad times; "because as why," says he, "would it not be the hardest thing in the world if a man could not arrest another for a just and lawful debt? besides, sir, you must be mistaken; for how could that ever be? is not liberty the constitution of England? well, and is not the constitution, as a man may say—whereby the constitution, that is the law and liberty, and all that—"

Booth had a little mercy upon the poor bailiff, when he found him rounding in this manner, and told him he had made the matter very clear. Booth then proceeded to enquire after the other

gentlemen, his fellows in affliction; upon which Bondum acquainted him that one of the prisoners was a poor fellow. "He calls himself a gentleman," said Bondum; "but I am sure I never saw anything genteel by him. In a week that he hath been in my house he hath drank only part of one bottle of wine. I intend to carry him to Newgate within a day or two, if he can't find bail, which, I suppose, he will not be able to do; for everybody says he is an undone man. He hath run out all he hath by losses in business, and one way or other; and he hath a wife and seven children. Here was the whole family here the other day, all howling together. I never saw such a beggarly crew; I was almost ashamed to see them in my house. I thought they seemed fitter for Bridewell than any other place. To be sure, I do not reckon him as proper company for such as you, sir; but there is another prisoner in the house that I dare say you will like very much. He is, indeed, very much of a gentleman, and spends his money like one. I have had him only three days, and I am afraid he won't stay much longer. They say, indeed, he is a gamester; but what is that to me or any one, as long as a man appears as a gentleman? I always love to speak by people as I find; and, in my opinion, he is fit company for the greatest lord in the land; for he hath very good cloaths, and money enough. He is not here for debt, but upon a judge's warrant for an assault and battery; for the tipstaff locks up here."

The bailiff was thus haranguing when he was interrupted by the arrival of the attorney whom the trusty serjeant had, with the utmost expedition, found out and dispatched to the relief of his distressed friend. But before we proceed any further with the captain we will return to poor Amelia, for whom, considering the situation in which we left her, the good-natured reader may be, perhaps, in no small degree solicitous.

{Illustration: no caption}

Chapter iii. — Containing some extraordinary behaviour in Mrs. Ellison.

The serjeant being departed to convey Mrs. Ellison to the captain, his wife went to fetch Amelia's children to their mother.

Amelia's concern for the distresses of her husband was aggravated at the sight of her children. "Good Heavens!" she cried, "what will—what can become of these poor little wretches? why have I produced these little creatures only to give them a share of poverty and misery?" At which words she embraced them eagerly in her arms, and bedewed them both with her tears.

The children's eyes soon overflowed as fast as their mother's, though neither of them knew the cause of her affliction. The little boy, who was the elder and much the sharper of the two, imputed the agonies of his mother to her illness, according to the account brought to his father in his presence.

When Amelia became acquainted with the child's apprehensions, she soon satisfied him that she was in a perfect state of health; at which the little thing expressed great satisfaction, and said he was glad she was well again. Amelia told him she had not been in the least disordered. Upon which the innocent cried out, "La! how can people tell such fibs? a great tall man told my papa you was taken very ill at Mrs. Somebody's shop, and my poor papa presently ran down-stairs: I was afraid he would have broke his neck, to come to you."

"O, the villains!" cries Mrs. Atkinson, "what a stratagem was here to take away your husband!"

"Take away!" answered the child—"What! hath anybody taken away papa?—Sure that naughty fibbing man hath not taken away papa?"

Amelia begged Mrs. Atkinson to say something to her children, for that her spirits were overpowered. She then threw herself into a chair, and gave a full vent to a passion almost too strong for her delicate constitution.

The scene that followed, during some minutes, is beyond my power of description; I must beg the readers' hearts to suggest it to themselves. The children hung on their mother, whom they endeavoured in vain to comfort, as Mrs. Atkinson did in vain attempt to pacify them, telling them all would be well, and they would soon see their papa again.

At length, partly by the persuasions of Mrs. Atkinson, partly from consideration of her little ones, and more, perhaps, from the relief which she had acquired by her tears, Amelia became a little composed.

Nothing worth notice past in this miserable company from this time till the return of Mrs. Ellison from the bailiff's house; and to draw out scenes of wretchedness to too great a length, is a task very uneasy to the writer, and for which none but readers of a most gloomy complexion will think themselves ever obliged to his labours.

At length Mrs. Ellison arrived, and entered the room with an air of gaiety rather misbecoming the occasion. When she had seated herself in a chair she told Amelia that the captain was very well and in good spirits, and that he earnestly desired her to keep up hers. "Come, madam," said she, "don't be disconsolate; I hope we shall soon be able to get him out of his troubles. The debts, indeed, amount to more than I expected; however, ways may be found to redeem him. He must own himself guilty of some rashness in going out of the verge, when he knew to what he was liable; but that is now not to be remedied. If he had followed my advice this had not happened; but men will be headstrong."

"I cannot bear this," cries Amelia; "shall I hear that best of creatures blamed for his tenderness to me?"

"Well, I will not blame him," answered Mrs. Ellison; "I am sure I propose nothing but to serve him; and if you will do as much to serve him yourself, he will not be long a prisoner."

"I do!" cries Amelia: "O Heavens! is there a thing upon earth—"

"Yes, there is a thing upon earth," said Mrs. Ellison, "and a very easy thing too; and yet I will venture my life you start when I propose it. And yet, when I consider that you are a woman of understanding, I know not why I should think so; for sure you must have too much good sense to imagine that you can cry your husband out of prison. If this would have done, I see you have almost cried your eyes out already. And yet you may do the business by a much pleasanter way than by crying and bawling."

"What do you mean, madam?" cries Amelia.—"For my part, I cannot guess your meaning."

"Before I tell you then, madam," answered Mrs. Ellison, "I must inform you, if you do not already know it, that the captain is charged with actions to the amount of near five hundred pounds. I am sure I would willingly be his bail; but I know my bail would not be taken for that sum. You must consider, therefore, madam, what chance you have of redeeming him; unless you chuse, as perhaps some wives would, that he should lie all his life in prison."

At these words Amelia discharged a shower of tears, and gave every mark of the most frantic grief.

"Why, there now," cries Mrs. Ellison, "while you will indulge these extravagant passions, how can you be capable of listening to the voice of reason? I know I am a fool in concerning myself thus with the affairs of others. I know the thankless office I undertake; and yet I love you so, my dear Mrs. Booth, that I cannot bear to see you afflicted, and I would comfort you if you would suffer me. Let me beg you to make your mind easy; and within these two days I will engage to set your husband at liberty.

"Harkee, child; only behave like a woman of spirit this evening, and keep your appointment, notwithstanding what hath happened; and I am convinced there is one who hath the power and the will to serve you."

Mrs. Ellison spoke the latter part of her speech in a whisper, so that Mrs. Atkinson, who was then engaged with the children, might not hear her; but Amelia answered aloud, and said, "What appointment would you have me keep this evening?"

"Nay, nay, if you have forgot," cries Mrs. Ellison, "I will tell you more another time; but come, will you go home? my dinner is ready by this time, and you shall dine with me."

"Talk not to me of dinners," cries Amelia; "my stomach is too full already."

"Nay, but, dear madam," answered Mrs. Ellison, "let me beseech you to go home with me. I do not care," says she, whispering, "to speak before some folks." "I have no secret, madam, in the world," replied Amelia aloud, "which I would not communicate to this lady; for I shall always acknowledge the highest obligations to her for the secrets she hath imparted to me."

"Madam," said Mrs. Ellison, "I do not interfere with obligations. I am glad the lady hath obliged you so much; and I wish all people were equally mindful of obligations. I hope I have omitted no opportunity of endeavouring to oblige Mrs. Booth, as well as I have some other

folks."

"If by other folks, madam, you mean me," cries Mrs. Atkinson, "I confess I sincerely believe you intended the same obligation to us both; and I have the pleasure to think it is owing to me that this lady is not as much obliged to you as I am."

"I protest, madam, I can hardly guess your meaning," said Mrs. Ellison.—"Do you really intend to affront me, madam?"

"I intend to preserve innocence and virtue, if it be in my power, madam," answered the other. "And sure nothing but the most eager resolution to destroy it could induce you to mention such an appointment at such a time."

"I did not expect this treatment from you, madam," cries Mrs. Ellison; "such ingratitude I could not have believed had it been reported to me by any other."

"Such impudence," answered Mrs. Atkinson, "must exceed, I think, all belief; but, when women once abandon that modesty which is the characteristic of their sex, they seldom set any bounds to their assurance."

"I could not have believed this to have been in human nature," cries Mrs. Ellison. "Is this the woman whom I have fed, have cloathed, have supported; who owes to my charity and my intercessions that she is not at this day destitute of all the necessaries of life?"

"I own it all," answered Mrs. Atkinson; "and I add the favour of a masquerade ticket to the number. Could I have thought, madam, that you would before my face have asked another lady to go to the same place with the same man?—but I ask your pardon; I impute rather more assurance to you than you are mistress of.—You have endeavoured to keep the assignation a secret from me; and it was by mere accident only that I discovered it; unless there are some guardian angels that in general protect innocence and virtue; though, I may say, I have not always found them so watchful."

"Indeed, madam," said Mrs. Ellison, "you are not worth my answer; nor will I stay a moment longer with such a person.—So, Mrs. Booth, you have your choice, madam, whether you will go with me, or remain in the company of this lady."

"If so, madam," answered Mrs. Booth, "I shall not be long in determining to stay where I am."

Mrs. Ellison then, casting a look of great indignation at both the ladies, made a short speech full of invectives against Mrs. Atkinson, and not without oblique hints of ingratitude against poor Amelia; after which she burst out of the room, and out of the house, and made haste to her own home, in a condition of mind to which fortune without guilt cannot, I believe, reduce any one.

Indeed, how much the superiority of misery is on the side of wickedness may appear to every reader who will compare the present situation of Amelia with that of Mrs. Ellison. Fortune had attacked the former with almost the highest degree of her malice. She was involved in a scene of most exquisite distress, and her husband, her principal comfort, torn violently from her arms; yet her sorrow, however exquisite, was all soft and tender, nor was she without many consolations. Her case, however hard, was not absolutely desperate; for scarce any condition of fortune can be so. Art and industry, chance and friends, have often relieved the most distrest circumstances, and converted them into opulence. In all these she had hopes on this side the grave, and perfect virtue and innocence gave her the strongest assurances on the other. Whereas, in the bosom of Mrs. Ellison, all was storm and tempest; anger, revenge, fear, and pride, like so many raging furies, possessed her mind, and tortured her with disappointment and shame. Loss of reputation, which is generally irreparable, was to be her lot; loss of friends is of this the certain consequence; all on this side the grave appeared dreary and comfortless; and endless misery on the other, closed the gloomy prospect.

Hence, my worthy reader, console thyself, that however few of the other good things of life are thy lot, the best of all things, which is innocence, is always within thy own power; and, though Fortune may make thee often unhappy, she can never make thee completely and irreparably miserable without thy own consent.

Chapter iv. — Containing, among many matters, the exemplary behaviour of Colonel James.

When Mrs. Ellison was departed, Mrs. Atkinson began to apply all her art to soothe and comfort Amelia, but was presently prevented by her. "I am ashamed, dear madam," said Amelia, "of having indulged my affliction so much at your expense. The suddenness of the occasion is my only excuse; for, had I had time to summon my resolution to my assistance, I hope I am mistress of more patience than you have hitherto seen me exert. I know, madam, in my unwarrantable excesses, I have been guilty of many transgressions. First, against that Divine will and pleasure without whose permission, at least, no human accident can happen; in the next place, madam, if anything can aggravate such a fault, I have transgressed the laws of friendship as well as decency, in throwing upon you some part of the load of my grief; and again, I have sinned against common sense, which should teach me, instead of weakly and heavily lamenting my misfortunes, to rouse all my spirits to remove them. In this light I am shocked at my own folly, and am resolved to leave my children under your care, and go directly to my husband. I may comfort him. I may assist him. I may relieve him. There is nothing now too difficult for me to undertake."

Mrs. Atkinson greatly approved and complimented her friend on all the former part of her speech, except what related to herself, on which she spoke very civilly, and I believe with great truth; but as to her determination of going to her husband she endeavoured to dissuade her, at least she begged her to defer it for the present, and till the serjeant returned home. She then reminded Amelia that it was now past five in the afternoon, and that she had not taken any refreshment but a dish of tea the whole day, and desired she would give her leave to procure her a chick, or anything she liked better, for her dinner.

Amelia thanked her friend, and said she would sit down with her to whatever she pleased; "but if I do not eat," said she, "I would not have you impute it to anything but want of appetite; for I assure you all things are equally indifferent to me. I am more solicitous about these poor little things, who have not been used to fast so long. Heaven knows what may hereafter be their fate!"

Mrs. Atkinson bid her hope the best, and then recommended the children to the care of her maid.

And now arrived a servant from Mrs. James, with an invitation to Captain Booth and to his lady to dine with the colonel the day after the next. This a little perplexed Amelia; but after a short consideration she despatched an answer to Mrs. James, in which she concisely informed her of what had happened.

The honest serjeant, who had been on his legs almost the whole day, now returned, and brought Amelia a short letter from her husband, in which he gave her the most solemn assurances of his health and spirits, and begged her with great earnestness to take care to preserve her own, which if she did, he said, he had no doubt but that they should shortly be happy. He added something of hopes from my lord, with which Mrs. Ellison had amused him, and which served only to destroy the comfort that Amelia received from the rest of his letter.

Whilst Amelia, the serjeant, and his lady, were engaged in a cold collation, for which purpose a cold chicken was procured from the tavern for the ladies, and two pound of cold beef for the serjeant, a violent knocking was heard at the door, and presently afterwards Colonel James entered the room. After proper compliments had past, the colonel told Amelia that her letter was brought to Mrs. James while they were at table, and that on her shewing it him he had immediately rose up, made an apology to his company, and took a chair to her. He spoke to her with great tenderness on the occasion, and desired her to make herself easy; assuring her that he would leave nothing in his power undone to serve her husband. He then gave her an invitation, in his wife's name, to his own house, in the most pressing manner.

Amelia returned him very hearty thanks for all his kind offers, but begged to decline that of an apartment in his house. She said, as she could not leave her children, so neither could she think of bringing such a trouble with her into his family; and, though the colonel gave her many assurances that her children, as well as herself, would be very welcome to Mrs. James, and even betook himself to entreaties, she still persisted obstinately in her refusal.

In real truth, Amelia had taken a vast affection for Mrs. Atkinson, of the comfort of whose company she could not bear to be deprived in her distress, nor to exchange it for that of Mrs. James, to whom she had lately conceived no little dislike.

The colonel, when he found he could not prevail with Amelia to accept his invitation,

desisted from any farther solicitations. He then took a bank-bill of fifty pounds from his pocket-book, and said, "You will pardon me, dear madam, if I chuse to impute your refusal of my house rather to a dislike of my wife, who I will not pretend to be the most agreeable of women (all men," said he, sighing, "have not Captain Booth's fortune), than to any aversion or anger to me. I must insist upon it, therefore, to make your present habitation as easy to you as possible—I hope, madam, you will not deny me this happiness; I beg you will honour me with the acceptance of this trifle." He then put the note into her hand, and declared that the honour of touching it was worth a hundred times that sum.

"I protest, Colonel James," cried Amelia, blushing, "I know not what to do or say, your goodness so greatly confounds me. Can I, who am so well acquainted with the many great obligations Mr. Booth already hath to your generosity, consent that you should add more to a debt we never can pay?"

The colonel stopt her short, protesting that she misplaced the obligation; for, that if to confer the highest happiness was to oblige, he was obliged to her acceptance. "And I do assure you, madam," said he, "if this trifling sum or a much larger can contribute to your ease, I shall consider myself as the happiest man upon earth in being able to supply it, and you, madam, my greatest benefactor in receiving it."

Amelia then put the note in her pocket, and they entered into a conversation in which many civil things were said on both sides; but what was chiefly worth remark was, that Amelia had almost her husband constantly in her mouth, and the colonel never mentioned him: the former seemed desirous to lay all obligations, as much as possible, to the account of her husband; and the latter endeavoured, with the utmost delicacy, to insinuate that her happiness was the main and indeed only point which he had in view.

Amelia had made no doubt, at the colonel's first appearance, but that he intended to go directly to her husband. When he dropt therefore a hint of his intention to visit him next morning she appeared visibly shocked at the delay. The colonel, perceiving this, said, "However inconvenient it may be, yet, madam, if it will oblige you, or if you desire it, I will even go to-night." Amelia answered, "My husband will be far from desiring to derive any good from your inconvenience; but, if you put it to me, I must be excused for saying I desire nothing more in the world than to send him so great a comfort as I know he will receive from the presence of such a friend." "Then, to show you, madam," cries the colonel, "that I desire nothing more in the world than to give you pleasure, I will go to him immediately."

Amelia then bethought herself of the serjeant, and told the colonel his old acquaintance Atkinson, whom he had known at Gibraltar, was then in the house, and would conduct him to the place. The serjeant was immediately called in, paid his respects to the colonel, and was acknowledged by him. They both immediately set forward, Amelia to the utmost of her power pressing their departure.

Mrs. Atkinson now returned to Amelia, and was by her acquainted with the colonel's late generosity; for her heart so boiled over with gratitude that she could not conceal the ebullition. Amelia likewise gave her friend a full narrative of the colonel's former behaviour and friendship to her husband, as well abroad as in England; and ended with declaring that she believed him to be the most generous man upon earth.

Mrs. Atkinson agreed with Amelia's conclusion, and said she was glad to hear there was any such man. They then proceeded with the children to the tea-table, where panegyric, and not scandal, was the topic of their conversation; and of this panegyric the colonel was the subject; both the ladies seeming to vie with each other in celebrating the praises of his goodness.

Chapter v. — Comments upon authors.

Having left Amelia in as comfortable a situation as could possibly be expected, her immediate distresses relieved, and her heart filled with great hopes from the friendship of the colonel, we will

now return to Booth, who, when the attorney and serjeant had left him, received a visit from that great author of whom honourable mention is made in our second chapter.

Booth, as the reader may be pleased to remember, was a pretty good master of the classics; for his father, though he designed his son for the army, did not think it necessary to breed him up a blockhead. He did not, perhaps, imagine that a competent share of Latin and Greek would make his son either a pedant or a coward. He considered likewise, probably, that the life of a soldier is in general a life of idleness; and might think that the spare hours of an officer in country quarters would be as well employed with a book as in sauntering about the streets, loitering in a coffee-house, sotting in a tavern, or in laying schemes to debauch and ruin a set of harmless ignorant country girls.

As Booth was therefore what might well be called, in this age at least, a man of learning, he began to discourse our author on subjects of literature. "I think, sir," says he, "that Dr Swift hath been generally allowed, by the critics in this kingdom, to be the greatest master of humour that ever wrote. Indeed, I allow him to have possessed most admirable talents of this kind; and, if Rabelais was his master, I think he proves the truth of the common Greek proverb—that the scholar is often superior to the master. As to Cervantes, I do not think we can make any just comparison; for, though Mr. Pope compliments him with sometimes taking Cervantes' serious air—" "I remember the passage," cries the author;

"O thou, whatever title please thine ear,
Dean, Drapier, Bickerstaff, or Gulliver;
Whether you take Cervantes' serious air,
Or laugh and shake in Rabelais' easy chair—"

"You are right, sir," said Booth; "but though I should agree that the doctor hath sometimes condescended to imitate Rabelais, I do not remember to have seen in his works the least attempt in the manner of Cervantes. But there is one in his own way, and whom I am convinced he studied above all others—you guess, I believe, I am going to name Lucian. This author, I say, I am convinced, he followed; but I think he followed him at a distance: as, to say the truth, every other writer of this kind hath done in my opinion; for none, I think, hath yet equalled him. I agree, indeed, entirely with Mr. Moyle, in his Discourse on the age of the Philopatris, when he gives him the epithet of the incomparable Lucian; and incomparable, I believe, he will remain as long as the language in which he wrote shall endure. What an inimitable piece of humour is his Cock!" "I remember it very well," cries the author; "his story of a Cock and a Bull is excellent." Booth stared at this, and asked the author what he meant by the Bull? "Nay," answered he, "I don't know very well, upon my soul. It is a long time since I read him. I learnt him all over at school; I have not read him much since. And pray, sir," said he, "how do you like his Pharsalia? don't you think Mr. Rowe's translation a very fine one?" Booth replied, "I believe we are talking of different authors. The Pharsalia, which Mr. Rowe translated, was written by Lucan; but I have been speaking of Lucian, a Greek writer, and, in my opinion, the greatest in the humorous way that ever the world produced." "Ay!" cries the author, "he was indeed so, a very excellent writer indeed! I fancy a translation of him would sell very well!" "I do not know, indeed," cries Booth. "A good translation of him would be a valuable book. I have seen a wretched one published by Mr. Dryden, but translated by others, who in many places have misunderstood Lucian's meaning, and have nowhere preserved the spirit of the original." "That is great pity," says the author. "Pray, sir, is he well translated in the French?" Booth answered, he could not tell; but that he doubted it very much, having never seen a good version into that language out of the Greek." To confess the truth, I believe," said he, "the French translators have generally consulted the Latin only; which, in some of the few Greek writers I have read, is intolerably bad. And as the English translators, for the most part, pursue the French, we may easily guess what spirit those copies of bad copies must preserve of the original."

"Egad, you are a shrewd guesser," cries the author. "I am glad the booksellers have not your sagacity. But how should it be otherwise, considering the price they pay by the sheet? The Greek, you will allow, is a hard language; and there are few gentlemen that write who can read it without a good lexicon. Now, sir, if we were to afford time to find out the true meaning of words, a gentleman would not get bread and cheese by his work. If one was to be paid, indeed, as Mr. Pope was for his Homer—Pray, sir, don't you think that the best translation in the world?"

"Indeed, sir," cries Booth, "I think, though it is certainly a noble paraphrase, and of itself a

fine poem, yet in some places it is no translation at all. In the very beginning, for instance, he hath not rendered the true force of the author. Homer invokes his muse in the five first lines of the Iliad; and, at the end of the fifth, he gives his reason:

{Greek}

For all these things," says he, "were brought about by the decree of Jupiter; and, therefore, he supposes their true sources are known only to the deities. Now, the translation takes no more notice of the {Greek} than if no such word had been there."

"Very possibly," answered the author; "it is a long time since I read the original. Perhaps, then, he followed the French translations. I observe, indeed, he talks much in the notes of Madam Dacier and Monsieur Eustathius."

Booth had now received conviction enough of his friend's knowledge of the Greek language; without attempting, therefore, to set him right, he made a sudden transition to the Latin. "Pray, sir," said he, "as you have mentioned Rowe's translation of the Pharsalia, do you remember how he hath rendered that passage in the character of Cato?—

———Venerisque huic maximus usus

Progenies; urbi Pater est, urbique Maritus.

For I apprehend that passage is generally misunderstood."

"I really do not remember," answered the author. "Pray, sir, what do you take to be the meaning?"

"I apprehend, sir," replied Booth, "that by these words, Urbi Pater est, urbique Maritus, Cato is represented as the father and husband to the city of Rome."

"Very true, sir," cries the author; "very fine, indeed.—Not only the father of his country, but the husband too; very noble, truly!"

"Pardon me, sir," cries Booth; "I do not conceive that to have been Lucan's meaning. If you please to observe the context; Lucan, having commended the temperance of Cato in the instances of diet and cloaths, proceeds to venereal pleasures; of which, says the poet, his principal use was procreation: then he adds, Urbi Pater est, urbique Maritus; that he became a father and a husband for the sake only of the city."

"Upon my word that's true," cries the author; "I did not think of it. It is much finer than the other.—Urbis Pater est—what is the other?—ay—Urbis Maritus.—It is certainly as you say, sir."

Booth was by this pretty well satisfied of the author's profound learning; however, he was willing to try him a little farther. He asked him, therefore, what was his opinion of Lucan in general, and in what class of writers he ranked him?

The author stared a little at this question; and, after some hesitation, answered, "Certainly, sir, I think he is a fine writer and a very great poet."

"I am very much of the same opinion," cries Booth; "but where do you class him—next to what poet do you place him?"

"Let me see," cries the author; "where do I class him? next to whom do I place him?—Ay!—why—why, pray, where do you yourself place him?"

"Why, surely," cries Booth, "if he is not to be placed in the first rank with Homer, and Virgil, and Milton, I think clearly he is at the head of the second, before either Statius or Silius Italicus—though I allow to each of these their merits; but, perhaps, an epic poem was beyond the genius of either. I own, I have often thought, if Statius had ventured no farther than Ovid or Claudian, he would have succeeded better; for his Sylvae are, in my opinion, much better than his Thebais."

"I believe I was of the same opinion formerly," said the author.

"And for what reason have you altered it?" cries Booth.

"I have not altered it," answered the author; "but, to tell you the truth, I have not any opinion at all about these matters at present. I do not trouble my head much with poetry; for there is no encouragement to such studies in this age. It is true, indeed, I have now and then wrote a poem or two for the magazines, but I never intend to write any more; for a gentleman is not paid for his time. A sheet is a sheet with the booksellers; and, whether it be in prose or verse, they make no difference; though certainly there is as much difference to a gentleman in the work as there is to a taylor between making a plain and a laced suit. Rhimes are difficult things; they are stubborn things, sir. I have been sometimes longer in tagging a couplet than I have been in writing a speech on the side of the opposition which hath been read with great applause all over the kingdom."

"I am glad you are pleased to confirm that," cries Booth; "for I protest it was an entire secret

to me till this day. I was so perfectly ignorant, that I thought the speeches published in the magazines were really made by the members themselves."

"Some of them, and I believe I may, without vanity, say the best," cries the author, "are all the productions of my own pen! but I believe I shall leave it off soon, unless a sheet of speech will fetch more than it does at present. In truth, the romance-writing is the only branch of our business now that is worth following. Goods of that sort have had so much success lately in the market, that a bookseller scarce cares what he bids for them. And it is certainly the easiest work in the world; you may write it almost as fast as you can set pen to paper; and if you interlard it with a little scandal, a little abuse on some living characters of note, you cannot fail of success."

"Upon my word, sir," cries Booth, "you have greatly instructed me. I could not have imagined there had been so much regularity in the trade of writing as you are pleased to mention; by what I can perceive, the pen and ink is likely to become the staple commodity of the kingdom."

"Alas! sir," answered the author, "it is overstocked. The market is overstocked. There is no encouragement to merit, no patrons. I have been these five years soliciting a subscription for my new translation of Ovid's Metamorphoses, with notes explanatory, historical, and critical; and I have scarce collected five hundred names yet."

The mention of this translation a little surprized Booth; not only as the author had just declared his intentions to forsake the tuneful muses; but, for some other reasons which he had collected from his conversation with our author, he little expected to hear of a proposal to translate any of the Latin poets. He proceeded, therefore, to catechise him a little farther; and by his answers was fully satisfied that he had the very same acquaintance with Ovid that he had appeared to have with Lucan.

The author then pulled out a bundle of papers containing proposals for his subscription, and receipts; and, addressing himself to Booth, said, "Though the place in which we meet, sir, is an improper place to solicit favours of this kind, yet, perhaps, it may be in your power to serve me if you will charge your pockets with some of these." Booth was just offering at an excuse, when the bailiff introduced Colonel James and the serjeant.

The unexpected visit of a beloved friend to a man in affliction, especially in Mr. Booth's situation, is a comfort which can scarce be equalled; not barely from the hopes of relief or redress by his assistance, but as it is an evidence of sincere friendship which scarce admits of any doubt or suspicion. Such an instance doth indeed make a man amends for all ordinary troubles and distresses; and we ought to think ourselves gainers by having had such an opportunity of discovering that we are possessed of one of the most valuable of all human possessions.

Booth was so transported at the sight of the colonel, that he dropt the proposals which the author had put into his hands, and burst forth into the highest professions of gratitude to his friend; who behaved very properly on his side, and said everything which became the mouth of a friend on the occasion.

It is true, indeed, he seemed not moved equally either with Booth or the serjeant, both whose eyes watered at the scene. In truth, the colonel, though a very generous man, had not the least grain of tenderness in his disposition. His mind was formed of those firm materials of which nature formerly hammered out the Stoic, and upon which the sorrows of no man living could make an impression. A man of this temper, who doth not much value danger, will fight for the person he calls his friend, and the man that hath but little value for his money will give it him; but such friendship is never to be absolutely depended on; for, whenever the favourite passion interposes with it, it is sure to subside and vanish into air. Whereas the man whose tender disposition really feels the miseries of another will endeavour to relieve them for his own sake; and, in such a mind, friendship will often get the superiority over every other passion.

But, from whatever motive it sprung, the colonel's behaviour to Booth seemed truly amiable; and so it appeared to the author, who took the first occasion to applaud it in a very florid oration; which the reader, when he recollects that he was a speech-maker by profession, will not be surprized at; nor, perhaps, will be much more surprized that he soon after took an occasion of clapping a proposal into the colonel's hands, holding at the same time a receipt very visible in his own.

The colonel received both, and gave the author a guinea in exchange, which was double the sum mentioned in the receipt; for which the author made a low bow, and very politely took his leave, saying, "I suppose, gentlemen, you may have some private business together; I heartily wish

a speedy end to your confinement, and I congratulate you on the possessing so great, so noble, and so generous a friend."

Chapter vi. — Which inclines rather to satire than panegyric.

The colonel had the curiosity to ask Booth the name of the gentleman who, in the vulgar language, had struck, or taken him in for a guinea with so much ease and dexterity. Booth answered, he did not know his name; all that he knew of him was, that he was the most impudent and illiterate fellow he had ever seen, and that, by his own account, he was the author of most of the wonderful productions of the age. "Perhaps," said he, "it may look uncharitable in me to blame you for your generosity; but I am convinced the fellow hath not the least merit or capacity, and you have subscribed to the most horrid trash that ever was published."

"I care not a farthing what he publishes," cries the colonel. "Heaven forbid I should be obliged to read half the nonsense I have subscribed to."

"But don't you think," said Booth, "that by such indiscriminate encouragement of authors you do a real mischief to the society? By propagating the subscriptions of such fellows, people are tired out and withhold their contributions to men of real merit; and, at the same time, you are contributing to fill the world, not only with nonsense, but with all the scurrility, indecency, and profaneness with which the age abounds, and with which all bad writers supply the defect of genius."

"Pugh!" cries the colonel, "I never consider these matters. Good or bad, it is all one to me; but there's an acquaintance of mine, and a man of great wit too, that thinks the worst the best, as they are the surest to make him laugh."

"I ask pardon, sir," says the serjeant; "but I wish your honour would consider your own affairs a little, for it grows late in the evening."

"The serjeant says true," answered the colonel. "What is it you intend to do?"

"Faith, colonel, I know not what I shall do. My affairs seem so irreparable, that I have been driving them as much as possibly I could from my mind. If I was to suffer alone, I think I could bear them with some philosophy; but when I consider who are to be the sharers in my fortune— the dearest of children, and the best, the worthiest, and the noblest of women——Pardon me, my dear friend, these sensations are above me; they convert me into a woman; they drive me to despair, to madness."

The colonel advised him to command himself, and told him this was not the way to retrieve his fortune. "As to me, my dear Booth," said he, "you know you may command me as far as is really within my power."

Booth answered eagerly, that he was so far from expecting any more favours from the colonel, that he had resolved not to let him know anything of his misfortune. "No, my dear friend," cries he, "I am too much obliged to you already;" and then burst into many fervent expressions of gratitude, till the colonel himself stopt him, and begged him to give an account of the debt or debts for which he was detained in that horrid place.

Booth answered, he could not be very exact, but he feared it was upwards of four hundred pounds.

"It is but three hundred pounds, indeed, sir," cries the serjeant; "if you can raise three hundred pounds, you are a free man this moment."

Booth, who did not apprehend the generous meaning of the serjeant as well as, I believe, the reader will, answered he was mistaken; that he had computed his debts, and they amounted to upwards of four hundred pounds; nay, that the bailiff had shewn him writs for above that sum.

"Whether your debts are three or four hundred," cries the colonel, "the present business is to give bail only, and then you will have some time to try your friends: I think you might get a company abroad, and then I would advance the money on the security of half your pay; and, in the mean time, I will be one of your bail with all my heart."

Whilst Booth poured forth his gratitude for all this kindness, the serjeant ran down-stairs for

the bailiff, and shortly after returned with him into the room.

The bailiff, being informed that the colonel offered to be bail for his prisoner, answered a little surlily, "Well, sir, and who will be the other? you know, I suppose, there must be two; and I must have time to enquire after them."

The colonel replied, "I believe, sir, I am well known to be responsible for a much larger sum than your demand on this gentleman; but, if your forms require two, I suppose the serjeant here will do for the other."

"I don't know the serjeant nor you either, sir," cries Bondum; "and, if you propose yourselves bail for the gentleman, I must have time to enquire after you."

"You need very little time to enquire after me," says the colonel, "for I can send for several of the law, whom I suppose you know, to satisfy you; but consider, it is very late."

"Yes, sir," answered Bondum, "I do consider it is too late for the captain to be bailed to-night."

"What do you mean by too late?" cries the colonel.

"I mean, sir, that I must search the office, and that is now shut up; for, if my lord mayor and the court of aldermen would be bound for him, I would not discharge him till I had searched the office."

"How, sir!" cries the colonel, "hath the law of England no more regard for the liberty of the subject than to suffer such fellows as you to detain a man in custody for debt, when he can give undeniable security?"

"Don't fellow me," said the bailiff; "I am as good a fellow as yourself, I believe, though you have that riband in your hat there."

"Do you know whom you are speaking to?" said the serjeant. "Do you know you are talking to a colonel of the army?"

"What's a colonel of the army to me?" cries the bailiff. "I have had as good as he in my custody before now."

"And a member of parliament?" cries the serjeant.

"Is the gentleman a member of parliament?—Well, and what harm have I said? I am sure I meant no harm; and, if his honour is offended, I ask his pardon; to be sure his honour must know that the sheriff is answerable for all the writs in the office, though they were never so many, and I am answerable to the sheriff. I am sure the captain can't say that I have shewn him any manner of incivility since he hath been here.—And I hope, honourable sir," cries he, turning to the colonel, "you don't take anything amiss that I said, or meant by way of disrespect, or any such matter. I did not, indeed, as the gentleman here says, know who I was speaking to; but I did not say anything uncivil as I know of, and I hope no offence."

The colonel was more easily pacified than might have been expected, and told the bailiff that, if it was against the rules of law to discharge Mr. Booth that evening, he must be contented. He then addressed himself to his friend, and began to prescribe comfort and patience to him; saying, he must rest satisfied with his confinement that night; and the next morning he promised to visit him again.

Booth answered, that as for himself, the lying one night in any place was very little worth his regard. "You and I, my dear friend, have both spent our evening in a worse situation than I shall in this house. All my concern is for my poor Amelia, whose sufferings on account of my absence I know, and I feel with unspeakable tenderness. Could I be assured she was tolerably easy, I could be contented in chains or in a dungeon."

"Give yourself no concern on her account," said the colonel; "I will wait on her myself, though I break an engagement for that purpose, and will give her such assurances as I am convinced will make her perfectly easy."

Booth embraced his friend, and, weeping over him, paid his acknowledgment with tears for all his goodness. In words, indeed, he was not able to thank him; for gratitude, joining with his other passions, almost choaked him, and stopt his utterance.

After a short scene in which nothing past worth recounting, the colonel bid his friend good night, and leaving the serjeant with him, made the best of his way back to Amelia.

Chapter vii. — Worthy a very serious perusal.

The colonel found Amelia sitting very disconsolate with Mrs. Atkinson. He entered the room with an air of great gaiety, assured Amelia that her husband was perfectly well, and that he hoped the next day he would again be with her.

Amelia was a little comforted at this account, and vented many grateful expressions to the colonel for his unparalleled friendship, as she was pleased to call it. She could not, however, help giving way soon after to a sigh at the thoughts of her husband's bondage, and declared that night would be the longest she had ever known.

"This lady, madam," cries the colonel, "must endeavour to make it shorter. And, if you will give me leave, I will join in the same endeavour." Then, after some more consolatory speeches, the colonel attempted to give a gay turn to the discourse, and said, "I was engaged to have spent this evening disagreeably at Ranelagh, with a set of company I did not like. How vastly am I obliged to you, dear Mrs. Booth, that I pass it so infinitely more to my satisfaction!"

"Indeed, colonel," said Amelia, "I am convinced that to a mind so rightly turned as yours there must be a much sweeter relish in the highest offices of friendship than in any pleasures which the gayest public places can afford."

"Upon my word, madam," said the colonel, "you now do me more than justice. I have, and always had, the utmost indifference for such pleasures. Indeed, I hardly allow them worthy of that name, or, if they are so at all, it is in a very low degree. In my opinion the highest friendship must always lead us to the highest pleasure."

Here Amelia entered into a long dissertation on friendship, in which she pointed several times directly at the colonel as the hero of her tale.

The colonel highly applauded all her sentiments; and when he could not avoid taking the compliment to himself, he received it with a most respectful bow. He then tried his hand likewise at description, in which he found means to repay all Amelia's panegyric in kind. This, though he did with all possible delicacy, yet a curious observer might have been apt to suspect that it was chiefly on her account that the colonel had avoided the masquerade.

In discourses of this kind they passed the evening, till it was very late, the colonel never offering to stir from his chair before the clock had struck one; when he thought, perhaps, that decency obliged him to take his leave.

As soon as he was gone Mrs. Atkinson said to Mrs. Booth, "I think, madam, you told me this afternoon that the colonel was married?"

Amelia answered, she did so.

"I think likewise, madam," said Mrs. Atkinson, "you was acquainted with the colonel's lady?"

Amelia answered that she had been extremely intimate with her abroad.

"Is she young and handsome?" said Mrs. Atkinson. "In short, pray, was it a match of love or convenience?"

Amelia answered, entirely of love, she believed, on his side; for that the lady had little or no fortune.

"I am very glad to hear it," said Mrs. Atkinson; "for I am sure the colonel is in love with somebody. I think I never saw a more luscious picture of love drawn than that which he was pleased to give us as the portraiture of friendship. I have read, indeed, of Pylades and Orestes, Damon and Pythias, and other great friends of old; nay, I sometimes flatter myself that I am capable of being a friend myself; but as for that fine, soft, tender, delicate passion, which he was pleased to describe, I am convinced there must go a he and a she to the composition."

"Upon my word, my dear, you are mistaken," cries Amelia. "If you had known the friendship which hath always subsisted between the colonel and my husband, you would not imagine it possible for any description to exceed it. Nay, I think his behaviour this very day is sufficient to convince you."

"I own what he hath done to-day hath great merit," said Mrs. Atkinson; "and yet, from what he hath said to-night—You will pardon me, dear madam; perhaps I am too quick-sighted in my observations; nay, I am afraid I am even impertinent."

"Fie upon it!" cries Amelia; "how can you talk in that strain? Do you imagine I expect

ceremony? Pray speak what you think with the utmost freedom."

"Did he not then," said Mrs. Atkinson, "repeat the words, the finest woman in the world, more than once? did he not make use of an expression which might have become the mouth of Oroondates himself? If I remember, the words were these—that, had he been Alexander the Great, he should have thought it more glory to have wiped off a tear from the bright eyes of Statira than to have conquered fifty worlds."

"Did he say so?" cries Amelia—"I think he did say something like it; but my thoughts were so full of my husband that I took little notice. But what would you infer from what he said? I hope you don't think he is in love with me?"

"I hope he doth not think so himself," answered Mrs. Atkinson; "though, when he mentioned the bright eyes of Statira, he fixed his own eyes on yours with the most languishing air I ever beheld."

Amelia was going to answer, when the serjeant arrived, and then she immediately fell to enquiring after her husband, and received such satisfactory answers to all her many questions concerning him, that she expressed great pleasure. These ideas so possessed her mind, that, without once casting her thoughts on any other matters, she took her leave of the serjeant and his lady, and repaired to bed to her children, in a room which Mrs. Atkinson had provided her in the same house; where we will at present wish her a good night.

Chapter viii. — Consisting of grave matters.

While innocence and chearful hope, in spite of the malice of fortune, closed the eyes of the gentle Amelia on her homely bed, and she enjoyed a sweet and profound sleep, the colonel lay restless all night on his down; his mind was affected with a kind of ague fit; sometimes scorched up with flaming desires, and again chilled with the coldest despair.

There is a time, I think, according to one of our poets, when lust and envy sleep. This, I suppose, is when they are well gorged with the food they most delight in; but, while either of these are hungry,

> Nor poppy, nor mandragora,
> Nor all the drousy syrups of the East,
> Will ever medicine them to slumber.

The colonel was at present unhappily tormented by both these fiends. His last evening's conversation with Amelia had done his business effectually. The many kind words she had spoken to him, the many kind looks she had given him, as being, she conceived, the friend and preserver of her husband, had made an entire conquest of his heart. Thus the very love which she bore him, as the person to whom her little family were to owe their preservation and happiness, inspired him with thoughts of sinking them all in the lowest abyss of ruin and misery; and, while she smiled with all her sweetness on the supposed friend of her husband, she was converting that friend into his most bitter enemy.

> Friendship, take heed; if woman interfere,
> Be sure the hour of thy destruction's near.

These are the lines of Vanbrugh; and the sentiment is better than the poetry. To say the truth, as a handsome wife is the cause and cement of many false friendships, she is often too liable to destroy the real ones.

Thus the object of the colonel's lust very plainly appears, but the object of his envy may be more difficult to discover. Nature and Fortune had seemed to strive with a kind of rivalship which should bestow most on the colonel. The former had given him person, parts, and constitution, in all which he was superior to almost every other man. The latter had given him rank in life, and riches, both in a very eminent degree. Whom then should this happy man envy? Here, lest ambition should mislead the reader to search the palaces of the great, we will direct him at once to Gray's-inn-lane; where, in a miserable bed, in a miserable room, he will see a miserable broken lieutenant, in a miserable condition, with several heavy debts on his back, and without a penny in

his pocket. This, and no other, was the object of the colonel's envy. And why? because this wretch was possessed of the affections of a poor little lamb, which all the vast flocks that were within the power and reach of the colonel could not prevent that glutton's longing for. And sure this image of the lamb is not improperly adduced on this occasion; for what was the colonel's desire but to lead this poor lamb, as it were, to the slaughter, in order to purchase a feast of a few days by her final destruction, and to tear her away from the arms of one where she was sure of being fondled and caressed all the days of her life.

While the colonel was agitated with these thoughts, his greatest comfort was, that Amelia and Booth were now separated; and his greatest terror was of their coming again together. From wishes, therefore, he began to meditate designs; and so far was he from any intention of procuring the liberty of his friend, that he began to form schemes of prolonging his confinement, till he could procure some means of sending him away far from her; in which case he doubted not but of succeeding in all he desired.

He was forming this plan in his mind when a servant informed him that one serjeant Atkinson desired to speak with his honour. The serjeant was immediately admitted, and acquainted the colonel that, if he pleased to go and become bail for Mr. Booth, another unexceptionable housekeeper would be there to join with him. This person the serjeant had procured that morning, and had, by leave of his wife, given him a bond of indemnification for the purpose.

The colonel did not seem so elated with this news as Atkinson expected. On the contrary, instead of making a direct answer to what Atkinson said, the colonel began thus: "I think, serjeant, Mr. Booth hath told me that you was foster-brother to his lady. She is really a charming woman, and it is a thousand pities she should ever have been placed in the dreadful situation she is now in. There is nothing so silly as for subaltern officers of the army to marry, unless where they meet with women of very great fortunes indeed. What can be the event of their marrying otherwise, but entailing misery and beggary on their wives and their posterity?"

"Ah! sir," cries the serjeant, "it is too late to think of those matters now. To be sure, my lady might have married one of the top gentlemen in the country; for she is certainly one of the best as well as one of the handsomest women in the kingdom; and, if she had been fairly dealt by, would have had a very great fortune into the bargain. Indeed, she is worthy of the greatest prince in the world; and, if I had been the greatest prince in the world, I should have thought myself happy with such a wife; but she was pleased to like the lieutenant, and certainly there can be no happiness in marriage without liking."

"Lookee, serjeant," said the colonel; "you know very well that I am the lieutenant's friend. I think I have shewn myself so."

"Indeed your honour hath," quoth the serjeant, "more than once to my knowledge."

"But I am angry with him for his imprudence, greatly angry with him for his imprudence; and the more so, as it affects a lady of so much worth."

"She is, indeed, a lady of the highest worth," cries the serjeant. "Poor dear lady! I knew her, an 't please your honour, from her infancy; and the sweetest-tempered, best-natured lady she is that ever trod on English ground. I have always loved her as if she was my own sister. Nay, she hath very often called me brother; and I have taken it to be a greater honour than if I was to be called a general officer."

"What pity it is," said the colonel, "that this worthy creature should be exposed to so much misery by the thoughtless behaviour of a man who, though I am his friend, I cannot help saying, hath been guilty of imprudence at least! Why could he not live upon his half-pay? What had he to do to run himself into debt in this outrageous manner?"

"I wish, indeed," cries the serjeant, "he had been a little more considerative; but I hope this will be a warning to him."

"How am I sure of that," answered the colonel; "or what reason is there to expect it? extravagance is a vice of which men are not so easily cured. I have thought a great deal of this matter, Mr. serjeant; and, upon the most mature deliberation, I am of opinion that it will be better, both for him and his poor lady, that he should smart a little more."

"Your honour, sir, to be sure is in the right," replied the serjeant; "but yet, sir, if you will pardon me for speaking, I hope you will be pleased to consider my poor lady's case. She suffers, all this while, as much or more than the lieutenant; for I know her so well, that I am certain she

will never have a moment's ease till her husband is out of confinement."

"I know women better than you, serjeant," cries the colonel; "they sometimes place their affections on a husband as children do on their nurse; but they are both to be weaned. I know you, serjeant, to be a fellow of sense as well as spirit, or I should not speak so freely to you; but I took a fancy to you a long time ago, and I intend to serve you; but first, I ask you this question— Is your attachment to Mr. Booth or his lady?"

"Certainly, sir," said the serjeant, "I must love my lady best. Not but I have a great affection for the lieutenant too, because I know my lady hath the same; and, indeed, he hath been always very good to me as far as was in his power. A lieutenant, your honour knows, can't do a great deal; but I have always found him my friend upon all occasions."

"You say true," cries the colonel; "a lieutenant can do but little; but I can do much to serve you, and will too. But let me ask you one question: Who was the lady whom I saw last night with Mrs. Booth at her lodgings?"

Here the serjeant blushed, and repeated, "The lady, sir?"

"Ay, a lady, a woman," cries the colonel, "who supped with us last night. She looked rather too much like a gentlewoman for the mistress of a lodging-house."

The serjeant's cheeks glowed at this compliment to his wife; and he was just going to own her when the colonel proceeded: "I think I never saw in my life so ill-looking, sly, demure a b——; I would give something, methinks, to know who she was."

"I don't know, indeed," cries the serjeant, in great confusion; "I know nothing about her."

"I wish you would enquire," said the colonel, "and let me know her name, and likewise what she is: I have a strange curiosity to know, and let me see you again this evening exactly at seven."

"And will not your honour then go to the lieutenant this morning?" said Atkinson.

"It is not in my power," answered the colonel; "I am engaged another way. Besides, there is no haste in this affair. If men will be imprudent they must suffer the consequences. Come to me at seven, and bring me all the particulars you can concerning that ill-looking jade I mentioned to you, for I am resolved to know who she is. And so good-morrow to you, serjeant; be assured I will take an opportunity to do something for you."

Though some readers may, perhaps, think the serjeant not unworthy of the freedom with which the colonel treated him; yet that haughty officer would have been very backward to have condescended to such familiarity with one of his rank had he not proposed some design from it. In truth, he began to conceive hopes of making the serjeant instrumental to his design on Amelia; in other words, to convert him into a pimp; an office in which the colonel had been served by Atkinson's betters, and which, as he knew it was in his power very well to reward him, he had no apprehension that the serjeant would decline—an opinion which the serjeant might have pardoned, though he had never given the least grounds for it, since the colonel borrowed it from the knowledge of his own heart. This dictated to him that he, from a bad motive, was capable of desiring to debauch his friend's wife; and the same heart inspired him to hope that another, from another bad motive, might be guilty of the same breach of friendship in assisting him. Few men, I believe, think better of others than of themselves; nor do they easily allow the existence of any virtue of which they perceive no traces in their own minds; for which reason I have observed, that it is extremely difficult to persuade a rogue that you are an honest man; nor would you ever succeed in the attempt by the strongest evidence, was it not for the comfortable conclusion which the rogue draws, that he who proves himself to be honest proves himself to be a fool at the same time.

Chapter ix. — A curious chapter, from which a curious reader may draw sundry observations.

The serjeant retired from the colonel in a very dejected state of mind: in which, however, we must leave him awhile and return to Amelia; who, as soon as she was up, had despatched Mrs. Atkinson to pay off her former lodgings, and to bring off all cloaths and other moveables.

The trusty messenger returned without performing her errand, for Mrs. Ellison had locked up

all her rooms, and was gone out very early that morning, and the servant knew not whither she was gone.

The two ladies now sat down to breakfast, together with Amelia's two children; after which, Amelia declared she would take a coach and visit her husband. To this motion Mrs. Atkinson soon agreed, and offered to be her companion. To say truth, I think it was reasonable enough; and the great abhorrence which Booth had of seeing his wife in a bailiff's house, was, perhaps, rather too nice and delicate.

When the ladies were both drest, and just going to send for their vehicle, a great knocking was heard at the door, and presently Mrs. James was ushered into the room.

This visit was disagreeable enough to Amelia, as it detained her from the sight of her husband, for which she so eagerly longed. However, as she had no doubt but that the visit would be reasonably short, she resolved to receive the lady with all the complaisance in her power.

Mrs. James now behaved herself so very unlike the person that she lately appeared, that it might have surprized any one who doth not know that besides that of a fine lady, which is all mere art and mummery, every such woman hath some real character at the bottom, in which, whenever nature gets the better of her, she acts. Thus the finest ladies in the world will sometimes love, and sometimes scratch, according to their different natural dispositions, with great fury and violence, though both of these are equally inconsistent with a fine lady's artificial character.

Mrs. James then was at the bottom a very good-natured woman, and the moment she heard of Amelia's misfortune was sincerely grieved at it. She had acquiesced on the very first motion with the colonel's design of inviting her to his house; and this morning at breakfast, when he had acquainted her that Amelia made some difficulty in accepting the offer, very readily undertook to go herself and persuade her friend to accept the invitation.

She now pressed this matter with such earnestness, that Amelia, who was not extremely versed in the art of denying, was hardly able to refuse her importunity; nothing, indeed, but her affection to Mrs. Atkinson could have prevailed on her to refuse; that point, however, she would not give up, and Mrs. James, at last, was contented with a promise that, as soon as their affairs were settled, Amelia, with her husband and family, would make her a visit, and stay some time with her in the country, whither she was soon to retire.

Having obtained this promise, Mrs. James, after many very friendly professions, took her leave, and, stepping into her coach, reassumed the fine lady, and drove away to join her company at an auction.

The moment she was gone Mrs. Atkinson, who had left the room upon the approach of Mrs. James, returned into it, and was informed by Amelia of all that had past.

"Pray, madam," said Mrs. Atkinson, "do this colonel and his lady live, as it is called, well together?"

"If you mean to ask," cries Amelia, "whether they are a very fond couple, I must answer that I believe they are not."

"I have been told," says Mrs. Atkinson, "that there have been instances of women who have become bawds to their own husbands, and the husbands pimps for them."

"Fie upon it!" cries Amelia. "I hope there are no such people. Indeed, my dear, this is being a little too censorious."

"Call it what you please," answered Mrs. Atkinson; "it arises from my love to you and my fears for your danger. You know the proverb of a burnt child; and, if such a one hath any good-nature, it will dread the fire on the account of others as well as on its own. And, if I may speak my sentiments freely, I cannot think you will be in safety at this colonel's house."

"I cannot but believe your apprehensions to be sincere," replied Amelia; "and I must think myself obliged to you for them; but I am convinced you are entirely in an error. I look on Colonel James as the most generous and best of men. He was a friend, and an excellent friend too, to my husband, long before I was acquainted with him, and he hath done him a thousand good offices. What do you say of his behaviour yesterday?"

"I wish," cries Mrs. Atkinson, "that this behaviour to-day had been equal. What I am now going to undertake is the most disagreeable office of friendship, but it is a necessary one. I must tell you, therefore, what past this morning between the colonel and Mr. Atkinson; for, though it will hurt you, you ought, on many accounts, to know it." Here she related the whole, which we have recorded in the preceding chapter, and with which the serjeant had acquainted her while Mrs.

James was paying her visit to Amelia. And, as the serjeant had painted the matter rather in stronger colours than the colonel, so Mrs. Atkinson again a little improved on the serjeant. Neither of these good people, perhaps, intended to aggravate any circumstance; but such is, I believe, the unavoidable consequence of all reports. Mrs. Atkinson, indeed, may be supposed not to see what related to James in the most favourable light, as the serjeant, with more honesty than prudence, had suggested to his wife that the colonel had not the kindest opinion of her, and had called her a sly and demure——: it is true he omitted ill-looking b——; two words which are, perhaps, superior to the patience of any Job in petticoats that ever lived. He made amends, however, by substituting some other phrases in their stead, not extremely agreeable to a female ear.

It appeared to Amelia, from Mrs. Atkinson's relation, that the colonel had grossly abused Booth to the serjeant, and had absolutely refused to become his bail. Poor Amelia became a pale and motionless statue at this account. At length she cried, "If this be true, I and mine are all, indeed, undone. We have no comfort, no hope, no friend left. I cannot disbelieve you. I know you would not deceive me. Why should you, indeed, deceive me? But what can have caused this alteration since last night? Did I say or do anything to offend him?"

"You said and did rather, I believe, a great deal too much to please him," answered Mrs. Atkinson. "Besides, he is not in the least offended with you. On the contrary, he said many kind things."

"What can my poor love have done?" said Amelia. "He hath not seen the colonel since last night. Some villain hath set him against my husband; he was once before suspicious of such a person. Some cruel monster hath belied his innocence!"

"Pardon me, dear madam," said Mrs. Atkinson; "I believe the person who hath injured the captain with this friend of his is one of the worthiest and best of creatures—nay, do not be surprized; the person I mean is even your fair self: sure you would not be so dull in any other case; but in this, gratitude, humility, modesty, every virtue, shuts your eyes.

> Mortales hebetant visus,

as Virgil says. What in the world can be more consistent than his desire to have you at his own house and to keep your husband confined in another? All that he said and all that he did yesterday, and, what is more convincing to me than both, all that he looked last night, are very consistent with both these designs."

"O Heavens!" cries Amelia, "you chill my blood with horror! the idea freezes me to death; I cannot, must not, will not think it. Nothing but conviction! Heaven forbid I should ever have more conviction! And did he abuse my husband? what? did he abuse a poor, unhappy, distrest creature, opprest, ruined, torn from his children, torn away from his wretched wife; the honestest, worthiest, noblest, tenderest, fondest, best—" Here she burst into an agony of grief, which exceeds the power of description.

In this situation Mrs. Atkinson was doing her utmost to support her when a most violent knocking was heard at the door, and immediately the serjeant ran hastily into the room, bringing with him a cordial which presently relieved Amelia. What this cordial was, we shall inform the reader in due time. In the mean while he must suspend his curiosity; and the gentlemen at White's may lay wagers whether it was Ward's pill or Dr James's powder.

But before we close this chapter, and return back to the bailiff's house, we must do our best to rescue the character of our heroine from the dulness of apprehension, which several of our quick-sighted readers may lay more heavily to her charge than was done by her friend Mrs. Atkinson.

I must inform, therefore, all such readers, that it is not because innocence is more blind than guilt that the former often overlooks and tumbles into the pit which the latter foresees and avoids. The truth is, that it is almost impossible guilt should miss the discovering of all the snares in its way, as it is constantly prying closely into every corner in order to lay snares for others. Whereas innocence, having no such purpose, walks fearlessly and carelessly through life, and is consequently liable to tread on the gins which cunning hath laid to entrap it. To speak plainly and without allegory or figure, it is not want of sense, but want of suspicion, by which innocence is often betrayed. Again, we often admire at the folly of the dupe, when we should transfer our whole surprize to the astonishing guilt of the betrayer. In a word, many an innocent person hath

owed his ruin to this circumstance alone, that the degree of villany was such as must have exceeded the faith of every man who was not himself a villain.

Chapter x. — In which are many profound secrets of philosophy.

Booth, having had enough of the author's company the preceding day, chose now another companion. Indeed the author was not very solicitous of a second interview; for, as he could have no hope from Booth's pocket, so he was not likely to receive much increase to his vanity from Booth's conversation; for, low as this wretch was in virtue, sense, learning, birth, and fortune, he was by no means low in his vanity. This passion, indeed, was so high in him, and at the same time so blinded him to his own demerits, that he hated every man who did not either flatter him or give him money. In short, he claimed a strange kind of right, either to cheat all his acquaintance of their praise or to pick their pockets of their pence, in which latter case he himself repaid very liberally with panegyric.

A very little specimen of such a fellow must have satisfied a man of Mr. Booth's temper. He chose, therefore, now to associate himself with that gentleman of whom Bondum had given so shabby a character. In short, Mr. Booth's opinion of the bailiff was such, that he recommended a man most where he least intended it. Nay, the bailiff in the present instance, though he had drawn a malicious conclusion, honestly avowed that this was drawn only from the poverty of the person, which is never, I believe, any forcible disrecommendation to a good mind: but he must have had a very bad mind indeed, who, in Mr. Booth's circumstances, could have disliked or despised another man because that other man was poor.

Some previous conversation having past between this gentleman and Booth, in which they had both opened their several situations to each other, the former, casting an affectionate look on the latter, exprest great compassion for his circumstances, for which Booth, thanking him, said, "You must have a great deal of compassion, and be a very good man, in such a terrible situation as you describe yourself, to have any pity to spare for other people."

"My affairs, sir," answered the gentleman, "are very bad, it is true, and yet there is one circumstance which makes you appear to me more the object of pity than I am to myself; and it is this—that you must from your years be a novice in affliction, whereas I have served a long apprenticeship to misery, and ought, by this time, to be a pretty good master of my trade. To say the truth, I believe habit teaches men to bear the burthens of the mind, as it inures them to bear heavy burthens on their shoulders. Without use and experience, the strongest minds and bodies both will stagger under a weight which habit might render easy and even contemptible."

"There is great justice," cries Booth, "in the comparison; and I think I have myself experienced the truth of it; for I am not that tyro in affliction which you seem to apprehend me. And perhaps it is from the very habit you mention that I am able to support my present misfortunes a little like a man."

The gentleman smiled at this, and cried, "Indeed, captain, you are a young philosopher."

"I think," cries Booth, "I have some pretensions to that philosophy which is taught by misfortunes, and you seem to be of opinion, sir, that is one of the best schools of philosophy."

"I mean no more, sir," said the gentleman, "than that in the days of our affliction we are inclined to think more seriously than in those seasons of life when we are engaged in the hurrying pursuits of business or pleasure, when we have neither leisure nor inclination to sift and examine things to the bottom. Now there are two considerations which, from my having long fixed my thoughts upon them, have greatly supported me under all my afflictions. The one is the brevity of life even at its longest duration, which the wisest of men hath compared to the short dimension of a span. One of the Roman poets compares it to the duration of a race; and another, to the much shorter transition of a wave.

"The second consideration is the uncertainty of it. Short as its utmost limits are, it is far from being assured of reaching those limits. The next day, the next hour, the next moment, may be the end of our course. Now of what value is so uncertain, so precarious a station? This consideration,

indeed, however lightly it is passed over in our conception, doth, in a great measure, level all fortunes and conditions, and gives no man a right to triumph in the happiest state, or any reason to repine in the most miserable. Would the most worldly men see this in the light in which they examine all other matters, they would soon feel and acknowledge the force of this way of reasoning; for which of them would give any price for an estate from which they were liable to be immediately ejected? or, would they not laugh at him as a madman who accounted himself rich from such an uncertain possession? This is the fountain, sir, from which I have drawn my philosophy. Hence it is that I have learnt to look on all those things which are esteemed the blessings of life, and those which are dreaded as its evils, with such a degree of indifference that, as I should not be elated with possessing the former, so neither am I greatly dejected and depressed by suffering the latter. Is the actor esteemed happier to whose lot it falls to play the principal part than he who plays the lowest? and yet the drama may run twenty nights together, and by consequence may outlast our lives; but, at the best, life is only a little longer drama, and the business of the great stage is consequently a little more serious than that which is performed at the Theatre-royal. But even here, the catastrophes and calamities which are represented are capable of affecting us. The wisest men can deceive themselves into feeling the distresses of a tragedy, though they know them to be merely imaginary; and the children will often lament them as realities: what wonder then, if these tragical scenes which I allow to be a little more serious, should a little more affect us? where then is the remedy but in the philosophy I have mentioned, which, when once by a long course of meditation it is reduced to a habit, teaches us to set a just value on everything, and cures at once all eager wishes and abject fears, all violent joy and grief concerning objects which cannot endure long, and may not exist a moment."

"You have exprest yourself extremely well," cries Booth; "and I entirely agree with the justice of your sentiments; but, however true all this may be in theory, I still doubt its efficacy in practice. And the cause of the difference between these two is this; that we reason from our heads, but act from our hearts:

——Video meliora, proboque;
Deteriora sequor.

Nothing can differ more widely than wise men and fools in their estimation of things; but, as both act from their uppermost passion, they both often act like. What comfort then can your philosophy give to an avaricious man who is deprived of his riches or to an ambitious man who is stript of his power? to the fond lover who is torn from his mistress or to the tender husband who is dragged from his wife? Do you really think that any meditations on the shortness of life will soothe them in their afflictions? Is not this very shortness itself one of their afflictions? and if the evil they suffer be a temporary deprivation of what they love, will they not think their fate the harder, and lament the more, that they are to lose any part of an enjoyment to which there is so short and so uncertain a period?"

"I beg leave, sir," said the gentleman, "to distinguish here. By philosophy, I do not mean the bare knowledge of right and wrong, but an energy, a habit, as Aristotle calls it; and this I do firmly believe, with him and with the Stoics, is superior to all the attacks of fortune."

He was proceeding when the bailiff came in, and in a surly tone bad them both good-morrow; after which he asked the philosopher if he was prepared to go to Newgate; for that he must carry him thither that afternoon.

The poor man seemed very much shocked with this news. "I hope," cries he, "you will give a little longer time, if not till the return of the writ. But I beg you particularly not to carry me thither to-day, for I expect my wife and children here in the evening."

"I have nothing to do with wives and children," cried the bailiff; "I never desire to see any wives and children here. I like no such company."

"I intreat you," said the prisoner, "give me another day. I shall take it as a great obligation; and you will disappoint me in the cruellest manner in the world if you refuse me."

"I can't help people's disappointments," cries the bailiff; "I must consider myself and my own family. I know not where I shall be paid the money that's due already. I can't afford to keep prisoners at my own expense."

"I don't intend it shall be at your expense" cries the philosopher; "my wife is gone to raise money this morning; and I hope to pay you all I owe you at her arrival. But we intend to sup together to-night at your house; and, if you should remove me now, it would be the most

172

barbarous disappointment to us both, and will make me the most miserable man alive."

"Nay, for my part," said the bailiff, "I don't desire to do anything barbarous. I know how to treat gentlemen with civility as well as another. And when people pay as they go, and spend their money like gentlemen, I am sure nobody can accuse me of any incivility since I have been in the office. And if you intend to be merry to-night I am not the man that will prevent it. Though I say it, you may have as good a supper drest here as at any tavern in town."

"Since Mr. Bondum is so kind, captain," said the philosopher, "I hope for the favour of your company. I assure you, if it ever be my fortune to go abroad into the world, I shall be proud of the honour of your acquaintance."

"Indeed, sir," cries Booth, "it is an honour I shall be very ready to accept; but as for this evening, I cannot help saying I hope to be engaged in another place."

"I promise you, sir," answered the other, "I shall rejoice at your liberty, though I am a loser by it."

"Why, as to that matter," cries Bondum with a sneer, "I fancy, captain, you may engage yourself to the gentleman without any fear of breaking your word; for I am very much mistaken if we part to-day."

"Pardon me, my good friend," said Booth, "but I expect my bail every minute."

"Lookee, sir," cries Bondum, "I don't love to see gentlemen in an error. I shall not take the serjeant's bail; and as for the colonel, I have been with him myself this morning (for to be sure I love to do all I can for gentlemen), and he told me he could not possibly be here to-day; besides, why should I mince the matter? there is more stuff in the office."

"What do you mean by stuff?" cries Booth.

"I mean that there is another writ," answered the bailiff, "at the suit of Mrs. Ellison, the gentlewoman that was here yesterday; and the attorney that was with her is concerned against you. Some officers would not tell you all this; but I loves to shew civility to gentlemen while they behave themselves as such. And I loves the gentlemen of the army in particular. I had like to have been in the army myself once; but I liked the commission I have better. Come, captain, let not your noble courage be cast down; what say you to a glass of white wine, or a tiff of punch, by way of whet?"

"I have told you, sir, I never drink in the morning," cries Booth a little peevishly.

"No offence I hope, sir," said the bailiff; "I hope I have not treated you with any incivility. I don't ask any gentleman to call for liquor in my house if he doth not chuse it; nor I don't desire anybody to stay here longer than they have a mind to. Newgate, to be sure, is the place for all debtors that can't find bail. I knows what civility is, and I scorn to behave myself unbecoming a gentleman: but I'd have you consider that the twenty-four hours appointed by act of parliament are almost out; and so it is time to think of removing. As to bail, I would not have you flatter yourself; for I knows very well there are other things coming against you. Besides, the sum you are already charged with is very large, and I must see you in a place of safety. My house is no prison, though I lock up for a little time in it. Indeed, when gentlemen are gentlemen, and likely to find bail, I don't stand for a day or two; but I have a good nose at a bit of carrion, captain; I have not carried so much carrion to Newgate, without knowing the smell of it."

"I understand not your cant," cries Booth; "but I did not think to have offended you so much by refusing to drink in a morning."

"Offended me, sir!" cries the bailiff. "Who told you so? Do you think, sir, if I want a glass of wine I am under any necessity of asking my prisoners for it? Damn it, sir, I'll shew you I scorn your words. I can afford to treat you with a glass of the best wine in England, if you comes to that." He then pulled out a handful of guineas, saying, "There, sir, they are all my own; I owe nobody a shilling. I am no beggar, nor no debtor. I am the king's officer as well as you, and I will spend guinea for guinea as long as you please."

"Harkee, rascal," cries Booth, laying hold of the bailiff's collar. "How dare you treat me with this insolence? doth the law give you any authority to insult me in my misfortunes?" At which words he gave the bailiff a good shove, and threw him from him.

"Very well, sir," cries the bailiff; "I will swear both an assault and an attempt to a rescue. If officers are to be used in this manner, there is an end of all law and justice. But, though I am not a match for you myself, I have those below that are." He then ran to the door and called up two ill-looking fellows, his followers, whom, as soon as they entered the room, he ordered to seize on

173

Booth, declaring he would immediately carry him to Newgate; at the same time pouring out a vast quantity of abuse, below the dignity of history to record.

Booth desired the two dirty fellows to stand off, and declared he would make no resistance; at the same time bidding the bailiff carry him wherever he durst.

"I'll shew you what I dare," cries the bailiff; and again ordered the followers to lay hold of their prisoner, saying, "He has assaulted me already, and endeavoured a rescue. I shan't trust such a fellow to walk at liberty. A gentleman, indeed! ay, ay, Newgate is the properest place for such gentry; as arrant carrion as ever was carried thither."

The fellows then both laid violent hands on Booth, and the bailiff stept to the door to order a coach; when, on a sudden, the whole scene was changed in an instant; for now the serjeant came running out of breath into the room; and, seeing his friend the captain roughly handled by two ill-looking fellows, without asking any questions stept briskly up to his assistance, and instantly gave one of the assailants so violent a salute with his fist, that he directly measured his length on the floor.

Booth, having by this means his right arm at liberty, was unwilling to be idle, or entirely to owe his rescue from both the ruffians to the serjeant; he therefore imitated the example which his friend had set him, and with a lusty blow levelled the other follower with his companion on the ground.

The bailiff roared out, "A rescue, a rescue!" to which the serjeant answered there was no rescue intended. "The captain," said he, "wants no rescue. Here are some friends coming who will deliver him in a better manner."

The bailiff swore heartily he would carry him to Newgate in spite of all the friends in the world.

"You carry him to Newgate!" cried the serjeant, with the highest indignation. "Offer but to lay your hands on him, and I will knock your teeth down your ugly jaws." Then, turning to Booth, he cried, "They will be all here within a minute, sir; we had much ado to keep my lady from coming herself; but she is at home in good health, longing to see your honour; and I hope you will be with her within this half-hour."

And now three gentlemen entered the room; these were an attorney, the person whom the serjeant had procured in the morning to be his bail with Colonel James, and lastly Doctor Harrison himself.

The bailiff no sooner saw the attorney, with whom he was well acquainted (for the others he knew not), than he began, as the phrase is, to pull in his horns, and ordered the two followers, who were now got again on their legs, to walk down-stairs.

"So, captain," says the doctor, "when last we parted, I believe we neither of us expected to meet in such a place as this."

"Indeed, doctor," cries Booth, "I did not expect to have been sent hither by the gentleman who did me that favour."

"How so, sir?" said the doctor; "you was sent hither by some person, I suppose, to whom you was indebted. This is the usual place, I apprehend, for creditors to send their debtors to. But you ought to be more surprized that the gentleman who sent you hither is come to release you. Mr. Murphy, you will perform all the necessary ceremonials."

The attorney then asked the bailiff with how many actions Booth was charged, and was informed there were five besides the doctor's, which was much the heaviest of all. Proper bonds were presently provided, and the doctor and the serjeant's friend signed them; the bailiff, at the instance of the attorney, making no objection to the bail.

{Illustration: Lawyer Murphy}

Booth, we may be assured, made a handsome speech to the doctor for such extraordinary friendship, with which, however, we do not think proper to trouble the reader; and now everything being ended, and the company ready to depart, the bailiff stepped up to Booth, and told him he hoped he would remember civility-money.

"I believe" cries Booth, "you mean incivility-money; if there are any fees due for rudeness, I must own you have a very just claim."

"I am sure, sir," cries the bailiff, "I have treated your honour with all the respect in the world; no man, I am sure, can charge me with using a gentleman rudely. I knows what belongs to a gentleman better; but you can't deny that two of my men have been knocked down; and I doubt

174

not but, as you are a gentleman, you will give them something to drink."

Booth was about to answer with some passion, when the attorney interfered, and whispered in his ear that it was usual to make a compliment to the officer, and that he had better comply with the custom.

"If the fellow had treated me civilly," answered Booth, "I should have had no objection to comply with a bad custom in his favour; but I am resolved I will never reward a man for using me ill; and I will not agree to give him a single farthing."

"'Tis very well, sir," said the bailiff; "I am rightly served for my good-nature; but, if it had been to do again, I would have taken care you should not have been bailed this day."

Doctor Harrison, to whom Booth referred the cause, after giving him a succinct account of what had passed, declared the captain to be in the right. He said it was a most horrid imposition that such fellows were ever suffered to prey on the necessitous; but that the example would be much worse to reward them where they had behaved themselves ill. "And I think," says he, "the bailiff is worthy of great rebuke for what he hath just now said; in which I hope he hath boasted of more power than is in him. We do, indeed, with great justice and propriety value ourselves on our freedom if the liberty of the subject depends on the pleasure of such fellows as these!"

"It is not so neither altogether," cries the lawyer; "but custom hath established a present or fee to them at the delivery of a prisoner, which they call civility-money, and expect as in a manner their due, though in reality they have no right."

"But will any man," cries Doctor Harrison, "after what the captain hath told us, say that the bailiff hath behaved himself as he ought; and, if he had, is he to be rewarded for not acting in an unchristian and inhuman manner? it is pity that, instead of a custom of feeing them out of the pockets of the poor and wretched, when they do not behave themselves ill, there was not both a law and a practice to punish them severely when they do. In the present case, I am so far from agreeing to give the bailiff a shilling, that, if there be any method of punishing him for his rudeness, I shall be heartily glad to see it put in execution; for there are none whose conduct should be so strictly watched as that of these necessary evils in the society, as their office concerns for the most part those poor creatures who cannot do themselves justice, and as they are generally the worst of men who undertake it."

The bailiff then quitted the room, muttering that he should know better what to do another time; and shortly after, Booth and his friends left the house; but, as they were going out, the author took Doctor Harrison aside, and slipt a receipt into his hand, which the doctor returned, saying, he never subscribed when he neither knew the work nor the author; but that, if he would call at his lodgings, he would be very willing to give all the encouragement to merit which was in his power.

The author took down the doctor's name and direction, and made him as many bows as he would have done had he carried off the half-guinea for which he had been fishing.

Mr. Booth then took his leave of the philosopher, and departed with the rest of his friends.
END OF VOL. II.

VOL. III.

BOOK IX.

Chapter i. — In which the history looks backwards.

Before we proceed farther with our history it may be proper to look back a little, in order to account for the late conduct of Doctor Harrison; which, however inconsistent it may have hitherto appeared, when examined to the bottom will be found, I apprehend, to be truly congruous with all the rules of the most perfect prudence as well as with the most consummate goodness.

We have already partly seen in what light Booth had been represented to the doctor abroad. Indeed, the accounts which were sent of the captain, as well by the curate as by a gentleman of the neighbourhood, were much grosser and more to his disadvantage than the doctor was pleased to set them forth in his letter to the person accused. What sense he had of Booth's conduct was, however, manifest by that letter. Nevertheless, he resolved to suspend his final judgment till his return; and, though he censured him, would not absolutely condemn him without ocular demonstration.

The doctor, on his return to his parish, found all the accusations which had been transmitted to him confirmed by many witnesses, of which the curate's wife, who had been formerly a friend to Amelia, and still preserved the outward appearance of friendship, was the strongest. She introduced all with—"I am sorry to say it; and it is friendship which bids me speak; and it is for their good it should be told you." After which beginnings she never concluded a single speech without some horrid slander and bitter invective.

Besides the malicious turn which was given to these affairs in the country, which were owing a good deal to misfortune, and some little perhaps to imprudence, the whole neighbourhood rung with several gross and scandalous lies, which were merely the inventions of his enemies, and of which the scene was laid in London since his absence.

Poisoned with all this malice, the doctor came to town; and, learning where Booth lodged, went to make him a visit. Indeed, it was the doctor, and no other, who had been at his lodgings that evening when Booth and Amelia were walking in the Park, and concerning which the reader may be pleased to remember so many strange and odd conjectures.

Here the doctor saw the little gold watch and all those fine trinkets with which the noble lord had presented the children, and which, from the answers given him by the poor ignorant, innocent girl, he could have no doubt had been purchased within a few days by Amelia.

This account tallied so well with the ideas he had imbibed of Booth's extravagance in the country, that he firmly believed both the husband and wife to be the vainest, silliest, and most unjust people alive. It was, indeed, almost incredible that two rational beings should be guilty of such absurdity; but, monstrous and absurd as it was, ocular demonstration appeared to be the evidence against them.

The doctor departed from their lodgings enraged at this supposed discovery, and, unhappily for Booth, was engaged to supper that very evening with the country gentleman of whom Booth had rented a farm. As the poor captain happened to be the subject of conversation, and occasioned their comparing notes, the account which the doctor gave of what he had seen that evening so incensed the gentleman, to whom Booth was likewise a debtor, that he vowed he would take a writ out against him the next morning, and have his body alive or dead; and the doctor was at last persuaded to do the same. Mr. Murphy was thereupon immediately sent for; and the doctor in his presence repeated again what he had seen at his lodgings as the foundation of his suing him, which the attorney, as we have before seen, had blabbed to Atkinson.

But no sooner did the doctor hear that Booth was arrested than the wretched condition of his wife and family began to affect his mind. The children, who were to be utterly undone with their father, were intirely innocent; and as for Amelia herself, though he thought he had most convincing proofs of very blameable levity, yet his former friendship and affection to her were busy to invent every excuse, till, by very heavily loading the husband, they lightened the suspicion against the wife.

In this temper of mind he resolved to pay Amelia a second visit, and was on his way to Mrs. Ellison when the serjeant met him and made himself known to him. The doctor took his old servant into a coffee-house, where he received from him such an account of Booth and his family,

that he desired the serjeant to shew him presently to Amelia; and this was the cordial which we mentioned at the end of the ninth chapter of the preceding book.

The doctor became soon satisfied concerning the trinkets which had given him so much uneasiness, and which had brought so much mischief on the head of poor Booth. Amelia likewise gave the doctor some satisfaction as to what he had heard of her husband's behaviour in the country; and assured him, upon her honour, that Booth could so well answer every complaint against his conduct, that she had no doubt but that a man of the doctor's justice and candour would entirely acquit him, and would consider him as an innocent unfortunate man, who was the object of a good man's compassion, not of his anger or resentment.

This worthy clergyman, who was not desirous of finding proofs to condemn the captain or to justify his own vindictive proceedings, but, on the contrary, rejoiced heartily in every piece of evidence which tended to clear up the character of his friend, gave a ready ear to all which Amelia said. To this, indeed, he was induced by the love he always had for that lady, by the good opinion he entertained of her, as well as by pity for her present condition, than which nothing appeared more miserable; for he found her in the highest agonies of grief and despair, with her two little children crying over their wretched mother. These are, indeed, to a well-disposed mind, the most tragical sights that human nature can furnish, and afford a juster motive to grief and tears in the beholder than it would be to see all the heroes who have ever infested the earth hanged all together in a string.

The doctor felt this sight as he ought. He immediately endeavoured to comfort the afflicted; in which he so well succeeded, that he restored to Amelia sufficient spirits to give him the satisfaction we have mentioned: after which he declared he would go and release her husband, which he accordingly did in the manner we have above related.

Chapter ii. — In which the history goes forward.

We now return to that period of our history to which we had brought it at the end of our last book.

Booth and his friends arrived from the bailiff's, at the serjeant's lodgings, where Booth immediately ran up-stairs to his Amelia; between whom I shall not attempt to describe the meeting. Nothing certainly was ever more tender or more joyful. This, however, I will observe, that a very few of these exquisite moments, of which the best minds only are capable, do in reality over-balance the longest enjoyments which can ever fall to the lot of the worst.

Whilst Booth and his wife were feasting their souls with the most delicious mutual endearments, the doctor was fallen to play with the two little children below-stairs. While he was thus engaged the little boy did somewhat amiss; upon which the doctor said, "If you do so any more I will take your papa away from you again."—"Again! sir," said the child; "why, was it you then that took away my papa before?" "Suppose it was," said the doctor; "would not you forgive me?" "Yes," cries the child, "I would forgive you; because a Christian must forgive everybody; but I should hate you as long as I live."

The doctor was so pleased with the boy's answer, that he caught him in his arms and kissed him; at which time Booth and his wife returned. The doctor asked which of them was their son's instructor in his religion; Booth answered that he must confess Amelia had all the merit of that kind. "I should have rather thought he had learnt of his father," cries the doctor; "for he seems a good soldier-like Christian, and professes to hate his enemies with a very good grace."

"How, Billy!" cries Amelia. "I am sure I did not teach you so."

"I did not say I would hate my enemies, madam," cries the boy; "I only said I would hate papa's enemies. Sure, mamma, there is no harm in that; nay, I am sure there is no harm in it, for I have heard you say the same thing a thousand times."

The doctor smiled on the child, and, chucking him under the chin, told him he must hate nobody 5 and now Mrs. Atkinson, who had provided a dinner for them all, desired them to walk up and partake of it.

And now it was that Booth was first made acquainted with the serjeant's marriage, as was Dr Harrison; both of whom greatly felicitated him upon it.

Mrs. Atkinson, who was, perhaps, a little more confounded than she would have been had she married a colonel, said, "If I have done wrong, Mrs. Booth is to answer for it, for she made the match; indeed, Mr. Atkinson, you are greatly obliged to the character which this lady gives of you." "I hope he will deserve it," said the doctor; "and, if the army hath not corrupted a good boy, I believe I may answer for him."

While our little company were enjoying that happiness which never fails to attend conversation where all present are pleased with each other, a visitant arrived who was, perhaps, not very welcome to any of them. This was no other than Colonel James, who, entering the room with much gaiety, went directly up to Booth, embraced him, and expressed great satisfaction at finding him there; he then made an apology for not attending him in the morning, which he said had been impossible; and that he had, with the utmost difficulty, put off some business of great consequence in order to serve him this afternoon; "but I am glad on your account," cried he to Booth, "that my presence was not necessary."

Booth himself was extremely satisfied with this declaration, and failed not to return him as many thanks as he would have deserved had he performed his promise; but the two ladies were not quite so well satisfied. As for the serjeant, he had slipt out of the room when the colonel entered, not entirely out of that bashfulness which we have remarked him to be tainted with, but indeed, from what had past in the morning, he hated the sight of the colonel as well on the account of his wife as on that of his friend.

The doctor, on the contrary, on what he had formerly heard from both Amelia and her husband of the colonel's generosity and friendship, had built so good an opinion of him, that he was very much pleased with seeing him, and took the first opportunity of telling him so. "Colonel," said the doctor, "I have not the happiness of being known to you; but I have long been desirous of an acquaintance with a gentleman in whose commendation I have heard so much from some present." The colonel made a proper answer to this compliment, and they soon entered into a familiar conversation together; for the doctor was not difficult of access; indeed, he held the strange reserve which is usually practised in this nation between people who are in any degree strangers to each other to be very unbecoming the Christian character.

The two ladies soon left the room; and the remainder of the visit, which was not very long, past in discourse on various common subjects, not worth recording. In the conclusion, the colonel invited Booth and his lady, and the doctor, to dine with him the next day.

To give Colonel James his due commendation, he had shewn a great command of himself and great presence of mind on this occasion; for, to speak the plain truth, the visit was intended to Amelia alone; nor did he expect, or perhaps desire, anything less than to find the captain at home. The great joy which he suddenly conveyed into his countenance at the unexpected sight of his friend is to be attributed to that noble art which is taught in those excellent schools called the several courts of Europe. By this, men are enabled to dress out their countenances as much at their own pleasure as they do their bodies, and to put on friendship with as much ease as they can a laced coat.

When the colonel and doctor were gone, Booth acquainted Amelia with the invitation he had received. She was so struck with the news, and betrayed such visible marks of confusion and uneasiness, that they could not have escaped Booth's observation had suspicion given him the least hint to remark; but this, indeed, is the great optic-glass helping us to discern plainly almost all that passes in the minds of others, without some use of which nothing is more purblind than human nature.

Amelia, having recovered from her first perturbation, answered, "My dear, I will dine with you wherever you please to lay your commands on me." "I am obliged to you, my dear soul," cries Booth; "your obedience shall be very easy, for my command will be that you shall always follow your own inclinations." "My inclinations," answered she, "would, I am afraid, be too unreasonable a confinement to you; for they would always lead me to be with you and your children, with at most a single friend or two now and then." "O my dear!" replied he, "large companies give us a greater relish for our own society when we return to it; and we shall be extremely merry, for Doctor Harrison dines with us." "I hope you will, my dear," cries she; "but I own I should have been better pleased to have enjoyed a few days with yourself and the children, with no other

178

person but Mrs. Atkinson, for whom I have conceived a violent affection, and who would have given us but little interruption. However, if you have promised, I must undergo the penance." "Nay, child," cried he, "I am sure I would have refused, could I have guessed it had been in the least disagreeable to you though I know your objection." "Objection!" cries Amelia eagerly "I have no objection." "Nay, nay," said he, "come, be honest, I know your objection, though you are unwilling to own it." "Good Heavens!" cryed Amelia, frightened, "what do you mean? what objection?" "Why," answered he, "to the company of Mrs. James; and I must confess she hath not behaved to you lately as you might have expected; but you ought to pass all that by for the sake of her husband, to whom we have both so many obligations, who is the worthiest, honestest, and most generous fellow in the universe, and the best friend to me that ever man had."

Amelia, who had far other suspicions, and began to fear that her husband had discovered them, was highly pleased when she saw him taking a wrong scent. She gave, therefore, a little in to the deceit, and acknowledged the truth of what he had mentioned; but said that the pleasure she should have in complying with his desires would highly recompense any dissatisfaction which might arise on any other account; and shortly after ended the conversation on this subject with her chearfully promising to fulfil his promise.

In reality, poor Amelia had now a most unpleasant task to undertake; for she thought it absolutely necessary to conceal from her husband the opinion she had conceived of the colonel. For, as she knew the characters, as well of her husband as of his friend, or rather enemy (both being often synonymous in the language of the world), she had the utmost reason to apprehend something very fatal might attend her husband's entertaining the same thought of James which filled and tormented her own breast.

And, as she knew that nothing but these thoughts could justify the least unkind, or, indeed, the least reserved behaviour to James, who had, in all appearance, conferred the greatest obligations upon Booth and herself, she was reduced to a dilemma the most dreadful that can attend a virtuous woman, as it often gives the highest triumph, and sometimes no little advantage, to the men of professed gallantry.

In short, to avoid giving any umbrage to her husband, Amelia was forced to act in a manner which she was conscious must give encouragement to the colonel; a situation which perhaps requires as great prudence and delicacy as any in which the heroic part of the female character can be exerted.

Chapter iii. — A conversation between Dr Harrison and others.

The next day Booth and his lady, with the doctor, met at Colonel James's, where Colonel Bath likewise made one of the company.

Nothing very remarkable passed at dinner, or till the ladies withdrew. During this time, however, the behaviour of Colonel James was such as gave some uneasiness to Amelia, who well understood his meaning, though the particulars were too refined and subtle to be observed by any other present.

When the ladies were gone, which was as soon as Amelia could prevail on Mrs. James to depart, Colonel Bath, who had been pretty brisk with champagne at dinner, soon began to display his magnanimity. "My brother tells me, young gentleman," said he to Booth, "that you have been used very ill lately by some rascals, and I have no doubt but you will do yourself justice."

Booth answered that he did not know what he meant. "Since I must mention it then," cries the colonel, "I hear you have been arrested; and I think you know what satisfaction is to be required by a man of honour."

"I beg, sir," says the doctor, "no more may be mentioned of that matter. I am convinced no satisfaction will be required of the captain till he is able to give it."

"I do not understand what you mean by able," cries the colonel. To which the doctor answered, "That it was of too tender a nature to speak more of."

"Give me your hand, doctor," cries the colonel; "I see you are a man of honour, though you

wear a gown. It is, as you say, a matter of a tender nature. Nothing, indeed, is so tender as a man's honour. Curse my liver, if any man—I mean, that is, if any gentleman, was to arrest me, I would as surely cut his throat as—"

"How, sir!" said the doctor, "would you compensate one breach of the law by a much greater, and pay your debts by committing murder?"

"Why do you mention law between gentlemen?" says the colonel. "A man of honour wears his law by his side; and can the resentment of an affront make a gentleman guilty of murder? and what greater affront can one man cast upon another than by arresting him? I am convinced that he who would put up an arrest would put up a slap in the face."

Here the colonel looked extremely fierce, and the divine stared with astonishment at this doctrine; when Booth, who well knew the impossibility of opposing the colonel's humour with success, began to play with it; and, having first conveyed a private wink to the doctor, he said there might be cases undoubtedly where such an affront ought to be resented; but that there were others where any resentment was impracticable: "As, for instance," said he, "where the man is arrested by a woman."

"I could not be supposed to mean that case," cries the colonel; "and you are convinced I did not mean it."

"To put an end to this discourse at once, sir," said the doctor, "I was the plaintiff at whose suit this gentleman was arrested."

"Was you so, sir?" cries the colonel; "then I have no more to say. Women and the clergy are upon the same footing. The long-robed gentry are exempted from the laws of honour."

"I do not thank you for that exemption, sir," cries the doctor; "and, if honour and fighting are, as they seem to be, synonymous words with you, I believe there are some clergymen, who in defence of their religion, or their country, or their friend, the only justifiable causes of fighting, except bare self-defence, would fight as bravely as yourself, colonel! and that without being paid for it."

"Sir, you are privileged," says the colonel, with great dignity; "and you have my leave to say what you please. I respect your order, and you cannot offend me."

"I will not offend you, colonel," cries the doctor; "and our order is very much obliged to you, since you profess so much respect to us, and pay none to our Master."

"What Master, sir?" said the colonel.

"That Master," answered the doctor, "who hath expressly forbidden all that cutting of throats to which you discover so much inclination."

"O! your servant, sir," said the colonel; "I see what you are driving at; but you shall not persuade me to think that religion forces me to be a coward."

"I detest and despise the name as much as you can," cries the doctor; "but you have a wrong idea of the word, colonel. What were all the Greeks and Romans? were these cowards? and yet, did you ever hear of this butchery, which we call duelling, among them?"

"Yes, indeed, have I," cries the colonel. "What else is all Mr. Pope's Homer full of but duels? Did not what's his name, one of the Agamemnons, fight with that paultry rascal Paris? and Diomede with what d'ye call him there? and Hector with I forget his name, he that was Achilles's bosom-friend; and afterwards with Achilles himself? Nay, and in Dryden's Virgil, is there anything almost besides fighting?"

"You are a man of learning, colonel," cries the doctor; "but—"

"I thank you for that compliment," said the colonel.—"No, sir, I do not pretend to learning; but I have some little reading, and I am not ashamed to own it."

"But are you sure, colonel," cries the doctor, "that you have not made a small mistake? for I am apt to believe both Mr. Pope and Mr. Dryden (though I cannot say I ever read a word of either of them) speak of wars between nations, and not of private duels; for of the latter I do not remember one single instance in all the Greek and Roman story. In short, it is a modern custom, introduced by barbarous nations since the times of Christianity; though it is a direct and audacious defiance of the Christian law, and is consequently much more sinful in us than it would have been in the heathens."

"Drink about, doctor," cries the colonel; "and let us call a new cause; for I perceive we shall never agree on this. You are a Churchman, and I don't expect you to speak your mind."

"We are both of the same Church, I hope," cries the doctor.

"I am of the Church of England, sir," answered the colonel, "and will fight for it to the last drop of my blood."

"It is very generous in you, colonel," cries the doctor, "to fight so zealously for a religion by which you are to be damned."

"It is well for you, doctor," cries the colonel, "that you wear a gown; for, by all the dignity of a man, if any other person had said the words you have just uttered, I would have made him eat them; ay, d——n me, and my sword into the bargain."

Booth began to be apprehensive that this dispute might grow too warm; in which case he feared that the colonel's honour, together with the champagne, might hurry him so far as to forget the respect due, and which he professed to pay, to the sacerdotal robe. Booth therefore interposed between the disputants, and said that the colonel had very rightly proposed to call a new subject; for that it was impossible to reconcile accepting a challenge with the Christian religion, or refusing it with the modern notion of honour. "And you must allow it, doctor," said he, "to be a very hard injunction for a man to become infamous; and more especially for a soldier, who is to lose his bread into the bargain."

"Ay, sir," says the colonel, with an air of triumph, "what say you to that?"

"Why, I say," cries the doctor, "that it is much harder to be damned on the other side."

"That may be," said the colonel; "but damn me, if I would take an affront of any man breathing, for all that. And yet I believe myself to be as good a Christian as wears a head. My maxim is, never to give an affront, nor ever to take one; and I say that it is the maxim of a good Christian, and no man shall ever persuade me to the contrary."

"Well, sir," said the doctor, "since that is your resolution, I hope no man will ever give you an affront."

"I am obliged to you for your hope, doctor," cries the colonel, with a sneer; "and he that doth will be obliged to you for lending him your gown; for, by the dignity of a man, nothing out of petticoats, I believe, dares affront me."

Colonel James had not hitherto joined in the discourse. In truth, his thoughts had been otherwise employed; nor is it very difficult for the reader to guess what had been the subject of them. Being waked, however, from his reverie, and having heard the two or three last speeches, he turned to his brother, and asked him, why he would introduce such a topic of conversation before a gentleman of Doctor Harrison's character?

"Brother," cried Bath, "I own it was wrong, and I ask the doctor's pardon: I know not how it happened to arise; for you know, brother, I am not used to talk of these matters. They are generally poltroons that do. I think I need not be beholden to my tongue to declare I am none. I have shown myself in a line of battle. I believe there is no man will deny that; I believe I may say no man dares deny that I have done my duty."

The colonel was thus proceeding to prove that his prowess was neither the subject of his discourse nor the object of his vanity, when a servant entered and summoned the company to tea with the ladies; a summons which Colonel James instantly obeyed, and was followed by all the rest.

But as the tea-table conversation, though extremely delightful to those who are engaged in it, may probably appear somewhat dull to the reader, we will here put an end to the chapter.

Chapter iv. — A dialogue between Booth and Amelia.

The next morning early, Booth went by appointment and waited on Colonel James; whence he returned to Amelia in that kind of disposition which the great master of human passion would describe in Andromache, when he tells us she cried and smiled at the same instant.

Amelia plainly perceived the discomposure of his mind, in which the opposite affections of joy and grief were struggling for the superiority, and begged to know the occasion; upon which Booth spoke as follows:—

"My dear," said he, "I had no intention to conceal from you what hath past this morning between me and the colonel, who hath oppressed me, if I may use that expression, with obligations. Sure never man had such a friend; for never was there so noble, so generous a heart— I cannot help this ebullition of gratitude, I really cannot." Here he paused a moment, and wiped his eyes, and then proceeded: "You know, my dear, how gloomy the prospect was yesterday before our eyes, how inevitable ruin stared me in the face; and the dreadful idea of having entailed beggary on my Amelia and her posterity racked my mind; for though, by the goodness of the doctor, I had regained my liberty, the debt yet remained; and, if that worthy man had a design of forgiving me his share, this must have been my utmost hope, and the condition in which I must still have found myself need not to be expatiated on. In what light, then, shall I see, in what words shall I relate, the colonel's kindness? O my dear Amelia! he hath removed the whole gloom at once, hath driven all despair out of my mind, and hath filled it with the most sanguine, and, at the same time, the most reasonable hopes of making a comfortable provision for yourself and my dear children. In the first place, then, he will advance me a sum of money to pay off all my debts; and this on a bond to be repaid only when I shall become colonel of a regiment, and not before. In the next place, he is gone this very morning to ask a company for me, which is now vacant in the West Indies; and, as he intends to push this with all his interest, neither he nor I have any doubt of his success. Now, my dear, comes the third, which, though perhaps it ought to give me the greatest joy, such is, I own, the weakness of my nature, it rends my very heartstrings asunder. I cannot mention it, for I know it will give you equal pain; though I know, on all proper occasions, you can exert a manly resolution. You will not, I am convinced, oppose it, whatever you must suffer in complying. O my dear Amelia! I must suffer likewise; yet I have resolved to bear it. You know not what my poor heart hath suffered since he made the proposal. It is love for you alone which could persuade me to submit to it. Consider our situation; consider that of our children; reflect but on those poor babes, whose future happiness is at stake, and it must arm your resolution. It is your interest and theirs that reconciled me to a proposal which, when the colonel first made it, struck me with the utmost horror; he hath, indeed, from these motives, persuaded me into a resolution which I thought impossible for any one to have persuaded me into. O my dear Amelia! let me entreat you to give me up to the good of your children, as I have promised the colonel to give you up to their interest and your own. If you refuse these terms we are still undone, for he insists absolutely upon them. Think, then, my love, however hard they may be, necessity compels us to submit to them. I know in what light a woman, who loves like you, must consider such a proposal; and yet how many instances have you of women who, from the same motives, have submitted to the same!"

"What can you mean, Mr. Booth?" cries Amelia, trembling.

"Need I explain my meaning to you more?" answered Booth.—"Did I not say I must give up my Amelia?"

"Give me up!" said she.

"For a time only, I mean," answered he: "for a short time perhaps. The colonel himself will take care it shall not be long—for I know his heart; I shall scarce have more joy in receiving you back than he will have in restoring you to my arms. In the mean time, he will not only be a father to my children, but a husband to you."

"A husband to me!" said Amelia.

"Yes, my dear; a kind, a fond, a tender, an affectionate husband. If I had not the most certain assurances of this, doth my Amelia think I could be prevailed on to leave her? No, my Amelia, he is the only man on earth who could have prevailed on me; but I know his house, his purse, his protection, will be all at your command. And as for any dislike you have conceived to his wife, let not that be any objection; for I am convinced he will not suffer her to insult you; besides, she is extremely well bred, and, how much soever she may hate you in her heart, she will at least treat you with civility.

"Nay, the invitation is not his, but hers; and I am convinced they will both behave to you with the greatest friendship; his I am sure will be sincere, as to the wife of a friend entrusted to his care; and hers will, from good-breeding, have not only the appearances but the effects of the truest friendship."

"I understand you, my dear, at last," said she (indeed she had rambled into very strange conceits from some parts of his discourse); "and I will give you my resolution in a word—I will do

the duty of a wife, and that is, to attend her husband wherever he goes."

Booth attempted to reason with her, but all to no purpose. She gave, indeed, a quiet hearing to all he said, and even to those parts which most displeased her ears; I mean those in which he exaggerated the great goodness and disinterested generosity of his friend; but her resolution remained inflexible, and resisted the force of all his arguments with a steadiness of opposition, which it would have been almost excusable in him to have construed into stubbornness.

The doctor arrived in the midst of the dispute; and, having heard the merits of the cause on both sides, delivered his opinion in the following words.

"I have always thought it, my dear children, a matter of the utmost nicety to interfere in any differences between husband and wife; but, since you both desire me with such earnestness to give you my sentiments on the present contest between you, I will give you my thoughts as well as I am able. In the first place then, can anything be more reasonable than for a wife to desire to attend her husband? It is, as my favourite child observes, no more than a desire to do her duty; and I make no doubt but that is one great reason of her insisting on it. And how can you yourself oppose it? Can love be its own enemy? or can a husband who is fond of his wife, content himself almost on any account with a long absence from her?"

"You speak like an angel, my dear Doctor Harrison," answered Amelia: "I am sure, if he loved as tenderly as I do, he could on no account submit to it."

"Pardon me, child," cries the doctor; "there are some reasons which would not only justify his leaving you, but which must force him, if he hath any real love for you, joined with common sense, to make that election. If it was necessary, for instance, either to your good or to the good of your children, he would not deserve the name of a man, I am sure not that of a husband, if he hesitated a moment. Nay, in that case, I am convinced you yourself would be an advocate for what you now oppose. I fancy therefore I mistook him when I apprehended he said that the colonel made his leaving you behind as the condition of getting him the commission; for I know my dear child hath too much goodness, and too much sense, and too much resolution, to prefer any temporary indulgence of her own passions to the solid advantages of her whole family."

"There, my dear!" cries Booth; "I knew what opinion the doctor would be of. Nay, I am certain there is not a wise man in the kingdom who would say otherwise."

"Don't abuse me, young gentleman," said the doctor, "with appellations I don't deserve."

"I abuse you, my dear doctor!" cries Booth.

"Yes, my dear sir," answered the doctor; "you insinuated slily that I was wise, which, as the world understands the phrase, I should be ashamed of; and my comfort is that no one can accuse me justly of it. I have just given an instance of the contrary by throwing away my advice."

"I hope, sir," cries Booth, "that will not be the case."

"Yes, sir," answered the doctor. "I know it will be the case in the present instance, for either you will not go at all, or my little turtle here will go with you."

"You are in the right, doctor," cries Amelia.

"I am sorry for it," said the doctor, "for then I assure you you are in the wrong."

"Indeed," cries Amelia, "if you knew all my reasons you would say they were very strong ones."

"Very probably," cries the doctor. "The knowledge that they are in the wrong is a very strong reason to some women to continue so."

"Nay, doctor," cries Amelia, "you shall never persuade me of that. I will not believe that any human being ever did an action merely because they knew it to be wrong."

"I am obliged to you, my dear child," said the doctor, "for declaring your resolution of not being persuaded. Your husband would never call me a wise man again if, after that declaration, I should attempt to persuade you."

"Well, I must be content," cries Amelia, "to let you think as you please."

"That is very gracious, indeed," said the doctor. "Surely, in a country where the church suffers others to think as they please, it would be very hard if they had not themselves the same liberty. And yet, as unreasonable as the power of controuling men's thoughts is represented, I will shew you how you shall controul mine whenever you desire it."

"How, pray?" cries Amelia. "I should greatly esteem that power."

"Why, whenever you act like a wise woman," cries the doctor, "you will force me to think you so: and, whenever you are pleased to act as you do now, I shall be obliged, whether I will or no, to

think as I do now."

"Nay, dear doctor," cries Booth, "I am convinced my Amelia will never do anything to forfeit your good opinion. Consider but the cruel hardship of what she is to undergo, and you will make allowances for the difficulty she makes in complying. To say the truth, when I examine my own heart, I have more obligations to her than appear at first sight; for, by obliging me to find arguments to persuade her, she hath assisted me in conquering myself. Indeed, if she had shewn more resolution, I should have shewn less."

"So you think it necessary, then," said the doctor, "that there should be one fool at least in every married couple. A mighty resolution, truly! and well worth your valuing yourself upon, to part with your wife for a few months in order to make the fortune of her and your children; when you are to leave her, too, in the care and protection of a friend that gives credit to the old stories of friendship, and doth an honour to human nature. What, in the name of goodness! do either of you think that you have made an union to endure for ever? How will either of you bear that separation which must, some time or other, and perhaps very soon, be the lot of one of you? Have you forgot that you are both mortal? As for Christianity, I see you have resigned all pretensions to it; for I make no doubt but that you have so set your hearts on the happiness you enjoy here together, that neither of you ever think a word of hereafter."

Amelia now burst into tears; upon which Booth begged the doctor to proceed no farther. Indeed, he would not have wanted the caution; for, however blunt he appeared in his discourse, he had a tenderness of heart which is rarely found among men; for which I know no other reason than that true goodness is rarely found among them; for I am firmly persuaded that the latter never possessed any human mind in any degree, without being attended by as large a portion of the former.

Thus ended the conversation on this subject; what followed is not worth relating, till the doctor carried off Booth with him to take a walk in the Park.

Chapter v. — A conversation between Amelia and Dr Harrison, with the result.

Amelia, being left alone, began to consider seriously of her condition; she saw it would be very difficult to resist the importunities of her husband, backed by the authority of the doctor, especially as she well knew how unreasonable her declarations must appear to every one who was ignorant of her real motives to persevere in it. On the other hand, she was fully determined, whatever might be the consequence, to adhere firmly to her resolution of not accepting the colonel's invitation.

When she had turned the matter every way in her mind, and vexed and tormented herself with much uneasy reflexion upon it, a thought at last occurred to her which immediately brought her some comfort. This was, to make a confidant of the doctor, and to impart to him the whole truth. This method, indeed, appeared to her now to be so adviseable, that she wondered she had not hit upon it sooner; but it is the nature of despair to blind us to all the means of safety, however easy and apparent they may be.

Having fixed her purpose in her mind, she wrote a short note to the doctor, in which she acquainted him that she had something of great moment to impart to him, which must be an entire secret from her husband, and begged that she might have an opportunity of communicating it as soon as possible.

Doctor Harrison received the letter that afternoon, and immediately complied with Amelia's request in visiting her. He found her drinking tea with her husband and Mrs. Atkinson, and sat down and joined the company.

Soon after the removal of the tea-table Mrs. Atkinson left the room.

The doctor then, turning to Booth, said, "I hope, captain, you have a true sense of the obedience due to the church, though our clergy do not often exact it. However, it is proper to exercise our power sometimes, in order to remind the laity of their duty. I must tell you, therefore, that I have some private business with your wife; and I expect your immediate absence."

"Upon my word, doctor," answered Booth, "no Popish confessor, I firmly believe, ever pronounced his will and pleasure with more gravity and dignity; none therefore was ever more immediately obeyed than you shall be." Booth then quitted the room, and desired the doctor to recall him when his business with the lady was over.

Doctor Harrison promised he would; and then turning to Amelia he said, "Thus far, madam, I have obeyed your commands, and am now ready to receive the important secret which you mention in your note." Amelia now informed her friend of all she knew, all she had seen and heard, and all that she suspected, of the colonel. The good man seemed greatly shocked at the relation, and remained in a silent astonishment. Upon which Amelia said, "Is villany so rare a thing, sir, that it should so much surprize you?" "No, child," cries he; "but I am shocked at seeing it so artfully disguised under the appearance of so much virtue; and, to confess the truth, I believe my own vanity is a little hurt in having been so grossly imposed upon. Indeed, I had a very high regard for this man; for, besides the great character given him by your husband, and the many facts I have heard so much redounding to his honour, he hath the fairest and most promising appearance I have ever yet beheld. A good face, they say, is a letter of recommendation. O Nature, Nature, why art thou so dishonest as ever to send men with these false recommendations into the world?"

"Indeed, my dear sir, I begin to grow entirely sick of it," cries Amelia, "for sure all mankind almost are villains in their hearts."

"Fie, child!" cries the doctor. "Do not make a conclusion so much to the dishonour of the great Creator. The nature of man is far from being in itself evil: it abounds with benevolence, charity, and pity, coveting praise and honour, and shunning shame and disgrace. Bad education, bad habits, and bad customs, debauch our nature, and drive it headlong as it were into vice. The governors of the world, and I am afraid the priesthood, are answerable for the badness of it. Instead of discouraging wickedness to the utmost of their power, both are too apt to connive at it. In the great sin of adultery, for instance; hath the government provided any law to punish it? or doth the priest take any care to correct it? on the contrary, is the most notorious practice of it any detriment to a man's fortune or to his reputation in the world? doth it exclude him from any preferment in the state, I had almost said in the church? is it any blot in his escutcheon? any bar to his honour? is he not to be found every day in the assemblies of women of the highest quality? in the closets of the greatest men, and even at the tables of bishops? What wonder then if the community in general treat this monstrous crime as a matter of jest, and that men give way to the temptations of a violent appetite, when the indulgence of it is protected by law and countenanced by custom? I am convinced there are good stamina in the nature of this very man; for he hath done acts of friendship and generosity to your husband before he could have any evil design on your chastity; and in a Christian society, which I no more esteem this nation to be than I do any part of Turkey, I doubt not but this very colonel would have made a worthy and valuable member."

"Indeed, my dear sir," cries Amelia, "you are the wisest as well as best man in the world—"

"Not a word of my wisdom," cries the doctor. "I have not a grain—I am not the least versed in the Chrematistic {Footnote: The art of getting wealth is so called by Aristotle in his Politics.} art, as an old friend of mine calls it. I know not how to get a shilling, nor how to keep it in my pocket if I had it."

"But you understand human nature to the bottom," answered Amelia; "and your mind is the treasury of all ancient and modern learning."

"You are a little flatterer," cries the doctor; "but I dislike you not for it. And, to shew you I don't, I will return your flattery, and tell you you have acted with great prudence in concealing this affair from your husband; but you have drawn me into a scrape; for I have promised to dine with this fellow again to-morrow, and you have made it impossible for me to keep my word."

"Nay, but, dear sir," cries Amelia, "for Heaven's sake take care! If you shew any kind of disrespect to the colonel, my husband may be led into some suspicion—especially after our conference."

"Fear nothing, child. I will give him no hint; and, that I may be certain of not doing it, I will stay away. You do not think, I hope, that I will join in a chearful conversation with such a man; that I will so far betray my character as to give any countenance to such flagitious proceedings. Besides, my promise was only conditional; and I do not know whether I could otherwise have

kept it; for I expect an old friend every day who comes to town twenty miles on foot to see me, whom I shall not part with on any account; for, as he is very poor, he may imagine I treat him with disrespect."

"Well, sir," cries Amelia, "I must admire you and love you for your goodness."

"Must you love me?" cries the doctor. "I could cure you now in a minute if I pleased."

"Indeed, I defy you, sir," said Amelia.

"If I could but persuade you," answered he, "that I thought you not handsome, away would vanish all ideas of goodness in an instant. Confess honestly, would they not?"

"Perhaps I might blame the goodness of your eyes," replied Amelia; "and that is perhaps an honester confession than you expected. But do, pray, sir, be serious, and give me your advice what to do. Consider the difficult game I have to play; for I am sure, after what I have told you, you would not even suffer me to remain under the roof of this colonel."

"No, indeed, would I not," said the doctor, "whilst I have a house of my own to entertain you."

"But how to dissuade my husband," continued she, "without giving him any suspicion of the real cause, the consequences of his guessing at which I tremble to think upon."

"I will consult my pillow upon it," said the doctor; "and in the morning you shall see me again. In the mean time be comforted, and compose the perturbations of your mind."

"Well, sir," said she, "I put my whole trust in you."

"I am sorry to hear it," cries the doctor. "Your innocence may give you a very confident trust in a much more powerful assistance. However, I will do all I can to serve you: and now, if you please, we will call back your husband; for, upon my word, he hath shewn a good catholic patience. And where is the honest serjeant and his wife? I am pleased with the behaviour of you both to that worthy fellow, in opposition to the custom of the world; which, instead of being formed on the precepts of our religion to consider each other as brethren, teaches us to regard those who are a degree below us, either in rank or fortune, as a species of beings of an inferior order in the creation."

The captain now returned into the room, as did the serjeant and Mrs. Atkinson; and the two couple, with the doctor, spent the evening together in great mirth and festivity; for the doctor was one of the best companions in the world, and a vein of chearfulness, good humour, and pleasantry, ran through his conversation, with which it was impossible to resist being pleased.

Chapter vi. — Containing as surprizing an accident as is perhaps recorded in history.

Booth had acquainted the serjeant with the great goodness of Colonel James, and with the chearful prospects which he entertained from it. This Atkinson, behind the curtain, communicated to his wife. The conclusion which she drew from it need scarce be hinted to the reader. She made, indeed, no scruple of plainly and bluntly telling her husband that the colonel had a most manifest intention to attack the chastity of Amelia.

This thought gave the poor serjeant great uneasiness, and, after having kept him long awake, tormented him in his sleep with a most horrid dream, in which he imagined that he saw the colonel standing by the bedside of Amelia, with a naked sword in his hand, and threatening to stab her instantly unless she complied with his desires. Upon this the serjeant started up in his bed, and, catching his wife by the throat, cried out, "D—n you, put up your sword this instant, and leave the room, or by Heaven I'll drive mine to your heart's blood!"

This rough treatment immediately roused Mrs. Atkinson from her sleep, who no sooner perceived the position of her husband, and felt his hand grasping her throat, than she gave a violent shriek and presently fell into a fit.

Atkinson now waked likewise, and soon became sensible of the violent agitations of his wife. He immediately leapt out of bed, and running for a bottle of water, began to sprinkle her very plentifully; but all to no purpose: she neither spoke nor gave any symptoms of recovery Atkinson then began to roar aloud; upon which Booth, who lay under him, jumped from his bed, and ran

up with the lighted candle in his hand. The serjeant had no sooner taken the candle than he ran with it to the bed-side. Here he beheld a sight which almost deprived him of his senses. The bed appeared to be all over blood, and his wife weltering in the midst of it. Upon this the serjeant, almost in a frenzy, cried out, "O Heavens! I have killed my wife. I have stabbed her! I have stabbed her!" "What can be the meaning of all this?" said Booth. "O, sir!" cries the serjeant, "I dreamt I was rescuing your lady from the hands of Colonel James, and I have killed my poor wife."—Here he threw himself upon the bed by her, caught her in his arms, and behaved like one frantic with despair.

By this time Amelia had thrown on a wrapping-gown, and was come up into the room, where the serjeant and his wife were lying on the bed and Booth standing like a motionless statue by the bed-side. Amelia had some difficulty to conquer the effects of her own surprize on this occasion; for a more ghastly and horrible sight than the bed presented could not be conceived.

Amelia sent Booth to call up the maid of the house, in order to lend her assistance; but before his return Mrs. Atkinson began to come to herself; and soon after, to the inexpressible joy of the serjeant, it was discovered she had no wound. Indeed, the delicate nose of Amelia soon made that discovery, which the grosser smell of the serjeant, and perhaps his fright, had prevented him from making; for now it appeared that the red liquor with which the bed was stained, though it may, perhaps, sometimes run through the veins of a fine lady, was not what is properly called blood, but was, indeed, no other than cherry-brandy, a bottle of which Mrs. Atkinson always kept in her room to be ready for immediate use, and to which she used to apply for comfort in all her afflictions. This the poor serjeant, in his extreme hurry, had mistaken for a bottle of water. Matters were now soon accommodated, and no other mischief appeared to be done, unless to the bed-cloaths. Amelia and Booth returned back to their room, and Mrs. Atkinson rose from her bed in order to equip it with a pair of clean sheets.

And thus this adventure would have ended without producing any kind of consequence, had not the words which the serjeant uttered in his frenzy made some slight impression on Booth; so much, at least, as to awaken his curiosity; so that in the morning when he arose he sent for the serjeant, and desired to hear the particulars of this dream, since Amelia was concerned in it.

The serjeant at first seemed unwilling to comply, and endeavoured to make excuses. This, perhaps, encreased Booth's curiosity, and he said, "Nay, I am resolved to hear it. Why, you simpleton, do you imagine me weak enough to be affected by a dream, however terrible it may be?"

"Nay, sir," cries the serjeant, "as for that matter, dreams have sometimes fallen out to be true. One of my own, I know, did so, concerning your honour; for, when you courted my young lady, I dreamt you was married to her; and yet it was at a time when neither I myself, nor any of the country, thought you would ever obtain her. But Heaven forbid this dream should ever come to pass!" "Why, what was this dream?" cries Booth. "I insist on knowing."

"To be sure, sir," cries the serjeant, "I must not refuse you; but I hope you will never think any more of it. Why then, sir, I dreamt that your honour was gone to the West Indies, and had left my lady in the care of Colonel James; and last night I dreamt the colonel came to my lady's bed-side, offering to ravish her, and with a drawn sword in his hand, threatening to stab her that moment unless she would comply with his desires. How I came to be by I know not; but I dreamt I rushed upon him, caught him by the throat, and swore I would put him to death unless he instantly left the room. Here I waked, and this was my dream. I never paid any regard to a dream in my life—but, indeed, I never dreamt anything so very plain as this. It appeared downright reality. I am sure I have left the marks of my fingers in my wife's throat. I would not have taken a hundred pound to have used her so."

"Faith," cries Booth, "it was an odd dream, and not so easily to be accounted for as that you had formerly of my marriage; for, as Shakespear says, dreams denote a foregone conclusion. Now it is impossible you should ever have thought of any such matter as this."

"However, sir," cries the serjeant, "it is in your honour's power to prevent any possibility of this dream's coming to pass, by not leaving my lady to the care of the colonel; if you must go from her, certainly there are other places where she may be with great safety; and, since my wife tells me that my lady is so very unwilling, whatever reasons she may have, I hope your honour will oblige her."

"Now I recollect it," cries Booth, "Mrs. Atkinson hath once or twice dropt some disrespectful

words of the colonel. He hath done something to disoblige her."

"He hath indeed, sir," replied the serjeant: "he hath said that of her which she doth not deserve, and for which, if he had not been my superior officer, I would have cut both his ears off. Nay, for that matter, he can speak ill of other people besides her."

"Do you know, Atkinson," cries Booth, very gravely, "that you are talking of the dearest friend I have?"

"To be honest then," answered the serjeant, "I do not think so. If I did, I should love him much better than I do."

"I must and will have this explained," cries Booth. "I have too good an opinion of you, Atkinson, to think you would drop such things as you have without some reason—and I will know it."

"I am sorry I have dropt a word," cries Atkinson. "I am sure I did not intend it; and your honour hath drawn it from me unawares."

"Indeed, Atkinson," cries Booth, "you have made me very uneasy, and I must be satisfied."

"Then, sir," said the serjeant, "you shall give me your word of honour, or I will be cut into ten thousand pieces before I will mention another syllable."

"What shall I promise?" said Booth.

"That you will not resent anything I shall lay to the colonel," answered Atkinson.

"Resent!—Well, I give you my honour," said Booth.

The serjeant made him bind himself over and over again, and then related to him the scene which formerly past between the colonel and himself, as far as concerned Booth himself; but concealed all that more immediately related to Amelia.

"Atkinson," cries Booth, "I cannot be angry with you, for I know you love me, and I have many obligations to you; but you have done wrong in censuring the colonel for what he said of me. I deserve all that he said, and his censures proceeded from his friendship."

"But it was not so kind, sir," said Atkinson, "to say such things to me who am but a serjeant, and at such a time too."

"I will hear no more," cries Booth. "Be assured you are the only man I would forgive on this occasion; and I forgive you only on condition you never speak a word more of this nature. This silly dream hath intoxicated you."

"I have done, sir," cries the serjeant. "I know my distance, and whom I am to obey; but I have one favour to beg of your honour, never to mention a word of what I have said to my lady; for I know she never would forgive me; I know she never would, by what my wife hath told me. Besides, you need not mention it, sir, to my lady, for she knows it all already, and a great deal more."

Booth presently parted from the serjeant, having desired him to close his lips on this occasion, and repaired to his wife, to whom he related the serjeant's dream.

Amelia turned as white as snow, and fell into so violent a trembling that Booth plainly perceived her emotion, and immediately partook of it himself. "Sure, my dear," said he, staring wildly, "there is more in this than I know. A silly dream could not so discompose you. I beg you, I intreat you to tell me—hath ever Colonel James—"

At the very mention of the colonel's name Amelia fell on her knees, and begged her husband not to frighten her.

"What do I say, my dear love," cried Booth, "that can frighten you?"

"Nothing, my dear," said she; "but my spirits are so discomposed with the dreadful scene I saw last night, that a dream, which at another time I should have laughed at, hath shocked me. Do but promise me that you will not leave me behind you, and I am easy."

"You may be so," cries Booth, "for I will never deny you anything. But make me easy too. I must know if you have seen anything in Colonel James to displease you."

"Why should you suspect it?" cries Amelia.

"You torment me to death," cries Booth. "By Heavens! I will know the truth. Hath he ever said or done anything which you dislike?"

"How, my dear," said Amelia, "can you imagine I should dislike a man who is so much your friend? Think of all the obligations you have to him, and then you may easily resolve yourself. Do you think, because I refuse to stay behind you in his house, that I have any objection to him? No, my dear, had he done a thousand times more than he hath—was he an angel instead of a man, I

would not quit my Billy. There's the sore, my dear—there's the misery, to be left by you."

Booth embraced her with the most passionate raptures, and, looking on her with inexpressible tenderness, cried, "Upon my soul, I am not worthy of you: I am a fool, and yet you cannot blame me. If the stupid miser hoards, with such care, his worthless treasure—if he watches it with such anxiety—if every apprehension of another's sharing the least part fills his soul with such agonies—O Amelia! what must be my condition, what terrors must I feel, while I am watching over a jewel of such real, such inestimable worth!"

"I can, with great truth, return the compliment," cries Amelia. "I have my treasure too; and am so much a miser, that no force shall ever tear me from it."

"I am ashamed of my folly," cries Booth; "and yet it is all from extreme tenderness. Nay, you yourself are the occasion. Why will you ever attempt to keep a secret from me? Do you think I should have resented to my friend his just censure of my conduct?"

"What censure, my dear love?" cries Amelia.

"Nay, the serjeant hath told me all," cries Booth—"nay, and that he hath told it to you. Poor soul! thou couldst not endure to hear me accused, though never so justly, and by so good a friend. Indeed, my dear, I have discovered the cause of that resentment to the colonel which you could not hide from me. I love you, I adore you for it; indeed, I could not forgive a slighting word on you. But, why do I compare things so unlike?—what the colonel said of me was just and true; every reflexion on my Amelia must be false and villanous."

The discernment of Amelia was extremely quick, and she now perceived what had happened, and how much her husband knew of the truth. She resolved therefore to humour him, and fell severely on Colonel James for what he had said to the serjeant, which Booth endeavoured all he could to soften; and thus ended this affair, which had brought Booth to the very brink of a discovery which must have given him the highest torment, if it had not produced any of those tragical effects which Amelia apprehended.

Chapter vii. — In which the author appears to be master of that profound learning called the knowledge of the town.

Mrs. James now came to pay a morning's visit to Amelia. She entered the room with her usual gaiety, and after a slight preface, addressing herself to Booth, said she had been quarrelling with her husband on his account. "I know not," said she, "what he means by thinking of sending you the Lord knows whither. I have insisted on his asking something for you nearer home; and it would be the hardest thing in the world if he should not obtain it. Are we resolved never to encourage merit; but to throw away all our preferments on those who do not deserve them? What a set of contemptible wretches do we see strutting about the town in scarlet!"

Booth made a very low bow, and modestly spoke in disparagement of himself. To which she answered, "Indeed, Mr. Booth, you have merit; I have heard it from my brother, who is a judge of those matters, and I am sure cannot be suspected of flattery. He is your friend as well as myself, and we will never let Mr. James rest till he hath got you a commission in England."

Booth bowed again, and was offering to speak, but she interrupted him, saying, "I will have no thanks, nor no fine speeches; if I can do you any service I shall think I am only paying the debt of friendship to my dear Mrs. Booth."

Amelia, who had long since forgot the dislike she had taken to Mrs. James at her first seeing her in town, had attributed it to the right cause, and had begun to resume her former friendship for her, expressed very warm sentiments of gratitude on this occasion. She told Mrs. James she should be eternally obliged to her if she could succeed in her kind endeavours; for that the thoughts of parting again with her husband had given her the utmost concern. "Indeed," added she, "I cannot help saying he hath some merit in the service, for he hath received two dreadful wounds in it, one of which very greatly endangered his life; and I am convinced, if his pretensions were backed with any interest, he would not fail of success."

"They shall be backed with interest," cries Mrs. James, "if my husband hath any. He hath no

favour to ask for himself, nor for any other friend that I know of; and, indeed, to grant a man his just due, ought hardly to be thought a favour. Resume your old gaiety, therefore, my dear Emily. Lord! I remember the time when you was much the gayer creature of the two. But you make an arrant mope of yourself by confining yourself at home—one never meets you anywhere. Come, you shall go with me to the Lady Betty Castleton's."

"Indeed, you must excuse me, my dear," answered Amelia, "I do not know Lady Betty."

"Not know Lady Betty! how, is that possible?—but no matter, I will introduce you. She keeps a morning rout; hardly a rout, indeed; a little bit of a drum—only four or five tables. Come, take your capuchine; you positively shall go. Booth, you shall go with us too. Though you are with your wife, another woman will keep you in countenance."

"La! child," cries Amelia, "how you rattle!"

"I am in spirits," answered Mrs. James, "this morning; for I won four rubbers together last night; and betted the things, and won almost every bet. I am in luck, and we will contrive to be partners—Come."

"Nay, child, you shall not refuse Mrs. James," said Booth.

"I have scarce seen my children to-day," answered Amelia. "Besides, I mortally detest cards."

"Detest cards!" cries Mrs. James. "How can you be so stupid? I would not live a day without them—nay, indeed, I do not believe I should be able to exist. Is there so delightful a sight in the world as the four honours in one's own hand, unless it be three natural aces at bragg?—And you really hate cards?"

"Upon reflexion," cries Amelia, "I have sometimes had great pleasure in them—in seeing my children build houses with them. My little boy is so dexterous that he will sometimes build up the whole pack."

"Indeed, Booth," cries Mrs. James, "this good woman of yours is strangely altered since I knew her first; but she will always be a good creature."

"Upon my word, my dear," cries Amelia, "you are altered too very greatly; but I doubt not to live to see you alter again, when you come to have as many children as I have."

"Children!" cries Mrs. James; "you make me shudder. How can you envy me the only circumstance which makes matrimony comfortable?"

"Indeed, my dear," said Amelia, "you injure me; for I envy no woman's happiness in marriage." At these words such looks past between Booth and his wife as, to a sensible by-stander, would have made all the airs of Mrs. James appear in the highest degree contemptible, and would have rendered herself the object of compassion. Nor could that lady avoid looking a little silly on the occasion.

Amelia now, at the earnest desire of her husband, accoutred herself to attend her friend; but first she insisted on visiting her children, to whom she gave several hearty kisses, and then, recommending them to the care of Mrs. Atkinson, she and her husband accompanied Mrs. James to the rout; where few of my fine readers will be displeased to make part of the company.

The two ladies and Booth then entered an apartment beset with card-tables, like the rooms at Bath and Tunbridge. Mrs. James immediately introduced her friends to Lady Betty, who received them very civily, and presently engaged Booth and Mrs. James in a party at whist; for, as to Amelia, she so much declined playing, that as the party could be filled without her, she was permitted to sit by.

And now, who should make his appearance but the noble peer of whom so much honourable mention hath already been made in this history? He walked directly up to Amelia, and addressed her with as perfect a confidence as if he had not been in the least conscious of having in any manner displeased her; though the reader will hardly suppose that Mrs. Ellison had kept anything a secret from him.

Amelia was not, however, so forgetful. She made him a very distant courtesy, would scarce vouchsafe an answer to anything he said, and took the first opportunity of shifting her chair and retiring from him.

Her behaviour, indeed, was such that the peer plainly perceived that he should get no advantage by pursuing her any farther at present. Instead, therefore, of attempting to follow her, he turned on his heel and addressed his discourse to another lady, though he could not avoid often casting his eyes towards Amelia as long as she remained in the room.

Fortune, which seems to have been generally no great friend to Mr. Booth, gave him no

extraordinary marks of her favour at play. He lost two full rubbers, which cost him five guineas; after which, Amelia, who was uneasy at his lordship's presence, begged him in a whisper to return home; with which request he directly complied.

Nothing, I think, remarkable happened to Booth, unless the renewal of his acquaintance with an officer whom he had known abroad, and who made one of his party at the whist-table.

The name of this gentleman, with whom the reader will hereafter be better acquainted, was Trent. He had formerly been in the same regiment with Booth, and there was some intimacy between them. Captain Trent exprest great delight in meeting his brother officer, and both mutually promised to visit each other.

The scenes which had past the preceding night and that morning had so confused Amelia's thoughts, that, in the hurry in which she was carried off by Mrs. James, she had entirely forgot her appointment with Dr Harrison. When she was informed at her return home that the doctor had been to wait upon her, and had expressed some anger at her being gone out, she became greatly uneasy, and begged of her husband to go to the doctor's lodgings and make her apology.

But lest the reader should be as angry with the doctor as he had declared himself with Amelia, we think proper to explain the matter. Nothing then was farther from the doctor's mind than the conception of any anger towards Amelia. On the contrary, when the girl answered him that her mistress was not at home, the doctor said with great good humour, "How! not at home! then tell your mistress she is a giddy vagabond, and I will come to see her no more till she sends for me." This the poor girl, from misunderstanding one word, and half forgetting the rest, had construed into great passion, several very bad words, and a declaration that he would never see Amelia any more.

Chapter viii. — In which two strangers make their appearance.

Booth went to the doctor's lodgings, and found him engaged with his country friend and his son, a young gentleman who was lately in orders; both whom the doctor had left, to keep his appointment with Amelia.

After what we mentioned at the end of the last chapter, we need take little notice of the apology made by Booth, or the doctor's reception of it, which was in his peculiar manner. "Your wife," said he, "is a vain hussy to think herself worth my anger; but tell her I have the vanity myself to think I cannot be angry without a better cause. And yet tell her I intend to punish her for her levity; for, if you go abroad, I have determined to take her down with me into the country, and make her do penance there till you return."

"Dear sir," said Booth, "I know not how to thank you if you are in earnest."

"I assure you then I am in earnest," cries the doctor; "but you need not thank me, however, since you know not how."

"But would not that, sir," said Booth, "be shewing a slight to the colonel's invitation? and you know I have so many obligations to him."

"Don't tell me of the colonel," cries the doctor; "the church is to be first served. Besides, sir, I have priority of right, even to you yourself. You stole my little lamb from me; for I was her first love."

"Well, sir," cries Booth, "if I should be so unhappy to leave her to any one, she must herself determine; and, I believe, it will not be difficult to guess where her choice will fall; for of all men, next to her husband, I believe, none can contend with Dr Harrison in her favour."

"Since you say so," cries the doctor, "fetch her hither to dinner with us; for I am at least so good a Christian to love those that love me—I will shew you my daughter, my old friend, for I am really proud of her—and you may bring my grand-children with you if you please."

Booth made some compliments, and then went on his errand. As soon as he was gone the old gentleman said to the doctor, "Pray, my good friend, what daughter is this of yours? I never so much as heard that you was married."

"And what then," cries the doctor; "did you ever hear that a pope was married? and yet some

191

of them have had sons and daughters, I believe; but, however, this young gentleman will absolve me without obliging me to penance."

"I have not yet that power," answered the young clergyman; "for I am only in deacon's orders."

"Are you not?" cries the doctor; "why then I will absolve myself. You are to know then, my good friend, that this young lady was the daughter of a neighbour of mine, who is since dead, and whose sins I hope are forgiven; for she had too much to answer for on her child's account. Her father was my intimate acquaintance and friend; a worthier man, indeed, I believe never lived. He died suddenly when his children were infants; and, perhaps, to the suddenness of his death it was owing that he did not recommend any care of them to me. However, I, in some measure, took that charge upon me; and particularly of her whom I call my daughter. Indeed, as she grew up she discovered so many good qualities that she wanted not the remembrance of her father's merit to recommend her. I do her no more than justice when I say she is one of the best creatures I ever knew. She hath a sweetness of temper, a generosity of spirit, an openness of heart—in a word, she hath a true Christian disposition. I may call her an Israelite indeed, in whom there is no guile."

"I wish you joy of your daughter," cries the old gentleman; "for to a man of your disposition, to find out an adequate object of your benevolence, is, I acknowledge, to find a treasure."

"It is, indeed, a happiness," cries the doctor.

"The greatest difficulty," added the gentleman, "which persons of your turn of mind meet with, is in finding proper objects of their goodness; for nothing sure can be more irksome to a generous mind, than to discover that it hath thrown away all its good offices on a soil that bears no other fruit than ingratitude."

"I remember," cries the doctor, "Phocylides saith,

Mn kakov ev epens opens dpelpelv ioov eot evi povtw
{Footnote: To do a kindness to a bad man is like sowing your seed in the sea.}

But he speaks more like a philosopher than a Christian. I am more pleased with a French writer, one of the best, indeed, that I ever read, who blames men for lamenting the ill return which is so often made to the best offices. {Footnote: D'Esprit.} A true Christian can never be disappointed if he doth not receive his reward in this world; the labourer might as well complain that he is not paid his hire in the middle of the day."

"I own, indeed," said the gentleman, "if we see it in that light—"

"And in what light should we see it?" answered the doctor. "Are we like Agrippa, only almost Christians? or, is Christianity a matter of bare theory, and not a rule for our practice?"

"Practical, undoubtedly; undoubtedly practical," cries the gentleman. "Your example might indeed have convinced me long ago that we ought to do good to every one."

"Pardon me, father," cries the young divine, "that is rather a heathenish than a Christian doctrine. Homer, I remember, introduces in his Iliad one Axylus, of whom he says—

  —Hidvos o'nv avopwpoloi
    pavras yap tyeeokev
{Footnote: He was a friend to mankind, for he loved them all.}

But Plato, who, of all the heathens, came nearest to the Christian philosophy, condemned this as impious doctrine; so Eustathius tells us, folio 474."

"I know he doth," cries the doctor, "and so Barnes tells us, in his note upon the place; but if you remember the rest of the quotation as well as you do that from Eustathius, you might have added the observation which Mr. Dryden makes in favour of this passage, that he found not in all the Latin authors, so admirable an instance of extensive humanity. You might have likewise remembered the noble sentiment with which Mr. Barnes ends his note, the sense of which is taken from the fifth chapter of Matthew:—

{Greek verse}

"It seems, therefore, as if this character rather became a Christian than a heathen, for Homer could not have transcribed it from any of his deities. Whom is it, therefore, we imitate by such extensive benevolence?"

"What a prodigious memory you have!" cries the old gentleman: "indeed, son, you must not contend with the doctor in these matters."

"I shall not give my opinion hastily," cries the son. "I know, again, what Mr. Poole, in his

annotations, says on that verse of St Matthew—That it is only to heap coals of fire upon their heads. How are we to understand, pray, the text immediately preceding?—Love your enemies, bless them that curse you, do good to them that hate you."

"You know, I suppose, young gentleman," said the doctor, "how these words are generally understood. The commentator you mention, I think, tells us that love is not here to be taken in the strict sense, so as to signify the complacency of the heart; you may hate your enemies as God's enemies, and seek due revenge of them for his honour; and, for your own sakes too, you may seek moderate satisfaction of them; but then you are to love them with a love consistent with these things; that is to say, in plainer words, you are to love them and hate them, and bless and curse, and do them good and mischief."

"Excellent! admirable!" said the old gentleman; "you have a most inimitable turn to ridicule."

"I do not approve ridicule," said the son, "on such subjects."

"Nor I neither," cries the doctor; "I will give you my opinion, therefore, very seriously. The two verses taken together, contain a very positive precept, delivered in the plainest words, and yet illustrated by the clearest instance in the conduct of the Supreme Being; and lastly, the practice of this precept is most nobly enforced by the reward annexed—that ye may be the children, and so forth. No man who understands what it is to love, and to bless, and to do good, can mistake the meaning. But if they required any comment, the Scripture itself affords enow. If thine enemy hunger, feed him; if he thirst, give him drink; not rendering evil for evil, or railing for railing, but contrariwise, blessing. They do not, indeed, want the comments of men, who, when they cannot bend their mind to the obedience of Scripture, are desirous to wrest Scripture to a compliance with their own inclinations."

"Most nobly and justly observed," cries the old gentleman. "Indeed, my good friend, you have explained the text with the utmost perspicuity."

"But if this be the meaning," cries the son, "there must be an end of all law and justice, for I do not see how any man can prosecute his enemy in a court of justice."

"Pardon me, sir," cries the doctor. "Indeed, as an enemy merely, and from a spirit of revenge, he cannot, and he ought not to prosecute him; but as an offender against the laws of his country he may, and it is his duty so to do. Is there any spirit of revenge in the magistrates or officers of justice when they punish criminals? Why do such, ordinarily I mean, concern themselves in inflicting punishments, but because it is their duty? and why may not a private man deliver an offender into the hands of justice, from the same laudable motive? Revenge, indeed, of all kinds is strictly prohibited; wherefore, as we are not to execute it with our own hands, so neither are we to make use of the law as the instrument of private malice, and to worry each other with inveteracy and rancour. And where is the great difficulty in obeying this wise, this generous, this noble precept? If revenge be, as a certain divine, not greatly to his honour, calls it, the most luscious morsel the devil ever dropt into the mouth of a sinner, it must be allowed at least to cost us often extremely dear. It is a dainty, if indeed it be one, which we come at with great inquietude, with great difficulty, and with great danger. However pleasant it may be to the palate while we are feeding on it, it is sure to leave a bitter relish behind it; and so far, indeed, it may be called a luscious morsel, that the most greedy appetites are soon glutted, and the most eager longing for it is soon turned into loathing and repentance. I allow there is something tempting in its outward appearance, but it is like the beautiful colour of some poisons, from which, however they may attract our eyes, a regard to our own welfare commands us to abstain. And this is an abstinence to which wisdom alone, without any Divine command, hath been often found adequate, with instances of which the Greek and Latin authors everywhere abound. May not a Christian, therefore, be well ashamed of making a stumbling-block of a precept, which is not only consistent with his worldly interest, but to which so noble an incentive is proposed?"

The old gentleman fell into raptures at this speech, and, after making many compliments to the doctor upon it, he turned to his son, and told him he had an opportunity now of learning more in one day than he had learnt at the university in a twelvemonth.

The son replied, that he allowed the doctrine to be extremely good in general, and that he agreed with the greater part; "but I must make a distinction," said he. However, he was interrupted from his distinction at present, for now Booth returned with Amelia and the children.

Chapter ix. — A scene of modern wit and humour.

In the afternoon the old gentleman proposed a walk to Vauxhall, a place of which, he said, he had heard much, but had never seen it.

The doctor readily agreed to his friend's proposal, and soon after ordered two coaches to be sent for to carry the whole company. But when the servant was gone for them Booth acquainted the doctor that it was yet too early. "Is it so?" said the doctor; "why, then, I will carry you first to one of the greatest and highest entertainments in the world."

The children pricked up their ears at this, nor did any of the company guess what he meant; and Amelia asked what entertainment he could carry them to at that time of day?

"Suppose," says the doctor, "I should carry you to court."

"At five o'clock in the afternoon!" cries Booth.

"Ay, suppose I should have interest enough to introduce you into the presence."

"You are jesting, dear sir," cries Amelia.

"Indeed, I am serious," answered the doctor. "I will introduce you into that presence, compared to whom the greatest emperor on the earth is many millions of degrees meaner than the most contemptible reptile is to him. What entertainment can there be to a rational being equal to this? Was not the taste of mankind most wretchedly depraved, where would the vain man find an honour, or where would the love of pleasure propose so adequate an object as divine worship? with what ecstasy must the contemplation of being admitted to such a presence fill the mind! The pitiful courts of princes are open to few, and to those only at particular seasons; but from this glorious and gracious presence we are none of us, and at no time excluded."

The doctor was proceeding thus when the servant returned, saying the coaches were ready; and the whole company with the greatest alacrity attended the doctor to St James's church.

When the service was ended, and they were again got into their coaches, Amelia returned the doctor many thanks for the light in which he had placed divine worship, assuring him that she had never before had so much transport in her devotion as at this time, and saying she believed she should be the better for this notion he had given her as long as she lived.

The coaches being come to the water-side, they all alighted, and, getting into one boat, proceeded to Vauxhall.

The extreme beauty and elegance of this place is well known to almost every one of my readers; and happy is it for me that it is so, since to give an adequate idea of it would exceed my power of description. To delineate the particular beauties of these gardens would, indeed, require as much pains, and as much paper too, as to rehearse all the good actions of their master, whose life proves the truth of an observation which I have read in some ethic writer, that a truly elegant taste is generally accompanied with an excellency of heart; or, in other words, that true virtue is, indeed, nothing else but true taste.

Here our company diverted themselves with walking an hour or two before the music began. Of all the seven, Booth alone had ever been here before; so that, to all the rest, the place, with its other charms, had that of novelty. When the music played, Amelia, who stood next to the doctor, said to him in a whisper, "I hope I am not guilty of profaneness; but, in pursuance of that chearful chain of thoughts with which you have inspired me this afternoon, I was just now lost in a reverie, and fancied myself in those blissful mansions which we hope to enjoy hereafter. The delicious sweetness of the place, the enchanting charms of the music, and the satisfaction which appears in every one's countenance, carried my soul almost to heaven in its ideas. I could not have, indeed, imagined there had been anything like this in this world."

The doctor smiled, and said, "You see, dear madam, there may be pleasures of which you could conceive no idea till you actually enjoyed them."

And now the little boy, who had long withstood the attractions of several cheesecakes that passed to and fro, could contain no longer, but asked his mother to give him one, saying, "I am sure my sister would be glad of another, though she is ashamed to ask." The doctor, overhearing the child, proposed that they should all retire to some place where they might sit down and refresh themselves; which they accordingly did. Amelia now missed her husband; but, as she had three

men in her company, and one of them was the doctor, she concluded herself and her children to be safe, and doubted not but that Booth would soon find her out.

They now sat down, and the doctor very gallantly desired Amelia to call for what she liked. Upon which the children were supplied with cakes, and some ham and chicken were provided for the rest of the company; with which while they were regaling themselves with the highest satisfaction, two young fellows walking arm-in-arm, came up, and when they came opposite to Amelia they stood still, staring Amelia full in the face, and one of them cried aloud to the other, "D—n me, my lord, if she is not an angel!"—My lord stood still, staring likewise at her, without speaking a word; when two others of the same gang came up, and one of them cried, "Come along, Jack, I have seen her before; but she is too well manned already. Three——are enough for one woman, or the devil is in it!"

"D—n me," says he that spoke first, and whom they called Jack, "I will have a brush at her if she belonged to the whole convocation." And so saying, he went up to the young clergyman, and cried, "Doctor, sit up a little, if you please, and don't take up more room in a bed than belongs to you." At which words he gave the young man a push, and seated himself down directly over against Amelia, and, leaning both his elbows on the table, he fixed his eyes on her in a manner with which modesty can neither look nor bear to be looked at.

Amelia seemed greatly shocked at this treatment; upon which the doctor removed her within him, and then, facing the gentleman, asked him what he meant by this rude behaviour?—Upon which my lord stept up and said, "Don't be impertinent, old gentleman. Do you think such fellows as you are to keep, d—n me, such fine wenches, d—n me, to yourselves, d—n me?"

"No, no," cries Jack, "the old gentleman is more reasonable. Here's the fellow that eats up the tithe-pig. Don't you see how his mouth waters at her? Where's your slabbering bib?" For, though the gentleman had rightly guessed he was a clergyman, yet he had not any of those insignia on with which it would have been improper to have appeared there.

"Such boys as you," cries the young clergyman, "ought to be well whipped at school, instead of being suffered to become nuisances in society."

"Boys, sir!" says Jack; "I believe I am as good a man as yourself, Mr.——, and as good a scholar too. Bos fur sus quoque sacerdos. Tell me what's next. D—n me, I'll hold you fifty pounds you don't tell me what's next."

"You have him, Jack," cries my lord. "It is over with him, d—n me! he can't strike another blow."

"If I had you in a proper place," cries the clergyman, "you should find I would strike a blow, and a pretty hard one too."

"There," cries my lord, "there is the meekness of the clergyman—there spoke the wolf in sheep's clothing. D—n me, how big he looks! You must be civil to him, faith! or else he will burst with pride."

"Ay, ay," cries Jack, "let the clergy alone for pride; there's not a lord in the kingdom now hath half the pride of that fellow."

"Pray, sir," cries the doctor, turning to the other, "are you a lord?"

"Yes, Mr. ——," cries he, "I have that honour, indeed."

"And I suppose you have pride too," said the doctor.

"I hope I have, sir," answered he, "at your service."

"If such a one as you, sir," cries the doctor, "who are not only a scandal to the title you bear as a lord, but even as a man, can pretend to pride, why will you not allow it to a clergyman? I suppose, sir, by your dress, you are in the army? and, by the ribbon in your hat, you seem to be proud of that too. How much greater and more honourable is the service in which that gentleman is enlisted than yours! Why then should you object to the pride of the clergy, since the lowest of the function is in reality every way so much your superior?"

"Tida Tidu Tidum," cries my lord.

"However, gentlemen," cries the doctor, "if you have the least pretension to that name, I beg you will put an end to your frolic; since you see it gives so much uneasiness to the lady. Nay, I entreat you for your own sakes, for here is one coming who will talk to you in a very different stile from ours."

"One coming!" cries my lord; "what care I who is coming?"

"I suppose it is the devil," cries Jack; "for here are two of his livery servants already."

"Let the devil come as soon as he will," cries my lord; "d—n me if I have not a kiss!"

Amelia now fell a trembling; and her children, perceiving her fright, both hung on her, and began to cry; when Booth and Captain Trent both came up.

Booth, seeing his wife disordered, asked eagerly what was the matter? At the same time the lord and his companion, seeing Captain Trent, whom they well knew, said both together, "What, doth this company belong to you?" When the doctor, with great presence of mind, as he was apprehensive of some fatal consequence if Booth should know what had past, said, "So, Mr. Booth, I am glad you are returned; your poor lady here began to be frighted out of her wits. But now you have him again," said he to Amelia, "I hope you will be easy."

Amelia, frighted as she was, presently took the hint, and greatly chid her husband for leaving her. But the little boy was not so quick-sighted, and cried, "Indeed, papa, those naughty men there have frighted my mamma out of her wits."

"How!" cries Booth, a little moved; "frightened! Hath any one frightened you, my dear?"

"No, my love," answered she, "nothing. I know not what the child means. Everything is well now I see you safe."

Trent had been all the while talking aside with the young sparks; and now, addressing himself to Booth, said, "Here hath been some little mistake; I believe my lord mistook Mrs. Booth for some other lady."

"It is impossible," cries my lord, "to know every one. I am sure, if I had known the lady to be a woman of fashion, and an acquaintance of Captain Trent, I should have said nothing disagreeable to her; but, if I have, I ask her pardon, and the company's."

"I am in the dark," cries Booth. "Pray what is all this matter?"

"Nothing of any consequence," cries the doctor, "nor worth your enquiring into. You hear it was a mistake of the person, and I really believe his lordship that all proceeded from his not knowing to whom the lady belonged."

"Come, come," says Trent, "there is nothing in the matter, I assure you. I will tell you the whole another time."

"Very well; since you say so," cries Booth, "I am contented." So ended the affair, and the two sparks made their congee, and sneaked off.

"Now they are gone," said the young gentleman, "I must say I never saw two worse-bred jackanapes, nor fellows that deserved to be kicked more. If I had had them in another place I would have taught them a little more respect to the church."

"You took rather a better way," answered the doctor, "to teach them that respect."

Booth now desired his friend Trent to sit down with them, and proposed to call for a fresh bottle of wine; but Amelia's spirits were too much disconcerted to give her any prospect of pleasure that evening. She therefore laid hold of the pretence of her children, for whom she said the hour was already too late; with which the doctor agreed. So they paid their reckoning and departed, leaving to the two rakes the triumph of having totally dissipated the mirth of this little innocent company, who were before enjoying complete satisfaction.

Chapter x. — A curious conversation between the doctor, the young clergyman, and the young clergyman's father.

The next morning, when the doctor and his two friends were at breakfast, the young clergyman, in whose mind the injurious treatment he had received the evening before was very deeply impressed, renewed the conversation on that subject.

"It is a scandal," said he, "to the government, that they do not preserve more respect to the clergy, by punishing all rudeness to them with the utmost severity. It was very justly observed of you, sir," said he to the doctor, "that the lowest clergyman in England is in real dignity superior to the highest nobleman. What then can be so shocking as to see that gown, which ought to entitle us to the veneration of all we meet, treated with contempt and ridicule? Are we not, in fact, ambassadors from heaven to the world? and do they not, therefore, in denying us our due respect,

deny it in reality to Him that sent us?"

"If that be the case," says the doctor, "it behoves them to look to themselves; for He who sent us is able to exact most severe vengeance for the ill treatment of His ministers."

"Very true, sir," cries the young one; "and I heartily hope He will; but those punishments are at too great a distance to infuse terror into wicked minds. The government ought to interfere with its immediate censures. Fines and imprisonments and corporal punishments operate more forcibly on the human mind than all the fears of damnation."

"Do you think so?" cries the doctor; "then I am afraid men are very little in earnest in those fears."

"Most justly observed," says the old gentleman. "Indeed, I am afraid that is too much the case."

"In that," said the son, "the government is to blame. Are not books of infidelity, treating our holy religion as a mere imposture, nay, sometimes as a mere jest, published daily, and spread abroad amongst the people with perfect impunity?"

"You are certainly in the right," says the doctor; "there is a most blameable remissness with regard to these matters; but the whole blame doth not lie there; some little share of the fault is, I am afraid, to be imputed to the clergy themselves."

"Indeed, sir," cries the young one, "I did not expect that charge from a gentleman of your cloth. Do the clergy give any encouragement to such books? Do they not, on the contrary, cry loudly out against the suffering them? This is the invidious aspersion of the laity; and I did not expect to hear it confirmed by one of our own cloth."

"Be not too impatient, young gentleman," said the doctor. "I do not absolutely confirm the charge of the laity; it is much too general and too severe; but even the laity themselves do not attack them in that part to which you have applied your defence. They are not supposed such fools as to attack that religion to which they owe their temporal welfare. They are not taxed with giving any other support to infidelity than what it draws from the ill examples of their lives; I mean of the lives of some of them. Here too the laity carry their censures too far; for there are very few or none of the clergy whose lives, if compared with those of the laity, can be called profligate; but such, indeed, is the perfect purity of our religion, such is the innocence and virtue which it exacts to entitle us to its glorious rewards and to screen us from its dreadful punishments, that he must be a very good man indeed who lives up to it. Thus then these persons argue. This man is educated in a perfect knowledge of religion, is learned in its laws, and is by his profession obliged, in a manner, to have them always before his eyes. The rewards which it promises to the obedience of these laws are so great, and the punishments threatened on disobedience so dreadful, that it is impossible but all men must fearfully fly from the one, and as eagerly pursue the other. If, therefore, such a person lives in direct opposition to, and in a constant breach of, these laws, the inference is obvious. There is a pleasant story in Matthew Paris, which I will tell you as well as I can remember it. Two young gentlemen, I think they were priests, agreed together that whosoever died first should return and acquaint his friend with the secrets of the other world. One of them died soon after, and fulfilled his promise. The whole relation he gave is not very material; but, among other things, he produced one of his hands, which Satan had made use of to write upon, as the moderns do on a card, and had sent his compliments to the priests for the number of souls which the wicked examples of their lives daily sent to hell. This story is the more remarkable as it was written by a priest, and a great favourer of his order."

"Excellent!" cried the old gentleman; "what a memory you have."

"But, sir," cries the young one, "a clergyman is a man as well as another; and, if such perfect purity be expected—"

"I do not expect it," cries the doctor; "and I hope it will not be expected of us. The Scripture itself gives us this hope, where the best of us are said to fall twenty times a-day. But sure we may not allow the practice of any of those grosser crimes which contaminate the whole mind. We may expect an obedience to the ten commandments, and an abstinence from such notorious vices as, in the first place, Avarice, which, indeed, can hardly subsist without the breach of more commandments than one. Indeed, it would be excessive candour to imagine that a man who so visibly sets his whole heart, not only on this world, but on one of the most worthless things in it (for so is money, without regard to its uses), should be, at the same time, laying up his treasure in heaven. Ambition is a second vice of this sort: we are told we cannot serve God and Mammon. I

197

might have applied this to avarice; but I chose rather to mention it here. When we see a man sneaking about in courts and levees, and doing the dirty work of great men, from the hopes of preferment, can we believe that a fellow whom we see to have so many hard task-masters upon earth ever thinks of his Master which is in heaven? Must he not himself think, if ever he reflects at all, that so glorious a Master will disdain and disown a servant who is the dutiful tool of a court-favourite, and employed either as the pimp of his pleasure, or sometimes, perhaps, made a dirty channel to assist in the conveyance of that corruption which is clogging up and destroying the very vitals of his country?

"The last vice which I shall mention is Pride. There is not in the universe a more ridiculous nor a more contemptible animal than a proud clergyman; a turkey-cock or a jackdaw are objects of veneration when compared with him. I don't mean, by Pride, that noble dignity of mind to which goodness can only administer an adequate object, which delights in the testimony of its own conscience, and could not, without the highest agonies, bear its condemnation. By Pride I mean that saucy passion which exults in every little eventual pre-eminence over other men: such are the ordinary gifts of nature, and the paultry presents of fortune, wit, knowledge, birth, strength, beauty, riches, titles, and rank. That passion which is ever aspiring, like a silly child, to look over the heads of all about them; which, while it servilely adheres to the great, flies from the poor, as if afraid of contamination; devouring greedily every murmur of applause and every look of admiration; pleased and elated with all kind of respect; and hurt and enflamed with the contempt of the lowest and most despicable of fools, even with such as treated you last night disrespectfully at Vauxhall. Can such a mind as this be fixed on things above? Can such a man reflect that he hath the ineffable honour to be employed in the immediate service of his great Creator? or can he please himself with the heart-warming hope that his ways are acceptable in the sight of that glorious, that incomprehensible Being?"

"Hear, child, hear," cries the old gentleman; "hear, and improve your understanding. Indeed, my good friend, no one retires from you without carrying away some good instructions with him. Learn of the doctor, Tom, and you will be the better man as long as you live."

"Undoubtedly, sir," answered Tom, "the doctor hath spoken a great deal of excellent truth; and, without a compliment to him, I was always a great admirer of his sermons, particularly of their oratory. But,

Nee tamen hoc tribuens dederim quoque caetera.

I cannot agree that a clergyman is obliged to put up with an affront any more than another man, and more especially when it is paid to the order."

"I am very sorry, young gentleman," cries the doctor, "that you should be ever liable to be affronted as a clergyman; and I do assure you, if I had known your disposition formerly, the order should never have been affronted through you."

The old gentleman now began to check his son for his opposition to the doctor, when a servant delivered the latter a note from Amelia, which he read immediately to himself, and it contained the following words:

"MY DEAR SIR,—Something hath happened since I saw you which gives me great uneasiness, and I beg the favour of seeing you as soon as possible to advise with you upon it. I am

"Your most obliged and dutiful daughter,

"AMELIA BOOTH."

The doctor's answer was, that he would wait on the lady directly; and then, turning to his friend, he asked him if he would not take a walk in the Park before dinner. "I must go," says he, "to the lady who was with us last night; for I am afraid, by her letter, some bad accident hath happened to her. Come, young gentleman, I spoke a little too hastily to you just now; but I ask your pardon. Some allowance must be made to the warmth of your blood. I hope we shall, in time, both think alike."

The old gentleman made his friend another compliment; and the young one declared he hoped he should always think, and act too, with the dignity becoming his cloth. After which the doctor took his leave for a while, and went to Amelia's lodgings.

As soon as he was gone the old gentleman fell very severely on his son. "Tom," says he, "how can you be such a fool to undo, by your perverseness, all that I have been doing? Why will you not learn to study mankind with the attention which I have employed to that purpose? Do you think, if I had affronted this obstinate old fellow as you do, I should ever have engaged his friendship?"

"I cannot help it, sir," said Tom: "I have not studied six years at the university to give up my sentiments to every one. It is true, indeed, he put together a set of sounding words; but, in the main, I never heard any one talk more foolishly."

"What of that?" cries the father; "I never told you he was a wise man, nor did I ever think him so. If he had any understanding, he would have been a bishop long ago, to my certain knowledge. But, indeed, he hath been always a fool in private life; for I question whether he is worth L100 in the world, more than his annual income. He hath given away above half his fortune to the Lord knows who. I believe I have had above L200 of him, first and last; and would you lose such a milch-cow as this for want of a few compliments? Indeed, Tom, thou art as great a simpleton as himself. How do you expect to rise in the church if you cannot temporise and give in to the opinions of your superiors?"

"I don't know, sir," cries Tom, "what you mean by my superiors. In one sense, I own, a doctor of divinity is superior to a bachelor of arts, and so far I am ready to allow his superiority; but I understand Greek and Hebrew as well as he, and will maintain my opinion against him, or any other in the schools."

"Tom," cries the old gentleman, "till thou gettest the better of thy conceit I shall never have any hopes of thee. If thou art wise, thou wilt think every man thy superior of whom thou canst get anything; at least thou wilt persuade him that thou thinkest so, and that is sufficient. Tom, Tom, thou hast no policy in thee."

"What have I been learning these seven years," answered he, "in the university? However, father, I can account for your opinion. It is the common failing of old men to attribute all wisdom to themselves. Nestor did it long ago: but, if you will inquire my character at college, I fancy you will not think I want to go to school again."

The father and son then went to take their walk, during which the former repeated many good lessons of policy to his son, not greatly perhaps to his edification. In truth, if the old gentleman's fondness had not in a great measure blinded him to the imperfections of his son, he would have soon perceived that he was sowing all his instructions in a soil so choaked with self-conceit that it was utterly impossible they should ever bear any fruit.

BOOK X.

Chapter i. — To which we will prefix no preface.

The doctor found Amelia alone, for Booth was gone to walk with his new-revived acquaintance, Captain Trent, who seemed so pleased with the renewal of his intercourse with his old brother-officer, that he had been almost continually with him from the time of their meeting at the drum.

Amelia acquainted the doctor with the purport of her message, as follows: "I ask your pardon, my dear sir, for troubling you so often with my affairs; but I know your extreme readiness, as well as ability, to assist any one with your advice. The fact is, that my husband hath been presented by Colonel James with two tickets for a masquerade, which is to be in a day or two, and he insists so strongly on my going with him, that I really do not know how to refuse without giving him some reason; and I am not able to invent any other than the true one, which you would not, I am sure, advise me to communicate to him. Indeed I had a most narrow escape the other day; for I was almost drawn in inadvertently by a very strange accident, to acquaint him with the whole matter." She then related the serjeant's dream, with all the consequences that attended it.

The doctor considered a little with himself, and then said, "I am really, child, puzzled as well

199

as you about this matter. I would by no means have you go to the masquerade; I do not indeed like the diversion itself, as I have heard it described to me; not that I am such a prude to suspect every woman who goes there of any evil intentions; but it is a pleasure of too loose and disorderly a kind for the recreation of a sober mind. Indeed, you have still a stronger and more particular objection. I will try myself to reason him out of it."

"Indeed it is impossible," answered she; "and therefore I would not set you about it. I never saw him more set on anything. There is a party, as they call it, made on the occasion; and he tells me my refusal will disappoint all."

"I really do not know what to advise you," cries the doctor; "I have told you I do not approve of these diversions; but yet, as your husband is so very desirous, I cannot think there will be any harm in going with him. However, I will consider of it, and do all in my power for you."

Here Mrs. Atkinson came in, and the discourse on this subject ceased; but soon after Amelia renewed it, saying there was no occasion to keep anything a secret from her friend. They then fell to debating on the subject, but could not come to any resolution. But Mrs. Atkinson, who was in an unusual flow of spirits, cried out, "Fear nothing, my dear Amelia, two women surely will be too hard for one man. I think, doctor, it exceeds Virgil:

Una dolo divum si faemina victa duorum est."

"Very well repeated, indeed!" cries the doctor. "Do you understand all Virgil as well as you seem to do that line?"

"I hope I do, sir," said she, "and Horace too; or else my father threw away his time to very little purpose in teaching me."

"I ask your pardon, madam," cries the doctor. "I own it was an impertinent question."

"Not at all, sir," says she; "and if you are one of those who imagine women incapable of learning, I shall not be offended at it. I know the common opinion; but

Interdum vulgus rectum videt, est ubi peccat."

"If I was to profess such an opinion, madam," said the doctor, "Madam Dacier and yourself would bear testimony against me. The utmost indeed that I should venture would be to question the utility of learning in a young lady's education."

"I own," said Mrs. Atkinson, "as the world is constituted, it cannot be as serviceable to her fortune as it will be to that of a man; but you will allow, doctor, that learning may afford a woman, at least, a reasonable and an innocent entertainment."

"But I will suppose," cried the doctor, "it may have its inconveniences. As, for instance, if a learned lady should meet with an unlearned husband, might she not be apt to despise him?"

"I think not," cries Mrs. Atkinson—"and, if I may be allowed the instance, I think I have shewn, myself, that women who have learning themselves can be contented without that qualification in a man."

"To be sure," cries the doctor, "there may be other qualifications which may have their weight in the balance. But let us take the other side of the question, and suppose the learned of both sexes to meet in the matrimonial union, may it not afford one excellent subject of disputation, which is the most learned?"

"Not at all," cries Mrs. Atkinson; "for, if they had both learning and good sense, they would soon see on which side the superiority lay."

"But if the learned man," said the doctor, "should be a little unreasonable in his opinion, are you sure that the learned woman would preserve her duty to her husband, and submit?"

"But why," cries Mrs. Atkinson, "must we necessarily suppose that a learned man would be unreasonable?"

"Nay, madam," said the doctor, "I am not your husband; and you shall not hinder me from supposing what I please. Surely it is not such a paradox to conceive that a man of learning should be unreasonable. Are there no unreasonable opinions in very learned authors, even among the critics themselves? For instance, what can be a more strange, and indeed unreasonable opinion, than to prefer the Metamorphoses of Ovid to the Æneid of Virgil?"

"It would be indeed so strange," cries the lady, "that you shall not persuade me it was ever the opinion of any man."

"Perhaps not," cries the doctor; "and I believe you and I should not differ in our judgments of any person who maintained such an opinion—What a taste must he have!"

"A most contemptible one indeed," cries Mrs. Atkinson.

"I am satisfied," cries the doctor. "And in the words of your own Horace, Verbum non amplius addam."

"But how provoking is this," cries Mrs. Atkinson, "to draw one in such a manner! I protest I was so warm in the defence of my favourite Virgil, that I was not aware of your design; but all your triumph depends on a supposition that one should be so unfortunate as to meet with the silliest fellow in the world."

"Not in the least," cries the doctor. "Doctor Bentley was not such a person; and yet he would have quarrelled, I am convinced, with any wife in the world, in behalf of one of his corrections. I don't suppose he would have given up his Ingentia Fata to an angel."

"But do you think," said she, "if I had loved him, I would have contended with him?"

"Perhaps you might sometimes," said the doctor, "be of these sentiments; but you remember your own Virgil—Varium et mutabile semper faemina."

"Nay, Amelia," said Mrs. Atkinson, "you are now concerned as well as I am; for he hath now abused the whole sex, and quoted the severest thing that ever was said against us, though I allow it is one of the finest."

"With all my heart, my dear," cries Amelia. "I have the advantage of you, however, for I don't understand him."

"Nor doth she understand much better than yourself," cries the doctor; "or she would not admire nonsense, even though in Virgil."

"Pardon me, sir," said she.

"And pardon me, madam," cries the doctor, with a feigned seriousness; "I say, a boy in the fourth form at Eton would be whipt, or would deserve to be whipt at least, who made the neuter gender agree with the feminine. You have heard, however, that Virgil left his AEneid incorrect; and, perhaps, had he lived to correct it, we should not have seen the faults we now see in it."

"Why, it is very true as you say, doctor," cries Mrs. Atkinson; "there seems to be a false concord. I protest I never thought of it before."

"And yet this is the Virgil," answered the doctor, "that you are so fond of, who hath made you all of the neuter gender; or, as we say in English, he hath made mere animals of you; for, if we translate it thus,

"Woman is a various and changeable animal,

"there will be no fault, I believe, unless in point of civility to the ladies."

Mrs. Atkinson had just time to tell the doctor he was a provoking creature, before the arrival of Booth and his friend put an end to that learned discourse, in which neither of the parties had greatly recommended themselves to each other; the doctor's opinion of the lady being not at all heightened by her progress in the classics, and she, on the other hand, having conceived a great dislike in her heart towards the doctor, which would have raged, perhaps, with no less fury from the consideration that he had been her husband.

Chapter ii. — What happened at the masquerade.

From this time to the day of the masquerade nothing happened of consequence enough to have a place in this history.

On that day Colonel James came to Booth's about nine in the evening, where he stayed for Mrs. James, who did not come till near eleven. The four masques then set out together in several chairs, and all proceeded to the Haymarket.

When they arrived at the Opera-house the colonel and Mrs. James presently left them; nor did Booth and his lady remain long together, but were soon divided from each other by different masques.

A domino soon accosted the lady, and had her away to the upper end of the farthest room on the right hand, where both the masques sat down; nor was it long before the he domino began to make very fervent love to the she. It would, perhaps, be tedious to the reader to run through the whole process, which was not indeed in the most romantick stile. The lover seemed to consider

his mistress as a mere woman of this world, and seemed rather to apply to her avarice and ambition than to her softer passions.

As he was not so careful to conceal his true voice as the lady was, she soon discovered that this lover of her's was no other than her old friend the peer, and presently a thought suggested itself to her of making an advantage of this accident. She gave him therefore an intimation that she knew him, and expressed some astonishment at his having found her out. "I suspect," says she, "my lord, that you have a friend in the woman where I now lodge, as well as you had in Mrs. Ellison." My lord protested the contrary. To which she answered, "Nay, my lord, do not defend her so earnestly till you are sure I should have been angry with her."

At these words, which were accompanied with a very bewitching softness, my lord flew into raptures rather too strong for the place he was in. These the lady gently checked, and begged him to take care they were not observed; for that her husband, for aught she knew, was then in the room.

Colonel James came now up, and said, "So, madam, I have the good fortune to find you again; I have been extremely miserable since I lost you." The lady answered in her masquerade voice that she did not know him. "I am Colonel James," said he, in a whisper. "Indeed, sir," answered she, "you are mistaken; I have no acquaintance with any Colonel James." "Madam," answered he, in a whisper likewise, "I am positive I am not mistaken, you are certainly Mrs. Booth." "Indeed, sir," said she, "you are very impertinent, and I beg you will leave me." My lord then interposed, and, speaking in his own voice, assured the colonel that the lady was a woman of quality, and that they were engaged in a conversation together; upon which the colonel asked the lady's pardon; for, as there was nothing remarkable in her dress, he really believed he had been mistaken.

He then went again a hunting through the rooms, and soon after found Booth walking without his mask between two ladies, one of whom was in a blue domino, and the other in the dress of a shepherdess. "Will," cries the colonel, "do you know what is become of our wives; for I have seen neither of them since we have been in the room?" Booth answered, "That he supposed they were both together, and they should find them by and by." "What!" cries the lady in the blue domino, "are you both come upon duty then with your wives? as for yours, Mr. Alderman," said she to the colonel, "I make no question but she is got into much better company than her husband's." "How can you be so cruel, madam?" said the shepherdess; "you will make him beat his wife by and by, for he is a military man I assure you." "In the trained bands, I presume," cries the domino, "for he is plainly dated from the city." "I own, indeed," cries the other, "the gentleman smells strongly of Thames-street, and, if I may venture to guess, of the honourable calling of a taylor."

"Why, what the devil hast thou picked up here?" cries James.

"Upon my soul, I don't know," answered Booth; "I wish you would take one of them at least."

"What say you, madam?" cries the domino, "will you go with the colonel? I assure you, you have mistaken your man, for he is no less a person than the great Colonel James himself."

{Illustration: Booth between the blue domino and a Shepherdess.}

"No wonder, then, that Mr. Booth gives him his choice of us; it is the proper office of a caterer, in which capacity Mr. Booth hath, I am told, the honour to serve the noble colonel."

"Much good may it do you with your ladies!" said James; "I will go in pursuit of better game." At which words he walked off.

"You are a true sportsman," cries the shepherdess; "for your only pleasure, I believe, lies in the pursuit."

"Do you know the gentleman, madam?" cries the domino.

"Who doth not know him?" answered the shepherdess.

"What is his character?" cries the domino; "for, though I have jested with him, I only know him by sight."

"I know nothing very particular in his character," cries the shepherdess. "He gets every handsome woman he can, and so they do all."

"I suppose then he is not married?" said the domino.

"O yes! and married for love too," answered the other; "but he hath loved away all his love for her long ago, and now, he says, she makes as fine an object of hatred. I think, if the fellow ever

appears to have any wit, it is when he abuses his wife; and, luckily for him, that is his favourite topic. I don't know the poor wretch, but, as he describes her, it is a miserable animal."

"I know her very well," cries the other; "and I am much mistaken if she is not even with him; but hang him! what is become of Booth?"

At this instant a great noise arose near that part where the two ladies were. This was occasioned by a large assembly of young fellows whom they call bucks, who were got together, and were enjoying, as the phrase is, a letter, which one of them had found in the room.

Curiosity hath its votaries among all ranks of people; whenever therefore an object of this appears it is as sure of attracting a croud in the assemblies of the polite as in those of their inferiors.

When this croud was gathered together, one of the bucks, at the desire of his companions, as well as of all present, performed the part of a public orator, and read out the following letter, which we shall give the reader, together with the comments of the orator himself, and of all his audience.

The orator then, being mounted on a bench, began as follows:

"Here beginneth the first chapter of—saint—Pox on't, Jack, what is the saint's name? I have forgot."

"Timothy, you blockhead," answered another; "—Timothy."

"Well, then," cries the orator, "of Saint Timothy.

"'SIR,—I am very sorry to have any occasion of writing on the following subject in a country that is honoured with the name of Christian; much more am I concerned to address myself to a man whose many advantages, derived both from nature and fortune, should demand the highest return of gratitude to the great Giver of all those good things. Is not such a man guilty of the highest ingratitude to that most beneficent Being, by a direct and avowed disobedience of his most positive laws and commands?

"'I need not tell you that adultery is forbid in the laws of the decalogue; nor need I, I hope, mention that it is expressly forbid in the New Testament.'

"You see, therefore," said the orator, "what the law is, and therefore none of you will be able to plead ignorance when you come to the Old Bailey in the other world. But here goes again:—

"'If it had not been so expressly forbidden in Scripture, still the law of Nature would have yielded light enough for us to have discovered the great horror and atrociousness of this crime.

"'And accordingly we find that nations, where the Sun of righteousness hath yet never shined, have punished the adulterer with the most exemplary pains and penalties; not only the polite heathens, but the most barbarous nations, have concurred in these; in many places the most severe and shameful corporal punishments, and in some, and those not a few, death itself hath been inflicted on this crime.

"'And sure in a human sense there is scarce any guilt which deserves to be more severely punished. It includes in it almost every injury and every mischief which one man can do to, or can bring on, another. It is robbing him of his property—'

"Mind that, ladies," said the orator; "you are all the property of your husbands.—'And of that property which, if he is a good man, he values above all others. It is poisoning that fountain whence he hath a right to derive the sweetest and most innocent pleasure, the most cordial comfort, the most solid friendship, and most faithful assistance in all his affairs, wants, and distresses. It is the destruction of his peace of mind, and even of his reputation. The ruin of both wife and husband, and sometimes of the whole family, are the probable consequence of this fatal injury. Domestic happiness is the end of almost all our pursuits, and the common reward of all our pains. When men find themselves for ever barred from this delightful fruition, they are lost to all industry, and grow careless of all their worldly affairs. Thus they become bad subjects, bad relations, bad friends, and bad men. Hatred and revenge are the wretched passions which boil in their minds. Despair and madness very commonly ensue, and murder and suicide often close the dreadful scene.'

"Thus, gentlemen and ladies, you see the scene is closed. So here ends the first act—and thus begins the second:—

"'I have here attempted to lay before you a picture of this vice, the horror of which no colours of mine can exaggerate. But what pencil can delineate the horrors of that punishment which the Scripture denounces against it?

"'And for what will you subject yourself to this punishment? or for what reward will you inflict all this misery on another? I will add, on your friend? for the possession of a woman; for the pleasure of a moment? But, if neither virtue nor religion can restrain your inordinate appetites, are there not many women as handsome as your friend's wife, whom, though not with innocence, you may possess with a much less degree of guilt? What motive then can thus hurry you on to the destruction of yourself and your friend? doth the peculiar rankness of the guilt add any zest to the sin? doth it enhance the pleasure as much as we may be assured it will the punishment?

"'But if you can be so lost to all sense of fear, and of shame, and of goodness, as not to be debarred by the evil which you are to bring on yourself, by the extreme baseness of the action, nor by the ruin in which you are to involve others, let me still urge the difficulty, I may say, the impossibility of the success. You are attacking a fortress on a rock; a chastity so strongly defended, as well by a happy natural disposition of mind as by the strongest principles of religion and virtue, implanted by education and nourished and improved by habit, that the woman must be invincible even without that firm and constant affection of her husband which would guard a much looser and worse-disposed heart. What therefore are you attempting but to introduce distrust, and perhaps disunion, between an innocent and a happy couple, in which too you cannot succeed without bringing, I am convinced, certain destruction on your own head?

"'Desist, therefore, let me advise you, from this enormous crime; retreat from the vain attempt of climbing a precipice which it is impossible you should ever ascend, where you must probably soon fall into utter perdition, and can have no other hope but of dragging down your best friend into perdition with you.

"'I can think of but one argument more, and that, indeed, a very bad one; you throw away that time in an impossible attempt, which might, in other places, crown your sinful endeavours with success.'

"And so ends the dismal ditty."

"D—n me," cries one, "did ever mortal hear such d—ned stuff?"

"Upon my soul," said another, "I like the last argument well enough. There is some sense in that; for d—n me if I had not rather go to D—g—ss at any time than follow a virtuous b—— for a fortnight."

"Tom," says one of them, "let us set the ditty to music; let us subscribe to have it set by Handel; it will make an excellent oratorio."

"D—n me, Jack," says another, "we'll have it set to a psalm-tune, and we'll sing it next Sunday at St James's church, and I'll bear a bob, d—n me."

"Fie upon it! gentlemen, fie upon it!" said a frier, who came up; "do you think there is any wit and humour in this ribaldry; or, if there were, would it make any atonement for abusing religion and virtue?"

"Heyday!" cries one, "this is a frier in good earnest."

"Whatever I am," said the frier, "I hope at least you are what you appear to be. Heaven forbid, for the sake of our posterity, that you should be gentlemen."

"Jack," cries one, "let us toss the frier in a blanket."

"Me in a blanket?" said the frier: "by the dignity of man, I will twist the neck of every one of you as sure as ever the neck of a dunghill-cock was twisted." At which words he pulled off his mask, and the tremendous majesty of Colonel Bath appeared, from which the bucks fled away as fast as the Trojans heretofore from the face of Achilles. The colonel did not think it worth while to pursue any other of them except him who had the letter in his hand, which the colonel desired to see, and the other delivered, saying it was very much at his service.

The colonel being possessed of the letter, retired as privately as he could, in order to give it a careful perusal; for, badly as it had been read by the orator, there were some passages in it which had pleased the colonel. He had just gone through it when Booth passed by him; upon which the colonel called to him, and, delivering him the letter, bid him put it in his pocket and read it at his leisure. He made many encomiums upon it, and told Booth it would be of service to him, and was proper for all young men to read.

Booth had not yet seen his wife; but, as he concluded she was safe with Mrs. James, he was not uneasy. He had been prevented searching farther after her by the lady in the blue domino, who had joined him again. Booth had now made these discoveries: that the lady was pretty well acquainted with him, that she was a woman of fashion, and that she had a particular regard for

him. But, though he was a gay man, he was in reality so fond of his Amelia, that he thought of no other woman; wherefore, though not absolutely a Joseph, as we have already seen, yet could he not be guilty of premeditated inconstancy. He was indeed so very cold and insensible to the hints which were given him, that the lady began to complain of his dullness. When the shepherdess again came up and heard this accusation against him, she confirmed it, saying, "I do assure you, madam, he is the dullest fellow in the world. Indeed, I should almost take you for his wife, by finding you a second time with him; for I do assure you the gentleman very seldom keeps any other company." "Are you so well acquainted with him, madam?" said the domino. "I have had that honour longer than your ladyship, I believe," answered the shepherdess. "Possibly you may, madam," cries the domino; "but I wish you would not interrupt us at present, for we have some business together." "I believe, madam," answered the shepherdess, "my business with the gentleman is altogether as important as yours; and therefore your ladyship may withdraw if you please." "My dear ladies," cries Booth, "I beg you will not quarrel about me." "Not at all," answered the domino; "since you are so indifferent, I resign my pretensions with all my heart. If you had not been the dullest fellow upon earth, I am convinced you must have discovered me." She then went off, muttering to herself that she was satisfied the shepherdess was some wretched creature whom nobody knew.

The shepherdess overheard the sarcasm, and answered it by asking Booth what contemptible wretch he had picked up? "Indeed, madam," said he, "you know as much of her as I do; she is a masquerade acquaintance like yourself." "Like me!" repeated she. "Do you think if this had been our first acquaintance I should have wasted so much time with you as I have? for your part, indeed, I believe a woman will get very little advantage by her having been formerly intimate with you." "I do not know, madam," said Booth, "that I deserve that character any more than I know the person that now gives it me." "And you have the assurance then," said she, in her own voice, "to affect not to remember me?" "I think," cries Booth, "I have heard that voice before; but, upon my soul, I do not recollect it." "Do you recollect," said she, "no woman that you have used with the highest barbarity—I will not say ingratitude?" "No, upon my honour," answered Booth. "Mention not honour," said she, "thou wretch! for, hardened as thou art, I could shew thee a face that, in spite of thy consummate impudence, would confound thee with shame and horrour. Dost thou not yet know me?" "I do, madam, indeed," answered Booth, "and I confess that of all women in the world you have the most reason for what you said."

Here a long dialogue ensued between the gentleman and the lady, whom, I suppose, I need not mention to have been Miss Matthews; but, as it consisted chiefly of violent upbraidings on her side, and excuses on his, I despair of making it entertaining to the reader, and shall therefore return to the colonel, who, having searched all the rooms with the utmost diligence, without finding the woman he looked for, began to suspect that he had before fixed on the right person, and that Amelia had denied herself to him, being pleased with her paramour, whom he had discovered to be the noble peer.

He resolved, therefore, as he could have no sport himself, to spoil that of others; accordingly he found out Booth, and asked him again what was become of both their wives; for that he had searched all over the rooms, and could find neither of them.

Booth was now a little alarmed at this account, and, parting with Miss Matthews, went along with the colonel in search of his wife. As for Miss Matthews, he had at length pacified her with a promise to make her a visit; which promise she extorted from him, swearing bitterly, in the most solemn manner, unless he made it to her, she would expose both him and herself at the masquerade.

As he knew the violence of the lady's passions, and to what heights they were capable of rising, he was obliged to come in to these terms: for he had, I am convinced, no fear upon earth equal to that of Amelia's knowing what it was in the power of Miss Matthews to communicate to her, and which to conceal from her, he had already undergone so much uneasiness.

The colonel led Booth directly to the place where he had seen the peer and Amelia (such he was now well convinced she was) sitting together. Booth no sooner saw her than he said to the colonel, "Sure that is my wife in conversation with that masque?" "I took her for your lady myself," said the colonel; "but I found I was mistaken. Hark ye, that is my Lord——, and I have seen that very lady with him all this night."

This conversation past at a little distance, and out of the hearing of the supposed Amelia;

when Booth, looking stedfastly at the lady, declared with an oath that he was positive the colonel was in the right. She then beckoned to him with her fan; upon which he went directly to her, and she asked him to go home, which he very readily consented to. The peer then walked off: the colonel went in pursuit of his wife, or of some other woman; and Booth and his lady returned in two chairs to their lodgings.

Chapter iii. — Consequences of the masquerade, not uncommon nor surprizing.

The lady, getting first out of her chair, ran hastily up into the nursery to the children; for such was Amelia's constant method at her return home, at whatever hour. Booth then walked into the dining-room, where he had not been long before Amelia came down to him, and, with a most chearful countenance, said, "My dear, I fancy we have neither of us supped; shall I go down and see whether there is any cold meat in the house?"

"For yourself, if you please," answered Booth; "but I shall eat nothing."

"How, my dear!" said Amelia; "I hope you have not lost your appetite at the masquerade!" for supper was a meal at which he generally eat very heartily.

"I know not well what I have lost," said Booth; "I find myself disordered.—My head aches. I know not what is the matter with me."

"Indeed, my dear, you frighten me," said Amelia; "you look, indeed, disordered. I wish the masquerade had been far enough before you had gone thither."

"Would to Heaven it had!" cries Booth; "but that is over now. But pray, Amelia, answer me one question—Who was that gentleman with you when I came up to you?"

"The gentleman! my dear," said Amelia; "what gentleman?"

"The gentleman—the nobleman—when I came up; sure I speak plain."

"Upon my word, my dear, I don't understand you," answered she; "I did not know one person at the masquerade."

"How!" said he; "what! spend the whole evening with a masque without knowing him?"

"Why, my dear," said she, "you know we were not together."

"I know we were not," said he, "but what is that to the purpose? Sure you answer me strangely. I know we were not together; and therefore I ask you whom you were with?"

"Nay, but, my dear," said she, "can I tell people in masques?"

"I say again, madam," said he, "would you converse two hours or more with a masque whom you did not know?"

"Indeed, child," says she, "I know nothing of the methods of a masquerade; for I never was at one in my life."

"I wish to Heaven you had not been at this!" cries Booth. "Nay, you will wish so yourself if you tell me truth.—What have I said? do I—can I suspect you of not speaking truth? Since you are ignorant then I will inform you: the man you have conversed with was no other than Lord—
—."

"And is that the reason," said she, "you wish I had not been there?"

"And is not that reason," answered he, "sufficient? Is he not the last man upon earth with whom I would have you converse?"

"So you really wish then that I had not been at the masquerade?"

"I do," cried he, "from my soul."

"So may I ever be able," cried she, "to indulge you in every wish as in this.—I was not there."

"Do not trifle, Amelia," cried he; "you would not jest with me if you knew the situation of my mind."

"Indeed I do not jest with you," said she. "Upon my honour I was not there. Forgive me this first deceit I ever practised, and indeed it shall be the last; for I have paid severely for this by the uneasiness it hath given me." She then revealed to him the whole secret, which was thus:

I think it hath been already mentioned in some part of this history that Amelia and Mrs.

206

Atkinson were exactly of the same make and stature, and that there was likewise a very near resemblance between their voices. When Mrs. Atkinson, therefore, found that Amelia was so extremely averse to the masquerade, she proposed to go thither in her stead, and to pass upon Booth for his own wife.

This was afterwards very easily executed; for, when they left Booth's lodgings, Amelia, who went last to her chair, ran back to fetch her masque, as she pretended, which she had purposely left behind. She then whipt off her domino, and threw it over Mrs. Atkinson, who stood ready to receive it, and ran immediately downstairs, and, stepping into Amelia's chair, proceeded with the rest to the masquerade.

As her stature exactly suited that of Amelia, she had very little difficulty to carry on the imposition; for, besides the natural resemblance of their voices, and the opportunity of speaking in a feigned one, she had scarce an intercourse of six words with Booth during the whole time; for the moment they got into the croud she took the first opportunity of slipping from him. And he, as the reader may remember, being seized by other women, and concluding his wife to be safe with Mrs. James, was very well satisfied, till the colonel set him upon the search, as we have seen before.

Mrs. Atkinson, the moment she came home, ran upstairs to the nursery, where she found Amelia, and told her in haste that she might very easily carry on the deceit with her husband; for that she might tell him what she pleased to invent, as they had not been a minute together during the whole evening.

Booth was no sooner satisfied that his wife had not been from home that evening than he fell into raptures with her, gave her a thousand tender caresses, blamed his own judgment, acknowledged the goodness of hers, and vowed never to oppose her will more in any one instance during his life.

Mrs. Atkinson, who was still in the nursery with her masquerade dress, was then summoned down-stairs, and, when Booth saw her and heard her speak in her mimic tone, he declared he was not surprized at his having been imposed upon, for that, if they were both in the same disguise, he should scarce be able to discover the difference between them.

They then sat down to half an hour's chearful conversation, after which they retired all in the most perfect good humour.

Chapter iv. — Consequences of the masquerade.

When Booth rose in the morning he found in his pocket that letter which had been delivered to him by Colonel Bath, which, had not chance brought to his remembrance, he might possibly have never recollected.

He had now, however, the curiosity to open the letter, and beginning to read it, the matter of it drew him on till he perused the whole; for, notwithstanding the contempt cast upon it by those learned critics the bucks, neither the subject nor the manner in which it was treated was altogether contemptible.

But there was still another motive which induced Booth to read the whole letter, and this was, that he presently thought he knew the hand. He did, indeed, immediately conclude it was Dr Harrison; for the doctor wrote a very remarkable one, and this letter contained all the particularities of the doctor's character.

He had just finished a second reading of this letter when the doctor himself entered the room. The good man was impatient to know the success of Amelia's stratagem, for he bore towards her all that love which esteem can create in a good mind, without the assistance of those selfish considerations from which the love of wives and children may be ordinarily deduced. The latter of which, Nature, by very subtle and refined reasoning, suggests to us to be part of our dear selves; and the former, as long as they remain the objects of our liking, that same Nature is furnished with very plain and fertile arguments to recommend to our affections. But to raise that affection in the human breast which the doctor had for Amelia, Nature is forced to use a kind of logic which

is no more understood by a bad man than Sir Isaac Newton's doctrine of colours is by one born blind. And yet in reality it contains nothing more abstruse than this, that an injury is the object of anger, danger of fear, and praise of vanity; for in the same simple manner it may be asserted that goodness is the object of love.

The doctor enquired immediately for his child (for so he often called Amelia); Booth answered that he had left her asleep, for that she had had but a restless night. "I hope she is not disordered by the masquerade," cries the doctor. Booth answered he believed she would be very well when she waked. "I fancy," said he, "her gentle spirits were a little too much fluttered last night; that is all."

"I hope, then," said the doctor, "you will never more insist on her going to such places, but know your own happiness in having a wife that hath the discretion to avoid those places; which, though perhaps they may not be as some represent them, such brothels of vice and debauchery as would impeach the character of every virtuous woman who was seen at them, are certainly, however, scenes of riot, disorder, and intemperance, very improper to be frequented by a chaste and sober Christian matron."

Booth declared that he was very sensible of his error, and that, so far from soliciting his wife to go to another masquerade, he did not intend ever to go thither any more himself.

The doctor highly approved the resolution; and then Booth said, "And I thank you, my dear friend, as well as my wife's discretion, that she was not at the masquerade last night." He then related to the doctor the discovery of the plot; and the good man was greatly pleased with the success of the stratagem, and that Booth took it in such good part.

"But, sir," says Booth, "I had a letter given me by a noble colonel there, which is written in a hand so very like yours, that I could almost swear to it. Nor is the stile, as far as I can guess, unlike your own. Here it is, sir. Do you own the letter, doctor, or do you not?"

The doctor took the letter, and, having looked at it a moment, said, "And did the colonel himself give you this letter?"

"The colonel himself," answered Booth.

"Why then," cries the doctor, "he is surely the most impudent fellow that the world ever produced. What! did he deliver it with an air of triumph?"

"He delivered it me with air enough," cries Booth, "after his own manner, and bid me read it for my edification. To say the truth, I am a little surprized that he should single me out of all mankind to deliver the letter to; I do not think I deserve the character of such a husband. It is well I am not so very forward to take an affront as some folks."

"I am glad to see you are not," said the doctor; "and your behaviour in this affair becomes both the man of sense and the Christian; for it would be surely the greatest folly, as well as the most daring impiety, to risque your own life for the impertinence of a fool. As long as you are assured of the virtue of your own wife, it is wisdom in you to despise the efforts of such a wretch. Not, indeed, that your wife accuses him of any downright attack, though she hath observed enough in his behaviour to give offence to her delicacy."

"You astonish me, doctor," said Booth. "What can you mean? my wife dislike his behaviour! hath the colonel ever offended her?"

"I do not say he hath ever offended her by any open declarations; nor hath he done anything which, according to the most romantic notion of honour, you can or ought to resent; but there is something extremely nice in the chastity of a truly virtuous woman."

"And hath my wife really complained of anything of that kind in the colonel?"

"Look ye, young gentleman," cries the doctor; "I will have no quarrelling or challenging; I find I have made some mistake, and therefore I insist upon it by all the rights of friendship, that you give me your word of honour you will not quarrel with the colonel on this account."

"I do, with all my heart," said Booth; "for, if I did not know your character, I should absolutely think you was jesting with me. I do not think you have mistaken my wife, but I am sure she hath mistaken the colonel, and hath misconstrued some over-strained point of gallantry, something of the Quixote kind, into a design against her chastity; but I have that opinion of the colonel, that I hope you will not be offended when I declare I know not which of you two I should be the sooner jealous of."

"I would by no means have you jealous of any one," cries the doctor; "for I think my child's virtue may be firmly relied on; but I am convinced she would not have said what she did to me

without a cause; nor should I, without such a conviction, have written that letter to the colonel, as I own to you I did. However, nothing I say hath yet past which, even in the opinion of false honour, you are at liberty to resent! but as to declining any great intimacy, if you will take my advice, I think that would be prudent."

"You will pardon me, my dearest friend," said Booth, "but I have really such an opinion of the colonel that I would pawn my life upon his honour; and as for women, I do not believe he ever had an attachment to any."

"Be it so," said the doctor: "I have only two things to insist on. The first is, that, if ever you change your opinion, this letter may not be the subject of any quarrelling or fighting: the other is, that you never mention a word of this to your wife. By the latter I shall see whether you can keep a secret; and, if it is no otherwise material, it will be a wholesome exercise to your mind; for the practice of any virtue is a kind of mental exercise, and serves to maintain the health and vigour of the soul."

"I faithfully promise both," cries Booth. And now the breakfast entered the room, as did soon after Amelia and Mrs. Atkinson.

The conversation ran chiefly on the masquerade; and Mrs. Atkinson gave an account of several adventures there; but whether she told the whole truth with regard to herself I will not determine, for, certain it is, she never once mentioned the name of the noble peer. Amongst the rest, she said there was a young fellow that had preached a sermon there upon a stool, in praise of adultery, she believed; for she could not get near enough to hear the particulars.

During that transaction Booth had been engaged with the blue domino in another room, so that he knew nothing of it; so that what Mrs. Atkinson had now said only brought to his mind the doctor's letter to Colonel Bath, for to him he supposed it was written; and the idea of the colonel being a lover to Amelia struck him in so ridiculous a light, that it threw him into a violent fit of laughter.

The doctor, who, from the natural jealousy of an author, imputed the agitation of Booth's muscles to his own sermon or letter on that subject, was a little offended, and said gravely, "I should be glad to know the reason of this immoderate mirth. Is adultery a matter of jest in your opinion?"

"Far otherwise," answered Booth. "But how is it possible to refrain from laughter at the idea of a fellow preaching a sermon in favour of it at such a place?"

"I am very sorry," cries the doctor, "to find the age is grown to so scandalous a degree of licentiousness, that we have thrown off not only virtue, but decency. How abandoned must be the manners of any nation where such insults upon religion and morality can be committed with impunity! No man is fonder of true wit and humour than myself; but to profane sacred things with jest and scoffing is a sure sign of a weak and a wicked mind. It is the very vice which Homer attacks in the odious character of Thersites. The ladies must excuse my repeating the passage to you, as I know you have Greek enough to understand it:—

Os rh' epea phresin esin akosma te, polla te ede
Maps, atar ou kata kosmon epizemenai basileusin,
All'o, ti oi eisaito geloiton Argeiosin
Emmenai. — {Footnote: Thus paraphrased by Mr. Pope:

"Awed by no shame, by no respect controll'd,
In scandal busy, in reproaches bold,
With witty malice, studious to defame,
Scorn all his joy, and laughter all his aim."}

And immediately adds,

——aiskistos de aner ypo Ilion elthe
{Footnote: "He was the greatest scoundrel in the whole army."}
"Horace, again, describes such a rascal:
——Solutos
Qui captat risus hominum famamque dicacis,
{Footnote: "Who trivial bursts of laughter strives to raise, And courts of prating petulance the praise."—FRANCIS.}
and says of him,

Hic niger est, hunc tu, Romane, caveto."

{Footnote: "This man is black; do thou, O Roman! shun this man."}

"O charming Homer!" said Mrs. Atkinson, "how much above all other writers!"

"I ask your pardon, madam," said the doctor; "I forgot you was a scholar; but, indeed, I did not know you understood Greek as well as Latin."

"I do not pretend," said she, "to be a critic in the Greek; but I think I am able to read a little of Homer, at least with the help of looking now and then into the Latin."

"Pray, madam," said the doctor, "how do you like this passage in the speech of Hector to Andromache:

——Eis oikon iousa ta sautes erga komize,
Iston t elakaten te, kai amphipoloisi keleue
Ergon epoichesthai?

{Footnote: "Go home and mind your own business. Follow your spinning, and keep your maids to their work."}

"Or how do you like the character of Hippodamia, who, by being the prettiest girl and best workwoman of her age, got one of the best husbands in all Troy?—I think, indeed, Homer enumerates her discretion with her other qualifications; but I do not remember he gives us one character of a woman of learning.—Don't you conceive this to be a great omission in that who, by being the prettiest girl and best workwoman of her age, got one of the best husbands in all Troy?—I think, indeed, Homer enumerates her discretion with her other qualifications; but I do not remember Don't you conceive this to be a great omission in that charming poet? However, Juvenal makes you amends, for he talks very abundantly of the learning of the Roman ladies in his time."

"You are a provoking man, doctor," said Mrs. Atkinson; "where is the harm in a woman's having learning as well as a man?"

"Let me ask you another question," said the doctor. "Where is the harm in a man's being a fine performer with a needle as well as a woman? And yet, answer me honestly; would you greatly chuse to marry a man with a thimble upon his finger? Would you in earnest think a needle became the hand of your husband as well as a halberd?"

"As to war, I am with you," said she. "Homer himself, I well remember, makes Hector tell his wife that warlike works—what is the Greek word—Pollemy—something—belonged to men only; and I readily agree to it. I hate a masculine woman, an Amazon, as much as you can do; but what is there masculine in learning?"

"Nothing so masculine, take my word for it. As for your Pollemy, I look upon it to be the true characteristic of a devil. So Homer everywhere characterizes Mars."

"Indeed, my dear," cries the serjeant, "you had better not dispute with the doctor; for, upon my word, he will be too hard for you."

"Nay, I beg you will not interfere," cries Mrs. Atkinson; "I am sure you can be no judge in these matters."

At which the doctor and Booth burst into a loud laugh; and Amelia, though fearful of giving her friend offence, could not forbear a gentle smile.

"You may laugh, gentlemen, if you please," said Mrs. Atkinson; "but I thank Heaven I have married a man who is not jealous of my understanding. I should have been the most miserable woman upon earth with a starched pedant who was possessed of that nonsensical opinion that the difference of sexes causes any difference in the mind. Why don't you honestly avow the Turkish notion that women have no souls? for you say the same thing in effect."

"Indeed, my dear," cries the serjeant, greatly concerned to see his wife so angry, "you have mistaken the doctor."

"I beg, my dear," cried she, "you will say nothing upon these subjects—I hope you at least do not despise my understanding."

"I assure you, I do not," said the serjeant; "and I hope you will never despise mine; for a man may have some understanding, I hope, without learning."

Mrs. Atkinson reddened extremely at these words; and the doctor, fearing he had gone too far, began to soften matters, in which Amelia assisted him. By these means, the storm rising in Mrs. Atkinson before was in some measure laid, at least suspended from bursting at present; but it

210

fell afterwards upon the poor serjeant's head in a torrent, who had learned perhaps one maxim from his trade, that a cannon-ball always doth mischief in proportion to the resistance it meets with, and that nothing so effectually deadens its force as a woolpack. The serjeant therefore bore all with patience; and the idea of a woolpack, perhaps, bringing that of a feather-bed into his head, he at last not only quieted his wife, but she cried out with great sincerity, "Well, my dear, I will say one thing for you, that I believe from my soul, though you have no learning, you have the best understanding of any man upon earth; and I must own I think the latter far the more profitable of the two."

Far different was the idea she entertained of the doctor, whom, from this day, she considered as a conceited pedant; nor could all Amelia's endeavours ever alter her sentiments.

The doctor now took his leave of Booth and his wife for a week, he intending to set out within an hour or two with his old friend, with whom our readers were a little acquainted at the latter end of the ninth book, and of whom, perhaps, they did not then conceive the most favourable opinion.

Nay, I am aware that the esteem which some readers before had for the doctor may be here lessened; since he may appear to have been too easy a dupe to the gross flattery of the old gentleman. If there be any such critics, we are heartily sorry, as well for them as for the doctor; but it is our business to discharge the part of a faithful historian, and to describe human nature as it is, not as we would wish it to be.

Chapter v. — In which Colonel Bath appears in great glory.

That afternoon, as Booth was walking in the Park, he met with Colonel Bath, who presently asked him for the letter which he had given him the night before; upon which Booth immediately returned it.

"Don't you think," cries Bath, "it is writ with great dignity of expression and emphasis of—of—of judgment?"

"I am surprized, though," cries Booth, "that any one should write such a letter to you, colonel."

"To me!" said Bath. "What do you mean, sir? I hope you don't imagine any man durst write such a letter to me? d—n me, if I knew a man who thought me capable of debauching my friend's wife, I would—d—n me."

"I believe, indeed, sir," cries Booth, "that no man living dares put his name to such a letter; but you see it is anonymous."

"I don't know what you mean by ominous," cries the colonel; "but, blast my reputation, if I had received such a letter, if I would not have searched the world to have found the writer. D—n me, I would have gone to the East Indies to have pulled off his nose."

"He would, indeed, have deserved it," cries Booth. "But pray, sir, how came you by it?"

"I took it," said the colonel, "from a sett of idle young rascals, one of whom was reading it out aloud upon a stool, while the rest were attempting to make a jest, not only of the letter, but of all decency, virtue, and religion. A sett of fellows that you must have seen or heard of about the town, that are, d—n me, a disgrace to the dignity of manhood; puppies that mistake noise and impudence, rudeness and profaneness, for wit. If the drummers of my company had not more understanding than twenty such fellows, I'd have them both whipt out of the regiment."

"So, then, you do not know the person to whom it was writ?" said Booth.

"Lieutenant," cries the colonel, "your question deserves no answer. I ought to take time to consider whether I ought not to resent the supposition. Do you think, sir, I am acquainted with a rascal?"

"I do not suppose, colonel," cries Booth, "that you would willingly cultivate an intimacy with such a person; but a man must have good luck who hath any acquaintance if there are not some rascals among them."

"I am not offended with you, child," says the colonel. "I know you did not intend to offend

me."

"No man, I believe, dares intend it," said Booth.

"I believe so too," said the colonel; "d——n me, I know it. But you know, child, how tender I am on this subject. If I had been ever married myself, I should have cleft the man's skull who had dared look wantonly at my wife."

"It is certainly the most cruel of all injuries," said Booth. "How finely doth Shakespeare express it in his Othello!

'But there, where I had treasured up my soul.'"

"That Shakespeare," cries the colonel, "was a fine fellow. He was a very pretty poet indeed. Was it not Shakespeare that wrote the play about Hotspur? You must remember these lines. I got them almost by heart at the playhouse; for I never missed that play whenever it was acted, if I was in town:——

By Heav'n it was an easy leap,
To pluck bright honour into the full moon,
Or drive into the bottomless deep.

And——and——faith, I have almost forgot them; but I know it is something about saving your honour from drowning——O! it is very fine! I say, d——n me, the man that writ those lines was the greatest poet the world ever produced. There is dignity of expression and emphasis of thinking, d——n me."

Booth assented to the colonel's criticism, and then cried, "I wish, colonel, you would be so kind to give me that letter." The colonel answered, if he had any particular use for it he would give it him with all his heart, and presently delivered it; and soon afterwards they parted.

Several passages now struck all at once upon Booth's mind, which gave him great uneasiness. He became confident now that he had mistaken one colonel for another; and, though he could not account for the letter's getting into those hands from whom Bath had taken it (indeed James had dropt it out of his pocket), yet a thousand circumstances left him no room to doubt the identity of the person, who was a man much more liable to raise the suspicion of a husband than honest Bath, who would at any time have rather fought with a man than lain with a woman.

The whole behaviour of Amelia now rushed upon his memory. Her resolution not to take up her residence at the colonel's house, her backwardness even to dine there, her unwillingness to go to the masquerade, many of her unguarded expressions, and some where she had been more guarded, all joined together to raise such an idea in Mr. Booth, that he had almost taken a resolution to go and cut the colonel to pieces in his own house. Cooler thoughts, however, suggested themselves to him in time. He recollected the promise he had so solemnly made to the doctor. He considered, moreover, that he was yet in the dark as to the extent of the colonel's guilt. Having nothing, therefore, to fear from it, he contented himself to postpone a resentment which he nevertheless resolved to take of the colonel hereafter, if he found he was in any degree a delinquent.

The first step he determined to take was, on the first opportunity, to relate to Colonel James the means by which he became possessed of the letter, and to read it to him; on which occasion, he thought he should easily discern by the behaviour of the colonel whether he had been suspected either by Amelia or the doctor without a cause; but as for his wife, he fully resolved not to reveal the secret to her till the doctor's return.

While Booth was deeply engaged by himself in these meditations, Captain Trent came up to him, and familiarly slapped him on the shoulder.

They were soon joined by a third gentleman, and presently afterwards by a fourth, both acquaintances of Mr. Trent; and all having walked twice the length of the Mall together, it being now past nine in the evening, Trent proposed going to the tavern, to which the strangers immediately consented; and Booth himself, after some resistance, was at length persuaded to comply.

To the King's Arms then they went, where the bottle went very briskly round till after eleven; at which time Trent proposed a game at cards, to which proposal likewise Booth's consent was obtained, though not without much difficulty; for, though he had naturally some inclination to gaming, and had formerly a little indulged it, yet he had entirely left it off for many years.

Booth and his friend were partners, and had at first some success; but Fortune, according to her usual conduct, soon shifted about, and persecuted Booth with such malice, that in about two

hours he was stripped of all the gold in his pocket, which amounted to twelve guineas, being more than half the cash which he was at that time worth.

How easy it is for a man who is at all tainted with the itch of gaming to leave off play in such a situation, especially when he is likewise heated with liquor, I leave to the gamester to determine. Certain it is that Booth had no inclination to desist; but, on the contrary, was so eagerly bent on playing on, that he called his friend out of the room, and asked him for ten pieces, which he promised punctually to pay the next morning.

Trent chid him for using so much formality on the occasion. "You know," said he, "dear Booth, you may have what money you please of me. Here is a twenty-pound note at your service; and, if you want five times the sum, it is at your service. We will never let these fellows go away with our money in this manner; for we have so much the advantage, that if the knowing ones were here they would lay odds of our side."

But if this was really Mr. Rent's opinion, he was very much mistaken; for the other two honourable gentlemen were not only greater masters of the game, and somewhat soberer than poor Booth, having, with all the art in their power, evaded the bottle, but they had, moreover, another small advantage over their adversaries, both of them, by means of some certain private signs, previously agreed upon between them, being always acquainted with the principal cards in each other's hands. It cannot be wondered, therefore, that Fortune was on their side; for, however she may be reported to favour fools, she never, I believe, shews them any countenance when they engage in play with knaves.

The more Booth lost, the deeper he made his bets; the consequence of which was, that about two in the morning, besides the loss of his own money, he was fifty pounds indebted to Trent: a sum, indeed, which he would not have borrowed, had not the other, like a very generous friend, pushed it upon him.

Trent's pockets became at last dry by means of these loans. His own loss, indeed, was trifling; for the stakes of the games were no higher than crowns, and betting (as it is called) was that to which Booth owed his ruin. The gentlemen, therefore, pretty well knowing Booth's circumstances, and being kindly unwilling to win more of a man than he was worth, declined playing any longer, nor did Booth once ask them to persist, for he was ashamed of the debt which he had already contracted to Trent, and very far from desiring to encrease it.

The company then separated. The two victors and Trent went off in their chairs to their several houses near Grosvenor-square, and poor Booth, in a melancholy mood, walked home to his lodgings. He was, indeed, in such a fit of despair, that it more than once came into his head to put an end to his miserable being.

But before we introduce him to Amelia we must do her the justice to relate the manner in which she spent this unhappy evening. It was about seven when Booth left her to walk in the park; from this time till past eight she was employed with her children, in playing with them, in giving them their supper, and in putting them to bed.

When these offices were performed she employed herself another hour in cooking up a little supper for her husband, this being, as we have already observed, his favourite meal, as indeed it was her's; and, in a most pleasant and delightful manner, they generally passed their time at this season, though their fare was very seldom of the sumptuous kind.

It now grew dark, and her hashed mutton was ready for the table, but no Booth appeared. Having waited therefore for him a full hour, she gave him over for that evening; nor was she much alarmed at his absence, as she knew he was in a night or two to be at the tavern with some brother-officers; she concluded therefore that they had met in the park, and had agreed to spend this evening together.

At ten then she sat down to supper by herself, for Mrs. Atkinson was then abroad. And here we cannot help relating a little incident, however trivial it may appear to some. Having sat some time alone, reflecting on their distressed situation, her spirits grew very low; and she was once or twice going to ring the bell to send her maid for half-a-pint of white wine, but checked her inclination in order to save the little sum of sixpence, which she did the more resolutely as she had before refused to gratify her children with tarts for their supper from the same motive. And this self-denial she was very probably practising to save sixpence, while her husband was paying a debt of several guineas incurred by the ace of trumps being in the hands of his adversary.

Instead therefore of this cordial she took up one of the excellent Farquhar's comedies, and

read it half through; when, the clock striking twelve, she retired to bed, leaving the maid to sit up for her master. She would, indeed, have much more willingly sat up herself, but the delicacy of her own mind assured her that Booth would not thank her for the compliment. This is, indeed, a method which some wives take of upbraiding their husbands for staying abroad till too late an hour, and of engaging them, through tenderness and good nature, never to enjoy the company of their friends too long when they must do this at the expence of their wives' rest.

To bed then she went, but not to sleep. Thrice indeed she told the dismal clock, and as often heard the more dismal watchman, till her miserable husband found his way home, and stole silently like a thief to bed to her; at which time, pretending then first to awake, she threw her snowy arms around him; though, perhaps, the more witty property of snow, according to Addison, that is to say its coldness, rather belonged to the poor captain.

Chapter vi. — Read, gamester, and observe.

Booth could not so well disguise the agitations of his mind from Amelia, but that she perceived sufficient symptoms to assure her that some misfortune had befallen him. This made her in her turn so uneasy that Booth took notice of it, and after breakfast said, "Sure, my dear Emily, something hath fallen out to vex you."

Amelia, looking tenderly at him, answered, "Indeed, my dear, you are in the right; I am indeed extremely vexed." "For Heaven's sake," said he, "what is it?" "Nay, my love," cried she, "that you must answer yourself. Whatever it is which hath given you all that disturbance that you in vain endeavour to conceal from me, this it is which causes all my affliction."

"You guess truly, my sweet," replied Booth; "I am indeed afflicted, and I will not, nay I cannot, conceal the truth from you. I have undone myself, Amelia."

"What have you done, child?" said she, in some consternation; "pray, tell me."

"I have lost my money at play," answered he.

"Pugh!" said she, recovering herself—"what signifies the trifle you had in your pocket? Resolve never to play again, and let it give you no further vexation; I warrant you, we will contrive some method to repair such a loss."

"Thou heavenly angel! thou comfort of my soul!" cried Booth, tenderly embracing her; then starting a little from her arms, and looking with eager fondness in her eyes, he said, "Let me survey thee; art thou really human, or art thou not rather an angel in a human form? O, no," cried he, flying again into her arms, "thou art my dearest woman, my best, my beloved wife!"

Amelia, having returned all his caresses with equal kindness, told him she had near eleven guineas in her purse, and asked how much she should fetch him. "I would not advise you, Billy, to carry too much in your pocket, for fear it should be a temptation to you to return to gaming, in order to retrieve your past losses. Let me beg you, on all accounts, never to think more, if possible, on the trifle you have lost, anymore than if you had never possessed it."

Booth promised her faithfully he never would, and refused to take any of the money. He then hesitated a moment, and cried—"You say, my dear, you have eleven guineas; you have a diamond ring, likewise, which was your grandmother's—I believe that is worth twenty pounds; and your own and the child's watch are worth as much more."

"I believe they would sell for as much," cried Amelia; "for a pawnbroker of Mrs. Atkinson's acquaintance offered to lend me thirty-five pounds upon them when you was in your last distress. But why are you computing their value now?"

"I was only considering," answered he, "how much we could raise in any case of exigency."

"I have computed it myself," said she; "and I believe all we have in the world, besides our bare necessary apparel, would produce about sixty pounds: and suppose, my dear," said she, "while we have that little sum, we should think of employing it some way or other, to procure some small subsistence for ourselves and our family. As for your dependence on the colonel's friendship, it is all vain, I am afraid, and fallacious. Nor do I see any hopes you have from any other quarter, of providing for yourself again in the army. And though the sum which is now in

our power is very small, yet we may possibly contrive with it to put ourselves into some mean way of livelihood. I have a heart, my Billy, which is capable of undergoing anything for your sake; and I hope my hands are as able to work as those which have been more inured to it. But think, my dear, think what must be our wretched condition, when the very little we now have is all mouldered away, as it will soon be in this town."

When poor Booth heard this, and reflected that the time which Amelia foresaw was already arrived (for that he had already lost every farthing they were worth), it touched him to the quick; he turned pale, gnashed his teeth, and cried out, "Damnation! this is too much to bear."

Amelia was thrown into the utmost consternation by this behaviour; and, with great terror in her countenance, cried out, "Good Heavens! my dear love, what is the reason of this agony?"

"Ask me no questions," cried he, "unless you would drive me to madness."

"My Billy! my love!" said she, "what can be the meaning of this?—I beg you will deal openly with me, and tell me all your griefs."

"Have you dealt fairly with me, Amelia?" said he.

"Yes, surely," said she; "Heaven is my witness how fairly."

"Nay, do not call Heaven," cried he, "to witness a falsehood. You have not dealt openly with me, Amelia. You have concealed secrets from me; secrets which I ought to have known, and which, if I had known, it had been better for us both."

"You astonish me as much as you shock me," cried she. "What falsehood, what treachery have I been guilty of?"

"You tell me," said he, "that I can have no reliance on James; why did not you tell me so before?"

"I call Heaven again," said she, "to witness; nay, I appeal to yourself for the truth of it; I have often told you so. I have told you I disliked the man, notwithstanding the many favours he had done you. I desired you not to have too absolute a reliance upon him. I own I had once an extreme good opinion of him, but I changed it, and acquainted you that I had so—"

"But not," cries he, "with the reasons why you had changed it."

"I was really afraid, my dear," said she, "of going too far. I knew the obligations you had to him; and if I suspected that he acted rather from vanity than true friendship—"

"Vanity!" cries he; "take care, Amelia: you know his motive to be much worse than vanity—a motive which, if he had piled obligations on me till they had reached the skies, would tumble all down to hell. It is vain to conceal it longer—I know all—your confidant hath told me all."

"Nay, then," cries she, "on my knees I entreat you to be pacified, and hear me out. It was, my dear, for you, my dread of your jealous honour, and the fatal consequences."

"Is not Amelia, then," cried he, "equally jealous of my honour? Would she, from a weak tenderness for my person, go privately about to betray, to undermine the most invaluable treasure of my soul? Would she have me pointed at as the credulous dupe, the easy fool, the tame, the kind cuckold, of a rascal with whom I conversed as a friend?"

"Indeed you injure me," said Amelia. "Heaven forbid I should have the trial! but I think I could sacrifice all I hold most dear to preserve your honour. I think I have shewn I can. But I will—when you are cool, I will—satisfy you I have done nothing you ought to blame."

"I am cool then," cries he; "I will with the greatest coolness hear you.—But do not think, Amelia, I have the least jealousy, the least suspicion, the least doubt of your honour. It is your want of confidence in me alone which I blame."

"When you are calm," cried she, "I will speak, and not before."

He assured her he was calm; and then she said, "You have justified my conduct by your present passion, in concealing from you my suspicions; for they were no more, nay, it is possible they were unjust; for since the doctor, in betraying the secret to you, hath so far falsified my opinion of him, why may I not be as well deceived in my opinion of the colonel, since it was only formed on some particulars in his behaviour which I disliked? for, upon my honour, he never spoke a word to me, nor hath been ever guilty of any direct action, which I could blame." She then went on, and related most of the circumstances which she had mentioned to the doctor, omitting one or two of the strongest, and giving such a turn to the rest, that, if Booth had not had some of Othello's blood in him, his wife would have almost appeared a prude in his eyes. Even he, however, was pretty well pacified by this narrative, and said he was glad to find a possibility of the colonel's innocence; but that he greatly commended the prudence of his wife, and only wished

she would for the future make him her only confidant.

Amelia, upon that, expressed some bitterness against the doctor for breaking his trust; when Booth, in his excuse, related all the circumstances of the letter, and plainly convinced her that the secret had dropt by mere accident from the mouth of the doctor.

Thus the husband and wife became again reconciled, and poor Amelia generously forgave a passion of which the sagacious reader is better acquainted with the real cause than was that unhappy lady.

Chapter vii. — In which Booth receives a visit from Captain Trent.

When Booth grew perfectly cool, and began to reflect that he had broken his word to the doctor, in having made the discovery to his wife which we have seen in the last chapter, that thought gave him great uneasiness; and now, to comfort him, Captain Trent came to make him a visit.

This was, indeed, almost the last man in the world whose company he wished for; for he was the only man he was ashamed to see, for a reason well known to gamesters; among whom, the most dishonourable of all things is not to pay a debt, contracted at the gaming-table, the next day, or the next time at least that you see the party.

Booth made no doubt but that Trent was come on purpose to receive this debt; the latter had been therefore scarce a minute in the room before Booth began, in an aukward manner, to apologise; but Trent immediately stopt his mouth, and said, "I do not want the money, Mr. Booth, and you may pay it me whenever you are able; and, if you are never able, I assure you I will never ask you for it."

This generosity raised such a tempest of gratitude in Booth (if I may be allowed the expression), that the tears burst from his eyes, and it was some time before he could find any utterance for those sentiments with which his mind overflowed; but, when he began to express his thankfulness, Trent immediately stopt him, and gave a sudden turn to their discourse.

Mrs. Trent had been to visit Mrs. Booth on the masquerade evening, which visit Mrs. Booth had not yet returned. Indeed, this was only the second day since she had received it. Trent therefore now told his friend that he should take it extremely kind if he and his lady would waive all ceremony, and sup at their house the next evening. Booth hesitated a moment, but presently said, "I am pretty certain my wife is not engaged, and I will undertake for her. I am sure she will not refuse anything Mr. Trent can ask." And soon after Trent took Booth with him to walk in the Park.

There were few greater lovers of a bottle than Trent; he soon proposed therefore to adjourn to the King's Arms tavern, where Booth, though much against his inclination, accompanied him. But Trent was very importunate, and Booth did not think himself at liberty to refuse such a request to a man from whom he had so lately received such obligations.

When they came to the tavern, however, Booth recollected the omission he had been guilty of the night before. He wrote a short note therefore to his wife, acquainting her that he should not come home to supper; but comforted her with a faithful promise that he would on no account engage himself in gaming.

The first bottle passed in ordinary conversation; but, when they had tapped the second, Booth, on some hints which Trent gave him, very fairly laid open to him his whole circumstances, and declared he almost despaired of mending them. "My chief relief," said he, "was in the interest of Colonel James; but I have given up those hopes."

"And very wisely too," said Trent "I say nothing of the colonel's good will. Very likely he may be your sincere friend; but I do not believe he hath the interest he pretends to. He hath had too many favours in his own family to ask any more yet a while. But I am mistaken if you have not a much more powerful friend than the colonel; one who is both able and willing to serve you. I dined at his table within these two days, and I never heard kinder nor warmer expressions from

the mouth of man than he made use of towards you. I make no doubt you know whom I mean."

"Upon my honour I do not," answered Booth; "nor did I guess that I had such a friend in the world as you mention."

"I am glad then," cries Trent, "that I have the pleasure of informing you of it." He then named the noble peer who hath been already so often mentioned in this history.

Booth turned pale and started at his name. "I forgive you, my dear Trent," cries Booth, "for mentioning his name to me, as you are a stranger to what hath passed between us."

"Nay, I know nothing that hath passed between you," answered Trent. "I am sure, if there is any quarrel between you of two days' standing, all is forgiven on his part."

"D—n his forgiveness!" said Booth. "Perhaps I ought to blush at what I have forgiven."

"You surprize me!" cries Trent. "Pray what can be the matter?"

"Indeed, my dear Trent," cries Booth, very gravely, "he would have injured me in the tenderest part. I know not how to tell it you; but he would have dishonoured me with my wife."

"Sure, you are not in earnest!" answered Trent; "but, if you are, you will pardon me for thinking that impossible."

"Indeed," cries Booth, "I have so good an opinion of my wife as to believe it impossible for him to succeed; but that he should intend me the favour you will not, I believe, think an impossibility."

"Faith! not in the least," said Trent. "Mrs. Booth is a very fine woman; and, if I had the honour to be her husband, I should not be angry with any man for liking her."

"But you would be angry," said Booth, "with a man, who should make use of stratagems and contrivances to seduce her virtue; especially if he did this under the colour of entertaining the highest friendship for yourself."

"Not at all," cries Trent. "It is human nature."

"Perhaps it is," cries Booth; "but it is human nature depraved, stript of all its worth, and loveliness, and dignity, and degraded down to a level with the vilest brutes."

"Look ye, Booth," cries Trent, "I would not be misunderstood. I think, when I am talking to you, I talk to a man of sense and to an inhabitant of this country, not to one who dwells in a land of saints. If you have really such an opinion as you express of this noble lord, you have the finest opportunity of making a complete fool and bubble of him that any man can desire, and of making your own fortune at the same time. I do not say that your suspicions are groundless; for, of all men upon earth I know, my lord is the greatest bubble to women, though I believe he hath had very few. And this I am confident of, that he hath not the least jealousy of these suspicions. Now, therefore, if you will act the part of a wise man, I will undertake that you shall make your fortune without the least injury to the chastity of Mrs. Booth."

"I do not understand you, sir," said Booth.

"Nay," cries Trent, "if you will not understand me, I have done. I meant only your service; and I thought I had known you better."

Booth begged him to explain himself. "If you can," said he, "shew me any way to improve such circumstances as I have opened to you, you may depend on it I shall readily embrace it, and own my obligations to you."

"That is spoken like a man," cries Trent. "Why, what is it more than this? Carry your suspicions in your own bosom. Let Mrs. Booth, in whose virtue I am sure you may be justly confident, go to the public places; there let her treat my lord with common civility only; I am sure he will bite. And thus, without suffering him to gain his purpose, you will gain yours. I know several who have succeeded with him in this manner."

"I am very sorry, sir," cries Booth, "that you are acquainted with any such rascals. I do assure you, rather than I would act such a part, I would submit to the hardest sentence that fortune could pronounce against me."

"Do as you please, sir," said Trent; "I have only ventured to advise you as a friend. But do you not think your nicety is a little over-scrupulous?"

"You will excuse me, sir," said Booth; "but I think no man can be too scrupulous in points which concern his honour."

"I know many men of very nice honour," answered Trent, "who have gone much farther; and no man, I am sure, had ever a better excuse for it than yourself. You will forgive me, Booth, since what I speak proceeds from my love to you; nay, indeed, by mentioning your affairs to me, which

I am heartily sorry for, you have given me a right to speak. You know best what friends you have to depend upon; but, if you have no other pretensions than your merit, I can assure you you would fail, if it was possible you could have ten times more merit than you have. And, if you love your wife, as I am convinced you do, what must be your condition in seeing her want the necessaries of life?"

"I know my condition is very hard," cries Booth; "but I have one comfort in it, which I will never part with, and that is innocence. As to the mere necessaries of life, however, it is pretty difficult to deprive us of them; this I am sure of, no one can want them long."

"Upon my word, sir," cries Trent, "I did not know you had been so great a philosopher. But, believe me, these matters look much less terrible at a distance than when they are actually present. You will then find, I am afraid, that honour hath no more skill in cookery than Shakspear tells us it hath in surgery. D——n me if I don't wish his lordship loved my wife as well as he doth yours, I promise you I would trust her virtue; and, if he should get the better of it, I should have people of fashion enough to keep me in countenance."

Their second bottle being now almost out, Booth, without making any answer, called for a bill. Trent pressed very much the drinking another bottle, but Booth absolutely refused, and presently afterwards they parted, not extremely well satisfied with each other. They appeared, indeed, one to the other, in disadvantageous lights of a very different kind. Trent concluded Booth to be a very silly fellow, and Booth began to suspect that Trent was very little better than a scoundrel.

Chapter viii. — Contains a letter and other matters.

We will now return to Amelia; to whom, immediately upon her husband's departure to walk with Mr. Trent, a porter brought the following letter, which she immediately opened and read:

"MADAM,—The quick despatch which I have given to your first commands will I hope assure you of the diligence with which I shall always obey every command that you are pleased to honour me with. I have, indeed, in this trifling affair, acted as if my life itself had been at stake; nay, I know not but it may be so; for this insignificant matter, you was pleased to tell me, would oblige the charming person in whose power is not only my happiness, but, as I am well persuaded, my life too. Let me reap therefore some little advantage in your eyes, as you have in mine, from this trifling occasion; for, if anything could add to the charms of which you are mistress, it would be perhaps that amiable zeal with which you maintain the cause of your friend. I hope, indeed, she will be my friend and advocate with the most lovely of her sex, as I think she hath reason, and as you was pleased to insinuate she had been. Let me beseech you, madam, let not that dear heart, whose tenderness is so inclined to compassionate the miseries of others, be hardened only against the sufferings which itself occasions. Let not that man alone have reason to think you cruel, who, of all others, would do the most to procure your kindness. How often have I lived over in my reflections, in my dreams, those two short minutes we were together! But, alas! how faint are these mimicries of the imagination! What would I not give to purchase the reality of such another blessing! This, madam, is in your power to bestow on the man who hath no wish, no will, no fortune, no heart, no life, but what are at your disposal. Grant me only the favour to be at Lady——'s assembly. You can have nothing to fear from indulging me with a moment's sight, a moment's conversation; I will ask no more. I know your delicacy, and had rather die than offend it. Could I have seen you sometimes, I believe the fear of offending you would have kept my love for ever buried in my own bosom; but, to be totally excluded even from the sight of what my soul doats on is what I cannot bear. It is that alone which hath extorted the fatal secret from me. Let that obtain your forgiveness for me. I need not sign this letter otherwise than with that impression of my heart which I hope it bears; and, to conclude it in any form, no language hath words of devotion strong enough to tell you with what truth, what anguish, what zeal, what adoration I love you."

Amelia had just strength to hold out to the end, when her trembling grew so violent that she

dropt the letter, and had probably dropt herself, had not Mrs. Atkinson come timely in to support her.

"Good Heavens!" cries Mrs. Atkinson, "what is the matter with you, madam?"

"I know not what is the matter," cries Amelia; "but I have received a letter at last from that infamous colonel."

"You will take my opinion again then, I hope, madam," cries Mrs. Atkinson. "But don't be so affected; the letter cannot eat you or run away with you. Here it lies, I see; will you give me leave to read it?"

"Read it with all my heart," cries Amelia; "and give me your advice how to act, for I am almost distracted."

"Heydey!" says Mrs. Atkinson, "here is a piece of parchment too—what is that?" In truth, this parchment had dropt from the letter when Amelia first opened it; but her attention was so fixed by the contents of the letter itself that she had never read the other. Mrs. Atkinson had now opened the parchment first; and, after a moment's perusal, the fire flashed from her eyes, and the blood flushed into her cheeks, and she cried out, in a rapture, "It is a commission for my husband! upon my soul, it is a commission for my husband:" and, at the same time, began to jump about the room in a kind of frantic fit of joy.

"What can be the meaning of all this?" cries Amelia, under the highest degree of astonishment.

"Do not I tell you, my dear madam," cries she, "that it is a commission for my husband? and can you wonder at my being overjoyed at what I know will make him so happy? And now it is all out. The letter is not from the colonel, but from that noble lord of whom I have told you so much. But, indeed, madam, I have some pardons to ask of you. However, I know your goodness, and I will tell you all.

"You are to know then, madam, that I had not been in the Opera-house six minutes before a masque came up, and, taking me by the hand, led me aside. I gave the masque my hand; and, seeing a lady at that time lay hold on Captain Booth, I took that opportunity of slipping away from him; for though, by the help of the squeaking voice, and by attempting to mimic yours, I had pretty well disguised my own, I was still afraid, if I had much conversation with your husband, he would discover me. I walked therefore away with this masque to the upper end of the farthest room, where we sat down in a corner together. He presently discovered to me that he took me for you, and I soon after found out who he was; indeed, so far from attempting to disguise himself, he spoke in his own voice and in his own person. He now began to make very violent love to me, but it was rather in the stile of a great man of the present age than of an Arcadian swain. In short, he laid his whole fortune at my feet, and bade me make whatever terms I pleased, either for myself or for others. By others, I suppose he meant your husband. This, however, put a thought into my head of turning the present occasion to advantage. I told him there were two kinds of persons, the fallaciousness of whose promises had become proverbial in the world. These were lovers, and great men. What reliance, then, could I have on the promise of one who united in himself both those characters? That I had seen a melancholy instance, in a very worthy woman of my acquaintance (meaning myself, madam), of his want of generosity. I said I knew the obligations that he had to this woman, and the injuries he had done her, all which I was convinced she forgave, for that she had said the handsomest things in the world of him to me. He answered that he thought he had not been deficient in generosity to this lady (for I explained to him whom I meant); but that indeed, if she had spoke well of him to me (meaning yourself, madam), he would not fail to reward her for such an obligation. I then told him she had married a very deserving man, who had served long in the army abroad as a private man, and who was a serjeant in the guards; that I knew it was so very easy for him to get him a commission, that I should not think he had any honour or goodness in the world if he neglected it. I declared this step must be a preliminary to any good opinion he must ever hope for of mine. I then professed the greatest friendship to that lady (in which I am convinced you will think me serious), and assured him he would give me one of the highest pleasures in letting me be the instrument of doing her such a service. He promised me in a moment to do what you see, madam, he hath since done. And to you I shall always think myself indebted for it."

"I know not how you are indebted to me," cries Amelia. "Indeed, I am very glad of any good fortune that can attend poor Atkinson, but I wish it had been obtained some other way. Good

Heavens! what must be the consequence of this? What must this lord think of me for listening to his mention of love? nay, for making any terms with him? for what must he suppose those terms mean? Indeed, Mrs. Atkinson, you carried it a great deal too far. No wonder he had the assurance to write to me in the manner he hath done. It is too plain what he conceives of me, and who knows what he may say to others? You may have blown up my reputation by your behaviour."

"How is that possible?" answered Mrs. Atkinson. "Is it not in my power to clear up all matters? If you will but give me leave to make an appointment in your name I will meet him myself, and declare the whole secret to him."

"I will consent to no such appointment," cries Amelia. "I am heartily sorry I ever consented to practise any deceit. I plainly see the truth of what Dr Harrison hath often told me, that, if one steps ever so little out of the ways of virtue and innocence, we know not how we may slide, for all the ways of vice are a slippery descent."

"That sentiment," cries Mrs. Atkinson, "is much older than Dr Harrison. Omne vitium in proclivi est."

"However new or old it is, I find it is true," cries Amelia—"But, pray, tell me all, though I tremble to hear it."

"Indeed, my dear friend," said Mrs. Atkinson, "you are terrified at nothing—indeed, indeed, you are too great a prude."

"I do not know what you mean by prudery," answered Amelia. "I shall never be ashamed of the strictest regard to decency, to reputation, and to that honour in which the dearest of all human creatures hath his share. But, pray, give me the letter, there is an expression in it which alarmed me when I read it. Pray, what doth he mean by his two short minutes, and by purchasing the reality of such another blessing?"

"Indeed, I know not what he means by two minutes," cries Mrs. Atkinson, "unless he calls two hours so; for we were not together much less. And as for any blessing he had, I am a stranger to it. Sure, I hope you have a better opinion of me than to think I granted him the last favour."

"I don't know what favours you granted him, madam," answered Amelia peevishly, "but I am sorry you granted him any in my name."

"Upon my word," cries Mrs. Atkinson, "you use me unkindly, and it is an usage I did not expect at your hands, nor do I know that I have deserved it. I am sure I went to the masquerade with no other view than to oblige you, nor did I say or do anything there which any woman who is not the most confounded prude upon earth would have started at on a much less occasion than what induced me. Well, I declare upon my soul then, that, if I was a man, rather than be married to a woman who makes such a fuss with her virtue, I would wish my wife was without such a troublesome companion."

"Very possibly, madam, these may be your sentiments," cries Amelia, "and I hope they are the sentiments of your husband."

"I desire, madam," cries Mrs. Atkinson, "you would not reflect on my husband. He is a worthy man and as brave a man as yours; yes, madam, and he is now as much a captain."

She spoke those words with so loud a voice, that Atkinson, who was accidentally going upstairs, heard them; and, being surprized at the angry tone of his wife's voice, he entered the room, and, with a look of much astonishment, begged to know what was the matter.

"The matter, my dear," cries Mrs. Atkinson, "is that I have got a commission for you, and your good old friend here is angry with me for getting it."

"I have not spirits enow," cries Amelia, "to answer you as you deserve; and, if I had, you are below my anger."

"I do not know, Mrs. Booth," answered the other, "whence this great superiority over me is derived; but, if your virtue gives it you, I would have you to know, madam, that I despise a prude as much as you can do a——."

"Though you have several times," cries Amelia, "insulted me with that word, I scorn to give you any ill language in return. If you deserve any bad appellation, you know it, without my telling it you."

Poor Atkinson, who was more frightened than he had ever been in his life, did all he could to procure peace. He fell upon his knees to his wife, and begged her to compose herself; for indeed she seemed to be in a most furious rage.

While he was in this posture Booth, who had knocked so gently at the door, for fear of

disturbing his wife, that he had not been heard in the tempest, came into the room. The moment Amelia saw him, the tears which had been gathering for some time, burst in a torrent from her eyes, which, however, she endeavoured to conceal with her handkerchief. The entry of Booth turned all in an instant into a silent picture, in which the first figure which struck the eyes of the captain was the serjeant on his knees to his wife.

Booth immediately cried, "What's the meaning of this?" but received no answer. He then cast his eyes towards Amelia, and, plainly discerning her condition, he ran to her, and in a very tender phrase begged to know what was the matter. To which she answered, "Nothing, my dear, nothing of any consequence." He replied that he would know, and then turned to Atkinson, and asked the same question.

Atkinson answered, "Upon my honour, sir, I know nothing of it. Something hath passed between madam and my wife; but what it is I know no more than your honour."

"Your wife," said Mrs. Atkinson, "hath used me cruelly ill, Mr. Booth. If you must be satisfied, that is the whole matter."

Booth rapt out a great oath, and cried, "It is impossible; my wife is not capable of using any one ill."

Amelia then cast herself upon her knees to her husband, and cried, "For Heaven's sake do not throw yourself into a passion—some few words have past—perhaps I may be in the wrong."

"Damnation seize me if I think so!" cries Booth. "And I wish whoever hath drawn these tears from your eyes may pay it with as many drops of their heart's blood."

"You see, madam," cries Mrs. Atkinson, "you have your bully to take your part; so I suppose you will use your triumph."

Amelia made no answer, but still kept hold of Booth, who, in a violent rage, cried out, "My Amelia triumph over such a wretch as thee!—What can lead thy insolence to such presumption! Serjeant, I desire you'll take that monster out of the room, or I cannot answer for myself."

The serjeant was beginning to beg his wife to retire (for he perceived very plainly that she had, as the phrase is, taken a sip too much that evening) when, with a rage little short of madness, she cried out, "And do you tamely see me insulted in such a manner, now that you are a gentleman, and upon a footing with him?"

"It is lucky for us all, perhaps," answered Booth, "that he is not my equal."

"You lie, sirrah," said Mrs. Atkinson; "he is every way your equal; he is as good a gentleman as yourself, and as much an officer. No, I retract what I say; he hath not the spirit of a gentleman, nor of a man neither, or he would not bear to see his wife insulted."

"Let me beg of you, my dear," cries the serjeant, "to go with me and compose yourself."

"Go with thee, thou wretch!" cries she, looking with the utmost disdain upon him; "no, nor ever speak to thee more." At which words she burst out of the room, and the serjeant, without saying a word, followed her.

A very tender and pathetic scene now passed between Booth and his wife, in which, when she was a little composed, she related to him the whole story. For, besides that it was not possible for her otherwise to account for the quarrel which he had seen, Booth was now possessed of the letter that lay on the floor.

Amelia, having emptied her mind to her husband, and obtained his faithful promise that he would not resent the affair to my lord, was pretty well composed, and began to relent a little towards Mrs. Atkinson; but Booth was so highly incensed with her, that he declared he would leave her house the next morning; which they both accordingly did, and immediately accommodated themselves with convenient apartments within a few doors of their friend the doctor.

Chapter ix. — Containing some things worthy observation.

Notwithstanding the exchange of his lodgings, Booth did not forget to send an excuse to Mr. Trent, of whose conversation he had taken a full surfeit the preceding evening.

That day in his walks Booth met with an old brother-officer, who had served with him at Gibraltar, and was on half-pay as well as himself. He had not, indeed, had the fortune of being broke with his regiment, as was Booth, but had gone out, as they call it, on half-pay as a lieutenant, a rank to which he had risen in five-and-thirty years.

This honest gentleman, after some discourse with Booth, desired him to lend him half-a-crown, which he assured him he would faithfully pay the next day, when he was to receive some money for his sister. The sister was the widow of an officer that had been killed in the sea-service; and she and her brother lived together, on their joint stock, out of which they maintained likewise an old mother and two of the sister's children, the eldest of which was about nine years old. "You must know," said the old lieutenant, "I have been disappointed this morning by an old scoundrel, who wanted fifteen per cent, for advancing my sister's pension; but I have now got an honest fellow who hath promised it me to-morrow at ten per cent."

"And enough too, of all conscience," cries Booth.

"Why, indeed, I think so too," answered the other; "considering it is sure to be paid one time or other. To say the truth, it is a little hard the government doth not pay those pensions better; for my sister's hath been due almost these two years; that is my way of thinking."

Booth answered he was ashamed to refuse him such a sum; but, "Upon my soul," said he, "I have not a single halfpenny in my pocket; for I am in a worse condition, if possible, than yourself; for I have lost all my money, and, what is worse, I owe Mr. Trent, whom you remember at Gibraltar, fifty pounds."

"Remember him! yes, d—n him! I remember him very well," cries the old gentleman, "though he will not remember me. He is grown so great now that he will not speak to his old acquaintance; and yet I should be ashamed of myself to be great in such a manner."

"What manner do you mean?" cries Booth, a little eagerly.

"Why, by pimping," answered the other; "he is pimp in ordinary to my Lord——, who keeps his family; or how the devil he lives else I don't know, for his place is not worth three hundred pounds a year, and he and his wife spend a thousand at least. But she keeps an assembly, which, I believe, if you was to call a bawdy-house, you would not misname it. But d—n me if I had not rather be an honest man, and walk on foot, with holes in my shoes, as I do now, or go without a dinner, as I and all my family will today, than ride in a chariot and feast by such means. I am honest Bob Bound, and always will be; that's my way of thinking; and there's no man shall call me otherwise; for if he doth, I will knock him down for a lying rascal; that is my way of thinking."

"And a very good way of thinking too," cries Booth. "However, you shall not want a dinner to-day; for if you will go home with me, I will lend you a crown with all my heart."

"Lookee," said the old man, "if it be anywise inconvenient to you I will not have it; for I will never rob another man of his dinner to eat myself—that is my way of thinking."

"Pooh!" said Booth; "never mention such a trifle twice between you and me. Besides, you say you can pay it me to-morrow; and I promise you that will be the same thing."

They then walked together to Booth's lodgings, where Booth, from Amelia's pocket, gave his friend double the little sum he had asked. Upon which the old gentleman shook him heartily by the hand, and, repeating his intention of paying him the next day, made the best of his way to a butcher's, whence he carried off a leg of mutton to a family that had lately kept Lent without any religious merit.

When he was gone Amelia asked her husband who that old gentleman was? Booth answered he was one of the scandals of his country; that the Duke of Marlborough had about thirty years before made him an ensign from a private man for very particular merit; and that he had not long since gone out of the army with a broken heart, upon having several boys put over his head. He then gave her an account of his family, which he had heard from the old gentleman in their way to his house, and with which we have already in a concise manner acquainted the reader.

"Good Heavens!" cries Amelia; "what are our great men made of? are they in reality a distinct species from the rest of mankind? are they born without hearts?"

"One would, indeed, sometimes," cries Booth, "be inclined to think so. In truth, they have no perfect idea of those common distresses of mankind which are far removed from their own sphere. Compassion, if thoroughly examined, will, I believe, appear to be the fellow-feeling only of men of the same rank and degree of life for one another, on account of the evils to which they themselves are liable. Our sensations are, I am afraid, very cold towards those who are at a great

distance from us, and whose calamities can consequently never reach us."

"I remember," cries Amelia, "a sentiment of Dr Harrison's, which he told me was in some Latin book; I am a man myself, and my heart is interested in whatever can befal the rest of mankind. That is the sentiment of a good man, and whoever thinks otherwise is a bad one."

"I have often told you, my dear Emily," cries Booth, "that all men, as well the best as the worst, act alike from the principle of self-love. Where benevolence therefore is the uppermost passion, self-love directs you to gratify it by doing good, and by relieving the distresses of others; for they are then in reality your own. But where ambition, avarice, pride, or any other passion, governs the man and keeps his benevolence down, the miseries of all other men affect him no more than they would a stock or a stone. And thus the man and his statue have often the same degree of feeling or compassion."

"I have often wished, my dear," cries Amelia, "to hear you converse with Dr Harrison on this subject; for I am sure he would convince you, though I can't, that there are really such things as religion and virtue."

This was not the first hint of this kind which Amelia had given; for she sometimes apprehended from his discourse that he was little better than an atheist: a consideration which did not diminish her affection for him, but gave her great uneasiness. On all such occasions Booth immediately turned the discourse to some other subject; for, though he had in other points a great opinion of his wife's capacity, yet as a divine or a philosopher he did not hold her in a very respectable light, nor did he lay any great stress on her sentiments in such matters. He now, therefore, gave a speedy turn to the conversation, and began to talk of affairs below the dignity of this history.

BOOK XI.

Chapter i. — Containing a very polite scene.

We will now look back to some personages who, though not the principal characters in this history, have yet made too considerable a figure in it to be abruptly dropt: and these are Colonel James and his lady.

This fond couple never met till dinner the day after the masquerade, when they happened to be alone together in an antechamber before the arrival of the rest of the company.

The conversation began with the colonel's saying, "I hope, madam, you got no cold last night at the masquerade." To which the lady answered by much the same kind of question.

They then sat together near five minutes without opening their mouths to each other. At last Mrs. James said, "Pray, sir, who was that masque with you in the dress of a shepherdess? How could you expose yourself by walking with such a trollop in public; for certainly no woman of any figure would appear there in such a dress? You know, Mr. James, I never interfere with your affairs; but I would, methinks, for my own sake, if I was you, preserve a little decency in the face of the world."

"Upon my word," said James, "I do not know whom you mean. A woman in such a dress might speak to me for aught I know. A thousand people speak to me at a masquerade. But, I promise you, I spoke to no woman acquaintance there that I know of. Indeed, I now recollect there was a woman in a dress of a shepherdess; and there was another aukward thing in a blue domino that plagued me a little, but I soon got rid of them."

"And I suppose you do not know the lady in the blue domino neither?"

"Not I, I assure you," said James. "But pray, why do you ask me these questions? it looks so

like jealousy."

"Jealousy!" cries she; "I jealous! no, Mr. James, I shall never be jealous, I promise you, especially of the lady in the blue domino; for, to my knowledge, she despises you of all human race."

"I am heartily glad of it," said James; "for I never saw such a tall awkward monster in my life."

"That is a very cruel way of telling me you knew me."

"You, madam!" said James; "you was in a black domino."

"It is not so unusual a thing, I believe, you yourself know, to change dresses. I own I did it to discover some of your tricks. I did not think you could have distinguished the tall awkward monster so well."

"Upon my soul," said James, "if it was you I did not even suspect it; so you ought not to be offended at what I have said ignorantly."

"Indeed, sir," cries she, "you cannot offend me by anything you can say to my face; no, by my soul, I despise you too much. But I wish, Mr. James, you would not make me the subject of your conversation amongst your wenches. I desire I may not be afraid of meeting them for fear of their insults; that I may not be told by a dirty trollop you make me the subject of your wit amongst them, of which, it seems, I am the favourite topic. Though you have married a tall awkward monster, Mr. James, I think she hath a right to be treated, as your wife, with respect at least: indeed, I shall never require any more; indeed, Mr. James, I never shall. I think a wife hath a title to that."

"Who told you this, madam?" said James.

"Your slut," said she; "your wench, your shepherdess."

"By all that's sacred!" cries James, "I do not know who the shepherdess was."

"By all that's sacred then," says she, "she told me so, and I am convinced she told me truth. But I do not wonder at you denying it; for that is equally consistent with honour as to behave in such a manner to a wife who is a gentlewoman. I hope you will allow me that, sir. Because I had not quite so great a fortune I hope you do not think me beneath you, or that you did me any honour in marrying me. I am come of as good a family as yourself, Mr. James; and if my brother knew how you treated me he would not bear it."

"Do you threaten me with your brother, madam?" said James.

"I will not be ill-treated, sir," answered she.

"Nor I neither, madam," cries he; "and therefore I desire you will prepare to go into the country to-morrow morning."

"Indeed, sir," said she, "I shall not."

"By heavens! madam, but you shall," answered he: "I will have my coach at the door to-morrow morning by seven; and you shall either go into it or be carried."

"I hope, sir, you are not in earnest," said she.

"Indeed, madam," answered he, "but I am in earnest, and resolved; and into the country you go to-morrow."

"But why into the country," said she, "Mr. James? Why will you be so barbarous to deny me the pleasures of the town?"

"Because you interfere with my pleasures," cried James, "which I have told you long ago I would not submit to. It is enough for fond couples to have these scenes together. I thought we had been upon a better footing, and had cared too little for each other to become mutual plagues. I thought you had been satisfied with the full liberty of doing what you pleased."

"So I am; I defy you to say I have ever given you any uneasiness."

"How!" cries he; "have you not just now upbraided me with what you heard at the masquerade?"

"I own," said she, "to be insulted by such a creature to my face stung me to the soul. I must have had no spirit to bear the insults of such an animal. Nay, she spoke of you with equal contempt. Whoever she is, I promise you Mr. Booth is her favourite. But, indeed, she is unworthy any one's regard, for she behaved like an arrant dragoon."

"Hang her!" cries the colonel, "I know nothing of her."

"Well, but, Mr. James, I am sure you will not send me into the country. Indeed I will not go into the country."

"If you was a reasonable woman," cries James, "perhaps I should not desire it. And on one

224

consideration—"

"Come, name your consideration," said she.

"Let me first experience your discernment," said he. "Come, Molly, let me try your judgment. Can you guess at any woman of your acquaintance that I like?"

"Sure," said she, "it cannot be Mrs. Booth!"

"And why not Mrs. Booth?" answered he. "Is she not the finest woman in the world?"

"Very far from it," replied she, "in my opinion."

"Pray what faults," said he, "can you find in her?"

"In the first place," cries Mrs. James, "her eyes are too large; and she hath a look with them that I don't know how to describe; but I know I don't like it. Then her eyebrows are too large; therefore, indeed, she doth all in her power to remedy this with her pincers; for if it was not for those her eyebrows would be preposterous. Then her nose, as well proportioned as it is, has a visible scar on one side. Her neck, likewise, is too protuberant for the genteel size, especially as she laces herself; for no woman, in my opinion, can be genteel who is not entirely flat before. And, lastly, she is both too short and too tall. Well, you may laugh, Mr. James, I know what I mean, though I cannot well express it: I mean that she is too tall for a pretty woman and too short for a fine woman. There is such a thing as a kind of insipid medium—a kind of something that is neither one thing nor another. I know not how to express it more clearly; but when I say such a one is a pretty woman, a pretty thing, a pretty creature, you know very well I mean a little woman; and when I say such a one is a very fine woman, a very fine person of a woman, to be sure I must mean a tall woman. Now a woman that is between both is certainly neither the one nor the other."

"Well, I own," said he, "you have explained yourself with great dexterity; but, with all these imperfections, I cannot help liking her."

"That you need not tell me, Mr. James," answered the lady, "for that I knew before you desired me to invite her to your house. And nevertheless, did not I, like an obedient wife, comply with your desires? did I make any objection to the party you proposed for the masquerade, though I knew very well your motive? what can the best of wives do more? to procure you success is not in my power; and, if I may give you my opinion, I believe you will never succeed with her."

"Is her virtue so very impregnable?" said he, with a sneer.

"Her virtue," answered Mrs. James, "hath the best guard in the world, which is a most violent love for her husband."

"All pretence and affectation," cries the colonel. "It is impossible she should have so little taste, or indeed so little delicacy, as to like such a fellow."

"Nay, I do not much like him myself," said she. "He is not indeed at all such a sort of man as I should like; but I thought he had been generally allowed to be handsome."

"He handsome!" cries James. "What, with a nose like the proboscis of an elephant, with the shoulders of a porter, and the legs of a chairman? The fellow hath not in the least the look of a gentleman, and one would rather think he had followed the plough than the camp all his life."

"Nay, now I protest," said she, "I think you do him injustice. He is genteel enough in my opinion. It is true, indeed, he is not quite of the most delicate make; but, whatever he is, I am convinced she thinks him the finest man in the world."

"I cannot believe it," answered he peevishly; "but will you invite her to dinner here to-morrow?"

"With all my heart, and as often as you please," answered she. "But I have some favours to ask of you. First, I must hear no more of going out of town till I please."

"Very well," cries he.

"In the next place," said she, "I must have two hundred guineas within these two or three days."

"Well, I agree to that too," answered he.

"And when I do go out of town, I go to Tunbridge—I insist upon that; and from Tunbridge I go to Bath—positively to Bath. And I promise you faithfully I will do all in my power to carry Mrs. Booth with me."

"On that condition," answered he, "I promise you you shall go wherever you please. And, to shew you, I will even prevent your wishes by my generosity; as soon as I receive the five thousand pounds which I am going to take up on one of my estates, you shall have two hundred more."

She thanked him with a low curtesie; and he was in such good humour that he offered to kiss

her. To this kiss she coldly turned her cheek, and then, flirting her fan, said, "Mr. James, there is one thing I forgot to mention to you—I think you intended to get a commission in some regiment abroad for this young man. Now if you would take my advice, I know this will not oblige his wife; and, besides, I am positive she resolves to go with him. But, if you can provide for him in some regiment at home, I know she will dearly love you for it, and when he is ordered to quarters she will be left behind; and Yorkshire or Scotland, I think, is as good a distance as either of the Indies."

"Well, I will do what I can," answered James; "but I cannot ask anything yet; for I got two places of a hundred a year each for two of my footmen, within this fortnight."

At this instant a violent knock at the door signified the arrival of their company, upon which both husband and wife put on their best looks to receive their guests; and, from their behaviour to each other during the rest of the day, a stranger might have concluded he had been in company with the fondest couple in the universe.

Chapter ii. — Matters political.

Before we return to Booth we will relate a scene in which Dr Harrison was concerned.

This good man, whilst in the country, happened to be in the neighbourhood of a nobleman of his acquaintance, and whom he knew to have very considerable interest with the ministers at that time.

The doctor, who was very well known to this nobleman, took this opportunity of paying him a visit in order to recommend poor Booth to his favour. Nor did he much doubt of his success, the favour he was to ask being a very small one, and to which he thought the service of Booth gave him so just a title.

The doctor's name soon gained him an admission to the presence of this great man, who, indeed, received him with much courtesy and politeness; not so much, perhaps, from any particular regard to the sacred function, nor from any respect to the doctor's personal merit, as from some considerations which the reader will perhaps guess anon. After many ceremonials, and some previous discourse on different subjects, the doctor opened the business, and told the great man that he was come to him to solicit a favour for a young gentleman who had been an officer in the army and was now on half-pay. "All the favour I ask, my lord," said he, "is, that this gentleman may be again admitted ad eundem. I am convinced your lordship will do me the justice to think I would not ask for a worthless person; but, indeed, the young man I mean hath very extraordinary merit. He was at the siege of Gibraltar, in which he behaved with distinguished bravery, and was dangerously wounded at two several times in the service of his country. I will add that he is at present in great necessity, and hath a wife and several children, for whom he hath no other means of providing; and, if it will recommend him farther to your lordship's favour, his wife, I believe, is one of the best and worthiest of all her sex."

"As to that, my dear doctor," cries the nobleman, "I shall make no doubt. Indeed any service I shall do the gentleman will be upon your account. As to necessity, it is the plea of so many that it is impossible to serve them all. And with regard to the personal merit of these inferior officers, I believe I need not tell you that it is very little regarded. But if you recommend him, let the person be what he will, I am convinced it will be done; for I know it is in your power at present to ask for a greater matter than this."

"I depend entirely upon your lordship," answered the doctor.

"Indeed, my worthy friend," replied the lord, "I will not take a merit to myself which will so little belong to me. You are to depend on yourself. It falls out very luckily too at this time, when you have it in your power so greatly to oblige us."

"What, my lord, is in my power?" cries the doctor.

"You certainly know," answered his lordship, "how hard Colonel Trompington is run at your town in the election of a mayor; they tell me it will be a very near thing unless you join us. But we

know it is in your power to do the business, and turn the scale. I heard your name mentioned the other day on that account, and I know you may have anything in reason if you will give us your interest."

"Sure, my lord," cries the doctor, "you are not in earnest in asking my interest for the colonel?"

"Indeed I am," answered the peer; "why should you doubt it?"

"For many reasons," answered the doctor. "First, I am an old friend and acquaintance of Mr. Fairfield, as your lordship, I believe, very well knows. The little interest, therefore, that I have, you may be assured, will go in his favour. Indeed, I do not concern myself deeply in these affairs, for I do not think it becomes my cloth so to do. But, as far as I think it decent to interest myself, it will certainly be on the side of Mr. Fairfield. Indeed, I should do so if I was acquainted with both the gentlemen only by reputation; the one being a neighbouring gentleman of a very large estate, a very sober and sensible man, of known probity and attachment to the true interest of his country; the other is a mere stranger, a boy, a soldier of fortune, and, as far as I can discern from the little conversation I have had with him, of a very shallow capacity, and no education."

"No education, my dear friend!" cries the nobleman. "Why, he hath been educated in half the courts of Europe."

"Perhaps so, my lord," answered the doctor; "but I shall always be so great a pedant as to call a man of no learning a man of no education. And, from my own knowledge, I can aver that I am persuaded there is scarce a foot-soldier in the army who is more illiterate than the colonel."

"Why, as to Latin and Greek, you know," replied the lord, "they are not much required in the army."

"It may be so," said the doctor. "Then let such persons keep to their own profession. It is a very low civil capacity indeed for which an illiterate man can be qualified. And, to speak a plain truth, if your lordship is a friend to the colonel, you would do well to advise him to decline an attempt in which I am certain he hath no probability of success."

"Well, sir," said the lord, "if you are resolved against us, I must deal as freely with you, and tell you plainly I cannot serve you in your affair. Nay, it will be the best thing I can do to hold my tongue; for, if I should mention his name with your recommendation after what you have said, he would perhaps never get provided for as long as he lives."

"Is his own merit, then, my lord, no recommendation?" cries the doctor.

"My dear, dear sir," cries the other, "what is the merit of a subaltern officer?"

"Surely, my lord," cries the doctor, "it is the merit which should recommend him to the post of a subaltern officer. And it is a merit which will hereafter qualify him to serve his country in a higher capacity. And I do assure of this young man, that he hath not only a good heart but a good head too. And I have been told by those who are judges that he is, for his age, an excellent officer."

"Very probably!" cries my lord. "And there are abundance with the same merit and the same qualifications who want a morsel of bread for themselves and their families."

"It is an infamous scandal on the nation," cries the doctor; "and I am heartily sorry it can be said even with a colour of truth."

"How can it be otherwise?" says the peer. "Do you think it is possible to provide for all men of merit?"

"Yes, surely do I," said the doctor; "and very easily too."

"How, pray?" cries the lord. "Upon my word, I shall be glad to know."

"Only by not providing for those who have none. The men of merit in any capacity are not, I am afraid, so extremely numerous that we need starve any of them, unless we wickedly suffer a set of worthless fellows to eat their bread."

"This is all mere Utopia," cries his lordship; "the chimerical system of Plato's commonwealth, with which we amused ourselves at the university; politics which are inconsistent with the state of human affairs."

"Sure, my lord," cries the doctor, "we have read of states where such doctrines have been put in practice. What is your lordship's opinion of Rome in the earlier ages of the commonwealth, of Sparta, and even of Athens itself in some periods of its history?"

"Indeed, doctor," cries the lord, "all these notions are obsolete and long since exploded. To apply maxims of government drawn from the Greek and Roman histories to this nation is absurd

227

and impossible. But, if you will have Roman examples, fetch them from those times of the republic that were most like our own. Do you not know, doctor, that this is as corrupt a nation as ever existed under the sun? And would you think of governing such a people by the strict principles of honesty and morality?"

"If it be so corrupt," said the doctor, "I think it is high time to amend it: or else it is easy to foresee that Roman and British liberty will have the same fate; for corruption in the body politic as naturally tends to dissolution as in the natural body."

"I thank you for your simile," cries my lord; "for, in the natural body, I believe, you will allow there is the season of youth, the season of manhood, and the season of old age; and that, when the last of these arrives, it will be an impossible attempt by all the means of art to restore the body again to its youth, or to the vigour of its middle age. The same periods happen to every great kingdom. In its youth it rises by arts and arms to power and prosperity. This it enjoys and flourishes with a while; and then it may be said to be in the vigour of its age, enriched at home with all the emoluments and blessings of peace, and formidable abroad with all the terrors of war. At length this very prosperity introduces corruption, and then comes on its old age. Virtue and learning, art and industry, decay by degrees. The people sink into sloth and luxury and prostitution. It is enervated at home—becomes contemptible abroad; and such indeed is its misery and wretchedness, that it resembles a man in the last decrepit stage of life, who looks with unconcern at his approaching dissolution."

"This is a melancholy picture indeed," cries the doctor; "and, if the latter part of it can be applied to our case, I see nothing but religion, which would have prevented this decrepit state of the constitution, should prevent a man of spirit from hanging himself out of the way of so wretched a contemplation."

"Why so?" said the peer; "why hang myself, doctor? Would it not be wiser, think you, to make the best of your time, and the most you can, in such a nation?"

"And is religion, then, to be really laid out of the question?" cries the doctor.

"If I am to speak my own opinion, sir," answered the peer, "you know I shall answer in the negative. But you are too well acquainted with the world to be told that the conduct of politicians is not formed upon the principles of religion."

"I am very sorry for it," cries the doctor; "but I will talk to them then of honour and honesty; this is a language which I hope they will at least pretend to understand. Now to deny a man the preferment which he merits, and to give it to another man who doth not merit it, is a manifest act of injustice, and is consequently inconsistent with both honour and honesty. Nor is it only an act of injustice to the man himself, but to the public, for whose good principally all public offices are, or ought to be, instituted. Now this good can never be completed nor obtained but by employing all persons according to their capacities. Wherever true merit is liable to be superseded by favour and partiality, and men are intrusted with offices without any regard to capacity or integrity, the affairs of that state will always be in a deplorable situation. Such, as Livy tells us, was the state of Capua a little before its final destruction, and the consequence your lordship well knows. But, my lord, there is another mischief which attends this kind of injustice, and that is, it hath a manifest tendency to destroy all virtue and all ability among the people, by taking away all that encouragement and incentive which should promote emulation and raise men to aim at excelling in any art, science, or profession. Nor can anything, my lord, contribute more to render a nation contemptible among its neighbours; for what opinion can other countries have of the councils, or what terror can they conceive of the arms, of such a people? and it was chiefly owing to the avoiding this error that Oliver Cromwell carried the reputation of England higher than it ever was at any other time. I will add only one argument more, and that is founded on the most narrow and selfish system of politics; and this is, that such a conduct is sure to create universal discontent and grumbling at home; for nothing can bring men to rest satisfied, when they see others preferred to them, but an opinion that they deserved that elevation; for, as one of the greatest men this country ever produced observes,

> One worthless man that gains what he pretends
> Disgusts a thousand unpretending friends.

With what heart-burnings then must any nation see themselves obliged to contribute to the support of a set of men of whose incapacity to serve them they are well apprized, and who do their country a double diskindness, by being themselves employed in posts to which they are

unequal, and by keeping others out of those employments for which they are qualified!"

"And do you really think, doctor," cries the nobleman, "that any minister could support himself in this country upon such principles as you recommend? Do you think he would be able to baffle an opposition unless he should oblige his friends by conferring places often contrary to his own inclinations and his own opinion?"

"Yes, really do I," cries the doctor. "Indeed, if a minister is resolved to make good his confession in the liturgy, by leaving undone all those things which he ought to have done, and by doing all those things which he ought not to have done, such a minister, I grant, will be obliged to baffle opposition, as you are pleased to term it, by these arts; for, as Shakespeare somewhere says,

Things ill begun strengthen themselves by ill.

But if, on the contrary, he will please to consider the true interest of his country, and that only in great and national points; if he will engage his country in neither alliances nor quarrels but where it is really interested; if he will raise no money but what is wanted, nor employ any civil or military officers but what are useful, and place in these employments men of the highest integrity, and of the greatest abilities; if he will employ some few of his hours to advance our trade, and some few more to regulate our domestic government; if he would do this, my lord, I will answer for it, he shall either have no opposition to baffle, or he shall baffle it by a fair appeal to his conduct. Such a minister may, in the language of the law, put himself on his country when he pleases, and he shall come off with honour and applause."

"And do you really believe, doctor," cries the peer, "there ever was such a minister, or ever will be?"

"Why not, my lord?" answered the doctor. "It requires no very extraordinary parts, nor any extraordinary degree of virtue. He need practise no great instances of self-denial. He shall have power, and honour, and riches, and, perhaps, all in a much greater degree than he can ever acquire by pursuing a contrary system. He shall have more of each and much more of safety."

"Pray, doctor," said my lord, "let me ask you one simple question. Do you really believe any man upon earth was ever a rogue out of choice?"

"Really, my lord," says the doctor, "I am ashamed to answer in the affirmative; and yet I am afraid experience would almost justify me if I should. Perhaps the opinion of the world may sometimes mislead men to think those measures necessary which in reality are not so. Or the truth may be, that a man of good inclinations finds his office filled with such corruption by the iniquity of his predecessors, that he may despair of being capable of purging it; and so sits down contented, as Augeas did with the filth of his stables, not because he thought them the better, or that such filth was really necessary to a stable, but that he despaired of sufficient force to cleanse them."

"I will ask you one question more, and I have done," said the nobleman. "Do you imagine that if any minister was really as good as you would have him, that the people in general would believe that he was so?"

"Truly, my lord," said the doctor, "I think they may be justified in not believing too hastily. But I beg leave to answer your lordship's question by another. Doth your lordship believe that the people of Greenland, when they see the light of the sun and feel his warmth, after so long a season of cold and darkness, will really be persuaded that he shines upon them?"

My lord smiled at the conceit; and then the doctor took an opportunity to renew his suit, to which his lordship answered, "He would promise nothing, and could give him no hopes of success; but you may be assured," said he, with a leering countenance, "I shall do him all the service in my power." A language which the doctor well understood; and soon after took a civil, but not a very ceremonious leave.

Chapter iii. — The history of Mr. Trent.

We will now return to Mr. Booth and his wife. The former had spent his time very uneasily ever since he had discovered what sort of man he was indebted to; but, lest he should forget it,

Mr. Trent thought now proper to remind him in the following letter, which he read the next morning after he had put off the appointment.

"SIR,—I am sorry the necessity of my affairs obliges me to mention that small sum which I had the honour to lend you the other night at play; and which I shall be much obliged to you if you will let me have some time either to-day or to-morrow. I am, sir, Your most obedient, most humble servant, GEORGE TRENT."

This letter a little surprized Booth, after the genteel, and, indeed, as it appeared, generous behaviour of Trent. But lest it should have the same effect upon the reader, we will now proceed to account for this, as well as for some other phenomena that have appeared in this history, and which, perhaps, we shall be forgiven for not having opened more largely before.

Mr. Trent then was a gentleman possibly of a good family, for it was not certain whence he sprung on the father's side. His mother, who was the only parent he ever knew or heard of, was a single gentlewoman, and for some time carried on the trade of a milliner in Covent-garden. She sent her son, at the age of eight years old, to a charity-school, where he remained till he was of the age of fourteen, without making any great proficiency in learning. Indeed it is not very probable he should; for the master, who, in preference to a very learned and proper man, was chosen by a party into this school, the salary of which was upwards of a hundred pounds a-year, had himself never travelled through the Latin Grammar, and was, in truth, a most consummate blockhead.

At the age of fifteen Mr. Trent was put clerk to an attorney, where he remained a very short time before he took leave of his master; rather, indeed, departed without taking leave; and, having broke open his mother's escritore, and carried off with him all the valuable effects he there found, to the amount of about fifty pounds, he marched off to sea, and went on board a merchantman, whence he was afterwards pressed into a man of war.

In this service he continued above three years; during which time he behaved so ill in his moral character that he twice underwent a very severe discipline for thefts in which he was detected; but at the same time, he behaved so well as a sailor in an engagement with some pirates, that he wiped off all former scores, and greatly recommended himself to his captain.

At his return home, he being then about twenty years of age, he found that the attorney had in his absence married his mother, had buried her, and secured all her effects, to the amount, as he was informed, of about fifteen hundred pound. Trent applied to his stepfather, but to no purpose; the attorney utterly disowned him, nor would he suffer him to come a second time within his doors.

It happened that the attorney had, by a former wife, an only daughter, a great favourite, who was about the same age with Trent himself, and had, during his residence at her father's house, taken a very great liking to this young fellow, who was extremely handsome and perfectly well made. This her liking was not, during his absence, so far extinguished but that it immediately revived on his return. Of this she took care to give Mr. Trent proper intimation; for she was not one of those backward and delicate ladies who can die rather than make the first overture. Trent was overjoyed at this, and with reason, for she was a very lovely girl in her person, the only child of a rich father; and the prospect of so complete a revenge on the attorney charmed him above all the rest. To be as short in the matter as the parties, a marriage was soon consummated between them.

The attorney at first raged and was implacable; but at last fondness for his daughter so far overcame resentment that he advanced a sum of money to buy his son-in-law (for now he acknowledged him as such) an ensign's commission in a marching regiment then ordered to Gibraltar; at which place the attorney heartily hoped that Trent might be knocked on the head; for in that case he thought he might marry his daughter more agreeably to his own ambition and to her advantage.

The regiment into which Trent purchased was the same with that in which Booth likewise served; the one being an ensign, and the other a lieutenant, in the two additional companies.

Trent had no blemish in his military capacity. Though he had had but an indifferent education, he was naturally sensible and genteel, and Nature, as we have said, had given him a very agreeable person. He was likewise a very bold fellow, and, as he really behaved himself every way well enough while he was at Gibraltar, there was some degree of intimacy between him and Booth.

When the siege was over, and the additional companies were again reduced, Trent returned to

his wife, who received him with great joy and affection. Soon after this an accident happened which proved the utter ruin of his father-in-law, and ended in breaking his heart. This was nothing but making a mistake pretty common at this day, of writing another man's name to a deed instead of his own. In truth this matter was no less than what the law calls forgery, and was just then made capital by an act of parliament. From this offence, indeed, the attorney was acquitted, by not admitting the proof of the party, who was to avoid his own deed by his evidence, and therefore no witness, according to those excellent rules called the law of evidence; a law very excellently calculated for the preservation of the lives of his majesty's roguish subjects, and most notably used for that purpose.

But though by common law the attorney was honourably acquitted, yet, as common sense manifested to every one that he was guilty, he unhappily lost his reputation, and of consequence his business; the chagrin of which latter soon put an end to his life.

This prosecution had been attended with a very great expence; for, besides the ordinary costs of avoiding the gallows by the help of the law, there was a very high article, of no less than a thousand pounds, paid down to remove out of the way a witness against whom there was no legal exception. The poor gentleman had besides suffered some losses in business; so that, to the surprize of all his acquaintance, when his debts were paid there remained no more than a small estate of fourscore pounds a-year, which he settled upon his daughter, far out of the reach of her husband, and about two hundred pounds in money.

The old gentleman had not long been in his grave before Trent set himself to consider seriously of the state of his affairs. He had lately begun to look on his wife with a much less degree of liking and desire than formerly; for he was one of those who think too much of one thing is good for nothing. Indeed, he had indulged these speculations so far, that I believe his wife, though one of the prettiest women in town, was the last subject that he would have chose for any amorous dalliance.

Many other persons, however, greatly differed from him in his opinion. Amongst the rest was the illustrious peer of amorous memory. This noble peer, having therefore got a view of Mrs. Trent one day in the street, did, by means of an emissary then with him, make himself acquainted with her lodging, to which he immediately laid siege in form, setting himself down in a lodging directly opposite to her, from whence the battery of ogles began to play the very next morning.

This siege had not continued long before the governor of the garrison became sufficiently apprized of all the works which were carrying on, and, having well reconnoitered the enemy, and discovered who he was, notwithstanding a false name and some disguise of his person, he called a council of war within his own breast. In fact, to drop all allegory, he began to consider whether his wife was not really a more valuable possession than he had lately thought her. In short, as he had been disappointed in her fortune, he now conceived some hopes of turning her beauty itself into a fortune.

Without communicating these views to her, he soon scraped an acquaintance with his opposite neighbour by the name which he there usurped, and counterfeited an entire ignorance of his real name and title. On this occasion Trent had his disguise likewise, for he affected the utmost simplicity; of which affectation, as he was a very artful fellow, he was extremely capable.

The peer fell plumb into this snare; and when, by the simplicity, as he imagined, of the husband, he became acquainted with the wife, he was so extravagantly charmed with her person, that he resolved, whatever was the cost or the consequence, he would possess her.

His lordship, however, preserved some caution in his management of this affair; more, perhaps, than was necessary. As for the husband, none was requisite, for he knew all he could; and, with regard to the wife herself, as she had for some time perceived the decrease of her husband's affection (for few women are, I believe, to be imposed upon in that matter), she was not displeased to find the return of all that complaisance and endearment, of those looks and languishments, from another agreeable person, which she had formerly received from Trent, and which she now found she should receive from him no longer.

My lord, therefore, having been indulged with as much opportunity as he could wish from Trent, and having received rather more encouragement than he could well have hoped from the lady, began to prepare all matters for a storm, when luckily, Mr. Trent declaring he must go out of town for two days, he fixed on the first day of his departure as the time of carrying his design into execution.

231

And now, after some debate with himself in what manner he should approach his love, he at last determined to do it in his own person; for he conceived, and perhaps very rightly, that the lady, like Semele, was not void of ambition, and would have preferred Jupiter in all his glory to the same deity in the disguise of an humble shepherd. He dressed himself, therefore, in the richest embroidery of which he was master, and appeared before his mistress arrayed in all the brightness of peerage; a sight whose charms she had not the power to resist, and the consequences are only to be imagined. In short, the same scene which Jupiter acted with his above-mentioned mistress of old was more than beginning, when Trent burst from the closet into which he had conveyed himself, and unkindly interrupted the action.

His lordship presently run to his sword; but Trent, with great calmness, answered, "That, as it was very well known he durst fight, he should not draw his sword on this occasion; for sure," says he, "my lord, it would be the highest imprudence in me to kill a man who is now become so considerably my debtor." At which words he fetched a person from the closet, who had been confined with him, telling him he had done his business, and might now, if he pleased, retire.

It would be tedious here to amuse the reader with all that passed on the present occasion; the rage and confusion of the wife, or the perplexity in which my lord was involved. We will omit therefore all such matters, and proceed directly to business, as Trent and his lordship did soon after. And in the conclusion my lord stipulated to pay a good round sum, and to provide Mr. Trent with a good place on the first opportunity.

On the side of Mr. Trent were stipulated absolute remission of all past, and full indulgence for the time to come.

Trent now immediately took a house at the polite end of the town, furnished it elegantly, and set up his equipage, rigged out both himself and his wife with very handsome cloaths, frequented all public places where he could get admission, pushed himself into acquaintance, and his wife soon afterwards began to keep an assembly, or, in the fashionable phrase, to be at home once a-week; when, by my lord's assistance, she was presently visited by most men of the first rank, and by all such women of fashion as are not very nice in their company.

My lord's amour with this lady lasted not long; for, as we have before observed, he was the most inconstant of all human race. Mrs. Trent's passion was not however of that kind which leads to any very deep resentment of such fickleness. Her passion, indeed, was principally founded upon interest; so that foundation served to support another superstructure; and she was easily prevailed upon, as well as her husband, to be useful to my lord in a capacity which, though very often exerted in the polite world, hath not as yet, to my great surprize, acquired any polite name, or, indeed, any which is not too coarse to be admitted in this history.

After this preface, which we thought necessary to account for a character of which some of my country and collegiate readers might possibly doubt the existence, I shall proceed to what more immediately regards Mrs. Booth. The reader may be pleased to remember that Mr. Trent was present at the assembly to which Booth and his wife were carried by Mrs. James, and where Amelia was met by the noble peer.

His lordship, seeing there that Booth and Trent were old acquaintance, failed not, to use the language of sportsmen, to put Trent upon the scent of Amelia. For this purpose that gentleman visited Booth the very next day, and had pursued him close ever since. By his means, therefore, my lord learned that Amelia was to be at the masquerade, to which place she was dogged by Trent in a sailor's jacket, who, meeting my lord, according to agreement, at the entrance of the opera-house, like the four-legged gentleman of the same vocation, made a dead point, as it is called, at the game.

My lord was so satisfied and delighted with his conversation at the masquerade with the supposed Amelia, and the encouragement which in reality she had given him, that, when he saw Trent the next morning, he embraced him with great fondness, gave him a bank note of a hundred pound, and promised him both the Indies on his success, of which he began now to have no manner of doubt.

The affair that happened at the gaming-table was likewise a scheme of Trent's, on a hint given by my lord to him to endeavour to lead Booth into some scrape or distress; his lordship promising to pay whatever expense Trent might be led into by such means. Upon his lordship's credit, therefore, the money lent to Booth was really advanced. And hence arose all that seeming generosity and indifference as to the payment; Trent being satisfied with the obligation conferred

on Booth, by means of which he hoped to effect his purpose.

But now the scene was totally changed; for Mrs. Atkinson, the morning after the quarrel, beginning seriously to recollect that she had carried the matter rather too far, and might really injure Amelia's reputation, a thought to which the warm pursuit of her own interest had a good deal blinded her at the time, resolved to visit my lord himself, and to let him into the whole story; for, as she had succeeded already in her favourite point, she thought she had no reason to fear any consequence of the discovery. This resolution she immediately executed.

Trent came to attend his lordship, just after Mrs. Atkinson had left him. He found the peer in a very ill humour, and brought no news to comfort or recruit his spirits; for he had himself just received a billet from Booth, with an excuse for himself and his wife from accepting the invitation at Trent's house that evening, where matters had been previously concerted for their entertainment, and when his lordship was by accident to drop into the room where Amelia was, while Booth was to be engaged at play in another.

And now after much debate, and after Trent had acquainted my lord with the wretched situation of Booth's circumstances, it was resolved that Trent should immediately demand his money of Booth, and upon his not paying it, for they both concluded it impossible he should pay it, to put the note which Trent had for the money in suit against him by the genteel means of paying it away to a nominal third person; and this they both conceived must end immediately in the ruin of Booth, and, consequently, in the conquest of Amelia.

In this project, and with this hope, both my lord and his setter, or (if the sportsmen please) setting-dog, both greatly exulted; and it was next morning executed, as we have already seen.

Chapter iv. — Containing some distress.

Trent's letter drove Booth almost to madness. To be indebted to such a fellow at any rate had stuck much in his stomach, and had given him very great uneasiness; but to answer this demand in any other manner than by paying the money was absolutely what he could not bear. Again, to pay this money, he very plainly saw there was but one way, and this was, by stripping his wife, not only of every farthing, but almost of every rag she had in the world; a thought so dreadful that it chilled his very soul with horror: and yet pride, at last, seemed to represent this as the lesser evil of the two.

But how to do this was still a question. It was not sure, at least he feared it was not, that Amelia herself would readily consent to this; and so far from persuading her to such a measure, he could not bear even to propose it. At length his determination was to acquaint his wife with the whole affair, and to ask her consent, by way of asking her advice; for he was well assured she could find no other means of extricating him out of his dilemma. This he accordingly did, representing the affair as bad as he could; though, indeed, it was impossible for him to aggravate the real truth.

Amelia heard him patiently, without once interrupting him. When he had finished, she remained silent some time: indeed, the shock she received from this story almost deprived her of the power of speaking. At last she answered, "Well, my dear, you ask my advice; I certainly can give you no other than that the money must be paid."

"But how must it be paid?" cries he. "O, heavens! thou sweetest creature! what, not once upbraid me for bringing this ruin on thee?"

"Upbraid you, my dear!" says she; "would to heaven I could prevent your upbraiding yourself. But do not despair. I will endeavour by some means or other to get you the money."

"Alas! my dear love," cries Booth, "I know the only way by which you can raise it. How can I consent to that? do you forget the fears you so lately expressed of what would be our wretched condition when our little all was mouldered away? O my Amelia! they cut my very heart-strings when you spoke then; for I had then lost this little all. Indeed, I assure you, I have not played since, nor ever will more."

"Keep that resolution," said she, "my dear, and I hope we shall yet recover the past."—At

which words, casting her eyes on the children, the tears burst from her eyes, and she cried—"Heaven will, I hope, provide for us."

A pathetic scene now ensued between the husband and wife, which would not, perhaps, please many readers to see drawn at too full a length. It is sufficient to say that this excellent woman not only used her utmost endeavours to stifle and conceal her own concern, but said and did everything in her power to allay that of her husband.

Booth was, at this time, to meet a person whom we have formerly mentioned in the course of our history. This gentleman had a place in the War-office, and pretended to be a man of great interest and consequence; by which means he did not only receive great respect and court from the inferiour officers, but actually bubbled several of their money, by undertaking to do them services which, in reality, were not within his power. In truth, I have known few great men who have not been beset with one or more such fellows as these, through whom the inferior part of mankind are obliged to make their court to the great men themselves; by which means, I believe, principally, persons of real merit have often been deterred from the attempt; for these subaltern coxcombs ever assume an equal state with their masters, and look for an equal degree of respect to be paid to them; to which men of spirit, who are in every light their betters, are not easily brought to submit. These fellows, indeed, themselves have a jealous eye towards all great abilities, and are sure, to the utmost of their power, to keep all who are so endowed from the presence of their masters. They use their masters as bad ministers have sometimes used a prince—they keep all men of merit from his ears, and daily sacrifice his true honour and interest to their own profit and their own vanity.

As soon as Booth was gone to his appointment with this man, Amelia immediately betook herself to her business with the highest resolution. She packed up, not only her own little trinkets, and those of the children, but the greatest part of her own poor cloathes (for she was but barely provided), and then drove in a hackney-coach to the same pawnbroker's who had before been recommended to her by Mrs. Atkinson, who advanced her the money she desired.

Being now provided with her sum, she returned well pleased home, and her husband coming in soon after, she with much chearfulness delivered him all the money.

Booth was so overjoyed with the prospect of discharging his debt to Trent, that he did not perfectly reflect on the distress to which his family was now reduced. The good-humour which appeared in the countenance of Amelia was, perhaps, another help to stifle those reflexions; but above all, were the assurances he had received from the great man, whom he had met at a coffee-house, and who had promised to do him all the service in his power; which several half-pay subaltern officers assured him was very considerable.

With this comfortable news he acquainted his wife, who either was, or seemed to be, extremely well pleased with it. And now he set out with the money in his pocket to pay his friend Trent, who unluckily for him happened not to be at home.

On his return home he met his old friend the lieutenant, who thankfully paid him his crown, and insisted on his going with him and taking part of a bottle. This invitation was so eager and pressing, that poor Booth, who could not resist much importunity, complied.

While they were over this bottle Booth acquainted his friend with the promises he had received that afternoon at the coffee-house, with which the old gentleman was very well pleased: "For I have heard," says he, "that gentleman hath very powerful interest;" but he informed him likewise that he had heard that the great man must be touched, for that he never did anything without touching. Of this, indeed, the great man himself had given some oblique hints, by saying, with great sagacity and slyness, that he knew where fifty pound might be deposited to much advantage.

Booth answered that he would very readily advance a small sum if he had it in his power, but that at present it was not so, for that he had no more in the world than the sum of fifty pounds, which he owed Trent, and which he intended to pay him the next morning.

"It is very right, undoubtedly, to pay your debts," says the old gentleman; "but sure, on such an occasion, any man but the rankest usurer would be contented to stay a little while for his money; and it will be only a little while I am convinced; for, if you deposit this sum in the great man's hands, I make no doubt but you will succeed immediately in getting your commission; and then I will help you to a method of taking up such a sum as this." The old gentleman persisted in this advice, and backed it with every argument he could invent, declaring, as was indeed true, that

he gave the same advice which he would pursue was the case his own.

Booth long rejected the opinion of his friend, till, as they had not argued with dry lips, he became heated with wine, and then at last the old gentleman succeeded. Indeed, such was his love, either for Booth or for his own opinion, and perhaps for both, that he omitted nothing in his power. He even endeavoured to palliate the character of Trent, and unsaid half what he had before said of that gentleman. In the end, he undertook to make Trent easy, and to go to him the very next morning for that purpose.

Poor Booth at last yielded, though with the utmost difficulty. Indeed, had he known quite as much of Trent as the reader doth, no motive whatsoever would have prevailed on him to have taken the old gentleman's advice.

Chapter v. — Containing more wormwood and other ingredients.

In the morning Booth communicated the matter to Amelia, who told him she would not presume to advise him in an affair of which he was so much the better judge.

While Booth remained in a doubtful state what conduct to pursue Bound came to make him a visit, and informed him that he had been at Trent's house, but found him not at home, adding that he would pay him a second visit that very day, and would not rest till he found him.

Booth was ashamed to confess his wavering resolution in an affair in which he had been so troublesome to his friend; he therefore dressed himself immediately, and together they both went to wait on the little great man, to whom Booth now hoped to pay his court in the most effectual manner.

Bound had been longer acquainted with the modern methods of business than Booth; he advised his friend, therefore, to begin with tipping (as it is called) the great man's servant. He did so, and by that means got speedy access to the master.

The great man received the money, not as a gudgeon doth a bait, but as a pike receives a poor gudgeon into his maw. To say the truth, such fellows as these may well be likened to that voracious fish, who fattens himself by devouring all the little inhabitants of the river. As soon as the great man had pocketed the cash, he shook Booth by the hand, and told him he would be sure to slip no opportunity of serving him, and would send him word as soon as any offered.

Here I shall stop one moment, and so, perhaps, will my good-natured reader; for surely it must be a hard heart which is not affected with reflecting on the manner in which this poor little sum was raised, and on the manner in which it was bestowed. A worthy family, the wife and children of a man who had lost his blood abroad in the service of his country, parting with their little all, and exposed to cold and hunger, to pamper such a fellow as this!

And if any such reader as I mention should happen to be in reality a great man, and in power, perhaps the horrour of this picture may induce him to put a final end to this abominable practice of touching, as it is called; by which, indeed, a set of leeches are permitted to suck the blood of the brave and the indigent, of the widow and the orphan.

Booth now returned home, where he found his wife with Mrs. James. Amelia had, before the arrival of her husband, absolutely refused Mrs. James's invitation to dinner the next day; but when Booth came in the lady renewed her application, and that in so pressing a manner, that Booth seconded her; for, though he had enough of jealousy in his temper, yet such was his friendship to the colonel, and such his gratitude to the obligations which he had received from him, that his own unwillingness to believe anything of him, co-operating with Amelia's endeavours to put everything in the fairest light, had brought him to acquit his friend of any ill design. To this, perhaps, the late affair concerning my lord had moreover contributed; for it seems to me that the same passion cannot much energize on two different objects at one and the same time: an observation which, I believe, will hold as true with regard to the cruel passions of jealousy and anger as to the gentle passion of love, in which one great and mighty object is sure to engage the whole passion.

When Booth grew importunate, Amelia answered, "My dear, I should not refuse you

235

whatever was in my power; but this is absolutely out of my power; for since I must declare the truth, I cannot dress myself."

"Why so?" said Mrs. James." I am sure you are in good health."

"Is there no other impediment to dressing but want of health, madam?" answered Amelia.

"Upon my word, none that I know of," replied Mrs. James.

"What do you think of want of cloathes, madam?" said Amelia.

"Ridiculous!" cries Mrs. James. "What need have you to dress yourself out? You will see nobody but our own family, and I promise you I don't expect it. A plain night-gown will do very well."

"But if I must be plain with you, madam," said Amelia, "I have no other cloathes but what I have now on my back. I have not even a clean shift in the world; for you must know, my dear," said she to Booth, "that little Betty is walked off this morning, and hath carried all my linen with her."

"How, my dear?" cries Booth; "little Betty robbed you?"

"It is even so," answered Amelia. Indeed, she spoke truth; for little Betty, having perceived the evening before that her mistress was moving her goods, was willing to lend all the assistance in her power, and had accordingly moved off early that morning, taking with her whatever she could lay her hands on.

Booth expressed himself with some passion on the occasion, and swore he would make an example of the girl. "If the little slut be above ground," cried he, "I will find her out, and bring her to justice."

"I am really sorry for this accident," said Mrs. James, "and (though I know not how to mention it) I beg you'll give me leave to offer you any linen of mine till you can make new of your own."

Amelia thanked Mrs. James, but declined the favour, saying, she should do well enough at home; and that, as she had no servant now to take care of her children, she could not, nor would not, leave them on any account.

"Then bring master and miss with you," said Mrs. James. "You shall positively dine with us tomorrow."

"I beg, madam, you will mention it no more," said Amelia; "for, besides the substantial reasons I have already given, I have some things on my mind at present which make me unfit for company; and I am resolved nothing shall prevail on me to stir from home." Mrs. James had carried her invitation already to the very utmost limits of good breeding, if not beyond them. She desisted therefore from going any further, and, after some short stay longer, took her leave, with many expressions of concern, which, however, great as it was, left her heart and her mouth together before she was out of the house.

Booth now declared that he would go in pursuit of little Betty, against whom he vowed so much vengeance, that Amelia endeavoured to moderate his anger by representing to him the girl's youth, and that this was the first fault she had ever been guilty of. "Indeed," says she, "I should be very glad to have my things again, and I would have the girl too punished in some degree, which might possibly be for her own good; but I tremble to think of taking away her life;" for Booth in his rage had sworn he would hang her.

"I know the tenderness of your heart, my dear," said Booth, "and I love you for it; but I must beg leave to dissent from your opinion. I do not think the girl in any light an object of mercy. She is not only guilty of dishonesty but of cruelty; for she must know our situation and the very little we had left. She is besides guilty of ingratitude to you, who have treated her with so much kindness, that you have rather acted the part of a mother than of a mistress. And, so far from thinking her youth an excuse, I think it rather an aggravation. It is true, indeed, there are faults which the youth of the party very strongly recommends to our pardon. Such are all those which proceed from carelessness and want of thought; but crimes of this black dye, which are committed with deliberation, and imply a bad mind, deserve a more severe punishment in a young person than in one of riper years; for what must the mind be in old age which hath acquired such a degree of perfection in villany so very early? Such persons as these it is really a charity to the public to put out of the society; and, indeed, a religious man would put them out of the world for the sake of themselves; for whoever understands anything of human nature must know that such people, the longer they live, the more they will accumulate vice and wickedness."

"Well, my dear," cries Amelia, "I cannot argue with you on these subjects. I shall always submit to your superior judgment, and I know you too well to think that you will ever do anything cruel."

Booth then left Amelia to take care of her children, and went in pursuit of the thief.

Chapter vi. — A scene of the tragic kind.

He had not been long gone before a thundering knock was heard at the door of the house where Amelia lodged, and presently after a figure all pale, ghastly, and almost breathless, rushed into the room where she then was with her children.

This figure Amelia soon recognised to be Mrs. Atkinson, though indeed she was so disguised that at her first entrance Amelia scarce knew her. Her eyes were sunk in her head, her hair dishevelled, and not only her dress but every feature in her face was in the utmost disorder.

Amelia was greatly shocked at this sight, and the little girl was much frightened; as for the boy, he immediately knew her, and, running to Amelia, he cried, "La! mamma, what is the matter with poor Mrs. Atkinson?"

As soon as Mrs. Atkinson recovered her breath she cried out, "O, Mrs. Booth! I am the most miserable of women—I have lost the best of husbands."

Amelia, looking at her with all the tenderness imaginable, forgetting, I believe, that there had ever been any quarrel between them, said—"Good Heavens, madam, what's the matter?"

"O, Mrs. Booth!" answered she, "I fear I have lost my husband: the doctor says there is but little hope of his life. O, madam! however I have been in the wrong, I am sure you will forgive me and pity me. I am sure I am severely punished; for to that cursed affair I owe all my misery."

"Indeed, madam," cries Amelia, "I am extremely concerned for your misfortune. But pray tell me, hath anything happened to the serjeant?"

"O, madam!" cries she, "I have the greatest reason to fear I shall lose him. The doctor hath almost given him over—he says he hath scarce any hopes. O, madam! that evening that the fatal quarrel happened between us my dear captain took it so to heart that he sat up all night and drank a whole bottle of brandy. Indeed, he said he wished to kill himself; for nothing could have hurt him so much in the world, he said, as to have any quarrel between you and me. His concern, and what he drank together, threw him into a high fever. So that, when I came home from my lord's—(for indeed, madam, I have been, and set all to rights—your reputation is now in no danger)—when I came home, I say, I found the poor man in a raving delirious fit, and in that he hath continued ever since till about an hour ago, when he came perfectly to his senses; but now he says he is sure he shall die, and begs for Heaven's sake to see you first. Would you, madam, would you have the goodness to grant my poor captain's desire? consider he is a dying man, and neither he nor I shall ever ask you a second favour. He says he hath something to say to you that he can mention to no other person, and that he cannot die in peace unless he sees you."

"Upon my word, madam," cries Amelia, "I am extremely concerned at what you tell me. I knew the poor serjeant from his infancy, and always had an affection for him, as I think him to be one of the best-natured and honestest creatures upon earth. I am sure if I could do him any service—but of what use can my going be?"

"Of the highest in the world," answered Mrs. Atkinson. "If you knew how earnestly he entreated it, how his poor breaking heart begged to see you, you would not refuse."

"Nay, I do not absolutely refuse," cries Amelia. "Something to say to me of consequence, and that he could not die in peace unless he said it! did he say that, Mrs. Atkinson?"

"Upon my honour he did," answered she, "and much more than I have related."

"Well, I will go with you," cries Amelia. "I cannot guess what this should be; but I will go."

Mrs. Atkinson then poured out a thousand blessings and thanksgivings; and, taking hold of Amelia's hand, and eagerly kissing it, cried out, "How could that fury passion drive me to quarrel with such a creature?"

Amelia told her she had forgiven and forgot it; and then, calling up the mistress of the house, and committing to her the care of the children, she cloaked herself up as well as she could and set out with Mrs. Atkinson.

When they arrived at the house, Mrs. Atkinson said she would go first and give the captain some notice; for that, if Amelia entered the room unexpectedly, the surprize might have an ill effect. She left therefore Amelia in the parlour, and proceeded directly upstairs.

Poor Atkinson, weak and bad as was his condition, no sooner heard that Amelia was come than he discovered great joy in his countenance, and presently afterwards she was introduced to him.

Atkinson exerted his utmost strength to thank her for this goodness to a dying man (for so he called himself). He said he should not have presumed to give her this trouble, had he not had something which he thought of consequence to say to her, and which he could not mention to any other person. He then desired his wife to give him a little box, of which he always kept the key himself, and afterwards begged her to leave the room for a few minutes; at which neither she nor Amelia expressed any dissatisfaction.

When he was alone with Amelia, he spoke as follows: "This, madam, is the last time my eyes will ever behold what—do pardon me, madam, I will never offend you more." Here he sunk down in his bed, and the tears gushed from his eyes.

"Why should you fear to offend me, Joe?" said Amelia. "I am sure you never did anything willingly to offend me."

"No, madam," answered he, "I would die a thousand times before I would have ventured it in the smallest matter. But—I cannot speak—and yet I must. You cannot pardon me, and yet, perhaps, as I am a dying man, and never shall see you more—indeed, if I was to live after this discovery, I should never dare to look you in the face again; and yet, madam, to think I shall never see you more is worse than ten thousand deaths."

"Indeed, Mr. Atkinson," cries Amelia, blushing, and looking down on the floor, "I must not hear you talk in this manner. If you have anything to say, tell it me, and do not be afraid of my anger; for I think I may promise to forgive whatever it was possible you should do."

"Here then, madam," said he, "is your picture; I stole it when I was eighteen years of age, and have kept it ever since. It is set in gold, with three little diamonds; and yet I can truly say it was not the gold nor the diamonds which I stole—it was the face, which, if I had been the emperor of the world—"

"I must not hear any more of this," said she. "Comfort yourself, Joe, and think no more of this matter. Be assured, I freely and heartily forgive you—But pray compose yourself; come, let me call in your wife."

"First, madam, let me beg one favour," cried he: "consider it is the last, and then I shall die in peace—let me kiss that hand before I die."

"Well, nay," says she, "I don't know what I am doing—well—there." She then carelessly gave him her hand, which he put gently to his lips, and then presently let it drop, and fell back in the bed.

Amelia now summoned Mrs. Atkinson, who was indeed no further off than just without the door. She then hastened down-stairs, and called for a great glass of water, which having drank off, she threw herself into a chair, and the tears ran plentifully from her eyes with compassion for the poor wretch she had just left in his bed.

To say the truth, without any injury to her chastity, that heart, which had stood firm as a rock to all the attacks of title and equipage, of finery and flattery, and which all the treasures of the universe could not have purchased, was yet a little softened by the plain, honest, modest, involuntary, delicate, heroic passion of this poor and humble swain; for whom, in spite of herself, she felt a momentary tenderness and complacence, at which Booth, if he had known it, would perhaps have been displeased.

Having staid some time in the parlour, and not finding Mrs. Atkinson come down (for indeed her husband was then so bad she could not quit him), Amelia left a message with the maid of the house for her mistress, purporting that she should be ready to do anything in her power to serve her, and then left the house with a confusion on her mind that she had never felt before, and which any chastity that is not hewn out of marble must feel on so tender and delicate an occasion.

Chapter vii. — In which Mr. Booth meets with more than one adventure.

Booth, having hunted for about two hours, at last saw a young lady in a tattered silk gown stepping out of a shop in Monmouth—street into a hackney-coach. This lady, notwithstanding the disguise of her dress, he presently discovered to be no other than little Betty.

He instantly gave the alarm of stop thief, stop coach! upon which Mrs. Betty was immediately stopt in her vehicle, and Booth and his myrmidons laid hold of her.

The girl no sooner found that she was seised by her master than the consciousness of her guilt overpowered her; for she was not yet an experienced offender, and she immediately confessed her crime.

She was then carried before a justice of peace, where she was searched, and there was found in her possession four shillings and sixpence in money, besides the silk gown, which was indeed proper furniture for rag-fair, and scarce worth a single farthing, though the honest shopkeeper in Monmouth-street had sold it for a crown to the simple girl.

The girl, being examined by the magistrate, spoke as follows:—"Indeed, sir, an't please your worship, I am very sorry for what I have done; and to be sure, an't please your honour, my lord, it must have been the devil that put me upon it; for to be sure, please your majesty, I never thought upon such a thing in my whole life before, any more than I did of my dying-day; but, indeed, sir, an't please your worship—"

She was running on in this manner when the justice interrupted her, and desired her to give an account of what she had taken from her master, and what she had done with it.

"Indeed, an't please your majesty," said she, "I took no more than two shifts of madam's, and I pawned them for five shillings, which I gave for the gown that's upon my back; and as for the money in my pocket, it is every farthing of it my own. I am sure I intended to carry back the shifts too as soon as ever I could get money to take them out."

The girl having told them where the pawnbroker lived, the justice sent to him, to produce the shifts, which he presently did; for he expected that a warrant to search his house would be the consequence of his refusal.

The shifts being produced, on which the honest pawnbroker had lent five shillings, appeared plainly to be worth above thirty; indeed, when new they had cost much more: so that, by their goodness as well as by their size, it was certain they could not have belonged to the girl. Booth grew very warm against the pawnbroker. "I hope, sir," said he to the justice, "there is some punishment for this fellow likewise, who so plainly appears to have known that these goods were stolen. The shops of these fellows may indeed be called the fountains of theft; for it is in reality the encouragement which they meet with from these receivers of their goods that induces men very often to become thieves, so that these deserve equal if not severer punishment than the thieves themselves."

The pawnbroker protested his innocence, and denied the taking in the shifts. Indeed, in this he spoke truth, for he had slipt into an inner room, as was always his custom on these occasions, and left a little boy to do the business; by which means he had carried on the trade of receiving stolen goods for many years with impunity, and had been twice acquitted at the Old Bailey, though the juggle appeared upon the most manifest evidence.

As the justice was going to speak he was interrupted by the girl, who, falling upon her knees to Booth, with many tears begged his forgiveness.

"Indeed, Betty," cries Booth, "you do not deserve forgiveness; for you know very good reasons why you should not have thought of robbing your mistress, particularly at this time. And what further aggravates your crime is, that you robbed the best and kindest mistress in the world. Nay, you are not only guilty of felony, but of a felonious breach of trust, for you know very well everything your mistress had was intrusted to your care."

Now it happened, by very great accident, that the justice before whom the girl was brought understood the law. Turning therefore to Booth, he said, "Do you say, sir, that this girl was intrusted with the shifts?"

"Yes, sir," said Booth, "she was intrusted with everything."

"And will you swear that the goods stolen," said the justice, "are worth forty shillings?"

"No, indeed, sir," answered Booth, "nor that they are worthy thirty either."

"Then, sir," cries the justice, "the girl cannot be guilty of felony."

"How, sir," said Booth, "is it not a breach of trust? and is not a breach of trust felony, and the worst felony too?"

"No, sir," answered the justice; "a breach of trust is no crime in our law, unless it be in a servant; and then the act of parliament requires the goods taken to be of the value of forty shillings."

"So then a servant," cries Booth, "may rob his master of thirty-nine shillings whenever he pleases, and he can't be punished."

"If the goods are under his care, he can't," cries the justice.

"I ask your pardon, sir," says Booth. "I do not doubt what you say; but sure this is a very extraordinary law."

"Perhaps I think so too," said the justice; "but it belongs not to my office to make or to mend laws. My business is only to execute them. If therefore the case be as you say, I must discharge the girl."

"I hope, however, you will punish the pawnbroker," cries Booth.

"If the girl is discharged," cries the justice, "so must be the pawnbroker; for, if the goods are not stolen, he cannot be guilty of receiving them knowing them to be stolen. And, besides, as to his offence, to say the truth, I am almost weary of prosecuting it; for such are the difficulties laid in the way of this prosecution, that it is almost impossible to convict any one on it. And, to speak my opinion plainly, such are the laws, and such the method of proceeding, that one would almost think our laws were rather made for the protection of rogues than for the punishment of them."

Thus ended this examination: the thief and the receiver went about their business, and Booth departed in order to go home to his wife.

In his way home Booth was met by a lady in a chair, who, immediately upon seeing him, stopt her chair, bolted out of it, and, going directly up to him, said, "So, Mr. Booth, you have kept your word with me."

The lady was no other than Miss Matthews, and the speech she meant was of a promise made to her at the masquerade of visiting her within a day or two; which, whether he ever intended to keep I cannot say, but, in truth, the several accidents that had since happened to him had so discomposed his mind that he had absolutely forgot it.

Booth, however, was too sensible and too well-bred to make the excuse of forgetfulness to a lady; nor could he readily find any other. While he stood therefore hesitating, and looking not over-wise, Miss Matthews said, "Well, sir, since by your confusion I see you have some grace left, I will pardon you on one condition, and that is that you will sup with me this night. But, if you fail me now, expect all the revenge of an injured woman." She then bound herself by a most outrageous oath that she would complain to his wife—"And I am sure," says she, "she is so much a woman of honour as to do me justice. And, though I miscarried in my first attempt, be assured I will take care of my second."

Booth asked what she meant by her first attempt; to which she answered that she had already writ his wife an account of his ill-usage of her, but that she was pleased it had miscarried. She then repeated her asseveration that she would now do it effectually if he disappointed her.

This threat she reckoned would most certainly terrify poor Booth; and, indeed, she was not mistaken; for I believe it would have been impossible, by any other menace or by any other means, to have brought him once even to balance in his mind on this question. But by this threat she prevailed; and Booth promised, upon his word and honour, to come to her at the hour she appointed. After which she took leave of him with a squeeze by the hand, and a smiling countenance, and walked back to her chair.

But, however she might be pleased with having obtained this promise, Booth was far from being delighted with the thoughts of having given it. He looked, indeed, upon the consequences of this meeting with horrour; but as to the consequence which was so apparently intended by the lady, he resolved against it. At length he came to this determination, to go according to his appointment, to argue the matter with the lady, and to convince her, if possible, that, from a regard to his honour only, he must discontinue her acquaintance. If this failed to satisfy her, and

she still persisted in her threats to acquaint his wife with the affair, he then resolved, whatever pains it cost him, to communicate the whole truth himself to Amelia, from whose goodness he doubted not but to obtain an absolute remission.

Chapter viii. — In which Amelia appears in a light more amiable than gay.

We will now return to Amelia, whom we left in some perturbation of mind departing from Mrs. Atkinson.

Though she had before walked through the streets in a very improper dress with Mrs. Atkinson, she was unwilling, especially as she was alone, to return in the same manner. Indeed, she was scarce able to walk in her present condition; for the case of poor Atkinson had much affected her tender heart, and her eyes had overflown with many tears.

It occurred likewise to her at present that she had not a single shilling in her pocket or at home to provide food for herself and her family. In this situation she resolved to go immediately to the pawnbroker whither she had gone before, and to deposit her picture for what she could raise upon it. She then immediately took a chair and put her design in execution.

The intrinsic value of the gold in which this picture was set, and of the little diamonds which surrounded it, amounted to nine guineas. This therefore was advanced to her, and the prettiest face in the world (such is often the fate of beauty) was deposited, as of no value, into the bargain.

When she came home she found the following letter from Mrs. Atkinson:—

"MY DEAREST MADAM,—As I know your goodness, I could not delay a moment acquainting you with the happy turn of my affairs since you went. The doctor, on his return to visit my husband, has assured me that the captain was on the recovery, and in very little danger; and I really think he is since mended. I hope to wait on you soon with better news. Heaven bless you, dear madam! and believe me to be, with the utmost sincerity, Your most obliged, obedient, humble servant,

"ATKINSON."

Amelia was really pleased with this letter; and now, it being past four o'clock, she despaired of seeing her husband till the evening. She therefore provided some tarts for her children, and then, eating nothing but a slice of bread and butter herself, she began to prepare for the captain's supper.

There were two things of which her husband was particularly fond, which, though it may bring the simplicity of his taste into great contempt with some of my readers, I will venture to name. These were a fowl and egg sauce and mutton broth; both which Amelia immediately purchased.

As soon as the clock struck seven the good creature went down into the kitchen, and began to exercise her talents of cookery, of which she was a great mistress, as she was of every economical office from the highest to the lowest: and, as no woman could outshine her in a drawing-room, so none could make the drawing-room itself shine brighter than Amelia. And, if I may speak a bold truth, I question whether it be possible to view this fine creature in a more amiable light than while she was dressing her husband's supper, with her little children playing round her.

It was now half an hour past eight, and the meat almost ready, the table likewise neatly spread with materials borrowed from her landlady, and she began to grow a little uneasy at Booth's not returning when a sudden knock at the door roused her spirits, and she cried, "There, my dear, there is your good papa;" at which words she darted swiftly upstairs and opened the door to her husband.

She desired her husband to walk up into the dining-room, and she would come to him in an instant; for she was desirous to encrease his pleasure by surprising him with his two favourite dishes. She then went down again to the kitchen, where the maid of the house undertook to send up the supper, and she with her children returned to Booth.

He then told her concisely what had happened with relation to the girl—to which she scarce

241

made any answer, but asked him if he had not dined? He assured her he had not eat a morsel the whole day.

"Well," says she, "my dear, I am a fellow-sufferer; but we shall both enjoy our supper the more; for I have made a little provision for you, as I guessed what might be the case. I have got you a bottle of wine too. And here is a clean cloth and a smiling countenance, my dear Will. Indeed, I am in unusual good spirits to-night, and I have made a promise to the children, which you must confirm; I have promised to let them sit up this one night to supper with us.—Nay, don't look so serious: cast off all uneasy thoughts, I have a present for you here—no matter how I came by it."—At which words she put eight guineas into his hand, crying, "Come, my dear Bill, be gay—Fortune will yet be kind to us—at least let us be happy this night. Indeed, the pleasures of many women during their whole lives will not amount to my happiness this night if you will be in good humour."

Booth fetched a deep sigh, and cried, "How unhappy am I, my dear, that I can't sup with you to-night!"

As in the delightful month of June, when the sky is all serene, and the whole face of nature looks with a pleasing and smiling aspect, suddenly a dark cloud spreads itself over the hemisphere, the sun vanishes from our sight, and every object is obscured by a dark and horrid gloom; so happened it to Amelia: the joy that had enlightened every feature disappeared in a moment; the lustre forsook her shining eyes, and all the little loves that played and wantoned in her cheeks hung their drooping heads, and with a faint trembling voice she repeated her husband's words, "Not sup with me to-night, my dear!"

"Indeed, my dear," answered he, "I cannot. I need not tell you how uneasy it makes me, or that I am as much disappointed as yourself; but I am engaged to sup abroad. I have absolutely given my honour; and besides, it is on business of importance."

"My dear," said she, "I say no more. I am convinced you would not willingly sup from me. I own it is a very particular disappointment to me to-night, when I had proposed unusual pleasure; but the same reason which is sufficient to you ought to be so to me."

Booth made his wife a compliment on her ready compliance, and then asked her what she intended by giving him that money, or how she came by it?

"I intend, my dear," said she, "to give it you; that is all. As to the manner in which I came by it, you know, Billy, that is not very material. You are well assured I got it by no means which would displease you; and, perhaps, another time I may tell you."

Booth asked no farther questions; but he returned her, and insisted on her taking, all but one guinea, saying she was the safest treasurer. He then promised her to make all the haste home in his power, and he hoped, he said, to be with her in an hour and half at farthest, and then took his leave.

When he was gone the poor disappointed Amelia sat down to supper with her children, with whose company she was forced to console herself for the absence of her husband.

Chapter ix. — A very tragic scene.

The clock had struck eleven, and Amelia was just proceeding to put her children to bed, when she heard a knock at the street-door; upon which the boy cried out, "There's papa, mamma; pray let me stay and see him before I go to bed." This was a favour very easily obtained; for Amelia instantly ran down-stairs, exulting in the goodness of her husband for returning so soon, though half an hour was already elapsed beyond the time in which he promised to return.

Poor Amelia was now again disappointed; for it was not her husband at the door, but a servant with a letter for him, which he delivered into her hands. She immediately returned up-stairs, and said—"It was not your papa, my dear; but I hope it is one who hath brought us some good news." For Booth had told her that he hourly expected to receive such from the great man, and had desired her to open any letter which came to him in his absence.

Amelia therefore broke open the letter, and read as follows:

"SIR,—After what hath passed between us, I need only tell you that I know you supped this very night alone with Miss Matthews: a fact which will upbraid you sufficiently, without putting me to that trouble, and will very well account for my desiring the favour of seeing you to-morrow in Hyde-park at six in the morning. You will forgive me reminding you once more how inexcusable this behaviour is in you, who are possessed in your own wife of the most inestimable jewel.

"Yours, &c.

"T. JAMES.

"I shall bring pistols with me."

It is not easy to describe the agitation of Amelia's mind when she read this letter. She threw herself into her chair, turned as pale as death, began to tremble all over, and had just power enough left to tap the bottle of wine, which she had hitherto preserved entire for her husband, and to drink off a large bumper.

The little boy perceived the strange symptoms which appeared in his mother; and running to her, he cried, "What's the matter, my dear mamma? you don't look well!—No harm hath happened to poor papa, I hope—Sure that bad man hath not carried him away again?"

Amelia answered, "No, child, nothing—nothing at all." And then a large shower of tears came to her assistance, which presently after produced the same in the eyes of both the children.

Amelia, after a short silence, looking tenderly at her children, cried out, "It is too much, too much to bear. Why did I bring these little wretches into the world? why were these innocents born to such a fate?" She then threw her arms round them both (for they were before embracing her knees), and cried, "O my children! my children! forgive me, my babes! Forgive me that I have brought you into such a world as this! You are undone—my children are undone!"

The little boy answered with great spirit, "How undone, mamma? my sister and I don't care a farthing for being undone. Don't cry so upon our accounts—we are both very well; indeed we are. But do pray tell us. I am sure some accident hath happened to poor papa."

"Mention him no more," cries Amelia; "your papa is—indeed he is a wicked man—he cares not for any of us. O Heavens! is this the happiness I promised myself this evening?" At which words she fell into an agony, holding both her children in her arms.

The maid of the house now entered the room, with a letter in her hand which she had received from a porter, whose arrival the reader will not wonder to have been unheard by Amelia in her present condition.

The maid, upon her entrance into the room, perceiving the situation of Amelia, cried out, "Good Heavens! madam, what's the matter?" Upon which Amelia, who had a little recovered herself after the last violent vent of her passion, started up and cried, "Nothing, Mrs. Susan—nothing extraordinary. I am subject to these fits sometimes; but I am very well now. Come, my dear children, I am very well again; indeed I am. You must now go to bed; Mrs. Susan will be so good as to put you to bed."

"But why doth not papa love us?" cries the little boy. "I am sure we have none of us done anything to disoblige him."

This innocent question of the child so stung Amelia that she had the utmost difficulty to prevent a relapse. However, she took another dram of wine; for so it might be called to her, who was the most temperate of women, and never exceeded three glasses on any occasion. In this glass she drank her children's health, and soon after so well soothed and composed them that they went quietly away with Mrs. Susan.

The maid, in the shock she had conceived at the melancholy, indeed frightful scene, which had presented itself to her at her first coming into the room, had quite forgot the letter which she held in her hand. However, just at her departure she recollected it, and delivered it to Amelia, who was no sooner alone than she opened it, and read as follows:

"MY DEAREST, SWEETEST LOVE,—I write this from the bailiff's house where I was formerly, and to which I am again brought at the suit of that villain Trent. I have the misfortune to think I owe this accident (I mean that it happened to-night) to my own folly in endeavouring to keep a secret from you. O my dear! had I had resolution to confess my crime to you, your forgiveness would, I am convinced, have cost me only a few blushes, and I had now been happy in your arms. Fool that I was, to leave you on such an account, and to add to a former transgression a new one!—Yet, by Heavens! I mean not a transgression of the like kind; for of

that I am not nor ever will be guilty; and when you know the true reason of my leaving you to-night I think you will pity rather than upbraid me. I am sure you would if you knew the compunction with which I left you to go to the most worthless, the most infamous. Do guess the rest—guess that crime with which I cannot stain my paper—but still believe me no more guilty than I am, or, if it will lessen your vexation at what hath befallen me, believe me as guilty as you please, and think me, for a while at least, as undeserving of you as I think myself. This paper and pen are so bad, I question whether you can read what I write: I almost doubt whether I wish you should. Yet this I will endeavour to make as legible as I can. Be comforted, my dear love, and still keep up your spirits with the hopes of better days. The doctor will be in town to-morrow, and I trust on his goodness for my delivery once more from this place, and that I shall soon be able to repay him. That Heaven may bless and preserve you is the prayer of, my dearest love, Your ever fond, affectionate, and hereafter, faithful husband, W. BOOTH."

Amelia pretty well guessed the obscure meaning of this letter, which, though at another time it might have given her unspeakable torment, was at present rather of the medicinal kind, and served to allay her anguish. Her anger to Booth too began a little to abate, and was softened by her concern for his misfortune. Upon the whole, however, she passed a miserable and sleepless night, her gentle mind torn and distracted with various and contending passions, distressed with doubts, and wandering in a kind of twilight which presented her only objects of different degrees of horror, and where black despair closed at a small distance the gloomy prospect.

BOOK XII.

Chapter i. — The book begins with polite history.

Before we return to the miserable couple, whom we left at the end of the last book, we will give our reader the more chearful view of the gay and happy family of Colonel James.

Mrs. James, when she could not, as we have seen, prevail with Amelia to accept that invitation which, at the desire of the colonel, she had so kindly and obediently carried her, returned to her husband and acquainted him with the ill success of her embassy; at which, to say the truth, she was almost as much disappointed as the colonel himself; for he had not taken a much stronger liking to Amelia than she herself had conceived for Booth. This will account for some passages which may have a little surprized the reader in the former chapters of this history, as we were not then at leisure to communicate to them a hint of this kind; it was, indeed, on Mr. Booth's account that she had been at the trouble of changing her dress at the masquerade.

But her passions of this sort, happily for her, were not extremely strong; she was therefore easily baulked; and, as she met with no encouragement from Booth, she soon gave way to the impetuosity of Miss Matthews, and from that time scarce thought more of the affair till her husband's design against the wife revived her's likewise; insomuch that her passion was at this time certainly strong enough for Booth, to produce a good hearty hatred for Amelia, whom she now abused to the colonel in very gross terms, both on the account of her poverty and her insolence, for so she termed the refusal of all her offers.

The colonel, seeing no hopes of soon possessing his new mistress, began, like a prudent and wise man, to turn his thoughts towards the securing his old one. From what his wife had mentioned concerning the behaviour of the shepherdess, and particularly her preference of Booth, he had little doubt but that this was the identical Miss Matthews. He resolved therefore to watch her closely, in hopes of discovering Booth's intrigue with her. In this, besides the remainder of affection which he yet preserved for that lady, he had another view, as it would give him a fair

pretence to quarrel with Booth; who, by carrying on this intrigue, would have broke his word and honour given to him. And he began now to hate poor Booth heartily, from the same reason from which Mrs. James had contracted her aversion to Amelia.

The colonel therefore employed an inferior kind of pimp to watch the lodgings of Miss Matthews, and to acquaint him if Booth, whose person was known to the pimp, made any visit there.

The pimp faithfully performed his office, and, having last night made the wished-for discovery, immediately acquainted his master with it.

Upon this news the colonel presently despatched to Booth the short note which we have before seen. He sent it to his own house instead of Miss Matthews's, with hopes of that very accident which actually did happen. Not that he had any ingredient of the bully in him, and desired to be prevented from fighting, but with a prospect of injuring Booth in the affection and esteem of Amelia, and of recommending himself somewhat to her by appearing in the light of her champion; for which purpose he added that compliment to Amelia in his letter. He concluded upon the whole that, if Booth himself opened the letter, he would certainly meet him the next morning; but if his wife should open it before he came home it might have the effects before mentioned; and, for his future expostulation with Booth, it would not be in Amelia's power to prevent it.

Now it happened that this pimp had more masters than one. Amongst these was the worthy Mr. Trent, for whom he had often done business of the pimping vocation. He had been employed indeed in the service of the great peer himself, under the direction of the said Trent, and was the very person who had assisted the said Trent in dogging Booth and his wife to the opera-house on the masquerade night.

This subaltern pimp was with his superior Trent yesterday morning, when he found a bailiff with him in order to receive his instructions for the arresting Booth, when the bailiff said it would be a very difficult matter to take him, for that to his knowledge he was as shy a cock as any in England. The subaltern immediately acquainted Trent with the business in which he was employed by the colonel; upon which Trent enjoined him the moment he had set him to give immediate notice to the bailiff, which he agreed to, and performed accordingly.

The bailiff, on receiving the notice, immediately set out for his stand at an alehouse within three doors of Miss Matthews's lodgings; at which, unfortunately for poor Booth, he arrived a very few minutes before Booth left that lady in order to return to Amelia.

These were several matters of which we thought necessary our reader should be informed; for, besides that it conduces greatly to a perfect understanding of all history, there is no exercise of the mind of a sensible reader more pleasant than the tracing the several small and almost imperceptible links in every chain of events by which all the great actions of the world are produced. We will now in the next chapter proceed with our history.

Chapter ii. — In which Amelia visits her husband.

Amelia, after much anxious thinking, in which she sometimes flattered herself that her husband was less guilty than she had at first imagined him, and that he had some good excuse to make for himself (for, indeed, she was not so able as willing to make one for him), at length resolved to set out for the bailiff's castle. Having therefore strictly recommended the care of her children to her good landlady, she sent for a hackney coach, and ordered the coachman to drive to Gray's-inn-lane.

When she came to the house, and asked for the captain, the bailiff's wife, who came to the door, guessing, by the greatness of her beauty and the disorder of her dress, that she was a young lady of pleasure, answered surlily, "Captain! I do not know of any captain that is here, not I!" For this good woman was, as well as dame Purgante in Prior, a bitter enemy to all whores, especially to those of the handsome kind; for some such she suspected to go shares with her in a certain property to which the law gave her the sole right.

Amelia replied she was certain that Captain Booth was there. "Well, if he is so," cries the bailiff's wife, "you may come into the kitchen if you will, and he shall be called down to you if you have any business with him." At the same time she muttered something to herself, and concluded a little more intelligibly, though still in a muttering voice, that she kept no such house.

Amelia, whose innocence gave her no suspicion of the true cause of this good woman's sullenness, was frightened, and began to fear she knew not what. At last she made a shift to totter into the kitchen, when the mistress of the house asked her, "Well, madam, who shall I tell the captain wants to speak with him?"

"I ask your pardon, madam," cries Amelia; "in my confusion I really forgot you did not know me—tell him, if you please, that I am his wife."

"And you are indeed his wife, madam?" cries Mrs. Bailiff, a little softened.

"Yes, indeed, and upon my honour," answers Amelia.

"If this be the case," cries the other, "you may walk up-stairs if you please. Heaven forbid I should part man and wife! Indeed, I think they can never be too much together. But I never will suffer any bad doings in my house, nor any of the town ladies to come to gentlemen here."

Amelia answered that she liked her the better: for, indeed, in her present disposition, Amelia was as much exasperated against wicked women as the virtuous mistress of the house, or any other virtuous woman could be.

The bailiff's wife then ushered Amelia up-stairs, and, having unlocked the prisoner's doors, cried, "Captain, here is your lady, sir, come to see you." At which words Booth started up from his chair, and caught Amelia in his arms, embracing her for a considerable time with so much rapture, that the bailiff's wife, who was an eyewitness of this violent fondness, began to suspect whether Amelia had really told her truth. However, she had some little awe of the captain; and for fear of being in the wrong did not interfere, but shut the door and turned the key.

When Booth found himself alone with his wife, and had vented the first violence of his rapture in kisses and embraces, he looked tenderly at her and cried, "Is it possible, Amelia, is it possible you can have this goodness to follow such a wretch as me to such a place as this—or do you come to upbraid me with my guilt, and to sink me down to that perdition I so justly deserve?"

"Am I so given to upbraiding then?" says she, in a gentle voice; "have I ever given you occasion to think I would sink you to perdition?"

"Far be it from me, my love, to think so," answered he. "And yet you may forgive the utmost fears of an offending, penitent sinner. I know, indeed, the extent of your goodness, and yet I know my guilt so great—"

"Alas! Mr. Booth," said she, "what guilt is this which you mention, and which you writ to me of last night?—Sure, by your mentioning to me so much, you intend to tell me more—nay, indeed, to tell me all; and not leave my mind open to suspicions perhaps ten times worse than the truth."

"Will you give me a patient hearing?" said he.

"I will indeed," answered she, "nay, I am prepared to hear the worst you can unfold; nay, perhaps, the worst is short of my apprehensions."

Booth then, after a little further apology, began and related to her the whole that had passed between him and Miss Matthews, from their first meeting in the prison to their separation the preceding evening. All which, as the reader knows it already, it would be tedious and unpardonable to transcribe from his mouth. He told her likewise all that he had done and suffered to conceal his transgression from her knowledge. This he assured her was the business of his visit last night, the consequence of which was, he declared in the most solemn manner, no other than an absolute quarrel with Miss Matthews, of whom he had taken a final leave.

When he had ended his narration, Amelia, after a short silence, answered, "Indeed, I firmly believe every word you have said, but I cannot now forgive you the fault you have confessed; and my reason is—because I have forgiven it long ago. Here, my dear," said she, "is an instance that I am likewise capable of keeping a secret."—She then delivered her husband a letter which she had some time ago received from Miss Matthews, and which was the same which that lady had mentioned, and supposed, as Booth had never heard of it, that it had miscarried; for she sent it by the penny post. In this letter, which was signed by a feigned name, she had acquainted Amelia with the infidelity of her husband, and had besides very greatly abused him; taxing him with many falsehoods, and, among the rest, with having spoken very slightingly and disrespectfully of his

wife.

Amelia never shined forth to Booth in so amiable and great a light; nor did his own unworthiness ever appear to him so mean and contemptible as at this instant. However, when he had read the letter, he uttered many violent protestations to her, that all which related to herself was absolutely false.

"I am convinced it is," said she. "I would not have a suspicion of the contrary for the world. I assure you I had, till last night revived it in my memory, almost forgot the letter; for, as I well knew from whom it came, by her mentioning obligations which she had conferred on you, and which you had more than once spoken to me of, I made large allowances for the situation you was then in; and I was the more satisfied, as the letter itself, as well as many other circumstances, convinced me the affair was at an end."

Booth now uttered the most extravagant expressions of admiration and fondness that his heart could dictate, and accompanied them with the warmest embraces. All which warmth and tenderness she returned; and tears of love and joy gushed from both their eyes. So ravished indeed were their hearts, that for some time they both forgot the dreadful situation of their affairs.

This, however, was but a short reverie. It soon recurred to Amelia, that, though she had the liberty of leaving that house when she pleased, she could not take her beloved husband with her. This thought stung her tender bosom to the quick, and she could not so far command herself as to refrain from many sorrowful exclamations against the hardship of their destiny; but when she saw the effect they had upon Booth she stifled her rising grief, forced a little chearfulness into her countenance, and, exerting all the spirits she could raise within herself, expressed her hopes of seeing a speedy end to their sufferings. She then asked her husband what she should do for him, and to whom she should apply for his deliverance?

"You know, my dear," cries Booth, "that the doctor is to be in town some time to-day. My hopes of immediate redemption are only in him; and, if that can be obtained, I make no doubt but of the success of that affair which is in the hands of a gentleman who hath faithfully promised, and in whose power I am so well assured it is to serve me."

Thus did this poor man support his hopes by a dependence on that ticket which he had so dearly purchased of one who pretended to manage the wheels in the great state lottery of preferment. A lottery, indeed, which hath this to recommend it—that many poor wretches feed their imaginations with the prospect of a prize during their whole lives, and never discover they have drawn a blank.

Amelia, who was of a pretty sanguine temper, and was entirely ignorant of these matters, was full as easy to be deceived into hopes as her husband; but in reality at present she turned her eyes to no distant prospect, the desire of regaining her husband's liberty having engrossed her whole mind.

While they were discoursing on these matters they heard a violent noise in the house, and immediately after several persons passed by their door up-stairs to the apartment over their head. This greatly terrified the gentle spirit of Amelia, and she cried—"Good Heavens, my dear, must I leave you in this horrid place? I am terrified with a thousand fears concerning you."

Booth endeavoured to comfort her, saying that he was in no manner of danger, and that he doubted not but that the doctor would soon be with him—"And stay, my dear," cries he; "now I recollect, suppose you should apply to my old friend James; for I believe you are pretty well satisfied that your apprehensions of him were groundless. I have no reason to think but that he would be as ready to serve me as formerly."

Amelia turned pale as ashes at the name of James, and, instead of making a direct answer to her husband, she laid hold of him, and cried, "My dear, I have one favour to beg of you, and I insist on your granting it me."

Booth readily swore he would deny her nothing.

"It is only this, my dear," said she, "that, if that detested colonel comes, you will not see him. Let the people of the house tell him you are not here."

"He knows nothing of my being here," answered Booth; "but why should I refuse to see him if he should be kind enough to come hither to me? Indeed, my Amelia, you have taken a dislike to that man without sufficient reason."

"I speak not upon that account," cries Amelia; "but I have had dreams last night about you two. Perhaps you will laugh at my folly, but pray indulge it. Nay, I insist on your promise of not

denying me."

"Dreams! my dear creature," answered he. "What dream can you have had of us?"

"One too horrible to be mentioned," replied she.—"I cannot think of it without horrour; and, unless you will promise me not to see the colonel till I return, I positively will never leave you."

"Indeed, my Amelia," said Booth, "I never knew you unreasonable before. How can a woman of your sense talk of dreams?"

"Suffer me to be once at least unreasonable," said Amelia, "as you are so good-natured to say I am not often so. Consider what I have lately suffered, and how weak my spirits must be at this time."

As Booth was going to speak, the bailiff, without any ceremony, entered the room, and cried, "No offence, I hope, madam; my wife, it seems, did not know you. She thought the captain had a mind for a bit of flesh by the bye. But I have quieted all matters; for I know you very well: I have seen that handsome face many a time when I have been waiting upon the captain formerly. No offence, I hope, madam; but if my wife was as handsome as you are I should not look for worse goods abroad."

Booth conceived some displeasure at this speech, but he did not think proper to express more than a pish; and then asked the bailiff what was the meaning of the noise they heard just now?

"I know of no noise," answered the bailiff. "Some of my men have been carrying a piece of bad luggage up-stairs; a poor rascal that resisted the law and justice; so I gave him a cut or two with a hanger. If they should prove mortal, he must thank himself for it. If a man will not behave like a gentleman to an officer, he must take the consequence; but I must say that for you, captain, you behave yourself like a gentleman, and therefore I shall always use you as such; and I hope you will find bail soon with all my heart. This is but a paultry sum to what the last was; and I do assure you there is nothing else against you in the office."

The latter part of the bailiff's speech somewhat comforted Amelia, who had been a little frightened by the former; and she soon after took leave of her husband to go in quest of the doctor, who, as Amelia had heard that morning, was expected in town that very day, which was somewhat sooner than he had intended at his departure.

Before she went, however, she left a strict charge with the bailiff, who ushered her very civilly downstairs, that if one Colonel James came there to enquire for her husband he should deny that he was there.

She then departed; and the bailiff immediately gave a very strict charge to his wife, his maid, and his followers, that if one Colonel James, or any one from him, should enquire after the captain, that they should let him know he had the captain above-stairs; for he doubted not but that the colonel was one of Booth's creditors, and he hoped for a second bail-bond by his means.

Chapter iii. — Containing matter pertinent to the history.

Amelia, in her way to the doctor's, determined just to stop at her own lodgings, which lay a little out of the road, and to pay a momentary visit to her children.

This was fortunate enough; for, had she called at the doctor's house, she would have heard nothing of him, which would have caused in her some alarm and disappointment; for the doctor was set down at Mrs. Atkinson's, where he was directed to Amelia's lodgings, to which he went before he called at his own; and here Amelia now found him playing with her two children.

The doctor had been a little surprized at not finding Amelia at home, or any one that could give an account of her. He was now more surprized to see her come in such a dress, and at the disorder which he very plainly perceived in her pale and melancholy countenance. He addressed her first (for indeed she was in no great haste to speak), and cried, "My dear child, what is the matter? where is your husband? some mischief I am afraid hath happened to him in my absence."

"O my dear doctor!" answered Amelia, "sure some good angel hath sent you hither. My poor

248

Will is arrested again. I left him in the most miserable condition in the very house whence your goodness formerly redeemed him."

"Arrested!" cries the doctor. "Then it must be for some very inconsiderable trifle."

"I wish it was," said Amelia; "but it is for no less than fifty pound."

"Then," cries the doctor, "he hath been disingenuous with me. He told me he did not owe ten pounds in the world for which he was liable to be sued."

"I know not what to say," cries Amelia. "Indeed, I am afraid to tell you the truth."

"How, child?" said the doctor—"I hope you will never disguise it to any one, especially to me. Any prevarication, I promise you, will forfeit my friendship for ever."

"I will tell you the whole," cries Amelia, "and rely entirely on your goodness." She then related the gaming story, not forgetting to set in the fullest light, and to lay the strongest emphasis on, his promise never to play again.

The doctor fetched a deep sigh when he had heard Amelia's relation, and cried, "I am sorry, child, for the share you are to partake in your husband's sufferings; but as for him, I really think he deserves no compassion. You say he hath promised never to play again, but I must tell you he hath broke his promise to me already; for I had heard he was formerly addicted to this vice, and had given him sufficient caution against it. You will consider, child, I am already pretty largely engaged for him, every farthing of which I am sensible I must pay. You know I would go to the utmost verge of prudence to serve you; but I must not exceed my ability, which is not very great; and I have several families on my hands who are by misfortune alone brought to want. I do assure you I cannot at present answer for such a sum as this without distressing my own circumstances."

"Then Heaven have mercy upon us all!" cries Amelia, "for we have no other friend on earth: my husband is undone, and these poor little wretches must be starved."

The doctor cast his eyes on the children, and then cried, "I hope not so. I told you I must distress my circumstances, and I will distress them this once on your account, and on the account of these poor little babes. But things must not go on any longer in this way. You must take an heroic resolution. I will hire a coach for you to-morrow morning which shall carry you all down to my parsonage-house. There you shall have my protection till something can be done for your husband; of which, to be plain with you, I at present see no likelihood."

Amelia fell upon her knees in an ecstasy of thanksgiving to the doctor, who immediately raised her up, and placed her in her chair. She then recollected herself, and said, "O my worthy friend, I have still another matter to mention to you, in which I must have both your advice and assistance. My soul blushes to give you all this trouble; but what other friend have I?—indeed, what other friend could I apply to so properly on such an occasion?"

The doctor, with a very kind voice and countenance, desired her to speak. She then said, "O sir! that wicked colonel whom I have mentioned to you formerly hath picked some quarrel with my husband (for she did not think proper to mention the cause), and hath sent him a challenge. It came to my hand last night after he was arrested: I opened and read it."

"Give it me, child," said the doctor.

She answered she had burnt it, as was indeed true. "But I remember it was an appointment to meet with sword and pistol this morning at Hyde-park."

"Make yourself easy, my dear child," cries the doctor; "I will take care to prevent any mischief."

"But consider, my dear sir," said she, "this is a tender matter. My husband's honour is to be preserved as well as his life."

"And so is his soul, which ought to be the dearest of all things," cries the doctor. "Honour! nonsense! Can honour dictate to him to disobey the express commands of his Maker, in compliance with a custom established by a set of blockheads, founded on false principles of virtue, in direct opposition to the plain and positive precepts of religion, and tending manifestly to give a sanction to ruffians, and to protect them in all the ways of impudence and villany?"

"All this, I believe, is very true," cries Amelia; "but yet you know, doctor, the opinion of the world."

"You talk simply, child," cries the doctor. "What is the opinion of the world opposed to religion and virtue? but you are in the wrong. It is not the opinion of the world; it is the opinion of the idle, ignorant, and profligate. It is impossible it should be the opinion of one man of sense, who is in earnest in his belief of our religion. Chiefly, indeed, it hath been upheld by the nonsense

249

of women, who, either from their extreme cowardice and desire of protection, or, as Mr. Bayle thinks, from their excessive vanity, have been always forward to countenance a set of hectors and bravoes, and to despise all men of modesty and sobriety; though these are often, at the bottom, not only the better but the braver men."

"You know, doctor," cries Amelia, "I have never presumed to argue with you; your opinion is to me always instruction, and your word a law."

"Indeed, child," cries the doctor, "I know you are a good woman; and yet I must observe to you, that this very desire of feeding the passion of female vanity with the heroism of her man, old Homer seems to make the characteristic of a bad and loose woman. He introduces Helen upbraiding her gallant with having quitted the fight, and left the victory to Menelaus, and seeming to be sorry that she had left her husband only because he was the better duellist of the two: but in how different a light doth he represent the tender and chaste love of Andromache to her worthy Hector! she dissuades him from exposing himself to danger, even in a just cause. This is indeed a weakness, but it is an amiable one, and becoming the true feminine character; but a woman who, out of heroic vanity (for so it is), would hazard not only the life but the soul too of her husband in a duel, is a monster, and ought to be painted in no other character but that of a Fury."

"I assure you, doctor," cries Amelia, "I never saw this matter in the odious light in which you have truly represented it, before. I am ashamed to recollect what I have formerly said on this subject. And yet, whilst the opinion of the world is as it is, one would wish to comply as far as possible, especially as my husband is an officer of the army. If it can be done, therefore, with safety to his honour—"

"Again honour!" cries the doctor; "indeed I will not suffer that noble word to be so basely and barbarously prostituted. I have known some of these men of honour, as they call themselves, to be the most arrant rascals in the universe."

"Well, I ask your pardon," said she; "reputation then, if you please, or any other word you like better; you know my meaning very well."

"I do know your meaning," cries the doctor, "and Virgil knew it a great while ago. The next time you see your friend Mrs. Atkinson, ask her what it was made Dido fall in love with AEneas?"

"Nay, dear sir," said Amelia, "do not rally me so unmercifully; think where my poor husband is now."

"He is," answered the doctor, "where I will presently be with him. In the mean time, do you pack up everything in order for your journey to-morrow; for if you are wise, you will not trust your husband a day longer in this town—therefore to packing."

Amelia promised she would, though indeed she wanted not any warning for her journey on this account; for when she packed up herself in the coach, she packed up her all. However, she did not think proper to mention this to the doctor; for, as he was now in pretty good humour, she did not care to venture again discomposing his temper.

The doctor then set out for Gray's-inn-lane, and, as soon as he was gone, Amelia began to consider of her incapacity to take a journey in her present situation without even a clean shift. At last she resolved, as she was possessed of seven guineas and a half, to go to her friend and redeem some of her own and her husband's linen out of captivity; indeed just so much as would render it barely possible for them to go out of town with any kind of decency. And this resolution she immediately executed.

As soon as she had finished her business with the pawnbroker (if a man who lends under thirty per cent. deserves that name), he said to her, "Pray, madam, did you know that man who was here yesterday when you brought the picture?" Amelia answered in the negative. "Indeed, madam," said the broker, "he knows you, though he did not recollect you while you was here, as your hood was drawn over your face; but the moment you was gone he begged to look at the picture, which I, thinking no harm, permitted. He had scarce looked upon it when he cried out, 'By heaven and earth it is her picture!' He then asked me if I knew you." "Indeed," says I, "I never saw the lady before."

In this last particular, however, the pawnbroker a little savoured of his profession, and made a small deviation from the truth, for, when the man had asked him if he knew the lady, he answered she was some poor undone woman who had pawned all her cloathes to him the day before; and I suppose, says he, this picture is the last of her goods and chattels. This hint we thought proper to give the reader, as it may chance to be material.

250

Amelia answered coldly that she had taken so very little notice of the man that she scarce remembered he was there.

"I assure you, madam," says the pawnbroker, "he hath taken very great notice of you; for the man changed countenance upon what I said, and presently after begged me to give him a dram. Oho! thinks I to myself, are you thereabouts? I would not be so much in love with some folks as some people are for more interest than I shall ever make of a thousand pound."

Amelia blushed, and said, with some peevishness, "That she knew nothing of the man, but supposed he was some impertinent fellow or other."

"Nay, madam," answered the pawnbroker, "I assure you he is not worthy your regard. He is a poor wretch, and I believe I am possessed of most of his moveables. However, I hope you are not offended, for indeed he said no harm; but he was very strangely disordered, that is the truth of it."

Amelia was very desirous of putting an end to this conversation, and altogether as eager to return to her children; she therefore bundled up her things as fast as she could, and, calling for a hackney-coach, directed the coachman to her lodgings, and bid him drive her home with all the haste he could.

Chapter iv. — In which Dr Harrison visits Colonel James.

The doctor, when he left Amelia, intended to go directly to Booth, but he presently changed his mind, and determined first to call on the colonel, as he thought it was proper to put an end to that matter before he gave Booth his liberty.

The doctor found the two colonels, James and Bath, together. They both received him very civilly, for James was a very well-bred man, and Bath always shewed a particular respect to the clergy, he being indeed a perfect good Christian, except in the articles of fighting and swearing.

Our divine sat some time without mentioning the subject of his errand, in hopes that Bath would go away, but when he found no likelihood of that (for indeed Bath was of the two much the most pleased with his company), he told James that he had something to say to him relating to Mr. Booth, which he believed he might speak before his brother.

"Undoubtedly, sir," said James; "for there can be no secrets between us which my brother may not hear."

"I come then to you, sir," said the doctor, "from the most unhappy woman in the world, to whose afflictions you have very greatly and very cruelly added by sending a challenge to her husband, which hath very luckily fallen into her hands; for, had the man for whom you designed it received it, I am afraid you would not have seen me upon this occasion."

"If I writ such a letter to Mr. Booth, sir," said James, "you may be assured I did not expect this visit in answer to it."

{Illustration: Dr. Harrison.}

"I do not think you did," cries the doctor; "but you have great reason to thank Heaven for ordering this matter contrary to your expectations. I know not what trifle may have drawn this challenge from you, but, after what I have some reason to know of you, sir, I must plainly tell you that, if you had added to your guilt already committed against this man, that of having his blood upon your hands, your soul would have become as black as hell itself."

"Give me leave to say," cries the colonel, "this is a language which I am not used to hear; and if your cloth was not your protection you should not give it me with impunity. After what you know of me, sir! What do you presume to know of me to my disadvantage?"

"You say my cloth is my protection, colonel," answered the doctor; "therefore pray lay aside your anger: I do not come with any design of affronting or offending you."

"Very well," cries Bath; "that declaration is sufficient from a clergyman, let him say what he pleases."

"Indeed, sir," says the doctor very mildly, "I consult equally the good of you both, and, in a spiritual sense, more especially yours; for you know you have injured this poor man."

"So far on the contrary," cries James, "that I have been his greatest benefactor. I scorn to

251

upbraid him, but you force me to it. Nor have I ever done him the least injury."

"Perhaps not," said the doctor; "I will alter what I have said. But for this I apply to your honour—Have you not intended him an injury, the very intention of which cancels every obligation?"

"How, sir?" answered the colonel; "what do you mean?"

"My meaning," replied the doctor, "is almost too tender to mention. Come, colonel, examine your own heart, and then answer me, on your honour, if you have not intended to do him the highest wrong which one man can do another?"

"I do not know what you mean by the question," answered the colonel.

"D—n me, the question is very transparent!" cries Bath. "From any other man it would be an affront with the strongest emphasis, but from one of the doctor's cloth it demands a categorical answer."

"I am not a papist, sir," answered Colonel James, "nor am I obliged to confess to my priest. But if you have anything to say speak openly, for I do not understand your meaning."

"I have explained my meaning to you already," said the doctor, "in a letter I wrote to you on the subject—a subject which I am sorry I should have any occasion to write upon to a Christian."

"I do remember now," cries the colonel, "that I received a very impertinent letter, something like a sermon, against adultery; but I did not expect to hear the author own it to my face."

"That brave man then, sir," answered the doctor, "stands before you who dares own he wrote that letter, and dares affirm too that it was writ on a just and strong foundation. But if the hardness of your heart could prevail on you to treat my good intention with contempt and scorn, what, pray, could induce you to shew it, nay, to give it Mr. Booth? What motive could you have for that, unless you meant to insult him, and provoke your rival to give you that opportunity of putting him out of the world, which you have since wickedly sought by your challenge?"

"I give him the letter!" said the colonel.

"Yes, sir," answered the doctor, "he shewed me the letter, and affirmed that you gave it him at the masquerade."

"He is a lying rascal, then!" said the colonel very passionately. "I scarce took the trouble of reading the letter, and lost it out of my pocket."

Here Bath interfered, and explained this affair in the manner in which it happened, and with which the reader is already acquainted. He concluded by great eulogiums on the performance, and declared it was one of the most enthusiastic (meaning, perhaps, ecclesiastic) letters that ever was written. "And d—n me," says he, "if I do not respect the author with the utmost emphasis of thinking."

The doctor now recollected what had passed with Booth, and perceived he had made a mistake of one colonel for another. This he presently acknowledged to Colonel James, and said that the mistake had been his, and not Booth's.

Bath now collected all his gravity and dignity, as he called it, into his countenance, and, addressing himself to James, said, "And was that letter writ to you, brother?—I hope you never deserved any suspicion of this kind."

"Brother," cries James, "I am accountable to myself for my actions, and shall not render an account either to you or to that gentleman."

"As to me, brother," answered Bath, "you say right; but I think this gentleman may call you to an account; nay, I think it is his duty so to do. And let me tell you, brother, there is one much greater than he to whom you must give an account. Mrs. Booth is really a fine woman, a lady of most imperious and majestic presence. I have heard you often say that you liked her; and, if you have quarrelled with her husband upon this account, by all the dignity of man I think you ought to ask his pardon."

"Indeed, brother," cries James, "I can bear this no longer—you will make me angry presently."

"Angry! brother James," cries Bath; "angry!—I love you, brother, and have obligations to you. I will say no more, but I hope you know I do not fear making any man angry."

James answered he knew it well; and then the doctor, apprehending that while he was stopping up one breach he should make another, presently interfered, and turned the discourse back to Booth. "You tell me, sir," said he to James, "that my gown is my protection; let it then at least protect me where I have had no design in offending—where I have consulted your highest

252

welfare, as in truth I did in writing this letter. And if you did not in the least deserve any such suspicion, still you have no cause for resentment. Caution against sin, even to the innocent, can never be unwholesome. But this I assure you, whatever anger you have to me, you can have none to poor Booth, who was entirely ignorant of my writing to you, and who, I am certain, never entertained the least suspicion of you; on the contrary, reveres you with the highest esteem, and love, and gratitude. Let me therefore reconcile all matters between you, and bring you together before he hath even heard of this challenge."

"Brother," cries Bath, "I hope I shall not make you angry—I lie when I say so; for I am indifferent to any man's anger. Let me be an accessory to what the doctor hath said. I think I may be trusted with matters of this nature, and it is a little unkind that, if you intended to send a challenge, you did not make me the bearer. But, indeed, as to what appears to me, this matter may be very well made up; and, as Mr. Booth doth not know of the challenge, I don't see why he ever should, any more than your giving him the lie just now; but that he shall never have from me, nor, I believe, from this gentleman; for, indeed, if he should, it would be incumbent upon him to cut your throat."

"Lookee, doctor," said James, "I do not deserve the unkind suspicion you just now threw out against me. I never thirsted after any man's blood; and, as for what hath passed, since this discovery hath happened, I may, perhaps, not think it worth my while to trouble myself any more about it."

The doctor was not contented with perhaps, he insisted on a firm promise, to be bound with the colonel's honour. This at length he obtained, and then departed well satisfied.

In fact, the colonel was ashamed to avow the real cause of the quarrel to this good man, or, indeed, to his brother Bath, who would not only have condemned him equally with the doctor, but would possibly have quarrelled with him on his sister's account, whom, as the reader must have observed, he loved above all things; and, in plain truth, though the colonel was a brave man, and dared to fight, yet he was altogether as willing to let it alone; and this made him now and then give a little way to the wrongheadedness of Colonel Bath, who, with all the other principles of honour and humanity, made no more of cutting the throat of a man upon any of his punctilios than a butcher doth of killing sheep.

Chapter v. — What passed at the bailiff's house.

The doctor now set forwards to his friend Booth, and, as he past by the door of his attorney in the way, he called upon him and took him with him.

The meeting between him and Booth need not be expatiated on. The doctor was really angry, and, though he deferred his lecture to a more proper opportunity, yet, as he was no dissembler (indeed, he was incapable of any disguise), he could not put on a show of that heartiness with which he had formerly used to receive his friend.

Booth at last began himself in the following manner: "Doctor, I am really ashamed to see you; and, if you knew the confusion of my soul on this occasion, I am sure you would pity rather than upbraid me; and yet I can say with great sincerity I rejoice in this last instance of my shame, since I am like to reap the most solid advantage from it." The doctor stared at this, and Booth thus proceeded: "Since I have been in this wretched place I have employed my time almost entirely in reading over a series of sermons which are contained in that book (meaning Dr Barrow's works, which then lay on the table before him) in proof of the Christian religion; and so good an effect have they had upon me, that I shall, I believe, be the better man for them as long as I live. I have not a doubt (for I own I have had such) which remains now unsatisfied. If ever an angel might be thought to guide the pen of a writer, surely the pen of that great and good man had such an assistant." The doctor readily concurred in the praises of Dr Barrow, and added, "You say you have had your doubts, young gentleman; indeed, I did not know that—and, pray, what were your doubts?" "Whatever they were, sir," said Booth, "they are now satisfied, as I believe those of every impartial and sensible reader will be if he will, with due attention, read over these excellent

sermons." "Very well," answered the doctor, "though I have conversed, I find, with a false brother hitherto, I am glad you are reconciled to truth at last, and I hope your future faith will have some influence on your future life." "I need not tell you, sir," replied Booth, "that will always be the case where faith is sincere, as I assure you mine is. Indeed, I never was a rash disbeliever; my chief doubt was founded on this—that, as men appeared to me to act entirely from their passions, their actions could have neither merit nor demerit." "A very worthy conclusion truly!" cries the doctor; "but if men act, as I believe they do, from their passions, it would be fair to conclude that religion to be true which applies immediately to the strongest of these passions, hope and fear; chusing rather to rely on its rewards and punishments than on that native beauty of virtue which some of the antient philosophers thought proper to recommend to their disciples. But we will defer this discourse till another opportunity; at present, as the devil hath thought proper to set you free, I will try if I can prevail on the bailiff to do the same."

The doctor had really not so much money in town as Booth's debt amounted to, and therefore, though he would otherwise very willingly have paid it, he was forced to give bail to the action. For which purpose, as the bailiff was a man of great form, he was obliged to get another person to be bound with him. This person, however, the attorney undertook to procure, and immediately set out in quest of him.

During his absence the bailiff came into the room, and, addressing himself to the doctor, said, "I think, sir, your name is Doctor Harrison?" The doctor immediately acknowledged his name. Indeed, the bailiff had seen it to a bail-bond before. "Why then, sir," said the bailiff, "there is a man above in a dying condition that desires the favour of speaking to you; I believe he wants you to pray by him."

The bailiff himself was not more ready to execute his office on all occasions for his fee than the doctor was to execute his for nothing. Without making any further enquiry therefore into the condition of the man, he immediately went up-stairs.

As soon as the bailiff returned down-stairs, which was immediately after he had lodged the doctor in the room, Booth had the curiosity to ask him who this man was. "Why, I don't know much of him," said the bailiff; "I had him once in custody before now: I remember it was when your honour was here last; and now I remember, too, he said that he knew your honour very well. Indeed, I had some opinion of him at that time, for he spent his money very much like a gentleman; but I have discovered since that he is a poor fellow, and worth nothing. He is a mere shy cock; I have had the stuff about me this week, and could never get at him till this morning; nay, I don't believe we should ever have found out his lodgings had it not been for the attorney that was here just now, who gave us information. And so we took him this morning by a comical way enough; for we dressed up one of my men in women's cloathes, who told the people of the house that he was his sister, just come to town—for we were told by the attorney that he had such a sister, upon which he was let up-stairs—and so kept the door ajar till I and another rushed in. Let me tell you, captain, there are as good stratagems made use of in our business as any in the army."

"But pray, sir," said Booth, "did not you tell me this morning that the poor fellow was desperately wounded; nay, I think you told the doctor that he was a dying man?" "I had like to have forgot that," cries the bailiff. "Nothing would serve the gentleman but that he must make resistance, and he gave my man a blow with a stick; but I soon quieted him by giving him a wipe or two with a hanger. Not that, I believe, I have done his business neither; but the fellow is faint-hearted, and the surgeon, I fancy, frightens him more than he need. But, however, let the worst come to the worst, the law is all on my side, and it is only se fendendo. The attorney that was here just now told me so, and bid me fear nothing; for that he would stand my friend, and undertake the cause; and he is a devilish good one at a defence at the Old Bailey, I promise you. I have known him bring off several that everybody thought would have been hanged."

"But suppose you should be acquitted," said Booth, "would not the blood of this poor wretch lie a little heavy at your heart?"

"Why should it, captain?" said the bailiff. "Is not all done in a lawful way? Why will people resist the law when they know the consequence? To be sure, if a man was to kill another in an unlawful manner as it were, and what the law calls murder, that is quite and clear another thing. I should not care to be convicted of murder any more than another man. Why now, captain, you have been abroad in the wars they tell me, and to be sure must have killed men in your time. Pray,

was you ever afraid afterwards of seeing their ghosts?"

"That is a different affair," cries Booth; "but I would not kill a man in cold blood for all the world."

"There is no difference at all, as I can see," cries the bailiff. "One is as much in the way of business as the other. When gentlemen behave themselves like unto gentlemen I know how to treat them as such as well as any officer the king hath; and when they do not, why they must take what follows, and the law doth not call it murder."

Booth very plainly saw that the bailiff had squared his conscience exactly according to law, and that he could not easily subvert his way of thinking. He therefore gave up the cause, and desired the bailiff to expedite the bonds, which he promised to do; saying, he hoped he had used him with proper civility this time, if he had not the last, and that he should be remembered for it.

But before we close this chapter we shall endeavour to satisfy an enquiry, which may arise in our most favourite readers (for so are the most curious), how it came to pass that such a person as was Doctor Harrison should employ such a fellow as this Murphy?

The case then was thus: this Murphy had been clerk to an attorney in the very same town in which the doctor lived, and, when he was out of his time, had set up with a character fair enough, and had married a maid-servant of Mrs. Harris, by which means he had all the business to which that lady and her friends, in which number was the doctor, could recommend him.

Murphy went on with his business, and thrived very well, till he happened to make an unfortunate slip, in which he was detected by a brother of the same calling. But, though we call this by the gentle name of a slip, in respect to its being so extremely common, it was a matter in which the law, if it had ever come to its ears, would have passed a very severe censure, being, indeed, no less than perjury and subornation of perjury.

This brother attorney, being a very good-natured man, and unwilling to bespatter his own profession, and considering, perhaps, that the consequence did in no wise affect the public, who had no manner of interest in the alternative whether A., in whom the right was, or B., to whom Mr. Murphy, by the means aforesaid, had transferred it, succeeded in an action; we mention this particular, because, as this brother attorney was a very violent party man, and a professed stickler for the public, to suffer any injury to have been done to that, would have been highly inconsistent with his principles.

This gentleman, therefore, came to Mr. Murphy, and, after shewing him that he had it in his power to convict him of the aforesaid crime, very generously told him that he had not the least delight in bringing any man to destruction, nor the least animosity against him. All that he insisted upon was, that he would not live in the same town or county with one who had been guilty of such an action. He then told Mr. Murphy that he would keep the secret on two conditions; the one was, that he immediately quitted that country; the other was, that he should convince him he deserved this kindness by his gratitude, and that Murphy should transfer to the other all the business which he then had in those parts, and to which he could possibly recommend him.

It is the observation of a very wise man, that it is a very common exercise of wisdom in this world, of two evils to chuse the least. The reader, therefore, cannot doubt but that Mr. Murphy complied with the alternative proposed by his kind brother, and accepted the terms on which secrecy was to be obtained.

This happened while the doctor was abroad, and with all this, except the departure of Murphy, not only the doctor, but the whole town (save his aforesaid brother alone), were to this day unacquainted.

The doctor, at his return, hearing that Mr. Murphy was gone, applied to the other attorney in his affairs, who still employed this Murphy as his agent in town, partly, perhaps, out of good will to him, and partly from the recommendation of Miss Harris; for, as he had married a servant of the family, and a particular favourite of hers, there can be no wonder that she, who was entirely ignorant of the affair above related, as well as of his conduct in town, should continue her favour to him. It will appear, therefore, I apprehend, no longer strange that the doctor, who had seen this man but three times since his removal to town, and then conversed with him only on business, should remain as ignorant of his life and character, as a man generally is of the character of the hackney-coachman who drives him. Nor doth it reflect more on the honour or understanding of the doctor, under these circumstances, to employ Murphy, than it would if he had been driven about the town by a thief or a murderer.

255

Chapter vi. — What passed between the doctor and the sick man.

We left the doctor in the last chapter with the wounded man, to whom the doctor, in a very gentle voice, spoke as follows:—

"I am sorry, friend, to see you in this situation, and am very ready to give you any comfort or assistance within my power."

"I thank you kindly, doctor," said the man. "Indeed I should not have presumed to have sent to you had I not known your character; for, though I believe I am not at all known to you, I have lived many years in that town where you yourself had a house; my name is Robinson. I used to write for the attorneys in those parts, and I have been employed on your business in my time."

"I do not recollect you nor your name," said the doctor; "but consider, friend, your moments are precious, and your business, as I am informed, is to offer up your prayers to that great Being before whom you are shortly to appear. But first let me exhort you earnestly to a most serious repentance of all your sins."

"O doctor!" said the man; "pray; what is your opinion of a death-bed repentance?"

"If repentance is sincere," cries the doctor, "I hope, through the mercies and merits of our most powerful and benign Intercessor, it will never come too late."

"But do not you think, sir," cries the man, "that, in order to obtain forgiveness of any great sin we have committed, by an injury done to our neighbours, it is necessary, as far as in us lies, to make all the amends we can to the party injured, and to undo, if possible, the injury we have done?"

"Most undoubtedly," cries the doctor; "our pretence to repentance would otherwise be gross hypocrisy, and an impudent attempt to deceive and impose upon our Creator himself."

"Indeed, I am of the same opinion," cries the penitent; "and I think further, that this is thrown in my way, and hinted to me by that great Being; for an accident happened to me yesterday, by which, as things have fallen out since, I think I plainly discern the hand of Providence. I went yesterday, sir, you must know, to a pawnbroker's, to pawn the last moveable, which, except the poor cloathes you see on my back, I am worth in the world. While I was there a young lady came in to pawn her picture. She had disguised herself so much, and pulled her hood so over her face, that I did not know her while she stayed, which was scarce three minutes. As soon as she was gone the pawnbroker, taking the picture in his hand, cried out, Upon my word, this is the handsomest face I ever saw in my life! I desired him to let me look on the picture, which he readily did—and I no sooner cast my eyes upon it, than the strong resemblance struck me, and I knew it to be Mrs. Booth."

"Mrs. Booth! what Mrs. Booth?" cries the doctor.

"Captain Booth's lady, the captain who is now below," said the other.

"How?" cries the doctor with great impetuosity.

"Have patience," said the man, "and you shall hear all. I expressed some surprize to the pawnbroker, and asked the lady's name. He answered, that he knew not her name; but that she was some undone wretch, who had the day before left all her cloathes with him in pawn. My guilt immediately flew in my face, and told me I had been accessory to this lady's undoing. The sudden shock so affected me, that, had it not been for a dram which the pawnbroker gave me, I believe I should have sunk on the spot."

"Accessary to her undoing! how accessary?" said the doctor. "Pray tell me, for I am impatient to hear."

"I will tell you all as fast as I can," cries the sick man. "You know, good doctor, that Mrs. Harris of our town had two daughters, this Mrs. Booth and another. Now, sir, it seems the other daughter had, some way or other, disobliged her mother a little before the old lady died; therefore she made a will, and left all her fortune, except one thousand pound, to Mrs. Booth; to which will Mr. Murphy, myself, and another who is now dead, were the witnesses. Mrs. Harris afterwards died suddenly; upon which it was contrived by her other daughter and Mr. Murphy to make a new

256

will, in which Mrs. Booth had a legacy of ten pound, and all the rest was given to the other. To this will, Murphy, myself, and the same third person, again set our hands."

"Good Heaven! how wonderful is thy providence!" cries the doctor—"Murphy, say you?"

"He himself, sir," answered Robinson; "Murphy, who is the greatest rogue, I believe, now in the world."

"Pray, sir, proceed," cries the doctor.

"For this service, sir," said Robinson, "myself and the third person, one Carter, received two hundred pound each. What reward Murphy himself had I know not. Carter died soon afterwards; and from that time, at several payments, I have by threats extorted above a hundred pound more. And this, sir, is the whole truth, which I am ready to testify if it would please Heaven to prolong my life."

"I hope it will," cries the doctor; "but something must be done for fear of accidents. I will send to counsel immediately to know how to secure your testimony.—Whom can I get to send?— Stay, ay—he will do—but I know not where his house or his chambers are. I will go myself—but I may be wanted here."

While the doctor was in this violent agitation the surgeon made his appearance. The doctor stood still in a meditating posture, while the surgeon examined his patient. After which the doctor begged him to declare his opinion, and whether he thought the wounded man in any immediate danger of death. "I do not know," answered the surgeon, "what you call immediate. He may live several days—nay, he may recover. It is impossible to give any certain opinion in these cases." He then launched forth into a set of terms which the doctor, with all his scholarship, could not understand. To say the truth, many of them were not to be found in any dictionary or lexicon.

One discovery, however, the doctor made, and that was, that the surgeon was a very ignorant, conceited fellow, and knew nothing of his profession. He resolved, therefore, to get better advice for the sick; but this he postponed at present, and, applying himself to the surgeon, said, "He should be very much obliged to him if he knew where to find such a counsellor, and would fetch him thither. I should not ask such a favour of you, sir," says the doctor, "if it was not on business of the last importance, or if I could find any other messenger."

"I fetch, sir!" said the surgeon very angrily. "Do you take me for a footman or a porter? I don't know who you are; but I believe you are full as proper to go on such an errand as I am." (For as the doctor, who was just come off his journey, was very roughly dressed, the surgeon held him in no great respect.) The surgeon then called aloud from the top of the stairs, "Let my coachman draw up," and strutted off without any ceremony, telling his patient he would call again the next day.

At this very instant arrived Murphy with the other bail, and, finding Booth alone, he asked the bailiff at the door what was become of the doctor? "Why, the doctor," answered he, "is above-stairs, praying with———." "How!" cries Murphy. "How came you not to carry him directly to Newgate, as you promised me?" "Why, because he was wounded," cries the bailiff. "I thought it was charity to take care of him; and, besides, why should one make more noise about the matter than is necessary?" "And Doctor Harrison with him?" said Murphy. "Yes, he is," said the bailiff; "he desired to speak with the doctor very much, and they have been praying together almost this hour." "All is up and undone!" cries Murphy. "Let me come by, I have thought of something which I must do immediately."

Now, as by means of the surgeon's leaving the door open the doctor heard Murphy's voice naming Robinson peevishly, he drew softly to the top of the stairs, where he heard the foregoing dialogue; and as soon as Murphy had uttered his last words, and was moving downwards, the doctor immediately sallied from his post, running as fast as he could, and crying, Stop the villain! stop the thief!

The attorney wanted no better hint to accelerate his pace; and, having the start of the doctor, got downstairs, and out into the street; but the doctor was so close at his heels, and being in foot the nimbler of the two, he soon overtook him, and laid hold of him, as he would have done on either Broughton or Slack in the same cause.

This action in the street, accompanied with the frequent cry of Stop thief by the doctor during the chase, presently drew together a large mob, who began, as is usual, to enter immediately upon business, and to make strict enquiry into the matter, in order to proceed to do justice in their summary way.

Murphy, who knew well the temper of the mob, cried out, "If you are a bailiff, shew me your writ. Gentlemen, he pretends to arrest me here without a writ."

Upon this, one of the sturdiest and forwardest of the mob, and who by a superior strength of body and of lungs presided in this assembly, declared he would suffer no such thing. "D—n me," says he, "away to the pump with the catchpole directly—shew me your writ, or let the gentleman go—you shall not arrest a man contrary to law."

He then laid his hands on the doctor, who, still fast griping the attorney, cried out, "He is a villain—I am no bailiff, but a clergyman, and this lawyer is guilty of forgery, and hath ruined a poor family."

"How!" cries the spokesman—"a lawyer!—that alters the case."

"Yes, faith," cries another of the mob, "it is lawyer Murphy. I know him very well."

"And hath he ruined a poor family?—like enough, faith, if he's a lawyer. Away with him to the justice immediately."

The bailiff now came up, desiring to know what was the matter; to whom Doctor Harrison answered that he had arrested that villain for a forgery. "How can you arrest him?" cries the bailiff; "you are no officer, nor have any warrant. Mr. Murphy is a gentleman, and he shall be used as such."

"Nay, to be sure," cries the spokesman, "there ought to be a warrant; that's the truth on't."

"There needs no warrant," cries the doctor. "I accuse him of felony; and I know so much of the law of England, that any man may arrest a felon without any warrant whatever. This villain hath undone a poor family; and I will die on the spot before I part with him."

"If the law be so," cries the orator, "that is another matter. And to be sure, to ruin a poor man is the greatest of sins. And being a lawyer too makes it so much the worse. He shall go before the justice, d—n me if he shan't go before the justice! I says the word, he shall."

"I say he is a gentleman, and shall be used according to law," cries the bailiff; "and, though you are a clergyman," said he to Harrison, "you don't shew yourself as one by your actions."

"That's a bailiff," cries one of the mob: "one lawyer will always stand by another; but I think the clergyman is a very good man, and acts becoming a clergyman, to stand by the poor."

At which words the mob all gave a great shout, and several cried out, "Bring him along, away with him to the justice!"

And now a constable appeared, and with an authoritative voice declared what he was, produced his staff, and demanded the peace.

The doctor then delivered his prisoner over to the officer, and charged him with felony; the constable received him, the attorney submitted, the bailiff was hushed, and the waves of the mob immediately subsided.

The doctor now balanced with himself how he should proceed: at last he determined to leave Booth a little longer in captivity, and not to quit sight of Murphy before he had lodged him safe with a magistrate. They then all moved forwards to the justice; the constable and his prisoner marching first, the doctor and the bailiff following next, and about five thousand mob (for no less number were assembled in a very few minutes) following in the procession.

They found the magistrate just sitting down to his dinner; however, when he was acquainted with the doctor's profession, he immediately admitted him, and heard his business; which he no sooner perfectly understood, with all its circumstances, than he resolved, though it was then very late, and he had been fatigued all the morning with public business, to postpone all refreshment till he had discharged his duty. He accordingly adjourned the prisoner and his cause to the bailiff's house, whither he himself, with the doctor, immediately repaired, and whither the attorney was followed by a much larger number of attendants than he had been honoured with before.

Chapter vii. — In which the history draws towards a conclusion.

Nothing could exceed the astonishment of Booth at the behaviour of the doctor at the time

when he sallied forth in pursuit of the attorney; for which it was so impossible for him to account in any manner whatever. He remained a long time in the utmost torture of mind, till at last the bailiff's wife came to him, and asked him if the doctor was not a madman? and, in truth, he could hardly defend him from that imputation.

While he was in this perplexity the maid of the house brought him a message from Robinson, desiring the favour of seeing him above-stairs. With this he immediately complied.

When these two were alone together, and the key turned on them (for the bailiff's wife was a most careful person, and never omitted that ceremony in the absence of her husband, having always at her tongue's end that excellent proverb of "Safe bind, safe find"), Robinson, looking stedfastly upon Booth, said, "I believe, sir, you scarce remember me."

Booth answered that he thought he had seen his face somewhere before, but could not then recollect when or where.

"Indeed, sir," answered the man, "it was a place which no man can remember with pleasure. But do you not remember, a few weeks ago, that you had the misfortune to be in a certain prison in this town, where you lost a trifling sum at cards to a fellow-prisoner?"

This hint sufficiently awakened Booth's memory, and he now recollected the features of his old friend Robinson. He answered him a little surlily, "I know you now very well, but I did not imagine you would ever have reminded me of that transaction."

"Alas, sir!" answered Robinson, "whatever happened then was very trifling compared to the injuries I have done you; but if my life be spared long enough I will now undo it all: and, as I have been one of your worst enemies, I will now be one of your best friends."

He was just entering upon his story when a noise was heard below which might be almost compared to what have been heard in Holland when the dykes have given way, and the ocean in an inundation breaks in upon the land. It seemed, indeed, as if the whole world was bursting into the house at once.

Booth was a man of great firmness of mind, and he had need of it all at this instant. As for poor Robinson, the usual concomitants of guilt attended him, and he began to tremble in a violent manner.

The first person who ascended the stairs was the doctor, who no sooner saw Booth than he ran to him and embraced him, crying, "My child, I wish you joy with all my heart. Your sufferings are all at an end, and Providence hath done you the justice at last which it will, one day or other, render to all men. You will hear all presently; but I can now only tell you that your sister is discovered and the estate is your own."

Booth was in such confusion that he scarce made any answer, and now appeared the justice and his clerk, and immediately afterwards the constable with his prisoner, the bailiff, and as many more as could possibly crowd up-stairs.

The doctor now addressed himself to the sick man, and desired him to repeat the same information before the justice which he had made already; to which Robinson readily consented.

While the clerk was taking down the information, the attorney expressed a very impatient desire to send instantly for his clerk, and expressed so much uneasiness at the confusion in which he had left his papers at home, that a thought suggested itself to the doctor that, if his house was searched, some lights and evidence relating to this affair would certainly be found; he therefore desired the justice to grant a search-warrant immediately to search his house.

The justice answered that he had no such power; that, if there was any suspicion of stolen goods, he could grant a warrant to search for them.

"How, sir!" said the doctor, "can you grant a warrant to search a man's house for a silver tea-spoon, and not in a case like this, where a man is robbed of his whole estate?"

"Hold, sir," says the sick man; "I believe I can answer that point; for I can swear he hath several title-deeds of the estate now in his possession, which I am sure were stolen from the right owner."

The justice still hesitated. He said title-deeds savoured of the Realty, and it was not felony to steal them. If, indeed, they were taken away in a box, then it would be felony to steal the box. — "Savour of the Realty! Savour of the f—talty," said the doctor. "I never heard such incomprehensible nonsense. This is impudent, as well as childish trifling with the lives and properties of men."

"Well, sir," said Robinson, "I now am sure I can do his business; for I know he hath a silver

cup in his possession which is the property of this gentleman (meaning Booth), and how he got it but by stealth let him account if he can."

"That will do," cries the justice with great pleasure. "That will do; and if you will charge him on oath with that, I will instantly grant my warrant to search his house for it." "And I will go and see it executed," cries the doctor; for it was a maxim of his, that no man could descend below himself in doing any act which may contribute to protect an innocent person, or to bring a rogue to the gallows.

The oath was instantly taken, the warrant signed, and the doctor attended the constable in the execution of it.

The clerk then proceeded in taking the information of Robinson, and had just finished it, when the doctor returned with the utmost joy in his countenance, and declared that he had sufficient evidence of the fact in his possession. He had, indeed, two or three letters from Miss Harris in answer to the attorney's frequent demands of money for secrecy, that fully explained the whole villany.

The justice now asked the prisoner what he had to say for himself, or whether he chose to say anything in his own defence.

"Sir," said the attorney, with great confidence, "I am not to defend myself here. It will be of no service to me; for I know you neither can nor will discharge me. But I am extremely innocent of all this matter, as I doubt not but to make appear to the satisfaction of a court of justice."

The legal previous ceremonies were then gone through of binding over the prosecutor, &c., and then the attorney was committed to Newgate, whither he was escorted amidst the acclamations of the populace.

When Murphy was departed, and a little calm restored in the house, the justice made his compliments of congratulation to Booth, who, as well as he could in his present tumult of joy, returned his thanks to both the magistrate and the doctor. They were now all preparing to depart, when Mr. Bondum stept up to Booth, and said, "Hold, sir, you have forgot one thing—you have not given bail yet."

This occasioned some distress at this time, for the attorney's friend was departed; but when the justice heard this, he immediately offered himself as the other bondsman, and thus ended the affair.

It was now past six o'clock, and none of the gentlemen had yet dined. They very readily, therefore, accepted the magistrate's invitation, and went all together to his house.

And now the very first thing that was done, even before they sat down to dinner, was to dispatch a messenger to one of the best surgeons in town to take care of Robinson, and another messenger to Booth's lodgings to prevent Amelia's concern at their staying so long.

The latter, however, was to little purpose; for Amelia's patience had been worn out before, and she had taken a hackney-coach and driven to the bailiff's, where she arrived a little after the departure of her husband, and was thence directed to the justice's.

Though there was no kind of reason for Amelia's fright at hearing that her husband and Doctor Harrison were gone before the justice, and though she indeed imagined that they were there in the light of complainants, not of offenders, yet so tender were her fears for her husband, and so much had her gentle spirits been lately agitated, that she had a thousand apprehensions of she knew not what. When she arrived, therefore, at the house, she ran directly into the room where all the company were at dinner, scarce knowing what she did or whither she was going.

She found her husband in such a situation, and discovered such chearfulness in his countenance, that so violent a turn was given to her spirits that she was just able, with the assistance of a glass of water, to support herself. She soon, however, recovered her calmness, and in a little time began to eat what might indeed be almost called her breakfast.

The justice now wished her joy of what had happened that day, for which she kindly thanked him, apprehending he meant the liberty of her husband. His worship might perhaps have explained himself more largely had not the doctor given him a timely wink; for this wise and good man was fearful of making such a discovery all at once to Amelia, lest it should overpower her, and luckily the justice's wife was not well enough acquainted with the matter to say anything more on it than barely to assure the lady that she joined in her husband's congratulation.

Amelia was then in a clean white gown, which she had that day redeemed, and was, indeed, dressed all over with great neatness and exactness; with the glow therefore which arose in her

features from finding her husband released from his captivity, she made so charming a figure, that she attracted the eyes of the magistrate and of his wife, and they both agreed when they were alone that they had never seen so charming a creature; nay, Booth himself afterwards told her that he scarce ever remembered her to look so extremely beautiful as she did that evening.

Whether Amelia's beauty, or the reflexion on the remarkable act of justice he had performed, or whatever motive filled the magistrate with extraordinary good humour, and opened his heart and cellars, I will not determine; but he gave them so hearty a welcome, and they were all so pleased with each other, that Amelia, for that one night, trusted the care of her children to the woman where they lodged, nor did the company rise from table till the clock struck eleven.

They then separated. Amelia and Booth, having been set down at their lodgings, retired into each other's arms; nor did Booth that evening, by the doctor's advice, mention one word of the grand affair to his wife.

Chapter viii. — Thus this history draws nearer to a conclusion.

In the morning early Amelia received the following letter from Mrs. Atkinson:

"The surgeon of the regiment, to which the captain my husband lately belonged, and who came this evening to see the captain, hath almost frightened me out of my wits by a strange story of your husband being committed to prison by a justice of peace for forgery. For Heaven's sake send me the truth. If my husband can be of any service, weak as he is, he will be carried in a chair to serve a brother officer for whom he hath a regard, which I need not mention. Or if the sum of twenty pound will be of any service to you, I will wait upon you with it the moment I can get my cloaths on, the morning you receive this; for it is too late to send to-night. The captain begs his hearty service and respects, and believe me,

"Dear Madam,
　　Your ever affectionate friend,
　　　and humble servant,
　　　F. ATKINSON."

When Amelia read this letter to Booth they were both equally surprized, she at the commitment for forgery, and he at seeing such a letter from Mrs. Atkinson; for he was a stranger yet to the reconciliation that had happened.

Booth's doubts were first satisfied by Amelia, from which he received great pleasure; for he really had a very great affection and fondness for Mr. Atkinson, who, indeed, so well deserved it. "Well, my dear," said he to Amelia, smiling, "shall we accept this generous offer?"

"O fy! no, certainly," answered she.

"Why not?" cries Booth; "it is but a trifle; and yet it will be of great service to us."

"But consider, my dear," said she, "how ill these poor people can spare it."

"They can spare it for a little while," said Booth, "and we shall soon pay it them again."

"When, my dear?" said Amelia. "Do, my dear Will, consider our wretched circumstances. I beg you let us go into the country immediately, and live upon bread and water till Fortune pleases to smile upon us."

"I am convinced that day is not far off," said Booth. "However, give me leave to send an answer to Mrs. Atkinson, that we shall be glad of her company immediately to breakfast."

"You know I never contradict you," said she, "but I assure you it is contrary to my inclinations to take this money."

"Well, suffer me," cries he, "to act this once contrary to your inclinations." He then writ a short note to Mrs. Atkinson, and dispatched it away immediately; which when he had done, Amelia said, "I shall be glad of Mrs. Atkinson's company to breakfast; but yet I wish you would oblige me in refusing this money. Take five guineas only. That is indeed such a sum as, if we never should pay it, would sit light on my mind. The last persons in the world from whom I would receive favours of that sort are the poor and generous."

"You can receive favours only from the generous," cries Booth; "and, to be plain with you,

there are very few who are generous that are not poor."

"What think you," said she, "of Dr Harrison?"

"I do assure you," said Booth, "he is far from being rich. The doctor hath an income of little more than six hundred pound a-year, and I am convinced he gives away four of it. Indeed, he is one of the best economists in the world: but yet I am positive he never was at any time possessed of five hundred pound, since he hath been a man. Consider, dear Emily, the late obligations we have to this gentleman; it would be unreasonable to expect more, at least at present; my half-pay is mortgaged for a year to come. How then shall we live?"

"By our labour," answered she; "I am able to labour, and I am sure I am not ashamed of it."

"And do you really think you can support such a life?"

"I am sure I could be happy in it," answered Amelia. "And why not I as well as a thousand others, who have not the happiness of such a husband to make life delicious? why should I complain of my hard fate while so many who are much poorer than I enjoy theirs? Am I of a superior rank of being to the wife of the honest labourer? am I not partaker of one common nature with her?"

"My angel," cries Booth, "it delights me to hear you talk thus, and for a reason you little guess; for I am assured that one who can so heroically endure adversity, will bear prosperity with equal greatness of soul; for the mind that cannot be dejected by the former, is not likely to be transported with the latter."

"If it had pleased Heaven," cried she, "to have tried me, I think, at least I hope, I should have preserved my humility."

"Then, my dear," said he, "I will relate you a dream I had last night. You know you lately mentioned a dream of yours."

"Do so," said she; "I am attentive."

"I dreamt," said he, "this night, that we were in the most miserable situation imaginable; indeed, in the situation we were yesterday morning, or rather worse; that I was laid in a prison for debt, and that you wanted a morsel of bread to feed the mouths of your hungry children. At length (for nothing you know is quicker than the transition in dreams) Dr Harrison methought came to me, with chearfulness and joy in his countenance. The prison-doors immediately flew open, and Dr Harrison introduced you, gayly though not richly dressed. That you gently chid me for staying so long. All on a sudden appeared a coach with four horses to it, in which was a maid-servant with our two children. We both immediately went into the coach, and, taking our leave of the doctor, set out towards your country-house; for yours I dreamt it was. I only ask you now, if this was real, and the transition almost as sudden, could you support it?"

Amelia was going to answer, when Mrs. Atkinson came into the room, and after very little previous ceremony, presented Booth with a bank-note, which he received of her, saying he would very soon repay it; a promise that a little offended Amelia, as she thought he had no chance of keeping it.

The doctor presently arrived, and the company sat down to breakfast, during which Mrs. Atkinson entertained them with the history of the doctors that had attended her husband, by whose advice Atkinson was recovered from everything but the weakness which his distemper had occasioned.

When the tea-table was removed Booth told the doctor that he had acquainted his wife with a dream he had last night. "I dreamt, doctor," said he, "that she was restored to her estate."

"Very well," said the doctor; "and if I am to be the Oneiropolus, I believe the dream will come to pass. To say the truth, I have rather a better opinion of dreams than Horace had. Old Homer says they come from Jupiter; and as to your dream, I have often had it in my waking thoughts, that some time or other that roguery (for so I was always convinced it was) would be brought to light; for the same Homer says, as you, madam (meaning Mrs. Atkinson), very well know,

{Greek verses}

{Footnote: "If Jupiter doth not immediately execute his vengeance, he will however execute it at last; and their transgressions shall fall heavily on their own heads, and on their wives and children."}

"I have no Greek ears, sir," said Mrs. Atkinson. "I believe I could understand it in the Delphin Homer."

262

"I wish," cries he, "my dear child (to Amelia), you would read a little in the Delphin Aristotle, or else in some Christian divine, to learn a doctrine which you will one day have a use for. I mean to bear the hardest of all human conflicts, and support with an even temper, and without any violent transports of mind, a sudden gust of prosperity."

"Indeed," cries Amelia, "I should almost think my husband and you, doctor, had some very good news to tell me, by your using, both of you, the same introduction. As far as I know myself, I think I can answer I can support any degree of prosperity, and I think I yesterday shewed I could: for I do assure you, it is not in the power of fortune to try me with such another transition from grief to joy, as I conceived from seeing my husband in prison and at liberty."

"Well, you are a good girl," cries the doctor, "and after I have put on my spectacles I will try you."

The doctor then took out a newspaper, and read as follows:

"'Yesterday one Murphy, an eminent attorney-at-law, was committed to Newgate for the forgery of a will under which an estate hath been for many years detained from the right owner.'

"Now in this paragraph there is something very remarkable, and that is—that it is true: but opus est explanatu. In the Delphin edition of this newspaper there is the following note upon the words right owner:—'The right owner of this estate is a young lady of the highest merit, whose maiden name was Harris, and who some time since was married to an idle fellow, one Lieutenant Booth. And the best historians assure us that letters from the elder sister of this lady, which manifestly prove the forgery and clear up the whole affair, are in the hands of an old Parson called Doctor Harrison.'"

"And is this really true?" cries Amelia.

"Yes, really and sincerely," cries the doctor. "The whole estate; for your mother left it you all, and is as surely yours as if you was already in possession."

"Gracious Heaven!" cries she, falling on her knees, "I thank you!" And then starting up, she ran to her husband, and, embracing him, cried, "My dear love, I wish you joy; and I ought in gratitude to wish it you; for you are the cause of mine. It is upon yours and my children's account that I principally rejoice."

Mrs. Atkinson rose from her chair, and jumped about the room for joy, repeating,

Turne, quod oplanti divum promittere nemo

Auderet, volvenda dies, en, attulit ultro.

{Footnote: "What none of all the Gods could grant thy vows, That, Turnus, this auspicious day bestows."}

Amelia now threw herself into a chair, complained she was a little faint, and begged a glass of water. The doctor advised her to be blooded; but she refused, saying she required a vent of another kind. She then desired her children to be brought to her, whom she immediately caught in her arms, and, having profusely cried over them for several minutes, declared she was easy. After which she soon regained her usual temper and complexion.

That day they dined together, and in the afternoon they all, except the doctor, visited Captain Atkinson; he repaired to the bailiff's house to visit the sick man, whom he found very chearful, the surgeon having assured him that he was in no danger.

The doctor had a long spiritual discourse with Robinson, who assured him that he sincerely repented of his past life, that he was resolved to lead his future days in a different manner, and to make what amends he could for his sins to the society, by bringing one of the greatest rogues in it to justice. There was a circumstance which much pleased the doctor, and made him conclude that, however Robinson had been corrupted by his old master, he had naturally a good disposition. This was, that Robinson declared he was chiefly induced to the discovery by what had happened at the pawnbroker's, and by the miseries which he there perceived he had been instrumental in bringing on Booth and his family.

The next day Booth and his wife, at the doctor's instance, dined with Colonel James and his lady, where they were received with great civility, and all matters were accommodated without Booth ever knowing a syllable of the challenge even to this day.

The doctor insisted very strongly on having Miss Harris taken into custody, and said, if she was his sister, he would deliver her to justice. He added besides, that it was impossible to skreen her and carry on the prosecution, or, indeed, recover the estate. Amelia at last begged the delay of one day only, in which time she wrote a letter to her sister, informing her of the discovery, and the

danger in which she stood, and begged her earnestly to make her escape, with many assurances that she would never suffer her to know any distress. This letter she sent away express, and it had the desired effect; for Miss Harris, having received sufficient information from the attorney to the same purpose, immediately set out for Poole, and from thence to France, carrying with her all her money, most of her cloaths, and some few jewels. She had, indeed, packed up plate and jewels to the value of two thousand pound and upwards. But Booth, to whom Amelia communicated the letter, prevented her by ordering the man that went with the express (who had been a serjeant of the foot-guards recommended to him by Atkinson) to suffer the lady to go whither she pleased, but not to take anything with her except her cloaths, which he was carefully to search. These orders were obeyed punctually, and with these she was obliged to comply.

Two days after the bird was flown a warrant from the lord chief justice arrived to take her up, the messenger of which returned with the news of her flight, highly to the satisfaction of Amelia, and consequently of Booth, and, indeed, not greatly to the grief of the doctor.

About a week afterwards Booth and Amelia, with their children, and Captain Atkinson and his lady, all set forward together for Amelia's house, where they arrived amidst the acclamations of all the neighbours, and every public demonstration of joy.

They found the house ready prepared to receive them by Atkinson's friend the old serjeant, and a good dinner prepared for them by Amelia's old nurse, who was addressed with the utmost duty by her son and daughter, most affectionately caressed by Booth and his wife, and by Amelia's absolute command seated next to herself at the table. At which, perhaps, were assembled some of the best and happiest people then in the world.

Chapter ix. — In which the history is concluded.

Having brought our history to a conclusion, as to those points in which we presume our reader was chiefly interested, in the foregoing chapter, we shall in this, by way of epilogue, endeavour to satisfy his curiosity as to what hath since happened to the principal personages of whom we have treated in the foregoing pages.

Colonel James and his lady, after living in a polite manner for many years together, at last agreed to live in as polite a manner asunder. The colonel hath kept Miss Matthews ever since, and is at length grown to doat on her (though now very disagreeable in her person, and immensely fat) to such a degree, that he submits to be treated by her in the most tyrannical manner.

He allows his lady eight hundred pound a-year, with which she divides her time between Tunbridge, Bath, and London, and passes about nine hours in the twenty-four at cards. Her income is lately increased by three thousand pound left her by her brother Colonel Bath, who was killed in a duel about six years ago by a gentleman who told the colonel he differed from him in opinion.

The noble peer and Mrs. Ellison have been both dead several years, and both of the consequences of their favourite vices; Mrs. Ellison having fallen a martyr to her liquor, and the other to his amours, by which he was at last become so rotten that he stunk above-ground.

The attorney, Murphy, was brought to his trial at the Old Bailey, where, after much quibbling about the meaning of a very plain act of parliament, he was at length convicted of forgery, and was soon afterwards hanged at Tyburn.

The witness for some time seemed to reform his life, and received a small pension from Booth; after which he returned to vicious courses, took a purse on the highway, was detected and taken, and followed the last steps of his old master. So apt are men whose manners have been once thoroughly corrupted, to return, from any dawn of an amendment, into the dark paths of vice.

As to Miss Harris, she lived three years with a broken heart at Boulogne, where she received annually fifty pound from her sister, who was hardly prevailed on by Dr Harrison not to send her a hundred, and then died in a most miserable manner.

Mr. Atkinson upon the whole hath led a very happy life with his wife, though he hath been

sometimes obliged to pay proper homage to her superior understanding and knowledge. This, however, he chearfully submits to, and she makes him proper returns of fondness. They have two fine boys, of whom they are equally fond. He is lately advanced to the rank of captain, and last summer both he and his wife paid a visit of three months to Booth and his wife.

Dr Harrison is grown old in years and in honour, beloved and respected by all his parishioners and by all his neighbours. He divides his time between his parish, his old town, and Booth's—at which last place he had, two years ago, a gentle fit of the gout, being the first attack of that distemper. During this fit Amelia was his nurse, and her two oldest daughters sat up alternately with him for a whole week. The eldest of those girls, whose name is Amelia, is his favourite; she is the picture of her mother, and it is thought the doctor hath distinguished her in his will, for he hath declared that he will leave his whole fortune, except some few charities, among Amelia's children.

As to Booth and Amelia, Fortune seems to have made them large amends for the tricks she played them in their youth. They have, ever since the above period of this history, enjoyed an uninterrupted course of health and happiness. In about six weeks after Booth's first coming into the country he went to London and paid all his debts of honour; after which, and a stay of two days only, he returned into the country, and hath never since been thirty miles from home. He hath two boys and four girls; the eldest of the boys, he who hath made his appearance in this history, is just come from the university, and is one of the finest gentlemen and best scholars of his age. The second is just going from school, and is intended for the church, that being his own choice. His eldest daughter is a woman grown, but we must not mention her age. A marriage was proposed to her the other day with a young fellow of a good estate, but she never would see him more than once: "For Doctor Harrison," says she, "told me he was illiterate, and I am sure he is ill-natured." The second girl is three years younger than her sister, and the others are yet children.

Amelia is still the finest woman in England of her age. Booth himself often avers she is as handsome as ever. Nothing can equal the serenity of their lives. Amelia declared to me the other day, that she did not remember to have seen her husband out of humour these ten years; and, upon my insinuating to her that he had the best of wives, she answered with a smile that she ought to be so, for that he had made her the happiest of women.

THE END.

Printed in the United States
144534LV00001B/2/P